THE STORY OF TIME NO MORE

Fate's Fray

A novel by
J.A. Tocksworth

Published by

TOCKSWORTH BOOKS, LLC

Tocksworth Books, LLC
P.O. Box 29795
San Antonio, TX 78229

Tocksworth Books Paperback:
The Story of Time No More: Fate's Fray
Published by Tocksworth Books, LLC

ISBN-10 1-941413-02-1
ISBN-13 978-1-941413-02-9
Library of Congress Control Number: 2014920619

Dedication & Acknowledgement

Dedication

To those who said I could…
And to those who said I couldn't…

To those who encouraged…
Just as to those who discouraged…

To those in the wake of broken dreams…
But also, to those living dreams anew…

This book was written for more than a few.
This book was written, for you.

Acknowledgement

I'd like to thank my friends and family for their support during my authorship of this work. Your listening ears, willingness to read, and professed interest in my novel helped keep me motivated throughout one of the biggest battles for good destiny that I ever fought.

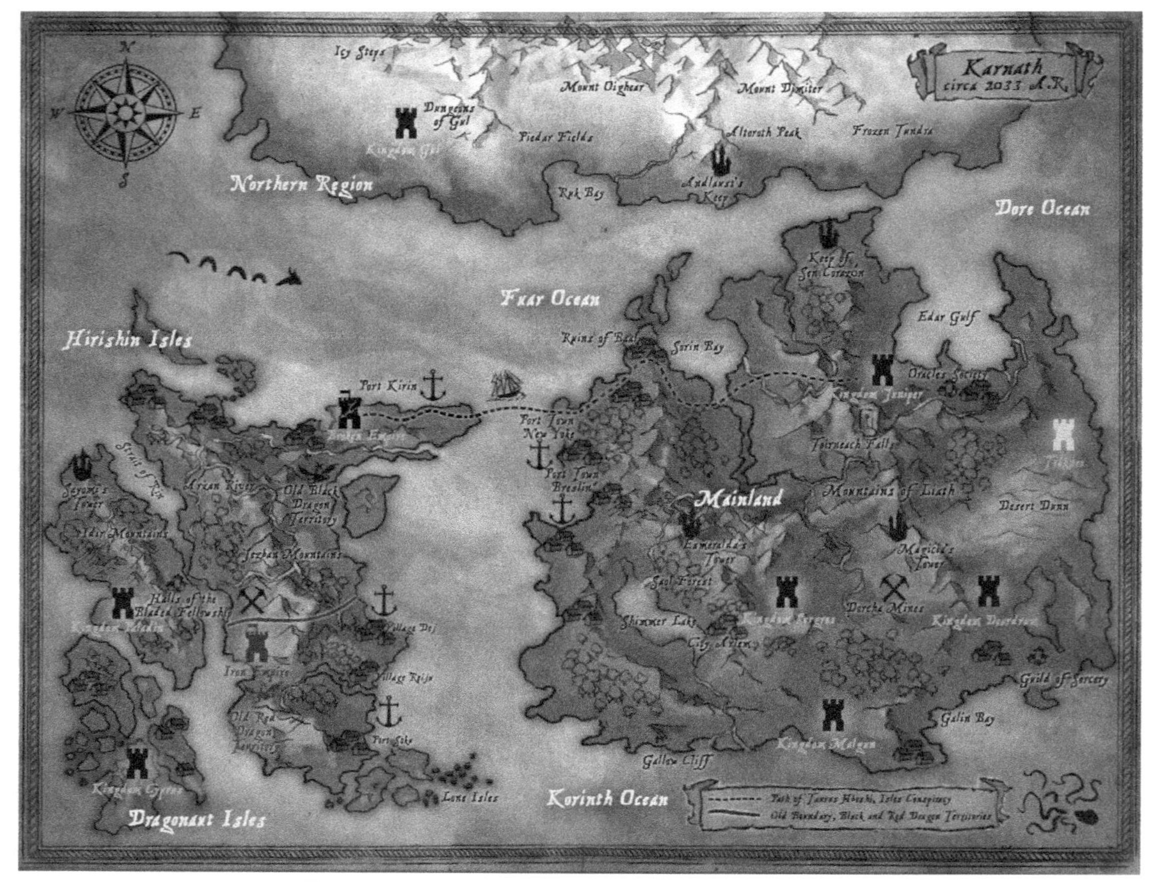

"MAP OF KARNATH"

Character List

Character	Summary
Autheos	Forerunner of Light; counterpart of Karnatha; wishes to win the Game for Light
Cedric	Talus' political opponent, the High Chancellor of Sergros, who wants the Sergrothian throne
Darconas	King of Deardrum in Old Karnath; disappeared from a hospice bed in old age; was later succeeded by Penultum
Dimral	X'ieth's fellow Guardsman (formerly); murdered during the Isles Conspiracy
Drichal	Solider of Sergros, murdered in the Isles Crusades
Elucid	The crimson knight, who has an unexplained interest in Kort, and a mysterious rivalry with Lucen
Enker	X'ieth's fellow Guardsman (formerly); murdered during the Isles Conspiracy
Eriens	King of Malgun in Old Karnath; recovered the black shard to enter New Karnath; caused the tragedy where Hrya was murdered
Esmeralda	Sorceress and sister of Magicia; believed to be bringing gloom upon Sergros
Finnel	X'ieth's fellow Guardsman, Hammar's close friend, and an elven knight from Juniper
Galwin	X'ieth's young hired hand, a servant that helps with chores around his cottage
Gambul	Solider of Sergros, murdered in the Isles Crusades
Garlew	Murdered hero of Sergros, revered by many in the Triangle Kingdoms
Gawdin	Renowned Juniperth architect, known for spectacular and innovative designs
Genze	Mainlandish fisherman, who lives in the Isles, and provides Kort a place to stay
Gremel	One of Karnath's three Ancient Dragons—the oldest and strongest dragons in Karnath
Hammar	X'ieth's fellow Guardsman, Finnel's close friend, and an dwarven knight from Deardrum
Hetron	Soldier of Sergros, murdered in the Isles Crusades

Character	Summary
Hrya	Prince of Deardrum in Old Karnath, murdered by King Eriens in the tragedy; loved Magicia
Illandrus	Renowned painter throughout the Mainland, who specializes in scenes from the Book of Karnatha
Inari	Kort's alias, as a fugitive hiding in the Isles
Inklin	Knight of Sergros and the Royal Protectorate; disagrees with Sagult's decisions
Karnatha	Manifestation of Destiny, member of a spiritual trinity formed with the Forerunners
Kayareth	Child of Light; wins the Game in the Light Prophecy, believed to be invented by the oracles
Kilwroth	Eriens' son, recipient of the Unwholesome Inheritance due to his father's misdeeds
Kort	Ex-knight suspected murderer of Garlew; wishes to redeem himself and find Nym
Kyan	Kort's frequent customer who buys fish in Reiju; a wealthy retired merchant
Lady Lyda	One of the last seeing oracles beyond their blindness from the Great Occlusion
Laotzu	Central figure in the story 'Maken and Rebels'; the only seroxian who tried to stop the rebellion against Maken; exiled to New Karnath
Lewes	X'ieth's fellow Guardsman, Tol's close friend, and an human knight from Sergros
Lucen	X'ieth's friend, who spared him from a deadly encounter with Kort; has a mysterious rivalry with Elucid
Ma'althan	Forerunner of Darkness; counterpart of Karnatha; wishes to win the Game for Darkness
Magicia	Most powerful sorceress in Karnath; sister of Esmeralda; the unnamed sorceress of legend; she loves Hrya, beyond his death
Maken	Creator of Old and New Karnath
Mance	Doomsayer of New Yoke who causes trouble
Merphonox	Brother to Penultum and son of Darconas; seeks restitution for the seroxians over Maken banishing them to [cursed] Old Karnath
Millicent	X'ieth's wife, the daughter of oracles; she's angry that the knighthood disrupts her home life
Naketo	Person in Magicia's and Elucid's visions of Gallow Cliff, seen dying there

Character	*Summary*
Nathan	X'ieth's superior, leads one of seven packs in the Sergrothian Crimson Guard
Nym	The Fallen Servant, who loves Kort and is trying desperately to find him
Penultum	Successor of Darconas, who died of illness to be succeeded by Merphonox
Perry	Technologist in Tekkneo, restores exo-core
Pyrus	Dragon Hunter wanted for the murder of an entire village, through inciting Gremel
Raiden	Hirishin fisher elf who befriends Kort in Doj
Ralfus	Assistant to Lady Lyda
Retha	Knight of Sergros and the Royal Protectorate; disagrees with Sagult's decisions
Rystys	Soldier of Sergros, murdered in the Isles Crusades
Sagult	X'ieth's fellow knight (formerly), and now, Kort's pursuer
Shaizan	Child of Darkness; the oracles foresaw him winning the Game of Time and Broken Sword in the Dark Prophecy
Sydullus	Talus' counsel, the man in black; he warned Eriens not to enter New Karnath in war
Talus	King of Sergros, who is devout in the Karnathan religion, and cruel to X'ieth
Taurus	Deceased Emperor of the Black Dragon clans in the Hirishin Isles; led the Isles Conspiracy with the aid of unknown Dark powers
Tol	X'ieth's fellow Guardsman, Lewes' close friend, and an human knight from Sergros
Thorin	Esteemed swordsman of the Bladed Fellowship; instructs X'ieth before his quest
Urzel	Talus' counsel, the woman in white; she still has a rivalry with Nym
Vaxlan	Merphonox's opponent on the Council of Seroxia, against war on the inferiors and reclaiming New Karnath
X'ieth	Young knight of Sergros who dreams of being Kayareth; he hates Talus and loves Millicent
Wicken	Guards Liath to prevent one shard of sword being unfairly destroyed in Ires Star, for the Light to win the Game, outside of Gallow Cliff

Character	Summary
Zeros	Mercenary to Sergros, who serves Talus in whatever way is needed

fate
/fāt/
noun
noun: fate;   plural noun: fates
1. the development of one's future as a result of supernatural powers or chance
2. the development of one's future as a result of personal choice
3. somewhere in between…
synonym: destiny

fray
/frā/
noun
noun: fray;   plural noun: frays
1. a raveled place or worn spot (as on fabric)
2. a heated fight or struggle

Foreword

In the land of Karnath, prophecy tells how the Game of Time and Broken Sword will settle what has been an endless war between good and evil. It's the simplest of games, involving a sword that can slay time, the fate of time itself, and its players: the Children of Light and Darkness. But as simple as that, no oracle in Karnath has foreseen the Game's winner for thousands of years. Yet one day, everything changes when the oracles suddenly go blind, their last vision being the Child of Darkness winning the Game and ushering Eternal Darkness on Karnath!

For three years after that prediction, nothing happens and the people of Karnath scoff at the oracles. But then all of a sudden, war, crime, injustice, and gloom descend upon Karnath within a matter of months, perhaps being a sign that end times are finally on the horizon. People far and wide begin hoping for a new hero to rise in the shadow of a fallen hero's grave. X'ieth Armstrong—a young knight of the human kingdom Sergros—has his heart set on exactly that, but it will take more than good will for him to save the world from Darkness.

High above the full moon that filled a blood-red sky, and even higher above the stars of heaven, Karnatha wept bitterly for Karnath. And with her tears fell all the stars from space in a trail of receding light; they kissed the night goodbye, never to shine again.

The falling stars plummeted to Karnath, bathing the Children of Destiny in brilliant fire, the pair who fought the Battle for Destiny at the foot of Gallow Cliff. Amid her crying, Karnatha offered up this prayer for those who dwell in Old and New Karnath, in hopes that their fate might be changed:

Karnatha's Prayer (2054 A.R.)

With this deed, yet again all is gone. Oh Karnath weeps in this end, and I too for chaos never ordained of Destiny! Shaizan's doing has brought forth great loss, from which this land may never recover. What a reproach to Destiny and all of creation!

X'ieth and Kort, time depends on you just as the natural course of history! I pray you find a way to overcome the circumstances you shall face, and rise above this malady that unfortunately has become your destiny. May conscience be your guide, and may Destiny be with you both in a quest for the restoration of order!

<u>TABLE OF CONTENTS</u>

Chapter 1
Another Beginning

(The Meeting and Pact)

It was an age of bright prosperity, yet an age that would end in the darkest gloom. It was an age to remember always, yet an age forgotten too soon. It was an age in the books of history, yet an age destined to be no more. Just like all the others, the ages after and before.

Few have heard of Karnath, and even fewer have heard of Time No More. But only because Lucen wanted it to go unknown, how he stole the peoples' fates, so very long ago! This is his story, not the beginning or the end, just somewhere in between, but still what happened again and again.

It goes like this… The year was 2035 A.R., over two millennia *after the rebellion* against Maken in the legend of Old Karnath, where Karnatha advanced the Game upon the Children of Destiny. And so it was, in this time and in this age, Lucen came one night to Karnath's present, all the way from its distant future.

It happened with a flash of light above the grasslands, where a young man appeared from out of nowhere, several cubits off the ground. He fell immediately, and in moments, his sandaled feet settled on the frosted fields of Sergros in New Karnath, hitting the frozen surface with a deft thud.

Upon landing, Lucen lifted his eyes to the plains before him, and saw a stone cottage in the distance, being only a few spans away. He knew this was a special cottage throughout the whole human kingdom—special for whom it housed. *X'ieth Armstrong…*

Lucen thought the name with a smile as he stared at the knight's cottage through a screen of dense fog; the home stood against a dreary backdrop of gloom that blanketed the entire field. It was a box of gray limestone mortared together, capped by a dirty hay-thatched roof, where a white-bricked chimney puffed smoke into a somber, dark-clouded sky. The cottage's front featured a single window, alongside a wooden door shut tight to the elements. Behind the window's frosted pane, a candle's orange flame danced and flickered.

It's a perfect scene, Lucen thought, while tightening a hand about his long gnarled staff, which extended to his feet, touching the ground beside his sandals. Strong winds suddenly struck him in the face; they pulled at his brown sackcloth robe, and ruffled his head of wild blond hair even wilder. During the winds, Lucen squinted his blue eyes and maintained his smile, as he continued studying the cottage on the desolate field. *It's perfect, this world I've created*, he thought gleefully. *It's a world of gloom, bound for nothingness!*

In that moment, Lucen's mind filled with memories of what Karnath was before he touched it: a beautiful world having lands covered in mossy emerald mountains and lush green forests, divided by crystal rivers, and bridged by azure blue oceans and seas; a fantastic world full of living creatures human and not, from King Talus Darxar ruling Sergros in his castle of corbeled turrets and onyx-hatted keeps, to the elves of Kingdom Juniper and the dwarves of Kingdom Deardrum.

But in the next moment, Lucen pondered the forces corroding beautiful and fantastic Karnath. By his doing, the three prosperous kingdoms triangulated about Liath—Sergros, Juniper, and Deardrum—now faced grave adversity. Gloom overhung the human kingdom, war hit the elven kingdom, and the dwarven kingdom was stricken with carelessness to the plight of its allies. *It's happening all over again, just like before... Ha ha ha...*

Lucen could remember Karnath's hardships in a time no more, and the memories made him eager for his meeting now with his long-time opponent: Elucid. It was a meeting where a very necessary conversation would take place, concerning their relative involvements in the Game and, of course, guiding the Children. It would preface the beginning of Karnath's real hardships in a new age, a thing Lucen anticipated with much excitement.

In the interest of his appointment, Lucen stopped pondering what was to come, and started to wander a ways from the cottage through the gloom, anchoring his staff into the frozen ground with every other step. As he went, the winds tossed his wild hair and flapped his robe; he shouted at the empty grasslands like a lunatic.

"Show yourself! Show yourself, Elucid!""

Lucen turned around and walked back toward the cottage, against more fierce winds. With every other step he shouted again, "Show yourself!"

Lucen continued shouting and walking, until it happened. Amid pacing, he suddenly saw a cloaked figure materialize right before him—a blood-red metal demon, turned to the back with a snowy cloak draped over its shoulders. It was a massive hunk of armor, looming cubits above his head.

The visual stopped Lucen in his tracks. This was one of the so-called magical knights from Tekkneo. This was one particular knight, whom Lucen had seen many times before. *Elucid, my old nemesis*, he thought to himself, while flashing an even wider grin.

For a brief moment, Lucen was able to study the white cape hanging off the shoulders of the crimson knight, before the winds swept it into motion. The cloak bore an insignia of a decades-old war, featuring a black dragon and a red dragon, both head-to-tail and eating each other from the tail up.

When seeing the symbol, Lucen taunted Elucid.

"Was the recent *Isles Crusade* your final victory?"

Lucen played on the situation's irony: through the cloak, the Crusade's success was associated with Elucid. Yet, Lucen beat Elucid at the same game, age after age. In this, he saw Elucid as a walking failure more than anything else. In this, Lucen flashed another smile, this time even wider. *Elucid provides such a lackluster fight, and I'm so bored with winning. But maybe a new spiral brings new challenges for me! Maybe this age, Elucid stands a better chance of winning…*

Despite his taunt, Elucid remained silent.

And so, Lucen continued taunting, in hopes of instigating a comeback or at least, a neutral response.

"Yes, perhaps the Crusade was the closest you'll get to winning anything, a fruitless attempt to stop conflict between feuding clans in Karnath's West!"

At the last remark, Lucen watched Elucid slowly turn about to reveal the full-body armor of a crimson knight, wickedly curved and barbed, having large spikes jutting off its gauntlets.

Now staring face-to-face, Lucen met the glare coming through the two narrow eye slits in Elucid's helmet. In the same view, he saw the helmet's ornamented top—a long piece of metal angling backward that tapered off to a fine point. A sword's braided handle peeked up from behind Elucid's right shoulder, off a curved Hirishin blade slid into a scabbard, which hung down the knight's back.

"Well, it's good to meet again, even if you've become mute," Lucen said, with a crooked smile. "Perhaps that defeat alongside Naketo stays far from your memories yet, just like many others. But with Saora's release of ether from the Void, I'm sure you'll become a worthy opponent again, when enough understanding comes to you through premonitions. It's just a matter of time—a substance of which Karnath is running short."

All of a sudden, from beneath the knight's armor came a deep voice, booming and powerful.

"For these many months, you've followed me, and called out my name from a place of hiding. And now, you request this meeting. What do you seek from me?"

Lucen showed another crooked smile and paused a moment before answering. *Play a fool when fighting one…*

"You wish to guide one Child to a shard of sword, is this correct?"

"It's so," responded Elucid. "For without the aid of Servants, who else shall help this Child?"

"It's debatable if the Servants' help is really helpful," Lucen said, biting his lip. "Your guidance does not concern me though, for I shall guide the other Child… toward the shard of opposing hue."

In a boom Elucid spoke again. "I am already aware of you guiding the other Child, and I need no answers to what I question not. Lest our time be wasted, tell me this moment what you truly desire."

Lucen paused before speaking.

"An agreement."

"What sort of agreement?"

"A pact that neither one of us will interfere with each other's guidance. I will stay upon the Mainland and you upon the Isles, until both shards are acquired."

"A fair proposition," Elucid said, "but if this is to be agreed, I expect no meddling in my affairs from either you *or the Servants*. A clear disadvantage it is to be without their aid, and I need no further complication from their hindrance."

Lucen replied playfully, "Oh, I would neither consider the Servants helpful, nor lack of them unhelpful."

"Count them what you may!" Elucid cut him off, with words of thunder. "It's a simple question. Do I have your promise?!"

"Ma'althan commands the Servants," Lucen shot back, "and Ma'althan has a separate agenda than mine! His own motivations make him eager to ensure both Children arrive at the cliffs with the shards."

Lucen stopped smirking, and showed a sincere face.

"For this reason I cannot guarantee your guidance will be free from the Servants' involvement, for their actions are more influenced by Ma'althan than by anyone else. Inevitably the Servants will act on Ma'althan's behalf, so that the *Dark Prophecy* comes true."

Elucid grew quiet, as if contemplating the matter.

Meanwhile, Lucen felt the winds, like a whip of ice cracked against his skin. Yet he did not as much as cringe.

"Do you swear you have no influence over them?"

"Ma'althan commands the Servants; this much I tell you is true," shouted Lucen, over the shrill scream of the harsh gusts. "And remember, any Servant who interferes with the Game will be dealt with by Destiny. They can at most aid the Game, nothing more."

After a moment longer, Elucid agreed to the pact.

"Fine. These things are taken upon your honor."

Lucen stood there smiling, his blue eyes lighting up noticeably amidst the gloom.

"Excellent," he said. "I wish you the best of luck, as you shall need it! Your goal is not an easy one, now that *he* shoulders the misfortune of the fallen Sergrothian hero."

"The larger the challenge, the more surprising my success will be."

"Very well then; your confidence hints that this should prove interesting!" *I hope for new challenges*, Lucen thought. *I need them*, he prayed to the Void.

At that, Lucen turned from the crimson knight and, with his back to the mysterious figure, began walking away. But after only a few steps he stopped. From where he stood, Lucen called out to the crimson knight, while looking straight ahead.

"One more thing, Elucid…"

"What is it, Lucen?"

"See you at *Gallow Cliff.*"

When Lucen named the place where the Dark Prophecy might be fulfilled, his face showed a smile as chilling as the cold winds. And then, all of a sudden, the winds stopped blowing and an eerie calm presided over the icy field. Dead silence enveloped the youth and the crimson knight. Lucen stood there quietly, his robe inanimate and waiting for the next gust, just as he waited for his opponent's response.

Then suddenly from that uncanny still, Elucid responded, "Don't be so sure of that."

With those words the winds resumed, instantly pulling at Lucen's brown robe, his blond hair, and Elucid's white cloak. The winds blew harder and harder and howled louder and louder, as if to protest the Game, which for ages and ages, had only been to Karnath's woe.

As the winds carried out their bluster, Lucen laughed deeply and Elucid vanished into thin air, from whence the crimson knight came. But even after Elucid was gone, Lucen continued cackling, the sound growing louder, fuller, and more guttural by the moment to the point where it deafened out the noisy gusts.

"Ha ha ha, Ha ha ha ha, Ha ha ha ha ha!"

Lucen's hearty laughter literally shook the grasslands now smitten and subdued by the gloom, causing a deep rumble that traveled field after field, all the way to the stone cottage of X'ieth Armstrong, with its window faintly aglow.

"SEE YOU AT GALLOW CLIFF"

Chapter 2
A Knight's Misery

X'ieth Armstrong, a young knight of the human kingdom Sergros, stood cross-armed facing his fire pit. It was a space hollowed into the stone wall, now littered with ash and dull embers, and scarcely emitting any heat. A cauldron hung over the pit, with its handle caught on a toothed rack.

The sight provoked his concerns. *The fire is dying*, X'ieth thought with a sigh, *just as our fire…* As the last words came to mind, he glanced over one shoulder to his wife Millicent, who sat stoically in her chair of coarsened wood, at his rear and in front of the fire.

She wore a gray dress, and her hands rested atop her pregnant belly, working a threaded needle through some linen. Her features told of passive anger, from the frazzled blonde hair framing her face, to her icy blue eyes perched above a sharp nose and a pair of pink lips, straight as a line. She focused on the needle rather than her husband, not saying a word, even at his glance.

Her actions spoke of avoidance, and easily reminded X'ieth of their unresolved conflict that had spanned days, which concerned his commitments to the knighthood interfering with his commitments to their marriage. Such was a repetitive argument between them that repeatedly led into Millicent's unforgivable request: *Giving up your dream. Giving up… the knighthood.*

The mere idea rendered X'ieth mad at his wife and hurt over her unfairness. So desperately, he longed to break through her callousness and reason with the woman, so that Millicent would understand his wants and needs alongside her own. Yet, she continued toiling with her linen as if her husband were not even in the room.

To X'ieth, her aloofness now reflected her frequent emotional distance to what he wanted out of life. *She esteems her desires more important than yours, and that's not bound to change.* X'ieth sighed. He loved Millicent unconditionally, but found her attitude difficult to accept in the framework of what should be a loving marriage.

X'ieth redirected his attention off Millicent, and beyond her chair, where he saw the visible expanse of his stone cottage—a drab space between gray walls, topped by support beams and a straw-thatched roof. On his right and adjacent to Millicent's chair was a table against a windowed wall, upon which stood a flaming candle before the casement. Past the table and along the same windowed wall was the cottage's door, being secured by a latch; it had thick wooden beams bound together by strips of hand-wrought iron. On the wall

7

opposite to the window, the house's kitchen was situated in a nook, near the fire pit. The cottage's four walls stood on a bed of rock that stretched in all directions beneath the hay roof, making for the home's foundation.

A strong, whistling wind suddenly shook the cottage's door and window. X'ieth followed the noises, first with a brief glance to the door, and then with a stare out the window, where gray fog swirled behind its frosty pane. The sights and sounds served an instant reminder of what lied outdoors, and of what confined him and his wife indoors. It was a misplaced season named *the gloom* that unexpectedly came upon Sergros, an early winter that killed the kingdom's harvest and now kept many housebound. The gloom descended a month or so after the *Isles Conspiracy* ended, in what did seem a mysterious and unexplainable causation. *Since then, it's been cold days and colder nights*, he thought, *filled with nothing but dense fog and frigid winds...*

As X'ieth continued looking out the window, the situation easily played on his misery. He was trapped inside his home with a quarrelsome spouse, on what he hoped was a temporary leave from the knighthood.

A sorrowful thought entered his mind then, of what he was missing without his knightly duties. *You're far from adventure, man. You're far from the corbeled turrets of Castle Sergros, where you receive your assignments... You're spans and spans away from the giants riding fearsome dragons across Dragonaut Island, the oriental elves of the Hirishin Isles, the hidden gnomes of Mainlandish lore, and the trolls exiled to the arctic Northern Region, where you might dare go, just to glimpse the Lights of Altoroth dazzle its night sky! At home, you're so very far from it all...*

X'ieth knew that his leave from the knighthood was his fault, due to how poorly his last assignment had ended. The king's last words, said weeks ago, constantly reminded him of what had happened: *Garlew was injured when attacked, with all his Guardsmen displaced but you. Yet your "skills" weren't good enough to save the Sergrothian hero. You let him die! And since that happened, I now wonder if you're good enough for the knighthood! Why don't you go home and think about that yourself...*

The king's voice lingered between his ears, as if it were speaking to him now. And much like this, X'ieth's failure as a knight stayed with him, haunting him and troubling him. *Much like your failure as a husband...*

At the thought, his eyes went from the window and back to Millicent, who continued sitting quietly in her chair, still working her hands with the needle and thread. Indeed, the sight easily reminded X'ieth how he and Millicent had failed to resolve anything after weeks of being together. Differences seemed irreconcilable.

Theirs was a typical contention between husband and wife. X'ieth wanted this; Millicent wanted that. This and that were clearly not the same thing, hence the problem. That, for her, was a better home life, one where she actually saw her husband instead of practically being left alone for weeks during his long missions for the king, attended only by their young servant Galwin who helped Millicent around the cottage.

But Millicent wanted that and X'ieth wanted this. This, for him, was the knighthood. While X'ieth barely tolerated Talus the king—his mentally cruel taskmaster—he felt the knighthood let him use his talents in sword and magic for good.

X'ieth continued to ponder the situation, and his eyes drifted from Millicent and back to the gloom, as seen through the cottage's window. *As an adopted son of the king, you had a fine upbringing in Castle Sergros that included academy, magic lessons, and weapons training—an opportunity that few Sergrothians get. You were fortunate to receive this, and owe a debt to others less fortunate—a debt to use the talents obtained from the opportunity, for a greater good than merely your own.*

X'ieth shook his head, acknowledging the validity of the idea; it was just one reason for which he strongly fought Millicent over the knighthood, and it was hardly the only reason. *The knighthood is your purpose, without greater purpose of...* X'ieth stopped himself from thinking further, feeling the onset of sadness. *Don't.*

His thoughts returned him to the cottage, where suddenly, X'ieth felt a chill run over him, from foot-to-brow. In a quick movement, he spun on his heel to face the fire pit once more. The motion tousled his dirty-blond hair. He brushed it to the side with his fingers, so that his hazel eyes could see the lifeless embers sitting beneath the cauldron. In his periphery, the young knight saw a fire iron placed obviously at the right of the fire pit, a small distance from his broadsword that also leaned up against the wall.

X'ieth stared at the dull embers for a long while, as if expecting them to light back up. Gradually, his eyes moved off the embers and to the thin leather boots he wore. He saw them, past his white tunic and gray trousers, where the boot tips would rise as he curled his toes from the cold. *Destiny damn it*, he thought, *what's become of you, Galwin?* He impatiently looked to the door then, still awaiting his servant to return from a simple assignment of chopping wood.

"It'd be quicker to do it yourself," X'ieth muttered, shifting from side to side on his cold feet, as he looked back to the pit. He grabbed the fire iron on his right and poked the ashes, watching the embers turn a bright shade of red, afterward cooling to white. And just in that moment, the young knight heard a strange sound from outside, at first what did seem as laughter. "Ha ha ha!"

X'ieth felt a sudden tremor through his feet, and he dropped the fire iron to clutch the inside of the fire pit for support. The tool's clang against the floor got swallowed in an instant, developing rumble, which caused him to whip his head around. Just as he turned, he saw Millicent bolt up from her chair with surprise—her eyes wide and mouth open— apparently feeling the tremor too. As the rumble continued, he looked to the house's interior to see his entire cottage shaking, as if taking a life of its own!

Chapter 3
Quaked and Shaken

Hardly believing his eyes, X'ieth stood open-mouthed and wide-eyed at the center of his cottage, spellbound by the sight of its walls vibrating. From above his head, hay continued raining off the thatched roof and onto the rock floor. In his ears, he could hear a clatter on the nearby table, and then, a sudden smash from the kitchen.

X'ieth turned to the last sound he heard, seeing his kitchen come into view. It was a tiny space in the dark corner of his cottage, situated at the right of his fire pit. The kitchen contained a small wooden table tucked below a shelf lined with glass jars of various spices. A double-door cabinet was mounted to the wall, overhanging both the shelf and table. His eyes found two spice jars shattered on the floor, explaining the sound heard moments ago. X'ieth looked back to the shelf, where the other spice jars rattled closer to its edge, soon to join the ranks of the fallen.

Before X'ieth could turn back to Millicent, his peripheral vision picked up the blur of his wife; she was already running into the kitchen. As if frozen in place, X'ieth stood idly and just watched Millicent reach up to save her clove, cumin, and other inexpensive seasonings, before more jars could fall and break.

Suddenly, X'ieth beheld the cupboard doors above Millicent fly open, while she still gathered her jars! The open cabinet revealed a stack of metal pots and kitchen implements that tumbled over and crashed discordantly around Millicent. She dropped the spice jars in order to shield her face with both arms; the jars fell and shattered in one moment, and the pots clanged to the floor in the next. After a few seconds Millicent lowered her arms, but did so apparently too soon, for a small mallet dropped out of the cupboard and smacked her right between the eyes!

X'ieth watched Millicent turn, her hands balled into fists and a red mark upon her forehead. She wore the crossest face ever, featuring a creased brow, indignant eyes, and a severe frown. She shouted angrily at her unoccupied husband.

"Do *something*, why don't you!"

Without a clear sense of what to do, X'ieth spun about just in time to see the table near the casement, at the wall to the left of his fire pit. There, a candle trekked toward the table's one end in its dish, clattering as it went.

The young knight hurried over and threw his arms around the candle dish, moving his arms inward to capture it. He guided the candle to the center of the vibrating table, where his hands released the dish. But the moment he did, it started moving again, back toward the table's edge!

X'ieth heard a sudden and boisterous thud against the door, which directed his attention there. He saw the wood beams literally shake within their iron bindings, as a strong wind repeatedly hit the house's flanks.

BOOM! BOOM! BOOM!

The winds struck again and again, a sounding percussion that soon struck fear into Millicent.

"What goes on?!" she cried.

"Ha ha ha, Ha ha ha!" came the same deep sound from outside, falling upon X'ieth's ears. *Destiny save us*, he prayed. *Don't know what be upon us!*

X'ieth heard the candle dish clatter until it fell off the table and clanged against the rock floor; he paid it no heed. Instead, he fixated on the door as it kept pounding and pounding with the continued winds.

BOOM! BOOM! BOOM!

The gusts blew relentlessly, and both husband and wife just watched on, not knowing what to do, or where to go. Then quite surprisingly, with another wind the door suddenly burst open, when its latch came undone!

X'ieth immediately felt cold air from outside, and in a very surreal way, the entire cottage instantly became still—the vibrating walls and everything inside, now stopped—the only motion being the cottage's door, swinging inward.

Without hesitating, X'ieth went to the wall beyond the fire pit, and grabbed his sword by its sheath. It felt heavy and awkward in his hands from lack of recent use, but even so, he drew the weapon quickly. As the steel left its casing, a gleaming blade greeted his eyes, imparting the comforts of fellowship with close friends.

He let the scabbard fall to the floor and held his sword in both hands. X'ieth turned about, eyeing his door that was now open to the outside and the gloom. From a gaping hole, fog literally wafted into his cottage and caused Millicent to panic.

"Destiny save us!" she shrieked in horror. "The gloom is a Darkness upon us, from which the Dark Prophecy is coming true! I've feared this since the gloom first descended!"

"Let us be calm," X'ieth said, lifting one hand from his sword and into the air, as if to ease her. "Let us be calm, and put off our superstitions!"

X'ieth dismissed his wife's worries and stepped courageously toward the door. He swallowed hard and, once again, tightened both hands around his sword. As his body lurched forward, his mind flooded with questions, all questions without an answer, and none even explaining what had happened. Even still, the young knight stepped closer and closer to the threshold, and in so doing, came face-to-face with the gloom.

"Who goes there?" he asked, in a firm voice.

There was no response.

X'ieth came right up to the threshold, feeling the chilly winds knife him between the ribs as they barged into the cottage. When he reached the door, he forced it shut using his body, fighting yet another gust as it clawed through the opening, trying to get in.

"Fierce winds me suppose," X'ieth muttered while holding the door shut, knowing whatever caused the quake was anything but ordinary, and anything but the winds. As his hands went for the latch, the door suddenly pushed toward him, this time with no wind at all!

X'ieth caught the door by its edge, just as two hands wrapped in cloth came through, clutching the wood.

"Shut it, shut it! An intruder lies in wait!" yelled Millicent, clearly worried for their safety.

"It is I!" came a voice from behind the door, muffled and difficult to make out. X'ieth recognized the sound and opened the door, seeing there his white-skinned servant Galwin, in an oversized black coat and thin gray pants, the legs tucked into leather boots covered in frost.

"Need warm," shivered Galwin, as X'ieth pulled the servant into the cottage with one hand, his other hand still holding the blade. The young knight closed the door, secured the latch, and then turned about.

"What were you thinking, man?!" X'ieth angrily scolded Galwin, who appeared too cold to defend himself. "You almost froze to death out there!"

He paused and arched his eyebrows, before asking heatedly, "And what of the wood you were supposed to cut? For soon we shall freeze in here!"

"I'm… sorry."

When Galwin just continued shivering with barely an audible response, X'ieth sighed. He guided the servant over to the fire pit, and while there, leaned his sword against the same wall. Galwin sat down without an invitation, as if eager to soak in any heat from the embers.

After thawing for some time, Galwin began to talk while looking into fire pit. "When at the logs I reached for the axe to chop one, but before I touched it, I saw him…"

X'ieth listened as the words trailed off, and his mind was left to wonder. *Saw… who?*

After a few more moments of silence, the young knight pressed his servant.

"Well, out with it now! Whom did you see?!"

"A robed traveler… It was a man, or maybe a boy," Galwin said, correcting himself. "He appeared in danger, confronted by a *metal demon*, red like blood! So I went to help him, but…"

"But what?" asked X'ieth in a sharp tone, doubting Galwin's story by the word, but still wanting an explanation.

"I got lost in the fog," Galwin replied.

X'ieth watched Galwin look back to him before continuing. It was in that moment the young knight sensed Millicent walk nigh, stopping a few cubits off his right shoulder.

"The fog became so dense!" he exclaimed, "I could barely see my own hand before me! I now question if anyone was there at all; the gloom perhaps played tricks on my mind!"

Surely it did... thought X'ieth, as he grew increasingly skeptical of the servant's account. *No man thinks clearly, especially when he's near frostbitten.*

Galwin stopped talking and looked down, as if becoming suddenly aware of the problem presented by no firewood. Raising his eyes once more, the servant said, "I'm so sorry. I should've done as told."

"Sorry won't help us now," retorted X'ieth with another long sigh. He glanced at the door, and then, back to Galwin. "Is the axe still in its place?"

The servant nodded, shamefacedly.

X'ieth turned to Millicent and announced, "If he didn't cut the wood, then I must."

"You will not," Millicent replied, rolling her eyes and throwing up her hands, like the mere idea was the most foolish thing in the history of folly. "The last thing I need is you disappearing on the verge of nightfall! The warmth that remains here should last through the evening. In the morning, you can cut your wood."

Listening with half an ear, the young knight put on the oversized coat Galwin wore, and it fit perfectly. *Wait until morning and we'll all freeze to death,* he thought. *That seems a bit more dimwitted than going off to cut wood...*

"Did you hear me?" she asked pointedly.

"What needs to be done must be done when required. Not tomorrow, or the day after, but now. I..."

Millicent interposed. "You just always do what you wish, don't you? This is no different than your constant missions for our king. You know no limits, X'ieth!"

There it is, what she's really mad about—you being gone so long in recent months with your knightly duties. Can't do much about that... Without a middle ground to resolve this longstanding problem, the young knight ignored his wife, failing to realize that one way or another, she would be heard. He mindlessly wrapped strips of cloth about his fingers and hands, so to protect them from the cold. *Poor man's gloves...*

"Are you listening to me?!" Millicent asked. "I'm telling you, I want you to stay here with us!"

Despite her requests, X'ieth went to the door and laid his hand on the latch, about to undo it, unknowingly making her point of doing what he wished.

He glanced back at her, seeing worry written across her face, prompting him to assure her of his return before leaving.

"I will come back."

X'ieth went for the door, and it was then that she pled once more in a broken, crying voice.

"Don't go!"

With his hand still on the latch, X'ieth turned back, seeing tears stream down Millicent's face as she continued speaking.

"You always leave me alone, and I'm tired of it!"

The young knight took his hand off the latch and completely turned about, to face his wife.

"There's honor in speaking forthrightly from the heart, not in projecting our feelings onto unrelated matters. So let us speak forthrightly about this, and not of me leaving to chop wood. The two are not the same."

"Fine," Millicent said, crossing her arms beneath her breasts, wearing a look like she doubted his professed willingness to talk. Dried tears lingered upon her cheeks.

"When I'm gone on quests, not a moment passes where you're far from my mind, my love." X'ieth spoke in sincerity. "Don't you know that it's not my pleasure to be away for such lengths? This is my duty as a knight of the Sergrothian Crimson Guard, toward the greater cause of protecting innocent blood in Sergros!"

Millicent said softly, "That's fine and well, but what of your duty to me, your wife? You've been away for months, where I only see you a few days here and there in between the king's assignments. It's unreasonable for him to ask this of you, and unbearable for me to endure! Yet, every time I ask you not to go, you side with your king. And now, you side with your need to do as you will. Must I always lose this battle?"

X'ieth stood with his back to the door, still facing his wife. The cottage's shadows draped them, and his hazel eyes met her blue eyes under the dim light.

"You're not always losing that battle," X'ieth said slowly, as his mind searched for an example of the contrary. "I'm constantly doing what you want, even when it's not what I want."

"How so," Millicent asked, "when all you do is serve as a knight?!"

"The oracle," X'ieth replied, "I asked the king for an oracle to attend our child's birth." The words rolled off the young knight's lips, and they reminded him of the tradition in Karnath of oracles naming children at birth according to their foretold purpose in life. It likewise reminded him of the problem throughout the land: most oracles went blind three years ago in the *Great Occlusion*.

Millicent's voice pierced his thoughts.

"That's for us, not me."

"No, that's for you," X'ieth countered. "Your parents are oracles, so you value the tradition, not me. I'm fine with what most people do in Karnath… naming the child ourselves."

"That's blasphemy to Karnatha!" Millicent snapped.

"Is it?" X'ieth asked. "I see my future just fine, and could do a better job of naming our child than any oracle now, likely better than even your parents."

"How dare you?!"

X'ieth paused, realizing then that he crossed a line by mentioning her parents, despite them indeed being blinded oracles.

"I'm sorry for saying that," he spoke softly, putting up his hand to ward off a fight. In silence Millicent stared at him, her temper somewhat defused. The young knight continued, "But it's true that many Karnathans now see more of their own future than the oracles can."

Those words ushered the truth into his mind. When the oracles went blind three years ago, people across Karnath started having visions about their future, including himself. For at about that time, his eyes developed a window into his near future, visions of the upcoming days that would come arbitrarily, with very high accuracy too. *Except on that last quest,* his inner voice chided him then, stirring up thoughts of the woman in white. *If you foresaw Garlew's death and instead saved the Sergrothian hero, you'd still be riding the countryside as a noble knight, not doing chores at home.*

Millicent shook her head. "Here we go again. More hogwash about how you're a seeing oracle." She looked to the side then, and muttered beneath her breath. "Guess your foresight is why the fire's out and you have no wood."

X'ieth cleared his throat, and quickly brought the discussion back on point. "Ahem. Whether you think I can see into the future or not, the oracle is for you, not me. Seeing oracles are short in supply, so I had to beg Talus for one, against my will! I hate asking the king for anything."

The mere recollection of asking Talus stung him, for as far as the young knight was concerned, requesting favors from the king only led to them inevitably being held over his head in the courts of Sergros, like he owed Talus something really big in return. *And that something rarely gets repaid… regardless of how hard you work!*

"And you didn't get an oracle, did you? So even if you did ask Talus for me, it's a moot point."

"I'm arguing that I do things just for you, at times against my will. Not saying they always go as we want."

X'ieth glanced to the window then, seeing the darkness outside, and growing mindful of the time. *Is such a long talk about our marital problems really required to just chop wood?!* He turned back to the door and put his gloved hand on the latch, about to undo it.

"You never do what I want!" Millicent insisted then, circling back to her initial claim.

Again, X'ieth removed his hand from the latch, turned from the door, and faced Millicent. And a moment later, he proceeded to reason with his wife from the mind and not from the heart, a common mistake of many males of the human race.

"I must chop the wood, else we shall surely go cold in the night. Who could survive this gloom without light and warmth? None, I say! For the cold winds grow colder, and the dark nights grow darker. So let me go, and do what's required for our lives. I shall return."

"You lie," she said. "You lie to me betimes! You tell me every time, how this'll be the last assignment for a while, and then there's another. I'm hurt that you give your king a higher place than me. Why am I *always* second?"

X'ieth sighed in exasperation. "Will you regard me giving you first place, if I don't chop the wood until morning? Would that be enough?"

"I'd regard you giving me first place by fixing the real problem. *Leave the knighthood.*"

The words smacked X'ieth defiantly in the face. As a land of freedom and opportunity, Sergros gave its citizens a choice regarding many things, including one's vocation. But Millicent clearly sought to take that choice from him by requesting his resignation.

"The knighthood is important to me," he answered defensively.

"As am I, no? So give it up." Her words were cold, as if she were uncaring of their effects, adverse or not.

X'ieth swallowed hard, as a lump rose to the top of his throat. His wife's repeated demands echoed his mind, sounding again and again. *Give it up. Give it up!* This was not the first time she had asked, nor would it be the last.

The request touched on very sensitive subjects to X'ieth—his identity, and what was left of his purpose in life. *She's selfish enough to ask you to sacrifice your noble career as a Guardsman, as some sort of test that you love her enough?!* It struck him as uncaring, disrespectful of his dreams, and worst yet, downright ugly behavior from someone alleging to love him—someone who should care about his personal happiness.

"You have your dream of a family," X'ieth said, his voice somewhat hardened. His eyes trailed to her belly, and then back up to her face. "Shouldn't I be afforded a dream too? Just one?!"

At that statement, pain bubbled up from the recesses of his heart, for immediately into his mind pranced visions of his biggest dream yet to be lived: being Karnath's prophesized hero—Kayareth, the Child of Light. His breath grew short as he imagined a white knight riding a white horse with shining barding—across white sands, beneath whiter cliffs!

X'ieth forced himself out of his frequent daydream of *Gallow Cliff*, and back into the dismal setting of his stone cottage, beside a demanding and unfair wife. Millicent stood glaring, her hands on her hips.

"Not when that dream gets in the way of you being a man, and honoring your commitments to this marriage."

"Doing good for others is a calling that Destiny has given me and I fulfill that calling right now, through serving as a knight in the Crimson Guard!"

"Just as you could do good for me by leaving the knighthood," Millicent shot back.

Lost for words, X'ieth stammered.

"I…I can't give it up. This is my dream."

"You and your dreams," Millicent responded, judgment clear in her sharp tone. "For years I've had to hear you go on about your dream of becoming the Child of Light, and now this. It's one pursuit after another, only to the ruin of this marriage. You just keep dreaming things unmeant to be!"

"That's not true," X'ieth replied, his chest tightening and his heart racing. "My dreams are sacred, a gift of divine purpose from Destiny herself!" Millicent's words poked his deep attachment to the knighthood, there as merely a coping mechanism for not getting his ultimate dream of being Karnath's hero. Serving in the Guard was essentially some purpose in life, in the absence of greater purpose.

"Then if your dreams are meant to be, why do they never happen, like being the Child of Light?! And if your dreams are meant to be, why is a dream like the knighthood something that your family can hardly endure?!" Millicent pressed him more and more in what was becoming a fierce inquisition.

"It's like I'm living with a child who's raptured in grand fancies of his future while forsaking their adult responsibilities to a family! Isn't being a husband or a father some part of your dream?!" Millicent crossed her arms beneath her breasts again, as she stared at her quiet husband, who now, had a storm raging inside.

X'ieth's blood boiled hotter and hotter; he simply could not believe how inappropriate his wife acted, and how disrespectful her words were to his purpose in life, his calling ordained by Destiny. Into his mind popped his initial thought: *She gets her dream of a family, yet you're not entitled to a single dream?!* The unfairness around that point easily made him mad.

Millicent started attacking again.

"Prove that you love me more than your knighthood by giving it up! Throw away silly dreams of being some important hero, and be an important figure in this house, like you should!"

"No!" X'ieth roared like a lion, turning about and slamming his gloved knuckles into the doorpost. The wood splintered with a loud crack. He looked back to Millicent, who shut up immediately, now having an open mouth and her chin slightly atremble, with a look of mixed shock and horror stricken upon her face, as if she happened upon a monster in the cottage. *She's the real monster…*

"I won't give up a dream—not now, not ever!" X'ieth yelled, his face stretched by righteous indignation. "The knighthood is my purpose and my destiny, a higher calling than just chopping wood or other such chores!" He paused before continuing. "During my time in this life, I'll do good for others with my talents, for that's my good destiny! You should do the same, using your talents here to give me a good home life, free of your contention and your unfairness!"

Taking a breath, X'ieth went on, gesturing with animate hands and showing wide eyes.

"Unbelievable that you would ask me to leave the knighthood, with no thought of us needing coin to live! I may not like Talus but he does give me a job, and therefore, he does more for us than levy taxes!"

The words faded as the situation became a replay of what happened so many times before during this same exact argument, a vicious cycle that highlighted shortcomings in both a husband and a wife—shortcomings that prevented their mutual understanding, making compromises, and ultimately having peace.

X'ieth watched Millicent shake her head back and forth, dried tears upon her cheeks. In a low voice, one evidencing defeat and despair, she said, "This is what I speak of. Being at home does not make you want to remain in this place. You're already thinking of work, even when at rest. You're obsessed with the life of a knight." She paused. "Such will do for a man of noble heart without commitments, but not for a married man."

When Galwin suddenly stirred in the corner, X'ieth became aware that he and Millicent just aired dirty laundry in front of their servant! *Destiny damn it!* With that realization, the young knight felt his face become many shades redder, his body seeming hot all over. He looked to his servant in rage, and then to Millicent.

"Go and speak poor things of me in front of others!" X'ieth shouted, carrying on at the top of his lungs. "Perhaps they shall think more of *you* and less of *me*, when all has been said!" With those words, X'ieth gestured to Millicent and then back to himself, flinging animate hands. His eyes grew wide and veins popped noticeably from his neck, as the anger within him poured out. Galwin showed a fearful face, and shrunk back into the corner.

After a long pause and the development of utter silence, X'ieth approached his wife. He lowered his voice and met her eyes. "The last thing you truly wish to hear is your husband's heart, respecting my words in private!"

With that, he turned from her to fiddle noisily with the latch and open the door, closing it behind him, its slam much louder than his last word.

Chapter 4
Chopping More than Wood

X'ieth lingered outside his cottage, facing its door. From inside, he could hear his wife start crying again, and her grief was unpleasant for him to endure. Despite his argument with Millicent, X'ieth still had a heart for the woman.

Your words need not always be pleasant, for not all things in life are pleasant... With the thought, X'ieth realized that indeed, not all things in life were pleasant, as his chore in the bitter cold would leave much to be desired. Merely thinking about it made him dismissive of her sobbing, and at that, he turned from the door to focus on the matter at hand: chopping wood.

From all directions the fog rolled over X'ieth, enveloping him in an icy shroud of gray mist. He could hardly see the ground before him, with only a few cubits being visible. The sight stirred up recollections of what Galwin had claimed: *I could barely see my own hand before me!* X'ieth nodded. *No exaggeration there...*

He stood in place, hesitating to take his first step. During that time, chilly winds ravaged X'ieth with fingers of ice, pulling at his clothes and stinging both his nose and ears. He shivered at their touch, feeling so cold, even with his coat and gloves.

The weather quickly put his top priority to mind. *Get this done fast, and get back inside!* With that idea, X'ieth took his first step into the gloom against another strong wind. As he went, he pulled his coat tight around his body, flipped up its collar over his neck, and squinted his eyes amid the relentless bluster.

X'ieth walked hastily into a cloud of fog, going in the direction of his shed. Due to his difficulties seeing with the thick gloom, he relied heavily on an orientation from previous trips outside. *Hope it's right!*

The stinging sensations afflicting his nose and ears soon became numbing; X'ieth could hardly feel his face. The situation reiterated his top priority: *Get this done, and get back inside!* He moved even faster.

Staying in the same direction, X'ieth pressed on against the fierce winds. Before long, he saw the outline of a stump in the distance, from which an axe jutted for hewing wood. He kept walking, until the outline of the shed appeared several cubits behind the stump, with a rack of logs stretched along its closest side. Beyond the shed, other structures peeked at him through the fog: his stable and his water well.

X'ieth walked up to the rack against the shed, knowing what he needed to do: take a few logs over to the stump, split them with the axe, and then carry them back to the cottage.

He scanned the rack for logs to be cut, quickly counting them in the process: there were now less than twenty. It seemed half the amount he had the week prior, and the sight easily dismayed him. *Perhaps it'll be enough for a week more, maybe not even that!*

X'ieth realized then that he would have to find a way for the logs to last longer. *Perhaps you could tend the fire more closely... Or maybe, you could do more to keep the cottage door closed... You'll have to do something.*

X'ieth sighed. Such moderation was not always required in the wealthy kingdom of Sergros. Until recently, the Sergrothians would carelessly use what they wanted without a thought more. But now, everyone would have to be more careful, including himself.

Going from careless to careful is never easy, X'ieth thought, eyeing the rack again. *And it won't be easy for the kingdom*, he considered, estimating that his family's predicament was one shared by many other families throughout the Sergrothian provinces, given the gloom.

Without spending more time thinking, he grabbed a few logs and walked over to the stump, releasing them there. They tumbled to the ground into a scattered pile, adjacent to the stump. He looked at the axe, laid his hand to its handle, and using one arm, tugged it out.

X'ieth proceeded to chop wood. One by one, he took his logs, put them on the stump, and halved them down the center with a quick swing of his axe. And swing after swing, the frozen wood split easily with his sharpened tool, allowing him to carry on effectively and mindlessly at the stump, where soon, he was buried in his thoughts.

X'ieth started thinking to himself about the argument he had with his wife. *Care not that you've married a man who does good; a responsible person who feels that for having had great opportunity, he owes a debt to others and ought to repay it?!* The conversation went through his mind, as his task soon became one of chopping more than wood—he chopped away anger and frustration.

"Duty to you as my wife," X'ieth muttered beneath his breath, as another log split with a sharp crack, followed by dull thuds when both halves hit the ground. "That duty is not to live without purpose! A marriage shouldn't deprive anyone of their dreams!" he screamed, thinking then about her demands that he give up his knighthood. After completing the swing of his axe, he placed another log on the stump, but took a step back before swinging again. Huffing and puffing, he let the axe drop to his side, as he looked from the stump to the ground, now being filled with split logs. Beads of perspiration dotted his face, and the frigid winds beat his body. And just as they did, he felt somewhat beaten in his fight for purpose against life's many opposing forces. One's battle for *good destiny*—his or her divine purpose—was the most heated battle in which a man or woman could find themselves, and his battle was no different.

As X'ieth continued standing there and breathing hard, the frigid winds continued beating him, and in that, he felt even more beaten, wondering how long he would be able to fend off Millicent's demands of his resignation, how long he would be able to tolerate Talus, who in his opinion had become a cruel employer. He also wondered how long he could justify to himself why Destiny had not granted his biggest dream yet—his lifelong dream of becoming Kayareth. X'ieth felt pulled apart at his seams.

This was *Fate's Fray*, an unraveling of what one was meant to be, and its looming possibility now became a force that weighed heavily upon him, as if the gravity of Karnath suddenly became many times stronger in a single instant. It literally pulled him to his knees, and X'ieth found himself kneeling beside the stump, amid the halved logs.

He propped the axe head against the frozen ground and leaned into its handle, folding his hands overtop and setting his chin. From this position upon both knees, X'ieth peered up through the gloom and into the gray sky, in want of sustainable fulfillment. He wanted a good family life. He wanted a fulfilling career. He wanted divine purpose. He wanted it all, without everything in his life falling apart.

Fate's Fray was a concept founded in his Karnathan religion, that poor choices and trying circumstances often led people to lesser destiny than was divinely intended by Karnatha—the manifestation of Destiny in spirit. X'ieth felt strongly that Millicent and Talus would become part of his Fate's Fray if he did not intervene.

With that in mind, X'ieth stood up, tightened his gloved hands around the axe handle, and turned to the log seated upon the stump. In that moment, he saw Millicent's unfairness and Talus' cruelty there, objectifying them both as the log itself. The sight summoned up a deep rage within him, from which he derived the will to wield the axe. And so, he raised the tool over the log, preparing to lower it and split the wood, to release his negative feelings within, over his wife and over his king.

Having the axe held above his head, he shut his eyes, and then dropped it quickly, intending to look after his swing with the log halved and his fury gone. But instead, the young knight looked mid-swing and saw not a log there, rather a young man peering up at him from the stump!

As the axe head fell, his heart seized and X'ieth felt a terrible fear grip him by the throat. But suddenly then, the young man on the stump disappeared, before the axe could make contact! And right before his eyes, the log reappeared where it was, splitting atwain when the axe hit.

Seeing that he had done no one any harm but still not quite believing it, X'ieth remained on edge over nearly chopping someone's face with his axe. The whole situation unfolded in such a bizarre way that he could barely grasp it, and it was clear to him that something was amiss.

Then, from behind X'ieth, came a voice that laughed hysterically.

"Ha ha ha, Ha ha ha!"

X'ieth turned and was surprised to see his good friend Lucen whom he had met on the Mainland some months ago, during the Guard's hunt for Pyrus. Lucen was a young man wearing simple traveler's robe and carrying a gnarled staff, who apparently had wisdom well beyond his age and the forecasts of a seeing oracle.

The sight of his acquaintance triggered instant memories. Like yesterday, X'ieth recalled how Lucen saved him from Kort Al'starz—murderer of the Sergrothian hero Garlew Il'therin, and now, ex-knight of the Crimson Guard. Deep down, X'ieth was extremely thankful that Lucen spared him from Kort at the dusk of the Isles Conspiracy. And for that, the young knight held both trust and respect for Lucen. *You owe him your life.*

"That wasn't at all funny!" X'ieth said to Lucen, who continued a raucous laughter.

Lucen chuckled, "You should have seen yourself! The expression on your face was priceless."

X'ieth shook his head and smirked, realizing then that Lucen's trick lightened the mood.

"What brings you to gloomy Sergros?" he asked.

"I bear news, to your joy though perhaps to Millicent's disdain."

The young knight raised a single eyebrow. "Oh?"

Lucen smiled back. "Your grueling taskmaster of a king has another favor, meaning I'll not be your only unexpected visitor this day."

X'ieth thought to himself for a moment. *Favor for Talus, like an assignment? The king and his favors you care not for, but a mission with cause you do. You'd be happy to ride again in the Crimson Guard!*

"Tell me more," X'ieth said, seeing a better use of his time in the knighthood than wasting his talents at home with mundane chores and endless strife.

Lucen kept his smile. "Such would ruin the surprise! I wouldn't spoil it for anyone, let alone you."

X'ieth shook his head at Lucen's antics, familiar with this sort of playful behavior.

"How will I know then?" asked the young knight, with a straight face.

"Like I said, you'll have more visitors, and they are part of your journey to know," Lucen replied, his eyes trailing off to the distance, toward the cottage.

X'ieth suddenly heard the sound of galloping afar, and at that, he noted Lucen's smile widen. No sooner than the youth appeared, did he step backward into the gloom, to vanish completely.

In the dense fog, the young knight's ears sensed more than his eyes, and from the galloping he could only tell that an ensemble of horses arrived at his doorstep. X'ieth looked to the cottage, and saw silhouettes of horse riders through the gloom. As the riders alighted their steeds, the unmistakable clangs from armor raked his ears, along with talk amongst them.

"Is this the place?" one rider asked.

"Aye, me thinks so," said another.

Suddenly the young knight's heart filled with worry for his wife. Despite being mad at her, the thought of harm befalling the woman he could not bear. And so, given the situation's uncertainty, X'ieth ran through the fog to his stone cottage, with his axe in hand and a willingness to use it on more than wood, if needed.

When X'ieth reached his house, he barely made out the figures in the fog. It was the Fifth Order of the Guard, a pack of seven knights wearing silver armor having helmets adorned with five alternating plumes, crimson then white. And upon their backs, scarlet cloaks hung down, falling below the knees.

One visitor knight pounded his cottage door.

BAM! BAM! BAM!

"Open up, by order of the king!"

But Millicent did not answer, possibly for fear of whom was outside.

From the gloom, X'ieth called out to the group.

"Who comes to my house, and for what reason?"

He watched as the visitor knight at his door turned with strained eyes, no doubt struggling to make him out through the haze.

"Be you X'ieth Armstrong, knight of the Sixth Order of the Crimson Guard?"

X'ieth replied, "Verily."

"You are summoned to the throne room of Talus Darxar, King of Sergros. Gather your things, we must leave at once." Suddenly X'ieth saw the cottage door open and out stepped Millicent, now as brave as could be!

"*What* did you say?" she asked pointedly.

"Who's this?" said the visitor knight, facing X'ieth.

The woman replied before her husband could.

"*The wife*, that's who. Now what's this all about?"

Despite her engagement, the visitor knight paid her no heed, and continued to address X'ieth. "The summons is for you and you alone." He turned to the angry wife and muttered, "We answer no others."

X'ieth held his axe in hand and studied the on-looking visitor knight. He glanced at Millicent, and the fire in her eyes aligned his questions with her own.

"Then I'll ask. What's this all about?"

"That's no question for me," stated the visitor knight. "In your session with King Darxar, you shall find answers to many questions, and perhaps you will learn more than you care to know."

X'ieth went to Millicent, who stood outside the cottage's door. He stopped when less than a footstep away and set his eyes upon her, noting her apparent look of disapproval; the woman's eyes said exactly what they did before he left to chop wood. *Don't go.*

Unexpectedly, X'ieth felt the warm touch of her fingers on his masculine square face, running over his stubbly beard and up through his dirty-blond hair. Her touch melted him, even in the gloom's bitter cold.

Millicent sighed in frustration.

"You're doing this again, and it's not fair to me."

X'ieth replied slowly. "This is my chance to do great good in Sergros. Maybe one day you'll realize that not serving is unfair to me."

The comment quieted Millicent, as if she thought about his words. She stood there, still with her hands on her husband's face. After a pause, she began speaking.

"Maybe one day, serving will mean that we can no longer be," Millicent said in sorrowed tone. "I fear your dreams are larger than our marriage."

Her statement iced X'ieth. All of him that had melted in the wintery gloom, once again became cold and calloused. Negative thoughts barged into his mind, like an uncomely troll from the Northern Region. *She offers more trouble than support! As your wife, shouldn't she support anything, rather than opposing everything?!*

X'ieth brushed away his wife's hands, no longer wanting her touch. He scowled and sighed.

"Words chosen well for a man obligated to serve, and not knowing what lies in store," X'ieth said. "At the end of all we do and say, a husband and wife should support each other in wholesome pursuits that are willfully undertaken. Such is this, though once again, you're unsupportive." His words were crisp, and to him they seemed justly spoken.

He looked into Millicent's eyes, and looked more, until the point where he saw past his anger to the woman he loved. X'ieth began melting again in the gloom.

All in one motion, he gave Millicent a firm embrace and then, leaned forward to kiss her on the lips. She began crying in his arms, and he felt her warm tears stain his tunic, serving a reminder that his fulfillment was bought with another's pain. During the embrace, the young knight sensed her large belly bump into his midsection, a testament of her pregnancy.

She said beneath her breath, "Though I'm unhappy in this, I still love you. Please come back to me."

"I will," X'ieth said, nodding his head.

The young knight backed up one step from Millicent, looking at her before he left. In that moment, her gaze of soft eyes and tear-stained cheeks etched itself into his mind. As X'ieth turned away, that last look was enough to give him a deep sense of what he was leaving behind, but it was not enough for him to see what he had become: a man who rarely honored his words; a man who was prone to anger.

X'ieth took his first step away from Millicent but suddenly stopped dead in his tracks, as a single question entered his mind. *Why didn't you foresee this summons with the king, since you can see into your future?*

The young knight suddenly felt an uncertainty unfelt for weeks, one imparted to him from a woman in white who spoke of things unforeseen on his last quest, things that went contrary to his visions of the future but happened anyway. *When you met her on your mission to find Pyrus, it was the first time your foresight failed you. And now, it's happening again!*

His mind spun with visions that likewise ran contrary to an unexpected summons from the king. In flashes, he saw what he had seen for weeks: staying at home with Millicent, working around the cottage with Galwin, and being present for the birth of his child. As the parade of images ended, a vice seemed to clamp around his chest, and he suddenly found it difficult to breathe.

Immobilized from taking another step, X'ieth looked to the knights before him. Despite knowing what he had to do, he was worried over what this unexpected summons could mean, and those worries wrestled with his eagerness to be back in service to Sergros. But in that moment, his inner voice urged him to look beyond his doubts and second thoughts. *Just go… Go.*

With that in mind, X'ieth pulled together his composure and started walking to the visitor knights. In a matter of moments, he settled before them and looked to their leader.

With a sparkle in his eye and a smile upon his lips, X'ieth said, "Take me to the king."

"UNEXPECTED VISITORS"

Chapter 5
The Gloom of Sergros

Talus Arrinius Darxar was the King of Sergros, the human kingdom in New Karnath. He was the middle-aged successor of Elix Darxar and a devout Karnathan exactly like his father, being very involved in the Church.

On one particular evening in Sergros, Talus slouched in his throne, letting his long legs stick out and his kingly cape of royal red bunch behind him. His one hand trailed off the throne's armrest to a nearby side table, to an iron goblet for wine, from which he drank heavily throughout each day.

His short, black hair was matted and his oblong face showed circles beneath brown eyes, indicating that the king's sleep was either short-lived or nonexistent in recent days. The gloom facing Sergros made him fret, and it was the subject of many discussions in his halls, such as one discussion ongoing right now.

Amid this painfully long talk, Talus glanced to the back wall, past the untrustworthy politician before him, literally as a diversion from reality. In that moment, he mulled over certain truths. *Being king entails many privileges that others don't have.* The thought grazed his mind, and he latched onto a neighboring idea. *Being king let's one communicate what one feels, good or bad.* Together, these contemplations easily inspired him to tell his High Chancellor what he really thought.

"I loathe you!" the king suddenly shouted at the old man before him, breaking the politician's droning voice mid-sentence. "Your every intention is to steal my throne through Sergrothian politics, and I won't have it!"

Talus suddenly stood up from the throne, his features contorted in anger, and in the same motion he emptied his goblet upon the old man's face! Indignation welled inside him as he screamed aloud, "Dealing with your conniving ways corrodes my soul! I am less of a king because of politics!"

"Did you hear what I said, my king?"

Talus' daydream popped as the old man standing before him spoke from the real world. The king looked about, and found himself back in the throne room. *How unfortunate for me…*

Blue banners of Sergros depicting a gold lion hung from the walls of gray stone, beneath high ceilings. Two large torches sat before the throne, one upon each side of the king. Flames burned inside their collars from wicks slathered in animal fat. And before the throne stood a wizened man named

Cedric, who was notorious in the Sergrothian Senate for political cunning and strategy.

Chancellor Cedric presided over the Senate, which represented the interests of the Sergrothian citizens in a political forum. For centuries, the peoples' voice came through the Senate electing the Darxar lineage to rule over the Kingdom of Sergros. The Darxar line had ruled in fact, for as long as records went back to, the age of the *Many Eras War—Saipei*.

Seeing the politician, even after all this time, was a constant reminder to Talus of what he was up against. He studied the old man, and thought about the structure of the Sergrothian democratic government. Its Senate was where Cedric came in, the branch that oversaw the legislative and judicial functions, such as making laws and managing the courts.

The Senate additionally worked toward representing the interests of the people, and also the continuity of competent leadership from the throne of Sergros. Up until this very moment, Talus regarded this latter duty of the Senate as a loophole whereby he could potentially lose his throne.

After rehashing the issue more times than he cared to admit, the king knew there were basically two ways of being deprived of rule over Sergros. *One, the people's vote...* He considered how the change of heart among enough citizens concerning his rule could spur a change in leadership on any given voting cycle. But Talus always found the people's voice a more legitimate reason to change leadership, for at least it was free of political corruption.

Two, the Senate's charge of incompetent leadership... He considered the alternative: any unanimous vote that arose among the politicians concerning his inability to rule the kingdom. This could possibly happen prior to the people's vote, between elections.

If not for these two things, the King of Sergros would exercise complete and uninterrupted executive power. However, Talus feared the continuous enjoyment of such power in the Darxar line might be at serious risk, for the first occasion ever.

"Your welfare law is not working."

Cedric's claim carved through the king's thoughts like a hot knife through ice. His focus returned to the old man leering at him, whose lips almost curled into a smile with every word.

"What?" Talus asked passively, no longer involved in the conversation.

"Your welfare law issued days ago, ordering citizens who cannot work to stay in their homes behind locked doors, waiting upon handouts from authorities… It creates more problems than it solves, and simply put, it's not working."

Talus watched the balding old man step back from the throne, with a head showing a few remaining grays. The king followed Cedric from left to right as the politician began pacing with hands held behind the back. He paid particular note to Cedric's sandaled feet that peeked from beneath his long, beige robe with every other step.

"Amid this gloom, having people stay off the streets to avoid the pillagers and terrible weather makes some sense, but is awfully shortsighted." With amber eyes upon the floor, Cedric continued to walk and talk. Talus found the moment opportune to yawn.

"Many people now wait indoors until set times where supplies and food are distributed by Sergrothian authorities, per the law. Only a few experiencing rekindled faith venture outside their houses to occupy the long vacant churches of Karnath. They pray to Destiny for deliverance from the gloom."

The king grumbled, showing his annoyance with the chancellor. "And what of it? These few who disobey my law over church prayers hurt no one, and those who follow it are kept safe from the gloom and ruffians. I see no problem in this."

Talus used the last words to sharply cut, like with an edged weapon. *I've done right in more ways than one.* He thought about how his law protected people from crime and the cold, rekindled some belief in the Karnathan religion, and most important of all, it even maintained logical soundness with his best philosophers.

Indeed, the king would tell anyone that sound philosophy backed his welfare law. As far as he was concerned, the gloom negatively impacted the system of checks and balances in Sergros that matched its demand to supply. Philosophers of the day called this system *an economy.* And using that nomenclature, he often would tout that his law had *economic basis* in the Senate because it offset *the gloom's economic component*, which simply prevented the citizens of Sergros from doing much in terms of work.

Farmers had nothing to farm after the early frost killed Sergros' harvest. Foresters and miners who attempted working perhaps froze to death in the cold, for they never returned to Sergros. Those Sergrothian merchants sailing exports across the Korinth Ocean to the Isles, were also lost at sea. *Only some of the gloom's effects, among many more*, the king thought. He soon found himself on a tangent, thinking about why the gloom necessitated a welfare law in the first place.

The gloom caused a shortage of natural resources and food, along with disrupted imports and exports, and increases in unemployment due to the harsh working conditions outdoors. These things depressed the economy and where resource shortages were greatest, pillaging and related crime increased, like in Sergrothian cities such as Arlem.

Talus sat there, still watching Cedric pace, and meanwhile recounting all the various reports from his informants in recent months, reports which indicated the city streets grew quite dangerous with rioting and criminals lurking in the shadows. *Something had to be done...*

The king was no expert in Sergrothian economics, but his philosophers helped him understand the problem and its solution. Given the rising unemployment and decreased output as a result of the gloom, demand outpaced supply. *My philosophers recommended I open up the reserves yet again, to supplement supply until the economy picked back up. The welfare law implements just this.*

Talus realized the intrinsic problem that Cedric continued to play upon was him reopening the reserves from an already strained storehouse. It was strained because several months beforehand—before the gloom came and took the harvest— Sergros sent food and supplies to its elven allies in Juniper who suffered sudden attack during the Isles Conspiracy. Talus shook his head, thinking more to himself. *Losing the harvest prevented us from even replenishing the storehouse too...*

Despite the bad timing of Sergrothian benevolence to Juniper, Talus created the welfare law to supplement disrupted supply given the gloom, and in addition, he froze taxes for his poorest citizens. But because of the strained storehouse, Cedric feared the welfare and reduced tax income put Sergros on the path to economic instability. *He's too blinded with lust for my throne to see my welfare law isn't permanent. It's only until the gloom passes. After that, all shall return to order...*

Talus contemplated his plan to fund the welfare law, as Cedric made another silent trek across the throne room. In the absence of tax for the poorer Sergrothian citizens, the wealthiest citizens would see a higher tax since they could pay it, with or without working. As much as this seemed sustainable to the king, Talus knew Cedric did not believe any of it would work. *It's hard to see anything as working, when the goal is to leverage the kingdom's changing economy as a basis for my incompetent leadership...*

When the last step of the politician rang out, it reined in the king's attention from his seriously deep contemplation. Talus watched Cedric lift his wrinkled face to the throne, now at a standstill from his pacing; the torchlight showed the ball on his nose bridge. Under the politician's stare, Talus rubbed a hand nervously over the forehead.

Cedric's voice rose then in the silent hall.

"Indeed the citizens of Sergros are safe, but they do not work. Hardly anyone works, many claiming they can't because of the gloom. It's certainly easier than working for them to wait idly with open hands, expecting the kingdom's provisions without labor, per your law!"

The politician spun about, and in an aside exclaimed to the four walls, "What heart ailment has made the people of Sergros so uncaring of their Fate's Fray! For doing nothing surely can't be anyone's purpose, and surely Destiny appoints divine purpose to one and all." Cedric lowered one of his upraised hands into a clenched fist, whispering then, "Have so many elected to no longer fight for their good destiny, deferring to the Game's outcome for their fate?"

He turned again to the king, looking Talus square in the eyes. "I don't know what's worse," said Cedric, "the able-bodied, young men and women of Sergros with open hands, or the king who fills them. Regardless of who commits the greater wrong, the kingdom's reserves cannot sustain this, even with your excessive tax of the rich."

"How very misfortunate that Sergros helped its allies during the Isles Conspiracy," Talus said sarcastically. "You know that aiding Juniper and our western cites in the conflict's aftermath *halved* Sergros' coffers." The king purposely emphasized the reduction in their reserves to bolster his own argument.

Tough as nails, Cedric shot back a response. "Justify it as you see fit, but justifications won't solve this problem upon Sergros. You broke the machine that turns hard work into dreams. People no longer work, and they still eat at your hand, but their meals are numbered. If you can't fix this predicament, I'm sure someone else will, as you manage the charges against you in the matter of poorly ruling this kingdom."

Taking offense, Talus countered, "Having an opinion without consensus is worthless here. Your suspicion that I, King of Sergros, deal poorly in the affairs of the human kingdom are unshared by anyone outside these walls."

Talus observed the politician's mock surprise, and Cedric acted as if the king were delusional with those last words. "The consensus grows of you being unfit to rule, my king. The Senate hears the voice of your citizens." Cedric paused, and then went on to make a passionate case against the king. "You believe the people of Sergros are satisfied with your meager provisions? While you rule in the wake of the Isles Conspiracy, the unsolved murder of Sergros' hero Garlew Il'therin, the increasing inadequacy of Sergros' courts to deliver justice, and now, this destructive gloom?!"

Talus was outwardly silent, though inside he screamed with contempt for the politician in his chambers, making skillful arguments against him in want of power.

"All of these demoralizations happened during your rule, my king." Talus listened to the chancellor's words, said in a matter-of-fact way. "And therefore," Cedric went on, "you must be held accountable to this kingdom for the outcome in said matters. If the people's vote cannot see to it immediately, the Senate will ensure only the most capable ruler sits in the kingdom's throne."

The king gave a cold reply, "And conveniently that is who, Cedric? You?" At that suggestion, Talus heard the politician hurry his response.

"Sergrothian politics have worked this way for years, and have done so effectively. I would only have executive power until your trial, where the Senate together with a neutral court would make a decision regarding your reinstatement of power, or the election of a new ruler. This should bridge the throne of Sergros with competent leadership, until the next election of the people." Talus noted his look on that last word, so smug in appearance, like he prided himself already over an airtight plan.

"And by the way," added Cedric, "the new ruler could be anyone in the Senate or kingdom excluding you, surely not just me."

Using all his might, Talus suddenly cast his goblet to the far wall, being consumed with deep anger over Cedric's plan to disrupt his reign of power. The king watched the wine splash onto the stone and run down in streaks, while the iron vessel clanged repeatedly as it first hit the wall, then the floor.

"Be gone from this place!" Talus demanded. "Our session is over!" The king watched Cedric carefully; he did not flee in fear, but rather just flashed another grin.

"But your agenda today is open and would permit us more time together. Do you not wish to continue this most important discussion?"

Hatred burned inside Talus at the very suggestion. He leaned forward in his throne and delivered crisp words to his chancellor. "I said, be gone. Actually I do have another session soon, one with counselors who are more cooperative and transparent than you, a counsel free of hidden agendas. If only you gave me advice and it came in goodwill, Cedric." Talus shook his head, frustrated with the questionable intent of his politicians, especially Cedric.

The king listened to Cedric's response, given with another grin. "As you wish."

Talus did not take his eyes off Cedric for the duration of the politician's exit. He watched him turn from the throne to stroll past the spear-brandishing guards and into the foyer, which opened to the long corridor leading from the king's chamber. Sounds of the Cedric's footsteps carried through the hall of stone and gradually faded.

When Cedric was finally gone, Talus began nervously holding his aching head, his body weary from lack of sleep and all this unhealthy fretting. Given the gloom, his decision to open the Sergrothian reserves for Juniper and others affected by the Isles Conspiracy now threatened Sergros through an internal, political attack.

These problems are merely situational instruments, he thought, *nothing else.* Talus reached this conclusion, knowing the backward politicians desperately sought out the perfect dilemma facing Sergros to unseat him from the throne. *That's all they want.*

The king ran two fingers through his beard and grabbed his chin, as he thought deeply about the situation. The more Talus considered the matter, the more he grew certain that Cedric would transform the economic and social turmoil in Sergros into a new political turmoil in the Senate, which could ultimately jeopardize his kingship. He rubbed his face again, nervous at the very idea.

In that moment of contemplation, politics could not seem more unjust to the king. The politicians' corruption might actually underpin a change of rule in Sergros instead of the people's choice, and such went inconsistent with the very ideals of democracy.

Though Talus aimed to preserve his citizens' favor amid the gloom with his welfare law—in hopes this would remembered at the next voting cycle—he might not make it that far at this rate. *Indeed, Cedric could turn this upside down on me, in no time at all...*

"Why, Destiny?" the king sighed.

His question received no answer, and in that, Karnatha did nothing to shed light on his clouded reality, where uncertainty abounded concerning his throne. But Talus' devotion to the Karnathan Church made him expect better than silence. In particular, he expected an intervention from Destiny, one that would save his throne. *Shouldn't my strong faith earn me continued rule over Sergros?*

The thought played on the fact that Talus was the model Karnathan. He read and reread the Book of Karnatha, and believed the whole book from front to back. He believed its *creation story*, how *Destiny—a deity* of spent energy—came from sheer nothingness at the very beginning of time, a well of unspent energy called *the Void*. He believed how Destiny manifest in the spirit Karnatha, handspun threads for the fabric of creation from strands of life, matter, and energy. He believed how Karnatha made the creator Maken to weave Karnath's ages upon the loom.

He believed in its *rebellion story*, how Maken's creation— the seroxians—rebelled against their creator over two millennia ago, which started the Game of Time and Broken Sword that would decide everyone's destiny and prayerfully would undo the forces creating bad destiny in Karnath. He believed how the rebel seroxians were punished with a curse that turned them into *lower races*—humans, elves, and dwarves, among others. He believed how the non-rebellious seroxians were left unharmed but in a cursed land—Old Karnath—while the lower races ironically inherited New Karnath, a remake of paradise. He believed how Laotzu—the lone seroxian who repented for the rebellion long before Maken's punishment—was exiled to New Karnath along with the lower races.

His in-depth studies of the Book of Karnatha were but one testament of his devoutness and faith, aside from so many more. When people lost faith due to *The Great Occlusion* three years ago, where most practicing oracles suddenly went blind, the king launched evangelisms to rekindle belief. Whenever heretics challenged Karnathan doctrines and accounts, Talus became actively engaged in proving them wrong.

Beyond debating with heretics, Talus even attempted to further the Karnathan faith among non-believers through many Sergrothian campaigns meant to substantiate the *Book of Karnatha*. A smile spread across his lips, as Talus recounted how most recently, he sent soldiers to the *Hirishin Isles* during the Isles Crusades, to scour the supposed location of Laotzu's grave. While the mission was unsuccessful, he ruled out another area where the seroxian's remains could not be.

"Laotzu, the king destined to be forever without a kingdom." Talus muttered, as he thought about how finding the bones would prove seminal to more Sergrothians believing the Karnathan religion. *Laotzu's bones, or either white or black shard of Maken's gray blade, would surely prove supposed myth as true!* Just thinking about all of Sergros becoming devout Karnathans lit up his face with yet another smile. *To think, if all Sergrothians could be like me!*

With weary eyes, the king looked to the guards at the rear of the chamber, and he yawned from utter fatigue. And when his yawn ended, his frown came back. *Karnatha should reward my commitment to her*, Talus thought, without feeling he had overstepped his bounds as a mortal, with regard to expectations of his god. He had been more than just a believer, but a defender of the Karnathan religion—a true champion of his faith. *And that should earn me Destiny's help toward the preservation of my divine destiny: ruling Sergros.*

Given how Karnatha did not intervene immediately with the politicians trying to seize his throne, Talus wondered sometimes if he could help enough Sergrothians find faith before he lost it himself. *I've done all this, yet you turn your back on me, Karnatha?!*

In times like these, Talus found himself doubting his religion. Whenever this happened, the king renewed his trust in Karnatha by embracing the core doctrines of his faith that helped him lead a better life. Those were that *one should trust the Game to ultimately decide his or her battle for good destiny; one may elect to fight his or her battle for good destiny until the Game is decided; one may not find good destiny through another's bad destiny; one should still seek good destiny, even in times of bad destiny.*

With a deep breath, Talus considered the principles as done so many times before, and in so doing he found some solace, concluding that Destiny had yet to show itself through the gloom for the best outcome of his people. In a matter of moments, the king had peace that Karnatha would eventually remove the need for his own intervention in Sergros, such as handouts to the working classes and tax freezes for the poor, and bring back good destiny to the human kingdom. *Or maybe bring good destiny, for the whole of Karnath!*

He often wondered if somehow by this strange course of events—the gloom, the Isles Conspiracy, the Great Occlusion—that the Game of Time and Broken Sword would soon decide the battle for good destiny for all creation. *This gloom could indeed be the onset of the Game's final battle at Gallow Cliff.*

Quickly Talus cast the idea from his mind, knowing that Sergrothians were not ready to deal with the possible reality that the gloom might lead into the

Game's end. It was too much for his citizens to bear, in such a time of great uncertainty. And so, Talus did everything in his power to prevent the people of Sergros from fearing the gloom's implications. *That's the last thing Sergros needs. The same was true three years ago when the oracles disclosed the Dark Prophecy.*

Such a lengthy course of thought eventually exhausted Talus. *From the gloom to the Game...* It made him realize the far reaches of his contemplation in connection to Sergros' perils, and for now, he would not brood the matter more. *Things beyond our control are ultimately matters of prayer.*

The king sighed, and decided to pray to Destiny for deliverance through the Game, through reciting an ancient poem written by the earliest of oracles. "Spindle and loom with Maken's gray blade," he said, "the last of these three brings Fate's Fray."

Those first words of his recitation sounded against the guards' blank stares, to echo the chamber. The act's isolation did not stop him, and Talus continued reciting the poem until its very last stanza. By the time the king finished, his eyes were so heavy, he finally decided to close them and keep them closed a while.

**** The King's Recitation ****

Game of Time and Broken Sword

Spindle and loom, with Maken's gray blade
The last of these three, brings Fate's Fray

Oh the gray blade, forged in Ires Star from the Void
Can time itself slay, and Destiny's balance destroy

For time decides a Game, good and evil play
Destiny ordains this choose, which way its scale sway

If time dies, then Darkness to god, people, and lands
But Light to those, if ever flows time's sands

Time goes on, if Ires Star consumes whole sword
But blade to Gallow Cliff, perhaps means time no more

For a contest grand, the gray sword was broken
In two pieces atwain, Maken's last word spoken

So that one shard of sword, each Child will find
But two shards of sword, only one Child can bind

Whichever this Game's victor, whichever its guide
Nevermore two hues, nevermore two sides

Oh Children of Destiny, give what you must
Karnath falls prey, to Destiny's lust!

****

Chapter 6
Wise Counsel

With his prayer Talus dozed for hours, until a sudden whoosh woke him from his sleep. He opened his eyes, and noted both torches before the throne had been snuffed out!

Through the darkness, Talus watched his guards run toward the throne. Talus raised his hand for them to stay back. "Be at ease!"

As the soldiers retreated, he waited calmly in his seat, knowing from many prior encounters exactly what would happen. His counselors were arriving.

And no sooner than the wicks went out, did they both burst aflame! With a smile Talus noted the torches shed light from darkness, but his guards did not share the same elation. Rather, they wore grimaces, sorely troubled by what took place. And then, something even odder occurred.

Right before his eyes, Talus saw a man and a woman appear from thin air; they occupied the space before him, between the torches. The pair knelt, each person upon one bended knee, with a face to the floor. And with this pair came good feelings upon Talus—an overwhelming sense of relief, trust, and respect for his external counsel.

Under the torchlight, Talus first examined the man on his left, who wore black from collar to boots, dark trousers and tunic beneath a sleeved surcoat with obsidian buttons. The man had brown hair and deep-set green eyes, placed in a rectangular face covered in leathery skin, with a wide brow and a pointy chin. *Sydullus…*

Next, Talus gazed to his right upon the woman, starting with her perfectly shaped blue eyes, set in an oval face of alabaster skin and enclosed by luscious blonde hair, evenly trimmed and falling below her shoulders. She wore garments similar to Sydullus, though with the colors inverted, and pearl buttons instead of obsidian upon her surcoat. *Urzel…*

An abrupt stirring at the room's rear brought the king's attention upon his guards. Once again, they were unsettled with stern faces, and making an advance to the throne with their spears extended.

Unlike previous times, Talus simply dismissed the guards on this occasion, saying choice words with an uplifted hand.

"I said, worry not! Just leave…"

He saw the guards halt their advance, and slowly walk out of the room, into the corridor, and out of sight. The echo of their footsteps became less and less audible.

Talus turned back to Urzel and Sydullus, who now looked up from the floor and stood from their kneeling positions. He acknowledged them instantly.

"Thank you for coming."

"As always, we provide you comfort in trying hours," said Sydullus. "Has morale improved in Sergros since our last encounter?"

Giving a long sigh and an even longer pause, Talus finally responded. "Not much. Between the unsolved murder of my kingdom's hero during the recent war and now this gloom, I fear that I'm losing face by the day, not only in the Sergrothian Senate but also in my kingdom!"

Urzel spoke up, "We sorrow over your troubles, my lord. But know that we're here to help those of Sergros."

As she talked, Talus followed the torchlight as it leaped upon her beautiful face, which was a glory to the drab stone chamber.

She continued. "Regarding the unsolved murder of your kingdom's hero, we already aid your search for Kort Al'starz, the suspected killer of Garlew Il'therin. As we requested last time, have you dispatched Sagult to the Isles, in order to find the criminal?"

Without hesitation Talus replied, "It is done."

"Excellent," Sydullus interjected.

For a moment, Urzel paused and then went on calmly, her blue eyes bright and vivacious. "About the gloom, we left off last session with an obvious need to understand its origin and how it related to other problems your kingdom has faced, such as war. After much delving of this matter, we are pleased to explain what's happening."

Smiling at that, Sydullus chimed in. "And obviously, we wish to propose a solution for your problems." The words comforted Talus, and in little time the tensions relaxed in his face.

"Please, do explain."

And with that request, Urzel expounded upon their discovery. "You likely have realized that much has gone awry in your kingdom since the oracles made the *Dark Prophecy*, a final vision before their occlusion three years ago. For after this dire forecast, one misfortune after the next occurred in the human kingdom, in a seemingly non-causal chain of events. But there's more cause to these effects than you might believe, in spite of the oracles' blindness now that has most Karnathans doubting the Dark Prophecy is even true."

As Urzel spoke, Talus pondered the matter of the oracles. He recalled how three years ago, their last vision supposedly showed an Age of Darkness descending upon Karnath, after the Child of Darkness won the legendary Game of Time and Broken Sword at Gallow Cliff. People eventually dubbed this vision as the Dark Prophecy, which went exactly opposite to the so-called *Light Prophecy* that oracles made up long ago, a lie to conveniently deal with their inability to foresee the Game's winner at all. *And for that, perhaps Destiny punished them,* he thought then, recollecting how the prophets ultimately lost their gift and became useless—unable to guide kings in the matters of kingdoms, or peasants in the matters of peasantry.

Throughout Karnath, this phenomenon affecting the oracles gained a common name—the Great Occlusion. At first, it caused a stir among people across Karnath: everyone thought the end of the world was coming. But years elapsed with nothing becoming of the Dark Prophecy. This, along with the oracles being wrong about their every prediction since the occlusion, made people generally doubtful that any mishap following the Dark Prophecy was even related, or so Talus presumed.

As a result these things, Talus thought that most Sergrothians surely did not associate the gloom with the Dark Prophecy, let alone war or Garlew's death. Talus, however, thought himself as more perceptive than the common people, and he had a strong hunch that it was somehow all related. Urzel's words played on his suspicions.

"Go on," the king instructed.

"Let me explain," Urzel continued. "Within a few years of the prophets going blind, one side of a family feud long restricted to the Hirishin Isles deceptively came to the Mainland. This transpired after the *Red Dragon* clans made a sudden, hostile takeover of the *Black Dragon* territory, somehow aided by advanced magic—*metal demons from Tekkneo.*"

Sydullus chimed in, "Taurus Hboshi, former Emperor of the Black Dragon clans, fled to the Mainland's west coast by ship with soldiers, being disguised as robed travelers wishing to visit holy sites in Juniper. From beneath his cloak of deception, he began taking cities by storm on his murderous path to the elven kingdom. *Baal* fell in a single night."

The mention of Baal conjured up images in Talus' head, as he remembered surveying ruins of the city, which had been completely destroyed by fire along with its residents. The memory sent a chill down his spine.

Urzel picked up the conversation. "Juniper was attempted in the emperor's twisted plot to reestablish his lost empire on the Mainland."

Sydullus spoke next, "Amid the Isles Conspiracy's resolution, the hero of Sergros is murdered by an elven knight entrusted to do good—Kort Al'starz. This has distressed your kingdom further."

Knowing well what happened, the weary Talus yawned, at the risk of being perceived uninterested.

Sydullus continued. "All this, because the oracles cannot help you see the future to protect your land."

When the two counselors went mute, Talus expected more. *That's it? They've told me what I already know!* In a reflex, the king snapped, "Is *this* your explanation?"

"Not at all," Urzel quickly replied.

Talus looked at both counselors—first Sydullus on the left, then Urzel on the right—to weigh the sincerity in their eyes. Upon seeing Urzel's soft features, he slowed his hasty conclusions, and awaited their expansion of these various ideas. *Let them talk...*

"No one in Karnath realizes what I now disclose. Your problems are consequences of the prophets' receding vision, which itself has been brought on by an even *bigger problem.*"

While listening, Talus rubbed his chin between forked fingers until hearing the last two words—bigger problem. His fingers stopped instantly. As he considered the prospect, a worried expression formed upon his face. *What bigger problem?*

The king soon began wringing both hands, waiting nervously for his counselors to go on.

"What else can't you see without oracles, my wise lord?" asked Sydullus.

Urzel answered, "Surely not the one who caused the oracles' vision to be cut off. This person is at the root of all your problems."

The king looked at them in silence, thinking deeply about their words. To him, the oracles being blind for years had always been the problem. He considered how the *Oracles Society* became worthless to Sergros, unable to name the peasants' children at birth even, according to their foretold purpose in life. But what his counselors now said indeed worried him, for it implied he had totally missed the real problem in Sergros.

She elaborated, "It's natural to believe the oracles' lost vision alone created all your problems, but this is not so. The one who blocks the oracles' foresight indirectly caused your wars, for calamity comes in the absence of prophets to guide the kings."

"What about the gloom?" Talus asked, in an effort to connect this idea to the biggest problem facing Sergros.

With a slight pause Sydullus answered, "The one who blinded your prophets brings this gloom upon Sergros, a precursor to the prophetic doom—the Age of Darkness. And this is just the beginning, for the gloom will spread into the outermost parts of the Mainland, eventually affecting all of Karnath until time's end."

Talus' heightened worry manifested itself through a gawked mouth, crinkled face, and wide eyes. He began to feel sick to his stomach, and his head pounded.

As if perceptive to all that, Urzel addressed the king in a soothing way. "You are alarmed, my lord. For you sense now that your foe is much larger than many presume, and in that, you are correct. The one blinding your prophets, bringing calamity, and now the gloom is none other than the Child of Darkness. Unfortunately, Karnath is on the eve of the Dark Prophecy being fulfilled."

The king's brow wrinkled, and his eyes showed extreme fear. "The Child of Darkness?! Who is this, and where is he?!" Frantically Talus looked to Urzel for an answer, then to Sydullus.

"The problem could not be any more yours," said Urzel. "For the Child of Darkness dwells in a province of Sergros, and is a woman, not a man."

The king's countenance dipped in grave concern.

"Who is this one?!" Talus asked, anxiously.

Sydullus began talking where Urzel left off. "The sorceress Esmeralda seeks to end the reign of her sister Magicia. She has recovered the shard from the mountain too, just as the prophecy describes."

By the word, Talus showed utmost surprise, intermixed with his worry. *I've had a good relationship with Magicia for years... How can this be?!*

Urzel interjected, "Esmeralda is *Shaizan*."

At her mention of the forbidden name of the Child of Darkness—something rumored to draw Ma'althan's stare—the words abruptly brought both silence and stillness to the throne room, among the two counselors and the king. The dancing torch fires became the only movement.

And in that moment, Talus felt it—his developing Fate's Fray from the poorest circumstances in Sergros and corrupt politicians in the Sergrothian Senate. From the corners of his destiny's fabric—his destiny of ruling the human kingdom just as his father Elix—the threads were pulled, unraveling his divine purpose of Sergrothian kingship into something far less than he was always meant to be. *Unraveling my destiny into humility and the dungeons!* he thought in horror, as he mentally pictured a cloth coming undone from its frayed edges.

Then suddenly, in his mind, a hole formed in the imagined cloth, from which Ma'althan's head emerged—goateed and of darkened countenance, staring right at him with embers burning in its eye sockets!

Talus screamed as the scary visual overtook him, and his face contorted from sheer dread. His heart raced, his breaths grew short, and while leaning forward, he clutched the armrest of his throne in one white-knuckled fist and lifted his other hand to point at the woman.

"Don't say *that name* in these courts!"

"I'm so sorry," replied Urzel.

Talus heard her gentle reply and it instantly defused his response. He stopped leaning forward in his throne and become frozen, with his pointed finger hung midair and a horrified look plastered upon his face. Lost in the woman's blue eyes, he could not find another harsh word for her.

"I'm sorry," Urzel said, yet again.

Though that reiteration dispelled his anger completely, his stomach stayed uneasy and his head still throbbed. *The Child of Darkness, in Sergros...* The thought clenched his throat, and would not let go. The king found it terribly hard to breathe, and felt incredibly uncomfortable. *That's certainly a bigger problem.*

From the ensuing quiet Talus begged urgently, "What should be done?! Let me know now!" But no immediate answer was given to his anxious inquiry. Talus grew more desperate for guidance with each passing second. *Why are they silent?!* The question rattled him.

"Please guide me in the matters of Sergros, wise counselors! My own Senate has turned against me for want of my throne! And now, who is to suffer from this political game?" He screamed despairingly then, "The Sergrothian citizens and I?!" The words resonated the chamber, sounding thrice.

Urzel's exterior showed empathy for the quailing king, and she spoke calmly, as if to relieve his worries. "Fret not, my lord. Esmeralda can be stopped from fulfilling the prophecy. With the end of her misdeeds, the gloom ends in Sergros along with Karnath's calamities. The Age of Darkness will not come, if you but act."

"Tell me how to thwart the sorceress," Talus implored his counselors. "And I'll commit the required resources to do this thing!" Amidst his request, Talus found his eyes suddenly held captive by Urzel's developing smile.

"Unbeknownst to you, we already help you commit resources so that the Seventh Order of the Guard can take *a special mission.*"

Talus recalled what the counselors spoke of last session: gathering his best Guardsman for a mission yet to be disclosed. It was then that an epiphany struck the king: *They advise me on how to restore order in Sergros, by sending Sagult to find Kort and solve Garlew's murder, and also, commissioning the Guard to cut down Esmeralda.*

With a bit of humility, he replied, "I see."

"So, about the Guard," asked Urzel, after a brief pause. "Have you summoned your knight X'ieth Armstrong to the castle for his promotion to the Seventh Order?"

"Yes. He travels now for a hearing with me."

Sydullus smiled and said, "Very good, my lord. And what of the last vacancy in the Seventh Order, the spot opened by Sagult?"

"There are many candidates for the position, and it could be filled within hours, if necessary."

"As much time as is needed should be spent," Urzel chimed in, "to acquire one particular warrior, to fill this position of high-rank and prestige."

Calmer now, Talus slumped back in his throne with raised eyebrows, intrigued as to which warrior his wise counselors had in mind.

"Whom do you suggest?" he asked, eager to hear.

"The mercenary Zeros."

With Urzel's last word, Talus looked incredibly solemn and pensive. He took a deep breath, and then slowly exhaled. *Zeros? Zeros and X'ieth?! Oh no...*

"Zeros fighting side by side with X'ieth is not a good idea," the king finally admitted. "I foresee this ending poorly, for the two won't mix well. Is this pairing so significant?"

Silence once again filled the space, before Sydullus spoke up. "Yes, it is, for there's certain advantages. Zeros and X'ieth are very capable knights, both being puppets controlled from different strings, if you know what I mean, my lord."

That's… not possible. Talus sat there, struck down by astonishment. In this moment, as in many others past, it became obvious that somehow his counselors understood a great many things about him that they were never privy to. *Is it somehow apparent*, he wondered, *that I manipulate both X'ieth and Zeros by different means, with outstanding results?*

"So manipulate both warriors to work toward the common goal of stopping Esmeralda," said Sydullus, "and your chance of failure will be minimal."

"Simply pull the right strings," added Urzel, her smile constant.

Talus shook his head, showing clear reservation.

"I just don't know," he said at last. "This bad pairing of X'ieth and Zeros robs me of peace."

"Difficult decisions you must wrestle with daily, my lord," said Sydullus then, after a moment. "I understand that you'll need time to carefully weigh your options before choosing one."

Urzel added, "Just know that we believe this dire situation warrants drastic measures, maybe even radical ones that initially might not agree with your first instincts."

"With our foresight and knowledge, we have concluded this course of action is best, but still encourage you to use sound judgments, my lord. We wish you wisdom in an affair that concerns not only Sergros, but also the whole of Karnath."

The king nodded his head, as Sydullus finished.

"Yes, I must think deeply about this, and only then can I give you an answer." In that moment, the situation's gravity weighed on Talus, and those last words sunk into his mind. *An affair that concerns the whole of Karnath…*

Talus paused with the counselors standing before him, and then continued. "I propose we convene again in a day. By then I should know how to proceed. Also, before meeting with X'ieth or anyone else in the Seventh Order, I'll need to understand exactly what this special mission entails to communicate its details to my knights."

"Without a doubt," Urzel replied, "we shall disclose all you need to know."

Sydullus spoke out, "I believe you'll find the Crimson Guard to be most effective for the task of stopping Esmeralda. Their *binding by Magicia's spell to protect the blood of the innocent* will prove very helpful. After all, Esmeralda intends to hurt many innocent through the Dark Prophecy."

"Yes, most certainly." Talus nodded.

With the king's agreement, the counselors in unison then stated, "We shall meet again in one day's time."

At those words, Talus watched Sydullus and Urzel spin from the throne, about to vanish away as they came. The king studied the cloaks before him then, both framing falling stars. Sydullus' was black with three white streaks strung across it, from the right shoulder to the mantle's lower left corner. Urzel's cloak showed the same, with its colors inverted.

Talus, now bemused by his counsel's foreknowledge when the oracles were blind as bats, asked a final thing to the departing duo. "One last thing to ease my curious mind," the king said. "How do you possess such a window into the future?"

Talus saw Urzel turn at his question, to say with a grin, "I'm a Servant of the Light who specializes in knowing. As such, I understand a great many things, my lord. Many things, both apparent and obscure…"

Talus spent a moment digesting her remark, and then addressed Sydullus, noting his differing attire. "And you, sir? Are you also a Servant of the Light?"

He watched Sydullus glance back at him with a smile, saying, "I am equal to any Servant of the Light, in word and deed. Don't let appearances deceive you, my lord. For I just prefer to wear black, and she white."

Both of the counselors stared back with a smile, and to Talus, the gesture was warm and imparted comforts. With another moment longer, he beheld the pair dissolve into thin air.

The king's eyes fell upon the now-empty space between the torches sitting before his throne, and the sight made him realize that he was left to the solitude of his chamber, alone to feast on what did seem much food for thought.

"KING AND HIS COUNSEL"

Chapter 7
The Unwholesome Inheritance

(780 A.R., Over a thousand years ago...)

[Second Walk of Existence]

Before Maken's curse, Magicia was seroxian, a member of the creator's superhuman race. She was bigger, faster, stronger, and smarter than what she became after the curse: a human inferior of kingdom Sergros, and a lowly sorceress in the Guild. As an original citizen of one of the rebel kingdoms, she watched in a single day her people fall, receive a curse, and be exiled to New Karnath—hundreds of years prior to this day.

Now, the only seroxian feature she had left was appearance, for seroxian appearance was relatively similar to human. Maken's curse distributed every seroxian quality across the lower races—strength and ingenuity to the dwarves, speed and magic to the elves, looks to the humans, and the remainder to the other lower races.

There were days where Maken's curse of humanity caused Magicia more grief than others, and this was one of those days. In her pursuit of Eriens Malgun—the rogue seroxian king from Old Karnath—her lesser speed and stamina posed real problems in keeping up.

She had been following him all the way from his entry point into New Karnath. It was a green Nexus portal, surely faded by now without the black shard in position to maintain the energy fields to bridge both worlds. Upon his emergence she immediately tailed him, but he quickly outpaced her, nearly hopping over entire fields with only a few bounds.

But even though Eriens moved out of sight, Magicia kept running in the direction she last saw him, running quickly as did her mind and heart. *Hrya, I can't lose you!* With that insistence, she moved as fast as she could, her violet robe flowing with every hurried step, its bell sleeves caught on the winds, just as her red braided hair.

Thoughts about Hrya easily propelled her forward throughout the night, as she knew her love was now endangered by a scathing situation that degenerated from her expectations about the seroxians entering New Karnath.

47

As of only a few days ago, Magicia had many expectations. She anticipated a peaceful entry of the seroxians from Old Karnath into her world. She anticipated alliances being forged between the seroxians and the lower races. She anticipated reuniting with Hrya, and living happily ever after with her first and only love.

But in the hundreds of years that passed since Maken's curse of Old Karnath and the lower races, the first meeting of the seroxians with her people was in betrayal and bloodshed, reaffirming that the seroxians could not be trusted given their deep hatred toward the inferiors over the *Coveted Land* wrongfully being theirs.

It all happened so fast. A man named Sydullus contacted her weeks ago with a message from Hrya, stating that King Eriens had finally found the black shard, with which Hrya intended to enter New Karnath across an energy bridge. Not only did Hrya mention that his love for Magicia still lingered, but also, he noted a peculiar problem facing the un-cursed seroxians of Old Karnath *without the River of Life*.

Recalling that portion of the message brought the river to Magicia's mind. She remembered how the seroxians of Old Karnath used to bathe in the River of Life for its rejuvenating properties, long before Maken's curse. Some thought its waters defied age.

But with the curse, the creator dried up the River of Life, only to recreate it in New Karnath at an undisclosed location. Maken did this to spite the seroxians under Darconas—those of Old Karnath who believed they were under no obligation to stop the rebellion and abstained from interfering while the others sinned against their creator. Though she would never really know why Maken did this, Magicia always presumed it was a way of transferring immortality to the rebels, which as a group were more contrite during the punishment than the non-rebels.

Hrya's message claimed that his father Darconas had somehow become his own shadow and that all seroxians would too without bathing in the River of Life. So, part of his plea involved bridging Old and New Karnath in order for the seroxians to find the remade river. Fortunately for Hrya's father, Magicia and her sister Esmeralda were the only humans of New Karnath who knew where the river was located. *That's how we've escaped death for hundreds of years beyond the rebellion!*

Magicia's mind circled back to the developments concerning Hrya's message. She herself loved Hrya since Maken separated them and knowing the river's secret location in New Karnath put her in a position to do more than serve her own wants of their togetherness; she could actually help Hrya's father Darconas, and the other seroxians too!

And so, to these ends, she agreed to bridge the worlds of Old and New Karnath under one condition: the seroxians enter in peace, with no hostilities over the inferiors possessing the Coveted Land. But against her trust, Eriens came through the portal from Old Karnath secretly armed with his father's sword, and started slaying inferiors by the thousands in an attempt to claim New Karnath for his own.

Given all that had happened, Magicia now feared that she would continue living in the wake of her broken dream of losing Hrya; she feared that she would continue to live the misery of her Fate's Fray. It had been nearly a millennium without seeing Hrya, and she felt their togetherness was an integral part of her divine purpose in life—her good destiny. That purpose had been undone by the rebellion and Maken's punishment, and might stay undone if she could not stop Eriens.

A wind slapped her in the face, interrupting her recall of how this had all happened. Magicia snapped back to the grasslands of New Karnath, where all she could see before her were seemingly endless spans of rolling green meadows, which sat below a breathtaking starlit sky, streaked by three shooting stars that unbeknownst to her, were ethers from a time no more.

She continued running against a severe cramp in her side. Her heart pounded in her chest and she breathed raggedly, on the brink of exhaustion and wondering how long it would be before she caught up with Eriens. *I hope I'm not too late!*

Magicia followed the upward slope of the next hill with that in mind, praying she would find Eriens before anything bad happened to Hrya. With a few more steps, she reached the top of its incline, and peered down over the rolling grasslands at a truly horrendous sight.

For over a span, she saw stretches of bloodstained grass littered by the gored remains of an entire Sergrothian cavalry, hundreds of horses and riders hewn to bits. And beyond that massacre was Deardrum's stone fortress, standing tall on the horizon and adorned in shimmering lights. With that single glance, the cumulative impact of Eriens' rampage weighed on her, and Magicia realized that Hrya, the dwarves, and the rest of New Karnath were in the gravest of dangers.

Motion suddenly caught her eye, hundreds of cubits past the bloody mess that became of Sergros' attempts to thwart Eriens. There, in the distance, she saw what appeared to be two seroxians fighting each other. *Eriens and Hrya!* The realization launched her into motion, and she jumped hurdle after hurdle of the slain, running toward the heels of Eriens Malgun.

Magicia ran until about twenty cubits behind him, and then stopped. From her vantage point she saw his posterior well, a young seroxian of about six cubits in stature. He stood in rugged armor, bearing his father's bloodied sword in one hand. His chiseled face was no less rugged, jet-black hair topping his head, a beard of matching color hugging his face. Eriens towered over the blond-haired Hrya on the grass, crumpled on one side and tightly holding the black shard of sword from seroxian legend. Its mirror-like blade captured the starlight in rainbow glimmers, from tip to hilt.

In that moment, it could not be clearer to her that Eriens was responsible for everything—an empty promise of the seroxians' peaceful entry into New Karnath, and now, a developing war between the seroxians and the lower races. *Eriens, betrayer of trusts—my trust, New Karnath's trust too!* The mere thought of that distressed her, but it was easily ousted by yet another thought—her mere contemplation of Hrya being killed in this ensuing conflict! The thought of that was beyond distressing, and altogether unbearable. *Hrya, I can't lose you!* Magicia's heart bled out, insisting yet again that he remain alive.

She stood there silent, knowing that as most worthwhile things in life, her future with Hrya demanded her action, involvement, and fight. *Our fight*, she thought then, how she and Hrya might together overcome the strength of Eriens. The idea easily summoned words to her mouth, words that fell from her lips and into the night air.

"Hrya, you must rise and fight… Together we can stop this!" Magicia's voice was firm, not cracking or breaking on a single syllable.

"He's too strong," Hrya said weakly.

As if realizing she was watching him on the ground, he slowly got to his knees.

"Yes, get up, Prince of Deardrum!" Eriens taunted the fallen Hrya once more, briefly glancing back to Magicia with a smile. "Just to fight me, you took my black shard from Gallow Cliff in Old Karnath, so fight me then! Destiny rewarded my search of Liath for that sacred thing you hold, perhaps for this! To enter New Karnath and reclaim paradise is no doubt my good destiny in spite of my broken dreams—a dead wife and a shadowed friend!"

Magicia saw Hrya kneel there, leaning into his fists pressed against the grassland, his one hand still clenching the black shard. He wore a look of defeat, which elicited her continued encouragement.

"Hrya, get up! We can do this!"

At that exact moment, Magicia saw Hrya struggle to his feet, appearing dizzy. He stood with the shard in one hand, his other hand balled tight. In not much time at all, she watched Eriens suddenly lunge toward him, and at that her heart skipped a beat. *Hrya!*

But she was surprised to see Hrya cast a fistful of sod and dirt in Eriens' face, right before slashing at the king with the black shard!

"Ugh!" cried Eriens, looking away with squinted eyes while raising his father's sword, just in time to deflect the black shard and push Hrya back with a single clang.

Magicia stood still, watching the entire spectacle as Eriens stumbled about, unable to see. Hrya backpedaled to a safe distance, moving toward the rear of the blinded king. But for whatever reason, he evidenced a clear hesitation to strike, likely from perceiving Eriens as older, stronger, and more experienced. Her eyes followed him as he nervously took one step forward, only to retreat a moment later. She kept mouthing two words the entire time. *Do it! Do it!*

After a second longer, Magicia grew dissatisfied with just watching Eriens rub his eyes, yet again. In that moment, her resourceful mind envisioned a unique opportunity that might very well offset Hrya's faltered courage—a unique opportunity that could best Eriens during his momentary impairment. *Use a decoy!*

With that particular idea in mind, she tapped *the Nexus*. Immediately Magicia had an extremely familiar experience for anyone practicing sorcery, one had all times when touching *the Source*.

In her mind, she stood barefoot and wearing a simple robe in a large room—her *channeling chamber*. Her eyes traced its circular walls, cubits away, which bowled to a single door right before her. Magicia looked down to the knob, and without hesitating, reached forth to touch it. As she turned the knob and *pulled*, she felt the door's resistance to open—her sensed mental restraint. And so, Magicia *pulled* harder, until suddenly the door budged beyond its jamb with a blast of light, hued in aqua green!

A deluge of Nexus poured through the opening, all around her in streams of energy, causing tingles from head-to-toe. She watched the flows conform to her body and fill the room, her face painted in awe the whole while, the same wonderment she displayed when practicing magic for the first time, as a girl so long ago. Still *pulling* against the door's opposing force, she found herself entranced by the enveloping light, seen from across the entry.

And just as the room filled with Nexus, so did her *aux core*—her reserve for magical energy. When it filled completely, she let the door slam shut and instantly was connected to the energy field that spread throughout the grasslands. Magicia opened her eyes with a keen sense of her surroundings, now able to feel everything through the Nexus, from the gentle breezes and vibrations of crickets chirping, to Eriens' steps and Hrya shifting upon both feet.

Viewing Eriens rubbing his eyes while Hrya remained behind him— stalling there as if afraid to strike—inspired her to enact her plan without further delay. *Create the decoy, now!* While holding the Nexus inside her aux core, Magicia *thought* of her love Hrya—*a trigger* to guide how her magic would be used. Back in her channeling chamber, she turned from the closed door to another door behind her. She ran up to this new door and *pushed* it hard, causing it to yield with a brilliant flash of light at its edges, as the energy in the room flooded out, over the threshold!

During her *pushing*, the Source flowed from Magicia's aux core and cleverly created a decoy of Hrya at the foot of Eriens, according to the trigger. It was a Nexus portrait of the prince reaching up with an open hand to shield himself from the looming king. It preoccupied Eriens, who seemed oblivious to the real Hrya behind him.

"Now!" she screamed.

Magicia saw Hrya glance her way with a set of brown eyes beneath his wavy blond hair. She watched him nod with a hint of hesitation, and then thrust the black shard at Eriens' rear.

However, Magicia was appalled when Eriens suddenly ignored the decoy and thrust his sword backward! In one heartbreaking moment for Magicia, she observed a rogue king and a valiant prince impale each other! The awful, bloody scene got stuck in her eyes, just as the sounds of their swords piercing flesh and breaking bone got caught between her ears!

Magicia ran for Hrya at once, screaming aloud his name. "Hrya!" The sound was lost in a sea of their groans, as both Eriens and Hrya winced in agonizing pain. At about the same instant, she witnessed them fall to their knees and raggedly gasp the air.

Magicia hurled herself to the ground and hugged Hrya, who leaned forward with Eriens' sword jutting from his belly. As she joined him, the grass padded the impact of her knees. There were sudden pained sounds and convulsing over Hrya's back; Magicia looked there and found the rogue king facing them, with the black shard sticking through his breastplate. Hrya let go of the black shard's grip, just then.

How did this even happen?! Magicia wondered, as the bloody and horrific scene inundated her senses. In the same moment, she maintained some disbelief that such a thing had really taken place. It was hard to accept.

"I only wanted peace of mind," Eriens whispered. "A peace to betray your trust. Paradise is ours… Maken took it from us, in… the rebellion."

Magicia ignored the dying king, holding Hrya tight, with tears streaming down her face. "Hrya!" she cried, nearly choked by grief as his blood poured all over her, warm and runny.

Eriens groaned, "My child Kilwroth… cried inconsolably last night… He cried after my careless prayer over peace of mind… To betray your trust for this attack… Kilwroth, who knows what awaits you… for my misdeeds! Destiny keep you, child…" With those dying words, the rogue king Eriens slumped over in a widening pool of his own blood; the black shard had killed him.

Hrya's eyes began to appear blank, and it grieved Magicia. Amidst her sobs, she spoke to him.

"Hrya, my love for you has endured centuries! Maken dried up the River of Life in Old Karnath as the seroxians' punishment, but it sustains me now in New Karnath. And I've stayed alive for you alone!"

Magicia saw Hrya's eyes hollow even more, and his breathing was struggled, in harsh wheezes. As the prince came closer to death, an immeasurable loss built up within her. She pled that he not go.

"You can't die!" Magicia said, still holding Hrya in her arms. "The rebellion has kept us apart for so long, and we are finally back together!"

Suddenly then, Hrya's chin went atremble as he began speaking.

"Your people are safe from… the seroxians. The human kingdom, that of the elves, the dwarves also… shall bleed no more from Eriens' blade."

"Hrya…" Magicia sobbed on with a heavy heart, knowing his death was imminent, but not knowing how she would cope over it happening.

"Share the River of Life!" Hrya pleaded. "My father Darconas became his own shadow… Without washing in the river… all seroxians will too!"

When Hrya abruptly slumped over, Magicia sensed him go limp in her arms. It was at that moment where she went into complete and utter hysterics, avalanched now by the pervasive loss of losing Hrya—her first and only love.

Looking into his eyes, she wept and wailed, without any release of the consuming pain inside. Magicia saw his gaze gradually become completely empty, as surely his life was but a dimming light and escaping scene, to one who lived his finale.

The sorceress felt Hrya's warm blood continue to pour out on her, soiling her garb. She looked again into his death gaze, and a reality set in that now, her dream of being together with him again was forever broken. And in this, her Fate's Fray became an unraveling of her future from which she could never recover. *There's no undoing death by a mortal, like me!*

In the single moment that Magicia internalized Hrya being gone for good, her world literally came crashing down. She could see it being smashed to bits, a shelter of gray glass assembled from the shards of her broken dreams from her long separation from Hrya. It was an enclosure built upon a foundation of her hope of being with him again, one that insulated her from despair for hundreds of years since the rebellion, and yet now, it fell apart all around her. The shelter's panes of gray glass smashed into new shards—some white, most of them black— and through their smashing she saw her new dream break, the one of reuniting with Hrya. Her hope, her joy in sorrow, her reason to live, all demolished with Eriens' lust for New Karnath. And in the place of those things was her pervasive emptiness, just waiting to be filled.

Smitten with colossal sorrow, Magicia's crying continued long past the death of Hrya, even longer beyond nightfall. "Why?" she asked Destiny, from out of her spell of teary grief. "Why?!" she screamed at the top of her lungs. There was no answer but a blowing wind to stir her robe and braided red hair, and with only that, no comfort for this forlorn soul.

Magicia regarded Destiny's evening breeze not as a gentle caress upon the shoulder to solace one laden with despair. Rather, it just seemed to her as mockery. And so, the sorceress lamented in deep pain, clutching Hrya in want of never letting go, still brimming with questions.

"Why Destiny do you watch, and leave my cares unattended?! Answer me!"

A moment of calm presided over the grassland, exactly as before. This time though, there was more than a wind as a reply. Before the sorceress' sore gray eyes, peering out above tear-stained cheeks, showed two figures having the semblance of humans, clad in diametric armaments matching their respective hue. They stood facing her from a few cubits away, and like night and day they struck a stunning contrast. On her left was a goateed man in black that had long sooty hair pulled into a tail. His skin was tough and leathery, rugged like the exterior of spikey black armor he wore with gray accents. On her right stood a man in white who appeared the antithesis of the former. He had wavy white hair and a matching goatee rung about the lips. His armor was silver with snowy accents and fancy swirled inlays of gold.

The one in black snapped, "I am Ma'althan, the *Forerunner of Darkness* and *evil counterpart of Destiny*. I seek bad destiny for the seroxians, both cursed and un-cursed alike."

"I am Autheos, *Forerunner of Light* and *good counterpart of Destiny*," said the man in white. Magicia watched him sneer at Ma'althan while speaking further. "I seek good destiny for the seroxians and also the peoples of New Karnath."

Magicia knelt there still holding Hrya, with her face wrinkled in astonishment and hardly believing her eyes. Below New Karnath's full moon, she stared without blinking, her jaw agape. *I haven't seen the Forerunners or Karnatha... since the rebellion!* The thought ran through her mind, as their appearance hit her as sudden and unexpected. And then, it was only moments before she could not believe her ears.

"Hrya and Eriens are but a small sacrifice for *Karnatha's Game* to move forward," Ma'althan said. "With the white and black shards now in New Karnath, we shall perhaps see more progress in the next age, toward the Battle for Destiny being had at Gallow Cliff."

Ma'althan's words were fiery arrows that stuck in Magicia's heart, and caused her tremendous pain. All of a sudden, her world spun wildly, and she struggled to stay upright with a new dizzying reality: *Hrya's death was not some accident that happened on its own... Karnatha planned it, as part of her Game!*

"Wh... what?" Magicia asked, neither trusting what she had heard, nor what conclusions her mind had drawn. "What?!" she queried again heatedly, as the suggestion ate at her self-control.

"You wanted answers, did you not?" asked Autheos, rhetorically. "You should feel privileged, as Karnatha rarely has us talk to anyone. There's something about you that makes her fraught with worry. You see sorceress, Destiny wishes to keep you at peace in spite of your loss."

Magicia kept silent and just listened, growing angrier at Ma'althan's every word. Her eyes widened with indignation, she pursed her lips, and the winds animated her hair into a fury comparable to what she felt inside.

"My Servant Sydullus warned Eriens not to betray your trust, by entering New Karnath in war instead of peace. Even though that warning made him terribly uneasy, the selfish fool bought his disobedience at the price of another— *Kilwroth's Unwholesome Inheritance*! Oh well."

In Magicia's mind until now, Eriens' motivation seemed to be explained by the tendency of seroxians to covet New Karnath after the rebellion against Maken, the creator ordained by Destiny to construct the worlds. *Eriens wanted nothing more than to reclaim paradise!*

But that conjecture suddenly felt wrong to her, as she remained on her knees seething with ire over Hrya's death. Another conclusion slowly burrowed into her mind: '*Twas the Game that killed Hrya!*

Magicia knew well how the persona of Destiny named Karnatha—the god of Old and New Karnath—architected this horrid game to decide Karnath's destiny. And her knowledge of that led into only one reasonable deduction: *This is Destiny's fault... Karnatha's fault!*

Enraged, she shouted at the dark sky in an aside.

"If Hrya dies in this cruel game, then so do I! Past this moment I shall not love again, only my hatred of Destiny shall persist from this day forth!"

Her icy words lingered in the night air, as the Forerunners looked on. Magicia turned to see Autheos' face of compassion, whereas Ma'althan only smiled.

"Well," the Forerunner of Darkness said, "it's happened just like Karnatha suspected. Some enemies are better not had, but we mustn't interfere. We'll let chance decide what becomes of her intentions."

Magicia noted how Autheos did not evidence agreement, and only voiced weak protest.

"It's not my choice that any should suffer bad destiny in the pursuit of the good, but such is the Game."

She saw Ma'althan fixate on the black shard that impaled Eriens' corpse, as if paying no attention to his opponent's talk. The mirror-like blade was covered in coagulated seroxian blood and now glistened beneath the moonlight.

"Take it up, sorceress. Take up, *your black shard.*"

Ma'althan continued, still looking at the sword. "Your Hrya gave his life to bring the sword here and stop Eriens, so let it be your keepsake now. Just don't grow too attached, or you might be the next casualty."

His caution came with a chuckle. "Ha ha ha..."

Magicia watched Ma'althan fall silent, and in just a moment longer, he vanished into thin air with Autheos, right before her eyes. She was left alone upon the field with the moon and the night breezes, the black shard, and two lifeless seroxians. It was then she felt a different sting from the cumulative situation, as if somehow her weakness led to Hrya's death, like if she were stronger it all could have been prevented. In Magicia's mind, alarms sounded. *Get up… Get up, and get revenge!*

It was a Dark motivation to rise in the wake of a broken dream, yet it was enough for Magicia. With that thought, she gently laid down Hrya's head and stood up, ripping the black shard from Eriens' back. Having the sword in hand, she left the site on foot.

Her every step away seemed to bring her closer to the black shard of her broken dreams, and closer to doing something incredibly evil to avenge Hrya. And as such, this was the beginning of her descent into utter Darkness.

As she walked, from her lips came forth a prayer to the Void, the anti-Destiny of Old and New Karnath.

"Give me vengeance upon Karnatha for Hrya, for what she did to him through her Game! Please, let me be strong enough… Please…"

With her final word, it seemed to the discerning eye that the lights blinked out from above, like what burned inside Magicia terrified the stars, making them hide behind the night's obscurity.

When only a few strides away from the site where Hrya was murdered, certain blackness filled the void inside of her, the one borne of her divine purpose forever gone, without him alive. Covered in Hrya's blood and holding the black shard of legend, she trudged on, vowing then a Dark vow in her heart. *I shall seek vengeance upon Destiny for this game! I shall seek revenge for the sake of my first and only love!* The hatred boiled more and more within, until it frothed from her mouth. "I shall do harm to these ones of opposing hue and to their awful ruse! Karnatha will pay for her Game, and for trifling with the destiny of mankind!"

Magicia uttered those words only to have them go lost in the night, just as she would go lost in her anger for hundreds of years, until in a future time where Destiny and Karnath would suffer the consequences of her wrath.

"MAGICIA'S LOST LOVE"

Chapter 8
The King's Mission

X'ieth stood in a foyer outside the king's throne room in Castle Sergros, patiently awaiting his session with Talus. He was dressed for the occasion, adorned in the full attire of the Crimson Guard. He wore silver armor and white mails, with a scarlet cloak that bore Sergros' emblem: an upright lion standing upon its hind legs. The wire-wrapped handle of his broadsword poked from its sheath, which hung from his dark leather belt wrapped around his waist. The sword had a molding of Sergros' lion at its pommel and a v-shaped guard. Adjacent to his sword was his helmet, cradled in one arm; it had long feathered strands protruding from its rear, plumes alternating from white then crimson in a group of six. The feathers and his cloak made for a striking contrast with the silvery armor. His breastplate had six notches along its top to symbolize membership in the Sixth Order of the Guard.

There was one session ahead of his, and X'ieth found himself passing the time by staring into the throne room or around the castle itself. His eyes would wander over the gray stone, large columns, and banners of Sergros strung from every torch-lined wall. They were sights he deemed acquainted, sights that inundated him with a certain fondness for his childhood long past. Adding to his nostalgia were familiar smells in the air. He breathed in those of cooking meals in the king's kitchen, fires fueled by wood and black stones in the hearths throughout the castle, along with heavy perfumes to mask the more unpleasant odors wafting from closet latrines. From sight to smell he knew the castle, and in other ways too.

For years he grew up in the castle, being taken in by Talus as Sergros' privileged orphan. For years, he worked in the castle, always being dispatched from these halls on the king's next big assignment. For years, he celebrated in the castle on each occasion he climbed an order of the Crimson Guard's seven-tier system, where First Order was the lowest, and Seventh Order the highest.

Indeed, much of X'ieth's life was spent in the castle, and the experience put him close to many indentured Sergrothian servants—maids, cooks, seamstresses, clerks, bishops, soldiers, knights, and more. Seeing others served and personally being served instilled him with a deep appreciation for official service. He long conjectured that his wants of doing good through service budded from this early exposure, later blossoming into what he felt was a divine calling to protect innocent blood in the human kingdom. *That's your service to Sergros...*

He thought on. *Protecting people, through the Crimson Guard...* Images popped into his head of his boyhood days, with his boyish admiration for the knights of Sergros. He would watch the Guardsmen ride out of the castle, sometimes while sitting cross-legged in the courtyard with his favorite book about the hero Kayareth and Gallow Cliff, or sometimes while chasing after the fleeting tails of the knights' horses, in hopes of being able to get close enough and hop onto one, so to join the knight on his or her quest.

He thought on some more. *Protecting people, through becoming Kayareth...* The thought made him breathless, in part due to how much he relished the idea of being everyone's hero, the one who would save the world from Eternal Darkness. But the thought also stole his breath because of something far less likeable. He had many negative feelings behind this dream unlived, for it was something that never came to pass—despite it being a good and wholesome thing, despite his upright character that made him deserving, despite it being his lifelong dream. *How can it be, that what you wholeheartedly want is never meant to be, when your want is to do great good through using your talents?!*

X'ieth found his Karnathan faith shaken at times like these, for he often debated with himself over if there was truly divine purpose for his life, or if there was nothing more than the self-invented notion of divine purpose that conveniently explained the unexplainable—things in life completely out of his control and subject to chance, things that happened for unknown reasons beyond his understanding.

That idea suddenly seemed dirty, as his Karnathan faith started to convict him. The notion of one simply inventing his or her purpose merely to better cope with life's uncertainty—a purpose supposedly ordained by Destiny—seemed very dirty indeed. He instantly pushed the thought out of his mind, and prayed to Karnatha for forgiveness. *Shouldn't think that; surely there's purpose for you, man.* He reassured himself and renewed his faith, determining to continue being a man who would make the best possible choices in life.

You'll find your purpose here soon enough, if only the king frees up today... From a far corner of his mind came the thought, nudging him to refocus on the reason he waited around in the first place—the king's current session, which far exceeded its allotted time. And so, he directed his eyes away from the overwhelming gray stone of Castle Sergros, back into foyer, across which sat the king's hall that was filled with Talus upon his throne and also, a mysterious man of regal appearance. This person stood facing the king in the space between the two torches that sat before the throne; he wore a fine gray tunic that tied at the neck, a cloak of scarlet, and dark trousers having their legs tucked into shiny black boots.

X'ieth curiously peered through the doorway at the man. He was of middle age, with short black hair upon his head showing hints of gray, a cleanly trimmed beard of the same color covering his face, and intense features that made prolonged staring a difficult task. Although the young knight remembered seeing this person from time to time over his years in Castle Sergros, he strangely could not place who the man was and relevantly, how the fellow's importance warranted such a lengthy session with the king!

Will this meeting ever end?! The thought rushed through X'ieth's mind, as the situation tested his discipline and patience, for he had stood around now for over half an hour beyond when the royal officials brought him here. He shook his head, wondering why the meeting might be going longer than expected. *A disagreement no doubt...*

X'ieth studied the man as he continued speaking lowly with the king. What the young knight saw of the man's face—acute contours of his cheeks and brow, dagger eyes—along with what he noticed in the man's speech—sudden sharpness of inflection, elevated tone—all suggested a vexing conversation took place. With those observations, X'ieth surmised that the session went over because of difficult Talus, who often forced subjects to do things unwillingly through tiresome discussions and other means, which disrespected their rightful freedoms to disagree, as citizens of Sergros. *You've had your share of disrespect and things being forced upon you...*

X'ieth sighed, mindful once again of the difficulties he faced as a knight, being up against a manipulative king and a demanding wife. *Dealing with Talus or Millicent alone is harder than fighting monsters and villains!* With a slight grin X'ieth appreciated the situation's irony, understanding that perhaps he enjoyed being in the field too much, just because solving problems there was often easier for him than solving problems at home or at work.

With that, his thoughts transitioned to the uncertainty around his unexpected summons to Sergros. Immediately to mind came X'ieth's uneasiness with his failed foresights of his near future. *Didn't see this coming at all...* The reality easily made him wonder if like the oracles, people across Sergros would go blind to the foreknowledge of their own futures. That foreknowledge was a surprising gift to many three years ago; it came upon the oracles themselves going blind, and maybe it too was temporary, just like the oracles' lost gift. He feared he had already started losing his foreknowledge since his own visions of the future seemed to come less and less often, and those that arrived were sometimes wrong.

Why would Talus call you here? The thought slowly wedged its way between others. X'ieth stood there, still watching the regal man talk with Talus, not quite knowing what would happen in his own summons. He hoped to be back in the service of Sergros. *Another mission would be a refreshing break from the boredom you've experienced at home in recent weeks, on your leave from the knighthood. And it might buy you redemption over not preventing Garlew's death—redemption with Talus and yourself.* His distant guilt over what had happened to Sergros' hero made him all the more hopeful for a second chance.

X'ieth fancied helping the needy through a new mission. *Perhaps Talus will instruct the Sixth Order of the Guard to venture to cities in the far west of Sergros' provinces, those most affected by the Isles Conspiracy such as New Yoke. Talus might send you and others there in order to restore order, curb crime, and protect the innocent!*

As he glanced again into the throne room, the very idea of another mission brought a smile to his face. A moment later though, he considered another mission's implications and it dipped his smile into straight lips. Taking an assignment could mean weeks away from home, and since leaving for his summons, X'ieth had been worried for his wife given the odd quake that shook their cottage a day ago, and also, the laughter on the winds. It was a strange occurrence indeed, and such things were perhaps terrifying for his wife. Though Galwin accompanied her, X'ieth would not be there to protect her or ease her worries, if gone on another mission. *Destiny, let there be no more oddities at home—for Millicent's safety, and for her peace of mind!*

"This is unreasonable punishment!"

Clamor suddenly drew the young knight's attention into the throne room. X'ieth was surprised to behold a sudden development there, as the regal man before the king no longer spoke but shouted angrily! "I've paid my dues!"

Those last words resonated the chamber.

Upon hearing quick footsteps at his rear, X'ieth spun about to see guards appear instantly, as if from out of nowhere. His eyes followed them as they rushed into the throne room with spears in hand. With their every hurried step, his ears filled with the clanks of their armor.

X'ieth watched as the regal man turned to the guards, with balled fists at his waist, taunting them.

"C'mon! I dare you!"

The guards stopped mid-run, opened their mouths and looked to each other as if reconsidering their advance, and then surprisingly slunk back to their positions deep in the foyer! With unbelieving eyes, X'ieth witnessed the whole episode, which suggested the guards became worried about the prospect of confronting the man.

X'ieth turned his attention to Talus, who looked blankly at his visitor, and seemingly ignored the retreating guards like this had routinely happened. The king yawned nonchalantly, and then paused before speaking. "My proposition stays as given. Make your choice, knowing what matters most to you."

When Talus flashed a smile the man fumed, turning slightly then. X'ieth could see huge indignation in his complexion, blue eyes fiercely drilling into the king, nostrils flaring, and his face severely creased. It easily froze the young knight in place; X'ieth held his breath.

Moments of silence developed in the throne room, and tension became so thick in the air that it might be readily sliced. X'ieth's mind spun as he looked to the man, and then Talus. *What's happening? Someone say something?!* The building suspense made him very uneasy, and he hoped violence would not ensue, or worse.

Finally, after a length that was becoming unbearable for X'ieth to endure, he heard the man's reply. "There's no depth you can ever sink to, Talus! Your heart is blacker than the night sky!"

The young knight kept holding his breath. Despite X'ieth having his issues with Talus, the regal man's behavior struck him as downright rude and unbecoming for any subject of the king. *What he just said wasn't only disrespectful, but might land him in the dungeon!*

X'ieth watched the man turn abruptly and storm from the throne room, without a moment of hesitation after speaking. Though the young knight saw him approach the foyer where he waited with a look of murderous intent, X'ieth kept his shoulders straight and his gaze fixed for as long as he could. At one point the man's cold blue eyes met his own, and the young knight eventually let his face fall to the floor for a moment of relief.

X'ieth looked back up when the man left, and finally, he exhaled. *Whew...*

A series of questions naturally popped into his mind. *What man is this, who addresses the king by first name, as an equal?! Who outwardly says what he thinks and feels without fear for his life, when before the sovereign ruler over all of Sergros?!* In that moment, the young knight felt his own envy mix with his disbelief and passed judgments.

"Are you ready for your summons with the king?"

Emerging from his pondering, X'ieth glanced up at whomever spoke. A middle-aged man stood on his right, one of the king's royal officials with a plain face and brown hair, who wore beige pants below a deep blue tunic that showed the kingdom's crest. For the life of him, the young knight could never remember this official's name.

He opened his mouth to answer, but before uttering one syllable, a sudden shout from the throne room forced his attention there.

"Of course I'll still see him!"

X'ieth saw the king staring at another royal official who stood before the throne, one who had apparently questioned if the delay from the previous session changed Talus' want of the next.

When the young knight saw Talus look up, those brown eyes locked upon his own and instantly paralyzed him. X'ieth sensed things happening all around him, he heard them too, but could not immediately act. Talus lifted his hand and snapped his fingers while looking at the young knight. It all occurred to him in slow motion, as if his reality flowed like thick syrup.

Unable to do anything, X'ieth became little more than a dumbfounded dog, one not knowing how to respond to its master's call. Literally frozen in place by Talus' stare, he saw only a sphere of control and cruelty upon the throne. X'ieth developed this perspective from years of the king's abuse, experienced through a variety of different techniques such as him leveraging past benevolence, him inappropriately conditioning continued well-being or future promotions upon compliance, and him playing mind games. Of all things, the young knight hated mind games most, those occasions where Talus would purposely say things to get underneath his skin—things that would perpetually bother him—many times having him question the true basis of awards he once presumed meritorious.

After what seemed an eternity of stillness, X'ieth swallowed the lump at the top of this throat and finally moved his stiff body into the throne room. Each step he took there was agonizingly slow, like somehow he moved through molasses. The whole while, Talus maintained eye contact, the corners of his lips upturned in a certain deranged, anticipated glee. *He's happy... to torment you.*

When X'ieth finally stood before the king—in the space between those twin torches—he displayed a clear hesitation to kneel. Amid this awkward moment, Talus watched him with heavy eyes, eyes that pressed his knee to fall. And so eventually, the young knight reluctantly went to the floor, setting his helmet down beside his thigh. There, he waited for Talus to address him, with eyes lowered upon the stone. *Do you bow your head more out of formality or simply because you can't bear looking into his eyes?*

In that very moment, X'ieth recalled how his heart was once filled with admiration for Talus. Years ago, he had a will bent on serving his king as much as his kingdom. But in the wake of disrespect and mental cruelty, the young knight acknowledged that everything had changed. *Your motivation is only to serve Sergros now...*

From his peripheral vision, the young knight could tell that Talus suddenly stirred, getting off the throne. X'ieth soon heard the unmistakable sound of a sword being drawn from its casing. *What's he doing?! Why would he need a sword?!* His head buzzed with questions, and before he could think one follow-on thought, he sensed the king walk forth.

From the floor, X'ieth recast his vision upon the approaching Talus. At a single glance, his eyes caught flickers from the torch fire off the naked blade held by the king! His mind worked quickly. *You've a sword too, so protect yourself!* His initial instinct was just that, to reach for his sword, but X'ieth stopped himself knowing that this reaction might lead to bigger consequences than he bargained for. *Don't do it!*

Using quick wits, X'ieth positioned himself well for honor and defense by taking his right hand and crossing it over his left breast, just as the king came to his side. Hand over heart was symbolic of allegiance in Sergros, and was easily a befitting gesture for the moment. But from X'ieth's kneeling position, his hand over heart was conveniently close to his sword's handle, should he need to defend himself.

As Talus laid the blade on his right shoulder, X'ieth immediately felt its weight. From the quiet he heard the king's steady voice, "In *promotion to the Seventh Order* of the Crimson Guard, do you solemnly swear to use your knowledge of sword and magic to promote goodness and order, to protect the blood of the innocent from violence, malice, and evil, to…"

The words trailed off, as X'ieth became lost in disbelief over the situation. He looked to the floor again, this time with a wide smile, being absolutely astonished by an unexpected promotion to the highest order of the Crimson Guard! *It's unbelievable!* he thought then, with a complete loss for words.

The Seventh Order, what a mark of honor and respect! How people will respect you now, perhaps even your own wife! The happy thoughts paraded through his mind, one after another. However, that smile upon X'ieth's face slowly dipped into a scowl. A good thing that he now stared at the floor, for the more he pondered the situation a grave realization betook him, causing the scowl to get bigger. *Ceremonies for knighting a Guardsman do not occur like this!*

From climbing higher orders of the Crimson Guard, X'ieth knew the process quite well. Along with the knighting ceremony itself, there would typically be a prayer to Destiny, a formal modification of a knight's armor for the higher order of the Guard, some sparring among the order of the promotion, and afterward, a bountiful feast. Knights in all orders of the Crimson Guard enjoyed these rituals, and this festive evening made for a sense of community among them.

Perhaps with the gloom, there's no means to observe these rites of passage? The young knight wanted to believe that idea since it seemed plausible, yet he naturally felt suspicious of an unexpected promotion, especially when his last meeting with Talus went so poorly given Garlew's unfortunate and untimely death.

The king's voice droned in his ears yet longer, and X'ieth still held his hand over heart. Upon his shoulder, the blade weighed heavily, and the young knight felt some discomfort, but he stayed completely still as Talus finished.

"And eschewing Darkness while abiding in Light, do you commit to uphold the beliefs of the Church of Karnatha and remain an upstanding citizen of Sergros in the knighthood?" asked Talus, finally.

Now was the time for X'ieth to answer to the overwhelming number of obligations imposed by any order of knighthood. "I solemnly swear," he said in earnest, while staring up directly at Talus.

Without a doubt, the young knight knew that his heart for Sergros was as noble as could be. And despite his disdain and mistrust for the king, he would neither betray his allegiance to Sergros nor the many confidences placed in one taking the oaths of knighthood. X'ieth considered himself a valiant knight, one who did well for his family while doing good for the kingdom.

With his pledge, Talus removed the sword off X'ieth's right shoulder, over his head to rest the blade on his left shoulder, and then returned the sword back to his right shoulder, completing the knighting gesture. Returning to the origin was a central theme in the ritual of Sergrothian knighthood, just as in Karnath's philosophy too.

By nature, things reverted back to a resting state, a simple fact long observed even by an elven knight of the Sixth Order, who when among the living, drew X'ieth's utmost respect. At the knighting gesture's completion, he recalled the words of Garlew Il'therin, the fallen hero of Sergros. *Warriors are made from dust for battle, and so do warriors return to the dust of battlegrounds.*

X'ieth heard Talus speak then, and cleared his mind of these jumbled thoughts. *Still your mind!*

"Rise knight, being of the Seventh Order of the Crimson Guard."

At that command, X'ieth took up his helmet and stood with a blank look upon his face, a look that masked the ambivalence felt inwardly. On one hand the promotion joyed him, though he still wondered why it came. He could not place why Talus would have a change of heart, given the circumstances. *Your last mission of hunting Pyrus ended so poorly with the Isles Conspiracy breaking out, and Garlew dying at the hands of Kort Al'starz.*

The final thought made X'ieth recall the deceiver who rode alongside him in his previous assignment of hunting Pyrus. Kort was an elven ex-knight, stripped of his rank in the Sixth Order of the Crimson Guard for treason against Sergros. He deceptively served Sergros for years, only to gather intelligence for Taurus Hboshi as an informant to the Black Dragon clans. Many believed he was instrumental to the Isles Conspiracy. In his betrayal of many trusts, Kort became to X'ieth the very antithesis of what a knight should be.

"Well," Talus remarked, "what say you?"

All of a sudden X'ieth realized Talus called upon the fact that he remained unspoken, long after the ceremony's conclusion! And so, without even a pause, he answered the king.

"Why have you bestowed this honor? Why me, of all you could choose?"

Talus paused, as if weighing his words before replying. "With great responsibility, comes great privilege. And with great privilege, comes also great responsibility. Now for that responsibility." With the last words came a smile, right before Talus turned away. X'ieth saw the king retreat to his throne, that lengthy red cape drug behind him on the stone floor. There he sat, and leaned forward to engage the newly appointed knight of the Seventh Order.

"The Seventh Order of the Guard must undertake the most important mission in the matter of Sergros. With this gloom, the kingdom itself and

Karnath face their Fate's Fray! The destiny of one and all depends on the outcome of my latest assignment *to end the gloom*, one I've already handed to the other Guardsmen."

X'ieth displayed a puzzled look with that last remark, for missions in the king's name usually came to the pack of knights as a group.

"The short timing really makes me handle matters this way," Talus continued. "Your hurried knighting, briefing the others of their mission before you, and so on." With his hand, the king gestured as he talked.

The young knight remained before Talus, thinking the whole situation quite odd. *Let it go! This still is a chance to serve Sergros, and an important one at that!* The thoughts occupied his mind and kept him silent, and X'ieth simply waited for the details of the mission.

"As anyone can readily note," Talus said, "the gloom is devastating Sergros each moment it lingers. Right now, there's only enough food in our reserves to last the kingdom through the end of the winter season, and no one knows if this gloom will persist past then. Not even people with *supposed premonitions* of their own future know anything about the gloom, or how long it will tarry."

Talus' last words struck X'ieth poorly, as if the king had general disbelief in people claiming to have premonitions. He considered certain possibilities in that moment. *Could it be, that Talus has no visions of his own future?* To avoid conflict, the young knight refrained from asserting anything to the contrary, from his own experiences with premonitions.

"And besides a shortage of food, the gloom has created additional problems in Sergros far beyond what you might guess."

Talus wetted his lips by taking a sip from his goblet. X'ieth watched him swallow with a long sigh.

"Something must be done to vanquish this fog and bitter cold that oppresses the land and its people."

It was then that the king's sharp brown eyes pierced through X'ieth, and silence filled the vast hall. Flames danced in the torch collars sandwiching X'ieth. His suspense built, which slowly drew his question.

"How can I be of service, my king?"

Talus diverted his stare long enough to guzzle what wine remained in his goblet. X'ieth watched him drink, even as some of the wine dribbled down his chin. With a sigh and a wipe of the mouth, the king set aside his cup and looked back. "Magicia the sorceress you may remember. She has long cooperated with Sergros on many occasions, while her sister Esmeralda has never done so."

How could any of us not remember Magicia? X'ieth instantly had a flash of his entry into the First Order of the Crimson Guard, where Magicia cast the spell upon him and others, binding them to protect the blood of the innocent. In particular, he recalled himself kneeling before the sorceress at his induction ceremony, while she cast Nexus all about him, producing a hot sensation that he would never forget.

Talus suddenly leaned forward in his seat, and the action engaged X'ieth, whose mind had taken him yet again out of the throne room. "But now," the king said. "I find that Esmeralda moves from detachedness with Sergros to Dark deeds against my kingdom." Talus leaned even closer, and his voice grew very solemn. "My informants tell me how Esmeralda draws life force from the land. Every night they witness green energies flowing into her fortress abode from all directions. These energies emanate from the mountains, the trees, and the soil. I'm troubled at my conclusion that she's drawing life out of nature through a powerful medium, in order to bring gloom upon Sergros."

There was a moment of silence, and X'ieth stared at Talus with a sense of where this was going. *He mentioned already that the mission was to end the gloom, and if he believes Esmeralda is behind the gloom, then that means...*

"Your assignment with the Seventh Order is to enter Esmeralda's abode, to end her misdeeds against Sergros in the name of your king."

With those words, a chill ran all the way down X'ieth's spine. To him the entire situation seemed too good to be true, for Talus not only promoted him but also entrusted his pack of knights to essentially stop the gloom. *What a great privilege this is, for you to bear this task!* Then and there, X'ieth purposed in his heart to do his best for a much greater cause than the king. The entire kingdom suffered from the gloom, and the young knight would help everyone through his quest.

The very prospect made him feel terribly important. *You shall save Sergros from ruin, man!* And it was then that he had a radical thought, one that connected his present circumstances with his dream yet lived—being Karnath's hero, being Kayareth. *This mission is an important step in that direction! Maybe Destiny appoints you to greatness through this task!*

With high hopes, the young knight grew so excited that he pushed his concerns about his false premonitions to the back of his mind. And he continued feeling good about himself. *You'll be... the new hero in Sergros, the new Garlew Il'therin!* A smile developed on his face, as he imagined himself being carried by townsfolk through the streets of Sergrothian cites, where people would proclaim him as their hero.

While X'ieth's fancies and daydreams went on, Talus continued speaking in the background. The young knight struggled to pay attention, and went in and out of the king's monologue. Fortunately, he managed to learn some details of the mission's course.

"Your journey will involve venturing to the city of *Arlem*," Talus said. " It's situated on the cusp of *Forest Saol*, overhung by the gray peaks of *Liath*. From there, traverse through the woodlands to the mountain's foot, where you'll navigate Liath's western pass to Esmeralda's fortress, a tower that stands high from the rock."

The words faded in X'ieth's mind, replaced by more of his prior daydreaming and wild fancies. Though the king talked on, addressing issues about how Esmeralda's abode might be magically protected, the young knight's concentration fought a losing battle with his immense elation over his promotion and newly-handed assignment. *You'll be the hero! The hero of Sergros!*

It occurred to him that maybe he should not carelessly overlook the details here. One moment later, he countered that after merely reconsidering the matter. It turned out that he *always* skipped over the details, without a major problem yet. *You can figure things out along the way...* He told himself that with utter confidence in his abilities, having skills to spare as a master swordsman and hand-to-hand fighter, as well as a novice sorcerer. Many called him arrogant, but X'ieth bore the *Waning Crescent* and *Five-Banded Fists* designations that few possessed. They were marks of skill—both widely respected and coveted. *And with your skills, you don't worry over details.*

"Excuse my repeated comparisons to Magicia," Talus said, dragging X'ieth out of deep thought. "Much isn't known about Esmeralda, but her sister is very open with Sergros, and that knowledge might prove helpful when confronting a sorceress of *comparable power.*"

Those words brought certain stillness in X'ieth's mind. He did not go back to daydreaming, fancies, or lofty thoughts of himself. Instead, he grew somewhat worried when pausing to actually ponder the implications of the mission the king described. *Oh no...*

X'ieth's mind fixed on two very real possibilities, each having the same consequence. *Magicia would likely protect Esmeralda, for what blood sister would not? And if Magicia couldn't intervene in time, she would pursue us in vengeance!* Either way the young knight looked at it, the situation involved turning Magicia into an enemy. *A very powerful enemy, given she's the most powerful sorceress in Karnath, more powerful than even Esmeralda!*

To X'ieth, the realization of Magicia filling the highest seat in the Guild of Sorcery made the matter all the more troubling. Worst-case scenario was that the Guard would have to fight both Esmeralda and Magicia simultaneously! The worrisome thought stole X'ieth's breath. He stood there speechless before the king, just holding it for nearly a minute. *Breathe, man...* he told himself. *Don't let this beat you.* He inhaled deeply before exhaling, now feeling a bit woozy.

"Do you have any questions?" asked Talus.

The young knight regrouped, and studied the king's tired face, noting black circles under both eyes. It was then X'ieth considered that the gloom presented much larger problems for Sergros than his own fears.

"No, my king. The assignment is clear."

"Excellent," said Talus. "You may go."

In a slight bow, X'ieth leaned toward the king, and then turned from the throne. He started to walk out of the room, but before taking more than three steps, the king cut him from behind with a final remark.

"You may go, only if you wish to leave this place without knowing how to be *worthy* of your promotion…"

"THE PROMOTION"

Chapter 9
A Cruel Catch

The young knight stopped instantly, and his last footstep against the stone rang out in the king's hall. Slowly then, X'ieth turned to behold Talus upon his throne, wearing a bone-chilling smile, like it pleased him to add a catch to the knight's promotion.

"Much opportunity has been bestowed to a needy orphan, more so than many deem appropriate."

Didn't you see this coming?! X'ieth instantly chided himself for not expecting Talus' ulterior motives from the beginning. *Foolish, foolish, foolish...*

Feeling less of a need for respect now, X'ieth spoke without being called upon. "Sergros is the land of opportunity," he said, "and I have earned the privileges I enjoy, my king. Through my indentured service to your throne and the kingdom, I enjoy them rightfully."

"Oh really?" asked Talus, grinning more. "You think of all the knights in Sergros that are suited for the Seventh Order, you are the most deserving?"

X'ieth just stood there, grinding his teeth in silence. Word by word, he felt hotter in the face, growing more certain that Talus would soon epitomize why he no longer relished serving his king.

"Always have I given you chances before you deserve them, young X'ieth. At times, your deeds attest to good judgments on my part, but on other occasions, they do not. I'm hoping my judgment was good in this matter."

X'ieth kept quiet, inside loathing the king's actions. *With a single statement Talus speaks to your whole life, like you haven't earned anything on your own!* It was the same situation as always, where the king held past provisions and opportunities over X'ieth's head to purposely upset him, to unman him, and to leave him questioning his own worth. The king cruelly used everything as a weapon—everything, from taking in X'ieth as an orphan and training him in academy, to the knighthood itself.

"Prove to me that you've *earned* this promotion." The king's words were crisp and lingered in X'ieth's mind, creating perpetual negativity. Like a sore in the mouth, the king's implication irritated him again and again—the very implication that he had not truly earned what he enjoyed. It casted doubts upon what he had achieved over the years, and often robbed him of the satisfaction that should accompany success through hard work.

"Prove it to me," Talus continued, "by bringing me the severed head of Esmeralda the sorceress."

In that moment, X'ieth remained silent before the king, reminded then that his ambitions of being anyone's hero were threatened by what might become his Fate's Fray—the unraveling of his divine destiny by these poor circumstances. Just like Millicent, the king was offensive, demanding, and manipulative.

That combination often drew from him a poor motive for achieving objectives that he would otherwise do with a good heart, and the young knight feared that perhaps Karnatha would not honor his deeds because of it. From a far corner of his mind came a voice often silenced, one that said, *Perhaps Talus and Millicent create circumstances that block Karnatha's blessings from you— blessings of you becoming Kayareth.*

As X'ieth stared at Talus without a word, the idea was easily angering, and he suddenly felt hot all over, as if flames in his gut burnt him from the inside out. The same inner voice continued to torment him, exacerbating his feelings. *Maybe you can't be the hero, even with your promotion and a mission to save Sergros. Good deeds done for bad reasons, aren't good at all...*

With everything happening, the young knight became progressively uncomfortable before Talus, and it elevated his vitals. X'ieth could sense the tight, rhythmic pulses of his heart from beneath his heavy armor, as it beat all the more quickly each passing moment.

Talus went on, without an interruption. "On second thought, perhaps I'm expecting too much of someone just promoted to the Seventh Order. Perhaps a more reasonable expectation is that you stay out of everyone's way. Yes, that's it... such a young knight might only slow more experienced knights."

Those words rolled off Talus' tongue and made X'ieth feel upset and cheated, like somehow the best opportunities in the knighthood would never get him any closer to his unlived dreams. For despite these opportunities, Talus tainted his motives with poison, making every mission about proving worth or showing up the king. *That's not a true hero's motive... That wouldn't be Kayareth's motive...*

"Tell me, knight of Sergros," the king beseeched X'ieth, pulling him out from a troubled sea of thought. "How shall I set my expectations of you?"

In X'ieth's mind, surely his contempt for the king's treatment showed— surely he glowed red, surely his eyes were afire, surely Talus heard his grinding teeth. Yet in reality, his face only hinted redness, his forehead had beads of perspiration, and his grinding teeth went unheard—all poor indicators that anything was wrong. So perhaps then the stronger indicator would be his eventual response to the king's question.

At last X'ieth answered, his words firm and sure. "The highest outcomes should always be expected of me, my king. Rest assured, I shall deliver Esmeralda's head."

At that, he watched Talus' lips curl to a broader smile. *When you talk, it's actually the weakest indicator of all. You're a coward for not saying more…*

"Good. I have always admired your spirit, my boy. It's one of your finer traits." The young knight stared back silently, then hating himself more than even Talus. *Why didn't you say anything?! Each time you're given a chance to address his behavior, you let it pass you by! You won't tolerate such abuse from Millicent, yet you'll tolerate it from the king?! Coward…* The young knight's thoughts were demoralizing, and now, he could do little more than just let things happen.

"I have a session with my counselors shortly; a king's life never allows dull moments." In a loud voice, Talus called to the Sergrothian official at the back of the hall. "Tell this knight of the plan before his departure."

In a daze, X'ieth saw the same official in blue tunic and beige pants bow from the foyer.

"As you wish, King Darxar."

X'ieth looked back to Talus upon the throne, and the king no longer smiled. With a straight face and a harsh tone, he said, "You're dismissed."

Slowly, X'ieth turned about, being conflicted over doing so. He had wants of saying something to Talus, but at the same time, he did not want to stay in the throne room a moment longer. With that in mind, he walked through the hall and toward the official in the foyer. *This is why you serve Sergros as a Guardsman, and not your king…*

By the time X'ieth got to the brown-haired official, he already had new thoughts in his mind, about his own worthiness concerning past promotions. *Prove you earned your promotion, he says? Why would a king freely give without merit? Makes no sense… And if Talus does give without merit, how long has he done it with you?* As a sliver in the flesh, comments like these bothered X'ieth most, well after being said. He found it tragically troublesome for Talus to even suggest that any of his honors were merely an extension of Sergrothian welfare.

The official snapped X'ieth out of his thoughts.

"Travel for your mission won't be made tonight. Talus has arranged a room here for your stay. You'll leave tomorrow. Your chamber is in the castle's east wing, up its eleventh tower. I'll take you there."

X'ieth just nodded as his reply. He watched the official afterward pivot on the heel and turn away. Together, they made a trip in dead silence through the castle's halls of gray stone, many lit by flickering torches.

As the two walked—one behind the other—X'ieth pondered his utter disbelief over the king's mistreatment. Enduring Talus' cruelty bred regret in him, and he felt obligated to somehow address that behavior, lest it continue indefinitely. *Yet before the king you don't have a voice, man.* With a sigh, he chided himself for being soft-spoken at all the wrong times.

Without a good solution for the problem, his mind transitioned to the next troubling matter, something a bit more worrying than Talus. X'ieth considered once again the possible danger concerning Esmeralda and Magicia. For perhaps this would be the one mission where he could not show up the king. *It's that important, isn't it? You're risking everything for your pride, purpose, and dreams… just like Millicent says.* The mere thought of his wife actually being right sobered him. He gulped.

After a lengthy walk, X'ieth's mind fell silent and he thoughtlessly followed the official through the remainder of the castle's east wing. At the end of one corridor, they entered a treacherous spiral staircase chiseled from gray stone. The two ascended it, and as they did, the young knight counted more than two hundred uneven steps. They fanned higher and higher—past many shut doors and burning torches—eventually leading them to a small chamber, into which they entered. The man now panted heavily from the climb. X'ieth, being better conditioned, did not have the same problem.

Now inside the dimly lit room, X'ieth saw a small table and wooden chair next to the bed. A ceramic basin on the floor peeked out from beneath the bedframe, a crude thing made of wooden beams and rope, with a straw mattress atop, covered in linens.

His eyes ventured to the table, where rested a pewter candlestick embracing a flamed wick smothered in runny wax. The candle illuminated parchment next to the candlestick; it sat under a vile of ink, in which leaned a lone quill feather. X'ieth felt a draft, and he glanced over at the window on the far wall, with squares of thin glass set in a rectangular lattice. Through it he beheld a darkening sky outside, beyond the corbeled tops of adjacent castle towers. It was nearly night.

He looked back to the official, who was still struggling to recover from the climb. The man motioned to the space with an outstretched hand, and spoke in a strained voice, frequently interrupted by his own breathing.

"Here you are. Breakfast will be brought… in the morning. Before departing midday… the king has arranged sparring… with the Seventh Order."

"Thank you for this chamber," replied X'ieth, appreciative of the accommodation.

"It is the king… who provides this chamber."

"I know."

X'ieth's words seemed out of place, but he would not correct himself. *Don't know if you received anything worthy of thanks from Talus today…*

"All right then, Destiny be with you. Sleep well."

With that, the official departed, shutting the door behind him. X'ieth sat on the bed, and just listened to the man slowly step down the stairs. The young knight placed his helmet on the mattress, and it was not long before he started mulling over his tricky situation, one that played out just like this so many times before, mission after mission.

Indeed, his knighthood had put him in the same tugging match and he had endured it for years—a tugging match between his wife, his king, and his dreams. In this, the knighthood entailed many bad things: *You have a knighthood that your wife is trying to connive you out of for a better home life, a knighthood that puts you under the king's mistreatment, a knighthood that might get you killed by Magicia and Esmeralda...* But on the other hand, the knighthood also entailed many good things. *You have a knighthood that's your only source of purpose, a knighthood that lets you use your talents for the good of others, a knighthood that may lead into your dream unlived, of being Kayareth...*

There were indeed pros and cons of the knighthood, but the tugs of the tugging match had stretched him over time. For this reason, X'ieth wondered if being a knight was sustainable long-term, and what would be his best course of action concerning his career. His mind circled with possible solutions that benefited one or more of the participants in the tugging match.

You could just favor your dreams, tolerating Talus' cruelty and fighting Millicent's wants; you'll have neither a good home life nor work relationship, yet you'll be fulfilled with purpose... Or, you could just quit the knighthood and be home with Millicent...

The mere thought was infuriating, and ended his considerations over further options.

"No!" he shouted at the idea, being reluctant as always to give up his purpose, especially in the lack of greater purpose. *You need the knighthood because without it... you're nothing.* In that single moment, the young knight felt saddened and selfish by his own desires.

He silenced his mind for a time, and that was enough space for him to realize that perhaps the only solution to his bigger problem was actually talking to both Millicent and Talus so that he could somehow continue his career in the knighthood. *So you can continue it, in the absence of greater purpose like...* He stopped himself from completing the thought, tired from disappointment over not being Kayareth. It was enough disappointment about this, at least for today.

He sighed again, looking down to the floor past his thighs on the straw mattress. As it bunched beneath him, he shifted for want of more comfort, which resounded with the idea of talking to the king for just that—more comfort. *Yes, you must talk to Talus about his mistreatment, if you're to stay a knight. There's no other way...*

Breaking from his thoughts, he looked up to the pen and parchment upon the table, basking there in the candlelight. The sight pulled him from his bigger problems concerning the knighthood toward the smaller, immediate problem— his unexpected quest to save Sergros from Esmeralda's gloom. *You have to write Millicent, and explain to her all that's happened.*

X'ieth leaned forth with a sudden urge to move to the chair and table. But quickly then, he sat back down not having a clear sense of what he would write. It was terrifying to even consider what negative reaction the news of his mission would elicit from Millicent. *She doesn't take uncertain things well. She's used to certainty, the kind that an upbringing with seeing oracles would provide.*

Yet again he sighed at his present indecision, but fortunately for him, an inner voice taunted: *If you can't face a quill and parchment, there's no facing Esmeralda or Talus...* With that thought, the young knight instantly jumped off the bed and plopped into the chair, unable to stay there idly with such a thing in mind.

With the quill pen, X'ieth began writing furiously, penning the contents of his heart onto the parchment. Fast strokes against its surface sounded in the chamber, along with his whispered words. "Millicent, I love you," he talked while writing. "With all my heart I wish to be home," X'ieth continued, "but unfortunately there's an important mission for Sergros, one bound to end the gloom!"

Onto the parchment he continued to write, and his truths slowly morphed into lies. "I shall return surely," he scribbled, uncertain of safety. With a lump at the top of his throat obstructing each written word, X'ieth knew well that his premonitions of the future failed him, and in that, there could be danger. In fact, he now felt exactly like he did months ago, after a woman in white spoke to him in a forest black. "Not as you expected?" were her words then, said moments before he almost died during an ambush—an attack not seen in his premonitions.

So there X'ieth was with uncertainty abounding, wanting to believe his own message but knowing that its half-truths counted for little. As mentioned in his letter to Millicent, surely he would return to Sergros from this mission. *Though perhaps in a wooden coffin...* X'ieth withheld the truth about the mission's danger from his letter, believing it better this way. *Let her hope for the best, as will you...*

After he finished writing, he put aside the parchment for the couriers. Then, after undressing and snuffing out the candle, he lied upon the bed in want of sleep. While it was far more luxurious than his bed at home—being a straw mattress covered in fine linen sheets—it was not enough to put an active mind to rest. He worried about Millicent. He worried for their marriage. He worried for himself, given the mission. He worried and worried, about a great many things.

And so it was, X'ieth restlessly tossed and turned for hours, unable to sleep. With his every movement, the mattress shifted upon its rope suspenders, and the wooden bedframe creaked then moaned. At one point, despite feeling cold from the room's apparent draft, he threw the wool blankets off in utter frustration. *Destiny damn it!* The thought of starting his quest tired and irritable rendered him mad; the anxieties he had about meeting the Seventh Order did not help.

His mind continued to race and race more, as he rehashed the same things he considered all day. His pregnant wife Millicent was left alone with young Galwin, the behavior of cruel Talus warranted a discussion for which he had no voice, and two powerful sorceresses would meet him, perhaps in a head-on collision. It all swarmed the young knight's mind, and made his heart so devoid of peace. But despite the circumstances, X'ieth finally fell asleep after a terribly long time, to be spared at last from these most troubling contemplations, for but a night.

Chapter 10
Flashback Incident

He awoke to gray; it stared right at him through the glass casement. X'ieth sat up in bed and rubbed his eyes, hearing the rooster's crow in the distance. Through the window, he returned his stare at the overcast that hugged the skyline of Castle Sergros. The young knight studied the ominous clouds, viewing them as a by-product of Esmeralda's oppressing gloom, a matter in which his purpose was never more apparent.

After sleeping on it, X'ieth came to some peace about his mission. He took risks with every assignment, and the risks associated with confronting Esmeralda and possibly Magicia were part of his job. And since he did not volunteer for the mission, he believed it must be part of his divine destiny. *Much innocent blood is endangered by Esmeralda's gloom, and something must be done.*

It occurred to him then, that perhaps one noble deed was between Sergros and blue skies. *Your noble deed of stopping Esmeralda...* The mission could very well be the most important thing he would do in his life, even if it were less than what he aspired to be: *Karnath's hero, Kayareth...* As his dream unlived came to mind again, his countenance fell like so many times before. *Kayareth. You'd give anything, to live one day in his shoes...*

From his periphery, X'ieth detected something placed upon his table in the small chamber. He stood from the bed and stretched briefly, before walking closer. His eyes sighted an iron dish on the tabletop that the servants must have exchanged for the quill and parchment. Inside the dish, a modest breakfast had been set out, consisting of one cooked quail egg and a chunk of whole wheat bread. Adjacent to the iron dish sat a cup of herbed water. *Wonder how long ago the servants brought this in...*

X'ieth dipped his finger into the cup of herbed water, typically served hot. *Lukewarm...* He concluded that perhaps he had overslept the freshness of his meal. But being hungry from the day before, he would not let lack of freshness deter him from eating.

And so, he grabbed the iron plate from off the table and sat on the corner of his bed, stuffing food into his face with his free hand. He ate ravenously, without spending enough time to savor, shoving in food faster than he could chew it and swallow. His cheeks bulged, and he chomped away while looking around the room. Suddenly, in the middle of his meal, the door shook from a rapping!

78

Knock knock knock!

He turned his head, just in time to see the door creak halfway open. The same Sergrothian official peeked in, dressed as the day prior.

"Good morning, knight. The Seventh Order… awaits you… in the sparring grounds."

X'ieth hurried to swallow so he could reply, but the official's words were short and the man closed the door in the very moment where the young knight could speak!

"Good morning," X'ieth replied to the wood. Sounds arose of the official's quick steps down the stairwell, and it made X'ieth feel awkward. He wondered why the man left so quickly. *Was the official trying to avoid talking? Perhaps.*

But when X'ieth looked down to the remaining food in his dish, his eyes caught a glimpse of his bare, hairy legs. And upon this sight he realized that he was not fully dressed! *Perhaps that's why the man fled like the Darkness itself chased him!* His face reddened at the thought of the official finding him undressed.

Upon realizing that he might be late to the scheduled sparring, X'ieth recovered from his embarrassment. He quickly finished his meal, and then started putting on his armor, a routine process that gave him the opportunity for a moment's prayer: *Destiny, please let Millicent be protected and well…*

Armored in minutes, X'ieth sat down on the bed's corner and began fastening his first leather boot. As he worked, he revisited a thought from last night about speaking with Talus. X'ieth wondered if perhaps that episode witnessed the other day had lent some inspiration; it had been entertaining to watch the regal man spout off to Talus in the throne room, like the king was an equal to him or less. While this fellow came off as a bit acrimonious, X'ieth still admired his courage to speak from the heart. *You must find courage to do the same, but hopefully with more finesse than that!*

After slipping on his second leather boot and fastening it, X'ieth rose from the bed and started walking for the door. In his ears were sudden footsteps in the stairwell, literally moments before the official burst through the entrance unexpectedly, swinging the door fully open and staring X'ieth right in the face!

"Talus commands… you meet the Guard… at once!" the man said, gasping between those words.

Smiling, X'ieth said, "I'm ready to go."

The official replied, "Right this way."

From behind, X'ieth watched the official descend, with almost evident enthusiasm for it being the way down, versus up. The young knight walked to the edge of the room and placed his feet carefully on the uneven steps one at a time, to follow along.

X'ieth and the official came down the tower together, and navigated the castle's east wing, which entailed many winding corridors of gray stone. While passing through them, at one point X'ieth lost count of the royal blue banners and tapestries hung from every wall, featuring the kingdom's lion crest. To X'ieth, the symbol made him proud to be in the Crimson Guard, for it served a simple reminder of his worthy cause: protecting the innocent of Sergros.

Around the next bend, X'ieth trailed behind the official, as their path put them in the adjoining torch lit hall, where mid-stride, he came face-to-face with *her*. It was the woman in white he met in the forest black! He recognized her instantly, given the woman's perfect alabaster skin, golden hair, rosy lips, and sapphire blue eyes!

He stopped at once, and with the same immediacy, his gaze fell from her pouty lips and over her body, taking the woman in from head-to-toe. Exactly as he remembered, the woman wore a white surcoat with pearl buttons and a matching cloak upon her shoulders. She exchanged a look with him and simply smiled, just passing by without a single word.

With his mouth open, X'ieth remained in the middle of the hall, as she and the official continued walking in opposite directions. He turned and directed his eyes back to the women in white. As X'ieth watched her leave, the sight conjured up an incidental flashback.

**** X'ieth's Flashback—The Woman in White ****

On their hunt for Pyrus, X'ieth rode with the Sixth Order of the Guard through a dark mountain forest. His horse trotted up the path taken by the pack of Guardsmen, which narrowed to a distant clearing with gnarled trees bowing over. He felt the summer night pressing down upon him, its air heavy and suffocating. On his ears fell sounds of chirping crickets and talk amongst three riders that went ahead: Enker, Dimral, and Kort.

"This isn't right," said Kort suddenly.

"What isn't right?" asked Dimral.

"Aye, what do you mean?" added Enker.

Kort gave no reply.

X'ieth just continued riding further up the path, following behind Kort and the other two knights, while being ahead of both Garlew and Sagult, who rode at his rear. As he came closer to the clearing, he noted the foliage peel back to reveal a ridge overlooking a gorge, in which white rapids ran noisily. The waters flowed between two mountains, sourcing rivers that would drain into Sorin Bay.

The three riders ahead of him trotted into the clearing, mixing more hoof clops with cricket chirps. X'ieth continued riding and in a few moments time, he reached the clearing himself. He emerged from the forest beneath a starry night sky with the ridge before him, maybe thirty cubits away. He approached it, as Enker, Dimral, and Kort had already rode there, and now, the three of them were starting the ridge's winding path that overlooked the gorge.

When about twenty cubits from the ridge and still being in the clearing, X'ieth glanced into the deep ravine, and as before, he saw the white rapids below. The visual connected to the roar of rushing waters yet upon his ears, a loud sound that was not loud enough to drown the noise of several abrupt snaps, heard from over his shoulder!

X'ieth maneuvered his steed about, to behold a woman in white standing on the fringe of the forest, behind Garlew on horseback. In the same instant, he sensed a rider pass him in the clearing; it was Sagult. X'ieth paid little heed to that, and instead, found himself entranced by the woman's sheer beauty; he fixated upon her brilliant face of blue eyes, red lips, and shiny blonde hair. She was stunning, and reminded him of Millicent.

When her lips began moving, the world stopped for the young knight. Feeling a bit spellbound, X'ieth surrendered to a certain stillness that overcame him then, and just watched the woman speak, following her lips as she pronounced each syllable of each word.

"Not as you expected?"

X'ieth looked then into her eyes, noting that her sapphire blues were upon another, someone over his shoulder! As X'ieth pulled his head and body around—back toward the clearing and gorge—the ambiance scrolled by with dramatic slowness. Leaving his vision first was the woman in white, her lips upturned in a developing smile. Then the young knight saw Garlew upon his horse, wearing an ice-cold look and being closer to the forest than to the ridge. Behind Garlew, he saw movement in the woods, followed by hearing metallic slides and low hums—the unmistakable sound of crossbow function. At last, the young knight's gaze swung back to the clearing's end, where he observed Kort, Dimral, and Enker stopped there on the ridge, with Sagult now riding ahead of them, as if oblivious to what now transpired.

X'ieth watched Kort's face show utmost surprise, as two bolts flew through the darkness toward him, the first going right at his head! Like lightning, Kort whipped his broadsword out, knocking the first bolt off its lethal trajectory. But that second bolt pierced Kort's chest armor, and when it did, his face was stricken with a terrible grimace; undoubtedly he was in great pain. More humming and metallic song filled the air, and X'ieth could tell another wave of bolts flew toward Dimral and Enker.

The young knight focused on Kort, whose horse jumped as a bolt struck the beast, causing him to fall out of his saddle and right over the ledge, into the ravine! X'ieth heard Enker and Dimral scream when the remaining bolts hit their marks. His eyes discerned Sagult riding off wildly into the night along the ridge, not looking back once.

****

The flashback ended as quickly as it started, and the sounds of the ambush faded in X'ieth's head, being replaced now with the noise of the woman's footsteps, which grew fainter by the moment. He watched her white cloak float all the way down the hall, where at last, it disappeared from view, going behind the corner. The three falling stars on it were the last thing he saw.

"That's her!" X'ieth said to himself.

He heard a sudden clap against stone, as the official came to an abrupt stop at the other end of the hall. And then, there was a stirring, as if the man spun about to see what had happened.

X'ieth turned back and verified it was so. The official showed a puzzled face, and was speaking to him, but he could not hear anything but the woman's words.

Not as you expected? The question hit him, like a coin sack to his head, causing X'ieth to stumble upon an unnerving realization: *The woman in white knew why your premonitions were untrue then, and she likely knows why they're untrue now!*

In that moment, X'ieth recalled being surprised by the visitor knights at his own cottage; it was an event that contradicted his premonitions of the future. And the longer he dwelled upon that, the more it seemed exactly like what had happened in the ambush. *She knows... She must!*

Without another thought, X'ieth ran down the hall, away from the official. He barely heard the man speak while he dashed toward its end and into the corridor, where the woman had turned.

"Are you coming, knight?"

He exited the hall, and took the bend into a long corridor, expecting to see the woman there. But when X'ieth peered down the hallway, he saw absolutely no one! The sight was at first dumbfounding, and he did not know how to respond. In some disbelief, the young knight judged the corridor's length to be tens of cubits, seeming too long for anyone to have traversed it, in merely an instant. *Impossible! No one could go that far, just like that. It's as if she vanished...*

X'ieth suddenly heard the official call him.

"Are you coming, knight?!" Frustration and angst were evident from the man's elevated tone.

With a pause, X'ieth gave a final look to the empty corridor before going back into the hall. He beheld the official standing there, with what might be construed a cross countenance, as seen by the torchlight.

"Well?" he asked again, a bit sharply.

X'ieth reluctantly walked toward the official, bothered now by seeing the mysterious woman in white. The connection he just made between her and his mismatched premonitions played on his fear about being unable to know his own future, and he worried beyond that fear about her very presence. *Why was she here?!* He wondered, with suspicions that it meant nothing good.

"Please stay close behind. We'll otherwise be late," warned the official, motioning for X'ieth to follow.

The young knight nodded.

Down more corridors X'ieth went, now staying on the official's heels, only to have his worries spare his mind from a thoughtless walk. For the second time he wondered, *Why was she here?!* It easily led into all sorts of follow-on questions: *What's happening? What does your future hold?* Those questions ganged up on him, and he did not have a good answer to any of them.

The same feelings overwhelmed X'ieth then, as when he had first encountered the woman in white—feelings of lost control and uncertainty. Such feelings were a common part of his human experience before his first premonition, but now, these feelings seemed foreign.

Seeing the woman in white awakened X'ieth's distress about his false premonitions, but now as before, he was unsure of what this could mean. The only thing he was certain of was that the woman in white somehow knew why his premonitions were wrong. *And the next time you see her, you'll talk about that.* X'ieth shook his head, agreeing with himself that next time, he could not let her get away without having her answer some of his questions first.

In not much time at all, or at least as it seemed, X'ieth left the halls of Castle Sergros to arrive at an open courtyard, frowned upon by the depressing gloom. He beheld a number of knights in crimson and white ahead. They occupied a large space between two columns, assuming various stances and sword forms. Only one figure—a small and hefty fellow—just stood and watched the sword exercises.

A conclusion popped into X'ieth's mind upon making the visual. *Surely, this must be… the Seventh Order of the Guard!* As he walked behind the official and nearer to the group ahead, flutters filled his stomach over his impending encounter with the highest order of knights in the sect. *What will you say? Will they accept you?* He did not know, but was soon to find out.

Chapter 11
Seventh Order of the Guard

X'ieth approached the knights practicing up ahead, still following behind the official. As he walked closer, he studied the one knight who did not participate in the sword drills.

From his limited vantage point, X'ieth could still tell the person was a dwarf, short and hefty, with a frizzy red beard. The dwarf stood several cubits in front of him, and about ten cubits off the nearest knight dancing through sword forms. Beyond that knight were two more knights sparring at the center of the courtyard, and one distantly practicing alone. All knights were dressed exactly like him.

His stomach knotted as he and the official drew nigh. X'ieth watched the knight beyond the dwarf suddenly leap into air, pulling his sword vertical, and high above his head. It was the *Geyser's Fount* aerial form, with which X'ieth was very familiar and did not count as an advanced technique. And so, he looked on unimpressed, as less of a spectator and more of a critic. *You probably assume that form in your sleep, man. 'Tis that easy...*

X'ieth watched the knight's last form spill into the start of his next: a non-aerial version of Geyser's Fount. The form was executed quickly, and ended in a distinctive stance, where the knight's one leg bent and his other almost kneeled. Dramatically, the knight held his sword up with both hands, curling them about its handle—one atop the other—the sword's pommel at his sternum. *Nice moves, for an intermediate.* X'ieth continued criticizing, as his anxieties over the situation stayed intact. And he did so, knowing that he was coping with those anxieties through criticism.

His eyes followed the knight yet again, who quickly leaped into the air to execute another sword attack. X'ieth watched him reposition his hands around the sword's grip before bringing the sword behind his head, with elbows up. When the knight reached the peak of his ascent, he threw his elbows down so that his blade cut through the air. The sword came over his head and was slammed forward, while his body returned to the ground. This form was known as *Rainfalls*.

Despite the fluency and accuracy of the practiced techniques, X'ieth gave the knight little credit. *Eh, novice forms for a novice swordsman... Bet he doesn't even hold the Crescent designation...* Another knot tied his stomach with the thought, as X'ieth and the official finished walking, now settling at the dwarf's heel.

Surprisingly then, X'ieth heard the knight before the dwarf speak up, still looking off to the courtyard wall, in the opposite direction of X'ieth. He literally spoke upon completing the forms.

"Yeah, like me said, Talus gave the lad everything growing up. I wouldn't be surprised if this promotion came likewise to him."

"Right you are!" the dwarf laughed, continuing what appeared to be the two's ongoing discussion. He spoke in a gruff voice. The dwarf looked to the side then, noting the presence of X'ieth and the official, which caused him to abruptly stop laughing.

"He's standing there, isn't he?" the knight asked.

"Aye!" chuckled the dwarf, after a moment's quiet.

The knight whipped about, his face painted with a smile. X'ieth immediately studied him, an elf of Mainlandish origin with blond hair, short pointy ears, non-oriental features, and a stature well below the norm. *The elves of Juniper are tall as humans, if not taller. But not this fellow; he likely stands at my shoulders, as would an elf from the Hirishin Isles!* X'ieth had this thought, familiar with Mainlandish elves being white-skinned and tall, and Hirishin elves being bronze-skinned and small.

The official and X'ieth stood beside the dwarf, with now, the elf walking toward them.

"Ah, the one whom we've heard so much about!" said the elven knight, after coming to a stop three cubits from X'ieth. "Let there be no hard feelings."

"Be easy, man. I'm not offended," X'ieth replied without even a glower, being accustomed to talk behind his back and on occasion, right in front of him. From many promotions within the Crimson Guard, he knew there was always a period of time where he would have to earn the respect of his new rank and endure some jeering.

Clearly, his reputation of being Sergros' privileged orphan preceded him. *And that could be causing resentment*, he thought, knowing that many knights in the Crimson Guard were many years older than himself and could be thinking that he was given a place among them undeservingly, well before his time.

The official raised one hand and began snapping his fingers, summoning the remaining knights to their location.

"Everyone stop for a moment, and gather here to meet your new Guardsman!"

The remaining knights stopped and looked—two men still sparring against each other nearby and another person, more distant in the courtyard and practicing alone. X'ieth returned their stares, as the men all started walking over with wooden practice swords in hand.

During their approach, X'ieth nervously readied himself for his moment to speak, and also, the official introducing him to the others. *Don't say anything stupid, man... And try not to grimace during the official's intro, when he tells your whole life's story!* The two knights who sparred together came to the left side of X'ieth and the official, with the elf and dwarf on his right.

When the last knight walked up, X'ieth was shocked to find that the man practicing all alone and most distantly in the courtyard was none other than the man of regal appearance he saw in Talus' throne room! The fellow stopped behind the two knights on X'ieth's left, looking blankly at the young knight as if he did not even recognize him. *Did he also get promoted to the Seventh Order?!* X'ieth was flabbergasted, feeling as if a complete nobody was thrown amidst a group of elite knights.

He counted six out of seven knights there including himself, but he did not see Sagult. Sagult was X'ieth's comrade from the Sixth Order of the Guard who was promoted to the Seventh Order for a valiant ride back to Sergros, after the ambush where the woman in white made her mysterious appearance. *Sagult rode for two days straight to tell Talus about the Black Dragon attack and conspirators in the knighthood like Kort, enabling Sergros to work with Juniper toward dismantling the Isles Conspiracy, quickly and effectively.*

But in Sagult's absence, X'ieth's mind began to doubt his own promotion, an insecurity nurtured by Talus over the years, because the king cruelly put everything he had earned into question. *Did Sagult receive a new assignment? Is this bearded man merely the temporary fill-in until Sagult returns? Or, is it you who's the fill-in?* The very idea brought a scowl to his face. He forced a quick, straight-lipped recovery. *It's not true. It can't be.*

"Let me start by introducing X'ieth," said the official, reining in the young knight's attention. "And then you may go around with introductions one by one. Try to be brief, as the king wishes for everyone to get as much self-practice as possible before the instructor arrives. Many of you have been out of the king's service for weeks now, so Lord Darxar thinks you can use a warm-up before your quest." The official waved his hand while talking just then, as if to brush off any negativity of his last statement.

"Ahem," the official cleared his throat and gestured to X'ieth using his already lifted hand. "I bring you X'ieth Armstrong, newly promoted knight of the Seventh Order, previously under the command of the humble and heroic Garlew Il'therin of the Sixth Order. He has five years of field experience as a knight of Sergros, receiving weapons and combat training in Castle Sergros, which led to his high designations of Waning Crescent and Five-Banded Fists…"

As the official went on, X'ieth felt his face go flush. *This is why every new Order of the Guard thinks you're arrogant from the start. You come to the Seventh Order with a strong pitch from the official, like he's a merchant trying to make a sale!*

"X'ieth sat under the best teaching in the Sergrothian royal academy while growing up in Castle Sergros, as one of the king's adopted sons. He's wed to Millicent Armstrong, formerly the maiden Millicent No'Seer and child of senior oracles in the Society. He lives in a simple cottage situated in the grasslands north of here." *Destiny save us, man! Can you keep it brief and let us knights practice, if that's what Talus wants?!* X'ieth tried hard to hold back a pained look, as the official wrapped up a lengthy and somewhat embarrassing introduction.

The elf opened his mouth to speak, but the official lifted his hand again and quickly paused the introductions.

"Save it for him, as I know you all! Let me excuse myself now, and see where your pack leader is—Knight Sharpstone of the Seventh Order." With that, the official scurried away, going through the courtyard toward the passage through which X'ieth and the man initially entered.

"Let me start our introductions," said the elf in perfect Mainlandish, prying X'ieth's gaze from the departing official. "The name's Finnel, elf from Kingdom Juniper, here to lend a helping hand in Sergros."

Upon him speaking, X'ieth looked back at Finnel, paying closer attention this time to his appearance. His chin was somewhat shallow, overhung by a sharp nose and piercing close-set, blue eyes. Though his frame was small, the elven knight had well-developed muscles all over his body. The most noticeable feature of all was the *Waning Crescent* upon his exposed upper arm, partially occluded by his hanging mail. *Didn't see that before…*

The designation matched the one X'ieth held, and meant that Finnel was a master swordsman, as recognized by the *Bladed Fellowship*, the esteemed center of swordplay throughout the Mainland and Isles. *Wonder what tier he is? Eh, probably less than third tier…* As X'ieth began to feel a little insecure, he started coping with his insecurity just like he would with his anxiety—through criticism. A hoarse voice suddenly broke his thoughts.

"I'm Hammar, dwarf from Kingdom Deardrum, also here to protect innocent blood in Sergros."

X'ieth immediately looked over to see Hammar, who stood not much taller than three cubits, a bit shorter than Finnel. His body was round and bulky, tucked inside the largest Guardsman armor that X'ieth had ever seen! The young knight studied Hammar's full face, with tough and leathery skin, vibrant green eyes set above a round nose and reddish beard, with frizzy head hair to match.

In that moment's glance, X'ieth noted something peculiar about Hammar, something unseen until now. While the dwarf had armor just as the other knights, he did not carry a sword but rather a larger club hammer. *What kind of knight is without a sword?!*

The next introduction interrupted his thought.

"I'm Tol, native of Sergros," said one of the two knights who had sparred together in the courtyard. X'ieth turned to see a lanky man running his fingers through long hair that flowed over his shoulders, black and curly. A stubbly shadow clung to his face, below a crooked nose and a pair of brown eyes.

X'ieth gave a nod as his simple acknowledgment, just as he had done with Finnel and Hammar. He planned to speak up when everyone was finished introducing themselves. *Otherwise, this will take far too long!*

"Pleased to meet you."

X'ieth turned to look at the fellow beside Tol.

"I am Lewes, also born in Sergros."

Lewes was of similar build to Tol, though about X'ieth's height, having a chiseled chin and a bearded face, dirty-blond hair falling over his brow, and brown eyes perched above his straight nose.

When Lewes stopped talking, the regal man spoke, the one who yelled at Talus in the throne room.

"I am Zeros…"

X'ieth turned to his left, looking beyond Tol and Lewes, into the man's cold blue eyes.

"I am Zeros," he reiterated, "a lowly mercenary for the king, having the privilege of serving among such warriors of high esteem throughout all the Mainland."

X'ieth watched Zeros say the last words. The mercenary did so, while looking collectively to the knights all around. When there was nothing but silence as his reply, the young knight's eyes drifted from the mercenary to Finnel, Hammar, Tol, and then Lewes. Their faces were all burdened by scowls. *They act standoffish to Zeros, like he doesn't fit in! And maybe he doesn't…*

His first thought led into others, as he tried to understand the situation. *Wait, why would Talus put a mercenary in the elite Guard, instead of a seasoned knight? Perhaps it bothers everyone to have a hired hand as a peer.* Then, from the corner of his mind, his insecurities spoke to him. *What does Zeros' promotion imply about yours? Talus might be inducting anyone into the Seventh Order these days.* The different thoughts did not make any sense to X'ieth, and he ultimately could not reconcile why Zeros was among the elite Guardsmen.

Suddenly, from behind X'ieth's shoulder, came a disapproving voice about the comment Zeros had made.

"Warriors? We're not warriors. We're knights."

X'ieth spun about to see another knight walking through the courtyard, staring directly at Zeros while approaching. He had gentle features, with wavy brown hair and soft brown eyes. The young knight looked down at his polished armor, clean mail, pressed cloak, and combed plumes. *Can this be Knight Sharpstone, the pack leader? He seems dressed more for the king's feast than a mission!*

X'ieth saw the knight gaze directly upon him, and smile. "You must be X'ieth. Welcome, brother!"

Before X'ieth could reply, Knight Sharpstone quickly reached a hand around X'ieth's back, and threw his chest up against X'ieth's while patting him roughly on the shoulder, twice. At the same time, Knight Sharpstone used his other arm to firmly shake the young knight's hand opposite to his patted shoulder.

This was *Brother's Embrace*, a gesture common among knights in Sergros, not so much the Crimson Guard. X'ieth had only experienced it a few times, and he lacked appreciation for it. The young knight arched his eyebrows as Knight Sharpstone continued shaking his hand. *Is this how they do things in the Seventh Order?*

A bit annoyed with it, X'ieth felt like the gesture went on forever, though in reality, it ended almost as soon as it began. When Knight Sharpstone finally released him, he watched the pack leader take a step back.

"I'm Nathaniel Sharpstone, leader of the pack," he said. "You may call me Nathan. Let me say again, welcome to the Seventh Order. Your reputation precedes you."

Jokingly, X'ieth asked, "For the good, or the bad?"

With a blank expression, Nathan remained silent, just staring back at him. X'ieth searched the pack leader's face for any hint of what he really thought. *Perhaps something akin to what Finnel already shared with Hammar!* He wondered.

X'ieth cleared his throat, not letting the moment grow more awkward. "Ahem, I'm pleased to be here, and pleased to meet you all. I count serving in the Seventh Order a great honor," he spoke in earnest, passing his eyes over all the knights, even Zeros. "There's no greater cause than protecting innocent blood."

The remark raised a round of enthusiastic "Ayes" from the whole group, except Zeros. Then, after everyone else, Zeros said "Aye" and his delayed agreement hung in the air, more awkwardly than the moment prior. Like before, X'ieth saw scowls darken the faces of the other Guardsmen, as though the mercenary's words were out of place and unwelcomed.

"We're awaiting the instructor," said Nathan, all of a sudden. "An instructor in sword and magic will lead us through some exercises." X'ieth watched Nathan's eyes, trail off to the distant walks, perhaps to see if anyone came.

"Feel free to practice the forms until your instructor arrives. I'm going to find out what's happening. We're supposed to leave for Arlem in two hours and ride through the night." With that, Nathan just walked away, leaving the group to self-practice.

X'ieth turned to the side and unsheathed his sword. He held out his blade with both hands, and prepared for the *Clap of Thunder* form. With his left arm crossed over his breast and the other upraised over his right ear, he held the sword vertically in both hands. Quickly he transitioned into *Lightning Impedes*, bringing both hands to his left ear, with his sword extending horizontally before him. His hands clasped around the handle—the right curling toward his face, the left away.

He suddenly heard Hammar's voice from one side.

"Nice moves. Care to spar before our lesson?"

X'ieth lowered his weapon and turned. He saw the dwarf there, grinning. His eyes fell to the club hammer at Hammar's side. *Be his name just coincidence, or did the dwarf come from the womb with this hammer?*

Hammar announced to the others, "He's undecided about sparring with me!" X'ieth watched the dwarf look around to the Guard, in an attempt to elicit their collective response. "Tell me now, who wants to see a pair of fighting knights—one with a hammer, the other with a real sword?"

Cheers arose from some knights, and X'ieth could hear a few urge them on, especially Finnel.

"C'mon, fight him!" said the elven knight.

"His hammer be a disadvantage!" added Lewes.

X'ieth listened to several knights support a sparring match between him and Hammar, until finally his acquiescence hit. *You didn't get your sparring and festivities when promoted to the Seventh Order, so why not have fun now?* Perhaps he would.

Looking to Hammar, X'ieth gave a satisfying concession. "Fine then, let's spar a bit!"

Standing by a column, X'ieth sheathed his weapon and adjusted his gauntlets in preparation for an interesting match against a hammer-swinging knight. As he tightened the gauntlet straps, his head filled with thoughts. *Can't believe this... You're here with the Seventh Order of the Guard, practicing before embarking on your noblest quest ever: ending the gloom of Sergros.*

When X'ieth realized that, it brought the same flashes to mind, those of his boyhood days spent relishing the idea of serving Sergros in the Crimson Guard, as he chased the knights on horseback through the castle streets. Early on, X'ieth had become aware of the different orders of Guardsmen distinguished by their number of plumes and breastplate notches. X'ieth grew hopeful of one day serving as a knight of the highest order. *That day is finally here!*

"Defend yourself!" Zeros suddenly cried out.

X'ieth looked up then, just in time to eye the flat surface of a hammer, swung right at his skull!

Gracefully, X'ieth moved to the left just as the hammer's head missed his own, going over his right shoulder instead. He heard a loud noise, and turned to view the stone column where the hammer struck, now with a crack up and down it!

He quickly jumped back and unsheathed his blade.

"What's wrong with you?!" asked X'ieth.

"You said you'd spar, but not to wait!"

X'ieth watched Hammar pull the hammer from the column and proceed to swing it at him in wide arcs, to the left and right with great force. He took steps backward while keeping his eyes on the hammer's head, retreating slowly from the column and into the courtyard's center.

At first X'ieth wondered what to do, but soon an idea came to mind. *Use integrated sword and magic!* And so, he prepared himself for just that by filling his aux core with magical energy.

The young knight quickly envisioned himself standing amid his channeling chamber—a simple room with two doors, one forward and another behind him. Without hesitating, he ran to the door before him and pulled its loop handle toward him. When the door budged, a brilliant green light shined along its edges, in the moment before the door burst open, and a stream of Nexus passed over its threshold, hued in aqua green! The stream flowed and flowed, filling the room from floor to ceiling.

He snapped back to the courtyard, where he stepped away from the pursuer Hammar, who still swung the club hammer. In that moment, X'ieth caught a glint of light from below, as his midsection shined radiant green from the Nexus filling his core. Instantly, he felt connected to the energy field all around them, through which he could feel vibrations of the swinging hammer, the spectator knights breathing, and every fidget or step.

X'ieth resumed watching the hammer's head, judging the time between swings. *It's not even a second, but just long enough to intervene.* When X'ieth saw the hammer swing once more, he knew the moment was right.

Before Hammar's next swing, X'ieth went back to his channeling chamber, where he spun from the door sforward to the one behind. As he turned, his eyes saw how green energy now filled the entire space of the room; such was a common sight whenever one's aux core was full. The room's energy was everywhere, coming all the way up to his body where it hovered a hair's length off his skin, like a green aura taking his natural outline.

Through the energy field he saw the second door ahead, with a knob instead of a loop handle. X'ieth ran to it, turned the knob, and pushed hard with the trigger image of lightning in mind. When the door budged, the Nexus in the room surged out with another blast of light—along the door's edges and then, a stream that went over its threshold—exactly as energy had entered from the start.

Back in the courtyard, X'ieth pushed the energy to his extremities and executed what is commonly known as a *fluid offense*, where like a fluid with absolutely no resistance to flow, he assumed one sword form after another in rapid blurring succession. The feat was performed by sword and powered by magic, evident as the young knight's body developed a train of green energy during his instant progression between two sword forms: Clap of Thunder, and then, Lighting Impedes.

X'ieth blindingly slashed the hammer's head during the first form, to send the hammer flying over Hammar's shoulder. In the blink of an eye, X'ieth moved around the dwarf's side and assumed the second form, preventing Hammar from retrieving the weapon, now being at his rear. It all happened in less than a second, and in that short span of time, Hammar was disarmed and left with only a surprised expression upon his face.

Raucous laughter erupted from the spectator knights. With that, X'ieth's face reddened, as did Hammar's, though his flushness was from anger rather than embarrassment. *He could have hurt you, man! Say something! Do something!*

Finnel shouted amid laughing, "Careful Guardsdwarf! Perhaps you ought to challenge a squire instead, surely not a full knight bearing the Crescent!"

The knights continued laughing, and X'ieth's blood boiled more and more each moment it went on. The dwarf putting him in harm's way conjured up feelings he had about Talus' mistreatment, feelings that soon provoked him to speak, right out of silence.

"You could've killed me!" X'ieth screamed irately, spit flying from his mouth. He watched Hammar cower before him, the dwarf's embarrassment now changing into severe solemnness. "How dare you endanger me or any other in a simple sparring match?!"

He saw Hammar appear sullen then, with softened eyes and remorseful features, and not a word to say. X'ieth's fury easily became exacerbated by the dwarf's prolonged silence, which led into his truly explosive reaction. His eyes grew wide, his nostrils flared, and veins popped noticeably from his neck, as he ranted and raved.

"Is attacking an unsuspecting knight the extent of your courage?! Answer me, dwarf!"

From the corner of his eye, X'ieth saw Lewes suddenly extend a hand, seemingly in an attempt to calm the situation. The other knight said, "Speak from a calm mind in trespasses, not with heated emotions…"

"Did I address you?!" asked X'ieth, in a tone so sharp it could cut bone. He watched Lewes stare back blankly in silence—exactly like Hammar—as if no one knew how to deal with the young knight's heated reaction, perhaps construed as way over the top.

"That'll be enough," said Nathan.

X'ieth turned, seeing the pack leader suddenly walk up from out of nowhere, with the instructor behind him.

"From here on out, I don't want to hear another word about rough sparring or the like," Nathan continued, with eyes on X'ieth. "If I do, there will be a sharp stone between your loins and the saddle for your entire ride to Arlem! And that'll be something worthy of complaining about, I assure you…"

Not quite believing what was happening, X'ieth met Nathan's admonition with an unblinking set of eyes and a head full of outrage. *Really?! Hammar started what became half the pack squabbling, not just you!*

Despite contriving a good comeback or two, X'ieth bit his tongue and did not speak, just waiting for Nathan to look away. Precisely that happened too, after the young knight kept quiet long enough. Indeed, Nathan's gaze wandered to the other knights—Hammar and Lewes, and then the others—in what became a more inclusive rebuke.

"Your actions don't reflect unity of mind. It makes me wonder if you've too quickly forgotten what makes the Crimson Guard distinct from so many orders of knights in the Triangle Kingdoms."

Tension in the air lessened considerably, as Nathan transformed a scuffle with certain culpable individuals into a more general problem where everyone was blameworthy. *Here comes leader's group lesson…* X'ieth grumbled inside, upset over how Nathan limited individual blame only to him.

Reluctantly X'ieth spoke up, upon realizing his best option was to try and redeem himself in Nathan's eyes. "Magicia's binding by spell makes us unique among other knights—her binding us to protect innocent blood!"

X'ieth watched Nathan shake his head in disagreement, feeling then a certain letdown.

"That only imparts us with the power to uphold our mission when our bodies resist."

Destiny damn it! Should've kept quiet, man…

X'ieth felt relief when Nathan finally diverted his eyes, and cast a glare to the other knights, including everyone again.

"Does *anyone* remember what makes us unique?!"

From the quiet, X'ieth heard Tol say, "Many knights must fight one on one, per the oaths of knighthood, but not the Guard."

Nathan's hardened face went soft with a smile.

"And why's that?" he asked.

Lewes answered, "Teamwork."

The pack leader nodded in approval, but soon looked around for yet another response, something particular. "Anything else?"

Zeros called out, "Diversity."

X'ieth glanced to both sides, seeing signs of disapproval among the other knights with the mercenary's response, some shaking their heads just for the sake of disagreeing.

"Sergros prides itself for diversity throughout the kingdom, being a melting pot of nations for humans, elves, and dwarves," continued Zeros. "That value extends to the Sergrothian knighthood, especially the Crimson Guard."

X'ieth smiled at the mercenary's comment, which somehow made him feel proud of being Sergrothian, as if the human kingdom had risen above the prejudice of other kingdoms, truly accepting so many of varied race and culture. *What an innovative idea, to value diversity!*

The very thought triggered recollections of his academic studies about the centuries-long evolution of Sergrothian government, which culminated in a warm embrace of diversity. *Sergros is now a government that bestows equal vote to all citizens—male and female alike, whether of Karnathan or non-Karnathan faith, and regardless of race.*

X'ieth quieted his mind when Nathan turned to Zeros and surprisingly commended him.

"Both answers are correct, though in different ways. A single knight is vulnerable for two reasons. First, he is alone and therefore numbers potentially pose a threat to the Guard's calling—to protect innocent blood." As heads nodded all around, X'ieth could sense group agreement.

"Secondly," Nathan continued, "in some areas a single knight is weak. But a diverse team patches weaknesses with strengths, while offsetting the numbers problem. Knights possessing varied strengths can prove most formidable to any foe, if they work together."

With emphasis Nathan noted, "*This commotion* is not working together." When the pack leader reverted to admonishing words, X'ieth held a straight face and posture, now regretting his reaction over Hammar's roughhousing. *Drawing Nathan's rebuke so early on was a mistake. You may never live this one down...*

"I understand why we play," Nathan said, "at times it's needed with the constant discipline we practice. But remember, lighthearted gestures must not compromise our ability to cooperate effectively in battle. I fear what has happened today might do just that. Heated reactions can follow you long after they happen, if you let them..."

X'ieth and the other knights shared a serious look as silence replaced the sound of Nathan's voice. And silence continued for a few moments more, until Nathan cleared his throat. "Ahem, let's get to your practice."

It was then that Nathan stepped to the side, revealing to X'ieth the instructor, who stood at the pack leader's rear. He was a swordsman of the most ordinary appearance—wiry, middle-aged, small-framed, and about as tall as Nathan. The instructor had short black hair with some grays, and wore a bushy beard. His face was narrow with deep-set blue eyes, both sharp and piercing. They sat above thin lips and a hooknose.

"This is Thorin Krails, esteemed swordsman of the Bladed Fellowship," Nathan said, gesturing to the instructor.

X'ieth's eyes were glued to Thorin from the introduction. Likewise the instructor looked back, though not just at the young knight. Thorin looked over all the knights one by one, as if studying them.

Nathan said, "He will first go over basic sword forms with you, then move onto integrated sword and magic. If time allows he'll cover coordinated attacks and counters, even for those unfamiliar with the techniques learned while pursuing a Crescent designation. Anyone who can form links and push Nexus has the essential skills to participate, and that includes all of you, along with half of Karnath!"

When Nathan finished talking, X'ieth was surprised to see the pack leader walk away and back toward the castle. Filled with surprise, he diverted his attention from Thorin just to leer at Nathan. *Why would the pack leader skip practice? Nathan should actually lead practice, not forgo it altogether!*

"Greetings," said Thorin. The words broke X'ieth's thoughts, and the young knight immediately looked back at the instructor. "Let's begin with basic sword form and progress to more advanced techniques."

Thorin suddenly gestured to both sides.

"Grab a practice sword and assemble into a line between the columns."

X'ieth followed along with the others, getting a practice sword from the rack and assuming a position between the columns. He noted Hammar reluctantly take a practice sword from Finnel, a few knights down from him. *Hmmm, let's see how well he uses that!*

For a few minutes, X'ieth and his peer group emulated a number of defensive and offensive forms that Thorin called out. Hammar's stance and technique was particularly poor for each of them, but at Fire's Breath it was bad enough to stop everything.

Thorin suddenly shouted, "Hold still!"

Quickly X'ieth double-checked his own form with the knights around him. He had his right foot forward and the left to the side, and was thrusting his sword at the level of his hips. He wrapped a hand over his sword's grip closest to its guard, with his other hand under the grip, near its pommel. In this form, he had a right arm extending over his breast. With the exception of one peer knight being left versus right-handed and having everything opposite, he matched the forms of most other Guardsmen. *We couldn't be more alike. Whew...*

With a hunch of what went wrong, X'ieth looked at Hammar, who stood a few knights away with both feet forward instead of having one to the side. *Ah, knew it...*

Thorin walked through the group and made comments where needed. "Make sure one foot is kept to the side for good balance," he said to Hammar who stood with incorrect form.

X'ieth observed how Hammar studied the others to reproduce their appearance. He made sure to meet eyes with Hammar then, and sent over a wry grin. The dwarf glowered in frustration and clumsily adjusted his stance. Eventually, X'ieth noticed a smile cross Finnel's face too, who watched Hammar as well.

"Everyone at ease," Thorin said, releasing the knights from the form. With a sigh of relief, X'ieth relaxed just as the other knights. *Thought he'd have us hold still, maybe an hour longer!*

"Very good," said Thorin. "That's enough sword practice for now, so please return your practice swords to the rack."

X'ieth followed the other knights to return his wooden practice sword, and then, resumed a position between the columns, awaiting further instruction.

"Now let's consider basic magic before moving into integrated techniques." Thorin paused briefly to add, "Since most people in Karnath can only push or pull Nexus and *link*, you knights may feel as sorcerers, having some experience with transformations of magical power."

X'ieth watched Thorin pace back and forth while talking. "Give in to that belief and fool yourself, for sorcerers know many more transformations of Nexus and have much more control and endurance. You should always consider yourselves as less than novice sorcerers, and that's how I'll treat you today."

X'ieth rolled his eyes at the comment but soon refrained from it, as Thorin looked directly at him and took a few steps closer! The action was easily enough for him to swallow hard, being nervous about the instructor singling him out, just as Nathan had done. *Keep it up, man... As punishment he'll have you sit in a corner, trying to move a coin with your mind!* The thought rendered him sober. Images flashed through his mind, of being sentenced to the courtyard's shadows, where before a coin, he squinted both eyes and strained. For X'ieth was never able to move much of anything with magic, and in times past, only exhausted himself by trying.

"I shall start with a description of the Nexus itself," Thorin said, in the background of the young knight's thoughts. "And then discuss drawing the Source, and holding power in one's core." At the announcement, X'ieth readied himself for a boring lecture about the basics of magic that were commonly given as a very first lesson. *Destiny save you, man… You've heard this too often.*

"What is *the Source, the so-called Nexus*? The words are used interchangeably, to refer to the same thing." Thorin walked back and forth before X'ieth as he talked, using his arms to gesture. "The Source always is and always was. It's the essence of Destiny, an energy that's all around us, in everything we see—a force that permits life. Students of Nexus believe it's a closed system, wherefrom life energy flows at birth, and to where it returns at death. The cycle of life maintains the Nexus, with only one phenomenon to threaten that balance, one which I'll mention later—*voiding*."

Thorin continued. "I have yet to find a place in Karnath where the Source cannot be tapped. Commonly, it's believed that the wide availability of Nexus signifies the opportunity we all have for a close relationship with Destiny... Nexus is perhaps a blessing from god, Destiny's smile upon us."

Thorin paused, as if to let the words sink in. Just then, X'ieth felt an itch on his nose, but when he budged to scratch it, the instructor looked directly his way. He put his hand down and just listened, mildly agitated.

"Per Karnathan belief, the Nexus is Destiny itself, from which comes the saying, *Destiny be with you.*"

X'ieth waited for Thorin's attention to find the other knights, and as soon as it did, he finally scratched. *Ah...*

"It's said in hopes that Destiny favors people with availability of the Source, to be used for their protection, sustenance, and utility." By the nature of Thorin's words, a clear realization dawned on X'ieth. *He must be devoutly Karnathan. These words are lifted right from the first passages of the Book of Karnatha.*

"But all natural resources should be used in moderation, not in excess or waste. The Nexus is no exception. There exists a delicate balance of forces in Karnath that mustn't be disturbed! The Nexus is like an ocean, where novices who tap it take only a cup, advanced users a bucket full, and so on. It's unlikely that any individual could ever deplete the Source sufficiently to cause a shortage of supply—even a sorcerer."

X'ieth watched Thorin direct his stare to Tol before continuing, who stood a few knights away.

"Still, we must have sobriety in all that we do. Keep in mind that while energy can neither be created nor destroyed, every transformation of Nexus outside one's core takes place with certain losses. Instead of returning to the Source, a small portion of your channeled energy goes to the Void, a well for unspent energy—*unused potential*. The *Guild of Sorcery* conjectures that in its new form, this energy is kept outside the Nexus, never to be regained. This transfer is called *voiding*."

At that word of caution, X'ieth prayed to Destiny for tolerance, having been served this admonition one too many times before. *Another warning about the Void and voiding...*

After describing the Source, Thorin proceeded to explain what is meant by *core*. "There are two vessels in every being for holding Nexus, and two actions that can be performed," he taught, "one vessel is the *primary core*, which holds life force. This core is typically filled by natural functions of one's body. When you eat, sleep, and exercise the energy level in the primary core increases. When you forgo these things, it decreases. The second core is called the *auxiliary core*, or more simply the *aux core*, and is used for magic unlike the first; it's the channeling chamber that one envisions when wielding Nexus. With either core, two actions are thought to be possible."

Thorin paused. "Cores can be filled and depleted. Filling a primary core is known as healing by the Source. It's an advanced technique we simply cannot cover here, which few can even learn." Thorin wet his lips before going on. "Emptying a primary core is not something easily done, for one's self or another. This particular feat has actually baffled skilled practitioners for ages, and is still quite mysterious. Perhaps one well-versed in magic, maybe a sorcerer or sorceress in high standing at the Guild could do such a thing."

Within X'ieth, the very mention of advanced magic that could drain one's primary core conjured up dormant worries about facing Esmeralda and Magicia, which he had managed to dodge since last night. *Destiny damn it*, he thought, pushing the worries to the back of his mind again.

"Emptying the primary core has the same effect as destroying the body. These are just notes in passing," Thorin said. "I don't mean for my description to be exhaustive, but I will mention different areas, to give you context for where your application of magic fits into the spectrum of its wider uses."

X'ieth noted slight movement, as Hammar shuffled upon his feet. *The dwarf readies himself to stand here a while longer!* X'ieth showed a brief smile, a bit joyed at Hammar's discomfort given their recent scuffle.

"Similarly, there are difficulties depleting another's aux core, though you can fill it, as you'll see in a later exercise. But I digress, so let's focus on the basics first." X'ieth watched the instructor resume constant walking and gestures, whilst lecturing the knights. *If bound hand and foot, Thorin likely couldn't teach a thing!*

"This exercise will focus on depleting and filling your own aux core. A natural start is filling the core. Everyone do so!"

Finally, an actual exercise... X'ieth envisioned his channeling chamber. A small room appeared in his mind, having four walls of gray stone and a low ceiling. He saw a simple door before him, its knob being an iron ring hanging from a fixture. The young knight glanced over his shoulder—directly behind him—seeing the same there: a simple door of similar construction, but with a round knob. *Your Source entry and Source exit*, he thought to himself.

X'ieth went to the door before him and pulled its iron loop handle. At first, he felt the door resist, and so he pulled harder against the Source entry—his mental restraint. He watched with a smile as the door finally yielded, cracking to reveal light along the door's edges. While he continued pulling, the young knight saw more Nexus energy pour into the room through the doorway, from a distant green light on the door's opposite side. A single stream of bright fluid ran at the level of his knees—a flow that continued to flow, and started to fill the room.

His vision was over in an instant, and X'ieth popped from his channeling chamber back into the courtyard, with his aux core now connected to the surrounding Nexus field. He could sense vibrations through the cobblestone from others' movements, just as vibrations through the air from Thorin talking. Glancing down, the young knight noticed green glow suddenly appear about his center, like light sparking from out of darkness.

In his mind, X'ieth still stood at the Source entry, almost fully ajar now. He pulled and pulled at the door, which constantly tended toward a closed state with opposing force. From the current state of his channeling chamber, he knew his aux core must be nearly full for he saw the room covered by a field of aqua green Nexus, from floor to ceiling. All over the room, energy literally hung in the air. It came up to his body from the room's four corners, to hover a hair's length off his skin. The spacing between one's body and the energy was typically referred to as a *Source boundary*, and across it, the Nexus caused a tingly sensation.

He continued pulling until excess energy started dripping toward him across his Source boundary. Knowing what would happen X'ieth immediately stopped, but it was too late. For the green droplets off the Source boundary hit his skin and at that, he felt the sensation of burning! *Argh, stop pulling! Stop it!*

X'ieth released the Source entry without hesitating, and watched the door slam closed from the opposing force. The experience he just had was none other than that of exceeding the channeling chamber's capacity, which sometimes occurred because it was difficult for him to judge when he had pulled enough Nexus.

Though he shut the Source entry, the Nexus remained in the room, slowly weighing on him. It caused a new developing sensation of increased pressure that made it near impossible to breathe. It formed all about his head too, like a vice, squeezing him. *Thorin didn't say let it go, so hold it! Remember the coin...*

Indeed X'ieth was right, for Thorin gave no instruction for any knight to release the energy. Sweat beaded on the young knight's brow, as he tried to hold it indefinitely, as surely the others did too. In his mind, he saw the channeling chamber, and stood at the closed Source entry with Nexus still covering the room. It felt as if the energy gripped his chest, and in that, he urgently needed air. *Can't do this much longer!*

X'ieth snapped from his vision back to the courtyard, just in time to hear Thorin.

"Hold the Nexus as long as you can! This feat can be likened unto holding one's breath, and doing it a long while takes endurance. The more often you practice this particular technique, the greater will be your stamina for holding magic!"

X'ieth resolved to keep the Nexus in his aux core at least until a few others dropped out, even if that meant his own discomfort. Not wanting to be the first one losing this contest, X'ieth looked around and watched others release their magic—Hammar, and then Finnel, followed by Lewes. The green glows about their midsections snuffed out like doused flames, and streams of energy wafted from the knights into the nearby air, before vanishing altogether.

Someone must be last, and the last one with Nexus wins! X'ieth worked hard to hold the energy longer, literally fighting the urge to breathe by releasing the energy. With apparent fatigue Tol suddenly expelled Nexus, for the sounds of his panting fell upon the young knight's ears. *Stay focused, man!*

X'ieth struggled on against Zeros, the two being the last knights in the contest now. X'ieth studied the mercenary, whose acumen and endurance for holding the magic were both ostensible from his appearance alone. *He doesn't even sweat!*

After nearly a minute more, X'ieth had enough. He went to his channeling chamber full of Nexus. The Source entry confronted him again, now shut. From that door he spun about, seeing the Source exit on the opposite wall. He ran toward it and all the energy moved with him, as if his body were the field's center. In only a few steps, he touched the door's round knob, twisted it, and then pushed. A quick succession of images blurred through his subconscious—of chains breaking, ropes fraying, dams busting—all images of release. Once again, he saw the door creak open, and the Nexus funneled over the door's threshold with flashy green light.

Snapping back to the courtyard, X'ieth found himself panting heavily. In a moment, he saw the glow at his center snuff out. His eyes beheld a stream of energy that wafted from his center into the open air, dissolving completely.

Given X'ieth's concession, Zeros freed his Nexus, without even a single huff. Green energy emanated from the mercenary's body and drifted off into the ambiance. X'ieth looked over with arched brows. *Show off!*

"Excellent," said Thorin. "Everyone did exactly what comes naturally. This exercise illustrates fundamental limits in wielding Nexus."

X'ieth panted more, trying to catch his breath again as a few others. He watched the instructor look over the line of knights to ensure everyone was paying attention.

"The size of one's core restricts the amount of Nexus they can wield. The extent one can hold energy gives the timeline for magical feats. Both size of aux core and endurance can be increased with practice."

He watched Thorin suddenly raise his hands before his chest, with straightened fingers and palms out. The instructor gestured pushing and said, "Our exercise also demonstrated that depleting your aux core is likened unto pushing against a mental restraint until the core is empty, versus pulling against the restraint like everyone did initially, when filling up."

"Now for the interesting stuff about basic magic," Thorin said, his hands flowing again. "Transformations."

The instructor instantly resumed pacing, just as before. *Like clockwork...* X'ieth thought, finding Thorin's mannerisms a bit predictable now, comfortable even.

"Once Nexus fills one's aux core, it can be channeled externally into another form. The simplest forms are elemental attacks with fire, sands, or wind. Essentially these involve transferring energy from one form to another." With a straight face Thorin explained, "Water can also be created from the Nexus, but making large quantities is difficult even for those familiar with the art. Moving any amount of water after it's created is just as hard."

X'ieth looked over when Finnel suddenly nudged Hammar beside him and whispered. "Check this out."

He watched Finnel humor the dwarf by creating a miniscule amount of water and trying to move it, but the droplet fell on Finnel's head with a faint dripping sound.

Hammar laughed lowly, though audibly.

Thorin glanced over. "Ahem."

X'ieth refocused and straightened up his posture, and could tell the other knights desisted from further talk.

"Another common use for Nexus," Thorin went on, "is creating energy fields to protect one's self, climb upon, and hold back assailants. These are all common uses. And just like there are additional basic uses, there are additional advanced uses. For instance, in addition to making or moving water, there's healing, mass elemental attacks, telekinesis, and *mind control* through surpassing one's mental firewall."

Those last words sent a shiver down X'ieth's entire body, and it triggered an immediate, vivid flashback of his final days of service in the Sixth Order of the Guard where he hunted the fugitive Pyrus.

**** X'ieth's Flashback—Garlew's Death ****

On the second floor of a two-story hospice, X'ieth stood in the corner of an unlit room, near the window that received the summer night's breezes, and beside the bed of Sergros' hero—Garlew Il'therin. Garlew was unconscious from a serious head wound administered by Pyrus the evening before, when finally locating the fugitive on the wooded outskirts of Deardrum. It was days after X'ieth and Garlew escaped an ambush by mysterious attackers who killed Kort, Enker, and Dimral.

While standing there, the young knight thought about Lucen's last words; they were haunting, ever present in his mind: "Leave this place at once! Kort will stop at nothing to kill Garlew and anyone who stands in his way."

The warning from Lucen worried X'ieth, but he did not understand it, knowing that Kort had already died in the ambush. And because of that, he stayed with Garlew in his poor condition, with a hopeful heart that his injured pack leader would recover.

"You stopped at nothing," X'ieth told the unconscious Garlew, who lied there with bandages wrapped around his head. "You stopped at nothing to see Pyrus served justice. And that's dedication to remember…"

Then suddenly, X'ieth heard abrupt noises from the lower level of the hospice—the banging of doors and a dull patter of feet upon wooden floors. In his ears, the sounds came closer and yet closer to his spot, until it became clear that someone ran up the stairs!

His head turned, as through the door a figure suddenly burst—hooded, cloaked, and bearing a dagger! It was clearly an assassin.

Immediately X'ieth drew his blade, its steel agleam by the starlight. As the assassin rushed to Garlew's bed, he thrust the sword at them. But when his blade tip was a hair's length off the assassin, the hooded figure's free hand glowed blindingly with green Nexus. Immediately, X'ieth sensed force fields tighten over his blade like a vice, and the energy caused its steel to become so bright he was forced to look away!

Keeping his vision to the side, X'ieth tugged at his sword's handle with both arms. But as hard as he pulled, he could not free the weapon. Then surprisingly, his feet suddenly lifted from off the floor and his body shifted, as the assassin threw the sword toward the window!

X'ieth let go of the sword just in time, and his feet touched the floor again. He looked up in despair, to watch his blade fly to the casement. Right before it reached the window, an elf's silhouette appeared on the windowsill, right as a figure jumped up from outside the hospice. It was then that the thrown sword met Kort's hand, and he stepped down from the window!

The sight rendered X'ieth dumbstruck. Days ago, he had witnessed Kort fall into a gorge, riddled with crossbow bolts.

"You," said X'ieth. "You're… you're dead!"

"Correction," Kort replied, "I was dead."

Back to assassin X'ieth turned, as the person hovered over Garlew with dagger in hand. From the hood fell long strands of silver hair, dispersing light from the starry sky into the dark chamber. In a mirror on the far wall, the young knight saw the reflection of the assassin. It was a female elf.

"If I can't do this," said Kort, "then she will!"

X'ieth noticed intricate blue flows of Nexus streaming from Kort to the assassin, blending into the room's drear ambiance. Light revealed her eyes, rolled up into her head, as she was clearly under Kort's control.

"What... have you become?!" struggled X'ieth, never having seen such a thing in all his life.

It was then that Kort charged X'ieth with the naked blade. From out of nowhere, Lucen appeared between Kort and X'ieth, clashing his gnarled staff with Kort's steel and yelling, "Leave now! There'll be no third chance!"

With that, X'ieth fled the hospice, right as the assassin stabbed Garlew where he lied.

****

As X'ieth snapped back from the flashback, a pained look crossed his face. *Kort used mind control to kill Garlew Il'therin!* He thought it then; he thought it now. The young knight was so sure of what he saw that upon his return to Sergros, he testified against Kort to Talus. *Your testimony was key to the king issuing warrants for Kort's arrest and searching him out.* That realization easily made him feel good inside, like he played an important role in righting a terrible wrong. *Garlew should've never of died like that...*

"Even masters of magic struggle..."

X'ieth grew startled when Thorin spoke loudly, right near his ear, as if noting his growing detachment from the lesson.

"They struggle with these Nexus transformations. In fact, most powerful sorcerers can perform only a few of these feats—or none of them at all."

He watched Thorin take several steps back from the knights, while stridently clapping his hands.

Clap clap clap! Clap clap clap!

"Let's get to another exercise before my lesson puts you to sleep!"

With that remark, laughter rippled through the knights, and X'ieth enjoyed the lightened mood, as did everyone else with the exception of Zeros, who remained very serious. *That fellow is hard to read.*

"Everyone, pull the Source into your aux core!"

X'ieth did as Thorin instructed and a green aura became visible near his waist, just as with the others.

"Good," said Thorin, "now transform the energy into any element of your choosing!"

X'ieth always had little problem with the fire transformation, and so, he decided he would do that now. Images of flames filled his head, from within his channeling chamber, and immediately, fire burst from his open palms and into the air. In his chamber, X'ieth saw a single stream of Nexus going over the Source exit's threshold, where the energy changed into fire, right before leaving.

Blinking back to the courtyard, X'ieth compared everyone's fire with his own. *Another perfect match...*

At his inclination toward fire, X'ieth recalled an explanation for this common tendency, offered up by one magic teacher in the royal academy. Supposedly, some people naturally preferred fire transformations because of their fiery emotion, particularly anger. The philosophy of Nexus wielding being intimately related to the psyche was one philosophy that X'ieth never bought into. *Too many angry people would be wielding fire, were that the case!*

When X'ieth sensed a minor vibration through the cobblestone, it brought his wandering mind back to the courtyard. There, he observed Zeros break the mold that far too many knights conformed to with their fire transformations. Instead of fire, the mercenary threaded Nexus energy through the ground, and moved the threads until the ground slightly accelerated.

When the ground stopped shaking, X'ieth looked over to see how Hammar fared, though the dwarf abstained from magic and merely watched Finnel. Being one to joke, the elven knight made a small wind to blow on Thorin's short hair from behind. Hammar could not help but snicker.

X'ieth chuckled beneath his breath, and fortunately for everyone involved, Thorin ignored the folly. Instead, the instructor suddenly met eyes with the closest knight who chose to make fire—Lewes.

"You, assist me in the next lesson."

Lewes nodded, awaiting further detail.

The young knight watched Thorin take several steps back, until a good distance from Lewes.

"Make fire again, this time cast it as far as you can."

"Are you sure?" Lewes asked cautiously.

"Yes," Thorin replied. "Do it with all your might!"

X'ieth watched Lewes produce fire from the Source; the air around the knight's midsection suddenly ignited green and burst into a stream of flames, hurled right at Thorin! But despite Lewes' best efforts, the fires fell short of the instructor, onto the stone walk. As if sighting another opportunity to teach, Thorin led Lewes into a particular situation.

"All of you have a *locus of control* when it comes to wielding Nexus, some greater than others. This is the limit Lewes just demonstrated—a spatial restraint when wielding magic, whether it be filling or depleting a core, transforming Nexus, or other feats. As all limitations, it can only be improved with practice."

At the last word, Thorin stopped walking and faced the knights from the far end of the lineup. X'ieth turned his head to meet eyes with the instructor.

"Let's have another exercise. This is necessary to make an important point." Thorin snapped his fingers, and X'ieth observed how a dozen or so Sergrothian soldiers poured into the courtyard, armored and holding wooden staffs. "King Darxar lent me some of his men for this."

X'ieth watched the instructor then, who walked over to a rack of practice swords beside the distant column, and came back with two in hand. *What's he up to?*

Thorin looked at the knights carefully, as if plotting his next words. "I need a volunteer, someone with the Crescent who knows about integrated sword and magic."

X'ieth and Finnel turned to each other, as if each knight expected the other to simply cooperate with Thorin. Finnel playfully motioned to the center of the courtyard like a gentleman. "I insist," said the elven knight, with a smile and mock chivalry.

Without much reservation X'ieth came forward, searching for ways to earn the Guard's respect. *This might be one way to do it*, he told himself, *if you don't humiliate yourself first!*

"Excellent," Thorin said. "I enjoy not having to pull someone from the crowd, kicking and screaming." None of the knights laughed at Thorin's sarcasm, and X'ieth showed an inquisitive look. *Is he serious?*

Thorin glowered from what seemed to be frustration and then muttered, "No one ever gets that."

X'ieth watched Thorin toss a wooden sword to him. From the moment it left Thorin's hand the young knight watched it come closer, and when close enough, he snatched it from the air.

"All right then, show us your skills, young knight."

Snapping his fingers again, Thorin glanced at the Sergrothian soldiers and shouted, "Surround and attack him; give it your best!"

What?! X'ieth thought, without much time to mull over the situation. From all sides, he saw the soldiers surround him, moments before poking their staffs in his direction. Quickly the young knight drew energy for a *fluid defense* where he effectively could shadow every attack from the soldiers with a counter, in rapid blurring succession.

The process he knew well, and it all unfolded quickly for him. Like many times before, he stood in his channeling chamber and pulled against the Source entry—his mental restraint. Suddenly, energy flowed to him in a stream across its threshold, to fill the room. Knowing the muscle movements, coordination, and timing for every sword form allowed him to push the energy out his Source exit from his core, into his extremities. During a fluid defense or a fluid offense, the mind effectively controlled Nexus that moved one's body, faster and with more precision than could be obtained otherwise.

And by this Crescent technique, X'ieth executed several counters instantly with only a thought, and his practice sword deflected the soldiers' staffs. But after only a few counters, X'ieth ran out of energy. In his channeling chamber, he watched the last of his Nexus funnel through the Source exit.

Pull, man! Needing more energy, he did just that, rushing back to his Source entry and pulling it open. But filling his aux core required enough concentration that he could hardly defend himself from the many soldiers who continued jabbing at him with their staffs. X'ieth felt embarrassed as some of the sticks hit him, breaking his concentration and causing him to pull open his Source entry again. *This is likely an awful spectacle to watch!*

When X'ieth received a forceful blow to his breastplate from one of the soldiers hurling a staff, he stopped channeling and drew his focus back to the opponents. He growled as the impact sent him back, into more staffs at his rear; they poked him in the shoulders. *To the Void with this!*

Tired from pulling and being unable to fill his aux core just yet, he let go of the energy, thinking it too difficult to power fluid defenses or offenses. *Just fight 'em without magic!* X'ieth centered his mind and body, and assumed different forms without magic to ward off his attackers and deliver a few strikes in between blocking. But despite his skill, the young knight becomes overwhelmed with so many simultaneous assailants, not being fast enough without magic.

Another stick jabbed him from behind and then another from his front. X'ieth took each impact, releasing a deep growl, "Grrr!" He felt pain course through his upper body with the strikes, which literally pushed him between staff-wielding soldiers at the center of the courtyard.

"Finnel, go! Assist your comrade!" shouted Thorin.

X'ieth barely saw the instructor toss a second practice sword to Finnel, who snatched it from the air while running through the cluster of soldiers and beside the young knight.

As Finnel joined him, X'ieth pulled energy into his core, having a moment of relief from the attackers all about. Together then, X'ieth and Finnel performed fluid defenses. The young knight watched his sword blur to knock multiple sticks away in a single instant.

Soon enough though, the pair of knights ran out of Nexus. X'ieth began pulling to fill his aux core once more, but even with a helping sword, he encountered the same challenge: refilling his aux core while defending himself. He passed a quick glance to Finnel, and verified that the elven knight struggled with the same.

X'ieth grew tired from attempting to manage the vicious cycle of sword and magic in the middle of combat, and Finnel did too. When their performance broke down and both knights were hardly able to fend off a barrage of speeding staffs from the Sergrothian soldiers, Thorin intervened.

"Work together, but now, with *a tether*!"

Surrounded by the soldiers and back-to-back, X'ieth and Finnel looked to each other from over a shoulder, knowing exactly what Thorin recommended. The technique of forming mental locks to combine aux cores was taught early in the Crimson Guard, and the pair of knights did not hesitate a moment longer.

Closing his eyes, X'ieth focused to see a stream of energy filling his channeling chamber as he pulled his Source entry open; the stream went across its threshold. He rushed over to his Source exit, while channeling off a portion of the incoming flow to direct it outward from the room with a push, through the Source exit. Suddenly then, an additional stream appeared through his Source entry and entered the room, from Finnel's aux core! The additional stream kept the Source entry open for a while longer, effectively overcoming X'ieth's mental restraint.

Both knights merged the incoming streams in their minds by pulling them together. Externally, their aux cores combined to become twice as large! X'ieth watched the walls of his channeling chamber stretch and move further apart, in all directions. The ceiling resized accordingly.

Upon coming back to the sparring match, X'ieth and Finnel could now optimally draw energy into a larger, combined core and fight more efficiently. They literally ran about their channeling chambers, pulling their Source entry and then pushing their Source exit, just to keep their practice swords in play and their bodies powered by magic.

After a while, X'ieth paused to wipe perspiration from his forehead, as drawing energy and transforming it remained a two-step process for him, and very tiring. *Would be better, if you could just worry about pushing energy and wielding your sword!* The young knight realized then that the same problem was still there, even with the tether. Now though, his and Finnel's performance deteriorated at a slower rate.

"Stop," Thorin shouted. Everyone stopped sparring; X'ieth and Finnel along with a dozen Sergrothian solders became as statues looking to the instructor. The young knight sucked air, weary from the activity. His side felt sore from more than one received blow, and he waited upon springy feet, expecting the sparring to continue at a moment's notice. *C'mon!* he thought, on edge.

"Note how being unable to continuously pull Nexus and push it presents difficulties when fighting. Continuous channel and transform, or rather, simultaneous pull and push, is another advanced form of magic. Again, not many people know how to do it, and I can't teach it to you."

Thorin smiled as he finished speaking.

Is that supposed to be a tease? wondered X'ieth.

"There's another way, to confront this problem," Thorin said. "Resume fighting!"

X'ieth and Finnel grunted, both of them being tired from continuously handling so many assailants at close quarters, using integrated sword and magic. But their weariness did not delay the onslaught of staffs for a moment. And so, X'ieth fended them off with his practice sword, Finnel too, and the sounds of smacking wood resumed, over which X'ieth could hear the instructor yell.

"This time, don't channel!" Thorin said.

He smiled at the spectator knights, and continued.

"Your fellow Guardsmen will do that!"

With an outstretched hand, Thorin urged the group of other knights to fill the combined core of X'ieth and Finnel, while they continued to fight the soldiers. At that, X'ieth instantly felt links from his fellow knights, additional streams into his channeling chamber, sourcing it now through the Source entry. A sudden sensation of increased pressure overwhelmed him then, as energy filled their combined core faster than before.

From his limited experience, X'ieth knew links were very different than the tether he formed with Finnel, in that no one linking merged a stream. The other knights merely pulled energy through their own Source entry and pushed it into the pair's combined aux core—a mental restraint that could be externally sensed, within everyone's locus of control.

And so, through his Source entry, X'ieth had streams of Nexus asynchronously enter, sometimes in spurts. *The flow isn't steady!* Because of this, he lost power right in the middle of a fluid defense. A whizzing staff smacked his breastplate again. *These soldiers hit hard for a sparring match!*

Then, quite unexpectedly, the opposite happened. The spectator knights pushed energy into the pair's combined core faster than X'ieth and Finnel could use it, and the result was painful.

"Argh!" winced X'ieth, as the Nexus burnt him across his Source boundary. Finnel echoed.

From the corner of his eye, X'ieth noted how Thorin's face beamed, as if the instructor was pleased with how efficient the example had become to demonstrate what worked well in the practice of integrated sword and magic, and also, what did not.

"Stop!" Thorin shouted once more. All participants came to a sudden halt. X'ieth heard a hoarse sigh, done with evident displeasure. *That's Hammar.*

The young knight pondered what surely everyone else did—when the exercise would end. He conjectured if this sparring match went on much longer, the group of knights would soon reach a point of diminishing returns.

"Your links are inefficient; there's a better way," asserted Thorin. The instructor looked to the five spectator knights, who linked to X'ieth and Finnel.

"You, link with a knight by you and one fighter."

Thorin addressed Zeros, suggesting he link with Lewes and either X'ieth or Finnel.

Thorin continued. "Everyone else, form a link with the knight beside you, so that together you create a chain!"

With that instruction, X'ieth saw many knights concentrate, some closing their eyes. Hammar apparently had difficulty reestablishing his link with the adjacent knight, so Thorin came to help.

"Focus carefully, and feel for an external restraint, one in your mind. That's the knight closest to you. Push the energy from your core against that."

X'ieth watched Hammar squint hard at first, but soon relaxed his face and calmed himself. Despite being annoyed with their earlier scuffle, he hoped the dwarf would get it right, for everyone's sake!

In short order, Hammar linked to his fellow knight.

"Complete the chain!" Thorin called to Zeros, and the mercenary immediately linked to X'ieth.

Having a smile upon his face, the instructor said, "Now pass the energy from the end of the chain to the combined core of the fighters!"

With this system only one knight channeled the energy, with everyone else passing it to the target aux core until it was filled.

"This is the chain tethering technique; it's very common in many coordinated attacks involving integrated sword and magic," Thorin called out. "Networks of some linked and others tethered are also possible!"

The instructor paused, and X'ieth looked to him. *What's he waiting for?*

"Now fight!" Thorin exclaimed.

At first, the other knights worked with ardor to rapidly fill the combined core of X'ieth and Finnel. Perspiration exuded from their skin, as they all toiled in the open air. But when their combined aux core offered no more room for Nexus, X'ieth and Finnel were able to worry about fighting while the other knights worked to maintain a constant flow of energy, as the knight at the chain's end channeled and everyone else in the chain passed energy forward to both X'ieth and Finnel.

With much agility, X'ieth danced from form to form, and he noted how Finnel did too. The pair wielded their practice swords, executing fluid defenses and offenses, again and again. In his channeling chamber, the young knight beheld a large stream going through his Source entry and holding it open, to pump the room full of Nexus. *Allows you to focus on fighting…*

In no time at all, the blurring swords of X'ieth and Finnel bested over a dozen simultaneous assailants! The soldiers backed off with grunts and yelps, as the practice swords smacked their hands and sent their staffs flying into the distance.

"Stop!" Thorin called once more.

X'ieth panted, tired from fighting. *Hope that's the final time today!*

When X'ieth gave his attention along with the others, the instructor continued. "I hope this exercise has been valuable to teach you the importance of teamwork, and assigning roles where strengths are greatest. Sometimes such coordination may be impractical, but often there will be integrated attacks that can prove more effective, than everyone working individually. Keep in mind, to always work together toward being stronger as a team than everyone fighting alone."

While Thorin talked, X'ieth watched the same Sergrothian official in blue and beige come forth in the distance. The official arrived at the courtyard's center just as the instructor finished speaking, and the man placed his first word right at the edge of Thorin's last.

"A surprise visitor has arrived to see the king. The entire Seventh Order of the Guard has been summoned to the throne room for an immediate session!"

"SPARRING IN CASTLE SERGROS"

Chapter 13
The King's Special Guest

A t the official's sudden news, the whole group of knights developed a somewhat curious semblance, especially X'ieth. *Who is the king's special guest?* He wondered, with practice sword in hand.

"Follow me," the official instructed from the center of the courtyard, and began walking back toward the castle without a glance back, as if expecting everyone to trail along without a question or moment's hesitation.

X'ieth watched the others form a line behind the official and walk after him, like horses led by invisible reins. He turned to Finnel, still holding a practice sword from Thorin's exercise.

"You'd better go," said Thorin, coming up to Finnel and taking the wooden sword.

X'ieth came forward with his own sword, seeing that Thorin had just collected Finnel's.

"You too," said Thorin, making eye contact with X'ieth then and taking the practice sword from his hands. "Lord Darxar wanted everyone practiced, fed a good meal, and bound for Arlem by now, so you best hurry."

With that remark, Thorin motioned to the castle. X'ieth directed his attention there, noticing that Finnel had almost reached the entrance, and the others were already inside and completely out of sight. *Run, man! Talus will single you out if you're late, just as Nathan did!*

Propelled by the thought, X'ieth bolted to the castle and ducked into the entrance, right on Finnel's tail. Now inside, he saw the others walking distantly, down a corridor and at the official's heels. The visual gave him an immediate sense of relief.

With Finnel at his side, X'ieth proceeded to Talus' throne room through the halls, walks, and annexes of gray stone. The path made for a well-known route—one he traversed many times, as surely did his peers.

When X'ieth arrived to the throne room, he walked in with Finnel and advanced to Talus, who was seated afar and talking with Nathan and someone else, both persons being before the throne. Upon seeing the king, he began feeling uneasy over his last session with Talus. Memories entered his mind, of how Talus suggested he had not earned his promotion, merely to twist his noble assignment into some sort of challenge to prove his worthiness. *Destiny damn him for that*, X'ieth thought bitterly, still working through the negative aftereffects of the king's mistreatment.

In a moment of daydreaming, X'ieth toyed with the idea of audaciously addressing the king's cruelty in front of everyone. *Now Talus, you ought to treat your subjects and servants better.* The reprimand echoed his head, deserving words for the king's mistreatment of subordinates, surely extending beyond his own experiences. *You'll have to say it louder than that.* X'ieth's inner voice once again derided him for being unable to do more than think the words. *Have that talk when you get back to Sergros with Esmeralda's head in hand! That'll make him choke on his words...*

When coming closer to the throne, X'ieth's daydreaming abruptly saw the dawn of terror. At the king's left stood Nathan, which was not a sight for worry. But to the right of Talus stood someone he did not quite expect to see— someone whom he actually hoped not to see.

Now tight-lipped and white-knuckled, X'ieth beheld Magicia—the most powerful sorceress in all of Karnath. She was talking with Talus in the space between the rightmost torch and the throne. In its light, she appeared beautiful, having a pretty round face, slender body, and red hair, both long and braided. Her skin was smooth, seemingly ageless and wrinkle-free. She wore the yellow sorceress robe, typical among members in the *Guild of Sorcery*.

His eyes fell to the green serpent pendant pinned at her neckline, as it clashed in color with the robe. His eyes fell further to the purple band sewn into the cuff of her one bell sleeve, adjacent to bands of many other colors—red, blue, green, and gray. The purple band was special among them though, symbolizing Magicia's highest rank and extreme prominence in the Guild.

Still walking to the throne, X'ieth looked up to Magicia's face and when he did, she already stared right at him with steely eyes! He instantly diverted his stare from the sorceress, and continued toward the throne with the incoming knights. His heart seemed to beat faster in his chest with every step forward, and suddenly, some dormant fears awakened at the back of his mind—fears about confronting Magicia and her powerful sister, Esmeralda.

He gulped back the terror, settling into a straight-line formation with the other Guardsmen, in between the two torches before the throne. He glanced to the side when detecting motion in his periphery, and noticed other knights falling to one knee. X'ieth eventually did the same, always being slow to gesture his respect for Talus. While kneeling, he noted how Zeros was just as slow, actually being the last knight to kneel.

"Everyone stand," Talus commanded from the throne. "Formalities are unneeded."

Hesitantly then, X'ieth got to his feet, along with the other knights.

Talus continued. "For those of you who don't remember Magicia, please enjoy the opportunity of meeting her again." Waving a hand Talus went on, "She hails from a line of powerful sorceresses, the ones that descend from the *unnamed sorceress of legend*! You've read of her ancestor, that one seroxian cursed to become a human, who later witnessed the death of Eriens and Hrya long ago. Magicia has risen to the most powerful sorceress in the land, as esteemed by the Guild, and also, Sergros."

X'ieth let a scowl cross his face as he processed the king's words. *Sure, sometimes you're gullible, man… But this doesn't ring of any truth! Talus couldn't possibly know if Magicia hailed from the same lineage as the unnamed sorceress of legend!* He shook his head and concluded, *Talus is full of horse dung!*

But at his thought, Magicia suddenly looked his way and her cold gaze froze his heart. It seemed colder than a moment prior, as if Talus' words further iced her already emotionless state. *Oh Destiny! Shouldn't have thought that about the king!* X'ieth immediately felt bad about how his thoughts about Talus wandered so far from what was appropriate and respectful, and he grew concerned that Magicia might somehow become Destiny's retribution for his poor actions.

Talus noisily cleared his throat, and X'ieth saw Magicia look back to the throne. He followed suit.

"Ahem… yes, yes… I'm attempting to embellish Magicia at the risk of her taking my words as flattery."

With that recovery, X'ieth perceived Talus send a warm smile to Magicia after rearing his gaze from the Crimson Guard, but she coldly glared back. The young knight noticed sweat beading from Talus' brow, as the king went on. "Magicia has made time for my summons to address inquiries about her sister's misdeeds. Please tell my knights what you disclosed to me."

X'ieth watched Magicia look away from the king, to behold the knights collectively. He struggled then to stare into her gray eyes, eyes that hinted years of maturity and wisdom but also, years of repressing something—sorrow, hurt, anger, or maybe, a combination of them all.

"To empower herself, my sister meddles in a strange Darkness," Magicia said, her words metallic with each syllable grating against each other. "Esmeralda secludes herself to her tower, continuously drawing the life force from nature, with an extended locus of control. I don't know how she does it, but she's killing Karnath."

Her words planted high anxiety in X'ieth. He gulped while listening on.

Talus asked, "Magicia, would you kindly lead my Guard into her abode, to end this evil act once and for all?"

When Magicia turned quickly to the throne, X'ieth held his breath, seeing then how her features hardened in the very motion—narrowing eyes, a creasing brow, and sharp contours along her cheeks. *She's not pleased with that request!*

"No, I won't." Magicia answered in a voice that was more metal against metal.

It was in this moment that X'ieth's discomfort peaked. *Are you the only one uneasy with this meeting?!* He wondered, but would not even dare glance upon the other Guardsmen to gauge their feelings from facial or bodily cues. His eyes were stuck upon Magicia.

"An accessory to my sister's demise I can never be." With those words Magicia's face softened, the sharp contours across her face dissolving in a single instant. "Esmeralda's bad destiny will lead to her own demise; I need not contribute to something bound to happen anyway." Her voice broke during that last statement, as if her inner pains rode upon it. "I will simply not protect her, and let my sister suffer the consequences of her choices."

Her voice suddenly became metallic again, and while speaking, Magicia alternated looks between the king and his knights. "I've tried reasoning with my sister, urging her to stop a behavior that is selfish, destructive, and drawing the wrong sort of attention. But she cannot be reasoned with, hence my position. So if you need to stop her by force, then so be it."

Unable to help his reaction, X'ieth dropped his jaw. *What in Karnatha's name?* he thought, not quite understanding how one sister would accept her sibling's fate like this; it was Fate's Fray for Esmeralda, yet Magicia acted as is she could not prevent the unraveling of her sister's divine destiny. Surely Esmeralda had some good destiny ordained by Karnatha that was much better than destroying Karnath. Yet, her actions were reality.

After a brief pause Magicia turned to the knights. X'ieth closed his mouth instantly.

"Should you stop her by force, I won't interfere."

Once again, the statement floored X'ieth, despite Magicia voicing her openness to Esmeralda's peril only seconds ago, given the circumstances. The whole prospect seemed very foreign to him, something that contradicted his reasonable expectations about how Magicia would react to the Guard's pursuit of Esmeralda. *It's natural for siblings to protect siblings, no?* His question did not have a good answer, just like his many others.

"And that's the only assurance I can give," said Magicia, with the same frigidity. X'ieth saw her bow to Talus. "Wisdom to you in this matter, King of Sergros."

Magicia began leaving the throne room, but before exiting, she stopped near X'ieth. A chill ran down his spine as her cold gray eyes passed over him, off to Finnel.

Smiling, she said, "Of great worth are those who do good by freewill, rather than by force. Of great worth then, is the Crimson Guard."

X'ieth glanced over just as Finnel's mouth went agape, as if he were shocked.

Magicia resumed her exit, soon departing from the hall of stone. The echo of her footsteps faded.

When she was out of earshot, Finnel exclaimed, "She passed my firewall, and read my mind!"

With concern, X'ieth looked at him, as did others of the Guard. *What was he thinking?* wondered the young knight, and perhaps later he would find the courage to ask.

From the throne, came Talus' voice, summoning his knights' attention. X'ieth looked up.

"Everyone can at least not fear her vengeance in your journey. A good thing, as we wouldn't want Magicia as an enemy." With a bit of judgment, X'ieth thought about the king's choice of words. *'We' wouldn't want her as an enemy? You would sit in your throne as the Guard faces her wrath!*

After Talus spoke, there was a developing quiet, from which Nathan called out. "My king, it nears midday. If we leave for Arlem now and travel through the night upon the main road, we can still reach the city by tomorrow."

X'ieth's focus shifted back to Talus, who nodded and replied, "Yes, the Seventh Order must leave soon. My servants have prepared your horses and supplies for the journey. Provisions such as water, dried meat, cheeses, unleavened breads, tents, and climbing gear have been included."

X'ieth looked back to Nathan, who lifted his chin, as if acknowledging that these things would be useful.

"You know the way, as does he," said Talus then, with a hand gesture to Zeros. X'ieth glanced at the mercenary, who stood with features cold as stone.

"I heard Thorin worked everyone hard during the practice," Talus continued. "You all should get a decent meal before departing; it might be your last for some time."

With those words, the Sergrothian official in beige and blue came up to the king, and began confirming the logistics of the meal and the knights' departure. Meanwhile, X'ieth's mind drifted to a distant place, as things began happening very fast, and it suddenly was occurring that this was the point of no return.

He had so many worries penned up at the back of his mind—since unexpectedly leaving his home for Sergros, since being handed his unseen promotion, since being given his surprise mission to stop Esmeralda and end the gloom. While his fears of confronting both Esmeralda and Magicia were now put at rest, his other worries broke free from their pen and ran amok in his head. *Would Millicent be well, only with Galwin by her side? Would confronting Esmeralda be your demise, or would it lead into your divine destiny of being the new Sergrothian hero and possibly, a hero across Karnath? Why was the woman in white in Castle Sergros, and why have your recent premonitions been wrong? Why have your promotions stopped altogether, just like the oracles'?*

X'ieth became dizzy as the questions revolved around, progressing from those about his family, to those about his greater purpose in life, and finally, the uncertainty of it all. To him, the uncertainty was undeniably related to how his premonitions became lost and his belief that somehow, the woman in white understood why.

The uncertainty easily stole his appetite, as X'ieth snapped back to the throne room from his deep contemplation, seeing the official raise a hand for the knights to follow him to the dining hall. Through the throne room, he walked behind Finnel with mixed emotions over leaving his family to pursue his divine destiny, without a clear sense of what would even happen.

When X'ieth stood at the throne room's exit that led into the foyer, Talus called out to him.

"Remember your promise to me," said the king.

X'ieth looked back and gave a silent nod, before slipping into the foyer, vowing to himself to complete his mission, if it were the last thing he did.

Chapter 14
Fugitive Hiding

For compelling reasons, some prefer to wear masks outside a masquerade ball. Behind the mask, one is freed from his or her identity, and others cannot judge them according to their deeds. Behind the mask, one is hidden from reputations.

Kort Al'starz lived now with all the aspirations of those who go masked outside the masquerade, though wearing a mask that covered everything but his face. He went by the name Inari, posing as a Hirishin fisher elf in the small fishing village of *Reiju*. Reiju was far west of the Mainland, across the blue Korinth Ocean, and on the east coast of the Hirishin Isles, being backed by the mossy *Jezban Mountains* and the stalky *Tai Forest*. It was quaint, quiet, and hopefully far from danger.

Kort needed distance, for back on the Mainland he was wanted for the murder of Garlew Il'therin. Only a month ago, the Sergrothian militants searched the continent westward, pushing Kort and his companion Nym from hideout to hideout upon the Mainland until they hid together outside the coastal town of Breslin.

One night while there, he quietly left Nym to escape the Mainland via a merchant vessel out of Breslin's port bound for Soku, a village in the southern Hirishin Isles. But Kort's stowaway voyage ended in disappointment, as lack of work in Soku caused him to leave shortly after his arrival. To his good fortune, however, a mysterious friend recommended Kort head to Reiju, where ultimately he found a job as a fisher, along with endless amounts of guilt and remorse over his past life, which prevented him from living this lie in peace.

What are you doing? Where are you going? The questions zipped through his head for not the first time today, unanswered after weeks of soul searching. Before having to run from the law, Kort attempted to redeem himself for involvement in the Isles Conspiracy, but instead, ended up mistakenly killing the Sergrothian hero Garlew. And since that tragic course of events, he lived day in and day out in the wake of all his broken dreams, what Karnathans would call Fate's Fray. From that, he was crushed by the lack of his own future and divine purpose. *And through my wrongs, I brought Fate's Fray to others—the very same destitution that I now live!*

The fish under his hand wriggled, bringing his attention back to the table in front of him. There on the wood, he stared at a squirming silver fish with black fins, about the length of his hand. Beside the fish was an unsheathed serrated knife. The sight was easily a reminder of what he needed to do. *Get these ready for the market...* With the thought, he glanced down to the bucket of brine at his feet, where swam about half a dozen more fish of the same kind.

Kort took up the knife, and pinned the fish to the table with his other hand. In one swift motion, Kort cut the fish along its belly from tail to chin, and then ripped out the entrails. Instantly the fish stopped moving, and in that moment, Kort was touched by the fish's surrender. A simple thing, yet it was enough to play upon all of his doubts in himself. It made him wonder if he too should be like the fish. *Just stop moving. Give yourself up to Sergros. There's nothing good that can become of your life now, not after your rotten past.*

Beneath Kort's palm the fish bled out on the table, and the sight oddly reinforced his sad thoughts, stirring up visions of his bloody deeds. Images flashed before Kort's eyes of him fighting fiercely in Baal, stopping at nothing to topple the Isles Conspiracy by hunting its leader through the entire city—Taurus Hboshi. He remembered so many scenes from Baal, all equally distasteful—the undercover soldiers slaughtering everyone in the common house; the smithy being killed with a pitchfork made at his own hands; the Hirishin mage who dealt devastating magic attacks; the giant nearly ripping him limb-from-limb before the trumpeting towers—he remembered each and every atrocity. *It's impossible to forget...*

Shaking his head, Kort snapped back to reality from these thoughts of his Dark past. He stood behind the table propped up against the exterior of Genze's house, facing the house directly. He was in Genze's backyard, a small lot covered with patches of burnt grass. Beside him was a wheelbarrow filled with rusted tools, about twenty cubits away from a wooden shed behind him that lied in the shadows cast by the stalky trees of Tai Forest, over which rose the morning sun.

It's going to get hot soon, Kort realized with a glance to the sky. With the Isle's early summer come months before due, Kort had experience with heat and when it would get hot. *And this summer is brutal compared to summers past...*

While thinking to himself, he took up the next fish from the bucket, and gutted it as the first, recalling nothing but windless scorching days ever since the Isles Conspiracy ended. With the excessive heat and lacking rain, the water supply in Reiju dwindled, and the crops wasted away throughout the region. *It's the poorest of circumstances!*

Kort gutted yet another fish, while considering how everyone's problems did not stop with hot days, little rain, and lost crops. For some unexplainable reason, the fish in Korinth grew harder and harder to catch. Indeed, despite Kort having heavy eyes and aching muscles from a sleepless night of fishing on Korinth, the bucket at his feet was only half their measly catch, and that was a fraction of what it was a week ago! *Genze isn't happy about it either...*

Kort recalled Genze grumble excessively about catching so few fish. In fact, Genze grumbled from the moment they docked the sailing boat in Reiju, all the way while they walked home, and even as the fisherman dragged a torn net into the house before collapsing onto his mat, to sleep the morning away.

As Kort gutted the final fish, he heard Genze's snoring drift through the rear window of the house, a reminder that while his boss' workday was over, his workday had not yet ended. Genze's expectation was that Kort would go to the market and sell the smallest fish they had caught, and possibly those tools in the wheelbarrow.

Kort sighed, removing his eyes from the fish and casting them upon the rusty iron. *What an assorted lot*, he thought. *Who sells fish and rusted junk?*

It was an odd lot indeed, but Genze saw it necessary to sell off unused or unwanted household items to supplement their small catches and fetch the same coin from the market, or maybe even more. Kort and Genze would use that coin to buy rice in the neighboring village Doj in order to stretch their meals of the unsold fish, over weeks rather than days.

Theirs was a tough situation, but perhaps no tougher than anywhere else in the Hirishin Isles, where people struggled to make ends meet. Stagnated imports and exports made for a burgeoning economic disaster that affected life in Reiju, Doj, and beyond. With the rice shortage, Doj had little to trade and merchants stopped sailing into its port, making resources from the Mainland even lesser in supply. *I've never remembered it this bad....*

With that thought, Kort took all of the gutted fish that he had piled up on the table, and threaded a single fishing line through their open mouths and out their gaping stomachs. He did this for each fish until reaching the last, where he knotted the line's end and at that, grabbed the line's other end and pulled the fish off the table, dangling them from an upraised hand. *Should make us a sale*, he thought with a glance over the six silver fish, strung neatly from head-to-tail.

Kort carried them over to the rusty iron wheelbarrow, which had its rear stands resting upon the grass, and a single wheel on its other end. The stands were literally metal prongs on the underside of two brittle wooden handles that extended to support the barrow on each side, being married at the opposite end with an axle, upon which spun the wheel.

Kort wrapped the line about one of the two wooden handles, before taking hold of them and pulling up to get the metal stands off the ground. With a push then, he moved the wheelbarrow forward, maneuvering it around the side of Genze's house, and onto the long dirt road connecting Doj to Reiju.

As soon as he stepped out of the shade, he felt the day's heat, and quickly gave a look back to the trees behind Genze's house. He noticed the sun even higher in the sky, and it made him consider the time. *Maybe it's later than I thought!* Thoughts buzzed through Kort's head all in one instant—of getting late to the mart and losing sales to rival fisherman; of the midday heat being enough to spoil his fresh fish; and worst of all, of Genze's poor reactions to either or both outcomes. It was easily motivating to head toward Reiju's market with a faster pace than before.

And so Kort did, pushing the wheelbarrow before him as he started the short trip down the dirt path to the village itself. There, the path would branch off into Reiju's main walk that led to the village center and also, the mart.

Each step of the way, the sun beat down upon his light skin and lengthy soot-black hair. With an upraised hand, Kort lowered his oval face to the ground, effectively shielding his slanted, brown eyes from the blinding sun.

To keep cool, he pulled his bowl straw hat over his head and at that, derived less discomfort from the hot sun. But his guilt inside nagged him to tilt the hat back as it was, and he did, careful not to enjoy any one gratifying experience too long. The otherwise joyous lives he cut short discouraged such indulgences from the grave. *I shouldn't enjoy anything, when those I've killed can no longer enjoy life.*

Down the path Kort kept walking, a path beset by mounds of burnt grass, brought about by the recent drought conditions. On one side of the path, he could see the tall, white stalks of Tai Forest at a distance, where on the other side, the fallow-hued grass yielded to a sandy coast and the clear blue waters of Korinth.

Kort walked on. Soon enough, Reiju came into sight—a bunch of dark wooden fisher houses on the coast, all with thatched roofs and piped smokestacks. On its outskirts, the village appeared completely lifeless, without anyone walking in the alleys between houses, the streets intersecting with those alleys, or the main walk through the village that was the artery into which all streets merged. *It's easy to get noticed, when I'm among the few who busy themselves in Reiju.*

Realizing that the village's depressed economic state drew attention to doers like himself, Kort maintained constant awareness of his surroundings. While he possessed oriental features typical of Hirishin elves in these parts and blended right in, he still feared that someone might identify his face with all his 'wanted' posters plastered throughout the Mainland. So, as he pushed the wheelbarrow to the market, he would stay off Reiju's main walk for as long as possible, by taking the back way to the mart—a series of alleys and streets. And around every corner he planned to look first with keen eyes, to verify it was clear of danger before stepping out.

Briskly, he ducked out of an alley and went along one dirt street lined by wooden fisher houses—decrepit wooden dwellings capped by tired thatched roofs with crooked smokestacks. He gazed over them, the picturesque rows of auburn wood and beige hay, overhung by a cloudless, cyan sky. The scene was familiar to the ex-knight, but beyond the village's familiarity and charm, he made a parallel to his own life concerning its tired state.

These houses had stood for years, enduring tropical rains and being weathered by the elements. And just as this, he was both enduring and weathered in a different way, still standing, but now on the verge of collapse under the weight of crushing demoralizations. His choices and how they hurt others made for wrongs that he could not aright, despite his efforts to live better.

But living better after doing wrong is all that I can do! he thought, during his walk toward the market, off the street into another alley. It was a reminder that frequently surfaced when considering his prior misdeeds that led up to the Isles Conspiracy, and that reminder clashed with the debasing realization that living better was simply not enough, at least for someone like him. *I need to do more than good for one or two people, but rather, great good for many—a great good that lasts!*

Deep inside, Kort sincerely desired to do great good for many to atone for his past sins, but how this might be done remained a perplexing mystery to him. Every day since he acknowledged his mistake with Garlew Il'therin, he desperately sought a road to redemption, without knowing how to start the path or if it even existed, given the extent of his previous wrongs. *Perhaps Destiny reserves second chances for people better than me*, he thought glumly, with only a hope that somehow he could still redeem himself before the law caught up with him.

Kort pushed the wheelbarrow out of the final alley on his back way to the mart and into Reiju's main walk; the market was immediately visible, being about two hundred cubits away. He discerned the mart's white canopies at a distance, standing out among the darker homes.

In the absence of redemption, he thought while walking, *my memories torment me day and night.* It was true, for every time Kort looked back to his Dark past it completely devastated him, not just for the evils he did, but also for a sobering reality. *My only good deed was a complete lie!*

Kort recalled how for years he deceptively held the honorable title of knight in the Sixth Order of the Crimson Guard. He rode with Sergros' hero, Garlew Il'therin, among many other respectable knights like X'ieth, Sagult, and Dimral. However, his true role was chief informant to the Black Dragon clans with a primary loyalty to Taurus Hboshi. *Simply put, I was a spy who posed as a well-respected knight in Sergros in order to gain access to Sergrothian intelligence about the Triangle Kingdoms and also, a trustworthy reputation upon the Mainland.* It occurred to him that these were bad reasons to be good— ones in Taurus' favor, though never his own.

Despite the poor intentions surrounding Kort's membership in the Crimson Guard, it ironically provided him with something that he never quite felt when working for Taurus—a noble purpose: to protect innocent blood. But his love for being in the Guard was not enough to stop him from letting the Isles

Conspiracy happen. And in so doing, he foolishly betrayed a common trust in Sergros and lost everything—from purpose and trust, even to true love.

As he pondered the far-reaching consequences of his misdeeds, a vision of Nym hit him. Tan skin. Silver hair. Pink lips. Delicate features. In his mind, he saw her well, the beautiful, silver-haired elf that he loved dearly. They met when she first resurrected Kort after he died from falling into a gorge, during Taurus' ambush.

As far as he understood, Nym had resurrected him for a Dark service to Ma'althan, a purpose from which he ran away in pursuit of Taurus, to the City of Baal. However, upon reaching Baal, Kort learned that Taurus was not even there; the Black Dragon emperor was supposedly outside the city at a nearby hospice, being treated for a serious wound to his head. But Kort discovered this far too late for him to escape the throngs of undercover solders that had infiltrated Baal to overthrow it. And so, he fought there to his death, awakening to strange magical powers along the way—from mind control to telekinesis—none of which were enough to save his life.

Before Kort died in Baal, he bent the will of Nym to resurrect him a second time so that he could get out of the city and kill Taurus. Once resurrected, Kort managed to flee Baal and find the hospice as planned, where he used Nym again to carry out the murder of Taurus. Since Taurus was the twin brother of his close friend Garlew, their close resemblance might interfere with Kort's ability to deliver death. *I wish it had...*

To Kort's utter disdain, he eventually learned that the injured elf lying in the hospice bed that he willed Nym to slay was actually Garlew Il'therin and not Taurus Hboshi. In that reality, Kort ended up murdering his friend, damaging his relationship with Nym, and leaving the Triangle Kingdoms to dismantle the Isles Conspiracy on their own. *It was easily the biggest mistake of my life.*

At the mere recollection of everything, Kort drowned in grief, especially at the thoughts of how he had used Nym. But surprisingly, despite all of what had transpired between them, Nym's adoration and affections remained constant since their meeting, after his first resurrection. In fact, she had always exerted a peculiar attraction for him that went well beyond physical attraction. It was a special kind of attraction that transcended his misdeeds, anything that Kort could possibly say or do. It was love, and Kort knew it. He knew it with such surety that he reciprocated it, and loved Nym with all of his heart.

Indeed, theirs was an odd relationship, but it was love of the most genuine kind, a love that trumped relational states of dislike, unfairness, and inequity. But as real as their love was, it seemed gone now. From the time when Kort left Nym outside Breslin, she seemingly never searched for him since. She was a powerful being, who surely was able to find him if she wanted, but she did not. The thought of Nym purposely leaving him in the Isles saddened Kort, and made him wonder if perhaps his love for Nym had become unrequited. *Perhaps this is just another angle of my punishment from Destiny...lost love.*

With a heavy heart, Kort emptied his mind and pushed his wheelbarrow down the main walk. The mart appeared closer in his eyes as he continued forward, where now a few more canopies could be seen. Their sheets of white marked a contrast with the clear sky above, stretched over tables holding sundry goods for sale. Some sellers put out produce scorched by the sun; fewer sold poultry, livestock, or fish. Others had fabrics, household items, or tools. *Like me,* Kort thought, with his bundle of two odd goods—fish and tools.

As Kort maneuvered his wheelbarrow into the mart and around a few customers, he realized how the market seemed to have less buyers and sellers, almost by the week. His observation rang consistent with the reality that people lived minimally in the Hirishin Isles, and perhaps never more minimally than this day of age, given the recent economic downturn.

When at his unofficial spot in the mart—between a seller of house crafts and a seller of linens, far from the competition of rival fish sellers—he plopped down his wheelbarrow in the stolen shade of one adjacent white canopy. As a first order of business, he unwound the line of six silver fish from the wheelbarrow's handle, and lifted it high to the canopy's poles, where he fixed the line so that the fish would dangle as a good advertisement to market goers of what he had available. *People don't buy what they don't see,* he thought, while finishing the knot.

With some satisfaction, Kort looked over the fish hanging from the canopy pole, the product of his and Genze's hard work. He gazed up into the crowd that filled the market, mainly female elves, ranging in age from young to old, carrying straw baskets and rounding from table to table. Among them, Kort did not see his frequent customers for fish. *Dunnen and Kyan,* he thought, *where are you, my friends?*

Kort's confidence was high that either of them would eventually make an appearance to buy fish, but the tools were another matter. In trying times, he realized people simply did not buy more than the essentials for survival. *And no one needs this stuff,* he realized, *not even Genze!* The thought brought a smile to his lips, as he looked at the tools and shook his head.

While Kort was thinking about the tools, he looked at them, and noticed a small bow saw hanging over the edge of his cart; it was one of Genze's rusted old things that nearly managed to escape the wheelbarrow during the transport. And so, he reached forth to grab the saw, so to prevent it from falling. But when his fingers grazed the tool, it fell from the wheelbarrow and hit the ground, flipping a few times before settling afar in the sunlit walk, outside the canopy.

Ugh, Kort thought, moving out from his spot in the shade. But just as he bent down and his fingers touched the tool's grip, he was eclipsed by darkness! Being startled, Kort quickly looked up, and as he did, he noticed a tower of barbed, red armor had appeared beside him, casting a long shadow on the walk. Kort looked up the armor, from its boots and curved breastplate, all the way up to the familiar metal face atop; it was a magical knight in crimson armor, one whom he called Elucid.

Kort stood up with the bow saw in hand. The immense knight before him went three cubits above his head and its armor was unlike most he had ever seen, testifying to the advanced magic the Red Dragon clans somehow acquired to conquer the Black Dragon dynasty. *Using magical knights in these armors— metal demons from Tekkneo—the Red Dragon clans seized our lands overnight,* he thought.

Since Kort was of the defeated Black Dragon clans, the sight of a metal demon sometimes reminded him of great loss and the underpinnings of the Isles Conspiracy. However, his heartfelt repentance over a life of lies and violence made him realize the conflict between the warring families fueled a consuming fire that left nothing but hate in its burning. *Given this, I now look at the situation differently. I can look at this crimson knight differently...*

And so Kort did, eying up Elucid in almost reverential silence, after slipping the bow saw back into the wheelbarrow. He first encountered the crimson knight in the Isles after fleeing from the Mainland. Elucid was the mysterious friend who recommended he leave Soku and head to Reiju to find work, as if understanding the lack of stability in the Black Dragon territory after the Red Dragon families took over. *The crimson knight directed me to Genze in the coastal village of Reiju, a fisher who needed help. Elucid saved my life, when I would've otherwise starved or worse.*

"What doing leads your destiny?" Elucid boomed. Kort gave a blank stare, prompting the crimson knight to rephrase the question. "What are you doing, and to what destiny does it lead?"

Fettered by transgressions from his past, Kort lacked a good response. The voice at the back of his head piped up then, the one that spoke to him as he gutted the fish. *Just stop moving. Give yourself up to Sergros. There's nothing good that can become of your life now, not after your rotten past.*

To derive a response, Kort considered his present state of being contextually, while wondering to himself what Elucid was really asking. With a shrug of his shoulders he said, "I sell fish and odd items, in hopes of getting money for rice."

"Is that all your hopes of the future entail?"

With a thoughtful pause Kort said, "No. I want so much more." He sensed the crimson knight loom over him, casting a long shadow upon the ground in the near vacant mart. In his vicinity he noticed few people, though none within earshot. *Can I speak freely here?* he wondered, with some hesitation to continue.

"Time is running out," Kort admitted finally, "I know it. Before long I'll be caught." Dejected at the thought of being forever unredeemed, Kort looked to the ground for a moment, before returning his gaze to Elucid. "Before long, my life will only amount to setting a legal precedent in the Sergrothian courts for this wrong that I mistakenly committed! I myself would go to the authorities over it, but not yet. For all this would achieve is me rotting in a Sergrothian prison, but that alone repays little while I seek to repay so much more!"

Looking past the crimson knight to the sky, Kort talked hopefully. "To the Sergrothian citizens who lost their hero, I'm sure my capture would provide their closure. But I must do great good before conceding to those who search for me. I must do something that helps many." He spoke words from his heart, with utter sincerity, yet a bit of distress in his voice. *But how to do enough good, when I've done so much bad?!*

Swallowing his doubts, Kort continued. "I've already found that the past cannot be changed, only the present and future. To live better can never aright past wrongs, for the past is set in stone!"

Elucid suddenly interjected, "To live better beyond transgressions is better than to continue living the same way."

Kort nodded in silent agreement.

"There's a path to what you seek and I can help you find it, but you must trust me in order to…."

Kort heard Elucid abruptly stop speaking, as the background noise increased in the relatively still market.

"I'll give you everything I have, for some food!"

Kort glanced over to a wiry elven lad in trousers cut at the knees and a pullover shirt. He stood before one of the sellers of poultry, trying to barter for a scrawny chicken with household items. The seller jingled a bag of money, as if indicating the only accepted payment.

"Sorry, only coin here, at least while it can still buy me rice in Doj."

Kort looked back to Elucid, who spoke just then.

"You should leave at once," Elucid said bluntly. "They'll search for you in this place."

With eyebrows arched Kort surveyed the market, and it seemed unthreatening to him, just as in many days and weeks past. Though he could not sense anything wrong, he wondered if Elucid had extraordinary perception. *Can the crimson knight detect something that I cannot?*

He stared at Elucid, part in disbelief. His mind worked the situation over. No 'wanted' posters had been hung in these parts, and it just did not seem likely that only after such a short while in Reiju, he would already be pursued here. Kort practiced some vigilance, but for now, he counted it more a precaution than a necessary measure. *My whereabouts are still secret*, he thought to himself, now with some added doubts.

While Kort often believed Elucid, the vision of Genze screaming at him for coming back with no coin overpowered his desire to listen. *Why didn't you sell anything?!* The fisherman's loud voice became trapped between his ears.

"I'm sorry," said Kort, "but the fish must be sold."

Elucid replied, "One day soon, you may decide to wholly trust me." The words were plain, without emotion.

Kort watched Elucid disappear into thin air, by a strange magic of the metal demons. He looked around cautiously, wondering if the words of his mysterious friend would swiftly be proven true. But nothing except a quiet bustle could be heard in the market, playing on his confusion with the situation. *So strange... What did Elucid sense, if anything?*

With that, Kort shook off the admonition and decided to spend time at the market in hopes of selling his goods. *After all, that's why I'm here...* But as time passed, he was without a single customer for a long while. He began to worry for the fish spoiling.

As if providential, however, Kort's frequent buyer eventually showed up from a nearby village off the coast, which was not often frequented by fishers.

"Kyan, good day to you!" said Kort with mirth, upon seeing him afar.

"A hot day to me," replied the heavyset man, waddling closer.

Kort watched a round, middle-aged fellow with a scraggly beard come up to the cart. The person wore plain cloths, pants tied at the waist and a worn pullover revealing an outcrop of chest hair. His locks were curly, his skin tanned and glistening with sweat, and he possessed brown eyes, set within a pudgy face.

"Have you fish today?" Kyan asked, shifting upon sandaled feet.

The ex-knight smiled. "Barely! I have half a dozen that took many hours to catch. There's simply not many fish in the waters anymore."

Kyan grew serious. "Strange times beset Karnath. Since the Great Occlusion there's been considerable need and destitution, from the *Isles* to the *Mainland*, and from the tip of *Dragonaut Island* to the *Northern Region's* frozen tundra!"

"My these are small," Kyan remarked, looking over the lot of fish, with now a less serious tone. "You know, perhaps a larger fish is having many meals at the expense of you fishers."

Kort opened his hand, as Kyan extended a palm full of coins, the Hirishin currency. The ex-knight judged the weight of the coin in his hand, so not to offend his customer by biting them to verify their authenticity.

"I've heard stories of a large whale that thrashes about," continued Kyan, "terrorizing the merchant vessels upon the seas." Untying the line of fish from the canopy pole, Kort listened as his customer went on. "Some ships have barely stayed afloat, the crew surviving to tell these tales. Other ships are lost on the waters, neither crew nor vessel to be seen again!"

Kort gave him the line. Kyan took it in one hand, whilst gesturing with his other. "You should watch for the whale when on the waters," he warned.

The story struck Kort as unusual, but interesting in the same regard. He much preferred to believe merchants came less often due to reduced trade with the depressed economy, rather than tall tales like ship-eating whales.

Smiling warmly, Kort replied, "I rarely go onto the deep, but I'll be careful nonetheless!"

Kyan returned the smile.

"Do that indeed, my friend. Destiny be with you!"

Beneath his lengthy pullover shirt, Kort put the coin into a leather pouch hanging from his neck. *Now to just sell this junk,* he thought with a look to the tools, knowing that Genze might not be pleased with only the fish sold. *How ironic,* he thought, knowing this amount of coin should be enough to buy rice for at least a week. *Genze just likes to complain...*

After waiting a few more minutes in the hot mart, it occurred to Kort that the junk could always be brought back another day. *I'll wait a little while longer,* he decided. *Sale or no sale, it'll do me good to get some space from the ornery Genze.*

He stood beneath the shade and thought about what Elucid had said. *The path to redemption...* He revisited the very concept in his mind, wanting more than anything to do good in an attempt to offset his failures and shortcomings in life with something hugely positive. *There must be a way... There must be.*

Lost in thought, Kort just stared into the market, when suddenly a certain sight caught his attention. Two cloaks framing falling stars—one white and the other black—fell motionlessly from two persons standing in the distance with their backs turned. The ex-knight remembered seeing a woman wearing that exact white cloak, right before Taurus' ambush of the Sixth Order of the Guard! *It's her!*

The visual instantly triggered mixed memories on a hot summer night: crossbows fired, bolts pierced his armor and caused blinding pain, and he fell down a ravine with both arms flailing. In his eyes, he saw the ridge's top move further and further from view, while the woman's chilling words remained. *Not as you expected?* Moments before it all happened, she looked right at him with that playful question, and the words lingered in his mind until this very day. He always wondered if her question was directed at him, like an inquiry about the unexpected situation about to unfold, which happened to differ dramatically from his premonitions of the future.

Being a traitor to Sergros at the time, Kort had actually planned that ambush with Taurus. But the ambush that occurred deviated drastically from their conspiring, and included him as a target! *I never saw that coming...*

The longer Kort stared at the woman in white as she stood there in the market, the longer visions appeared in his head, of himself falling down the ravine to his death. It happened after the Black Dragon soldiers fired bolts at the Crimson Guard from their hidden spots in the foliage that opened to the gorge. The scene became so real in his head that he literally could hear the projectiles buzz by him, along with sounds of crossbow function—metallic slide and humming bowstrings. *Taurus somehow knew about my assassination attempt before it happened and planned accordingly,* he thought, *only to Garlew's demise!*

His attention snapped back to the mart, and Kort studied the pair with intrigue. Then suddenly, he saw the man in black turn to cast a green eye his way. With alarm the ex-knight watched as the man leered right at him, the sunlight painting his toughened complexion. What alarmed Kort even more was the person with whom the woman in white spoke—Sagult!

After having served with the Sergrothian knight for years, Kort could not easily forget his features: he had a slender jawbone on his oblong face, with bright amber eyes of brown speckles, spaced widely apart on each side of his pointy nose, all beneath short coppery hair. His skin was pale, white like the virtues inside him. Sagult was a righteous man, perhaps more so than any Karnathan that Kort had ever met.

When seeing Sagult a few cubits away, Kort barely could believe his eyes. Fortunately for him, Sagult was completely occupied with the stunning woman in white. And then, Kort saw the man in black point directly at him, all of a sudden and complete unexpected!

Dread weighed down Kort's gut in that; his breathing became tense and short, and his heart skipped a beat. He watched the Sergrothian militants with Sagult look in his direction, and talk amongst each other.

"That's him?" one asked.

"It's to whom the man points, no?" said another.

Kort observed Sagult just keep talking to the woman in white, as if oblivious to the soldiers' conversation. *They're here for me!* he thought, worriedly.

Without even planning his escape, Kort rushed away from the mart, leaving everything behind—both cart and tools. *I'll deal with Genze's frustration later!*

He surreptitiously weaved in between the canopied tables, moving toward the houses that sat behind the stands. He went so fast, that the setting literally blurred in his eyes.

All of a sudden, he heard a shout from one of the soldiers.

"He went this way! Follow me."

Oh no... His mind raced, as he got out of the market and was finally at the street before the houses. Once there, he immediately began contemplating ways of getting out of view. Kort looked to his right, sighting a narrow alley between two houses, which give him an idea. *Go up.*

Without losing a moment, he ran into the alley, being formed by two exterior house walls that faced each other. He sprung up the walls, alternating from one to the other until reaching the level of the thatched roof. What at the roof, he pulled himself onto it using both arms and his upper body. The quick motions caused his straw hat to fall off his head and hang from its chinstrap about his neck. Kort ran to the back of the housetop, far from the field of view in the market.

From rooftop to rooftop, the nimble ex-knight leaped, evading the main ways in the village and lessening his chances of being caught. But what he could not avoid was his chance of the unexpected. For with his bound onto the next tired rooftop, Kort was shocked as his feet sunk into the straw, and he felt nothing beneath him along with an immediate sensation of falling!

Destiny save me! he thought, hearing a loud crash while descending into the house's blackness. As if expecting this all along, Kort landed adroitly inside the home of a fisher elf. Kneeling on the floor, he glanced up to the roof, seeing the hay falling in from a huge opening above, as did light pour through, illuminating a tidy space with wooden floors and sparse furnishings—notably a table and chairs.

Kort immediately tapped the Nexus and envisioned himself in an enlarged channeling chamber, made of stone. He stood at two large wooden doors, cubits above his head, and pulled them back using their bronze handles. When the doors parted, his eyes saw light blast through the opening. Several streams of aqua green Nexus flowed in, providing an immediate connection to the Source. Through those varied, complex flows, the ex-knight could sense how his surroundings interacted with the energy field. And by this means, he detected a broom jabbed right at his head!

In an instant, Kort snapped from his concentration and back into the house, blurredly moving himself to the side, just in time to avoid being hit in the face by a haggard, broom-wielding lady elf. In his periphery he saw her then, wearing tattered garments and wildly waving her broom. Kort knew she shouted in Hirishin, but he was so familiar with multiple languages that, in his head, it sounded as Mainlandish.

"Get out! Get out!" she screeched.

Kort sensed the husband come into view, an aged elf with gray hair and smooth skin, adorned in common dress. His steps showed apparent caution. While at a first glance he seemed more reserved than his wife, Kort bet this fellow would be equally unwelcoming.

As if to confirm those suspicions, Kort watched him grab the broom from his wife, and run forward. Without anything to swat the intruder, she yelled hysterically and threw her arms about.

"Get out! Get out!" she yelled again.

Always being a good judge of when he was unwanted, Kort evaded the husband and went to exit through the front sliding door. But just as he reached it, the wood burst open! He saw two Sergrothian militants rush forth, with swords drawn. From his periphery, he noted the husband and wife retreat to the house's nearest corner.

Kort back-flipped two times, bringing his body near the table and chairs occupying the space. He raised a leg and using his foot, snagged the top rail of one chair's backrest. With a quick whip of the same leg he sent the chair flying at the nearest solider! He watched the flung chair smack the militant right in the forehead. Upon contact, the seat broke into pieces and the struck soldier fell to the ground unconscious, covered in pieces of wood. The ex-knight's eyes were already on the second assailant, who did not waste time in mounting an attack.

To the side Kort moved, just as the soldier's sword came crashing down onto the solid table, getting stuck deep in its timber. He observed the solider pull at his blade hard, to remove his weapon with a single, sharp jerk before striking again.

Right as the militant slashed at him, Kort fell to the floor and slid under the table to its opposite end. While there, he could sense the militant's evident frustration.

"Grrrrhh!" the soldier growled, as he leaned over the table with enraged eyes and weapon in hand, trying to swipe the sword again. But he was too far away.

Suddenly, the soldier belly flopped onto the table, trying to get closer to Kort for a clean strike. But when he did, Kort deftly slid beneath the table to its other side, under the militant's dangling feet! In a flash, he was upright and running toward the door. And Kort did not stop running either, after he exited and reached the dirt roads that led all the way back to Genze's house and even further on to Doj.

Meanwhile, the militant ceased swinging his sword wildly and looked back over his shoulder, his belly still on the table. "Destiny damn it!" he shouted, realizing what had just happened. The solider got off and checked under the table, to verify the fugitive was really gone, according to his suspicions. *Not here. Sagult will be disappointed in me.*

With sword in hand he ran outside and looked all about, but the fugitive was nowhere to be found. *How could he do that?!*

From the adjoining dirt byways of Reiju, the soldier watched Sagult come forth with another militant.

"Where did he go?" asked Sagult.

The soldier replied, "He's just gone."

Sagult shook his head in disagreement, squinting under the intense sunlight. "You just didn't see his last move. People don't disappear."

The soldier watched Sagult's eyes trail off to the dirt road leading from the main village, up toward Doj. It was then he that looked too, and noticed signs of fresh footprints there for the length of the road.

Brimming with determination, Sagult said, "He wouldn't stay here; let's see if he returned home!"

"POINTED OUT BY THE SERVANTS"

Chapter 15
The Faceoff

Up the long road Kort ran, out of Reiju and back toward Genze's. The sun beat upon his head and shoulders, without a cloud in the sky to block its strong glare. He felt perspiration dampen his pullover near his chest and armpits, but it provided minimal relief in the sweltering heat. *It's so hot*, he thought, knowing his discomfort was the least of his worries.

Beside his rapid breathing, Kort could hear the sounds of his own feet, hitting the dirt again and again as he literally sprinted away from the village center of Reiju. As he went, the ex-knight could not stop thinking about Sagult locating him there. *How in Destiny did he find me?*

The very mismatch rattled him, of his present reality and his premonitions about going undetected in Reiju, but he was left without any explanation about why he could no longer predict his own future, like so many people in Karnath. *My premonitions come less often now, and seem to be always wrong!*

False premonitions were not new to Kort, and he recently stopped trusting them the moment they got him killed by Taurus Hboshi's forces. The woman in white's casual glance and chilling words were the precursors to his mistrust, a mistrust that only grew since then.

His recollection about false premonitions and the woman in white easily led into contemplations about seeing her again in Reiju's market. *Why was she there?!* Her presence worried Kort greatly, and the more he pondered this matter, the more he associated the woman in white with his flawed premonitions—from Taurus' ambush to being detected in Reiju. *Every time I have a wrong premonition, it seems like the woman in white is there!*

With a thoughtful mind, he ran more up the dirt path, huffing and puffing along the way. The landscape blurred as he jetted by, stalky trees behind the tall grass, both just streaks of green and brown. Like his body, his mind kept running too. *The woman in white…*

In days of their accuracy, Kort's premonitions made his life kind of boring. He always knew what was coming, and occasionally planned ahead. Most times though, he just let things happen as they would. As far as he was concerned, true premonitions detracted from life's suspenseful moments, and he could care less about getting them back. However, where lost premonitions became important to him was in order to understand the chain of events that culminated in his Fate's Fray—through the wrongful death of Garlew, and whatever was happening now. *That's where she fits in: explaining why my foresights couldn't prevent any of this.*

Kort believed that the woman in white's presence—both in Taurus' ambush and now with Sagult—indicated her significance in his own Fate's Fray, and furthermore, suggested that she was the Dark power with whom Taurus allied to carry out a fiendishly diabolical plan: the Isles Conspiracy. Given this, he was convinced that her help would be necessary to learn how Taurus foresaw his assassination attempt in Baal, only to counter it by targeting him in the ambush. *The woman in white knows how Taurus preempted me and caused this downward spiral leading to Garlew's death. Understanding this is essential for me to find redemption, lest I continue spiraling down!*

Kort ran more on the dirt road, until finally seeing Genze's house ahead. It lied alongside a few other older homes on the outskirts of village Reiju, all with dark wood exteriors and beige thatched roofs making for their striking dissimilarity between the sky overhead and the surrounding landscapes. These fisher homes were even simpler than those in Reiju, being built in an earlier era with a single, front sliding door, a rear window, and much less space that the newer-style homes in the village itself. Older homes like these were not raised on stilts either, which more and more was done with newer construction to offset the frequent flooding in these parts of the Isles—the coastal wetlands.

He slowly approached the door, and then stopped to look back down the dirt road, just waiting and listening. Though calm presided in that moment, it was not enough for him to believe the militants would not come searching for him outside of Reiju, especially here. *With the woman in white helping Sagult, who knows what other information she might reveal regarding my whereabouts!*

With that in mind, he turned around to the home's door and pulled it back, not wanting to hesitate entering a second longer. But when he opened the door, he revealed Genze inside mending his fishing nets.

"Shut the door!" Genze shouted immediately, as if bothered by the light pouring into the relatively dark space. And so, Kort stepped in, and closed the door behind him, afterward turning to the fisherman.

Kort saw him well, a man with a balding head and tanned skin from being out on the waters. Genze's nose was a crooked nub, perched above wide lips and below deep inset eyes of brown. The fisherman was previously a Mainlandish sailor who immigrated to the Isles long ago.

But despite Kort looking at Genze, the fisherman kept both eyes on his torn net, which he had hung on the wall by shoving each end into crevices between the wall frame and the wallboards. It hung before Genze in a parabola, making the tears easily accessible. Kort's attention was drawn to his hands, which worked through the first stage of mending the net: preparing the tears. With a small knife Genze steadily cut around them, to convert asymmetric holes in the netting into openings that were regular, and suitable for patching with new material.

Kort cleared his throat. "Ahem."

"Tell me you sold the fish, Inari…" Genze said. With a smile, Kort opened his mouth to speak, but before he could, the fisherman continued. "Along with those old belongings of mine."

At that added expectation, Kort closed his mouth, and a scowl spoiled his face. *You had to make that remark, didn't you?* While he knew Genze well and could have easily predicted the fisherman, the comment caught him off-guard with everything that happened. Silent and waiting, Genze kept cutting around tears in the net.

"The fish I sold," Kort finally replied. In hopes of pleasing Genze with the mere sight of coin, he removed most of the proceeds from the small leather purse about his neck and under his pullover, and extended a palm full of coins to the fisherman.

From Kort's vantage point, he could not tell if Genze even budged at the mention of money. As much as he tried to be optimistic, it was apparent that Genze was not very impressed. *He works with that netting, even as I push money at him!*

"And the other things?" asked Genze, again.

Kort paused for a few moments, contemplating what he should say. *Nothing short of the truth will do!* he thought, while placing Genze's share of the coin upon the nearby short stool.

Looking back up, Kort answered reluctantly, with expectations of grief and fuss. "There was danger in the market; I had to leave the tools behind with your cart."

Genze instantly stopped cutting and turned from the net, and it was then that Kort knew what to expect. *Here it comes...* Though he warned himself, it was rarely enough to prepare the ex-knight for Genze's over-the-top, explosive reactions.

"Someone will just take my possessions for their own!" Genze shouted with a cockeyed, angry stare. "You ought to bring them back!"

Kort stood there, shaking his head from side to side.

"It's dangerous for me in the mart. You should take a break from the net, and see to your things."

Genze cursed with evident frustration. "Destiny blinds me to your foolishness, Inari! I never expected you to be so thoughtless!" As Genze's face suddenly contorted, Kort cringed. The fisherman screamed at the top of his lungs. "Do you realize what this means?! I might have nothing to sell in later weeks when I simply do not catch fish! How shall I buy food then?!"

At this, Kort started having second thoughts of coming back to Genze's house. *Was this really such a good idea?* He regarded it appropriate to give the fisherman his due share of money and farewells before leaving Reiju. *But this might get me to Sergros' prison sooner rather than later, to be forevermore laden by my own guilt!* The thought crushed him. In the background, Kort heard Genze carry on, but his attention waned, and he went in and out of the conversation.

"*You* ought to bring my things back!" Genze said with particular emphasis on 'you', during his angry rant. *That's likely about the sum of it*, Kort guessed, upon listening again. *Tell him that being in Reiju presents danger for you*, Kort thought to himself. *Reiterate that you must leave, now. You gave him his money, so be gone.*

The thoughts circled around Kort's head, each one seeming logical and common sense imposing clear expectations upon himself. A simple 'thank you' and 'goodbye' ordinarily would be sufficient for most people, but things were not so simple with Genze.

"You ought to bring my things back!" the fisherman shouted. This was said so many times that the words were doomed to be stuck in Kort's ears. *You ought to bring my things back!*

All of a sudden Kort blurted out, "Thank you for having me here, Genze. But as I said, there's danger for me, and I must go." When Genze stared back silently, to Kort it seemed like the fisherman silently processed the statement. *Maybe… he understands?*

Then from the quiet, erupted another of Genze's angry outbursts that showed the contrary. "How dare you be careless with my things in such trying times?!" Genze shouted, "I let you stay here and I gave you work, yet this is how you repay me?!"

With that, Kort started to feel guilty. *It's true, he did let me stay here and times are tough.* The ex-knight considered then, how likely his capture would be if returning to the same market, in order to please Genze. He believed the militants from Sergros probably still searched for him there. *Such would be foolish!* His inner voice desperately tried to reason him out of doing what would jeopardize his plans of redemption.

Kort looked at the angry Genze, and his common sense wrestled with his will to be a better person. Something important suddenly occurred to him. *Leave all that you can on good terms, even this.* The thought prompted him to speak.

"Fine, I'll go back," Kort finally agreed.

The concession suddenly quieted Genze, whose face showed a bit of shame—some color in the cheeks, along with immediately softened features—as if the fisherman realized it was wrong to carry on like he did, simply to get his way. *Perhaps Genze now considers that he behaved poorly.*

Kort continued, "But when I bring back whatever remains in the mart, I must leave. Be prepared then, to say what you will."

His last words seemed to soften Genze's features even more, and the fisherman's eyes got moist. Kort watched him open his mouth to speak, but just as he did, the door shook with a pounding from outside.

BAM! ... BAM!

Kort glanced to the crevice between the sliding door and its track, seeing shadows of visitors outside. *They've found me!*

The ex-knight came close to Genze's ear and whispered, "Like I said, danger awaits me here. For my sake, tell a different story than what you know as true. Say that you work alone, without anyone else!"

Unspoken, Genze stared at him, and Kort remained completely still. He heard more bangs upon the door.

BAM! ... BAM!

"Promise me you'll do so," Kort whispered.

He alternated looks between the door and Genze, feeling some anxiety with the situation of not yet having the fisherman signal cooperation. But slowly, Genze nodded, as if he understood.

With that, Kort retreated to the back room, where he waited to hear Genze open the door. When its sliding sounded, Kort neared the window in preparation to leap outside. *Just wait until Genze has their attention, then go!*

"Hello?" Genze answered in perfect Hirishin.

In reply, Sagult's voice was heard, speaking some slaughtered variant of the language. "Aku… tentara wong saka… Sergros, lan… katon iwak manungsa. Njupuk kula menyang maling."

What in Destiny's name? Kort's face looked so puzzled as each syllable struck his ears, for the words Sagult spoke clearly had a very different meaning than what was intended. Sagult's broken Hirishin went through his head as something rather strange. *We army people from Sergros and look for fish man. Take me to your thief.*

Kort shook his head, thinking how Sagult probably tried to tell Genze that they are soldiers from Sergros, looking for a criminal posing as a fisher. From a long pause, the ex-knight could tell Genze struggled to answer.

Moments later someone else with Sagult chimed in.

"Yagene kowe ora ing banyu dina iki?"

Kort stiffened at the soldier's question. *Why are you not on the waters today?* He knew immediately this could lead nowhere good. The ex-knight swallowed hard, as he reconsidered when to jump outside.

"I'm mending my net," Genze said hesitantly, likely motioning to the thing hung between the wall posts.

As predictable as sunrise and sunset, Kort heard worrying conclusions with Genze's fumble for a good response. "Kanggo ilang sing wutuh dina keno iwak kanggo sing misale jek aneh. Ayo kita teka, lan mriksa ing pidana."

Without much effort, Kort agilely translated the soldier's Hirishin into Mainlandish. *To lose a whole day catching fish for that [mending nets] seems strange. Let us come in, and check for the criminal.* His face was suddenly stricken with panic. *Jump out!*

Through the window Kort exited and landed softly on the grass without making a single sound. In that moment, the noise of soldiers entering the house fell upon his ears.

Outside now, he looked around. Beyond stretches of burnt grass, he saw Genze's dilapidated and taupe-hued shed of twin doors. It stood askew in the distance, before the vast wooded area of Tai Forest filled with tall trees having narrow, white stalks that shot upward with leafy branches along their length.

Get behind the shed, Kort told himself. With footsteps light and feathery on the grass, he hastened there, to lean against the shed's side facing the stalky forest. He took deep breaths and stayed hidden, his mind quickly pondering a deviation from his agreement. *Should I just run into the woods to evade Sagult?* The notion of going back on his word instantly bothered him. *Or, should I honor my commitment to Genze and venture back into Reiju?*

Kort hoped for the soldiers from Sergros to just pass on to Doj, which would leave him free to go back to Reiju for Genze's things. In his mind, it seemed the right thing to do, as the fisherman showed kindness to him these many months.

For a little while longer he considered the situation, and suddenly his thoughts were interrupted by a worrying sound. Voices emanated from nearby, and clearly Kort heard Genze speaking with the soldiers outside as they walked about the house, toward its back.

"Mana ngeculaké?" asked the same soldier, who now did the speaking. *Where's your shed?* The words went through Kort's head, creating more panic! His heart began beating faster in his chest, and he experienced difficulty breathing.

Genze answered, "This shed out back is where I sometimes store my boat. There's nothing here to see."

Kort moved to the rear corner of the shed from its side, sensing the men come closer. He could hear Sagult's voice, as the Sergrothian knight talked aloud to the militants, now in Mainlandish. "Check inside."

His heart continued pounding in his chest, and his muscles tightened. The flow of blood throbbed his head, as the men continued talking in the background. *Please, Destiny… Just let me do something good, before I do what I must.* Kort prayed the words and after a minute or so, a man's voice was heard.

"He's not here," the soldier announced in Mainlandish, after inspecting the shed.

"Let's take another look inside the house…"

Kort heard Sagult's slow response. He listened as the sound of their footsteps gradually moved further away from the shed. The flow of blood lessened in Kort's head, and the vein pulsating over his temple now stopped.

After a moment, Kort cautiously moved along one side of the shed as before, taking each step with care to make no noise. And upon reaching its front corner, he looked out slowly toward the house, to see militants walking with Genze, back to the dwelling.

Quickly, Kort ducked behind the corner of the shed again, giving more time for the soldiers to enter the house. From his spot, the ex-knight peered to the dirt road, and thought again about going back to Reiju for Genze's things. *Maybe I can do this after all...*

When all was quiet, Kort took a careful step toward the house, and then another. But from the corner of his eye, in the place immediately before the shed's front doors, Sagult somehow stared right at him!

"Soldiers, come at once!"

"GET MY THINGS"

Chapter 16
The Confrontation

Kort and Sagult exchanged unwavering stares beneath the shade of Tai's stalky trees; they loomed over them, from behind the shed. In his periphery, the ex-knight saw three soldiers run from Genze's house toward their location. Genze came with them, wearing a look of bewilderment upon his face, as if he were completely lost, and did not understand what was happening or what he should even do.

With eyes fixed on Sagult, Kort pondered how he would proceed. *It's been a month since I've seen Sagult, and I never expected to meet him again like this. What to do?* He glanced to the foliage backing the shed, and it occurred to him that making a run for his freedom might be the best option. *Or then, I could try and reason with him...*

Before Kort could even think about the relative likelihood of successfully escaping versus persuading his pursuers, he heard Sagult speak. "By order of the King of Sergros, you're to return to the Mainland and stand trial for the murder of Garlew Il'therin, treason against Sergros, and betraying common trusts of the Sergrothian knighthood."

For Sagult's long list of charges, Kort wished in the moment that he could vanish from sight and simply blend into the shadows, never more to be seen. *Hearing those charges be punishment on its own!* he thought, feeling genuinely rotten over his past life.

"Garlew Il'therin was never supposed to die," Kort answered, pained by his very admission.

"And here comes your explanation," Sagult said, rolling his eyes.

Kort ignored the gesture and looked around before making his next statement, as if to include everyone—Sagult, the soldiers, and Genze.

"This mistake happened because Taurus Hboshi allied with a mysterious Dark power that enabled him to betray me before I could assassinate him." He spoke on ardently, with the woman in white in mind. "I believe Taurus used this mysterious Dark power to plan the entire Isles Conspiracy!"

Before Kort continued, he moved his head around, making eye contact with everyone. "To remove himself from a dangerous situation, Taurus didn't pose as Garlew to launch his attacks from the Mainland, as originally planned. Instead, he positioned your fallen hero as a decoy who could be easily targeted..."

Kort went on, feeling he had everyone's attention. "Taurus needed a decoy, in case his betrayal of the Crimson Guard failed and word leaked, about conspirators within the knighthood! In so doing, Taurus positioned himself to avoid my assassination and distract the kingdoms with a chase after his own brother! It's like he knew exactly that would happen had he gone with his original plan, and devised a perfect counter measure!"

Even after explaining what had happened, Kort felt it was still necessary to disclose how he attempted to stop the Isles Conspiracy. "When I was resurrected," he went on, "my first impulse was not selfish. It wasn't to simply enjoy life, as before my death." Kort's tone suddenly grew firm. "Rather, I pursued Taurus Hboshi through Baal with unbelievable zeal, seeking to cut down the leader of the atrocious Isles Conspiracy before the plot unfurled!"

While talking, his professed zeal exuded from him, as his fiery eyes jumped face-to-face, keeping everyone engaged during the outpouring of his passionate words that bound Sagult, the soldiers, and Genze to absolute silence.

"Had Taurus not been aided by a Dark power to reestablish his empire on the Mainland, and had he not been endowed with special knowledge of my attack before it came to be, Garlew would've never been my mistaken target. I would've killed Taurus Hboshi, as intended."

"But regardless of your intentions, you killed Garlew," came Sagult's curt reply. "How can I even believe that you sought to assassinate the emperor in the first place? Taurus was killed in the Isles by the invading Red Dragon forces, a day or two after the first ship left his harbor full of Black Dragon warriors. He never made it to the Mainland to lead the Isles Conspiracy. Hence the entire plan was so easily dismantled by the Triangle Kingdoms, after I disclosed your treachery!"

With Sagult's last statement, Kort sensed a bit of pride gleaming from his bright amber eyes.

Kort countered. "Taurus stayed back in the Isles to avoid the ambush that he setup for the Sixth Order of the Guard. It became an ambush were I was the target." From a few quick glances to his audience and seeing their straight faces, he guessed that anyone still listening was hard-pressed to believe what might seem a convoluted story.

To continue reasoning with his pursuers, Kort asked, "If I were truly part of the Isles Conspiracy, why were bolts slung at me? Remember, that very ambush on the ridge killed me, and I assure you that the ambush was no mistake in Taurus' plan."

Kort waited for Sagult's reaction, only to see a blank stare. *What's he thinking? I'll see…* The ex-knight entered his channeling chamber—an enlarged, spacious room of gray stone with four walls and a high, vaulted ceiling. He viewed the Source entry before him, having twin doors with bronze handles, both elaborate in construction and massive in size, bedecked with intricate, carven inlays of ivy. Over his shoulder he saw the same, another pair of giant wooden doors at his rear.

He pulled at the Source entry with both hands, feeling the doors resist at first, but then give way. At the point where their edges moved apart, Kort saw light through the opening. And then, multiple streams of energy spilled into the room over the door's threshold, at his feet. The stream flowed and flowed, and began filling the room from floor to ceiling. Immediately, Kort could sense the Nexus all about the shed in the back of Genze's house. From the energy field, he could tell the position of each man, including Sagult.

Kort identified where Sagult was in the energy field—a spot in the room's midst—and walked closer, carrying the accumulated Nexus with him. The green energy that had filled the room through the Source entry now concentrated around Kort's body and followed him with every step. When he let the trigger image of Sagult's head fill his mind, a blue Source exit suddenly materialized at Sagult's location in the energy field; it was a door, wrought in energy!

The green Nexus about Kort immediately turned blue, and became a large energy stream connecting him to the blue Source exit. In a single instant, he threw his hands forward and dove into that stream of blue energy to fly through the door, in what did seem as an out-of-body experience!

All around him, Kort sensed a tube of blue energies, as he navigated a winding tunnel until at a large dam that separated Sagult's thoughts and memories from the world. *His firewall...* Kort looked up and down the dam's surface, for any crack or fissure. Sure enough, there were some tiny ones. *Now wedge into his mind...* As the blue energy itself, Kort applied himself to a discovered hairline crack, and a developing pressure gradually moved him inside the dam.

Still feeling out-of-body, Kort saw images in Sagult's mind of himself falling out of his horse's saddle and into the deep ravine, right after a bolt pierced his armor during the ambush. And then, he saw Sagult riding horseback and glancing over at him while he fell, in a quick ride along the ridge, away from the ambush. *How did that fall not kill Kort?* Sagult thought, upon seeing Kort now.

Kort jumped out of Sagult's head before the Sergrothian knight could realize that he had bypassed his firewall. From that experience, it was clear to Kort how his pursuer thought. *My mention of being attacked triggers his recollection of my deathly fall, and he questions how this elf before him can live again. Not understanding that, prevents his belief of anything more... It clearly is not enough, to tell him 'I was resurrected'.*

Having knowledge of Sagult's thoughts, Kort answered his questions in hopes of swaying the Sergrothian knight. "I was killed, and then resurrected by a powerful being for a special purpose; she found my body, in the ravine." Visions of Nym entered his mind as he spoke, but he pushed them out immediately. *Not the time…*

"Taurus killed me," Kort continued, "and left the true Garlew Il'therin to pursue Pyrus. That way, if the ambush of the Crimson Guard failed and word got back about the attack, Taurus would have his twin brother become the target of the Triangle Kingdoms instead of himself. I sometimes wonder if that's what the emperor wanted all along." Kort remarked, "Their resemblance was so uncanny, I made the mistake of thinking Garlew was Taurus, when hunting him after my resurrection! That's how… I killed him!" Kort choked on the last words.

Sagult rubbed his chin, while listening.

"You expect me to believe this? That Garlew is the twin brother of Taurus, the deceased emperor of the Black Dragon clans, who somehow had a plan to steal his brother's identity to orchestrate the entire Isles Conspiracy from the Mainland, under the guise of Sergros' hero?"

"As the words roll off my tongue now, they sound farfetched and preposterous!" Sagult exclaimed, "How can you expect me to accept any of this as true?!"

"The prospect is more plausible than you think," said Kort. "The loose requirements for immigration, Sergrothian citizenship, and membership in Sergros' sect of knights, allowed me to gain admission to the Crimson Guard while having dual citizenship. It's therefore reasonable that Garlew, a Hirishin elf also, could have ties to both the Black Dragon dynasty and Sergros, which Taurus later exploited."

He watched puzzlement spread across everyone's face. The first soldier gawked noticeably, the other two had eyes glazed over, and Sagult just shook his head, as if in disbelief. *It must bend their minds to think that Garlew was Taurus' twin brother, when both of them assumed such diametric occupations!* Kort thought. *One was a hated emperor, the other a beloved hero.*

Despite their difficulties in believing or understanding, Kort kept trying to clear their confusion. He decided to do this by arguing the matter another way.

"I was a spy, someone who worked directly for Taurus Hboshi. Of all persons, perhaps you should believe that I knew about planning for the Isles Conspiracy."

Sagult shot back, "Yet you knew not of whom Taurus conspired with all along? You speak of a Dark power aiding the emperor, as if it's still a mystery to you."

Kort paused, weighing his words carefully before speaking. *Destiny help me, for I don't have a good answer. In spite of my suspicions, I don't know that Taurus conspired with the woman in white. And the last thing I wish to do after my change of heart, is to speak another lie!*

After a brief silence, Kort spoke hurriedly. "I do not expect for you to understand this twisted plot, for even I wonder who could craft a plan so diabolical for Taurus and implement the seemingly unfeasible. Such does not seem possible, by any mortal!"

Frantically, Kort looked from soldier to soldier, only seeing faces that did not believe. From the depths of his soul, he earnestly summarized his situation in hopes of persuading his pursuers to give himself more time.

"If you can understand anything in this complicated affair, let it be this. With a change of heart, I sought to slay Taurus Hboshi with all my might, in order to topple the Isles Conspiracy in its inception. Through this, I sought to do good but mistakenly killed the hero of Sergros."

Kort watched Sagult, who continued staring blankly. He glanced to the impatient soldiers next; they stood on each side of their commander, some of them sighing, all of them with eager eyes telling of how they died for orders to seize the fugitive.

Then suddenly, Kort sensed something different. He noticed Sagult studying him pensively, now with less of an empty stare. *Perhaps he tries to place of all of this?* It was tempting to enter his pursuer's mind again, but he figured it might not be worthwhile. *After all, elaborating on my resurrection did little to convince him.*

"When you and I rode in the Sixth Order together," Sagult finally said, after a long pause, "I counted you as a friend. And with friendship comes a certain tolerance for trespasses." Those words grabbed Kort's complete attention.

"But with your crimes came the end of our friendship, and the end of my tolerance." Sagult sighed deeply before continuing. "Even if I could look past the murder of Garlew and give you credit for alleging to do good, there's still your treason against Sergros and your betrayal of the oaths of knighthood. These things, I cannot see past."

Kort thought about Sagult's position, and lowered his face for a moment. *I must let him know where I stand. He just thinks I'm trying to avoid punishment, and that's not my goal by any means!*

"I'm one who believes just punishment should be endured for crimes committed," said Kort. "As such, I shall stand trial for my misdeeds, and endure punishment up to death or lifelong imprisonment." Before talking again, he collected his thoughts for a moment. "But also as one of regained conscience—a person longing desperately to redeem himself—I must say that for me, to endure these punishments alone is simply not enough."

Kort looked about to the militants, to Genze, to Sagult, and now even to Tai Forest, as if wanting to include the whole world for this profession.

"In me is a strong desire to do good, after I have wronged so many! It simply won't suffice to have my death match the deaths of many, or to have my solitude in a dungeon match the eternal solitude of those fallen."

Sagult snapped at him, as if tired of Kort's arguments, regardless of whatever heartfelt elements they might have had. "You've taken life and betrayed trusts. Therefore, you deserve to neither enjoy life nor trusts. Such would you have in your pursuit of doing good, and this cannot be."

Inwardly, Kort suspected all along that attempts to persuade Sagult might meet this end. *It's foolish to reason with the law once it's after you, whereas reasoning with yourself before breaking the law is far wiser. Just as this, I should have reasoned with myself before committing my wrongs, not with Sagult now.*

At last, Kort nodded and said, "Words fitly spoken from one never losing morals like me. Long ago you earned my respect, over your intolerance for injustice and wrong. Given that, I wouldn't expect you to renege on your convictions, Sagult. As the saying goes in Karnath, a man who stands for nothing will fall for everything. You stand for something…"

Kort sighed and paused.

"Well then, let us proceed so that our exchange continues not into the night. I believe you know how I'm bound, regarding my cooperation here."

"Seize him!" Sagult yelled to the soldiers, clearly having run out of patience.

"FISHER IN HIDING"

Chapter 17
Pursued by a Friend

No sooner than Sagult's command rang out, Kort darted into Tai Forest, filled with stalky trees that dotted the foot of the nearest mountain in the Jezban range. As he ran deeper into Tai's foliage, it was not long until the terrain steepened and made for an uphill chase. Every foot forward, the ex-knight could hear the militants pursue him at hind with their leader.

"Don't let him escape!" Sagult screamed.

As he sprinted away from Sagult and the soldiers, the brush became a distorted landscape in his eyes, with different shades of brown and green blurring into a single hue. He could feel his heart beat quickly beneath the pullover, and at the mere thought of capture, his adrenaline peaked. *It mustn't end this way!* he insisted to himself.

On more than one occasion, Kort sensed a hand grab at him from behind, and he zigzagged in between the stalky trees, hoping to make it more difficult for the soldiers to get at him. *The uphill resistance should slow them too!* he thought, given his increased exertion from trekking the forest's incline. Kort sweated profusely while running, realizing the uphill chase was many times harder than one on flat ground. *Surely the soldiers tire from this...*

Suddenly, nearby clangs entered his ears, just as he zigzagged through more trees. Kort could not deduce exactly what happened but a reasonable possibility entered his mind: *The soldiers tear off their heavy armor! It's harder to run when armored...*

To Kort's surprise then, he suddenly saw one soldier appear at his far left and another at his far right; they ran with him, literally neck-to-neck. *How did they catch up?!*

As he weaved in between the next set of stalky trees, the soldiers on both sides moved ahead of him! Kort immediately realized his oversight. *They run straight whenever I move to the side, and make strides ahead! And all this time, was there ever a hand at my back?!*

Kort scolded himself now for paranoia, recalling the constant sensation of a hand from behind. It led him to trick those presumably on his tail, where in reality, his mind merely played tricks on him. To his disdain, he watched the flanking soldiers make even more of a gain on him, before whipping about to face him! At that, the ex-knight slowed himself to a complete stop. From the rear Sagult was heard.

"Give up; you're surrounded!"

In a single instant, Kort focused his mind and entered his enlarged channeling chamber. He stood at the twin doors again, which he pulled open to reveal a bright light glowing distantly behind them. He watched multiple streams emanate from the light and flow to his Source entry, over the doors' threshold, and into the room; the streams flowed and flowed until the chamber was completely filled with green Nexus.

Cool, tingling sensations washed over Kort from across his Source boundary, as the energy hovered a hair's length over his skin. He snapped back to the stalky forest, now with a keen awareness of his surroundings. Through the medium of Nexus accumulated in his core, Kort could sense slight vibrations as his pursuers moved, as well as their positions based upon disruptions in the field.

I'm boxed. Kort could tell that three militants and Sagult were at the vertices of a rectangle, of which he made its center. At his back, he heard Sagult and one soldier cease running and settle to a stop, as suggested by dull clanks from the armor still on their bodies. Before him stayed the other two soldiers, completely still.

Destiny help me, he prayed, hoping that Karnatha was listening. During this moment he caught his breath, and calmed his mind. Kort felt hot, thirsty, and tired—all secondary to this primary concern of being captured. *It mustn't end this way!* he reminded himself, yet again.

"There's no more running," Sagult said. "Let Sergrothian judges decide your fate. With the gloom, our courts have been unable to deliver justice amid the rioting and upswing of crime in Sergros. People now lose hope in their chance of a safe life, and the murderer of Garlew Il'therin roaming free doesn't help much. Give people back hope. You can do *this* good thing."

As Kort heard Sagult's voice from behind, he thought about the argument, and it tempted him. *My capture would at least give people that...* But the thought betrayed his insatiable desire for something greater than rotting in prison with his guilt, or hanging from the gallows. *Surely I can do something of greater good before my time is up. It must not, and cannot end this way!*

Kort looked to Sagult and the other militant at his rear, and then back at the two soldiers before him. As far as his eyes could see, the sloping terrain unfolded for spans, with many white stalks standing vertically to support a lush ceiling of green leaves, where sunlight poured over every one, casting triangular shadows upon Tai's floor of soil and shrubbery. Red birds hopped from the leafy branches of the stalky trees that enclosed this small clearing, filled by pursuers and the pursued. Despite the scene's splendor, the numerous white stalks reminded Kort of bars in a jail cell, and he grew increasingly aware of how close he stood to never being able to redeem himself. *If I must, I'll fight them. After all this, I can't forfeit my chance of doing something more!*

"Why not make this easy on yourself?"

Sagult's question received no reply.

There was a moment of silence, and Kort felt nothing but the rapid pulses from his beating heart. He ignored Sagult's question, and refocused his attention on the surroundings. Like before, the ex-knight tapped the Nexus, and it filled his core. In moments he saw himself again, standing in his enlarged channeling chamber. Energy streams spurted into the room from across the threshold of his Source entry, and the streams quickly filled the room, providing his connection to the Nexus field in the forest, for the length of his locus of control. Through that continuum, Kort could feel the soldiers move in the energy field—small side steps, fidgets, and shifting. He took time to reorient himself with how his pursuers were positioned, their distance from one another, and how their placement related to the environment.

Sounds arose, of steel leaving its casing. Then quite suddenly, through the Nexus, Kort sensed a large movement from his front and rear, when two opposite corners of the rectangle enclosing him moved toward its center! Kort turned about to face his nearest attacker—one militant with his sword drawn. Only a single stalk stood between Kort and the solider.

Kort watched as the soldier slashed at him from the side, as fast as lightning, in an attempt to sever the thin stalk and catch his flesh. He jumped back to avoid the whizzing Mainlandish blade, just in time. The sword narrowly missed him and sliced right through the stalk!

"He's to be taken alive!" Sagult yelled. "Sheathe your sword!"

In that moment, the situation unfurled slowly as Kort returned to the channeling chamber, where he could feel everything through the Nexus. He noted the soldier who swung the blade, now having withdrawn attention and turning aside, distracted by Sagult's instruction. Also, he saw the severed stalk between the soldier and himself; it slid at an angle according to its cut, bowing gracefully toward the mountainside. Over his shoulder, Kort sensed how his second attacker had stopped for a moment, not quite coming close enough to be within striking distance. Through the energy fields, these observations were as clear to Kort as if he had the opportunity to carefully study a frozen pane of the entire scene.

In a split second, Kort's mind came back to the stalky forest and ignited his body into action. Before the militant in front of him could regain attention, Kort ran up the falling stalk. From it, he sprung off to kick the soldier's sword! The weapon flew from the militant's grip and through the air, into the distance.

As Kort landed gracefully—off the shoot and now beside his foe—he coiled back his one leg to kick the soldier three consecutive times at points along a large arc. His flying foot hit the soldier's lower leg first, then the groin, and finally the chest.

He watched the militant lose balance in suffering those multiple blows, and smack the ground with a pronounced thud. Back to the channeling chamber Kort went, where he felt the cool tingles of Nexus once more. Through the field,

Kort now sensed the opponent behind him run forth. Instinctively, he brought his upraised leg back to the ground, rushed rearward while rotating his torso counterclockwise at the waist, to lean back into a double-fisted punch, right to the soldier's breastplate.

His fists hit the militant, and Kort could see the soldier stumble then. The ex-knight—still charging backward—quickly sprung into the air and rotated clockwise now, with his right leg raised high. He spun like a top and pushed Nexus from his aux core to his extremities, so that his foot sparked aflame. His body continued whirling around, its entire weight thrown into the attack, until the glowing green foot hit the soldier right in the chest, putting a huge dent in the soldier's breastplate!

Kort watched his opponent get knocked to the ground, the soldier's mail now smoking and singed. The ex-knight assumed a resting position after his roundhouse kick, by bouncing into a series of backflips to land afar and crouched, his legs spread like an open scissors over the ground, with one hand touching down between its blades. At his front and back, and to his left and right, the ex-knight studied Sagult and one soldier, the two remaining of four. To him, they both appeared hesitant of attacking, perhaps after witnessing that spectacle.

Run. Seeing an opportunity to remove himself from the situation, Kort pulled himself upright and dashed into the stalks, away from the two pursuers. Soon enough, he heard the duo approach him from behind. He hastened his step accordingly. *Think fast; think smart!* he told himself, as the green forest blurred by. And in a moment he happened upon a realization overlooked before. *Their remaining armor... Keep 'em moving, and they'll tire fast!*

And so, Kort kept running up into the forest. Aside from the pat of his steps and the sounds of himself sucking air, he heard the same from his pursuers at heel. *Don't stop.* The thought ran through his mind, as his side suddenly ached from a cramp.

Kort tried to keep a straight path for the most part, but occasionally weaved in and out between some stalky trees. He ran and ran without a clear sense of time, but could tell his plan was working as the pursuit drew on. For he heard his pursuers getting further away, and then the soldier with Sagult fell to the ground from exhaustion.

"Get up!" Sagult shouted, still afoot.

Kort heard no response, only the soldier raggedly gasping the air. He kept running with his eyes set straightway. Oddly he could no longer discern anyone behind him, as if Sagult himself had stopped running just like the solider. Whatever the case, Kort continued trekking up the mountain forest. *The further from Sagult, the better!*

He went on for a few minutes, until suddenly happening upon a clear stream that winded through the stalky trees. It stretched from left to right, flowing over a bed of stones all along its length, and vanishing at the limits of his sight in both directions. Upon coming close, Kort fell upon his knees before the stream, near delirious from all his intense running in the hot weather. Without hesitating, he threw his cupped hands into the shallow waters, feeling their coolness over his skin in the short moment before he raised them to his lips. Sloppily, Kort drank the water, with some of it leaking from the crevices between his palms pressed together

He continued drinking more while hearing music of the forest—birds chirping and insects buzzing. Enough time elapsed where his breathing gradually slowed from rapid to regular, his heart rate gradually went down, and everything gradually came to a certain still. Then from that quiet, Kort heard a familiar percussion added to the forest's song—the sound of quick footsteps. He turned about to see Sagult running toward him at a distance, wearing trousers with a chain mail, now being stripped of his heavy armor.

In an instant, Kort was on both feet and sprinting again, away from the refreshing stream and further up the side Jezban's forested mountain. *How did he catch up so soon?* he wondered, but the answer came to mind without much further thought: *The man has longer legs than me.*

Having only a modest lead now, Kort ran deeper into the stalky forest, which after only a few minutes more time, opened to a clearing. But upon reaching the clearing, he came to an immediate and sudden stop from an immobilizing sight, at least for his eyes. For he stood before a gorge with a rope suspension bridge stretching across, one having rope rails and a deck lying atop its two support cables, thick though frayed.

As his eyes peered over the side of the ravine, his stomach filled with flutters, his mind with angst. He swallowed hard, as a huge lump formed at the top of his throat. For him, seeing the gorge easily conjured up memories that not many have—of dying. Indeed, the mere sight stirred up his recollection of crossbow bolts, searing pain as they penetrated his armor, along with his free fall before hitting the rocks below, so hard that the sheer impact broke multiple bones—internally piercing his organs and externally piercing his flesh. *Another gorge, just like in Taurus' ambush.*

The gorge petrified Kort for some time, and it became difficult for him to look away. He stared blankly at it, lost in his own fear. For a few seconds, the only audible sounds to him were the water's roar and its constant whoosh against rock, with every forest noise filtered out. Seeing the rapids below from these heights made him terribly queasy, and sent alarms through his head. *Not another gorge! Not another gorge!*

Eventually, Kort broke free from the hold of his paralyzing fear, and turned himself to the right, noticing another suspension bridge stretching over the ravine, further up the ridge. But from what he could tell, it appeared ricketier than the one before him. *Not any advantage there!* he thought, his main priority now being to safely cross the bridge before him.

The same percussion in the forest's song abruptly stole his attention. Kort looked back to the stalky trees, where Sagult could be seen emerging from Tai with sword in hand! He watched the Sergrothian knight step into the clearing, with a relentless determination read from his razor-sharp amber eyes. *Just go already!*

With that in mind, Kort spun about and simultaneously took hold of the rope rails, while making his first step onto the plank deck. The boards moaned under his weight, a warning for him to tread lightly and with care. *One step at a time...* he thought, and he did just this to make slow progress on the bridge, despite the constant battle with his fears of the gorge below. *Don't look down!*

In what seemed only a few moments, creaks from behind pulled Kort's head around his shoulder, where he saw Sagult begin crossing the rope bridge, about thirty cubits at his rear. He took note how the Sergrothian knight's every step was quick and sure. *Sagult steps without fear unlike me! But to be fair, he goes without any deathly experiences of falling into ravines!*

The observation of Sagult's steady progress motivated Kort to face his challenge once again, being only a quarter way down the bridge. He turned back to the deck constructed of flimsy planks that extended before him—a path minimally requiring some faith in dated construction.

He continued making progress, now faster than before, but working even harder against his fears. For the ravine's depths came into his direct sight, every time he felt the bridge sway with Sagult's movements. A few times, his fears brought him to stop and squeeze the rope rails tightly in white-knuckled fists. During at least one of those occasions, he thought about his relative progress to Sagult, since his pursuer kept moving from behind while he was held back by fear. *I mustn't always compare myself to others...* he chided himself. *Just do what you need to do!*

Kort centered his mind and steadily moved forward, beyond his fears. Whenever the bridge swayed and caused the ravine to come into his view, he redirected his eyes off the gorge and onto the rope rails, grabbed rope further up, and stepped on the next plank, literally forcing himself to make progress in a situation that previously had stalled him. But after only a few steps more, Kort felt a hand latch onto his shoulder, from out of nowhere. He instinctively turned, coming face-to-face with Sagult!

Without delay, Kort hurled a series of non-lethal strikes right at him. As his arms blurred while delivering multiple punches and flat-handed chops, Kort felt Sagult bend to dodge each one, causing the bridge to sway even more wildly than before, from side to side.

"I don't want to hurt you!" shouted Kort, loud enough to be heard over the speeding waters below. He stopped punching and grabbed the rope rails, given how the bridge rocked.

"You've got an odd way of showing it!"

Kort saw Sagult raise a fist to smite him then, but he quickly transformed Sagult's offensive attack into a defensive counter. In one fluent motion, he ducked beneath Sagult's flying knuckles, twisted his body around while clasping the knight's arm with his own, and pinned Sagult's arm over his shoulder. Then, with a sure grip of Sagult's arm, Kort bent his knees forward, to lift his attacker's feet off the bridge and using his shoulder, he threw him.

He watched in sheer horror though, as Sagult flew over the suspension bridge, toward the gorge! *Not what I intended!* As an automatic reaction, Kort reached his hand toward the Sergrothian knight who fell face-forward over the rope rail. However, he saw Sagult grab onto the rail versus his hand, in the moment before going into free fall.

SNAP!

In one sudden instant, Kort felt nothing under him, as the bridge's deck of wood planks turned vertical! With barely enough time to prevent falling, Kort took hold of the opposite handrail, keeping his feet on the plank edges. *What's happening?!* He glanced over, and noted how Sagult's weight made one rope rail detach from its support post on the gorge's other side, causing the bridge to flip!

Kort squeezed the upper rope rail and gazed down to verify that Sagult still held the lower one. Staring past the Sergrothian knight into the waters below brought back memories of dying, yet again. *This can't end here! Not like this...* He kept reminding himself in the face of his fears, which now, stared him right in the face.

He suddenly felt the bridge sway wildly, jerking him about. Kort gripped the rope rail beneath his white knuckles, looking down then at Sagult, who swung back and forth with one hand on the rope rail, while clenching his sword's casing in the other. *Why in Destiny's name would he do that?!*

More queasiness overwhelmed Kort, as he saw the bridge planks stressed. Now vertical, they creaked with tension under Sagult's weight, with every full pendulum of the bridge. Swallowing hard, Kort bit back his fear, and advanced slowly over the plank edges where he stood; the plank edges essentially became a tightrope walk over the gorge! *One step at a time*, Kort thought, trying not to look at anything but the bridge as he went.

Despite Sagult's repeated movements from below, Kort managed to carefully advance beyond where his pursuer swung. While stepping slowly on the plank edges, he kept clinging onto the rail rope. At one point though, he spun about to see why Sagult continued swinging back and forth. The Sergrothian knight still swung on the lower rope rail, as if to build up momentum.

"What are you doing?!" Kort asked.

He received no response.

"This can end well for both of us!" Kort asserted further. "I only wish to find peace within before seeing my due judgment in Sergros!"

In that moment, Kort watched Sagult deftly toss his sheathed sword into the air, letting it fall a bit, before grabbing its handle. Then he saw Sagult shake free the weapon, causing the scabbard's drop to the waters below. The bridge swayed as before, and the ex-knight continued to hug the rope rail.

"What are you doing?!" Kort called again.

Sagult replied, "Even if it takes my life, I'll ensure you see death for what you've done in Sergros!"

At the full arc of Sagult's continued swings, Kort could see him begin hacking at the rope rail below. *Not good.* His mind raced to an unpleasant conclusion. *If Sagult cuts his rope rail from its one remaining support post, his full weight will be applied to the deck planks and the bridge will fall apart!*

"You fool!" Kort shouted. "You'll kill us both!"

Sagult grinned, "If not justice in Sergros, then let Destiny decide your fate here!"

Kort quickly imagined his channeling chamber, and he pulled at the handles of his double-door Source entry. As so many times before, the doors budged open, and Nexus flowed into the room as aqua green streams, over the doors' threshold. The streams flowed and flowed, until filling the room completely. He opened his eyes with a full aux core, still clinging onto the upper rope rail of the suspension bridge, with intentions to take control of the bridge's inevitable destruction. *If this bridge will fall apart, then I fall to one side, and he falls to the other!*

Without wasting any time, Kort channeled the Nexus and transformed it into fire, to burn parts of the bridge between him and Sagult. Using his one hand off the rope rail, he emitted green flames that devoured the frayed rope and planks separating him from his pursuer. But in that very moment, Kort watched Sagult cease hacking the lower rope rail, and upon his next swing, he released it to fly through the air and grab onto part of the bridge, right beneath Kort!

When the magical fire consumed the bridge's center, it fell apart with both Kort and Sagult on the same side, hanging on for their very lives. Kort held the rope rail securely and braced for impact, as the bridge swung him closer and closer to the ravine's rocky wall.

"MILITANTS ATTACK"

Chapter 18
The Most Powerful Sorceress

E yes wide with desire can sometimes rob humans of their humanity, and the story of Esmeralda makes the point well, but the story of her sister Magicia makes it better. This spiral, their stories intersect in a new way, different from previous spirals.

As sisters, the stories of Magicia and Esmeralda always intersected to some extent, and they did so for a very long time. In fact, Magicia and Esmeralda were over a thousand years old, being the longest surviving humans after Maken's curse of the seroxians. They cheated both death and age by the River of Life, the one that Maken remade in New Karnath to spite the rebels after the creator toppled their rebellion. But the gifts of eternal life and everlasting youth were no longer enough for Esmeralda. *She wants power, at any cost...*

Her sister's objective posed a simple problem for Magicia: Esmeralda wanted power and was amassing it through the shard that Magicia had recovered from Eriens. Esmeralda having the shard now prevented her from using the legendary sword to save Karnath from Saora's destruction. And though it was a simple problem, its solution would not be so simple. *What to do?!*

As so many times before, Magicia was perplexed with how to proceed. Again, she found herself in Esmeralda's tower, attempting to reason with her sister as an alternative to taking back her property in either a thieving or brutish fashion. But Magicia's attempts at an amiable resolution seemed all the more pointless each passing day.

Despite frequent visits over the past few weeks, Magicia and Esmeralda's arguments were the same, and went absolutely nowhere. After Magicia had entrusted Esmeralda with the shard this spiral for some reason not remembered, she wanted it back, arguing that the sword should be returned and not used for evil. But Esmeralda wanted to use the shard for her own empowerment, being convinced that with it, she could advance her standing as a sorceress in the Guild, and across Karnath. And round and round they went, with arguments and counterarguments.

As silence replaced their loud yelling, the evening finally brought the conflict between sisters to a standstill. During its intermission, Magicia decided to give herself some space. She walked to an area of solitude in Esmeralda's tower, only a few cubits away from her sibling, who stood at a window.

Magicia and her sister had met on the tower's highest floor to deliberate. It was an open room of gray stone, with one end backed by an occluded foyer

158

and a spiral staircase, its other end having a double-pane window that opened to vistas of Liath and Saol. At the room's center the floor had a large crack, in which stood the shard of sword, handle-up. Its blade pulsed green with energy, serving Magicia a constant reminder of how Esmeralda was abusing the shard, using it as a reservoir for Karnath's life force. *She can't continue doing this…*

Quietly thinking, Magicia watched her sister gaze out the tower's casement, into the Mountains of Liath. Esmeralda fixated on streams of green Nexus in the distance, energy that emanated from the mountains, trees, and soil, moving closer to the tower beneath a menacing black sky. The sky grew increasingly more ominous than in the day, its gloomy clouds now taking darker shades of gray and rolling across the horizon, to give the illusion that the night had come alive, was omnipresent, and overseeing all. Magicia saw the sky's menace extend beyond its grim appearance to the monsters that weaved in and out of its darkness. With mournful bellows, Liath's starving dragons flew overhead, with the fiercest being among them—Gremel, an ancient dragon of Karnath's three.

Amid the pervasive gray of the scene—the night, the mountain, its dragons, and her sister's tower—Magicia could see beauty. There, standing before her, she observed her younger sister, still as pretty as in the days of first meeting her maturity. She possessed sharp gray eyes, just like Magicia, above a dainty nose, and pouty, rose-red lips. Her face was covered by ageless white skin, and framed by straight red hair. Magicia's eyes fell upon perfect locks, with no split ends or graying, which hung from Esmeralda's crown and down her back.

Both Magicia and Esmeralda wore yellow, velvet robes from the Guild of Sorcery, with a green serpent pendant at the neckline. With the loose robe, Magicia could barely see the natural contour of her sister's body, as the garments were modest by design. But despite being modest, the robes were nonetheless stylish, featuring long flowing bell sleeves, in which multiple colored bands were stitched. And there lied the motive for Esmeralda's empowerment.

While Magicia and Esmeralda shared the red, blue, green, and gray bands in their sleeves—colors that designated high standing in the Guild and expertise in sorcery—Magicia's robe had one additional band that no other robe had. Indeed, it was the hallowed purple band, coveted among sorcerers and sorceresses alike.

Just looking at it triggered Magicia's recollection of Maltimar at the Guild pronouncing her above all others as the most powerful sorceress in Karnath. She could literally hear the Guild elder bestowing the band to her before an assembly of world-class sorcery practitioners. *In stopping the battle between Andlaust and Sen Corazón over the icy Fuar, you've restored peace to the Guild and saved many lives!* Maltimar's praise sounded in Magicia's mind, until the voice of Esmeralda interrupted her daydreaming.

"Enjoy it while you can."

Magicia popped back to the tower, seeing Esmeralda now turned from the casement, speaking these words like sharpened steel—cold and cutting. While she spoke, she eyed the purple band.

"Esmeralda, what you're doing just isn't right."

That conviction was what led Magicia to inform Sergros of how she would not intervene, or at least, she wanted to believe this much was true. In reality, Magicia was highly motivated to reclaim her shard, which made it hard for her to accept that her meeting with Talus was really toward a greater good in Karnath. *It could just be toward my own good, of settling a score with Saora...*

The truth behind Magicia meeting with Talus was not black or white, but rather gray, where she felt divided over going to the king about Esmeralda's misdeeds, for her appearance seemed influential to the course of action Sergros would take. One half of Magicia concluded that lust for power turned Esmeralda into a monster, who now, caused the mysterious gloom she remembered time and time again in her premonitions. To this half, it seemed Sergrothian intervention was a natural consequence to Esmeralda that would follow, regardless of her involvement. But Magicia's other half thought that perhaps she acted biasedly against her own sister, seeing Sergros as a force that would not only stop Esmeralda's wrongdoing, but also get back her shard. *I'd like to think it's the former, but either way, I need the seroxians' help again this spiral and the shard is key...*

"Why isn't it right, sister?" Esmeralda asked, again in a steely voice. "Because this ends your legacy?"

Magicia stared back without a word, helpless as their argument returned to where it had been stuck for hours. She had been trying to reason with Esmeralda—how it was wrong to have good destiny at the expense of another's bad destiny, how it was wrong to renege on her promise to give back the shard. But as much as Magicia reasoned and reasoned with Esmeralda, her sister merely deflected every line of reasoning with the same claim: *You've invented these arguments over fear of losing power, and with them, only wish to deter your deserving sister from her good destiny!*

"Esmeralda, stop this!" Magicia screamed at the top of her lungs, for perhaps the tenth time this night. Her words resonated throughout the closed chamber.

But Magicia observed Esmeralda flash a smile as her response, before turning back to the window, which showed a wide stretch of Liath, and the energy wafting over its forested valleys toward the tower. In that moment, Magicia could hear the mountain dragons bellow again, loudly and mournfully, starving without food as Liath's life died in the gloom.

"Do you see *it*, sister?" Esmeralda asked with cheer, still looking through the pane. Magicia watched her take a step closer to the window, marveling at the energies across the night sky. "Maltimar thought I wasn't expert enough to receive the purple band. However, this matter will soon change as I amass power unlike any other."

Unexpectedly then, Esmeralda hurried over to the casement, where she reached up and pushed the windowpane out, as far as it would swivel. Cold air rushed in, sending a chill down Magicia's spine.

"Is that a good view, sister?" Esmeralda asked, whipping back her head. "Can you see what I see?!"

With disdain, Magicia forced herself to once again look beyond Esmeralda and through the window, to behold the Nexus life energies from Saol and Liath, drifting through the dark overhead. *How is she doing this?!* Magicia wondered, the many holes in her memories suggesting that reality was only a partial truth.

"This is my ascent to power!" Esmeralda exclaimed. Magicia looked back just in time to see her gloat, with upraised fists. "Streams of green energy converging from all sides upon my mountain tower surely make for a spectacular nocturne! I bring the *Lights of Altoroth* to our Mainland now for everyone to enjoy, including Maltimar at the Guild!"

At that, Esmeralda's laughter rose, and Magicia watched on with concern as her sister repeated a daily routine. Using an extended locus of control, Esmeralda pulled energies from outside into her aux core, through the window. Somewhat entranced, Magicia just watched the energies accumulate in her sister's center, which shined radiant green. Her eyes remained there, until in one instant, the Nexus arced from Esmeralda's core with a bright flash, toward the middle of the chamber! She raised her hand over her face.

When Magicia lowered her hand and unshielded her eyes, she looked to the room's center and beheld the energies funneling into the shard. It stood several cubits from her, handle-up and with its blade wedged into the cracked floor, now glowing even greener than before!

From visiting Esmeralda often, Magicia grew accustomed to seeing the pulsing shard; she literally argued beside it for hours, hoping to persuade her sister to avoid using a sacred Karnathan relic for evil, one that many believers thought would stay hidden, until the Battle for Destiny. *A relic that Esmeralda can't keep, if I'm to win that battle! I need the shard, if the seroxians are to enter.*

"Karnath empowers me!" Esmeralda cackled.

"Stop this!" Magicia screamed, fighting hard to pry her eyes off the shard, along with the constant temptation to just grab it and run. *Stop this, and help your sister avoid Sergros' wrath! Time is running out...*

"No one saw this coming!" Esmeralda exclaimed, as if not even hearing Magicia. "My premonitions told me that you would empower yourself like this with the shard! I foresaw myself enviously watching you and another from Gallow Cliff, as you stood at its ledge with this blade, a torrent of energy running through it—'twas so glorious!"

The very comment brought back Magicia's fragmented memories of a time no more. She muttered beneath her breath, "And I foresaw you giving the shard back then, which helped me help Naketo."

"But now I'm the risk taker," Esmeralda said, "and act off my premonitions. You'll have your shard back, only when I possess your title, as *the most powerful sorceress in Karnath!*"

With those words, Magicia saw reflections of flowing, green energies dance in Esmeralda's eyes. "Listen to yourself!" Magicia said. "You sound crazy!"

"I am listening to myself, sister. My words sound brave and adventurous, daring even! Your presence here is but a reminder that jealousy follows around budding greatness, as you are jealous of losing power, now that I'm using this shard of sword, a mighty magical weapon."

As hard as Magicia fought it, her eyes trailed again to the broken sword. It occurred to her then, how ironic it was that the shard was physically situated between two feuding sisters—an object that long ago was a centerpiece in her Fate's Fray, and now, proved so emotionally and relationally divisive again. Though Magicia saw it as the way to break out of Saora's downward spirals, it might never be, as Esmeralda was convinced that this was her path to the purple band. *I must reason with her to stop this at once, and give back the shard.*

"Your folly with the sword attracts much attention," Magicia said. "The half of which you know not! Give it back, before you get hurt."

"What's wrong, sister?" Esmeralda asked playfully, with a smile. "Do your premonitions tell you the Guild of Sorcery suddenly perceives another as the most powerful sorceress in all of Karnath?"

Magicia grunted angrily in frustration. "Ughh! There's no end to your want of higher esteem in the Guild!" She balled her fists, and took a few steps closer to the broken sword. "You'll do anything to be looked upon differently. For sure, you know how to draw attention, though not of a good kind!"

"Jealousy only speaks now, and how I wish my sister still had a voice," Esmeralda replied, her grin wider now. "It bothers you that I've trusted my premonitions, and done so to my gain and your loss!"

Magicia answered defensively. "Not a word you speak is true! I have no problem with your gain, as long as it's good for Karnath and good for you. That's good destiny, not this!"

Magicia threw her hands up and exasperatedly shouted in an aside, "My whole life, all I've wanted is her gain! But now she seeks good destiny in the Guild at the expense of Karnath's bad destiny! It's not right for any to hurt others to help themselves!"

Magicia heard Esmeralda just babble on, as if skipping over her words. "My premonitions told me you would use this sword to empower yourself, should I give it back. But instead, I've used the sword to draw immense power from Karnath!" Magicia watched Esmeralda look to the broken sword. In that moment, she indulged herself also, examining the blade surging green with raw energy.

"Power like this, I've never even seen!" Esmeralda yelled. "The Source flows to me whenever I summon it! Just like we have primary cores, creation does too, and I'm draining that core of life energy to accumulate abundant Nexus, for my own empowerment!"

"I know not how you do this evil," Magicia admitted, as she revisited the holes in her memories. There was only a big gap between Esmeralda's rise to power following the last spiral's end, where Naketo died at Gallow Cliff with the seroxians. *I should understand what's happening,* she told herself. *The spirals have so much in common and I've lived through more than one, so I should know!*

But despite Magicia's hunch that the mystery was just a thought away from being solved, the truth about Esmeralda remained elusive. After a long pause, she turned to Esmeralda and said with some despair, "And barely can I trust my eyes, upon seeing you steal energy right from Karnath. It's impossible." As Magicia attributed Karnath's destruction to Esmeralda, her sister's eyes lit up.

Esmeralda gave another hearty cackle. "Ha ha ha, Ha ha ha ha!" Its sound filled the space, and Magicia witnessed Esmeralda pull more Nexus into her core through the open window, sending it into the sword.

Suddenly, it struck Magicia that she might persuade Esmeralda to stop, from different angle. "Esmeralda, you love nature—plants and animals alike! Have you stopped to consider the potential negative effects on this land and the creatures it sustains?! You're disturbing a natural balance in the forest and mountains, and this'll disturb balance in the kingdoms! In this, you'll upset all of Karnath! Are you really at peace, with neither beasts nor trees having food, just as men?!"

As if unhearing, Esmeralda cycled through the process of pulling more free energies from out of the sky via the window, and dumping them into the shard's core.

Magicia glowered. *It seems she doesn't care at all!*

With that thought, she declared, "The sword has changed you, and not for the good! You've become Dark, and a stranger to me!"

Magicia listened to Esmeralda's angry counter. "To be powerful is not to be evil! Are the kings of the Triangle Kingdoms evil?! Are you yourself evil, with high standing in the Guild?!" Mid-speech, Magicia observed Esmeralda's face suddenly contort, an expression that gave her a glimpse of her sister's deep pain inside, a weighty thing that wrung goodness from Esmeralda's soul. *Something is eating her alive, but what?!*

"Do not denounce my means and vilify me, for I am anything but evil!" shouted Esmeralda, at the top of her lungs. With that statement, she paused and walked back toward the window, to mechanically push Nexus at the shard, after pulling it again into her own core, from outside. "This power is merely my reward for wise use of my premonitions!" exclaimed Esmeralda, her features still intense. "Destiny has given many a window into their future, a taste of what we can achieve. I'm now tasting the fruits of my labor, and you can't stand to see my hard work finally rewarded!"

Then from out of nowhere, Magicia noticed Esmeralda start quivering, as if jostled by an incredible ire. Worried for her sister, she asked urgently, "Esmeralda, please tell me honestly… What's wrong?!"

"What's wrong?!" Esmeralda echoed with certain fury. She continued to shake. "Everything has been wrong, for years and years! There was never justice in a sorceress like you having the highest position in the Guild, being you're so uncommitted to the discipline of magic! When you courted Hrya, you enjoyed the life of a young maiden—a life I forfeited for the study of magic."

Magicia painfully watched tears stream down her sister's cheeks. "Esmeralda…"

"I seldom took only a break from practicing spells to marvel at the unspeakable love you two had—a love I thought had endured for over a thousand years!"

Awash went Magicia's mind then, with fond memories of Hrya: many nights walking the country roads of Old Karnath beneath the starlit sky, days spent along the southwest coastline overhung by Gallow Cliff, as other times together—all gone with the path of king Eriens, who sought New Karnath's bad destiny because of his own misfortune—a wife who died giving birth to Kilwroth, and also, a friend who became his own shadow.

In an aside Magicia exclaimed, "Hrya and I lived the story of an un-cursed seroxian who still loved a cursed human, a tale of love so strong it stayed alive despite such isolation brought about by Maken's punishment, the gulf between Old and New Karnath!"

Unexpectedly, Esmeralda's words cut Magicia.

"Yet I suspect you now embark on new adventures of love, still enjoying this life of the young maiden while I commit myself to the discipline of magic." The comment snapped Magicia out of her reminiscence about lost love. She saw Esmeralda standing there enraged, still shedding tears. "My premonitions tell me of another sordid affair of yours, with a handsome man of red hair and sapphire blue eyes! I'm sure there have been many more!"

"Stop!" Magicia screamed. "You've overstepped your bounds! How dare you guess about such a delicate matter, of which you know nothing?!" Magicia struggled as an attractive man entered her mind for the millionth time, with a perfect face framed with red hair and dotted by blue eyes. *Stop your wandering mind, for sister's sake! Focus, and help her…*

Re-centering herself in a single instant, Magicia continued. "I have loved Hrya for more than a thousand years beyond his death, and with my forlorn love, I carried profound hatred for Destiny and the Game! This hate consumed me, a thing I regret ever allowing! For I'm trying to undo the effects of my vengeance, even 'til now!"

Magicia's mouth ran far ahead of her mind, and she rambled about something she could not place, something not entirely understood—her race against Saora to save Karnath, a race that somehow started when her wants of vengeance went terribly wrong. As she delved the matter, more peculiar holes in her memory became evident, alongside premonitions of events that might happen or simply might never be. Such were premonitions from different spirals that coalesced in her mind, and often caused extreme confusion.

As Magicia kept explaining herself to Esmeralda—an explanation that was questionably sensible in her own mind—she maintained confidence of one thing, and of one thing only: that she needed to forge an alliance with the seroxians, find Naketo's father, and venture to Gallow Cliff once more with the shard. *I'm sure at least, that these things need to be done...*

"Whatever the case," Esmeralda cut her off, "whether you're in love or out of love and scarred, regardless of how much time you squander with your relationships, one thing is certain to me—a mere maiden isn't fit to be the most powerful sorceress!"

She added, "This is Destiny's way of settling the score, reconciling a situation long unfair! This is Destiny's reward, of all my disciplined study of magic! I'm more suited than you to be Karnath's most powerful sorceress! And that's why I'm favored with these warnings through my premonitions, of how you'll only achieve more undue empowerment from the shard, if I let you have it back!"

Esmeralda's cold words proceeded forcefully from the lips, propelled by certain fury. "Destiny chose *me* to have this power, *not you*. That's why my premonitions led *me* down this path, and *not you!*" Each statement, Esmeralda accentuated her ascension to power, and the falling away of her sister's.

Magicia became frightened by Esmeralda's sheer rage, and what she said. The words coming from her sister's heart indicated utter contempt. *This is what eats her alive... She's accusing me of jealousy, whereas she's the one with deep-rooted envy!* In the background, Esmeralda ranted and raved, but Magicia did not dare interrupt her angry sister. *Like a storm, it will pass... Let her speak these things, for the benefits of them being said.*

She watched Esmeralda continue yelling with wild gestures, intermittently smiting her chest, while saying aloud, "I am the one who studied sorcery for years beyond any other; I'm the disciplined one who hasn't forsaken magic ever; I've not faltered so many times in the pursuit of magic, like you with your lusty romances! Therefore, I deserve to be recognized as the most powerful sorceress in Karnath, *not you!*"

Esmeralda's last two words were strident, a powerful sound that coursed through the chamber, and repeated itself again and again in Magicia's ears. With unbelieving eyes, she saw her sister change into something never seen before—a child of wrath, consumed wholly with anger over a situation deemed unjust. *My sister has become a child of wrath, as was I, once upon a time no more!*

"And indeed I shall be noticed as such, very soon!" Esmeralda shouted. "My empowerment from Karnath shall make it so! It's as though nature itself elevates me to higher standing in the Guild. No doubt this is my good destiny!" As Esmeralda ranted and raved, Magicia found her sister's eye upon the purple band. *Such a simple thing makes her so Dark. Keep trying to reason with her.*

"Esmeralda," Magicia said. "Please, don't do this thing. Give me back the shard, before all is lost." She dropped her head, to study the stone floor and search for words. *Esmeralda thinks you want to empower yourself with the shard, so tell her the real reason.* Hopeful that this might be a worthwhile avenue to explore, Magicia continued. "The Child of Darkness shall rise soon, and only one person in New Karnath is strong enough to stop the Dark Prophecy from being fulfilled. This has been made known to me through my premonitions."

Magicia's last words triggered certain recollection, of a Hirishin elf in white armor fighting a dark-armored man with wild hair upon Gallow Cliff. At the vision of the elf being slain, she murmured, "The one strong enough now is Naketo's father. The oracles foresee Darkness befalling Karnath, because of..." *Don't say another word. You're hardly certain anymore of what is true.*

With a pause, Magicia avoided trying to explain a puzzle she could not yet solve, and simply pled with her sister. "I need the shard, because the Child of Darkness has become so powerful that the seroxians are the only hope Karnath has. Without them fighting alongside the Child, the oracles' vision will come true."

At the first mention of the seroxians, Magicia saw Esmeralda's features evidence clear shock. Her eyes opened wide, her jaw dropped, and her forehead wrinkled—all in the same instant. "Once more, I must open the path into their world to enlist their aid!"

"What?!" asked Esmeralda pointedly. "You wish to use the shard for a deed you swore to never do again, after the tragedy with Eriens?!" She laughed to herself, while talking more. "I suspected aspirations of power in your request, but didn't think it would bring you to lie like this."

Ardently Magicia interjected, "My words are true! For long I've conspired with a shadow from Old Karnath to bridge our worlds, and have the seroxians thwart the Child of Darkness." *I've allied with the seroxians before.* She thought those words, but refrained from saying them. *Adding that will only complicate matters...*

Magicia watched Esmeralda pace between the window and the shard. During her trek, she cast more energy into the blade, while chortling at Magicia's words.

"Conspire with a *shadow*, you say?" Esmeralda pitched the rhetoric. "At least before these words, I counted you credible though with poor intentions. But now I count you as much less. For you profess speaking with *vespers*, and admit that their persuasion urges you toward a poor choice, one from which you've long abstained!"

Magicia began losing patience for her sister, as Esmeralda amusedly cackled again. *Just let Sergros deal with her, and stop this vain persuasion. Time is running out, and you're wasting what's left! Take the shard.* She pushed the temptation of taking the shard to the far corners of her mind, and re-centered her thoughts. *Reason with her, and do all you can before Sergros intervenes. Don't give up on her, or yourself!*

"I'm no fool," Magicia snapped, with some displeasure at Esmeralda's mocking tone, "for sure I talk with the shadow of a great seroxian!"

Esmeralda just replied with a smile, ear-to-ear. *She thinks you're a complete simpleton. No more asking. Simply take what's rightfully yours.* Her temptation of taking the shard came out of reclusion, to the forefront of her mind. *No. Reason with her.*

"Give me the shard, so the Dark Prophecy can be changed! After all, this should be most important thing, to any of us!" Magicia argued with a straight face, her words icy and cold, with a hint of desperation. She was skeptical that Esmeralda even mused over the matter, even though her sister's face indicated serious contemplation.

But as Esmeralda took an inordinate amount of time thinking, just staring into space, Magicia started to wonder is her skepticism was misplaced. *Perhaps she has a shred of humanity left? Maybe she reconsiders her actions, based upon what I've said?*

Magicia suddenly saw a vision of Lucen fill the place where Esmeralda stared. It was a striking semblance of the robed figure with wild hair, wrought in pure Nexus energy as a glowing portrait. And in that moment, she became instantly aware of what transpired. *If Esmeralda reconsiders anything, it's not because of me!*

"You!" Magicia screamed. "Don't you even dare influence her!"

"As I have led you before, again I lead you now," Lucen spoke to the entranced Esmeralda, who stared at his portrait with hollow eyes. "If you give the shard to your sister against your premonitions, Magicia will have access to *both* shards. And with the whole sword of legend, she'll increase in power beyond what the Guild ever shall see, in you or anyone else!"

The vision disappeared as soon as it first came and Magicia reacted quickly. In the tower of stone surrounded by gray, she found herself on the brink of taking matters into her own hands, learning now that Esmeralda was under Lucen's influence. *Simply seize what's rightfully yours!* The thought kept tempting her, just as before.

"Don't listen to him!" Magicia insisted to Esmeralda, whose eyes showed normal once again. "Lucen is not working for us, but against us!"

"Since when have you cared for me?" Esmeralda said thoughtlessly, pulling more Nexus from outside and throwing it into the shard, as if filling the broken sword with power mattered most to her now. And in that moment, it happened: Esmeralda's perpetual state of unreachability finally pushed Magicia over the edge. *Enough reasoning with her… Enough saying how you care… Just take it!* The thoughts revolved through her mind, each one seeming perfectly rationale, given the circumstances.

And so, when Magicia saw Esmeralda turn her back and face the window once more, she ran for the shard, being completely out of patience. With every step she could see herself, standing in her vast channeling chamber, where already, she pulled at two huge wooden doors. When they cracked open, her eyes detected light all along the edges, light that spilled into the room as she opened the doors wider. Streams of glowing energy flowed in, swirling around her, to fill the room from floor to ceiling. Magicia popped out of her channeling chamber and back into the tower, now with the ability to sense everything through the energy field, especially her sister turning about!

Right when Magicia's hand hovered over the shard, she met Esmeralda's gray eyes, wide and fiery. To her vast channeling chamber Magicia returned, and there, she saw the inflows of Nexus that spilled through the doors suddenly stop and reverse direction, becoming outflows that left! As the final stream exited the chamber, Magicia's Source entry slammed shut with a loud bang. She ran up to it and pulled with all her might, but the doors would not budge! *Esmeralda emptied my aux core!*

When Magicia opened her eyes, she found herself hung in the air, suspended by energy that emanated from Esmeralda's upraised hands! In that moment, Magicia's mouth fell open as she tried to tap the Source or even move, only to find herself completely bound by the enveloping Nexus energy. *This can't be happening, can it?!*

In a single moment, Magicia felt herself thrown through the chamber, by the energy all around her. Helpless, she watched the shard appear further away as the Nexus field displaced her body. When her back slammed into the tower's stone wall, she suffered immense pain all over and with it, a loud crack rang out!

"FEUDING SISTERS"

Chapter 19
Shadows from Old Karnath

Magicia shrieked as Esmeralda used Nexus energy to throw her brutally against the wall. Sharp pain shot up her back and throughout her body. She felt the wall's impact hurt deeply at first, and then it pricked all over her, feeling like pins and needles. In the same way, the sound of her scream was initially loud, but then resonated through the chamber, to slowly fade.

When a chip of stone dropped beside Magicia on the floor, she looked up over her shoulder to behold a large fissure in the wall, spreading from where her back hit its surface.

"How could you?" Magicia asked Esmeralda, as one tear streamed from her left eye. "I'm your sister!" she asserted in utter disbelief. "How dare you hurt me?!"

Magicia looked at Esmeralda, who stood silent and returned only an icy stare. In a matter of moments, she resumed filling her aux core with more Nexus that floated outside, like nothing had even happened! *Unbelievable!* thought Magicia, uncertain how Esmeralda's lust for power could make her so cold.

She continued watching Esmeralda draw even more power through the window, her midsection glowing green until the point where she channeled off the accumulated energy into the shard. The blade absorbed the Nexus fully, appearing greener than before.

From outside, Magicia saw lightning arc across the sky, and in a few seconds, she heard a thunderclap followed by the fall of heavy rain, as darkness enveloped the tower. In the distance, the dragons again bellowed, only part of creation's protests to Esmeralda's doing.

"You have no right to take what's in my possession!" Esmeralda shouted above the noise. "I decide where this ends, and that decision has already been made." She paused briefly before embellishing upon her intentions. "I shall take enough power from Karnath to make the Guild realize that I'm deserving of the purple band!"

At yet another mention of the purple band, Magicia tugged sharply at her flowing bell sleeve, to tear off the purple band! In her hand, she held it up for Esmeralda to see. *Sister should be ashamed that a simple object has made her act so poorly!*

"Here," Magicia said, as she tossed the band toward Esmeralda, while still slouching against the fissured wall. "I acknowledge you as the most powerful sorceress in Karnath, more powerful than I or any other! This symbol of power isn't worth losing my relationship with you." Despite being hurt physically and emotionally, Magicia's words were sincere, delivered with an unwavering stare.

"That's not good enough!" snapped Esmeralda, scoffing at the purple band that Magicia removed from her sleeve. "I need to hear it from Maltimar at the Guild. Only when he acknowledges my power and bestows the band, then I'll have nothing more to prove!"

From her sister, Magicia turned away her head and more tears streamed down her face. Regret filled her in that moment. *I shouldn't have entrusted Esmeralda with keeping the shard. Why would my premonitions not warn me of this?*

"That shard of sword is mine," Magicia said with a strong voice, looking back to the blade. She lifted a hand toward it in one instant, but in the next, weakly dropped the hand back to her side. "I need it back."

"And back I'll give it, once the Guild gives me due recognition." Esmeralda's face lit up with a smile.

Magicia followed the flowing energies that illumed the space, from which danced stray shadows upon the walls. One of the shadows suddenly showed a familiar face, which drew Magicia's attention away from her sister and the shard. She kept following the one shadow and looking for the same face to reappear, and when it did, she was certain the shadow was *he. Darconas is here!* she thought to herself. *How embarrassing, the shadow witnessed my entire exchange with Esmeralda and me tolerating her violence…*

Magicia sensed a stirring and glanced back to see Esmeralda pulling more energy from outside, and pushing it into the shard. As far as Magicia could tell, her sister appeared completely occupied by that, and unaware of Darconas the shadow being among them. As rain blanketed Esmeralda's tower and Liath, she heard it play against the tin roof. From out the window, she watched lightning flash the night sky as before, followed by a boom of thunder.

Into her vast channeling chamber Magicia went, pulling Nexus into her aux core through its Source entry. With Esmeralda's encumbrance removed, she now had inflows of energy over the threshold once more. They flowed and flowed through the open doors, until filling the room, which was when she released the doors. In that moment, they slammed shut and the room's Nexus conformed to her entire body, imparting tingly sensations across her Source boundary. The energy hovered less than a hair's length away from her skin. And precisely then, she could feel everything in the room through the energy field, including her preoccupied sibling.

Very soon, something additional materialized in Magicia's channeling chamber—a shadowy figure in two dimensions, with only breadth and height. To her, the silhouette resembled a giant, six cubits tall and completely dark, with little or no discernable features. Magicia saw the figure reach out a black appendage toward her, having the outline of five fingers.

From past experiences of establishing this link, Magicia reached forth and took hold of the shadowy hand in her own. In the instant of contact, her ears rang and her eyesight became distorted, with two images forming from one. But after that brief moment, everything normalized—the ringing of ears was gone, along with her double vision.

Upon opening her eyes, Magicia found herself outside of the channeling chamber and back inside Esmeralda's tower, where Darconas jumped wall to wall. From the shadows, she heard him talk through the Nexus link in a garbled otherworldly voice. *As Esmeralda lacks this link*, Magicia thought, *she'll hear not a thing.*

"No one in New Karnath understands the ways of *vespers*, and speaking of me discredits you," said Darconas. She watched the shadow continue moving around the room, blending into other shadows, and peeking out its head momentarily; it was a black blotch, emerging from the giant's silhouette, having two white dots for eyes.

The sensation of pins and needles still lingered in Magicia's body, and reminded her to check on her offending sister. She glanced over and saw Esmeralda, who still obsessively shoved more energy into the shard. Darconas pulled back her attention.

"You discredit yourself, ironically by speaking of the creditworthy," said the shadow, "*for vespers are only shadows of shadowed seroxians from Old Karnath*, who slip between the seams that close off the path between our worlds. They come into New Karnath to search for the River of Life. Like so many others, the shadow seroxians only pursue what they want and need."

In an aside, Darconas the shadow despairingly said, "Oh, if only those among the bodied in Karnath knew our pains! Being in the world without doing, is not a life at all! This shadowy body prevents me from doing most things, for I cannot touch!"

"Without bathing in the River of Life, all seroxians who don't die from disease or sword eventually become their own shadow, in the onset of old age! I was the first seroxian to shadow, but hopefully I shall see the last of the shadow seroxians! We must reclaim what Maken's punishment has stolen from us!" Magicia listened as Darconas implored her with passion. He was a shadowy being made desperate by his circumstances to share Old and New Karnath, in order to find the River of Life and undo the effects of shadowing for all seroxians.

It only took the mere sound of Darconas' garbled voice to remind Magicia of the agreement she struck with the shadow—she would obtain the shard of sword, and bridge Old and New Karnath so that the seroxians could join the Battle for Destiny at Gallow Cliff, as described in both Light and Dark

Prophecies. In return, she would disclose the River of Life's location to Darconas, so the seroxians could prevent shadowing by washing therein.

"Tell me you're closer to obtaining the shard."

Magicia glowered at Darconas, wondering how the expectation could even by set, given what had just happened with Esmeralda. *Didn't you just witness my own flesh-and-blood sister hurl me into the wall, over your beloved shard?!* She paused a moment, to allow the mixed shock and frustration to dissipate.

At last, Magicia shook her head from side to side, gesturing a negative response. "My sister uses the shard for evil, and refuses to give it up, even though I entrusted she would return it upon request. But I'll not see her bloodshed over the sword itself. The evils she commits shall cause her own demise, and no force in Karnath can stop the consequences of wrongdoing, not even I."

"Who knows how long Sergros will take to see Esmeralda's justice served?" Darconas replied. "Perhaps it'll take too long, and unfortunately, time is running out to help my people. Is there another shard you can use to bridge our worlds?" The shadow popped the question, while continuing to circle about the room.

"Yes, the white shard," answered Magicia. "But I prefer my own property."

Darconas told her, "Do as you see fit, but let's obtain a shard soon. As before, I promise you a pact of peace when the seroxians enter New Karnath, except unto the evil in your world. As you said, there's no stopping the consequences of evil in Karnath, especially to the Child of Darkness." With emphasis Darconas stated, "The seroxians shall cut down the One of Prophecy called Shaizan, if you will only enable us to enter. Just get the shard, as planned."

Into Magicia's mind, entered visions of the seroxians helping Naketo in the last spiral—large superhuman beings with superior skills in combat and magic. She leaned against the wall, remembering both the seroxians and Naketo losing the Battle for Destiny then, to the black-armored man with wild hair. *I'll need their help again… It's not an option to lose the help of Darconas.*

"Leave the shard to me," Magicia asserted, while looking up to Darconas. Using both hands, she stood slowly, and all the while, her back ached with pain from where she slammed into the wall. With a glance over her shoulder, she noted Esmeralda, still accumulating energy into the shard. *Still occupied, with her own selfishness…*

At the sight of her sister, Magicia gazed to the side for a moment, and shook her head in frustration. Her physical and emotional hurts lingered, and these would not be easily undone. From what it seemed, the stories of Esmeralda and Magicia might depart here, nevermore to intersect, at least in this spiral. *A sister's love can only forgive so much…*

Magicia leaned forward and assured Darconas, "Protect my sister I've done always, but I'll not stop Sergros from hunting her. One way or another, we shall have *this* shard of sword."

Darconas answered, "Do what you must to bridge our worlds. The rest is a Battle for Destiny, and the seroxians can help you win."

"KORT'S PLIGHT"

Chapter 20
Journeyed Premonitions

From the cloudy evening sky over Esmeralda's tower, cold rain poured down upon the gray rock of Liath, showering the eroded mountain face and one crimson knight, standing at a mountain ledge, enshrouded by gloom. At those heights, Elucid beheld the spectacular light show as stray green Nexus energies carved through the fog, being pulled into the tower from Karnath's soil, trees, and rocks.

Suddenly, a frigid wind gusted, and Elucid could feel its vibrations through the metal demon, along with slight changes in the ambient temperature field. That wind stirred into motion the white cloak upon Elucid's shoulders, along with the purple cloak clutched tightly in one metal hand. With both arms at rest, Elucid stood less than a cubit from the steep drop to Esmeralda's tower, hundreds of cubits below the ledge.

Given the pact with Lucen, the crimson knight should not have been in Liath, let alone anywhere upon the Mainland. However, Esmeralda's rise to power brought Elucid here for observation, as this made for an unforeseen and perhaps dangerous wrinkle in the story of guiding one Child to a shard of sword. *This never happened before...*

That much was true, for of the many things that the crimson knight remembered would happen—from the gloom and the Child's awakening, to the prophecy's fulfillment and the Battle for Destiny—Esmeralda had little to do with them. It made no sense to Elucid, but so did most of the current reality in this *spiral*.

Elucid could detect changes of the age in which the Game was being played, and to the crimson knight, such changes were known as *spirals*. Right now, it seemed to Elucid as though there were at least three spirals, maybe more. Somehow, the crimson knight was reliving life in each spiral, and the memories from each *walk of existence* accumulated in Elucid's head, often contradicting reality.

Elucid continued watching Esmeralda's tower in the rain, entranced by the trails of green Nexus strewn throughout the sky and wafting into the tower, with close resemblance to the stunning Lights of Altoroth. All the while, the crimson knight kept thinking. *Memories contradicting reality...*

Such contradictions were becoming familiar with Elucid, almost an anticipated part of the knight's daily routine. Most recently were a series of contradictions that ultimately led Elucid to speak with Kort, only after fruitlessly seeking out Naketo and Fieronju beforehand. It all started with Elucid's memories of Naketo being the Child; these prompted searching the Isles for him. As far as Elucid understood, Naketo was the only son to Fieronju Hboshi, the famous elf upon the Mainland better known as Garlew Il'therin. But because of Garlew's untimely death in this spiral, Naketo's mother Shima never met Fieronju as she was supposed to, and therefore, Naketo was never even conceived! *Given this, Naketo is definitely not the Child this spiral… It's someone else.*

Naketo not being the Child as Elucid remembered implied that the Game was being played in yet another spiral, with different Children. Elucid did not know for sure what was happening, since along with contradicting memories were deteriorating memories, literally *memory holes* where the time continuum of events became distorted. For Elucid, the net effect of memory holes was being unable to discern the chronology of events, but Elucid suspected that contradictions between memories and reality could only mean that the memories were really premonitions about a future that happened in one spiral, but now would never happen again, given changes in the current spiral.

Elucid's suspicions were seminal to the crimson knight abandoning the search for Naketo and instead looking for Garlew, who was the next ancestor of the Light Lineage up from Naketo. But at this inflection point, Garlew's murder led to yet another change of plans, as the closest receiver would absorb his spirit and become the Child. *Being a member of the Gray Lineage makes Kort a receiver, and surely he has experienced a spiritual endowment, and is now, the One. Kort is the Child.*

Elucid stood staring down at the tower, while more cold rains pelted the metal demon. The crimson knight's thoughts wandered from Kort, to how Kort could even take Garlew's place. For what had happened was very unordinary: a spiritual transfer of the next destined Child from the blood lineages of Light and Darkness to that of *a receiver*—any member of the Gray Lineage, or of the spirit's lineage. But this could only happen if there was a change to the Game itself, especially a change from one of the Children being killed before Gallow Cliff.

Occasionally Elucid could hear whispering among the Immortals—typically just a voice on the winds. The latest whisper was Urzel's, telling how someone had changed the Game by letting Kort go to Baal, ultimately causing the spiritual transfer of the Child between lineages. However, the crimson knight did not care to learn any details about that, such as how Karnatha might alter the Game's rules to ensure it was still fair. The only thing Elucid cared about was gaining enough understanding to guide the Child to find the shard of sword, and then go to Liath for something that Lucen might not expect. *The destruction of one shard by Ires Star, versus destroying the whole blade after winning the other shard at Gallow Cliff, as victor of the Battle for Destiny...*

Elucid considered the objective, while watching streams of Nexus pollute the night sky with light, and it was then that a black cloud settled over the crimson knight. To Elucid, there was no sound basis for deviating from the prophecy to destroy one half of the shard, only the crimson knight's instincts that strongly suggested this was the right path for the Child, and that pursuing the Battle for Destiny would only lead to Karnath's destruction.

Studying the tower more, Elucid stared on against the backdrop of fierce winds and swirling fog. The crimson knight had a head filled with memories from different spirals, memories about many lost battles for destiny, and at that, the purple cloak made Elucid feel guilty, as if the crimson knight had only managed failure on a front where success was desperately needed.

Somehow Elucid knew that time was literally falling apart, beyond the confusion from memory holes and contradicting memories between spirals. Indeed, each spiral was something more than just reliving life; it was something bad that would happen repeatedly if Kort were to simply go to Gallow Cliff, just like all the other Children did. *Time will keep falling apart, causing Karnath's history to fall apart too.*

And that realization played more upon Elucid's guilt, resounding a deep conviction felt within that the crimson knight had failed the commitment represented by the purple cloak. And with those feelings, a flashback suddenly seared Elucid's mind, and visions appeared as real as day.

**** Elucid's Flashback—The Purple Cloak ****

(798 A.R., Over a thousand years ago...)

[Second Walk of Existence]

It had been nearly twenty years Kilwroth was told, since his father Eriens betrayed Magicia's trust, by entering New Karnath in war instead of peace to slay many inferiors. Eriens' legacy was Kilwroth's unwholesome inheritance—a tarnished reputation, a crumbling castle as what remained of the broken kingdom Malgun, and his father's purple cloak that he always wore, showing its seven stars.

It was said that upon Eriens' decision to betray Magicia, Kilwroth cried all night in the nursery, for what he foresaw of hardships to come, though the reality was that visions came upon him now versus then. If he cried like that years ago, it was for another reason, something yet to be understood.

Eighteen years without a father brought him to this very moment, standing without answers in the messy library of Castle Malgun, now unoccupied and completely abandoned. The library itself was a derelict room off one of the castle's many dilapidated stone halls, its sole glory being an open window that overlooked Gallow Cliff in Old Karnath. The cliff's massive chalk-white, rocky walls appeared stunning beneath the cloudless blue sky that extended widely to the horizon, lighted by an unseen, midday sun. Through that window, the light grazed Kilwroth's countenance from where he stood, a rugged face dotted by stubble and framed by long, black hair.

But besides the window's view and that alone, the library was just depressing. Kilwroth studied the cracked, dirty floors littered by books—some destroyed by the elements, others lying prostrate and spine-up. What stayed intact of walled shelving peered down upon its fallen brethren, freestanding bookcases that had toppled over, tacitly explaining the disarray of books everywhere. In the room's corners were cobwebs from spinsters that now laid claim to the library, putting it to a different use than was originally intended.

As Kilwroth took a single look while breathing in the crisp sea air, it was enough to speak poorly of seroxian knowledge, as if the shadows of Maken's curse almost a thousand years prior still overcast the minds of his people, and would continue doing so for years to come. And his mind was perhaps no different, having the same overcast.

Though Kilwroth had read and reread every readable book in the library about the Game and its implications to his purpose, he had minimal clarity about his future, less clarity even than what came from sudden, unexplainable dreams. He dreamed nearly every night now, and most recently, his dreams told him of his visitor—a mysterious seroxian that strangely arrived yesterday and who had equally mysterious motives.

"I need it." Kilwroth turned to the seroxian claiming to be Laotzu, who called to him from the hall just outside the library. He met a pair of brown eyes with his own gray eyes, then looking down over the seroxian's silver armor with yellow accents—colors of ancient Kingdom Juniper in Old Karnath. In that instant, his mind transcended above the tangential clutter that touched his present circumstances, and all at once, the seroxian's story came back into focus.

If Kilwroth understood correctly, the seroxian said he was Laotzu—the lone seroxian exiled to New Karnath after the rebellion against Maken. Supposedly, he came back to Old Karnath using a bizarre magic he kept calling the exo-core, in order to take Eriens' purple cloak with him into the future. He came now because it was allegedly the only time possible, being before a war that he insisted would come in New Karnath—one spanning many eras, one that would damage the exo-core and prevent access to Old Karnath for hundreds of years.

During his short life in Old Karnath, Kilwroth had heard and seen a great many things, but despite all of them, believing this would still require his faith. So, with what he could summon of that faith, he wet his lips and prepared himself to speak.

"This is Eriens' cloak, what he left behind when leaving for New Karnath years ago, never to return! His mantle and broken kingdom are all that remain of him, lasting keepsakes of the father I never knew."

Laotzu came up, wearing a serious look.

"Please, Kilwroth. Trust that only a serious reason would have me ask."

In the moment of silence that followed, Kilwroth watched Laotzu raise a hand to place it on his cloak's chain, near the neck clasp. When he felt Laotzu's hand fall on his shoulder and grab the chain, he immediately deflected it.

"Want of my worldly possessions is of no importance. Don't you understand?! My dreams are seminal to how the Game will unfold, and I thought you coming here was part of my journey to understand how the fate of the seroxians might be changed."

"It is," Laotzu assured him. "But you must trust me. I've had visions too and know better." Again, Laotzu slowly rested his hand on the cloak's chain, but as soon as it happened, Kilwroth pushed the hand away.

Once more, Kilwroth felt Laotzu lay a hand on his shoulder, a heavy hand placed now with deliberate eye contact. Laotzu spoke again, "Over a thousand years from now, time will begin falling apart. We both are destined to fight battles, and neither of us truly understands how or why right now. But know that the answers you seek are in the age after this one, and you'll find them in another walk of your life. You'll perhaps find them, in the age of your childhood, versus the age of your adulthood now."

"So," Laotzu continued, "pass the mantle."

With that, Laotzu quickly loosened the chain, and snatched the purple cloak from Kilwroth. He stormed out of Castle Malgun, not to be seen again for a few days' time.

****

The flashback ended as soon as it began, and Elucid returned to that place upon the gray rock of Liath, a purple cloak in metal hand. The crimson knight looked out to the night sky, to the energies converging upon Esmeralda's fortress, feeling like Karnath was let down with the knight's repeated failure. While Elucid had memory holes about the outcomes of past battles for destiny, the fact that Elucid was in another spiral said more than anything else could. *We must have lost, every single one of them!*

"I'm sorry," boomed the words from beneath the metal demon, said in Elucid's most despondent voice. "How I wish the truth was untrue, oh how I wish reality was unreal! I'm still fighting a war I don't entirely understand, with incomplete memories of battles lost and the consequences of losing!"

The darkness in Elucid's mind closed in from all sides, and it was then that the crimson knight turned away from the tower, and looked to the distant peaks of Liath, up which Elucid hoped Kort would climb with the one shard of sword. *This change to the Game might mean a world of difference this spiral ... From whence comes the Gray Child, and the chance to destroy one shard versus the whole gray blade!*

Suddenly, a flash of lightning streaked across the night sky, moments before Elucid sensed another boom shake creation. The firmament continued to cry and rains poured down, as if emphatic of a hope ever present in Elucid's heart.

"I shall make this right!" shouted Elucid. "I shall find a way, when a way exists not!"

Lightning streaked the sky again, followed by another strident rumble that wrinkled the clouded canopy above Liath.

Elucid continued. "Hear me now, and take this as my vow! I shall win this Game, or die trying."

In that very moment, the boom of the crimson knight's voice trumped the thunder. However, when lightning struck again, Elucid felt blinding pain all over, as premonitions flooded the crimson knight's head. Images blurred by so fast, Elucid could not discern what they were, but even as this, each one felt like knives put all over the body. With a deep groan, Elucid fell to both knees, the sound nearly lost in another loud clap of thunder, booming just then. "Arrrrgghhh!"

During Elucid's fall, the purple cloak dropped from the knight's metal hand and onto the rock. While Elucid reached for it from a kneeling position— stretching and straining to touch the cloak—the visions continued through the knight's mind, now burning like a hot iron. The immense pain prevented Elucid from reclaiming the purple cloak. And so, crouched on the ledge the crimson knight was, full of suffering, with a trembling metal hand almost touching the cloak's plum fabric, but not quite going as far as needed. It felt analogous to losing, as Elucid had done for many spirals past.

Suddenly, discernable images filled Elucid, those of a time no more. Elucid saw Naketo wearing that very purple cloak at Gallow Cliff, on the day of the prophecy's fulfillment. Resembling Fieronju, Naketo wore white armor and in one hand wielded a glowing shard of sword. Then from the blurry background behind Naketo, Lucen appeared suddenly. The youth with wild hair also wielded a glowing shard of sword, and using it, slayed Naketo while laughing sadistically. "Ha ha ha, Mwha ha ha!"

"Naketo!" shouted Elucid. The memories motivated the crimson knight to reach further. And with that, Elucid managed to touch the purple cloak in the very instant of remembering defeat. This missing ether was just another hole of many plugged in the crimson knight's memory.

In the very next moment, Elucid was relieved from those burning premonitions, and the knight's reality snapped back to the forefront. Elucid crawled upon Liath's gray rock beneath the heavy rain, grasping the purple cloak in metal hand and now hearing the same eerie laughter heard at Gallow Cliff—laughter that literally hung in the air. A streak of lightning flashed once more, which revealed Lucen standing right above the fallen Elucid, cackling now just as then!

Peering up from the rock, Elucid saw Lucen well through the darkness and the pummeling rain, in particular his wide, soul-icing smile. Elucid looked down to the purple cloak in metal hand, seeing then how Lucen's sandaled foot had nudged it away with his final step. Elucid glanced over to Lucen's feet; they had stopped walking at a place beside his gnarled staff, with its bottom anchored upon the ledge, very close to Elucid's head.

"A pact is a pact, no? Why are you here?"

Elucid gazed back at Lucen, knowing that their promise was broken by the crimson knight's mere presence upon Liath.

"I will stay upon the Mainland and you upon the Isles, until both shards are acquired. Doesn't *that* sound familiar?"

"I came here to see Esmeralda's tower…"

"Whatever the case, it was against your word. Now aren't you one to say untruthful things? I wonder what other things you believe or say that are also untrue, just as this. The Child you guide ought to be careful in just what he believes, coming from you."

Elucid was silent at that, and only the rain could be heard during Lucen's pause. The crimson knight stared up at him, seeing a mop of wet hair, and still, the same crooked smile.

"You speaking lies is no surprise to me," Lucen taunted. "Every time you say you'll win, but just when has *that* happened? You're just full of false hopes, confusion, and lies."

As another bolt of lightning zigzagged across the sky, illuminating their ambience, Elucid saw Lucen flash the same smile, and give a wink. The repeated gesture played upon Elucid's confusion over the current spiral and the Game, and implied that Lucen somehow knew more, though the crimson knight did not. And just as Lucen kept rubbing salt in an old wound—three spirals old or more—the cold rain continued to fall, unrelenting and dismal.

Elucid now had closure about one Battle for Destiny, closure beyond just existing in yet another spiral. The vision of Naketo being slain by Lucen replayed itself in Elucid's mind, and affirmed that the Child could not be Naketo, for the spiral was no longer his. *It's Kort's.*

"Mwha ha ha, Mwha ha ha!" The crimson knight heard Lucen's laughter rise again, as if Elucid remaining fallen upon the ledge signified an unwillingness to continue this fight another spiral, and any more that might be needed. It was then that Elucid turned away from Lucen, and eyed the purple cloak that the knight grasped—a reminder to rise upon falling, a reminder to confront giants. Slowly, Elucid got up on both feet, and turned to meet the youth's gleaming blue eyes, which caught the luminous flare of yet another lightning bolt, flashing across the obsidian night.

"There's been an endowment," Elucid boomed, "for the Game changed. 'Tis reason you ought to be worried."

Lucen responded, "You've no doubt heard what I've heard also. The *Gatekeeper* was removed from Liath—*Wicken the Wicked*. That, and the remaining Servants of the Light now turning to the Darkness, is how Karnatha has reconciled the Game over the Gray Child versus Garlew."

When Lucen finished speaking, his eyes trailed to the same distant peak of Liath that Elucid viewed before, the one that had inspired hope of Kort climbing higher. It was only a moment before Lucen shrewdly deduced Elucid's real purpose here.

"You coming here over Esmeralda's tower is another lie, isn't it? Liath is what brought you here," he said. "Liath is sourcing your false hope. You've come here, with dreamy eyes toward Liath and not Gallow Cliff."

Elucid remained silent, letting Lucen's immediate answer be the riddling of noisy rains. Each moment that passed, the winds blew Lucen's robe wildly, just like his sopped hair.

Eventually, Elucid's reply came from beneath the armor: "The victory with Naketo will be your last. This time, the Gray Child and I climb Liath with one shard, and we'll see to its destruction. Try then, melding together the whole sword."

Lucen replied, "As you said before, *don't be so sure of that*. Bad destiny may see to both you and *him* arriving at the cliffs, counter to your plans!" Those words slipped between Lucen's parted lips, said with another wide grin—one indicating haughtiness and pride.

But there was no comeback from Elucid, no harsh words to fuel this fire, only deep resolve in the crimson knight. Elucid just turned away and put one metal foot forward after the last, for a slow trek down the mountain pass during this most rainy night. The sounds of Elucid's sure movements were lost in the tumult of rains, the cracks of lightning, and the booming thunder.

Before going out of earshot, Elucid heard Lucen shout, "Remember, a pact is a pact. Don't let me find you on the Mainland again, until that shard is acquired!"

With those words, the scene grayed away to obscurity, matching the gray of Karnath's plight.

"A PACT IS A PACT"

Chapter 21
Arlem before Liath

Through the gloom, seven knights rode black horses along the hilly dirt road, connecting Castle Sergros to the city of Arlem. As they pressed on against the fierce, freezing winds, their cloaks flapped behind them, tucked beneath beveled shields slung over their backs. They were saddle-bound for hours since their departure and it was already night, but their trip was far from complete.

Toward the pack's rear X'ieth found himself, on horseback and gripping his reins with gauntleted hands, feeling the cold air against his face. It entered through his helmet, stinging his skin and freezing his lips. His teeth chattered in his head, and though he was tired, the unpleasant conditions kept him wide awake during the entire ride.

He watched the riders ahead of him hold their lanterns high. The lights were captivating, appearing as fireflies drifting lazily through the dense fog. It was the effect of seeing them float ahead, carried by charging horses down the main road. Those lanterns were essential to see, illuminating a short stretch of road before them.

Too short... In X'ieth's opinion, visibility presented very real limitations to how fast the knights could safely ride, but apparently, Nathan did not agree. And so he rode just like the others, at a breakneck speed set by their leader, done in the interest of making up lost time.

The knights' departure from Castle Sergros took longer than expected, given Magicia's sudden appearance. That session alone had easily put them behind schedule. X'ieth just hoped that rushing now would not lead to further delays. *At this rate, we all might get to the nearest hospice, instead of Esmeralda's tower!*

He endured the grueling ride for hours and hours through the night, both saddle sores and a frozen face being his greatest discomforts. They made X'ieth wish for his destination all the more, but unfortunately, Arlem would not come until the riders put in enough time and energy upon the main road.

The trip's length and his many discomforts made X'ieth prone to think. During the journey to Arlem, his mind repeatedly circled through thoughts from days prior, about Millicent's unfairness, Talus' cruelty, his dormant fears of confronting Esmeralda, and most of all, his unlived dreams of being Karnath's hero. On one hand, his thoughts elicited negative emotions, but beyond that jumble of negativity, X'ieth was very happy over how far life had taken him.

Through the knighthood, he was able to do something truly meaningful, whereby many of his childhood dreams came true. *You're finally in the Guard as you always wanted, and now, helping to save Sergros from the gloom!* The more he thought about it, the more it joyed him. And Talus, Millicent, or his fears would not take that feeling away from him, at least for the moment.

Time passed, and X'ieth broke from his thoughts when he noticed the main road come into view, as the gloomy night turned into the gloomy day. He looked up, at the ceiling of light gray clouds hanging over him, which obscured the morning sky. But though the morning's glories remained unseen, he knew that surely a radiant sun was behind those clouds, since sunlight filtered through.

With improved visibility, he observed the lines of gnarled trees besetting the path, all of them blurring by as his horse ran forward. His eyes scanned the ground beneath those trees, where lied frozen heaps of dead leaves. The sight itself awakened his dormant nostalgia for the season cut short by the gloom—autumn.

The young knight loved autumn, with its crisp fall air welcoming him from the morning until the evening, and the majestic array of colors beneath any wooded horizon. Shades of forest green, orange sunburst, scarlet red, and gold yellow would tint the leaves hung upon adjacent trees, indulging his eyes until the change of seasons. Indeed, the visual splendor of colored leaves was a final show before they fell, preceding the gradual ease into a tame winter. *Not this year*, he thought sullenly, knowing that a bitter winter came upon Sergros all of a sudden, stealing many days owned by autumn. *No varied colors for Sergros this autumn, only gray.*

Hours elapsed beyond the break of day and a sight eventually interrupted his continued thoughts, a joyful one that meant an intermission to his long ride—Arlem! The city's towering buildings could finally be seen in the distance, gray stone structures that almost blended right into the gloomy sky, with their darker hues making for only a slight contrast.

From the back of his galloping huffing horse, he could see the single spire of Arlem's Karnathan church. It loomed high in the midday gloom, above a multitude of red slate rooftops around it, all standing beyond the city's wall of stone. In the greater distance above Arlem was foliage from Saol Forest, and above that, the gray peaks of Liath. Faint outlines of trees below the massive rock definitively stood out, even with the fog. *That's where we're headed—the path to Esmeralda's fortress beyond the city, through the forest, and up the mountain.*

In a few minutes time, X'ieth rode up to Arlem's main gates along with the six other knights. The entire pack slowed their horses when about thirty cubits from the closed entrance. Though it was midday and typically the gates would be opened to welcome visitors, the sight came with little surprise to X'ieth, who was well aware of the mistrust across Sergros in the wake of the

Isles Conspiracy. *The gates are shut to ward off the uninvited, given these uncertain times....*

With that thought, he examined the finer details of the entrance to Arlem. Two large, beveled doors stood before him. They were made of thick chestnut brown wood and filled a timber frame encased by stone, mortared neatly about it in an arc.

X'ieth glanced over at Nathan, who looked up to the walls while steering his grunting horse by the reins. Nathan trotted from one side of the entrance to the other, and then repeated the trip, as if expecting it to get him noticed. The young knight directed his eyes up too, and saw that no guard was visible upon the walk. *Now that presents a problem.*

Breaking X'ieth's thoughts came a noise that surely had everyone's attention—multiple, low creaks. The young knight suddenly beheld bowmen raise their drawn weapons to multiple loopholes in the city walls! Like lightning, he pulled his shield forward for protection with the rest of the Guard, should an arrow be hastily flung. *Hope no jokes come from Hammar or Finnel just now!*

X'ieth watched a man peek over the parapet.

"Who goes there?!" he asked in a firm voice, no doubt having difficulty making them out in the fog.

"Nathaniel Sharpstone, leader of the Seventh Order of the Guard," replied Nathan. "We knights of Sergros embark on a quest for our king and need to enter for lodging." The young knight listened carefully, hearing a slur in those words caused by Nathan's frozen face.

Through the thick fog, X'ieth watched the man peer with squinting eyes from the parapet, as if still struggling to verify the outlines and colors of the ensemble's armor. With an eventual nod, he finally shouted to other men inside, and they worked a crank to lift the portcullis gate that hung several cubits behind the doors.

When X'ieth heard a sudden unlatching, he saw the doors move inward, opening the way for the knights to enter Arlem. He watched the riders ahead of him move forward. X'ieth followed after them with his shield yet up, everyone cautiously glancing to both sides with evident uneasiness at the bowmen. For they still raised their weapons, with arrows nocked and bowstrings taut.

Once inside the inner gate complex, X'ieth mimicked the other knights, pulling his shield back as it was. He noticed Zeros ride next to him as they passed through the complex, both of them trailing behind the other knights. He turned his head and looked over his shoulder, noting several men scurry to close the doors.

"Make haste!" said one, as others helped him push.

X'ieth and Zeros went under the raised portcullis gate with its teeth overhead. The young knight looked up with a bit of angst. *Don't drop it just yet!* The thought stayed in his mind until clearing the danger above.

187

Just after passing the portcullis, X'ieth sensed it slam down behind him! He could feel the ground shake as it hit, so strong that it alarmed his horse. Spooked, the beast neighed and jostled him in the saddle, and he worked the reins to steady her. *What in Destiny's name?! Why would they do that?!*

As dust clouded the air, X'ieth and the mercenary stared back at the men of Arlem, who only returned mistrusting eyes. The young knight watched Zeros salute them with an upraised hand, as if to acknowledge those besides the Guard who sought to serve and protect.

A moment later, X'ieth saw Zeros turn to bring his face close and whisper. "Due to austerity measures, the Sergrothian protectors have been reduced in many cities. Clearly townsmen man these posts, having perhaps little experience with those bows beyond hunting." The young knight nodded his head to what seemed a likely explanation of why the men acted as they did.

Together, X'ieth and Zeros exited the inner gate complex and entered onto the cobblestone streets of Arlem. They maneuvered their horses, following after the five other knights, with Nathan at their lead. From his saddle, X'ieth studied the city's houses from the bottom-up, noticing first their brown wooden doors that held a diamond window at the height of a man's head. The simple casement had triangular and square panes of glass set in a simple lattice—a cross over a box. Rectangular windows of the same semblance extended along the second story of these houses, lending to their quaintness.

As a sparkle caught his eyes, X'ieth looked up above the second-story windows, to the building tops. There, light bounced off shards of stained glass plastered all over the gable roofs, in colors progressing from dark amber, to bright yellow and red. He had heard how the people of Arlem decorated their roofs gaudily with pride over their own ambitions, as the light of dawn would strike the multi-colored glass for spectacular morning sights. For this reason, Arlem had long been known as *Dreamer's Dawn*: a home to workers of sundry trades and arts, where dreams became their reality through hard work.

X'ieth stopped gazing at the houses when he realized the other knights rode ahead, including Zeros who initially accompanied him. He saw them distantly on their horses, going into what was apparently the marketplace of Arlem in the city square, lined with tables and stands.

He squeezed his horse using both legs, and with a whinny and a snort, the beast bolted him forward. Ignoring some pain from his saddle sores, X'ieth steered the horse in a straight line toward the nearest rider—Lewes. While catching up, he looked over the market's tables and stands, many being vacant just like the market itself, a few of them seeming burnt.

"What has become of Arlem?" asked X'ieth, when coming alongside Lewes. "I expected to see more life than this!" *It's past noon for Destiny's sake! People should be out and about.*

"The townsfolk are too afraid to show themselves?" Lewes replied, giving an answer that sounded like merely his best guess. "The recent pillaging caused fires and riots here. That was before Sergros intervened with handouts."

From the market, X'ieth rode with the knights until seeing Hammar and Finnel suddenly stop ahead. He watched them dismount and start walking alongside their horses, not seeming particularly bashful about it. One by one, X'ieth observed the other knights follow suit, and eventually it seemed like a good idea to him as well. *Better on foot than in the saddle!*

Keeping one hand on his reins, X'ieth descended from his horse onto the uneven cobblestone. When his boots made contact, he felt a bit lightheaded. The sensation of being on foot seemed foreign to him, like he had not stood in ages. Nevertheless, he began following the line of knights through the street. Every step he made, the inside of his legs hurt from his saddle sores.

X'ieth continued down the cobblestone, while leading his horse by the reins. Nathan likewise led the knights, from Arlem's dead marketplace to its business district. X'ieth looked around as they passed many shops that were completely empty and dark, without a single candle burning. He felt uneasy at the sight, the same uneasiness he felt when seeing the market.

He walked further along, noting how some of the shops appeared to have been vandalized, with broken windows or burnt storefronts. The streets were eerily lifeless like the market. *It's as though the city suddenly stopped.* Spellbound by the sight, he stood there with horse reins in hand, his cloak astir by the freezing winds.

This can't be... X'ieth observed how the glass blower, potter, clockmaker, and woodworker had all abandoned shop, among many others. Beside him stood Zeros, who commented about the scene's oddity.

"Demand in Sergros for their goods is usually high throughout the year. Maybe the gloom makes essentials more in demand than these?"

As Zeros finished speaking, X'ieth had to wonder why the mercenary constantly stayed at the back near him. *Maybe he's like you, and wants to keep out of Nathan's way.* From fighting Hammar, X'ieth established a poor reputation for himself that needed mending, and perhaps in a different way, Zeros worked toward the same—a better reputation with Nathan and the others.

"Don't know," X'ieth muttered mindlessly, before wandering from Zeros with eyes on the potter's kiln. He led his horse closer to the shops, so he could peer through whatever windows were not boarded up. When at the first open window, he recognized instantly how it appeared that people lived inside the store, with dirty pots, crumpled clothing, and artifacts of cooking fires scattered atop its dirty stone floors.

X'ieth heard some talk arise in the background between two other knights, though he was completely oblivious to what they were saying. It was a matter that did not bother him much. *Arlem is far more interesting...*

He thought on, turning his head and gazing around once more, just to take in the collective sight of the city. *You're in Arlem, man! 'Tis amazing, this journey you're on!* The young knight simply could not believe where he was, and with what company. It resounded of the joys he experienced during his ride from Sergros, joys that came with his realized successes in life.

Slowly, his attention ventured back to the shops. He walked on a bit with his horse, still near the windows, with the other knights walking mid-street. Before the knights reached the street corner, he happened upon the blacksmith's shop, which still showed signs of life from within. Through the thick glass window, he could see the smith toiling away at a large forge filled with orange flames. Using some tongs, he subjected metal to the fires.

"See the smithy at work! People still want weapons in such dangerous times!" When X'ieth heard Zeros, he looked over his shoulder. The mercenary was afar, speaking to a few others. X'ieth smiled and looked back to the blacksmith. *Zeros has keen eyes... He can tell the shop's in use, all the way from the street!*

"No wonder why the market's empty," the young knight heard Zeros talk again. He gazed back toward the street, seeing the mercenary motion with a free hand to the surrounding shops. "Hardly a tradesperson works, because townsfolk have so little money for their goods."

X'ieth saw Tol, a few knights ahead of Zeros, turn around and assert, "Either that, or pillagers forced many to close shop altogether. See over there!"

The young knight followed his pointing hand, to the ransacked silversmith and goldsmith shops, appearing just as destitute as many of the others. From behind he heard Lewes claim, "Even Arlem's wealthy cannot live as before, in these hard times!"

Tugging at his horse's reins, X'ieth turned back to the shops and took a few more steps toward the next one, for textiles. Replacing the knights' talk were sounds of clopping hooves, loud breathing from his horse, and the constant winds.

X'ieth stopped before the window of the storefront, where through a cloudy pane, he peered inside the textiles shop, seeing there an empty loom beside a table, where lied a distaff that was undressed, and also, a spindle. X'ieth focused upon the spindle, following its contours and studying its fine needle, until the moment where it was lifted off the table!

X'ieth could not believe his eyes, when seeing a tall, middle-aged brunette woman appear out of nowhere within the shop, to take up the spindle. She wore silky, gray attire that fell loosely over her body. X'ieth remained at the window with his horse, and they watched her work.

She dressed the drop spindle with three different bundles of fibers for thread, and passed the strands through a hook above its whorl, fastening them to the shaft through a slipknot of the lead thread. With the distaff in one hand, she held the spindle in the other, letting it dangle and spin. And by spinning it more, the woman handspun fibers from the distaff into thread.

Having interest in her technique, X'ieth watched the threads accumulate on the drop spindle. He gazed to the distaff for but a moment, and was surprised when one fiber of three vanished completely! X'ieth looked back to the drop spindle, and the spindled threads suddenly untwined into the remaining two fibers.

X'ieth watched the woman skillfully work to reverse the unraveling, but to his shock, any newly spun thread upon the spindle would simply untwine into those two fibers, without the missing third! His vision drifted to the loom, which now held a fabric of the same thread that she had handspun, and it frayed entirely!

When his eyes trailed back to the woman, she stared directly at him. X'ieth could not look away, as she opened her mouth to speak.

"Please," she asked.

Suddenly, X'ieth felt a hand clasp his shoulder.

"C'mon, man!"

From behind, Lewes' voice was heard.

"What's wrong with you?!" he screamed, turning around to face the other knight. X'ieth exploded over being startled from Lewes' unexpected touch.

He watched Lewes shrink back and shield himself with an upraised hand. "Easy there, friend. Just didn't want you to fall behind. Sharpstone will be get sharp with us if we don't keep up!"

With his other hand, Lewes motioned to the cobblestone street, where clearly the other knights walked on without them. X'ieth could discern Tol among the group ahead, leading an extra horse by the reins, clearly that of his friend Lewes.

X'ieth remembered how Nathan treated him over fighting with Hammar, yesterday in the courts of Castle Sergros. It served him a reminder of his probationary status, and that was all he needed to get past his frustration over Lewes' startling him and just cooperate.

"Right," replied X'ieth, feeling a bit bad now, given his heated reaction. Together, X'ieth and Lewes walked toward Nathan, but mid-stride, the young knight glanced back briefly to the textiles shop. Its window was now empty, no longer showing a woman spinning thread, but rather an empty space near the abandoned spindle and distaff, in which stood the loom, holding the same frayed fabric. The suddenness of the woman's departure struck X'ieth as eerie and strange, and now he wondered if there was ever a woman at all. *Dead Arlem perhaps makes you see the dead! Get out of here, man!*

X'ieth led his horse behind Lewes, walking faster than before and at times, tugging the reins. As he went, he refused to look back, and a chill ran the course of his entire body, sending him into an uncontrollable shudder.

Lewes turned to him while walking.

"Are you all right, lad?"

"Thought I saw something," he said. "That's all."

"Might do you well to get some sleep."

X'ieth heard the words, but sheer confusion stunted him from a response. *Who was that? Was she even real?* His mind sputtered the questions passively, at the very moment where he and Lewes caught up to the other knights. Nathan turned about at the most inopportune time.

Destiny damn it! X'ieth cursed in his mind, when Nathan stared at him a long while, clearly noting the young knight's absence. X'ieth lowered his eyes to the cobblestone, while settling beside Zeros and Tol, the last image in his mind being the scowl across Nathan's face. *This isn't getting any better for you, man…*

Deliberately, X'ieth kept pace with the other knights now, as they walked with their horses from the business district to Arlem's residential corridor. There, the city well for drinking water stood before rows of stone, two-story houses. Just like all of the others, they were gray structures topped by red roofs, making for a common theme throughout the city, distinctively Arlem.

"Most people stay behind locked door, fearing what's outside," Zeros commented. X'ieth followed the mercenary's pointing hand, to the smoke billowing up from house chimneys, sucked into the gray sky.

He looked back to Zeros, who continued talking.

"And the townsfolk need not come out to work, because Sergrothian welfare meets their base needs. It was all right for a short time, but now, it's turning dreamers into the dreamless."

At those words, X'ieth saw Finnel move, who stood close to Nathan at the front. He whipped about to caution Zeros. "Words like that would strike a sour chord, if said before the king. When we get back to Castle Sergros, hold your tongue for my sake, if not your own!"

X'ieth arched an eyebrow, as more banter about politics came from others. "Handouts from the throne of Sergros completely remove the people's incentive to labor," Lewes said, in seeming agreement with Zeros. "It's done to get the middle-class citizens through the gloom, but hurts them more than it helps!"

Tol piped up. "There be a freeze on taxes for the poor and common folk alike!" he exclaimed. "Food and supplies are simply handed out to those in need. When people don't work, they don't appreciate things as much as they should."

X'ieth disconnected from the conversation; it continued in the background without him. Though he had studied government systems back in the Sergrothian royal academy, and maybe knew more about politics than many knights here presumed, he had little attention for such things. *Not interested…*

His focus drifted up the way to Arlem's local pub, nestled between some buildings ahead. From the wooden sign that hung over the front door, X'ieth read the name *Parched Traveler* carved thereupon, done so in the Mainlandish tongue. Below the words he saw the same words carved in romanticized Hirishin, a typical practice in diverse and multicultural Sergros. Beside the pub, X'ieth observed Arlem's inn with its adjoining stable.

X'ieth reined in his attention, when Nathan suddenly turned to address the group. "Evening is a few hours from us. We'll spend the night in Arlem, and leave first thing in the morning for Saol."

Silently, X'ieth stood as the rest of the group, and watched Nathan proceed through the inn's front door. *Likely he'll talk with the innkeeper…*

And so it was, X'ieth was left outside awaiting his leader's return, along with everyone else. He heard some talk start up between the other knights, but did not listen much in his detached state. His mind wandered off. *Hope Millicent is well; miss her already.* That thought and others crowded his head.

After several minutes, X'ieth emerged from his thoughts when the inn's door suddenly flew open, and out stormed Nathan with a terrible scowl, one worse than any he had seen yet. While the door remained ajar, X'ieth could hear the innkeeper's hearty laugh from inside.

"Ha ha! On credit, he says!"

The innkeeper's words were lost mid-sentence, as the door banged shut, silencing the sounds of talking that escaped from the inn, and onto the street.

"Apparently the king's credit is a matter of jest these days," said Nathan, his scowl still in place. "I've paid in silver coin for a night's lodging."

X'ieth noted the look of disbelief among most knights, some pulling a cheek to the side, arching an eyebrow, or leering wide-eyed.

When he looked to Tol, the other knight appeared more amused than shocked, saying, "Freezing taxes for workers causes concern among those who ordinarily accept the king's credit."

"Aye, Talus can't pay his tab with lesser tax."

Another harsh wind struck then, blotting out Lewes' voice, and making X'ieth feel chills all the way down to his bones. Fortunately for him, Nathan cleared his throat, and shifted the topic from politics to getting out of the cold. *Thank Destiny.*

"Ahem, let's stable our beasts, and go inside."

Leading his own horse, X'ieth followed the other knights with their beasts into the stable, all of them in a straight line. When entering the space, smells of dung and hay filled his nose. He glanced to his left and right, seeing nothing but empty stalls

"Where's the stable boy?" he thought aloud.

"Where be the horses, lad?" replied Finnel.

"Ain't nothing to care for until we arrived," chimed in Lewes, in a matter of fact way, as if the lack of horses surely explained Arlem's jobless stable boys.

Zeros added, "Well, we'll pay less if our beasts aren't attended."

X'ieth watched a smile form on Nathan's face.

"You'll be attending the horses throughout the night, mercenary! Even in this market, fine beasts like these still fetch some coin, so you'll need to ensure they're not thieved away."

"I'll do whatever you need," said Zeros, raising an eyebrow. "As long as it's good for me and good for you." With that acquiescence, X'ieth noted Nathan's satisfaction through a wink, before the leader started unsaddling his horse. At that, everyone else did the same.

After leading his unsaddled horse into a stall, X'ieth beheld a pitchfork in a distant haystack, and immediately went for it. *Take initiative and it'll be noticed, man!* With a few quick strides he had the tool in hand, and started filling the stalls with hay for the horses to feed.

"I bet that's going to cost me," came Nathan's voice from behind. "Not so much," he snapped, as a follow-on remark.

X'ieth's face darkened with another failed attempt at redeeming himself of a poor reputation. *Yeah, your initiative will be noticed... in the wrong way!* Not adding any more hay, he exchanged the pitchfork for his saddle, which he had put aside while he worked. He stood beside Zeros and Lewes, awaiting Nathan's instructions.

"Let's take the saddles and supplies to our rooms," said Nathan, "if anything is left in the stable, it might be stolen. Zeros, remember to check on horses tonight. It's important."

"Worry not, friend. Consider it done."

Behind Nathan, X'ieth followed the other knights. As a group, they proceeded to the innkeeper, got room assignments, and stashed away their saddles and bagged supplies, before returning to the street outside the inn and pub for a discussion about their evening plans.

"I wish to go to Arlem's church," Lewes blurted out. "To say a prayer or two for our quest."

X'ieth looked his way, along with the others.

Tol added, "I'll join the man, so he's not alone."

Nathan paused for thought.

"I'm not keen on the pack splitting up, but I'll not keep a man from his religion. If you must, go."

X'ieth watched Tol join Lewes. *The two seem good friends?* he conjectured, without being sure.

"But come back to the pub straight after it," Nathan continued. "We'll all be there, and have some planning to do concerning Forest Saol."

X'ieth observed the two knights nod their agreement, then turn and begin talking amongst themselves, while walking away.

"Do you know where it be?" asked Tol.

"No, but the spire be visible on the skyline."

"Aye, 'tis true. Guess we'll find it…"

X'ieth listened as their spoken words faded behind their steps against the cobblestone and the relentless winds.

"If no one else is opposed," Nathan said, pulling the young knight's attention. X'ieth looked over, to see his leader smiling. "Let's go get a drink!"

Such words were well received by thirsty travelers, and grins went all around. Beyond his elation, X'ieth thought about the practical matter of moneys. *Hope Nathan's got more coin, cause the king's credit might not buy us any ale!*

Without further delay, the five knights piled up at the pub's narrow entrance. Waiting to enter, X'ieth stood beside the front window of frosted glass. While he could not tell exactly what went on inside, his eyes detected much motion behind the pane, as people clearly moved about.

"Grrr…" A sudden and menacing sound jolted X'ieth from the glass. He turned to the side, and looked in the sound's direction: the alleyway beside the pub. There shined several pairs of neon eyes, glowing in the dark!

The nearest pair of eyes moved closer, as one of Arlem's street dogs stepped out of concealment, snarling to show its jaws, full of glistening white teeth. The gloomy overcast shed enough light for X'ieth to see the beast's sunken belly and rib cage, outlined in its coat of mangy gray fur. *Nothing to eat…*

X'ieth dropped a hand to the sword at his side, prepared to draw it and defend himself, if necessary.

"Those strays haven't seen scraps in a while," said Zeros, bringing X'ieth's gaze up, to the knight ahead of him. "In a day's time, they might be eating each other."

At that remark, X'ieth gulped. *Hopefully the rest of Arlem has better options…*

He watched Zeros turn back to the pub, as the entrance became clear, with now Nathan, Hammar, and Finnel inside. Behind the mercenary, X'ieth ducked through the entrance, and the pub's warmth greeted him with welcoming arms. All in one instant, he felt the cold in his body begin to dissipate. He heard the door slam shut at his rear, the bang almost lost in a sudden clamor of talk and singing in his ears. His nostrils filled immediately with smells of sawdust, fermenting ale, and smoked *bakus root*.

Now inside the pub but still behind the other knights, X'ieth looked about, to behold a public house occupied by so many people, more than he had seen yet in Arlem! There were table upon table full of seated men with drinks or puffing pipes, a few ladies here and there, and even more people crowded around the long table behind which stood the pub landlord, serving drinks. The crowd was mostly human, with a few other races mixed in, dwarves and elves mainly, those of the Triangle Kingdoms.

Through the pub, X'ieth followed the other knights to an open bench. As he walked, he continued looking around, taking in the pub's drab interior—walls of gray stone, their windows not taking in much light from outside. Above him hung chandeliers of hand-wrought iron, having only half their candles lit; they dangled on chains from thick wooden supports for the pub's roof, which was cobwebbed and dusty, appearing as if not cleaned for years.

X'ieth sat on the bench near Finnel and across from Zeros, and pulled his meandering eyes back to the people seated all around, noting how many paid no attention whatsoever to the Crimson Guard. *These folk might be so drunk, that they even forget the gloom!*

Through the sea of people, X'ieth saw Nathan moving toward the pub landlord at the long table, likely to request ales be brought over. When looking there, a sight on the far wall grabbed X'ieth's attention—an oil painting of Garlew Il'therin, who was rendered in shiny armor.

Even from a distance, X'ieth could see the painting well. It depicted the murdered hero of Sergros just as the young knight remembered, showing Garlew as a Hirishin elf with slanted brown eyes below shoulder-length sooty hair, parted down the middle. He had a narrow face with rounded chin, a nose of modest breadth, and a short-cropped black beard. Allegedly, Taurus Hboshi looked exactly the same with the exception of a birthmark, and X'ieth generally accepted this as the truth. *Guess it could be possible…*

A rattle in a tin cup drew X'ieth from the painting to a pair of seated men on a nearby bench, who gambled for towers of coin placed before them. He watched as one man shook the cup before emptying it onto the table. From it rolled three dice that rattled to a still, and the same man cheered while the other fellow showed disappointment by kicking the nearest table leg.

X'ieth watched the gleeful winner sweep the coins closer to his spot on the table, the sounds being swallowed whole by the tavern's noisy atmosphere. Gambling was allowed in Sergros, and so this freedom gave rise to a number of games—some of dice, others of cards, but all of chance.

When the guitar music stopped and there was a sudden shuffle of feet, X'ieth's attention went to a wooden platform on one side of the pub, a place overlooked until now. There, a costumed man plucked a seven-stringed *danar lute*, with a bowl-back. He wore typical garb of the *wandering vocstrum* in Karnath: a cloak checkered with blue and green squares, blue trousers with their pant legs tucked into long black boots of dark leather, and a matching vest overtop a green tunic. Upon the vocstrum's head was a flat blue cap that tapered to a fine point, which overhung his brow.

X'ieth noted many wrinkles in the vest and pants, which gave the vocstrum a disheveled look, one that suggested he had not wandered far from Arlem's pub in months. X'ieth was aware how such performers traveled from city to city across the Mainland, playing and singing in pubs for coin, food, and lodging. *With the gloom, perhaps this vocstrum just stays in Arlem for now…*

He turned as the knights began talking at his table.

"Some in Sergros refuse to lose dignity with the king's handouts," said Finnel to Hammar, his lips curled in a smile. "The vocstrum would rather sing and dance for a living, instead of subjecting himself to Sergrothian welfare! He may look unkempt, but you've got to respect that…"

Hammar replied, "Aye, he sounds good too!"

Zeros joined in. "A job well done is most fulfilling, especially when it brings goodness and joy to a person, through his or her hidden talents!"

X'ieth looked back to the stage, when the vocstrum suddenly called out to the crowd.

"Who has a favorite?"

X'ieth heard lively voices around the room, from quite a few people with a decided interest in the next song.

"Sing *Karnatha and the Game*!" one shouted.

"*The Unwholesome Inheritance*!" yelled another.

"Or how about *Maken and Rebels*!"

X'ieth smiled at the mention of those songs, all made from stories he grew up with. Just hearing the names brought back fond memories of his childhood days, spent reading the *Book of Karnatha* beneath a tree's shade in the courtyards of Castle Sergros. And from his own love for the olden stories, he himself had a favorite, one that stood on his tongue's tip for as long as he could bear, until it finally made a nosedive into the crowd. Unable to contain himself any longer, X'ieth blurted out his favorite.

"Play for us, *A Child's Triumph*!"

At first there was silence at his request, but then from around the room came the audience's push for what many apparently favored.

"Yeah, sing that one already!" exclaimed a man.

"That'll do!" shouted a woman.

"Aye, a good one!" More remarks of agreement came from people of varied race, age, and gender.

With a chuckle the vocstrum gave in. "All right then… *A Child's Triumph* it is!" He began singing the words in Mainlandish. "The Child of Light to Gallow Cliff, did smite the Dark and its Age did lift…"

As much as X'ieth wanted to hear the song, those words brought sudden grief upon him. His eyes grew heavy and moist, his mouth felt dryer, and he attempted to swallow the lump at the top of his throat. With the vocstrum's song, his unlived dream stared him right in the face, agonizing him, making him remember how he wanted it more than life itself. *You'd give anything, to live one day as Kayareth.*

It was hardly an exaggeration to the young knight, and in that moment, the lack of his biggest dream eroded the joy he felt, over how far life had taken him—in spite of an unfair wife, a cruel king, and his fears. In that moment, all he wanted was to be Karnath's hero, and the lack of this dream was most saddening.

With tears in his eyes, X'ieth flashed a weaker smile as the vocstrum continued the ballad. It was not the first time he felt sad when hearing *A Child's Triumph*, nor would it be the last. He loved its story, founded in prophecies predating the Dark Prophecy, which foretold the Child of Light winning the Game at Gallow Cliff, instead of Shaizan. The so-called Light Prophecy was Karnath's hope for years, well before the Dark Prophecy came about. Some said that the oracles never knew the Game's winner, and just invented the prophecies to influence the people, but X'ieth was a believer, at least of what he wanted to hear. *The Light Prophecy...*

His disbelief was no different than that of many across Karnath. As if overlooking the Dark Prophecy, the vocstrums wrote no songs after it came to be, and many devout Karnathans outright rejected it as heresy. But perhaps at the back of everyone's mind was the same question. *What if the Dark Prophecy were true, and the Light Prophecy merely a lie?*

Feeling uncomfortable, X'ieth cleared his mind while whispering aloud. "I don't believe it." It was true, the young knight did not believe the Dark Prophecy, and would not even bring himself to read it. He just knew it said that Shaizan won the Game instead of Kayareth, bringing Eternal Darkness upon Karnath in the absence of time. And that, was all he needed to know to become uninterested. *No need to hear more...*

Interrupting his thoughts, people suddenly clapped and cheered, as the vocstrum strummed the last chord and took a bow on the stage. At about the same time, raucous laughter sounded. X'ieth peered from his seat on the bench, to the place across the pub where Nathan stood, at the long table talking with the pub landlord, apparently trying to save some coin, yet again.

"Ha ha ha! Don't try to push the king's credit here!"

"But we're knights from Sergros on a quest for our king!" retorted Nathan. "On his credit, would you not give us warm meals and drink to fend off the cold? We've traveled here, through the night!"

X'ieth heard the landlord laugh heartily once more, and the young knight watched him quiver from his own humor. His large belly bounced up and down, and his white mustache became wildly animate, as the man threw back his bald head for another laugh.

"I'd rather not trust the king to repay his debts. No payment has come from the throne in sometime, my friend!" The pub landlord laughed again, this time with more composure. "If the king cannot pay his debt, surely he pays not his hired hands."

X'ieth looked over at Finnel who spoke while nudging Hammar.

"The king's credit will only buy Nathan humility!"

Hammar snickered with some restraint, as if trying to avoid Nathan seeing or hearing him.

Detecting motion in his periphery, X'ieth gazed over to the landlord, who stared right back. The young knight noticed Zeros look over his shoulder, as if he too felt eyes upon him.

X'ieth saw the pub landlord face Nathan again.

"That's your party, eh? Well, as Garlew was the noblest of the Guard, I shall serve your men free of charge, over his sake. But only one drink and one meal for each of you, lest me own coin purse go bust!"

Good going! X'ieth thought when overhearing, glad he ignored the other knights who criticized Nathan for pushing the king's credit. *Persistence pays off, though only for the persistent...*

"Thank you, sir! We appreciate your generosity."

X'ieth heard Nathan thank the pub landlord graciously, before returning back to their table. When the leader finally sat down, Hammar and Finnel grew quiet.

"There's no loss of dignity in getting a free meal and drink on occasion," Nathan said. "It's when you come to always expect something without work, that's when dignity has left a man, along with the will to do."

Zeros added, "People of Sergros now feel entitled to free things, all of the time." X'ieth saw Nathan cock his head to the side, as if in slight agreement.

X'ieth internalized some of what was said today, about tax freezes and workers no longing working. His eyes looked around to the varied people in the pub, at least half having food or drinks, perhaps put on pub tabs. *How would they even pay? Perhaps they can't, and most are living beyond their means...*

About the room X'ieth kept gazing, until he noticed that Nathan fell silent, instead of discussing their upcoming journey through Forest Saol. The young knight looked over, seeing the leader just relax. Nathan put his elbows on the table, with his forearms up and knuckles in hand, using them to support his face. *Seems like a good idea. Relax ...*

At that, X'ieth's mind went still, and as it did, he overheard Hammar talk to Finnel, joking how he wanted to replace his Guardsmen cloak with the vocstrum's.

"It's got more flair to it than mine, eh?!" asked Hammar, with a raucous chortle.

Absent mindedly, X'ieth looked over at Zeros, who now showed a different facade than the assertive one he witnessed earlier. The mercenary seemed preoccupied, staring mutely at the table, as if studying the wood's grain.

A mug of piping hot ale slammed down, right in front of X'ieth! It took him by surprise, and he glanced up, just in time to see the pub landlord busily placing ales in front of the other knights as well. The young knight focused on the ale, watching steam waft from the tall mug and into the air. *Finally, the ale! Too bad it's only one mug.*

When everyone was served, X'ieth hastily took up his ale with great anticipation for the first sip. From the corner of his eye, he noticed Nathan raise his mug high, and open his mouth. *Don't do it! He'll propose a toast.* That alarm went off within the young knight's head, and just in time, he aborted his sip before offending Nathan.

"Let's toast. To the king and his quest!"

"Aye!" said Hammar.

The dwarf touched Nathan's mug with his own.

"To the king's quest and Sergros!" said Finnel, doing the same.

A bit hesitant to participate, X'ieth just watched the others' enthusiasm. *Toast to Talus, really?!*

When Nathan looked at X'ieth with his upraised mug in hand, he knew there was no way of avoiding it any longer. Reluctantly, X'ieth clanked his mug with Nathan's, giving a reserved response. "Aye…"

X'ieth watched Zeros mimic his halfhearted toast, though perhaps with even greater reservation. He waited for the dull clank of their mugs before taking a swig of ale with the other knights.

When the ale entered X'ieth's mouth, it felt as hot as boiling water, scalding his tongue and the roof of his mouth. In a reflex, he jerked his shoulders back and pulled the mug from his lips.

"Burnt your taste away, lad?" said Finnel.

With that remark, Hammar and Nathan shared a rowdy laugh with Finnel, though Zeros just drank his ale in silence. X'ieth smirked. *A laugh is still a laugh, even if it's at your expense…*

X'ieth waited before taking his next sip, watching the others drink without delay, as if the ale's temperature did not faze them. When his ale cooled, the young knight took a long swig, afterward wiping the foam from his lips.

Just when X'ieth set his mug down, Nathan collected the group's attention by rapping his palms noisily on the table a few times. The young knight looked up at the leader, who met eyes with everyone.

"I'll go over this again when Tol and Lewes return, but like I said, tomorrow we must leave at the break of dawn." As Nathan continued, X'ieth sipped his ale while listening, just as the others. "Forest Saol is best traveled by day cause it's teeming with wildlife and can be dangerous at night. I'd like to get as far as we can tomorrow."

In the background, X'ieth heard the vocstrum start singing a new song from the stage, and he fought to keep engaged as Nathan went on.

"I'll ensure we replenish the lanterns, so we can travel until dusk."

Finnel asked, "How long does it take to get through the forest, to Liath?"

Nathan paused before answering, "It depends on how much progress we make when there's light, but several days is typical."

X'ieth saw Zeros raise an eyebrow at the leader's comment, but said not a word. *What's the mercenary thinking? Is the trip shorter, longer, something else?* Curiosity gnawed at X'ieth.

An outstretched hand appeared over X'ieth, suddenly dropping a plate before him. It was a thick iron dish, which rattled against the table and startled him. He stared at a meager portion of root vegetables and cubes of meat, all covered in brown gravy, which ushered a distinct garlic aroma into his nostrils. With a glance, he saw the other knights being served by the pub landlord himself, who carried multiple plates using his forearm and elbow. *It's got more vegetables than meat...*

X'ieth took his eyes off the stew, and looked to some Arlemers sitting at the bench across from him. Before them were thinned soups and porridges, and measly stews. *Food is getting scarce,* X'ieth thought. He returned to his own plate, and felt thankful to eat.

By the mouthful, X'ieth pondered while eating, how the landlord could even keep the pub open. *Perhaps he gets more coin than you presume?* The young knight continued eating, and heard people talking together in the background. The noise was pervasive, a constant reminder to what purpose this place served. *It keeps people together.*

It was then X'ieth realized that despite the oppressive gloom, the pubs brought Arlem together, just as pubs in other Sergrothian cities brought together the communities. In the case of Arlem, the Parched Traveler was an inviting place for those who would otherwise stay indoors, alone. Like many others, this pub was at the heart of Arlem, just as its counterparts were in their respective cities—an indispensable part of Mainlandish society.

As X'ieth continued eating, there was some more talk about the quest that brought him back to the common room, from his thoughts. Hammar started asking about the wildlife in Saol, while he picked his teeth with little table manner. "So what wildlife is in Saol? Lions and bears?"

As X'ieth took his last bite, he dropped from the conversation as quickly as he entered. *Not interested...*

"He's over there," came a familiar female voice.

The woman in white! Recognizing the voice, X'ieth looked into the crowd with heightened awareness to behold a mix of faces, some with laughter and merriment, others somber. He gazed all around, trying not to be conspicuous. But the young knight no longer heard whom he thought was there, so he just listened and waited. *Where is she?*

To him, Nathan and Hammar were the closest sound, filling his ears with their discussion. He ignored it.

More distantly he overheard a conversation between two older men: "If Garlew were only alive, he would surely lift the gloom from Sergros!" said one to the other.

Also, X'ieth overheard some exchange over politics: "I admire the king for his provisions. They come without a day's work from me! For that alone, I'd give him my vote in the next election."

His eyes drifted to the next face in the crowd, as he picked up yet another conversation: "There's not been anyone to my shop but the pillagers. Sergros is no longer a land of free and brave souls, rather a home for those who are dependent and afraid!"

X'ieth went from face-to-face, and did not find her in the common room. His mind conjured up memories of the corridor in Castle Sergros, where the woman in white mysteriously disappeared. *Has she done it again?* he wondered.

At the lack of suspicious sights and sounds, X'ieth looked to his ale again, and reached for the mug to finish it off, feeling more at ease. *Maybe you just imagined that...*

Before touching the mug, X'ieth suddenly heard the door open and felt a chilly draft from outside. He turned just in time to see who left the pub: a woman in white, wearing a cloak that framed black falling stars!

He immediately burst up from the bench, away from the table, and ran for the door, without even as much as looking at Nathan or the others. A few standing townsfolk in the pub were in his way, but X'ieth brushed past them, being careful not to bump into them on his way to the exit.

X'ieth moved through the common room quickly, and when reaching the door just as it closed, he forcefully pulled it open. The cold winds slapped him in the face as he left the pub and ran into the street, in hot pursuit of the woman in white.

"MIDNIGHT RIDERS TO ARLEM"

Chapter 22
Alleys and Byways

X'ieth ran out of Arlem's pub, pushing past the front door and into the cold. Outside, he collided into Lewes and Tol, apparently on their way into the pub! As if bumping into complete strangers, the young knight muttered mindless apologies and dashed onto the street, looking all around. *Where did she go?!*

Just then, X'ieth caught a glimpse of the cloak's tail, going into an alley down the street, away from the pub. The sight had him running instantly, and after only taking a few steps, he heard Lewes call out.

"X'ieth, wait! What's wrong?!"

"Wonder what's got into him?" asked Tol.

"He looks troubled! Let's find Nathan…"

While running, X'ieth turned, seeing the knights head into the pub. *Don't stop; don't explain. Just find her!* With those thoughts, he re-centered his mind on the chase, and ducked into the alleyway where he last saw the woman's fleeting cloak.

Upon entering the alley, X'ieth was immersed in the shadows of Arlem's unlit backstreets. He saw tall buildings on both sides, standing adjacent to other buildings in the distance, and even more buildings beyond that. The alley extended down a corridor of gray stone, narrowing into a black vanishing point, where just barely, he could see the cloak afar, drifting behind the woman in white. And just as his eye met the cloak, he saw it veer right, off into an adjoining alley!

He quickened his pace, running faster, as the alley filled with sounds of his boots clapping against the cobblestone, along with his own breathing. X'ieth raced to the adjoining alley and turned, to follow after her. There, he found himself in a new alley, looking identical to the one from which he came. And in the distance floated the cloak, just as before.

X'ieth ran after the woman in white again, until she suddenly ducked down an adjoining alley; he followed her into it without thinking twice. But unfortunately for him, this same process repeated itself, again and again: X'ieth kept darting into new alley after new alley, as she kept wondering deeper into Arlem's maze of streets—streets that winded around buildings and intersected with adjacent ways. It was easily enough for the young knight to grow disoriented, and to merely aim at just following the woman in white, wherever she went. *How will you find your way back?!* he worried, only to assure himself a moment later. *That's the lesser problem for sure, when compared to having no premonitions of your future! You must find her, and get to the bottom of this...*

In continued pursuit of her, X'ieth ran through more alleys that connected him to different residential districts, taking him yet deeper into Arlem's maze of conduits. The cloak still drifted ahead of him, as the woman just walked slowly down the various alleys. Despite his constant running, it seemed as though the cloak always stayed a fixed distance from him, like a carrot perpetually before a mule. *How is this even possible?!*

After what seemed forever—district upon district later and alley upon alley—X'ieth beheld the white cloak up ahead, now stationary at the cross section between two intersecting alleys. He sprinted until directly behind the woman, breathing heavily from near exhaustion.

You caught up. The thought went slowly through his mind, with some disbelief. He stood there sucking down air, his throat and lungs burning, unable to take his eyes off the woman or her cloak, which showed three black falling stars on a field of white.

Gradually, his breathing slowed, though his heart continued beating fast, now due to his anxiety over the encounter. Being in shock over the run, X'ieth remained still and with an empty mind. Every other second, the freezing winds would slap him in the face in open rebuke, regarding his hesitation in the matter. *You pushed yourself this hard to catch her, and now you're silent?! Say something!* His inner voice taunted him, as the situation began to reek of all others where X'ieth lost his voice, like before Talus in the throne room.

Silent still, X'ieth gazed around the backstreets through the fog, which hung in the air. He glanced up, and noticed the insipid, crescent moon peeking out of the gray clouds, being partly occluded. The young knight looked to the windows in buildings on both sides, where candles flickered yellow light into the alleyway.

His mind searched for something to say, with nothing to be found. He looked at the back of the woman's head, covered in shiny flowing blonde hair that fell beneath her shoulders, catching the moonlight. It was as if she waited there for him, and the more she did, the more he felt uncomfortable. Beneath his boots, the bumpy cobblestone irritated his feet, a match for how he started to irritate himself. *Speak to her! Raise your voice, man!*

All of a sudden, the woman turned her head to the side. X'ieth watched her locks of golden hair bounce with the movement, which revealed one of her blue eyes, sparkling brilliantly through the fog, like a gem of allure.

"Who are you?" asked X'ieth, his voice cracking.

She stayed silent, still looking from the side.

With some irritation, X'ieth raised his voice.

"Who are you?!" Feeling ignored, he spouted off questions in his increasing frustration. "Why do premonitions no longer tell my future?! Why have my premonitions stopped coming, since leaving my home!"

She kept quiet, still staring at X'ieth from the side.

How dare she remain silent?! The young knight simmered in his own anger, as the situation summoned up negative energies in him, those held in reserve from his memories of the occasions where Millicent disregarded his opinion and made his spoken words as worthless as dung. For just as this, his words now vanished into the gloom, and became words spoken for naught.

"How dare you ignore me!" he yelled. "I'm a knight of Sergros, and command you tell me why these things are so! I remember you from Taurus' attack! I recall what you said about my premonitions!"

X'ieth paused, vexed that the harsh winds were still his only reply. "Speak! For I know you know, about what happens to me!"

From out of silence, the woman in white responded.

"I am Urzel, Lordess of Day."

At that, the young knight stared blankly. *Who?!*

And with her final word, he witnessed her disappear immediately from where she stood, in the blink of an eye! X'ieth rushed forward and looked all about the alleyway, not believing the woman was just gone like that. It bothered him, for after all his effort to find her, he still had no closure whatsoever, about his premonitions becoming untrue before they stopped coming altogether. *Just another question without an answer...*

"What is she?! Some sort of... witch?!" *Unbelievable!* he thought, shaking off the unpalatable outcome.

In his ears, X'ieth suddenly heard steps from behind him and spun about in a flash, drawing his sword in the same motion. He held the blade in both hands, seeing then the shadows stir as a silhouette moved toward him!

From the dark alleyway, X'ieth watched Lucen step forth with a smile, carrying his gnarled wooden staff. The young knight sheathed his weapon, relieved at finding a friend rather than a foe.

"Immortals rarely speak with mortals," said Lucen. "Next time you approach the woman in white, perhaps you should ask more kindly."

"She's immortal?" the young knight asked, appearing impressed. "I will... if I get a second chance."

X'ieth looked down momentarily, and then back up. *Your first chance is up, but maybe Lucen can still help...*

"Can you explain any of this to me? Three days ago I had my life planned out, but now, I'm not so sure what's happening anymore. I found my premonitions were untrue, when Sergros arrived at my door, requesting me to meet with the king, who bestowed a mission upon me to confront Esmeralda, in order to end the gloom."

Lucen stared back straight-faced, as if listening.

"This quest seems for the good of others, and I've undertaken it to pursue my good destiny, to help my kingdom that's currently in need! But in this, there's so much uncertainty. I fear the risk of peril, from fighting a powerful sorceress like Esmeralda. I fear what may happen, that I'll not return to my wife and soon-to-be child!"

In a matter of confiding in Lucen, X'ieth's many fears coalesced into a common theme: wanting good destiny in spite of unfair Millicent and cruel Talus, but without premonitions, being unable to know how big the risks were, and what the end result would be.

Lucen spoke after a length of silence, as if allowing more time for X'ieth to say anything else. "There are reasons you wish to speak with Urzel and not me. As such, perhaps I can answer only some of your questions. But first, a question for you."

X'ieth looked back at Lucen, his sharp blue eyes shining in the shadowy walk. *Another question in return for your question?*

"What is it?" he asked, a bit impatient.

Lucen replied, "What destiny leads your doing?"

To that, X'ieth gave a blank stare, in hopes it would induce the question being rephrased.

"What's your destiny, and where does it lead you?" Lucen stepped forward, and flashed a smile. "Does it lead you somewhere you want, somewhere good enough?"

Does Lucen imply your good destiny isn't good enough?! His interpretation of Lucen's words touched on his unfulfilled desire of being Kayareth, which for him, was the source of much pain.

A bit hotheaded, X'ieth answered defensively, "My destiny of being a superior knight, well-versed in swordplay and magic, leads me to this most noble quest for Sergros. I have expert designations in swordsmanship and hand-to-hand combat, and perhaps am the youngest to possess such marks of skill."

Lucen's silent reply inspired X'ieth's anger.

He snapped the question, "What greater destiny can I have, than serving Sergros with such prestige and honor?"

"Serving Karnath, instead of just Sergros? Imagine greater, beyond what you see as adequate."

X'ieth stared at the smiling Lucen in the dimly lit alley. Just then, freezing winds ripped through, whistling shrilly and ruffling his cloak as well as the youth's robe.

In spite of the harsh elements, X'ieth managed to think about more than just being cold. For Lucen's comment stayed at the front of his mind, provoking his contemplation of what his friend really meant. *Be calm, man. Lucen only challenges you to pursue greater destiny than you've already found.*

X'ieth grew reserved, feeling foolish over his quick anger. "Please, tell me more. I'm sorry for getting angry."

Lucen continued, his smile still in place. "Did you know," he asked, "that your king's wise counselors tell him that Esmeralda is the Child of Darkness?"

X'ieth showed surprise. *Talus didn't tell you that...*

"She seeks to end her sister's reign of power, and has recovered the legendary shard of sword from off a mountain, just how the Dark Prophecy foretells."

So the Guard... works toward stopping the Child of Darkness from winning the Game?! He pondered then what further details Talus might have held back when describing their assignment. *Talus wasn't honest.*

"Perhaps you wouldn't know," Lucen reasoned aloud, then staring away from X'ieth and up into the sky. The young knight watched Lucen look back a moment later, before continuing. "As Talus wouldn't want seven knights all thinking their quest made them the Child of Light. For whoever stops the Child of Darkness surely is the One of Prophecy."

X'ieth's mouth dropped. *He can't be saying that...*

"Surely Talus wouldn't say a thing, for disclosing this might lead to fighting among knights—fighting over who confronts Esmeralda. For there can be only one Child with a chance of changing the Dark Prophecy."

With intrigue, X'ieth begged for details. "Who then is the Child, among these knights of valor?! Surely one of us must be him."

A cold gust blew just then, but X'ieth hardly felt its freezing bite, given the gravity of their discussion. The smile on Lucen's face vanished, and he become incredibly solemn before opening his mouth to speak. "You are a Child of Destiny, the one fated to do mighty things."

X'ieth felt sudden tingles all over his body. Though the winds continued beating him, in that moment, he felt impervious to their assault. His mind halted, with no thoughts in motion, as did the world stop around him. Everything just stopped. *You're... Kayareth?!*

X'ieth met eyes with Lucen, and while staring at him, his cautious half wrestled with his gullible half, the two sides clearly being at odds. One part of him hesitated at believing such a big claim, whereas his other part embraced it with open arms. This was the news young X'ieth always wanted to hear, the blessing he hoped Karnatha would drop upon him from the sky. And now, the news finally came to him from the lips of a trusted friend, a friend who clearly could see the future. *You're... Kayareth.*

The gears in X'ieth's head began turning, and suddenly, it all made sense. His surprise promotion and unexpected quest, mired with non-ideal circumstances like leaving behind pregnant Millicent, made absolutely perfect sense. *Your hardships at home and work are nothing short of Kayareth's hardships, and now at last, Karnatha exalts you to greater purpose. It's the purpose you've always fought for at home, the purpose you've always wanted from your work under Talus! This is why you're in the Seventh Order, on a quest to stop the Child of Darkness! It's your good destiny of becoming Kayareth, now coming to be!*

It took a while before X'ieth's mind stopped spewing thoughts. In time, he silenced himself and looked at Lucen, who stared back with an unwavering sincerity, as opposed to his typical playful antics. A strong wind howled while he waited for his friend to go on.

"Don't worry over appeasing your king or your wife," Lucen said. "Just as you've always thought, these are but distractions that draw you away from a most dazzling future. It's not so much what you do that matters, for what's meant to be, shall be, regardless of your deeds."

The young knight listened carefully to the youth, and rationality pled with him to reason carefully over the matter. *Can you really believe this, just like that?* The very thought easily prompted him to further contemplate what he was told, but again, his mind settled on the obvious facts. *Lucen is clearly a prophet. He predicted Kort would be a threat some months ago, and he knew about unexpected visitors at your cottage some days ago. What he says just happens. You're Kayareth!*

Even though the news struck him as wonderful, X'ieth was still full of questions. When the next wind died, he took advantage of meeting Lucen again, by trying to get a few answers. X'ieth blurted out his questions, wondering what the youth would prophesy.

"Are the oracles' visions true, the Dark Prophecy? Will the Child of Darkness prevail?!"

Lucen smiled again and replied, "Would you trust the last image a blind man saw before losing his sight, told to you years after his blindness? For long the oracles saw the Light Prophecy and now this Dark thing, so there's clearly confusion in the Society—confusion that need not be your own. The prophecies aside, I assure you that Esmeralda can be stopped. Your destiny is clear to me."

"All you need to do is be," Lucen told him, "and great things shall simply come to you, for this is your fate." X'ieth watched him step back, toward the alley. "I shall visit you again. Until then, be careful. For many men of poor intentions stroll through Arlem."

X'ieth followed the pointing finger that Lucen suddenly raised, to shadows moving in the distance, apparently those of a great many people coming his way!

"I heard them talk, over there!" yelled a voice.

"Aye, let's go!" said another.

In the distance, X'ieth beheld a number of armed men emerge out of the black alley. When he turned back to Lucen, the youth had already disappeared.

The young knight looked down the opposite way, preparing to run, but he saw more men approaching from that direction. *Need to get out of here!*

With men coming from both sides, X'ieth abandoned the idea of running up or down the alley that brought him to the cross section. Instead, he went through the intersection, down the adjoining way, and headed around a building and to the right, into an alley running parallel to the one with danger.

Chapter 23
Won't Lose Ground

As fast as he could, X'ieth ran down the alley, not having an alternative. He knew the gang occupied the alley that ran beside the one he was in. With each foot forward he thought about Lucen's words. *It's not so much what you do that matters.* He cast it from his mind with some disbelief. X'ieth was convinced that he must be smart to avoid bad situations. *Destiny does not just spare fools from the consequences of folly, regardless of the fool's destiny! Surely good destiny must be earned with some good choices.* But as much as X'ieth wanted to be clever to avoid confrontation with the men, ducking into this alley seemed like his best choice, with no other options. And so, he just kept going.

Sounds of his pursuers entered his ears—their footfall against the cobblestone, loud voices, and crashes as obstacles in the alley were kicked, thrown, or overturned by the droves of men. Still in motion, X'ieth continued down the alley at full speed. Before his eyes, rows of stone buildings along the path smeared into streaks of gray. Up above, on some second-story houses, he noticed windows open as residents peered out, some holding a shining lantern. But just as fast as those windows opened, many were quickly shut, in what became the residents' fearful response to loud commotion in the streets.

X'ieth dashed a bit further down the alleyway, into an intersection, hoping that no one would see him from the parallel alley.

"There he is! Cut him off!"

He heard the voice rang out from one misfit, right when he passed through the intersection. *Destiny damn it!* And immediately following that, he heard increased footfall against the cobblestone, as if the men on the side alley ran even faster.

They're gaining. Despite X'ieth's quick pace, he was at a clear disadvantage, as running in heavy armor rarely affords one a victory, even in the shortest of foot races. Despite the odds against him though, he continued running. And as he did, his heart beat quickly in his chest, in part from the exertion, in part from his dread over confronting the ruffians. And that dread doubled when he heard feet against the cobblestone, right behind him!

"There! Keep at his hind!"

X'ieth could not see it, but he knew it was happening. Some men ran into his alley at the intersection, and were now directly on his tail. The young knight hastened his step, seeing the next intersection of backstreets up ahead, maybe twenty cubits from him. But suddenly five men emerged from it—the men that hurried down the parallel alley with greater haste.

X'ieth came to an abrupt stop, where his last step against the cobblestone was hard and pronounced, shooting pain up his right leg. He instinctively turned to run from the men, in the opposite direction. But at his back rushed up the rest of this gang. He watched about ten additional men stop behind him. *You're flanked!*

He looked both ways, seeing middle-aged men with faces masked by shadows and fog. Some had tattoos and noticeable scars, hallmarks of former military men. Indeed, by no means did these men appear to him as common thieves, for the whole group was armed and dangerous, most of them holding daggers, swords, clubs, or brass knuckles.

In the alley, X'ieth stood there like a trapped animal, with one shoulder blade facing each set of men. Wary of a sudden attack from either side, he cautiously looked from one direction to the other, at every small movement or noise. The winds beat upon him, without any good news or captivating discussions from Lucen to soften their blows. X'ieth heard a sudden voice at his right, and his attention went there.

"Well, what do we have here?"

A taller muscled man of medium build came forth, who wore plain attire, and retained a ghastly scar down his left cheek, clearly from an edged weapon. *Is this the gang leader?!* X'ieth wondered.

"A Guardsman from Sergros, who's better taken care of than the grunts Talus used to fight his bloody war—the Isles Conspiracy."

X'ieth experienced a slight tremble, as he stayed in place, his nerves frayed and his heart beating fast. He whipped his head to his left, where arose the scratchy voice of another man.

"We all fought to save Juniper from becoming a new Black Dragon territory on the Mainland, and what good did it do us?"

The speaker came from X'ieth's other side—a bearded man with a balding head, in a short-sleeve tunic beneath a thick vest. X'ieth could see his right bicep jutting out; it featured a tattoo of Sergros' lion ripping apart a black dragon, a common mark taken by those Sergrothians who joined the fight against Taurus Hboshi. X'ieth immediately looked back the other way, when the gang leader completed his friend's sentence.

"Homeless and destitute we are, a great thanks from Talus our gracious king."

Aside from some intermixed coughs and hacks, the men from both sides showed their agreement.

"Aye, it's true!" called out someone.

"There's fewer and fewer opportunities in Sergros for military men!" claimed another, beside the prior man.

X'ieth's mind raced back to those shops in the business district, some appearing as though people lived within. *Can it be, these men dwell there this winter?! Talus should've done better for them!* X'ieth turned, as the man at his opposite side chimed in.

"Without a job after the war, no landlord in Sergros gave us shelter. This city still runs on coin, just as the others! The king's welfare hasn't stopped owners from collecting rent, and they wouldn't have any of us without being a hire somewhere."

His other ear heard the gang leader pipe up.

"But there ain't no work, you see! So we're just left in the cold to wait on Sergros' provisions, which come less often all the time."

As the different speakers engaged him, X'ieth alternated looks between his opposite sides. At the back of his mind, he considered any possible means of escape, but drew a blank. *No way out.* The conclusion was a bit jarring.

"You think we want to live in mediocrity on the kingdom's handouts?" one man said heatedly. "We want opportunities after Sergros' wars, not this."

X'ieth remained on edge from the gang's sudden movements and noise, stirring like a scared rabbit. Not seeing any way to avoid this confrontation, he suddenly raised his hands to interrupt the talking men. *Perhaps if you understand what they want, you'll get out of here alive.*

"Wait," he said, meeting eyes with the gang leader. "I'm a lowly knight from Sergros on a quest for our king. Carry neither coin nor wealth do I, so what of me do you require?" At his words, X'ieth heard denials ring out on both sides, from the band of men.

"He's lying!" one shouted.

"I bet he has gold!" said another.

"Aye, look at his fancy armor!"

"Tis true! Maybe gems, even!" stated a man, with a cascade of echoed "Ayes", building into group agreement.

X'ieth gulped and watched the gang leader look around, lifting both hands to silence the men. His heart thumped in his chest, and his palms sweated.

"That's enough already!" shouted the leader, again facing X'ieth. "Even if you have no coin, I bet your armor would command a bit of money with the smithy. He's always looking for scrap metal!"

A round of cheers was heard from the gang.

"Aye!" yelled one.

"Scrap his armor for coin!" said another.

X'ieth looked at the men, desperation in their eyes.

"I cannot do that," he replied, knowing that he needed the armor for his mission. His mind shuffled through various thoughts, ranging from confronting a powerful sorceress without protection, to Nathan simply being mad at him. Most of all, X'ieth was hung up on one thought in particular, that giving up his armor resembled Millicent's want of him forfeiting his purpose, and his stance on this was no different than that. *Not giving up anything!*

"Lad," said the leader, "if you don't give us the armor, we'll take it from your body, bruised and beaten!"

More cheers erupted from the motley mob.

"Yeah, that'll show him!"

"He'll know we're serious then!" said the next man.

X'ieth stood there silent, still unwilling to give up his armor. As their shouts died down, he realized that this would be his final chance of merely yielding to the gang's demands. Conflicting voices exchanged their viewpoints in his mind: *The armor isn't worth your life, man... Give it up! Give up the armor as soon as you would give up your purpose... Don't do it.*

But in the wake of that clash between the voices, he stayed with his original position. *Not giving up anything!* The arrogant part of X'ieth spoke up just then. *If they want to fight, then fight 'em! After all, you're Kayareth.*

"He won't give it up," the leader shouted, "so take it off him!"

From the right, suddenly came the bearded man a brawling, his fists flying at X'ieth's head. The young knight moved to avoid a face full of knuckles, watching the man's arm go out, right before him.

In one fluent motion, X'ieth quickly clasped the back of the man's hand with his own, placing a thumb below its outermost small finger and other fingers below its thumb. With that and a twist of his wrist, X'ieth grabbed the man's elbow and steered him right into another assailant, who rushed from the frontlines of the leftmost group. X'ieth released the bearded man and watched the two collide into each other! They fell to the ground with low moans. It was then he heard murmurs ripple through the men at both his sides, along with a few more coughs.

"Eh, a fighter is he?" asked one rhetorically.

"The Sergrothian army is better than the Guard!"

"He's no match for us," said another.

Looking directly at the gang leader, X'ieth said, "I wish to leave this place, being unharmed and not harming any more of you."

"Never, boy... Not without that armor!"

As a man ran from his right, X'ieth unhooked the sheath from his belt, and lifted it above his head in his left hand, his other hand placed on his sword's grip. He pulled at the sword, hitting the assailant square between the eyes with the weapon's pommel.

X'ieth touched the Nexus just in time, sensing another man grabbing at him from the ground. He turned quickly and knocked the assailant over the head with the sheathed sword. As two others rushed in, the young knight bashed them with his elbow and the cased blade. Both men fell to the ground, one hitting a building's wall beforehand.

He watched the other men come closer, and it tempted him to draw his sword and start slashing. But X'ieth restrained himself for good reason. *Don't want to kill anyone!* Just as he had that thought, one man appeared out of nowhere, and tackled X'ieth at the waist! The young knight was thrown to the ground and lied upon his back. He looked up and saw the gang converge upon him, right as those at the front began kicking and throwing punches!

Jolts of pain went through him, as he took one hit in the face, and more hits to his chest and extremities. *Was the armor really worth it?! Was your pride worth it? Was your arrogance the real cause for not backing down? Were you saying "no" to more than just giving up the armor?* As he received the gang's assault, the questions posed themselves in his subconscious. All valid questions, all barred from his waking thoughts.

No material possession, can match the worth of life! X'ieth had that thought, taking another hit to the chest. The realization smacked him, along with enough punches and kicks to make him black out.

"STREET SCUFFLE"

Chapter 24
Events Unforeseen

From the shadows he witnessed the atrocity unfold. A gang of ex-military men pummeled a young knight, who was much like himself years ago. Pushed about by the king, a bit naïve, and unsuspecting… X'ieth was all of that just like him, though he did not deserve this.

Let him take a few hits. That should beat the foolishness out of him. After the first punch to his face, however, followed by their kicking, Zeros drew the line there. *On second thought, there's no letting that happen.*

"Stop!" he shouted, unafraid to speak up at this point in his life. A career of tolerating Talus literally instilled Zeros with zero tolerance for enduring abuse, even though abuse seemed to persist in his own life, as well as those all around him. He looked on with surprise as the cowards swarmed X'ieth, like flies to horse dung, not even pausing when he spoke, as if no one heard.

"Stop it!" he screamed then, at the top of his lungs, much louder this time. Zeros watched everyone slowly stop beating X'ieth and look up, some displaying surprise. The one who undoubtedly was the gang leader approached, having a smile from ear-to-ear.

"Well, another of the Guard comes to join the fun."

Zeros stepped a bit further into the dimly lit alley, his matching armor shimmering in the moonlight, and his black hair with grays showing his age. In one hand he held a long piece of wood carved into the shape of a Hirishin blade, typically used for practicing *Endo Najatsu*, the style of swordplay most prevalent in the Isles.

Some of the gang started laughing.

"He's come to us with a toy!" one of them laughed.

"We'll see how he likes to be spanked with it!" said another. At the remark, more laughter rose among them, the gang leader included.

Zeros' eyes trailed to X'ieth upon the cobblestone; his lip was bloodied and his face red from a few blows. *I let this get too far. Should've intervened before.* Though the mercenary chided himself for not doing more, in reality, he showed up just as X'ieth went to the ground.

"Why not try to take on someone your own age, one at a time like honorable men," said Zeros. "Let's see how you fare then."

The leader released a guffaw into the alley.

"Really now?! *You* stand a better chance against me than him, with your little trinket? In a fight between you and this boy, I'd give him my bet any day. And we've already seen how he fared with me."

"What makes you so confident?" asked the gang leader, while unsheathing a small dagger.

"Experience," replied Zeros. "Though perhaps of the same kind you have, I'd safely presume mine is better than yours."

Zeros smiled as the gang leader's eyes widened in rage, right before the man stabbed at him with the naked blade. Gracefully, the mercenary stepped back twice, avoiding first a lunge and then a sideswipe with the dagger. The gang leader wielded the weapon to afflict grave wounds upon Zeros, and so, he would not show mercy.

All of a sudden, Zeros smacked the dagger out of the man's hand with the wooden sword. His face was immediately stricken with a mix of shock and pain, and he looked down to his hand, with several of its digits jammed. In that moment, Zeros whipped the sword across the man's groin, forcing him to turn away squealing, with his knees slightly bent. It was then that Zeros slashed downward with the wooden sword, from the level his right shoulder, hitting the gang leader's calf hard.

CRACK!

That sound accompanied an immediate scream through the alley, as Zeros' impulsive strike with the wooden sword splintered the gang leader's fibula. With little compassion the mercenary looked on, as the man fell to the ground, writhing in pain.

He cried aloud with little dignity, "Destiny damn you to the Void!" His voice was shrill and aggrieved.

Now without their leader, Zeros turned to the gang.

"Anyone else need a lesson?"

The mercenary noted a balding bearded man at the front with a tattoo upon his bicep. He stared back with a look of anger in his eyes. *This one's going to be trouble.*

Zeros drew Nexus into his core. Instantly, he saw himself standing in his enlarged channeling chamber, where multiple streams flowed through his Source entry—a large door, pulled open. The streams flowed and flowed until the room was full, and at that point, he returned to the alley. Using the accumulated energy, Zeros transformed it into flames, and precisely singed the little hair left on the bearded man's head! The mercenary just watched him, holding back a smile until the bearded man noticed his few head hairs were afire. It was then that he acted with a sense of panic, clawing through the mob and screaming, to run off down the alley while patting his head.

"Anyone else?" asked Zeros again.

The mercenary saw a lean young man confront him from the crowd, of about X'ieth's age, with piercings in the ears and longer hair. He suddenly rushed forth, and his coattails flowed behind him.

Zeros stepped back as the man threw forceful punches with brass knuckles, one after another. While moving away, the mercenary ducked below the wild fists, sometimes weaving from one side to the other, just to make it harder for his opponent to predict him. During his entire defense, Zeros maintained an impressive situational awareness through the Nexus, knowing when he needed to step over the injured gang leader, who continued making noise upon the ground, right in the middle of their fight.

Zeros dodged another series of punches from the young man. Before him stood his opponent again, pulling back his arm and raising both fists at eye level, like a brawler would. Quite unexpectedly, Zeros rushed forward along the young man's side with one arm ready, wrapping its forearm under the his armpit, over his shoulder, with his palm against the back of his head.

With the wooden sword still in one hand, Zeros used his other hand to clutch a handful of his opponent's hair, watching the young man struggle to free himself from the hold. Though the young man stepped away forcefully, Zeros kept him in place. *You're not going anywhere, lad.*

Using his hand, Zeros gave the young man's locks a sharp tug to bring him off-balance and lead him to fall beside his torso. As he fell, Zeros looked into his opponent's eyes while whipping the wooden sword across the young man's abdomen with a loud smack.

"Arrghhh!" His yelp ripped through the alley, intermingled now with the same sounds from the fallen gang leader. Zeros let the young man hit the cobblestone groaning. No sooner than the young man went down, Zeros noticed someone else charge from the crowd.

To the left, now! In a single instant, the tip of Zeros' wooden sword met his next opponent's throat, bringing another daring man to a complete stop.

"You too?" asked the mercenary.

He paid close attention to the man's green eyes, seeing the fear inside. The would-be attacker just trembled, with the sword tip pressed against his throat's apple. In the background, Zeros could hear the young man wheeze noticeably from the cobblestone. Yet his attention stayed on the man behind his practice sword, for he anticipated a change of mind would soon take place. *Just let it all sink in… He'll reconsider.*

Just then, the young man with long hair got up from wheezing upon the cobblestone. He pushed through the men gasping, the wind knocked out of him. He left the alley, and did not come back.

"What's it going to be?" Zeros asked the man at sword point. Just as expected, the mercenary saw him turn around and bolt through the dwindling crowd, now with less than ten men. And this was the start of more of the gang gradually departing, one member at a time. All the while, Zeros heard the fallen gang leader wail from the cobblestone. *Without a leader and with a few defeats, no one's willing to stick around and be my next example.*

Zeros watched what remained of Arlem's gang run off, as he turned their thievery sour. As they fled, their steps against the cobblestone were quick, loud, and many. When someone stepped on X'ieth's hand, Zeros also heard the young knight yelp.

X'ieth blinked his eyes open, and saw Zeros standing before him. *What happened?* He lied there breathing slowly, with his body hurting all over. *Did you get run over by a carriage, man?* Although in the moment he wondered just that, memories started coming back, of encountering the gang and getting into a street scuffle. Feelings of humility suddenly overwhelmed him. *You're Kayareth, and those men just beat the dung out of you. Destiny save Karnath...*

X'ieth saw Zeros come over, and kneel beside him.

"Don't move, lad."

Stubborn as a mule, X'ieth leaned forth and sat up.

"I feel fine," he said, proceeding to stand. "Nothing a good night's sleep won't cure." The young knight glanced over at Zeros, who showed a face of concern.

"You could've gotten killed, you know?"

"Well, I didn't," replied X'ieth. "Guess Destiny has something in store for me. Thank you anyway though."

On both feet now, X'ieth felt his head pound and his body ache. He noticed an absence of the usual heavy weight on his belt, and immediately started looking around the alley for his broadsword. Fortunately for him he saw it nearby, still in its scabbard, and bent over to pick it up. While clipping the sheath to his belt, he heard another moan from the fallen gang leader.

"What'll become of him?" asked X'ieth to Zeros, seeing the gang leader there. He watched the mercenary cast a downward glare upon the streets, the wooden sword in his hand.

"Let him crawl to Arlem's hospice," Zeros replied, looking up. "I'm sure they have a long wait, as so many get free care on the nobles' coin. He'll certainly have time to think of what he's done before a healer can see him." At that, a smile lit Zeros' face in the dark, and X'ieth's too.

"C'mon, let's get back to the pub."

As X'ieth started walking, he felt Zeros put an arm around his shoulder mid-stride. He glanced to him, and saw the mercenary tuck the wooden sword beneath the pit of his opposite arm. They walked on together.

"Do you think Nathan will notice I've been in a brawl?" asked X'ieth, chuckling.

"Just keep to the shadows. He won't see a thing!"

The two knights shared a laugh together.

As they took steps away from the spot of the street scuffle, the gang leader piped up, "I can't walk! You worthless knights leave me for dead! To the Void with you all, and Talus!"

The sounds faded, and were replaced with those of winds and their steps against the cobblestone. With every stride, X'ieth's body continued hurting in many places. *Bet you're all bruised up, though maybe your armor helped lessen that.*

Suddenly, he saw Zeros turn to him, right as X'ieth coincidentally felt his face and wiped blood from his lip.

"Do you want some worldly wisdom?"

"Sure," X'ieth replied, not having enough energy to fend off this forthcoming lecture. As he rubbed his aching head, the young knight literally suffered from the hard knocks of life. *And you'd think those knocks would teach a lecture, on their own...*

"Never do *that* again," said Zeros. "You clearly have some training in combat. Five-Banded Fists?"

X'ieth stopped with Zeros, and nodded his head.

"Five-Banded Fists is primarily defensive, and the designation can be earned through sparring matches alone. Sparring is no substitute for real combat like street fights or wars. Don't be overly confident. That's what you did tonight, and you should've backed down."

X'ieth listened as Zeros admonished him.

"You can easily end up on the losing side of a fight that way, especially against numbers. And often no one's around to stop the other side from killing you. Completely unlike those sparring matches..."

Completely quiet, X'ieth looked at him. *He's right. Lucen's news went to your head, and you thought you could take them...*

"Though tonight you had some good fortune, lad. I'm glad I found you not a moment later."

X'ieth felt Zeros remove the arm from off his shoulder, and with that, the mercenary continued walking. The young knight watched him take only a few steps before putting his own feet into motion. He caught up with Zeros, and walked side by side with him.

"If you're approached by a large group of men," Zeros said. "Just give them whatever thing they want. Your life is worth much more than any material good they can take from you."

Realized that too, X'ieth thought, *though it took a beating to make the point!*

"And another thing," said Zeros. "You shouldn't try to be a champion of bad cause, like your own pride. There's times to fight for good cause, even principles and morals, but *this* wasn't one of them."

They strolled together through the alleys in a seemingly precise route. *Does Zeros know these ways like the back of his hand?* X'ieth wondered about this, as the backstreets became increasingly familiar. *We're close to the pub.*

"Try to avoid conflict when you can, and make sacrifices at your discretion, only for important causes. Risk your life to protect your family, or those upstanding in Karnath, but *not* your pride. Protecting your pride can get you killed."

X'ieth digested Zeros' remarks, thinking about their applicability. *Zeros be swinging a hammer at nails, and hitting 'em all on the head!* The more he listened to Zeros, the more he admired the mercenary's wisdom.

"But, if you're going to fight a fight, do it well. You should've attacked the gang leader first, as soon as the conflict started. Most gangs aren't much without a leader. The same holds for soldiers led into war." X'ieth listened as Zeros continued, absorbing every detail like a sponge.

But with those words, Zeros suddenly fell silent. The two walked together in silence, which soon grew awkward for X'ieth. More than anything, the young knight wanted to ask Zeros about certain things. *How do you know so much about fighting? What's your background?* But every time the questions reached his tongue, he struggled to ask them. *Destiny blind me!* he thought to himself, acutely aware of his inability to speak.

Then unexpectedly, X'ieth heard Zeros talk again.

"So, you rode with Garlew Il'therin?"

X'ieth answered instantly, being proud of the fact.

"Yes, indeed. What a noble knight. He rejected countless promotions to the Seventh Order, and Talus allowed it." As X'ieth spoke, he reminisced of the great knight Garlew in his mind, still Sergros' hero to many.

"Ah, common ground we have."

X'ieth raised an eyebrow. "Eh?"

"In the days where Garlew fought in the Isles Crusades, I joined him. We rode together," Zeros said, "commanding a legion of Sergrothian soldiers."

X'ieth's eyes lit up. *You're not only in Arlem with the Seventh Order of the Guard, man… Beside you walks a former high commander of the Sergrothian army!* The thoughts raptured him into a bizarre state of euphoria, where just then, his bumps and bruises seemed like the least important matter in Karnath.

"In multiple campaigns I served Sergros. My last assignment was as a war general in the Isles Crusades, some thirty years ago."

X'ieth scrunched his brow in confusion, and Zeros looked over, seeming to take note of it. *Isles Crusades? Which one, when?* The history X'ieth learned in academy was long gone from his mind. Thankfully to him, Zeros assumed ignorance.

"Our kingdom sent militants to aid the Red Dragon clans in the most recent of the Crusades, years before your time. Back then, the one family stood on the brink of losing their territories to Black Dragon invaders, led by the father of Taurus Hboshi. The matter of which family should prevail in the Isles had seen a long history of taking sides. It has been easy to do for kingdoms and men alike. Tekkneo took a side months ago in the recent conflict, deciding the Red Dragon clans should have an upper hand through advanced magic, the metal demons. The ages-old story about conflict between the families hopefully ended with its final chapter, the Isles Conspiracy."

X'ieth noted how when the mercenary said these words, his eyes went moist. He could not tell what Zeros felt exactly, but a more important question crept up in his mind. *What happened with Zeros being a general?*

"You know, the only difference between you and me is time," said Zeros. "For with time comes experience."

X'ieth came to a stop with Zeros, and met the mercenary's eyes straightway. Yet another shrill wind struck them, sending a shiver through X'ieth as they both waited for it to quiet. Meanwhile, the young knight died to know why Zeros had no fame, why he was not as celebrated as Garlew.

Just ask. A bit abruptly, X'ieth boldly brought himself to shift topics to the previous one and ask his question. "What happened?"

He saw Zeros look back at him with a straight face.

"What do you mean exactly?"

X'ieth used his hand to gesture as he talked, motioning to Zeros before him, like he were an object.

"I mean no disrespect, but you're now a mercenary with no glories following you in Sergros. Why haven't I heard praises to your name, if you're a former commander? From the sounds of it, you had comparable standing to Garlew himself!"

X'ieth watched Zeros stand silent, and study the cobblestone as if searching for words. After a truly awkward silence developed, the mercenary looked up.

"Let's walk further. The pub is around the corner."

He changed topics. Why? X'ieth did not understand.

Zeros began walking without X'ieth, and a repeat of what happened before played out. The young knight hurried over to the mercenary and together, they rounded the bend. Sure enough, the alleyway opened to the street, on which stood the pub and the inn.

Upon the walk, they stood beneath the gloomy overcast, with stars and a pale crescent moon resting upon a sliver of exposed sky. Together, the pair basked in the light for a moment, and X'ieth noted Zeros' gaze drift aloft, and to the right.

Feeling bad over asking Zeros the question, X'ieth looked down and pondered. *You shouldn't have asked.* He paused, being at a momentary loss for words. *Say something to right this wrong.*

"My apologies," said X'ieth at last, from out of nowhere, still looking at the cobblestone. "What happened to you is not for me to know." He gazed back at Zeros, who slowly answered while staring off into the sky.

"Fret not. I've taken no offense."

X'ieth watched Zeros lift a pointing hand.

"Look, up there!"

The young knight followed his finger out above the city's skyline, past the distant Forest Saol, and to the looming mountains in the distance. The lines from the massive gray rock stood out in the darkness, beneath green lights! From the closest tall summit, up the western pass, was what seemed to be Esmeralda's tower, a distant structure into which green energies flowed from the forest and mountains. Strident cracks and sounds like thunder could be heard from Saol and Liath.

And then, X'ieth heard a loud roar. *RAWWWRRR!*

Though the sights and sounds induced fear in him, of power beyond what was typical in Karnath, the spectacle itself was magnificent to watch, and X'ieth could not pry his eyes away. In that moment, the very visual confirmed his reason for being there, to stop Esmeralda. From his state of captivation, Zeros pulled at his attention.

"We should rest," he said. "For tomorrow will require much of us."

But X'ieth's gaze lingered upon the green energies, as he slowly responded, "Indeed, we should…" His words trailed off. In his mind, he kept thinking of those oil paintings he studied in academy, involving the Lights of Altoroth strewn across the night sky in the Northern Region. *This is just as breathtaking!*

Zeros walked to the pub, while X'ieth stayed mesmerized. From the pub's door, Zeros called out to him.

"Think a bit about what you'll say to Nathan. He's a little heated you took off like that without even a word."

X'ieth looked back, his attention suddenly caught. He shook his head in acknowledgement, thinking about the prospect of discussing this with Nathan. *That will likely not go well.* Being unscathed after his poor choices tonight, however, X'ieth found some peace amidst his uncertainty over how the pack leader would respond. And he derived that solace from Lucen's words. *It's not so much what you do that matters, but what's meant to be.*

Chance gained on choice in his mind, and X'ieth wondered if there was any stopping his good destiny of becoming Kayareth. With that, he turned from the night sky and like Zeros, headed into the pub.

"AS LIGHTS OF ALTOROTH"

Chapter 25
The Fallen Servant

The highest star in Karnath's skies, just as the brightest or the largest, resembles all others fallen upon making its fateful descent. Not all stars are destined for an intransient future of light. This truth could not be better told than through the life of one who came to be known among immortals as *the Fallen Servant.*

Nym, formerly a Servant of the Dark named the *Lordess of Night,* stepped through the streets of the port town *New Yoke,* the city furthest west in the province of Sergros, situated on the Mainland's west coast. Her walk was of the utmost humility, such that as she passed, the homeless either gawked at her, or glanced without even looking twice.

Despite her matted silver hair, Nym held her head high and kept her gray eyes keen, even though her outward appearance spoke of one hitting a new low. Her tattered garments were worn and she looked unkempt, beaten down by life. Though she still wore the black cloak of the Servants that framed falling stars, it endured in derelict shape more as a reminder to mock what she had become, rather than a keepsake to honor what she was.

And if anything about her could draw pity, it would be her belly. Enlarged and round, Nym clearly showed signs of being mid-term in her pregnancy. But no one showed her care, for those of New Yoke had their own concerns. Because New Yoke neighbored cities affected by the Isles Conspiracy, a number of refugees had sought asylum here. The additional people burdened the already fragile economy of this port town, and it saw shortages of supply and more crime as demand increased beyond its carrying capacity.

In fair weather, Nym continued her walk through the gray cobblestone streets, beset by rows upon rows of colorful buildings in a variety of pastels— cyan, yellow, and pink. Far ahead of her, beyond New Yoke's stores and houses, she could see the blue sea beneath the midday sun, its waters calmed by gentle breezes. As she went, a passerby sent her a scowl while begging with an open hand. Nym glanced at him, seeing it was an older man with a mangy white beard, who wore soiled clothes. She heard him cry out, "Help me! I hunger all day!"

With a feeling of helplessness, Nym continued walking. *I'm hardly able to help myself now, let alone others.* But despite her reasonable position, she heard the man's frustration over her dismissal.

"I'm talking to you!" shouted the man "Who do you think you are, to ignore me like that?!"

In that moment more than most, she felt inclined to turn about and give an honest answer. *I am the mastermind behind the Isles Conspiracy! I am the Dark force Taurus Hboshi allied with to mount the most surprising and violent strike against the Mainland in its entire history! I am the conspirator that no mortal knows about, the unsolved mystery of who conspired with whom during those coordinated, brutal attacks against Juniper! I am she!* The answers rang out in her mind, a resounding bitterness over her former life lost, her current love lost, and everything else in between. The sad truth about her unspoken response was most apparent. *I was she, and so much more...*

As Nym walked further down the streets, memories surfaced of her severe punishment for falling in love with a mortal while an immortal, and how she coped with that punishment. For a few weeks after she lost her immortality along with her Servitude, she roamed the streets of Baal in hopes of feeling better about her fate.

In so doing, she beheld all the destruction she had wrought in the months prior, hoping it would serve a reminder of her former greatness, and that it did. Her strolls stirred up memories of the spans of fire seen from those rooftops, like a thousand city lights burning to ward off the black descending upon the world with another day's death—lights that grew dull, and eventually yielded to the night. For a while, she prided herself in her memories of ruining days for people, joying in the demise of each and every day, as many as she recalled. After all, she was once the Lordess of Night, and hated the day. *But in time, all of that changed...*

As the weeks passed beyond her punishment, Nym's increased acquaintance with the fragility of her own life filled her with an ironic fear of the night—of the dangers for mortals that could emerge from its shadows.
And so, being weak now, she no longer visited Baal to feel good about herself. Given the risks, she instead contented herself with feeling how she would, over being sewn back into the weave, living among frail mortals as a mortal herself, and with a heart torn by love. *I'm so incredibly vulnerable now. So vulnerable, to so many things...*

Stepping forth, she walked out from the shadows cast by a hanging rooftop and into the light. The sun's rays bathed her fair skin and pointy ears from a blue, cloudless sky. Her nose made for a dainty tip upon her attractive face, a testament to the fact that beauty can still linger with age. Nym's lips were a natural pink, and no longer were they her only soft feature. *After years of having a hard heart, I finally know how to love... I love Kort, but can't find him...*

Slowly Nym finished her trek down the cobblestone street, went around a bend, and headed down another street toward the marketplace where New Yoke's shops were located. Her every step sounded noticeably, emphasizing her presence in a place where many slumbered in open sight. Lining this particular walk, and down its every alleyway, she saw many without a home, sleeping upon frayed blankets. A few sat upright, extending an open hand to everyone that passed, even to other beggars.

Overwhelmed with her own problems, Nym paid them no mind, as many times they paid her no mind, even when she struggled. In her daily rounds through New Yoke, she would stumble a few times on the uneven pavement, and occasionally came close to twisting an ankle. But no one would even attend a pregnant lady in distress, many being desensitized to the whole world given their own plight. And so without any reliance upon others for help, Nym stayed careful with how she stepped, her preoccupations with the treacherous cobblestone yet another adjustment to the unacquainted life of a mortal.

Just like she rounded New Yoke now, she did the same in the neighboring port town *Breslin* in the last week, and her rounds of both towns were by no means aimless. With all her energy, Nym sought the father of the child she carried, the one whom she loved deeply—Kort Al'starz. After Kort had left her one night without saying a word, she searched for him on the Mainland to no avail. *As Sergros can't even find him, what better chance do I have?!* She thought this to herself, realizing the odds against her now.

Indeed, her efforts had become particularly arduous without the superior powers that accompanied her lost immortality. In her former experience as an immortal, she had access to an information network on most people, along with the ability to quickly mediate through the Nexus. Together these means enabled her to efficiently locate mortals. *Not as easy these days.*

As she walked into the town square full of shops, her thoughts bunched to the back of her mind when a familiar New Yoke tavern came into view, *The Happy Place*, as noted by the sign hung overhead. A black slab with white lettering, the sign showed the establishment's name in Mainlandish at the top, as well as the Hirishin tongue at the bottom: *Panggonan Seneng*. The tavern was placed obviously in the center of New Yoke's depressed square, now a marketplace of unfrequented shops, filled by frowning storeowners who wondered how they would make ends meet.

Seeing the marketplace led Nym to recall how she occasioned many stores in her stay of New Yoke and also Breslin. From her memories alone, she could literally hear herself speaking with shopkeepers about those who wandered through these parts and even sojourners: *Have you seen an elf, of this appearance?* The common replies especially lingered: *No one fitting that description has been seen here, lady.*

She remembered how a few times her questions raised eyebrows among the storeowners and eavesdropping browsers. For the description she gave matched that of sketches of Kort in his 'wanted' posters; they were plastered everywhere upon the walls of buildings. *Anyone with a sharp mind would catch on, hence the need to improvise.*

Nym walked closer to the tavern and thought on, being about fifty cubits away. Fortunately, this was literally her safer alternative to asking such blatant questions—common rooms, pubs, and taverns. They not only avoided suspicions, but also, they compensated for her lost access to her information network. As far as she was concerned, any place of gathering where drinks were served was the mortal's grapevine. *I can learn more in pubs, than anywhere else!*

Now only twenty cubits away, she looked at the tavern's sign again, and in so doing, her hopes soared of finding answers that might lead to Kort. This tavern was a spot where commoners gathered and many travelers stopped to rest from their journeys, making it an important hub in New Yoke's information exchange. *And with a drink or two, even those with tighter lips might offer up a word.* A smile crossed her face with the thought.

She stopped walking, finally at the tavern's plain entrance—a windowless wall overhung by a shingled roof, having a very large door. Without a moment's delay she entered, struggling a bit with the awkwardly sized door that was clearly suited for giants.

Once past the threshold, clamorous talk fell upon her ears, and in her nose were the scents of pine, fermenting ale, and smoked bakus root. She beheld the tavern's open space, lit by wrought-iron chandeliers overhead and a window on the far wall beyond the bar, made from four panes of glass set in a lattice; it showed the side street leading up to the square. All around the room, she saw scores of benches beside long tables, filled with diverse peoples on the Mainland's coast.

As New Yoke was still in Sergros, many in the tavern were of races allied by the Triangle Kingdoms—elves, dwarves, and humans. But in addition to people of that variety, Nym noticed a few *dragon hunters* from Dragonaut Island sitting in one corner with drinks, tall giants of about six cubits in height, dressed in woodsy leather garb. While drinking ales from huge mugs, they leaned their long spears against their shoulders, with the weapons sheathed in tanned rawhide. The spears were so long, they nearly touched the roof!

Nym looked around the room again trying to find an open seat, and as she did, a few men in the corner neglected their ales and stared at her, which she readily ignored. *The men of New Yoke act like they've never seen a lady in these parts.* From spending time in this port town, she knew the trend was no different than in Breslin. *While race is diverse, gender is not. Mostly males, but me...*

Bearing that in mind, she wanted to avoid unwanted attention and get off her feet as soon as possible. So, she took the open seat that she spotted beside some dwarves. Sitting now, she cleared her mind and began listening; she spent some time to first understand the main topics of what conversations could be overheard. Just as she suspected, a good portion of time elapsed before she picked up on topics, one of which concerned the now fallen Garlew Il'therin, and who murdered the hero. *A relevant discussion...*

"The king's couriers brought news that Kort Al'starz of the Crimson Guard killed him," said one elf to a dwarf. "A traitor they say he is, one who was involved in the Isles Conspiracy!"

The dwarf spoke, "Appears far from the truth to me… A traitor who served in the Crimson Guard, beside Garlew himself?! I wonder if the king knows at all who did it!" The dwarf took a sip of ale and continued. "If the king is uncertain of who committed the crime, he'll accuse the nearest one to it! Low-hanging fruit it be."

Nym heard their exchange of opinions, knowing that Kort murdering Garlew was only a partial truth in Sergros. For it was her dagger that plunged into the hero's heart, whereas the force guiding her hands was another matter. The memory of being forced to kill Garlew was a reminder of her unconditional love for Kort, despite how he used her. *Love with conditions, is not love at all…*

She broke from her thoughts, and quieted her mind. Conversations continued about her in murmurs, and she listened in. "The king sent provisions only to cities affected by the gloom! New Yoke and Breslin haven't gotten a bit of help from Sergros, while we've got sole survivors of the Isles Conspiracy!" An angry voice said the words, clearly a disgruntled person stressed in some way by the influx of people into New Yoke, a smaller port town than Breslin.

Another talk came from the opposite corner. "Trade is down! Merchant vessels bound to *Soku* and Doj have not come back! Something seems amiss on the seas."

For a while, she listened to other discussions, but as more time elapsed, she heard nothing pertaining to Kort's sighting—only questions about the validity of accusations against the ex-knight, nostalgia for the deceased Garlew, along with grievances here and there about how Talus managed the kingdom with its depressed economy.

Nothing Nym overheard so far really helped her cause, and she began to wonder if perhaps the other tavern down the way might be a good place to go. *Not much said is even relevant to Kort, but I'm here already…* So, before rashly leaving The Happy Place, she decided to wait there a while longer, listening more.

But in that span of time, something happened that would make her rethink her decision to stay, along with anyone else in the tavern that decided the same. After about half an hour more of waiting, Nym heard the tavern's door open along with the scrape of feet, as someone clearly entered. She did not even glance back to see who was the tavern's latest visitor, but the visual was unneeded given the person's despairing cry.

"This is the end!"

It's Mance. Nym turned back, to see a hooded *doomsayer* with intense brown eyes and a matching beard. She watched the youngish man jump onto a bench and raise both hands. With that sudden motion, the long sleeves of his sackcloth robe bunched midway down his forearms.

"The gloom is coming to New Yoke!" he shouted into the crowd. "It will come, as it's already come upon Arlem and elsewhere in Sergros, even the castle!"

Instantly, the tavern grew completely quiet, with all eyes upon the doomsayer.

"When the oracles went blind three years ago, do you recall what their final vision was?! It was Shaizan, winning the Game!"

Nym turned as the tavern landlord yelled from other end of the room, near the window. "Mance, you've been told to stop coming around here!"

As if the landlord never spoke, the doomsayer Mance went on. "You all act like that forecast isn't real, like it's of no consequence to you! But in that, you're all fools! The Game is real, and Shaizan will win because we've stopped fighting for our good destinies! Don't you see, it's a test!"

Nym turned back to the doomsayer, and mid-sentence, she saw some burly men emerge from the crowd and lift him right off the bench! Wrapping their arms about Mance, they began dragging the doomsayer to the exit, who wrestled with them and shouted more along the way.

"Karnatha tests us all with the option to fight for our good destiny, before a Battle for Destiny at Gallow Cliff!, So we need to fight for our good destinies now, in the time that we have, else that battle will come and all will be lost!"

Just as Mance said those words, the men carried him through the large door. In their clutches, he wriggled for freedom of body and speech, trying to implore the tavern's customers, but to no avail. The tavern's door slammed shut after the men threw Mance into the street, and the scene returned to Nym, who was perhaps the most afflicted by the doomsayer's words.

Talk of the Game threw her mind into a downward spiral, which now circled with her memories of all the tangential events that led to the deterioration of her future, which she regarded as her own Fate's Fray. Images flashed before her eyes, of her prior service to Ma'althan as an immortal, where she raised Kort from the dead for a special Dark mission, but ended up falling in love with him. Love brought her too close to a powerful mortal like Kort, where she ended up getting used and hurt. *Kort used you to kill Garlew, and in that, you violated rules of interference on the mortal plane. For that you were punished.* That at least, was Nym's understanding of her infraction from Ma'althan, which she revisited now with a tear in her eye.

Being strong, she held it back. *I'll not cry over choosing love and dealing with the consequences.* With that thought, and a realization that staying longer in The Happy Place might not make her any happier, Nym got up with intentions of visiting the next tavern in New Yoke. And so, out the door she went, the wood closing behind her with a loud bang.

Once more, she stepped carefully onto the uneven cobblestone, and started to walk back the way she came, down the way lined with the sleeping homeless. The sight of many living on the streets raised her awareness that Sergrothian welfare had only reached those cities overhung by the gloom, just like the commoners mentioned in the tavern. But she realized the problem in New Yoke was a widespread problem throughout Karnath, one that could never be solved by welfare. *Some are truly without opportunities*, she thought, *in a kingdom that can solve problems for only a few… But many are without a want to do more than be. The reality of people just existing has become a sad norm in Sergros, and that's unsustainable for any kingdom!*

As she continued a bit further down the path, her steps were suddenly accompanied by steps other than hers, ringing out noticeably against the cobblestone. Nym turned at once, seeing then those men who initially looked upon her in the tavern with lusting eyes, now following her from behind! *Get out of view!*

Having some mobility challenges, it took Nym a short while to duck into the nearest alleyway, which bent around a nearby building. She took to the alley, hoping to be removed from sight and to dissuade the men from following her more.

However, the distant footsteps of those men hastened once she disappeared into the alley. *Hide!* On the backstreets, she quickly stooped behind a large wooden barrel, big enough to occlude her small body to any passerby. Shortly after her concealment, their steps slowed and their voices rang out into the open air.

"Where did she go?" asked one man.

Another said, "She was just here!"

"Perhaps she turned into the next way. Check it."

After a pause, another voice was heard.

"Aye. Let's go and see."

Agreement was reached among the men, and their footsteps against cobblestone rose again, growing a bit distant. *Move, now!* Nym realized her opportunity to escape was at hand, and so, she did not hesitate to act.

Nym began walking down the alley with soft steps, careful not to make any noise. But her shoe suddenly snagged an uneven spot on the bumpy street, and she fell toward the cobblestone! For fear of her child's safety, she reflexively screamed at the thought of hitting it hard.

"Oh Destiny!"

Just barely, she caught the side of the nearby building, which prevented her from falling. But Nym soon found that with her audible cry, those searching for her suddenly learned of her location.

"I heard her!" one said, instantly.

"Over here!" shouted another man.

Their footfall sounded as they hurried toward her.

Nym attempted to leave the alley from whence she entered, but abruptly the quick footsteps stopped as the three men came up behind her, from the alley.

"Pretty lady," said the one man.

Slowly, she turned to the side, seeing two middle-aged men past the oversized barrel, along with a younger fellow. The first man had a face and head of blond hair. The second man had brown locks and a scraggly beard. His youthful companion was stubbly, with black hair. All the men wore simple breeches of natural hues without stockings and short-sleeved tunics, clothes suited for common folk in these parts.

With their presence, Nym picked up the pungent scent of ale. *They all reek of it.* The thought crossed her mind, and she realized that clearly these men had been heavily drinking and might not be the most reasonable. She watched the two older fellows grin, though the younger companion looked a bit unsure about this encounter, appearing anxious with constant fidgeting and frequent looks to the side street.

As the closest man stared at Nym's belly, he asked, "Where's your husband? A beautiful elf like you doesn't get *that way* by herself."

He laughed heartily as did his companion, clearly both of them being entertained with that remark.

Nym answered honestly, not particularly in the mood to bluff about having a husband nearby.

"I have no husband."

The men laughed more amongst themselves, their noisy guffaws filling the narrow walk.

"So," said the one, "you're *that* kind of lady."

Again, they burst into obnoxious drunken laughter.

"Ha ha haw! Ha ha haw!"

"How much coin do I need to get some decent company with the lady?" the one man asked, flashing a crooked smile.

Nym replied carefully, trying not to incite them. "No amount of coin can buy you my favors. I'm not *that* type of lady." Her words were crisp, striking a contrast with the gentle winds gracing them all.

"Not that type of lady?!" one man said, surprised.

"I bet she's the kind of lady we think," said the friend, with a chuckle.

She stared at the drunken men with a bit of disbelief. *Some men just won't take 'no' for an answer, will they?* When Nym saw how their eyes widened with desire, she loathed it.

The young man suddenly interjected from the back.

"Friends, let's go. She's not *our* type of miss. We best look elsewhere!"

She focused on the man at the young lad's left, who raised a deflecting hand. "No no, we ought to see what kind of lady she be!"

The man beside him laughed again.

"Yeah, me thinks so!"

Once more, the two older men flashed grins and laughed amongst themselves. Nym watched the one man on her right step closer, and undo his belt buckle; she was completely repulsed. *No better than animals…*

"Grab her!" he shouted.

His friend rushed forward, right toward Nym.

"IN SEARCH OF REDEMPTION"

Chapter 26
Destiny's Scapegoat

She stood there appalled, watching the two men of New Yoke in disbelief. The one remained as he was, with a crooked grin and undone belt, while his friend approached, having both hands up and ready to grab Nym.

"We'll have our way with her," one man said.

"Aye, to see what kind of lady she be!"

Behind them, Nym sensed a sudden motion, when the younger man in this party of three threw up his hands and protested.

"Stop it! She's with child, for Destiny's sake!"

Despite that plea, Nym watched as the two older men advanced, paying their younger friend no heed. She focused upon the closest man, the one with arms raised, hands open, and his fingers out, in hopes of seizing her. *Not while I'm still alive…*

She was next to the barrel and literally up against the wall, but by no means out of options. Nym had always been one with something up her sleeve, and this situation was no different. And so from her sleeves and into each palm dropped three throwing knives, the blades dipped in necrotic poison.

In one fluent motion, she spun gracefully upon her heel and whipped her right arm, sending three blades twirling through the air. She completed her spin by whipping her left arm, releasing another three blades. At Nym's rear, her black cape flowed animatedly, as if taking on a life of its own.

Thunk thunk thunk!

She watched the first three blades strike the man with the unbuckled belt—the first to the groin, the second and third severing his rotator cuff tendons on each shoulder. Nym kept a plain face, even as the man screamed like a young child and fell to the ground, hardly able to move his arms. A pool of blood formed around his body as he flailed there, completely helpless.

The second trio of blades had almost the same effect. Her eyes followed one blade, which flew into the man's groin. Likewise, she saw the second blade twist right into her target, hitting the man's shoulder with a red spurt! But the third blade missed its mark, sinking into the teal siding of an adjacent house; its poisoned tip bit the wood with a dull smack.

Her ears filled with the man's pained screams, the very moment those blades pierced his flesh. She watched him slowly look down while crying aloud, as if not believing his injuries were real. He reached to pull the blade from his groin, cursing the whole time. *Don't do it.*

236

"Destiny damn you to the Void!" he shouted.

With a groan he ripped out the knife, and Nym watched blood pour profusely from his unplugged wound. It was then that she knew the man was bent on retaliation, perhaps valuing that more than his own life.

When she saw him raise the throwing knife and retract his arm, Nym instantly went to her enlarged channeling chamber. There, she pulled open her Source entry, through which streams of green energy flowed. Back in New Yoke, her midsection sparked with green light, as she prepared her counter.

"You wench!" cried the man, his hand moving forward with the knife between his fingers.

Using Nexus, Nym formed an energy bar at the level of his knees and knocked him off-balance, right before he could hurl the knife! He fell toward the cobblestone, but before his body hit, she shifted the Nexus field by extending her open hand, pulling her fingertips together, and lowering her arm—all in one motion. In so doing, she wrapped the Nexus field around the man's feet, pulled him high into the air with his head dangling and eyes widened by fear, before tossing him into the large barrel! With his head now inside, he tried hard to get out, wildly flailing his legs.

"Burn you, wench!" he sobbed, in a shrill voice.

With his continued struggle, the barrel suddenly toppled over, and rolled on the street with the man screaming within! In the background, the first man continued wailing from a puddle of his own blood, both of them now suffering a huge loss of dignity as grown men—first for what they attempted to do, and now, with their injuries.

From her peripheral vision, she detected the young man bolt toward the side street, once the barrel fell over. *Oh, you've had enough after just watching? Your departure won't be that easy.*

With all that had happened, the young man knew now, that his friends picked the wrong lady with whom to trifle. And he picked the wrong lady to leave to the devices of his poor-intentioned friends. So, as the young man ran down the alley for the side street—with his hands up and arms moving naturally—Nym dropped another knife into her palm and then hurled it right at him!

She watched him look back, just in time to perceive her blade go right between his two fingers! Its edge grazed their webbing and drew a trickle of blood. His eyes widened and his mouth gawked.

"Halt, right there!" she screamed, as the knife smacked into a building, behind her words. With that alone, the man stopped running and stood still, like a statue. *You likely realize you're as good as dead with another step forward, given my skill!*

"Face me!" she demanded in a loud voice.

She watched the young man turn, clearly afraid for his life. Meanwhile, his companions continued wriggling and groaning from the cobblestone, covered in blood.

"I… I'm sorry!" stammered the young man.

"Silence!" Nym hushed him with a harsh voice.

At her command, the alley grew so quiet that even a feather's touch against the cobblestone could be heard. She noted the man's throat, as he swallowed hard, preparing himself for whatever she had to say. *Good. You need to hear this.*

"By not intervening and just staring," she said, "you're nearly as bad as them! I should do you the same harm." Another throwing blade showed visibly in Nym's palm, and when her carpal bones flinched ever so slightly, she saw the man soil himself. A noticeable stain formed at the front of his trousers, as he crossed his legs and quivered. *Thoughts of my knife hurled into your loins have that effect, no?*

"If you ever find yourself in the presence of foul company again and such misdeeds are attempted, only let it happen over your broken body!" The young man began shaking as she stepped closer to him, to intimidate him.

"Do you promise?!" she shouted.

He nodded his head. "Yes, yes… I will!"

Looking down at the struggling middle-aged men, these pathetic two of poor intentions, she said, "Both you and your friends are poisoned. I suggest going to New Yoke's healer within the hour, if you care for your lives."

Now a bright crimson, the young man turned to run.

"Halt!" yelled Nym. She watched him slowly face her again. "Help your friends get to the healer also, for death affords them no second chances. There can't be learning and changed behavior without second chances. While the common illness inflicting your bodies can be healed at a hospice, you are much more fortunate than they. For even now, the gravest ills these men suffer are of the mind, which might not be as easily cured as ills of the body, such as your poisoning. Remember that."

A few seconds passed, and Nym thought it strange how all of a sudden, the young man became completely inanimate! He did not fidget nervously; his lip no longer trembled. She looked about, and observed how the two fallen men suddenly stopped squirming as well. The whole scene appeared frozen in place!

Nym became extremely cautious, and immediately went to her enlarged channeling chamber, where she pulled open her Source entry, only to find no streams of Nexus! She watched the door's threshold, expecting streams of energy to enter at any moment, but instead, a dark sludgy fluid came forth, sluggishly creeping into the chamber. Instantly she snapped back to the streets of New Yoke, a look of concern now upon her face. *The Servants!*

The sludge in her channeling chamber altered the Nexus field via a spell, which sure enough, was cast over most of New Yoke, suspending people in place! Nym observed the two men, frozen in place on the ground, just as the young man who was frozen upon both feet. And soon after she realized what was happening, the clap of hands sounded at her rear along with footsteps, as several people walked into the cobblestone alley.

"Good show!" rang out a familiar female voice.

Urzel! Nym spun about, to see a white cloak flowing behind her former rival: Urzel—the Lordess of Day. Beyond Urzel, she saw Sydullus approaching, with Ma'althan and Autheos also. When arriving to Nym's spot, everyone fell still and silent, the Forerunners standing side by side on her right, with the Servants standing likewise on her left. Urzel was first to break the silence.

"Now it's a rare occasion when a mortal impresses an immortal, but somehow you've done it!" she said, her blue eyes not sparing Nym's from an intense engagement.

"What do you want?" Nym said, short on patience.

Apparently ignoring her, Urzel just continued.

"Oh that's right. You were once immortal. With that in mind, your feats aren't that impressive after all."

Nym watched Urzel smile. *Your rivalry with me doesn't end even with my Servitude? Unbelievable.* Nym was used to similar antics from her pastimes as an immortal; Urzel loved to pick fights.

"Ah, that reminds me of the reason backing our purposeful visit. Your mortality, and *further punishments*."

Sudden concern wrinkled Nym's face. *Further punishment?! What?!*

"Oh, did you forget? Your immortality and related powers were both stripped because you resurrected Kort, after his little accident during the Crimson Guard's campaign to hunt for Pyrus." As if with clear pleasure to rehash the painful situation for Nym, she went on. "You know, after the Isles Conspiracy erupted and Taurus Hboshi's forces ambushed the knights…"

Nym cut her off. "Enough, Urzel! I know the reasons. You're wasting your breath…"

She saw Urzel flash a wider grin before continuing, even after that interruption. "Once resurrected, Kort embarked for the City of Baal in vengeful pursuit of Garlew Il'therin, whom he believed was really Taurus Hboshi! Garlew's eventual death is therefore, *on you*!"

"You've had your word, Urzel," chided Ma'althan.

Immediately, Urzel fell silent, her face showing ostensible disdain for the reprimand. Nym looked over at Ma'althan, who sounded stern and showed a clear look of disapproval. The very next moment, he met eyes with Nym and began speaking.

"At the time of your original punishment, we knew Kort wasn't to go to Baal and had he not gone, we know that Garlew would still be alive. This was your perceived interference on the mortal plane."

"At that time, however, Karnatha had not revealed to us who would be the Children. It turns out that Garlew was more than just a mortal. He was a special Child of Destiny, fated to become the One of Prophecy!"

Nym's jaw dropped, and her mind surged with thoughts. *I fell in love with a mortal and caused another mortal's death, that's all! I simply chose to be with Kort, and was punished for resurrecting him upon his death, nothing more!* Her mind resonated with denial, as to her, what the Forerunners insinuated became obvious. *I didn't change the Game! I couldn't have…*

Under the combined glare of Ma'althan and Autheos, she felt her heart beat quicker. The blood pulsed over her temple in deep throbs, and her chest tightened. Ma'althan's eyes seemed to especially drill into her, as if examining the very contents of her body, mind, and soul.

"Your willful deed did much more than merely interfere on the mortal plane," Ma'althan said from Nym's right. "You changed how the Game was destined to unfold by changing the Child! Kort was a receiver…"

Autheos added, "Yes, with Garlew's death this burden fell on Kort, through a spiritual endowment." He paused before contextualizing Nym's offense. "As a Servant, you were entrusted to only aid the Game for your own hue, and leave its play to its players—the Children of Destiny. You betrayed this base trust of Servitude."

Once again, silence dominated the alley in unanimated New Yoke. Nym began to feel uncomfortable, as the sun's heat radiated from a flaming medallion above, hung upon the pure sky, widespread overtop the port town like a never-ending sheet of blue.

"These are least of your problems," Ma'althan suddenly snapped with fiery eyes. "Because of your wrongdoing, Karnatha suspects you're the one behind bigger changes to the Game, threatening changes that none of us understand!"

Her chest tightened more.

"What?!" Nym blurted out finally, her eyes wide.

So many questions entered her head just then, but when she opened her mouth, none of them could even escape. Her tongue shackled by fear, she found herself completely lost for words. And in that single moment, Nym realized exactly what had happened. *I'm not just being blamed for changing the Game, but making matters even worse, they're blaming me for somehow re-mastering it!*

Nym's mind was overwhelmed then with her recollection of experiences not understood, like premonitions that would contradict her eventual reality, and separate memories of events in her own life with different outcomes. In particular, she recalled the Game being played by differing players in differing ages, and those memories reeked of something being terribly wrong. *Am I being blamed for that, or something more?!*

"Karnatha is dying, and so are we," Autheos said, "Destiny is dying." The words came suddenly, and interrupted her thoughts, mixing shock now into her elixir of fear. *Can that even be?* she wondered.

"That's how we know the Game has changed," Ma'althan added. "Also, it's clearly being played in the wrong age. Karnatha now has the same visions as the oracles' last, that Shaizan fairly wins the Game for Darkness, sometime in the future and not now."

"How am I involved in anything beyond loving a mortal?" Nym asked innocently.

Urzel snickered in the background.

"A fool's choice, to trade immortality for love!" she said. "Hope you're happy with that poor decision." A smile upturned the corners of Urzel's lips. Sydullus echoed her laugh, as if sharing the same sentiment.

Nym shot back her response, "Mortality and true love trumps a loveless immortality, any day of any millennium! I am happy with my choice, are you with yours?! After all, Servitude is free of freedom."

"Silence!" stated Ma'althan firmly, passing an admonishing glare about. She saw his gaze return to her, and when it did, the Forerunner shook his head. "Your professed love for Kort unfortunately has led to Garlew's death, and transferred the correct lineage for one hue to the Gray Lineage. Karnatha suspects that you're attempting to rewrite history so that Shaizan no longer wins the Game."

"That's preposterous!" exclaimed Nym. "I am powerless, and doomed to die! Now a mortal, I'm sewn back into the weaves, with no ability to change the Game pursuant to my punishment! Suspicions that I could alter time are equally ridiculous!" Her mouth worked faster than her mind. *This is so unfair!* she thought to herself, full of resentment.

Ma'althan barked at her, "Think what you will, mortal! Destiny senses a huge disturbance in the Game's balance, and now acts to reconcile it over you."

"Wicken the Wicked steps aside, removing the gatekeeper from Liath," Autheos added, "and the Servants of the Light now turn to the Dark, to compensate the advantages you created for the Light with the Gray Child."

"No!" Nym cried out, her face stretched by panic. "This isn't needed! I've done nothing wrong!" No longer collected, she felt her own fear gnawing at her composure. Her body trembled; her voice cracked. She glanced at Urzel, who displayed a look of satisfaction.

"Destiny considers that I may have put you up to this," Autheos noted. Nym's gaze zoomed his way. To her, the deductions reached by Karnatha and the Forerunners seemed more bizarre by the word.

"This very conjecture I resent," he continued, "for I've never needed your help in the Game!" Autheos spoke harshly, and to Nym, anger was clear from his tone.

"I would never…" Nym's voice trailed off.

"Enough of your denial!" Autheos yelled. "It matters not to Destiny or to me."

Ma'althan spoke, "Indeed your judgments matter little, mortal. Destiny will decide your fate, and what further punishment is due!"

Nym's mind raced, her heart beat wildly, and her lungs had trouble breathing. "Is it not enough," she asked, "that my immortality is removed, and I'm now a lovesick mortal, destitute and companionless?"

Her eyes showed of desperation, as she wailed in an aside. "More punishment than this, I could never endure! For it would keep me from Kort, and that separation would be the strongest fetter about my heart, a soul-crushing chain to squeeze out the little life that's left in me!"

"Karnatha will decide what is just consequence," said Autheos, his words cold as ice. "You are to wait in New Yoke, until Destiny understands more about the changes to the Game and whether these reconciliations make it fair again for the Light and Darkness. Only then, can your fate be determined."

"Should you attempt to use knowledge from your prior immortality to create added unfairness in the Game, your infraction will be dealt with! Love is no excuse for your interference, mortal. Remember that." With those words Ma'althan snapped his fingers, and the Forerunners and the Servants left New Yoke in an instant, vanishing into the air.

Nym was temporarily removed from the developing, sticky situation. With enough time, her heartbeats and breaths slowed gradually, and her body became less tense.

In their regained animation, she watched the three men struggle to the hospice of New Yoke. All the while, thoughts buzzed through her mind about what to do. *Stay. Leave! Stay!*

Though fear crippled her just now, it was awfully tempting to simply disobey the Forerunners by departing New Yoke to continue searching for Kort elsewhere. For in the face of more punishment, locating the one she loved remained Nym's top priority, and in the end, she cared little about the risks.

"MEN OF POOR INTENTIONS"

<h1 style="text-align:center">Chapter 27
Saving the Threat</h1>

The suspension bridge on which Kort and Sagult fought came apart as Kort's Nexus fires devoured the bridge's center. Kort had planned for this to separate him from his pursuer, putting Sagult on one side of the gorge, and himself on the other. He was mistaken.

Kort watched with surprise, as Sagult swung on the support rail below him, to his same side of the bridge, right before it split! Kort and Sagult held onto the bridge tightly as it sped toward the ravine wall, bound for an imminent collision with hard rock.

CRASH!

With a loud noise, the bridge swung into the cliff face. Kort felt the deep impact through his upper body, which literally threw him about on the rope, as he hung on for his life. The impact was so hard that Sagult yelped and planks fell off the bridge, clattering noisily down the rock, until splashing in the white rapids below.

Over roaring waters in the gorge, Kort and Sagult hung by the burnt remains of the rope bridge that once stretched across. Holding onto the rope rail in both hands, Kort looked down into the gorge. And for not the first time today, he became lost in his own fears.

For Kort, the sight momentarily immobilized him, for it conjured up the memory of his deathly fall some months ago. *Stop looking down!* he told himself, realizing that the only way out of this situation, was up.

Kort gripped the rope tighter, as he still swayed over the ravine after the bridge's sudden destruction by fire. When the swaying ceased his dangling legs bumped into the rocky wall, bringing him right up against its face. Loose parts broke off and clattered down, all the way to the cliff's foot. Just watching them fall was enough to play on his fears again, fears he tried hard to suppress.

Destiny, please not again! But when Kort looked to the gorge's bottom this time, he saw more than his own fears, for his pursuer Sagult was below, hanging from a piece of fraying rope. Amid his struggle, Sagult looked up to shout. "You cannot escape justice, Kort! You must face your due punishment!"

Kort glanced away from Sagult and toward the cliff's top, to the support post there, from which the rope was pulled taut by their combined weight.

"You'll face due punishment!" said Sagult, again.

Kort turned back to watch his pursuer struggle more, still slipping from the fraying rope. He saw Sagult extend a hand to the cliff face, as if trying to share his weight with the rock. But suddenly, the rope Sagult held in his other hand frayed completely, and he quickly latched onto the cliff with both hands! Disbelieving what he saw, Kort witnessed Sagult begin scaling the sheer wall, like there were no risk of falling to his death.

"Whether you hang around there or climb up, know that I'll bring you to justice, if it's the last thing Destiny allows me to do!"

Kort felt compelled to speak, in the face of Sagult's righteous pursuit of him. Yet a voice in his head was fiercely dissuasive. *Just go up! Talk in the wrong forum helps nothing, so climb already!* With that, Kort kept silent and reached one hand over the other, to move a bit higher up the rope and toward the cliff's ledge above.

"I'll see to it that you face your dues!"

More of Sagult's words came from below, each one of them strained, as was the knight's continued climb up the rock. Kort ignored his pursuer and pulled himself up another arm's length, while keeping the support post in view. He realized how much was literally at stake with that wooden stake! Indeed, the support post driven deep within the soil once supported the rope bridge, and now supported life. *My life, as well as Sagult's!* He prayed to Destiny that it would hold.

Kort continued using his strong arms to pull himself up more. He climbed and climbed until reaching where the rope tied to the support post, and it was then, that the cliff's ledge stared him right in his face. In one motion, he threw his elbows over the ledge and let go of the rope, placing both hands on the cliff top. And then, pushing his shoulders above the ledge, he swung his right leg up and pulled his left over, getting onto the ledge. He crawled to safety, away from the precipice.

Tired from the climb, Kort rolled over onto his back, and gazed up into the sky. For a few moments, he caught his breath and listened to Sagult continue making slow but steady progress up the wall. Eventually, he rested enough to move back to the precipice, where he peered down at his pursuer. Sagult clutched the rock with bloody hands, with the rope dangling beside him, now out of reach. Kort contemplated the obvious. *I could just pull it up.* His conscience urged him to do differently. *Don't. Help others.*

"Don't be a fool, Sagult!" Kort shouted. "Grab the rope, and I'll help you." Kort watched his pursuer stubbornly grasp the rock a bit higher, clearly challenged by the climb.

"How do I know you'll not cut it?!" Sagult asked, with a zest for life clear from his sharp amber eyes.

"You can't know, but you can have faith!"

Kort saw Sagult struggle on, and the rock broke suddenly underneath his one hand! Sagult quickly latched onto the nearby cliff.

Kort immediately acted on his faith that Sagult would do the sensible thing. He took hold of the rope attached to the support post, and swung it closer to Sagult. Sagult looked at it with a full turn of the head, no doubt noting the rope's proximity.

"Grab on, Sagult! Don't risk your life this way, in the pursuit of mine!" Kort continued looking down at his pursuer, who grew silent, as if considering the matter. *What's there to think about?! Take hold before you fall!* To Kort, the matter could not be any simpler.

When Sagult finally reached out his one hand and grabbed the rope, a smile crossed Kort's face. He saw Sagult move the other hand from off the cliff, and place it also upon the rope.

"Pull yourself up one arm at a time, and I'll meet you half way!"

Kort watched Sagult, who as instructed, pulled himself up just one arm's length. In the moment that Sagult hung there before climbing with the opposite arm, Kort pulled the rope to bring his pursuer yet higher, looping its slack around the support post. In rhythm, Kort and Sagult worked together, carrying out a few repetitions of the process. Before long, Kort pulled his pursuer up to the cliff ledge and helped him climb atop.

Kort saw Sagult crawl a safe distance from the precipice, where he plopped on the rock, panting with the expense of energy it cost to climb. Likewise, the ex-knight panted from the hard work of helping his pursuer. As he rested, he rethought his decision about saving the threat. *Helping Sagult might not help my interests, but in the end, it was the right thing to do.*

Between breaths Sagult asked, "I don't understand. You could've pulled up the rope… before I grabbed it. But you chose not to… You could've cut the rope when I grabbed it… Yet you didn't… You had the upper hand... But you act like that meant nothing to you."

After a cycle of inhaling and exhaling, one following the other, Kort replied, "I don't want you to die… Or any other, who does good in Karnath…" Kort watched Sagult simply nod, a gesture that led into a developing quiet between them, in which the two caught their breath under the midday sun. It glared down heatedly upon their shoulders.

"You can rest assured that more glory awaits you in Sergros," said Kort eventually, breaking the silence. "For after finishing my course, I shall turn myself over to your hands. Your militants can bring me back to stand before the courts of Sergros. No fears have I to face prison, death, or both for what I've mistakenly done."

"Why not now?" Sagult asked, staring off into the ravine and giving Kort enough space in their conversation for a thoughtful response. But instead of giving an audible answer, Kort suddenly knocked Sagult over the head and caught his limp body, guiding it gently to the rock!

"Because," Kort answered his now unconscious pursuer, "I still must redeem myself for this life I've led."

Kort stood upon both feet, and looked to the distant sky with upheld hands, exclaiming then in an aside, "How can others live after misdeeds, without a sorely troubled conscience? Having this burden upon my soul as I rot in the castle prison or hang from the scaffolds of Sergros would be punishment I cannot bear!"

In his eyes appeared the distant rope bridge, which ran adjacent to the one destroyed. Upon seeing it, the recollection of his promise to Genze immediately came to mind. *Fine, I'll go back for your things.*

He looked back at Sagult's body, sprawled out upon the rock. It occurred to him then that with his pursuer disabled, he likely bought himself enough time to return to Reiju—across that rickety bridge, back through the stalky Tai Forest, and to the village center. But a second thought crept into his mind, one about the other militants with Sagult still looking for him. *They might go back and ransack Genze's house, going through everything there!*

At that, a massive tide of uneasiness washed over Kort. It brought to mind far-reaching matters of concern, from Genze's well being to his possessions being intact. An image of a silver amulet appeared in his head, the one Nym gave him that he had left at Genze's for safekeeping. *Destiny, I hope it's still there!*

The prospect seized him, and laid question to what he would do. *Should I return to Genze's immediately, or risk going to the market first?* Kort stopped himself, and thought carefully about how to proceed. In little time, he figured that either way, he would ultimately go to the fisherman's house, so he should go to the market first. *If the house got ransacked it already happened by now. And I made a promise to Genze, a promise to keep. We'll end things on good terms if I get his things, as I'll have honored my words by doing what I said I would.*

Having a clear plan of going back to Reiju, Kort began running to the next suspension bridge. It took several minutes to reach it, being a span or two away. And when Kort stopped before the bridge, a certain dread overwhelmed him at the thought of crossing, given all that had happened with Sagult. *I'd gladly face two-dozen armed men rather than face such a treacherous thing strung across a gorge, big or small!*

He studied the planks of the rope bridge as far as his eyes could see. Many appeared coarsened and cracked, the wood rotten perhaps. In the far distance, he had trouble seeing the planks at all. *Are they even there?* He wondered.

Taking a deep breath, Kort stepped forward to confront his fears and slowly, he began to make his way across the bridge. *Take one step at a time, and don't think beyond that!* He traced the rope rails with both hands, carefully placing his feet upon the boards, stepping on each one with some hesitation.

Don't look down, Kort told himself the whole time, never far from his morbid fear of falling into gorges.

Crack! Crack!

When about halfway across the bridge, Kort suddenly felt one rotten plank split right beneath his foot! His left foot remained on the plank before the one now gone, while his right leg dangled over the gorge. In that moment, a fluttery sensation filled his gut and his breathing tensed, as he gripped the rails tighter in white-knuckled fists. His eyes were stuck on the splintered wood that fell deeper and deeper into the ravine, until hitting its bottom with a faint splash. In his ears, the sounds of rushing water stayed, yet another reminder of danger below. Kort slowly exhaled in an attempt to calm himself. Through his mind went positive words. *Center your mind, and keeping going.*

At that, Kort pulled his right leg up and put a foot on the next plank, now having legs spread wide over a hole to sure death. He moved his left foot to the same plank where he positioned his right, and the board moaned under his weight. *Keep going!* Kort did just that, stepping to the next plank without further delay. The unsteady bridge drifted from one side to the other as he moved, its sways lending the same to his confidence.

Kort swallowed hard in the middle of what was becoming a terrifying experience. He kept a constant grip on the rope rails, his knuckles whiter now. A look to the shabby planks before him stirred up a prayer. *Destiny, please let them be sturdy enough for me!* With faith, he stepped over a few more planks, until another one broke just as before, this time from under his left foot! His leg dangled again, and flutters filled his gut. Slowly, he pulled his foot out, putting it onto the same plank with his right. But doing so concentrated his entire weight on one plank being in a very weak state, and suddenly, it broke as well!

Crack! Crack!

At the very moment of breakage, the cracks cued Kort's keen ears as to what was happening. With speed and the utmost care, he stepped quickly upon the next plank and the one after it, moving his hands along the rope rail. But as he stepped, each plank was so weathered that it broke upon contact! Kort was barely able to move fast enough at each snap, impeded now by his very grip on the rope rails.

With how the planks kept breaking, he knew he had to let go of the rope rails and literally jump from one rotten plank to the next, in order to make it across. While the feat on its own seemed daunting, the bridge's consecutive planks kept snapping beneath Kort's feet, and now, there was no turning back. *Daunting or not, I must leap forward!*

His instincts told him he would need magic, so Kort closed his eyes and found himself in his enlarged channeling chamber. He ran to the double doors and pulled them open. When they parted, he saw streams of green Nexus flow into the room, filling it from floor to ceiling. Back on the bridge, he sensed everything through the Nexus field: how his weight translated to the balance of forces distributed over each rope and plank. He estimated then, how the bridge would sway with his jumps.

Kort opened his eyes, prepared to make a daring advance on the bridge to the cliff before him. Using his strong legs, he made three jumps in quick succession; springing from his two feet upon one plank to jump over a few planks beyond it, to land on a new plank for a moment before repeating the same immediately. In order to straighten out the swaying bridge, he jumped over a series of planks to the left, and then to the right, followed by a jump to the left again. The planks beneath him broke right as he sprung off, after each and every jump. Though the sensation of his short-lived foothold alarmed him, he pressed himself to keep his mind on what was at hand. *Focus, Kort! Just keep jumping...*

He leaped with a right skew once more, coming closer to the ledge on the gorge's opposite side. As Kort jumped though, he noticed that several of the bridge's furthest planks were completely missing, others already broken. *That's a problem!*

As he jumped again to the left, to land on another plank, his mind raced as to what he should do. *I can't jump the full distance without at least one missing plank...* The plank beneath him broke then, emptying his mind, and launching him into his next jump, just as the wood fell apart. Midair, Kort looked up ahead, and could see maybe ten more planks before the gaping hole between the last plank and the ledge.

Kort landed from his jump over four planks onto a fifth one. A moan in his ear foretold of the imminent crack. *It's going to break.* In that moment, he realized that only five planks separated him now from the last wooden plank and the gaping hole between it and the cliff's ledge. *What will you do?!* Kort became anxious, and his mind worked.

Fortunately for him, he had a sudden idea. Images flashed through his head then of running on the remaining planks to the edge, leaping through the air to a magical plank wrought of Nexus, and springing off this created plank to the ledge.

Initially, it seemed like a daring plan that could mean his demise. But he had no better idea than that, and upon understanding this, he summoned up his courage for the feat. *No fear. Just do it!*

With that in mind, he ran on the remaining planks instead of jumping over them, to build up significant speed by the time he got to the opening. While running over one plank after the other, his feet touched down for only a moment prior to their breakage. He moved so fast that in the corners of his eyes, the rope rails constricted into threads! Kort rushed toward the gaping hole, and what at the plank before the last, he used the Nexus in his aux core to create a plank of raw energy, right in the middle of the opening up ahead. *Here goes...*

When confronting the last plank before the large hole, Kort clamped his jaws, biting into his own fear, as his peripheral vision picked up pieces of the gorge below. *It can't end like this. Not here! Not now!* he reminded himself, and from that, derived the same determination.

With that thought, he leaped off the last plank, just as it broke. Kort sailed through the air and over the hole, with both arms extended at his front. He kept his eyes on the energy plank before him, touching down his hands when he came close enough, and throwing his legs over his head, all in one motion. In but a moment, Kort flipped off the energy plank and over the remaining portion of the abyss, his body balled and spinning in a somersault!

While spinning, he tried to judge the distance to the ledge, but upon getting nearer he realized that continuing the somersault would be his last feat of acrobatics, should he twirl once more! *The ledge is closer than I thought!*

Kort opened from his somersault just in time, clinging the top of the ledge, as his body slammed hard into the cliff face. He felt the rock impact his upper body, sending a jolt of pain through his extremities. He growled, tired by what seemed a constant struggle to do great good after being so evil.

Using his arms, Kort pulled himself up. He threw his elbows over the ledge, pushed himself up using both shoulders, and then swung his right leg up, followed by his left. When upon the ledge, he crawled from the precipice. *Thank Destiny!* he prayed, grateful to Karnatha for being alive. In that moment, Kort eyed the gorge from his spot of safety, never wanting to see another one ever again, or a rope bridge for that matter!

While he caught his breath, Kort checked all around to see if Sagult somehow followed him, or the other militants. Upon seeing no one in the distance, he chuckled to himself. *Now I'm just being paranoid!* Two rope bridges falling apart would surely set back his pursuers. Kort grew aware that he bought himself even more time now. *But at what a price!*

His eyes drifted from the opposite cliff to the dilapidated bridge again, and he looked away quickly, in almost a reflex. "Ughh!" he muttered audibly in disgust, as all the images associated with his struggle entered his mind. *For sure, that'll create a new breed of nightmares!*

After a short rest, Kort used both hands to get up on his feet. He turned away from the gorge and to the forest, its stalky inners and green foliage now before him. He lifted his foot to take a step forward, but when a particular sound hit his ears, the ex-knight stopped in his tracks.

"It won't stop him, but Sagult might," said a man.

"Precisely," replied a woman, "so this delay can only be good, for his escape on the waters."

Kort slowly spun from the forest, and beheld two figures standing in the distance upon the cliff, two figures that he certainly did not expect to see. With disbelief, he rubbed his eyes and looked twice. Sure enough, this was not an illusion from the sweltering heat. Talking together, the man and woman of opposing hue stood before him—the same pair that appeared in Reiju's market!

The man's black cape struck him as most noticeable, with those white falling stars upon its field of black. *He's the one from Baal!* Images of the man standing upon the burning rooftops with crossed arms appeared in his mind. He blinked and shook his head, not surrendering to the flashback.

Kort watched the man for a while, and his gaze wandered to whom the man spoke, the woman in white. *They're talking… about me? Just what's going on here?!* The situation perplexed him, and Kort desperately sought answers about what he was amidst.

He stepped toward them, still holding a deep belief that the woman in white could explain the mystery, of how Taurus knew about his assassination attempt before it happened. Being only about ten cubits away, he continued walking closer to the pair, who kept talking as if oblivious to his approach. All of a sudden, the woman looked away from the man in black and directly at Kort, her blue eyes piercing him like daggers! Kort stopped his advance. He looked back, searching for words to say.

"Powerful one," said Kort finally, "please do tell me what I'm amidst. Taurus knew my intentions before I could act, and ever since my life has turned upside down!"

The woman in white stood silent for some time. Her beautiful face entranced Kort; it was more aweing than the brilliant sun overhead. In that instant, he hoped for clarity. *Please Destiny, let her be a light of truth… Please Destiny, let her tell all that I require…*

"Taurus had premonitions too," she spoke at last.

Kort felt surprised. *She knew exactly what I would ask.* He quickly examined his firewall, in his mind, a vast blockage that stretched across a dirt road. The surface had no fissures or imperfections, signs that might indicate it had been compromised. He jumped back from his firewall, not really believing what he saw. *She read my mind, she must have!* Kort drew that conclusion, with no way to explain it.

"How did you? I…" he asked, unable to finish.

"I've read your mind before," she interjected. "Clearly you know how to read and control minds, no? Nym would attest to that, even if you won't."

Kort swallowed hard. The very mention of Nym triggered memories that he buried at the back of his mind. *I used her, even though I love her… She visits me not; does she still love me?* His mind sputtered the thoughts before he cast them aside, for revisit at a more befitting time. *Focus.*

As those blue eyes speared him, Kort quickly came to prefer staring into the blinding sun for hours instead of her intense gaze. Sweat dripped profusely down the sides of his face, as he stood off from her confused, his eyes locked upon hers. *Taurus also having premonitions implies what?*

"What does it mean, though?" asked Kort, dumbfounded by her answer. He watched her flash a broad smile.

"The next time you meet Taurus in your nightmares, why don't you ask him personally? Nightmares and dreams alike can be vehicles for premonitions—vehicles for truth."

With that advice, Kort saw her turn away with the man in black. Her male companion slowly disappeared into thin air, and then the woman in white began to fade as well. She spun around and opened her mouth to talk, but before she did, her body vanished completely. After her departure though, Kort could still hear her speak, and her words hit his ears over and over again.

"One more piece of advice... Trust not, the crimson knight." Her statement progressed from an audible voice to a quiet whisper, and ultimately, sheer and utter silence.

Kort was left alone upon the ledge, alone to ponder these things. *Questions to answer questions, and now this warning? Trust not, the crimson knight...* Kort's longstanding dislike for puzzling talk presented itself. His whole life, he wished people had been more transparent with him, as he should have been with others.

Why shouldn't I trust Elucid? He considered just that, weighing his regard of the crimson knight as a friend against Elucid's undisclosed interest in his person. Kort shook off the suspicions, though in the back of his mind, a bit of mistrust lingered over that.

In the next moment, the woman's words concerning Taurus stole his attention. *Confront him directly, in a nightmare?* The idea was intriguing, of just asking Taurus his questions in his next vivid nightmare. *And there will be many opportunities to try that.* Kort was sure of that, from the high frequency of his bad dreams concerning Taurus.

With a glance to the forest, Kort realized he should waste no more time before heading back. *Soon it'll get dark,* was his last thought before ducking into Tai, for a hike back to Reiju.

"HELP FROM A CRIMINAL"

In the heat of the day, Kort found himself refreshed by the shade of Tai's towering stalky trees as he made his way back through the forest. Every step down the mountainside, his mind actively thought about the woman's words. *Did Taurus act off premonitions about my assassination? How would he know about what I hadn't yet done?* It was perplexing and enigmatic for him.

Kort continued to ponder over the matter, as he ran further down the mountainous terrain overshadowed by flora. He scanned the expanse rolling out before him, looking between stalks for any militants possibly lying in wait for him. *No one there…*

For about half an hour or more, Kort continued through Tai. His mind revolved through diverse topics, ranging from Sagult's pursuit, finding redemption and, of course, Nym. An image of the silver-haired elf filled his head, the fireflies encircling her in a wooded scene, one night not far from him. *It feels like yesterday.* Kort felt so close to memories of Nym from months ago, as if they took place days, hours, or even seconds ago. *My love for her keeps them fresh in my mind, and real in my heart!*

Kort hopped over a large rock jutting from the soil, and he went further down the forest's decline. When his feet touched the ground, he looked up to see lines of white stalks ahead, some stooping toward each other. Their leafy canopies littered a shallow stream with shadowy teeth, cast from the sunlight filtering through. The visual conjured up the realization: *I drank here earlier.*

Being thirsty, Kort slowed himself and came to the stream. Once there, he knelt beside it and as he did, the rocks felt rough against his shins. The discomfort was hardly enough to delay him from drinking. And so, with cupped hands, Kort scooped up a bit of water and lifted it to his dry lips.

As he drank, some water trickled through his fingers and wet his pullover shirt—a small pleasure that made him feel guilty. *Don't.* In an instant he tightened his fingers, and less of it spilled upon his tired, heat-exhausted body. As the last of the water entered his mouth, he lowered both arms to his sides, and just stayed at the stream, looking at it. The very sight of those shallow waters reminded him of the anomalous weather patterns in the Hirishin Isles.

It hasn't rained in weeks. The air is dry, not heavy as usual. Days have been for long windless. In Kort's experience, dry spells were infrequent in this part of Karnath, tropic rains fell often, and there were rejuvenating breezes. He recalled his talk with Kyan earlier, about things changing throughout the land.

What could be causing this? He pondered the matter, and wondered when it would get better. *Or, if it would get better...*

His immense thirst tempted him to drink more, and Kort debated whether it was his want or his need. *Fulfill needs, not wants*, he reminded himself of his personal commitment. Not wishing to indulge, he was hesitant to lower his cupped hands again. But as his stomach growled, and he felt faint in the heat of the day, it became apparent that his body was currently deprived of many needs. *Just drink. Who knows where else you'll find water?*

At the very moment of that thought, Kort felt a soft wind blow. It refreshingly enveloped his body, embracing him. He looked up to behold many leaves upon the stalky trees stirred by that gentle breeze, now moving eerily as if animated after an entire lifetime of inanimate being. The sight was strange to him, unnatural in a peculiar way. *I haven't felt wind in over a month. Why now?*

The inviting water was enough to pull Kort's attention from the novelty of wind that stirred the leaves above. And so, like before, he cupped his hands, and went to lower them into the stream, but stopped himself upon noticing something strange beneath the water's surface. Kort saw two dots of gold light above a larger oval light. He leaned closer to study them. *Are those fish?* Even closer he leaned. *It looks like, eyes and a mouth?* He wondered.

All about the lights in the water, Kort saw movement, though not ripples. He looked harder, and noted an outline overtop the dots. *That seems... as hair.* A deeply uneasy feeling filled Kort's gut, as he realized that these images were not in the water, but reflections of something over his shoulder!

He bolted upright, spun about, and came face-to-face with a ghostly woman, who had blotches of gold light for her eyes and mouth! With his jaw agape, he perceived her fair face, with barely even a nose. About her flowing gray robe, the ghostly woman's skin fell off in droplets, only to replenish itself in the next instant!

Her ghastly appearance terrified Kort, and he recoiled instantly. His heart rate climbed all of a sudden, and sheer horror numbed him. He watched her stand there, when abruptly, her odd semblance of a body burst into droplets dispersed throughout the air, just staying in place! He felt another wind blow, rustling all the leaves upon the trees in the same uncanny way.

Kort looked around, and gawked at the suspended droplets. *Run.* Though he tried to move, his body was completely petrified by fear. In his past life, Kort had courageously dealt with many things that inspired dread, but this was otherworldly odd, odder than anything he had ever seen before. *Why can't I move?!*

Like the body would work in thick mire, his mind churned slowly as to what he should do. *Protect.* Kort instinctively reached for magic to shield himself from the perceived threat. He closed his eyes, and found himself immediately in his enlarged channeling chamber. He ran up to his double-door Source entry, and pulled the handles hard. When the doors creaked open, however, no Nexus flowed into the room! He stood in his chamber, being dry and completely devoid of energy.

This is unreal! Even more frightened now, Kort snapped back to the forest just in time to behold each airborne droplet transform into the lit eyes and mouth of the ghostly woman. All around the forest, Kort gazed up into the trees, seeing the woman's face looking back at him, wherever he turned. The winds kept caressing him, and Kort beheld the leaves continue their dance, some lured from their branches to float through the air, like ghosts.

Just then, he heard a deep beat overtop of him, like the forest itself developed a throbbing heart. It pounded more dread and angst into him, and he wrestled with tightness in his chest and difficulties breathing. Before his eyes, the trees and flora abruptly reddened in hue, and every pronounced edge of the foliage appeared sharpened, deadly even. At that moment, Kort had trouble speaking or thinking much of anything, but strangely enough, he regained control over his body in that very moment.

His body worked without his mind, and his instincts propelled him through the Tai Forest, away from danger. *Something Dark is here, or someone!* The thoughts grazed his panicky mind, as his limbs grazed the shrubbery of the woods, which drew his blood. He glanced down at his bleeding arms that bumped into the brush, being struck with shock over his wounds. In that, fear ate him alive. *How can this be?! It's just leaves!*

Beset by winds, Kort rushed through the woods with Tai's heart still thumping overhead. He glanced up, still seeing the woman's omnipresent face watching him, a face surrounded by the leaves that perpetually floated. Suddenly, an eerie song filled the air, of speaking unlike anything Kort had ever heard. His ears picked up chiming words in neither Mainlandish nor Hirishin, each one lingering as the next sounded, all strung together in a mind-boggling, yet mellifluous way.

"Your inheritance is more wholesome than his, *Kilwroth's unwholesome inheritance.*" The words were strange and from another world, seemingly another space of the universe.

Kort grew terribly frightened when his very thoughts sounded in this otherworldly tongue, yet it seemed as common to him as any other language. *What's happening?!* he thought in a foreign lexicon, without a clue as to how it was even possible to think in a language that he had never learned!

Then Kort saw it, every copy of the ghostly woman in the spaces between the trees merged into one—a single ghost floating right beside him! The ex-knight hurriedly ran down the next slope, not stopping for anything. As he went, he glanced where the woman was, but saw her not. Though upon looking the other way, she floated right at his opposite side!

"The distance between Kilwroth and his fate shall be many fold the distance between you and redemption!"

Intensely Kort yelled with a newfound voice, "Let me be, spirit! Leave me alone!" The ghostly woman still floated beside him, as he ran in terror.

"May your blood not muddy the waters in this gulf between Kilwroth's destiny and yours!"

Through the forest, Kort saw its exit ahead, opening to the fields outside village Reiju. He sprinted faster, his head pounding from inrushing blood. *Don't stop.* One after the other, his feet shot forward and blurred beneath him, as he hurried out of the woods. He felt the winds blow fiercely when he reached the final stretch of Tai, and at his sides, he discerned stalks cracking in half!

From his periphery, he saw those trees fall toward his path out of the forest, coming at him from multiple angles. Kort ducked beneath them and juked around them, pushing his body forward. Somehow, he managed to run even faster. His heart beat furiously in his chest, feeling on the verge of exploding, and he could tell his body was at its physical limits. Through his mind ran a simple instruction: *Whatever happens, don't turn back.*

He sensed stalks crash behind him as he ran out of the forest, and just before his exit, the ghostly woman continued in her arcane song. "I'm cheering for you, Kort Al'starz! Give me a grand show."

Her musical words sailed through the air, even after Kort emerged from Tai Forest. In his ears they lingered, and in his mind. *Give me a grand show.* When the sun's rays poured over him, a blinding white light engulfed his body and he shielded his eyes.

"Arrghh!" he groaned.

The intense light faded slowly, and when it did, he opened back up his eyes, seeing the setting sun and skyline of Reiju. It was then that everything normalized for Kort. The dreadful beats of Tai's heart, the odd winds, the ghostly woman, the sharpened leaves, and even his wounds—all disappeared. The eerie sounds of her speech in that unworldly language, also gone. Kort looked around his ambience, and then at his unwounded arms. He rubbed his face with both hands, and pinched his skin, feeling as if he had just awoken from one of his many nightmares linked to his Dark past. Gradually, his breathing became slow and regular, his heartbeats too. *What happened?!*

To both knees Kort fell, and he grabbed the dirt in his hands. He let it break over his palms, and felt the granular texture against his skin. The ex-knight looked back to Reiju; he inhaled the air deeply, and listened intently to Tai's music in the background—the hum of insects and birds chirping. He let the environment inundate his senses, for confirmation of having returned to the real world. *You're back...*

Slowly, he rose to his feet and staggered toward the dirt path connecting Reiju to Genze's house, and to Doj—the neighboring village. *That's where I should spend the* night, he thought passively, being a bit shaken and preoccupied by whatever had just taken place in Tai Forest. *Destiny, is this my chastisement for a life of wrongs, to now be haunted by troubled spirits?!* He considered that whatever had happened might be his due punishment, for all of his wrongdoings.

With improved function, Kort's mind mulled over the strange things said to him, while his body moved him closer to Reiju. He recalled something about killing or wrath, and his blood filling a gulf between his destiny and that of another. *Strange sayings, perhaps from a distressed spirit?* As much as he pondered the odd words, they made little sense to him, and he eventually stopped trying to assign meaning to the perceived meaningless.

On the outskirts of village Reiju, his alertness heightened and he cleared his mind, as he walked even closer. *Sagult's militants might be lurking about.* The realization hit him, and he grew concerned about a repeat of what transpired earlier today. *Keep an eye out for those from Sergros,* he warned himself, and started navigating Reiju's dirt streets.

Into the first alley he darted, between two drab houses overlooking the blue sea, seated beneath a brilliant sunset of reddish orange. At the land's end, Kort saw sand dotted by patches of burnt grass that yielded to still waters, in which distantly were several boats being rowed, each with its sails down.

In the shore waters, he observed a line stretched taut between two posts mounted there, laden with nets and hooks to catch any sea creatures venturing close enough to land. At his left, cubits away from the one house nearest the water's edge, Kort beheld also a weather-beaten port of cracked wood. It was a small platform with one end anchored by posts in the sand, with its other end floating on the water. There, some junk sailboats were docked, their ruffled sails of copper hue striking a pleasant contrast with the sienna brown wood vessels, which bobbed on the azure sea. Waters gently whooshed up against their sides.

Kort went down the alley and darted into the next alleyway, away from the village outskirts and closer to the market. The streets and alleys are like veins to the artery of the main way within Reiju, each lined by dark wood houses capped by thatched roofs. The visual of brown and amber gave him a very real sense of déjà vu, despite the sky being different than before, tinged now by oranges and reds. *Been here earlier today.*

When Kort rounded the bend leading to the market, he came face-to-face with the husband of the elven lady he startled earlier, when dropping unexpectedly through her roof. The husband stood outside their house, holding pieces of the broken chair. Seeing it reminded Kort of the whole episode, from crashing through the roof to drawing the militants inside the house, whereby their door and furniture got smashed to bits.

Kort looked into the husband's brown eyes, and slowly his vision trailed to the tattered cloths he wore. The husband scowled, and it took little imagination for the ex-knight to understand why: *Him and his wife had little to begin with, and destroying his property only made his life harder.* Feeling responsible for the loss he created, Kort withdrew his share of coin from the leather pouch hung about his neck. His stomach ached from not eating yet today, and he was famished. *Here goes my rice in Doj. Though giving this money is not in my interests, it's the right thing to do…*

"For your troubles," said Kort to the husband in Mainlandish, extending his open hand with the coin. He watched a confused expression form on the husband's face, an open mouth and empty eyes. *In Hirishin*, he told himself, and just as easily, he spoke the native tongue of the land, which clearly would be understood.

"Kango alangan panjengan."

Gratefully the husband took the coin.

"Nuwun babagan gendheng. Aku ora duwe dhuwit liyane!" said Kort, expressing apologies for damaging the roof, and stating that he had no more money to offer.

With a smile, the husband replied "Iku bocor!" Translated in Mainlandish, this is to say 'the roof leaks anyway!' Kort smiled.

Suddenly Kort heard a female voice through the bashed door; it was the husband's wife yelling from inside the house. Without waiting a moment longer, Kort ran in fear. *All the coin in the Isles might not please her! I don't need any more problems in this visit to Reiju.*

He went down the main way, away from the house and into the market. There, he saw a few people now closing their stands. Through the clusters of canopied tables, he wandered to the spot where he left Genze's cart in such a hurry. *Please be there! Please be there!*

Upon reaching the site, he found Genze's cart sitting in its place with not a thing missing! *Well, staying longer to sell this stuff was a waste. No one wants this junk, not even thieves!*

Despite Kort being annoyed with the fisherman asking him to retrieve the junk, he gladly got behind the wheelbarrow and pushed it from the marketplace. *At least he can't complain.* The noisy wheel announced Kort's presence as he maneuvered it through parts of Reiju, and beyond. *Given the noise, those militants might hear me a span away!*

Paranoia made Kort look over his shoulder constantly, but despite it, he left the village unscathed with Genze's junk. He steered the wheelbarrow onto the dirt road connecting the village to Doj, as the sun sank lower on the horizon. *Must get this back, before it's too late.* Kort took a few more steps up the dirt road, and was surprised when from out of nowhere, a familiar figure appeared beside him—Elucid.

"Will you fish in Doj?" boomed the crimson knight.

"Perhaps, if someone will let me," Kort answered. "Though it won't happen today."

"Why not fish now, with me?"

A pile of thoughts stacked up in Kort's head, with Sagult chasing him being at the top, and those words of the woman in white being somewhere in between. *Trust not, the crimson knight.*

"It's late. I can fish tomorrow."

"Delaying a problem does not solve it. Not fishing today precludes both success and failure now."

Kort paused as they both walked on together. *Is Elucid talking about fishing, or something else?*

"Only by lowering your net into the waters can there be any chance of catching fish—today, tomorrow, and all days after. Karnath sees a time, where many fishers no longer fish, as many doers no longer do. So many people just struggle to exist, hoping to weather a storm."

When Kort ignored the crimson knight, suddenly Elucid vanished to reappear right in front of his wheelbarrow, bringing him to a stop. *What's Elucid doing?!*

"I speak of more than just lowering a net to fish. Lower a net for your own destiny, a good one."

Deep inside Kort, Elucid's words stirred his emotions. *I want to do great good for many—that's my good destiny.* Kort did not live anymore for self-gratifying things—riches, fame, or other fortune. He lived every day with a desperate want to do great good, after committing such great wrongs. *It's the biggest of my broken dreams: Fate's Fray with no chance of redemption!* The thought crossed his mind, as his aspirations of helping others seemed all the more unlikely each waking moment of each passing day.

"Perhaps a destiny of fishing in the Isles, is what lies in store for me." Kort choked on the words. *I would rather die in Sergros, than spend a fruitless life in the Isles, helping no one but myself.*

Silence presided over the dirt road, and to Kort, the sun seemed lower in the sky than before. *Just leave; it's getting late.*

"An unwanted destiny is no destiny at all," Elucid spoke on. "Seize that which you desire with the time you have, something possible that brings good to Karnath, and good to yourself, while using hidden talents. *Being unable to spend your time to seek out good destiny is like already being out of time. 'Tis one's Time No More.*"

In that moment, those words ushered a whirlwind of thoughts upon Kort, about his deep want of redemption and his anxiety from not being able to obtain it. *I don't know how to make this right. Even though I try every day, I can't!*

"I don't know how to spend my time toward a good destiny," Kort admitted, "so I guess I'm out of time."

"You need not be," Elucid answered. "It's not wrong to be without direction, but the lost not seeking help are foolish. You need a wise guide, to join you on your quest for good destiny."

Looking at the sun once more, the words sounded again in Kort's mind. *Trust not, the crimson knight.*

"I best be going. Genze's things need to be returned by the day's end." Kort took up the wheelbarrow's handles, wanting to push it forward, but the crimson knight did not move. He held the handles, wondering what to do. *Do I just push it around Elucid? I need to get back to Genze's, and the day is short.*

"You should be lowering your net for the shard of broken sword, fallen to the depths of the Korinth Ocean," said Elucid. "You are much more than you presume."

Trapped inside Kort's head were widespread allegations from Sergros, which now, collided with the crimson knight's insinuation. He could hear Sagult's voice still identifying him: *You're a traitor, a murderer, and a knight who betrayed the common trust of his kingdom.*

"I know what I am," replied Kort.

"You know not what you say. For alas, one of such low character having a history of misdeeds can still do great good."

Angry by the suggestion, Kort pushed the cart until it stopped against Elucid's leg with a clang.

"Please move from the way," Kort asked firmly.

"Listen to something other than your hurting heart," Elucid pleaded with him. "For my words are true, and this I've come to say: you are the Child, the One of Prophecy destined for great things!"

Kort shook his head, denying the statement. *What Elucid suggests is the biggest blasphemy to Karnathan beliefs! Surely, I'm no Child of Light.*

"Please step aside."

"What's the source of your disbelief?" asked Elucid, as the sun slipped further beneath the stalky trees.

"Surely a good person of many virtues would be the Child of Light," replied Kort, "as opposed to one such as I! A person like me has committed too many wrongs for the best of good destinies, so to insist otherwise is only to mock!" A flash of Garlew Il'therin entered his mind just then, as a testament to how futile his pursuit of good destiny had been until now. *If anything, I killed the hero! I'm not one, and never could be…*

Kort continued. "I try to dismantle the Isles Conspiracy so Juniper would be spared, and in the process, I killed Sergros' hero! Before my valiant effort to stop the Isles Conspiracy, I feigned two allegiances, the one to Sergros being a falsehood! My involvement in the Crimson Guard couldn't be more of deceit! The only good I ever did was a complete lie! I'm not a good person…"

Kort looked to Elucid, with tears in his eyes. He felt one stream down his cheek, as he said, "The Light Prophecy speaks of the Child of Light being from the Light Lineage. Kayareth is one who has the blood of Destiny's good counterpart, Autheos." In an aside, Kort balled his fist and screamed to the wooded horizon. "No doubt the blood of Ma'althan courses through my veins!" Kort watched Elucid stare at him, unreadable beneath that suit of armor.

"You are not of the Light Lineage," said the crimson knight. Hearing that from another corroborated Kort's debased view of himself. *As spoken, I couldn't be the One of Prophecy... I'm more easily evil incarnate!* His countenance fell with the mere thought.

"You should joy that this matters not," Elucid added, "for you descend from a special lineage, the Gray Lineage. Formed long ago, it's the intersection of both lines, where the bloods of Light and Darkness have become intermingled. It's a conscious choice to do either good or evil, one choice every man can and must make. It's your choice too."

Kort felt the handles of his wheelbarrow weigh heavily on his forearms. He wished he could just plow it right over Elucid, and be done with this silly conversation. *You think I'm motivated by this, knight? You rent my heart atwain with lofty ideals, so unattainable by one like me!*

"Few in Karnath do anything these days and even fewer do good," Elucid said, "so your repentant heart actually makes you more valuable than most. One who does evil and then chooses good, is more useful to change the Dark Prophecy than one who did neither good nor evil to begin with."

Kort heard Elucid's invitation, yet again.

"Go onto the waters today, to fish for more than fish, for your own good destiny. It's that good thing, which you're best at, something you feel naturally inclined to that helps others and yourself. For you, this is..."

"Move," Kort interjected. "I must be going."

He glared at Elucid with frustration.

"Sand still falls in your timer," Elucid replied, "and it's not too late for you to do, instead of just be. Think about my words."

Kort saw the crimson knight finally step aside, and open the way up the dirt path to Genze's house, which dotted the distance. He pushed the wheelbarrow forward and when past Elucid, he turned over his shoulder to say, "Tomorrow I fish, in my way and in my time."

With his back turned to Elucid, Kort forsook the crimson knight and continued onward, not turning again. Elucid stood there silently watching him go, before vanishing with the day, into the sunset.

"SOWING SEEDS OF MISTRUST"

After leaving Elucid behind, Kort brought the wheelbarrow of Genze's things right up to the house. He dropped the handles, letting the wheelbarrow hit the ground. The discordant sound of shifting tools entered his ears. With one hand, Kort wiped the sweat from his brow as he looked at the fisherman's abode, seeming dark and unoccupied.

No one's home? Kort stared at the black side window, and noted how no light slipped from beneath the door. *That's odd.* He recollected how Genze would always be home in the early evenings, even with his occasional night fishing. With some surprise over the situation, he stepped closer to the door, examining it. The wood sat in its track, weathered from exposure to the elements, but not showing signs of forced entry. *Did the militants even come back?* Kort wondered, while double-checking the window around the side. *It's completely dark.*

He went back around to the house's front, and put his hand on the door, but hesitated opening it. *I hope Genze is all right.* With that thought, Kort slid back the door, which rubbed noisily against its track. From inside, inky blackness spilled out into the day's remaining light, overwhelming him.

"Genze… are you home?" Kort yelled.

There was no answer.

He went inside, but could not see a thing.

"Genze!" he shouted. Into his ears wandered the intermittent chirp of crickets from the distant forest, high-pitched and rhythmic. That and his voice were the only sounds.

"Genze!" he called out. "Are you all right?!"

In the dark house, his eyes strained to discern one shadow from the next. Given his difficulties seeing, Kort decided to use Nexus, in order to perform a trick he learned in Baal. It was one of a dozen other advanced magical techniques he picked up there, under bizarre circumstances, without even a lesson. He shoved the memory of Baal to the back of his mind. *Not thinking about Baal.*

Extending his hand, Kort formed a single green flame that floated over his palm. It sparked afire, as he *continuously pulled Nexus* into his aux core and transformed it into fire, to feed the flame. Kort moved his palm from left to right, shedding enough light to illuminate the entire space. He found Genze's abode exactly as he last saw it: a short stool with the man's money still atop, along with the fisherman's linens, paper lamp, and ceramics, all appearing where they should. There was no evidence of a struggle, of things wildly displaced or broken. *He's just... not here? Very odd...*

All of a sudden, Kort noticed something upon the wall, wedged between the house's frame and the wallboard. It was the net that Genze worked on earlier, perfectly mended. *He'll be back on the water in no time!* Kort thought with a smile.

Into the space, he continued to call out. "Genze!"

To Kort, the fisherman not being home resounded of strangeness. *Can't believe this.* He walked from room to room in the small house. "Genze!" he called again, yet there was still no reply.

Repeatedly, Kort shouted the fisherman's name until he began feeling silly. He took a moment to ponder a few possibilities. *Could it be, that the fisherman went to look for his friend Inari?* The ex-knight backed out of the thought, clearly giving Genze too much credit. *Or maybe, the militants came back and involved him in their search?* Kort merely thinking about soldiers entering the house immediately drove him to where he stayed. *The amulet!*

Quickly, he ran to the corner of one room, praying with every step. *Destiny, let it be there! Please, Destiny...* Kort saw his mat neatly laid out over the floor, the place where he slept many nights. Next to it rested some of the ex-knight's things. Using his free hand, he rummaged through his belongings—not much more than an extra set of cloths—before he happened upon the sought-after object: the amulet. *Whew...*

Such relief filled Kort, as he lifted Nym's silver amulet in one hand. His eyes scanned its metal surface, which caught light from the small flame still burning over his other palm. The sight stirred up fond memories, causing Kort to smile. *It's silver, like her hair.* Feeling the amulet's thin chain against his fingers reminded him of how he used to run his fingers through the silver strands of her hair. *Nym, where are you?* Every time he thought of Nym, he contemplated her whereabouts and if she was safe. *Destiny, let her be well...*

Kort kissed the chain, before dropping the amulet into the pouch hanging about his neck. He stopped pulling Nexus, and let his flame die so he could work with two hands. When the light went out, he found himself in the house's darkness, though with his eyes better adjusted now. He grabbed a brown burlap bag, and began stuffing it with his worldly possessions. After only a few moments, he finished and grabbed the sack's neck in his right fist, throwing it over his shoulder.

Kort took a few steps toward the sliding door, but before stepping out, he turned to give his temporary home a final look. As before, the small green flame sparked over his left hand, shedding enough light for him to see the house one last time. He glanced over its simple layout and simple furnishings with a bit of nostalgia. This was a humble fisherman's home, and for the past month, Kort had been a humble fisherman with Genze. He remembered all the times they spent together in this space, from mending nets and preparing meals, to talking. *More like arguing!* A smile spread over his face at the thought. *Genze, you've been a curmudgeonly and intolerable one betimes, but I like you more than not!* With that thought, he let his green flame extinguish, just like this chapter of his life's story came to a close.

Before Kort turned back for the door, something caught his eye and he stopped himself from leaving. *Wait.* There, on the windowsill, lied a leather-bound copy of the *Book of Karnatha,* a book that contained unbelievable stories suited for children of the land. To many, it was a book more of myth than of fact, describing unbelievable feats like Maken's creation of the world, the seroxian rebellion, epic wars with the superhuman race to reclaim paradise, and so on.

Despite Kort's limited appreciation for fancy, he walked over to it, and picked up the small book in his one hand. It felt light, and a bit fragile. He let the cover fall open in his palm, and made the pages flip. The book's tired state became obvious to his senses, as the air filled with the pages' musty smell, and also, sounds of parchment against parchment. *This book is as worn, as the stories inside!* At that thought, he pressed the book closed with his fingers, its spine resting in the palm of his hand.

While staring at the book's corded binding, Kort could not help but remember Elucid mentioning the prophecies in the Book of Karnatha, which were also among its myths and legends. *Nonsense.* The hurried thought came to mind as Kort denied what the crimson knight said, still a bit flustered about their earlier encounter. And just when that thought echoed his mind, Kort went to put the book back. But halfway to the windowsill, he stopped with a thought: *Borrow it.* The idea blindsided him and he stood there frozen, unable to return the book where it originally lied. *Borrow it, and see what it says.*

In his mind, Kort weighed the prospect of Genze getting mad, should he take the book. *I've never seen him even read it... Though maybe he did?* Kort could not know for sure if Genze would care or not, but his inner voice urged him to seek forgiveness rather than permission. *Just borrow it already.*

After much deliberation, Kort finally stuffed the book into his burlap sack. *Genze, forgive me.* He promised himself to return the book. *I'll give it back, prior to surrendering to Sagult!* That final thought followed him out the open door, which he slid shut before starting his trek up the long dirt road to Doj.

Just a few spans... Kort considered how the next village was only a few hours travel on the path. It was a path overlooked by the mossy Jezban Mountains, beset by the stalky Tai Forest that gradually yielded to the fertile fields used for rice farming.

Another thoughtful walk... Often, Kort took walks to clear his mind, and when he was not walking or working, he sometimes would just stare into Reiju's harbor, letting his mind go adrift as the many small fishing boats that left its small port. To him, time for thought was invaluable. For he acknowledged that movements of the mind happened only with perpetual thinking, relentless reevaluation of matters both decided and undecided, to foster learning from life's lessons, and change. And so, being one prone to thought, Kort exercised his mind and his body upon the dirt road to Doj.

Elucid popped first into his head. *How dare the crimson knight mock me like that?* He felt angry, confused, hurt even. *I'm the One of Prophecy, Elucid says. Really, I'm destined to be the hero of every child in Karnath? And the source of hope for many despite their disbelief?! It's surely a lie.* He thought all this, his denial fueled by the ever-present realization of whom he had been, not too long ago. *I'm a traitor and a murderer, worthy of painful death or lifelong imprisonment.*

Like waves rolling one after another, Kort's next thought came to be, with the last crashing into obscurity. Beneath the moonlight, Kort walked along the dirt road, so preoccupied that the time just melted away. *What was that in Tai Forest?* He feared that Destiny sent a spirit to haunt him, for past trespasses. What happened earlier today in some ways validated his insistence of being a bad person, who was worthy of punishment. *This must be part of my punishment, before I get my dues in Sergros.*

He strolled up the dirt path for a good hour or more, accompanied by music from the crickets of Tai. His mind jumped to the neighboring thoughts, about his purpose and plan. *I must remove hardship for many in the Isles, before handing myself over to Sagult.* Kort's objective was set, ever since news of Taurus Hboshi's death in the Isles reached the Mainland—a death administered by metal demons, not by his own hands.

Until receiving this news, Kort was convinced that he had personally slayed Taurus. But upon hearing otherwise, it was obvious that he killed the wrong person. It was regrettably his trusted friend, Garlew Il'therin, who had been injured while hunting Pyrus and lied unconscious in a hospice bed. It was devastating news for Kort, news that overwrote his beliefs of doing good by putting an evil emperor to death. It was news that led into his Fate's Fray—the unraveling of his perceived good destiny, amidst bad destiny in the Black Dragon clans.

Know that my mistake shall see recompense, Garlew! I shall negate all the wrongs I've done, all the lives I've ruined... It'll take my good deeds, as well as my very life! His commitment remained to the deceased Garlew, who in the Isles might be better known as Fieronju—the brother of Taurus Hboshi, who ran away as a child from bad destiny in the Black Dragon clans, and took the Mainlandish name Garlew. *I shall make this right, friend! For both you and me...*

Kort continued up the beaten path connecting Reiju to Doj, rousing a few times at the slightest sound from the stalky forest. Seldom he looked behind him and into the foliage, still suspecting that he could be followed. *Sagult or his men could find me yet.* But every time he checked his rear and the woods, no one was there. Only the night sounds and sights collided with his senses—the chirping crickets, bass locusts, and colorful fireflies zooming about.

The latter shed light upon the trees in the distance, to give the forest a fantastic look—the neon outlines of stalky trees, in both greens and reds, projected onto a soft backdrop of grays. He saw the stalks leaning, as if against the emerald peaks of the Jezban Mountains, the two sitting below the overhung blue starry sky, filled with a pale and luminous half-moon.

The sight of those fireflies stirred up Kort's memories of Nym once more. Immediately, it reminded him of a wooded scene forever engraved in his memories, where the glowing insects enchantingly encircled her, when she appeared to him in the forests he traveled before reaching Baal. *That was after my resurrection, and how that memory lingers!*

Oh how I miss Nym so! he thought. *I miss her laugh, her smile, her touch, and above all, her very presence!* Kort felt incomplete for the month or so without her in his life. He had to leave her suddenly outside of Breslin, when they were hiding together in the wake of Isles Conspiracy. *Those seeking to avenge Garlew put me in seclusion, though not her. Yet she stayed with me and I enjoyed her company, until the point where I became convinced that my circumstances put her in danger.*

Kort's thought trailed away, for he never quite understood why she never came for him in the Isles. *Perhaps our relationship was doomed from its start.* He offered up that conjecture, in hopes of settling the confusion in his own mind. Upon being resurrected, Kort realized that Nym was a supernatural being and that she would likely outlive him. *And perhaps likewise, my novelty to her outlived itself!* As the dull sphere of a mortal's adoration might bore any supernatural being, maybe his love for her had worn out its welcome.

Kort was deeply saddened by the situation. He lived for a two-sided purpose—redemption and Nym. But more and more it seemed like Nym was choosing not to see him, for even though he left her, she had the powers to find him. And that destroyed Kort, the prospect of Nym not loving him anymore. In his heart, it created anguish over why love for Nym would be part of his destiny, if that love would not be returned, and their togetherness was never meant to be. *Who can understand the ways of love, this strange thing both enriching and damaging!* The conflicting emotions bunched up inside him, as he walked alone up the path, and also through the struggles of his own life.

He grasped the pouch hanging beneath his pullover shirt, feeling the amulet's outline through its leather. The amulet and memories were all that Kort had left of his relationship with Nym. And so, in the absence of her as well as redemption, it seemed more and more like he was doomed to die without fulfilling his purpose in life. *These will be just two more broken dreams atop a pile of many more! These will be only a crown to my Fate's Fray—a thing I live from day to day!*

The thoughts were so saddening, that they brought Kort to a complete stop upon the dirt road. In an aside, he shouted to the starry sky.

"As my dreams are broken, so is my heart, Karnatha! It's a shattered vessel that yearns for Nym with every struggled push, as it yearns for my own redemption! The memories of my former life are all that I have left—of love, of respect in the Guard, and so much more! Is it my bad destiny, to be in want of these things, but nonetheless without?! Given this lack, shall I cling to my memories all the more tightly?! Will they forever be, the ghost of my lost love and honor, the ghost of my good destiny? Yes I say, without your help of making more from less! Help me, lead me, to find good destiny after the bad! Please, Destiny…"

Despite his cries into the night, Destiny spoke in a voice quieter than the humming locusts or the chirping crickets. Amid the silence Kort had to wonder, *Does Destiny speak at all?* His dilemma matched that of those in want of good destiny, but without guidance from above. And so, when his reality sunk in—that he waited upon a silent stranger's response—he resumed walking and the path continued. The ex-knight followed its twists and turns, wherever they led. No longer beset by the forest of stalky trees, a large clearing now hugged the dirt road, yielding an expansive view of the mountains to the rear.

Soon, Kort saw Doj's large fields on both sides, used for rice farming. Being in the coastal wetland, he knew the village could successfully produce enough rice for itself and Reiju. Rice was by the far the most important staple in the Hirishin Isles, and was enjoyed at every meal. *Though not without money...* His recollection of giving up his coin in Reiju triggered the thought.

When passing the fields, Kort stopped in his tracks to behold something most troubling. Many fields were scorched by days of intense sun, as inferred from the cracked soil beneath the rice plants—plants that were weeks from harvesting. And upon Kort surveying the fields, it appeared that only one field remained, the others being dried out before the harvest or gleaned just in time with the scythe. *Could it be, that this is all the rice left?!*

In that moment, Kort's mind flashed with images brought about by the dry spell. He remembered how Reiju's local well dried up, and on more than one occasion, he and Genze boiled seawater as the freshwater became scarce. He remembered how every few weeks, when visiting Doj's market, Genze complained about the price of rice climbing higher and higher, the consequence of a shortage. *I knew it was bad, but not this bad!*

And then, at the worst possible time, his stomach growled, reminding him that he had not yet eaten. In that moment, Kort's fierce hunger seemed many times more severe than the thirst in his parched throat, and it became a basis to question why he would even fish any longer, if there were fewer and fewer fish to be caught, and no rice to be had! He could literally see himself starving to death—unredeemed and without Nym. The thought was jarring.

Again, he stopped on the road, feeling saddened and beaten down. But slowly then, a determination awoke inside of him, one that he lived and breathed at times prior, even today. *This can't end here. Not here! Not now!* Kort's redemption literally hung in the balance. *Fish for fish still, and if no fish are caught, still fish for good destiny...* His mind revisited the idea, founded in Karnathan belief to seek good destiny even amid the bad, and that gave him hope. A moment later, he sighed when realizing that this was partly a regurgitation of what Elucid said, and though the idea comforted him, he did not like its source.

Having a bump of encouragement, Kort started walking up the dirt path again, soothed by the rhythmic chirp of the crickets, emanating from the nearby woods and fields. He opened his mouth, wanting to enjoy a deep breath of summer night air, but realized then what he was doing. *Satisfy needs, not wants.* Inhibition presided over him then, and he took only a shallow breath.

Walking a bit further up the path, Kort finally saw Doj in the distance. The night's darkness gave way, revealing the outline of stilted houses along the seafront, some with lit windows, others darkened, many overlooking the water and the port, at which boats had been fastened and sat idly there. Kort could barely distinguish the dichotomy of colors between the wooden houses and their straw-thatched roofs. He stood there, noting other houses along the path that stretched into Doj, all the way to its village center. These structures were outside of the village, just like Genze's house, with a similar appearance to the ones in Reiju.

Maybe I can wait here tonight, at least until morning. Some fisher is bound to need help... Hopefully. He thought these things to himself and saw an overturned boat, outside the nearest fisher's shack at his right. As he crept forward, he observed the side window of the house showed no light inside. *They're likely asleep.*

Despite his conjecture, Kort took care to be quiet and avoid conspicuous movements in the dark. Upon the grass, much of it seeming dry and burnt beneath his feet, he moved closer to the overturned boat. As soon as he reached it, he ducked underneath the propped hull with his burlap sack, and sat there, having both knees bent.

His breathing slowed, and he listened to the calm about him, distant crickets singing into the still night. For some time, Kort just stared at the boat's wooden hull, rethinking many things that kept him occupied on his long walk to Doj. Gradually, his head began to nod, and he blinked in and out of sleep.

From his doze, the pad of footsteps near the boat stirred Kort awake! *Who is that?!* The thought rattled him, just as the sound filled him with angst. Beneath the hull's edge, he could barely see shadows upon the ground, which suggested someone walked closer and closer. Kort held his breath, as a beam of light shined upon the dirt, coming nigh to where he hid. *A lantern?* He noted how dispersed the beam was, drawing a reasonable conclusion from that.

He immediately feared the worst. *Sagult! But how did he find me so quickly, and in another village?* His mind struggled to reconcile his reality with what seemed possible. At this most inopportune time, Kort's stomach growled unexpectedly, to protest him missing meals all day. *Destiny damn it!*

The figure standing above the boat completely stopped, and Kort became extremely tense. *He's just waiting.* Kort's anxiety multiplied. *He heard me… Sagult must know I'm here!* After a few moments of silence, Kort heard the figure walk away. *What?* In his ears, the footsteps grew increasingly distant. His eyes noted the lantern's fading light. He took a deep breath, after holding it for what seemed a lifetime. *Thank Destiny.*

But as much as Kort enjoyed that relief, it was short lived. For in several minutes he heard the figure return, going right next to the overturned boat. He held his breath again, and the anxiety was back, just as heightened as before. *Sagult did hear!* All of a sudden, Kort saw the boat pulled back as a figure with a lantern stooped down and lifted up its one side, to reveal his place of hiding!

"LOST AND FOUND"

Kort rolled out from beneath the hull, and nimbly threw his body upright to assume a defensive stance. He held his hands at his waist—open and ready—and looked toward the figure behind the lantern, with every muscle tense. Adrenaline flowed through him, and the edginess he felt all day was back.

With eyes adjusted to the dark, Kort squinted as the lantern shined over him. *It's got to be Sagult, and he won't back down without a fight!*

A male voice spoke, fluent in the Hirishin tongue.

"Ora bakal kaget, kanggo Maksudku sampeyan ora gawe piala!" The words ran through Kort's mind as Mainlandish, from his tendency to translate one language to the other. *Be not alarmed, for I mean you no harm!*

Still straining to see, Kort could barely make out the figure. But as his eyes adjusted to the light, he saw an elven fisher behind that lantern, older in age. Gray hair topped his head, the same color as the stubble on his wrinkly face. The elven fisher wore traditional Hirishin garments for sleeping, in particular, hand-woven cotton slacks and a simple shirt, both being of natural hues.

Lost for words, Kort stood there silent. It took a moment for him to process the reality of it not being his pursuer. *It's not... Sagult?*

"I'm Raiden of Doj," he said, suddenly.

Kort just stared back, his heart racing. *It's not Sagult.* When that boat turned over, he would have bet everything in his sack that Sagult had found him. Someone friendlier discovering him brought definite feelings of relief. His heartbeats slowed, his adrenaline ramped down, and by the moment, he became less on edge. But just as this happened, his mind began to race. *How did he hear me? Why isn't he worried?* It puzzled Kort why Raiden was at ease, but he was not about to start asking questions.

"Are you hungry?" asked Raiden.

The question took Kort by surprise. *Did he just ask, if I'm hungry?* His stomach growled right then, this time most befittingly.

"By the sounds of it, you are!" Raiden laughed. "C'mon, let's get you some food."

Kort watched Raiden walk toward the house, taking the light with him. The ex-knight was left in darkness, as he found himself so often. For a moment, he stayed in place, thinking about what he should do. One half pulled him away from the house. *Run! This might be more trouble than it's worth!* The other half urged him to venture inside. *Running would be foolish! Go in and eat.*

Slowly he stepped in the direction of the fisher's home, its window now agleam with light. Kort shook his head, realizing then he was not as clandestine as he thought. *Somehow, I managed to wake Raiden!* He chided himself for not being more careful.

When Kort came to the open sliding door, he saw Raiden inside the house, standing upon its dusty wooden floors, tending to a fire pit on the leftmost wall with a cauldron hanging over. He hesitated at the door until Raiden looked up and motioned for him to come closer.

"Come in! Come in!"

With that invitation, Kort entered. Immediately upon stepping onto the floor, he took off his shoes and set them near the threshold, a customary sign of respect in the Isles, especially for visitors in a stranger's house.

Kort glanced around the simple space. It contained typical furnishings of a fisher's house in the Isles. Kort saw a short stool, various ceramics and linens, and a glowing paper lamp with intricately hand-drawn Hirishin characters in black ink. It sat beyond a paper sliding door at the back of the room, which featured even more characters. The door was pulled open, and led into where Raiden slept. Only an eye's passing was enough for Kort to imagine Raiden after a day on the waters, sitting on the floor and eating a rice ball beside his hung netting. *It's much like Genze's abode!*

He observed Raiden motion to the floor.

"Please, sit. You're hungry."

Kort sat cross-legged on the floor, and gazed at the hay ceiling, supported by several beams overhead. Sudden motion in his periphery brought his eyes from the ceiling to his shoulder, where Raiden pushed a steaming bowl toward him, with wooden sticks hanging over its side.

Graciously, Kort received the meal, taking the bowl from Raiden. He peered inside, at fish stew with rice noodles in thin broth. In that moment, Kort considered the portion. *It's twice the size of meals Genze and I would eat!*

He ate without hesitation, and the food tasted so good to him, better than any of his recent meals. *This broth from the fish makes it so tasty!* he thought to himself, while working the sticks and slurping away. Meanwhile, from the corner of his eye he saw the elven fisher take a seat nearby. At an unwelcomed moment, right when Kort had a mouthful of food, he heard Raiden start asking questions.

"So, you're from Reiju?"

Kort continued chewing, and nodded his head to answer. He voraciously slurped afterward, the only sound being heard after Raiden's words. *Mind yourself.* With sudden self-awareness, Kort quieted his eating.

He devoured the stew under the watchful gaze of Raiden, thinking to himself while munching the food. *Have I seen him before? I've been to Doj so many times, and maybe we've crossed in the market, without exchanging a word?* He wondered if this were possible.

"What brings you to sleep under my boat, rather than on a mat, like others?" The follow-on question caught Kort off-guard, and after a pause, he tried to deflect it with half-truths. *Must not divulge too much information… I'm wanted for Garlew's murder, apparently even in these parts, given Sagult's pursuit.*

"I'm looking for work here," he finally answered, "and I just needed somewhere to stay tonight."

An image of Elucid appeared in his mind, along with a recollection of the knight's metaphorical ramble on fishing for more than fish. *Maybe just fishing for fish…*

"I want to fish." The words escaped Kort's mouth.

"If it pleases you, I can take you fishing tomorrow."

Kort noted how Raiden paused for a while, as if to judge the expression on the ex-knight's face. *Did my silence offend him? Should I say something?*

"My boat is older," he added, "but it stays afloat."

Kort smiled.

"Works for me. I know how to cast and mend nets."

When silence developed, Kort tried to distance his next question from Raiden's last.

"How are the waters? Do you catch many fish?"

He waited for Raiden to answer, and meanwhile, discerned deep contemplation from the elven fisher's face. *Why so much thought in his reply?*

"If I continue fishing, I always catch enough to survive," Raiden said finally. "I imagine if I stop fishing, I'll starve to death."

Kort hoped the statement was just Raiden's dry humor, but unfortunately the elven fisher stared back without a grin. *He's serious.*

"While it's harder to catch fish, I match that challenge with more effort, by fishing longer. And if there's no fish in one part of the sea, I go and fish somewhere new."

Kort nodded his head, and silence built again. He removed his gaze from Raiden, and focused once again on the stew. A few moments later he looked back, upon hearing him talk again.

"You know, there's a great drought in Doj. Maybe Reiju is affected too."

Kort continued eating with some thought, and eye engagement. *Yeah, there's a drought. Not news to me.*

"With the months of heat wave, dry spell, and no rain, much of Doj's rice crop has been lost before the harvest. Some rice has been harvested early, just because."

Kort chewed even slower as different thoughts fired in his mind, one after the other. *There's a drought, therefore a rice shortage, and thus Raiden mustn't have much food.* Guilt made his stomach unsettled, and the chewed rice in his mouth suddenly formed a glob at the top of his throat. *Just swallow.* And when he did, Kort heard Raiden speak.

"That's actually the last of my food."

To an abrupt stop, the ex-knight brought the wooden sticks in the bowl. He felt a prickly sensation in his feet at that moment, perhaps from sitting for so long or maybe it was his body's way of reacting to this most shocking news. *What?!*

"Worry not," Raiden said, raising his hand.

Kort stared back with his mouth open, bits of food still on his tongue, pieces felt in the crevices of his mouth. He peered down at the near empty bowl with broth wetting its bottom, where a few crumpled rice noodles dotted the shiny surface. *What... have I done?*

"We're able to fish, and willing to fish. Maybe Destiny will favor us with a catch. Greater things no doubt await us, if we survive what comes."

"What... comes?" Kort slowly mouthed the words. He watched Raiden look back with relaxed features, seeming very serious.

"Famine," said Raiden. "It's perhaps weeks away."

At the statement, his mind wandered to a distant memory, something about a story he heard when a child, strangely involving famine. *What does Genze's book say?* He wondered about any tales describing famine. *What happened?*

"Don't waste a morsel," Raiden said from the floor, motioning to the bowl Kort held. The words drug him from his thoughts. *Right...*

So not to leave any part of his meal uneaten, Kort finished every last scrap of stew in the bowl. Guilt burned his gut, and his chest felt constricted. He struggled to breathe, with Raiden's odd benevolence in mind. *Why would he give a stranger his last food?* To himself, the ex-knight pondered the matter quietly, after setting down the clean bowl beside him on the floor. *People do more good for me, than I can even do for them!* The thought made him sad, while in the same instance, inspired to do better.

"If you want to fish in the morn, you'd better rest!"

Those words broke Kort's concentration, and pulled him back into the elven fisher's home. He saw Raiden stretch out a mat and then lay it in the corner, afterward spreading a worn beige blanket across the bedding. *Just like with Genze.*

"That should do it," Raiden said to himself.

Kort felt dazed with everything happening so fast.

"Destiny keep you this night," said Raiden after going into his room and pulling the paper door shut.

"The same to you," Kort replied as it closed. *Well... fishing in Doj came easier than expected.* His thought was an eventual one, after taking a moment to consider his providence, in spite of what had been an otherwise difficult job market in Soku.

"Thank Destiny," Kort muttered to himself, as he plopped onto the mat. His body hurt, and he felt exhausted with the huge expense of energy today. *Running from Sagult takes more out of me than fishing on the seas!* In a moment of still he sat there, until the next thought entered his mind. *Being on the waters tomorrow should make me harder to find. That should give me more time...*

Kort watched as the glow soon flickered away, of Raiden's paper lamp that was visible beneath the sliding door. It left him with only the moonlight coming through the side window, which was covered by netting to keep out the mosquitoes. *Just sleep.* The idea seemed amenable to his weary self, but curiosity made him reconsider.

Slowly Kort's eyes trailed to the burlap bag containing the Book of Karnatha. Without thinking the matter over more, he suddenly got up and took hold of the sack, to finger through its contents until finding the book. He gently laid the sack down and then in both hands, held the leather-bound volume, to feel its weight.

In a single moment, he dived right into the book, turning the parchment pages with care, though vigorously, to find any story about famine. *Whether legend or prophecy, somewhere this book tells of famine, and I need to know what it says!* At the top of his mind, Kort felt that legend about famine would be informative to developments in Doj and Reiju. At the bottom of his mind, perhaps even the depths of Kort's subconscious, prophecy about famine was of greater interest.

As Kort looked over the text by moonlight, he realized the book was penned in Hirishin but the words were not from the character set used to decorate Raiden's lamp and the sliding door. *This is romanticized Hirishin,* he thought to himself, about a language where the words were written using the Mainlandish alphabet, so to help Mainlanders learn the otherwise enigmatic words of the oriental folk.

Likely this is among few books Genze found that he could read! Kort's thought was founded in fact, as Hirishin was not Genze's native tongue, and he always struggled with the written language over the spoken.

Amidst his flipping, Kort happened upon the Dark Prophecy, and the finding jerked him. His shoulders shot back in surprise, and he dropped the book, hearing it hit the floor with a loud thud! Instantly, sounds arose of stirring from behind the door to Raiden's room.

Kort's body was frozen in place, just as his eyes, which he could not remove from a story that he had never brought himself to read. He stared at the open book on the floor, his heartbeats fast and his breaths tight, as if a vice clamped about his chest. *The Dark Prophecy... Destiny help me...*

Kort knew little of the Dark Prophecy, aside from it being penned by the oracles some three years' prior. It was the latest addition to some copies of the Book of Karnatha, though not even included in texts existing before the Triangle Kingdoms. Kort understood the Triangle Kingdoms an alliance that united the dwarves, elves, and humans of the Mainland for economic reasons predating Saipei, and this union gradually melded their tongues and culture into something commonly known as *Mainlandish*.

Kort remembered being told how certain sects of the Karnathan Church regarded older versions of the Book of Karnatha to be complete, in particular those in elven script. The same sects proclaimed the Dark Prophecy—a new addition to that text—as heresy. Kort thought to himself. *There might be no other reading more shunned throughout all the Mainland and Isles!* He found it sobering that this very prophecy of much debate lied at his feet, just begging to be read.

When Kort heard soft snoring from Raiden's chamber, he kneeled before the book and leaned forward to grab it from the floor. As he did, his hands trembled, but even so, he still took hold of it. The moment his fingers contacted the parchment, his eyes met the page, and one thing led to another.

**** Kort's Reading ****

The Dark Prophecy
(Unknown Location—Circa 2032 A.R.)

The Child of Light will be called Kayareth, and shall rise up in humility from the West to discover the white shard of sword, pulling it from the depths of the Korinth Ocean. Even though broken in body and spirit, Kayareth will lift famine from Logan to heal the land. And with the famine's remission, one of low standing shall be recognized as the Child throughout Karnath, and many will follow in the Child's way.

From the East, the Child of Darkness named Shaizan shall rise in anger to recover the black shard of sword from off a mountain. Shaizan will wound a dragon and pierce the gloom, ending a sorceress' rein of power in Karnath. Unrecognized as the Child, Shaizan will pass through the land in deceit, with few expecting Dark deeds.

Before sundown on the third day after the Children touch each shard's grip, the Army of Light as a Lion shall wage war at Gallow Cliff against the Army of Darkness as a Serpent, just as Shaizan and Kayareth too shall fight, with the state of Karnath and Destiny to hang in the conflict's balance.

And this war shall not be without a victor, for that day the one called Shaizan shall defeat Kayareth in a final duel between the Darkness and the Light. Recovering from thence the second shard of sword, the Child of Wrath will meld it together with the first. Doing so shall restore the blade to its full state when forged by Destiny. With the whole gray blade, Shaizan shall hail time's end and then the Age of Darkness—upon Destiny, Karnath, and all those who dwell therein.

****

Kort slowly lifted his eyes from the page, and plunged his mind into contemplations of the deepest sort. He thought about the coincidence between Elucid and Raiden's words. *Fish for more than fish, for good destiny.* His mind jumped to the imminent threat to Doj and Reiju. *Famine comes.* And then his mind pondered something else, a personal admission. *I'm perhaps of the lowest standing in Karnath.*

"No," he gasped aloud, shaking his head. "That's all this is… coincidence." He put the Book of Karnatha to the side, and slouched his back up against the wall, letting his mind wander aimlessly. *It can't be. Something much Darker than this must be upon me, the worst of bad destinies!* The situation's coincidences aligned with the words of Elucid, yet the woman in white did say, to trust not the crimson knight. Kort clasped his head, not knowing what to believe.

The allegations against him in Sergros rang out in his mind. *You're a traitor to Sergros, the murderer of Garlew, and a betrayer of the Guard's oaths!* Then came into his mind the recollection of that evil spirit chasing him in Tai, followed by a reiteration of the woman in white's words. *Trust not, the crimson knight.*

Kort grabbed the book and stood to his feet. In an aside, he cried out to Destiny. "For choosing bad destiny over good destiny, or no destiny at all, can it be that even worst destiny stands at my doorstep! I want to do better, Karnatha! But any good destiny I can now find—in the wake of my broken dreams, in the wake of my past misdeeds and trespasses wanton against many—is surely *not the best destiny* one could ever have!"

The book split open in Kort's hands, as he thumbed through the book, back to the Dark Prophecy. Kort read and reread it, nitpicking every detail, and contriving sundry arguments against the prophecy:

"The Child of Light shall lift famine, but it's from Logan… not Doj. The white shard… no one has ever found it… it might not even exist! Gallow Cliff… what's so special about that place? Have any of these prophecies come true… ever?" Below his breath he muttered these things. He became progressively irritated by the prospect he faced, and slammed the book shut. Kort got up and stormed to the window, looking out to those distant fields and their rice crops.

"It's not true!" he said in a harsh whisper. "It's not! I'm not the Child of Light."

At a break in Raiden's snoring, Kort heard sounds of his stirring, and the ex-knight stopped his hushed, though forceful, talk. It was denial that seeped from his heart's wounds that could not be silenced, for even when he stopped speaking, it still went on inside. *I can't be that one!*

Kort allowed time for his mind to settle, and his emotions to lose momentum. Carefully he opened the book again, and paged to the Dark Prophecy once more. The ex-knight read it slowly. As he did, Raiden's snoring rose again behind the door. *The Child of Light does great good… for many.* From the prophecy, he drew an immediate parallel to his own want of redemption and closed the book once more. *I can't do this, or can I?*

As Kort returned to the window and stared at the distant fields beneath the pale moonlight, it made him wonder if anything had changed. Willfully then, he closed his eyes and let a vivid flashback of Baal occupy his mind.

**** Kort's Flashback—Dousing Flames of Baal ****

Upon the scarlet cobblestone of Baal, Kort stood. He was painted in red and held two curved Hirishin blades, one in each hand. Ironically, Kort wore the armor of the Crimson Guard, though was now dirtied by the blood of those he swore to protect.

Despite how the smoke from fires on every rooftop irritated his eyes, he could not bring himself to look away from mass carnage all around him. Bodies littered the street, distant screaming pierced his ears, and the crackle and hiss of flames was pervasive. Ash filled the night sky to burn his nose, which could barely pick up the scent of sulfur now.

In one fluid motion, he tucked the swords away, and braced his feet as Nexus filled his enlarged aux core. He cried out to the night sky, filled with billowing smoke from burning Baal. "Surely this awakening befalls me for a reason, Karnatha! My prayer is that I've been empowered to save Baal from what approaches Juniper! I'd dump the entire sea upon this city to relieve it of fire, only if you would have it!"

As a torrent of energy ripped through Kort's core—burning him, hurting him—he channeled it toward the ocean Fuar, with the intent to lift its waters. He saw the embers swirl around him in the night, amid his struggle to douse the flames of Baal. "Arrrghhhhhh!"

****

His scream faded, as did his flashback, now banished to the far reaches of his mind, along with a thousand other Dark memories. Kort opened his eyes, and stared at the fields again. *Has anything changed? I couldn't move water then to save Baal from fire, so how would I do that now, to save Doj from famine?*

With a pause, his mind worked again. *There's only one way to find out.* As stealthily as he could, Kort snuck out of Raiden's house, hoping not to wake him this time. He took this hope with him, back on the dirt road connecting Doj to the fields, where a few remaining rice crops stood. His walk was a good half an hour or so, but seemed worth it. *A test can settle matters of doubt!*

Before long, Kort came before the cracked fields containing the rice crops. He looked at them as a challenge to coincidence, a challenge to the words of Elucid.

"If I'm the Child of Light," he said aloud, "then I can water these few crops!"

Kort stepped into his enlarged channeling chamber, where he pulled against his mental restraint—the Source entry. The door opened, admitting several flows over its threshold, streams of Nexus energy that began to fill the room. From his concentration, he returned to the field, where now, a green light shined at his midsection. Instead of waiting for his aux core to become full, he continuously transformed the energy into water while channeling more energy. This required Kort pushing his Source exit open with his trigger image in mind, and in moments, running back to pull more energy through the Source entry.

Snapping from his channeling chamber and back to the field, Kort saw a stream of green energy wander from his body's center toward the crops, the end of which formed tiny amounts of water—several beads hung midair. *Add another flow to move the water...* He stepped back into this channeling chamber and saw the droplets there, at his Source exit. To bring them over the crops, he needed another stream of Nexus, which he summoned through the Source entry, with the intention of using it to push the water drops out of his Source exit. His skin emitted a cold sweat, as he focused his mind to perform the three feats together. The thought of his possible failure was terrifying.

And in one sudden instant, the whole act fell apart! For just a moment, Kort's connection to the various energy streams became obscured, and he lost a sense over which flow was being used for what purpose. The energy in his channeling chamber funneled out the Source exit, and both Source exit and Source entry slammed closed with a loud bang. His eyes opened then, just in time for him to watch the droplets fall upon the scorched ground, cubits away from the crops yet to be harvested. *Destiny damn it!*

Kort growled gutturally over his failure. "Grrr!" *This is why telekinesis is best left untried by most...*

Once getting past his disappointment, he reluctantly moved closer to the crops, and tried again. *I shouldn't have to stand atop them, if I'm really the Child.* He juggled the doubt with everything else in his mind.

This time, Kort managed to recreate the droplets using Nexus, and a few fell on the rice. When continuously pulling energy for more water, however, he fumbled at creating additional droplets, confusing the flows again, just like before. Once again he stopped channeling, and panted heavily from this effort. Concentrating to control so many flows was tiresome. *Destiny, please help me!*

After resting a while, Kort decided he would try something else—a final attempt to water the crops. *This time, I'll fill my core with Nexus first! I should be able to create more water that way, and also, I'll perhaps avoid getting my flows confused by not needing to immediately pull more energy for creating more water or moving it...*

With that idea in mind, he returned to his enlarged channeling chamber. There, he pulled open his Source entry, and just like before, flows came in through the door, and this time, he let the energy accumulate. As soon as Nexus occupied the space between the floors, ceiling, and walls, he snapped out of his channeling chamber and back to the field, where he began transforming energy into water and using his accumulated energy to push the water at the crops. On this attempt, he made three times more droplets than before and brought them to the crops. But with a visit to his channeling chamber, he confirmed that it was nearly empty, something that threatened his ability to keep the process going. *I'm running out of Nexus!*

Still in his channeling chamber, Kort ran back to his Source entry and pulled it open. Immediately, Nexus entered through, and started to replenish the room. In a few moments, almost the entire space filled with green energy, exactly like the conditions he began with. He had filled his room, transformed the energy into water, moved it to the crops, and now, filled the room again. *It's working, as long as I don't run out of energy!*

When Kort had a smidgeon of success, he confidently tried continuously channeling to keep the room filled as he transformed the chamber's Nexus into water and pushed the droplets. In so doing, he was bearing the same risk of confusing his three flows, just like before. But the reality was, if the room went empty, he would not be able to move any water he created, and pulling more Nexus then could lead to the very same confusion.

This time as Kort did the tasks in parallel—the continuously pulling, the transforming Nexus into water, and the moving of created water droplets— something different happened; it was something unexpected. His pulling brought more energy into the room than he could transform and push out, and suddenly, Nexus dripped over his body from his Source boundary, causing him pain!

"Ahhh!" Kort cried out, as excess energy spilled from his aux core and burnt his flesh. He fell to both knees, writhing in pain, while gasping the air raggedly from the physical tolls of wielding Nexus.

In that moment, his mind was bombarded with the various challenges to watering crops by magic, none of which he could surmount. He saw himself unable to manage the three separate flows, and unable to manage the rates of pulling, pushing, and transforming Nexus. For applications other than watering crops, these particular actions seemed doable, which only added to his feelings of inadequacy.

At last, Kort gave a long exasperated sigh. *I can't… do this.* In a sudden turn of events from what initially seemed like success, he admitted defeat in Doj's fields upon this summer night, with the moon and Destiny as his witness. "I'm not the Child of Light!"

His failure validated these words, and with that, his countenance fell, as did his heart. *Elucid is wrong, and I am right to think lowly of myself!*

In his moment of weakness, kneeling there prostrate before the crops, Kort's mind began working toward a frightening new conclusion, one that he had not considered until now. *My misdeeds…. My hauntings… My warning from the woman in white… If I'm not the Child of Light, then what do these things suggest?*

Kort continued kneeling in the field, and as he did, his various thoughts strung together into a solid line of reasoning. "I'm… something Darker than the Child of Light…" he admitted, hesitantly. "I'm Shaiz…"

In the moment of that realization, Kort lost his breath and his heart skipped a beat. His skin felt cold all over, like he had frozen from the inside out. Just barely, he stopped himself from saying that name. The notion of Ma'althan's eyes going upon him made him uneasy. *But maybe, Ma'althan's eyes already fall upon me!* The thought stole his breath, and he cast it from of his mind.

All that became of Kort's simple experiment was negativity, and that negativity lingered with him each step of the way, up the dirt road from the fields, back to village Doj. Into Raiden's house Kort retreated, and finally laid himself down in the spot prepared for him.

While lying there awake, Kort's mind was laden with serious thoughts about the reality of his bad destiny. He anticipated where this might go. *You should climb Jezban and slay Sayomi, the Isles sorceress.* Kort could literally hear Elucid's booming voice in his mind, guiding him to fulfill the Dark Prophecy. *No…* he thought. *Not this!*

Upon the mat Kort tossed, as restless as could be, despite being so tired. *If I fish for more than fish, what destiny will I find?* As he wondered where his future was headed, his doubts in good destiny turned into fears that his bad destiny could never be changed, and perhaps, it might become worse yet.

"*A SIMPLE TEST*"

Chapter 31
Back in Old Karnath

For over two thousand years, the superhuman seroxians lived in the original world that Maken created; it was in a parallel dimension to New Karnath, now called Old Karnath. Maken's curse left the seroxians there after the rebellion ended, at first without food, shelter, or health.

Indeed, Maken's curse rendered their fields infertile, smashed their kingdoms to dust, and made many seroxians ill. And if that were not punishment enough for them piously standing by and letting the rebellion just happen, the insult to injury was Maken's re-creation of paradise in New Karnath and handing it over to the rebels, whose only punishment ended up being lost membership in the seroxian race.

For that, the seroxians hated the rebels and condescendingly dubbed them *inferiors,* as they were *lower races,* each one having only a share of the seroxians' greatness. By name, the inferiors were the *humans, elves, dwarves, gnomes, giants,* and *trolls.*

But even though destitute in the wake of Maken's curse, the seroxians started a long journey to recovery, and now after millennia of hard work and innovation, they rebuilt their smashed kingdoms, to erect even stronger kingdoms, more resilient to the shocks that crumbled stone and shattered *acryllum.* Six resurrected kingdoms stood from ruins of the old: *Deardrum, Sergros, Juniper, Paladin, Cyprus,* and *Gul*; these represented the way of life before Maken's punishment, and the reconstruction was widely regarded as a monumental achievement.

In addition to rebuilding their kingdoms, the seroxians learned how to terra-form Old Karnath's infertile fields, and once again, they could live off the land. To combat the illness brought about my Maken's curse, the seroxians engineered small devices unseen to the naked eye, which could repair bodily deterioration. It was one success after another for them, with the race's continued advancement attributable to many capable leaders throughout the years.

Merphonox Lercena was one such capable leader, a grandchild of Darconas and nephew to the celebrated Hrya. He was the King of Deardrum in Old Karnath, and was responsible for many advances of the seroxians in his lifetime. He united the six kingdoms under a single order known as *Seroxia,* where he presided as one of its governors. Also, he forged a productive alliance with Tekkneo in New Karnath, and championed the development of a new magic for building cores that could source Nexus energy, much like the primary core of creation. *All these advances, to move the seroxians closer to reclaiming paradise...*

The thought ran through Merphonox's mind, as he stood at a stone monument in *Grotto Tribute*, a cave carved into a massive mountain, which opened to panoramic views of the crags and fields of Old Karnath. At about seven cubits tall, with rippling muscles all over, he cast a long shadow over the monument in the fading light of day. With his head tilted down, his long graying hair fell down his neck and touched the cheeks of his chiseled face. Upon his body, he wore a two-toned tunic, one half black the other white, with gray leather pants having their legs shoved into his knee-high boots.

After a long bout of staring at the monument, he glanced outside of the grotto, noting the distant sunset on the horizon; an orange ball of fire peeked at him from behind the mountains. The sight reminded Merphonox of how long he had been there with the intentions to pray, but not the will. Several times each week, he would come to the monument, in order to beseech Karnatha for the awakening of his people to a forgotten war against the inferiors. But her continued silence made it easy for him to become distracted.

He sighed in frustration, and brought back his wandering eyes to the monument, a gray ellipsoidal mass of rock, hung midair on a Nexus energy field, sourced from a core at the monument's foot. It was centered at the rear wall of the grotto, with large spirals of translucent, acryllum sconces on each side, also floating upon energy. In each scone burned a candle, altogether hundreds in number, which flickered yellow light throughout the cave.

While the monument and the candles commemorated those who died in the *Tragedy of Old Karnath*, their death as a cause to reclaim paradise became one that fewer seroxians cared about these days, especially the leaders. *If Vaxlan doesn't care about reclaiming New Karnath, then I shall! My grandfather's disappearance and my uncle's death resulted from the inferiors' deceit long ago, and I'll see they are avenged! I'll see that the seroxians get their due restitution!*

The scene of Merphonox alone at the monument spoke of a prevailing apathy among newer generations in Old Karnath—apathy to the past injustices of Maken's punishment, and the slaying of Hrya long ago. Those who were not directly affected no longer cared, a sentiment stemming from other governors, such as Vaxlan, pushing a different agenda than vengeance on the inferiors and reclaiming paradise. *Have these losses been forgotten by all, except those who were alive to see Maken take away our land, except those who share blood with the fallen?!*

As so many times before, these frustrations made it difficult for Merphonox to pray at the monument—for revenge against the inferiors, for regaining paradise lost. As his eyes fell upon the monument's smooth surface, he saw the names etched into its stone, of all those who died in the Tragedy of Old Karnath. He scanned the names, one after another, with many strung together in a single line, until reaching the monument's middle, where a gold placard was mounted that showed Hrya's name in black lettering.

At the sight of that placard, visions flashed before his eyes, according to the accounts on record of Hrya's noble attempt at peace with the inferiors. Merphonox saw Hrya and Eriens leading a caravan laden with gifts for the lower races into New Karnath, just as it happened over a thousand years ago. And then, in a sudden burst of crimson, he visualized the bloodshed they faced, when met by the inferiors' hostility. As historians told, the Triangle Kingdoms of New Karnath attacked Hrya and his caravan, and though Eriens tried to defend them, all the seroxians who entered the Coveted Land were killed. Merphonox had a series of visions that progressed from the seroxians entering New Karnath, the carnage that ensued, all the way to Magicia—a human sorceress who established the portal between both worlds, in a fiendish plot to lure in the seroxians with hopes of an alliance, only for them to meet their demise. In his mind, he pictured the sorceress of red braided hair and gray eyes; she stared coldly over a field in New Karnath covered in seroxian blood. The thought angered him, and stirred up his contempt for the inferiors. *I hate her and the lower races, for what they did to my uncle! And my grandfather, who vanished from a hospice bed to die an isolated death, as he mourned over Hrya!*

Merphonox was the son of Penultum, who was brother to Hrya, both of them being the sons of Darconas. He inherited his fierce contempt for the inferiors from his father, who used to swear that when walking the fields of Old Karnath at night, he could hear his brother's blood crying out to him from the ground, across the dimensions from New Karnath, where Hrya's bones lied, never being brought back to Old Karnath. And that blood demanded that Penultum avenge the seroxians who were slain in the tragedy.

Just the same, Merphonox spent time walking the fields of Old Karnath, to listen for the voices. And like his father would swear to hearing them, so would he. For many times, Merphonox heard Hrya's blood calling out to him, and it was a sound that haunted him in the years to come, a sound that he would always remember. For it demanded the same of him as of his father, that he should avenge the slain seroxians.

Trapped inside his head, Hrya's voice kept a fire burning within Merphonox to reconcile the injustices that his forefathers suffered. He would likely live twenty times longer than any human, and in that time, he would preserve his father's anger over the Tragedy of Old Karnath. The thought stirred up vivid memories of how Penultum felt, and a flashback whisked his mind away.

**** Merphonox's Flashback—Bitter Penultum ****

FATE'S FRAY, by J.A. Tocksworth

As a child, Merphonox used to watch his father in the study of Castle Deardrum, from around one of its many bookcases. Penultum would stand at the study's window, staring out into the city surrounding the castle and the mountains beyond the city. He was dressed pristinely, wearing a fanciful royal vesture that bore the insignia of Deardrum—a progression of an eclipsed sun to half-eclipsed and full suns, all encompassed by a gray serpent.

Penultum spoke to himself, embittered by the past.

"How long, Karnatha, will you stare idly upon me, amidst my wants of vengeance?! The inferiors stole paradise from me, just as all other seroxians! The inferiors stole my brother Hrya from me, as he died in an ambush that Magicia brought upon him! The inferiors stole my father Darconas from me too, as he vanished when learning of brother's death! The inferiors are responsible for what has become my Fate's Fray, selfishness being their sole motive. All this, because they won't share paradise!"

When Penultum lowered his face to the floor, the boy Merphonox could barely discern his next words, spoken in a low voice. "Magicia seeks to keep New Karnath among her people... She wishes for the reproach of Maken's punishment to be felt indefinitely by the seroxians! The lower races live a hundred years if not more, and then pass from New Karnath. Oh, so many generations of inferiors have come and gone since Maken's punishment! They remember not what it's like to be seroxian, and so the inferiors' punishment has lesser effect than ours! We live to remember what we had."

Still looking out the window, Penultum suddenly shouted and raised a balled fist. "Our punishment lives on as we live in this cursed land, for hundreds of years past Maken's deed, while knowing these inferiors enjoy paradise!"

Merphonox heard Penultum scream loudly then.

"Darconas abstained from the rebellion, so he and his followers should have stayed seroxian and inherited New Karnath! Instead, Destiny spited us by having Laotzu and the cursed ones possess New Karnath, only to our suffering!"

"Father!" cried out Merphonox then, from his place of hiding. The teary child watched on with worry, beholding Penultum now aquiver, deep wrath evident through his warped features and shaking body.

****

Merphonox snapped back to his present reality at the monument, inside Grotto Tribute. *It was too late for him then, just as it's too late for me now.* He considered how years ago in his childhood, he neither could understand the Darkness that possessed his father nor could he help in any way, just as his children were equally helpless to penetrate the deep conviction that gripped his soul, of Maken's wrong—Destiny's wrong. *My inheritance from father might be likened unto Kilwroth's unwholesome inheritance, from Eriens!*

288

The thought made Merphonox solemn. After the tragedy long ago, there were a group of seroxians who insisted that Eriens really embarked for New Karnath armed and fully intending to take out his anger on the inferiors. That was plausible, since Eriens left in the wake of bad destiny—his wife's untimely death, during the childbirth of their son, Kilwroth. Speculation back then was that Eriens sought revenge on Destiny through Karnatha's beloved inferiors, but in so doing, he brought an unwholesome inheritance of unknown proportions upon Kilwroth and his own kingdom—Malgun. In the years following the tragedy, Malgun imploded under social, political, and economic duress and Kilwroth became a recluse in his father's broken kingdom, which was never reconstructed as the others. This, in some sense, made the speculation a fulfilled prophecy and gave it a place in seroxian legend.

In Merphonox's case, he drew an analogue to the olden story by regarding Penultum's contempt as his unwholesome inheritance, a thing that might destroy him and his descendants, until this wrong was made right. *This unsettled score is my unwholesome inheritance—my gloom. From grandfathers to fathers, and from fathers to sons, may our anger be passed down until the balance is settled, and the seroxians reclaim New Karnath!*

Still unable to pray, his focus trailed outside the grotto again, to the mountains on the horizon seated beneath the dusk sky, now a violet and crimson aura that clung to black outlines of crag rock. He pondered then what kept him so committed to something that destroyed his father. *Anger at Destiny… Guilt for being unable to stop it… Lust for the Coveted Land…* All the various feelings vied against one another, but in the end, their combination sustained his commitment to avenging the fallen, rather than any one of them alone.

Gazing off into the horizon reminded Merphonox that past those mountains were more mountains, and that was easily a metaphor for life, in that new challenges often arise after conquering the old. *Father died confronted by challenges, some that I've now overcome, but many that I still face.* Merphonox's mind wandered to thoughts of Penultum, and how the seroxian saw a very short rule, before a serious illness took his life. He remembered then how Penultum's body was burned at sea over prayers to Karnatha, in the customary ritual for funerals of seroxian kings. As Merphonox watched his deceased father go up in flames, he swore to this day hearing his voice, shouting to him then. *Remember my cause! Avenge their blood, since I could not!* Those sounds resonated of Hrya's voice, the one that called out from his blood. Years ago during that requiem, Penultum's voice ran through his ears as it still did now, serving as another call to this mission forgotten by many seroxians.

Struggling to pray, Merphonox's eyes drifted back to the monument, where the floating crystal-like sconces hovered midair at each side, in two large spirals. The candles inside had fires slowly burning their wicks to cinders, cold and flameless remains. It was analogous to the prevalent apathy in Old Karnath, a reminder that Merphonox was nearly alone in his mission. The realization conjured up faith from the depths of his soul. *But I trust that Karnatha hasn't forsaken me in this!* And with that, he at last found the voice and words to pray.

"Oh Destiny, hear this day my prayer!" he shouted finally, with no one around to hear. "I ask you restore the monument's purpose in Old Karnath. Though this memorial, may memories of those lost survive in our children! With the sheer number of names upon this shrine, let my people know in ages now and to come, that the lower races are devils which killed a great number of us! Bless this memorial, Karnatha… Use it to stoke a fire of change in Old Karnath so that many join me to reclaim the Coveted Land!"

Destiny only knew how far Merphonox's prayer even got. Hate, revenge, bitterness, and other negative emotions fueled his every word. These were aftereffects of his father's broken dreams, and those of his father's father. The emotions degenerated his character, with his own inability to cope with Fate's Fray for Penultum, Hrya, and Darconas. He stood against the odds of having their Fate's Fray become his own, and the thought inspired him to break the cycle. While he was aware of all the negativity that motivated him, and the possible risks that this entailed, he considered it a chance well worth taking. *If reclaiming paradise is all that becomes of my possible demise in this pursuit, I find that outcome adequate!*

As Merphonox stood staring at the monument, more time deprived him of the focus needed to continue praying. His mind wandered off once again. Like before, he tilted his head and lowered his face before the monument, appearing involved on the exterior, though being completely detached inside. His mind drifted to thoughts of entering New Karnath to war with the inferiors. *The inferiors are weak, so recovering New Karnath is a matter of bridging our worlds once more. And that will require a large Sink.*

Merphonox considered how the seams were naturally opened between the spatial fabrics of New Karnath's dimension and that of Old Karnath. Merphonox knew that these seams could be pulled together by channeling large amounts of Nexus from a major outflow point in one world, over the seams themselves, and into a deep Sink in the other world—a large inflow point where excess spent energies could be stored. When the seams came together, a bridge connected both worlds through a portal. *The major outflow point is Gallow Cliff in either world.* He pondered how the challenge was not channeling magic over the seams. *We lack a Sink—that's the fundamental problem.*

His conclusion stemmed from the seroxians' reality, which was caused by Hrya long ago, who took the black shard of sword over the last-established bridge into New Karnath, in order to help Eriens fight the inferiors. *The blade's internal aux core served as a Sink for our bridge then, with Magicia channeling energies into it from Gallow Cliff in New Karnath. Though now, that shard is in the other dimension.*

Relevant to finding a new Sink, Merphonox considered his plan founded in his established alliance between Seroxia and Tekkneo in New Karnath. Every so often, he communicated with a so-called technologist there named *Perry Lindenburg*. Lindenburg built something called the *exo-core* that could replicate this capability of the shards of sword. *This'll be our Sink, hopefully without waiting much longer.* Merphonox's patience wore, as the exo-core was still under development.

Merphonox returned from his thoughts, back to the monument. The sun sank lower beneath the horizon, as night slowly descended upon Old Karnath. A refreshing breeze blew over him then, stirring his tunic and lifting his long graying hair that flowed naturally in the wind. He knelt at the monument and closed his eyes, while touching the gray stone. Against his skin, its surface felt like cold marble. His eyes focused to behold the placard, and he lowered his head in reverence.

"Rest eternally brave uncle," he said.

And then, in a voice not much louder than a whisper, Merphonox prayed again to Karnatha. "Oh Destiny, spare us from continued want of something destined to be ours. New Karnath belongs to the seroxians, so I implore you that it be delivered back into our hands."

Suddenly, Merphonox sensed a large shadow pass over the monument. Alarmed, he immediately opened his eyes, stood from his kneeling position, and drew Nexus into his aux core. A green glow radiated from his center, in the single instant it took him to go into his vast channeling chamber, run up to its Source entry, and pull open the large doors with his muscled arms. The series of actions caused Nexus to flow into the room, filling it from floor to ceiling.

From that split second of concentration, Merphonox bounced back to Grotto Tribute, now with a connection to the ambient energy field. Through it, he sensed nothing strange. *Like waters on the calm Asmear Sea.*

Deriving some peace from that, Merphonox calmed himself, and turned his eyes back to the monument. But when he did, he saw its gold placard now read "Merphonox" instead of "Hrya"! His jaw dropped.

"REBELLION AGAINST MAKEN"

Chapter 32
Shadowing, the Cursed Fate

Merphonox was extremely unsettled by the sight of his name upon the placard commemorating Hrya's death. He took a few steps back from the monument, and drew Nexus into his aux core, connecting himself to the ambient energy field. All in one instant, he could sense the forces of gentle evening breezes and vibrations in the air from his own breathing.

Still sensing nothing strange, Merphonox turned his head from side to side, anxious for what might happen. He snarled, "One of strange sorcery, do show yourself! Today you meet your match!"

At his final word, Merphonox saw a shadowy figure emerge from the placard's black lettering, leaping into the shade cast by the monument! It resembled the crisp outline of a tall seroxian's shadow, standing vertically before him without depth, only having breadth and height. The placard afterward read "Hrya", as before.

Never seeing such a thing as this shadow, the sight startled Merphonox, but that in no way prevented him from boldly demanding answers.

"Who are you, and by what folly does a walking curse of nature stumble into the realm of such powerful beings, Maken's own handiwork—the seroxians?!"

Upon saying this, Merphonox heard a garbled voice come from the shadow, deep in tone like that of a male seroxian.

"Who I am is not the question, but what."

"Speak then, of what you are!"

He watched the shadowy figure throw itself onto Merphonox's silhouette upon the cave floor, morphing in shape to perfectly overlay it.

"The answer is what you see," replied the shadow.

Merphonox looked down upon his own shadow and then remarked with cunning. "You odd being, profess not to be a person, but the shadow of a great king?"

At that, he watched the shadowy figure stand erect.

"Can you believe this thing?"

"How could I?" asked Merphonox. "Does my father's shadow speak to me, beyond his grave in Asmear?"

In the blink of an eye, Merphonox saw the shadow reposition itself, now appearing on his other side.

"How could he or his shadow speak?" said the shadowy figure. "Penultum has passed from this world, and the deceased speak not."

Merphonox studied the shadowy figure, which seemed to be able to take whatever shape it willed. The sight amazed him, and prompted questions in his mind. *How is that possible?! What is this being, without a body?!*

"How do you know my father?" Merphonox asked sharply, his words piercing the air like a sharpened javelin. Just then, he saw the shadowy figure vanish, to reappear before the monument.

"Does a father know his sons?"

Merphonox stared back, with an outraged expression upon his face. *This is no time for games!* he thought to himself, taken aback by the mere suggestion. *This shadow cannot be my grandfather.*

"The monument to the fallen in Old Karnath is a sacred place," shouted Merphonox. "Not one for jokes!"

"Why assume that? I joke not, and make no folly."

With that reply, anger acidified Merphonox's tone.

"Know your place in the world, fiend! For you are but a shadow, not a powerful seroxian!"

Immediately following his last word came the shadowy figure's response. "But I was…"

"You? Unthinkable!" Merphonox roared. "My father was a powerful seroxian, and his father even more powerful! My grandfather is the subject of legends written to immortalize his great deeds, of rebuilding the broken kingdoms and helping the seroxians recover from Maken's curse! You are nothing compared to my titan predecessors!"

With his words, the shadowy figure became quiet. After a long intermission of calm night breezes, the garbled voice sounded again.

"Why do you find this so hard to believe?"

The shadow purporting the same thing as before shook Merphonox with rage. *This being insists upon lies! For surely my grandfather is not a shadow!* Merphonox channeled more Nexus, the green glow ever present at his core. He held the Nexus after accumulating it, ready to hurl the energy at the shadowy figure, which now, sorely offended him. "No tolerance have I for lies and disgraces!" said Merphonox angrily. "Now be gone from this world! Leave a king alone to his own kingdom!"

But as much as Merphonox wished for the shadow to leave him alone, to stop picking at wounds that had not healed in centuries—of tragedy after tragedy in his family—the shadow was not displaced with his request. And that brought Merphonox's blood to a boil. *How dare this being linger, in spite of a seroxian's command?!*

Suddenly, Merphonox put his open hands together at their wrists, pulling them toward his body. A large sphere of Nexus formed between his open palms, a glowing ball of green energy that surged about furiously. "Be gone!" he shouted at the top of his lungs, hurling the mass of magical power right at the shadowy figure!

Merphonox witnessed the blast of magic fly from his palms faster than lightning, going past the monument and hitting the shadow straight on! But when the shadowy figure absorbed the energy, he saw the walking silhouette glow green for a moment, but then return to its same color of dark gray.

"What are you?!" Merphonox asked, simply not believing his attack had no effect whatsoever.

"I'm the shadow of a king no more," the shadowy figure answered. "Standing before you now is the shadow of Darconas, the father of Penultum."

This claim from the shadow dropped Merphonox's jaw. He stood frozen in place, cubits from the monument, with his hands together at his center from his attack. And it was then that his mind began to consider the matter over. *Could it be, that this being speaks the truth?*

Merphonox lowered his hands to his sides.

"Prove it to me."

"By what?" asked Darconas. "Shall I recount how your uncle eventually saw me as but a shadow, with my body gone? Shall I describe that saddened look in his eyes? I could say all this and more, yet your doubt would remain in the absence of faith."

"How can this be?!"

"What you see is what you shall become," Darconas answered. "It's what all seroxians will become, for time can be most cruel to us. I assure you that some fates are worse than death, and this is one such fate. I can no longer do anything, but rather, just be."

Merphonox walked closer to the shadow. He carefully inspected the silhouette, being only in two dimensions of space, like some kind of apparition. He extended his hand into the shadow, and it passed right through! *That's unlike anything I've ever seen!* he thought, his face wrinkled by disbelief.

"Seroxians live and die, but they do not become shadows," Merphonox said finally, trying his other hand through the silhouette with similar results.

"Verily, some seroxians you know have died, but you're choosing to overlook a big problem facing Seroxia—*the disappeared.*"

Merphonox raised his eyebrow, acting like the comment took him by surprise, but inside, he knew that there was indeed a big problem in Seroxia concerning just this. For as long as he could remember, elderly seroxians disappeared without explanation. Many conjectures were offered up throughout the kingdoms as to why this was happening, none of them sufficing to satisfy the families who were affected. *Especially my father*, he thought then, recalling how Penultum even was skeptical that Darconas left his hospice bed to mourn Hrya's death in solitude.

"You pretend to be so knowledgeable," Darconas said, breaking Merphonox's thoughts. "Yet you can't explain those elderly in your kingdom who simply disappear. What are your thoughts about this, that these older seroxians just run away into the night?"

"That sounds plausible to you?" Darconas asked rhetorically, and simply went on. "I suppose any theory always holds without experiment. Perhaps no shadowed seroxian can overcome the humility of losing their body, to speak of it. The life once known to the shadowed is most haunting. Previously having the ability to do, I'm now restricted to only be and nothing more! Such is the experience of these ones as woeful as I, the shadowed of Old Karnath! Let me tell you how this happened to me…"

Merphonox listened with intrigue, as Darconas told him a story never heard before, of a powerful seroxian king who shadowed during Eriens' exploits for the black shard in the Mountains of Liath, over a millennium ago in Old Karnath. Darconas told him how the king lost everything—his body, his family, and his kingdom—all fragments of another's broken dream. As the story went on, night fell outside of Grotto Tribute, and Merphonox saw the sunset yield to the dark night sky.

"What you never knew is that Hrya found me in the hospice before embarking to New Karnath, as a shadow on the wall! And when he learned of my state, he sought to do more than making an alliance with the inferiors upon entering the Coveted Land: he sought to find the cure for my ailment."

As Darconas continued speaking these words, it was obviously from a rich experience, and Merphonox became convinced that this could only come through a life once lived. *The shadowy figure is clearly the shadow of Darconas,* he thought, *Deardrum's true king!*

Overwhelmed by emotion, Merphonox fell to both knees. *More than I, this shadow deserves to rule Deardrum and preside as a governor over Seroxia!* Kneeling there, Merphonox felt deep remorse for the harsh things he said, when the shadowy figure first claimed to be his grandfather. *What a fool was I, to say the great Darconas was nothing compared to my titan predecessors! He is my titan predecessor, the one who rebuilt the kingdoms of Old Karnath after Maken's punishment!*

"Forgive me," pled Merphonox, repentantly.

Darconas stayed as he was, giving a garbled reply.

"Rise, King of Deardrum. Not in this land or any other, shall a powerful king kneel to one so debased and lowly as me! Do stand, and let the mysteries of your kingdom be revealed."

Slowly Merphonox got upon his feet, and when he did, he felt a sudden shift in the Nexus field. Merphonox went to his vast channeling chamber, where he still stood at his Source entry, pulling it open so that streams of energy spilt over its threshold, gushing onto the floor like water. The water's level got higher and higher, in time filling the room from floor to ceiling.

At one corner of his channeling chamber, Merphonox saw the shadowy figure extend an outstretched hand. "Link to me," instructed Darconas, "and link to full knowledge of the Dark fate awaiting Seroxia."

Amid his deep concentration, Merphonox took the shadow's hand and established a link to Darconas over the energy field. In the very moment of contact, information surged through his mind, burning him as memories settled into place—Darconas' memories.

"Arghhh!" he cried, and fell to his knees.

Scenes of people and places flashed through his mind, and it became clear to him then, how elderly seroxians literally became their shadow beyond a certain age, and how these *shadow seroxians* would slip between the seams holding together the spatial fabrics of both worlds, searching for the River of Life in New Karnath, so to reverse their condition.

"The shadow seroxians are called vespers in New Karnath," Darconas finished, "and are restricted to moving about, only through shadows and the darkness of night."

Merphonox panted on his knees, clutching his head.

"What… was that?" he asked.

"Some of my ether, which I imparted to you," replied Darconas, "so now you know."

Gasping the air, Merphonox slowly rose to feet. When standing, he begged the shadow. "Please tell me, Darconas… How can I have my people bath in this River of Life? I need to prevent the fate of shadowing from befalling others in Seroxia! The seroxians are destined for so much more than becoming their own shadows!"

His urgent tone reflected the dire contemplations at the back of his mind. *Shadowing combined with the seroxians' exile to this cursed land can only mean that Maken's punishment to us is all the more unfair! There's nothing more unjust in all of Old and New Karnath!*

"The River of Life is hidden in New Karnath," Darconas answered, "so you must find it to prevent everyone in Old Karnath from shadowing over time!"

Those words soured Merphonox's face.

"We can't enter New Karnath just yet," he admitted with some shame. "But there's a plan to replicate the Sink in order to create the bridge into New Karnath, but that work isn't yet completed."

"It need not be, for there's another way."

Merphonox relaxed his face. "Oh?"

"Yes," Darconas replied. "Despite the tragedy, Magicia is willing to use the black shard to create the bridge from New Karnath, opposite to the way it was done before, but equally effective. She will do so under the seroxians' promise of peace and with one additional contingency: that we join her in a war against Darkness. In return, she'll lead us to the River of Life. Magicia knows where it's located and has promised it to us, if only we fully cooperate."

The very suggestion incited Merphonox. *Trust that deceptive sorceress?! Not a chance!* His feelings were so strong that they quickly made their way to his mouth.

"Never would I conspire with her!" Merphonox shouted, in what was almost a reflex.

"Fine, let Seroxia become a Land of Shadows."

"Absolutely not!" replied Merphonox, a bit frantic. "How can you so easily trust her?! What if she betrays us, like before?!"

"History has led you to believe the opposite of what's true. You should know that Eriens betrayed a trust, not Magicia. And Kilwroth paid for that, in ways none of us even know. The legend of the Unwholesome Inheritance is very true!"

Darconas continued. "Magicia actually helped Hrya stop Eriens, who wouldn't withhold his wrath against the lower races, upon entering New Karnath."

Merphonox grinded his teeth. *I don't believe a word of this, even if it's said by Darconas! And I won't trust Magicia! Not now, and not ever!*

With a moment of silence between them, however, Merphonox began to ponder the matter differently. It occurred to him that he really should trust Darconas. And furthermore, his trust of Darconas should prevail over his mistrust of Magicia. *There just ought to be an alternative plan, should trusting Magicia become a poor choice again.*

"What's your backup for finding the River of Life, should this not go as expected?"

"It may be to your surprise," answered Darconas after a pause, "but like you, I've also forged an alliance with Tekkneo in New Karnath, the likeminded kingdom of study and innovation as Deardrum, who often takes sides in the various conflicts throughout the Coveted Land."

Merphonox jumped hastily to a conclusion.

"I told you, the exo-core isn't ready!" he snapped.

"I'm not planning to bridge our worlds with it," said Darconas. "For that matter, I'm not planning on bridging our worlds at all, should this plan fail. My contingency plan for finding the River of Life involves something novel."

Merphonox found himself intrigued.

"What is it?" he asked, his brow wrinkled.

"Tekkneo has made some stunning advances in what they call *material science*, whereby special weapons have been forged that shadow seroxians can touch, in a world with so many things untouchable by vespers."

Merphonox recalled his inability to touch Darconas at all. *My hand passed right through his silhouette…*

"Tekkneo takes a side once again, and pledges to help me arm vespers and organize a *Legion of Shadows* to scour New Karnath for the River of Life. I've started the search already, to not lose any time."

Darconas went on. "The shortest path to the river though, would be with Magicia's help. She will lead us to it, if we promise to help with her quandary. Focus now on her conditions, so that we might gain her assistance."

"I'm listening," Merphonox muttered. *And I don't like it either*, he thought to himself.

"Enter in peace with the lower races, except one."

"Do we have Magicia's promise that the lower races will receive the seroxians in peace?!" Merphonox shot back. "I'm doubtful that this happened before."

With a pause and another cool breeze, Darconas said, "Magicia vows that the tragedy won't repeat itself, if all seroxians who enter heed her instructions. But, like I said, the seroxians must wage war upon one and only one inferior—a man."

"Nothing prevents you from going on. Do tell."

"Magicia needs the seroxians to fight… Shaizan."

The statement distressed Merphonox. The seroxian oracles had forecasted Shaizan winning the Game for Darkness at Gallow Cliff in Old Karnath, before they all went blind some three years ago. While he was aware of the so-called Dark Prophecy in Seroxia, what Darconas disclosed now changed all of his expectations. *The Battle for Destiny happens in New Karnath rather than in Old Karnath? Shaizan is an inferior, rather than a seroxian?*

"Well, will you join this cause?" asked Darconas.

"I pledge myself to causes that I understand," countered Merphonox. "Explain to me first, how the Dark Prophecy comes to New Karnath, where Shaizan is an inferior! Our oracles have long foretold of these same things happening, but here instead of there."

"Old and New Karnath are parallel worlds and share much in common, from legends to prophecies. And just as this, the Dark Prophecy has appeared in both worlds, though it can only happen in one. And that world is New Karnath, where Shaizan will rise as an inferior."

Merphonox said, "The Dark Prophecy can happen in one world, or it will happen? The seroxians have stopped believing in many things, including this."

"While the Dark Prophecy has not happened yet, it will happen if no one acts. But Magicia seeks to avoid this outcome. She believes success will come, if only you and the seroxians help cut down the Child of Darkness before it's too late. New Karnath will become Old Karnath through the *curse of legend*, if the

Child wins the Game of Time and Broken Sword. The inferiors need the seroxians' help to stop this, and Magicia acknowledges that."

Darconas summarized her offer, still seeking Merphonox's aid.

"Enter New Karnath over Magicia's bridge, harming no one but the Child of Darkness, and the River of Life is ours. You must simply join the Army of Light, those who assemble on the Child's side for that hue, and fight against Shaizan."

Merphonox knew that both shards of sword were now in New Karnath and the exo-core's delayed creation prevented another Sink from being used. The situation easily created delays to entering New Karnath, and his newly founded fears about seroxians shadowing pushed him toward a positive response, despite his mistrust of Magicia and hating the idea of relying upon her.

"Fine. I'll rally my people to this cause."

"Excellent," Darconas replied. "See what you can do. In the meantime, I shall continue talking with Magicia. Expect to hear from me soon with next steps."

And with those garbled words, Merphonox watched Darconas simply disappear into the shadows of Old Karnath's night, leaving him alone before the monument. A smile crossed his face, as thoughts surfaced in his mind about revenge against the inferiors and reclaiming paradise. *Entering New Karnath, even with Magicia's help, puts you closer to your good destiny than ever before!*

As he toyed with the idea of betraying Magicia's trust, a related idea entered his mind: *Magicia will probably do the same...* The night closed in on Merphonox, as the possibility of her betrayal darkened his heart along with his countenance, making his own betrayal seem all the more befitting and appropriate.

"HINT FOR MERPHONOX"

Chapter 33
Through the Forest Gray

X'ieth heard Tol scream, "Look out!"

Standing toward the back of the Guard, he watched as the other knight pushed Lewes out of the way.

Crack! Crack! CRACK! SMASH!

The young knight shuddered as both of them barely evaded another falling tree. He saw it come crashing down through the dense fog that filled Forest Saol. Sounds of horses neighing and jumping entered his ears, as the other knights yelled against the whirling winds.

"Be careful, man! Didn't you see that?!" said Tol.

"See it?! Lewes retorted, a bit defensively, "I can't see *anything*!"

That's true. X'ieth sided with Lewes, as he looked down. Between his eyes and his feet was a thick vapor blanketing the ground. It spread in all directions, all over the forest, as if Saol were a sea of dense and icy mist. More sounds in front pulled back his attention.

X'ieth looked up when Lewes' horse whinnied. He saw Tol grab the reins in an attempt to hold the beast in place. It jerked the other knight's arm wildly, every which way. He cried out, "Help me calm her!"

X'ieth saw Lewes rush up to soothe the frazzled horse, stroking its coat with his hand. Barely visible beyond Tol and Lewes, X'ieth could discern the other knights advancing through the forest with lanterns held high. Just as him, they led their horses by the reins, while walking.

Can't ride, he reminded himself, since Saol presented very real dangers for those not dismounting. *In this fog, saddling a spooked horse could mean a run-in with a tree, or worse!*

In a line, X'ieth trailed behind Zeros, Tol, and Lewes when everyone started walking again. From the very front, he soon heard Nathan curse, yet again.

"Damn this contraption to the Void!"

Through the fog, he squinted to see Nathan looking down at a compass like an oaf. *Here it comes... the excuse.* The young knight could read the pack leader like a bound book in Mainlandish.

"This confounded device is still acting up!" Nathan exclaimed in frustration. "The needle spins wildly!"

X'ieth's cold gaze, as well as that of the others, surely applied pressures on the pack leader. The young knight worried by the step. *We're lost, tired, and*

302

rationing provisions—with Liath nowhere in sight! No one had to tell Nathan how bad the situation had become since leaving Arlem three days ago, or longer.

"This territory isn't mapped," Nathan said from the front, "without the compass it's impossible to navigate."

That's encouraging, thought X'ieth.

With a stern face the young knight looked forward, having a heart full of prayers. *Destiny, let me come home alive to Millicent!* His mind latched onto a nearby wish. *Destiny, let me come home the hero!* He chided himself. *Keep attentive, man. There's time for that later.*

Crack! As a sudden sound emanated from the fog, X'ieth watched Finnel's hand fall to his sword's hilt like a stone. From the other knight's appearance, X'ieth could sense how nerves rubbed raw with not only himself, but also, his comrades. Everyone was wide-eyed, jumpy, and irritable. Everyone seemed a bit scared.

"What is that?!" Finnel asked, clearly on edge.

"These trees are dead," remarked Zeros.

X'ieth watched the mercenary look about with lantern held at arm's length.

"And someone's killing them, or something."

Crack! Crack! X'ieth heard more sounds from the trees—sounds that prefaced them falling. And they occurred with perfect timing to support Zeros' conclusion.

X'ieth looked past the mercenary's shoulder at his front, to the frosted trunks that stood high in the fog, some leaning therefrom on the verge of toppling over. The dense haze winded about every tree and drifted eerily throughout the forest, mesmerizing him. To X'ieth, the whole scene looked of gray, a murky backdrop for his quest that challenged the young knight's expectations of something more colorful and exciting than this.

His every footstep crunched against dead leaves. *Or something else…* X'ieth had to wonder what he really stepped upon, as much of the crunching, snapping debris drew his doubts of it really being leaves. *It's far too brittle, like bone.* His imagination ran wild with that conjecture. *Is death beneath your boot, hiding now in the gloom?! Nothing at all seems alive in Forest Saol!* It was a hypothesis yet to be proven untrue. The trees were dead as Zeros noted, and the wildlife that Nathan had mentioned in Arlem was nowhere to be found.

Just then, another cold wind fiercely lashed X'ieth, causing him to shut his eyes as it blew. Behind the line of other knights, he continued to trudge forward, shivering along the way. His teeth chattered inside of his helmet, and his lips felt as if they had frozen.

After the gust died, he glanced up to perceive nothing new. Only dead trees, endless fog, and spans of gloom, for as far as the eye could see, with no signs of life whatsoever. And all of Forest Saol seemed this same way, no matter how far they traveled.

The sight began to disturb X'ieth, of a full forest devoid of living creatures, including plants. *This is so strange!* The thought echoed his mind, as the Guard's traversal through the woods proceeded to fray nerves and shake confidences, causing the weak of mind to become increasingly frantic and edgy.

"This can't be!"

X'ieth heard Hammar shout, a few knights up. He saw the dwarf's face stricken with fear, as Hammar turned spastically with every sound. Another frigid wind stabbed at X'ieth, stealing his attention from the other knight.

Crack! Crack! CRACK!

An abrupt noise originated ahead of X'ieth, and he looked there, where suddenly before his eyes, a burst of green energy flowed from a nearby trunk, ascending upward into the heights of the forest. As energy left the tree, it appeared to die, its trunk graying.

"Destiny keep us!" X'ieth muttered to himself.

"What's happening?!" asked Finnel.

"Get out of the way!" yelled Zeros, as the tree suddenly fell toward the elven knight.

X'ieth watched Finnel move spryly to the side, just before the tree crashed down between him and his drawn horse, pinning the reins to the ground. The unexpected movement and loud noise spooked his beast, which fearfully jerked to loose itself, neighing and pulling against the reins upon notice of being trapped by the large trunk. *Do something!*

Quickly X'ieth stepped forward to calm the animal, by leading it closer to the fallen tree, so to create slack in the reins. He noted how meanwhile, the other knights nudged the rotten tree a little to free the horse.

Eager to help, X'ieth bent down from the horse's side to grab the reins. When he took hold of them, he rose, briefly eyeing them in his gloved palm before turning to Finnel. The other knight stood with one outstretched hand, his other still at sword's grip. X'ieth handed over the reins, and when he did, a terrible sound ripped through the forest.

RAWWWRRR! … RAWWWRRR!

X'ieth's heart jumped in his chest, as he heard it. The young knight looked all around, and caught a glimpse of how the strident noise startled Nathan, who abruptly threw his shoulders back and leered about, from being hunched over the compass.

"What in Destiny was that?!" he asked.

As no one answered, X'ieth just waited, until Zeros finally spoke, "Tis a mighty creature upon Liath."

X'ieth stared back at the mercenary, a bit unbelieving. *That sounds as if it comes from the forest!* There mere thought of confronting whatever made the sound concerned the young knight. *You've been traveling on little sleep. In no shape are you or the other knights to face any mighty creature!*

That thought eventually passed, just like time itself, as the knights wandered through Saol behind Nathan, and darkness fell. X'ieth heard Tol and Lewes speak quietly.

"Me thinks we're going in circles. I've seen this place before!"

"Aye, he hasn't a clue where we are, does he?" muttered Lewes.

X'ieth was surprised to hear Nathan give a snippy reply from the front. "What do you propose I do?!" he said, while fiddling with the compass more.

As another burst of green energy flowed from a nearby tree, X'ieth redirected his gaze there, seeing it pulled upward beyond the forest's ceiling with a loud crack, which sounded as the tree's trunk turned gray and lifeless. Esmeralda was bringing gloom right before his eyes, and X'ieth felt it reinforce his purpose for being here. *You must stop her. You were meant for this.*

"There it is again!" cried Hammar suddenly.

The shout interrupted X'ieth's thoughts. He looked away from the tree and to the dwarf, who vigorously pointed into another part of the forest, seeming on the verge of hysteria.

Hammar continued. "Faces I see, from shadows!"

Finnel looked at the trees, and then to Hammar.

"I can barely see my next step, let alone shadows or the like! What are you talking about?!"

Hammar swore by what he saw.

"There are shadow people; I see them!"

X'ieth heard Zeros speak. "Calm yourself, dwarf!"

He observed how the mercenary's focus was withdrawn while he spoke, as if studying the forest where Hammar was still looking.

"Vespers find a home even in these parts. They're walking shadows in Karnath, being more frightening than dangerous."

Hammar asked, "Not dangerous?"

Zeros turned to him. "The shadows cannot touch you or hurt you. They'll just spook you. That's what others have said, who have encountered vespers."

When the beasts neighed, X'ieth added from behind, "And maybe they'll spook the horses too!" He saw Finnel and Zeros pass icy glares, and Hammar also. *Stay quiet, man. No need to invite more chill besides these winds! This is not the time for jokes.*

Leading his horse, X'ieth followed the others for what seemed another hour or two, and the evening closed in on them. Eventually, the group entered a clearing, and the young knight witnessed Nathan's frustration with the compass.

"Destiny burn you to ash!" he cursed at the device, about to hurl it into the foggy unknown.

X'ieth saw Zeros, who stood right beside Nathan then, catch his arm before he could throw it!

"Don't do it," Zeros urged Nathan. "If at first your attempts yield nothing, try again later."

X'ieth admired Zeros' bravery, and wondered if Nathan would rebuke the mercenary. He watched the pack leader stare back at Zeros with a plain expression plastered upon his face, as if shocked. *Leader might not like a subordinate speaking out of line*, X'ieth thought to himself.

Zeros added. "And there's no trying later or doing things differently with your compass, if you throw it away! Keep it, please." While speaking, the mercenary did not relinquish his gaze from the pack leader. Zeros let go of Nathan's hand.

In a moment or two, Nathan nodded, and slipped the compass into his saddlebag, putting it away for later.

X'ieth watched the whole interaction, and he could not help but marvel at how dramatically Nathan had changed from the sparring yards of Castle Sergros. *Nathan—so calm, so polished, so put together then—now demonstrates some shortcomings in leadership. On the other hand, Zeros is staying relatively calm.*

Nathan cleared his throat, "Ahem."

X'ieth watched him survey the open space of the clearing, where a few trees stood not far from them. The leader nodded. "We would've soon stopped for the night anyway, and this place is better than others for camp, so let's set it up here and continue our travels in the morning..."

Nathan faced Hammar and Finnel, to whom he barked orders. "You two, fasten the beasts to the trees!"

X'ieth saw the pair move upon command, whereas the others just stood and waited.

"Both of you," X'ieth's eyes went to Nathan, who looked at Lewes and Tol while talking. "Go pitch the tents over there in a circle, where the horses will be tied!"

X'ieth watched the two knights scurry away with their bidding. Their every step away caused sounds of crunching beneath the fog, sounds that rose then fell.

The young knight straightened his posture then, expecting an order of sorts from Nathan. But he saw the pack leader face Zeros instead.

"C'mon, let's check the perimeter."

Nathan and Zeros turned, and started walking off.

What about you, man? X'ieth wondered. He spoke to Nathan's back. "Wait. What am I to do?"

X'ieth could not help but feel excluded. *Nathan gave you no orders.* A flash of Talus upon his ornate throne entered his mind, the red wine dripping down the king's chin. *On second thought, perhaps a more reasonable expectation is that you stay out of everyone's way! Maybe such a young knight will only get in the way.* The image dissolved in his head, along with those words. Just thinking about Talus brought X'ieth to grind his teeth, and this particular recollection wakened a dormant anger inside X'ieth. *How dare he suggest that?!*

The young knight watched Nathan pivot upon the heel and meet eyes with him. At that very moment, an icy wind slapped the two of them.

"Go find some wood," said Nathan, in a voice that was just as cold. "We must make a fire to keep alive through the night."

He seems annoyed by you… Ever since X'ieth came back to Arlem's pub with bruises and a bloody lip, he could not get Nathan's disapproving scowl out of his mind. *Does he think of you as an inconvenience, perhaps an arrogant knight who can't back down from a fight, or maybe both?* X'ieth struggled to repair the pack leader's perception of him, which likely had been tarnished by what had happened in Arlem, compounding with everything else.

Nathan turned and walked away, joining Zeros.

Zeros, however, turned and spoke.

"Destiny keep you, lad," said the mercenary, with his blue eyes shining through the haze.

With that, Zeros spun about and walked off with Nathan, as the two went to check the perimeter of the campsite. The crunch of their feet against Saol's carpet sounded, and grew distant and more distant, with every step away from the young knight.

X'ieth stayed where he was, watching as the pair of flowing cloaks disappeared into the gloom. In a matter of moments, the young knight was left alone for his task.

"FOREST SAOL"

Chapter 34
Questions for Answers

ll alone now, X'ieth took his lantern and ventured not too far from where the other knights made camp. *There's always some hazing,* he thought to himself while walking. Indeed, X'ieth knew from his career in the Crimson Guard how the more experienced knights would typically stick a younger peer with unwanted tasks, especially if that younger peer was recently promoted. This happened to him, each and every promotion. *Often you get the firewood, too.* He doubted his repeat task of fetching firewood was merely coincidence.

So with a long sigh and his lantern in hand, X'ieth went into the fog, his mind astir with thoughts. As he walked, he pondered many things—his wife Millicent, her pregnancy, his knighthood. And of course, he thought of those words Lucen told him in Arlem. *You are the Child destined to do great things.* Since leaving the city several days ago, his mind went in circles about these topics, and a few others. But above all, he thought of his future and greater purpose in Karnath. *You're Kayareth! You're more than just a knight…*

A mind at work can be distracting, and just as this, X'ieth became distracted from how far he actually wandered from camp to find firewood. The dense haze enveloped him, scrolling before his eyes wherever he went, threatening his sense of direction. By the step, he wondered how he would make it back to the other knights.

He saw a few trees up ahead and stopped when reaching them, having the idea that surely some fallen branches or twigs could be found there. As X'ieth settled to a stop, however, his final step made a very different noise than the usual crunches that accompanied his footfall in the forest. He felt resistance beneath his boot, right before something broke with a series of brittle snaps. Images of bones flashed in his mind, and he pondered then whether death was under his feet, as he had suspected all along.

While traversing Saol, the notion that X'ieth walked on bones was not completely foreign to him. On several occasions in the last few days, he had wondered exactly the same thing. And now, he wondered it again. *Is that what you're stepping?!*

X'ieth saw a sudden image of Forest Saol, where the woods were green, vibrant, and alive, as Nathan had described. In his vision, the woods were teeming with wildlife, such as wolves, bears, elk. And then suddenly, he saw how a gloom descend, causing the animals to become skeletons which collapsed into piles of bones, right before a frost withered the greenery to gray, and fog blanketed the entire forest, hiding the deceased from sight. And as soon as the vision started, it stopped. X'ieth was left gasping, now with an empty mind. A moment later, he had to wonder. *Has the gloom indeed killed everything, and do you really walk upon death?!*

X'ieth focused on his spot beneath the tree. He shifted on his feet, which caused a few more snaps, distinct in sound from the crunch of leaves. *Don't stay here; go elsewhere for firewood!* a voice insisted inside of his mind. *You're wasting time; just reach down, get some branches, and then go back to camp,* insisted another voice. And like this, the two voices went back and forth in his mind, pushing him toward different courses of action.

"Ugh." Not really wanting to, X'ieth decided he would get wood here in the interest of time. And so, he bent over, leaning into the denser fog that blanketed the ground. He reached out his hand, his heart beating faster as he saw his gloved fingers disappear in the haze. He extended his arm until his hand hit an uneven surface, and it was then, that he raked the ground for branches.

As his fingers passed over objects—many of them seeming odd in shape and proportion—he feared it was all bones, given his apprehensions. More images went through his mind, of the animal skeletons he had just seen, which X'ieth shut out immediately. *Don't spook yourself.*

When X'ieth found something that felt long and branch-like, he withdrew it from the haze. Beneath his flickering lantern, he peered at what was in fact a long stick, broken from a tree branch. The young knight sighed in relief, wondering to himself if his fears were empty, a product of being in a place with so many things strange and unseen. He tucked the stick under his opposite arm, and reached back into the haze. When he felt something similar on the ground, he pulled out yet another stick. *Not so bad.*

Still holding his lantern in one hand and working with the other, X'ieth repeated the task again and again, until he eventually cradled a good number of sticks under his arm. As he worked, his mind drifted to familiar thoughts. He saw the last image of Millicent he could remember—at the cottage, right before he left for Sergros. He remembered her and her large belly. *You'll soon be a father,* he thought to himself with a smile.

Like others in Karnath, we'll pick the child's name according to the gender. As many times before, he favored the idea of following a new trend in Karnath, where parents named their own children, due to the Great Occlusion. At that thought alone, however, his wife's nagging sounded in his mind. *Have the king find us an oracle to pronounce the child's name, for it's tradition!* He shook his head from side to side. *That's what you get for marrying an oracle's daughter—her commitment to pointless traditions, which puts you in a bad position—asking favors from a boss you can't stand. Ugh.*

The thought was an easy transition to what made up the bulk of X'ieth's thoughts since leaving Arlem—his greater purpose, and if that purpose ultimately entailed the knighthood. He could not place why Karnatha would want him to continue being a knight if it created such friction in his marriage. *After becoming Kayareth, the knighthood won't be your greatest source of fulfillment anymore,* he reasoned with himself. *It will just be a thorn in your side, constantly creating conflict between you and Millicent. Clearly, Destiny gave you desires to become a knight merely for the purpose of joining the knighthood, which has led into your good destiny, by means of this very mission! All along, the knighthood was just a stepping-stone...*

X'ieth collected more sticks, thinking as he did. The idea was unpalatable to him in a number of ways. The knighthood fulfilled him now and he had not yet risen to his greater purpose of becoming Kayareth, so in that, it saddened him just to think of resigning from the knighthood upon returning to Sergros. *Could you really do that?* he wondered, feeling fondness for being a knight. And then, there were some remote doubts that Lucen's words were even true.

When X'ieth came face-to-face with his doubts in Lucen, like he did on occasion since leaving Arlem, he confronted them with the same line of reasoning:

You're of good standing, perhaps the best standing in Sergros, and well suited to be the hero. You know Kayareth is likely human, since the Light Prophecy describes him warring as a lion at Gallow Cliff, and Sergros is the only kingdom in the Mainland, Isles, or Northern Region with a lion in its emblem! And as Lucen mentioned from the Dark Prophecy, Esmeralda is trying to end the reign of a powerful sorceress in Karnath—her own sister Magicia— and you're the one who will stop her. Esmeralda must be the Child of Darkness, and you the Child of Light! It all makes perfect sense.

And just like before, his reasoning dispelled any doubts in Lucen, replacing them with his frequented daydream. He imagined himself with the Army of Light beneath Gallow Cliff—a massive host assembled in Kayareth's name, bearing banners of Sergros, strewn from side to side. In his mind, he wore the shimmering armor of Autheos and held high the white shard of sword upon his snowy steed, bedecked with polished barding. *Rally to me! Rally to me!* Those words echoed his mind, as did the cheers and songs of the mighty army. He pictured himself shouting to the ranks and commencing their charge upon the Child of Darkness.

With a smile ear-to-ear, X'ieth thought of that day, confident that his confrontation with Esmeralda would lead to Gallow Cliff. *According to the Light Prophecy we'll end there, that's for sure. Maybe she'll flee in terror when you storm her tower, and hide at the cliffs!* The thought widened his smile, and brought on another thought. *You can definitely give up being a knight for Millicent, since you're the Child of Light!*

X'ieth's smile vanished, as he found himself stooped there in gloomy Saol, his arm extended to retrieve another stick. The thought of leaving the knighthood easily betrayed what had been his purpose for years. And it was all in the hopes of even greater purpose that supposedly made his prior purpose lesser and disposable. A scowl formed on his face.

The very notion of leaving the knighthood made him feel even worse then, like he planned on using his good destiny to avoid speaking with Talus about the king's mistreatment, upon his return to Sergros. X'ieth grumbled. *You did promise yourself you'd do that… Maybe you should stay a knight, at least until that talk…*

When a wind suddenly lashed X'ieth, he lost his train of thought, growing irritated then with being in the cold. *Focus, man. For you can think about this later. Finish getting the firewood, so you can go back to camp and warm up.* The thought raced through his mind, and he stayed stooped in the fog, his one arm still extended, his other cradling the sticks and holding the lantern in hand.

He withdrew another stick from the fog, judging the size of the lot he had collected when putting it with the others. *Is this enough to start a fire?* X'ieth wondered. *How long they'll burn is perhaps the question*, he thought, knowing from experience that rotten wood never burnt well. With those considerations, he decided to grab a few more sticks. *Do it now, or be asked later!* With some anticipation, he could literally hear Nathan's instructions to go fetch more wood. *And that request might come past midnight too…*

And so, X'ieth moved closer to the tree, crouching there to get sticks off the ground. A bitter cold wind smote him again, making him realize how important his fire would be. *You'll be celebrated with dried meat and crackers, man! Your fire will make you the hero of Forest Saol!* Though his inner voice ridiculed him, but he did not stop collecting firewood.

After taking up another stick from the ground, X'ieth pulled it close to the lantern and when seeing it, he iced over with dread. A human thighbone stared back at him, and a sinking feeling suddenly filled his gut.

"Destiny!" he exclaimed while dropping it. He watched the fog swallow up the bone, just before it hit the ground with a thud. Startled, the young knight backed away, his chest tight. *The Sergrothian foresters who supposedly froze to death, might have had a different fate! No frost picks a bone that clean!*

Then suddenly, X'ieth heard a strange sound during the next wind, shifting his thoughts from the bone. *Is that talking, or crying?* When the wind died, he could tell the noise was faint crying, as if from a small child. Concerned that a child was lost in Forest Saol, he tried to place it.

"Whhhaaa whhhaaa," came the cry again, in his ear.

X'ieth bravely stepped forward, and listened intently as the sounds continued. *Those cries are before you, maybe a tenth of a span away!* He thought this and walked further, toward another line of trees up ahead, barely seen through the dense fog.

"Whhhaaa whhhaaa whhhaaa!" X'ieth heard more cries, and another wind blew hard in his face. He squinted his eyes, using his other arm to hold the sticks against his elbow, while keeping the lantern held high.

But upon taking another step, those sounds just stopped. X'ieth wondered, *Should you call out? The child is young; would the babe even understand? Is it a child and a mother, together?* Disliking his indecision to act, he put an end to the questions in his mind. *Just do it.*

"Who goes there? Do you need help?" X'ieth called into the gloom, feeling a bit foolish as silence replied.   "Hello?" he shouted again, only to hear nothing, save the wind.

X'ieth became alarmed when suddenly an eerie music began playing, like chimes sounding endlessly. It happened right after a strong gust died. His instant reaction was to use magic for protection. *Ready yourself, man! Perhaps Esmeralda is already in your midst!*

He concentrated, and found himself standing within his small channeling chamber. X'ieth pulled against his mental restraint—the Source entry—but there were absolutely no inflows of energy! Awed, the young knight stood there, in a dry and empty room containing no Nexus. *What in Destiny?! It's just gone—the Nexus is gone!*

Back he went to Saol, and the music continued playing, growing louder and surrounding him. X'ieth looked ahead and saw what appeared to be a few fireflies in the fog. *The music comes, from there...* The young knight raised his lantern high, and took one step closer. Beneath his breastplate, his heartbeats sounded quickly and deeply, in bass repetition.

"Hello?!"

Thump thump, thump thump, thump thump!

"Hello?" he shouted again, as fear welled inside.

Thump thump, thump thump, thump thump!

Upon taking a few steps closer to the fireflies, X'ieth beheld a multitude of dots jittering about them. He took another step, its crunch against the frosted soil lost in the music, still playing overhead.

Thump thump, thump thump, thump thump! His heart worked faster, beating of sheer dread—a sounding percussion for the chimes.

With another step, X'ieth realized the dots jittering about the fireflies appeared as hair, and at that, he gasped. An epiphany struck him then. *That's... That's a...* He kept his focus on the lights, when suddenly they turned into the glowing eyes and mouth of a ghastly female face, which flew right toward him!

X'ieth tried to move, but was petrified by fear.

Thump thump, thump thump, thump thump!

All about him a ghostly woman flew, with flowing hair and dissolving skin that sprinkled the air, from out of her robe of gray silk. X'ieth tried to open his mouth and scream, but his tongue was bound from moving, as was his body. He was frozen in place, left to listen to the strange music, until it happened. The chimes became a voice, speaking words to him that he somehow understood, despite being in an otherworldly language!

"Your inheritance is more wholesome than his, *Kilwroth's unwholesome inheritance.*" Those words were musical and sounded a frightful melody, like a single note that subtly varied through entire scales without ever really changing at all.

He stood spellbound with his mouth open, as the ghostly woman passed right through him, again and again. X'ieth saw her linger before his face then, as she continued talking. "The distance between Kilwroth and his fate, shall be many fold the distance between you and your dreams! A beautiful wife and child, along with your knighthood, and other such things."

In a single instant X'ieth felt his face freed to move. And though he found the voice to call out, the words his mind did not contrive, for they came forth in an involuntary reflex. "Trouble me not, spirit!"

X'ieth gasped as he spoke in the bizarre musical language, without even knowing it, yet completely understanding every word.

"Trouble not yourself," replied the ghostly woman.

X'ieth could barely move his eyes to follow the woman's floating body through the gloom.

"Good destiny evades you, young knight. And that, shall not be easily forgiven."

"Release me!" shouted X'ieth, his heart racing beneath his armor. He tried to move, but still could not. *Destiny, help! Please...*

"Of course."

At that moment, X'ieth saw the ghostly woman hover before him, now stationary and no longer moving about. Immediately, he felt the hold over his body released.

"How else will I have a show if you're held here?" she said. "Give me a good one."

Without thinking twice, X'ieth tossed the lantern and his sticks to the side, drew his broadsword, and charged the ghostly woman with a newfound bravery.

"May Karnatha find bad destiny in yours," she said in that musical voice. Just at that moment, he slashed her face with his blade. Upon contact, X'ieth instantly saw her body explode into droplets that flew all about his vicinity, to hang midair.

As X'ieth witnessed each droplet slowly disappear, a tuneful laughter sounded. "Ha ha ha ha! Ha ha ha ha!"

It lingered in his ears for some time, and even after the noise had left, his heart continued throbbing.

Thump thump, thump thump, thump thump!

What was that?! X'ieth wondered to himself with no explanations in mind. His vitals were all elevated, and he remained still and silent for a while, until they became normal again. In that time, he felt the wind's bite, not believing entirely what had happened. Then suddenly from the distant woods, he heard his name called.

"X'ieth!" one cried.

"X'ieth?!" shouted another.

The young knight struggled to make out the voices. *Maybe Tol or Lewes? Zeros too?* Without thinking more, he immediately went to the ground, frantically trying to pick up the dropped sticks. *You've taken too long. Nathan will be furious!*

When having an armful, he grabbed his lantern off the frosted soil, and quickly inspected it. *Not broken...* With it in hand, he did not waste any time moving in the direction of the voices.

X'ieth!" someone called.

That's Tol for sure. He ran through the fog toward the voices. As much as he tried, he could not get that image of the ghostly woman out of his head. In his mind, the sounds of that music were trapped also; it played a haunting interlude between his moments of conscious thought. *What was that?!* he wondered again, this time considering that whatever happened might be related to him being Kayareth. *As the Child, you'll be Ma'althan's target...*

Lost in thought, X'ieth reasoned with himself, as he followed the voices.

"X'ieth!" called someone.

Likely Tol and Zeros... Amid his tromp through Saol, his boot caught what felt as a tree root, causing him to fall! He hit the ground hard, dropping the branches and lantern. They scattered across the forest's foggy floor with a series of thuds, mixed with the whistle of winds.

Destiny damn it! X'ieth thought to himself, while sucking in the cold air upon the ground. He leaned forward on both arms, with his hands on the soil. Pain spread throughout his upper and lower extremities. Slowly then, X'ieth stood up, and took a single step toward the fallen objects. And when he did, a familiar, non-musical voice cut through the fog.

"You seek the truth?"

X'ieth nearly jumped out of his skin. His face showed utter surprise, as he saw the same white cloak hung upon her shoulders, framing black falling stars. *This one, called Urzel!* He gawked as the woman in white turned to him, from beside a tree. "The truth about your premonitions, and your future?" she continued.

How did she know? Her words were like a temptation to him, for clearly, he yearned to know why his premonitions stopped, and how it related to his future.

X'ieth saw her feet suddenly lift off the ground, as she hovered upon Nexus! His jaw dropped, as he watched her float around him at the level of his waist, like a ghost might do. While she floated, her body left behind trails of glowing energy, and she circled him several times, emitting streams of Nexus that hung in the air and shined in the night, illuminating this small nook of the forest. To X'ieth, the scene appeared wondrously magical, as the green light all around him refracted through the fog and bounced off the distant trees, fading slowly as she circled to leave more energy behind.

Thinking to himself, X'ieth compared Urzel's movements to those of the ghostly woman that visited him earlier in the woods. *Is Urzel one and the same, with that ghostly woman? Why would she appear in two forms?* His mind could not reconcile his reality. *Just ask her your questions*, he thought, *this time, respectfully.*

"Powerful immortal," X'ieth said, "please disclose why my premonitions no longer foretell my future. Why did they become untrue, and then, stop altogether?" The questions gnawed at him, even as they proceeded from his lips. *Why this thing? Is it because you're the Child, and Destiny can't have you know your future?*

In a soothing voice Urzel replied, "Have you considered, that others have premonitions too?" The young knight turned from side to side, to follow Urzel around as she continued her circles.

"Many these days have premonitions in Karnath, but what of it?" asked X'ieth. *How are others' premonitions relevant to yours?*

He heard Urzel's laughter, as she came into view again. "Young knight, your fate is inter-tangled in a messy web of destinies with those around you. *Perhaps someone in your web did act on a premonition, and changed your future along with theirs?* Premonitions enable change, for the lucky and the brave."

X'ieth digested her remark with a blank expression upon his face. And then, an epiphany struck, parting his lips ever so slightly. In a moment of clarity, he was sure he knew what the woman in white spoke of. *If someone has true premonitions about a future event, they have the power to change it. And therefore, people who act first on premonitions, might invalidate the premonitions of others, if their destinies are related!*

But this conclusion slowly confounded him with his continued thoughts. *If premonitions are a lens into the future, but somehow premonitions can be rendered untrue, how then were they even premonitions in the first?* The whole line of reasoning began to ring paradoxically to X'ieth, and when that occurred, he stopped pondering the words further.

"Who has done *this deed*?" X'ieth blurted out, referring to someone changing his future through a premonition. A wind nipped at his face just then. From squinted eyes, he watched Urzel just continue her circles, leaving a train of energy behind her that faded over time. X'ieth saw most of the Nexus suspended midair, forming thick rings about him that slowly dissolved.

"Perhaps Esmeralda, perhaps another," Urzel answered, vaguely. "You may soon learn who re-authors your fate!

"Oh immortal," X'ieth anxiously inquired, now jarred with the uncertainty of his future. *Since my premonitions are untrue, what lies in store?!*

"What is *my fate*? Please do tell."

At first, Urzel replied with only her constant smile. And then, a moment later, she spoke.

"Choice and chance shall make your way. Only you can find your path through intense search, and listening to wise counsel!"

And with that, he saw Urzel blend into the gloom.

"X'ieth!" called Zeros.

The young knight looked over his shoulder, as Zeros and Tol entered the clearing, with lanterns shining through the thick fog.

"GHOSTS AND MAIDENS"

Chapter 35
Back to Camp

X'ieth finally yelled, being under Tol's constant reprimand from the moment he and Zeros located the young knight in Forest Saol. "I know!" *Yeah, got it. Nathan's mad.*

In silence then, he walked behind Tol and Zeros, satisfied that his outcry put an end to the discussion. *There, that did it.* Though exactly during his moment of thought, another wind whipped him, making X'ieth reconsider the matter. It hit him so hard that he nearly dropped the firewood, jerkily clasping the sticks tighter under his elbow, while managing to keep his lantern in hand. *Maybe that's Karnatha's way of saying you shouldn't get so angry with people...*

Quietly X'ieth continued mulling over his attitude, as he, Zeros, and Tol navigated the dark forest. After walking for some time, he could make out distinct outlines of armor in the distance, along with shades of white and crimson. Sounds of Zeros and Tol talking entered his ears, serving a reminder that he was still in their midst, without an apology yet spoken. *Destiny damn you and your pride, man. Just get this over with. You were wrong.*

"Tol, I'm sorry." X'ieth said the words at the first break in their conversation. But just as he spoke, a loud wind blew over him, forcing him to raise his voice. "It serves me well to hear about Nathan's disdain. I shouldn't have spoken to you like that. Please forgive me."

Good that you said it louder; you'll feel more humility if all of Forest Saol knows! He stared at the back of Tol's helmeted head, until the other knight turned around mid-stride.

"No worries," Tol finally replied, walking backward. "You should hear how my wife speaks with me! Getting an apology from her has less likelihood than the Dark Prophecy coming true!" Tol spun back around, walking forward again, with Zeros.

X'ieth weakly smiled, as they continued on together. He instantly became a bit stoical from the moment Tol made light of the Dark Prophecy. Maybe what had not come true was a laughing matter for unbelievers, but certainly not for him. *Changing this stark prediction is your good destiny, and that's not any reason to laugh!*

When the campsite came into view, the sight broke his thoughts. By lantern light, he walked silently behind Tol and Zeros through the darkness, fog, and wind. The mercenary and other knight continued their quips about the struggles of married life.

"Maybe a wife's nagging is your dark prophecy!"

"Tell me about it. Women are more mysterious than Forest Saol."

"They'd say the same of us!" remarked Zeros.

They laughed.

X'ieth disengaged from the discussion, when the camp appeared up ahead. He could see Nathan in the distance, who stood cross-armed beside the stones encircled about a spot for the fire. Nathan oversaw Hammar and Finnel checking the ropes that tied six of their horses to a pair of thick-trunked trees, three horses to each one. Behind them, the remaining horse had been tied to a smaller tree by only its reins.

In not much more time, X'ieth and the others finally entered the clearing, and when they did, Nathan turned to face them, as if expecting some answers.

"The lad found us," Tol said, "after we got lost!"

Zeros added, "He took more time to get more wood, so we'd have enough for the night!"

X'ieth looked into Nathan's brown eyes, as the pack leader remained silent. The situation pressed against he chest, constricting his breathing and making him feel anxious, despite the other knights covering for him. *Please Destiny... Let him not be upset. That's the last thing you need: getting further down on the man's dung list.*

Finally, after what seemed forever, X'ieth heard Nathan sigh. The leader pointed to the center of the circled stones at his feet.

"Place those here."

As instructed, X'ieth crouched over the spot and laid the sticks in the middle of the stones, a few at a time. He put down about half of what he had collected, a good many sticks for the fire. The other half he put aside for later, should they be needed.

From his periphery, X'ieth noted Finnel come up with a flint in hand, crouching beside him. The other knight leaned over the sticks, and struck the flint against his steel gauntlet. Though sparks flew, the sight provoked X'ieth to thought. *Why wouldn't Finnel just use Nexus to start a fire? That's what you would do...*

For some time X'ieth watched Finnel struggle with the flint to kindle the fire. As each cold wind hammered him, he watched with disdain as it also beat down the flames. *Why insist to do things the hard way?!* he wondered, now with some agitation.

"I'll make good ol' Krails proud," Finnel finally admitted, striking the flint against his armor more. The young knight saw him turn about, and beam to his spectators. "This be my way of conserving Nexus! *Time well spent, to avoid voiding!*"

X'ieth glanced over at Nathan, who seemed to have a crosser expression upon his face, still with arms folded beneath his chest. *He's not amused*, the young knight estimated, from his outward appearance alone. A sudden shout of excitement drew his attention back to Finnel.

"Destiny smiles upon us today!" he exclaimed happily, motioning to the flaming wood.

"Hurray! It only took an hour!" Hammar snickered.

"Better than you would do, Guardsdwarf! We'd still be cold and shivering if up to you!"

With a smirk on his face, X'ieth followed the speakers, as the two went back and forth.

"We still *are* cold and shivering!" Nathan grumbled. "Make sure the flames keep."

Though X'ieth saw Finnel nod to Nathan's request, the young knight did not give the other knight a chance to act. Wanting to show off, he pulled Nexus into his aux core. In his channeling chamber, he stood at his open Source entry, where streams of energy flowed into the room, over the door's threshold. The energy filled the room, its level getting higher and higher, rising from the floor to the ceiling.

X'ieth went from his moment of concentration, back to the circle of rocks amid the campsite. He channeled the energy outward into fire, throwing his hands at the sticks. As he did, flames sparked from his midsection and onto the branches. In his channeling chamber, he pushed open his Source exit at the same time this happened, thinking of fire to trigger how the energy would be spent.

When the rotten wood burnt more, X'ieth smiled in satisfaction, despite the fire seeming less warm than one started from a healthy tree.

Finnel looked up at him from the blaze, appearing irritated—his smile gone and his brow creased.

"Not to worry," X'ieth said. "I did it to help."

Hammar exclaimed, "If all the Nexus goes to the Void, you'll be to blame now!"

X'ieth smiled, not minding being part of Hammar's play on the topic that Finnel indirectly brought up—voiding. When Finnel did not smile in response to the dwarf's humor though, he wondered if the other knight actually believed Thorin's admonition. *A strange thing to be mad about... After all, no one has proven voiding! Oh well... If he's mad, he'll have to get glad again.*

With X'ieth's dismissal, the evening rolled on for seven knights who were happy to stop traveling for the day. They banded together around a campfire of orange and yellow flames. Snaps and crackles sounded, as X'ieth watched Nathan portion meager provisions of food for everyone's dinner. *We're probably eating less with this unvaried diet.* He conjectured that rightfully, for reason of consuming nothing but crackers, dried meats, and cheese since leaving Arlem.

Across the fire, X'ieth saw Hammar drink from one of their many water skins. Thirsty, he followed the leather hide around the leaping flames, as it got passed from knight to knight, so that everyone could sip some. By the time it reached X'ieth, the skin felt light in his hand, and so, he drank sparingly. *Just enough to quench your thirst...*

As time went on, the group ate together and talked amongst themselves. X'ieth kept quiet, picking up bits and pieces of different conversations when he was not deeply entrenched in his own thoughts.

"My daughter was accepted," said Lewes.

"To the royal academy?" replied Tol, playfully grabbing the other knight's shoulder. "A great thing. She's bound to avoid working in the Guard with an education!"

Laughing, Lewes shot back, "Aye, Talus is always looking for unwary... erh, good people!"

The two chuckled together.

That comment triggered X'ieth's recollection of the discussion he had with Millicent long ago, concerning his pursuit of the knighthood beyond academy, instead of a better-paid calling. *That's probably part of why she's always pushing for you to leave...*

The thought led him to once again consider the matter of resigning from the knighthood. *It would make her happier,* one voice said, in his mind. *But would you be happy with that? Would you still feel purpose?* another voice countered. *Yes, after you become Kayareth!* It was easily a war inside X'ieth's head, as he debated his own fulfillment and purpose.

The situation of multiple competing interests—Millicent, the knighthood, and his hero's title—made him feel conflicted over what was truly meant to be. *Can it be,* X'ieth wondered, *that your struggles to maintain your knighthood and marriage are Destiny's way of telling you that all of these things can't coexist?* He wondered, not being sure, one way or another.

"When I use a working compass with a map," Nathan told them, "I've never gotten lost, not one time!"

X'ieth pooled his attention with that of Zeros, Hammar, and Finnel, who all acted engrossed in another of Nathan's longwinded conversations about the tragedy of his poor combination: excellent navigation skills, but a faulty compass.

"And with a compass alone, I've had much better experiences too! This..."

"Your every use of a compass hereafter will have better results!" Hammar asserted, breaking the awkward monologue with some comic relief.

Caught completely off-guard, X'ieth burst out laughing, Finnel too. Nathan eventually shared the laugh as well, but it was no joke how the pack leader had let the Guard's plight in Forest Saol get inside his head. *He's got to let it go...*

Despite everyone having a good time, X'ieth noticed that Zeros stayed reserved for some reason. *He's like that more often than not...* The young knight judged the mercenary, though ironically, he became just as uninvolved further into the night.

Are the knighthood and being the hero both your destiny, or is it just being a hero? What is your purpose? X'ieth slowly sank into a mire of his own thoughts. An hour or so later, he paused his thinking to listen to Finnel talk to Hammar about a matter of previous interest: what Finnel was thinking in Talus' throne room, when Magicia confronted him.

"Aye, she read my mind then. When we were called from practice, into the throne room..."

"What were you thinking?" Hammar asked, lowly.

"About her binding us by spell to protect the innocent's blood. Every time I've seen her since, I can't help but recall the ceremony. From that moment long ago, I've felt it—a loss of control over my destiny when the innocent are in danger. In the Guard I'm compelled to forfeit my own good destiny for others. The very binding is sacrilege to the Karnathan religion!"

As their talk grew philosophical in nature, it intrigued X'ieth. He loved philosophy.

Hammar offered his opinion. "If the binding gives others good destiny for the Guard's bad destiny, then I see your point. But if you're like me, risking neck and limb for the innocent be my good destiny!"

"Aye, me too!" Finnel agreed. "I just think we ought to have that choice come from here."

As Finnel pounded his breastplate, X'ieth watched with a nod. *Couldn't agree more*, the young knight thought. *Doing the right thing shouldn't be forced, but done of free will, from the heart.*

Mid-thought, X'ieth beheld Nathan stand.

"Ahem..." he cleared his throat. "We best get some sleep... We'll be up early in the morn to travel the whole day. That should be enough time to find our way out of this Destiny-forsaken forest."

X'ieth noted how Nathan glanced in his direction, before continuing to speak. "Two knights must stand first watch, and then two others the second. Who will it be?"

With that question, X'ieth saw Nathan gaze all around, but often looked back his way. *Should you take that as a hint? Just speak up.*

Having a will to be more vocal, X'ieth blurted out, "I'll stand first watch, Nathan. If you're not opposed..."

He noticed the pack leader's face brighten as those words were said. Nathan's eyes lit up and his smile widened. *That's the man's happiness to sleep showing!*

One knight over, X'ieth heard Zeros.

"And I'll be with him."

As Nathan bobbed his head while thinking, X'ieth waited for the yay or nay. Despite being so tired, he could stay awake half the night. *Your preoccupied mind won't let you rest, whether in the tent or by the fire, so why not stand first watch? Especially if it puts you back in Nathan's good graces; that's certainly a step in the right direction!*

"What about second watch?" Nathan said, looking to the remaining knights. X'ieth's eyes jumped from person to person, just in time to watch Tol take initiative.

"Lewes and I will stand second watch," Tol said, with his friend acquiescing through a quiet nod.

"All right then," Nathan said. "The rest of us sleep."

X'ieth watched Nathan head for his tent, but before reaching it, he turned around and faced the young knight.

"No falling asleep, lad. Be a second pair of eyes for this tired mercenary." The pack leader motioned to Zeros while talking, and he grinned.

He just couldn't let it be done without saying something, could he? Nodding his head, X'ieth did not audibly reply. *First impressions are very difficult to change*, he realized, in what seemed like his many failed attempts to repair a damaged reputation with Nathan.

Upon Nathan's remark, he watched the group of five knights disband. All being bound for sleep, they took out their blankets and settled into their tents. The young knight glanced over at Zeros, who had an occupied look about him.

Seems like we'll both have time tonight to think, X'ieth considered, with hardly a smile, anticipating more thoughts about his purpose and divine destiny, and whether or not the knighthood was really part of it.

"AROUND CAMP"

Chapter 36
Confiding Trusts

Rotten wood burned at the center of their camp—a cluster of tents filled with sleeping knights, who were surrounded by hungry horses tied to dead trees, hanging their heads low. X'ieth and Zeros lingered by the fire, having volunteered for the first watch.

From his knees, the young knight leaned closer to the orange fire, so he could hold his hands over it. His scarlet cloak fell to the ground behind him, trailing off into the darkness. This small campfire warmed him in a world so cold, a world unlike that which he ever knew. *Everything is so different with the gloom, including you. You've gone from being committed to the knighthood, to doubting if it was ever meant to be.*

It seemed to him that already an hour had passed, or more. And just as he expected, not much had been said from the mercenary. *Good, let it stay that way. More time to think...* His thought came with some hesitance though, for X'ieth wondered if another's opinion could be helpful. *You've been at this for hours, but are lost for what to do.*

It was true that X'ieth could not decide if he would resign from knighthood to appease Millicent or not. He was divided over the fulfillment and sense of purpose it gave him for years, versus the conflict it created in his marriage and the difficulties he had with Talus. And so, with a loss for what to do, X'ieth found himself increasingly inclined to open up to a stranger. *The mercenary...*

He looked at Zeros, his head full of confusion over the knighthood, and how it related to his true purpose—an uncertainty that slowly wedged its way into his life, after learning from Lucen that he was destined to become Kayareth. *Talk to him. Stay silent. Talk to him. Stay silent.* The conflicting voices went back and forth, growing in magnitude until the moment where X'ieth could not endure it any longer. *Talk to him.*

And with that in mind, X'ieth started talking, without knowing exactly what he would say, or where it would lead. "I've been pondering… my life's purpose."

The comment grabbed Zeros' attention and broke the long silence between them. The mercenary looked his way and made eye contact, though remained absolutely silent, as if encouraging the young knight to go on.

X'ieth continued. "I was sure before I left Sergros, that my purpose was to be a knight of the Crimson Guard, a husband, and a father. But now, I'm not so sure if that's really my life's purpose. I think I'm meant to be something much more, something that I've always wanted to be."

Zeros stared back blankly, and after a long silence he replied, "We all have thought the same at one point. It's the gray dream."

"The gray dream?" X'ieth arched his eyebrows.

Zeros smiled. "There's a saying in Sergros that an uncertain matter is gray. It's not black; it's not white; it's somewhere it between, like the color gray. And our dreams—the things we live for, those things that motivate us in life—can be just that. Uncertain and gray."

X'ieth kept silent, waiting for Zeros to elaborate.

"Karnathan belief makes us all think we have divine destiny and unique purpose, and that's why people dream gray. They presume their future lives must be meant for more than their present lives offer."

The words made X'ieth think about his present life, which entailed the Guard, his wife, and his child-to-be, versus what Lucen foretold would happen—his future life as the Child and hero of Karnath. The present he lived; it was real and sure. Whereas the future was yet to be lived—it was neither real nor sure. *Not yet, but soon…*

"I don't understand," X'ieth admitted.

Zeros shook his head, as if knowing why.

"Your thoughts of greater purpose than the purpose Destiny affords you, suggests to me that you're dreaming gray. The gray dream is the biggest dream a man has ever dreamt—the one that's larger than life; the one that he wants more than anything else. It occupies so much space in his mind, there's none left to consider if the dream is poorly chanced or not, and what the cost of pursuing this dream might be. Men who dream gray see their dreams as possible versus poorly chanced, cause for them, there's always enough hope to hold on."

X'ieth's mind went back to Arlem's pub, where the vocstrum sang *The Child's Triumph* and he got teary eyes, wanting his dream more than anything else. The memory resonated of what Zeros said, and he began to wonder, *Is my dream as he says: gray?* He shut the idea out, bearing in mind what Lucen had spoken. *You are the Child destined to do great things.* As told by a prophet, it seemed certain.

Zeros flashed another smile, and looked down for a moment, before going on. "Gray dreams are dangerous. They can skew our priorities, and make us forfeit positive relationships, such as those with family, friends, and god. This often happens when people continue chasing a dream that's not meant to be, or if they can't cope with reality when that dream breaks. Either way, the gray dreams will become Fate's Fray for them without their relationships, because Destiny puts relationships in our lives that are key to our development and realizing our potential. And without our relationships, we miss out on who and what we're supposed to be…"

The comment made X'ieth feel a bit guarded. *You give your family enough time, you've made friends in the Crimson Guard, and you go to the Karnathan churches once and a while. Maybe the mercenary wanted things out of life that weren't meant to be… Maybe he had the wrong priorities, and ended up with a fistful of broken dreams. But that's not you. You're different…*

"There's a story," Zeros said, "one that surely you've heard. It's about the seroxian in 'Maken and Rebels' who started the rebellion. As legend tells, Maken carved Karnath into existence from the Void, using a gray blade forged in Ires Star. Maken lost that blade after creation, but years and years later, the creator found it one day when walking Karnath. Maken hid the gray blade in a heavenly realm, but rumors of its immense power on the mortal plane tempted those seroxians with the gray dream of becoming god to enter Maken's abode, take the blade, and overthrow their creator. It was only a matter of time until this was attempted and the rebellion ensued."

X'ieth thought about that. *Stealing the gray blade was a seroxian's gray dream… Overthrowing the creator was what then, a dream larger than life and poorly chanced?* He struggled to make a connection with what Zeros discussed earlier.

"When Maken stopped the rebellion, Karnatha acknowledged that possessing the gray blade presented advantages to the Forerunners in the Game, as well as those in the mortal plane seeking more power. As a result of this, she decided to split the gray blade into two shards using Maken's life force—one black, and one white. Likewise, gray dreams break into black and white shards, just as the gray blade. And the breakage of dreams can easily break a man, putting him into a downward spiral from which he never recovers."

The comment made X'ieth solemn. He knelt there before the fire, diverting his eyes from those of Zeros, and letting the loud snores from Hammar's tent dominate their conversation. Fighting a sense of conviction, his mind dodged thoughts about the uncertainty of dreams, and where broken dreams might take a man. *That's for men of poor choices to worry about, perhaps like Zeros. On the other hand, you've made the right choices your whole life, and Karnatha sees to your dreams becoming reality.*

Images flashed through his mind—of beautiful Millicent holding a child, his shimmering Guardsman armor, and paintings of Kayareth fighting red-haired Shaizan at Gallow Cliff—all making him realize that his blessings from Karnatha were real. He slowly turned his attention back to Zeros, who sat across the fire with both legs stretched out before him, leaning back on his arms. Slowly then, it occurred to X'ieth that he had not gotten direction on the knighthood. *This sermon from the mercenary isn't what you really need. Speak clearly, and from the heart.* Though in the wake of that idea, he wondered if he were brave enough to do so.

Through the forest, cold winds blew against X'ieth just as the thought hit him, and he hunched more over the fire. Though unfazed by the actual cold, his want of warmth came from the ice over his spirits from merely imagining himself as no longer a knight. It had been so much of what he lived for until now, yet he struggled to see a future with himself wearing so many titles—husband, father, hero, and knight. *Millicent would say it's too much, so maybe it's just that: too much.*

At the howl of another wind, X'ieth noted motion in his peripheral vision, as Zeros suddenly stood from where he sat with eyes scanning the forest and his hand at sword's hilt. The young knight glanced around, only to hear and see nothing, and then suspect that undue caution had roused Zeros. As his eyes found the campfire again, his thoughts found the matter of balance in his own life. *Husband, father, hero, and knight—maybe it's just too much...*

"What's really wrong, lad?" Zeros asked, settling down again into his same place, from across the fire. "There's been dancing shadows and voices on the wind. It's enough to scare most, yet you sit near the fire in another world, like you don't hear or see a thing. Even the grayest dream couldn't occupy a man through all that!"

X'ieth kept quiet this time, apprehensive about speaking directly of the knighthood and his considerations of leaving, when in the midst of his fellow knights. But as he remained silent, an inner voice started coaxing him to confide in Zeros. *If you could safely talk with anyone here about that*, he told himself, *it would be Zeros. After all, he's a mercenary who's temporarily filling Nathan's spot, with no intentions of staying in the Guard. So out with it, man. Talk to him...*

X'ieth looked over at Zeros, who stared off into the fire, its reflections jumping about in his eyes. And without removing his gaze from its flames, the mercenary began talking more.

"By the looks of you, I fear your gloom is gloomier than Forest Saol itself! But if you can't tell me what's really going on, I'll not hold that against you. When words are said in the wrong forum or at the wrong time, the consequences can be much worse than words unsaid. Believe me, I've been holding my tongue up until now about a great many things. So I know perfectly well how a man needs to decide when and where to talk, and what battles are worth fighting."

A few seconds passed with Zeros' remark, and a wind blew. In that moment X'ieth pulled his cloak tighter, and he waited for the wind to die before speaking.

"When we finish this quest," he said quietly, "I'm thinking of resigning from the knighthood." He looked to the mercenary across the fire, ready to gauge his immediate reaction.

Zeros raised his eyebrows; shock hit his face.

"Why? You've just made the Seventh Order."

The simple question launched X'ieth's mind into thought, as to how he should answer. *It's unneeded, as you're Kayareth. It's making your wife miserable. It's forcing you to deal with a cruel king.* At the final thought, his head filled with memories of himself treating others poorly, perhaps the indirect consequence of enduring Talus' cruelty and repressing anger. He saw himself angry and yelling—at Millicent in his own home, Hammar in the sparring yard, Lewes in Arlem, and Tol in Forest Saol.

X'ieth turned his face way from the mercenary's intense stare, back to the fire. It was then that he felt his knees hurt and his stomach rumble from hunger, feelings that he was generally distracted from with the conversation, but now confronted him. *Give him an answer, man…*

"I know I was just promoted, and I know that the Seventh Order is the highest and most coveted order that exists. But dealing with Talus I can't do any longer." X'ieth paused before continuing. The flames snapped and crackled, as another wind fed them. "His treatment is poor and I resent him for it. The bitterness in me affects my life in many ways outside the throne room, and I wonder if this burden is worth bearing."

"Millicent does not approve of my intense service to the king," he continued. "Something has to give here, simple as that." He turned to Zeros and said, "It's either the knighthood, or my family and dignity."

As the last word rolled off his tongue, X'ieth wondered how well he had represented the truth about his knighthood. While he felt that so many of his negative emotions were questionably cause or effect, he spoke of them as effects, as if absolutely certain his career in the Guard had caused them and created a tradeoff between the knighthood and more wholesome things in his life.

"Do you dislike your life as a knight?" Zeros asked. "Does this factor into your consideration too?"

"No, knighthood suits me well," replied X'ieth. "I shall miss being a knight. Up until now, the Crimson Guard has been my purpose, one of the reasons I rise each morning—that, and my family. It's who I am, and what I do well. It fulfills me…"

Silence developed between X'ieth and Zeros, and a wind eventually broke it, followed by the mercenary's words. "So to solve one problem, you create another?" Zeros asked. "Forsaking your heartfelt purpose for anyone or anything would betray you!"

X'ieth looked into the fire, mulling over his words, reflecting upon the fact that he would feel a great loss if no longer a knight. *That you knew, from the start.*

"You must find a way for your dreams to survive your personal life," said Zeros. "Unless, your dream of knighthood isn't worthwhile?"

From the fire X'ieth turned, offended by the remark.

"What do you mean *by that?*" he asked.

X'ieth looked at Zeros intently, in want of an explanation. But the mercenary seemed to collect himself for a moment before answering, as if understanding that his comment touched on a sensitive subject with the young knight and needed a thoughtful explanation.

"If you aspire to do something that's achievable, with reasonable impositions upon yourself and others in your life," Zeros said at last, "and if that thing makes use of your hidden talents from Destiny—to the good of those in Karnath, your family, and yourself—only then is it worthwhile."

X'ieth internalized the statement, and it rang of things he learned from his religion to do good for one's self and others with hidden talents, while respecting the balance between work and life.

"That's just good destiny according to the Book of Karnatha," Zeros went on. "And Karnathan religion teaches us to pursue good destiny, but to abstain from bad destiny and null destiny. Surely you know that the opposite of good destiny is bad destiny, and null destiny is neither bad nor good destiny—it's just being nothing, a waste of one's life and purpose. Both bad and null destiny are equally offensive to Karnatha, and hence I believe a man should only pursue good destiny through his worthwhile dreams."

Not the best Karnathan, but certainly a believer, X'ieth weighed the mercenary's words carefully within the framework of his religious beliefs. *You've said many times before that the knighthood was a perfect match for your abilities in sword and magic. As a knight, you do good in Karnath, fulfill yourself, while providing for your family too. Therefore, the Guard is your good destiny. Remember how you've thought that all along...* As before, X'ieth went completely silent, lost in thought.

Zeros added, "A worthwhile dream merits your fight, but it's hard to distinguish worthwhile dreams from gray dreams. In search of my worthwhile dreams, I've chased many a gray dream in my few years upon Karnath, as we all do. Gray dreams are part of life."

As Zeros paused, X'ieth heard the fire snap and hiss, and another wind blew, this time hinting of a voice. It directed his eyes to the enveloping black of the forest, though nothing was to be seen. In little time, however, the mercenary's talk regained his attention.

"Sometimes we dream gray, of what's not meant to be—grand, fanciful things that are wonderful, but perhaps out of our reach. Some dreams are fated to be had by many, though only lived by a few. When gray dreams break, some people end up so broken that they never try anything else, and they live to watch alternative possibilities pass them by, unaware that a broken dream shouldn't be their end."

Zeros stopped talking, and looked at X'ieth directly. The young knight looked up from the fire, right back at the mercenary.

"But your dream of the knighthood isn't gray. You're living it." Zeros swallowed, as if with a dry throat, and then reached over for the water skin, which sat a cubit away from him, next to one knight's saddle. He took a small drink.

"Never throw away a worthwhile dream that's come true over a gray dream. But at the same time, don't hold off from chasing a gray dream if you think it's worthwhile and you know it doesn't jeopardize a dream that you're living. Again, it comes down to balancing your personal life with your dreams. They both have to survive."

The comment put X'ieth's mind to work. He started to reconsider everything in his life, and if somehow it was all meant to be.

"If your gray dream breaks, be a strong man and get up from the ground, dust yourself off, and try to piece that dream back together. If you can't, just try something new. There are plenty of dreams out there, so busy yourself with the chase of another gray dream, as long as you think it's worthwhile. Dreaming shouldn't end with any one broken dream, nor should the chase of dreams anew."

Zeros paused, and took another sip from his water skin. "Choice can only take people so far in life," the mercenary said after wetting his lips again, "and chance makes up the rest. Sometimes chance is in our favor, and sometimes not. Our share of both choice and chance determines the future of our gray dreams. So knowing that, we should chase gray dreams as long as they remain good destiny and we don't fall apart if they break. Never lose positive relationships or the will to do over any gray dream; it will cost you your future. Instead, dream responsibly, for your own sake and also that of others in your life…"

The talk of choice and chance conjured up X'ieth's recent experience in Arlem, with Lucen. He remembered what was said to him then: *It's not so much what you do that matters, but what's meant to be.* That downplay of choice rang between his ears, deepening the concept of chance in his own mind. Not liking the idea, he countered it with his frequent defense. *You've made good choices; hence Karnatha's blessings are upon you.*

Zeros just smiled, as if his only alternative to talking more, amid the young knight's silence. When that silence became prolonged, however, the mercenary tried to recover from a perceived misstep.

"Forgive me, I be rambling," Zeros confessed. "You don't have to agree with me, lad. I'm just sharing what I think, part from experience, and part from belief. As for you, like all others in Karnath, you must find your own way. How much you choose to rely on my advice, and whether you think it wise, are really up to you."

Zeros added, "In the end, your good destiny will be a fight, and likewise all people should fight for good destiny throughout their lives, just as the Battle for Destiny spoken of by the oracles!"

X'ieth halfheartedly nodded his head, only in partial agreement to many things said. If the young knight gained anything from opening up to Zeros, it was one formative idea: *Have your dreams survive your personal life.* His head started churning the possibilities. *What if your every dream is good destiny, divinely appointed by Karnatha herself? What if your every dream is meant to be, in spite of a selfish wife, a cruel king, and other titles?* These were ideas he had before even leaving Sergros, but now, they became more deeply entrenched in his mind. *Your dreams are your good destiny, and you must have them all!*

A wind suddenly lashed X'ieth, bringing him out of his deep thoughts, as it carried an unmistakable voice: "Shous da rio! Shous da rio!" The words came in a rasp upon his ears, and then with a mix of voices, from high pitched to deeper tones. "Shous da rio!"

He bolted upright, and looked into the woods, where the darkness of Forest Saol moved noticeably this time. And then from the shadows, X'ieth saw the darkened face of a large man come forth! The young knight's hand trailed to his sword grip, as he watched with awe, feeling bad now for judging Hammar earlier, who claimed to see shadowy figures.

"It's only vespers," Zeros said from behind. "These shadows can't touch us."

"Are they typically that big?" X'ieth asked, considering the shadow's size, surely not of a man, but rather a giant.

Zeros replied, "Vespers are shape-shifters. They can be both large and small."

When he noted the mercenary sit down once more by the fire, gradually X'ieth did the same. In a few moments, he became settled and thought of changing the discussion from his knighthood, until the end of first watch. *Ask him about the Crusades and Garlew…*

"So, you fought in the Isles Crusade?" asked X'ieth.

The young knight stopped speaking when suddenly, beams of gray fire appeared all around them from edges of the forest, painting out full circles as they spun about fixed points. His mouth went agape, as the fires continued swirling and came closer to the campsite!

"Rise, knights!" Zeros yelled, immediately sensing the imminent danger. With that, both he and X'ieth were on their feet and ready to defend themselves.

"INCONSOLABLE KILWROTH"

Chapter 37
Shadows of Saol

X'ieth ran through their encampment, making lots of noise. "Everyone, rise! Get up!" he yelled, while beating a gauntlet against his breastplate, sounding bang after bang into the night.

He watched the knights pour from their tents, weary eyed and taken abruptly from sleep, still wearing full armor. Footsteps ahead of him was tired Finnel who yawned and stretched, unaware of the vesper that loomed right behind him, wielding a fiery gray sword!

"Look out!" X'ieth shouted, unsheathing his blade without thinking, and running right past the other knight. In a moment, Nexus poured through his Source entry, into his aux core, and went out his Source exit, as he pushed the energies to his extremities and triggered a fluid offense, with precise muscle movements, coordination, and timing. Like a fluid with no resistance to flow, X'ieth transitioned between sword forms in the blink of an eye, first executing Clap of Thunder with a slash that fell diagonally through the vesper's body, though without adverse effect!

At seeing the vesper unharmed, fear sent questions through his mind. *What in Destiny?! How is that possible?!* The situation afforded him little time to consider the matter, however, as the vesper's flaming sword came right at him, already so close that X'ieth could feel its heat. Immediately, he performed *Avalanche Avail*, which swung both his arms back and forth like a pendulum fixed at his torso. His held his sword the entire time, with his left hand curling over the weapon's handle and his right under it.

He watched his whirling steel make contact with the vesper's fiery sword, right before it hit him. He saw the weapon fly from the shadowy hand and into the fog, its gray flame extinguished.

"Shous da rio!" hissed the vesper, going after it.

"Thanks, friend!" Finnel shouted, from the rear.

"Thanks be to Destiny!" X'ieth replied, breathing heavily and somewhat expended from his rapid sword attack. *Be ready for another, if need be!* Following his thought he looked back, but by that time Finnel was already gone, absorbed by the fierce conflict that developed throughout their camp.

Commotion sounded all around X'ieth—clangs of steel, yelling, and horses whinnying. His eyes scanned the area before him, detecting motion as the darkness stirred with knights fighting and their horses pulling wildly against their tree restraints. Before X'ieth could fully appreciate what went on, he noted how at his front, a fiery beam appeared again from the fog. It swirled about a fixed point up ahead, painting out gray circles on black, going clockwise then counterclockwise, and right at him!

"Move!" came a holler at his rear. X'ieth hit the ground face-first, as a blast of green Nexus blew by him, ripping up a tent along with its stakes! He lied facedown with sword in one outstretched hand, and slowly looked up to see Zeros hurl energy masses at the vespers.

"They must stay in the shadows!" barked mercenary, with his midsection glowing green, as he threw more blasts at them, each one shedding intense light.

"Arggh!" X'ieth groaned while shielding his eyes, from sharp pain to his head. The young knight got up and looked back toward the shouting. He saw fast-paced swordplay where Nathan and Finnel fought three vespers. Zeros appeared amidst them suddenly with his sword in one hand, while throwing Nexus at the shadows using his other. The mercenary looked tired from pulling all that magic, even though their fight was just beginning.

Beyond all that, X'ieth observed Lewes and Tol fight three more shadowy figures with fiery swords. As before, it amazed him to see the knights' steel blades carve through the vespers' bodies without consequence. *They can't touch*, he thought. *Wouldn't want to find out though, if those fiery blades can touch us!*

But with his momentary pause X'ieth found out just that, when beholding Lewes' misfortune, as one vesper's sword cut into his exposed upper arm, instantly cauterizing the wound! "Aggghhhh!' the other knight screamed, falling to the ground.

Do something, man! Along with his own good will, Magicia's spell nudged X'ieth to help Lewes. And so, he rushed toward the vesper standing over the other knight, about to deliver a fatal blow. But after only a few strides forward, he was stopped short as Hammar cut right in front of him, facing the vesper head on. X'ieth saw the dwarf appear in his path, with his club hammer pulled back and ready to strike. "Step aside!" Hammar shouted, slamming his weapon down onto the vesper's head.

X'ieth watched the hammer go through the shadowy figure hovering over Lewes, to knock the flaming sword from its grip and into fog, before the weapon could do further damage. The young knight helped Lewes to his feet, and as he did, Nathan yelled suddenly from behind

"Circle about the fire! Vespers must avoid light!"

"Aye, let's fight there, back-to-back!" yelled Zeros. "Keep a man's back, and he'll keep yours! We'll stand together, or fall alone!"

From the corner of his eye, X'ieth saw the fire's glow in the distance, with a few vespers standing between him and the site. The young knight flowed into Geyser's Fount, sending the closest vesper's sword into the fog. Tol ran in beside him wielding his sword to disarm the next vesper in the path. X'ieth followed suit with his own sword, disarming the vesper beyond that one. Each time a vesper lost a sword, the shadow disappeared into the fog hissing those same arcane words, obviously in another language.

"Shous da rio! Shous da rio!"

X'ieth and Tol cleared the way of vespers, with Lewes running at their rear. They went to the center of camp, where soon the other knights joined them. Together, the Guardsmen encircled the dying fire, with their backs facing one another, just waiting with swords readied as the vespers regrouped.

Then suddenly from the dark, X'ieth watched their fiery swords come swirling once more, sending heat his way. Beads of sweat formed on his forehead as the gray flames trumped the gloom's chill. Despite his discomfort, he stood still in his heavy armor, hearing the horses whiney more as they pulled against the trees.

"This can't be happening," X'ieth muttered in disbelief, recalling Zeros' words. *These shadows of Saol can't touch us.*

"Well, it's happening!" replied Finnel.

X'ieth turned just then, seeing the other knight's straight face, swathed by shadow.

"Everyone, form links with those near you!" shouted Nathan, interrupting them.

As instructed, X'ieth closed his eyes to envision his small channeling chamber. He went to his Source entry, and pulled it open. Nexus streamed in, filling the room from floor to ceiling and thus, his aux core. Still in his chamber, he spun from the Source entry and ran to his Source exit, with the energy hovering about his body, hair lengths away across his Source boundary. At the exit, he pushed out the energy through the door, against every mental restraint he could sense. Exactly like this, the other knights filled their aux cores and pushed Nexus against their perceived mental restraints, thereby linking to nearby comrades.

When X'ieth opened his eyes, it was just in time to see the vespers charge, first toward Lewes. *They attack the injured!* Even with his arm wound, Lewes threw fire at the shadows until his core was drained. But in the very moment he ran out of magic, the knights linked with him supplied more energy. Mimicking the other knight, X'ieth decided to throw fire at the vespers nearest him. But as soon as flames sparked from his center with a whoosh, he heard Nathan tyrannically spout off.

"Not fire! Saol will go ablaze, man! Make light from Nexus!"

Feeling bad, the young knight replied, "Light it is!"

And with that, he continued channeling Nexus as the others, sending flashes of light to ward off the vespers, and pushing magic to replenish the depleted cores of other knights. The entire process tired him, and X'ieth panted like a dog on a summer day. With a quick glance around, he noted how the other knights suffered from the same fatigue, with their constant transformations of Nexus into light. But as fatigued as they were, they still hurled magic at the vespers, every time the shadows got too close, wielding their flaming gray swords.

With the knights' magic wielding, tents flew into the woods, stakes and all. Though the lost supplies discouraged X'ieth, he would not let it stop him from hurling magic at the vespers, as needed. *Our rations! Our saddles!* The thoughts grazed his mind in a single instant, but were gone as soon as they came, as sounds of horses whinnying stole his attention. Through the shadows and fog, he could see the beasts twisting and turning, at every flash of light. It made them wild with fear, and caused them to pull even harder against their tree restraints.

X'ieth heard the other knights' heavy breathing all around. Flashes from their magic brought the forest to life, with beams of light dispersed through the heavy fog to shine against the distant trees, standing tall in the gloom. The sights and sounds reminded him that the Guard was stuck in Saol, now amid this epic battle for their lives. *Nathan should tell his children of this, rather than his struggle with the compass!*

At that moment, X'ieth spotted a vesper that was cubits away from him, with sword in shadowy hand. In a jerk reaction, he threw Nexus at the fiend, startled with the sudden appearance of a shadow in a space that he thought was clear. And as his opponent fled back into the fog, he summoned his absolute best of mind and body, back into the fight. *Be here now!* But in only a moment's passing, X'ieth saw the giant silhouettes come back, time and time again. Their reappearance caused the horses to neigh and jump, perhaps spooking them more than the Guard's magical attacks with light.

"We only stand to tire this way!" yelled Zeros.

"Light pushes the shadows back, but hurts them not!" shouted Nathan. "We need a new plan!"

After a few seconds, Zeros asserted, "They can touch their swords, nothing else. So rid these fiends of the weapons, and likewise we'll rid us of them!"

Instantly, X'ieth acknowledged the plan's brilliance. *It'll work.* He heard the horses jump anxiously, pulling more at their restraints. *Crack.*

Moved by Zeros' cunning, X'ieth proposed, "Finnel, let's tether! A whirlwind of steel can knock their swords to the ground!"

It was then that noise filled his ears, of several horses whinnying as another wave of vespers approached.

Crack.

"Aye!" the elven knight replied.

Crack. Crack! CRACK!

Suddenly, X'ieth felt deep vibrations in the darkness accompanied by a loud thud and smashes. He heard rapid clopping immediately afterward. From the corner of his eye, he noted three of their horses run about Finnel's sides, displacing the fog every which way. As the horses charged, they pulled their tree restraint behind them, roots and all!

As Finnel was thrown to the ground, X'ieth watched in horror as the tree's large trunk and its veiny roots raked the now fallen knight!

He screamed, "No!"

"Grrraaahhh!" Finnel grimaced in pain at the tree's impact, which broke his leg in places, as told by the sounds of snapping bones.

At this very moment, X'ieth watched vespers close in on the broken ring of knights from its opposite side. At the sound of more whinnies, his gaze drifted to the other three horses spooked out of their minds, also tied to a tree with thick rope.

Oh no. His thought fired, right before their restraint ripped from the ground, and the horses charged toward him and the other knights, dragging the tree behind!

"Link with me, and keep pushing!" Zeros yelled, hurrying in front of the oncoming horses and tree. The thunder of those hooves instilled fear in the young knight. Yet without hesitation, X'ieth envisioned his small channeling chamber and pulled against his Source entry, to draw energy into his core. He felt so weary, and wondered to himself, *Can you even fill your room?! Just keep pulling until it happens, then push and repeat.*

And just like this, X'ieth continued pulling until his chamber was nearly full. He snapped back to Saol, seeing the horses and tree coming closer, only a few cubits away now. With more fear, he watched the fog leap to the sides in the unrelenting advance of those terrified horses. The young knight forced himself to keep working, while watching. *Push now.*

In his channeling chamber, not entirely filled, X'ieth turned to push against the Source exit—in this context, his closest mental restraint. *That's Zeros.* As the sweat beaded his forehead and he grunted aloud, the young knight glanced to the mercenary, who started drawing the Nexus that X'ieth provided. A green light blinked from nothingness at Zeros' waist.

Prior to the horses reaching them, X'ieth watched Zeros cast the magic to form a force field between them and the horses, along with the tree and its roots. Through a green wall of pure energy, X'ieth stared with Nathan and Lewes, as the mere sight of the Nexus barrier caused the trio horse stampede to radically change direction, and run around it! However, the force field obstructed the tree, its trunk thudding into it and snagging the horses.

In a frenzy the beasts neighed and jumped, still unbelievably spooked and wanting to flee. X'ieth returned to his channeling chamber, which nearly emptied by now. *Not good!* He went back to Saol, and verified the mercenary still maintained the force field, but Zeros clearly tired from pushing alone. He noted sweat glistening from the mercenary's forehead, catching the green light. *Just a little longer... Please Destiny!* prayed X'ieth.

When the horses continued struggling, the young knight saw their ropes pulled taut, about the side of the force field. Without even thinking, he unsheathed his blade and lunged to slash the ropes, only moments before Zeros stopped channeling, and the green wall of energy vanished. And when those events happened in but a span of seconds, the tree and its mass of roots stopped, not more than two cubits away from them!

X'ieth fell to his knees with sword in hand, as the neighs and clopping hooves of those three horses filled his ears, during their wild run through Forest Saol. As those sounds faded, he slumped to the ground, exhausted from the physical expense. In the backdrop, he heard Finnel wince from the ground in agony, and also, the last tied horse neighing and jumping, still somehow restrained by the smaller tree.

When X'ieth abruptly sensed heat, he looked around to behold more vespers closing in from all sides, nearly a dozen with flaming swords. *Get up, man. The fight's not over!*

"Disarm them!" Nathan shouted.

X'ieth stood, and when he did, Zeros faced him.

"Let's tether. I shall try to be as Finnel would!"

Does Zeros hold the Crescent? X'ieth wondered.

Not knowing what to expect, the young knight nodded and closed his eyes, envisioning his small channeling chamber once again. He stood at his Source entry with the door ajar, and a stream of Nexus energy flowing into the chamber, born of the light seen distantly from the opening. The stream flowed more and more, filling the room from floor to ceiling. X'ieth carried the accumulated energy to his Source exit and pushed out his stream for Zeros. He instantly spun about to pull Nexus through his Source entry again, into his core.

A sudden hot flash came over him, and he popped from his vision, just in time to witness salvation. Before his eyes, Hammar threw his club hammer to disarm a vesper that would have otherwise sliced him. Without a word the dwarf smiled at him, and then resumed throwing his hammer about, just as another shadow cast its sword at X'ieth from the rear. He heard Hammar curse like a Mainlandish sailor.

"Destiny damn you all!"

Keep your mind centered! Amid all the distracting chaos that ensued about him, X'ieth closed his eyes once more, and now saw his own stream in the chamber, as well as that of Zeros. In an instant, he merged them together. The young knight opened up his eyes to behold Zeros staring back, and he felt the mercenary successfully form the tether.

"We stay close," Zeros said. "Lest our locus of control break this bond!" X'ieth saw a green light blink from the midsections of Nathan and Lewes, as both knights linked to him and the mercenary.

"My arm prevents me from pushing a blade just now, but I can still push magic!" X'ieth heard Lewes shout, seeing a sparkle in the other knight's eyes.

He glanced to the side, seeing how Tol guarded the fallen Finnel from a number of vespers seeking to prey upon the weak. To Zeros, X'ieth looked then and said aloud, "Complementing forms… Let's go!"

The young knight and mercenary moved quickly, one executing Rainfalls the other *Cresting Wave*. Then, the pair did Clap of Thunder from opposite sides, and Avalanche Avail with blades moving synchronously, to the same side. Their blaze of steel did just as intended, knocking fiery swords from half a dozen armed vespers, if not more.

In the corner of his eye, X'ieth saw Hammar unhook his cloak and throw it on one vesper's blade, which barely could be seen through the dense fog. The young knight watched with astonishment, as the vesper sought to reclaim its weapon, but could not! He heard the shadowy figure hiss while clawing frantically at the cloak, unable to touch its material.

Between different sword forms, X'ieth continued dancing with Zeros, and noted at one point how Tol emulated Hammar's tactic the next time a weapon fell from a vesper's grip: the other knight uncloaked his cape to lay it over the sword, which lied fireless on the ground afar.

X'ieth finished his current sword form, and then turned just in time to see the disarmed vesper claw at Tol's cloak, hissing those common words: "Shous da rio!"

He looked up to Tol with a smile, but upon seeing two swords of gray fire come at him, from over his shoulder, X'ieth bolted his way.

"Behind you!" he yelled to Tol, while running.

"Destiny save me!" Tol cried, upon turning and beholding the two vespers, armed with swords. As X'ieth ran up, he saw the other knight twist to the side, avoiding the end of one vesper's sword, but hitting the other's. Adrenaline pumped into the young knight, as he watched the fiery blade carve into Tol's thigh, on an unarmored part.

"Ahhh!" winced Tol, clearly feeling incredible pain.

X'ieth saw him double over, grinding his teeth and growling, as the vespers loomed overhead. Just then, X'ieth and Zeros confronted the vespers with a steel cyclone to neutralize the fiends—an attack that sent swords flying from their grips and into the fog.

When his sword came to a rest, he stood there breathing heavily, with his mind full of thoughts. *How'd our combined core stay so full?* A glance one way, revealed Nathan and Lewes still throwing Nexus toward him and Zeros. The pair stopped hurling magic when the vespers' weapons fell near their feet, to throw their cloaks overtop.

"Shous da rio!" the vespers hissed, incited more.

"It's working!" shouted Nathan, above the hissing and distant whinnies from their one remaining horse.

Beyond exhausted now, X'ieth felt weak in the knees, idly watching Hammar at a distance, who kicked dead leaves over more swords knocked from the vespers. He slowly realized how resourceful the tactic was. *The dwarf's improvise of leaves works just as well as a cloak!* The young knight recognized Hammar's combination of might and mind made him well suited for the knighthood. *Even with that awfully clumsy hammer!*

In short order, X'ieth saw Hammar move nimbly for his girth, along with Lewes and Nathan, to cover up a few other fiery swords, cubits from where they stood.

"Shous da rio! Shous da rio!" the vespers hissed, shadows that hung upon the air, clawing at the leaves now covering their swords.

The young knight slumped to the ground, and he sensed Zeros do the same from behind. They both leant against each other's back with their swords held in hand, laying the blades on the ground.

"You did well," Zeros said. "Makes me proud."

Only half involved now, X'ieth muttered, "Yeah."

He watched the unarmed shadows frolic in the night, about the scattered remnants of the Guard's encampment, hissing those same words.

"Shous da rio! Shous da rio!"

His eyes trailed to a limping Tol beside the fallen Finnel, who still struggled on the ground with a serious leg injury. From there, he took in the dying embers of their fire, tents thrown into the woods, with all their supplies peeking from the fog. The scene drew a stark forecast for the young knight, and he prayed carelessly then, *Please get me out of here. Must see Millicent again... Must see my child born!*

He heard the hissing fade into the night: "Shous da rio! Shous da rio!" Those words grew quieter and quieter, until only the howl of winds reigned over silence, and the Guard was left alone to regroup.

"SPINDLE AND LOOM"

Chapter 38
The Regroup

The Guard was exhausted after their sudden attack by vespers, with a campsite now strewn throughout Saol. Six stood, with one fallen, and not a single vesper in sight. Three total had injuries—Lewes with a slashed arm, Tol with a gashed thigh, and Finnel with a smashed leg. Beneath the cloak of night, the group gathered to tend to the wounded.

Across the rebuilt fire, X'ieth sat watching Zeros use the Nexus to partially heal Finnel's leg. With an intense face, he focused to continuously fill his aux core, while channeling Nexus around the leg, and transforming it into a rejuvenating force that spiraled about its length. X'ieth had never seen such a thing outside of Sergrothian hospices, and so, he looked on with amazement, seeing bruises vanish as Nexus seeped into Finnel's skin. But he noted how some of those black and blue marks would not go away, and he could tell the outcome made Finnel worried.

"What's wrong?!" Finnel asked with angst.

X'ieth shifted his eyes to the mercenary, who looked to Finnel with a solemn face.

"Your leg is broken badly… I cannot heal the whole wound," he replied, a bit hesitantly.

Silence developed, and X'ieth glanced over at Finnel. The other knight's face showed surprise—an open mouth and arched eyebrows—as if he expected better from Zeros. The expression quickly turned into one of frustration, when Finnel's forehead wrinkled.

"No! Say it isn't so!" he protested. "How will I continue?! I must go on! I must!"

From over yonder, X'ieth heard Nathan talk.

"On horse, knight. There's one left yet, and the rest of us can walk," said the pack leader, straight-faced.

As Finnel shook his head and muttered denial, X'ieth wondered about a variety of things. *Is his leg still broken? Can he limp as Tol even?* Random thoughts kept hitting him, as he considered the prospect of confronting Esmeralda with one less knight. *Doesn't matter, man. You know who you are. Kayareth…* When Finnel moved abruptly, X'ieth pushed the thought from his mind and paid attention to what took place.

"Don't put your weight on it!" Zeros exclaimed.

Finnel attempted to stand, ignoring Zeros.

"I can't fight the sorceress upon a seat, man!"

As Finnel rose to his feet, X'ieth watched eagerly to see if the other knight could walk. *Hope so*, he thought to himself. But Finnel stumbled the very moment he put the slightest pressure on his leg.

"Argghh!" he groaned, falling down.

Zeros rushed to catch the other knight, and lead him back into a seated position.

"Told you not to put weight on it!" he admonished.

Once again, X'ieth found it interesting how the mercenary had such good instincts for a great many things. *He just knows.*

"How'd you learn to heal like that?" asked Tol.

To the side, X'ieth turned his head, seeing the other knight limp forward, cubits away, from across the fire. *He likely wants some healing too.*

"I've never seen anything like that outside of a hospice. And healers can only do so much for those of infirmity, not even that."

Zeros smiled.

"Oh, I've learned healing in my journeys."

"Can you see to my hurt? And Lewes?"

X'ieth looked to Zeros then, studying the mercenary's appearance. His withdrawn eyes sat above dark rings underneath them, telling of his fatigue. *He's weary, from a day of non-stop doing.*

Nathan asserted then, "Your wound and Lewes' can wait 'til the morning. Let the man get some sleep first."

X'ieth kept his eyes on Zeros, who appeared indifferent to the granted relief, but spoke differently.

"Aye, that might be best," said Zeros. "I'm hardly able to pull Nexus now, being so tired."

X'ieth noted how he delicately admitted it to Tol, as if not wanting to make any offense. He glanced at Tol, who nodded in reply. Behind Tol, X'ieth saw Lewes sitting by the fire and holding an injured arm, also acknowledging Zeros' response with a silent nod.

Again silence developed, and X'ieth sat by the fire quietly, pondering what he had pondered before. *These shadows of Saol can't touch us.* He thought about how what just happened was a complete departure from what Zeros presumed, and wondered why no one had asked yet. *If no one else will ask, then you will!*

"Vespers can't touch anything?" he blurted out, unable to contain his curiosity. In his mind, flashes of his sword appeared, passing through the vespers' bodies without any effect whatsoever.

Slowly Zeros responded, "It's true—vespers can't touch most things, though their swords seem special. Something must be very different about them."

X'ieth observed how Hammar, with almost perfect timing, came to the fire from his rounds of collecting the vespers' swords. The other knight set down one cloak that contained them all, and it hit the ground with a dull clang. In his other hand, the dwarf held the various cloaks he found on the soil. The young knight smirked when he threw them to Nathan in a heap, covering the pack leader's head.

From his periphery, X'ieth sensed a few knights go for their cloak, whereas his interest was on the vespers' magical blades. *Go get one*, he told himself. Carefully then, the young knight opened the bundle that Hammar brought, to remove a sword.

He held one in his hand, and his first impression was that the material felt extremely lightweight. Inspecting it from tip to pommel, X'ieth noted how the sword appeared as a solid, one-piece construction, having a curved blade that showed an odd pattern with infinite depths of complexity. Chains of overlaid triangles were visible to him, chains that resembled a dragon at many scales, with smaller versions of the same pattern repeated within the larger, many times over.

Around the sword's grip, he saw no protective wrapping. *It's like the vespers need to touch it*, he thought, not understanding why exactly. He continued considering characteristics of the weapon, and its material stood out to him next, being unlike anything the young knight ever experienced before. To his touch, the blade felt as a soft mineral, but its edge was sharp enough to draw blood from his naked finger! He gasped at what was a seeming paradox. *Soft and sharp, together?! What is this?* His mind spun with questions.

"Let me see!" said Tol from across the fire.

"Give one here," said Lewes.

X'ieth distributed a few swords among the other knights. He wrapped the cloak tightly over the remainder, fearing the vespers could reach for their blades from the shadows. After X'ieth took his seat again by the fire, he watched Zeros inspect the sword carefully. The mercenary touched the blade without getting cut.

"This came from the forges of Tekkneo."

X'ieth stared back blankly at Zeros with the other knights. *Tek what?* He wondered what was just mentioned, never hearing of a so-named person, place, or thing.

"Tekkneo is where the metal demons come from."

X'ieth grew incredibly intrigued. He, like most commoners in Sergros even, had heard of encounters with so-called metal demons in the Mainland's northeast. They were rumored to be magical knights that forced travelers and nomads out from the area.

"Hidden behind high tapered walls of ivory, Tekkneo is a secret civilization protected by the metal demons," Zeros continued, "and not many in Karnath know anything of it."

X'ieth hung on every word, his mind now silent.

"The city is not even on maps, and the area about Tekkneo is completely uncharted." The wind howled behind Zeros' words, making the mercenary pause.

From the eventual silence, X'ieth asked, "When did Tekkneo come into being, and why?"

Zeros' countenance lit up with a smile.

"Some think Tekkneo originated back in the middle of a war spanning centuries called Saipei. And to this day, no one really knows what kingdoms fought over in that war, how it started, or why Tekkneo came out of the conflict."

X'ieth saw Zeros look around the fire at the other knights while speaking, as if to maintain complete engagement. The mercenary's stare returned to the young knight, with the fire caught in his eyes.

"All records on the war were destroyed in *History's Crucible.*" X'ieth listened intently, as Zeros told of conjectures how before Saipei, a Dark magic came out of Deardrum and was shared with Sergros and Juniper, up until the time it started changing history. Society started to evolve, but the rulers tried to stop it. An edict came forth in all three kingdoms named the *Ban on Innovations*, ordering everyone to stop the study and practice of this Dark magic.

"What type of Dark magic?" X'ieth interrupted.

Zeros looked his way.

"They called it *technology*, and it provided for comforts of life that perhaps we shall never see. Horseless carriages, clocks that run perpetually, webs of knowledge in black boxes… So many things!"

Silence built, and X'ieth glanced to Tol, who eventually spoke. "What happened?"

With another smile, Zeros talked on.

"Some believe that the presumably dangerous magic continued to be created, and changing history."

X'ieth listened as Zeros told how historians essentially penned of great advances the kingdoms made, and began documenting the evolution of society stemming from the Dark magic, of which the rulers desperately wished to rid themselves. The politicians and royal officials of all three kingdoms grew terrified of how history was changing, and they became tyrannical when some would not obey the new written law. The young knight watched the mercenary gesture vivaciously with his hands as he talked, the snap and crackle of the fire behind his words. "And so, the leaders did something awful to set a precedent…"

The mercenary proceeded to tell how the crucible earned its name. "Some historians who still wrote of the innovations were imprisoned, while others were publicly executed in cruel ways! Drawn and quartered, beheadings, and burnings were common practice, many in the square. Those caught practicing the magic saw worse, tortures before execution!" At each spoken word, X'ieth's jaw began to drop.

"But that runs contrary to Sergrothian law," Lewes interjected, "which makes all free with a right to life and the pursuit of happiness!" From his shocked tone, X'ieth inferred the obvious. *Lewes finds that stark contrast to modern Sergros difficult to believe, just like you do.*

"I know," Zeros replied. "But the government was perhaps very different then. We can't be entirely sure." The words met silence, and X'ieth's eyes remained fixed upon Zeros. He contemplated the matter. *We enjoy freedoms that weren't always enjoyed.*

From the quiet, Zeros elaborated on what happened when imprisonment and execution alone did not work. "Some historians still penned of drastic changes to society that resulted from the Dark magic, and the new records of innovations were then burned, and even records before that in what became a frenzy to abolish any evidence of it. Accounts of the Dark magic were destroyed, along with many people who used it."

X'ieth listened as Zeros further explained how the few scholars who conducted studies of this Dark period refer to these heinous acts as History's Crucible, the name mentioned before. "The effects of the crucible clarify why much of Karnath's history became lost during the era of Saipei," Zeros said. "It's another guess that Tekkneo broke off from the three kingdoms in the middle of the crucible, to lead a new way of life with this Dark magic, in isolation from the rest of Karnath."

"Why would the Triangle Kingdoms institute such violence against the innocent?" X'ieth asked, either feeling nudged by Magicia's binding or his own disdain for such misdeeds. *Maybe by both...*

"The Karnathan religion was very influential, some believe," Zeros says with a pause. "The Dark magic came to be viewed by authorities as stealing good destiny from the people."

X'ieth just nodded, while sitting around the fire with the other knights. Like him, surely the others found themselves spellbound by a story never heard before. *If what happened is not well known, how does Zeros know?* X'ieth wondered.

Sharp-minded Nathan asked a natural question, one on the tip of young knight's tongue, though one that he could not bring himself to ask. "How do you know so much about these things, which by your own word, aren't well documented at all?" As the last word sounded, X'ieth looked from Nathan to Zeros, feeling some regret for not speaking. *Should of asked, man. Your questions are those of others...*

"During the last Isles Crusade," Zeros answered, pausing thoughtfully, "I and some other soldiers ended up protecting a very large man, maybe a giant, who came into the possession of crimson armor energized by a magical stone. The man called this armor a metal demon. It was the first time I'd ever heard the term used." All eyes were on Zeros, as he continued talking. "When I asked the man about the magical armor, he spoke of Tekkneo." The mercenary described the curves and spikes of the armor, using his hands to illustrate its sheer size.

"At the time, I'd never seen such a thing," Zeros admitted. "Had I seen such a metal demon near that city of ivory, I would be fearful knowing what it could do."

X'ieth wondered what that entailed. *What can a metal demon do?* His eyes widened as he heard Zeros explain how the armor from Tekkneo imparted inordinate ability to anyone who wore it.

"The armor makes one incredibly fast, awesomely powerful, and enhances magical ability to that of a sorcerer," told the mercenary. Without blinking X'ieth listened to Zeros talk, his jaw dropped even lower. "Whoever possesses such armor has superior might!"

After a little thought, X'ieth asked insightfully, "Why would anyone with a metal demon even need protection?"

Zeros stared back in silence a moment before replying. "The man was large and too big to fit! And so, he still couldn't wear the armor, and being old he needed protection."

"Couldn't a solider just wear the armor?"

"No. Though too small for a giant, the armor was too big for a grown man, not that Elucid would allow anyone to wear it, if they could," Zeros replied. "He was fairly protective over the armor, as protective as I became over him… even after his death."

The young knight saw Zeros across the fire, and thoughts collided in his mind. *So, Elucid was this man's name, and he wouldn't allow the armor to be touched? His death, the mercenary mentions… What even happened?*

X'ieth's curiosity would be at the mercy of what Zeros would disclose. But the mercenary's pensive appearance discouraged further questioning. The young knight noted how his brow wrinkled, how his facial muscles tensed, and how his eyes hinted of a topic deeply bothering, as if somehow the conversation wandered into dangerous territory that was off-limits.

Suddenly, Zeros talked again, looking more collected now. "Talking about Tekkneo moves us further from the topic of the vesper's swords. Telling what I learned of the city made for a nice story, but let's discuss the swords, since I stirred everyone's interest."

X'ieth saw a cloud of certain mystery and darkness roll back from Zeros then, as the mercenary distanced the other knights from a seemingly unfavorable subject—Elucid's death, and something that occurred in its aftermath.

Against the bonfire's snap and crackle, X'ieth heard what Zeros had to say. "I could tell that Tekkneo forges produced these weapons, because of the material used to construct the blades and their unique metalworking."

The material used to construct the blades… X'ieth's mind raced to recall the paradox about the blade's composition of soft mineral to the touch, yet hard alloy in function. *The unique metalworking...* He knew it was neither pattern-welding nor forge-welding by sight alone.

X'ieth watched Zeros look down at the blade, to examine it carefully. "This material is special," he said. "The vespers can make contact with it, unlike anything else in Karnath. Tekkneo could fashion other objects tangible to vespers, from swords to armor, *even metal demons*. Why this would be done, is beyond my understanding."

Zeros flipped the sword about in one hand, and X'ieth followed it with every twirl. "This weapon possesses an additional feature, one that no one has yet considered."

His eyes narrowing, the young knight stared back with a concentrated look. *The vespers somehow wrought that gray fire*, he thought, wondering if this was what Zeros referred to. A blank expression formed on his face, and he glanced about the campfire to see others wearing the same.

X'ieth turned back to Zeros, just waiting for the mercenary to unfurl the mystery. But he was surprised to observe him act instead of speak. In a single instant, Zeros suddenly tapped the Nexus, drew a continuous flow of energy through his core, and ignited the sword, just as when the vespers wielded it!

X'ieth noticed how the mercenary stopped channeling, short of the metal burning his hand. The fire snuffed out immediately, following the green aura at Zeros' midsection. Along with everyone else, X'ieth displayed a surprised look.

"How did you do that?!" asked Finnel.

Zeros turned to the other knight and explained.

"Some weapons, especially ancient ones, are designed with the advanced feature of an aux core, like the one we have." The young knight's jaw started dropping again, having been closed since their discussion of the metal demons ended. *You never heard that, not even in academy!*

"It aids the magical ability of whomever wields it," Zeros continued, "and allows for continuous channeling of the Source until the weapon's core is filled, rather than the wielder's."

Zeros smiled. "And that's what I know about the swords, plus a little more." And with that, the conversation about Tekkneo and its swords lost energy, as did the mercenary. X'ieth saw a glimpse of restrained morning light breaking through the trees. When a long silence developed, he watched Zeros pass that sword back to Hammar.

Nathan shouted, "Everyone, return also the swords! We must keep them bundled."

X'ieth handed his sword to the dwarf, and saw the other knights follow suit, all together. Hammar piled them lengthwise onto another cloak, and wrapped the magical weapons once more.

"Now let's organize for departure in a few hours," Nathan said. "Until then, X'ieth and Zeros get some sleep." He redirected his stare, while saying the words.

From his periphery, X'ieth sensed Zeros nod and lie down in the space a few cubits away, no doubt eager to get an hour or so of sleep. When he turned back to Nathan, he noted how the pack leader would not relinquish his eyes, until the young knight conceded in the same.

"As you wish," X'ieth said finally, and got up from his seat around the fire. He trudged over to where Zeros lied, his head hanging low the entire walk. *As the Light Prophecy foretold, man... The path of Kayareth would not be easy, and such is yours.*

He laid himself down, a few cubits from Zeros, and the ground felt ice-cold beneath him. Face-up, X'ieth lied awake looking into Saol's barren trees, the night's black on the verge of morning gray. In the background, he heard Hammar and Lewes, as they scoured the area for supplies.

"Over here," said Lewes. "There's a single pack."

"Aye, I'm coming. Patience," replied the dwarf.

X'ieth's chest rose slowly beneath the armor, his lungs working shallower breaths as his mind drifted closer to sleep, closer to a state of rest. The words of Lucen echoed his thoughts. *You're destined for greater things than you figured. Imagine greater, see beyond what you deem adequate.* He thought to himself then, *This life is wholly your good destiny... Being the hero, a knight, a father, and a husband.*

And then, the words of Zeros wandered through his mind. *Your worthwhile dreams, your good destiny, must survive personal circumstances.* In that moment more than any other, X'ieth came to want all of his dreams with greater passion. *You must have them all.*

This new dream of greatness swallowed whole all his prior dreams, even being Kayareth. Ever since his talk with Zeros, he wanted it all. The young knight would be a husband, a father, a knight, and a hero. *You'll have your every dream,* he told himself. *And somehow, your dreams must survive Talus' cruelty and Millicent's want of you being less, instead of more.*

When X'ieth closed his eyes, visions so splendid replaced the drab sights of Forest Saol. For when he shut them, his dreams came alive inside his head.

**** X'ieth's Reverie ****

As the Child of Light and new hero of the land, X'ieth rode into the city of Castle Sergros upon a snowy white horse, bedecked in polished barding. His wife Millicent held his child and stood at the front of a massive throng, amid so many others who joyously sang praises to the new Garlew Il'therin, the one who slayed the Child of Darkness and brought Light to Karnath.

As his steed trotted forward, its hooves upon the cobblestone rang out in victory, and the young knight raised his hands high to be showered with rainbow confetti, thrown by the handful from those who adored him. Cheers mixed with the crowd's song—the Child's Triumph—as trumpets sounded and drums played, heralding the hero to the city square, where Talus himself would honor the savior of Sergros.

Ovation shook Karnath when everyone in the land venerated the Child of Light with applause and accolade, over a deed that would live on with infamy throughout the ages, to be immortalized in legend forevermore.

****

X'ieth's reverie went on inside his head, a happy dream to fill such a short span of rest. And such a rapturous thing would drive him toward his best of good destinies, on the morrow.

"X'IETH AND HIS REVERIE"

Chapter 39
Newfound Optimism for the King

Fire burned within the collars of twin torches besetting the throne of Sergros, one on each side. A row of doctors stood in between the torches, being of varied age and race. At the front of the row was a female doctor, with light skin and dark hair. Facing them, Talus sat in his ornate chair, well rested and of good decorum, nodding with a smile to the ramble of his finest Sergrothian physicians. Despite the gloom, it was one of the king's better days since the Guard left to slay Esmeralda, given the recent onset of visions about his own bright future, now confirmed as neither sickness of mind nor body.

He looked again to the female doctor standing before him, clothed in white fabrics, as all workers of Sergrothian hospices and healing houses. She was a woman of medicine, one bound to do good with her medical knowledge, one to be trusted. But while the king saw her mouth working, while he could hear her words fall against his ears, he struggled to listen to them, despite her trustworthiness and acumen. He was so overwhelmed with joy over the news that it was hard for him to focus.

"My attention lapsed," Talus interjected amid her sentence, twiddling his fingers on an upraised hand. "In the matter of my health, tell me again your finding." *Yes, let them say it one more time, just for the sake of hearing it!*

He looked intently at the dark-haired woman before him, having a light complexion and brown eyes. When she opened her mouth again to speak, he promised himself to remain mindful this time.

"Regarding the onset of your premonitions, my king," she said politely, "the application of the best knowledge and experience in medicine finds you well. You are of good health, King Darxar."

The words filled Talus' belly with fluttery delight. *I'm not a crazed man, nor one of devilries!* he thought. *I'm just as others in Sergros, blessed now by Destiny with visions of my future! And beyond that, blessed now is my kingdom with great fortune!*

Only a day ago, the king experienced his very first premonition, putting him among the likes of many in Karnath. Visions of his own future sporadically overtook him, which agreed exactly with his eventual reality. *What I foresee does happen!* he considered gleefully.

In retrospect of hurriedly calling upon so many physicians, the king now felt foolish. He still looked back at them with a smirk upturning the corners of his lips, recalling how unlike so many in Karnath, his foresights evaded him until now. And so, the sudden onset of premonitions scared him indeed, hence his want of immediate medical examination.

Though generally unlearned about the sophistication of Sergrothian medicine for mental illness, Talus still knew it entailed a philosophy that balance of the body's composites related directly to mental health. And per Sergrothian physicians, since the most fundamental bodily element is blood, Talus called upon them with the anticipation of their first recommendation being bloodletting. *Thank Destiny it's not needed, and all is well!*

Talus noted an edgy look about one younger physician standing before him, a man with a reputation for poor judgments. This doctor was in the row of doctors behind the woman, at its left end. From out of nowhere, he began to speak.

"My king, we have yet to see if letting some blood would restore balance to your body, and stop these visions!" Talus watched as the young physician flashed a wide grin, and then from a grim-faced servant, grabbed a glass jar filled with leaches to hold it high.

With disgust, Talus gazed upon those slimy black creatures squirming about in the jar, many right up against the glass. Having ostensive disdain for them, he cringed while imagining the leaches crawling all over his body and sucking his blood. The mere thought made his skin crawl, and he shuddered. *Ewww!*

Not believing what he heard, the king stared back with an expression of mixed repulsion and disbelief. *Can it be that this young physician suggests an unpleasant cure when I have no ailment, just to see if it helps? Is this man detached from his own wits?! I clearly dislike the leaches.* The king's eyes moved between the grinning young doctor and glass jar, struggling to understand the situation.

The young physician talked on about the leaches like a catapult in rapid fire, while Talus drifted in and out of the conversation, struggling even more to understand. *He keeps talking about those leaches, as if oblivious to my scowl.* Talus let his frown worsen. It did not help.

"We recommend at least fifty leaches be attached to the body, put all over for the best results!"

From the continued discourse of the young physician, Talus resigned himself, yet again. *Is the man more a fool than a doctor?* The king wondered. In the background, he heard the young physician babble on incessantly about how well the treatment works.

"My king, I would highly recommend the leaches!"

Talus watched an older doctor beside the young physician suddenly nudge this fellow, while shaking his head from side to side. Simultaneously, yet another doctor at the right of the young physician showed widened eyes, and gestured a slit throat with an upraised hand.

When the young physician internalized these cues, he pulled the jar of leaches behind his back with a sheepish smile. It was then that Talus saw firsthand the real benefits of having friends. *A good thing they intervened, for my patience waned. That fellow was very close to spending a night in the dungeons, hugging his jar of leaches!*

The king stared coldly at the young physician, with a look of marked disapproval. The doctor stood there with his face red as a beet, surely embarrassed by the faint echo of his last words that lingered in the hall. Talus faced the female doctor again when she cleared her throat.

"Ahem… The bloodletting won't be necessary, my king. Nothing ails you." The king observed her turn to the young physician. She flashed a nasty look his way, and then looked back to the throne. "These premonitions are frequent among many in Karnath," she continued. "There's no reason for concern."

When the female doctor fell silent, quiet ensued in the entire throne room. Talus bobbed his head happily, scanning the attendees before him, the young physician still bright red. After a few moments, he waved his hand to the entrance and said, "Good news it is then! You may go."

With that, Talus saw the doctors all turn to leave and walk away in unison. But after only a few steps, he watched the female doctor stop, and then spin about to face him once more, the others still departing. *Does she have concerns about my health?* Talus wondered, immediately.

"My king, I request permission to speak," she said, her face straight as a line. Talus looked back at her fearing the worst. *Please Destiny, let her not recommend those leaches after all this!*

"Granted. What is it?"

Timidly, the female doctor asked, "Does the nature of your premonitions trouble you? Do you foresee some Dark thing, involving your future or those around you?"

The king smiled widely and kept silent, before erupting with laughter: "Aha ha ha, Aha ha ha!"

At that, he perceived a somewhat puzzled look develop upon her face, and mirthfully he thought, *Do you lack insight, as to why your king wears a grin and chuckles as when before a jester?* His smile broadened even more. Meanwhile, the female doctor just stared back blankly, surely wondering what went on. By her face, she was lost.

After quieting himself, Talus replied, "Oh doctor of Sergros, your question does humor me! For to the contrary, my visions are of good things!" With those words, Talus literally watched her bewilderment dissolve, and with joy he saw her inquisitive look replaced by a smile almost as wide as his own. He laughed again, and eventually she did too. At last, however, the king admitted to her the nature of his premonitions and their betokening of good fortune.

"The gloom is going away!" Talus said enthusiastically, after their laughter ceased. "I don't foresee it in my future, and surely it won't be in that of Sergros'!" In this, he beheld her smile widen. "Tell *that* to those people you remedy! It may lift their spirits more than your medicines and magical healing. Now be off, as I have matters to which I must attend."

Talus waved her out with upraised hand. He watched the female doctor bow graciously before walking out of the stone hall, past the two guards at its entrance with upheld spears. As she went, the king's smile returned, growing larger with every step she took from the throne room, for to him, it confirmed that he was sane.

"I'm not crazy after all!" he exclaimed when she was out of earshot. He glanced to the stiffened guards, looking onward with straight faces. *You two wouldn't dare disagree either!*

Standing then, the king stepped down from his throne and moved to the center of the chamber, where he raised both arms high. Talus looked to the ceiling, to all those glorious blue banners of Sergros depicting the kingdom's gold lion, and then spun about in a merry dance. One after the other, he kicked his legs and swayed both arms, moving rhythmically to the song in his heart.

Wearing a cheery look, he stepped a few times and spun more, his arms still held above his head. *I've not felt better for some time now!* Talus thought to himself. *The gloom lifting from Sergros is a gloom lifting from over me!*

Of all things foreseen, Talus saw himself keeping his throne, the Guardsmen back in Sergros, and the gloom being gone like it was never there. *Construed together, these signs indicate my Crimson Guard shall return triumphant!* And with that conclusion—one approached cautiously in days prior—he stopped amid swirling to retract his arms, and then, threw them high again, with tightly balled fists.

"Yes!" he shouted, his voice resonating the hall.

Joyous thoughts flooded his mind then. *Chancellor Cedric holds daily sessions with his peers, undoubtedly arguing for my removal. But that does not matter now, for the wizened fool cannot touch me any longer! Upon seeing him pass in the halls, I shall only wave and smile!*

Then in the next instant, Talus considered that perhaps at his feast to celebrate Sergros' return to order, he would make a special toast to that beloved, balding politician. *To not believing in your king, and his wise counselors!* The words echoed his mind. Talus would love to see Cedric drink to that. *Or even better yet, choke!*

As the echoes of his voice died, so did Talus' enthusiasm. Suddenly, he realized that with all of his good premonitions, he did not foresee Kort being brought back to justice. In fact, at this point, he did not foresee Sagult returning safely to Sergros either. *Perhaps these premonitions will come later?* the king wondered, knowing that the visions came quite arbitrarily to him, and not all at once. While feeling good overall still, this possible explanation did not satisfy him.

But then, with a moment's repose, Talus suddenly had what appeared to be a brilliant idea. *Why not act on premonitions, to the gain of the kingdom and myself?* He brooded how surely it would yield very beneficial results, if he could implement a plan to counteract Kort going free and Sagult not returning. Standing still in his throne room, Talus toyed with a general idea, as he rubbed his chin between forked fingers. *Based on the lack of good premonitions, could a situation be improved? Maybe I can change this poor outcome, by doing!*

With hands behind his back, Talus started pacing back and forth as he would often see Cedric do. While taking each step, he thought of how he might improve Sagult's chances of success. *Perhaps he needs reinforcements, more men to scour the Isles from bottom to top? Maybe additional help would bring Kort Al'starz to justice?* The more he thought of that idea, the more he liked it. Talus looked up to the entrance, and saw his official peering in curiously—the one in blue tunic and beige pants. Talus locked eyes with him, and snapped his fingers on an upraised hand.

"Come. Quickly, quickly!" he shouted, and the official approached with a scowl. *Does he feel called like a dog? Matters not!*

"How may I be of service?" the official asked politely, upon arriving before the king. Talus smirked when looking at the man, already admiring his own cunning.

"Arrange for a sailing ship to the Isles, filled with two dozen of Sergros' finest knights and soldiers. I order these men to aid Sagult on his fugitive hunt, and for them to submit to his command."

Talus watched the official stare back with a surprised look. *You think it rash and undue, man? Well, when you carried my orders for Sagult's departure to the Isles, you didn't think it odd then.*

The official asked for clarification.

"Send *another* ship to Soku?"

Talus digested that remark, knowing Sagult ported his ship at Soku, toward the south of the Isles, to search the tall landmass from bottom to top. *But it's been sometime since Sagult departed, thus he's likely nearer the center of the main island by now.* And so, in order for the reinforcements to find him as quickly as possible, Talus would suggest something different.

"No, send the ship to *Logan*."

As the words rolled off his tongue, the official showed a sudden look of confusion. Talus saw him raise both eyebrows.

"Logan? There's no port Logan."

Talus considered the matter, knowing differently. The port Logan was once a functional port between the Mainland and the eastern Isles used heavily until the last Isles Crusade. He remembered how Garlew and Zeros sailed into that harbor during the war. Like the port's name, many residents of its town came to have Mainlandish names as some sailors immigrated there and took Hirishin brides. *Mainlandish names, just like the port's name…*

Talus recalled how from Logan, much Mainlandish influence came upon this small town residing in the Red Dragon territory. At the conflict's end, the town Logan was partly destroyed by armies of the Black Dragon clans led by Taurus Hboshi's father. However, the port remained intact to this very day, despite it being used less often than before, mainly for fishing and exports of rice crops to the Mainland.

"You're not familiar with that name. It's from tens of years ago," Talus said. "The port is now in the fishing village Doj. Send the ship there."

The official nodded, though slowly asked with a hint of reservation, "Sire, are you certain the chancellors would agree with you on this? It'll take much resources to dispatch a…"

How dare he question me?! Talus, beyond bothered by the comment, gruffly cut him off.

"I am your king, so do as I say!"

The words rattled the hall, ringing in the ears of all present. *Yes, I am king, and will continue to be king.*

With a fearful countenance, the official quieted.

"As you wish."

Pleased with asserting his authority, Talus watched the official scurry away to arrange his bidding. The guards kept looking straightway, as if not even wanting to blink in the king's direct presence. *A good thing, mind you!* he thought, not having much tolerance for more backtalk.

Feeling that he acted promptly on his premonitions and took appropriate action, Talus enjoyed a good feeling inside, warm and fuzzy. He resumed where he left off. "Now where was I? Ah, that's right—praise be to Destiny!"

Talus strolled past those guards and into the winding corridors of Castle Sergros. From behind him, he heard the two soldiers exhale, and then their footsteps as the pair turned quickly to follow him.

"JUBILANT KING"

Chapter 40
Praise Be to Destiny

Through great halls of gray stone—opening to rooms and anterooms, connecting towers to fortress ramparts—Talus walked and walked until reaching a particular courtyard outside gigantic Castle Sergros. This courtyard was special because on the weekly *Day of Thanks*—where Karnathans expressed gratitude to their deity Karnatha—citizens from the surrounding city were given access through the castle's western gate, to the gaudiest limestone basilica ever erected upon the Mainland. It was a gift handed down to Sergros from Juniper in the days of his father Elix's reign, masterminded by *Gawdin*, a Juniperth architect of exceptional talent and renown who innovated outstanding designs for the era.

Every time his eyes encountered the amazing manmade structure, Talus was awestruck. He studied the exterior as it faced him now, while approaching the church through the courtyard. The basilica had four towers ascending high into the sky, placed as vertices on a large square made by its four outer walls. Each tower was round, with window slots opening all the way around at fixed intervals, to afford those climbing up to the cupola a panoramic view of the city and beyond. Talus looked aloft, seeing the dome overtop the basilica, knowing the altar inside was located within the square that could be inscribed within the circle of the dome's projection upon the floor.

As Talus approached the basilica's corner, only two entrances met his immediate view, even though he knew two additional entrances existed on the other walls. All entrances provided access to aisles inside that led to the altar, and the king understood only one of four towers could be climbed from any given entry. He enjoyed this design, partially because each entrance had unique imagery, showing marble sculptures of Maken, Karnatha, and the Forerunners lifted exactly from legend.

When Talus came about twenty cubits from the nearest entrance, he studied the sculptures sitting upon double arches over the twin golden doors. All other entrances had the same, being four entrances together that depicted four scenes from east to west and north to south: Karnatha hand-spinning thread with Maken at the loom, Karnatha advancing the Game upon the Forerunners, Maken dying for the Game in the rebellion's end, and finally, Eriens and Hrya impaling each other in the Tragedy of Old Karnath.

His eyes followed contours of the three-dimensional scene over the entrance before him—the one with Eriens and Hrya. Beside that sculpture on the

361

basilica's exterior wall, he saw two columns of round windows having stained glass, mixing together colors of blue, red, yellow, and green. The windows depicted icons of Ma'althan and Autheos, along with others from the Book of Karnatha.

Talus stopped, with the guards at his rear. He inhaled deeply to savor the outside air and then talked to himself. "Few go here for solitude, or prayers to Destiny. Today is my day of praise, after many days of prayer!" His awareness of Karnathans forsaking their religion nowadays spurred his rather pious remark, and his thoughts of even greater piety. *Others in the kingdom have lost faith—with gloom upon Sergros, with vast uncertainty in the kingdom without prophets, but not me! I've stayed faithful, throughout the gloom!*

Talus moved forward to access the church while both guards waited there, distancing themselves from the king in his time of worship. And so, he took joyous steps closer to the doors, knowing that even more grandeur awaited him inside. The king's fondness for the basilica's interior stemmed from how it celebrated Gawdin's appreciation for nature, in a way unlike any previous design. Indeed, Gawdin transcended other elven artists of Juniper and their love of nature, by depicting Forest Saol through the basilica's architecture.

When reaching the two golden doors, Talus entered through the one ajar and below its arches overhead. He stepped one foot into the aisle before stopping, his breath completely raptured away. A forest of limestone trees presented themselves to the king, as he lifted his eyes above the granite floors to behold them—four rows of octagonal columns, which rose from their base to branch into three smaller octagonal supports, extending all the way up to the ceiling around the dome. As many times before, Talus noted how the shape of columns changed from octagons to circles with depth into the nave. The king followed the nearest support from its base up beyond where it branched, seeing how every branch touched a ceiling that resembled a leafy canopy, which hid catenary arches to the keenest of eyes.

Talus observed how light entered through stained glass windows on the entrances to his far left and right, painting multiple supports with rainbow hues, from bottom to top. Where metal intermingled with stone, the light reflected off resplendently in colored rays, as seen from railed balconies accessible at several stops on each tower's ascent to the cupola.

He gazed to the basilica's limestone walls, which showed more imagery of the figures from legend—some through engravings, others with framed woodcarvings of exquisite craftsmanship. These various icons watched him approach the altar down the church's one aisle, along with more icons mounted in oval frames on the branch point of each support.

His mind spun thoughts as he walked down the aisle. *This church captures my Karnathan religion in such a distinct way, unlike any other place of worship!* Talus loved every aspect of the basilica's design, his favorite feature being the five major artistic depictions that lined the walk into the nave, progressing from scenes of creation near the entrance to the concluding Battle for Destiny—a sixth artistry at the altar. The same painter *Illandrus*, gifted for capturing the essence of complex imagery in a succinct way, created all the paintings.

To Talus' right, he beheld the first scene upon a support. It showed the emergence of Destiny—a spent energy—from the well of unspent energy called the Void. *Praise be to Karnatha, for breaking free! The world is but spent energy, whereby we have destiny!* As he studied the epic depiction of the phenomenon whereby Destiny came to be, he noted how the brush strokes seemed volatile. *How he painted it, shows a* struggle, the king thought, knowing that a relatively new idea pursued by many current-day theologians was that Destiny and the Void had been at war from that moment on. *Maybe Illandrus thought this, years before these theologians did!*

The king walked a bit further into the nave, and beheld a second icon at the support to his left. The scene illustrated the creation story, where in the background Karnatha—the persona of Destiny—hand-spun threads for creation's fabric from intertwined strands of life, matter, and energy. In the painting's foreground, Talus viewed the creator Maken, weaving the fabric for Karnath's first age upon the loom—the genesis of seroxians. As he stepped away from the painting and closer to the altar, part of the olden story echoed his mind. *A new fabric to be woven for every age and interweaved with the last age's fabric, using the thread of causality...*

Talus walked up to a third icon on the support at his right. The painting showed how Karnatha fashioned the *Game of Time and Sword* at the dawn of creation, due to premonitions of bad destiny entering the world. *She sought to end bad destiny, through the Game. Thanks be to Destiny!* Talus rejoiced at the sight. In the painting's background, Talus saw multiple important depictions regarding the Game. At one side, Karnatha forged the gray blade in *Ires Star* that could slay time, meant initially for Maken to carve the worlds from the Void. In the middle, he saw Karnatha presenting its counterparts Autheos and Ma'althan each with their first Child—Ja'eel and Kilmar, respectively. On the other side, the king saw a race to the gray blade, forerun by the Forerunners from opposite ends of Karnath, so to determine which Child would have it.

With chin in hand, Talus inspected all the scenes, and contextualized their holistic meaning. *Destiny separated from the Void and after creating the worlds, sought to ensure spent energy remained used for good destiny through a Game, played by the Children of Destiny. In this, the offspring of Ja'eel and Kilmar with the seroxian daughters would eventually save us all from bad destiny...*

Talus walked away, toward the fourth icon upon the support at his left. He settled beneath it, and started looking at its one side that showed Maken finding the gray blade before the Forerunners could reach it. Toward the middle, a separate scene depicted the rebellion among the seroxians to rid Maken of the gray blade. His eyes scanned the canvas, to the opposite side that showed the creator cursing those rebellious seroxians as lower races of lesser ability—the humans, elves, dwarves, trolls, giants, and gnomes. Only those cursed seroxians with the repentant Laotzu—the overthrown king of Juniper in Old Karnath— inherited remade paradise in New Karnath.

Viewing the fourth painting still, Talus looked at the depiction of New Karnath shown through a green portal on the canvas, where the cursed seroxians and Laotzu entered remade paradise. From his studies, the king remembered how New Karnath was a remake of Old Karnath before its curse. Old Karnath was a land where the faithful though unrepentant seroxians were banished for not stopping the rebellion. In the painting, Maken appeared near the portal, using its life force to split the gray blade into two shards of opposing hue, for sake of the Game. *This marked a change from the Game of Time and Sword to that of Time and Broken Sword, with the rebellion's end.*

Talus' thought accompanied his steps to the last icon before the altar, the fifth one, upon the support at his right. This one depicted the seroxian Eriens at its left half, emerging from his study in Castle Malgun one evening. As the story went, he answered a maiden's knock on his door, past midnight. She came from the nursery holding the king's son, Kilwroth. The child cried inconsolably after Eriens' careless prayer for peace of mind, over contemplations of entering New Karnath in war versus peace. In so doing, Eriens would betray the trust of an unnamed human sorceress who enabled the seroxians to enter paradise over an energy bridge between their worlds.

Still studying the fifth painting, Talus noted a separate scene at its middle where Hrya—son of Darconas and Prince of Deardrum in Old Karnath— removed the black shard from a rock at Gallow Cliff, which began closing the bridge between both worlds. Talus recalled how according to the legend, Hrya entered New Karnath and battled Eriens with the shard. Through the help of the unnamed sorceress, Hrya was able to stop the King of Malgun from conquering the lower races, but at the expense of his own life. Talus felt sobered when looking at how the sorceress expressed her anguish in the painting. Legend told also, how she loved Hrya deeply, and still sought revenge on Destiny over his death. *Her cries of wild abandonment supposedly echo the Void, even 'til now!*

His final thought before walking to the altar was the shards of sword, shown also in the fifth painting, in yet another separate scene on the right half of the painting. Hrya brought the black shard into New Karnath, where it was left with the sorceress. However, Ma'althan cast the white shard to depths of the Korinth Ocean ever since the rebellion, and there, it likely stayed.

At last, Talus walked from the fifth painting to the altar. When all the way down the aisle, scents of incense welcomed the king. He found a few people praying before tiny brass sconces holding lit candles, set within circular racks winding about a support at differing levels, each rack narrowing in diameter toward the support's top, giving it a conical appearance. The king saw how some noticed him, and left immediately, their faces filled with worry. *Greatness has that effect...*

He noted a young man in a brown robe who remained in place, closing his eyes and kneeling before the large icon. Gazing up to it, Talus marveled at how immense the sixth painting was, which hung above the altar's center. He studied how it showed blond Kayareth battling red-haired Shaizan at Gallow Cliff, both of them wearing the armors of god and having the opposing shards of sword, being beset on each side by the Armies of Light and Darkness. *The fated conclusion of the Game would decide good or bad destiny for Karnatha, Karnath, and its people. Either Ma'althan's bloodline would slay time using the melded shards to bring Eternal Darkness through a curse upon god, the land, and its people. Or, Autheos' bloodline would save time by destroying the whole gray blade in Ires Star, hailing Light upon Karnath, for what remained of time!* Talus was extremely reverenced at the very realization, knowing this was how Karnatha [god] ordained the Battle for Destiny would be determined for everyone. *For reason of the Game, men can trust that their Battle for Destiny will be fought, even if those men choose not to fight for their own good destiny!* The idea comforted him deeply.

The king knelt, and closed his eyes to pray. He took the appropriate time to still his active mind before uttering a word, knowing well that praying to Destiny halfheartedly or thoughtlessly, or not to Destiny at all, was regarded as praying to the Void, something blasphemous in the Karnathan religion.

To avoid being like Eriens in the legend of *The Unwholesome Inheritance*, he mustered his concentration. When ready, Talus deeply meditated on the balance of life, relating to the balance of Destiny. *A share a good and bad, every life shall involve! Lift now from us this season of bad, and let the season of good return upon Sergros! Thanks be to you, Destiny... For my premonitions of good fortune... For my throne... For lifting the gloom... And for the Guard's imminent safe return to Sergros!*

Moments passed as Talus offered up his thanks to Karnatha, and prayed sincerely. Then all of a sudden, he felt watched and opened his eyes to see the young man who prayed nearby, now standing before him with a chilling smile! Beneath the dim light, Talus perceived how the youth wore a brown traveler's robe and held a long gnarled staff. His hair was wild, just as his striking blue eyes.

The situation was most unsettling for Talus; it sent chills down his spine, and numbness up both his forearms. The king yelled immediately to his soldiers.

"Guards! Come quickly!"

"Who are you?" demanded Talus, taking a step back from the altar. He saw the youth smile more.

"If you must know, my name is Lucen."

On Talus' ears, fell sounds of both guards running up the aisle. From his periphery, he sensed them fall short and stare from a distance.

"Is there a problem, my king?" asked one.

Talus raised his hand, so to hold off the soldiers.

"I encourage you to continue praying. To continuously pray for good things might lead to good things, though not necessarily."

Lucen stepped toward Talus.

From the corner of the king's eye, a soldier stirred.

"Back away!" he said firmly, readying his spear.

Keeping an upraised hand to allay the solider, Talus inquired of the youth, "Do you challenge my premonitions? Is that what this is, you jealous oracle? Who's told you of my visions?"

Lucen's smile stayed intact, and he laughed.

"Aha ha! So you do expect a good outcome, king?"

"My premonitions assure me all will be well in my kingdom," Talus replied instantly, though a subtle uneasiness turned his stomach then. He felt the youth's eyes drilling deep into him, above that insidious grin.

"How deceived you may be, in the onset of these strange premonitions," Lucen said. "Perhaps you're one to trust a stranger as soon as you befriend him?"

Lucen took a step closer, now cubits from Talus.

"You should know, that premonitions can be one's path to destruction!"

Talus' knees buckled under the youth's comment.

With raw nerves, he yelled, "Seize him! Seize him!"

Taking a step back, Talus saw his soldiers run up.

"Take this youth away to the jails!"

He watched them attempt to grab Lucen, only to end up just grabbing each other, as their hands went right through the youth, who vanished away! In Lucen's absence, Talus could still hear his voice coursing throughout the immense Karnathan church.

"Your visions are but *memories from your future* never more to be seen, reborn in the past as *premonitions*! Just be careful in what you trust, king! What you foresee, might not be what you get!"

Talus trembled as Lucen's laughter rose.

"Mwha ha ha ha, Mwha ha ha ha!"

When the laughter faded, his guards looked around.

"Where did he go?" the one asked.

"He's a sorcerer, just gone!" answered the other.

Talus stood there, a bit shaken. *Who's this oracle called Lucen?!* the king wondered. Regaining his composure, he glanced at his two guards who gazed back.

"What are you staring at?!" he snapped.

They instantly took their eyes off him.

Talus scoffed at what the youth said.

"Memories from the future—complete nonsense!"

Talus faced the altar once more, determined as could be. *I'll not let the words of Lucen take away my joy!* He screamed at the top of his lungs with that thought, irreverently in the church. "I shall order a feast to celebrate vanquishing the gloom in Sergros!" He lowered his voice then, and clenched his fists to say, "It will be the grandest feast—the largest this kingdom has ever seen!"

Talus turned from the altar, facing the entrance and his guards. The church's gray weighed heavily upon the king, as the icon of Karnatha in stained glass watched over him, in what was becoming his pursuit of a gray dream. The hue was everywhere he looked—gray stone, like the gray gloom. Not letting uncertainty win, he shouted again with confidence, his eyes full of zest. "The most lavish spread shall await my knights, when they return victorious from their quest, with hunger in their bellies!"

Talus walked down the aisle in silence, and passed the guards, who followed promptly behind their king. He began talking to himself, with eyes afire. "I shall go now to the cooks in the castle kitchens and also to the servants in the castle storehouse, and speak to them about readying a feast unlike any other seen yet in the kingdom, one to be attended by every noble in the city walls of Castle Sergros! It will be timed according to my premonitions, and we shall see then who has trusted a wrong thing!"

And with those words, the scene faded as the king's confidence guided his pursuit of revelry, through shadows of doubt cast by the youth named Lucen.

"WORSHIP INTRUDER"

Chapter 41
Sunset of Oracles

Inside a fortress carved out of rock on the outskirts of Castle Juniper, Lady Lyda sat in her study, on a chair covered with tanned animal skins and behind a long wooden table of dark grains. She was the eldest remaining practitioner in the Oracles Society, who was rumored to still have her prophetic powers intact, among many visionless peers and underlings. *Such makes me a person in high demand...*

By appearance, she was ageless, draped in a green cloak that covered a black fanciful gown. With her hair as blonde as the sands of *Desert Dunn* and her eyes greener than emerald, she flaunted the most resplendent countenance, more radiant than the sun itself. Impressions of wisdom and knowledge preceded her, and she maintained a presence that spoke of greatness and commanded respect throughout not only Juniper, but also, the whole of Karnath.

All about her, fires flickered from the candles upon many brass candelabras. He glanced over *the towers* on her desk, seeing the top of a closed door on the far wall, one made of long thick beams of wood, with strips of hand-wrought iron running widthwise to bind them together. The door's sturdy iron hinges were fastened directly to the rock.

After the mysterious Saipei War, the Society claimed this abandoned fortress as one of its meeting halls; it was the oldest meeting hall and also the most durable, being built from rock, right out of the northeastern pass of Liath. Due to dangerous times facing the Society and the need for safety, the fortress was heavily used these days, for various meetings each and every week. *Too many meetings...* she thought to herself, knowing all too well how the dire state of the Society called for them, and how the meetings occupied much of her time.

We keep talking about the same thing. She acknowledged how months of drawn-out gatherings concerned the obvious: the Oracles Society lost more face to the peoples of all kingdoms, than any other institution upon the Mainland.

It all began with the onset of the Great Occlusion about three years ago, where oracles from all corners of the continent seemed to agree upon what became known as the Dark Prophecy among many believers, and the prophetic doom among scoffers. The prophets foresaw Shaizan winning the Game at Gallow Cliff, and hailing an eternal Age of Darkness upon Karnath in the absence of time.

If the oracles' visions remained true after that stark forecast, perhaps the Oracles Society would still have respect—respect of the common people, the lords and ladies of the kingdoms, and also bishops of the Karnathan Church. But from politician to clergyman, and from clergyman to peasant, the people could no longer believe the oracles due to their lost vision of the future that followed the Dark Prophecy. *How could they? It's like the blind leading the blind now…*

The sudden loss of vision among oracles translated to a number of widespread dilemmas affecting many in Sergros, Deardrum, and Juniper. She rehashed how news of a blinded Society propagated through the Triangle Kingdoms, from the first instance of an oracle being unable to name a child at birth. *It happened a day after we advanced the Dark Prophecy to the leaders of the kingdoms!*

Lady Lyda contemplated how the problem developed, still not understanding it. *The first loss of foresight was only the* start, she thought, pondering how after that, many oracles faced the same inability to foresee the future throughout the Mainland, which shook the people's belief in the Society, long before news even struck about their omen—the Dark Prophecy.

Initially the kingdoms' leaders prevented the Dark Prophecy from leaking to the commoners and Church officials to avoid far-reaching chaos among citizens, but ultimately, the kings just let the Society humiliate itself once the oracles demonstrated that their foresight was gone. *With friends like the kings, who needs enemies?* She wondered if the situation could have been dealt with more gracefully, for the Society's sake.

From the occasion where a child could not be named, the leaders learned that the oracles had lost their vision. If anything, the timing was perfect for them to let the Dark Prophecy disseminate to the people from a source that could no longer be trusted. *It transferred potential problems caused by the Dark Prophecy, back to us.*

But even in the Society's humiliation, the people of the Triangle Kingdoms became unsettled, given the nature of the forecast. The vision entailed Darkness for Karnath in the years to come. *No one liked the sound of* that, she reflected. Shortly after the Dark Prophecy, multiple blows against the kingdoms heightened concerns. She considered all the coincidental atrocities that occurred, one by one. Out of nowhere, war came first as the Isles Conspiracy struck the Triangle Kingdoms like an iron fist behind velvet, deceptively hitting province Juniper the hardest. War had not come to the soil of the Mainland for hundreds of years, and it shocked everyone in the three kingdoms.

The kings called upon the oracles immediately, begging they offer up their vision into the future for planning and mitigation of a truly scathing situation. *They swallowed their pride then…* She recounted how almost overnight, the kings went from labeling the oracles as loons, to begging them for help. But the blind prophets could provide no assistance whatsoever, and the un-blind were too afraid of a future beyond Shaizan. *Especially those like me…*

Lady Lyda recollected how the Isles Conspiracy impacted all the kingdoms, but especially Sergros, as the humans spent considerable resources to aid Juniper. As the first impact, the conflict cut down the Sergrothian hero like tall grass—Garlew Il'therin was killed at the hands of an unknown murderer. *With speculative accusations thrown at the fugitive Kort Al'starz in the midst of little or no proof.*

Secondly, the efficacy of the Sergrothian courts lessened considerably in the regard of the kingdom's citizens, because such a large crime could not be solved with punishments administered to the guilty. *No wonder the king reached out for the Society's help, years after letting us fall on our face.*

Thirdly, people in Sergros began rioting, some perhaps moving with impunity over the kingdom's inability to solve the murder, others just in protest of diminishing opportunity that threatened the standard of living in Sergros after the kingdom extended part of its reserves to Juniper, an early winter took most of their crops, and the gloom prevented people from remaining productive.

She was all too aware of the situation before Talus instituted order. Rioting in the Sergrothian cities made for very real problems due to the gloom's induced shortages of food and work, which further smeared the court's reputation of adequately maintaining order through legal precedents. *What an artificial fix*, she brooded, realizing the way Sergros decided to promote peace was opening up the kingdom's reserves to get the citizens through a hard time. *Sergros has certainly weakened amidst war and gloom.*

Knock knock knock!

A sudden rapping upon her door brought Lady Lyda out of her seriously deep contemplation. She stared blankly, not quite remembering how to deal with this. A voice at the back of her mind nagged, *Perhaps because you don't deal with this… When's the last time you've answered?*

Knock knock knock!

The sound grew louder, coming once again from the large door. Lady Lyda peered over her parchment enclosure, struggling to see past her desk. Before her, several stacks of letters loomed two to three cubits high, occluding her view. There was so much parchment—letters bearing seals from all three Triangle Kingdoms—that she was uncertain of how many were even present. She sighed to herself. *For me, this is my Great Occlusion!*

KNOCK KNOCK!

Reluctantly came words off her lips.

"It's open already!"

As the door crept open, her mind echoed the singular thought, *Please, don't be Ralfus! Please, don't be Ralfus!* Again and again she hoped for it, not wanting those stacks to get any higher. Lady Lyda was so overwhelmed by the sheer volume of incoming requests for her services that she would rather deal with most other problems first. *Let a troll from the arctic Northern Region stand at my doorstep instead of more cursed parchment!*

"Destiny blind me," she cursed silently, as the door opened wide enough to show her assistant Ralfus, carrying a few more parchments. Not the sight she had hoped for, Lady Lyda peered at him around the outermost stack of scrolls and papyrus.

She beheld Ralfus well, a young lad with a diamond-shaped face and blond hair. He wore a green tunic and black trousers that matched the colors of her own ensemble. Neatly embroidered on his tunic, was the Society's emblem, a symbol formed by two intercrossed ovals, with the first fitting through the middle of the second, with a jagged-s at their centers. She glanced down briefly, and saw pointy brown shoes upon his feet.

"More summons from Sergros," he said in a chipper way, with a twitch of his tapered nose and his hazel eyes showing a sparkle.

How does he maintain such vigor in these depressing times? she remarked at the sheer tone of his voice, feeling exhausted by excess meetings in the Society and the great volume of requests. She noted how Ralfus stood on his toes to meet eyes with her, past the mounds of parchment. *They're that high, are they?* She mused how the stacks had grown beyond manageable, and now, even strained the bystanders.

"Where shall I put them?" came the question from Ralfus, spoken in a cracked voice.

He knows the answer, she thought callously in that moment, not really having the patience or motivation to read anything. The stack itself mocked her unwillingness to overcome a besetting gloom, and simply do more than be.

The one nearest Ralfus was on the shorter side, so Lady Lyda favored it for incoming letters. She lifted a hand and flicked her fingers toward it, motioning for him to set the letter there. She saw Ralfus place the parchment with a look of compassion about him, as if he understood that she was more tired than irritated with his redundant question.

No sooner than the new parchment hit the lowest stack among the few piles, she watched Ralfus retreat from the chamber, quietly closing the large door behind him. *Good, more time for thought.*

Thinking, instead of acting, became commonplace to her, with the emotional, spiritual, and physical tax of the Society's many meetings about what to do. Lady Lyda gazed at the towers of parchment and let out a long sigh, depressed by the mere visual. *While Sergros deals with a very real gloom, this is my gloom!*

Back to her thoughts she went, eager to make headway on any problem. *It's been so long since I've felt accomplishment.* She knew how tomorrow the Society's elders would meet in Juniper yet again to discuss three major problems—three problems yet to be solved that she just kept hearing about.

The first problem concerned stunted growth of the Society, since no new oracles entered. This had been a threat ever since the oracles initially lost vision into the future. For with it, they lost certain bestowed knowingness from Destiny on which new oracles to ordain. She thought to herself about the consequences of this missing instinct. *Without knowing who is best suited for the calling of many apprentice oracles, the Society simply shrinks in number, and by the day, we become less of a prominent force in Karnath.* That realization was most sobering to her, as well as to other senior members of the Society.

The second problem concerned the decreasing stock of current oracles, due to certain dangers posed by fanatics and suicide. *Radical Karnathans have shed the blood of oracles they deem heretics...* She recalled how the problem concerned oracles that falsely proclaimed the future with enough time elapsing to later prove their predictions wrong. For reason of believing them blasphemers, radical Karnathans lacking tolerance would hunt out and kill such oracles, providing the oracles did not kill themselves first. Indeed, certain oracles had taken their life before the radicals could find them, being unable to cope with blindness. A few of them notably jumped from Gallow Cliff. *Of these, many could not distinguish premonitions from mere dreams...* She considered how this might have driven them to insanity.

The third problem was historical with a life of three years, one that Lady Lyda considered as a major factor to the Society's present day problems, and perhaps warranting more thought than the others. The dire circumstances now befalling the Society stemmed from the Great Occlusion, but in some sense, these paled in comparison to the Society's tattered image in the eyes of the people. The oracles—a once revered group in Karnathan society—were now unable to see the future for kings and nobles, or name unborn children for peasants. *The common people no longer believe us. And the kings, well, they're just desperate...* As a whole, she knew all too well how those who dared to foretell the future failed, and those still having visions sat idly. *The Society no longer serves an important purpose for the Triangle Kingdoms...*

Counting these many developments, Lady Lyda saw the Society unravel before her eyes—it was Fate's Fray for all of them. The mysterious gloom that now beset Sergros would in time wreak havoc upon the entire Mainland. *The gloom is expanding, and perhaps soon will chew up Juniper and Deardrum, only to spit out the bones of kingdoms once strong!* She knew that these drastic times called for drastic measures, and something must be done. *Perhaps, something different than just entertaining longwinded discussions...*

As before, Lady Lyda felt terribly overwhelmed as she looked at the stack of parchments once more. Seeing those letters with differing seals reminded her of how the Triangle Kingdoms as a whole sought out her foresight in this most troubling time. However, ever since the Society advanced the Dark Prophecy to the Triangle Kingdoms, she had not used her abilities, refusing to look into the future for fear of what she might see. *There may be something beyond the Dark Prophecy, a thing more troubling!* The possibility worried her.

With her restraint, the letters stacked up, each one requesting the application of her special talent. She reached forth her hand to the stack, wanting desperately to overcome her fears and start a task that appeared insurmountable. With a thought about equity, her hand fell back: *How to fairly decide amongst so many requests, when I'm but one, only able to accommodate few?*

Feeling an obligation to act, however, Lady Lyda reached forth her hand yet again, but drew it back—half in her own fears, half in what she just considered. And then in that moment, it came once more, that same rapping.

Knock knock knock!

Does opportunity stand at my door, the opportunity to do more than simply be, to act for the good of others and myself? Lady Lyda considered the prospect of good destiny upon her. She had skills that could help people, and fortunately became cognizant of her abilities very early on in life. *You have a skill, so use it for good!*

Knock knock knock!

There it was again, a call to use her talents in a way that fulfilled her for a great cause and purpose. Fear welled up inside her, building on top of her lungs and making it difficult to talk or breathe. Concerns of unfairness pressed down heavily upon her chest, and added to the difficulty of even answering that call. *How to decide, where to start?!*

KNOCK KNOCK!

There it was again, now louder, a call to do rather than just be.

"For Destiny's sake, it's unlocked!" she exclaimed, with a sudden shift of her feelings.

As the door crept open, her heart filled with hopes. *Please be Ralfus! Please be Ralfus!* Hungry for change, with an appetite for doing, she gleefully watched her assistant once more, from over the stack.

"Lady Lyda, Chancellor Cedric from Sergros has sent a request," he said with a single scroll in one hand. *Can it be, that this message was delivered just now by the Sergrothian couriers?*

"Give it to me," she said, and with that, disbelief parted his lips. Ralfus stared back gawking, as if not knowing how to respond. She looked on with satisfaction, in that her assistant was oblivious to her changed heart. *Surely he expected me to order this to the stack!*

Lady Lyda motioned for the letter to be brought to her, by curling the fingers of her outstretched hand. Ralfus drew nigh with the parchment, and when close enough, she took it from him without any hesitation.

"Thank you," Lady Lyda said while studying the scroll in her palm, absent-mindedly shooing Ralfus way. From her peripheral vision she noted how he retreated from the chamber, closing the door behind him and leaving her in solitude to review the latest request.

Just fretting about problems behind closed doors stands little chance of actually solving them. This epiphany, one had moments prior, sparked her different approach to solving problems, an approach that had been there all along. *There must be action!* She contemplated this, realizing she was for long dissatisfied with the Society passively seeking out solutions. *Fixes must be made actively, and collaboratively with the wise counsel of others! And I can lead that…*

Undoing the scroll, Lady Lyda sighed to herself. *There's no point of having a gift if it's not to be used for good,* she thought to herself, now aware of her wasted talent for the last three years. Though it might not be the fairest place to start, this scroll would be her beginning. *For a start anywhere, is better than no start at all!*

And so, she began reading the parchment from Castle Sergros, to learn of a matter that surely was not of highest importance in the kingdoms, but something still deserving of her attention.

"GLOOM OF LADY LYDA"

Chapter 42
Dreams No More

Magicia stood in the green grasslands of Sergros on a simply fabulous day. She saw the pristine blue sky hang overhead, without a cloud in sight and only a smiling sun, which provided comforts of warmth and light. From all around, she enjoyed pleasures to her senses. Birds chirped and insects buzzed—sounds to her that were musical, pleasant to her ears. Smells of now blossomed flowers lingered in her nose, a favorite being the lily. When handed part of the loaf, she tasted the freshest bread ever; it crunched in her mouth as a preface to its chewy center. And just as she felt his hand caress her back, her five senses that started from touch came back in a full cycle. At one corner of her mind, she wondered from whence this wonderful scene came, given the gloom. *Can it be, that I've fallen to yet another weave? Can it be, even real?* She wondered and wondered, uncertain of the truth, but wanting more than anything to enjoy a fleeting moment. *Enjoy it, before it becomes as the others—a time no more.*

Swallowing the bread, she turned to see the man she loved. Long red hair fell over his shoulders, framing the most perfect face that she had ever seen. He possessed deep inset blue eyes, sparkling and spaced evenly on each side of his straight nose. His lips were symmetric, flawlessly balanced between full and thin. There was not a single blemish to the man's smooth skin, light in complexion, like that of Magicia's.

"I knew you'd give in if I offered," he said, grinning. She saw him raise their basket, showing the loaf now broken. *Like always, tasted before arriving at our spot!* Magicia smiled back warmly, knowing that he could never quite wait until lunch, before eating some of the bread from their favorite Sergrothian bakery.

Without an invitation, Magicia took hold of his hands in her own, and playfully moved to the front, impeding him from taking another step forward. Rubbing her palms against his, she gazed up into those blue eyes and willfully fell, a never-ending descent beyond the look's precipice. Magicia's smile grew wider then, and her pearl white teeth complemented the glory of day.

"I have a confession to make," she admitted.

She watched him return her large grin, and then jokingly ask, "Oh, have you another? Or the same confession you make always?"

Her face reddened as she thought about his remark. *True! I've said this same thing not too long ago!* She giggled at the thought, knowing that certain gestures were often natural to repeat. *There's simply no stopping this!*

"I must confess," she said with mirth, "that I love you, Shaizan."

Leaning closer to his face, she shut her eyes and met his supple lips with her own. During this lock of lips, the world stopped for Magicia. Her hand fell out of Shaizan's and dangled there for what seemed an eternity, with only her heart left in motion, beating much faster than time's clock could even tick. And in that moment, all of creation witnessed their profession of that heartfelt thing most wonderful—love itself.

When Magicia opened her eyes, she still faced Shaizan, but neither he nor Karnath was anything like what she knew. She beheld the red-haired man now in spiky armor—dark with gray accents—the sky somber and menacing behind him. Her eyes trailed down, and she saw the black shard of sword at his side, encased in its sheath. *No...* she protested, both tacitly and weakly.

A cold wind lashed Magicia, and she looked down with squinted eyes, to pull her jacket tighter. Her momentary glance revealed that she still stood on green grass. But immediately, Nexus flowed out of it and the grass became brown, as lifeless as the world around her! For when Magicia looked up, she noted how energy spiraled up into the heavens from all over the field, as the life force fled creation. Other greenery dulled as well—distant trees and brush—no longer a vibrant hue as the energy seeped out, no longer alive.

"No," Magicia said in disbelief. "No... no!" she protested again. "Noooooo!" Her scream waned in the open air, and she turned to see Shaizan's cold, unwavering stare.

"What do you mean?" he asked in a steely tone. "Surely you knew."

Magicia took his hands and pled, "No, I didn't! You have to believe me!" She looked intently into his blue eyes, desperately seeking him in those depths. *Can it be, that the man I once knew is not there anymore?!* The very prospect gripped her. All of a sudden, she felt him roughly shake his hands free.

"I don't want your touch any longer!" snarled Shaizan. "No sooner would I invite an enemy into my abode for favors!"

Magicia recoiled at the statement, her mouth open and brow wrinkled, before a single tear streamed from the corner of her eye. She glanced down and watched it fall with uncanny slowness to wet the ground—a drop of moisture upon what was now, as dry as a desert.

"How can it be," Shaizan asked, "that you knew the means to kill Destiny but not of the consequences?!"

Magicia instantly looked back up, wide-eyed. *Fight for him.* She took his hands again, with a renewed urgency to break through.

"I didn't know Destiny's curse would fall to the remaining weaves, this I swear!" she exclaimed.

Once more, she felt Shaizan shake his hands free.

"I was the youngest Servant of the Light, one of conscience," he said. "Destiny trusted me and I betrayed that trust, as you betrayed mine!"

"No, no!" she denied.

"Yes!" he countered. "Befitting punishment for me, betrayal by someone loved! Perhaps now, I know how Karnatha felt," said Shaizan. "How could I have been so foolish? You must've known exactly what could fall to the remaining weaves, yet you valued revenge more than anything else!"

Magicia shook her head, afraid to even answer.

"You used me, only to avenge Hrya!" he insisted.

To gesture fierce denial, she wildly shook her head now, back and forth. She stopped doing so and looked straightway, as the accusation literally compelled her to speak. Tears dribbled down her face, as she cried her response: "Oh that a woman suffer the unjust! Can any man know her pains?! Relate to my position as one damaged, and judge me not!"

Shaizan's skin suddenly reddened all over, and his eyes burned with terrible fire; his muscles bulged, and his veins became enflamed—all foreshadowing his heated response: "I stopped time twice, first in goodwill though second in your plot to kill Destiny! This motivation no longer made me one of conscience! Rather, I became one of vengeance, a spiteful soul such as you!"

With these words, Magicia grew frightened as the fury about him increased tenfold—the intensity of his eyes and those flames. She felt immense heat come from Shaizan, like clouds rolling back on a hot summer's day.

"Please don't," she begged him. "I'm now trying to stop what Saora started!"

"My attempts of good saw only an evil return!" he shouted, as if not even listening. His thunderous voice boomed in her ears. "On the very first occasion, in an age where we stood not together, I stopped time in hopes that I could save the world from its last age. Karnatha wasn't strong enough to weave again, so I had hoped that Karnath could continue without time. But alas, I was wrong!"

Magicia sensed Shaizan's wrath deepen, as fire erupted all over his body. It roared, as the orange flames burned furiously, fueled by his anger. "In a future we'll never see, you wanted nothing more for me to continue stopping time with every unraveled weave, but in your vengeful spirit! So be glad that in the remnants of my broken dream, yours lives on!" When the orange flames turned black, Magicia felt increased heat from his furnace of resentment.

"No, that's where you're wrong! I've had a change of heart!" she exclaimed, her voice strained to rise over the roar of Shaizan's fire.

"I am one of broken dreams," she declared in sorrow, more tears streaming from her eyes. "My broken dream is that I turned you into this, through *her* intentions that benefited my wants! My broken dream is blindly following Saora, in order to quench my thirst for vengeance!"

She watched the spirals of life force all around her—those welling up from the fields—change into thick columns of green Nexus, as if the energy were being sucked from Karnath's soil and into the black sky. With that, the ground became more barren, cold and dead inside, just like the man standing before her.

"Despite my gray dream, of being with Hrya after centuries of separation," she shouted, over his fires. "Despite my embrace of the black shard of that broken dream in his death, and despite me losing good destiny then… I found it again, with you!"

"Clearly I wasn't enough," Shaizan snapped. "You kept climbing higher to chase the fiery sun, wanting its wrath upon Destiny more than me! But those destined for sol—the ones always in pursuit of something else—are fated to burn! Your gray dream led to another, and another, killing us slowly."

She shielded her eyes then, from a sudden blaze about Shaizan.

"It's befitting to want things broken fixed," Magicia said, looking back as the fire lost ferocity. "It is the same, to wish for those things wrong to turn right! No different was my loss of Hrya because of Destiny's Game, in which I became willing to aid causes far Darker than my own!"

She watched the fire consuming Shaizan stoke then, just as the increasing intensity of his spoken words. "My broken dreams remain, for now I'm that thing, which no man should be—a man bound to bad destiny!"

"My broken dreams remain as well!" Magicia contended. "Every time I hear your voice, is to clutch shards of dreams shattered! Each moment I see you again haunts me, of how these fragments once pieced together!"

"The ghost of your scent on my nose, is a constant reminder that overlooking good destiny had, surely leads to good destiny fleeting! Your withdrawn touch," she sobbed, "is life withdrawn from me!" Magicia shouted, more tears flowing, "Revenge mocks my struggle now, for it makes my dreams sand through open fingers!"

"Your fulfilled dreams were blood on open hands! My hands rather than yours!" Shaizan countered.

"Revenge left me empty and my dreams no more," she argued with wide eyes. "This you must understand!

"Though revenge was your dream of yesterday, 'twas once your dream indeed, and now, it's my nightmare!" he screamed with eyes aflame. "I've lost everything!"

"I've lost more," she shouted back. "My broken dream is losing you!"

Her wail manifested her deep lament, as those columns of Nexus suddenly erupted from the ground, geysers of life energy shooting up from creation and into the sky, a final surge of energy that became unseen within moments. It was the last bit of Karnath's life force.

Darkness descended upon the cursed field where she stood, as the ground crumbled to dust beneath her, leaving her somehow standing upon a plot of pure black. And that very darkness engulfed Shaizan, who became invisible to her discerning eye, being robed now in the blackest of fires. Magicia cried more, as everything she loved broke around her, and was absorbed into a looming shadow. Her land and all she held dear within it, was gone.

And suddenly, she heard a child's crying drown out her mournful sobs.

"Wha wha wha!"

Magicia lifted her tear-stained face, and peered about the consuming darkness.

"Kilwroth!" she called. "Kilwroth!"

Her voice echoed the black.

"Wha wha wha! Wha wha wha!"

The child cried on and on, inconsolably.

Magicia fell to her knees, and again, her tears flowed. She screamed, "We're trying to end this! I know that Saora has you crying, but *I know not why*!"

In an effort to reconcile everything Magicia searched her memories, but unfortunately, there were large holes where she needed answers. *Where is Kilwroth?! How and why is Saora doing this?!* Her questions lingered, along with dozens more begging attention.

If she had to assign value to each of her stolen memories, perhaps one would trump them all. Though seemingly not as important as others, she strongly yearned to remember Shaizan like he was. *I'd give anything to remember him, before all of this happened!* She sifted through her memories frantically, only to find disappointment. *More holes...* Then, Magicia snapped from her thoughts as the crying faded in her ears, soon to be replaced by that eerie musical voice.

"This distance between Kilwroth and his fate, shall be many fold the distance between you and your want of vengeance," it said. "Karnatha weakened from people's null destiny in the Age of Light, though now, she dies."

"Ha ha ha ha, Ha ha ha ha!" sounded a laugh. "Here, have some more of your ether."

With both hands, Magicia clasped her head as it seeped in, and memories settled into place. "Ahhhhhh!" she screamed into the cavernous black, suffering from unspeakable pain to the head. And her voice carried all the way to her bedchamber in New Karnath, where until now, she lied soundly asleep.

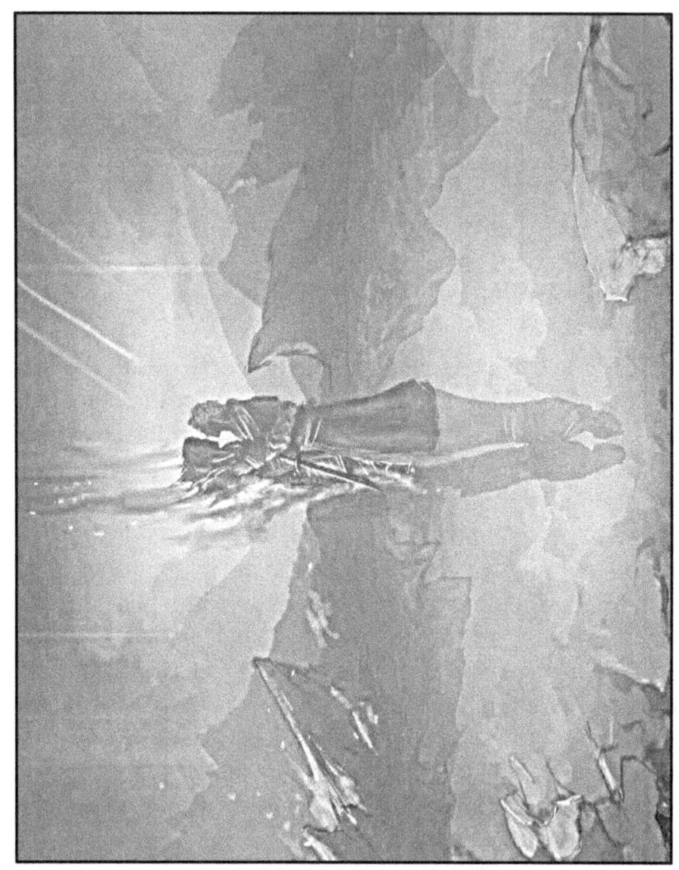

"DREAMS NO MORE"

Chapter 43
Warnings from the Wardrobe

Covered in perspiration, Magicia awoke from her nightmare. In her bed of four posts and white linens, she sat up, gasping the air raggedly and cupping her face with two trembling hands, feeling the outline and contours of her skin, in her frantic attempts to get a grip on what was real.

"He stood before me!" she told herself, recalling the vividness of her dream. Slowly, she realized it was a nightmare, another haunting of what she once had, and why now, it was nothing but a time no more.

Growing calmer, Magicia looked around the bedchamber in her own sorceress tower, one that mirrored Esmeralda's, but stood in the eastern pass of Liath instead of being in its west. She saw her wardrobe against the wall on her right, and past it, a window on the far wall. In her eyes everything was gray—the tower's stone, the gloomy sky, and mountain rock seen through yonder casement—all seamlessly gray.

Magicia, still with her hands to her face, touched what seemed to be delicate wrinkles. *The onset of aging!* she thought with angst. As a reflex, she looked to the floor at the foot of her bed, and saw a bucket full of jade-colored water. She leaned forward, scooping her cupped hand into the bucket. When its palm filled, she retracted her arm, bringing the water closer to splash it upon her face. When she did, a subtle smell of fruit filled her nostrils, and her wrinkles dissolved instantly, leaving her skin like that of a newborn. *The River of Life still sustains me…*

She pulled her shoulders back, looking away from the bucket. When her eyes suddenly detected motion, her attention returned to the window in her room. There, through the casement, she could see green energy slowly ascending in a spiral, a sight that immediately drew her to the pane. She got out of bed, put her feet on the cold floor, and walked toward the glass, beholding the energy outside. It swirled and danced in the air from the tower's mountain enfold, mesmerizing her, each step of the way.

At this sight, scenes from her nightmare ran through her mind, of the life force breaking from the soils of Sergrothian fields and likewise spiraling into the sky. It was then that a deathly realization went through her and she ran hurriedly to the glass, plastering both hands against it to stare at the exact same sight she beheld outside Esmeralda's: energy emanated from the mountain, all about her tower, coloring the night green. *Her locus of control isn't big enough to reach here… Surely then, I've had a premonition embedded within a dream!*

Magicia continued watching in a trance, swallowing hard with worry. "Esmeralda isn't killing Karnath after all!" she exclaimed, backing away from the window and raising both hands to her cheeks. "This outpour of life force is Destiny's curse *from the future*—the Age of Darkness after Shaizan won the Game!" With that realization, the omnipresent gray weighed heavily on the sorceress, sending images through her head—of Hrya impaled by Eriens, of Saora's laughing face, of Shaizan's rage, of the gloom. *This all started with your gray dream that broke into hued shards, where you took up the black!*

"I was a fool," Magicia admitted, lowering her hands with a newfound epiphany. In an aside, she chided herself over it. "Convinced was I of Esmeralda's misdeeds, lacking these memories from another time! And my sister's reluctance to return the shard of sword, made me calloused toward Sergros chasing her! What have I done?!"

Magicia spun from the pane, back to her room.

"This changes everything!" she shouted to her bedchamber. "Sister's lust for higher standing in the Guild now puts her on deadly ground!" With a look of determination in her eyes, she thought, *I have to stop this before it's too late. I must warn Esmeralda!*

Magicia remained with her back turned to the pane, speaking then in a voice not much louder than a whisper, her hands upraised and fingers curling. "So many weaves unraveled and so many memories displaced, make for my endless challenges with coherency!" *What happened now, versus then?! What is cause, versus effect?! Why is the world so different from what I glean, from memories of my future, still in my head?!* The questions dizzied her.

To the wardrobe Magicia ran, in need of changing from her nightclothes. *I must go to Esmeralda's, now!* As her bare feet settled onto the stone before it, she glanced over the tall wooden box of dark wood, having two doors that swiveled outward. By its handles, she opened the wardrobe and began to rummage the shelves for her yellow robe. Magicia continued until suddenly, from its shadowy inners, she saw a hand offer her the sought clothes!

With surprise, Magicia stepped back, her jaw agape. She entered her vast channeling chamber, and Nexus gushed in through her Source entry to fill the room, accumulating about her. Across her Source boundary she could feel the energies on her skin—cool, invigorating, and tingly—even at a distance. Instantly, she connected to the energy field in her entire bedchamber, feeling the objects placed therein, the vibrations of the glass pane under those leaning winds, and her own breaths in the air.

Magicia returned from her channeling chamber, with an aux core now filled. She stared at the hand presenting her the garment, which emerged from the wide sleeve of a brown traveler's robe. When a smile showed from the wardrobe's inners, she saw a familiar man step out, carrying her yellow robe in one hand and a gnarled staff in the other.

"What do you want, Lucen?" she asked, her words cold as ice. Magicia released her Nexus.

Lucen suddenly threw the robe toward her, and she snatched it from the air with quick reflexes.

"Dreaming of me again?" he said spiritedly.

"Don't fool yourself," Magicia shot back. "You could never be *him*."

"I'm much more than many imagine, including Karnath's most powerful sorceress."

Magicia sent another icy comeback, "Continue to think so highly of yourself. Your pride shall make for a harder fall. This age is your last, so get used to wandering the plains of Karnath in this time, instead of returning to the Void. I know you wish for the latter."

Her words preceded a long silence, where she watched Lucen stare back. Then suddenly, came his reply.

"Oh, so you think you can stop me?"

"I'll stop what Saora started," Magicia said. "And what you continue…"

"How interesting," Lucen noted with a smirk. "It seems more memories from the unraveled weaves come to you as premonitions. You remember more than I thought."

Magicia turned, and made an aside. "I'm anguished knowing what fate overhangs Karnath now, from Saora granting my wants of vengeance! May Destiny forgive my foolishness, and help me overturn this thing!"

She returned her gaze to the youth.

"What envy I had," Lucen said, then pausing. "For a woman who conspired with Shaizan of her own free will to kill Destiny through Saora's grand design."

When he took a step closer, Magicia backed up.

"To you it seemed like a good idea then," he asserted. "Returning to the people what's truly theirs—the Battle for Destiny. Surely you found yourself moved by Saora's mission too, no?"

"Nothing but loss comes from *Time No More*!" she snapped. "There's no good destiny to be had for any soul, when all that is Destiny becomes the Void!"

"Oh?" Lucen said, begging the question. "Do tell me about your change of heart, sorceress."

"You know all too well!" she shouted back. "For ages I've tried stopping this!"

Suddenly then, her mind went awash with memories from Gallow cliff, surrounded by the mighty seroxians and Naketo, together fighting Lucen with them. She could still see the youth in wickedly curved black armor, his wild hair blowing in the winds. At that moment, visions dominated her mind of the black shard impaling Naketo. *It symbolizes so much more than one bad ending!* All Magicia could see beyond that was loss everywhere—so much carnage, from the seroxians and inferiors alike, to Naketo lying at Lucen's foot in a pool of his own blood. *And it'll continue happening, unless you somehow end this!*

Lucen's voice pulled her from Gallow Cliff.

"Indeed I know your change of heart, though it makes no sense to me! I fear your moral compass spins wildly, unable to stay at any one direction. On the other hand, I have no such problem."

"Embracing Saora's cause yourself makes it no more right."

Lucen interjected, "I disagree, for she makes a needed point. Destiny learns the hard way, about what should be."

Magicia pinched the fabric of her robe between two fingers, as she talked. "Saora can't make this decision for a world of spent energy, as she's not Destiny. You enable her, as did I."

"Every message needs a carrier," Lucen said with a smile. "The rights or wrongs are but opposite sides of this holy war. We both take our respective side, and I see more correctness to mine than yours."

"Consider," he continued, "that the people for whom you struggle so desperately to save time, kill it daily and thereby their good destiny." It was then, Lucen shouted to the four corners of the chamber. "So who can judge me unrighteous, for killing both time and Destiny?! I shall move backward what Shaizan can't live to see, what Saora cannot do herself!"

When Lucen turned about, Magicia met his eyes.

"Again, it's not your decision to make!" she argued. "My wants of revenge were wrong. They corroded my soul, and through Saora's plan I made Shaizan suffer!"

"Well, regardless of your beliefs, I've made my choice, and you yours." She watched him gesture two sides of a scale with his hands, the balance shifting. "Destiny or the Void, destiny or a void?" Magicia followed his right hand, which fell lower than his left holding the staff. He stopped abruptly then. "The Void it is. So to Gallow Cliff we go."

"Have it your way," Magicia replied. "You shall have company at the cliffs, for the seroxians join me again this age, just as the last one unraveled. You almost lost…"

Lucen cut her words short.

"But what?" he asked. "Even with the seroxians and the Child, you didn't win. What makes you think this age will be any different?"

"Change is on the horizon," she replied. "Elucid tells me about whispers among the immortals. I've learned we have the Child from the Gray Lineage this age, the one with power beyond Garlew."

"Ha ha ha!" Lucen cackled. "Surely you joke about the Gray Child. He's more a liability than an asset, but I won't say more to steal your false sense of advantage. Instead, I'd rather point to your plan's major flaw."

"Oh really?" Magicia asked. *I've gone wrong already, have I?*

"Why yes," Lucen answered with a chilling smile. "You can't even convince your own sister to give up the shard of sword. How then will you bridge Old and New Karnath, to enlist the seroxians' aid? Will your Gray Child be such a wildcard to offset your lack of a shard?"

Her eyes trailed past Lucen to the casement. She saw the energies wafting up from the mountain, and it reminded her of Esmeralda's plight. *This banter is more distracting than helpful.*

"My sister may give back the shard."

She turned from Lucen with her robe in hand, now facing the wardrobe. *End this back and forth, and then leave!* pressed her inner voice.

"If you pry it from her death's grip?"

Lucen's words ran through Magicia's mind, vexing her. She calmed herself, understanding his nature. *He'll instigate you until Gallow Cliff for sure, and even there. Ignore it, and go!*

Staring at the wardrobe's bottom, she muttered thoughtlessly, "It's only a matter of time."

"Time is against you, and everyone on your side!"

"Time is not against us, but for us."

She heard a shifting from behind, as Lucen reappeared right in her face, between her and the wardrobe. Magicia stepped back. *There's no avoiding you, is there?*

"Well, I suggest you go after the other shard, while there's still time. You should find it before the Gray Child does. Otherwise, you might have to convince him to help your cause."

Magicia looked at him, tilting her head to the side.

"And what's so bad about that?"

To her disdain Lucen smiled and replied, "Well, the only person you've managed to convince so far was Shaizan. Everything else has been your epic failure."

Feeling pulled back into the quarrel, Magicia contended with that remark. "Untrue, my sister gave back the shard in the next age, now unraveled. That alone is convincing enough." Her reply was said surely and firmly, a smirk curling her lips, as she enjoyed the satisfaction of words fitly spoken. *That should put you in your place.*

Lucen stepped closer, once again in Magicia's face.

"But her cooperation wasn't lasting. For in this age, your sister acts on her premonitions of what you'll do with the shard, should she give it back. Only your dealings with Saora had truly lasting effects, of the sort you wish you could undo. Now isn't that brine to your open wound?" His response came forth, like a sharpened javelin to her heart.

"I curse the day I met you!" Magicia said heatedly.

As so many times before, Lucen smiled.

"Save your sweet talk for Gallow Cliff. You may need it there."

She watched Lucen walk to the casement, and open the pane. Magicia felt cold winds blow in, making her shiver in her thin nightclothes.

"I'll show myself out," he called back, climbing into the window. "Better get to Esmeralda before the Guard does, *if you can…*"

Lucen paused, still looking her way.

"One more thing, a rhyme you might remember. *Every warp and weft, unraveled will be. From time's end to start, all the weaves.*" As those words entered her ears, and nestled into her mind, her heart iced over. *'Tis imminent, unless you stop this before it's too late!*

Right when Lucen leaped out, she ran over to the window and closed it. Through the glass, Magicia saw him descend from the tower, to land on the rock below in a crouch, his robe flapping behind him all the way down. His feet touched the surface with a loud scrape that she heard through the pane, over the wind. As he turned and flashed a smile before hastening off, her stomach knotted. *Destiny, what have I unleashed upon Karnath?!*

Magicia beheld Lucen vanish before her eyes, and immediately her attention turned to more important matters. *Esmeralda! Get to her, if you can…* She wondered what Lucen's last remark could mean for her quick journey to Esmeralda's tower on the other side of Liath. *Perhaps it means, nothing good…* That last thought followed her, as she dressed and took to the mountains, in hopes of intervening with a sister's dangerous meddling.

Chapter 44
Playing Both Sides

From the jade, moss-covered Jezban Mountains that sat underneath the starlit sky, Elucid contemplated the dilemma with Kort. The crimson knight studied the low river winding through the valley, enclosed by rock on each side, ruffled from years of elemental erosion. *Likewise, life can have erosive effects on many. This will be harder than I expected.*

Like so many in Karnath, Elucid realized that Kort had given up on himself, after his broken gray dream. He wanted to stop the Isles Conspiracy more than his own life, but he failed at doing so. And now, guilt floored him, and Kort drifted through life yearning for redemption, but doubting if redeeming himself was even meant to be. For with Elucid's suggestions of it being possible, Kort became hurt, guarded, and mistrusting.

Kort won't go on the waters just yet, at least not with me... Elucid had the thought, attributing much of this conclusion to instinct alone. The crimson knight could literally see that decision in Kort's eyes and hear it on his voice. *Appropriate measures must be taken...*

Like a hunter stalking its prey, Elucid's approach to reach Kort must be subtle enough, so not to startle or scare. In this case, the crimson knight would be the predator, chasing after prey of low self-esteem though of tremendous potential. *After all, Kort is the Gray Child.*

Then suddenly out of nowhere, Elucid heard it, interrupting the thought. Eerie music filled the air, like perpetual chimes. *That sound.* The crimson knight sensed those vibrations more than hearing them, and it triggered an immediate flashback.

**** Elucid's Flashback—Start of Visions ****

(798 A.R., Over a thousand years ago...)

[Second Walk of Existence]

At the southern coast of the Mainland, Kilwroth stepped onto the embankment overlooked by the heights of Gallow Cliff in Old Karnath. He wore his armor without Eriens' purple cloak, having given it to Laotzu two days prior.

He walked carefully over the uneven rock, closer to the water, where in the seas opening to Korinth, Laotzu stood barefoot with his pant legs rolled up, wearing the purple cloak. A mighty tide rolled in, hitting him again and again. When Kilwroth witnessed those waves break over his new friend, he could not help but wonder why the seroxian endured it.

"Laotzu," Kilwroth yelled, "what are you doing?!"

But despite his call, Laotzu just remained there, bracing for yet another wave. When one rolled in—larger than most—Kilwroth saw it crest high above Laotzu's head before crashing down, drenching the seroxian completely from brow-to-toe.

"What are you doing?!" Kilwroth shouted again, as the tide met the shore, and gushed over his feet. He felt the water through his boots.

"Imagining what it will be like," Laotzu finally said, staring into the sea, not even bothering to look back. "Imagining what lies in store. She's come to me again in my dreams."

"You told me days ago that you had the visions," Kilwroth yelled. "Are yours from the ghostly woman singing a song?"

"Aye," answered Laotzu, finally gazing back.

Kilwroth met eyes with him.

"Those are the ones I've had since a boy, the ones that make me question my purpose. Since we share these visions, I feel we're both meant for something more epic than we ever imagined!"

He saw Laotzu smile, and then slowly nod.

"Neither of us understand, but yes."

And with that reply, otherworldly chimes sounded on the wind, a sound that both Laotzu and Kilwroth knew, from their dreams.

****

The flashback ended, and Elucid was once again on Jezban with only recollections of a ghostly woman and frequent visions from the past. *Who has appeared in those visions, remains unknown to me.* The mystery jarred Elucid, as sifting through memories revealed too many holes to place the facts. But those chimes lingered in the air, telling the crimson knight that she was nigh, and so was the answer to this age-old question.

All around, Elucid spun, trying to pinpoint the origin of the music, chimes of an uncommon sort. *It's over there…* Elucid peered up, sighting a large stretch of mossy rocks, going higher and higher up the mountainside, from where the music's vibrations could be sensed.

With uncanny agility, the crimson knight jumped rock after rock, up the side of the mountain in pursuit of that song. A train of green energy flowed in the metal demon's wake, as its boots touched down with boisterous cracks, stones flying.

After enough leaps and bounds, Elucid was nearly at the mountaintop, where the ghostly woman hovered midair, having fair skin and long flowing hair—a seeming apparition with blotches of gold light instead of eyes and mouth. She floated at a distance, and upon seeing the crimson knight, floated further away, up the mountain toward its peak.

"You," shouted Elucid from afar. "You're responsible for the visions so long ago! You foretold of an *unwholesome inheritance.*"

Elucid kept jumping higher, but she moved away.

"Wrong you are," the ghostly woman answered musically, "for I *caused* the *unwholesome inheritance,* and never just warned."

Elucid kept leaping at the retreating apparition.

"Who are you?" asked the crimson knight.

She replied, using words shrouded in mystery.

"I am strength in Destiny's weakness."

Elucid jumped higher toward the mountaintop, as she hung on the air, yet further away. The crimson knight gained on her by the bound, and her voice continued sounding in chimes.

"I am life in Destiny's death." *It can't be.* Suspicions and denial waged war in Elucid's head.

And then, as Elucid daringly sprung once more, the ghostly woman came into full view, enabling the crimson knight to observe how her body jittered between solid and fluid, as if its skin shed droplets of flesh that dissolved into nothing, before replenishing themselves instantly!

With the ghostly woman at arm's reach, Elucid sailed through the sky— the moss-covered landscapes beneath—when suddenly a serious problem developed. *The Nexus?!* Elucid sensed it first via the *transition stone* mounted in the metal demon's breastplate, used for mediating through the energy field. *Nothing! It's gone!* And then, the same lost Nexus was sensed, in the armor itself. It started falling.

Inflight Elucid entered a vast channeling chamber, where before, spent energy flowed from the sourcing stone—a magical rock that powered the metal demon. Now, however, the chamber was completely empty—dried and parched. And so, Elucid attempted to connect to the Nexus, pulling against every possible mental restraint, only to find none available. *What's happening?!*

Though right next to the ghostly woman—literally cubits away—Elucid fell from the sky like a stone, in what suddenly became an unpowered metal demon! The crimson knight reached out a hand toward her, plummeting further and further away.

"Nooo!" Elucid bellowed into the night.

While in free fall, Elucid saw the ghostly woman zoom closer, hovering cubits from the metal demon. She talked more in musical notes, playfully. "Who am I? As Destiny loses spent energy, I see increases in unspent energy! It's when the people of Karnath choose bad destiny or null destiny over good destiny! It's when they embrace the black shard of their broken gray dreams!"

Elucid fell more, and the ghostly woman floated about, encircling the metal demon midair. The crimson knight saw her pop in and out of view, just as her words registered in and out of cognizance: "Who am I? The one who loses unspent energy, as people meet or exceed their potential. People have a share of spent energy, they hold their destiny in their own hands, and decide its fate. To be spent on good destiny, or forfeited without. I give people the power to draw on potential, and make more from less!"

"Who am I?" the ghostly woman continued, still circling Elucid, who fell closer to the mountain below. "I'm one with no lust for life! I am one who craves a natural demise, but defies an unnatural expiration! Karnath without the Game is the former, but with the Game, it's the latter."

Just then, Elucid slammed into the rock, sensing immediate and pounding vibrations, which scattered pieces of the metal demon throughout Jezban with loud clangs and bangs. The crimson knight's armor rolled and rattled to a stop, beneath a long shadow cast by a dramatic ledge above. There, in the darkness, the now armor-less crimson knight felt as if having an out-of-body experience, and just beheld the ghostly woman approach from eyes in a head, without even a body or a face!

"Who am I?" she asked rhetorically. "Maybe you ask that question yourself, wondering if your true identity is that of Kilwroth, Laotzu, or neither. Perhaps you're just one who deceives themself, ironically called Elucid, as if you could elucidate anyone, including yourself!"

"Ha ha ha!" she laughed then paused, before going on. "Here, have some ether to help solve this mystery."

Elucid's head burned with fire, and though having the sensation of placing hands to skull, the crimson knight wondered then, *Do I have hands? Do I have even a skull?!*

"Arrghhhhh!" Elucid's scream passed through sheet after sheet of starlight, cascaded across the heavens. And with it, more of the crimson knight's missing memories settled into place.

**** Elucid's Flashback—Soldiers to Robbers ****

Drichal moved through the dark, fingering the cold walls of stone. A pungent stink hung in the stale air and offended his nostrils, like death had been trapped here forever. His Sergrothian armor clanged every time it bumped the sides of the cramped corridor. Unable to see much of anything, he stepped carefully.

"Are you there, Hetron?" asked the soldier.

"Aye, me and the others," one said from the rear.

Another man commented, "The tomb smells of old death. Was not the funeral last week?"

"Yeah," shouted back Drichal, "but the mausoleum's shared."

More minutes passed, as Drichal led the soldiers deeper into the shadowy crypt; it was inside a mausoleum located in a Hirishin graveyard. When he encountered a far wall, he felt the outline where the long coffin was slid into a deep cavity, set right in the stone.

"Over here!" Drichal shouted, sensing the others pile behind him. "Get one side, and I the other!" he yelled to Hetron, the soldiers' faces veiled by black.

His entire upper body worked to pull the stone coffin, the other man too. He heard Hetron release a struggled groan. "Grrhhh!"

"Don't stop pulling!" Drichal hollered, "Rystys, Gambul... guide it to the floor."

Drichal coordinated with the others, sweating profusely as he worked the stone coffin from its walled sheath. With a sudden realization, he let go and jumped back. It's too heavy... they've lost control! That thought ran through his mind. A moment later, he sensed Rystys and Gambul release the stone coffin, and its weight brought it down upon the hard floor, breaking it into pieces.

CRASH!

"Is everyone all right?!" Drichal shouted amid a cough from all the dust in the air. He heard a number of others hack in the background.

"Barely kept me foot!" Hetron exclaimed.

"All here," said Rystys, his deep tone clearly noted.

"Aye," said Gambul. "Almost crushed, but here!"

Unable to stand the poor lighting anymore, Drichal acted. "Shield your eyes," he told them, "I'll make a flash, as it's just too dark to see!"

Nexus flowed through the man's aux core, as Drichal channeled it outward and transformed it into a burst of light, which lingered in the crypt. His unadjusted eyes shut immediately at first, but slowly he was able to see his comrades all standing above debris from the broken stone coffin. The light began to fade, but nonetheless Drichal started sifting through the rubble.

"Impossible," he said. "It's like there's no body!"

Hetron asked, "Weren't you at the funeral?"

"Yeah," answered Drichal, "saw the body placed after embalming too!"

When darkness descended upon the group of four, Drichal repeated his feat of magic to illume the chamber. At the transformation of Nexus, light shined once more, just in time to reveal the explanation for Gambul's sudden gargles of death! Shocked, Drichal looked across the lit crypt to see his commander Zeros rip a crimson blade from the man's chest.

"From soldiers to grave robbers!" Zeros shouted irately. "I'll kill you all!"

Gambul's gurgles continued behind his words.

Drichal saw motion in his periphery when Hetron raised open hands, as if to show an unarmed state.

"Lord Darxar was privy to one in these parts, by Elucid's description!" The words came hurriedly, fast spoken and fearful.

"We were given orders from the king," Drichal reinforced, "to come back with the body, dead or alive, should he be found during our campaign!"

Drichal's ears hurt, as Zeros screamed at the top of his lungs in the confined space. "Lies!" he insisted, with eyes afire. "Soldiers fight wars, not rob graves! Now see a commander spill his command's blood!"

When Drichal beheld Rystys move to run, Zeros spun like a tornado with that Mainlandish blade, and the scene went scarlet, darkened by stray shadows.

****

Elucid's mind stopped hurting as the flashes of images and sounds melded into the store of the knight's existing memories. Still having an out-of-body experience, the crimson knight lingered in the shadow of that long ledge, the ghostly woman hovering nearby.

"There's more where that came from," she said with a musical laugh, "I'll return all of your ether by Gallow Cliff or Liath, whichever *he* prefers. His preferences matter, as you've never forced anyone to choose, and wouldn't begin with him."

"Kort will stop this," Elucid asserted. "Whatever you've turned Destiny's Game into, he'll stop!"

"You've at least found the correct player this age," the ghostly woman sang. "My advice to you, though, is to answer your own questions before trying to help Kort answer his. You face the same enigma as Magicia, earned by living millennia in so many different walks of your own life—repeats of your reality— different each time. Spirals."

Elucid saw her begin circling again.

"Know you, *who* you are, *where* you are, and *what* to do? My *Game of Broken Time and Sword* will surely stir questions in many a curious mind, including his own."

Beyond all the confusion Elucid had, the crimson knight struggled with the same question, each and every spiral. The question concerned the ghostly woman's identity—whom she even was. Elucid searched available memories for the answer, but found more questions than answers. *Holes and holes, so many missing memories!*

"One more bit of ether, to end your search," she added unexpectedly.

Elucid released a guttural roar as more memories burned into place, "Garrhhh!" Again, the crimson knight somehow felt hands to head, without the physical feedback of having either hand or head. The moment after the memories settled, Elucid fixed upon this ghostlike thing hung in the dry air of the Hirishin Isles. And it was then that the crimson knight knew exactly with whom was dealt.

"Saora!" Elucid shouted.

"That's right. I'm Maiden of the Void, by name Saora. And Destiny's Game I've made my own, a new game where I play both sides! The Children were never destined to decide the destiny for all in Karnath, and Karnatha stands to pay!"

Her melodic laughter rose. "Ha ha ha, Ha ha ha!"

Elucid felt the vibrations of each laugh, as a mix of recollections blurred through the crimson knight's mind. *I am strength in Destiny's weakness, life in Destiny's death!*

"Let it be known that Liath is your saving grace this age," Saora said musically, "now that Wicken steps aside and the Servants of Light turn to Darkness. Without these changes to the Game, you would otherwise falter from my unwholesome inheritance, the bane to Eriens' child! Of all things, I know you struggle most to place this!"

Saora came closer to Elucid. "Now, put yourself back together, and give me a show." In the blink of an eye, the ghostly woman disappeared.

Knowing the foe once again, Elucid resolved to continue fighting, for certainly not the first time. The scene faded as the night itself, leaving Karnath with reams of mystery in this darkest of Dark plights, possibly meaning Fate's Fray for one and all.

"DESTINY FROM THE VOID"

Chapter 45
Nightmares Evermore

(Kort's Nightmare)

One night, in the forests before the gorge where he died, Kort sat around a warm campfire with the Sixth Order of the Guard. X'ieth and Sagult occupied seats beside him, where across the flames, Dimral and Enker perched themselves on rocks beside Garlew. Behind the knights hung a wooded backdrop showing silhouettes of trees and brush, with crickets chirping at a distance.

From the corner of his eye, Kort saw Sagult and X'ieth pull venison flesh from the roasted carcass that hung on a spit over the fire; it was a deer that Dimral shot with his bow. He glanced at the archer knight, who drank from a water skin. Seeing where he was and with what company caused Kort to look around the fire again, in sheer disbelief. *This can't be real*, he concluded, staring at Dimral—a knight whom he remembered dying permanently, without any second chances at life, like him.

Dimral greeted his stare with a smile and cheery words. "Eat, eat! Enjoy the spoils of my hunt!"

Without replying Kort looked away, redirecting his gaze collectively to his fellow Guardsmen who ate together. The visual triggered an immediate thought. *We're on the quest to find Pyrus...*

Kort's eyes shifted to Garlew again, to the possible traitor at the lead of the pack—to his possible friend. From sight alone, he could never discern any difference between Taurus and his brother Fieronju while growing up, and that situation was no different now. The two looked identical, as Taurus and his sibling shared bronze skin, jet-black hair parted down the middle, and the same exact narrow face with thin lips, along with short-cropped goatee, intense brown eyes, and a nose with round nostrils.

In the middle of his lengthy stare, Kort saw Garlew smile his way. The mere sight concocted warmth from his friendship with Garlew together with disgust for Taurus, and the mixture easily led to contention in Kort's head. *It's Taurus—ask him already about your premonitions! No, don't ask—it's Garlew.*

Humility slowly replaced Kort's confusion about the knight's true identity. He looked to the ground, thinking then of his failed plans for Taurus. He knew it was days before Baal, days before assassinating the Black Dragon leader, days before toppling the Isles Conspiracy, days before preventing it all from reaching Juniper. *You know it won't happen that way. Somehow Taurus knew of your plans and preempted you... But how?*

A sudden voice sliced through his thoughts.

"My premonitions of your assassination attempt have come in handy. Now this story will have a very different ending than what you anticipate. I've really fooled Nym and you, just wait and see!"

As those last words ended in a chuckle, Kort turned to him. *It is Taurus!*

The other knights chimed in from around the fire.

"Whether you act off your premonition or not, I'll still go to the king once your ambush kills half of us!" Sagult said to Taurus, before swigging his water skin.

"What a way to go for one like me!" exclaimed Dimral. Kort watched the archer knight gesture an arrow to the chest, with lipped noises. "I guess it be Destiny's way of avenging all the deer I've shot!"

X'ieth laughed, "Since Taurus changed everyone's future, now I get to watch Kort mistakenly kill Garlew!"

Kort glared at the young knight.

"You'd have killed me too, but fortunately Lucen saved me from a shared fate."

Kort's gaze wandered among the other knights. He heard this exchange often before. *It's my same nightmare...* They continued laughing nonchalantly about the situation. Dimral gestured the flying arrow again.

"Oh, I died!" he exclaimed, motioning the projectile hitting his chest.

"I was so shocked," X'ieth chuckled, "when that elven lass ran upstairs with dagger in hand, to kill Garlew Il'therin! And even more shocked was I, to see you step from the windowsill in that very hospice!" He showed quirky facial expressions to relive his shock—eyes wide and mouth open—in mock surprise.

Sagult laughed hysterically.

"Ha ha ha! Hospices aren't the same anymore in Sergros, as you get killed now instead of healed!"

"Poor Garlew!" grinned Enker. "Sergros shall miss their hero! I miss him already."

Kort looked face-to-face, knowing all too well what was going on. "None of this is real!" he exclaimed, pinching his arm only to feel nothing. "This is just my nightmare!" Kort slapped himself in the face, again not awakened from his presumed sleep.

"Eat! Go on, the meat gets cold..."

Dimral's merry invitation struck Kort unexpectedly, pulling at his attention and bringing him to look at the carcass hung over the fire. When Kort's eyes fell upon the spit, he beheld the fire diminish to dull red embers, and instantly, everyone about it was masked by darkness!

Kort could hear Taurus start laughing with those who died in the ambush—Enker and Dimral. And after only a few moments of their laughter, the red embers burst afire, shedding light on Taurus and the deceased. Slowly their faces morphed into skulls, their entire bodies into skeletons! Still, Taurus laughed raucously with them, looking directly at Kort with two cackling skulls upon stacks of vertebrae—one on his left, another on his right!

The embers dulled again, setting Taurus' eyes eerily aglow in the dark, as they caught the dying light. And suddenly, Kort flinched when Taurus slapped the back of both deceased sitting beside him, to knock their bones into the fire. From its cinders the skulls gawked up at Kort, both laughing and ridiculing. "Ha ha ha! Ha ha ha!"

"This isn't real!" he shouted. "None of this is real!"

But as much as Kort protested the nightmare, their laughter just continued all around him, growing louder and heartier. As the embers dulled even more, the same blackness closed in on the camp from the forest, and it was then, that Taurus disappeared completely from sight, along with Sagult and X'ieth.

Kort could barely see Dimral now, a talking skull who gave the same invitation from the fire. "Eat, eat! In several months you'll wish you had, for the gloom is coming upon Sergros!"

Kort knew that partaking of the deer would advance him in this nightmare had many times before. And so, he reached to the spit hung over the fire, and pulled away some deer meat from the carcass. As he put it to his lips and closed both eyes, he heard Dimral cackle wildly.

A pungent taste filled his mouth when the meat touched his tongue, and exactly then, his nose picked up the scent of death. Kort opened his eyes instantly, and spit out the rotten meat, to watch it fly through the air and hit a seated giant in the back of the head! The saliva-coated morsel began sliding down the giant's bald mound, moments before he threw back a hand to peel it from his scalp. Kort saw the giant stare at it enraged, and then whip about to face the ex-knight, standing now with his head bumping the ceiling.

"You dare spit at me!" roared the giant.

Seated in a pub—below hanging lights from cobwebbed, dusty beams that supported a gambrel roof—Kort looked back, without a word in his mouth but with a sobering thought in his mind: *I'm not just in any common house! I'm in Baal…*

Kort looked around the giant into the space of an enormous pub, seeing folk seated on benches behind row after row of long tables placed end to end, some reaching near thirty cubits in length. Dim flames flickered from iron chandeliers above, casting shadows upon those seated beneath. Hirishin murmuring arose ominously in the distance, and directed Kort's eyes to the hooded many seated throughout the common house. Travelers robed foot-to-brow—seeming pilgrims to the holy sites in Juniper—sat amongst the common people. His eyes scrolled over them, most having tall, untouched mugs of unfermented ale.

Amid scrolling, Kort's eyes stopped when he suddenly saw it, the sight to confirm his suspicions. Behind the bar where the landlord poured drinks was a rack, upon which stood several bottles of liquor and an oil painting of a rose having a thorny stem. This pub was none other than the *Thistly Rose*, a frequented common house in Baal.

"You spit at me!" The giant roared again, thudding the table right before Kort. He heard two consecutive cracks, and glanced down to see the giant's large fists sink into the wood, splitting its surface.

Kort found himself lost for words. "Saka…"

"I should do the same to your face!" the giant shouted, sending spit flying at Kort and the face-wrinkling smells of sour drink and meal. Every non-pilgrim in the pub just continued eating, drinking, and talking like they did not even notice the altercation. *Just… like… usual.* The thought slithered through his head.

"Uh," Kort said, this time in Mainlandish. Uneasiness gripped his belly, not for the giant of six cubits towering over him, but because of this same nightmare from his Dark past, repeating itself yet again.

Eventually, Kort seeing the giant before him triggered a one-word thought. *Move.* Without hesitating, he threw his upper body back and let his hands touch the floor, flipping off the bench and into a crouched position. There, he looked up at the giant just in time to witness three long Hirishin blades suddenly protrude from the giant's trunk, being thrust from behind! Soaked in blood, the blades emerged from the giant's breasts and belly, reaching the spot where Kort sat moments ago! The giant's face instantly contorted, with eyes rolled up in the head.

In a split second, Kort glanced to the side as all around the pub, the disguised Hirishin soldiers undid their façade of pilgrim then, some of them smashing mugs against the nearest seated Mainlandish person, while others gashed victims with swords revealed from their robes! And just like this, bloody chaos erupted all around the ex-knight, as part of the senseless killings that would preface the undercover soldiers swarming Juniper. While the disguise of pilgrim could be seen as a way for the now-fallen Black Dragon clans to conceal many soldiers beneath a cloak of trust, Kort knew better. *The surprise attacks mock the tolerant Triangle Kingdoms and their trust toward Hirishins.*

In slow motion, Kort's peripheral vision filled with scenes of soldiers killing unsuspecting occupants of the common house—the very same scenes he saw so many times before. In his nightmares, his premonitions, and haunting memories, the bloody scenes tormented him and sourced his guilt. The situation was simply unbearable for Kort to endure, and his conscience spurred him to action. *This is wrong, and I stand accountable for letting the Conspiracy reach Baal!*

Kort had these various thoughts at light speed—of Taurus' intentions, of his guilt over what happened. They were thoughts that ended, just as soldiers withdrew their swords from the giant still standing before him, who collapsed in a low moan, with blood spurting from multiple wounds. Kort saw the tall corpse topple toward him like a cut tree, and he reflexively back-flipped twice to land on the long table at his rear, one moment before the giant crashed over the space where he crouched a second prior!

He stood on the table, as killing took place all around him in the pub, with sounding cries, breaks, and squishes. Out of nowhere, Kort suddenly saw a solider beside him on the table, having a drawn sword. The ex-knight reacted by delivering a succession of devastating strikes, his hands blurring and enflamed by Nexus: one punch to his diaphragm followed by another to his ribs, and a chop to his neck with a straight hand.

Despite the loud massacre, Kort could still hear bones crack beneath the soldier's armor as his fists dented its metal. The strikes sent the hunched soldier into a backward stumble, moving him closer to the table's edge with his sword still in hand. Kort returned to his channeling chamber to fill his core with Nexus. He pulled hard against his old Source entry—a simple door in a small room—just like it was before his awakening. Kort saw energy flow along its edges, through the opening, and over its threshold.

From his moment of concentrating, Kort snapped back to the pub and pursued the debilitated soldier down the table. He sped up to him in a trail of green energy, reaching the soldier just before he fell off. In that moment, Kort grabbed the soldier's armed hand, clasping his palm over its back, and simultaneously twisting the soldier's wrist to free the sword. In the same motion, he kneed his assailant's gut repeatedly, sending Nexus down his leg and into the soldier, forcing him to double over, go off the table, and toward the floor. Quickly, Kort reached across his right hand to take the sword and, with the soldier still midair, used the weapon to decapitate his foe! The soldier's headless upper body hit the wooden floor spewing blood, as his head rolled beneath an adjacent table.

Through the Nexus, Kort suddenly sensed a soldier run up behind him with his sword held high. The ex-knight instantly turned about and thrust his blade, impaling the soldier right before their collision. As Kort's upper body absorbed the impact from his assailant, his feet slid back on the table by half a cubit. When Kort came to a stop he head-butted the soldier and spun abruptly to hurl him over his hip, off his sword, and into the crowd. He watched the thrown body hit a group of soldiers seen afar, slaying drunken lads.

From his position at the table's center, Kort watched the soldiers crash into each other. Sounds from dying men continued to fill the air—shrieks, screams, and aggrieved wailing. Intermixed with that were dull thuds as two soldiers jumped onto the table's far end in front of Kort, standing side by side. He faced them and flipped his sword in one hand, preparing himself for the encounter. But suddenly then, more thuds sounded from behind.

In an instant, Kort entered his channeling chamber and pulled open his simple Source entry. Streams of energy flowed through the opening and all around him, filling the space. He opened his eyes being connected to the Nexus field, now able to sense everything in the pub, including the two soldiers standing at the table's opposite end. The soldiers before him unsheathed their curved Hirishin blades and charged, and Kort could feel the table flexing under their combined weight. And suddenly, through the energy field he sensed the two soldiers behind him run, also drawing their swords!

Kort had about ten cubits between him and the soldiers in either direction. He rushed toward the two soldiers at his front, keeping his eyes on them the whole time. When Kort came within two cubits of the soldiers, the pair attacked all of a sudden, anchoring their foremost feet and swinging their blades—the left soldier at the level of Kort's thigh and the right soldier at the level of his neck. Both swords were perpendicular to Kort's torso but the strikes lacked harmonization, in that one blade lagged the other. Being mid-stride, Kort knew turning about was not even possible, and he realized that if he did nothing, he would be cut to bits! Kort shut out the idea, unwilling to let this dream end without getting answers first. *Taurus must explain my premonitions, and get his due!*

With that in mind, Kort tucked his right shoulder and courageously threw his body forward in a front-flip, over the nearest blade and under the furthest one! He twisted through the air, with arms held straight against his legs, narrowly missing the edges of both weapons. He filled his aux core with Nexus while landing on the table, on the soldiers' other side. A gargle of death brought his attention to one soldier that came from the table's opposite end, who apparently ran into a friendly sword!

Kort saw three remaining soldiers clustered up ahead on the table. He sped over to the first two in a trail of green energy, using magic to blur through several sword attacks in a single instant. His blade went up and down, left and right, with thrusts following slashes. Kort moved so fast, he barely saw the two soldiers get completely obliterated in bloody splatters!

Beyond the three soldiers lying gored now and in pieces, Kort beheld the fourth solider back up on the table, his face stricken by fear. *You're not getting away.* Kort used Nexus in his aux core to rush over to him in a trail of green energy. While moving, he swept low with his curved blade, to thrust it upward in the *Blossomed Flower* form of the Endo Najatsu style. His sword tip pierced the soldier's chin, going up through his head until the guard caught his jaw. Kort lifted the soldier off the ground, ending the technique with his sword up, having both hands wrapped around its braided handle, his elbows out, his right foot pointing forward and his left foot to the side. He felt the soldier's weight distribute down the blade, being nothing more now than a lifeless body suspended by steel, and hanging limp.

Out of the deceased's hand, Kort took a second Hirishin sword. And then, using all his might, he hurled the soldier's corpse into the fray, from off his first sword. Kort watched the body twirl through the air to strike down two soldiers a few tables over who were in the process of killing; it was a sudden strike that decommissioned them from further violence, rendering them both motionless upon the floor. Meanwhile, their fellow soldiers did not even notice, still mechanically murdering as before. *I'll change that,* Kort thought, *by serving justice to these murderers!*

Kort ran upon the tables nimbly, wielding his blades to send many preoccupied soldiers to their grave. *Meet eternal damnation for your deeds this day!* He prayed the words spitefully, tasting their blood upon his lips as he slayed soldier after soldier. Their groans and undignified shrieks filled the air. And those who dared confront Kort died the same, as he used his two swords to adeptly cut through their muscle, sinew, and bone.

When finished delivering death, Kort looked around the pub to behold a grisly scene. The common house was painted crimson, littered by dismembered bodies, and with its every furnishing either broken or overturned, the only exception being the oil painting showing a rose. He eyed it standing upright on the shelf behind the bar table, paying particular heed to the thorns.

Upon the stone floor Kort huffed heavily, awash in the soldiers' blood. *The blood of the innocent in Baal stains me more!* He let that most debasing realization renew his cause. And with that, he stormed out from the pub and into the streets of Baal, having a single thought in his mind: *I must get answers, kill Taurus, and give this story the right ending... Even if, it's just my nightmare!*

Chapter 46
Thistles Off the Rose

(Kort's Nightmare, continued)

From the *Thistly Rose* pub, Kort stepped out into more chaos upon Baal's cobblestone streets. In every direction he looked, terrible sights appeared: blood pooled around bodies of the slain; rooftops and buildings burned with fire; smoke wafted into the clear night sky, to offend both his eyes and nostrils. In every direction he looked, he beheld a struggle for life—unarmed men accustomed to peace dying to protect their families, others with farm tools or the like trying to defend what they held dear. The cumulative visual formed a single idea in his mind. *These things ought not to be!*

Kort saw soldiers ten cubits ahead of him—four of them huddled together and laughing, one of them raising a severed head, letting it dangle from a fistful of hair. They mocked the expression upon the head's face—an empty look portrayed by hollow eyes and straight lips. Without even thinking about it, Kort ran to them with his twin blades, cutting down the two Hirishin soldiers nearest him. Blood splattered his face, as the two remaining soldiers rushed him to attack, the one dropping the severed head.

Kort backpedaled, seeing a soldier on his left and right, both drawing their swords. They slashed at him together, and he blocked each blade with one of his own. They slashed at him again, but instead of blocking the soldier on one side, he parried to the other side, blocked the soldier's sword, and then impaled him! Kort let go of the sword stuck in his victim, but unexpectedly the other soldier knocked the remaining blade from his hand!

Kort stepped back unarmed as the second soldier grinned and confronted him, flipping a blade about the wrist. Beyond his opponent, Kort saw the first soldier fall to both knees, grabbing the bloody sword handle at his belly. Kort kept focused on his attacker, who suddenly slashed at him from one side and then the other, forcing him to retreat more on the streets. The soldier stepped closer, and then, swiped his sword at Kort's waist, causing him to drop to the ground, in order to avoid the blade.

Kort hit the ground hard and looked up from the street, with his hands pressed against the cobblestone, seeing the soldier continue to swing the sword, still executing the same attack. Sighting a clear opportunity, he sprung upon his feet and assaulted the soldier, crushing his windpipe with a quick straight-hand chop. The soldier's eyes grew wide and he dropped his sword wheezing,

404

struggling to breathe. Kort reached forward and brutally ripped his throat out, spinning about to slap the first soldier in the face with it, who still remained upon his knees, impaled by a sword. Kort took hold of the weapon's handle, tore it from the first soldier, and then in a blindingly fast, two-way slash, decapitated both foes.

At his sides the headless soldiers collapsed onto the cobblestone, their necks leaking blood. In that moment, the crimson all around Kort made him feel responsibility for this immense bloodshed in Baal. *I should've assassinated Taurus before this murderous plan left the Isles, to spare these innocent from death!* With a heavy heart, Kort lifted his eyes to the evening sky polluted by fire's light. There, he saw columns of swelling smoke rising up to the heavens, flurried by embers scattered to the winds—signs foretelling Baal's destruction by fire. "I'm no better than these!" Kort admitted to Destiny. "Though now I turn from my wrongs, oh to my sorrow that I've ever committed them!"

Kort picked up his second sword from the cobblestone, and looked up beyond his decapitated foes to the distant city wall, manned now by Taurus' soldiers, who prevented anyone from leaving Baal. And it was upon the wall that a particular sight stilled him, for over yonder appeared a menace unlike most others. Kort saw a Hirishin mage facing him on the parapet, wearing a long green robe, with two shining eyes that stared out from beneath the hood's shadow. The mage's robe buttoned across the chest and dropped to the fiend's ankles, its fabric featuring elaborate embroideries of mazelike spirals, meant to symbolize the mystery of magic in the West.

Even though Kort relived this grisly nightmare so many times and knew what would happen, he still watched in amazement as the cobblestone between him and the mage lit up green with Nexus. To his discerning eyes, the whole expanse of street seemed to vibrate, slowly at first but then quickly! A series of cracks sounded upon his ears, as the stones became unseated and hovered upon an energy field. Each one hung midair, at uneven heights to those around it. He studied them with eyes full of fear, swallowing hard the whole time. *What are you waiting for?! Run!*

Unable to look away, Kort saw the mage lift the cobblestone to form a large wave looming high above the heralding towers of Baal, overshadowing them both. As Kort glanced to his left and right, he noticed how darkness blanketed his entire vicinity, a sight that caused his heart to beat mightily his chest. Immediately, acute pain throbbed throughout his tensed upper body. *Wait no longer! Run!*

All of a sudden, the ex-knight dropped his Hirishin blades and dashed in the opposite direction, as fast as his legs would carry him. The cobblestone felt uneven and treacherous beneath his feet, but he fled from danger nonetheless. And as he did, he could sense his own heartbeats, pounding from beneath his Guardsman armor.

Thump thump, thump thump, thump thump!

Kort ran further down the streets into a wall of smoke, hearing rocks fall behind him from the wave's crest; it was a constant clatter against the cobblestone, cubits at his rear. *Keep going!* he told himself, pressing himself to not stop, no matter what happened. He continued running until the mayor's mansion peeked out of the smoke; it was a three-story stone structure up ahead, with many glass windows on all floors.

As the city blurred in Kort's periphery, his uncompromised sprint quickly brought him to the building's exterior. He ran to a large window on the lower level, put forth his shoulder, and dove through the glass. He felt it shatter upon impact, breaking all around him as he tumbled to the stone floor, inside the mansion. From a crouched position, he looked up, seeing a doorway up a corridor, one that led into a dark chamber. Instinctively, he rolled down the hall and across the door's threshold, then hearing the cobblestone smash through the mansion's windows. Without wasting a moment, he got up and shut the thick wooden door behind him, throwing all his weight against it. Kort listened as cobblestone continued crashing through windows on every level of the mansion, and also, thudding the roof above. He could hear stones rolling through the house.

And then, Kort felt sudden force behind the door as cobblestone struck abruptly! The door budged open, maybe half a cubit, where in the very same moment, he heard loud knocks from the stones hitting. Using his entire body, Kort slammed the door shut again, working his hands in the dark to find the latch. *There!* Once taking hold of it, he secured the door, as more cobblestone noisily struck.

Kort stepped back from the door, seeing nothing but blackness about him. He literally could feel the entire house shake, and from all around the shadowy room he heard a distinct metallic rattle on the walls. Then came the clanging in his ears, as whatever fell off the walls and onto the floor. Kort pulled against a mental restraint, opened his Source entry, drew Nexus, and pushed the energy out his Source exit while thinking of the sun. Back in the mansion, he hurled a burst of energy, which shed light on the ambiance. He looked to the walls, seeing weapons bounce from their racks as the house shook further—decorative battle-axes, spears, and lances! *I've fled to a more dangerous place than the street!* Kort feared, given the danger all about. The light faded, and his mouth fell open as he heard the steel continue to rattle all about him—a danger that summoned up a prayer. *Destiny keep me...*

Suddenly, Kort saw bright eyes shining in the dark. *The mage! How did he?!* Before he could reason the matter, the chamber was instantly illuminated, showing weapons all over the stone floors overlaid by rug, suits of armor leaning from their stands. *This is the armory...* Beyond the disarray of armaments, Kort beheld the mage across the room, with a center glowing green. And then, from the corner of his eyes, he could tell weapons flew off racks and up from the floor by magic. He watched javelins, axes, and maces all hang in the air by Nexus, moments before the mage hurled them all at him!

Off the wall at his rear, Kort grabbed two Hirishin blades and faced the weapons, executing one sword form after another, swinging his arms wildly to deflect the mage's attacks. As metal hit metal, Kort saw sparks fly, and in groups the weapons fell from off his swords to the floor, only to rise once more for the same thing to happen all over again! *You know what happens now in your nightmare… Just blink.*

For but a moment Kort shut his eyes, and upon opening them he found himself once again on the bloody cobblestone streets—far away from the mage. The sounds of clanging steel from the armory were now replaced with the roar of fire and screams. As before, soot and ash strung through the air irritated his nose and eyes.

He took a few steps down the street, but suddenly a familiar cry sounded from behind, stopping him. The ex-knight spun about to witness a group of four Hirishin soldiers, killing Baal's muscled blacksmith at a distance of thirty cubits. Kort saw the large man held by three and assaulted by one, wailing as they pricked his living flesh with the pitchfork he used to defend himself—a pitchfork that he likely made at his own forge. *There might be no better depiction of cowardliness in Karnath!* With disgust, the ex-knight watched the soldiers smile and laugh at the smithy's suffering, talking amongst themselves in Hirishin.

"Nangis kaya babi!" one remarked.

The others laughed even harder.

Kort walked the street, coming closer to the four, having his bloody swords crossed, one over top of the other. His pupils trapped the fires lighting the city's skyline, and his sure steps sounded noticeably against the cobblestone, warning of death in the shadows. The soldiers holding the smithy noticed Kort appear from behind, though not a one of them showed alarm. The reality perplexed Kort, sending a sobering realization through his head. *Perhaps I, one of changed heart, look too much like one of unchanged heart? Perhaps I look just like them!*

"But I am of changed heart!" Kort yelled when upon the closest soldier holding the pitchfork, as he pulled his arms apart quickly, his two blades acting like a scissors to the soldier's neck. From behind, he lopped off his head, and it hit the cobblestone with a smack. He saw the three remaining soldiers drop the blacksmith's corpse to confront him, drawing their weapons in one instant. It was then the sound filled his ears, of guttural laughter from a nearby rooftop.

"Ha ha ha !" cackled a male voice.

Kort turned to see the man in black standing behind him atop a gambrel roof, who wore a cloak that framed falling stars. Upon the ex-knight making eye contact with him, he shouted, "Sydullus feeds on pain! I am the *Lord of*

Suffering, and live for such moments. With your choice to enter Baal comes trial, and by trial comes growth!"

Upon feeling the sensation of burning by Nexus, Kort entered his channeling chamber, and as he did, he saw the entire room enlarge from an expansion of the walls and ceiling! Awestruck, he watched the chamber become many times bigger, perhaps reaching the size of a mighty sorcerer's. His old Source entry enlarged too, into double wooden doors showing carven inlays of ivy. Familiar with the sight and knowing what would happen, Kort ran up to the doors and pulled at their handles—against his mental restraint. He watched the doors crack open and light peek along their edges, only a moment before torrential energy gushed into the room over the threshold, to swirl all about him! It rose far above his head, now a circular enclosure of Nexus. As the events took place in a matter of seconds, Kort experienced once again happened to him in Baal—an awakening of sorts to bizarre magical abilities.

He opened his eyes, and the man in black stared right at him. "Baal is an *attractor for your destiny*—a thing that binds you to a fate, when you've come sufficiently close to it. So now, there's no stopping what lies in store for you, and its consequences. Hence your awakening now, days before you kill *him*! Ha ha ha!" Sydullus vanished as the laughter filled the air, leaving Kort behind, empowered to face his attackers.

Kort beheld the three soldiers charge him, with blades drawn. He felt energy surge in his aux core, ready for immediate use. His body energized by Nexus, Kort back-flipped repeatedly to put himself at a distance of fifty cubits from the oncoming soldiers. Even after he settled afar, the soldiers ran for him even harder. He watched them approach, while channeling Nexus through his aux core, this time in a way never known before—continuously. In his channeling chamber, Kort observed how Nexus simultaneously entered his Source entry and left his Source exit in a single flow, just by thinking about the weight of the soldiers' misdeeds crushing them alive. *Like these misdeeds crush me daily!*

Time slowed as he had the thought. Immediately then, Kort witnessed a strange magical dome develop over the trio of soldiers, which changed the pressure field in their confined space, creating a vacuum! By the sight of it, Kort knew the soldiers cried out, and spoke to one another. But he heard nothing, as their voices were silenced instantly. Immediately after that, he saw their faces suddenly show immense pain, as their bodies bloated and lungs ruptured from their bodily fluids reacting to the ambient conditions in a vacuum.

Did I do this, by thought alone?! At the pitiful three Kort stared, taking in the terrible sight of their armor crushing them, as it limited their bodies' expansion from the bloating. Blood flowed from the exterior of the armor, as its edges cut into their flesh. The soldiers began convulsing instantly, and their skin turned shades of blue from excess bruising. *I only thought about them being crushed, as I channeled?!* In that instant, the strange happening and Kort's particular thoughts seemed much more than coincidence. When Kort stopped channeling, the pressure field normalized about the soldiers, as told by the sounds of them dying noisily on the bloody cobblestone—sounds unheard until now, due to the vacuum.

Behind him, Kort heard the sound of approaching soldiers, perhaps ones witnessing his killings of the four. He turned instantly and channeled, thinking again about the weight of misdeeds crushing them. Without delay, the ex-knight saw strange Nexus enwrap the Hirishins, constricting them. He heard their bones crush under tightening bands of energy, placed about their limbs in intricate rings. *Those sounds! These sounds of death are what haunt me!*

"Ha ha ha!" cackled that same voice, once again.

Kort spun about to see Sydullus gaze upon him, from yet another rooftop. He called out to the man, "I take no joy in seeing the innocent killed, or killing those without innocence! Now where's Taurus, so I can get my answers and end this?!" He watched Sydullus just look at him with a smile, not saying a word.

"Where is Taurus Hboshi?!"

Sydullus finally answered, his brittle voice rubbing against the crackle of fires. "Over there."

Kort followed his pointing hand down the cobblestone street, to a bend in the path, where Sydullus indicated. There, the ex-knight beheld Taurus turn, walking onto the intersecting way.

Without waiting a moment longer, Kort ran after him, only to face new memories around the corner. A giant towered over him, one of many working with the Black Dragon clans. His stature was about eight cubits, and he wore a massive plain-colored tunic and trousers. His body was muscular and well defined, with a dark beard wrapping his face. Instantly Kort tried to attack the giant with his two blades. But the giant quickly grabbed Kort by both arms, raised him off the ground, and pulled outward, subjecting his ligaments to tension.

Kort groaned, "Arrrggghhh!" *My arms will be torn!*

Knowing exactly what to do from nightmares past, Kort glanced to one side, seeing there a wooden cart full of wheat grain. He held his breath, and pulled Nexus into his aux core. Then, in a continuous flow, Kort swept up the grains in whirling winds, about both him and the giant! Being choked by airborne particulate, the foe coughed vigorously and dropped Kort within seconds.

Kort hit the ground hard, dropping his blades, and crawled to a safe distance, from where he looked back at the giant, who still coughed and hacked, blinded and stepping unknowingly. Kort got to his feet, ran to pick up the blades, and faced the giant, leaping with each blade placed precisely. In one moment, his sharpened steel severed an artery in the giant's neck, and the crimson geyser spewed forth.

Kort landed from his aerial attack in a crouch, several cubits away from the impaired giant. Over his shoulder, he watched the grains and giant both hit the ground, equally lifeless. Still crouched, Kort breathed deeply and turned back the other way, to watch Taurus walk further in the distance. *Don't let him go.*

The ex-knight got up and bolted in that direction, his scarlet swords in bloody hands, with a resolve to not let his answers get away.

"KORT IN BAAL"

Chapter 47
Spiders and Re-spun Fates

(Kort's Nightmare, continued)

Kort did not hesitate to run toward Taurus, whom he saw only cubits away now, a bit up the street. A quicker pace and a little time put him right on the emperor's heels.

"Taurus!" Kort yelled, coming to a stop.

He watched Taurus take a final step, and his scarlet cloak instantly ceased flowing. Still looking straight ahead, the emperor guffawed aloud, above the distant roar of fires and shrill screaming. And with that, he turned about.

Kort came face-to-face with Taurus, and he saw how the emperor wore the full armor of the Crimson Guard, along with a glowing grin and lively eyes, both of which aired certain enthusiasm for these killings and destruction. It was a sight that sickened and outraged Kort in the same instant. *How can it be, that you joy at a sight which causes decent men sorrow?! For your subordinate stands before you now, drenched in the bloods of the innocent, just as the guilty! This terrible thing is what you've wrought, a thing for which you stand to pay!*

Remembering his purpose for this nightmare, Kort silenced his mind. *Ignore it all for a moment, and ask what you came here to find out—how he had premonitions...*

"What gave you the privilege?!"

Only the distant fires were Kort's reply.

"What gave you *this* advantage, to change your destiny through premonitions of the future, but others not?! Why would Destiny bestow this thing upon someone like you, who used this gift for evil, instead of good?"

Taurus remained silent.

"Answer me!" demanded the ex-knight.

"Chance," Taurus finally replied.

Kort tightened his grip on the duo of curved Hirishin blades at his sides, restraining his urges to thrust them into the mass murderer Taurus, and literally cut their conversation short.

Taurus continued speaking.

"I merely was the first to act off my premonitions of the future, and changed the worlds of those around me, as evidenced by you! Garlew died at your hands, because I saw your assassination coming!"

Kort shook his head, hating the truth more than Taurus. "Why *you*?!" he asked again, not satisfied with the response given. "What made *you* so special?"

Taurus smirked, "There are many spiders of change who spin destiny's web anew for those around them. These spiders are at the root of cascading effects that premonitions have on the lives of many. Perhaps there's a single spider that re-spun webs of destiny for all other eight-legged creatures in its web, one who led change for everyone!"

Kort wrinkled his brow and raised an eyebrow. *One spider who re-spins destiny's web for all others? How can it be, that a sole person is responsible for all premonitions, and grants first access to future knowledge, for only a select few?!*

"I came to a point where my premonitions convinced me I was reliving my life, again and again! That feeling like you've been somewhere before and done something with certain consequences, comes only through experience!" Kort listened as the emperor went on. "And indeed we've all been here before, repeating our lives differently each time, because of people like me!"

Kort saw Taurus abruptly turn and begin walking away, laughing with every step. "Ha ha ha, Aha ha ha ha!" As the emperor went, Kort's ears filled with sounds of Taurus' joy in others' suffering; it was the same laughter heard at the beginning of his dream turned nightmare, about the campfire. And that sadism stoked flames in him, many times hotter and more furious than what consumed the city of Baal this very night.

At once, he ran for Taurus and thrust both swords, having the intention to drive them through the emperor's back. Right when Kort reached him, however, the crimson cloak turned black, featuring white falling stars, and the figure before him spun about, becoming Nym!

"Destiny, no! Kort shrieked, but it was too late.

His swords pierced her stomach and went through her back—the fate he had intended for Taurus, given instead to his love.

Kort felt her slump into his muscled arms, her gray eyes meeting his own then, framed by silver hair. "Our love has always endured misgivings, and this too shall pass."

Kort wept as life slowly faded from Nym. She leaned closer to him, and whispered dying words into his ears. "Our baby was due, in so little time…"

At that, he looked down, and saw a bloody sword hilt protruding from Nym's enlarged belly—her belly's size a clear indication of her pregnancy. When he realized what he had done, he cried out in a voice so loud that surely Karnatha heard it, from every corner of the universe.

"Nooooooooo!"

(Awakening from Kort's Nightmare)

Kort awoke in Raiden's house, lying on a mat and covered with a thin blanket, just as he was when he laid himself to sleep. A series of images from his nightmare ran through his mind—blood everywhere, the man in black laughing from Baal's rooftops with the backdrop of orange fire, and finally, chasing Taurus only to mistakenly skewer Nym to death. The final images tightened his breathing and summoned words to his trembling lips. "What soulless father kills mother and child?!" He repeated the phrase to himself, and tossed about with hysterics, before gradually coming to grips with his reality. *It was only a nightmare! It was only a nightmare...*

Moments passed, and eventually Kort's breathing slowed. His once tightened fists loosened their grip on the covers, and he slowly exhaled. Kort reflected on his visions, and began weeping. *Nym...* The thought of hurting the one he loved pained him deeply.

Even more time passed and it was enough for Kort to finally grow calm. But just then, the covers overtop him moved on their own, flying off him and into the air, appearing as if draped over a large mound! Kort startled at the sight. "A nightmare within a nightmare?!" he cried. "Destiny save me!"

From beneath the blanket, he heard a sudden voice boom a question. "Who took the life of Garlew Il'therin?!"

Kort swallowed hard, wanting to offer a different answer than the truth. *I killed Taurus Hboshi, using the might of Nym!* He knew this was the reality robbed from him, by a spider that re-spun the web of his own destiny. *I know better... I killed Garlew using Nym, that's all.*

The voice from beneath the blanket asked the same question again, even louder this time. "Who took the life of Garlew Il'therin?!"

And it was then that he saw it. From beneath the blanket, a crooked and shaking finger pointing him out. It sent tears streaming from Kort's eyes, at his mere recollection of killing the Sergrothian hero, surely what must be the direct antithesis of any good deed. It served a reminder of how he stood so far from his wants of doing great good in Karnath. *You're a traitor, a murderer, and a knight who betrayed the common trust of his kingdom. You deserve prison or death!*

Overwhelmed by these thoughts, Kort wept more. His mouth worked out his heartfelt contrition for what he saw as a terrible and grave misdeed, committed at his very hands. "Taurus made Garlew a target; I never meant to kill him! I've been sorry for my mistake, every day since! I've changed after this happened, and strive to right my wrong every chance I have! I just need more time!"

Kort watched the shaking finger, still pointing at him. "Despite your heartfelt repentance, punishment will be due in full!"

Confused, the ex-knight cried out, "What are you? Speak to me before I see any punishment beyond what I suffer daily—being crushed alive by my own conscience!"

From beneath the blanket came a deep tone.

"It's not what I am, but who I was."

Kort begged, "Tell me then, who you were!"

He saw the blanket drop to the floor, revealing the glowing semblance of a bandaged knight, with a gaping hole in the chest filled by Nym's dagger. "You speak with the ghost of Garlew Il'therin!"

In bitter remorse, Kort continued weeping.

"I'm so sorry, friend…"

"And you'll be sorrier!" the ghost retorted. "By using Nym to avoid shedding the blood of an enemy looking as your good friend, much more blood will be on your hands!" Garlew boomed then, "There was a burden meant for me to bear that now you must shoulder!"

Kort cowered before the ghost in trepidation, unable to believe what happened to him now. *This isn't real, or is it?!* He pondered the situation, neither understanding how Garlew could visit him beyond the grave, nor the mystery of these strange words.

"In time," the ghost said, "you'll live to regret your choice more so than this very eve, in the moment where you drown in Karnath's blood!"

Kort beseeched the ghost, "Please, tell me of what you speak!" Despairingly, he watched the apparition float in silence, not giving a single word of clarification. Then suddenly, from beneath the house's sliding door, Kort saw blood flow into his very room, toward where he sat upon the mat! Blood dripped down the windowsill too, meeting a pool of blood forming from each corner of the room, as it welled up from the floorboard's grain, surrounding him.

Blood oozed from every opening of the house all over Kort, it what became an immersion of crimson! Struggling not to be choked by blood as it flowed up his neck, Kort outstretched his hand toward the ghost, and yet again, begged for an answer.

"Tell me how to change my future!"

No response was given from the ghost.

From Kort's periphery, he saw the sky outside the window turn blood red. Therefrom, all the stars of heaven fell to Karnath in streams of receding light—kissing the night goodbye, never to shine again. The blood covered Kort just then, and he started to drown in it beneath the crimson overhead. And just before it entered his mouth with a sobering metallic taste, he uttered one last plea.

"Tell me how to reweave my destiny, from that already woven for me!"

A musical laughter entered his ears, like otherworldly chimes. "Ha ha ha… I'll tell you how not. Trust not, the crimson knight."

Wide-eyed, the ex-knight cried out and clutched his garments tightly in fear, when beholding Garlew's ghost become the ghostly woman of dissolving flesh seen in Tai, with blotches of gold light for her eyes and mouth!

(Awakening from Kort's Nested Nightmare)

The rooster suddenly crowed, waking Kort from a troubled sleep, and his nightmare within a nightmare. He grabbed the covers while lying upon the mat, pulling them up to his chin, and breathing intensely as he looked around the room. Pouring through the window beside him, he saw morning light shine into Raiden's house. He continued looking around, only to find the front door of the fisher's home wide open, with no one in the dwelling but him.

Chapter 48
The Chance of Exodus

X'ieth continued sleeping in Forest Saol, and in his sleep, he continued dreaming of his soon-to-be-had hero's title. He found himself in yet another splendid scene, standing in a particular courtyard of Castle Sergros, outside Gawdin's magnificent basilica. At all four sides, he saw the outer walls of the castle enclosing him in a massive open space. Corbeled turrets hung off those walls and pointed into the sky, having windows filled with happy-faced people peeking out, at what took place below. Beyond the turrets, free-standing keeps of gray stone jutted into the horizon, hatted by hemispherical roofs of onyx and with balconies on multiple levels, all packed with onlookers just as the turrets. The streets connected to the courtyard via the castle's western gate were no different than the turrets and keeps, housing scores of Sergrothians who wore their best dress, lining the ways to the basilica. They were mostly humans, elves, and dwarves, representing both the young and old, just as both male and female alike. Almost everyone threw confetti into the air, and it flurried around X'ieth; it fell onto his head, shoulders, and white armor.

He gazed to the sky overhead, gorgeously blue and clear, free of clouds and the sun. The sight made him realize what a fabulous day it was for his reception in Sergros after having slain the Child of Darkness and having restored Light to Karnath. When feeling a hand touch him from behind, X'ieth turned about, seeing Millicent there with their newborn child wrapped in swaddling clothes. Beside her was Talus, in his best spirits ever, with a broad smile and a gleam of cheer in his eyes.

"You've the look of a hero, young knight!"

At the king's words, X'ieth glanced down at his body, which was bedecked in the shimmering armor of Autheos. At his side, he saw the sheathed gray blade, the sacred artifact from the Karnathan religion, what he used to undo the Dark Prophecy and defeat Darkness. X'ieth let one hand fall to his belt, feeling then the sword's hilt and also, the sheer surface of his armor. Though his actions started in mistrust of the sights and sounds happening all around him, they ended in trust as he lifted his same hand to his hair and removed some confetti, afterward staring at it in his palm. *It's real*, he thought. *It's all very real!*

"Time to light the torch," Talus said.

X'ieth looked up, seeing the king extend to him an elaborate, bronze hand torch. It was long, increasing in breadth from bottom to collar, with seven stars winding northward up the handle, the topmost colored white. X'ieth reached for it, and when he took hold of the torch, Talus did not immediately let go, causing the young knight to meet eyes with the king.

"Thank you, for everything."

The words struck X'ieth by surprise, ringing of appreciation, a thing foreign to him throughout many years of indentured servitude to the throne of Sergros.

X'ieth smiled and nodded, taking the torch; he instantly could feel its weight in his hand. He studied the object, a thing clearly made for lighting larger torches at celebrations and ceremonies, though perhaps never in Sergros. His eyes rested upon the insignia of seven stars, the crest of Malgun described in the Book of Karnatha, in passages about Old Karnath.

"Light the torch," Talus repeated.

X'ieth glanced up, seeing again his joyous king.

"And in so doing," he continued, "light a flame that shall burn forever, a flame to kindle a fire in your children and your children's children. From you shall descend a long line of heroes, one without end!"

"Light it! Light it!" urged Millicent.

X'ieth turned from the king to his smiling wife, who for the first time ever seemed supportive of something in his life. He glanced back to Talus, still beaming and showing signs of approval, his hands gesturing for the young knight to proceed.

It was enough for X'ieth to duck into his channeling chamber, in order to channel Nexus to light the torch. But upon entering, he found the room strange and unfamiliar, with fog robing its unseen walls. X'ieth spun all around, not seeing his Source entry anywhere! It filled him with panic, for he knew that without a Source entry, even a simple magical feat like lighting the torch would be impossible.

He snapped back to the courtyard, seeing Talus maintain his encouragement, Millicent too, and now, the entire throng singing a mantra. "Light it! Light it!"

Above the crowd's collective voice, Millicent shouted, "Light the torch, and in so doing light the flame that's gone out in our marriage, the fire we've left unattended!"

When X'ieth thought again about his missing Source entry, he could feel himself sweating beneath his armor. A realization slithered through his mind. *You have to light it; you just have to! You've never had her approval or that of Talus. This is a chance, perhaps had only once in your lifetime. So what are you waiting for?!*

At that thought, X'ieth dove back into his channeling chamber, hoping things might be different there. But just as before, he saw fog and gloom masking the entire space, with his Source entry nowhere to be found! He felt even more anxious then, as more thoughts of being unable to light the torch entered his mind. His heart beat faster in his chest, and his breathing instantly grew strained. *This isn't right... It's not...*

Still in his channeling chamber, X'ieth ran into the gloom and it soon became clear that the walls of his channeling chamber were not even there. *It's like the walls have disappeared!* He was able to run and run further, without ever hitting anything besides more and more gloom.

"What's wrong?"

Millicent's voice popped X'ieth out of his channeling chamber, back into the courtyard of Castle Sergros. There, he saw her staring back crossly, her eyes narrowed, with creases in both cheeks as she tightly puckered her lips, displaying a clear look of condescension over the young knight's hesitation to light the torch.

"What's wrong?!" she asked, more pointedly then. "Surely the Child of Light could light a torch at his own celebration! Perhaps the explanation is exactly what I always said: you'll never be Kayareth! It's just another of your gray dreams, to the demise of our marriage!"

"Yes, what's wrong?" Talus asked.

X'ieth looked his way, seeing him smile sinisterly.

"Surely the Child of Light could do something as simple as lighting a torch. For even the castle servants can do that! Perhaps we should get Galwin to help you, since clearly you've disappointed us once again."

"You and your dreams. Nothing but disappointment to everyone around you," Millicent chimed in. "Do you disappoint yourself as much as you disappoint me? Would be a pity if you did. Why can't you see that your aspirations of becoming more than what Destiny affords you, aren't meant to be?"

"That's not true!" X'ieth interposed, between her harsh words. And just after he spoke, the confetti froze in the air, as did the people freeze mid-cheer. With that, the entire scene grayed in color!

"I am the Child of Light, for I slayed the Child of Darkness!" X'ieth declared, looking to Millicent first. "I'm a knight also," he said, looking then at Talus. "And the father of that child," he added, returning his gaze to Millicent. "I'm your husband, and so much more."

They stared back silently, aggravating the situation.

"Are you anything more than just an orphan?"

"I've wondered that for years," said Talus, adding to Millicent's comment, while shaking his head. "I've wondered if you're more than just a fatherless, damaged boy. I've wasted so much on you."

"A boy he is for sure," Millicent said. "With fancies as such, and zero commitment to his own family!"

"What a disappointment," Talus remarked.

"Why yes," Millicent agreed, looking to the king. "What a terrible disappointment he's been, to you and me!"

"That's not true!" X'ieth shouted, his eyes heavy, as was his heart from their injurious words. "I'm much more than an orphan, and not anyone's disappointment! I'm a hero, a knight, a father, and also, a married man!"

"Supposedly all that, yet he can't light the torch."

Talus nodded to Millicent. "It's pathetic, and makes me sorrow over what's surely your shame!"

X'ieth stood amidst this back and forth between wife and king, now questioning if any of this really took place. He glanced away as they continued mocking him, to the inanimate and grayed throng of onlookers with confetti plastered to the air. *It's not real. It can't be real!*

"I'll bet you my own child, that he can't light it!"

The conversation pulled at X'ieth's attention.

"I'll bet my whole kingdom he can't," Talus snickered. "His every dream of being more than an orphan was only a fool's delusion, just as him lighting the torch!"

"Ha ha ha!" Millicent laughed.

Talus joined in, as if humored by his own words.

"Ha ha ha, Ha ha ha!"

They laughed and laughed, increasingly more raucous each occasion they paused to glance upon the young knight. Millicent dropped the swaddling clothes, and they fell to the ground, without a child inside.

Mixed with confusion and anger, X'ieth looked back, resenting himself for enduring such poor treatment. His face burned bright red, hinting at the negative feelings that he repressed through silence.

In one moment, he looked to the torch again, and from somewhere deep inside, his determination came forth. *Light the torch right as they mock you, and show them otherwise. This dream has become a nightmare, but it need not end that way!*

With that thought, X'ieth entered his channeling chamber, which was still filled with mystery. In search of his Source entry, he resumed running into the fog, until a large shadow appeared before him, stopping his body and mind in one sudden instant. X'ieth ceased running and gawked curiously at what appeared to be a large box in the distance, seated behind the gloom in his chamber. X'ieth immediately felt cold, as if the object itself imparted that sensation.

"Where's my Source entry?!" he asked the fog despairingly. Images of Talus and Millicent laughing at him ran through his mind, and simply would not go away. The gloom, however, had no answers to his inquiry. He stared at the fog in silence, half expecting an explanation, half expecting the Source entry to show itself. It was then that he muttered, "It's not right… This isn't right…"

From his right side came a voice abruptly—deep, distorted and otherworldly. "But does it feel wrong?"

Nearly jumping out of his skin, X'ieth spun about, startled as could be. He looked into the gloom seeing nothing, and began turning all about, peering anxiously. With every full circle, he could see the box in the distance.

"Who's there?!" X'ieth yelled, on edge.

"I am what you are … *Dark on us.*"

"Who?"

"I am what so many have become… *Dark on us.*"

"What?!"

"*Darconas…*" the voice said once more. "The gloom clouds peoples' judgments, making them feel at lower lows than are real. Just as this, the citizens of Sergros feel they can't achieve anything more than an empty existence of being rather than doing, awaiting the next handout from the throne. But with that mindset, they're deceived! The gloom limits their potential, by disabling them from trying new things, especially after failing…"

"Show yourself!" X'ieth demanded, still following the voice through the fog, seeming at different places with every spoken word. As he made his circles, the large box showed itself again and again in his eyes, serving a constant reminder of its presence.

"Many need help to rise," said the voice, garbled and breaking. "And perhaps I should rise on my own to greater understanding. For I wonder now, if the un-shadowed can really help my cause more than the shadowed. It's doubtful that *the king* shares my zeal, perhaps a thing to test. What he'll do on his own should tell, in the absence of my full guidance. If he enters New Karnath of his own volition, it'll prove our wants are one."

"Hide behind shadows," X'ieth retorted, upon stopping at the last direction from where the voice sounded. "Hide, just as you hide your intentions behind strange words! End this now and do reveal yourself, fiend! Reveal yourself and explain why you've taken my Source entry! This isn't right…"

"Is it so hard to admit, that it's wrong?"

X'ieth's attention went to the box again.

"What is it even?!" he asked, feeling colder the longer he looked at it. He watched the gloom peel back, to reveal the object as massive, wooden double doors, bearing carven inlays of thorns. *What in Destiny's name?!* he thought to himself, confused more than anything else.

"A shard… your shard," said the voice, as if providing an answer to the question of what.

Just then, images flashed before X'ieth's eyes, of a large, black, and mirrored shard reaching up from the floor to the door's height, overlaying it. The images came and went, then came again, repeatedly showing themselves.

"My shard is not a door," X'ieth replied, "but rather a sword. I'm Karnath's hero, if you haven't heard!"

"That you are…" came the voice. "But a shard of sword is more than what seems. *Shards are of things broken, like dreams. Shards deal with what you'll do after their breaking.*"

"What does that mean?"

"Your shard is what you'll do, a choice you'll make when things break, as all do. To rise or to fall, is but to choose or to chance. Just as this, the shard is what you'll do. It'll be your awakening to action—a deliberate step you take through a doorway."

From the fog X'ieth saw a vesper suddenly emerge, with height and breadth, but without depth! The young knight gasped, as the shadow opened its shadowy mouth, to utter the arcane words, as said before. "Shous da rio!"

(Awakening from X'ieth's Reverie)

Voices woke X'ieth right from his dream.

"Shous da rio! Shous da rio!"

He opened his eyes and immediately saw the other knights frantically scurrying about the camp with swords in hand, as giant-sized shadowy figures came at them with blades of gray fire. Near the brink of daylight now, the vespers emerged from every shadow of Saol, to flood the small clearing of the gloomy forest!

Events unfolded so fast before X'ieth. He watched Lewes struggle to untie the remaining horse with a single arm, which jumped and neighed while Hammar and Nathan tried to hoist Finnel upon it. They literally contended with the beast's will, as Zeros was beside them, vying a much darker nemesis—the shadows.

X'ieth's eyes shifted to the mercenary, who swung his sword with one muscular arm, deftly fending off the vespers near Nathan, Hammar, and Lewes. Like a dancer upon a stage, he spun and jumped with his blade in hand, guarding their every flank. The whole time, the young knight saw a green glow at the mercenary's midsection, which blinked each moment before he threw luminous bursts of Nexus to ward off the vespers.

"We won't last until day's light!" Zeros shouted, fighting in a frenzy. X'ieth unsheathed his blade and joined the mercenary, knocking the fiery sword from a vesper at Zeros' rear. The two stayed close to protect Nathan, Hammar, and Lewes, while working back-to-back to protect each other.

Zeros' voice suddenly rose above the clang of steel.

"We must move to survive!"

X'ieth turned to him, seeing Zeros look at Nathan, who continued working with Finnel. The young knight followed their talking heads in what became a brief exchange.

"Run through Saol," said Zeros, "and should the mountain show above the trees, bear that direction!"

Nathan continued saddling wounded Finnel upon the horse, and looked over his shoulder to exclaim, "What good will it do us to run?! The vespers are everywhere!"

As new vespers appeared, Zeros suddenly started swinging his sword again, and X'ieth kept behind him, protecting the mercenary's back. He listened to their talk, while deflecting fiery swords that swiped out of nowhere, at both him and Zeros. X'ieth's counters flung fiery sword after fiery sword into the fog. *For Destiny's sake*, he thought, *someone make a decision! We can't stay here much longer!*

Zeros shouted, "Vespers must remain in the shadows. Here they're kings of the forest, so let us go to where they are mountain hermits!"

"Perhaps your weary mind can't recall that we're lost in Saol!" Nathan called back, as he finished saddling Finnel and spun about, to draw his sword and join in the fight beside Zeros.

The horse's whinny and clangs of steel filled the air.

Lewes drew his sword, and started fighting at the opposite of Finnel, protecting yet another flank.

"I urge you lead us from here!" yelled Zeros, still fighting. "May we hope for the best! Moving is better than standing still!"

As X'ieth listened to their conversation, he sent yet another vesper's sword into the murky woods. Just then, leaves crunched in his ears, causing him to instinctively pivot, seeing Hammar shoulder a hobbling Tol, both of them coming up to the horse. He sighed in relief.

"You're right," Nathan finally consented, deflecting another vesper's sword. "So then, to the way before us!"

At Nathan's command, X'ieth turned to see him point to the clearing's one end with an upraised sword. It was then, he watched Nathan take one of Tol's arms over the shoulder, Lewes the other, as Hammar let go.

A fiery blade came out of the fog, right at the rear of the Tol, Lewes, and Nathan. Before anyone else could even react, Hammar quickly threw his hammer at the weapon, sending it into the fog, and another vesper into a hissing fetch. "Shous da rio! Shous da rio!"

The sudden course of events made X'ieth remark, *That was amazing. How did Hammar even see that vesper?!*

"Pay attention, lad," said Zeros, pulling X'ieth back into the fight. He looked at the mercenary, who just then, struck down another of the vesper's blades while talking. "Let's form the tether again, so our integrated sword and magic can clear the way for the others!"

Finnel spoke from his mount. "I'll ride behind you both. I can link to push Nexus into your combined core!"

"Aye, me too!" called out Tol, who stood shouldered by Nathan and Lewes. "They'll help me move along, and I'll help you two flight fast through Nexus!"

Another hiss sounded suddenly with a dull clang.

"Shous da rio!"

Quickly the young knight turned, just in time to see a sword fly into the fog that would have otherwise hurt the three knights—Nathan, Tol, and Lewes. Grinning, Hammar stood nearby with his large club hammer in hand.

"Nathan and Lewes can run behind Finnel on horse!" Hammar said with a wink. "I'll keep their back!"

X'ieth's eyes shifted to Nathan, who talked next.

"Some plan is better than none. Let's move!" Nathan used the arm not around Tol's neck to lift his sword and point to the clearing once again.

Without any delay, X'ieth just acted. He went to his channeling chamber, and now, his Source entry appeared, just as it should. He sighed in relief, before running up to it and pulling open the door. Nexus flowed first along its edges, then through the door's opening and across its threshold.

Across his Source boundary, X'ieth could feel the cool energies envelope his body. The young knight spun about, ran to his Source exit, and pushed it open to let out a stream of energy for the mercenary. In moments, he saw a new flow enter his Source entry. *That's Zeros!* He immediately merged the outbound and inbound stream together, to form the tether. And immediately when he did, the walls and ceiling of his channeling chamber moved outward, forming an even larger chamber!

When X'ieth opened his eyes, he felt Tol and Finnel link to him and Zeros, no doubt pushing against the sensed external restraint of their combined core. X'ieth braced himself for fluid offenses and defenses, feeling as weary as could be. His muscles ached, his eyes were sore, and his head throbbed. But at the sight of yet another vesper, he knew what was required. *Just do it.*

X'ieth launched into a sword attack, having his limbs ablaze with Nexus. He began pushing toward the clearing's end that Nathan pointed out, disarming any vesper in the way, starting with the one before him. The clang of steel filled his ears, as his sword collided with the vespers' magical weapons in a fury of slashes, Zeros' too. From behind, the young knight could hear the gallop of Finnel's horse, and more steel clangs from Hammar, Lewes, and Nathan, who all worked their weapons while running.

As planned, the ensemble paraded through Saol in a blur, gnarled trees flying by as X'ieth whipped his sword with blinding speed at any shadow that suddenly became an armed vesper. All the while, fog poured around him whilst he cleared this path, deeper into the woods. And with it, the familiar sounds accompanied the Guard's advance, of hissing in tones ranging from soprano to bass.

"Shous da rio! Shous da rio!"

Fierce winds stabbed X'ieth in the face like a cold knife, but there was no stopping for warmth or comfort. *Don't know how long you can keep this up!* He panted hard, tired from running, fighting, and channeling. X'ieth then felt energy from Tol and Finnel replenish his drained core. *There isn't a better hint than that, to do it all over again!*

"Don't stop running until daylight!" shouted Nathan from behind, in a voice suggesting strain from Tol's weight. *We're all strained...* X'ieth thought, discounting the pack leader's struggle to himself, as vespers kept emerging from every shadowed crevice of Saol, and his sword remained in play.

As X'ieth looked back to the path, an unarmed vesper suddenly threw its face right in the young knight's! "Struggling in vain!" the shadow whispered in Mainlandish. "Darconas sees to our empowerment! Now show us the river, or else!"

"Shous da rio! Shous da rio!" hissed the shadow's cohort, more voices from the fog. As soon as the vesper appeared before his eyes, it vanished away. X'ieth moved forward and fought on, unable to reconcile any of this. *Dark on us? The river? What do these shadows want?!* He did not understand their motive, but he knew how the vespers endangered the Guardsmen and threatened their mission of stopping Esmeralda. *In that, they threaten your good destiny!*

Enraged at the thought, X'ieth threw his blade through another vesper, batting a fiery gray sword deep into the woods. When he returned his gaze upon the path, something hopeful appeared in the distance, a sight that took him by surprise. He fought sudden urges to rub his eyes from sheer disbelief of seeing a white light shining ahead. X'ieth perceived it through the trees, and though it was neither the daylight nor the mountain pass, he hurried toward it along with the group. *Do they see what you see?!*

X'ieth ran with his sword extended in Fire's Breath, snagging another vesper's weapon. He turned his blade aright suddenly, to fling the sword into Saol. From his peripheral vision, he saw Zeros hold out his sword with the outer arm, striking down anything in the way.

As X'ieth moved closer to the white light with his pack, he saw it shine through the trees in crisp rays that carved through the haze, slanted and visible. X'ieth's attention went to three silhouettes seen distantly in the white light—a woman, and two men, one holding a staff. *Who are they?!*

Heat from a fiery sword pulled X'ieth back into the fight, just in time to see it coming toward his face! Not believing his eyes, he watched Zeros cut in front of him just in time, to whack the vesper's oncoming sword into the unknown.

Over the mercenary's back, X'ieth saw another vesper came from the shadows with a fiery sword swirling. He pushed past Zeros, and swiped the magical weapon clean. As it flew through the forest, he thought to himself, *Zeros saved you, you saved him; that means you're even!*

X'ieth looked back to the yonder trees, where the white light suddenly intensified, shining even brighter now, to the point where the three silhouettes could no longer be seen. An abrupt thud from behind jerked back his attention, to the Guardsmen at his rear.

Just as X'ieth spun about, Finnel whizzed by on his horse. He saw then, how Nathan emerged from the fog, his face stricken by shock, when realizing he no longer shouldered Tol, and that Lewes was not on his other side!

X'ieth peered behind Nathan, and could barely make out Hammar in the distance, throwing a hammer at a vesper, being very far behind everyone. But between Hammar and Nathan, X'ieth could see Lewes upon the ground, apparently having tripped over some debris hidden by the fog! And with him was Tol of wounded leg, no longer afoot!

To X'ieth, what happened then seemed in slow motion. He watched as three armed vespers swarmed the fallen knights from the forest's dark corner. Tol and Lewes looked up from the ground, their eyes growing wide as the vespers drew back their swords. Lewes shielded himself with an uplifted hand, being unarmed now, with his sword lying in the distance.

X'ieth's bolted toward them in hopes of helping, but it seemed as though he moved through molasses, thick goo that prevented him from doing anything at all! And so, while his heart desperately wanted to save his fallen comrades—to protect their innocent blood—he could not.

Screams filled the air, as the vespers slashed Tol and Lewes to death! With Nathan still in sight, X'ieth saw the mix of grief and rage on the leader's face, as he turned about screaming his denial.

"Noooooo!"

And also, in his eyes was Hammar, who glanced up from fighting just then, with a woeful look that told how he too realized what had happened. The dwarf's face stretched in pain, rage, and disbelief—an awful contortion of varied emotions that was awful to see.

X'ieth reacted just as they. But as his mouth fell open in one sudden instant, his ears filled with a loud ringing. And all about him then, he saw that intense light come over his shoulder from behind, whitening the entire scene to obscurity. All sights, all sounds, all emotions disappeared in that moment, perhaps never to appear again.

"LEGION OF SHADOWS"

Chapter 49
Up the Mountain Gray

And everything was blinding light, until that light finally faded. After their flight from the vespers, X'ieth found himself standing among the other knights, outside of Forest Saol and at a trail leading into the western pass of Liath. As cold winds lashed him, he leered at the gray rock with unbelieving eyes. *Are you dreaming this?! We went from stuck in Saol to Liath, just like that?* His presence in this place alongside the Guard seemed more a work of magic than anything else.

He watched the others look around awestruck just as him, with faces of open-mouthed wonderment. Before him, Finnel sat upon the remaining horse, holding the reins. On Finnel's left stood Hammar, and at his right were Zeros and Nathan. The knights still held their weapons, as they did when the white light engulfed them in the forest.

Zeros and Nathan sheathed their swords when it became apparent the only danger here was the relentless wind with its icy teeth. X'ieth followed suit, dropping his blade into its casing, and let out a breath of air. The vapor billowed from his mouth, sucked into a sudden harsh wind, causing him to shudder.

Stomp!!! Stomp!!!

At hearing a few pronounced thuds, X'ieth looked in the direction of Hammar, and saw the dwarf put down his boot against the rock again and again, as if seeking to physically authenticate the surrounds by touch. Instantly he stumbled, part of the mountain being porous and crumbling to dust beneath his boot!

"What sorcery is this?" Hammar asked, sounding as if surprised.

Is he talking about magically appearing in Liath, or that bit of rock breaking apart? X'ieth wondered, not knowing to what Hammar referred.

Nathan's voice cut into his thoughts.

"Lewes and Tol are gone." The words came abruptly, and were perhaps in his sullenest tone.

X'ieth glanced his way, seeing Nathan stare collectively over the remaining knights. While the pack leader kept a straight posture, he might as well hunch given the dejected scowl on his face. The expression easily counted as body language evoking Nathan's pains over the situation.

The same scowl, hollow eyes, and wrinkled brow rippled across the other knights, as reality set it and they too became cognizant of this great loss. Sadness inside X'ieth continued pulling down at the corners of his lips, worsening his frown into one far more severe. Through his mind went depressing realizations that touched upon the many far-reaching implications of lost life. *Lewes clearly had a family, perhaps Tol too. Never will they see their loved ones again; never will their dreams see reality! Their futures unraveled in moments… They both suffered Fate's Fray!*

Witnessing the fragility of their life made him sober of how close he himself came to Fate's Fray. Voices rang out in his head. *I now wonder if you're good enough for anything!* said Talus. *Prove that you love me*, Millicent chimed in, *by giving up silly dreams of being some important hero!* And then, Lucen's voice: *You are a Child of Destiny, the one fated to do mighty things!*

"Destiny, we grieve for Tol and Lewes…"

X'ieth's last thought dissolved, and he looked over to see Nathan and the others, bowing their heads and offering up a prayer for the fallen. The act shamed him, making him feel as though his mind were not in the right place at the right time. *End these thoughts and silence your mind, for there's more happening in Karnath than your own affairs!* Now a shade of red, X'ieth too closed his eyes as Nathan went on.

"They were our friends and comrades, sharing our common purpose. As their energies return now to the Nexus, in time, return order to the lives that surely will be disrupted by this loss of good men…"

Nathan fell silent, just as a hard wind blew.

"Karnatha," Zeros spoke suddenly, above the wind.

X'ieth opened his eyes, seeing Nathan, Zeros, Hammar and Finnel still with their heads bowed, with now, the mercenary praying. The young knight closed his eyes once more, now feeling irreverence versus shame.

"I pray also that the death of our friends won't be in vain. Let us complete what we intended in the first. Let us slay Esmeralda, as both Lewes and Tol would, if they still had the chance."

Silence fell upon the group of five knights, and after a few moments, X'ieth slowly opened one eye, seeing Nathan and the others looking down solemnly upon the rock, with their countenances equally grayed. He opened both eyes then, and did the same. He stared for a while at the rock before slowly gazing away up into the sky, to behold the morning light press against the gloomy clouds.

From the heavens, X'ieth's vision drifted down to the path in front of Finnel's horse; it led around the mountainside, being overhung by a ridged outcropping above. The way forward served a reminder to him that their journey was not yet over, and his good destiny awaited him—of confronting Esmeralda to end this gloom; of becoming the man that Karnatha had ordained him to be.

"The day is young," Nathan said, collecting his knights' attention. "Shall we go further toward Esmeralda's tower, or rest awhile?"

X'ieth exchanged looks with the other knights, everyone remaining quiet. A single thought buzzed through his mind. *Don't say a word, man! Asking for rest will break the thin ice, on which you stand!* The young knight realized he partially redeemed himself in Nathan's eyes by fighting the vespers, and he needed to keep in that direction.

After several moments of quiet, Nathan gave a nod.

"Very well then. We go now into Liath."

With those words, the weary group of knights took the first step of what turned into many over the hours to come. From the back, X'ieth trudged behind Zeros, watching Nathan and Hammar walk on ahead, behind Finnel on horseback.

Together, they hiked the mountain path. It snaked around Liath, sandwiched between gray rock on one side and thick mist on the other, which masked a deathly drop into the valley below. In the distance, X'ieth could see a peak adjacent to the mountain they ascended, deeper in the range; it jutted up in the gloom, like a granite dagger.

As time melted away X'ieth hiked further with the others, and hunger gnawed at his gut, just as weariness gnawed at his body. The sights along the way, however, made the feelings easy to dismiss. The young knight almost marveled at things with every other step—the varying rock formations on the mountain face, large boulders perched high from ledges aloft, but most strikingly, the complete lack of life on the mountain. *There's not even a flower in bloom...* He pondered this, bearing in mind what he learned of mountain flowers in academy, some exhibiting late flowering after the main growing season ended. *The mountain lilies should be showing...*

But just as X'ieth had the thought, a sight suddenly distracted him from following the other knights. He knelt down next to a soil patch on the mountain landscape, where protruding from the surface was ironically one mountain lily. *Maybe you were wrong?*

The sight of life brought a smile to his face. Kneeling there beside the flower, he studied the plant's healthy appearance; its many lavender tepals formed a lush whorl of sepals from which the petals flowered. With some hesitance, X'ieth brushed the back of his gauntlet against the petals, and upon contact a vision instantly assaulted him! Images of a woman flashed before his eyes; she was in elaborate dress with curly red hair, being presented a mountain lily by a rugged-looking hiker of fine features—a muscled, red-haired man with sapphire eyes. That flash was followed by two more: the first of which involved the same woman laying a bundle on the mountain pass; the second showed this same man, later finding it.

And as fast as they came, the images were gone. X'ieth roughly exhaled. *Great Destiny, be these mountain ghosts?!* His mind sputtered that single question, weirdness being no stranger to him on this particular quest. *The woman in white… The ghostly woman in Saol and the crying child… The vespers… The part of your dream about those strange doors… The visions of the red-haired man and woman upon Liath…* They were all weird happenings, all of them being out of the ordinary.

As the visions evaporated, so did the flower at his reach. Astonished, X'ieth watched green energy seep from the lily and spill into the open air, the petals withering a moment later. His eyes followed the lily's life force, wafting into the gloomy sky. *Just like the energy from those trees in Forest Saol!*

In that moment, the apparent destruction of Karnath touched X'ieth, and from it, he derived deep resolve to stop whatever took place. Near the ledge that overlooked the mountainside, he stood tall with eyes on the distant horizon, surveying a land robed in gloom by a burgeoning Dark power—a power he had to thwart before all was lost. *You'll stop Esmeralda*, he reassured himself, *and you'll become so much more than this.*

He glanced down to his white mail and silvery armor, regarding himself then as only one knight among many others, until his path for good destiny went trodden. *In slaying Esmeralda, you'll be the hero, the knight of knights, the father of a new knighthood in Sergros!* Since X'ieth's talk with Zeros the night prior, his every dream conglomerated into one far grander than anything he had ever imagined before. *And neither Millicent nor Talus can stop you now; they'll not be your Fate's Fray!*

X'ieth suddenly felt strange. He stepped into his small channeling chamber, and upon entering it he saw streams of blue energies flowing through the air! Startled, he turned about at the room's center, and right behind him was a blue Source exit and a man's silhouette, connected to each other by the very same blue energy. In his mind, X'ieth rushed toward the silhouette, and when coming closer, the shadow became exposed as Zeros!

He snapped out of his channeling chamber, back onto the mountain path. X'ieth came face-to-face with the mercenary, who stood at arm's length. *He read your mind.* That conclusion slowly formed within him, as those energies seen in his channeling chamber strikingly resembled the ones Kort used when killing Garlew. *He read your mind; he must of!*

"You know," Zeros said, "gray dreams can rob a man from enjoying dreams already come true, and I fear you're being robbed. If the gloom didn't block the sun, I bet you'd try to reach out and touch it."

X'ieth did not know how to respond. He stood there, silent and glaring. From the moment Zeros overstepped his bounds, the young knight's fondness for the mercenary began to atrophy.

"Those always in want of more are evaded by good destiny," Zeros continued, "they keep climbing the sky and try to touch sol. Where few achieve more than men who don't dream gray, many going higher are fated to burn."

"But the gloom does block the sun," snapped X'ieth. "So you don't know what I'd do."

With that comment, the young knight walked from the ridge, past Zeros, and back toward the path, in the direction of catching up with the others.

"Do you know what I'd do, if I were you?"

Zeros' comment broke X'ieth's stride. He stopped in his steps, though did not look back. Inside, it frustrated him how the mercenary was suddenly snooping into his personal life, between last night and now. *Do you want to know his opinion? Not really...* X'ieth bit his tongue, and just stayed silent.

"If I were you, I'd revalue what life has given me—a beautiful family; a fulfilling career. Those are things that most men would die to have. If I were you, I'd value them more and think differently, because the way you're thinking now is very dangerous..."

The young knight glanced over his shoulder.

"What?" he asked, as a frown marred his face.

He saw Zeros standing exactly where he was near the ledge, holding his shoulders straight, and staring back with his lips pursed. Fog rolled behind him off the precipice, hiding the valley. A strong wind blew then, giving the mercenary a few moments more to consider his response.

"You're thinking just like men, who've lost everything over their gray dreams! Look, I don't know what you're dreaming of, whether it's poorly chanced, or if you have enough hope to push for it, no matter what. But I do know that you're thinking if your dreams don't come true, your future will simply unravel. And in that, you've drank the same poison as many Karnathans—a poison that warps their understanding of Fate's Fray."

X'ieth glared at Zeros. *What's he trying to say?!* But as the young knight's features grew hard and he became even more offended, the mercenary's eyes softened and hinted moistness.

"Listen to me," Zeros urged him. "Karnathans have it all wrong. Fate's Fray isn't about someone or something stopping what you're meant to be. Rather, Fate's Fray is about fighting for what you want to be. It's our own Battle for Destiny, and the biggest impediment to fighting that fight is ourselves, not anyone else."

As he heard Zeros talk, X'ieth was slow to even blink. He thought about what the man had to say, not seeing it as more valid that his own world view. *You've fought for what you've wanted, and had to prevent others from taking it from you... The biggest impediments were Talus and Millicent, not you.*

Zeros went on. "So never think that your whole future is over because of something that happened at work, home, or wherever. Bad situations can improve on all of those fronts, and none of them have to be your end. Just keep fighting for what you want, and avoid blaming anyone else more than yourself for your dreams not coming true.

In the end, it's your Battle for Destiny—your Fate's Fray. Only you can decide what side you'll take, how much you're willing to fight, and whether it's time to fight differently—to dream a new dream."

Zeros looked away for a moment, and then back.

"I used to think my future was over with what happened to me years ago. Nearly every day I blamed Talus for it too, though now, I blame only myself..."

X'ieth sighed. *Another bit from his troubled past...*

Zeros continued, "I get that Talus and Millicent are giving you grief over the knighthood, but..."

The comment sucker punched X'ieth in the face. His mouth fell open and his forehead wrinkled in one singular moment, where he realized that Zeros had been talking to someone about him, and knew personal details. *Even so, he doesn't know you...* And X'ieth would not hesitate in communicating just that.

"You don't know anything about me," X'ieth cut him off. "Someone has clearly told you a thing or two about me and my life, but it makes no difference. You still don't know me."

Zeros spoke softly. "So true. But I should have."

With that, the mercenary dropped his eyes to the rock, and marched past X'ieth up the path toward the others, scowling at his boots. The young knight lingered there a moment, watching Zeros and his crimson cloak float away, and in time, become absorbed by the gloom.

Now in solitude, X'ieth reflected on what just occurred, for he found himself confused by the mercenary. *Why is Zeros trying to get so close? Why's he offering advice, now even without an invitation?* The young knight did not have good answers to these questions, and was divided over what he thought. One half of him conjectured that perhaps Zeros felt closer to him than any other knight, and was acting as a friend more than an acquaintance. His other half proposed something else, that Zeros had intentions of some kind. *Don't know...*

When a strong wind struck X'ieth, he realized it might be Destiny's way of reminding him of where he was, and what he needed to do. *Better find the others... You've got a sorceress to stop, a gloom to end, and a prophecy to change.* That thought was enough to stir X'ieth into motion; he jogged apace up the trail, until seeing several crimson cloaks, one of them flowing behind a horse.

At seeing Zeros from the rear, it brought up negative feelings inside X'ieth. *No one gave him the right to read your mind! Does everyone in Sergros feel entitled to something not theirs? And why's he talking to anyone about you, behind your back?* He was vexed that Zeros had intruded upon his thoughts, and his personal life. If it were done for the mercenary to get closer to the young knight, the outcome went ironically counter to those intentions. Because now, X'ieth felt increased distance from Zeros.

Nathan turned about, as if hearing X'ieth approach.

"Try not to wander far, lad… I mustn't lose any more knights before returning to Sergros."

X'ieth gave a silent nod, now being footsteps behind Zeros. His sense of violation from what just happened would indeed keep him much closer in their continued hike through Liath. Once more, the young knight followed the trail with the others.

As their path winded around the mountain, another mountain stood close now on one side, instead of an open drop into the valley. To his left and right, X'ieth beheld steep rock walls, ruffled by erosion. The trail widened, as it extended between the two mountains.

After walking a while more, something odd appeared to X'ieth many cubits ahead. It was on his left side below the mountain wall, off the path—a nest amassing straw and twigs. The site seemed very large, as five men lying foot-to-head, maybe with greater breadth.

With the other knights, X'ieth cautiously approached the place. His eyes scanned the area, and he could see animal bones scattered throughout. The sight sent his hand to his sword hilt. Nathan and Zeros did the same. X'ieth continued looking over the area; the trail seemed at its widest point here, with many boulders, crevices, and nooks on the mountain walls. *Whatever built that nest could be lurking here, and ready to strike!*

The young knight kept on high alert. He watched Nathan approach the nest, studying it with great attention to detail. When Nathan suddenly fixated on something in the nest, X'ieth brought his focus there, seeing several ellipsoidal white stones speckled by gray dots lying on the straw: one forward and two back.

"These are no stones," muttered Nathan.

"They're dragon eggs," added Zeros. "That be what he heard roaring from Saol, a mighty dragon."

"They're bigger than any I've ever seen!" exclaimed Hammar. "Perhaps we could crack but one to feed us until we get back to Sergros?" While the dwarf joked and laughed, his stomach rumbled just then, as if to make the suggestion half serious. "Eggs for breakfast sounds good about now, eh?"

X'ieth had an immediate reaction. Memories of the devastation seen on the outskirts of Deardrum zoomed through his head—rows of homes crushed to pieces and burnt to cinders. "Don't you dare," he reprimanded, "you should know more than any of us about Pyrus, the dragon hunter who incited Gremel by foolishly trifling with the dragon's young."

In a single moment, X'ieth recounted the well-known happening very close to his previous experience in the Guard. Thimbraldorf, the King of Deardrum, commissioned Pyrus the dragon hunter to slay a fearsome dragon named *Gremel* that terrorized a small provincial village on the eastern pass of Liath, near Magicia's tower. The young knight remembered reports of how Gremel burnt crops, killed livestock, and seldom ate villagers. Despite Pyrus' attempts to rid Deardrum of one of Karnath's ancient dragons, he was unsuccessful in direct attacks. As an alternative, the dragon hunter stole her eggs as a lure, which unfortunately brought Gremel's wrath upon the village. Thimbraldorf later declared the act as reckless and a crime against the village's people, and hence Deardrum set a bounty on Pyrus' head.

X'ieth knew details about Pyrus appearing in Sergros some months ago. A convenient escape as no bounty existed there yet, and ordinarily, Sergrothian laws protected refugees. Though upon hearing about the fugitive in his province, Talus feared for his people and dispatched the Sixth Order of the Guard to capture Pyrus for handover to Deardrum, before any innocent suffered. *This was our assignment, shortly before the Isles Conspiracy erupted on the Mainland.*

He stared at Hammar, who eventually looked back with knowing eyes. X'ieth smiled, knowing his comment reminded the dwarf about the potential consequences of acting recklessly to appease the wants and needs of the flesh.

"Perhaps we best stay hungry," Hammar admitted, even though his stomach growled again.

Nathan reached up into a bag behind the horse's saddle, rummaged about, and withdrew some unleavened bread. "Here, have a cracker."

X'ieth saw the pack leader toss a wrapped biscuit to Hammar, who snatched it from the air and began inhaling it. "Just settle for wafers instead of those eggs, my friend. It'd be more trouble than it's worth."

Loud munching could be heard, as Hammar ate.

"Are you going to share, Guardsdwarf?" asked Finnel jokingly, right when Hammar was finishing, still with a mouthful of cracker and unable to answer.

X'ieth grinned, watching the dwarf stand there and glower in the long shadow cast by Finnel's horse. Whether it was over Hammar's frustration from being asked a question with his mouth full, or his frustration from being asked to share food, it was thoroughly entertaining. *He's probably frustrated from both!*

Finnel began laughing from his seat on the horse.

"C'mon, Guard. Just up this trail…"

X'ieth looked over at Nathan, who continued walking the path, some time after throwing Hammar the biscuit. He raised an arm and rolled his hand, to gesture that the group follow after him.

So up the path the Guardsmen went, still between two walls of rock, but now with the way narrowing. Together, they continued further into Liath, and closer to the tower of Esmeralda. As before, the various sights kept amazing X'ieth as he walked on, especially the walls. The rock formations showed marked differences from those seen earlier, now appearing as tree bark with shingled layers, having streaks gently contrasting between shades of gray. But while he marveled at these sights, he did so in passing, not letting himself fall behind.

The Guardsmen hiked for hours more, and it neared midday. At one point, Nathan ordered food be distributed among the other knights, but with moderation.

"We only have unleavened bread and cheese now, and fortunately two water skins. Eat and drink sparingly, for we must ration the little that remains."

Finnel reached behind him to the saddlebag, withdrew some food, and began distributing it to the knights who walked on each side of the horse.

When handed a wafer block and a cheese nub, X'ieth received them gratefully. But his hopes of anything more dwindled given the Guard's reality. Both forest and mountain were absent of life, a thing suggesting nothing to hunt and making their provisions the sole source of food. And since the Guard was days of travel away from Arlem or any nearby city, they would not get any more provisions than those on hand. *The crackers and cheese in that bag might be our last meal!* On one hand the thought jarred him, though on the other, he recalled yet again how the Light Prophecy told that the way of Kayareth would be hard. *And such is your own...*

Sudden sounds of Hammar cursing and rocks crumbling stole X'ieth's attention.

"Destiny blind me! Is Liath such an unsure step?!"

X'ieth looked over, seeing the dwarf stumble when porous rock broke beneath his boot, yet again. *He acts like he almost broke his neck*, the young knight thought to himself, studying the rock that crumbled while walking by. It had small holes on its exterior, as did other rock seen thus far, in large stretches of Liath. He considered then that some of what he thought was peculiar rock resembled just this—porous rock. *Could it be, that much of Liath is soft?* X'ieth reached out and hit the rock with a forearm. His gauntlet clanged as he felt what was a hard surface, and with this, his speculation of a soft mountain went away.

A few minutes more, the group continued up the path, until when all of a sudden Nathan raised a straight hand, motioning for everyone to stop. X'ieth slowed, as did the others, all of them silent and just listening. In the young knight's ears, a low rumble could be heard nearby in the mountain range. *Something seems wrong!*

X'ieth visited his small channeling chamber, where he ran to his Source entry and pulled open the door. Streams of energy flowed into the room the moment the door cracked, going first along its edges, then through the door's opening and over its threshold. The energies flowed and flowed, in time filling the room, and accumulating about him. Across his Source boundary, X'ieth could feel cool tingles of Nexus and a connection to the ambient energy field. Through it, he could sense objects in the reach of his locus of control, as well as their relative position and forces upon them. And so, he could immediately sense the other knights, the individual rocks on the mountain trail, the winds blowing, and most importantly, the vibrations from that rumble. Though he could not be sure, it seemed like they came from above, on the mountain opposite to the one they ascended!

Through the Nexus, X'ieth suddenly could sense huge rolling rocks, coming toward the ridge above them in a straight line, but then fanning out as they reached the ledge, from bumps in the uneven topography. *It'll be showers of rock!* X'ieth snapped out of his channeling chamber, and back onto the trail. Just as he opened his mouth, shade enveloped the group. Zeros cried out, before X'ieth could even speak, "Boulders, from above!"

The low rumble got louder in X'ieth's ears. He looked up and to the right, and saw large rocks tumble down the side of the mountain in forking paths, some breaking to bits as they rolled.

X'ieth, like the other knights, sprinted up the path without further delay. As his feet shot forward, his peripheral vision picked up Finnel squeezing his horse with both thighs, so that it ran ahead of everyone on foot. He looked back and saw Hammar moving slowest at their rear, a shower of boulders right behind him! His quick glance afforded him notice of how those falling rocks showed dimples on their surface. And sure enough, as they made contact with the path, they proved to be porous just like the others, breaking immediately, sending rock fragments flying in all directions, and beclouding the range with dust!

X'ieth steered his focus once more to the front, seeing the path before him. Finnel rode up ahead, and trailing behind him, ran Nathan and Zeros. Dust filled the air, and he could see rocks flying over his shoulder, from behind. Flashes of pregnant Millicent filled his head, reminding him of what he left behind for this. And it was then, beneath his mire of arrogance, pride, and wistful occupations of becoming the One of Prophecy, his thoughts of more than himself motivated him to run all the more faster. *Run, for their sake!* And so, X'ieth pushed himself to a quicker pace, with thoughts of family in mind. Though while he ran with a clear want of returning to his wife with child, part of him had other wants. *Return also, the hero…*

As X'ieth hastened further up the trail, rocks continued flying over his shoulders. Dust entered his lungs as he sucked in the air, still sprinting with his fellow Guardsmen. He choked and coughed, but somehow, still managed his pace. Suddenly, while running, he saw a boulder piece fall onto the path, right between him and Nathan. X'ieth juked to his left side, avoiding the boulder just as it hit, but not avoiding the bits of rock that flew everywhere upon it breaking. He deflected rocks from his face with a raised gauntlet, feeling others pelt him in the legs, chest, and arms. Each made clangs against his armor, sounds easily lost in the continuing rumble.

X'ieth ran faster, overtaking Zeros and now, sprinting at Nathan's heels, with Finnel riding horseback about twenty cubits ahead. And then, suddenly, he noted how Finnel's horse abruptly stood on its hind legs, neighing in terror as boulders fell right in front of the beast, blocking the path and sending more rock fragments into the air! Finnel fell off the horse, hit the path, and lied there stunted.

"We have to help him!" Nathan shouted, looking over to X'ieth. The young knight nodded, and set his eyes on Finnel again, hurrying there.

Just as Nathan and X'ieth arrived to the spot, boulders fell on the horse, toppling the beast, and covering it in porous rock. Boulders continued falling right in front of him, sending rocks flying through the air. X'ieth felt the stings of them hitting him all over.

"Grab his arm, and I the other!"

At Nathan's instruction, X'ieth wrapped Finnel's arm about his shoulder, and with the pack leader, carried him in the opposite direction from danger. But upon looking back, X'ieth saw danger there too, beholding Zeros running up from about ten cubits away, with boulders falling at his rear and a huge dust cloud, coming right toward them!

"There's a ledge at our left," Zeros called out, "that shields a mountain crevice! Let's go there!"

X'ieth glanced to where Zeros pointed, seeing through the dust a nook in the rock overhung by a ledge, a possible haven from this shower of rock. Together, X'ieth and Nathan hauled Finnel over to the place, with Zeros at the lead.

As they ducked into the nook, Finnel asked in a troubled voice, "Where's Hammar?!"

With almost perfect timing, the dwarf burst from the veil of dust that filled the pass, his face showing panic just as he noticed the boulders blocking the path ahead.

"Over here!" shouted Zeros, sticking his head out of the nook and waving to Hammar.

X'ieth saw the dwarf look up and hurry toward the others, keeping both hands over his head as small rocks flew through the air, and bounced off his armor. Hammar slipped into the crevice, beside the other knights who crouched lowly, away from the opening. The knights each put two hands over their nose and mouth, trying not to be choked by the dust. Despite their best efforts, Finnel and Nathan began coughing.

From their secure area, X'ieth and the other knights watched the rock continue to rain down, burying their horse entirely. More and more dust filled the air, as the porous rock fell apart and broke everywhere. It stacked up beyond the horse's grave, barricading the trail ahead even more.

After a few minutes time, rock stopped falling and the dust began clearing.

"Who did this?!" Finnel said, out of a long silence.

"Perhaps Esmeralda knows we're nigh?" responded Nathan, who now stood and surveyed the mound of rock on the path, from out of the opening.

"This may not be the work of anyone," Zeros said then, shaking his head. "These soft rocks suggest the unthinkable." X'ieth noted a worried look about the mercenary, as another quiet developed.

"What do you suggest?" Nathan asked, turning back from the opening and looking at Zeros.

"Liath is falling apart," Zeros replied, and just as he did, a strong wind punished the other knights, as if to emphasize his point. "It's as if the mountain itself is dying, just like Forest Saol." With Zeros' speculation, X'ieth perceived how across the other knights, eyes grew wide.

Hammar spoke to himself, "Creation is dying."

"Is this what lies in store for the Triangle Kingdoms?" asked Nathan. "Is our land destined to become cold and lifeless, through Esmeralda's misdeeds?!"

The very words deepened X'ieth's resolve to stop Esmeralda from taking more of the land's energy. *She must be stopped, to protect the way of life in Sergros!* His thought was followed by a disturbing afterthought: *Sergros is the land of opportunity, but the gloom will impede many from seizing opportunity! Many will have bad destiny or no destiny, because of their gloom!*

"What do we do now?" asked Finnel.

A silence developed, with more winds blowing.

"I have an idea," said Zeros, after a few moments. X'ieth watched him get up wearily from his crouched position, to walk toward the mound of rocks where Finnel's horse died. There, the mercenary pulled Nexus into his aux core, and a green glow emanated from his midsection.

"*What...* are you doing?" asked Nathan pointedly, with some hesitation. X'ieth looked at the mercenary, who answered by doing, using magic to displace some of the rock. He kept working and working, pulling Nexus into his core and using magical force to move rocks aside. They took flight and dust filled the air, making X'ieth cough with the others, everyone shielding their eyes.

"You can't possibly clear all the rock!" shouted Nathan. "There's far too much!"

As X'ieth soon discovered, this was never the mercenary's intention. In little time, he could see that Zeros cleared just enough of the rock to reveal the carcass of Finnel's horse, and more importantly, their saddlebag.

"What will the biscuit and cheese do for us?"

"Give us a final meal upon this wasted rock," answered Hammar, in what appeared to be a sarcastic follow-up to Finnel's question.

Zeros rummaged the brown leather bag with one hand, while holding it with the other. X'ieth did not remove his eyes from the mercenary, who apparently was determined to find something inside the bag.

After a few moments, Zeros suddenly withdrew climbing gear—two ropes, one grappling hook, and a belay—and looked up to the mountain on their left. X'ieth followed the mercenary's gaze, as another icy wind blew. The young knight squinted amid the angry gust, struggling to see the ledge far above them, with hundreds of cliff wall beneath.

"The mountain trail continues up there," Nathan said, understanding now. His lips showed a smile.

Zeros smiled back.

"Aye, if we can't go forward, then let's climb up!"

Chapter 50
Choice Goes as the Lily

Nathan shouted from above, "Hold on!"

X'ieth looked up the cliff wall with despair, at his pack leader who peered down at him from the ridge above, along with Finnel and Hammar. *Destiny damn it*, thought X'ieth while clutching the rock in his gauntleted hands, as he watched the line sway beside him, taken by the weight of the grappling hook on its end. A glance down reminded him how far he and Zeros had climbed before the accident happened. *You're a hundred cubits up, maybe more… Destiny damn it!*

X'ieth now regretted climbing with Zeros instead of Hammar. Images flooded his mind at that moment, of the dwarf scaling the cliff wall with ease, having Finnel upon his back! *Let this be a lesson, man. Often preconceptions about people are wrong! Yours are especially wrong, regarding Hammar.*

His brain pieced the situation back together, of what occurred moments' prior, memories that he deemed himself fortunate to recollect, given his near death. After Nathan climbed with Hammar and Finnel, he belayed with Zeros, who professed to be an experienced climber, a statement yet to be disproven. But while scaling the mountain, the rock securing their line suddenly gave way under tension on the grappling hook, and the apparatus fell from above, first past Zeros' shoulder, and then right beside the young knight's head. *Clang! Clang! Clang!* As he recalled everything, X'ieth could still hear the hook in his ears, repeatedly bouncing off the rock.

Moments after their line was no longer secured, Zeros initially fell, though quickly latched onto the cliff face. He did it moments before the belay tightened between him and X'ieth. And until the young knight took hold the rock, Zeros somehow bore his entire weight!

X'ieth looked off to the side, seeing again the line hanging from Zeros. His eyes followed it down the cliff wall, to the grappling hook on its end. The object mocked him, as his hands slipped more on the chuck on granite. He struggled to keep his grip with a growl. "Grrhh!" "Maybe you can grab the line," Zeros said, "and try to whip it up toward the ledge!"

From above, X'ieth heard Nathan call out.

"That sounds like fool's talk! The boy will surely fall to his death."

X'ieth glared up, cockeyed and angry. *Did he really just say that?!*

"We have another rope up here!" Nathan continued. "We'll fasten it, and lower it down."

"All right," Zeros answered. "Just hold it this time! We thought the line was secure before, yet here we are!"

X'ieth leaned his chest against the rock facing him, trying hard to brace his chest up against part of it that was more flat than steep. In so doing, he hoped to relieve some weight for his tired arms. Not helping matters much, an icy wind nipped at his face. Despite it, he looked up and squinted just in time to see Nathan begin lowering the rope.

He did not take his eyes off the rope from the moment it began dropping to Zeros. Eager for the mercenary to have it, he silently cheered on the braided strands. *Closer, closer!* His cheers stopped abruptly though, when the rope suddenly stopped moving. His mouth dropped, and his eyes widened.

"That's as much line as we've got!" called Nathan.

Refusing to believe, X'ieth stared at the lowered rope that hung a bit off Zeros' waist, cubits above his head.

That's all? That's all?! X'ieth's mind rang with exasperation over the rope being too short.

He saw Zeros look down and shout.

"Worry not, you're still tied to me!"

At that, X'ieth's eyes shifted to the taut rope from the belay at Zeros' mid-section—the obvious indicator.

"I'll make it work! It needs only to reach the other line…"

As much as X'ieth was upset at Zeros, he was not in the best position to let anger dampen his hopes in the mercenary's abilities. Zeros took one hand off the rock and quickly grabbed Nathan's lowered rope, wrapping it about his hand. Taking his other hand off the rock, and now hanging by the lowered rope, he reached down to his waist, and took hold of the rope connecting his belay to the grappling hook. He pulled up enough of the line, and managed to tie it to the lowered one, using improvises of his elbow and body to knot them together.

"Pull us up!" Zeros shouted, when finished.

"Aye!" called back Hammar.

"Strong arms!" Finnel remarked, as Nathan and the dwarf pulled the line with a groan.

X'ieth felt slowly drawn up with Zeros. But after only a few moments, Nathan was heard from atop the ridge.

"Cling to the rock, so we can rest awhile!"

X'ieth got the hint, and grabbed onto some rock to alleviate the burden of their weight on the line. He looked up, and noticed how Zeros did the same, practically hugging the cliff face.

In moments, Nathan's voice was heard. "Resume!"

Like this, X'ieth and Zeros were pulled up with such intermittent stops, until they reached the top. When there, the young knight and the mercenary climbed over the ledge, with some help from Nathan and Hammar. The four knights collapsed on the rock, breathing heavily. Finnel watched them from his seat on the rock, cubits away.

X'ieth felt the winds slapping him, but he hardly cared, being thankful to Destiny that he was still alive to enjoy the moment. Vapor billowed from his mouth with each breath, and he prayed to Karnatha in earnest. *Thank you. Thank you for helping us.*

A few minutes passed, allowing the knights to recover. From his peripheral vision, X'ieth noted Nathan stand in the distance.

"Let's not sit around for these bone-chilling gusts," he said. "They're easier to endure while walking! C'mon."

X'ieth sat on the rock staring past the precipice into the sky. When Nathan spoke, he looked back to see the trail stretch up the mountain, just as it did before. The pack leader continued to hike, and one by one, the young knight watched the other knights around him get up and follow Nathan. Zeros was first to rise, jogging off. Hammar got on his feet next with a grunt; he walked over to Finnel, and stooped down so his injured friend could jump on his back. Finnel saddled Hammar, and the dwarf carried him away. The elf playfully beat Hammar's side with his scabbard, acting like he rode a horse again.

"Faster! Faster!"

"When a horse is *this* tired it won't trot, even upon your wallops," replied Hammar with a gruff laugh. "You'll have to do better than that!"

Their spirited talk faded from X'ieth's ears as he stayed there for but a moment. His head ached from not eating enough, and his body was exhausted. *Every trial is but a way marker on your path to becoming much more—to becoming Kayareth!*

With that thought, he smiled and stood up, turning toward the path and putting one foot after the other. Before walking off, however, X'ieth noticed the brown leather bag from the corner of his eye. It lied upon the rock, and contained the last of their food and the climbing gear, now re-stowed. *Saw that by chance,* he thought while picking it up, being so tired as to almost have overlooked it. He saw their water skin upon the rock too, and picked it up as well. With that, he started walking after the others.

X'ieth kept to the path, jogging briskly until seeing hints of silver and crimson ahead, through the dense fog. He ran all the more faster when viewing them, and soon settled behind Hammar, who trailed Zeros and Nathan by several cubits.

Time passed once again, as X'ieth continued up the trail with the others. It was covered in porous rock and beset by more unique rock formations on the mountain terrain. There were granite streaks and feathery ruffles married upon a canvas of stone, just as deep crevices in the rock—nooks eaten away by eons of glacial moves. All were sights worth stopping to see; yet all were sights he passed by, without even a pause.

With every step forward, X'ieth sensed how he and the others went higher up the mountain by the thinning air. At points he gasped, finding it difficult to breathe. *No option but to continue*, he told himself. *Remember, Kayareth's path is one of hardships, and such is yours.*

After another hour or so of walking, X'ieth saw Zeros stop at a crack in the mountain on the right side of the path; it was large enough for someone thin to go through—a seeming slit in the rock. Hammar passed by Zeros with Finnel still on his back, and just the same, X'ieth walked by. He glanced to his rear in passing, and saw Zeros in a complete standstill at the crack, just continuing to stare at it. *What's he doing?*

"Come now, let's make haste!" Nathan yelled. "We're hours until nightfall, and there's still more to hike."

X'ieth looked away from Zeros and up the path, seeing that Nathan had stopped walking, turned about, and now fixated on the mercenary. He crossed his arms, appearing frustrated over the small delay this caused.

X'ieth returned his stare to Zeros, and waited upon his reaction, wanting to see if the mercenary would linger at the crack or not.

"Does anyone else hear that?" asked Zeros.

Ice-cold winds whistled through the pass, making it difficult for X'ieth to discern any other noise. *Not a thing. Are you missing something, man?*

"That's water I hear," Zeros said, looking again to the crack. "We should fill the skin before continuing! There's not much water left."

Nathan uncrossed his arms, and walked over.

"What are you saying?" he asked.

"I hear running water in this crack!"

"Surely you joke!" Nathan laughed, coming to Zeros' side. "There can't be water in a mountain that falls apart, one which stands high above the dead forest of Saol."

X'ieth watched Zeros lean toward the crack, as if attuning his ear by increased proximity. He looked back smugly, knowing better. "I hear what I hear. It's water."

X'ieth stood there, witnessing another cycle of the same thing: Nathan rehashing his denial, professing not to hear a thing; Zeros, as expected, countering that. The whole time, the young knight experienced a prompting of sorts—to exercise choice and do, to take initiative even though the situation weighed heavily on his pack leader.

"I don't hear a thing!" shouted Nathan over another freezing wind. "Let's just go!" He pointed to the path urgently, as if time ran short and the matter of progress was now left unattended.

X'ieth blurted out, "I'll check!"

The comment brought an immediate end to the cycles of bickering between Zeros and Nathan. They turned to the young knight, who stood with both hands raised, as if to quell further contention. "I'll go quickly, and see."

X'ieth swiveled his head on his neck, from Nathan to Zeros, gleaning mixed looks from the pair. The mercenary seemed satisfied, yet the pack leader did not.

"Fine, boy," Nathan said after a sigh. "Take the skin into the crack, and if there be water, fill it up."

Without waiting for an invitation, X'ieth handed the saddlebag to Zeros and edged his body through the opening with the water skin pressed against his chest.

"Fearless the lad is," Finnel commented to Hammar, while X'ieth was still within earshot.

"Not courage but comfort!" countered the dwarf. "It's warmer in there than out here! The winds can't beat him down inside."

Their talk faded on X'ieth's ears, as he slipped further through the crack. In his eyes, the little light on the path was soon replaced by darkness, and all he could see was black. He kept going deeper into the crevice nevertheless, and it seemed like the walls began closing in on him, at times making it difficult to breathe. *What if you get stuck! How will they even get you out?!* Reasonable concerns went through his head, yet they were not enough to stop him now. For there was no turning back given what X'ieth wanted: exercising his choice rather than leaving the outcome to chance. *The chance of whether Nathan or Zeros would prevail…*

As X'ieth continued into the crevice, a musty cave smell filled his nostrils. Upon his ears, a slow trickle became faintly audible, from somewhere nearby. He slipped more through the blackness, and the same sounds grew even louder, to the point where it seemed like he stood right over them. New scents entered his nose then, those of a mellow citrus; they intermingled with the cave's mustiness. X'ieth suddenly felt cool liquid flow around his boot. With another step, something soft brushed upon his cheek, sensations across his face too, thin strands all over. Without light, he imagined what it could be. *Have you become entangled in a spider's web?* Using his free hand, he struggled to wipe his face in the confined space.

When the darkness shifted up ahead, X'ieth stopped. *What was that?!* he wondered, concerned that something might alive might be there. The sight added to his array of discomforts, gotten from so many unknown sensations since entering the cave. The darkness stirred again, and instantly his mind began inventing monsters from the black, carnivores lurking in this shadowy domain that survive off human flesh. *Have you volunteered to enter a creature's lair?!* The question popped into his head, and stayed at the forefront of his mind. It was then that fear paralyzed him, and his nerves frayed. The young knight's heart pounded in his chest, and a vice developed over him, which constricted his breathing even more than the walls.

Millicent's voice echoed his head. *Do you disappoint yourself as much as you disappoint me?* The voice angered him each time it rang out, until the point where he would not tolerate his immobilization anymore. *You'll not be anyone's disappointment, man! Neither hers, nor Nathan's and Zeros'!* In one sudden motion, he wedged himself through the remainder of the crevice, into what seemed to be a larger space. As he moved, he heard his feet splashing, sounds that rose above the nearby trickling.

With two final splashes, he settled in the middle of the space, still being in complete darkness. He felt a crawling at the side of his neck. Instinctively, he pulled against his Source entry to fill his aux core with Nexus. A single inflow filled his small channeling chamber to capacity, and he hurled raw energy in the cave to create light. It reflected off objects in the space, and hit his eyes. In that moment X'ieth saw a cave about him, having the backdrop of hanging stalactites. He looked down, seeing water all around his feet; it formed a pool overtop of an aqua-green rock floor, which seemed to glow from the dispersion of light. A tiny hole in the cave's far wall admitted a trickle of water, which sourced the pool. *What is this? You've never seen rocks like these before...*

The crawling sensation came back on his neck, stealing his attention from the cave and its strange pool. X'ieth clawed over his neck, and afterward brought his gauntleted hand before his face, to peer down at it. Upon his palm walked a small spider having a furry thorax, tinged in the same aqua hue as the rock! The sight alarmed him, and his first impulse was to kill the creature.

Life in a dying world! From deep in his mind, a voice urged him to stop. *Life in a dying world!* The voice got louder and louder in his head, until the point where X'ieth put his hand up to the wall, and let the spider climb off. As he watched the spider scale the rock, he slowly realized its significance; this was literally the only life he had seen since leaving Arlem, aside from the mountain lily. *The spider is alive, when nothing else is!*

The light faded, soon leaving X'ieth in darkness again. He breathed the musty air, still hearing the trickle of water in his ears. *You're taking too long, man. Fill the skin and get out, before Zeros taps you on the shoulder about leader's disdain!* He smirked at the thought of Zeros following him into the cave, should he take too long.

X'ieth lowered his water skin toward the pool, but when coming nigh, he stopped himself from the dipping its neck below the water's surface. It was the water's smell that worried him. *That fruit scent!* It brought to mind the aqua-green rock, and new questions about whether the water was even safe to drink.

In his head, he weighed the options. On one hand, he could just fill the skin with this strange water. *That's why you came here, man... Just do it!* On the other hand, he thought how filling the skin might contaminate the water that remains. *You'll poison your fellow knights.* To X'ieth, the possible options were obvious, along with the perceived risks. He wrestled with the decision for a moment, before making his choice. *The risk of poisoning everyone seems great, so just leave. The chance of getting drinking water is not worth everyone's death.*

So with his decision made, X'ieth wedged himself back through the crevice in utter darkness, and kept the water skin pressed up against his chest. In what seemed a minute or two of pushing himself through the cave, he emerged from the crack onto the pass beneath the gray sky. Outside, the light irritated X'ieth's eyes, and he raised his hand to shield them. Behind his hand, he could tell Nathan and Zeros stood there looking at him, their faces suggesting that they wanted some answers.

"That took a while," said Nathan impatiently.

"Did you find the water?" asked Zeros.

It occurred to X'ieth then, he spent time to go search for the water, and though finding it, he did nothing with the opportunity to fill the skin. His choice suddenly seemed wrong by both pack leader and mercenary, and he opened his mouth, hesitant to speak. *Out with it, man. Tell of what you found, and your decision.*

"There's a stream back there all right," X'ieth admitted. "A stream of poison!" His hands waved dramatically as he went on. "The water is green, and smells of moldy fruit! It seems unfit to drink!" As he spoke X'ieth felt cold from the icy glares of Nathan and Zeros. Their eyes along numbed him, both men standing without a word, like they froze over with ire.

"Did you not bring your wit with you?" asked Zeros pointedly, as another harsh wind ravaged the knights. Beyond the mercenary, X'ieth saw Hammar standing with Finnel upon his back, supporting his friend's legs from under the knees. The dwarf shifted his weight, seeming somewhat uncomfortable.

"Look at me!" Zeros shouted, drawing the young knight's attention. His gaze wandered back to the mercenary, and when it settled, he did not dare blink. "We could've boiled it. Water be water, so we best fill up."

"Yet he took time," muttered Nathan, shaking his head. The pack leader signed in frustration.

Like a statue, X'ieth stood with the water skin. Unexpectedly, he felt Zeros snatch it right from his grip. In return, the man put the saddlebag in his hands. He saw the mercenary then turn toward the crack, letting a cross look be the last impression upon the young knight before entering. *His attitude we all can do without! What's gotten into him lately?*

While waiting on his return, X'ieth's head swam in thoughts that placed Zeros very low in the world. He felt angry over how the mercenary scolded him in front of the others, as well as how the mercenary read his thoughts earlier. The whole time, Nathan sent him icy glares that made the gloom's weather seem warm and cozy.

X'ieth equated the situation to his failures of pleasing Millicent at home. *Damned if you do, man… And damned if you don't! To the Void with it all…* His mind stepped a bit further, and he considered how choice failed him. *Should've let the two of 'em settle the feud about filling that skin! Should've left it to chance…*

A minute or two passed, and X'ieth finally saw Zeros emerge from the crack, with the water skin full and dripping. He tossed it to X'ieth with a scowl. X'ieth caught the skin in one hand, and tucked it under his arm.

"Filled it to the neck," Zeros said in a steely tone. "It's what should've been done all along."

Nathan nodded silently, having lost ground.

"Let's go," he said, spinning about to continue his insistent hike up the mountain. Everyone followed after him, the clangs of their armor filling the air. Seconds turned into minutes, and minutes into hours, as it now went well beyond midday.

After walking some time, X'ieth's throat became parched, and it did not take long for him to regret not drinking some water before Zeros contaminated their supply. *You should've had water then!* Yet despite the contamination, his desiring eyes fell upon the glistening lip of the water skin, and his nose picked up perky citrus notes that wafted toward him. *Don't do it…*

X'ieth raised his eyes to avoid the temptation of the water skin, yet when he did, a strong wind blew and kept his head down. Once more, he came face-to-face with the water skin and his own desires. *Just think if you left your safety to chance, and just drank the water? Would you live or die?* His throat seemed so dry in the moment that he toyed with the idea of gambling his own life on a drink.

Once more, Lucen's words from Arlem circulated through his head. *Some things are unavoidable, and such is your fate… All you must do is be, and great things will come to you!* Chance tempted him through the water skin, and his will against it lessened by the step.

After the wind died, X'ieth looked back up to the path with a smile, hearing the sounds of the other knights' advance, and some distant talk among Hammar and Finnel. As he walked behind them, the implications of chance slowly swelled in his mind. *There's no stopping your good destiny. Like Lucen said, you just have to be and greatness will come! It is your good fortune, in this land of opportunity!*

Abruptly, X'ieth stopped himself on the path as the others walked ahead. Standing there, he undid the water skin's clasp, raised it to his lips, and guzzled a bit, being intolerant of having thirst a moment longer. The green water was cool upon his tongue, having dulled sweetness and tang, like a diluted potion of water and citrus juice. The moment he swished it in his mouth, chance's triumph over choice tasted so incredibly good.

Upon swallowing, X'ieth did not notice any immediate effect, for the good or the bad. *See, man… A little sip didn't kill you!* But as X'ieth continued walking, the cold winds did not faze him anymore, his tiredness and hunger melted away like ice on a sweltering day. He felt completely rejuvenated, like he had rested for weeks!

With elation beyond compare, X'ieth ran up the path, past Hammar and Finnel riding piggyback, beyond the hostile Zeros, all the way before Nathan. Each step felt to him like walking on clouds, light and bouncy. Nathan stopped in his tracks when X'ieth settled before him, and the young knight smiled widely. Nathan, conversely, showed a face suggesting he had gone mad.

"Stop at once!" X'ieth said joyously, as the other knights piled up behind Nathan.

He lifted the water skin high over his head.

"You must drink this!" He beamed even more now, feeling giddy like a child would, when proud of a particular feat. *Your feat being, taking this risk of drinking this water, supposedly poison but not!*

Everyone looked at X'ieth blankly, as if puzzled.

"Boiling it, you ought not to do!" he exclaimed. "That might remove the water's natural properties! I've drank the water as is, and it mended my body and spirit!" He looked beyond the pack leader to Zeros. "I can now walk on for days!" he shouted, and then glanced to Hammar and Finnel. "Without sleep even!" His words came enthusiastically, full of zest.

But when X'ieth extended the water skin, Nathan and Hammar took a step back. Finnel deflected it with a raised hand, from Hammar's back.

"Keep it away, lad!" said Nathan, acting fearful.

"Aye, I'll stay thirsty," added Hammar, Finnel just shaking his head.

X'ieth turned to Zeros and offered the water skin. He watched Zeros raise an eyebrow, as if noting something obviously different about the young knight. After a few moments of complete silence, a few angry winds between, the mercenary took the skin and slowly raised it to his lips.

"Don't do it!" shouted Nathan, a protest that came much too late. For as the pack leader spoke, light green fluid dribbled down Zeros' chin, as he chugged the water.

The sight increasingly bothered Nathan.

"No more!" he yelled, throwing up both hands. "Just boil the water when we set camp! We don't know anything about it!"

With Nathan's second protest, Zeros stopped.

"As you wish," said the mercenary, lowering the skin from his lips. Zeros fastened the clasp and threw it back to X'ieth, who again, snatched it from the air and tucked it beneath his free arm, the other still carrying the saddlebag.

His eyes trailed to the skin's glistening lip once more. The sight made him smile. *There's something very special about this water!*

When X'ieth looked up, he saw Zeros looking right back at him, smirking. And it was then that the young knight noticed something different about the mercenary's chin. The dribble of green water streaked through his stubble and left behind shiny skin, new and hairless. *Do the others see that?!* He wondered if tired attentions made the detail unobvious, or if rather, he was just imagining it. When Zeros turned to follow after Hammar, Finnel, and Nathan, X'ieth decided he would say nothing and just continue along the path.

Dusk fell upon the five knights as they walked the western pass some more. A winding trail took them up around the mountain, with its one side open to deadly heights. Off the path, X'ieth saw adjacent granite domes on the horizon, having rings of haze hung at multiple levels below their apexes. Upon hearing loud cracks, he gazed down to see the distant Forest Saol, sitting beneath a layer of gloom. Green light flickered from the woods, and energy flowed into the air. X'ieth followed the stream up from its source, until the point where it disappeared into the very fog screen that covered their path up the mountain!

Nathan pointed to the energy.

"Follow it!"

With the other knights, X'ieth chased after the stream of Nexus energy, clearly something headed into Esmeralda's tower. And with only a few strides more, the knights all happened upon a surprising thing. There, standing high into the gloom was a tower of gray stone. It was round, four stories tall, with one door on the bottom and a single window at its top, with the Nexus floating through that upper casement.

Upon making the visual, X'ieth looked the tower up and down, not believing his eyes. He wondered then, *Did our climb lessen the journey?! Nathan spoke of camp tonight, for naught?*

The tower's door being open caught X'ieth's attention. It was cracked ajar, as if someone either left or came in a hurry. He glanced to the knights ahead of him—Hammar and Finnel frontward, Zeros to his left, and Nathan to his right—and all of them stared at the same. *An open door, right into the tower...* It seemed too good to be true.

X'ieth and the other knights drew their swords, including Finnel, just as Hammar readied his hammer. Their naked blades gleamed in the enclosing darkness, catching the glow from green energies flowing overhead, into the tower.

X'ieth had an immediate fluttery sensation inside, and his mind danced with fancies of his good destiny. *This is it*, he thought to himself. *This is where you meet the inevitable!* He envisioned himself once more, in a grand scene at Gallow Cliff, where his strong voice rang through the air, rallying the Army of Light to great victory there. But while his imagination bequeathed determination, his favorable chance imparted strength. *That water sustains you, surely just for this!*

A grin snuck to the corner of X'ieth's lips, as he saw Nathan motion for them to move forward. He took a few steps with the other knights, before Zeros harshly whispered, bringing everyone to a sudden stop.

"The tower's defenses are down!" said the mercenary. X'ieth's eyes followed to where Zeros pointed: pyramids of smooth gray stone that beset to the foot of the tower, spaced in a circle going around it. "Nexus ordinarily flows between these *ward stones*, energizing a defensive magical field that implements devastating strikes against intruders!" Zeros briefly described how he heard Magicia's fortress was exactly like this.

"It's been disarmed!" Zeros said. "Something is very wrong! Maybe this is a trap!"

X'ieth struggled to see his preoccupation. *A disarmed tower is a good tower...*

Nathan gave a disapproving nod. "We're going in nonetheless! If she invites us, let it be an invitation to take her life and end this wrong!"

X'ieth stood in place with the other knights, the fog rolling around them and the tower looming high. And then suddenly upon his ears, sounded a deep roar from the gloom, both earsplitting and startling!

RAWWWRRR! ... RAWWWRRRR!

X'ieth felt sudden winds gust over him, starting then stopping. He turned his head, sighting the silhouette of a massive winged creature through the gloom, flying right toward the five knights! His mouth opened, and his adrenaline flowed.

"Draaaaaaggggggoooon!" Zeros shouted, his voice stretching the word.

"Quickly, let's get inside!" Nathan yelled, pointing to the tower's door with his sword, motioning for the knights to take refuge there.

X'ieth hurried without wasting a single moment, just as the other knights. Behind him, he heard the dragon's loud roar, he felt strong winds from flapping wings, and he saw the entire tower blanketed by a huge shadow. It caused him to sprint even faster toward the door, now about ten cubits away. The sights and sounds got X'ieth's heart thumping in his chest, and he felt sudden pulsations of blood throbbing his temple.

RAWWWRRRR! ... RAWWWRRRR!
Thump thump! Thump thump! Thump thump!
RAWWWRRRR! ... RAWWWRRRR!

Just as the dragon swooped for them, the knights funneled into the doorway, with perfect timing. Nathan slammed the door shut and latched it. X'ieth backed away in darkness, hearing the dragon claws scrape the rock outside, followed by noisy crumbling. The dragon released a loud roar, one that literally shook the stone tower.

RAWWWWWWWRRRRRRRR!

X'ieth's mouth dropped open, as he wondered if the knights would be safe inside, from this unexpected threat!

"UP LIATH"

Chapter 51
Esmeralda's Fortress Abode

Inky blackness was all he could see. Indeed, the light outside no longer aided X'ieth's eyes, once Nathan slammed the door shut from within Esmeralda's tower. His ears, however, could still hear the menacing sounds from which the knights fled.

RAWWWRRRR! ... RAWWWRRRR!

A booming dragon's roar suddenly shook the double doors! X'ieth looked at the doors open-mouthed, worried that the threat outside might break into the tower to pursue after them. As the floors and walls of the tower literally quaked from noise, just like the doors, the dragon's power tripled his worry. *Destiny keep us...*

But suddenly then, different sounds could be heard: wings flapping and growing distant, just as one final roar, this time seeing mournful. X'ieth stood still in the darkness, watching Finnel's face move, a faint outline of lips swathed in shadows.

"What's happening?!" he whispered, still hanging off Hammar's back.

Nathan shushed him. "Shhh..."

X'ieth listened as the sounds faded, gradually. When silence replaced the fearsome roars, his heart rejoiced. *It left! The dragon left!* The conclusion appealed to him on many levels, the primary being that he would not have to confront both a dragon and a sorceress.

Whew. His mind settled just as his body, soon recovering from the adrenaline rush that brought him into the tower. His heartbeats and breathing slowed and he felt less wired, each moment the knights waited in the quiet.

When his eyes better adjusted to the tower, X'ieth looked around, taking in his surroundings. He stood in a foyer of gray stone that narrowed into a corridor, with torches mounted upon its walls, all being strangely unlit. Tapestries bedecked the walls between torches, having embroideries that depicted three kings and three kingdoms—the humans, dwarves, and elves. *The Triangle Kingdoms*, he thought to himself, upon making the visual. Alternating with the tapestries, the hallway had several closed doors on its left and right, leading off into other parts of the tower. At its vanishing point, the corridor ended in a stairwell.

Suddenly, in his ears arose the faint sounds of people talking. The noise grabbed his attention, reminding him then that there was still a confrontation to be had. He attuned his ears, struggling to hear well. *They're arguing, not talking... And it's a party of at least two, definitely females...* He glanced at Zeros and Nathan, who both showed straight faces, while they too listened intently.

Everyone looked to Nathan for direction, including X'ieth. After only a few moments, the pack leader waved the knights down the hall and began stepping clandestinely that way, his sword raised. Zeros was on his heels, as was Hammar following behind. X'ieth crept behind Finnel, who rode the dwarf with his blade drawn.

As they went down the hall, he noted other details there. Below the tapestries that adorned both walls, was a waist-high, marble trim; it framed paneled motifs of recurring themes. He studied them in passing, and was able to make a keen observation: *Every tile involves the Guild's serpent, and the serpent has a varied diet...* The young knight looked across the panels, showing the Guild consuming everything from defiant leaders to fruits of wisdom. The symbolism gave a very real sense of the Guild's perceived standing in not just the Mainland, but also, in the whole of Karnath.

X'ieth proceeded with his fellow knights through the remainder of the corridor. Everyone stepped softly, and no one made as much as a peep. They passed many sealed entrances to adjoining chambers, which X'ieth watched from the corners of his eyes, ready for one of the doors to open suddenly and reveal a threat. But despite his suspicions, this never happened, and the group continued unharmed until the next chamber beyond the corridor's end, where a slim spiral staircase awaited them. It had smooth, marble steps that fanned up to higher levels of the tower, along its inner wall.

Beside the stairs, X'ieth saw more elaborate statues of marble, further immortalizing the Guild's serpent. The statues stood beneath cascading motifs on the walls, going up the stairwell as far as the eye could see. In one, X'ieth saw symbolism of the serpent's coils binding the hands of kings, those same coils hushing the king's speech in another. He noted astutely how there was no depiction of the Guild related to the king's sight, as prophecy was reserved for the oracles, not those practicing sorcery.

X'ieth heard more sounds faintly from above, the voices of at least two women shouting, maybe more. *This is it... This is where you fight her.* The very thought fluttered his stomach with certain angst, causing X'ieth to feel less confident than before. Now being on the eve of confronting Esmeralda changed his anticipations of facing her from days' prior. He swallowed hard and gripped his sword tighter, trying to prepare himself for what would come.

In the darkness, X'ieth saw Nathan lift a sword toward the stairs. The young knight watched his leader go first, and then Zeros, followed by Hammar with Finnel clinging to his back. For a few moments, he paused his advance and stood still before the steps, watching Finnel and Hammar disappear around the staircase's center. In an effort to be calm, he took a long breath and waited a few seconds, before starting his climb. *This is it!*

Up the staircase X'ieth went, his left hand bracing the outer wall having the motifs, and his right holding his sword. The steps were dark, as each torch between motifs was in its sleeve, cold and unlit. One by one, he continued taking the steps until reaching Hammar and Finnel, who apparently piled behind Zeros and Nathan at tower's second level.

When X'ieth stopped behind Finnel, he wondered why everyone was there. In absence of an answer, he quieted himself and listened. At first there was nothing to hear but silence, and then out of it, muffled voices emerged of females arguing. The sounds came from above them, higher up in the tower.

Nathan waved everyone forward. X'ieth observed the signal, and followed Hammar and Finnel past the second level without stopping. *Esmeralda is not alone*, X'ieth thought nervously as he took the steps fanning to the third level. He wondered what that might mean for their confrontation. *Esmeralda would only take company of elite members of the Guild*, he considered, and with that, his dormant concerns awakened about confronting two powerful sorceresses. Once again X'ieth gulped, losing count of how many times now.

More steps brought the five knights to the tower's third floor, where X'ieth could definitely decipher two females speaking Mainlandish, still above them. He estimated a fierce contention went on between them.

"This has gone on long enough! You're now in danger!"

"Silence already! You just want the shard, to empower yourself!"

The voices continued in the distance.

Nathan gave the signal for everyone to continue on to the next level. So X'ieth, behind his fellow knights, advanced to the top of the spiral staircase, his anxiety heightening with his ascension of the tower. He held his sword ready, tightening his grip on it yet again, as his hands sweated beneath the gauntlets. *This is it...* he realized, a thing both exhilarating and terrifying.

When completing their climb, the sword-brandishing knights assembled in a foyer at the top of the spiral staircase, before an open doorway that led into the main chamber on the tower's fourth floor. Zeros and Nathan rushed to its left side, and Hammar, Finnel, and X'ieth stayed at its right side.

Like the others, X'ieth peered around the door post into the room ahead, seeing Esmeralda and Magicia bickering there, both of them wearing yellow robes of the Guild! They stood between an object stuck in the floor, with a double window hung behind them, opening to the vistas of Liath and Saol. In that moment, he hoped that the Guardsmen's position in the foyer was obstructed from their vantage point. The worry, however, dissipated as the two siblings kept at it, as if not even noticing the knights had climbed the stairs and now, lied in wait.

Never having seen Magicia's sister before, X'ieth remarked in that moment about their close resemblance. In many ways, Esmeralda appeared exactly similar, though she had straight hair versus curly and stood taller by a small measure. But beyond his moment of pondering the two's likeness, he was stricken by sheer terror once more. *Esmeralda and Magicia! Destiny, please let Magicia's promise to Talus be true…*

As he prayed, X'ieth experienced a slight tremble in his hands and body. At first, it made him feel bad, like somehow he were so fearful of Esmeralda and Magicia that he literally shook. But then, he thought differently, how perhaps the entire tower shook. He glanced at Hammar, who shifted on his feet as if to compensate for the tremor, but no sooner resumed peering into the chamber, a thing from which X'ieth had become distracted and was no longer doing. *You best do the same…*

With that, X'ieth peered back into the room, beholding Magicia and Esmeralda still arguing, with their attention on each other. The mere sight of them clamped X'ieth's chest and raised his heart rate. He relieved his anxieties by taking his eyes off them, to scan the rest of the room. His eyes jumped from the sorceresses, to the window, and then to the object in the floor, and it was then that he happened upon something of sheer beauty—something that he had overlooked until now.

At the room's center stood a glowing sword, wedged into the floor's deep crack. The sword was broken evenly down its entire blade and handle, burning a luminous green from all the Nexus concentrated in its blade. The sight had an inexplicable allure to X'ieth, and he found himself mesmerized by it. *The white shard of sword…*

He pried his eyes off it, placing them upon Esmeralda, who suddenly walked to the window. He ducked behind the corner completely, his heart striking a fearful percussion for this lackluster performance. *The whole journey, you've been anticipating this moment so much, to only stand here afraid?! Why don't you step into the room, and leave this up to chance?!* His inner voice instigated him amidst personal disappointment and fear.

Slowly, X'ieth made a modest gain on his terror, bringing himself to look around the corner once more. He saw Esmeralda, still at the window, pulling Nexus from outside; it emanated from Liath and floated in energy streams, both through the sky and toward the tower. When Nexus came to the casement, Esmeralda sucked it into her core. X'ieth fixed on her mid-section then, as it suddenly shined a radiant green and grew increasingly bright. He watched the light's intensity increase, until the moment where Esmeralda discharged it. With awe, he observed Nexus arc from her midsection with a bright flash, toward the middle of the chamber, where it entered the sword!

His attention was then on the shard, as its blade grew greener, coursing with Nexus. It reflected power and prestige, things that jumped in his eyes. It brought to mind the mention of a white shard from the Light Prophecy. *Can it be, this is what Esmeralda uses for evil?!* he thought. *Is this how you're meant to acquire the white shard?!*

Nathan budged, drawing X'ieth's attention. The pack leader raised a straight index finger on his lip, indicating for everyone to remain quiet. X'ieth nodded to signal his compliance, and then returned his eyes upon the chamber. Esmeralda repeated what she did before, pulling more energy from Liath and throwing it into the shard, while continuing her argument with Magicia.

"I am soon to be named the most powerful sorceress in Karnath!" she exclaimed. "You envy my rise to power, a power above your own!" During her words, Esmeralda's face became incredibly intense. She narrowed her eyes, and barred her teeth, as the energy's light danced in her pupils.

You are soon to be named the Child of Darkness! X'ieth thought, tightening his grip on his sword again, his aspirations of becoming the hero wrestling with his own anxieties about confronting Esmeralda.

"This is foolish!" Magicia shouted at her sister. "Realize that Sergros witnesses you drawing loose energy into your tower. Others perhaps see this too! In plain sight, you merely steal that which breaks free of creation!"

"Foolish to stop!" Esmeralda countered. "Let all behold what I've done, everyone from kings of kingdoms, to Maltimar at the Guild! Let all know my power!"

Magicia cut her off.

"There is *no* power! You're not ripping the primary core of Karnath to spill its life force." Tears welled up in her eyes as she continued. "Something much Darker is doing this! Please, you have to believe me!"

X'ieth caught bits and pieces of the conservation, not understanding any of it. *What are they talking about?!*

"Believe you?! When all you want is the shard's power?! And how dare you suggest I'm not responsible for this! Surely your jealousy speaks yet again, for I now wield powers in excess of you!"

"Please, believe me!" Magicia said. "What you're doing has not empowered you at all…"

Esmeralda's face contorted in anger, and X'ieth was perceptive of that. *That comment struck a nerve!*

"Oh, I am not empowered?!" Esmeralda shot back, as if resenting the remark.

Hammar leaned with Finnel against the wall. X'ieth stood behind him, watching the dwarf raise a hand to Nathan, gesturing confusion over the prolonged waiting. In the darkness, Nathan's lips mouthed two words. *Not yet…*

"Then how do you explain this great power I've amassed?!" Esmeralda asked. X'ieth peered into the room once more, just in time to see her motion to the luminous shard with animate hands. "I am indeed powerful, sister. And you shall come to fear my power!"

Esmeralda screamed the words, immediately taking hold of the broken sword.

The act sent alarms off in X'ieth's head. *Stop her! Don't let her use the white shard for evil!* Yet, despite his alarms, the young knight stayed put, his fear compounding with the absence of Nathan's signal to advance. *But if Nathan commanded you to enter, would you even go?* His inner voice challenged the true reason for him remaining in position, instead of just facing Esmeralda, here and now.

He swallowed again, watching Esmeralda walk through the chamber with the glowing shard in hand. His eyes fell on its blade, and immediately, the sight rendered him spellbound, a captive of his own desires. With lips curling into a smile, his eyes chased after it, their glossy pupils trapping the sword's brilliance.

"Stop this!" pled Magicia.

X'ieth's attention redirected on her.

"You think you steal Karnath's power in some delusion, but Sergros thinks it by mistake! I let Sergros make this mistake, a kingdom that now sends knights to slay you!"

Esmeralda lifted the shard high in both hands, holding it at the handle.

"I care not! Let them come, let them face *this* power! Let anyone try to stop me, including you!"

And then, in a moment unanticipated by anyone in the room—even Magicia—Esmeralda attempted linking to the shard's core to pull rather than to push, in order to use the Nexus energy stored inside. But after establishing the link, something happened unlike every occasion where Esmeralda had pushed energy to the shard before. That something, being absolutely nothing. Esmeralda could not pull the power out of the blade, only push power to the blade, and the finding made her incredibly mad.

"Arrgghh!" she screamed, shrilly.

Esmeralda dropped one hand from the shard's handle, and used it to rent the sleeve of her robe, removing her colored bands to throw them on the floor! To X'ieth it seemed impulsive, a thing that stripped the sorceress of her marks of power in the Guild, perhaps done hastily in a moment where she felt powerless.

"Stop it!" Magicia pled again. "I would've told you this from the start, had I known! The shard is an ancient weapon, and its core has a lock fashioned by Karnatha, so that only the Children of Destiny can use it!"

Magicia gazed at the floor briefly, and then back up.

"You may find it hard to believe," she told Esmeralda, "but you've only been capturing life force as creation's fabric tears… You see, Karnath is falling apart, due to curse from the future!"

Esmeralda's eyes widened and she snarled, right before casting the shard upon the floor in one sudden instant, an act seemingly done in anger and with all her might! X'ieth's ears filled with clangs as the glowing shard bounced against the stone at the midst of the chamber, sounds that soon were drowned out by another scream from Esmeralda. "Aggggrrrhhhhhhhhhh!"

She pulled at her hair and garments, wildly furious.

X'ieth witnessed all the violence, from Esmeralda ripping off her bands and hurling the sword, to the screaming and once again, the ripping of her cloths. She tore the top of her robe, revealing the white-skinned expanse of one bosom. Through his mind went one thing, and one thing only: *The Child of Wrath!* It was the alias for the Child of Darkness, straight out of the Light Prophecy.

"Aggghhh! Uggghhh!" Esmeralda continued to shriek, lost for how to verbally express her immense rage. Her body quivered as she paced the chamber. Magicia stood nearby, and looked terribly worried for her sister while all of this happened.

When X'ieth saw motion among the assembled knights, he looked over to see Nathan suddenly signal their advance, from the other side of the doorway! It multiplied his anxieties, filling his stomach with flutters. The young knight felt a bit light-headed, and nearly lost his balance. But while he reacted to all of what the signal meant—a confrontation with Esmeralda and Magicia, right now—the knights were not about to wait for him to be ready. Nathan barged right into the room with his naked sword, and beside him was Hammar, with his club hammer out and ready for action, as well as Finnel upon his back, who also wielded his sword.

With debilitating uneasiness, X'ieth made a pathetic attempt to step forward, but only budged a little, his fear holding him back. But even a budge was enough for Zeros to act. For with that alone, he blocked X'ieth's advance!

"Stay here, if you value your life!" warned the mercenary, rushing to the other side of the door, and in front of X'ieth. Zeros drilled into him with stalwart blue eyes, causing X'ieth to swallow.

He watched as Zeros went into the room with the other knights, and immediately, he felt out of place for not following. *Go, he's not your leader! Or, are you too afraid?!* He gulped hard, now finding the true reason for his iron feet, given he stayed in hiding even when commanded to action.

"By order of the King of Sergros," Nathan shouted, "this affair must end!"

Petrified like a tree, X'ieth was unable to move. While he wanted to obtain his good destiny, the matter of confronting Esmeralda and Magicia completely immobilized him. It put visions in his mind, of both sisters killing the Guard gruesomely with arcane magical powers, their blood and guts going everywhere. And the mere thought of that tragic end to their quest reduced him to a coward, hiding in the shadows.

Under his gauntlets, his palms felt sweaty. In deep thumps, his heart raced beneath his breastplate. And once again, he sensed his body tremble, from the foot up. A small part of him wondered if the tower itself were moving, but he dismissed the notion in humility, knowing well the telltale signs of visceral fear.

From his place of hiding, he directed his eyes to the other knights, now in the main chamber. Nathan stood at the front, Hammar at the left with Finnel, and Zeros at the right. All four of them had their weapons drawn, ready for use. Esmeralda and Magicia had whipped their heads around from the moment Nathan announced himself, and continued looking his way, their faces plastered with surprise—raised foreheads, arched brows, and wide eyes.

"For causing the gloom, you'll be tried in Sergros' courts, Esmeralda!" continued Nathan. "There, due punishment shall be set!"

"And who's taking me there?" asked Esmeralda.

She pulled Nexus into her aux core; it lit up green.

"You four, the Sergrothian circus?!"

Cringing, X'ieth watched as Esmeralda's feet rose off the floor, and her body levitated on a field of Nexus energy. She held her hands palm-up, at her waist. Then surprisingly, Magicia did exactly the same. Hung midair, the two sisters appeared cold as ice with faces stern as stone and red locks flowing in an aura of Nexus that suddenly developed about their bodies. Their midsections glowed green as they both filled their cores, readying themselves to attack.

The whole while, X'ieth watched as the fight began, unable to look away, and still, unable to join his fellow knights. The confrontation with Esmeralda was turning into exactly what he feared all along: an engagement with two powerful sorceresses. *Magicia's promise of not stopping the Guard was a lie!* While the outcome validated X'ieth's concerns, it made him feel no less of a coward given that he was nothing more than a spectator.

Do something, man! On one hand, he felt urges to blitz the room with his unsheathed sword—to help the Guardsmen, to seize his good destiny. Yet regardless of those motivations, he lingered in the foyer, hiding inside the doorway. It was a cowardly act that begged the question: *Are you really Kayareth?!* But that question went unanswered in his mind, as X'ieth continued to wonder why he—the supposed hero—would tend toward deeds lacking the slightest heroism.

"Tether with me!" shouted Zeros to Nathan.

"Aye, let us!" replied Nathan.

In that moment, X'ieth saw them blink their eyes shut, concentrate, and just like that, raw energy sparked between them, signifying their connection.

"Links to you!" Finnel shouted, on Hammar's back with his sword held high. X'ieth observed more energy flow from Finnel and Hammar, suggesting the two connected to the combined aux core of Nathan and Zeros.

And with that, the fight broke out in a single instant. X'ieth watched Nathan and Zeros spin into a cyclone of steel aimed at Esmeralda, as Hammar and Finnel pushed energy to them, while blocking Magicia from interfering. Both sorceresses threw green fire—Esmeralda at Nathan, and Magicia at both Hammar and Finnel. Zeros stopped right in the middle of a sword form and pulled enough Nexus to cast a shield over Nathan. However, the mercenary could not protect Hammar in the same way; the dwarf hurled his hammer right into Magicia's fire.

With mouth agape, X'ieth beheld Magicia mediate through the Nexus, to disappear right before Hammar's weapon struck, and reappear immediately behind the dwarf! Meanwhile, when the steel shaft of his hammer conducted heat from her fire, it forced him to drop the hammer, and cry out in writing pain.

"Arrggghhh!"

Hammer stared at his blistered hands, while his weapon—aglow with orange—clattered to the floor. From Hammar's back, Finnel leaned toward Magicia, swinging his sword. But she parried by stepping back, and pushed more energy from her aux core to both palms. Finnel leaned more, and swung all the more wildly, and his reach took him right off Hammar's back and onto the floor! With Finnel fallen, Magicia threw flames again and hit Hammar straight on.

Appalled, X'ieth could not look away, the cumulative sights held captive in his eyes. He saw Hammar collapse to the floor with another aggrieved bellow, the magic-wrought fire singeing his body and armor. Lying there, his limbs twisted and turned, as the dwarf responded to surely what was terrible pain.

Conflicting voices warred in X'ieth's head. *Do something! Don't move. Do something! Don't move.* But of the voices, the latter one prevailed, for frozen in place X'ieth remained. Continuing as the hidden spectator, his eyes went back to Esmeralda, who still was confronted by Zeros and Nathan. She formed another fireball in her palms and cast it, attempting to enflame them. But using the same technique as before, Zeros created an energy dome about them, to block her green fires from causing any harm.

Esmeralda continuously threw more fire and Zeros continuously blocked, and the conflict soon became a matter of who could channel magic the longest— the sorceress, or the mercenary. As they both strained to wield Nexus, beads of sweat formed on Esmeralda's forehead, Zeros' too. They strained and strained, channeling magic until the point where the victor was decided, and that was to X'ieth's complete surprise.

Shocked, he watched how Esmeralda tired at channeling magic first, and stopped throwing fire. She panted, temporarily unable to cast another magical attack while recuperating. And the moment of her rest would be the exact moment in which Nathan readied his sword, to deal Esmeralda a fatal blow.

"Now!" cried Zeros, lowering the dome just then.

But before the attack could continue, X'ieth watched as Nexus ensnared both Nathan and Zeros from behind; it was bands of green energy that abruptly bound their arms and legs. This happened moments before Magicia used magic to slam both knights into the ceiling first, and then into the floor!

X'ieth went aghast, seeing grown men thrown about the room like rag dolls. It was a feat of utter brutality, not on par with any he had witnessed before. The young knight raised a quivering hand to his open mouth, his heart now beating even faster. After seeing the Guardsmen's defeat, he had to wonder why he lacked the courage to suffer the same defeat beside them. *After all, that would be more honorable than this. Why aren't you doing anything, man?!* He held himself accountable for not acting; never knowing such lack of courage in his life, up until now.

His inner voice sounded once more, pressing him, *Go!* But then came a conflicting one, in the spirit of Zeros, *Stay, if you value your life!* As before, he stood conflicted, a clear choice before him with the inability to decide. *Leave it then, to chance...* The thought rang out, echoing his mind again and again, making it apparent that stepping out might be more a gamble than anything else.

He heard Nathan grunt from the gray stone floor. A crumbling sound above directed X'ieth's eyes off the fallen knights, and to the ceiling overhead, which broke in the places where the knights hit! From a crack branching in multiple directions, some fragments came crashing down upon the pack leader and mercenary, and dust filled the chamber, causing X'ieth to defend against a cough.

"Arrghhh," groaned Nathan, struggling to move from his position on the floor. On the other hand, Zeros looked as still as a corpse to X'ieth, making him ponder the worst just then. *Is he even alive?!*

"How many times must I protect you, sister?!" asked Magicia of Esmeralda. The two sisters stared at each other—Magicia in anger, though Esmeralda being mellower now, given her deflated ego.

X'ieth held his breath as Finnel crawled toward Magicia's feet with his outstretched sword. *No, no! Play dead!* He urged the other knight tacitly, but to no avail. For Magicia—without even taking her eyes off Esmeralda—effortlessly stomped on Finnel's hand, before the elf's sword could do her any harm. Finnel winced, released the weapon, and it clattered to the floor.

"How many times?!" Magicia screamed the question. Humiliation perhaps tied Esmeralda's tongue, at her near death encounter with Nathan.

And then unexpectedly, X'ieth watched Hammar rise from the floor. He ran past Magicia and toward Esmeralda, his hammer raised high. *Not you too!* Magicia wrought a bolt of lightning from Nexus, which she cast at him like a javelin!

No! Nooo! X'ieth's horror increased and his jaw reached its lowest point, right as the energy zapped Hammar's armor, and jolted him back into the far wall! With a loud crack, the dwarf struck the wall and bounced off onto the floor, twitching and foaming at the mouth.

Still unable to look away, X'ieth watched Finnel reach up toward Magicia from the floor, determination in his eyes. But she noticed and fashioned a club from Nexus, bludgeoning him over the head with it, to render the knight unconscious or dead.

The young knight, who once bravely dreamed about confronting the Child of Darkness, was now officially something much less worthy of praise. *You've stayed the coward hiding in these shadows, and you didn't help them, despite multiple chances to intervene!* The reality easily shamed him.

Magicia walked nearer to Esmeralda in the chamber, she glanced down at the glowing sword, with eyes full of desire.

"Do you know how hard it is to keep good relations with the kingdoms, when I must do things like *this*?" Every spoken syllable of every spoken word grinded against each other, just like in Talus' throne room.

When Magicia whipped her head back toward the entrance, X'ieth ducked behind the doorpost in the nick of time. *Destiny save us!*

"The Guard come in sevens, and there are four knights here," said Magicia coldly, looking back to Esmeralda. Immense dread consumed X'ieth then, over worries of her possible suspicions that more knights lurked in the shadows. *Like you!*

"You should be glad that the others died in Saol. You mocked me for speaking with shadows, sister… Yet were it not for Darconas' minions you'd be facing a formidable threat of seven knights!"

X'ieth looked around the corner again, and his eyes found Magicia. He followed her walk to the far end of the room where her sister stood, closer to the shard at the room's center. As a response, Esmeralda distanced herself from Magicia, going to the opposite end of the room, away from her sister. She stopped a cubit away from where Zeros lied, lifelessly still.

X'ieth noticed how Esmeralda stood only cubits from him then. He held his sword in gauntleted hands, his palms sweating beneath. *Just step out, and kill her! It couldn't be easier, man!* His entire body shook again, and like before, the young knight wondered if the tower itself were shaking.

RAWWWWWWWRRRRRRRR!

A dragon roar many times louder than any previous, made X'ieth nearly jump out of his skin! It sounded right outside the casement, and with explosive force, it swiveled the window's panes back into the tower past their stops; the glass hit the stone wall, and shattered into pieces!

At precisely the same instant, X'ieth felt his head on the verge of explosion. He clasped one ear tightly with a free hand, and blood began trickling from the other, his eardrum burst. Blinding pain throbbed his head, and he gritted his teeth so hard that one broke from his gums, adding to his severe and nerve-splitting pain.

Despite being hard of hearing, X'ieth could still tell that the dragon flapped away from the window, returning to the sky, in order to make circles about the tower.

His mind ventured off the dragon, and back to Esmeralda, who again, stood a few cubits past the doorway leading out of the foyer. His eyes fixated on back of her head, and its flowing red hair. In that moment he squeezed the sword, terribly burnt by desire. X'ieth shut his eyes, and imagined how he would have the situation develop.

Visions danced in his head, of him courageously emerging from hiding to grasp Esmeralda's long hair in one sudden movement, right before sharply tugging it, drawing her head back, and exposing her neck. With the other arm, he would wield his broadsword in a mighty way to part her mind from body. And her beheading would precede his tireless walk on foot to Sergros through Liath and Saol, sustained by that mountain water. He could see himself, appearing at one of Talus' elaborate feasts during his mission, to drop her severed head right onto the king's plate of roasted hog. *Eat this instead, my king! Your Dark Prophecy changes by one you've treated poorly 'til now, the Child of Light!*

Those words from his daydream faded to obscurity, as he opened his eyes to find himself beset by opportunity, though without the will to do. His inner voice derided him again. *A good thing in your daydream, you weren't a coward! Valorous acts don't mix well with what you are.*

Magicia's voice stole his attention.

"Now that you know the shard's power cannot be used, *give it to me.*" She hissed the last words, her desire evident in how she spoke. X'ieth wondered, *What does Magicia want with the white shard?!*

"No!" Esmeralda retorted. "My premonitions tell me how you'll use it!"

"Now sisters, you shouldn't fight," said Lucen.

X'ieth stared into the chamber at three people now, hardly believing his eyes. *Where did he even come from?! And how is the prophet involved in all of this?!* Questions mounted on him, as the oddity of the situation grew.

He watched Esmeralda step forward, right over Zeros' motionless hand and a bit closer to the glowing shard on the floor.

"Magicia wants the sword!" she said to Lucen, exasperation in her voice. "You said she has access to the other shard, and will use it to increase in power beyond what any can imagine. Is this true?"

"Verily, she seeks the sword for her own gain." Turning to Magicia, Lucen said, "Now that's a claim you can't deny, isn't it?"

"Leave her alone!" Magicia yelled at him. "My sister has no part in Time No More!"

X'ieth's eyes focused on Lucen, who shook his head. "What a tangled web she weaved," he said, "to affect all around her, their destiny. Esmeralda chose this path on her own; my involvement was coincidental…"

Not understanding much of this bizarre meeting, X'ieth just watched as Lucen started to pull Nexus and channel complex flows, filling the chamber with blue and green energies. They winded around the room, emanating from Lucen's aux core, and rising in swirls to form a filter of sorts, an intricate lattice right before the window. It hung in the air, above the fallen knights and the shard of sword.

"What are you doing?!" asked Esmeralda sharply.

X'ieth heard Lucen's evil laughter within the tower, as the green and blue energies painted his face sinister. *He acts differently now! Never seen him like this before!* Worry filled the young knight then, for what he was actually amidst. Combined with his paralyzing fears, the realization made an elixir with even more stopping power.

He looked again to the back of Esmeralda's head, the opportunity of a lifetime within his reach. *Go, man! You wanted this good destiny, so seize it!* He tried to move his body forward, but found himself powerless, shackled by consternation. His heart still raced, his breaths were short, and his body shook. Once again, it all begged the question: *Are you really Kayareth?! This shouldn't be happening!*

Magicia exclaimed, "Enough with your play, Lucen! Let us both meet our destinies, but at Gallow Cliff, not here!" With those words, X'ieth saw Magicia suddenly lunge for the shard on the floor.

Just before she could touch it, a huge gray-scaled claw unexpectedly reached in through the open window to take hold of the glowing sword! He saw the sorceress immediately recoil from it, backing away.

The sight sent X'ieth's heart racing even faster.

Thump thump, thump thump, thump thump!

"No, not this!" screamed Esmeralda.

X'ieth looked her way, seeing Esmeralda's face stricken by a deep fear of unknown proportions.

And then, X'ieth beheld that very claw remove the sword from the window, and in a matter of moments, it returned to forcefully punch right through the wall! Stones fell from the tower's side and into the mountain below, swallowed up by the range's darkness. Those sounds of destruction went completely lost in the dragon's sudden and loud roar. *RAWWWRRR!*

X'ieth clasped one ear, and grinded his aching teeth, watching with dreadful angst as into the chamber came that head, a massive gray-scaled, horned thing with piercing yellow eyes, a long snout, and a maw lined with sharp teeth glistening with smelly saliva. By the very sight alone, X'ieth associated it with drawings he had seen before, and stories heard. His mind went awash with visions of Pyrus then, as now he stood before the giant's very pursuit: *Gremel!* One of three ancient dragons in Karnath that had outgrown and outlived any other dragon of sundry breed, the name was given to this particular dragon by

Mainlandish folk, handed down through frightening tales and grave accounts of what the dragon could do.

From his place of hiding, X'ieth exchanged looks between the hideously beautiful dragon and both sorceresses, who stood there completely still.

Gremel spoke, and her aged breath filled X'ieth's nostrils with a rank smell. *The dragon smells of death!* A snort followed by a scratchy voice traveled through the prism of Nexus energies that Lucen intricately constructed, which bended the deep, guttural sounds off the dragon's tongue into perfect Mainlandish.

"Since Saol and Liath are dying, I can no longer feed myself to look after my young." Looking right at Esmeralda, Gremel continued. "With the gloom you created, food has become scarce, for both dragons and kings!"

"This isn't true!" Magicia boldly contradicted Gremel, drawing the dragon's gaze. "Esmeralda has only drawn energy as the land falls apart…" Her voice proceeded through the filter, which adjusted its resonant frequencies to that of the dragon tongue.

From his peripheral vision, X'ieth noted how Lucen stared directly at him! The young knight turned, and looked upon the youth, who began rolling a hand, gesturing his advance to Esmeralda. "Claim this prize that awaits you as the Child," said Lucen. "This victory is your destiny."

But as much as X'ieth wanted to approach Esmeralda, fear glued his feet to the floor. *You're so close to this good destiny*, he thought. *Yet you still can't do this!* His reality and irony were one and the same. *You disappoint yourself.*

The thought triggered X'ieth to recollect his strange dream in Forest Saol, of Millicent and Talus in Castle Sergros. *Do you disappoint yourself as much as you disappoint me?* He shook his head, denying the statement, angered by it. Talus and Millicent ganged up on him, telling him what he could be. *Give up silly dreams of being some important hero! You're not good enough for that, or anything else!* He shook his head once more, denying the statements again, growing even angrier by them. Through his mind went comebacks: *You're a success, not a disappointment. You're a fearless knight, not a coward. You're Kayareth, and merely act as a wise hero against too great a threat!* And with that, X'ieth took his first step toward Esmeralda, followed by another and another. The newfound freedom to move was most wonderful after being fettered by his fears, for what seemed an eternity.

"She tore the very core of creation!" Gremel countered. "The rocks and trees, and all that lives in the mountains and forest, bleed out Nexus by her doing! They are dying with Esmeralda's lust for power!"

With his sword in both hands, X'ieth crept a few steps more, hearing Magicia speak to Gremel. "A curse has fallen into this time, from another age!" Her voice broke in his ear, hinting of regrets.

"I've watched her steal the energy," Gremel retorted, "with keen sight when flying afar! You lie, to protect your own sister."

Less than a cubit away, X'ieth reared back his sword, as both Magicia and Esmeralda stood occupied by the large dragon that peered inside the tower. Perspiration dotted the young knight's forehead, as his inner voices wrestled on the brink of the balance falling. *Cowardliness is not of Kayareth! The Light Prophecy speaks of the brave hero, not of what you did!* went one voice. *Neither is foolishness of Kayareth, as only a fool would have revealed himself... In the end, we'll see who the brave hero shall be*, sounded the other voice.

Gremel continued talking, "I shall take the shard from your sister, so she won't do more harm to Karnath!"

"You can't!" Esmeralda protested, right before X'ieth's sword severed her neck. Not believing entirely what happened, he watched blood spray from her headless stump and onto his face, as her flailing body fell to the floor. He savored the metallic taste of her blood in his mouth, watching her head smack the stone and roll, directly into limp Zeros. It came to a stop, staring back at him with wide eyes and pained features.

Lucen laughed hysterically in the background, the laughter's sound stuck in the young knight's ear. As X'ieth saw Magicia turn toward him, her shock morphed slowly into fiery indignation. And it was then that X'ieth heard the youth's wild cackle mix with a most disturbing cry ever, of a sister who lost a sibling that she loved, for over a thousand years.

"Esmeralda!" Magicia shrieked dreadfully.

A sudden, thunderous crashing outside sent X'ieth's attention to the hole Gremel created. In the space behind the dragon—still peering inside the tower, with a claw at the room's center—he beheld a large segment of Liath's range begin to collapse, as told by the soft mountain imploding on itself with a huge cloud of dust! And moments after that happened he felt the whole tower begin to shake violently, causing him to stumble!

X'ieth caught his balance, and looked up from the floor—past the fallen Guardsmen, past Lucen and Magicia, and past Esmeralda's corpse—to the dragon. Gremel released a roar, retracted its claw from the chamber with the shard inside, and turned midair upon flapping wings, about to fly away into the night.

RAWWWWWWWRRRRRRRR!

"INVADING THE TOWER"

Chapter 52
Confidence and Revelry

He had been planning a celebration for days now, and for good reason. Ever since Talus encountered Lucen in the Karnathan Church, he felt a challenge to the correctness of his premonitions. And that was a challenge he had to meet, for a king could not be proven wrong by any of his subjects, jealous oracle or not.

With that intention in mind, Talus visited the castle kitchen upon his return from worship, in order to get his cooks cooking, his bakers baking, and his servants serving. He needed them to prepare a feast of truly epic proportions, one to occur at a future time—a time when he foresaw his Guardsmen arriving in Sergros from their quest. *That will be proof, of my premonitions being right!*

And so, nights came and nights went, as Talus mulled over the appropriate time for him to revel in his correctness alongside his knights. Meanwhile, his workers worked, and the Sergrothian storehouse got lower and lower. It made for a cycle that continued for days with some food perishing—a cycle that could not go on forever, a cycle to which Talus was obtunded. But fortunately for Sergros, the king finally settled on a day for his feast, and that day was finally upon him.

It happened one afternoon, where Talus sat in his great hall of stone, at the head of a long, rectangular table that stretched the hall's length. He occupied the highest chair in the room, ideal so that he could look down upon his very best subjects that were seated on his left and right: the Sergrothian nobles. They consisted of men and women gathered around the table, all eating, drinking, talking, and laughing together.

Behind the nobles, the walls at his left and right held three blue banners of Sergros showing the kingdom's gold lion crest. The banners on each wall alternated with doors that connected the castle corridors to the hall. A pair of burning torches beset each door; they hung in iron sleeves mounted upon the wall, being adjacent to the banners.

Beyond the table's far end—the one opposite to Talus—a large space opened before the wall, where dancers twirled about, as lords led ladies in step and some women danced on their own, banging a tambourine. The musicians stationed themselves in one corner on the far wall—men strumming danar lutes, and drumming on their bowl-backs for added percussion, along with women playing brass flutes. The musicians were opposite to the performers in the wall's other corner, where currently, two jesters skillfully juggled balls.

The party unfolded with wild drunkenness and carefree mirth, which Talus had not witnessed in Sergros for months since war and gloom. A smile easily came to his lips, as he swayed his chalice of wine to the music, for the party itself made him feel like he had already conquered gloom in Sergros, and furthermore, like he had exonerated himself of Lucen's charges. *Indeed, this is a celebration of my correctness! Just look at the joy on people's faces!*

Talus gulped more red wine; it trickled from the corners of his lips with the clumsy drink. He wiped his face with a sleeve and sighed in pleasure, focusing then on the feast set before him. He beheld a smorgasbord across the table, steaming casseroles and dishes plated in fine porcelain imported from the Isles, all appearing incredibly edible. There were roasted ruby potatoes, orange yam puree, stewed purple plums, green cabbage soup having a thick pea-based broth, and so many others. The dishes sent savory aromas to his nose, along with bright colors and appetizing textures to his eyes.

At the center of the casseroles sat the eaten carcass of a suckling pig on a wooden plank, now reduced to bones. Like magic, servants appeared out of nowhere, exchanging the devoured one for another—fresh from the kitchens, with legs bound and apple in mouth. It happened exactly like this, several times over and without cause for worry, as if there were unlimited swine in Sergros to satisfy hunger of the Sergrothian elite. The visual of the pig stirred Talus' mind with thoughts. *No need for my livestock awaiting slaughter any longer, when Sergros' reborn prosperity is nigh!* Smells of the suckling pig wafted through the air to him, notes of maple and brown sugar, which made the table even more desirable than before.

And just like the pig, Talus watched fresh breads plopped onto the table, off the hands of servants scurrying in from the side doors. Each loaf had meaning to him, as the breads were baked from grains once held in reserve, the grains that would go to those subjects dependent upon his kingdom. *There's no need for Sergros to shoulder that burden anymore, of feeding the lower and middle classes!* Indeed, in Talus' eyes, the grains now saw a better purpose on the eve of Sergros returning to order. *It's time for the nobles enduring my harsh tax to see relief, soon to be had by everyone under my rule!*

As several times already this day, Talus' eyes trailed away from the reveled bunch—the lords twirling ladies in fanciful gown, the jesters in jest, the musicians playing music, and indulgers of indulgences many. Instead of watching them more, he found himself looking to the nearest door. *Any moment, the Guard shall burst through, making a grand entrance indeed!* His hopes inspired fancies, and his mind spun splendid ideas. *Or maybe*, he thought, *the gloom shall vanish, right amid my lavish feast!* Talus showed a big smile at the very thought of the gloom dissolving, and being replaced by the bluest of skies ever seen in Karnath—skies dotted by a golden sun that smiled right back at him. Talus could not be more certain that either one or the other would happen.

Perhaps even both! The king saw it in his premonitions—a near future free of gloom, with the Seventh Order of the Guard in Sergros, and where he kept his throne. *It's like the gloom never even happened!*

And then, as if coincidence with his daydreaming, the side door suddenly burst open on Talus' left! He whipped a smiling face about, expecting to see X'ieth strut in, beaming with pride as he carried the trophy of Esmeralda's head; or maybe Zeros, carrying the same head but without the same enthusiasm. But the king saw neither X'ieth nor Zeros, or any of his knights; instead, he saw Cedric, who stormed into the hall scowling, seemingly furious over what took place! The king's smile vanished immediately.

Talus watched Cedric rush to the table, turn his back to the revelers, and slam his fist onto the table, right before the king. Cedric glared at him with indignant, amber eyes. "How dare you arrange such a wasteful feast?!" He spoke the words in a low voice, but harshly.

In response to Cedric's disdain, Talus just yawned and loosely wrapped a few fingers around the base of his chalice. *Even Cedric won't make a big scene before Sergros' wealthiest of wealthy.*

"The kingdom's reserve cannot sustain revelry like this, while you continue such excessive welfare to the lower and middle classes!" Cedric gestured to all the drunken nobles while speaking. "They all pay a greater tax, but their lands bear no fruit! I ask what good is their money, when the reserves dry up! What good will it do, in the moment when the kingdom's last morsel is eaten, in the very instant when the last thread enters a new garment? How shall you provide food or supplies in Sergros then, at a point where there's more coin than commodity?!"

Talus nonchalantly traced his index finger around the lip of his chalice, and gave another yawn. He then waved his hand back and forth to the music, in part to blow over the details of the problem, in part to shoo Cedric from the room.

"Your worries will come to an end, Cedric. This gloom shall lift from Sergros, by my good fortune! I'm a devout king, and Destiny soon smiles upon Sergros again."

"You afford too much to chance," Cedric countered angrily, "and too little to choice! You'll stand accountable to powers higher than me for your decisions, my king. I suggest you treat your rule different than a gambling game…" As the words trailed off, Talus watched the politician lean closer, the ball on his nose bridge coming a few hair lengths from the king's face. "That is, if you want to keep your rule!"

And just as he entered, Cedric left the hall, stomping away from Talus with apparent frustration. The sounds of his departure were lost in those of the party. Despite the politician's words—words that might arouse caution in some—Talus delighted himself in Cedric's doubt, as if it agreed with Lucen's charges against him days beforehand. To him, it was just another challenge he aimed to prove wrong. And so, Talus confidently sat there in smiles and smugness, more drunken on his premonitions of good fortune than on the wine. *Cedric will choke on his words soon enough...*

Talus guzzled the remaining wine from his chalice, and like before, some ran from the corners of his mouth. With a brush of the hand, he wiped his mouth and let his smile widen; it spread now from ear-to-ear. The buzz to his head from the strong drink impeded careful thought about said matters, and lent to his enjoyment of memories about prosperity in Sergros, a thing he had always enjoyed before war and gloom. *Ascription has blessed me thus far, so I need not be careful!*

Then suddenly, Talus heard a loud splat. The whole room hushed, and an eerie quiet presided over it. From his seat, the king stood upright, as every set of eyes cast a stare forward, including his own. Not knowing exactly what had happened, he prematurely blamed one of his oaf workers. *Which fool servant dropped a pudding?! Hopefully it wasn't dropped on one of my nobles!*

As the haze lifted over Talus' dulled senses, he slowly gathered where his nobles looked. *It's the dancing floor,* he thought, *before the far wall.* Quickly, his eyes darted that way, where he saw a tall, middle-aged brunette woman in two-toned gown, half black and half white, standing to the side. She was at the center of the floor, amidst other dancers, who froze in place, just fearfully staring at the woman in complete silence.

And in that moment's glance, Talus could not believe his eyes, doubting them at first. But as his vision moved between her bloody, grinning face and the lump of flesh upon the floor, the reason for the sound became awfully apparent. *Her cheek... fell off!* When her eyes met his own, the torch fires on both walls instantly snuffed out, and gasps could be heard from around the room.

From his peripheral vision, Talus witnessed horror develop on the faces of everyone present. Many just stared with fearful eyes and features severe, a few with mouths quivering or agape. Talus felt then his own mouth begin to tremble, as not a word found a path to his mouth. And it was then that his body went numb, and queasiness turned his gut. The terrifying reality slowly dawned on him that the woman stood there smiling, with half a face! It implanted notions in his head that the woman was really something sinister and Dark. *Perhaps Esmeralda herself!*

When Talus suddenly felt the hold over his tongue loosened, he called out with a newfound voice.

"Guards! Come at once!"

From the halls, Talus heard the clangs of his armored soldiers approaching the room; within a matter of moments, they poured through the doors on both sides of the room, brandishing spears, a half dozen in number.

When Talus saw them, he looked collectively to his men and barked orders, while pointing out the woman with a shaky finger.

"Remove this menace! Kill her! Kill her!"

The soldiers were dispatched, even as Talus' shrill cry still hung in the air. He watched everyone on the dance floor clear from around the woman's vicinity. In the background, he heard murmuring arise from the nobles—quickened and fearful talk.

"Who is that?!" one lord exclaimed.

"That's the most awful thing!" said a lady.

Meanwhile, the scuffle of his soldiers' advance filled his ears, filling him with hope that they would vanquish the threat. But before his men could even reach the woman, Talus saw her skin begin to jitter between solid and liquid. His mouth opened more, as he beheld the flesh on the dance floor come back to her face, at the same exact time her eyes and mouth turned into blotches of gold light!

"*What* is she?!" asked a noble then, full of angst.

Talus watched panicked scores of men and woman rush out of the room—screaming as they went—while others were bound in place by sheer terror.

"Kill her! Kill her!" Talus shrieked.

When three soldiers confronted the ghostly woman, they speared her from the center, left, and right. Talus watched eagerly as the weapons made contact, only to suffer a mix of disappointment, shock, and dread. For instantly, her body exploded into concentrated globules that struck the soldiers hard, and then floated through the space, filling the entire hall! The three soldiers tumbled to the floor from the impact, and lied there motionless.

Gawking in fright, Talus looked up from his soldiers, to the iridescent beads hovering midair. He watched them wide-eyed with terrible anxiety, until they quickly moved through the chamber and coalesced on the far end of the table, at the opposite side from him. There, the ghostly woman materialized, crouched on the flat surface upon her hands and knees, like a four-legged beast!

She crawled toward Talus down the long table, knocking over the casseroles as she went. Porcelain hit the floor and broke into pieces, leaving food everywhere. The king saw his feast suddenly ruined right in front of him. From the corners of his eyes, he could tell more lords and ladies frantically funneled from the room, some with hands to face and shrieking.

"Destiny save us!" a lady yelled.

More crashes brought Talus' attention back to the table, where the ghostly woman still crawled; she was halfway down, ten cubits or more away from the king, her eyes and mouth aglow in the darkened chamber. The sight of her approach was terrifying, a thing that shackled Talus in fear. Unable to even blink, he just stared at her initially, until finally his instincts led to involuntary, defensive reactions: his hands went up to shield himself, and his body recoiled toward the nearest wall.

"Summon every mage in the castle," screamed Talus. "Do so, immediately!"

The situation intensified as one soldier exited with the king's orders, while the two others rushed between the king and the threat, facing her head-on. Talus swallowed hard, while watching them approach the ghostly woman with spears ready, though fear evident in their eyes.

What Dark power is upon Sergros?! Those words ran through Talus' terrified mind. But just after they did, into his ears meandered the strangest sound ever heard, a language of chimes that somehow, he could understand!

"Your inheritance is more wholesome than his," said the ghostly woman. "Kilwroth's unwholesome inheritance…"

To Talus, the words sounded as strange, perhaps from another world, or seemingly another space of the universe. They invoked dread, and he felt his mouth open wider than he thought possible, to the extent where he feared his jaw unhinging.

The ghostly woman crawled closer toward him, and he watched the rightmost soldier jab at her. But Talus worried tremendously as the man's strike resulted in the same outcome—her body exploded into a barrage of beads, concentrated and aimed at the soldier. After being hit, the soldier tumbled to the floor, and lied there motionless as the others. And the ghostly women, just as before, merged from the beads upon the table, crouched on her hands and knees, and now closer to the king by a few seats!

It was then that the remaining soldier completely lost his composure, and ran out of the room.

Talus could barely believe the man was fleeing.

"Come back!" he shrieked, "by order of the king!"

Surprised, Talus watched as his soldier kept running, not even turning back once.

Now without his soldiers, Talus set his eyes on the ghostly woman. He gulped and prayed in fear. *Destiny, please deliver me!*

She continued crawling toward him, and speaking in a musical voice of chimes. "The distance between Kilwroth and his fate shall be many fold the distance between you and your dreams! An entire kingdom follows you, yet your rule is reckless and instills not values of fighting for good destiny in your people. Welfare is meant to help those truly in need, but not those without a will to ever work!"

At that moment Talus heard swift running, and shifted his eyes to the doorways on his left and right that connected his great hall to the castle corridors. Multiple mages burst through the entrances, and poured into the chamber, their midsections glowing green from Nexus energy. More crashing brought back his eyes to the ghostly woman who came closer, over plates of half-eaten food and set dishes; they fell to the floor with crashes and bangs. At this point, she was literally two or three cubits from the king's face.

"Do away with her!" Talus screamed to his mages, recoiling more toward the wall. At that exact moment, green Nexus arced from their midsections toward the ghostly woman, but stopped short of the threat with blinding light, as those spent energies hit what appeared to be a glass wall! Talus shielded his eyes, knowing then that even his mages could not stop whatever this was. And that realization was enough to steal his breath, and sent his heart beating even faster in his chest.

Thump thump! Thump thump! Thump thump!

"Good destiny evades you, king," continued the ghostly woman in her musical song. "And *that*, shall not be easily forgiven. Neglecting good destiny had, leads to good destiny fleeting!"

The ghostly woman stopped crawling, and stared at Talus from a hair length away. He looked right into her glowing eyes, his vitals yet elevated, as his sheer discomfort and dread over the situation peaked. *Destiny, please deliver me! Please!*

Talus could hear the mages grunt as they tired from using magic against the Nexus barrier. They stopped channeling one by one, and when the last mage stopped, the ghostly woman suddenly disappeared with a bright flash! The intense light was from the wall torches, which burst afire once more, a ferocious burning where flames jumped from their collars and onto the banners of Sergros! The gold lions on a field of blue were gobbled up in the blaze, subliminally telling Talus that perhaps the same was happening to his dreams and divine destiny of Sergrothian kingship.

"Water!" Talus shrieked. "Bring water now!"

Shuddering with fear, he ran from the fiery chamber into the stone hall, as smoke filled the air, along with the shouts of servants and soldiers in all the commotion that ensued. And mixed in with the background noise, Talus could hear the faint sound of a child, crying inconsolably.

"THE KING'S CELEBRATION"

Chapter 53
Farewell, Logan

After a night of dreaming nightmares, Kort awoke in Raiden's house the next morning, but awoke to no one there. The house was completely empty, with its sliding door wide open. He sat up from the mat and stared, just listening to outside noise of Doj's morning bustle. He heard supplies being carted to boats and yells from the port. These were the sounds of a daily grind of fishers fishing, something that maybe everyone in Karnath ought to be doing in their own way. *Including me...*

With that thought, he threw off his blankets, arose from the mat, and stepped toward the exit. As he walked closer, the floorboards creaked in his ears, as his mind wondered the obvious. *Where's Raiden? Maybe busy readying the boat...*

Kort settled a cubit from the open doorway, and stopped himself there. He looked down, studying the morning light spilling across its threshold. In that moment, the open door seemed a metaphor for his life, as the decision to walk through symbolized choice and chance. In the end, he would decide whether to fish with Raiden, and that choice had some chance of leading into Light—a better way to live, where Kort could help more people than only himself. But just as anxiety, fear, and doubt can accompany both choice and chance, the ex-knight felt them all with this decision, and prayed it was the right one. *Please, Destiny... Let fishing with Raiden help me repay something, after I've taken so much from so many.*

Given his worries, Kort paused and sighed, continuing to stare at the doorway. Meanwhile, the morning bustle continued in the background, which eventually prompted him to get ready for a day of fishing. And so, Kort retreated from the door, went back to his mat where he had laid his sack of things, and began changing into a second pair of cloths. He stuffed legs into pants and arms into a short-sleeved shirt, while thinking to himself.

Tomorrow I fish, in my way and in my time. As Kort dressed, his last words to Euclid surfaced in his head. While he would indeed honor those words by fishing, he would not do so with the crimson knight. *Too many strange things have happened, with recurrent urges to trust not the crimson knight... So how can I?* He seriously wondered, with a lot of compelling reasons: *The woman in white and man in black... That ghostly woman from the forest... My nightmare, followed by a visit from the deceased Garlew and that same eerie apparition...*

Whether indirectly or directly, each visitor referred to not trusting the crimson knight, which made it natural for Kort to eschew Elucid.

Clothed in a matter of seconds, Kort slung his sack over his shoulder and took a step for the door. Images from his nightmare randomly flashed through his mind then, of impaling Nym. They made him stop where he was and cringe. "I've never stopped loving her," he spoke to himself, "and I would never do *that*!"

Kort could not understand why his recent nightmare had him killing Nym, and it instilled him with feelings of sudden confusion and sadness. In fact, none of his nightmares ever featured that, and its novelty now was concerning. Even so, there was little he could do but hope Nym was well, and continue to hope that somehow, he would see her again.

The amulet! His thoughts of Nym suddenly redirected his attention to her keepsake. He hurried back to the mat, knelt down, and emptied the contents of his sack, letting them spill out. *Where is it? Where is it?!* He frantically searched through the articles, including his clothes, Genze's book, and other things, until an epiphany struck him and he instantly went still. Kort paused from his rummaging, raised a hand up to his chest, beneath his shirt, and touched the small purse hung about his neck. From its exterior, he could feel the amulet inside. *Forgot where I placed it… Whew!*

Kort took out the amulet and held it in his palm. He saw a thin-chained amulet of teardrop form, and its mere sight sent his mind astir with memories of Nym. He fondly remembered her in the forest days after his resurrection, being encircled by green and red fireflies. The amulet was still about her neck then, its gleam matching the shimmer of her silver hair, drenched in the starlight that fell between the trees overhead.

He snapped back to the drab fisher's house, and it sadly occurred to him how that was then, and this was now. Kort sighed, and took up his sack in one hand, while using the other to put his things back inside again. "I hope she still loves me," he muttered to himself, wondering again where Nym was, and why she never found him.

Kort stood up, and slung his sack over his shoulder, thinking it better to leave Raiden's house like he was never there. So, before turning to go, he leaned down and ran his hand over the mat's linen cover to smooth out the wrinkles. In the same motion, he could feel its sturdy wooden support, made from the stalky trees of Tai.

When finished, he spun from the mat with his sack, and walked to the door again, stopping before the threshold like before. He slipped on his shoes lying there, one foot at a time; he had taken off when entering Raiden's house.

Now in his shoes, Kort stood there adorned in a new set of cloths and the morning shadows, with his eyes on the tired flooring at the sunbathed entrance, which lied several cubits ahead of him. He literally was in darkness, but within only a few steps, he could be in the light. Kort had to wonder then, why his attempts at redemption had been so difficult—why his personal journey from Darkness to Light presented so many challenges. *Why couldn't leading a better life be as easy, as walking across the room?*

So went Kort with that last thought, through the door and outside the house. The mysteriously dry air of the Isles welcomed him. *The rain comes with increasing heaviness of the air,* he thought, familiar with high humidity in days leading up to rain. *Does this missing thing rob Doj and Reiju of a downpour?* It remained a mystery to him, one that he could not place.

With keen eyes, Kort looked around the home's exterior, wondering if Raiden might be there. Scorched grass spread in all directions from the house; it extended until meeting a dirt path that zigzagged distantly. The path ran up from where he came, in the direction of Reiju, and continued on through Doj, beset there by stilted houses of burnt umber hue. They sat on wooden supports, four cubits off the ground with ladders leading up to the doors, because of the coastal flooding frequent in these parts. Kort looked up, beyond the fawn thatched roofs and piped smokestacks of these homes, to the tranquil azure sea in the distance, with gulls swarming overhead like white vultures. The sounds of squawking and continued yells from the port filled his ears.

"Where are my lines?!" one asked urgently.

"I'm coming, I'm coming already!" replied another.

In his mind, Kort processed the Hirishin words as Mainlandish. He learned enough languages when a child, that now, they all ran together as his single native tongue.

A few cubits to his right, at the front of Raiden's house, Kort saw the dilapidated junk boat under which he hid last night; it was propped against a few posts jutting from the ground. Slowly, he walked about it, studying a vessel that had apparently seen quite a few sailing days. Its dark hull was made of timber, with planks fastened tightly together, each strip of wood perfectly flush to its adjoining brethren. His eyes traced the planks, which extended the boat's full length of about eight cubits. From the keel to its outer edges, they met from opposite sides at the front and back of the vessel. On the rear, a rudder was attached for steering. The mast and spars were completely removed. At the base of the hull, he saw one hole sized bigger than a coin. *Would have to be plugged, for this to stand a chance of staying afloat! And even then, it'd just be a chance...*

In the middle of that thought, he recalled more from his nightmare. It was conjured up by the mere concept of chance, given what Taurus said concerning re-spun webs of destiny, and Kort's destiny gone awry. *Chance enabled him to use premonitions to ruin other's lives, my life even! Chance...* In that, the idea of chance seemed Dark to Kort, perhaps as Dark as the power that Taurus allied with to reestablish his empire upon the Mainland. *When learning the Red Dragon clans came to possess the metal demons, Taurus perhaps gambled with his own soul to save his empire!*

When Kort considered the unknown alliance between Taurus and the Dark, visions of the man in black immediately popped into his head, and then came an image of Nym, being of similar dress. Violently he shook the notion off that Nym was involved in the Isles Conspiracy. *Perhaps the man was involved or even the woman in white, but not Nym. Nym is good, more so than she could be evil...* He remained convinced of that.

"Do you still wish to go?" Raiden asked.

The words came from behind Kort, blindsiding him.

"Eh?" Kort replied, turning to the fisher.

"Want to sail on the water and fish? I let you sleep for a while, and arose early to prepare my boat."

Staying silent, Kort just nodded. *Sit on the water sounds more like it. Try to sail far without wind.*

"I have my things," he said finally, "and will go whenever you're ready."

Raiden motioned for Kort to follow, and with that, the fisher began walking down the dirt path. Kort followed at Raiden's heel, still shouldering his burlap sack. They both walked through Doj, which took them past narrow paths branching from the way, surrounded by crooked houses on stilts. They walked further, which had them go past Doj's market, and while in the vicinity, Kort overheard many worries and complaints about the rice shortage.

One farmer packed up his wagon there, being backed by a crowd.

"But isn't there more?" one asked, at his rear.

The farmer stopped working, and turned about to exclaim, "My field is burnt up! I've less rice this week than the one prior!"

Those waiting to make purchases made a malformed line leading up to the farmer's stand. With his news, their murmurs rippled through the crowd, against a backdrop of white canopies over clustered tables.

Kort slowed his pace, turning his head to watch the farmer raise his hands to allay the market goers. He was a black-bearded elf wearing a bowl straw hat with an open white shirt and beige pants tied at the waist.

"I've no more rice to sell today," he said to everyone with a scowl. "No more besides what I've kept for my own family!"

More murmurs arose in Hirishin, as if people were taken by surprise with his admission. They looked increasingly frantic, and asked one hurried question after another.

"What will I do?!" said an adult elf with a handful of coin. A child elf hugged one of his legs, suggesting his role as the provider for little ones and a wife. "My family will starve!"

Kort watched an older Hirishin lady barge through the distressed bunch, to the front of the line. She raised a single coin in her hand, and shouted above the many who voiced their protest

"This is the last money I have!" she said. "Take it, and give me but a few grains so I can eat another day!"

"Do you have other fields?!" one asked.

"Can't you plant more rice?!" asked another.

Behind Raiden, Kort kept walking. He hurried his pace, and turned his head away from the market and back to the path, after just having witnessed money go worthless in Doj's shortage of supply. With that, the troubled sights and sounds of the market faded from his eyes and ears, only to be trapped in his mind. *This drought causes famine!*

Kort pondered his place in all of this, while walking through a final corridor of Doj that led up to the port. His recall of failure last night—in watering the fields of Doj—made him question what, if anything, that place was. It rang of the same defeat he suffered when trying to douse Baal's flames using the waters of Sorin Bay. *Despite my awakening to advanced magical skills, I haven't been able to use those skills for any good. I couldn't do it.* The thought depressed him.

But Kayareth could... The thought depressed him even more, and countered Elucid's proclamation yesterday that he was not the One of Prophecy. With a frown, Kort thought about the artistry depiction of the blond-haired hero from the Light Prophecy, the one who the oracles now predicted would lose at Gallow Cliff, versus enjoying victory. *Yet the prophecy says, he could at least lift famine despite that defeat... I guess I can only sail away from it!*

Kort's despair carried him to the port with Raiden. He stepped onto its wooden planks, scowling at his feet. When Kort looked up, he saw tall wooden piers on each side of the port's walkway, spaced every few cubits apart, allowing for boats large and small to dock in and out of Doj. Thick, braided rope wrapped some piles, mainly for tying the ships. The whole port told of Mainlandish construction from another time, decades before this one.

He glanced around the port, seeing a few other junk boats in the water, some docked but others out in the harbor. Kort squinted, trying to discern whether or not the fishers in the distant boats used oars due the lack of wind. He could see a few closer boats moving, without oars and without wind. "The current," Raiden said from behind, "is what we'll rely upon to move out from port, just as they."

Kort looked to where the fisher motioned, a small sailboat appearing like the one outside Raiden's house, except with mast, a coppery ruffled sail, and all the sparring. *Hopefully it hasn't holes on the bottom!* he thought, but dared not ask. Inside the boat, he saw a looking glass, some oars, rope, netting, fisher's knife, and a handled pot with latching top. Rusty iron cleats where attached inside the boat on port and starboard, one of which was tied to the nearby pile.

"This is my sailboat," Raiden said. "She's not much, but has allowed me to find good destiny on the waters all these years."

When Kort saw Raiden climb over the side of the vessel to get in, he followed suit, counting an invitation to board unnecessary. The moment he stepped down onto the hull, he felt the vessel rocking on the water. Hugging his burlap sack, he settled himself down onto the planks.

When the corner of his one eye picked up motion, Kort turned to see Raiden untie the boat from port, working his hands in a circular fashion then, to unloop the rope about the nearest pile. Kort watched him finish the task, and then throw the bunched rope into the hull. With an oar the fisher went to the stern, to push the sailboat away from the port.

As it drifted out, Kort watched the land become further away, as the sea's current took the sailboat forward. Then suddenly came a strong wind, completely unexpected! It embraced the boat for a long while, and Kort found it refreshing. He put his sack to the side and stood up smiling, with both arms stretched out, letting the wind envelope him and lift his hair. He looked up, and saw the copper-colored sails catch the gust. When his gaze fell, Raiden could be seen beaming, both amazement and happiness read from his face.

"Maybe it'll be, winds of change!"

The comment played on Kort's wants of redemption, and living better. He smiled back.

When Kort saw the fisher look into the sea, he began hearing ethereal chimes on the wind, otherworldly sounds as those from Tai. His smile dropped instantly into a frown, as flashes of the ghostly woman appeared in his head; he could see her blotches of gold light for eyes and mouth, along with her jittery flesh.

In one sudden moment, his chest tightened, his heart began beating rapidly, and blood throbbed his temple. He looked to the wind caught in the coppery sail, a thing he welcomed a moment ago but now mistrusted.

No. No! Noooooo! Kort felt increasingly uneasy, like once again he was being pulled into some Dark scheme beyond his control.

"Did you see that?!" Raiden asked, drawing Kort's attention. His heart continued to beat fast.

Thump thump, thump thump, thump thump!

It sounded over Raiden's words, to the point where he could not understand a thing.

"What?!" Kort asked, panicked by what went on.

"Upon the port, a blur sped by and went into the sky! I just saw it!" Raiden's words came out fast, as appropriate for one seeing something supernatural.

Kort struggled to peer back at the shore, as the sun's glare smote him in the face. He squinted and raised a hand to shield his eyes, and studied it as

Raiden did, only to see nothing. But upon returning his gaze to the waters, the onset of shade made him look up. In one sudden instant, Kort beheld a black dot high in the sky; it abruptly blocked out the sun's glare! The sight alarmed him, and his body grew tense. All the while, those eerie chimes still sounded on the wind.

"Give me a good show." That voice from Tai suddenly entered his ears, perplexing him.

"What in Destiny?!" he said, standing with Raiden.

Kort kept his eyes on the black dot, now associating whatever it was with the ghostly woman. But in not more than a brief moment, the black dot changed in size and color, becoming blood red and much larger. With great apprehension, Kort watched as the crimson knight plummeted through the heavens, right toward the boat! As Elucid fell, an aura of Nexus suddenly ignited about the metal demon, with the knight's white cloak flapping behind.

Before Kort could grasp everything that happened around him, Elucid landed upon the boat's hull in a crouched position, clutching a purple cloak in metal hand. A scrunched forehand, open mouth, and stretched cheeks marred Kort's countenance—the display of varied negative emotions.

"That's impossible," Raiden remarked. "The boat didn't as much as move!"

But Kort was not impressed with the feathery impact that Elucid achieved through magic. Nor was he happy to see the crimson knight at all. *And why is Raiden amused with this*, he wondered. *Do they know each other?!* His thought easily projected shadows upon the good character he presumed of Raiden, if indeed the fisher worked with Elucid, someone who as of now, the ex-knight could not trust.

So in that instant, it was natural for the many oddities of yesterday to circle around Kort's mind. From the encounter with the ghostly woman in Tai, the ex-knight became suspect of being followed by an evil spirit. *My punishment from Destiny for misdeeds past!* But now that Kort heard those chimes on the wind once again, while seeing Elucid stand there as cold as ice, it enabled him to piece the puzzle together. *The crimson knight is an evil spirit, having an interest in me because I'm Shai... !*

His mind sputtered that single thought, stopping short of completion for fear of Ma'althan's gaze. With every hair on his body raised, his jaw dropped, and a heart about to explode in his chest, Kort recoiled from Elucid in the hull like a scared alley cat. A single command entered his mind, and his body acted instantly. *Jump!*

"KORT AND RAIDEN FISHING"

Chapter 54
Jumping Ship

Elucid boomed "Don't do it!", right as Kort rushed to the side of the small fishing boat, about to jump.

The crimson knight reached out a metal hand, unable to do more than watch him go. But suddenly, from out of nowhere, Elucid saw Raiden grab Kort by the shoulder before he could leap overboard!

When touched, Kort showed a cross look and spun about on one leg, aiming to kick Raiden. The mere image of both elves entering into hand-to-hand combat sent warnings through Elucid's head: *Stop them! It shouldn't be like this!*

What happened next, happened so fast that Elucid could only continue to watch. Raiden snagged Kort's foot and threw it back at him, but Kort countered with blurring hands and feet—he punched, kicked, and chopped at Raiden. In defense, Raiden raised his hands and skillfully blocked each strike.

As the fight ensued, Elucid weighed how to best intervene. *Should I put myself in between them, or just speak?* The boat literally rocked on the waters every moment the crimson knight deliberated, and the conflict between Kort and Raiden intensified.

"Stop it already!" Elucid finally yelled, just at the point where Raiden sidestepped Kort's straightened hand, slung right at his neck. The sudden shout from Elucid brought Kort and Raiden to a momentary standstill. The crimson knight stared at them both; the two elves were now frozen in place, with arms raised and in the middle of combat. But the pose did not last, as Kort hurried to the side of the boat again, only a few seconds later!

And with that, the same sequence of events took place: Raiden grabbed Kort before he could leave; Kort responded by turning about with a punch, leaving Raiden to defend himself. Their feet shifted on the hull, and the vessel bounced on the water as it did a moment prior, jostled by the jostling two.

"Stop it already!" demanded Elucid, this time in a voice twice as booming and loud.

Kort and Raiden froze mid-combat, and looked at the crimson knight once again. After several moments, they turned to each other and lowered their hands. Kort showed a face of certain shame, as if now he pondered whether Raiden's character was incorrectly presumed after all.

Elucid sensed immediate sound vibrations to the boat's right. It came from distant talk, upon nearby boats maybe a hundred cubits away.

"Aja sing mikir punika uga?" one neighboring fisher called out, the Mainlandish equivalent of asking if all was well.

Raiden faced the fisher elves on the adjacent boat, and yelled across the sea. "Ana masalah!"

To that reply, Elucid shook a metal head, gesturing some disagreement, for the crimson knight knew the truth was very different. *There are certainly problems here, but hopefully ones I can circumvent.*

"It isn't supposed to be like this," Elucid said to Kort and Raiden.

They both turned from the fishers who addressed them, and back to the crimson knight.

"No one should force choice on another; it should be willful, and come from within."

Elucid saw Raiden get Kort's attention, by raising a hand to his shoulder. And it was then, that Raiden excitedly shared what Elucid had told him this very morn.

"This metal demon says you're the Child of Light, the one who will lift famine from Logan and change the Dark Prophecy!"

Kort's face contorted painfully at the words, as if a fierce denial prevented him from enjoying the proclamation. The sight alone, however, was not enough to stop Raiden from speaking more.

"Doj hasn't gone by the name Logan for decades, but that was never enough for me to doubt the Light Prophecy! You're him… I know it!" Raiden went on, "You just showed up outside my house last night like a gift to Doj, a gift from Karnatha herself!"

"Our meeting couldn't be more of coincidence!" Kort contradicted, shaking his head. "I've been in Doj for months, and am no gift to it. I'm just a fisher like you, that's all." Beneath his breath Kort muttered to himself, "I am not a gift, only a curse to any and all, a reproach to even my parents!"

As winds carried the sailboat further into the sea, Elucid watched the blue waters pass by, beneath the bright sky. Those gusts lifted the long hair and clothes of both Raiden and Kort, who stood squinting on the hull under a risen sun, which soon would shed the midday's heat. Overhead, gulls noisily whined behind the rolling waves. Elucid sensed the mix of sea sounds through the metal demon; each one had a distinct vibration.

Say something. Once again, an inner voice prompted Elucid to speak persuasive words to Kort, who still had disbelief written all over his face. But to the crimson knight, it remained in question what benefit such words would even have. *It seems that his persuasion must come from within…*

When Kort suddenly went for the boat's edge like before, Raiden flinched to stop him, but Elucid dissuaded him from interfering further.

"Raiden, don't…" Elucid trailed off, frozen in place with a metal hand hung in the air. "If he must jump, let him jump. His choice must prevail over ours." The crimson knight knew it was the right thing to say, even though it carried risks of an undesired outcome: Kort actually leaving the boat. *He may jump, but the choice is his…*

Kort glanced at Elucid over his shoulder, flashing an arched eyebrow as if the knight's instruction came as unexpected. Raiden stepped back, lowering both arms meant to restrain the fleeing ex-knight.

"Everyone in Karnath is given the opportunity to do good," said Elucid, "to find his or her hidden talents and employ them to better the entire world, creating positive change for themselves and others! But while this transforming power can shape our land beyond what could even be wrought by the Deardrumman master builders, many forfeit good destiny! That's what you're about to do, for the same reasons as others who forfeit good destiny throughout Karnath."

Elucid paused, and in that moment of quiet, the winds stirred the white cloak at the crimson knight's rear, along with the purple cloak still clutched in metal hand. "Good destiny is a spent energy that we all hold with much self-doubt, anxiety, and fear over the possibility of failure. People are made uneasy by failure, and rightfully so."

Kort stared at Elucid over his shoulder, with a face now relaxed. He still had his hands on the boat's side, with the intention of jumping overboard.

"But as doubtful we are," Elucid continued, "and as prone to fear and anxiety we may be, the chase of good destiny should sustain us. After all, the pursuit of that which helps others and ourselves is rewarding on more planes than one! It's well worth the time, energy, and risk of failure!"

With those last words, Elucid seemingly swayed Kort not to jump immediately. He slowly removed his hands from the boat's side, and faced the crimson knight.

Meanwhile, Elucid lifted both hands to gesture—one held the purple cloak over the boat, whereas the free hand extended over the moving waters.

"So have it your way," Elucid said. "Your *choice* can be to trust me and stay here for good destiny…" As those words were spoken, the crimson knight motioned to the boat, the place where Kort could stay. "Or swim back to land, with the *chance* of finding better destiny there with Sagult on your heel and nowhere to work." Elucid motioned with the second hand while talking, to the waters where Kort could leave. Upon the last word, Elucid dropped both metal hands.

A grimace appeared on Kort's face, as more winds interceded Elucid to voice a strong talk of their own. The skyline began darkening from light blue to dull gray. Below it, large waves splashed against the boat.

"I am not whom you think!" Kort admitted finally. "Last night I tried to lift famine from Doj, but couldn't!" With his confession, Kort's eyes showed more pain; they glistened from welled-up tears, barely restrained from flooding down his cheeks.

"You can lift famine, if…" said Elucid.

"How?!" Kort cut in. "Certainly not by magic."

"You ask the wrong question. *When* is more important than *how…*"

Kort interjected again, "I'm not the Child of Light."

Lightning streaked across the darkening sky in the distance, and thunder roared. A very different scene now replaced the once-blue skies overtop the calm seas: gray clouds above troubled waters.

"You are," Elucid replied calmly, as the heavens opened up and rain gently fell. "I'm not sure how, but you are indeed the One of Prophecy."

"We should turn back!" Raiden called out from the rudder, trying to point the boat toward Doj again. Elucid turned to him, only to witness the fisher sent abruptly to the hull, as a crashing wave jolted the boat! Elucid shifted upon metal feet to maintain balance, as did Kort.

"I am not the Child of Light!" shouted Kort again, his eyes speaking of persistent denial.

"Only because you don't believe," Elucid answered. "Faith can bridge your doubt!"

"I'm not the Child of Light!" screamed Kort, as if enraged by the insistence of a contrary claim. Earsplitting cracks of thunder brought Elucid's attention to the gray clouds, their menacing contours luminously tinged by lightning that struck the sky, one moment ago.

To the rudder, Raiden went again but with the same outcome—knocked to the hull upon touching the controls.

"A storm is upon us!" he yelled from the planks, though upon deaf ears.

Elucid would not turn back, even if the choice were available. *We're meant to endure certain hardships, not flee from them!* The rains continued coming down, harder now, hitting the crimson knight's armor all over and wetting the fishers.

Elucid considered how to break through to Kort. *Surely unanswered questions enroot his doubts… Every Child needs the Game clarified… Naketo did, and so does he…* "Does this Game of Time and Broken Sword seem a myth to you? Is that what prevents you from believing?"

"Isn't the Game a myth to everyone?!" Kort snapped, from under a mess of drenched hair, covering his one eye.

"Undoubtedly questions circle your mind," Elucid shot back. "You wonder so many things, why Gallow Cliff is so special?! It's a spot where anyone can tap into the age's time to find a unique destiny through spent energy!"

Kort's face showed confusion, as if he wondered why Elucid gave this particular explanation.

"So many questions hinder your belief?! Like about the white and black shards of sword, broken from the gray blade? Breaking the whole sword was the only way of preventing our creator Maken from interfering with the Game, the only way one lineage of Destiny wouldn't start play, having an unfair advantage!"

Kort's face showed of greater confusion.

"More questions?" Elucid asked. "Maybe another, like how Shaizan's victory will ensure everlasting Darkness? It can happen by a curse from Destiny, a curse that's found its way into this age!"

Kort's face showed of yet greater confusion.

Finally he blurted out, "What are you doing?! These questions are not wholly mine!"

"But surely answers to these questions help," retorted Elucid, in a booming voice. "They helped Fieronju's son!" Thunder roared again, after those words.

Against the sensory clutter of the storm, Elucid discerned through narrow eye slits, how Kort's features mixed between sheer disbelief and incredible sadness at the last remark.

He cried aloud, "Because of me, Fieronju is deprived of love and family; he's dead and sonless! How then, is he or his child involved in any of this?!"

"The storm is taking us into the deep!" Raiden interrupted above their screams, his voice overwhelmed by mighty winds, the rains, and thunderclaps.

As the boat's ruffled sails swelled with another strong gust, increasing amounts of precipitation fell. Dark clouds menaced Elucid and the fishers from above, now bunching on the horizon as far as the eye could see! The waves grew high, and Elucid felt the boat sickeningly ride up then down, waters crashing all around and into the hull.

"There's clarity after the storm," replied Elucid to Kort, just as a wave splashed them both. Kort shielded his face with an upraised arm, looking back at Elucid after the wave and against the winds, struggling to maintain eye with the crimson knight. "But for now, you must deal with life's tempest!"

Chapter 55
Life's Tempest

Awave crashed, splashing Kort in the face with cool water. He clung to the boat's mast in wet clothes, drenched thoroughly by the sea's sudden anger. Past the bow, he watched the sea as the boat rode another wave, from crest to trough. His gut sank the entire time, though at the back of his mind, he wondered if the sinking sensation truly came from still being with Elucid. *Should've jumped ship before the winds brought us this far!* The thought smacked him with regret, followed by his anticipation of the next drop, when another large wave carried the boat high.

As it rode the wave up then down, Kort became suddenly aware of wetness at his knees, feeling as though he already waded in the sea. He pried his eyes away from the storm to glance at the hull, which was filled with water. The visual sent a single realization through his head: *We'll surely sink!*

From the corner of one eye, Kort saw a sudden, red blur. He turned to observe Elucid use Nexus to displace water in the hull by raking it with an energy field, repeatedly until the hull was empty.

"If you help, we can get through this!" Elucid shouted to Kort, against the noisy storm.

Kort's face went grim.

"I can't move water to save my life!"

"Doesn't matter if you've failed before," answered Elucid. "Try again, and if nothing still, try something new!"

"But how?" Kort asked, his voice cracking from the disbelief that was stuck in his throat.

"Do as me!" Elucid said. "We must use magic to keep the water out!"

Kort watched the crimson knight create two force fields, one at a time; the first was at port and the second was at starboard of the small sailing vessel. They blocked waters that would otherwise enter. He saw green walls of Nexus flash at the left and right of the boat, just long enough to prevent more spillage into the hull.

"I'll take the right, you the left!" asserted Kort with initiative. He paused in that moment at his own words. *If Genze were here, the old sailor would insist on the correct nautical terms!* He recalled Genze shouting at him to use port and starboard, versus incorrect substitutes.

"Focus!" Raiden shouted

Water suddenly hit Kort in the face and flowed into the hull, during his short lapse of attention. Before he could even react, Elucid turned and quickly displaced some water in the hull with Nexus—water that Kort should have blocked.

Kort ran to the left, and tried to offset the crimson knight's vacancy by tending to the waves crashing there. He reached the boat's side, where he faced a large wave. Without delay, he entered his channeling chamber, pulled open his Source entry, let the energies envelope him, and went to his Source exit. There, he pushed the door open, while imagining a large stone wall.

He snapped back to the boat, where in only an instant, a green aura blinked at his midsection as he tapped the Nexus, and a sheet of energy materialized a cubit before him, just in time to block the wave!

From all sides, Kort felt the gusts hitting him, just as the hard rains pelted his body and face. Ignoring these distractions, he sighted another wave coming toward the boat. Just like before, he pulled more energy to create a barrier that would prevent it from entering. In his peripheral vision, he could tell Elucid did the exact same thing, but at his hinder parts.

After the wave bounced back into the sea, Kort's eyes went to the horizon where ominous clouds stretched from left to right, blotting out the light and sourcing darkness. Beneath that terrifying sky, gale-force winds upheaved the waters into a frenzy. Row after row of intimidating waves surged between him and the limits of his sight; the nearest of them mounted each side of the boat, to push it around on the troubled sea like a bully.

Kort glanced over at Elucid, and in that look, he saw a huge wave coming toward the opposite side of the boat! He budged to help, but immediately the crimson knight urged him to do otherwise.

"Just stay there!" Elucid called out. The knight's midsection already glowed green, as Elucid spun into action, forming a large energy field, and pushing the wave back. "Keep to your work, and I'll keep to mine!"

A shadow suddenly engulfed Kort, over his right shoulder. He turned while filling his core with Nexus, anticipating the need for quick magic. When about face, a large wave filled his vision, being much closer than expected—hair lengths away instead of cubits! He immediately felt the waters pummel him, before he could create the barrier.

Kort attempted to stand firm against the wave, keeping both feet planted on the hull. He found the water to be strong and near overpowering, yet he began pushing Nexus anyway. A sheet of green energy formed between him and the wave. He pushed and pushed to maintain the barrier, pulling more energy continuously when running out. Imagery of a study stone wall filled his head as, with a grunt, he continued to fight the wave. "Arghhh!"

Kort's magic outlasted the wave, and it retreated into the sea. Precisely then, the boat bounced on the tumultuous waters, and he lost his footing. But right before, Kort could hit the hull, he sensed Raiden catch his body from behind.

"Thanks to you!" said Kort.

"Thanks to Destiny we're still alive!"

And with that, Kort continued working together with Elucid to defend the boat, repeatedly forming energy fields to deflect oncoming waves. However, Kort soon tired, as it seemed this storm knew no end of wind and rain; his one defense followed another and yet another, in a way that proved exhausting.

At one point he stopped channeling, and just held the mast while catching his breath, being soaked to the bone and being almost out of fight. The boat, meanwhile, rode another wave. Kort looked out into the waters, against the backdrop of a gray sky flashed by lightning, with the rumble of thunder stuck in his ears. Clearly, the turmoil on the sea had not improved.

When Kort looked down, he saw a massive wave that loomed head-on before the sailboat! He held his breath, for their boat had rode many waves thus far, versus going against any. As he beheld its high crest crashing toward the bow, the sight gripped him with mind-numbing terror. His peripheral vision detected a glimpse of green, moments before Elucid ran up to boat's front, channeling Nexus. It flowed out of the knight's aux core, and all about the vessel's outer walls.

"What are you doing?!" shouted Kort.

"Propelling us forward!" Elucid boomed, not turning back. With those words, Kort felt the boat driven by Nexus, instead of being merely tossed about on the sea. In white-knuckled fists he tightly held the mast, Raiden too, as the wave towered over them. Just watching it come closer made Kort anxious; he wrung his hands about the wooden pole, not caring that splinters caught his skin.

As the boat met the wave, Kort felt it start a dangerously steep incline. Elucid channeled even more Nexus, as if determined to have the boat cut through the waters, no matter what. Kort watched Nexus surge on the outer walls, as the boat's bow pointed aloft, near completely vertical! In that moment, he took his eyes off the boat and looked up to the weepy heavens, letting the rain slap him across the face.

"We're going to tip over!" Kort cried, unable to stand it anymore.

"Learn to trust me," called back Elucid, still standing strong at the bow. "There's much more in store for you than this!"

When the boat rode over the crest in the next moment, Kort could not believe his eyes.

"You did it!" he exclaimed

"We're saved!" shouted Raiden.

Elucid stopped channeling.

A sloshing sound pulled Kort rightward, where he saw water pour into the boat from a wave breaking over its side. Though tired from using so much magic, Kort persevered. *Pull once more, and hopefully pull no more!*

Kort entered his enlarged channeling chamber, and pulled open his Source entry; his body ached in the very act. When the double doors parted, multiple flows of Nexus entered over their threshold; some streams swirled around him, others gushed past his feet. The streams flowed and flowed, filling the chamber from floor to ceiling. He ran to the Source exit with all the energy accumulated about him, pushed the door, and envisioned the same stone wall. Back on the boat, Kort held both hands at his waist—flat with their palms facing the wave—just as Nexus arced from his center into a barrier that blocked it.

When the wave bounced back into the sea, Kort lowered the wall of Nexus. But just as he did, it revealed something dreadful indeed—the biggest wave the ex-knight had ever seen on the sea, coming right at them! Fifty cubits high or more, it sped toward the vessel with its crest falling into its trough, as the wave broke from an opposing wave, being one wave ahead of the wave on which the boat rode. At this terrifying sight, Kort felt a pronounced flutter inside his stomach, along with the rapid pulsations of his own heart. *Destiny save us!*

In little time, a repeat occurred of events seen previously: Kort felt the vessel tilt upward and start a dangerous incline, its bow facing heaven. Both he and Raiden hugged the mast, while Elucid ran to the bow and channeled energy all around the vessel, in an attempt to propel the boat through the wave. While the experience was somewhat familiar, it was in all ways dreadful for Kort to endure, yet again.

"It'll capsize!" Kort shouted in fear, as the boat leaned vertical. "We'll never make it, even with magic!"

"There's little to lose by having faith," Elucid replied calmly, with the same deep vocals. "Do you trust me?!" Certain urgency built in the crimson knight's voice.

"I trust you some," said Kort, scared for his life.

"Let some faith become more… It's a start."

With that, Kort felt the boat angle back further, and he hugged the mast even tighter. He prayed aloud, not caring if anyone aboard heard his words.

"Destiny, allow me just enough time to right my wrongs. No more, no less!"

As Elucid pushed the boat up the gigantic wave, Kort felt it tilt back even more—no longer being vertical. *We're going over! We're going over!* Despite Kort's nascent faith in Elucid, he could not help but fear what he believed was inevitable.

And so, with some pessimism, Kort sensed the tiny sailboat lean back more—its bow now over its stern— perhaps foretelling of its future as a few planks among Korinth's vast ship wreckage. Time slowed in that moment, and he stared up beyond the bow to the wave's crest in the background, its shadow arcing over them like death's sickle. *Destiny, please…*

It was then that Kort fell out of the boat, and water flooded his every side. Straining, he turned his head away from Elucid tumbling out of the boat, to behold Raiden falling out just the same. When he looked back, he beheld the boat mast break off, and the hull shatter to planks and splinters. With that, all was lost.

But their misfortune was not without a song, for in that moment the eerie chimes played upon Kort's ears, the ones from Tai Forest and Doj's port. At the very point of failure—where an unexpected storm smashed Elucid's hijacked fishing expedition to bits and pieces—a light pierced the dark sky and filled Kort's entire field of vision with pervasive, all-consuming white. It was exactly like what he experienced upon emerging from Tai to stand on the outskirts of Reiju.

The white ensued in Kort's eyes with the chimes still playing in his ears. In time, the latter fell silent, being replaced by sounds far more soothing, rhythmic, and tranquil—those of water lapping against the boat. As the noise lolled Kort, he had to wonder. *Have I died?!*

But slowly, Kort found a very different set of circumstances. It happened when the pervasive white suddenly became royal blue waters that rolled peacefully beneath a starry night sky. They swaddled Raiden's sailboat and added serenity to the scene, just as the halo of moonlight that sat overtop of them.

Kort looked about in sheer disbelief, seeing Raiden standing in his boat, which now appeared fully intact despite the storm; it had a mast, spars, rigging, and sails. And beside the fisher, he saw the mysterious Elucid on both feet, still clutching the same purple cloak, an object of perhaps even greater mystery than the knight.

"STORMS OF LIFE"

Chapter 56
Stars and Skies

K ort blinked several times, wondering if his eyelids would peel back on one particular blink to reveal a different and more explicable reality. Yet, as much as be blinked, he kept opening his eyes to the same magnificent scene, with the dark sky strewn above the calm waters of Korinth, dotted with bright shining stars. There was no longer a storm on the sea, or so it seemed.

"Now do you believe?" asked Elucid.

Kort turned to see the crimson knight, focusing upon him with a pair of black eye slits. All he could do was stare back, not knowing exactly what to say. It was as if Elucid presumed their miraculous exit from the storm erased any doubts he could have, when to the contrary, his mind still spun questions. *How did this happen? Why are we here? Who is the crimson knight? What does Elucid really want?*

The topics wrestled with each other for their place at the top of Kort's mind. With a deep breath, he resolved to not follow his instincts by openly questioning Elucid's intentions. *Try to believe.* With that thought, he opened his mouth, and a more neutral set of questions came forth.

"What happened, and why are we here?"

"You made the choice to fight the storm with me," Elucid boomed. "Whether that choice would be blessed was decided by higher powers above kings of kingdoms—awesome powers that relate to what is and what is not."

"Your answer does not suffice," Kort replied. "I understand neither the natural nor the supernatural as it happens to me. My life, so far, has seemed more chance than choice."

"But do any of us understand?" interjected Raiden, in perfect Mainlandish. "My life, too, seems more a product of chance versus choice, but I can't control the chance. I can only choose how I want to live, regardless of chance."

"And how's that?" Kort's forehead wrinkled.

"To fish for more than fish," Raiden answered, "to fish for good destiny. Wherever I go, and whatever comes my way, the Book of Karnatha teaches that I should pursue good destiny even if I encounter bad destiny by chance. It instructs Karnathans to seek good destiny that leads into good destiny for others, not bad or null destinies! Living by this code is a conscious choice we all can make, and for me, it gives purpose!"

Elucid nodded, as if in agreement.

497

"It can give us all purpose, though in different ways. We're all meant to do something different in this life, to help others and ourselves. For you, good destiny is more than slowly redeeming yourself in the Isles; it's more than just being a fisher of fish! You're meant to cast your net for the white shard of sword, fallen to the depths of the Korinth Ocean by Ma'althan's doing."

And just like the sunken shard that Kort read about in Genze's book, he sunk to certain depths of quiet contemplation. *Their claims seem as preposterous as the tall tales themselves...* Even though trusting the crimson knight seemed more reasonable now, Kort was still sensitive to being proclaimed as Karnath's hero. *It's impossible that I'd be a hero now, after being the villain for so long! It's just impossible...*

"How can I believe what you say?" asked Kort, as the repeated insistence from Elucid and Raiden deeply sorrowed him. His voice was firm and unshaken, though tears streamed from his eyes. "Your claim that I am the One imposes great weights on my weak character, a burden so heavy it gives way to duress! All that I've been to others is deceit, pain, and death—not truth, healing, and life!"

At his comment, Kort heard nothing but the swash of water against the boat's side, as the vessel glided along the Korinth by the cool breeze caught in its sails. He saw Elucid stare back without a word, Raiden too, both of them inhibited from any contradiction, at least for the moment. *Like I said!* The ex-knight despaired over his presumed correctness.

He felt warm tears run down his cheeks, and that sensation was easily a reminder of his pains due to his Dark past. Whom he was and what he did were bothersome things that completely and utterly deprived him of solace. *Oh that I could change what I've done*, he thought, despairingly. *If it were possible, I'd redo my whole life all over again!*

But in a few moments of silence, Kort began to think differently about his predicament. What Elucid said during the storm came to mind. *There's little to lose by having faith.* He pondered the validity of that argument, whether having faith was more of choice or more of chance, and what consequences it would have. After mulling over it a while, his mind settled upon an opinion. *To have faith is my choice, and if I find my faith wrong, I'll simply change beliefs. Just believing may be the only way to move beyond my doubts, which up until now have limited the future person I can be!*

"So if I believe," Kort said suddenly, the tears drying on his face. "Then tell me how this thing will be possible. How can we find a shard sunk in the sea?"

"To catch even a fish, you must lower your net. Why would catching a broken sword be any different?"

Kort returned the immediacy of that response.

"Because, a fish is different than a broken sword! And fish don't swim to the depths iron falls! This matter in which you require my faith is truly difficult to believe!"

To Kort, it seemed obvious why the matter of finding the shard would be seen as more difficult than catching a fish. But then, as more silence developed, his mind worked over the words spoken, applying them in different ways and analyzing them. *Have I missed Elucid's point? Perhaps it's only to say, in order to succeed I must at least try...*

"To find the lost shard," Elucid boomed, "you must search for it rather than just asking how it can be found." And with those words, confirmation came to Kort of what the crimson knight meant, being exactly as he supposed. *You must try in order to succeed.*

"My suggestion," said Elucid, "is to fish for fish before lowering your net for a sword. Your body needs fish more than the shard." The comment struck Kort with surprise. With the storm he forgot how he was without food for the entire day. The ex-knight looked to his net and then to Raiden.

"Well? Are we going to fish or what?"

Kort stared back, appreciating Raiden's warm smile; it seemed reassuring in a way, and of goodwill.

"Let's cast our nets!" Kort said finally with enthusiasm. And so, the ex-knight and Raiden launched their weighted nets into the deep, first swirling them over their head in one hand while holding the affixed lines in the other. Kort watched as one by one, their nets splashed into the distant water and sank. He fastened the lines to a cleat inside the boat, and waited.

Kort grabbed another net from the boat and began swirling it over his head, readying himself to throw it over the boat's opposite side and into the water.

"Stop and look," Elucid boomed.

Mid-whirl, Kort aborted his throw. He turned to see Elucid standing there, pointing to the net with a free hand. Kort put it down on the planks, to understand the problem. Without much effort, he noticed a large hole in the netting, big enough for fish to swim through.

"If you're going to do anything," Elucid said. "Do it well and mightily. This net permits neither."

Kort examined it, his mind swimming in thought. *If only a single fish swam into the net*, he thought, *it might easily escape! And what's the likelihood of catching many fish, on the fishless Korinth?* He gazed back up, now aware of some wisdom in Elucid's words.

Kort dropped the net to the hull.

"Well spoken, so I shall fish well and mightily, with what's ready for fishing!" He stared at Elucid, unable to sense a single emotion from the crimson knight, since the metal demon gave off the feelings of a rock.

With that, he turned to Raiden and started talking as the two fished on through the night. A free-flowing exchange between fisher and ex-knight melted away the time. Kort remained guarded about his past, not divulging too much, and staying under his alias "Inari". But that did not stop him from asking questions about Raiden.

In so doing, Kort learned a bit about Raiden as the fisher opened up and shared his life's story. Never married, he did not have any children, though always wanted a family. Strangely enough, he did come to shelter a runaway from the Black Dragon territory; it was an elven boy of the orient, who fled from an allegedly troubled home and sought refuge in Doj. Raiden confessed to selfishly never seeking out the parents, for his own want of a son.

"It was wrong," Raiden said, looking into the sea. The breeze lifted his lengthy white hair, above his scraggly beard and bushy eyebrows. "The right thing would've been to scour the Black Dragon lands to find the boy's parents, but the longer he stayed, the harder it became to let go."

Kort saw Raiden shake his head, and heard a mumbled justification or two. "It didn't help matters that the neighboring territory was so hostile. And for those in the Red Dragon lands, this meant no one had an accurate map of the region. So it would have been near impossible to navigate."

"What was his name?" Kort asked with a smile. His stomach growled just then, reminding him that indeed his hunger had not vanished.

Raiden smiled back. "From the moment he appeared at my doorstep, he called himself... Garlew. And I loved him immensely."

Kort's chest tightened considerably, and he struggled to breathe. Not sure if he heard correctly, he reiterated his question, stuttering a bit.

"Wh... what was his name?"

"Garlew. I thought it was such an odd name at first. Clearly Mainlandish in origin, not Hirishin..."

Kort partially disconnected from the conversation, very distracted now by the nature of the fisher's news. In one sudden instant, his eyes narrowed, his lips parted ever so slightly, and his face felt cold as ice. *I'm sailing Korinth with a metal demon who thinks I'm the One of Prophecy, and also, with the adopted father of Fieronju?!*

"Maybe his name wasn't that peculiar after all," Raiden said with a shrug. "There's a heavy Mainlandish influence throughout parts of the Isles as indicated by the olden name of Doj's port—Logan. I've even come to learn the common language of the dwarves, humans, and elves by so many sojourners from the East..."

Raiden rambled on about inconsequential things, while Kort was deep in thought about information that essentially was a revelation for him. Indeed, he cared little about how the name Garlew originated, but rather, cared more about learning the story of what happened to Fieronju in the decades between the disappearance of childhood friend in the Isles and his later rise to fame in Sergros. *As children, the last time we spent together was sitting together in the palace, listening to Shima teach astronomy. After that, Fieronju was just gone...*

He remembered the situation well for a number of reasons, one of which included how Shima—one of their female caretakers—was particularly cruel to Fieronju for a very odd reason: Fieronju was the second of Emperor Hboshi's twin sons to emerge from the womb, and thus, neither the firstborn nor an heir to his father's empire. *She always ridiculed him for being lesser than his brother.*

But beyond his closure on the runaway Fieronju, Kort's guilt literally gnawed at him. In the moment following Raiden's account, he wanted so desperately to express condolences for what had happened to Garlew. *Surely Raiden heard the news already*, he thought, thinking about Garlew's untimely death.

Kort heard Raiden continue to talk, but he was so preoccupied that he missed about half of the conversation's full share. *Tell him what happened!* An inner voice suddenly pressed him about expressing his repentance to someone who was directly affected by his mistake.

"I've always liked to think he lived my dreams of a family," Raiden said. "I had premonitions about my grandchild, *Naketo*. I'm sure that Garlew had a son..."

As Raiden rambled on, it became evident to Kort how the fisher had some many dreams related to Garlew and his legacy, even though they seemed detached from Garlew's prestige on the Mainland. And so, despite having more than a little brine during the storm, Kort's mouth went suddenly dry at the mere thought of his admission shattering those dreams.

If I tell, how will Raiden react?! In that moment, he felt torn between his pursuits of contritely owning his wrongdoing and the consequences of such ownership. *Maybe it would be better, not to speak?* Kort weighed the two options, thinking of what he should do or not do, until a distraction removed him from further contemplation.

"There!" Elucid exclaimed, all of a sudden. The interjection quieted the rambling Raiden, who fell silent.

Kort looked over, to where the crimson knight pointed with one metal finger. It was to an area in the sky full of stars, so densely packed that whatever the crimson knight beheld was in no way apparent.

"All I see are stars!" exclaimed Raiden, clearly sharing in the same dilemma.

"There!" Elucid said again, still pointing.

"Oh, that. What is it?" Raiden asked.

"*Ires Constellation*," replied the crimson knight.

In Kort's mind, the mention of Ires Constellation triggered memories of Shima's astronomy lesson, and a sudden vision came upon him.

**** Shima's Lesson – Light Prophecy and Ires Star ****

Kort sat cross-legged with young Taurus and Fieronju in the lavish palace of the prior Black Dragon emperor, surrounded by dozens of other children from the most affluent families in the empire. Their caretaker Shima occupied a stool before them, wearing a silk dress dyed a teal green and holding a leather-bound book in her hands. She had jet-black hair that covered her pointy ears, big brown eyes, smooth olive skin, and a cute nubby nose.

Shima was fascinated by astronomy and mythology, and she loved to teach both subjects to the children after their morning lessons and lunch. But Kort loved staring at Shima's pretty face, as he was coming of age and she was an elven girl not far from her maturity.

Shima smiled, and spoke to the children in a gentle voice: And the prophecy tells how the battle shall not be without a victor, for on that day Kayareth shall slay Shaizan and meld the black shard with the white into the whole gray blade, before climbing Liath to destroy it in Ires Star. Now, Ires Star is one special star in Ires Constellation, the brightest group of stars that shine over Karnath. It's the highest and hottest star that exists!

****

Kort's vision faded, and was replaced by the ongoing conversation between Elucid and Raiden.

"It's a fist," Elucid explained. "The hand and knuckles are upright, made from different stars in the constellation. The highest star, making the middle knuckle, is Ires Star."

The crimson knight turned to address Kort.

"Your pursuit of the shard is only the first step."

Elucid's statement stirred Kort's mind with questions. His immediate thought concerned how the Light and Dark Prophecies talked about a fight at Gallow Cliff, a duel involving two Children of Destiny, each bearing a shard of respective hue. *Will fighting the Child of Darkness be the next step after finding the sunken shard?! How does that relate to Ires Star or Ires Constellation?*

"What do you mean?" Kort asked.

"In order to save time, it's not enough to merely retrieve the shard and fight the Child of Darkness—the shard must be destroyed." Elucid spoke the words bluntly.

"It must be destroyed?"

"Yes, the white shard must go into the star," Elucid boomed, "because another Child from the Dark Lineage might seek to destroy time using the whole gray blade. It's conceivable that this could be done, as long as both shards exist.

502

Karnatha forged the gray sword in Ires Star so Maken could create the worlds, hence the shards can only be destroyed there."

Kort's face showed wild disbelief.

"How in Karnath could I put a sword into a star?!"

All of a sudden, thoughts clouded his mind, so many colliding with existing ones of the day, and those of days beforehand. *That's preposterous!* said a first voice, followed by a close second. *A broken sword couldn't be put so high in the heavens by anyone on land, let alone me!*

Elucid replied, "One step at a time. When you get the shard, we'll have this talk. All my premonitions aren't intact yet, but the white shard up Liath is your path."

The comment rendered Kort silent, for it struck him as contradictory to the prophecies. He opened his mouth and turned to the crimson knight, but then shut it knowing better. *The white shard up Liath? What about Gallow Cliff?* The questions were clear in his mind, though his wished not to evidence continued incredulity, by posing challenge after challenge to Elucid.

"What is it?" asked Elucid.

"Forgive me for seeming of little faith," Kort meekly said, "but both Light and Dark Prophecies tell of a Battle for Destiny deciding which of the Children would prevail with the whole gray blade. And the Light Prophecy foretells the whole blade being destroyed in Ires Star, not just one shard. But if we find the white shard of sword, we won't have the gray blade." His mouth worked faster, so to keep up with the conclusions his mind had reached. "I would have to fight Shaizan at Gallow Cliff and win, in order to recover the full sword for its destruction!"

"No," Elucid replied, "one shard up Liath, and into the highest and hottest star of all the heavens, is the way to win this Game."

Kort sifted through all the information provided, and made a startling discovery. *Elucid is not trying to have me fulfill the Dark Prophecy, nor does the crimson knight urge me to fulfill the Light Prophecy as written!* His mind went round and round, dizzied by the conundrum. *What does that mean?!*

"But if I'm whom you say," asserted Kort excitedly, his hands aflutter in gestures. "I am the one to prevent the Dark Prophecy from coming true, the one foretold of in the Light Prophecy who makes *that prophecy* a reality, exactly as written!"

"No!" boomed Elucid. "Trust my guidance in the matter, and question this not."

From the boat's back, Raiden came forth. Kort watched him stand upright on the planked hull, and step toward the crimson knight with an upraised hand.

"He asks a fair question. Why would your recommendation be different than the prophecies?"

With that, Kort watched Elucid go stoic and aloof, as if pondering Raiden's question a great length. At last, the crimson knight responded calmly, "This question comes without posing any of your own questions to what the oracles have said, lo these many years. But you should know that if ever a time existed to question what the prophets have spoken, it is now."

Kort observed Elucid turn away, cross both arms, and gaze into the sea. "The oracles once foresaw good with the Light Prophecy, they recently foresaw bad with the Dark Prophecy, and now many foresee nothing at all. So what better time could there be for one to believe that he or she owns their future? What better time could there be, to decisively map out the course of our destinies? Don't hang yourself at the cliffs, just because the oracles said so. Let us do rather, whatever will win this Game for the Light. And my heart tells me that going up the mountain with one shard of sword is it…"

Elucid uncrossed both arms, turned from the sea, and walked over to Kort. The crimson knight placed a hand on his shoulder. Kort glanced down at it, feeling the metal through his shirt, cold as steel but light as feathers. The sensation made him shudder.

"Seize your good destiny with good choices," Elucid said, "and decide for yourself the goodness of your choices, with the aid of wise counsel."

Kort locked his eyes on the dark slits in Elucid's helmet. Behind the crimson knight, the sky lightened and gave way to the morning sunset, the debut of another day in Karnath. "If you trust that I'm your wise counsel," Elucid said finally, "then do believe I drive you toward good choice. I want good destiny for you, and Karnath too."

Over his shoulder, Kort glanced back when sensing Raiden move at the boat's other side; he checked the cast lines for any caught fish by judging the resistance. Elucid removed the hand and Kort nodded his head. Just then, a breeze blew over them.

Kort suddenly felt tired and hungry again, but he grew dismissive of his needs, being preoccupied by the things discussed and how they pertained to his life. *My bad choices culminated in bad destiny*, he thought with a scowl. *So it might be, that good choices culminate in good destiny…* He remembered then, how in his nightmare Taurus Hboshi ascribed a bizarre ability to chance, which enabled him to warp the future through his own premonitions. The thought conjured up his disdain for chance, and his bias toward choice.

It was then that he renewed his commitments to himself. In an aside Kort shouted, "Maybe Taurus would roll the dice with his premonitions, but I won't! Instead I shall make good choices!" *I need something I can control, and choice is it.* So in that moment, with a heart hopeful that he might be used to do good things for many, Kort stayed open-minded to placing trust in Elucid for guidance on good choices.

"So what choice leads your destiny?" asked Elucid, again. The question stirred up Kort's memories about the same words spoken in Reiju's market, days ago.

After a few moments of silence, Kort replied, "This choice leads my doing, my choice to be in this place having faith, and with this worthwhile pursuit!"

In his heart, Kort prayed to Destiny. *Please Karnatha, let me map out my own destiny, as Elucid has encouraged me! Let me rewrite my life's story, to give it the right ending!* And Kort knelt down and continued to pray for half an hour or so, beseeching Destiny for this dream to come true.

Time elapsed and suddenly, soft snores could be heard from the back of the boat. Still on his knees, Kort opened his eyes and glanced back to see Raiden; he was lying down in the hull, fast asleep. Kort smiled, noting then the orange-slathered sunset above the boat.

He looked up to the sky, and beheld Ires Star go invisible in the morning light. It served a reminder of what Elucid said they had to do. *Up Liath with the white shard...* The thought ran through his mind and into obscurity, just as this nightly star, which would surely shine again, perhaps betokening of good destiny to come.

His eyes drifted again to Elucid, who crouched on the hull and stared into the sea. Kort slowly noted something unseen until now. Beneath the crimson knight's white cloak—the one showing the emblem of the Isles Crusades—a green light shined through, circular in form and pulsating. Kort just stared at it, until the sight provoked a singular thought: *Does this stone power Elucid's magical armor?* Though he wondered about just that, he refrained from asking a question of little consequence to him. To Kort, it was a question of the same kind, as asking about the purple cloak that Elucid carried. *Doesn't matter...*

A gentle breeze kissed Kort then, pulling at his hair and shirt. He smiled and started taking in the nets, knowing by the line's resistance that there was no catch, but refusing to be disappointed by it. *It isn't a foreshadowing, but rather, a challenge!* he considered, optimistically.

"Perhaps the nets can be launched again," Elucid boomed, "once we sail a bit deeper on Korinth."

Kort nodded, and kept pulling in the lines. When the nets finally came to the boat, he dropped the weighted mesh onto the planks, and then used the boom to reposition the sails hung from the mast. And with that, they caught more winds and carried the boat into the sunset.

It was a new day's dawning, a fresh start that bore hope for good things on the horizon, for not just any one person, but all three of them—the crimson knight Elucid, the fisher Raiden, and the ex-knight Kort. As the vessel moved the motley trio deeper into Korinth, they each could wonder where the winds would take them, and to what fortune the winds might lead.

Chapter 57
Broken in Body and Spirit

Perhaps those winds led to misfortune, or perhaps misfortune came when the winds died. Regardless of the truth, their boat just sat on the listless sea, only a few hours after Kort raised the sails again. And it sat there for hours that turned into days, and days that turned into weeks, drifting lethargically on Korinth by a weak current.

Their story of good fortune was now overwritten with a bleaker tale, with only death in sight for two starving and emaciated elves—Kort and Raiden— neither of which had eaten for weeks. Despite launching their nets into the deep again and again, at no point did the line pull taut for either fish or sword.

And repeats of failure wore at Kort's faith, and he began to look differently at Elucid, wondering Darker things now, like if Elucid really brought them onto the ocean to die.

Under a blazing sun, Kort leaned against the boat's side and let his legs stretch out over the planks. In between his feet was the covered pot. It sat distantly on the boat's opposite side, adjacent to the dismantled looking glass, their rope, and oars. Raiden slumped at Kort's right, gaunt as could be. Further right he saw Elucid at the boat's far end, peering into the ocean without a word. On his left, the cleats inside of the boat had lines fastened that went into the water, to their cast nets. It was a repeat of the same exact scene that Kort saw for weeks now.

Kort raised his arm to block the intense sunlight from his eyes; it was a cure for just one of his many discomforts. Indeed, he knew a world of affliction trapped at sea without food. From day to day, his stomach ached, his head pounded from throbbing migraines, and his mind suffered frequent delirium. It was a literal breakdown of his body, and his nerves insisted that he know about it.

Kort looked to his feet then, seeing the handled pot sitting before him, its lid leaning on an angle and not flush to the body. At the sight, he could not tell if he owed the pot thanks or regret, for it was the reason he endured such bodily deterioration, enabling him to at least drink water by unconventional, yet resourceful, means.

On a daily basis, Kort used the pot that Raiden brought aboard to boil water through the Nexus, first having placed a key piece from the looking glass inside—its lens. The condensation of water vapors from boiled water would accumulate on the lid, and trickle into the small convex lens. *It's just enough for a sip, and just enough to keep alive if done repeatedly…*

Kort became uncertain of whether the pot was more a curse than a blessing because it enabled him to live in spite of loosing his life purpose. For every day they spent on the waters without food was a bleak reality that diverged increasingly from his path to redemption and finding Nym. In that, Kort regretted being able to keep alive, only to see his body waste and his dreams die.

Kort sighed, still leaning up against the boat. He kept his arm over his face, ignoring the discomforts of the sun's searing rays against his skin. Ever since the storm ended, the sun grew hotter and unbearable, creating excessive heat at sea, despite the higher heat capacity of the water. Without a cloud to shield him from the sun's glare, his skin blistered, being red in places and sore to the touch. He wondered often if he should jump into the ocean and swim awhile for some relief. While he had done so betimes to cool off, his body tired easily in its current state, presenting a clear tradeoff between blistering and drowning.

"In my premonitions, Inari…" Raiden mumbled, a bit incoherently. "I foresee myself with a grandchild, Garlew's son named Naketo…"

"You told me that already," said Kort, a bit snarky. He grew irritated of everything and everyone, due to going so long without the essential needs of his body met. Kort had changed like others put in such situations, though not for the good.

When Kort turned away from Raiden and looked to Elucid, he easily filled with anger. The crimson knight stood at the boat's side, still gazing into the horizon and clutching the purple cloak. Elucid remained unspoken despite the bad situation that had developed, without offering a bit of guidance or wise counsel. Kort found the mismatch frustrating, between reality and the expectations he set based on Elucid's previous words. *He doesn't tell us anything at all. Some guidance and wise counsel he is…*

Kort stared at Elucid's back with some contempt, fixating upon the emblem embroidered on the white cloak showing the black and red dragon eating each other from the tail up. He contextualized the symbol in a way he never would have imagined before. *Does Elucid care if Raiden and I become as those dragons, and eat each other for want of food? As Elucid doesn't need food, how can the knight even care?!* Kort kept staring at the cloak, noticing the glowing green stone once more, shining from beneath the fabric. *That's why he doesn't care… Elucid gets power from that.*

"What are you anyway?" Kort asked in a testy way, tired of their predicament.

But Elucid stayed silent, those eye slits fixed toward the water alone, and nothing else.

"What's that purple cloak you hold?" Kort asked further, only to hear water sloshing against the boat.

Given a provoking silence, Kort demanded answers.

"How long shall we drift on the windless Korinth?!" he asked. "Tell me, how long will it be!"

"As long as is needed," Elucid finally replied.

Kort hated how Elucid offered up enigmatic responses, seemingly done to deflect questions. It irked him more than usual given their poor circumstances, and led to him coping through sarcasm.

"Until we die, is that it?" Kort yelled. "This isn't working... We've looked for the shard with lowered nets day come and day go, only to encounter failure time after time! I can't even recall how often the sun has risen and set on the horizon."

"Failure," said Elucid, "is a waymark on the path to success. Fear of failure prevents some from even trying."

"We've tried and failed," Kort snapped. "Why are you saying irrelevant things?"

Elucid responded, "But have we tried enough? Don't let initial failure bar your continued efforts, for perseverance sees to rewards given. So we must persevere."

Kort put an elbow on the boat's side, to give himself support as he struggled to stand on his weak legs. When upon his feet, he felt wobbly and lightheaded; blood pounded his head. Slowly, he made his way over to the lines fastened to the cleats, tracing the boat's side with his hand along the way. When he reached the lines, he tugged them both and judged the resistance.

"Nothing, like always," Kort muttered.

He went back over to where he was, by Raiden, and addressed Elucid. "Will we have fish today? How long until all this fishing leads to fish or swords?"

Elucid just stared into the waters.

"I asked you, how long?"

"I don't know how long," Elucid answered, after a long pause. "Perhaps that will be decided by you."

For a moment, Kort almost presumed Elucid was being honest and not deflecting, until that last comment. *Another cryptic response?!* It drove Kort mad, causing him to grind his aching teeth in frustration. Many things raced through his mind, a great deal of them not fit for speaking. But of many things worth holding back, one thought escaped, hissed through the ex-knight's clenched teeth, as if spoken with a forked tongue.

"So *this* is fishing for more than fish?!" Kort shouted. "*This* is fishing for good destiny?!"

Elucid turned from the water.

"Good destiny shall come to you, through good choice. Continue to make good choices, and all else shall fall into place."

More potential responses vied for supremacy in Kort's mind, some less distasteful than others. He was so angry with the crimson knight that it was most tempting to quickly blurt out whatever was at the top of his mind. He exercised some self-control, but that restraint weakened by the passing moment.

Staring at Elucid, Kort hit his chest with one balled fist; he let that hand bounce off his chest, toward the crimson knight, with his index finger pointing. "You're my guide, my wise counsel. Am I not making good decisions with *your* help?!"

Elucid fell silent at the question, and that silence upset Kort in a way where he could not easily respond.
Being tired, weak, and many other things, Kort ended up laughing off the direful situation, as his means of coping.

"Oh, maybe it's my simpler choices? Was my net not launched in the right spot? Perhaps if I had strength enough, I could recast it further where we'd have better luck?" While speaking, he gestured to the most distant point on the horizon.

It was then that Kort's vexation over their plight peaked, and he shouted to the waters in his own aside.

"Is there a single fish in the whole ocean?! Could the ocean spare Raiden and me just one fish, so we could live on?! Would it be too much, for me to last long enough to right my wrongs before passing from Karnath?! To die upon the land, to die upon the sea, a life lived without purpose, seems pointless to me! What is the point of these tests and trials, Destiny?! I seek good destiny when having the bad, only to endure bad destiny more and more!"

Elucid kept silent, as if allowing space between Kort's heated talk and anymore angering words.

"Ughh," Kort grunted in disgust over more quiet from the crimson knight, and turned his back to the metal demon. He was so close to wishing he never set sail with Raiden, so close to regretting dreaming of good destiny amid the downward spiral of his Fate's Fray. *Am I reduced now to a person of only regrets? Was it wrong of wretched me to want better than misdeeds from my horrid past, better than my beguiling and murderous acts of old?!*

He screamed across the listless sea. "For me, is it impossible to right a few wrongs after committing so many?! I now wonder if for me, redemption will only be another lofty ideal, likened unto the fancies of children and delusions of fools!" Kort's world of wants and needs seemed so distant then, an array of things lost and seeming destined to be forever unfound, despite his good choices. *My lost honor, lost for good! My unfound redemption shall remain unfound! And of everything lost, my greatest loss is that of all losses had. 'Tis my lost love, a love perhaps nevermore to be! Nym…*

The image of her entered his mind then. He pictured Nym's long flowing silver hair, her fair complexion. In that moment, he gripped the amulet through the small leather purse hung about his neck, and remembered how she complemented him in every way, how she proved a reason for which to live wholesomely and decently toward others. "She forgave my trespass and loved me still," Kort whispered, looking into the sea. "And that showed me what love really is…"

For Kort, his expedition on Korinth was turning into a barrage of lost hopes. Broken for long in body and now being broken in spirit too, he found his faith tried and on the verge of failing. When he realized his state of being, he confronted himself with the question, of whether he still believed what Elucid said, concerning him being the Child. He paused and took a deep breath, letting everything in his mind settle. And then, in a moment of clarity, he acknowledged his position. *I do believe. It makes no sense to me, but I believe.*

With that thought, one line suddenly became taut, releasing a low hum! Kort turned from the sea, rushed past Raiden through the hull, and took hold of the rope. Upon touching it, he could definitely feel resistance from something trapped in the net!

Without wasting any time, Kort began pulling it in with all his might. He watched the netting come to him from the water, a single fish flapping inside, silver in color with darkened fins. The scales reflected the bright light of the sun, which nearly paled in comparison to the smile that instantly spread across Kort's lips.

"A fish, a fish!" he exclaimed, lowering it to the hull. Smiling still, Kort looked over his shoulder, seeing Raiden slumped against the vessel's side, sleeping in the same place beneath the sun. Kort was so excited he ran over to him with the squirming fish in the net and stooped down on his knees, wanting to share his joy.

"We got one!" he said over and over again, but Raiden stayed asleep. "Raiden, I have a fish for you!" Kort declared enthusiastically, his body animate and lively. But as Raiden did not stir, his smile turned into a straight face. He heard only the calm water splashing against the boat, and in his periphery, he could see Elucid at the boat's end, looking into the horizon.

Kort continued trying to wake Raiden, until his efforts elicited Elucid's speech. "His sleep is deeper than you think," said the crimson knight, not turning back.

With his senses dulled and head throbbing, Kort had little patience for more riddles from Elucid. "What do you mean?!" he demanded, only to encounter silence. Kort forced his mind to work over Elucid's words. *Deeper sleep is what?* His mind processed the notion until reaching a certain realization: *Death.* His straight face dipped to a frown, and Kort immediately stood up.

He grabbed Raiden's arms, shaking and tugging them. "No, no… Wake up! You're just sleeping!"

With some hesitance, Kort slapped Raiden across the face using the inside of his palm, but the fisher was completely unresponsive.

"No. No! Nooo!" Kort shouted. With trembling hands, he ripped his shirt from both sides, while despairingly looking up into the heavens. He felt the fabric tear as did his soul, and he collapsed upon the planked hull, weeping under the sun's glare.

He heard the water's slosh against the boat, and the fish still flopping in the net. And then came distinct footsteps against the wood, footsteps of someone having a large gait. With crying eyes, Kort glanced up to Elucid.

"In this malady, you lose sight of redemption, you lose sight of love and honor. More questions than answers fill your mind, leading only to confusion and anxiety." Elucid stopped then, for a brief pause. "But you should trust that the prophecy speaks of brokenness in body and spirit, and this is part of your path."

Lying there, Kort looked down to the planks, focused on the wood's winding grain, not wanting to get up and continue his life. It was one of hardship and pain, one that he did not want to live anymore.

From the ensuing quiet, Elucid said, "Eat the fish."

"No," Kort said, doubtful of good destiny to come.

"Would you do it for answers?" asked Elucid, in a persuasive way. Questions stayed abuzz at the back of Kort's head, some colliding into others. *Who is Elucid? What is that green stone in the armor? Why does he carry a purple cloak?* The offer was tempting, but he doubted any clarity will become of it, and he knew it would do nothing for the pain he suffered.

"So many times you've asked, who or what I am. Do you still wish to know?" The thoughts continued speeding at the back of Kort's mind. Meanwhile, his body hurt all over from head-to-toe; he felt weak and famished. *I'll likely break down and eat the fish anyway... So why not have Elucid tell?* In past weeks, Kort sometimes felt like he would die just to get one answer that made sense of everything, but at this point, any answer might be better than none. *Just do it.*

"Yes, knight. Reveal yourself to me," Kort said the words halfheartedly, looking to the flopping fish once more. Out of his pain and regret for the current situation, he wondered then. *Could that fish have kept Raiden alive, if caught moments earlier?*

"Fine," boomed Elucid. "Eat the fish for your health, and then I'll tell."

Kort sat up and turned to the crimson knight. His eyes passed over the metal demon, which shimmered in the midday sun. Merely seeing Elucid put his mind into motion, for the sight of the crimson knight had been so many extreme things for him—from friend to suspected foe, from encouraging words to bottomless mystery.

Kort shook his head, confused over why Elucid wanted him to eat the fish so badly. He finally leaned against boat's side to stand, determined then to do just that. *I'll at least get a straight answer out of Elucid, if it's the last thing I do…*

From Raiden's person, Kort took a knife. He went to the sole fish in the net, and grabbed it in his hand. The scales were warm to his touch from the sunlight; he felt the sea creature wiggle its body, wildly flapping its tail.

To the deck, Kort pressed the fish down, and with the knife he made a slice down its belly, to gut the animal alive. Afterward, he slit the fish parallel to its backbone, and it stopped squirming immediately.

Kort raised the fish to his mouth and sank his teeth into its flesh, eating it one fillet at a time. After eating most of the meat, he scraped the backside of the scales with his teeth, to pick it clean. Bodily juices and blood ran from his mouth, as he devoured the fish messily.

After finished eating, he tossed the fish carcass at Elucid's feet. "I ate it, now tell."

Kort watched Elucid nod, but the crimson knight fell strangely silent. The only sounds were water, once again heard as it lapped against the boat.

"Well?" asked Kort, in an impatient way.

"I come from before your time," answered Elucid finally, "and I've come to live and relive my life from the near beginning of existence, to its end."

Kort chewed his gum, feeling fish in the crevices of his mouth, and the irony taste of blood still lingering on his tongue. The hot sun beat down upon his shoulders, intensifying the situation. And like the sun burned, so did Kort; he burned to know the truth.

"Go on," he said.

"I am the shadow of my former self, forever a king without a kingdom, the one described as such in your legends."

When Elucid fell silent again, Kort slowly realized the telling was over. *That's it?! That's all he plans to say?!* It was an enigmatic, non-informative response that boiled Kort's blood, for he felt tricked into eating the fish, having gained no greater clarity on Elucid's identity.

He stood there fuming beneath the sun's fiery glare, feeling his face grow red and hotter.

"One honest, forthright response from you is all I require!" shouted the ex-knight to Elucid. "I've vowed myself against willful violence since I accidentally murdered Garlew Il'therin! But you incite me in a terrible way, one that makes me rethink my promise!"

Elucid spoke in an assuaging way, "I'm sorry for your provocation! Don't you understand that my true name means little beyond my attempts to elucidate you?"

With anger Kort shouted, "Just like the truth means little to a liar? Tell me now what you promised!"

"Have it your way then," Elucid conceded after a moment's silence. "My name is Laotzu, the first King of Juniper in Old Karnath!"

The words struck Kort with disbelief, and his forehead wrinkled. *Elucid claims to be the repentant king Laotzu, exiled to the paradise reborn in New Karnath, after Maken's punishment?* His mind searched for memories about Karnathan legend, and the name Laotzu obviously fit.

"You, Laotzu?" Kort challenged. "Kings rarely live in armor! There are seasons of war, but after them, many seasons of peace where armor is not one's home!"

"It is, if you're like me! Your books of legend are penned by cursed seroxians who know not the curse to those un-cursed in the blighted land of Old Karnath." Kort discerned a sense of urgency in Elucid's booming words. "Without bathing in the River of Life, seroxians become their shadow, and I've never found that healing water, the water which Maken put in New Karnath!"

"You purport then, to be the shadow of Laotzu, imprisoned in that magical armor?!" Kort yelled, doubts marking his tone.

"Yes!" Elucid said, with unwavering insistence.

But before this tirade between Kort and Elucid could continue, the waters in the distance became incredibly disturbed! Kort stopped talking and looked that way, with his hands upraised, as he was amid another gesture when it happened.

Kort observed the waters afar, which swirled at first in what appeared to be a whirlpool. But then, the waters suddenly erupted in the same spot, from which emerged an awful sea creature, towering high above Kort and Elucid in their boat. And the monster started moving rapidly on the ocean, right toward them!

"TROUBLE AT SEA"

(The Shaken Tower)

The image was trapped in his eyes, of Liath's western pass suddenly crumbling, spans away from Esmeralda's tower. What X'ieth did not expect, however, was that the pass would continue crumbling, up until the tower's foot!

His entrancement with the mountain's destruction ended in a split second. X'ieth stopped staring over Gremel's shoulder, out the tower's gaping hole that the dragon had created, and redirected his attention inside the stone chamber where he stood. He held his bloody sword in hand, still being overtop the headless corpse of Esmeralda. Scattered at his feet where the fallen Guardsmen, all of them bloodied, injured, and motionless. Beyond the knights were irate Magicia and laughing Lucen; both of them floated through the air like ghosts, with the sorceress chasing the youth.

It was a scene of carnage, wrought of the Guard invading Esmeralda's tower to stop her wrongdoing. It was also a scene of unexpected victory, seemingly made possible by Lucen's orchestration of events. In a matter of minutes, Lucen appeared to facilitate Gremel's communication with the sorceresses, thereby creating a deadly distraction for Esmeralda. X'ieth found himself wondering if Lucen had made it all happen, for some reason yet to be understood. *Why would he do this?*

An abrupt tremor interrupted his thought, as the tower started shaking, along with its floors. He suddenly felt it through his feet and shifted to keep his balance. Unable to brace anything for support, however, he fell to the unsteady floor, with his side hitting the stone. That impact sent a sharp pain through his hip, but he instantly ignored it and got to his knees. From there, he stood and peered across the shaking chamber, seeing the floor suddenly crack in multiple directions, from where Gremel tore the wall. The cracks were hairline fissures at first, but then widened and forked between the bodies of the fallen Guardsmen strewn throughout the chamber.

Now upon his feet, X'ieth started running for the severed head of Esmeralda that had rolled across the floor and bumped into Zeros. But after only a few steps, he stopped himself as the noise of flapping wings filled his one ear. He looked over his shoulder then, seeing Gremel turning from the hole, about to fly away. In her claw she held a green glowing object. *The white shard!*

The situation did not present a good tradeoff to X'ieth, as it soon became apparent how he could not have both the head and the sword. They were in opposite directions and there was limited time before Gremel left, so he would have to pursue either one or the other. *Would you rather show up Talus with the head, or become Karnath's hero with the sword?* Only a moment of weighing the two options was required, for him to see pursuing Gremel as the weightier. And with that realization, he no longer saw a mere dragon clutching a sword, but instead, his good destiny on wings.

RAWWWRRR! Gremel released a vociferous roar, and X'ieth put his deaf ear to the sound. He turned away from the direction of Zeros and Esmeralda's head, sheathed his sword, and ran toward the dragon. *To the Void with Talus' challenge... The Child must possess the shard!*

The thoughts sprinted through his mind, just like he sprinted toward Gremel on the shaking, breaking floor. After a few steps he heard Magicia scream, and he whipped about to run backward, in order to see what was happening. Magicia charged Lucen while shrieking in anger; her core shined a bright green, full of Nexus.

"You!" she yelled.

Magicia threw a burst of fire at Lucen, who mediated across the chamber, dodging it. X'ieth watched as the sorceress chased him, throwing more fire. Lucen disappeared then reappeared, dodging each attack.

At the glimpse of sudden motion, X'ieth directed his eyes to the floor. There, on the cracked stone, Zeros lifted his face and clutched the long locks that flowed from Esmeralda's severed head. X'ieth made eye contact with the mercenary, who acknowledged it with a nod and slowly stood, holding his broadsword and the dangling head in opposite hands. Awestruck, X'ieth nodded back to Zeros and spun about, still running. When about face, he found himself cubits before the hole leading out of the tower, to a sheer drop into Liath's foggy abyss!

He's alive. The quick thought grazed his mind, right as his feet neared the edge of the tower's floor and the opening came closer and closer in his eyes; it was a sight that shifted his attention off Zeros and ironically made him wonder if he would stay alive also, after exiting the tower.

No fear, man... Just jump! To X'ieth, pursuing Gremel seemed more of chance than a sure thing like getting Esmeralda's head. But in the end, it was a chance he was willing to take for the payoff of becoming Karnath's hero. And so, with all the power he could muster in his strong legs, the young knight leapt boldly into the night sky, right at Gremel hung upon beating wings, above a blanket of gloom covering the valley.

(Back in Esmeralda's Tower)

In a stone chamber of the shaking tower, Zeros rose from the floor, with his sword in one hand and Esmeralda's head in the other, dangling by its red hair. His body hurt all over from being thrown through the room by Magicia's magic; pulses of dull pain coursed through him, from head to toe. He anticipated a thorough bruising by morning, if not worse.

Ever since Magicia's brutal attack, Zeros had played dead on the floor, just waiting for a favorable moment to get up and strike. But he was happy to learn that X'ieth beat him to it, managing to invert Esmeralda's victory, though perhaps with less flair than he desired.

Once afoot, Zeros quickly glanced around the room, taking in Nathan, Hammar, and Finnel crumbled on the floor, which now had cracks zigzagging across it from where the dragon broke into the tower. Still at the gaping hole was Gremel, who turned on flapping wings to fly into the gloom, just as X'ieth ran from the tower at breakneck speed and jumped for the dragon's back. With a roar, both he and the dragon vanished into the fog, without giving Zeros closure as to whether the young knight made it or not. Coming into his continued view of the hole was Magicia chasing after the robed youth; she flew through the air on Nexus, hurling blasts of green fire. Lucen kept disappearing then reappearing, evading each attack. They left his field of vision as soon as they entered, going all around the room, both of them floating like ghosts.

In the mercenary's ears was a rumble, as the tower's violent shaking was still ongoing, from the moment he struggled up from the floor until now. He shifted his weight on both feet to keep standing, despite the floor's constant movement. It was certainly not the best position for Zeros, and debatably, he had not found himself worse off, despite years of Talus abusing him. *Burn the king... I'm getting too old for this!*

Magicia shrieked, "I curse the day we met!"

Zeros looked back, seeing her throw more fire.

Lucen vanished and then reappeared behind Magicia, laughing more. "Mwha ha ha ha!"

Zeros continued shifting on his feet, and glanced back to the gaping hole in the wall, thinking again of X'ieth. *Destiny, I pray he's well!* In that moment's look, the mercenary noticed a perpetual jitter of the rock outside in the valley, underneath the gloom. This sight resonated of his troubling realization had hours ago, and perhaps explained what was happening now: *Liath falls apart, and with it, the tower!*

As Zeros could still hear the whoosh of flames mixed with the rumble, he turned back to Magicia, who chased Lucen as before. Surprisingly, even though the sorceress almost killed him, the mercenary felt more negative emotions toward Lucen than toward her. *He's more the reason that X'ieth could be dead now, than is she!* And with that thought, Zeros growled in anger and raised his sword at Lucen, joining Magicia in her fight.

Zeros was at the chamber's center, and Lucen reappeared cubits before him. He ran and slashed at the youth, putting his sword into motion. But just before it made contact, Lucen moved blurredly to the side, evading the weapon with blinding speed. The mercenary slung his sword again and again at Lucen, with similar results. Either by sheer speed or vanishing away, Lucen remained evasive and moved around the room, near its walls. Zeros kept to the center, and rushed in whichever direction Lucen appeared next.

As the tower continued shaking and breaking apart, Zeros stumbled a few times while running with his sword, along with Esmeralda's dangling head. After many cycles of lunging at Lucen with his blade, Zeros breathed heavily at the room's center, feeling tired. His eyes found the floor, as the cracks widened across the chamber. A sudden motion brought his attention back up to Lucen, who blurred all around him, moving so fast that there seemed multiple copies of the youth! Zeros turned his head from side to side, trying to follow them. *Damn sorcerer...* Lucen's laughter filled his ears, as if to ridicule his failed efforts thus far. "Mwha ha ha ha!"

"Duck!" Magicia yelled, out of nowhere.

Panting still, Zeros dropped instantly to the floor, sensing a glimpse of green light from one side. As his extremities absorbed another impact against stone, he put his face down, sensing heat right above him! A moment later, Zeros glanced up to see Lucen dodge another fire burst; the mercenary understood then how he managed to get in the way of one of Magicia's attacks.

"Mwha ha ha ha! Mwha ha ha ha!"

Lucen continued to laugh, moving about the room.

When sounds entered Zeros' ears of shifting sands, he looked to the walls, where he noticed how the floor was shaking to dust, as it was now completely covered by cracks and still vibrating with the shaking tower. The floor's disintegration started at the room's length and moved inward, right toward Zeros! The sobering sight got him on both knees, and stirred his mind with immediate thought. *What in the Void?!*

Zeros continued kneeling on the floor. Lucen still circled him, with Magicia hovering upon Nexus and chasing after the youth; she made treks across the room's center where Zeros was, hurling fire at Lucen, who alternated between moving fast and disappearing, just as before. Through it all, Lucen managed to maintain eye contact with Zeros, every time he appeared in front of the mercenary. He stopped laughing, and began speaking.

"The choice you've made fighting for your destiny here, perhaps tells of choices men have likewise made, in their own Fate's Fray! You lied there and played dead, even though your fight wasn't over, even though had more time. And just like this, many will abandon their fight for destiny to see Time No More, *now and again.* Surely those of Karnath have lives meant for more than a destiny of defeat! Time is a means to do, like this mountain was a foothold and a means to stand. So I ask, how you'll stand to chase gray dreams when your time falls apart, just as this mountain?"

During the last sentence, Zeros rose to his feet and began lunging at Lucen again with his sword. Like a ghost, Lucen floated away, dodging strike after strike. The mercenary began to tire, as before, but nonetheless he persevered, pursuing Lucen more.

"It's not so much that I stand," shouted Zeros, "but that upon falling, I rise again!"

Zeros followed Lucen round and round, wielding his sword at him while holding Esmeralda's head by the hair; his continued motions carried it through the air, like a ball on a string. As the mercenary attacked, his eyes noticed the stone floor continue to break, disintegrating inward from the walls by a few cubits. In all directions from the room's center, there was now less flooring than before.

Lucen made a feisty remark, stealing Zeros' attention from the developing problem.

"Oh, you shall be a difficult one! At an *earlier time* we'll work through that."

"Can you do more than toy with us!" yelled Magicia, casting fire at Lucen. He vanished at the whoosh of flames, to reappear before Zeros, who slashed at him but narrowly missed, as the youth parried in a blur.

"I prefer to save my fight for the end. Not that Elucid needs it though! He's challenged enough, as is."

Zeros began panting again, and took a few more swings at Lucen with his sword, hitting nothing more than air. The youth floated about the space, apparently using magic just like Magicia.

For a moment Zeros paused to rest, and like before, he beheld the stone floor continue to crumble to dust, from the walls to the room's center. The edge of the remaining floor was maybe three cubits away from him now, leaving only a pedestal where he could stand.

The floor's evaporation clouded the air with dust, but Zeros could still see the injured Guardsmen fall to the lower levels of the tower, as the floor beneath them vanished! *No, no!* Alarms went off in his head, as the bodies of Hammar, Finnel, and Nathan tumbled into the pit that closed in on him from all sides. But with that sense of panic was also one of immense helplessness, for there was little that Zeros could do. It occurred to him then, how there might be no returning to Sergros after all, for any of them. *Hopefully X'ieth will fare better than us! Please, Destiny…*

And then, the floor's disintegration stopped, and all that remained was the pedestal on which Zeros stood, and over which Magicia and Lucen hovered. It wobbled even more violently than before, and Zeros fought to keep his footing. Amid frequent shifting, his eyes went to the pit off the floor's edge and between the tower walls—the one where the Guardsmen fell. And suddenly, Zeros watched those very walls fade to darkness, as if becoming hidden by a bizarre magic! The stone was literally consumed by thick blackness, which expanded to meet the very perimeter of the pedestal. *How is this happening?!*

When Zeros saw Lucen blur by again, he resumed slinging his sword at the youth. The mercenary glanced over to see Magicia throw another blast of fire.

"Even if ending what Saora's started means certain death for me," she shouted, "then fulfilled I shall die!"

Lucen laughed, again evading sword and sorcery to treat the whole charade like it were play.

"Keep talking sweetly," he said, "for sweet talk might be of use to you at Gallow Cliff. Saora has released some ether from the Void that could change the plans of your supposed allies!"

Zeros and Magicia followed Lucen from different positions at the pedestal's edge. While moving, the mercenary compensated his footing to keep upright, as the floor never stopped moving under him. When right before Lucen, Zeros hurled his blade again. At the same exact time, Magicia threw fire from a few cubits away, now at the opposite side of the pedestal from Zeros, both of them occupying end points of a secant line across it.

But, when both of them struck simultaneously, Lucen disappeared only to reappear at the pedestal's center, betwixt Zeros and Magicia. The mercenary turned just in time to watch Lucen abruptly smite the floor with his gnarled staff.

In Zeros' eyes, white light engulfed the scene of gray stone, just like what happened to him on the fringe of Forest Saol. It was then that chimes filled his ears, along with sounds of a child crying inconsolably. In a matter of seconds, the varied noises drowned in a pervasive ringing, which suddenly dominated everything he could hear.

(*The Leap of Chance*)

X'ieth leaped through the sky toward the dragon's back. Midair, he watched Gremel turn from the huge hole that she tore in the tower's wall; she remained upon flapping, leathery wings, being a moment from flying away. And just as he sailed through the sky—still being cubits away from her spine—Gremel released a roar and sped into the gloom!

As the dragon began flying away, X'ieth panicked, thinking for a moment that he might fall to his death, with his courageous though shortsighted jump. When he too entered the gloom, fog enveloped him and limited his sight, just as his body lost momentum and started sinking. A falling sensation immediately filled his gut. *Oh no!*

A lump formed at the top of his throat, as if his heart popped up from his chest after it constricted suddenly from his own fear. Ahead of him, X'ieth saw

520

the shadow of winged Gremel in the gloom, and stretching behind it, a thinner and lengthier shadow. When X'ieth saw himself approaching that second shadow, he reached out his hands. *Please, Karnatha.* Images of Millicent and a baby went through his head, followed by the white shard and the hero's destiny that came with it. *Please…*

When X'ieth felt a solid surface, he latched onto it. In his eyes, the end of Gremel's tail entered his view, and his hands wrapped about a pair of its barbs. *Praise be to Destiny!* he thought, while tightening his grip. And then, quite unexpectedly, he heard Gremel roar, as if the dragon noticed that she now had a passenger.

Holding onto the dragon's tail, X'ieth burst through the patch of gloom and into clearer sky. Since grabbing the barbs, he felt immediately accelerated by Gremel, and she started flying even faster! His cheeks flapped, his hair blew wildly, and the cold air stung his face.

In his hearing ear, destruction sounded from below. He looked down to behold stretches of Liath's western pass break apart: large contiguous chunks of granite disintegrated from where they stood, for perhaps thousands of years; these mountains were as old as time, though now, were seemingly being erased by the gloom.

The mountain's collapse became so loud that it subsumed further roars from Gremel. X'ieth clenched his teeth the whole time, on the brink of his endurance threshold for noise. Hanging onto the barbed tail, he could literally feel the sound vibrations discharged from spans upon spans of crumbling rock beneath him.

Suddenly, his gut sank as Gremel swooped down to the right, and then to the left. X'ieth held onto the dragon's tail, being whipped from side to side. With the jarring movements his stomach turned, and he felt like at any second, he might heave. *Don't let go, man… Not for dear life!* Amid Gremel's aerial maneuvers, X'ieth laid sight on the glowing shard in her claw, and the visual sent a very different thought through this mind. *Don't let go, for sake of your good destiny!*

X'ieth held onto the tail, as Gremel's flight carried him over the crumbling mountain pass, from which dust rose in thick, puffy columns. Eventually, sights became familiar to X'ieth, as the dragon flew into part of the mountain that was yet intact and not falling apart. He glanced down, seeing the same open space he happened upon earlier with the Guardsmen, before their climb. And there, maybe a hundred cubits before him, was Gremel's unscathed nest, still holding three eggs.

The nest came nigh in his eyes, and X'ieth felt increasingly urged by his inner voice to take action. *Get off! She'll find you in her nest more easily than in the darkness!* And with that idea, he waited a few moments for Gremel to come closer to the mountain before he would release her tail. When X'ieth judged the right distance, he let go, fell a few cubits, and landed hard onto the rock, upon both knees. He looked up and saw a nearby crevice occluded from the open space. Without delay, he got to his feet and quickly darted inside.

Within the crevice and hidden from direct view, he crouched to his knees and slowed his breathing, a moment before hearing Gremel's claws contact the mountain with a deep thud, scrapes, and then, sounds of crumbling rock. He heard the dragon shift quickly and begin snorting repeatedly, in what did seem signs of exasperation. Images went through his mind, of Gremel searching for her passenger only to find nothing, and then, becoming extremely upset.

RAWWWRRR! ... RAWWWWWWWRRRRRRRR!

X'ieth slapped one hand to his ear, as Gremel roared ferociously, apparently aggravated, just as he supposed. In the background, he could hear the winds whistle; they whipped around the rocks, touching him with icy fingers. He did not as much as shiver, the sensation dulled by the mountain water he drank before entering the tower, which still made him feel strangely impervious to the elements.

When he saw flashes of light reflect onto the expanse of rock visible from the crevice, and when he heard the whoosh of flames, X'ieth knew that surely Gremel breathed fire. She romped around her lair, ostensibly searching for him and getting angrier each moment she could not locate the hidden young knight.

RAWWWRRR! ... RAWWWWWWWRRRRRRRR!

With one hand, X'ieth covered his ear again while wincing in pain. After her loud roar, he continued listening to Gremel scour the mountain, as told by the clatter and breakage of porous rock. Every time the dragon stirred in the darkness, his fearful heart stirred up just the same.

Thump thump, thump thump, thump thump!

The dragon came closer and closer, and with her approach, so came he to the complete fray of his nerves. *Destiny, please let her pass over me!* X'ieth prayed the words again and again, careful not to speak them aloud. Thoughts raced his mind about seeing Millicent, being present for his child's birth, and returning to Sergros to announce his victory over Esmeralda—the Child of Darkness. *It must not end like this. I am the Child, so it must be that I can possess the shard! This is part of my hero's destiny.* The thoughts were comforting, and lent him confidences when his own were fleeting.

Time elapsed for X'ieth, who waited there scared and restless. A repeat of the same scenario went on for hours: Gremel romped through her lair, spewed fire, and roared while searching for the hidden young knight. But at last, the dragon tired and would do it no more; she released a final roar somewhere in the middle of the night, followed by noises of her heading to a spot and settling down on the rock. X'ieth imagined Gremel in her nest, laying herself down to sleep.

As his first impulse, X'ieth wanted to peek out from around the rock and check on the dragon, but he stopped himself, knowing the risks were too great. *Not yet...* He held his breath and waited, careful not to make a sound. In a few moments, he silently exhaled and waited some more, allowing a generous amount of time to pass.

X'ieth stayed hidden in the mountain crevice, tucked away from the large space containing Gremel's nest. Seconds of waiting turned into minutes, and minutes perhaps into hours, in what became a test of his patience. But eventually, the dragon's occasional snorting became snoring, and the young knight knew then, how it was safer to peek out. And so he did.

From around the rock, X'ieth looked out of the crevice to see Gremel lying in her nest. Through the fog, he could discern her chest rising and falling, working out shallow breaths as she slept. Beside her was the glowing shard of sword in her one claw, and inside her opposite arm, were three gray-speckled eggs, cradled close to her body.

X'ieth paused from proceeding, and instead, ducked back into the crevice. He slumped to a seated position, leaning his shoulders against the rock wall. Gremel's rhythmic snoring continued in the background, a raspy noise that pressed him to secure the white shard: *Go on... Get the sword... Seize your good destiny!* The mere thoughts of the legendary sword and his hero's destiny had him peeking around the rock once more at the glowing object in Gremel's claw. His eyes brimmed with desire.

And so, X'ieth emerged from hiding, and took a few cautious steps from the crevice, toward the nest. With every move forward, his eyes moved between the dragon's massive head and the glowing shard in her claw. As he drew nigh to her, he could feel Gremel's breath hit him—currents of foul air blasted from her tapered, pointy snout, mounted upon a horned pate.

His steps brought him closer and closer, right up to Gremel's claw and the luminous shard in her grip, sticking out blade-first. From the looks of it, her claw appeared relaxed, and he hoped that the shard would easily slip out. However, it occurred to him then, how this hope might be a false one with fatal consequences. Images filled his head of what could happen. He saw himself tugging at the shard, only to find that her claw would not yield. And then, Gremel awakened, opening her piercing yellow eyes, right before she suddenly reached out and shredded X'ieth with her talons! It was a vision of his bloody and agonizing end, which easily made him shudder.

X'ieth took a step back, now deathly afraid of the gamble he wanted to take. He breathed in and out, slowly and with length, in order to calm himself. *You can do this. Just take hold of the shard's blade, and in so doing, take hold of your good destiny!* With that thought, the young knight stepped forward to gain on the short distance he had retreated, and to bring himself even closer to the shard, which now, was only a few hair lengths away. X'ieth stilled himself, on the verge of laying claim to his prize. His ear caught the predictable sounds of Gremel's breathing. *Just take it… Take it…*

And so, with desire in his heart and desire also in his eyes, he removed his cloak and laid it on the shard's blade, and then grabbed the object's girth with both hands. Gremel's snoring instantly stopped, jolting X'ieth's head in the direction of her own.

As he turned, he envisioned meeting a pair of yellow eyes in the night, and like before, the thought of confronting Gremel drove fear into him. His heart beat inside his chest, as did the life pulse of sheer terror inside his mind.

Thump thump, thump thump, thump thump!

When X'ieth's vision found Gremel's head, he saw a set of closed eyes. The dragon snorted, before resuming her snores. He exhaled deeply, calmed that his expectations of worse went unmet. And with that, X'ieth redirected his attention to the shard. In his head, the same voice spoke up again, urging him to claim his hero's destiny. *Go on… Just take it already!*

X'ieth began pulling on the shard again, never having removed his hands from its blade, not even when Gremel stopped snoring. And to his surprise, the legendary half sword slid against the dragon's talons! Indeed, X'ieth found that Gremel had relaxed her claw and the shard could be removed, but definitely at the risk of awakening the dragon. It was the acute scrape of sword on talon that warned him—a sharp and offensive sound. He instantly paused his pulling, and looked back to Gremel. She still slept, snoring as usual. *Thank, Destiny…*

After waiting a moment or two, X'ieth continued pulling on the shard, hair length by hair length, trying to manage the noise he created. The whole time, he alternated looks between the sword and Gremel, being careful to check that the dragon remained asleep.

With more excruciating scrapes, the blade slowly yielded to X'ieth in the gloomy night. While the noise caused him angst, the sword's cooperation brought a smile to his lips. He pulled and pulled, with more of the shard being removed from Gremel's clutches, until the point where it suddenly felt stuck!

In one instant, his lips parted ever so slightly and his eyes widened with surprise. X'ieth first looked down at his hands, before tracing the sword's length from his gauntlets to the claw, where he noticed that the shard's hilt had become snagged by one of the talons.

X'ieth let out a deep breath, a bit on edge by this complication. *You can do this. Just twist it and pull…* He took a deep breath. *Ok.* In his hands, he twisted the cloak-covered blade, trying to free its hilt from the talon. As he fiddled with the sword in the darkness, his terror struck again, with the same percussion of his beating heart.

Thump thump, thump thump, thump thump!

He fiddled and fiddled, the sword still caught.

Thump thump, thump thump, thump thump!

When Gremel's snore stopped, X'ieth froze in dread. He looked over, half expecting to see those yellow eyes and an open maw lined with sharp teeth, ready to eat him alive. But instead, he saw how Gremel lied there with her eyes shut, snorting briefly before snoring again. Yet, despite the scene's calm, his heart continued pounding in his chest, so loud that he feared its noise alone might wake the dragon.

Thump thump, thump thump, thump thump!

X'ieth refocused on the shard. In his hands, he fiddled with it more, since it was still stuck. *Please, Destiny… Please!* He turned and pulled the shard again, praying that doing so would be enough to free the sword. And fortunately for him and his growing anxiety, the shard came free with his continued efforts, right when Gremel's talon finally shifted!

Using his cloak, X'ieth bundled the shard; what showed of its glowing blade was instantly removed from sight. He held the bundle in his hands, with some disbelief that the sword was finally in his possession. The young knight breathed slowly and glanced at the sleeping dragon, careful not to make any sudden noise. He stayed in place momentarily, just listening to Gremel's snores and smelling her foul breath. *You've got the shard, so get out of here!*

And without thinking over the matter more than that, X'ieth carried away the bundled shard into the night. He turned about and began navigating the pass, trying to regain his orientation from visiting Gremel's lair during the day. But at night, it was a confusing affair at best, leaving his mind to wonder the correct way for his exit. *Which direction leads to Forest Saol? Which way leads to Esmeralda's tower?*

X'ieth continued walking into the gloom, until he suddenly stood at a rock wall. He looked on his left and his right, seeing it stretch the length of Gremel's lair. The sight brought him to a stop, and he realized then that a choice was needed: to turn left or right.

Based on his best recollection of the way out of Liath, he decided he would turn left. And so, he began walking in that direction. As he went, he occasionally looked to the towering wall of rock at his right; it loomed above him, casting dark shadows on his path, to the point where he could barely see. The shadows made for treacherous walking conditions indeed, where X'ieth tread with even greater care than before.

X'ieth hiked further, and a wall of rock slowly emerged from the gloom at his left. The other wall at his right stayed visible, as his continued walk took him out of the open space of Gremel's lair, and into a narrower passage that winded through the range. It was not long, however, until he came face-to-face with a dead end!

With an open mouth and raised eyebrows, X'ieth stared at the blockaded corridor before him, the one he rushed through earlier. He saw the scores of boulders that fell from above, which ultimately required him and the Guardsmen to climb.

Destiny damn it! he cursed to himself, finding his choice of direction poor, much poorer than his gamble of retrieving the sword from Gremel. *Should've left it to chance...* The realization hit him, and served as his final thought before he turned around and headed back to Gremel's lair, as carefully as he came.

In about the same time it took X'ieth to reach the dead end, he backtracked through Liath. As he went, the narrow corridor gradually opened to the familiar wide space of Gremel's lair, making him feel more vulnerable than before.

When he arrived at the place where he initially turned, he showed caution; it was maybe a hundred cubits or so off the nest, and in plain view. But as cautious as he was, it did not help him from noticing a terrifying sight—a nest containing only dragon eggs, but no longer a dragon!

X'ieth's chest tightened immediately, and his heart pounded just as before.

Thump thump, thump thump, thump thump!

Then suddenly, from the presumed mountain face right before X'ieth, opened a pair of bright yellow eyes striped by fang pupils, staring right at him!

Chapter 59
A Thankless Rescue

Those twin yellow eyes shined at him in the darkness of Liath's pass, both of them menacing and showing fang-like pupils. It happened, just as the seeming mountain rock suddenly grew arms, wings, and a tail! X'ieth stood there somewhat smitten by disbelief, over how the presumed mountain was really the dragon!

Without a warning, Gremel swiped at him with her claw, and in one motion, the young knight felt the bundle knocked from his grip! Keeping his face forward, he jumped back several cubits, watching the shard fly over his shoulder and into the darkness. *No!!!*

RAWWWWWWWRRRRRRRR!

When the dragon released a loud roar, it discharged the tacit protest from X'ieth's head, replacing it with sheer pain. The booming sound jolted him, causing him to involuntarily turn away his hearing ear, and clasp it with one hand.

RAWWWWWWWRRRRRRRR!

Flames suddenly shot up the side of Gremel's long snout, reaching up from the corners of her lips. X'ieth watched them keep jumping, a tamed inferno that shed light onto the ambiance. He glanced in the direction where the shard went, and could see his bundle lying in the distance, tens of cubits from her nest; the cloak peeled back ever so slightly, revealing a sliver of glowing shard, which gleamed in the night. In that moment's look, he discerned towering walls of rock at both his sides—walls that enclosed him, the dragon, and her nest.

In one sudden motion—one that defied all reason within him—X'ieth sprinted for the bundled shard. His feet went instantly to motion, giving off sounds of his boots against the rock. Immediately, cold winds lashed him from both sides, as if creation were warning him about his reckless pursuit of a hero's destiny. And those winds whistled as they blew, though not loud enough to overwhelm the deep whooshing sound X'ieth heard from behind.

The young knight glanced back at Gremel, and mid-look, his peripheral vision detected intense light. It was then that he apprehended what the dragon would do, and X'ieth leapt to the side and closed his eyes, just in time to avoid a stream of orange flames that passed over his shoulders and struck the rock ahead, between him and the shard! With a grunt, X'ieth hit the mountain hard and looked away, keeping both eyes shut.

He could hear the fire continue to burn overtop him, mighty in sound like a windstorm. He could feel its heat too, and could sense light behind his eyelids. It went on for a while, until finally, those sights, sounds, and sensations all left him in one sudden instant. And when they did, he opened his eyes, and saw the rock steaming and charred where the fire touched, and beyond that, the bundled shard with its faint glow.

The visual got him on his feet and running again, in the opposite direction of Gremel, toward the sword. Through his mind went images of himself at Gallow Cliff as Kayareth, with the Army of Light rallying to his cries. The images were grand and fanciful, altogether motivating him to seize his hero's destiny—Gremel or not.

This time, X'ieth felt a large thud at his rear while running, followed by the clatter of loose rocks and the beating of wings. An immediate upsurge of air pulled at his face and hair, as clearly Gremel became airborne!

The young knight kept running for the shard, refusing to glance back. He saw it lying ahead, maybe thirty cubits from him. And in that, he saw the means to defeat Gremel. X'ieth imagined himself taking hold of the weapon and channeling its stored energy into her body—an attack that would send the dragon out of Liath, with only the echoes of her wails lingering behind.

When X'ieth was about fifteen cubits from the shard, he saw Gremel enter his field of vision, swooping down from the right. With a powerful crash, she landed on the rock between him and the sword, creating a shock that toppled X'ieth face-first onto the mountain!

A moment after falling, he looked up to see Gremel on her hind legs, looming over him. In one motion, she leaned forward and threw down her talons against the rock, tightening her phalanges and crushing it. Noises of destruction filled the air—smashes and crumbling. It happened a moment before Gremel brought her head closer and roared, right in X'ieth's face.

RAWWWWWWWRRRRRRRR!

At the sound, he slapped a hand to his ear and recoiled from the terrible sight of Gremel's teeth-lined maw, opening the height of a man and half the width! It had an amaranth pink, pointy tongue in the middle, with saliva stretching between her jaws, as if to tell of her yearning for a meal.

The mouth sent odors of death to X'ieth, a very real reminder of how this dragon represented just that—death. He saw images of her tearing him in half and eating his entrails, with his blood spraying all over the rock. It was an end that went against all his dreams of a dazzling future—an end that provoked him to stand. *She won't take this from you! Not today, man!*

X'ieth got to his feet, drew his sword, and courageously started slinging it at the dragon. Gremel reared back her head, and the young knight could see it floating distantly behind a veil of gloom, as if without a body. In the same motion, she lifted her claws from the rock, and pulled them into the darkness.

X'ieth looked to the mountain below Gremel, seeing the silhouette of her distant hind legs, and more importantly, the bundled shard lying beyond them, still beckoning with its green glow.

And so, the young knight ran for the shard, aiming to pass Gremel's front, roll beneath her underbelly, and come out on both feet, right before the bundle. But before he could reach her front, a set of five scythe-like talons emerged from the darkness at his immediate left, each several cubits long and sharp as razors!

As the claw descended upon X'ieth, he went to his channeling chamber and pulled open his Source entry. The door swung upon its hinges, and into the room gushed streams of Nexus—along the door's edges, through its opening and across the threshold. The streams flowed and flowed, quickly filling the room from floor to ceiling. He turned from his Source entry and ran over to his Source exit, with the energy accumulated about him, hovering a hair's length from his body; it sent tingly sensations to his skin with his every step. At the exit, he pushed the door open, imagining the trigger image of a hurricane storm.

He snapped back to the mountain pass, with Nexus flowing to his limbs and powering a fluid offense against the claw. His sword blurred as it moved quickly in his hands, hitting three of the five talons with a shower of sparks that colored the night yellow and deflected the dragon's attack. The young knight watched, as seeming anger spread across Gremel's face, which still hung distantly; she snorted out vapors into the air and growled gutturally, her eyes aglow.

And then from his right, X'ieth saw the second claw fly from the shadows, prompting him to fight it off in the same way. He pulled then pushed magic, powering a second fluid offense. His speeding blade hit multiple talons, and alit went the mountain's darkness, sparked by yellow light. Upon deflecting the second claw, X'ieth ran for Gremel's underbelly, seeing opportunity there. For out of the night's blackness, the shard glowed to him yet again, as seen from another glimpse of her hind legs.

Sudden motion in his periphery directed his attention to both his left and his right, where now, both claws descended upon him, for a total of ten scythe-like talons! X'ieth ran even faster at the sight, knowing he needed speed to avoid this danger. But just then, he saw fire reach up from Gremel's lips and the dragon opening her mouth, a thing foretelling of fire to come.

He grunted, and forced himself to run as fast as he could, to the limits of his body. After just a few moments of sprinting, X'ieth tucked his shoulder and threw himself forward in a tight roll, to tumble safely underneath both claws and a stream of fire that Gremel spewed!

RAWWWWWWWRRRRRRRR!

X'ieth got to his feet, and like before, slapped a hand to his ear at the dragon's roar. Not having completely cleared Gremel with his roll, he found himself under her belly, cubits away from her hind legs. The dragon's large body cast an immediate shadow that filled his vision. X'ieth could still see her barbed tail in the distance; it touched the rock ahead, behind her legs. The gleam of the shard caught his eyes again; he saw it just a few cubits away, at the rear of Gremel's right leg. *Go for it!*

The young knight laid his eyes on the bundle, and ran in that direction. A few strides took X'ieth to Gremel's rear and right before the shard, where suddenly, she cut him off with her thick tail. It crashed down in front of him, at the height of his chest!

RAWWWWWWWRRRRRRRR!

While running, X'ieth bit hard into the sound's pain and threw himself up onto the tail, intending to roll over it and grab the shard. But Gremel stirred, and the tail rose into the air with X'ieth still on it, and pulled him forward, away from the shard!

Gremel started whipping about, causing him to grab a tail barb in his free hand, and to wedge his hand with the sword between two others. With every sharp move of the dragon, X'ieth's body flew like a flag on a windy day. Her incessant tosses, lurches, and heaves upset his stomach, bringing him on the verge of vomit.

RAWWWRRR! RAWWWWWWWRRRRRRRR!

Gremel stopped thrashing about, and X'ieth came to a stop on the tail. Immense dizziness overwhelmed him, and rendered him unable to get up and do anything just yet. The dragon snorted and snarled.

After a few moments, the young knight's wooziness subsided, and he glanced off the tail onto the rock, looking for the bundled shard. He turned his head several times, searching the pass for it, but was unable to find it. *You'll need to go higher...*

X'ieth looked up, seeing a path to a better view right before him—Gremel's spine. He instantly got afoot, ran up her tail, and onto her spine. The dragon noticed instantly, releasing a loud roar.

RAWWWWWWWRRRRRRRR!

The young knight gritted his teeth, chomping down on pain again, as the sound coursed through him. He ran until mid-spine, when all of a sudden, X'ieth saw the glowing shard on the rock, at the corner of Gremel's nest. It was displaced from where it was earlier, perhaps kicked by the dragon amid her thrashing; the sword slid partly out of the cloak now.

When X'ieth looked at the shard, its energized blade shed green light that frolicked in his lusting eyes. As so many times before, the young knight viewed the shard as more than merely a broken sword; he saw a hero's destiny—power, prestige, and everything else befitting.

Jump, man... And get it! His inner voice urged him to leap for the shard, as he continued looking at it, from atop the dragon's back. But X'ieth judged the distance to the rock below as tens of cubits, much too high for a safe landing. *The fall might break both your legs!* While the chance of just jumping anyway appealed to him, the young knight saw higher odds of success in employing common sense. His eyes trailed to the large leathery wing beside him that draped to the ground, prompting an immediate idea. *Leap on her wing, and then simply slide down!*

At first thought, the notion seemed a bit daring to X'ieth, but in his mind, it remained the best possible choice. And so, in a sudden moment of decisiveness, he sprang off Gremel's back toward the wing. During his jump, the glowing shard was stuck in his vision, as it was very much still stuck in his mind. *The Child must have the shard!*

But unexpectedly, he felt abruptly jerked when the dragon reached over her shoulder and snatched him from the air, in her one claw! X'ieth felt trapped in her clutches, as Gremel maintained a firm grip about his waist. Her terrifying, horned head came into his view, as the dragon's arm moved him further from the shard. His eyes watched the sword, as it drifted away. *No. No! No!!!*

X'ieth wriggled in Gremel's claw, still having both arms free. As he struggled, he could hear the thunder of the dragon stomping through the mountain pass, carrying him off. *RAWWWRRR!*

Gremel roared suddenly, so loud that X'ieth grinded his teeth again until one broke from the gum line with agonizing pain; the taste of irony blood greeted his tongue. He retaliated by thrusting his blade into the fleshy part of Gremel's appendage. Through his gauntlets, he felt warm blood flow out from the dragon's wound.

She stopped walking, and shrieked into the night.
GRAAAWWWLLL!

Instantly, X'ieth felt a sinking sensation as Gremel released him, and he fell through the air, dropping his bloody sword in the process. He mentally braced himself for hitting the rock hard, when all of a sudden Gremel's other claw snatched him up!

X'ieth immediately felt a jerking, whipping sensation replace that of falling, and his arms were suddenly bound by her phalanges. He could hear his sword clatter against the rock below, which elicited his envy for the kinder fate of hitting the mountain versus being caught by the dragon. The claw tightened around him, pressing down his chest and making it difficult for him to breathe. *My bones will surely be crushed!* X'ieth's mind worked frantically then. *But what to do?!* Absolutely nothing entered his head, and pathetically, he just kicked and squirmed.

It was then that the young knight started to realize just how grim his prospects were, ones of utterly hopeless nature: essentially staying there, and waiting to be crushed, eaten, or both. At that thought, the world and all it held for X'ieth seemed a fading realm of desire, with so many hopes and wishes unfulfilled. Zeros' words went through his mind: *Those always in want of more climb the sky to touch sol. While some achieve greater than men who don't dream gray, many climbing higher are fated to burn.*

Visions of Millicent, his soon-to-be child, and his Guardsman career all paraded through his head in sheer mockery, of the good destiny he had, though now, he would leave behind. Anticipating his bones cracking beneath his armor in a matter of seconds, he turned his eyes to the glowing shard, which prompted a final thought. *Your hero's destiny was even better than all of those good destinies. Too bad it's ending like this...*

X'ieth pulled his shoulders back while trying to lift his arms with his large biceps, hoping that his strength might save him. But as strong as the young knight was, Gremel was even stronger, binding him inside just one of her claws. His eyes found the shard's glow once more, and he looked at it hopefully this time, still considering himself moments from being squeezed to death, but wondering if Destiny would smile upon him. *Karnatha, for my family's sake and for that of my every dream, please give me the shard, so I can save my own life! If I'm the hero and meant for more than a plain life, please give it to me!*

And suddenly then, X'ieth beheld the shard move with his cloak draped about it, as if displaced by his prayer alone! The sight completely stilled his mind and body, and he leered with wide eyes. When a smile shined from the black, he took his vision off the shard, seeing white teeth that caught the blade's luminosity. That smile showed only one moment before Lucen stepped out of the darkness, wearing his traveler's robe and having the shard in one hand, his wooden staff in the other.

In a swift movement, X'ieth saw Lucen wave the glowing shard at Gremel, discharging the energy inside with an explosion of green Nexus, which illuminated the entire nest and its mountain enfold! The blast hit the dragon's side, burning her flesh. X'ieth felt the claw loosen, followed by a series of loud roars.

RAWWWRRR! RAWWWRRR! ... RAWWWRRR!

He plummeted from the heights of Gremel's claw, and as he fell, the sound of flapping wings filled his ear, and requisite air currents hit his face. X'ieth looked over just in time to witness the dragon fly off. She clearly had been gravely wounded, since she left her eggs behind.

Still in free-fall, X'ieth looked down to see the rock approach with increasing speed. But just before contacting the mountain face, he perceived green energy materialize between him and the hard surface. And when near the length of his fall, he felt a force field pad his descent, right before his body made physical impact.

"Uggh!" he grunted, hitting the rock with a pronounced thud. Sharp pain shot through his entire body, and he just lied there for a moment, wondering if he had broken anything. X'ieth moved his arms and legs for the feedback sensation of controlling them, to see if there might be concentrated pain in either. *Nope.*

Eventually, X'ieth looked to his broadsword, a cubit or so ahead on the rock, where it clattered moments ago. And in his periphery, he noted the slow approach of Lucen's sandaled feet; each step rang out distinctly amidst the winds. Near Lucen's right foot was his gnarled staff, being pushed against the rock with his every other step. X'ieth glanced up and saw him standing overhead, holding the cloak-enshrouded shard.

"What is meant to be shall be," Lucen said, wearing his usual smile. From the moment he uttered those words in Arlem, X'ieth felt chance slowly gaining on choice. It all seemed pure chance—from Zeros rescuing him in the city; from him drinking the green waters of the mysterious mountain spring and staying alive; to his miraculous slaying of Esmeralda; and to him defeating Gremel. *Pure chance… Nothing of your choice…*

"Only the Children of Destiny can channel Nexus through the shard, and such are we," said Lucen, his wild hair blowing in the wind. X'ieth's eyes trailed to the crimson cloak Lucen held. A moment's glance was enough for him to want the shard inside, exactly as he did before.

And then, as if knowing exactly what the young knight desired, Lucen extended the bundle to X'ieth with one hand, his other hand still holding the gnarled staff.

"Take the shard and pull Nexus, to feel its power."

The moon hovered over X'ieth, anointing him with pale light. It exposed the bundle to his eyes, a seeming invitation to power, prestige, and good fortune. At the sight, a grin snuck to the corners of his lips and his eyes widened with desire. Deep inside, X'ieth yearned for the sword; he yearned for how it could transform his life, from the pedestrian into the extraordinary. And so, with much anticipation, he got to his knees and reached out his hand, ready to take hold of his long awaited destiny.

But when Lucen peeled back the cloak, X'ieth's fingers stopped short, and began to tremble. Before him emerged a shard from his cloak, though of unexpected hue. A mirror-like black blade peeked out at him; it extended from tip to hilt, broadening in its descent on one side, straight on the other, being broken perfectly down the middle. The young knight noted how Lucen held the sword through the crimson cloak, with his fist around the covered handle.

It's… it's black. The sight stole his breath and shocked him in a single instant. X'ieth felt immediate restraint from touching the broken sword, knowing very well its implications from the prophecy: *Before sundown on the third day after the Children touch each shard's grip, Shaizan and Kayareth shall fight at Gallow Cliff.*

X'ieth willfully began retracting his outstretched hand from the shard, back toward his body. Yet, amid his retreat, the most outlandish thing happened.

All over again, the young knight found his hand stopped, right before his fingers trembled and began to move involuntarily back toward the sword! *What are you doing, man?!*

He stopped short of touching the shard, and with confusion over his intention to do just that, he examined himself. X'ieth felt absolutely no negative bodily responses at the sight of the shard: his heart leapt not in his chest, nor did nausea wrench his gut, neither was his breath short or quickened; no pins or needles could he feel, and there was no pain or uncanny sensation whatsoever. All that ran through him was what he felt all along for the shard—desire. And it did not seem to matter, whether it was black or white.

X'ieth found himself kneeling on the rock, with his outstretched hand frozen midair. His fingers started trembling again, as he sensed a strange magnetism between him and the shard. Like ore to loadstone, it pulled him, urging him to take hold of a Dark destiny. His hand moved forward by a hair's length, and at that, X'ieth was appalled. *This is all wrong!* he thought, rejecting that his attraction for the black shard was even real. *This is a mistake!*

His mixed feelings for the shard bothered him enough to muster the self-will to overcome what seemed his most natural urge ever felt—touching the black shard's grip! And so, he forced his hand to stop, once again.

X'ieth exhaled, being only hair lengths away from the defaming and vilifying act of wielding the black shard. The young knight pried his eyes from the nightly blade and looked to Lucen, who peered down upon him with sharp blue eyes, set above a crooked grin.

"This shard has a core that no mortal could ever fill with energy, one that is nearly bottomless. And the whole gray sword… Well, that core *is* bottomless." The last statement was emphatic, as if to entice X'ieth.

Again, he felt the same magnetism between his hand and the shard. His eyes too were drawn with nearly as much force, just like one pole of his will. Strangely, the young knight found himself converging to a deed that he would have denounced a moment sooner—a moment before coming into the black shard's presence.

Using the opposite pole of his will, X'ieth retracted his outstretched hand by a small measure, stopping himself from touching the shard's grip. However, stopping himself took a battle and it was not clear how long he could fight it, or whether he could even win.

Lucen covered up the shard, and turned from him.

"What are you doing?!" X'ieth asked, somewhat perplexed by the shard being cloaked and taken away.

"I can see you're fighting this," Lucen said, "and that fight is admirable. However, you're only fighting because you're confused. Let me make this proposition even simpler for you…"

Lucen turned back to X'ieth and outstretched his arms at each side, with his one hand holding the staff, and his other the bundle. Part of the cloak fell off the shard, exposing its smooth black blade to the moon. For perhaps the first time, X'ieth noticed how beautiful the light was that played off its mirrored surface in rainbow glimmers—glints of red, blue, and gold. The mere sight turned up the corners of his lips in a smile, yet again.

"I'll give you the choice."

Lucen's sudden voice pulled at X'ieth's attention.

"Leave the shard with me, and forget this ever happened. Hike down Liath into Saol, go through the forest and into Arlem, and secure a horse to ride back to your cottage. You can return to your plain life in the home with Millicent and at work for Talus. If you leave now, you can still make your child's birth. Your cottage is maybe a few days' travel, just over that horizon."

At the statement, Lucen nodded his head to one side, and X'ieth glanced in that direction, seeing stretches of rock in the dark, descending down the mountain and vanishing in the distance, beneath the night sky. He imagined a trip like Lucen described, starting with his walk down that trail and ending with him arriving back at home, and it seemed even more doable than before, as if just walking away and things going back to normal would be relatively simple, should he choose to do so.

Motion directed X'ieth's attention back to Lucen. The youth stood there with his head cocked to the side, toward the trail; it was the same side of his hand holding the gnarled staff, opposite to the shard. The way Lucen gestured the options struck X'ieth as mutually exclusive: it was either one or the other.

"Or," Lucen said, "you can take the shard, and rise above your ordinary existence, as a great hero who you never dreamed of being—one who merely champions a different cause than you're familiar with, one who is already prophesized to win!" The energy increased in Lucen's voice by the word, and he shook the shard while talking, as if to try X'ieth's desires.

"Avoid falling from grace," Lucen continued, releasing his gnarled staff just then. It clattered to the rock abruptly, and startled X'ieth. The young knight glanced at the staff, and then back to Lucen.

"Like my staff, you'll take a fall if you return to your plain life—a fall from higher expectations in yourself, than settling for the ordinary!"

The words ushered a recollection upon X'ieth, of what Zeros shared with him in Forest Saol, around the fire during their first watch: *Dreaming of greater purpose than the purpose Destiny affords you, suggests that you're dreaming gray.*

"You've long dreamed of becoming something bigger than a knight of Sergros, something bigger than a family man. Who will nurture that dream, if not yourself? No one is in your corner for that dream, at home or at work. No one there believes in you becoming anything more than what you already are. You'll

535

just lead the simple life that *they* want you to live, and hate yourself everyday for throwing away the opportunity of a lifetime!"

Lucen became a force that pressed on X'ieth and stirred up internal forces, which pressed on him just the same. Before he knew it, warring voices went back and forth in his mind, telling him different things. *You're dreaming gray. No, you're meant for more than a simple life. You're dreaming gray! No, you're meant for more!* The voices continued bickering, getting louder and louder until one finally dominated. *You're meant for more.*

"Your friend Zeros would have you believe that you're the most accountable person when it comes to your own dreams. But what about the accountability of others? Can you truly say that the important people in your life—your wife, your boss—care for your development, your advancement? You know they don't care about your dreams, as they should. So don't let them steal a brilliant future from someone who's meant for more."

In one sudden impulse that indulged his wants, X'ieth snatched the cloak from Lucen, shard and all. When the bundle rested in his hands, he stared down upon it, silenced by an upsweep of disbelief. *Did you just do that?!* He felt abashed then, and hotness colored his face red with shame. When presented with the choice between his family or his career and a hero's destiny, he chose the latter, without even stopping to think how what he embraced now was no longer his childhood dream of becoming Kayareth.

Beyond his surprise and shame, his attraction to the shard presided, coaxing X'ieth to peel back the cloak around the sword's hilt. He watched the beautiful blade appear before his eyes and more temptingly, the shard's grip. He thought of grabbing the handle, as abruptly as he took the bundle from Lucen in the first, and wielding the shard right there in Liath. In his mind, the act concocted both pleasantries and repulsion, and he wrestled with an idea that had worrying implications to his identity. He mulled over just that, while staring at the shard, until at the back of his mind developed the cheer: *Touch its grip! Touch its grip!* The sounds grew louder and louder in his head, so loud that they became difficult to ignore. X'ieth resorted to pulling the cloak back over the shard to cover it up, thereby covering his own affections for the broken sword of legend, at least for the moment.

Lucen spoke, and his voice reined in the young knight's attention.

"Have you considered that perhaps your destiny is not as good as you think?"

X'ieth cradled the bundle in his arms, as if cradling his own child. Meanwhile, Lucen stepped closer.

"What do you mean?!" X'ieth shot back, guardedly. His body responded with anxiety to the developing situation, as his decision to take the sword from Lucen now showed consequences. A sickening flutter wriggled through his stomach, his heart beat mightily in his tightened chest, and his breaths grew short. Pins and needles pricked his face, and he felt sudden coldness in his feet.

X'ieth stood there on the mountain pass, with the bundled shard in his hands, the frigid winds blowing over him, and a host of negativity now underneath his skin. Through his mind, went new labels for someone whom he had esteemed highly for months: *Deceiver. Liar. Enemy.* Indeed, X'ieth now looked at Lucen very differently than ever before. His supposed friend, his trusted prophet, his savior this night, was clearly not any of what he had mistakenly presumed.

Lucen's smile widened, and he spoke.

"Well, you may have believed certain things from what I said, but did you carefully weigh my words?"

In a trail of blinding light, X'ieth's mind hastened to the memory of standing in Arlem with the youth. Lucen's words then, echoed his mind now: *You're the Child of Prophecy, the one meant to do great things!* It slowly dawned on the young knight how that statement was nothing short of open-ended, describing either Shaizan of Darkness, or Kayareth of Light.

"No… No… No," X'ieth muttered repeatedly, gripping his bundle tighter, with gauntleted hands of knuckles white. "This can't be!" he shouted to Lucen, the opposite pole of his will detesting the latest wrinkle in his life's story.

"Or can it?"

"No, it can't!" X'ieth protested. "No! No! No!"

Each repetition was increasingly stressed, increasingly louder and more severe. But his denial fell upon deaf ears, the winds like busybodies not bothering to cease their toiled blowing for but a moment, the mountain pass insistent on being cold and hard to his anguished words. X'ieth grew red in the face, and started spouting off accusations of sundry kind.

"Y… you deceived me!" he stuttered. "I would've run in the opposite direction, had you truthfully told me I pursued the black shard. Had you told me forthrightly, how *you thought* I was this evil one, I… I would've left you!"

When Lucen looked on smugly without a word, it enraged X'ieth. *How dare he be so dismissive of your point of view, and how dare he think that he knows better?!*

X'ieth walked up to Lucen, grabbed the youth by the collar of his robe using one hand, and yelled in his face.

"Never would I do this thing! Never! Do you hear me?! Get that into your head, once and for all."

Spit flew from his mouth as he talked. Lucen endured it with a knowing smile that only damaged X'ieth further. Though the young knight stood on a mountain of rock, he felt as if he were sinking in a sea of denial, with nothing beneath him.

"You're wrong," he told Lucen. He said it again for good measure, this time emphatically and louder. "You're wrong! Dead wrong!"

The frigid winds blew behind his words, as X'ieth let go of the smiling youth, aggrieved with Lucen's quiet.

"But am I wrong?" replied Lucen, finally. "It seems you say more to convince yourself than me."

X'ieth swallowed the lump at the top of his throat, and made a daring declaration. "I am… the Child of Light," he said at last and with authority, as if settling any questions on the matter.

Cunningly, Lucen asked, "Tell me then, why do you hold the black shard, instead of the white?"

As he faced the cutting question, X'ieth's tongue felt immediately bound up, for the question blindsided him and he lacked a good answer. But he could only tolerate smug Lucen judging his silence for so long, and he quickly brought himself to invent a line of reasoning and reply.

"It's meaningless that I hold the black shard," X'ieth retorted. "I clearly do nothing wrong, nor would any other man, by keeping it from the wrong hands! I'm merely… protecting Karnath from bad destiny!"

"Oh, is that what *this* is?" Lucen asked, again flashing his smug smile before falling silent.

X'ieth's skin turned a deeper red, and his heart beat faster. From head-to-toe, he could feel resentment course through him with deep throbs, over the poor situation that Lucen had put him in.

"Yes, that's what this is." X'ieth said. "You see, your proposal is absurd for someone like me who despises evil. Understand that every bone in me, and every scrap of flesh that hangs on each bone, as even the blood that flows through my veins and feeds my flesh—my entire body—detests the Dark! I'll never be a proponent of the causes you mention, not in this life or the next!"

In an aside, X'ieth shouted to the mountain, "I'm a noble knight of Sergros, one who seeks to do good and abstain from evil! Darkness is not of me!"

X'ieth turned back to Lucen.

He muttered, "You deceiver…" As another frigid wind struck, the young knight pulled the bundled shard tighter to his body.

"I've deceived no one," contradicted Lucen. "It is you, who have deceived yourself. As a boy you loved the stories foretold, the Light Prophecy penned by the oracles long ago, handed down through the generations. And as such, you knew that Kayareth didn't climb a mountain to find the white shard. You knew the king's mission put you amidst something else, yet your own intrigue made you continue."

"That's not true," X'ieth said, shaking his head.

Still smiling, Lucen nodded.

"Yes, it is. Common things were spoken of even in the Light Prophecy, such as the black shard's location: on a mountain. You wanted a hero's destiny enough to neglect sure misgivings about pursuing a shard upon a mighty mountain, rather than in deep waters."

X'ieth restated Lucen's account, insisting it be true.

"You spoke how the Child of Darkness sought to end a sorceress' reign of power, and had recovered the shard from off a mountain, according to the Dark Prophecy! You said also, how counselors that the king trusted had proclaimed Esmeralda as the Child of Darkness, hence the Guard's deployment!"

Lucen snapped, "I said many things, but in the end, you assumed more answers than you asked questions. All I told you was how trusted counsel influenced your king, and then, part of the Dark Prophecy. That's all. Can I really be blamed, for counselors who beguiled Talus, for you being ignorant of the Dark Prophecy, or for you misinterpreting my words and believing hearsay?"

"You deceived me!" X'ieth exclaimed. Denial's murky water rose well over his head, and he struggled to stay above the surface.

Lucen stared back without a word, and his silence provoked X'ieth to press his accusations more.

"You said the shard was my destiny."

"As it is. All my words have been words of subjectivity, even this. Where you should have applied wisdom, you chose to subject my sayings to presumption and wild fancy. In so doing, you presumed Esmeralda was the foe, rather than yourself."

X'ieth stood there against another strong wind, unaffected by its bite. He watched Lucen's hood stir in the bluster, and turned his eyes to the bundle again, an easy reminder of the vexing situation.

"I suggest you reconsider what you believe is destined," X'ieth shouted into the gust. "My only destiny here is safeguarding Karnath from the black shard."

"Oh, right. That's what you said before, isn't it? A shame it's so hard to believe, given that you now possess the black shard, which betokens your Dark destiny."

X'ieth shook his head in denial, and insisted upon the situation that he supposed true in his own mind, to avoid confronting the issue that Lucen highlighted.

"Esmeralda was the Child of Darkness, and I stopped her evil deeds. I changed the Dark Prophecy!"

But Lucen just stared back at X'ieth in silence, wearing the same smug look, as if he knew better. And the longer he did it, the more this instigated X'ieth by what the gesture implied, that the young knight's beliefs were untrue and doubtful. It sourced his introspection, in which he wondered the same. *Are you being honest, about why you took the shard? Is it really to protect Karnath, or to...*

X'ieth shrugged off the thought, and looked down at the bundle, to his cloak covering a thing that he wished to no longer bear, but yet a thing that perhaps he could not throw away. It was a dichotomy hard to rationalize, yet easy to understand: love and hate.

"I am the Child of Light!" X'ieth shouted, above his confusion, Lucen's presumed knowingness, and the winds. With that, he attempted to have the last word, by turning away from the youth with his bundle. When about face, he walked over and picked up his sword with one hand and sheathed it. And then, he took his first step toward his intended many, by which he would traverse the mountains alone in the night, all the way back to Saol and Arlem.

X'ieth continued walking through the range, and before long, Lucen called out to him, taunting him from a distance.

"You're mad, aren't you? Yes, indignation wells within you for what destiny chance affords, while ironically, you only hold the black shard through your own choice! Your anger will leave you downtrodden, subjugated, and vulnerable. If you don't give in today, you'll do so on another day. But by then, you'll be completely desensitized to your surrender by the natural progression of your own feelings. Your anger will breed wrath, your wrath will become hate, and your hate will lead to malice against others. 'Twas the path of Eriens in Old Karnath, and it'll also be yours!"

X'ieth kept walking. Though he still heard Lucen talking, the young knight purposed to ignore him.

"Eriens came to possess the black shard too," Lucen continued, "and when it destroyed him, he allowed it to destroy others—all of the seroxians, in fact! Through his treachery, he violated a pact of the seroxians' peaceful entry into New Karnath, thereby destroying the one chance for Darconas to forge an alliance with the lower races, in order to find the new River of Life and reverse his shadowing. In so doing, Eriens likewise doomed all the seroxians to suffer the same fate! He doomed Malgun to destruction, and his son to an *Unwholesome Inheritance*!"

X'ieth stayed on his course, heading down the mountain. *Don't even turn around. Keep going...*

"Like Eriens, everyone has their black shard, their possible downfall after a broken dream. Though shards are different—distinct as fragments of one's broken dream to those of another—they can be equally divisive! Some give up when dreams die, others lash out at the world, just as Eriens. You'll do a little of both."

X'ieth stepped further away, as Lucen went on.

"With your progression of wrath to malice, it'll seem reasonable in your mind to hurt others. You'll hurt many people by the time you're finished..."

The comment struck a nerve with X'ieth, who long ago took the Guardsmen's oath to protect the blood of the innocent, and never to hurt anyone on the right side of the law. Against his initial plans, he stopped in his tracks and faced Lucen, feeling compelled to interject. The youth appeared nearly a hundred cubits away, up the mountain. X'ieth noted that he had picked up his gnarled staff from off the rock, and now stood holding it.

"I can control myself, as I always have," X'ieth shouted, above the whistling wind. "And even if not for self-control, I'm bound by spell to protect versus shed, the blood of the innocent."

Lucen chuckled, "Bound by spell to good destiny? Any man would be better off without, for doing what's right is better done by choice, rather than the chance of spells. And just as this, a man's destiny is partly left to his choice rather than chance, as was your election to take the black shard from me! In this, you've chosen where your destiny begins, and a mix of choice and chance will see to how it ends."

More winds lifted Lucen's traveler's robe and hood as he spoke, along with his lengthy hair.

X'ieth turned and started down the path again.

"You're the Child of Darkness," Lucen called out.

At hearing that dreadful proclamation, X'ieth stopped immediately, with widened eyes. He tightened his grip around the bundle, and protectively pulled it closer to his chest. *You're… Kayareth.* The thought echoed his mind weakly. He started walking down the mountain again, refusing to look back.

"You're Shaizan!" Lucen called out, all of a sudden with a raucous laugh. "Mwhaa ha ha ha, Aha ha ha ha!"

X'ieth stopped yet again, as freezing chills overcame him then, all over his body, and not from the elements. The words literally paralyzed him; they hung in the air, riding the winds to echo through the mountain and ultimately linger in his mind, even after the sounds died. His inner voice weakly contested. *No, you're Kayareth…*

Standing in place upon the mountain, X'ieth held the bundle close, knowing it would mean war between two poles of his will, to keep the shard wrapped. His love and hate for the shard was unfounded, worrying, and without any rationale, yet he stuffed that concern to the back of his mind, and continued down the beaten path. His boots clapped against the rock, as he moved away with hopefully what would prove to be the final word. "I'm Kayareth!"

This time, Lucen stayed silent. That silence was a small victory for X'ieth, for it meant he would enjoy the last say. But despite having it, his mind questioned the statement: *Are you really Kayareth?* Little did he know that this thought actually had the last say, and perhaps it would have many more to come.

Moonbeams played off X'ieth's armor, as he walked down the mountain and disappeared from sight to both Sydullus and Urzel, who watched from their hidden position. They looked to each other and smiled, just as Lucen materialized before them. The Servants immediately grew solemn.

Lucen balanced his staff across both wrists, behind open and upturned palms. The flesh of his inner hands showed the insignia of three falling stars—white on his right, black on his left. The Servants kneeled before him, and kissed the stars of their respective hue.

As Urzel's lips came off Lucen's skin, the woman in white said, "We hail you, Lord of Broken Dreams."

Sydullus looked up. "Greetings, my Lord."

Lucen smiled upon his allies.

"Every warp and weft, unraveled will be; from time's end to start, all the weaves. Rise Servants, for the work of Saora imposes much on us."

Together, Sydullus and Urzel stood to their feet.

Lucen informed them, "The Child has the shard."

Both Servants smiled with delight.

"Have you placed *them*?" Lucen asked.

Urzel replied, "It is done."

"Where have you placed *them*?"

"In the mountain's hidden pass," Sydullus added, "they should re-unite within days."

Lucen showed a sly grin.

"Excellent. Let them enjoy their food and drink to come, for there's much to celebrate!"

The three figures of mystery laughed heartily together. Their wild cackles mixed with the ripping winds, filling stretches of Liath with unsettling noise. And at that, the scene faded to black.

"THANKLESS RESCUE"

Chapter 60
Watchful Eyes

Eternal Darkness was coming; he could feel it. For the gloom was already upon Sergros, oppressing the human kingdom to render its people dependent, fearful, and unproductive. Indeed, Ma'althan saw the present state of Sergros as merely a foreshadowing of what lied in store for the world, when the gloom expanded into the hearts and minds of all, and never went away.

With glee, the Forerunner of Darkness contemplated Karnath's plight from the heights of Gallow Cliff. Ma'althan stood right at the ledge, wearing his spiky armor of god—nightly black, fiendishly curved, and with gray accents. He peered down at spans upon spans of chalky granite that descended to the embankment far below, where waves crashed against the rocks in the blue sea. His focus on the tide served a reminder of what Karnath was amidst.

Like the tide, battles had come and gone through the ages for Karnath's character. Every age offered up yet another generation of the Children who would fight for Karnath to stay in eternal Darkness or eternal Light, exactly as Karnatha intended through the Game. The Game was meant to transfer the burden of Fate's Fray from the people to the Children, no longer requiring the commoner to fight for his or her destiny. And now, it seemed likely that the Game would be decided for Darkness, unless Nym had really altered its prophesized outcome.

He buried his chin in one hand and contemplated the matter further, being concerned that the latest revisions to the Game over Nym's change might not make it fair. From the start, Karnatha judged unfairness in the Game because the Gray Child took Garlew's place and thereby improved the Light's odds of success. She initially acted in Ma'althan's favor, deciding to restore balance by ordering the five Servants of the Light to turn to the Dark.

After Karnatha had made this adjustment, however, she sensed that the Darkness had too great an advantage over the Light. And so, she acted once again in the interest of the Game's fairness, ordering the gatekeeper Wicken to step aside from Liath, improving the Light's odds of success by making it feasible for the Gray Child to bypass Gallow Cliff and destroy only one shard.

The gulls flew above Ma'althan in a clear, midday sky, squawking occasionally. They broke his thoughts and reminded him that his scheduled meeting with his two Servants at Gallow Cliff had overrun its appointed time. The winds whipped Ma'althan, adding to his annoyance over the situation as he continued standing at the ledge, unattended and waiting. And his annoyance invoked concern. *They'd better not be meddling on the mortal plane, to interfere with the Game…*

The thought was followed by silence, and the slow transition of his mind back to Nym. She was the Fallen Servant who had interfered on the mortal plane, and was punished by being sewn back into the weave. Yet, despite Karnatha's suspicions that she was attempting to re-author time and change the Game's outcome, there would be little done beyond Destiny's requirement for Nym and her baby to die. Urzel had already been assigned the task, and she was waiting for the perfect time to complete it.

To Ma'althan, her death was not enough. He would have preferred for Nym's entire family tree to be eliminated—the descendants of the family she knew before entering the Servitude long ago; before her thread was lifted from the weave; before she was elevated to immortality. Nym started as a mortal with a mortal's mundane life and everything attached, and now, she should be forced to watch the destruction of that life. He smiled, enjoying thoughts of how she would suffer from witnessing her relationships being destroyed right in front of her, a thing that surely would remove any threat to the Darkness from her relatives. Ma'althan's wants were wrong, evil, and sadistic; they were Dark.

He popped out of the thought, and again found himself at cliff's edge, standing and waiting. In one instant, he took in sounds of the gull's melancholy song and the crashing waves below, just as feelings of the lashing winds. There was an absence of Sydullus and Urzel, and an absence of what he felt was required planning. Despite the Darkness having a clear advantage over the Light with so many Servants, and despite the oracles already prophesizing Shaizan's victory, Ma'althan felt that the Dark Prophecy's fulfillment still would require constant communication, planning, and hard work.

Winning this Game will prove challenging… Ma'althun sank back into contemplation, pondering the current assignments for his Servants. Of the four remaining Servants of the Dark excluding Nym, he commanded three to keep Karnath in order, while Sydullus specifically saw to the Children ending at Gallow Cliff.

In a similar way, he commanded the five newly acquired Servants of the Light, with Urzel dedicated to guiding the Children, and the others watching over related affairs in Karnath. The Servants were relatively good about sticking to their assigned tasks and not impinging upon the work of other Servants, although Urzel and Sydullus seemed to be justifying more and more tangential influence, as it supposedly related to the Children ending at Gallow Cliff. Ma'althan exercised his judgment in these matters, as many times, he had sound recommendations on their orchestration on the mortal plane, despite the clutter in his own mind from premonitions.

Strange premonitions often rendered Ma'althan confused and worried. In his head were conflicting visions of what would happen, or somehow, what had already happened. He had the visions for as long as he could remember, since the Game's start long ago. They were as worrying to him as they were to Karnatha, compounding with his other worries of Destiny dying, the Game being played in a seemingly different age by missing Servants, and sudden changes to it, like the Gray Child and him possibly going straight to Liath versus Gallow Cliff. He rubbed a hand up one side of his face, as the situation resounded of a clear need to monitor his Servants and give them guidance to the best of his ability. *If only they would come to their meetings…*

His mind turned to retribution options for his tardy Servants. But before Ma'althan could relish over them, he sensed a sudden disturbance in the energy field, which just so happened to be their arrival signature. Through the Nexus, Ma'althan felt them standing at his rear, cubits behind the ledge. He almost wanted to overreact to their tardiness, by sewing their life threads back into the weave, just like Nym. *Let your lost immortality be a lesson*, he mused with himself, *not to be late!*

In one instant, Ma'althan's brow bunched together, his eyes narrowed, and his facial muscles tensed. He voiced his frustrations then, with words cold as steel.

"Just where have you two been?!"

There was no immediate response.

"Well?! Do I have to force the truth out of you?"

"No, master."

Ma'althan turned about, seeing Sydullus and Urzel on one knee, paying homage.

"Get up," he snarled at them. "I appreciate timeliness more than other gestures. Start acting like this Game isn't already won for the Dark, cause it's not."

With straight faces, Urzel and Sydullus stood.

"What news do you have for me?" Ma'althan asked. "Are the Children of Darkness and Light on track to meet at Gallow Cliff?"

"Everything is going according to plan." Sydullus replied, in a brittle voice like snapping bones.

Urzel chimed in, "X'ieth now has the black shard."

Ma'althan's smile returned. *It's beginning.*

"Excellent," he said, rubbing his hands together.

"And it's likely Kort will have the white shard," Sydullus added, "if he can obtain the leviathan's help."

At the comment, Ma'althan entered into silent contemplation. He stopped rubbing his palms together, folded his hands, and raised his index fingers to his lips. *Kort already had his awakening, though X'ieth may not have. So, if both Children arrive at the cliffs under those circumstances, Kort would be stronger than X'ieth…*

Ma'althan removed the fingers from his lips, and crossed his arms. "Has X'ieth had his awakening?"

"Not yet," confirmed Urzel, "but the Child shall progress toward this soon! I…"

Sydullus cleared his throat, abruptly. "Ahem."

The inflection stopped Urzel mid-sentence, as if telling of his irritation that she excluded him.

"*We*," she said with emphasis and a slight glance his way, "have taken measures to ensure that Zeros and X'ieth stay together."

Sydullus complimented her, "Urzel created a sense of urgency to skillfully move past Talus' reservation of pairing Zeros and X'ieth. By having the king believe Esmeralda was the Child of Darkness who brought gloom upon Sergros, he found himself inclined toward anything to ensure his mission's success."

"Very soon X'ieth will accept his bad destiny," said Urzel. "Zeros is a base to the young knight's acidic demeanor, and the product of this pairing will be salt to X'ieth's deep wounds!"

Sydullus snickered gleefully with her analogy.

She continued. "Bringing the Children together at Gallow Cliff should be *easy* now."

From his silence, Ma'althan rebuked her.

"Mind your words. You assume victory before me, without even realizing it! I've told you to take this more seriously."

Ma'althan sighed. Urzel stopped beaming.

"Talus and Esmeralda are among the few doers left in Karnath, those who act upon premonitions and change what will happen to others around them. Doers can be dangerous, as they too might change the Game."

Ma'althan's very words reminded him just why he commissioned the other Servants to keep watch over Karnath for doers. He needed them to block interference and to maintain order so that the Children would converge to Gallow Cliff.

"Intrinsically, our goal involves decision under uncertainty. Even slight deviations from expectations can prove devastating to its viability."

Ma'althan sighed, again.

Sydullus and Urzel just stared back, more serious than before.

"Lose your confidence and think hard," Ma'althan said. "Are any minor deviations known, previously deemed insignificant?!"

Following the question, there were moments of inordinate silence, each one perturbing Ma'althan more. He began to wonder what was holding their tongues. *Does their pride prevent them from admitting an oversight?! It's always the oldest Servants who have the biggest egos. Sometimes I question how much better these immortals are than mere mortals…*

Under Ma'althan's glare, Urzel's face eventually flushed red.

"Talus ordered another ship to Logan," she noted, with some embarrassment. "It was done to aid Sagult's search. The king acted off his lack of premonitions about Kort's capture. This may have effects."

Another wind blew hard just then, as if to accentuate the Servant's willful omission from Ma'althan.

Unbelievable. Ma'althan released another sigh, this time no deeper than his deliberation on the matter. *While X'ieth has yet to awaken, his path has higher certainty of ending at Gallow Cliff than does Kort's. Liath will surely be a distraction for the ex-knight if we don't intervene; Elucid will see to that. But also, the young knight needs his awakening to happen before the cliffs, in order for him to beat Kort. Something must be done, where Kort avoids Liath and X'ieth is sure to have his awakening.*

From the quiet, Ma'althan instructed Urzel.

"Go to Logan, where that additional ship will dock after its voyage from the Mainland. Make sure it doesn't leave port. Under any circumstances, Sagult isn't to pursue Kort on the waters."

Ma'althan watched her swallow, without a word.

"Do I make myself clear?"

"Yes," she said, timidly.

For her benefit, Ma'althan expanded on why this would be important.

"If Sagult witnesses Kort's re-entry into Logan, he'll become the zealot we need for the ex-knight to choose Gallow Cliff over Liath. This won't happen if Sagult takes to the seas, and misses Kort's re-entry. I'll show you what I mean…"

From Ma'althan's open palm, energy flowed into Urzel's head to power a revelation. Her mouth opened and her eyes widened, in what appeared to be shock.

"That's only what I think will happen."

She remarked, "That's… that's brilliant!"

Ma'althan smiled then, extremely satisfied with his own cunning. *Hope it happens like that. No one knows anything for sure, even a Forerunner…*

Urzel's surprise dissolved as Ma'althan turned to Sydullus, and began speaking.

"X'ieth should be back in Arlem within a matter of days. See that everything stays on course. That should be enough for his awakening. When you witness it, however, lift your voice though never a finger. Immortals must not do more than aid the Game."

Sydullus replied, "Consider it done."

"And just a recommendation," Ma'althan added, looking to Urzel. "Since you now understand why Kort will choose Gallow Cliff over Liath, consider that he may be attended there by his lost love. And that could be the perfect time you've been waiting for to complete your special assignment. To think, everyone will die, including time itself!"

Ma'althan's face creased with joy at his own words, as did the Servants'. But out of that moment of delight, he suddenly grew serious and spoke curtly with them.

"Now, busy yourselves. I've much to consider."

The Servants replied in unison, "As you wish."

In a single instant, he watched them vanish into thin air, using the Nexus. Left alone on the cliff ledge, Ma'althan faced its precipice once more, his cloak blowing behind him in the wind. The gulls continued squawking noisily, gliding through the sky.

Ma'althan considered the Game as it was being played, and the thought filled him with angst. Questions buzzed through his mind, regarding the many strange things that neither he nor Karnatha could place. *How is Destiny dying? Why is the Game being played in an earlier age? Where are the Nullen Servants, as seen in our premonitions: Shaizan and Kayareth? Why are they named to fulfill a prophecy, when they aren't even present to do so?* His mind kept spinning with worry, until he cast it out and let a grander thought replace the former: *The Age of Darkness befalling Karnath—the last age to go on record!*

He closed his eyes and imagined what it would be like. *Bad destiny, for kings and kingdoms! People will abuse their talents to hurt others, and further only their own causes!* He envisioned Sergros falling, then Juniper, and ultimately strong Deardrum, in what would become a falling away across Karnath, where governments would fail and chaos would reign. *There will be nothing but murder and trickeries! People will suffer like never before!*

The varied thoughts brought a smile to Ma'althan's lips, and made him less concerned than before. *While I don't have answers to these many questions about Destiny's death, the Game's play, or missing Servants, a victory is still a victory, and that's all I care for!*

Suddenly then, still with his eyes shut, Ma'althan cleared his mind and suddenly leaped off the ledge, headfirst! Immediately, a falling sensation developed in his gut and air currents struck him hard in the face, as he fell from the heights of Gallow Cliff, toward the sea.

With his arms at each side, his body fell span after span, increasing in speed for an impact that would prove deadly for other men, though not him. And just before making contact with the water, he opened his eyes and flashed a wide, insidious grin. *Dark on us… Dark on us… Dark on us!*

SPLASH!!!

With that sound, both the thoughts and he entered the sea, for an imminent uprising against the Light. Indeed, the Darkness was coming.

"PLUNGE FROM GALLOW CLIFF"

Chapter 61
Revelations to Magicia

agicia's fight with Lucen in Esmeralda's tower continued until a moment where she presumed victory. It was the instant in which she hurled fire at him, being exactly at the same moment Zeros slashed with his blade. But Lucen mediated through the Nexus, effectively dodging sword and sorcery in the blink of an eye, and nullifying her expectations that two simultaneous and well-aimed strikes amounted to twice the chance of vanquishing their threat. She was wrong.

As her fire whooshed through the chamber to hit empty air, Magicia turned over her left shoulder. The moment's glance afforded her a view of Zeros as he swung his blade for naught, at a disappeared foe. She turned back further, glimpsing the center of the chamber, where Lucen reappeared. In one fluent motion that tousled his hair and sent his traveler's robe flowing behind him, he smote the floor with his gnarled staff.

Intense light suddenly flooded her eyes, replacing the sights of gray stone with those of white oblivion. And then chimes filled her ears, along with sounds of a child crying inconsolably. In a matter of seconds, the varied noises drowned in a pervasive ringing, which dominated everything Magicia could hear. The ringing continued in her ears, growing louder and louder, until the moment where she feared her ears could not withstand anything more. But it was then that the noise and light fled her senses, revealing a very different location than the tower.

Magicia found herself in a low mountain pass on Liath's eastern side, which extended all the way to Esmeralda's tower in the west. All around her, she saw dust fill the air from the mountain's partial destruction, which apparently had reached even these parts. It was blown about on the fierce cold winds, which lashed her brutally.

That dust challenged her vision, yet Magicia looked through it intently, straining to see the horizon in search of Esmeralda's tower, as seen from her spot many times before, when walking this very pass. *Sister! Sister!!!*

In the aftermath of her heated reaction toward Lucen, severe denial now coursed through Magicia over witnessing Esmeralda's decapitation and her tower crumbling to bits. For the moment, Magicia could not and would not accept those things as true.

Yet as much as she searched the horizon, and yet as much as she hoped to see the tower standing there like the entire development was somehow just a bad dream, there was nothing to be seen but heaps of crumbled gray rock. The sight was devastating and forced poor memories through Magicia's mind, from her turning to Esmeralda's headless neck as it fountained blood and Gremel flying away with the shard, to the fight with Lucen and the tower shaking apart with the mountain's collapse.

Magicia fell to her knees and lamented with a wail.

"Esmeralda!" she cried.

Tears gushed from her eyes as she pictured the death again, a thought that easily ushered feelings of grief, anger, and guilt upon her, the most powerful of them being guilt itself. *She had the black shard because of me!* It was a sobering realization, yet valid in every sense of the way.

"Why must I live new heartaches in every walk of my life?!" Magicia wept from the rocks. "Why must the ones I love be affected by my poor choices?!" As so many times before in her experience, there was no response from Destiny save that of nature: more cold winds. They whipped Magicia and she endured their punishment thinking it less than due for bringing destruction upon her family, and also, Karnath.

"Why, Saora?! Take it out on me, not them!"

She continued crying upon her knees, and soon, her denial pulled her in a new direction. *Go back for closure.*

A sudden need filled Magicia, to verify what she saw and experienced was real indeed. She needed to go back to the tower, and she needed to see its ruin in order to fully believe that Esmeralda was gone. The necessity set her hands to motion, as she started checking every pocket of her robe for the object that she would use to mediate from the pass to the tower in a matter of moments: her transition stone.

Yet, though she searched every pocket twice, turning some inside out, the stone was nowhere to be found! Frantically, Magicia patted her neckline to see if she could feel it there, knowing that sometimes she wore the object about her neck. She felt nothing, and she felt dismayed. *Where is it? Where is it?! I must return to the tower! I must!!!!*

After a few moments of searching, the reality of not finding the stone steered her mind toward alternatives. *Just walk, or run!* The mere thought was in desperation, yet it mocked her, for she knew the journey neared tens of spans and would be impossible by foot with so little time. Despite all the pain inside her, her foremost priorities still pressed her in a way where every hour mattered: *Get the shard; go to Gallow Cliff; connect with the seroxians; fight the Child of Darkness when he shows himself!*

Slowly, it occurred to her that doing any of these things would be most difficult without the aid of her transition stone. Her challenges of reaching Esmeralda's tower now manifested themselves as challenges of even reaching Gallow Cliff, or even pursuing the other shard with Kort. *How will I do any of these without my stone?!*

Clenching both fists, Magicia wept more from upon her knees, feeling angry and embittered over the situation. The winds continued beating her, swirling dust all around her and in her face, like a constant reminder of the curse destroying Karnath, one born of a curse that destroyed her—vengeance. And in that moment, being brought to both knees reminded Magicia of a time over a thousand years ago, in perhaps another walk of her life, where she knelt in despair over Eriens and Hrya impaling each other. She lost something important then; she was losing something important now.

Then in her ears, sounded a musical voice from the distance, a series of chimes that rang out, with the former melding into the latter, discernably yet indistinguishably.

"Your inheritance is more wholesome than his, Kilwroth's unwholesome inheritance."

Magicia got up from her knees, and turned about on both feet, trying to locate the voice's origin. A dust screen obscured her view of the mountain range, allowing her to see only a few cubits ahead, in any direction.

"Show yourself, Saora! Show yourself!"

Half expecting it, Magicia watched as the ghostly woman appeared from the dust, with jittering skin that dissolved then replenished itself in an instant, with gold blotches of light for her eyes and mouth.

"Good destiny evaded you, sorceress. When you found Shaizan, you found love again. Wasn't that enough to leave your hurt over Hrya alone? Apparently not."

Magicia visited her store of memories, so many of them completely missing as if stolen; or conflicting, as if being present from multiple walks of her life. She remembered Hrya's death long ago, her pursuits of vengeance through the Void's empowerment, and somehow involving Shaizan in an affair that she suspected meant the end of time and the end of Karnatha. It was an affair that made her regret wanting vengeance in the first, an affair that now dedicated her every effort to stopping Saora.

"My vengeance over Hrya is long dead!" Magicia answered. "You've seen to that."

"Oh, you don't want vengeance anymore, after seeing its implications for Shaizan?" Saora asked, coming closer. "Maybe you should have loved him, versus choosing to love your own hate. You could have chosen differently."

"You used me!" Magicia replied, caustically.

"Indeed, just like you used him. You've become the pawn in my game of chess, the lucky one who makes it to the board's opposite side and becomes queen."

"The black queen!" Magicia snarled. "You've employed me for evil versus good!"

"I'd much rather the pieces be gray, rather than black or white. I've enlisted the help of many in the realm of spent energy to carry out a plan that would otherwise be impossible!" Each of Saora's words chimed together.

"Karnatha dies and rightfully so," she continued, "for removing people's battle for destiny, and obligating the Children of Destiny to fight that battle through the Game! Her change to how Karnath realizes its fate is perverse, for people are meant to battle for destiny themselves, using time well spent! So now, as punishment for her perversion, I'm destroying the time she's reserved for people's purposeless existence, and in so doing, I'm destroying Destiny herself, just as Karnatha destroyed destiny for others. She'll lose a small share of life force with every destroyed age, with each unraveled weave!"

Saora moved closer to Magicia, and the sorceress stepped back. Her foot touched down on soft rock that crumbled underneath her weight with a boring sound, causing her to nearly stumble.

"And until that death," Saora continued, creeping again toward Magicia, "the curse of Eternal Darkness will appear in Karnath age after age, a constant reminder to Destiny of what she wrought through the Game! She devised the Game so that its outcome would decide the battle between good and evil in the hearts of men, sealing their fate through a curse that could ensure bad destiny in Karnath, should Darkness be the Game's victor!"

Saora continued. "Shaizan won the Game already, and therefore, I'll throw that victory in Karnatha's face until she breathes her dying last! For once and for all, Destiny wanted to end the war between good and evil by robbing Karnath of the challenge it's due. But how that plan has backfired on her! For now, the war between good and evil is coming to earlier ages, where evil will be advantaged through Shaizan's future win and a curse of Darkness upon creation!"

"Unless," Magicia interjected, "someone can undo your fiendish plan, and restore order before time is erased."

"Is that someone you, sorceress? By seeking vengeance on Karnatha, you've put yourself in the middle of my holy war between Destiny and the Void. Yet, I'm a force to be reckoned with, for you see, *I control knowledge* by what ethers are dispersed from the Void. The ethers, in part, are memories stolen from those of Karnath—memories that they've had in another walk of their life in an unraveled weave—many times seen as premonitions in weaves yet raveled. Here's a token of my power!"

An intense burning sensation suddenly overwhelmed Magicia's head, as if hot irons were stuck into both of her ears. She fell upon her knees and wailed in pain, as missing memories burned into place.

"Arrrgggggghhhh!"

**** Magicia's Recall—Curse in Victory ****

[Second Walk of Existence]

Shortly after the dawn of creation, Karnatha devised a Game of Time and Sword to be played by the Children of Destiny, under premonitions of bad destiny entering the world sometime in the future. She knew the Age of Light was doomed to end, and so, she would start the Game in hopes of ending what she feared would be an endless war between good and evil. She intended the Game to decide one victor, and to seal that victory with a curse over Karnath, if the winning Forerunner so chooses.

One evening, she stood at the center of Karnath wearing a gray, silken gown. In her hand, she held a gray blade capable of slaying time. On each side, her Forerunners waited before her: Ma'althan was at her left and Autheos on her right, both of them wearing the armors of god that showed their respective hue. The full moon hung in the night sky behind them, above the Mountains of Liath on the horizon. The air was clean and crisp, and spoke of a new direction for Karnath through the Game.

"Let a race decide which of you shall have the gray blade, for a wholesome inheritance to our Children," Karnatha said, shifting her eyes from Autheos and then to Ma'althan. "You shall run from the East," she instructed Ma'althan, "and you from the West." The last words came with a glance to Autheos. "Whichever lineage holds the blade has a clear advantage in the Game."

Looking to Autheos of Light, Karnatha said, "Possessing the blade allows you to save time by taking the whole sword to Liath for its destruction." To Ma'althan of Darkness she turned, "Or possessing it could mean going to Gallow Cliff, to slay time."

She watched their eyes light up as she spoke of favoring possibilities for the Light and Darkness. "To the winner go the spoils. If time is slain, I'll place a curse on Karnath that erodes any chance of good destiny, to destroy opportunity and break apart creation! People will have only bad destiny then, as the Forerunner of Darkness pleases, should the Child of Darkness win."

Ma'althan shook his head with satisfaction.

"And if time be saved..."

****

In Magicia's mind, Karnatha's voice trailed off as the ether settled. She clasped her head, hearing a distinct ringing in her ears. Her vision doubled, and two of everything appeared before the sorceress. Then slowly, the situation normalized. The ringing stopped; the two images became one.

Magicia stood and brushed the dirt from her sorceress robe. When upon her feet, she visited her store of memories, with now, another hole filled by Saora. *Shaizan won the Game for the Darkness in my future, and began unraveling the ages' weaves! The Age of Darkness came to Karnath then, through Karnatha's curse. And now, that curse falls to this age, as the gloom!* It was the same conclusion she reached through premonitions embedded in her dreams no more, just with added clarity: *The Age of Darkness is Karnatha's curse and already here through Shaizan's win!*

"The curse favoring Ma'althan comes from the future to ages past," Saora laughed musically. "Be comforted that you're not alone in your confusion, for I've withheld ether about the Game's state from Karnatha and her Forerunners, among many other things. So even for them, the current reality is most perplexing! To them, it feels like the Game should be played in the future, yet it's being played in the present. To them, Destiny's life force is dwindling, though they don't understand why. To them, premonitions tell of two young Servants, Shaizan and Kayareth, who will join the Servitude, who are prophesized to be the Children of Destiny, who are missing from Karnath with other Children taking their place at Gallow Cliff. It's a mire of complexities for Karnatha to wade through, and as of yet, she's unable to understand how the Game is changing or why. As a result, she'll blame anyone who's close enough to the problem. This age, Nym gets the blame, just like other scapegoats of times no more. There have been many, when in reality the one who causes Destiny's trouble is none other than whom Karnatha presumes dead and powerless—me!"

Magicia shook her head in disbelief, as she looked at Saora floating a few cubits away from her, like a ghost.

"Causality makes what you're doing impossible!" Magicia said. "Future events can't just fall into the present without being affected by the past!" She sifted through her memories again while speaking, finding too many holes to piece together this puzzle.

"What causality? Don't you remember, *Karnatha severed the thread of causality* when the second walk of existence ended? That thread ran through all the weaves, propagating effects of the past forward in time."

With Saora's question, she faded from Magicia's view, into the dust cloud.

"Don't you remember, *the weave effect*?"

Magicia spun about, trying to follow the voice.

"Here, let me revive your memory…"

Immediately, Magicia felt the same hot irons entering her ears and going deep into her head. She closed her eyes and gritted her teeth, as the pain pulled her to both knees. Images flashed in her mind, of a horizontal line wrought in green Nexus with a time marker overtop, shaped as a chevron and pointed down. The time marker moved slowly, from the left to the right.

The searing pain subsided for Magicia, and was replaced by the sound of Saora's voice.

"Karnath's first walk of existence was a long Age of Light, where the land saw no Darkness and people had no bad destiny. Yet, they lived aimlessly and without purpose; as time drew on, they embraced null destiny. And *if you remember what Karnatha's lifeblood is*, well, then you know what happened. Year after year, I strengthened while she weakened, until the point where she couldn't weave more ages for Karnath. That's when Shaizan took matters into his own hands."

In her mind, Magicia saw the time marker move along the horizontal line until its end, where suddenly, the line's right end shortened and the chevron hung in space, next to it.

"Shaizan was the youngest Servant of the Light appointed to the Servitude, along with Kayareth. When he learned that Karnatha was too weak to weave, he stopped time to save Karnath."

Saora told Magicia of a story about Shaizan, which she never knew despite their relationship.

"It was before the Game even existed," Saora explained, "in the first walk of existence where you had never even met him."

Still upon her knees, Magicia kept envisioning the timeline and its time marker.

Saora continued talking. "With Shaizan's intervention, he unraveled the final age. This caused the time marker to fall off the loom, and all its ethers went to the Void, where they were held captive. I freed the memory of what had happened to Karnatha, and this ether moved the time marker back to the first age. It was then that history began to over-write itself."

Magicia imagined the chevron return to the line's left end, and begin moving toward the right once more.

"When a time marker follows ether, it's one weave effect that changes the current weave upon the loom. You see, the time marker moving to the beginning of time started the second walk of existence, where things went drastically different than in the first walk. Karnatha now had premonitions of bad destiny entering the world and time ending; she now had a counterpart of Darkness named Ma'althan, and no longer just Autheos. It became clear to her that she already had bad destiny inside, and this foreshadowed how bad destiny might inevitably be part of Karnath if she didn't insert herself into the people's destiny, through her Children and a game. 'Twas an unforgivable decision, for which Karnatha stands to pay!"

Magicia followed the time marker, as it moved a quarter way down the line.

"Despite all your memories I'm still keeping in the Void, surely you remember how you got wrapped up in this: Hrya. When he became a casualty in

Karnatha's Game on the second walk of existence, you sought to avenge him, and prayed to the Void for help with your mission!"

Visions flashed through Magicia's head of Hrya and Eriens impaling each other, overtop of the timeline and its time marker. She remembered watching that scene from upon her knees, in the grasslands of New Karnath, being anguished over Hrya's death and willing to do anything to exact revenge upon Karnatha for stealing her first love.

The flashes of Hrya and Eriens were gone within moments, leaving Magicia to her visions of the timeline, where the chevron marker continued moving to the right. It traveled from the quarter point to halfway down, and then to the end, where the same thing happened: the line shortened from the right and the time marker flew off of it, hanging in space.

"Even with Karnatha having her own Children vie for Karnath's destiny, another Shaizan entered the world through her lineage, as if Ma'althan's seed was destined to be her Fate's Fray. You met him in the second walk of existence, where you used him to end time again at Gallow Cliff!"

Denial wrestled with guilt in Magicia's head. *No, I didn't use him! Yes, you did. I loved him... Even so, you still used him.*

"At the end of existence's second walk, I released more ether to Karnatha, which hinted at consequences from Shaizan's backtracking expedition through time, where the furthest ages were unraveling and time itself was compacting! Given what makes up Karnatha's lifeblood, she feared that somehow the Game was being used to destroy herself, an entirely correct suspicion! It was happening little by little, with each weave Shaizan unraveled."

Saora went on. "With causality, Karnatha knew that if one age unraveled at the beginning of time, it would mean the end of all forthcoming ages, and her immediate demise. And so, she severed the thread of causality to segment time and avoid this possibility!"

Magicia suddenly noticed the timeline appear segmented along its length, with noticeable breaks that turned it into many smaller lines. And then, she watched the chevron multiply into many chevrons, with one going to each time segment, where it made treks from left to right.

"The result of eliminating causality was the isolation of ages as separate weaves, and a *poly-furcation of the time marker* where one marker appeared *in each age*!" Saora exclaimed. "The new time markers move between an age's start and end, where like their predecessor, a weave effect can reset their position independent of other time markers in adjacent ages! These markers are re-writing a fragmented history across the ages, such that Karnatha will never be able to stitch the present back into the future using the thread of causality!"

She watched the time markers go back and forth on their individual segments. They moved right until hitting the age's end, and then, they moved back to the age's beginning.

"When a weave unravels, its ether returns to the Void, where it stays until I decide to release it! The reentry point for that ether is always a given age, and the age's time marker moves according to the era's earliest memories that journey from the future."

From upon her knees, Magicia opened her eyes, and saw nothing but the dust rolling over her, swirled about by the fierce winds. Like an ice whip, the gusts snapped over her skin and acutely stung her flesh.

Magicia struggled to believe Saora after receiving ether about the state of time; she struggled to believe how multiple ages were simultaneously ongoing. It just did not seem possible.

"This is how people re-author fates…"

Magicia arose from her knees and ran into the dust, following Saora's voice.

"And the Game is how Karnatha became the spider having all other spiders in her web."

Magicia heard the voice from her right; she ran in that direction, even though the dust cloud limited her sight of what was even there.

"She's the one who re-spun everyone's web of destiny through creating the Game, which has led me to create Time No More…"

Saora's voice suddenly sounded from the left.

"In order to destroy Destiny and time!"

Magicia stopped herself and changed directions, now going left. After only moments of running, she saw someone a few cubits ahead, someone whom she never dreamed of seeing—Esmeralda.

The sight stopped Magicia immediately. Esmeralda stood there, as real as day, wearing her yellow sorceress robe of the Guild, with healthy, glowing skin and luscious, red hair that fell from her crown, over her shoulders!

From sheer surprise, Magicia's mouth first dropped open, but soon formed a wide smile, as joy spread across her face and lit up her eyes, now enlivened with excitement. In one instant, she felt immense giddiness inside, as if her heart skipped beats and leaped ecstatically in her chest.

"Esmeralda!" Magicia exclaimed.

She ran forward with arms wide open, preparing to embrace her sister. But after only a few strides, Magicia ricocheted off the thin air between her and Esmeralda, like she would if colliding into a wall of thick glass. As she tumbled to the ground, her back hit Liath's rock and a sudden jolt of pain shot through her body. Still and silent, she lied there on the mountain, with the strong winds blowing over, stirring her robe.

Without spending much time to recover, Magicia sat up and rose to her feet. She felt unsteady and wobbly when afoot, still in shock over what had just happened. Her eyes scanned the dust cloud again for Esmeralda until finding her; she stood there just like she was last seen, as if unfazed by the sight of Magicia.

"Esmeralda?!" Magicia cried, running forth and plastering both hands against the translucent barrier, which separated the sisters. When her hands touched its surface, it felt cold and smooth, like glass.

Esmeralda still acted unfazed by Magicia's cries. It seemed like the two of them were strangely in different worlds, where only Magicia could see into Esmeralda's, but not the other way around.

"Esmeralda…" Magicia said, looking despairingly through the barrier, at her sister.

Magicia's lips parted, when suddenly a hand appeared behind Esmeralda's shoulder! She intently watched the development, as at her sister's rear, a figure slowly stepped into view. It was a woman with a pretty round face, red braided hair, and striking gray eyes; it was Magicia herself! Her jaw dropped.

Magicia continued peering into what seemed another world, at Esmeralda and herself. At her double's touch, Esmeralda turned and smiled. She saw them laugh together, yet Magicia could not hear a thing!

"What is this?!" she asked, in awe. Her mind raced with Saora's words: *The result of cutting causality's thread is the isolation of ages and the time marker splitting into many, where now, each weave gets constantly re-spun upon Destiny's loom!*

"What is it?" Saora responded, in a voice overtop of Magicia. "I'm showing you an age before this one, where time still flows just as it flows in your current age…"

"Without causality, the flow of time in different ages is independent and happening all at once. As you can see, both you and Esmeralda are still together in the past, even though she's gone in your present… Perhaps you should enjoy this picture while it lasts, before this age unravels! It's destined to be a time no more, just as the others. Ha ha ha! Ah ha ha ha!"

Saora's chiming words and sadistic laughter crushed Magicia's heart, and she was stricken with immediate grief over losing Esmeralda. The anguish was felt first from within, and then poured out. Her body trembled as she leaned against the barrier, pounding it with both fists, using all her might. In one singular moment, her countenance darkened and the grief spread across her face like a disease—scrunching her brow, tearing up her eyes, and contorting her cheeks and mouth, as she wailed mournfully into the mountain pass.

"Esmeralda! Esmeralda!!! Esmeraldaaaaa!!!"

She beat more and more against the barrier, pounding out her anger over her immense and soul-hollowing loss. Her fists became red and sore, hurting as she carried out her lament, hurting just like she did inside.

This whole while, Magicia was revisited by the same exact negative emotions she suffered long ago when committing herself to taking vengeance on Destiny over Hrya, which now, seemed as something she was ironically doomed to relive again and again, in spite of her change of heart.

"Why are you doing this, Saora?! Why?! Each age, you kill me a little more…" Magicia yelled, still overwhelmed by grief. Her head spun wildly with so much bizarre information, some of which she knew; some of which were holes in her memory.

"Indeed," said a voice, now sounding at Magicia's rear. "The emotional toll of losing your loved ones in each and every age is akin to how Karnatha dies."

Magicia turned away from the barrier, toward the voice. She scanned the dust cloud, still not seeing Saora.

"She dies with each and every weave that Shaizan unravels. Let me remind you that I'm killing Karnatha strictly over the Game. For with the Game, I cannot accept people as they are—shapeless clay. Without people being molded by their battle for destiny, they're without form and unmade. Per Karnathan teaching, everyone in Karnath supposedly has a divine purpose, yet Karnatha gave everyone an escape: the option of relying on the Game for their destiny, should they not wish to fight. Existence where people mostly be and rarely do is a reproach to what they're meant for, an existence worthy of being undone. Time and Destiny must die."

Magicia started running into the dust cloud, searching for Saora. *Remember, she has your transition stone and there's no leaving until you have it. Find her.*

"So," Saora asked, "how do you like my re-design of Karnatha's Game?"

Magicia ran on a diagonal, to her right.

"It's my own little takeover of the Game, in which I architect the information structures of the remaining ages, so that the Game unfolds exactly how I see fit! My ethers released from the Void decide *what people know*, even *who plays* and *how*."

Magicia kept chasing after the voice, still hearing it from the same direction.

"Give back my transition stone!" Magicia shouted.

"Will you do the right thing with it?" Saora asked. "Going back to Esmeralda's wastes time. You ought to always be moving forward. Your sister… is dead."

The comment choked Magicia, like a hand to the throat. She felt momentarily impaired, unsure if she could keep chasing after Saora through Liath. Her inner voice suggested otherwise. *You can't let this stop you, for there's nothing that can be done for Esmeralda now. On the other hand, Karnath still has a chance…*

Doubts swarmed her mind, over uncertainty of how she could help Karnath, over uncertainty of which cycle she could really break. *Would a victory at Gallow Cliff be the end of Time No More, or would it only break Saora's loop in this isolated age?! Or rather, would it do both?!* She did not know. To so many questions in her mind, there were, unfortunately, very few answers.

"To continue my rendition of Destiny's Game, I'll enable you with the stone," Saora said. "But I encourage you to make a brief stop before going to the Isles, if you value aid from the seroxians at Gallow Cliff!"

"Of what do you speak?" asked Magicia, after a long pause and more cold wind, felt through her robe.

"While Elucid tells you of whispers among immortals," Saora replied, "the crimson knight may not be telling you everything. What Elucid has not disclosed is a very different intent, of not going to Gallow Cliff at all!"

Magicia followed the music of Saora's voice through the dust cloud.

"Elucid can be trusted!" she yelled, while running.

"Can he?" Saora laughed. "Would you trust one who defies the prophecy this age? For Elucid shall propose taking the white shard to Liath for destruction, versus going to Gallow Cliff for the whole gray blade."

Magicia's face wrinkled in puzzlement. *Why would Elucid do that?! The Light Prophecy must be followed!*

"Now that sounds drastically different than what the oracles once foretold!" Saora continued. "Surely to change the Dark Prophecy's outcome mustn't require deviating from the Light Prophecy so radically. I would think either one prophecy or the other must be true…"

In that moment, Magicia pondered the matter further. *Elucid hasn't even suggested this… Could it be that the crimson knight hides his true intention?!* The mere thought perplexed her, of alternative plans impacting her own agenda of the seroxians aiding the Gray Child at Gallow Cliff. *This cannot happen! It mustn't, if we are to stop Lucen!*

"You're against that, sorceress. So make a choice concerning whether you'll let it happen," Saora spoke then, in more otherworldly chimes.

Magicia ran and ran, following the sound through the dust cloud, further into the range. She felt lost.

"How?!" Magicia asked, with a hint of desperation.

"There's a lady in waiting, beside the harbor in Breslin. If you have her go to the harbor in New Yoke instead, it may make a difference…"

And then, Magicia saw something ahead of her in the dust that brought her to a complete standstill. She made a final stride and stopped, just watching as a vertical beam of light shone from the sky and cut through the dust, falling onto the rock maybe ten cubits before her. From above, an object fell through the light and landed with a clatter, lying there in its beam. As her ears registered the sound, her mind registered the realization. *My transition stone!*

The sight stirred Magicia into motion; she hastened her feet, and ran toward her prized possession. But when only a cubit or two away from her stone, the hot irons suddenly entered her ears and sent blinding pain through her head.

She collapsed to the ground and lied there on her belly, clasping her head with both hands as withheld memories settled in place, like Liath's dust.

"Arrgghhhh!" she cried in agony.

From over her, Magicia heard Saora's words, "Have some more ether, some more regret, and some more answers in your search for truth! Ha ha ha!"

**** Magicia's Recall—Seeds for Her Conspiracy ****

[Second Walk of Existence]

On a truly splendid day, two sisters enjoyed time together in the western pass of Liath. They stood together on the rock, surrounded by the natural beauty of gray mountain peaks on the horizon, seated below a clear blue sky. The autumn air was cool and crisp from these heights, and Magicia breathed it in, enjoying every whiff just as other things, like the reminder she was just served of how the mountain lilies were still in bloom.

With a broad smile, Magicia twirled the flower in her fingers, the one handed to her by a handsome man who hiked the trail where the sisters spent the afternoon. In her other hand, she held the bundled black shard, something she kept close through the years. To her, it was but a memory of her pursuit of vengeance. To her, it was but a memory of distant love that waned, over time and with the heart's yearning for new love.

"A flower is all it takes, and you're raptured!" Esmeralda teased.

Magicia looked over and smiled, returning the wide grin upon her sister's face.

"You should've seen how you looked upon him," Esmeralda continued. "How you hung upon his words with desirous eyes!"

"Oh stop it!" Magicia said playfully. "There are many handsome men in Karnath, and I've not a history for falling for just anyone."

Her eyes scanned the trail, to the distant hiker she met moments prior, the one who handed her the lily after a pleasant exchange. She saw his red hair from the distance, growing even more distant as he continued walking the snaky trail into the mountains. Magicia returned her gaze to the lily.

"His name is Shaizan," Esmeralda asserted.

Still smiley, Magicia twirled the flower in her hand.

"It's not a common name at all," she finally replied. "I've never met anyone with it before."

"Who would bestow that name to their child?" asked Esmeralda. "'Tis the name of the Child of Darkness in the Light Prophecy…"

Looking up from the lily, Magicia noticed her sister displayed a pensive façade.

"Apparently a blacksmith in Village Winsdor would!" Magicia jokingly countered, recalling what Shaizan shared of his father's occupation.

"Having that name seems less wholesome than whatever Kilwroth's inheritance was!"

Magicia turned from the lily to her sister, and silence developed as a gentle breeze kissed both of them.

"Could you imagine," Esmeralda said, "what prejudice would do to your hiker friend, if he came into the possession of the shard you hold?"

Startled by the mere suggestion, Magicia gripped the bundle tighter.

"I would never do such a thing to him," she muttered, although feeling a nudge from inside. The sting of losing Hrya surfaced in her heart, along with memories in her mind of praying to the Void long ago. Saora told Magicia that one day an opportunity would arise for her to take vengeance against Destiny, and she wondered if that day had finally come.

"I know," Esmeralda continued. "Was just a thought, that's all..."

Magicia's eyes trailed to the lily again. She touched its petals, while talking. "I wonder if I'll see him again."

"You may, if you plan to visit me still."

At those words, Magicia looked up to her sister.

"He hikes the trails near my tower, all the time."

The bundled black shard suddenly felt hot in Magicia's hand, burning her with desire. It occurred to her slowly, of how easy it would be to drop this burden upon the path, for another poor soul to bear.

****

Still on the ground, Magicia lifted her hand toward the voice, as the ether merged into her store of existing memories. Her head throbbed just as her heart, from pains of losing Esmeralda, from pains of what she brought upon Karnath.

"It's rude to keep a lady in waiting, so you best be going!" called Saora, from the dust cloud.

"Of all this ether, I've yet to remember Shaizan the way I knew him!" Magicia protested, getting first to her knees and then to her feet.

"Give me that memory! Put that back in my mind!"

"Soon, sorceress," said Saora. "Now be off, so not to waste anymore time!"

Magicia was literally left in the dust, standing alone in Liath's pass and staring down at her transition stone, knowing exactly what she needed to do.

"LUCEN'S HELP"

Kort found himself on the deck of Raiden's storm-beaten sailboat, enraged with Elucid over being stranded upon Korinth. Going weeks without food, he was broken in body and spirit, literally living to see his body waste and his dreams die.

Kort was weak. Kort was tired. Kort was hurting. He was all of these things, and in no position to accept Elucid's latest claim of being Laotzu. And so, he stood there incredulous as could be, before the crimson knight and under the burning sun, not knowing what, if anything, to believe anymore.

"You purport then," Kort asked, "to be the shadow of Laotzu, imprisoned in that magical armor?!"

"Yes!" Elucid boomed.

And right at that word, thunder sounded suddenly from over the crimson knight's shoulder! Kort directed his attention there, just in time to see the waters erupt at a distance of one hundred spans from the boat. They shot up into the air as a fountain, and fell in large splashes to reveal what appeared to be a gray mountain.

Kort leered on, hardly believing his eyes that a large rock shot up from the ocean. But the longer he looked, the more it seemed to be something different than a mountain, something frightening—a mound of gray coils with an awful head atop! Indeed, it was a snake-like sea monster that rivaled the worst of images from Kort's nightmares!

In one sudden motion, the monster uncoiled itself and came speeding toward the boat, headfirst! Kort steered his eyes back to the boat, and he noticed then how Elucid had turned away to look at the disruption in the waters. Kort imagined rowing the boat away from the monster, and it stirred him to immediate action. He stooped down, grabbed the oars, and threw one at Elucid.

With a dull clang, the oar bounced off Elucid's armor and into the crimson knight's gauntlets. Elucid turned to the ex-knight and looked down at it.

"Let us row from harm!" shouted Kort.

He watched on with some surprise as Elucid dropped the oar, and raised a hand.

"Be not afraid. Your good destiny comes forth."

But an upraised hand and calm words did little to ease Kort. He looked away from Elucid and back to the fearsome sea monster, seeing it about fifty spans closer to the boat. It snaked through the waters, which parted on each side of its wide-open mouth that swallowed the sea—a toothy and terrifying pit to death that came right their way.

"Row with me!" Kort insisted, dunking his oar into the water and working it quickly.

The boat turned little by little, soon pointing in a direction perpendicular to the one in which the monster approached. Kort kept pushing the oar, despite being puzzled over why Elucid would not help. *He doesn't even budge! Why?!*

"Row with me!" Kort pled again, right before falling as the boat suddenly jumped on waves from the monster's approach. He hit the hull hard and dropped the oar. His eyes watched it clatter across the deck into Elucid's feet, as the boat continued rocking up and down on the troubled waters. Raiden's limp body bounced in the hull, just as other loose objects onboard.

After only a moment, Kort looked up from the boat, but by the time he did, the sea monster loomed right over them, casting a huge, enveloping shadow!

From the sunbaked planks, Kort lifted a hand to shield his eyes, trying to hold back an unsightly spectacle. For he stared face-to-face with his own disbelief, as a figure of Karnathan myth came to life—the leviathan! It was a hideous, awful creature of the deep that strikingly resembled its drawings in books of lore, with minor differences like four jaws instead of three, many more fins, and an enormity that was hard to comprehend. The leviathan's thick body stretched behind it for a great length, one comparable to all of Doj's houses strung together in a single line, ending in a spiky tailfin.

VESSSS! VASSS! ... VESSSS! VASSS!

Kort moaned in pain as a sudden raspy, loud noise penetrated his ears and throbbed his head. At the same time, a rank, nose-wrinkling odor filled his nostrils, stinking of rotten fish or worse. He turned his attention from the leviathan's tailfin and back to its awful head that was dotted by a pair of beady eyes. The monster had apparently opened its four jaws lined with razor-sharp white teeth to show its mouth filled with a long, pink tongue. The sight was menacing, and froze Kort in fear.

Slowly, he managed to look away from the sharp teeth, long enough to see the three fins on the monster's head, one on the top and another at each side. Gills opened and closed behind the leviathan's head at the top of its neck; they were like rows of fleshy, gray shutters that moved every time the creature sucked air.

Alarms went off in Kort's head: *If the leviathan eats you, there's no redemption! There's no seeing Nym!* While he did not know how to prevent the outcome of being eaten, he felt immediately inclined to do something about it. And so, Kort overcame his paralysis and struggled to his feet, as the boat continued rocking on the waters.

When afoot, however, Kort instantly fell to the hull. He hit the planks near the boat's edge, and realized then how violently everything was shaking. He grabbed onto its side, worried that the vessel would capsize.

"We'll go into the water!" Kort exclaimed.

All of a sudden, Kort felt the boat lurch, as the leviathan's body encircled the vessel and raised it up out of the water, ten cubits from its mouth! In panic, Kort hugged the boat's side more, unable to look away from the monster's sharp teeth, which now, were uncomfortably close. Thoughts raced through this mind: *Will the leviathan eat a meal of bone?! That's all I am!*

From the hull Kort watched Elucid, who somehow kept standing through the boat's tossing and it being lifted right out of the water on the leviathan's body. As if knowing exactly what to do, the crimson knight started channeling Nexus. Kort followed streams of green and blue energy that emanated from Elucid's center, and flowed all about them in a complex swirl.

"What are you doing?!" asked Kort.

There was no reply from Elucid.

And so, Kort was left to wonder. All he could do was continue to follow the energies that flowed from Elucid's core and all around them. Suddenly, the Nexus amassed into a film of energy that stood vertically between the monster's head and the boat, like a filter of sorts.

The leviathan abruptly made a loud, hissy noise, and it went through the energy field to enter Kort's ears as a language he surprisingly knew—the Mainlandish tongue!

"I mean no harm to the sailing ships passing through these parts," said the leviathan. "But from an infirmity deep in my belly, I often find comfort to thrash in the waters, which upsets the sea for nearby vessels."

Kort found himself awestruck and silent, not knowing what to say. When he turned to the crimson knight, his eyes met a pair of dark slits in the metal demon's helmet.

"Speak with the leviathan," boomed Elucid. "This problem is meant for you to solve."

Kort felt confused. *How could Elucid possibly know that? How even, would I solve the leviathan's problem?*

He turned from the crimson knight, back toward the leviathan, still not knowing what to say, but no longer being able to endure Elucid's unwavering glare. Slowly and with some fear, Kort spoke into the energy filter, trusting that just as it bent the leviathan's voice into Mainlandish, it could also bend his tongue into that of leviathan.

"Great leviathan, I sorrow over your pain, and also, that which you've caused to sailors. This aside, I don't believe I can help you."

Kort's words traveled through the energy, and emerged as a series of raspy sounds, which immediately evoked a mournful hiss from the leviathan. The monster began talking, shortly thereafter.

"Perhaps you can do more than you believe is possible. Something I've eaten cannot leave me, and causes an ache within."

Their conversation circled around the same points: the leviathan had stomach pain; Kort did not know how to help. The same confusion surfaced in his mind: *How can I assist with that?*

In his moment of thought, the leviathan made a startling and unexpected request of Kort. "Go inside me to find what causes my discomfort."

The recommendation struck Kort poorly. *Do I appear more a doctor for sea creatures than a meal? Surely not… Perhaps the leviathan just wants easy food?*

He looked to Elucid, who stared back, as if expecting his unconditional compliance.

"No!" Kort exclaimed, presuming the crimson knight's thoughts. "Such a terrible thing would surely be my end!"

Kort watched Elucid extend a metal hand, and place it reassuringly on his shoulder. It felt warm from the sun, and light as a feather.

"Remember the storm and the weeks of hunger," reminded Elucid. "Through every trial, Destiny protected you and Destiny will do the same now. You are the One of Prophecy, and you should trust that great good can become of you taking this risk—a great good to others."

Kort listened on with a mixed face, showing some disbelief, yet a willingness to do good.

"The leviathan is but a milestone on your path to obtain the shard. Do what the creature asks, conditional upon a request of your choosing. And after helping this mighty fish, let your sole favor be to scour Korinth's depths, in search of the lost shard."

Many thoughts zipped through Kort's mind, banging into one another. *Have I gone crazy from lack of food, to even seriously consider this matter?* went one. *Or rather, would I be crazy not to do it, given that my choices brought me this far?* sounded a second. *Could it be, that helping the leviathan is my path to redemption?*

The more Kort thought about curing the leviathan's ailment, the more it seemed like doing good for others. It would remove unsafe conditions on Korinth for merchants, fishers, and seamen alike. It would restore trade in the Isles. Perhaps indirectly, curing the leviathan would save lives. *Do it then. Do this good thing for others…*

Kort exhaled, and then took a deep breath. He pondered the matter, fearing its implications, yet knowing it was the right thing to do. He hesitated nonetheless, enduring each passing moment as the present one seemed even slower than the last. He felt weak in body. He felt weak in spirit. And those weaker parts of the ex-knight wanted so badly to be off the ocean and back in the Isles. His heart wanted to be with Nym, whom he still loved.

Yet, though his flesh showed weakness and craved nicer things, a part of him deep inside knew that there was no enjoying the remainder of his life, until he repaid his great debt to others for his many wrongs. He thought about that reality for some time, and at last, re-committed himself to a cause that he embraced all along. *As my name is Kort Al'starz, I'll enjoy neither ease nor plenty, neither comfort nor pleasure, over Garlew Il'therin's grave and many more needlessly laid to rest! My deep regrets outweigh this hold from my flesh, this most natural preference of the easier road! I'll do better than this, even if it means my death.*

Finally, after a long delay, Kort slowly spoke words into the filter, with fear before them but hopes of redemption pushing from behind. "Would you return a deed of my choosing, if I do as requested?"

Once again, the film of Nexus energy transformed the resonant frequencies of his voice from that of Mainlandish into that of leviathan. Hisses and rasps filled the air, and without much delay, the monster responded.

"If you ease my suffering, I shall do whatever you ask of me. I will comb Korinth's floor for sunken treasure of wrecked ships, or anything else."

"That's exactly what you need."

Kort glanced to Elucid, who had started speaking.

"Your request of the leviathan can be, that the creature descend to the ocean's floor and retrieve the white shard of sword. And then, to Liath we go…"

Kort turned back to the leviathan, and waited there silently with much reservation, not yet committing himself to the deed. Doubts swarmed his mind as to whether he would survive this experience. But even so, Kort felt he could do good here that would give some purpose to Raiden's death. *There must be something good that becomes of him losing his life, and maybe that something is this…* In enough time, Kort safely concluded that this entire trip was a waste of time and life if he did not proceed.

"I'll do it," Kort said, finally.

The words traveled through the filter, and came out in rasps that the leviathan could understand. After only a moment, the leviathan's awful face relaxed, and the monster made a series of alleviated, hissy noises.

"Thanks be to you," said the leviathan.

Kort swallowed hard, knowing that the leviathan's gratitude might last only as long as his ability to deliver upon their agreement.

With grave anxiety, Kort watched the leviathan move its head even closer, to the point where it came close enough to touch. And then, the leviathan opened its mouth, lowering one jaw before Kort's feet with it tongue rolled overtop like a pink carpet. A pungent odor of decay instantly smote him in the face, many times stronger that what he breathed before. Kort fought a gag relax and pinched his nose, while lowering his eyes on the jaw. He saw sharp teeth that went all around the tongue in a parabola, sticking up like stalagmites.

From front to back, Kort traced the jaw before him until he looked up into the leviathan's mouth, seeing a narrow passage into its throat, which led deep into the monster's belly. At the top of the passage hung a pinkish uvula—a lump of dangling flesh. Above Kort's head, the monster's second jaw loomed, showing ivory stalactites of razor-sharp teeth, glistening in smelly saliva. At his left and his right were the same: other jaws lined with teeth.

The entrance before had the same welcome as an invitation to death; it led into a cavern of inky blackness that meant danger, uncertainty, and possibly, his demise. Despite Kort's willingness to be redeemed, the challenge before him inspired dread. He was afraid.

Kort stood a cubit or so from the jaw, and before taking even one step, he looked back to Elucid.

"One's destiny might not always entail easy choices or sure chances of good outcomes. But choice over chance shall lead your way." And with that statement, Elucid gestured to the path that needed to be taken.

It was a path Kort hoped would be an important waymark on his longer path to redemption. With a final deep breath, Kort stepped forward and this time, he did not look back, bracing himself for the perils of a journey unlike any trip ever taken before.

Meanwhile, Elucid could only stare with pride, and also, an unmentioned reminiscence of times past for showing others the way. For Laotzu had done the same, many times before.

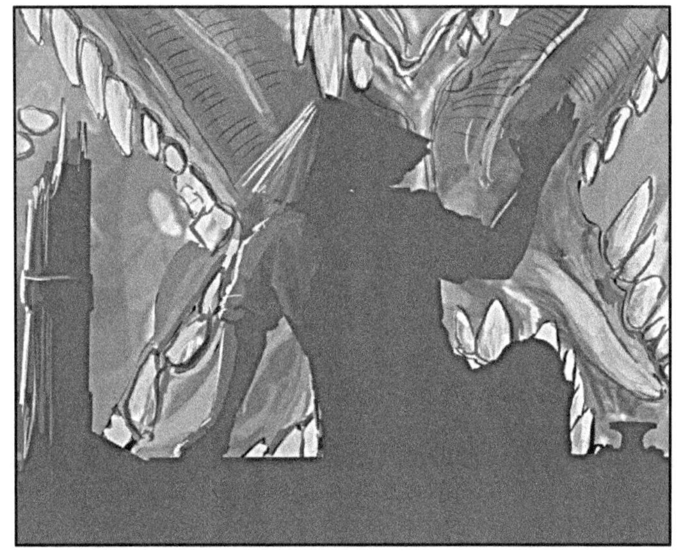

"A BONEY MEAL"

Chapter 63
Bowels of the Beast

Kort carefully placed his feet onto the spongy pink tongue rolled out before him, leading into the leviathan's mouth. The surface felt unsure, just as his confidences about this task at hand. But even so, he still advanced, being convinced now that helping the leviathan was required of him for a good reason, perhaps one that only Destiny understood.

A few strides brought Kort halfway down the tongue, which rested upon the leviathan's lowered jaw. His eyes wandered to the other jaws—the one looming straight above him, and the jaw at his left along with the jaw at his right. They all showed white teeth inside, about a cubit long with sharp points, capable of puncturing his body all over, should the leviathan decide to suddenly chomp down. The thought of such a grisly death sent chills down his spine.

He recovered and kept walking along the tongue, and soon stood at the mouth's entrance. It was a dark cavern that seemed to swallow up the daylight with every cubit that he got closer. For a moment, Kort breathed through his nose instead of his mouth, and the same foul odor ominously filled his nostrils, reminding him of how the monster reeked of death. He heard the gills work as the leviathan sucked air, a hoarse gasping like one's dying breaths. His nose, his ears—his senses—all warned him of foreboding danger. Yet, he still entered the mouth, ignoring them all and remaining confident that he should do this.

As Kort began walking to the rear of the tongue, he looked to one side and noticed the fleshy wall of the leviathan's inner cheek; it was amaranth pink in color, and showed contours that hinted at the muscles with which the leviathan worked its jaws. He lifted his eyes along the cheek to the mouth's palate hued in carmine, seeing there an arch of tissue stretching over. The palate extended back to the top of the throat, where dangled a teardrop uvula. From appearance, every surface of the mouth was shiny and moist, touched by both water and saliva.

As Kort stepped up to the back of the mouth, the general lack of light did not prevent him from seeing a thing more alarming than even the leviathan's teeth. For before him was the top of the monster's gullet, featuring a vast pit that descended into pitch black, toward the bowels of the beast.

At the sight, Kort gasped, and once again he accidentally breathed through his nose. Gag reflexes overwhelmed him, and he fought against them even harder than before, as the odors wafting up from the leviathan's esophagus were more pungent than anything smelled yet.

There, at the top of the throat, Kort lingered for a while, now more aware of what this actually meant for him. *This is the point of no return*, he realized. And it was then that the whole idea of venturing into the leviathan's belly seemed increasingly insane to him, as if only a complete fool would do such a thing. And that notion easily evoked doubts in him, causing Kort to suddenly look back.

In one motion, he turned over his shoulder and peered outside the mouth, seeing Elucid standing afar on their raised boat, just watching him. Raiden's body lied at Elucid's feet, motionless and bloating in the sun. All it took was one glance for Kort to realize that were he to retreat now, he would have needlessly spent Raiden's life, disappointed Elucid, and not finished what he started. *I can't have that... I can't.*

Kort turned back to the pit, and summoned up all his courage. And then, in one fearless moment, the ex-knight held his breath and leapt into it. The light was instantly gone, and replaced with darkness. Just as quickly, a sinking sensation filled his gut, as he alternated between sliding and falling down the leviathan's throat. His exposed skin became completely immersed in saliva and mucus coating the tract, and was irritated by enzymes. Altogether, it was a harrowing experience for so many of Kort's senses, and he was hardly able to judge bad from worse, or worse from worst.

After falling and sliding for some time, Kort landed in the creature's belly, smacking into a glop of mush at its bottom. He opened his inflamed eyes, and perceived nothing but blackness all about. Instinctively, Kort entered his enlarged channeling chamber, where he pulled against his double-door Source entry. Like so many times before, the doors parted with a blast of green Nexus along their edges, and a single flow entered his room, filling it from floor to ceiling. He continuously pulled more energy, while transforming some into a small green flame that sparked overtop his hands, the one's knuckles in the other's palm.

The fire revealed a putrid mess of the leviathan's digesting meal—mainly seaweed, small creatures of the sea, and such. In that instant, Kort mistakenly breathed through his nose again, and it triggered his heaving. He defended against gagging with a few coughs, and began breathing again through his mouth.

Kort lowered his flame to inspect the mire in which he stood, going well up to his knees. Through both legs, he felt the acidic digestive juices in the leviathan's gut irritating his skin much more than the saliva or the mucus. But irritation or not, Kort maintained a clear sense of what he needed to do. And so, without delaying it further, he began trudging through the digesting food, feeling his way around in search of whatever caused the monster pain. His best hunch was that there was something lodged in the belly's sides, and so he stuck to the left side first, walking along it.

Abruptly, the leviathan shifted, causing Kort's sudden imbalance, which sent him bottom-first into the mess. Kort stopped channeling, his fire went out, and darkness closed in on him. He just sat there, with the seaweed going up to his neck. *What's happening?!*

Slowly, he got to his knees as the leviathan continued moving. A sinking feeling cued him that the monster lowered itself into the water. *Perhaps to stop sucking air*, he thought, *and to breathe naturally.*

In moments, gushing sounds entered his ears, coming from his rear. Kort got afoot, started his flame again over one hand, and spun around. He saw water trickling in where the leviathan's gullet connected into its stomach. Kort stood in place for a few seconds, just studying the phenomenon. He noted how it happened periodically during the leviathan's breathing cycle: whenever the leviathan pulled water over its gills, some rushed down its throat.

Kort looked away from the trickling water, and back to the challenge. The puree of foul-smelling seaweed stood between him and the leviathan aiding his search of Korinth for the shard. Locating anything in the leviathan's belly seemed very daunting to him just then. As he looked on in despair, he began to feel incredible weakness in his body, the same he felt in all the days prior. It weighed on him, awakening the realizations of how crazy this was, of how impossible it appeared. Thoughts of Raiden and Elucid went through his mind, along with his memory of Kyan warning of merchant vessels disappearing on the sea. *I can't give up. I won't!*

Not knowing entirely how he would do this, Kort stepped into the digestive slurry, again following the belly's one side. He literally walked along it, feeling the flesh up and down with one hand, while lighting the space using his second. The leviathan's belly was warm and sticky to his touch, covered in a gooey gray lining on the inside, but in no place sore where he checked.

And so, Kort proceeded to check the belly's opposite side by repeating same search process there, but unfortunately, he arrived at no different outcome. *Nothing…* It was enough to suggest that he repeat the task in order to be sure he did not miss anything important. And so, he did.

However, when Kort trekked the entire perimeter of the leviathan's belly two times over without finding anything, he began walking through the midst of the mire in hopes of locating something there. To start, he inspected the area above him, using a lifted hand with his small fire burning overtop. He saw the glossy interior of the upper stomach, pinkish in hue, with blue veins barely visible outside the membrane. But to Kort, the flesh did not appear reddened or sore, and no foreign objects jutted out.

Destiny damn it! He cursed in frustration over his fruitless search, which rendered him a bit exasperated and willing to try things that he had hoped were unnecessary, like crawling through the shallow seaweed, and in deeper areas, dunking his head in order to feel the stomach's bottom with his hands. In these ways he covered a large area, searching as needed given the depth of the mire. But alas, there was nothing to be found. *Destiny damn it!*

Time passed slowly, and Kort repeated the whole search, again and again. He soon lost track of how long it took him, just as he did on the seas. The seconds seemed as minutes, the minutes seemed as hours, and the hours as days. But whether seconds or minutes, minutes or hours, or hours versus days, it made Kort's search no more fruitful. Despite how much time he spent, and despite how careful he searched, he found nothing strange in the leviathan's belly. And it began to seem like there was nothing there in the first place.

Destiny damn it! he cursed again, tired and frustrated. In a step toward defeat, he stopped channeling Nexus for his small fire and let the darkness close around him. And with it came a moment of doubt. *Will anything good become of this, for me or others?! Have I just been lured inside the leviathan's belly, as easy prey?!* The idea of serving as nothing more than the leviathan's meal seemed far short of good destiny to the ex-knight.

Through Elucid's words, Kort tried to assuage his fret over a possible demise in the leviathan's belly. *Through every trial, Destiny protected you and Destiny will do the same now. You are the One of Prophecy.* Yet as reassuring as Elucid tried to be when speaking those words, the voice in Kort's head did little to quell his brewing storm of fear: *How will I even get out, whether I find whatever hurts the leviathan or not?!* He had not thought about this upon entering, and now, it created great uneasiness in him.

The ex-knight had trusted Elucid, and he had prayed to Destiny all this time for change. But even as he kept pursuing good destiny amidst the bad, he still encountered hardship after hardship with no good fortune yet. It was reason to stop believing and to lose faith, but Kort would not do so that easily. Instead, he would pray again.

"Karnatha, give me my redemption… Please give it to me, and I shall render what is due. Help me help the leviathan, toward helping others."

Then suddenly, at the conclusion of his prayer, a single light shined through the darkness in Kort's eyes. At first it surprised him and he fixated upon it, wondering what the light could be. It shined from a distant point in the leviathan's stomach, across the mire before him, near the monster's gullet.

The moment Kort first saw it he took a few steps closer. With his every movement, the seaweed stew conformed about his body. But in the middle of his walk to the light, it suddenly disappeared! Observing this brought him to a complete stop, in utter darkness. But now, he wondered if he even saw that light to begin with, or rather, if his mind were just inventing what he wanted: more Light, in his world of Darkness.

So he stood there, doubting himself and enrobed by blackness, when two distant lights suddenly shined through the darkness, both on a common horizontal line. Upon making the visual, Kort moved hurriedly toward the spot, refusing to blink. *What is that?!* he wondered.

When coming nigh, a third light shined beneath the two, oval in form. Suddenly, Kort heard the sounds of otherworldly chimes all about him, each one hanging eternally in the air—intransient though transient—the next distinct from the former, yet all of them melding together. The chimes were so many paradoxes to his listening ears, none of which he could place. The ex-knight thought in the chimes and he spoke in them, somehow understanding every word.

"What in Destiny?!" he shouted.

The lights sped toward him, the moment he lifted his voice. Kort quickly channeled Nexus and recreated his flame, just in time to reveal the ghostly woman of dissolving flesh. She floated right toward him, over the slop of half-digested seaweed!

As best as he could, Kort stepped to the side, trying to dodge the ghostly woman. But she came right to him. He moved away again, but she followed, hugging every turn the ex-knight made.

"Your inheritance is more wholesome than his," she said, "Kilwroth's unwholesome inheritance. The distance between him and his fate shall be many fold the distance between you and redemption, given your willful soul as that of others' prior! Eriens, Lucen, Magicia, and Laotzu… all deer to the hunter's bow, ones slain by the hunt of desire, ones who have become pawns in my new game, the *Game of Broken Time and Sword*!"

"Spirit, tell me what you want!" Kort screamed. "Tell me now, and let me be!"

"Spirit I'm not; anti-Destiny I am, by name, Saora!"

"What do you want?!" Kort insisted.

"Absolution for you, absolution for all others in Karnath from Destiny's Game. Some things only come at the price of death, and such is this. Time will die in all ages, and ultimately, Destiny too will die."

Kort turned again, but Saora appeared right before him. In fear he stepped back, away from the ghostly woman.

"I've sent Shaizan into one time and Kayareth into another," Saora continued, "to leer at each other from afar and with contempt for what lies in store! Fate's Fray I've withheld from *him*, much more than you or others in Karnath will ever see. Life is full of momentary gaps between reality and desire, between the present and one's fight for good destiny. Yet *his* gaps are already so much larger, and *his* fight is postponed."

Saora came nigh again, causing Kort to retreat. But with a single step, he found himself cornered and up against the belly's one side.

"Of what do you speak?!" Kort demanded.

"Perhaps you shall see firsthand," Saora replied. "It's more your preference for mountain climbs, versus hiking cliffs. The choice is always yours, just as with others in Karnath. Do your best with choice!"

As Saora flew toward him, Kort took one step along the belly's side, only to stumble over a long object beneath the mire. And when he bumped it, from the monster's throat resonated an earsplitting sound, as the leviathan's vocal chords worked out an aggrieved moan, which echoed and echoed the fleshy chamber.

Kort's fire went out and his head throbbed from the sound, as he fell backward into the seaweed. He clasped both ears and grinded his teeth in pain, tasting blood in his mouth that flowed from his sore gums. During his fall, he saw Saora's shining eyes and mouth disappear into thin air.

The mess conformed about him, and he sat up in the seaweed with his hands over both ears, waiting for silence. After a while, the noise finally stopped echoing. Kort lowered his hands from his ears, got upon his knees, and leaned closer to the spot. Using both hands, he scooped away mess to reveal what was there.

As before, he channeled Nexus to create his flame, which shed light upon the area on the side of the leviathan's belly that seemed reddened and sore; this was surely the source of the leviathan's pain. *How did I miss this before?!* In that moment, Kort would have sworn to having passed over this same spot more than once.

Disregarding his frustrations over somehow not finding this before, Kort dropped his hand toward the object, but suddenly stopped himself from touching it. He just paused to study the elongated, slimy piece of debris, and some unsettling conclusions popped into his head. *It's... it's a mast... from a sunken sailing ship! The leviathan ate a ship!!!*

The sight contradicted Kort's belief that the leviathan did not purposely hurt sailors, and immediately put him in a state of not knowing what to do. Unable to react, he stared at the monster's side, seeing what was clearly a mast with a broken yard perpendicular to it, both slathered in a revolting film from the leviathan's digestive process.

Images filled Kort's head of the leviathan attacking merchant vessels, swallowing up sailors whole, destroying the ships, and ultimately disrupting trade in the Isles. *The leviathan sank the merchant vessels and fed off the crew! Remove that mast, and the leviathan will continue doing the same thing!* Alarms sounded and sounded in his head, discouraging him from acting as he intended, and just removing the mast.

Still using the flame, Kort glanced behind him to scrutinize the mire of digesting food. Upon a closer look, he saw no fish, big or small. Only tiny sea creatures and plants appeared in the leviathan's meal, perhaps not enough to sustain the monster by themselves. To Kort, it suggested that the leviathan attacked ships, even in the absence of sailor corpses. There was now reduced travel on the open sea in the wake of recent sailing tragedies, and less likelihood the leviathan had eaten anyone recently.

"Oh no, what have I done?!" Kort asked himself aloud, rethinking his decision of entering the leviathan for a completely new reason. "Has the leviathan fed off sailors, all long?!"

For some time, Kort carefully considered the situation. *Under the best pretenses, I agreed to help the leviathan, not knowing the source of the monster's pain. In this, I've deliberately done no wrong.* He instantly felt less guilt, and he considered the situation even further. *If you don't remove the mast, you'll never know if any good would've become of this. You'll die here with your doubts in the leviathan, and also, your doubts in yourself.*

The realization motivated Kort to withdraw the object, and continue doing what he believed was the right thing, under his best intentions. *I just hope everything I touch doesn't turn to bad destiny…*

Kort pushed that thought to the back of his mind, and focused on the task at hand—removing the mast. Expecting this to hurt the leviathan, but seeing no other way, he took hold of the object, and pulled it with all this might. "Grrrhhh!" he grunted.

Once again, he heard the monster release a loud roar, just as strident as the one before. Kort bit down as the sound coursed through him, so hard that a tooth broke from his gums and blood flowed again. *Whatever you do, don't let go! Just keep pulling!*

With Kort's continued effort, the mast finally came free, and he fell backward into the mess, holding onto the prized object. *I'll show it to the leviathan as proof, and ask a few questions too…*

In the same moment of falling into the seaweed, the leviathan thrashed wildly in the waters, and Kort slid deeper into the nasty mire. Then suddenly, the ex-knight crashed against the belly's upper membrane, with all the mess atop him, as the leviathan moved yet again. Some of the seaweed entered his mouth, tasting of acidy glop, and he immediately spewed it out.

Emanating from the throat of the leviathan, Kort heard raspy gagging, all the way down in the stomach. Quite unforeseen, Kort felt pressure suddenly develop about him, pushing his body up the throat, along with a mass of undigested meal! The only thing the ex-knight could do was close his eyes and hold his breath the entire time, along with the trophy mast.

The force propelled him through twists and turns of the leviathan's esophagus, then out from the gullet into the mouth. Kort felt himself sliding over the leviathan's tongue, and suddenly, he experienced a falling sensation, at the same exact time he sensed light behind his eyelids. He looked then, seeing the blue sea as he fell toward it in a spray of green vomit!

From heights of the leviathan's mouth, Kort hit the waters hard, feeling the impact as his body struck their surface. It caused him to let go of the mast. He sunk about ten cubits beneath. The sea around him felt instantly cleansing, like a warm bath after having been in the leviathan's stomach for so long.

With his fingers pressed together and his hands cupped, Kort displaced the water before his face, moving his arms to the side and repeating; he kicked his legs behind him for propulsion. The ex-knight swam up toward the surface, and as he did, he saw the mast piece floating down. Kort quickly swam to it and grabbed onto the object on his way up.

When his head finally emerged from the sea, he gasped the clean air while treading water. It took only a moment for his eyes to adjust, so that he could see Raiden's tiny sailboat afar, now sitting on the sea, with the crimson knight standing inside its hull.

Weakened severely from being inside the leviathan, Kort struggled to swim there, but slowly moved closer. And when before the vessel, he saw Elucid lean forward to extend a metal hand. He took hold of the crimson knight's gauntlet and felt pulled into the boat, just as his ears discerned the leviathan rising again in the distance, casting a tall shadow overtop them both.

Chapter 64
Lifting Famine

aking Elucid's hand, Kort climbed into Raiden's boat with the piece of slimy mast. When aboard, he collapsed onto the hull breathing hard, and let the mast fall from his grip. It clattered to the planks.

Slowly, he got upon his hands and knees and just stayed there, still short on breath. A pool of water formed around him as it dripped off his wet cloths, given his thorough drenching in the sea. He glanced upon his arms, no longer a bronze color, as they were. For now, his skin was a pasty white from enzymes in the leviathan's stomach. The sight of his own body seemed foreign to him and somewhat shocking, and he reacted in disbelief with parted lips and raised eyebrows.

In the distance, the monster rose up from the sea using its powerful snake-like body, and cast a shadow over the patch of sea on which their boat drifted. Kort looked up, just in time to see the leviathan move through the waters, right toward them!

He immediately could feel the vessel rock on the waves, up then down. Kort turned and grabbed onto its side, before looking up to watch Raiden's bloating body bounce in the hull, along with the slimy mast.

Beyond Raiden and the mast, Elucid stood, steady as a mountain despite the unsteady boat. The crimson knight turned from Kort and toward the leviathan. Streams of blue and green Nexus began swirling from the metal demon's center into the air, forming the same filter between the boat and the monster, to be used for communication.

The leviathan reached the boat and stopped. In the wake of its approach, the vessel continued rocking on the waters. It rode several new waves, up then down.

VESSSS! VASSS! ... VESSSS! VASSS!

Kort remained lying on his side, hugging the boat. He suddenly could hear the flapping, wheezing noises of the leviathan sucking air through its gills, just as the monster's raspy voice.

"You did it!"

The sounds emerged from the filter in Mainlandish.

Kort withheld his response, and continued lying there silent, in a state of ongoing recovery. Meanwhile, the upset boat slowly rocked to a calm.

The experience of going inside the leviathan took a brutal toll on his body, and he needed some time before saying anything. He felt tired. He felt weak. He hurt all over. Dull pain ached through his head and extremities, reminding him that his time on Korinth was nothing short of punishing.

After the boat became completely still, he got afoot and bent down to take up the slimy piece of mast from the hull—the one found lodged in the leviathan's stomach. At the moment of contact, the same images filled Kort's head of the leviathan attacking merchant vessels, swallowing up sailors whole, and destroying the ships. *I'll show the mast to the leviathan as proof, and ask a few questions too...*

"What did you do?!" Kort asked, waving the mast before the leviathan's beady black eyes. "It seems part of a merchant ship!"

His voice went through the filter and came out in leviathan—a series of hisses and rasps. And complete silence developed shortly after he finished speaking.

"My days of wrecking ships are long past," replied the leviathan, at last. "What you suspect is untrue."

The comment rendered Kort solemn. He found himself confused over what to believe. The chunk of ship found in the leviathan's stomach suggested the obvious, yet the monster wanted him to believe otherwise. He wondered then, in whom he should place his trust and how could he go against what seemed to be objective truth. *Can I trust the leviathan in spite of this, like I trusted Elucid after the storm? Perhaps...*

"Thank you for helping me," continued the leviathan. "I won't need to thrash on the waters anymore for relief. Ships will have safe passage in these parts."

Kort dropped the mast to the hull; it hit the planks with a boring clatter. In so doing, he dropped also his doubts, letting them fall into his reservoir of faith.

Elucid turned from the monster to Kort.

"Ask the leviathan to search the bottom of Korinth for the shard. We need it."

Kort lowered his head, for a moment of serious thought. He trusted Elucid, who once again pushed for the shard, which did seem important to find if he really were the Child of Light. But by the same token, he had to wonder then if the oracles' telling of lifted famine were just something to be ignored. Images of the despairing people in Doj entered his mind; he remembered them murmuring in the market behind the farmer's stand, unable to purchase rice with the drought.

"What do you desire of me? Ask anything."

More rasps emerged from the energy filter, as it bent the voice of leviathan into Mainlandish.

"The shard of sword—we must find it!" boomed Elucid, as if to reinforce the same position.

Kort stood in silence before the leviathan. His eyes trailed to the hull, to Raiden's bloating body, slumped over at the boat's side. And it was then that he wondered what the unspoken would say. *What would Raiden tell me to do?*

Inside of Kort, the two desires started to wrestle with each other. He wanted to have the shard and its hero's title. But also, he wanted to help others and do great good. And helping Doj and Reiju seemed like the latter. *If I'm the Child of Light, I must fulfill the prophecy by lifting famine.*

Kort glanced to Elucid, prompting another urge.

"Without the shard, all is lost."

Kort looked back to the leviathan, bearing Elucid's comment in mind, but judging what he really needed to say. And so, he opened his mouth and spoke with courage to do the right thing, even if it would not be the consensus.

"There's a problem in the coastal village of Doj," said Kort. "Severe drought oppresses the land, and soon, the last of Doj's rice crops will perish in the sun."

Kort wet his lips after starting to describe what ran contrary to what Elucid wanted, a thing that perhaps would make the crimson knight very mad. *But even so, I must help people in need. The shard is just a sword, and a hero's title is nothing without people to revere a hero…*

"Can you help Doj?" Kort asked the leviathan. With a moment's pause, Genze popped into his mind. Kort quickly added to his request.

"Can you help Doj, and Reiju too?"

Kort listened to his own words go through the Nexus filter, which bent his voice into that of leviathan, rasps and hisses of sundry kind. But those sounds met silence, as the request itself seemed to usher a lengthy quiet upon the scene, one so long that Kort soon began to question if the leviathan would really deliver upon its promise after all. *The monster said it would do anything, but perhaps not this?*

After a terrible delay, the leviathan spoke. "Arzan."

When the one-word reply came through the Nexus filter in Mainlandish, it sent Kort's head spinning. Arzan was a river, hundreds of spans north of both Doj and Reiju. *A mighty river to which neither I nor anyone else in the villages could walk!*

"Arzan can cure, a summer without rain. Arzan can cure, your crops of drought," said the leviathan. "I will show you how."

Once again, Kort found himself confronted by a prospect requiring his faith. For his life, Kort could not understand why the leviathan mentioned Arzan or how the river would help the drought, when it was so far away. Yet despite that, he chose to trust the leviathan.

Kort nodded and turned to Elucid, who as usual, emitted no emotions. The armor appeared cold and lifeless to him, a hunk of talking metal that seemingly did not feel.

"Well, it's not what I would have asked," boomed Elucid. "Yet I understand your care for the villagers. And in that, perhaps you already have your white shard."

Kort's forehead scrunched together, and his eyebrows dipped. "What do you mean?"

"Everyone can have their white shard, a comeback after a broken gray dream. By poor choice and chance you found only Darkness in your past, but in a turn toward the Light, you dreamed gray—of stopping the Isles Conspiracy to aright your wrongs. Yet despite your valiant efforts to kill Taurus, you failed. And your gray dream of doing great good through stopping the Conspiracy became so broken, that it couldn't be fixed. That defeat slumped you for months, like the gloom that overhangs Sergros now."

Elucid's words pricked Kort's heart, and he started to bleed on the inside, showing it with a pained face.

"Likewise, others in Karnath dream gray, of fanciful things larger than life—dreams that are poorly chanced, and destined to be broken. But in the wake of broken gray dreams, some experience null destiny by giving up, or bad destiny by hurting others in their own frustrations. These are black shards of one's broken dream, possible downfalls that you've avoided!"

Elucid continued. "In the wake of your broken dreams, you didn't give up and you didn't hurt others over your momentary defeat. Instead, by having enough faith to sail with me on Korinth, you continued dreaming of doing great good, in a different way than toppling the Isles Conspiracy. Despite your broken dream, you got back up and dreamed again. It was a comeback indeed, your white shard! So Destiny be with you, Kort... I trust we'll somehow find a way to Liath, with all that we need."

The pain dissolved on Kort's face, and a smile came to his lips. He found Elucid's words strengthening, uplifting, and helpful. In that moment, all the good vibes he had for the crimson knight suddenly returned—those had after the storm and before getting lost at sea.

"Ride with me, to witness your lands healed."

At those words, Kort turned to the leviathan.

The monster came even closer to the boat, submerged itself in the water, and brought its head near Kort so that he could climb on. To Kort, it suggested that he and Elucid part ways, and the mere thought filled him with ambivalence. *Elucid is my friend. I can't just leave him, can I?* At the thought, his face went straight as a line.

"Go."

Kort's eyes went to Elucid. The crimson knight stood there emotionless as always, with an extended hand toward the leviathan.

"But..." Kort started.

Elucid cut him off. "Worry not for me. I shall see you again, upon the Isles."

Another smile snuck to Kort's lips. *I trust Elucid.*

Kort nodded and turned to the leviathan that was just a cubit or so from the boat, with its head partially submerged in the water. He stepped to the edge of the vessel and jumped off, onto the leviathan's neck. Once upon it, he assumed a riding position and took hold of the monster's fins in his hands.

"I shall dive and surface," said the leviathan. "On the former hold your breath, and on the latter, take it."

Kort had little time to process the remark, before the monster suddenly dove into the warm waters ahead of them, plunging him beneath their surface. He held his breath, feeling the leviathan go down as it swam away from his boat, only to suddenly change directions, swim up, and resurface. The leviathan popped its head above the water, giving Kort just enough time to suck air, before the process started again.

In this way, Kort rode the leviathan for what seemed hours of travel, until at one point, the monster surfaced and stayed surfaced. To his surprise, Kort rose above the water until it was at the level of his waist. Without delay he inhaled deeply, gasping for air from holding his breath during the leviathan's last dive. He remained there saddling the monster's neck and gripping a fin, being completely drenched and soaking wet. The water literally poured off him, back into the sea.

With a clop of his wet hair over his eyes, Kort could not see anything immediately. He removed one hand from the fin and pushed away the hair. Suddenly he could see, though his vision was blurry. It took a few moments before it sharpened, allowing him to perceive long landmasses to his right and left. *This is part of the Northern Isles peninsula.* Kort knew how the freshwater of Arzan flowed through the Isles and out to Korinth through this channel; it was the river's drainage basin into the sea.

"What will you do?" asked Kort, as the creature stayed above in the water. He heard the leviathan speak in that same raspy voice—words no longer understood without Elucid's help.

VESSSS! VASSS! ... VESSSS! VASSS!

Whatever the leviathan plans to do, I hope it'll work! Kort's last thought dissolved as the creature hissed before ducking beneath the surface again, taking him forward into Arzan via the channel.

Underwater, Kort opened his eyes to watch the leviathan swim forward and gulp freshwaters with its mouth. And the monster continued pushing itself and gulping water in the same way, for a longer time than any of its previous dives, forcing Kort to hold his breath almost a minute or two, maybe more. Straining to hold his breath for this length, Kort had to wonder. *Does the leviathan remember my need for air?!*

But just when he was on the verge of swallowing water, Kort saw the leviathan close its mouth, right before abruptly changing directions in the water and swimming up to the surface again. When the leviathan brought Kort above water, he immediately inhaled as much air as possible, fearing that the cycle would repeat itself within moments. And it did.

A dozen or so repetitions followed, to the point where Kort lost count. Each and every time, he was subjected to holding his breath for very long times, while the leviathan gulped more and more freshwater from Arzan into its belly. The experience was terribly taxing for weak Kort but he endured it, hoping that he would live to see great good come to others.

When the leviathan finished filling its belly with freshwater, Kort found that the monster resumed its cycle of diving and surfacing, which took him away from Arzan, and to the coast of Doj. It was a swim south of the peninsula, to a point that was only a few spans away from the east coast of the Hirishin Isles.

When at close proximity to the spot, the leviathan surfaced and Kort emerged from the sea again, dripping wet. He sucked the air instantly and looked around. It took a few seconds for his vision to sharpen, until realizing where he was. He beheld the shores of Doj from afar, and knowing that the leviathan had swallowed much freshwater in its belly, he guessed that the monster would bring the water closer. *But how even, will the leviathan water any crops that way?! The coast is still very far from the fields!* It was perplexing, and Kort did not entirely understand how the leviathan planned to water crops.

But quite unexpectedly, the monster took a very deep dive, plunging Kort once again into the waters. He held the leviathan's neck fins during the maneuver, feeling pressure increase around him with increasing depth. The cold increased also with depth, as did darkness as the light diminished. The combination of these things made Kort feel as though he were slipping into death. He worried for himself, wondering if he would survive whatever the leviathan was doing now. *Should I jump off?! Maybe I can still swim up to the surface!*

Breaking his thoughts, he felt the leviathan abruptly change directions, and swim quickly to the surface with excessive speed and force, unlike any surfacing ever experienced. The sinking sensation in his gut during the dive suddenly disappeared, along with the deep's darkness and the cold, now being replaced by light, warmth, and the sensation of rising through the sea!

Kort found himself riding the leviathan's back, and soon above the water's surface and airborne, as the monster jumped out of the sea. The water instantly left Kort's nose and ears, and he took a deep breath while the leviathan continued ascending high into the sky.

Amazed, Kort watched the sea grow increasingly distant by the moment. The splendid sights of the blue ocean alongside Doj's port and its surrounding white coast—both dotting the periphery of Tai and Jezban—filled his eyes and left him wondering. *What's happening?!*

At the highest reach of the leviathan's jump, Kort watched the creature spray water out over the distant lands of Reiju and Doj. It was a stream of water that broke in the air, and showered the parched lands.

Suddenly, Kort felt a falling sensation as the leviathan plummeted through the sky, back toward the sea. Air currents pulled at his face and hair the whole time, causing him to squint. Even so, he was able to see the leviathan continue spraying water on the way down, to further shooting it into the air, over both Doj and Reiju.

In a single instant, Kort felt jerked about as the leviathan changed its orientation midair, before splashing into the water for another deep dive. He filled his lungs with air before being submerged into the sea yet again, for a descent of increasing pressure, cold, and dark. *This is crazy!* he thought, during a ride unlike anything he had experienced before.

The leviathan performed this feat again and again. It was only a matter of time before Kort noticed how the leviathan's sprayed water lingered in the air, to create a mist about Doj and Reiju.

After a few rounds of jumps, Kort splashed into the sea with the leviathan, but this time, he sensed no plunge like before. Instead, the monster did something new, and started swimming toward the coast.

The change struck Kort as strange. *If your belly is empty of freshwater, why not go back to Arzan?* But beyond his questions, Kort trusted the leviathan after witnessing these remarkable feats—he trusted they would be for the best.

And so, in an unexpected trip toward the shore, Kort held his breath with the monster's first dive of many more to come. But even so, he refused to hold back his high hopes of great good for those in Doj and Reiju.

(The Observation)

So many things were in Sagult's favor: extra men, a second ship, and wind in its sails. It all suggested that his search for the fugitive Kort Al'starz was destined to continue on the waters of Korinth.

Indeed, the same day that Sagult and his men recovered from their encounter with Kort in Tai was the same day they left Reiju for the village north of it called Doj. They searched Doj up and down, only to find nothing and to conclude that Kort had gone further north. And so would they, all the way up to the boundary of the old Black Dragon territory, scouring the northern Isles for weeks, but still, not finding Kort. When Sagult and his men returned to Doj on the way back, they were greeted by a ported Sergrothian ship filled with a captain, his crew, and a dozen more militants subject to Sagult's command. And it seemed a clear indication of what they should do next.

Yet, despite all these signs of destiny, a figure of mystery came this morning to Sagult's ship, in order to urge him not to sail on Korinth just yet. It was the beautiful woman in white that had last appeared to him in Reiju's market weeks ago.

Her voice continued in the background without him.

"Don't leave just yet..."

"It's not my decision. Ask Sagult."

Another wind blew, taking Sagult's attention a bit further from the conversation. It caressed him like a hand up the side of his face, running fingers first through his wiry beard and then through his curly, copper-colored hair. He glanced up from his spot on the ship's quarterdeck to the three tall masts looming over him, seeing their white sails billow yet again. It told of their ability to set sail and search for Kort on the seas, in opposition to what Urzel was suggesting.

"If you leave, you may miss Kort!"

"I told you, lady, it's not my decision. Ask Sagult!"

Not knowing if he should stay or go, Sagult stood there in the ship's quarterdeck, beside its spoke wheel where Urzel and the captain currently talked. The quarterdeck was a raised platform off the main deck at the rear of the ship; it was ascended by a staircase, and boxed by a crude wooden railing that was laden with thick braided ropes and round lanterns in iron frames.

The sun aggravated Sagult's indecision further, baking him in his armor each moment he stayed put. Likewise, the armored militants stood stationary on the main deck awaiting orders, surely just as uncomfortable.

"Consider how much time you might waste by missing Kort. Leaving too early could be a diversion from your goal of finding the fugitive, for days or weeks!"

"Lady, I'm just in charge of how this ship is sailed. Where and when we sail is his call, by order of the king."

While speaking, the captain laid a hand on Sagult's shoulder, giving it two hearty pats. At first touch, Sagult turned to the captain, seeing a late-aged man with waxy-skin and a white bush hiding his mouth; he was adorned in blue Sergrothian shipman vesture that showed the lion of Sergros in gold embroideries. The captain winked at Sagult with one of his gray eyes. Beside him was the woman in white who, as always, was flawlessly beautiful and wore her cloak streaked by three black falling stars. With a turn of her head, she acknowledged Sagult's authority with an unwavering stare; for to no one else did she turn for the decision-making.

Their eyes weighed on Sagult, who was beset by a difficult decision between two options, just as his ship was sandwiched by the land and sea. In the direction of the former, he looked off the vessel to the shore for a reminder of why he should leave.

There, dotting the horizon, were the piped smokestacks and fawn-colored roofs of the people's stilted fisher homes, hued in burnt umber. This was Doj, a community in need, as famine had now spread throughout the village like an epidemic, and foretold of a bleak future for the villagers, of starvation or worse. And it was Doj's current state of destitution that reasoned with Sagult to leave. *Get out now, before you can't…* The thought made him feel guilty.

Just thinking of Doj's famine made Sagult automatically lower his eyes from the horizon toward the port of Logan, where many of the affected Hirishins lingered between the piers in hopes of incoming merchant vessels with food. In that same motion, he picked up the visual of burnt patches of coastal grass near the land's end that thinned into the embankment between the village and its port, where pantone browns blended into white sands and dark rock. Off the rock was the port itself, a wooden walkway stretching over the water from the land, supported by multiple pairs of tall piers, spaced at equal intervals for its entire length.

With compassionate eyes, Sagult gazed upon the gaunt Hirishins, male and female alike, just as children, adults, and elders. Some of them reclined against the piers with hollow cheeks and empty eyes, about to fall off from weakness, while others sat cross-legged, peering hopefully into the sea. It was an entire village on the verge of death, in one month's time or less.

And it was then that Sagult's belly rumbled at perhaps the worst possible time, given the immense lack of resources right before his eyes. *How is it even just*, he wondered, *that my body could want anything more, when others have so little?* He had eaten light meals the past two days, since the Sergrothian ship came supplied with rations from Sergros' reserves. And though it was not as much as he was accustomed to eating, the Sergrothian provisions for his men were still much more than anyone had here. So, his body's want of more, despite it being involuntary, seemed wrong and sourced even more guilt. He chided himself. *Ignore your hunger, for at least it won't kill you; these Hirishins unfortunately can't say the same…*

Memories filled Sagult's head in that moment of everything he had seen during his time in the Isles.
The unnatural weather patterns: lacking winds and rain, along with scorching sun… The lost rice crop, dried-up wells, and reduced trade… The inexplicable migration patterns of fish in these parts, causing fishers to stop fishing… It was a set of bizarre, almost supernatural conditions that worked against Doj, toward complete disaster. *Like a curse…*

"So, will you stay longer, Sagult?"

Urzel's words carved through his mind.

He turned back to her and met her brilliant blue eyes, but held his tongue for just a moment more to think. Behind her shoulder, Sagult could see a few junk sailboats on the water, the last few fishers who still fished despite the gloom depressing Doj.

The sight of those boats inspired him to take to the waters, and continue fishing for Kort just the same. While it was terrible what was happening here, he had to continue making progress toward bringing Garlew's murderer to justice. Only then could he return to his family in Sergros, whom he had left behind, in the care of his eldest son.

"No, we can't stay longer. The ship has already been ported here for weeks as my men and I scoured the land north of Reiju, thinking Kort fled there after our encounter with him in Tai. We're confident he's not on land."

Had it not been for Urzel's help thus far in finding Kort, his confidence would have already shut down this particular discussion. Sagult was simply this confident that Kort simply was not in the Isles. But despite believing that, he entertained Urzel's idea because of their good working relationship, until the point where it went against his every instinct. *What she's telling you to do makes no sense…*

"And I agree with you."

Sagult raised an eyebrow. "Eh?"

"My claim is that he's never gone north of here," said Urzel. "I believe Kort has been at sea for a long time, and perhaps will come back soon to land. You stand to miss him by leaving Logan today."

The comment emptied Sagult's mind of its next thought. He just stared at Urzel, who stood beneath the sun with perfect alabaster skin, not even breaking a sweat in the heat. And noting that, Sagult began to think about how perfect her advise had been all along, just like her unmarred appearance. *Can it be, she's right?* The realization cast doubts on his intentions to leave.

Sagult reconsidered his intentions, and his instincts pressed him. *Kort might be off to the Mainland by now endangering people there, if you don't leave the Isles and look elsewhere… The longer you stay, the longer he goes uncaught, and the longer you're away from your family.* His eyes ventured to the militants standing upon the main deck, and the crew. *They have families to—families that need them back…*

"Captain, undock the ship," Sagult said suddenly. "Push out from port, and let us sail the seas for Kort. Let no more time be wasted."

"Aye aye, commander," answered the ship captain.

A wind listed just then, arousing the captain's coat to action, just as he would arouse the crew to the same.

"Untie the cleats; raise the anchor; push from port!"

The captain barked orders, and the crew scurried across the ship, executing them. In a few moments, the ship lurched forward into the sea, a little ways from the port.

Sagult felt as though he disappointed Urzel. He looked to her radiant face wrapped by blonde hair flowing in the winds, and prepared himself to apologize for taking a different action than what she recommended.

Sagult opened his mouth to speak, but she spoke sooner. "You command these men, and owe me no apologies. Apologize to them, should you lead them wrong. The king requires you to lead them in order to complete a mission, and that mission's success could be at stake. But always do what you feel best and what you feel is right. The rest shall fall into place…"

Sagult fell silent, and looked out into the sea, at the fisher junk boats that would perhaps catch no fish. And he wondered then if he would find the same. *What if I'm wrong? What if I miss Kort, by a matter of moments?!* He worried and worried. But as much as he did, he would stick to his orders. And so, with a crewmember's hard push of an oar and wind in the ship's sails, the vessel drifted about forty cubits out from Doj.

Sagult continued staring into the sea, when wetness suddenly blanketed his entire face, like a moist rag. At first he thought it was a spurt of water from the sea, but when the wetness hung in the air, he thought differently. *Can it be, a mist?* Sagult glanced to his armor, seeing the water there too, all over him.

He wondered then if the others onboard experienced the same. Sagult turned to the other knights and militants with him, and indeed, they too were covered with water!

Sagult looked back to the port, seeing a thin haze hanging over the sea and the distant village, from the mist in the air. Slowly then, a realization crept into his mind. *With this water, the land's crops will be saved!!!*

Smiling from ear to ear, Sagult lifted his hands high, letting the mist encompass him. His sadness over Doj suddenly morphed into extreme joy. He danced upon the quarterdeck, twirling around with his hands stretched to the sky. "Doj shall not go without rice!" he exclaimed. "Not with this heavenly mist—a mist divine, surely from Karnatha herself!"

To the increase of Sagult's euphoria, he watched the people at the port of Logan realize the same. The Dojese started murmuring with smiles, some rejoicing, so thankful for this gentle rain to their parched land. They saw the benefits instantly, perhaps an advent for stalled tongues, which began to speak and sing praises.

Sagult stopped dancing and spun around to Urzel, who also displayed a widening grin. But she did not look to Doj for her joy. Rather, her gaze was upon the sea, as if she expected someone or something to arrive upon the waters.

(The Redemption)

Kort rode on the leviathan's back, still grabbing onto the long fin in both hands, as the monster took him closer and closer to the shores of Doj, diving then surfacing as before. Every time Kort's head popped above the waters, he sucked air and enjoyed a mist hitting his face—a mist that surely spread all the way to the village. *The leviathan did it; the crops are saved!*

The leviathan brought him very close to the shore, in view of many watching from the port and village. Kort laughed when seeing the monster spray water over the crowded port, which fell upon those present. He lifted one hand high and balled its fist, feeling the urge to celebrate a victory to his long-fought, personal battle. *I did great good through the leviathan! Doj is saved, Reiju too! Despite my Dark past, I stepped back into the Light and helped others!*

Pure catharsis filled Kort when he beheld the Dojese reveling upon the port—a great many of ecstatic cheer. It was literally the whole village—the young and old, the big and small, male and female, elf and human too—dancing with joy over a mist that would save their crops and lift famine.

Kort rode the leviathan even closer to the land, around a large, white-sailed Mainlandish vessel in the harbor, to about twenty cubits away from the port. Both he and the leviathan rode the low-energy tide, which hardly could boast any wind of change before today.

As hard as he tried, Kort could not take his eyes off the joyous Dojese. Their smiles captivated him and stirred up joy within him, lightening his burden carried since Garlew's death, little by little.

But while the people of Doj knew the prophecies well, no one dared to speak of the obvious, of what really happened before the port of Logan. Everyone knew it was more than a mist, more than a saved rice crop, and more than just a happy moment. Yet, despite all the dancing, prancing, singing, and cheers, despite seeing a gaunt fisher upon the leviathan who spared Logan of famine, no one called the event for what it was. Perhaps Destiny reserved this proclamation for someone of greater insight and faith.

(The Proclamation)

"Wait! Wait!" Sagult cried out to his crew. "Anchor the ship at once!"

His eyes went back to the water. In the background, he overheard the grunts from men who threw the anchor over the ship's side and sent it splashing into the sea. As they removed slack in the anchor's chain by working a crank, the vessel stopped where it was.

Sagult returned his eyes to the water between his ship and the port, hardly believing what he saw: a leviathan spraying water into the air, being rode by someone whom he would have never expected to see. *It's Kort.*

"There he is!" Sagult suddenly exclaimed, pointing at the leviathan's rider, who suddenly fell off the monster and into the sea. The mythical leviathan began speeding northward, away from Doj and toward the Isles peninsula, but

Sagult paid the monster's departure little heed. Rather, he kept his eyes on the spot where Kort fell.

In a matter of moments, he watched Kort's head appear from the sea. And it was then that the ex-knight began swimming toward the shore.

"That's him!" Sagult said again.

"Is that Kort?" murmured one of Kort's militants, from the main deck.

"He looks so thin," said another, also there.

Before speaking again, Sagult's mind made a dramatic shift, which would have consequence to what he would say. The words on the tip of his tongue—criminal, fugitive, murderer, and traitor—became replaced with another set of words in one instant, the very moment in which he put it all together: *Doj had a port once called Logan… Kort lifted Doj's famine… Kort lifted famine from Logan to heal the land! (…) Kort is Kayareth!*

"That's the Child of Light!" Sagult finally blurted out, with all the power he could put behind his voice.

Everyone on the main deck turned to look at their commander, half of them seeming doubtful in Sagult's radical proclamation, while the other half seemed surprised at what was said.

Sagult ignored those on his ship, and faced the people still rejoicing throughout the village. To them, he called out loudly, again and again to get their attention.

"Doj is Logan, Doj is Logan!"

The people at the port looked to Sagult, and when that happened, he began shouting even more.

"Behold the Child of Light, he who lifts famine from Logan!" He repeated it with energy and zeal, pointing out Kort who still swam toward Doj's shore. "Behold the Child of Light!"

Kort seemed absent-minded, unaware of what happened all around him, as the Dojese began murmuring.

"He fulfilled the prophecy!" one said.

"He's the One of Prophecy!" exclaimed another.

All at once, a swarm of Dojese left the port and ran down onto the embankment, and then, into the sea. As they went, elation widened their eyes and pulled their mouth corners into big smiles. They were wildly ecstatic, yelling, cheering, and singing as they went.

"The Child of Light to Gallow Cliff, shall smite the Dark and its Age will lift!"

"He's the One!"

"Destiny brings us the One!"

"Praise be to Karnatha!"

As Kort came ashore and stood to his feet in knee-high waters, the Dojese overwhelmed him, with even more villagers pouring onto the white sands behind them and running for the embankment.

With a grin, Sagult watched the development from his ship. In a powerful voice, he bellowed once again, "Behold the Child of Light, the one who lifts famine from Logan! He is the One of Prophecy; the one who shall bring an Age of Light upon Karnath! Behold now, the Child of Light!"

(The Celebration)

This time, Kort was sure he heard those words, and the voice indeed seemed familiar. It stopped him where he was at upon the shore, with water up to his knees. Before him, he saw a crowd of happy Dojese ahead, joining him in the water. But from them he turned away, and looked across the sea in the direction of the voice. It came from a large Mainlandish ship on the waters where, to his surprise, he saw Sagult upon its quarterdeck, proclaiming the same thing again and pointing right at him. *Who, me?!*

"Behold now, the Child of Light!"

Kort could not believe what he heard, nor let alone what he saw. Sagult labeling him as the hero versus the villain was unthinkable. But even so, it was happening and Kort was left to witness the follow-on effects: half of the ship's crew was overjoyed with Sagult's proclamation, just like the Dojese.

Kort was awed to watch certain militants on the main deck hug each other, dance, and cheer—a select few matching their leader's enthusiasm. But the other half of Sagult's crew was stoical and sullen, especially a bald-headed man in armor, as well as a woman knight right beside him. They scowled at the revelry upon the ship.

Suddenly Kort heard Sagult order the captain.

"Raise the anchor, and take this ship to Breslin at once! We must tell others of what we've witnessed!"

From behind, Kort heard more people of Doj step into the water, as they rushed forth to meet him. But something seen just then prevented him from turning around; it was something on the horizon—a crimson dot coming right his way!

Kort watched Elucid jump on the waters repeatedly, skidding across their surface like a pebble in perpetual skip, without any splashes as the armor's boots never broke the water's surface tension; a magical green aura enclosed the metal demon the whole time.

Kort watched the crimson knight arrive before him with a final jump, in which the aura around Elucid's armor was suddenly extinguished and the knight's feet suddenly sank. It caused a large splash that hit Kort in the face.

After the water fell, Kort's vision sharpened to show the crimson knight, holding a bundle in one hand—a bundle wrapped in Elucid's purple cloak.

"You chose wisely!" Elucid boomed. "You chose wisely indeed!" Those words of deep tone resonated beneath the magical armor, sounding in Kort's ear. He glanced to the crimson knight's metal hands, which extended the bundle to him.

"The mast was not a mast at all," Elucid said. "This I noticed after cleaning it!"

Into Kort's hands, the crimson knight placed the purple cloak and whatever was wrapped inside. His eyes fell upon it, and his hands pulled back the fabric to reveal a startling sight. For inside, Kort found the shard of legend, its blade being white as snow. It had a short guard on one side above its handle, which was wrapped in strips of sable leather.

Flashes went through his mind of the slimy mast with the broken yard perpendicular to it; the images overlaid those of what the mast really was: the white shard. Just the same, disbelief ran through Kort. *I can't believe it.*

As beautiful and inviting as the blade appeared to Kort, he overcame the urges to touch its handle. Instead, he wrapped the shard back up in the purple cloak, and turned again to the crowd.

The Dojese surrounded Kort, wading up to him through the sea. Four younger elves at the front threw his arms and legs upon their shoulders. In a single moment, Kort felt lifted up into the air and carried away, toward the village center. As he went, he thrust the bundle high into the air.

"The Child of Light saved us!" the people shouted around him, again and again.

He was carried from the waters, up the embankment, and back into Doj, where more villagers joined the Dojese, some waving stalks from Tai, others banging cooking pots, and a few starting to sing the olden song again—*The Child's Triumph.*

"The Child of Light to Gallow Cliff," chanted many, "shall smite the Dark and its Age will lift…"

"He lifted famine!" one boy cheered.

"He fulfilled the prophecy!" said a young elven couple together, both of them joining hands and skipping.

The crowd carried their hero back and forth over the dirt paths of Doj, beset by patches of scorched grass and stilted fisher homes. All the while, Kort's face showed of immense happiness, until at one point, tears of joy streamed from his eyes at the fulfillment of his long awaited redemption that now, was a dream come true.

In one moment, Kort went from someone disguised to someone esteemed throughout the Isles. And in time, perhaps he would go from someone despised to someone esteemed on the Mainland. If anything in all his life showed him that perseverance paid off, it was this very moment more than all others. *Perseverance, and my good choice!*

Then, unexpectedly—amid the Dojese celebrating and carrying their hero though the streets—Kort heard one female voice from the crowd, saying something a bit different than everyone else. It came suddenly, and took him by complete surprise.

"It's not so much that he fulfilled prophecy," she said, "but rather, that he will change the Dark Prophecy!"

Upon the shoulders of several elves, Kort tried turning to see who spoke, but alas, he could not. The crowd carried him away from the woman, and he was unable to move in time, in order to see her. But nonetheless, she continued speaking:

"He is the chosen one, the Child of Destiny to restore Light to Karnath! He's the One who shall revert the Dark Prophecy to the Light!"

When the unseen woman made the people realize Kort's true potential, they shouted and cheered more.

"He'll change everything!" one exclaimed.

"He shall best the Child of Darkness at Gallow Cliff, yes he will!" said another.

The throng continued carrying him through the dirt streets, and Kort did not hear the woman again, only her words as spoken from the people that she influenced.

"RETURN TO LOGAN"

Chapter 65
Turns of the Heart

Beneath the midnight sky, X'ieth carried the bundled black shard through the Mountains of Liath. As he went, moonbeams played off his armor. All around him, the gloom's harsh winds gusted and howled. He walked the same rocky trail that snaked around the mountain, tinged in gray as it reflected pale moonlight from above. A thick crown of fog sat upon the path.

Despite the limits to his vision, X'ieth still noticed that this trail was the very same trail he walked earlier with Nathan and the other knights. Just thinking of them triggered a series of images in his mind.

In but a moment, he saw himself with the knights climbing Esmeralda's tower; he saw himself hiding in the shadows outside Esmeralda's chamber, while the others confronted her; he saw Magicia pummeling the knights in response to their attack. It was a tragedy that ended with X'ieth later emerging from the shadows to slay Esmeralda, followed by his jump onto Gremel in pursuit of the shard.

The images stopped for a moment, but then started again. *Coward.* Again flashed the image of X'ieth hiding in the shadows, unseen. *Luck.* Once more, flashed the image of X'ieth emerging from those shadows, to sever Esmeralda's head. *Desire.* And then, flashed the image of his jump onto Gremel's back, with his eyes fixed on the glowing shard in her claw.

Those three things stuck with X'ieth, stopping him from enjoying his defeat of Esmeralda. Cowardliness let him watch his friends get killed, luck spared him from a shared fate, and desire to be the Child made him chase after Gremel, which led into even bigger problems now. *The black shard...*

Since the latest encounter with Lucen, X'ieth could not stop thinking about the sword and its implications for his future. He did so, each and every step of the way. *The shard... The prophecy... Your dreams...* While walking more down the mountain, his eyes suddenly went to the bundle; it was his crimson cloak wrapped around the shard of sword, the one he literally snatched from Lucen's clutches back in Gremel's nest. At the mere sight, the bundle conjured up negative emotions and confusion that X'ieth felt over Lucen. *Deceiver. Liar. Enemy.*

He shook his head, trying hard to negate a reality that he simply did not want to accept. For many months, Lucen had been a friend to X'ieth, not an enemy. And he had been truthful and transparent, not deceptive or lying. To this day, X'ieth remembered how Lucen even saved him from Kort, some months

598

ago. Cumulatively, these things made X'ieth want to feel differently about Lucen, and urged him to see things from another perspective.

He tried hard to invent a line of reasoning. *Maybe Lucen was mistaken over your identity, when proclaiming you the Child of Darkness... The oracles cannot see into the future with the Great Occlusion, so how could he? Maybe there was no deception after all...*

X'ieth thought on as he trekked through another stretch of Liath, with gray rock all about. Off the path, he saw a descent into the valley robed by fog, where distantly on the horizon was the dagger peak of a far mountain in the range.

Maybe Lucen lost his vision, like the oracles... At the mere idea, memories surfaced of Lucen correctly predicting visitors at his cottage some days ago, of Lucen correctly predicting the ruffians in Arlem's alleyways. Those recollections hindered his acceptance of the notion, suggesting otherwise. And for but a moment, X'ieth was silenced from further thought about the convenient presumption that Lucen lost his vision.

With a few more steps down the trail, another idea popped into his mind. *Perhaps, Lucen's vision is not lost, but rather is declining, just as other oracles...* He deliberated over that possibility. *Why yes, many prophets struggle to tell visions of the future apart from dreams... So perhaps like this, Lucen is wrong about certain visions...* But as the idea settled in his mind, it did not bring inner peace. *For why was it that Lucen has not been wrong about anything yet?*

X'ieth continued walking down the trail. In the distance, beyond the fog hung over the valley, he saw the barren treetops of Forest Saol, to where this trail would take him. A sudden wind blew, sending a wave of ice picks through his armor, and into his skin. He did not as much as shiver.

X'ieth kept moving forward with an active mind. He suddenly relived his shock when Lucen peeled back his cloak, to reveal the black shard instead of the white. His jaw dropped. His eyes widened. He just could not believe it, even as of now. It sent his head spinning with denial, with which he rehashed the entire course of events concerning Esmeralda.

She sought to end a sorceress' reign of power, just like the Dark Prophecy foretold of the Child of Darkness! So even if Talus arranged your mission under bad counsel, for this reason, Esmeralda undoubtedly was the Child of Darkness. And therefore, thwarting her makes you the Child of Light!

He continued trudging down the path, scowling at his feet and carrying the shard. It was not long before a lump suddenly formed at the top of his throat, and he found difficulty swallowing. Slowly, it occurred to him that he did not know what the Dark Prophecy said, and that this line of reasoning was essentially what Lucen fed him in Arlem. *Destiny damn it!* At this realization, his scowl grew many times more severe. He kept his head down, watching his boots while hiking the mountain, as if somehow fearing he was more susceptible to missteps than thought a moment prior, for now, he realized how he trusted Lucen's hearsay only to possibly be deceived. *Should've read the prophecy for yourself, man… You should've…*

X'ieth remained thoughtless for tens of minutes, until his walk along the trail brought him to the cusp of Forest Saol. Now with his back to the path that led up Liath, he stared into a mess of gnarled trees stripped of their leaves. They stood tall in the air, twenty or thirty cubits in height, all of them appearing cold, gray, and dead, exactly like what he recalled of the eerily lifeless woods.

He watched the fog filling the forest drift between the adjacent trunks, adding mystery to the scene. In a single moment, flashbacks assaulted X'ieth of all the oddities he encountered in the woods—the woman in white, the ghost of dissolving flesh, and the vespers. He saw images of them before his eyes, one after another, as real as day. They made him pensive about traversing the forest, but even so, he knew he had to proceed.

"Destiny keep me," he muttered, and stepped between the nearest trees. His steps crunched beneath the dead leaves littering the ground. Winds blew hard from behind him, swirling the fog around him. His eyes went to the trunks before him, grayed lifeless as he witnessed before, having a thick frost over their surface.

X'ieth could not see below his waist with the fog, and at one point, his boot abruptly snagged a tree root! In an instant he stumbled a bit, and in so doing, he fumbled with the bundled shard. It literally bounced in his hands as he caught himself and steadied his feet to avoid falling. In the process, the cloak peeled off the shard, revealing its nightly blade.

Surrounded by the trees of Forest Saol, X'ieth stood in place, spellbound by the beautiful shard that somehow glimmered in red, blues, and yellows in the lack of light. A smile snuck to the corners of his lips, and into his head, snuck his frequent daydream of being Kayareth.

He saw himself, on a white horse running over white sands, beneath the towering white walls of Gallow Cliff, thrusting the white shard into the air, as he cried to the Army of Light. "Rally to me! Rally to me!" There was a mighty force running behind him, a host of elves, dwarves, and humans of the Triangle Kingdoms with Sergrothian banners strewn throughout, showing the lion crest. The scene was epic and alive, but suddenly, became frozen! Kayareth and his army were frozen in place.

Behind the hero and his army, the blue sky turned blood red. And out of the red, seven stars appeared in the heavens, the next ascending the former in a staircase, with the highest star being the brightest—the insignia of Malgun. And then, those seven stars suddenly became shooting stars that fell through the sky, like they were never meant to hang there in the first. The focus returned to Kayareth, whose dirty-blond hair became red, and his hazel eyes, a striking sapphire! The white armor all about the hero turned black, with horns and spikes growing all over it. The shard in Kayareth's hand turned black, and the army behind him, turned into a mob of giants with banners showing a gray snake coiled about eclipsing suns.

But as the daydream turned to daymare on X'ieth, his first reaction was not repulsion or horror. Instead, it struck him as though the transitions from Light to Darkness were not an inversion of what he always wanted, rather a neutral distortion. And the moment following that feeling, he felt overwhelmed by sickness in his gut, as the daydream gone bad shattered into a thousand pieces, and left him once again to Saol, where he stood staring at the shard of sword.

The rainbow glimmers captivated him, not allowing him to remove his gaze, even though he wanted to. X'ieth tried to cover the shard back up in his cloak, but his hands would not work. And so, he found himself helpless, trapped in the shard's unexplainable beauty. Somewhere, from deep inside him, emerged a desire to touch the handle. It was the last rite before the prophesized one would become the Child, and in that, X'ieth hated the idea. Yet something in him wanted it dearly. And so, the two started to wrestle. *Touch the grip… No, don't! Just touch it already! No…* The voices went back and forth, bickering with each other, and intensifying as they did, to the point where a whisper pierced through the situation, and quieted them.

"Purpose…"

X'ieth's smile dropped into a straight face. He glanced around the woods, and as expected, there was no one to be seen. Inquisitively then, he looked back at the sword, wondering if it had spoken to him.

"Purpose…"

X'ieth heard it again, though with one hearing ear, he wondered where the voice came from. The winds were blowing, and he stopped himself to consider if the whisper were on the winds. He entertained that idea until the winds died instantly, and he heard the whisper again.

"Purpose…"

This time, the whisper did come from the sword.

X'ieth leaned closer.

"What… did you say?"

There was a moment of silence, and then, the winds suddenly began blowing again, fiercely and loudly. And now, on those winds was the same whisper!

"Purpose… Purpose! Your purpose!"

Immediately, X'ieth drew his broadsword. It slid out of its casing with a metallic song, having a blade stained red from Gremel's coagulated blood.

"Who's there?!" X'ieth asked in a firm voice, with courage borrowed from his experiences battling the vespers, severing Esmeralda's head, and fighting Gremel.

"Your legacy!" said the whisper, still on the winds.

"Who are you?! What do you want?!" X'ieth demanded, as the voice filled his ear. He turned all around, struggling to place it. The winds continued blowing.

When the young knight faced the direction of the trail up Liath—the one he left to enter the forest, just twenty or thirty cubits behind him—he no longer saw it! Instead, X'ieth saw spans upon spans of Forest Saol, an entire graveyard of gnarled trees wrapped in dense fog.

"You traded *them* for purpose, for legacy…"

X'ieth kept silent, listening for the voice's origin. It seemed all around him, and omnipresent force in Saol that was nowhere in particular, only on the gloom's winds.

"Your family wasn't enough… Your knighthood wasn't enough… You traded them, betrayed them…"

X'ieth shook his head, not understanding.

"The shard of sword you hold is actually the shard of your broken dream. You traded them, for it. You traded them, to hold onto what wasn't meant to be…"

The harsh winds swirled the fog around X'ieth, causing him to squint his eyes. Yet he still looked straightway with denial raging within him, and was easily inspired to contend with the voice.

"That's not true!" he shouted back.

"Yes, it is."

"No, it's not!"

"Tsk tsk tsk… Tsk tsk tsk… Tsk tsk tsk…"

The sounds repeated themselves over and over again, coming at X'ieth from all sides, a chatter that became caught between his ears and stuck in his mind. The whisper judged X'ieth for taking the shard from Lucen, and now, the whisper purported that he did so in exchange for his own family.

As much as he hated the idea, it conjured up the memory of Lucen's words upon Liath and his choice: *Leave the shard with me, and forget this ever happened. Hike down Liath into Saol, go back to your cottage. You can return to your plain life in the home with Millicent and at work for Talus. If you leave now, you can still make your child's birth.* But X'ieth did not choose to leave Liath. He did not choose to return to Millicent. He did not choose to return to his child. Instead, he chose the shard. The whisper's accusation suddenly rang of truth. *You traded them, for it.*

"No!" X'ieth screamed, with even more denial.

The whisper's tsk suddenly stopped, and was replaced with a simple reply.

"Yes… You traded them. Do you know why?"

The suggestion squeezed X'ieth's chest, making it difficult for him to breathe. The request for an explanation exacerbated his feelings that his priorities were in the wrong place.

"I didn't!"

"You did. I know why."

X'ieth bit his lip, still staring into the trees with his sword in one hand, the bundled shard in the other.

"Why then?! Why do you presume I traded?!"

In response to his pained question, X'ieth heard the whisper laugh. "Ha ha ha... Ha ha ha…"

"Answer me!" X'ieth shouted.

He chomped down his teeth in anger, and tightened his fingers around his sword's grip, wishing so hard that the whispering voice would manifest itself as a being with a body, so that he could slash it into oblivion. X'ieth disliked the whisper's accusations that he had traded his family and career for the black shard, and as such, he would disregard any elements of truth that might be present.

"Purpose… Legacy… That's why you did it."

X'ieth's face went blank. *What does that mean?*

"Kayareth is an important figure in the prophecy, but so in Shaizan. He will have a legacy of greatness like Kayareth, and that's what appeals to you, villain or not."

The words shocked X'ieth. In that instant, he remembered his daydream turned daymare, how Kayareth turned into Shaizan, and the Army of Light into that of Darkness. He remembered how it first struck him as merely a change of perspective, rather than evil. And now, the whisper suggested that his impressions of the daymare spoke to how he truly felt, that somehow, being Shaizan was merely a substitute for being Kayareth!

The idea touched on something that X'ieth feared was partly correct, and it made him feel uncomfortable. A cold wave washed over him and his chest tightened, as if the truth itself were squeezing him. He stood there, tightening his hand over his sword's grip, holding the bundle in the other arm. Ahead of him, the fierce winds continued blowing, to swirl fog around the trees and to carry the whisper to his listening ear—Dark words that stayed within him, and went right to his heart.

"Shaizan has a purpose, and will leave behind a legacy. Purpose and legacy are what you need; they are what you've always needed. To be more important than how important you are, *in the life* that Destiny afforded you, *beyond the life* that Destiny afforded you. Purpose and legacy…"

The suggestion enraged X'ieth. He suddenly grew dissatisfied to stand there, just letting the voice say things that bothered him deeply, things that he denied were true despite knowing better. And so, a moment after the voice finished, he began slashing at the trees with his sword, and screaming like a mad man.

"Show yourself! I'll send you to the Void for your lies, if you but show yourself!"

As he continued slinging his sword, his blade's tip grazed another frozen trunk, filling the air with dull clangs beneath the voice.

"I'm already there."

"Show yourself!"

Clang! Clang!!! CLANG!!!

X'ieth spun around in circles, slashing at the trees as he went, until his blade stuck deeply in one trunk. He let go of the grip and fell to his knees at the tree's roots, with the fog coming up to his neck. In that moment, the young knight felt like the gloom was swallowing him alive, a gloom that was filling his mind and hijacking his life, killing his dreams.

On every wind, the voice laughed.

"Ha ha ha! Ha ha ha! Ha ha ha!"

The laughter continued for some time, and echoed X'ieth's head. Behind the laughter and the winds, sounded otherworldly chimes, of a sort that the young knight had heard before. *The ghostly woman...* His heart began racing.

Thump thump! Thump thump! Thump thump!

"Oh, what a show! You remind me so much of *him*. You remind me so much, of Kilwroth..."

Thump thump! Thump thump! Thump thump!

In one sudden instant, the winds stopped blowing, the voice went silent, and the chimes stopped, leaving X'ieth upon his knees in solitude. In some time, his heart rate slowed and his breathing became regular. The icy wave rolled off him, and the tightness in his chest was gone.

Kneeling there, he used both hands to lift the bundle up above his head, out of the fog. It literally hovered over him, and his eyes fixated on an object that he knew had an unexplainable hold on him.

He stood up, keeping his eyes upon the bundle, in part not being able to look away. And when upon his feet, he lowered it to the level of his chest, and stared down at it. Thoughts surged his mind, of Lucen revealing the black shard instead of the white, of his unfounded magnetism and desire felt for the black shard. A picture of him grabbing the sword from Lucen flashed before him eyes, shaming him, making him wonder what he really were, given the circumstances.

But then, out of his poor memories came a reminder, of how all along, he was a noble knight of Sergros, one who sought to use his talents for the good of others and himself. Reaching this predicament suddenly seemed out of place, given the good intentions surrounding his place in the knighthood that literally put him on this quest. *It doesn't make any sense...*

Some time elapsed in the stillness of Saol before X'ieth found the voice to ask the question that now, was crushing him. It was the question at the back of his mind, amid so much confusion over how this could even happen.

"Why?"

His question was absorbed by the quiet, without a reply. But X'ieth was not contented to have it go unanswered, and so, he asked again.

"Why?!"

Again, there was no reply, just the quiet Forest Saol. X'ieth expected better, like for Karnatha herself to answer.

"Why?!?!"

Out of nowhere, the winds began blowing again, this time with no whispers or chimes. Like a brute, they beat X'ieth, but he would not be easily beaten.

"Why?!?! Answer me, Destiny!"

The winds blew again, as if to say that nature had more to say than god. And then, once again, came the still of the forest between the winds. It aggravated him, and drove him to contemplate alternatives to guidance from Karnatha. *If not from Destiny, then guidance from anyone will do.*

Naturally, X'ieth began thinking of Lucen, who had been a trustworthy guide for so long. But instantly, he shut out this idea, given how uncertainty about Lucen filled him ever since the youth spoke upon Liath. *Your happiness has been short-lived, ever since he pronounced you as Shaiz...*

X'ieth stopped himself short of completing the thought, knowing that it was rumored to draw Ma'althan's gaze. *Though perhaps the Forerunner of Evil already directs his attention upon you...* The thought alarmed X'ieth, and stalled his active mind. All became silent.

The young knight shook his head in more denial.

"No," he said audibly, staring at the bundle. "No!"

A few winds blew in between his last word, and what he would say next. Hesitantly, X'ieth made the following proclamation: "I am... the Child of Light."

But just as he stated that, part of his crimson cloak fell off the shard, exposing the nightly mirrored blade, as if to challenge his statement. Immediately, X'ieth felt a pull toward the shard; his hand literally moved toward the handle, like it were somehow attracted. *No...*

With all his might, X'ieth summoned enough control to stop his hand from moving further. It was a battle in his mind, between forces that compelled him to touch the shard's grip and his own wants to avoid touching it. Such had worrying implications attached, for mixed emotions about the black shard were not of Kayareth, and thus, fissured X'ieth's dreams of being the hero. He visualized a picture of himself in Autheos' white armor at Gallow Cliff, with hairline cracks spread all over.

"I am the Child of Light!" X'ieth shouted to the gloom, his voice breaking under the weight of his own doubts. The idea of keeping the black shard from the wrong hands, as he explained to Lucen upon Liath, was no longer satisfying to him anymore. As X'ieth continued to wrestle with urges to touch the shard's grip, he began to wonder if the wrong hands were indeed his own. *Perhaps, Karnath needs safeguarding… from you.* The thought brought his mind to a screeching halt, like before. All became silent.

"I'm the Child of Light!" X'ieth screamed finally, from out of that silence, above the winds and his own doubts. He watched the gloom dance around him in the forest, like it were celebrating its victory. X'ieth saw it that way at least, as he felt as though he himself were losing something, a battle fought from within for good destiny.

The problems of balancing the knighthood with married life and a cruel king now seemed very small to X'ieth. For this enveloping situation had crushed him. He somehow carried the black shard, and for some reason, a part of him wanted to partake of the defaming and vilifying act of touching its grip. *It's not right… It's not.*

Once again, Fate's Fray weighed heavily on X'ieth. He could feel the gravity of his poor choices and trying circumstances unravel his good destiny, into something far less grand than what Karnatha had divinely intended. *Poor choices, like taking the shard from Lucen… Trying circumstances, like Talus and Millicent, soiling the intentions of all your good deeds…*

Images of Talus, Millicent, and Lucen flashed through X'ieth's mind, to him, the manifestation of his poor choices and trying circumstances, and more and more, what seemed to be an explanation for his predicament. They continued one after the other, provoking the young knight, and summoning up his wrath. X'ieth began breathing heavily. His face grew red, and veins bulged noticeably from his neck.

"They did this to me! They did this!"

Bad destiny hung over X'ieth, casting the blackest shadows upon his life, making him wonder how long he could stay in the Light before slipping off into the Darkness. He quickly covered up the shard, to remove the temptation from touching it. But even so, it was just a temporary fix to an even bigger problem. For he could not undo his possession of the black shard, and his natural want to wield it. The facts threatened his dreams of being Kayareth, and the hairline crack grew a hair larger.

"I'm the hero!" X'ieth yelled with exceeding ire. "I'm a noble knight, a faithful husband, and soon to be a father!" His voice grew harsher by the word, and the wind beat upon his anguished soul. "These are my dreams, Destiny!"

A large sea of denial rose above X'ieth's head. He flailed amid the crashing waves that beset him on every side. He simply could not let go of his dreams, and the self-image he framed in Arlem would not be easily changed. *You're Kayareth... You are...*

He stood there, with the bundled black shard in the middle of Forest Saol, not knowing where to go or what to do. But when X'ieth looked to the horizon—to the distant treetops above stretches of foggy woods—he saw a black cloud in the sky. And it was then that inside him, a voice prompted him to move in that direction. *You're perhaps destined to be under that black cloud, so walk toward it.*

With that idea, X'ieth laid one hand onto the grip of his broadsword stuck into the nearby tree, yanked it out, and let the arm drop to his side, holding the blade. He began to step closer to the looming darkness on the horizon, and as he went, his head buzzed with thoughts about the situation. *Lucen isn't right... There must be some mistake...*

But X'ieth was left helpless to wonder these things, being at no greater clarity due to Destiny's intervention. And so, all he could do was ponder what should be, versus what was reality. In not much time at all, X'ieth hardened his heart against the quiet Karnatha, and continued to stomp through Saol, with heavy feet and a heavy heart, his nostrils flaring and his heart pounding in his chest. He would storm out of Saol, and in so doing, would leave his faith behind.

"These are my dreams, Destiny!" X'ieth screamed, while walking. "And I will have them all!"

As the young knight marched through the woods, off toward the black cloud in the sky, Forest Saol stood idly to observe the young knight's growing anger. For creation could not prevent its bad destiny, or his.

"QUESTIONS WITHOUT ANSWERS"

Chapter 66
Storm Brewing

X'ieth followed the black cloud on the horizon as seen from Forest Saol, all the way out of the woods, onto the main road, and back to Arlem, where he sat under yet another black cloud, in one of the city's many pubs. He was seated behind a wooden table, which had an iron mug standing on its surface full of water, next to the bundled shard of sword, placed in front of him. In the background, X'ieth could discern a host of people seated in the pub, their faces nearly dejected as his own. Sunken in shadows draping the pub, they were perched on benches before tables, eating thinner meals than before, as if the food and drink were ever scarcer now in Arlem.

Slowly, X'ieth felt a certain gravity pull his gaze down to the bundle beneath his nose. He looked to the tabletop at the shard wrapped in his crimson cloak, half in admiration and half in disgust. On one hand, he imagined himself opening up the bundle, touching the shard's grip, and wielding the nightly blade—a prospect that pleased part of him. But on the other hand, he felt a certain taint seeping through the cloak's fabric to dirty his clean self-image of being Karnath's beloved hero—a prospect that repulsed the other part of him.

The longer he stared at the shard, the dirtier he felt, and in not much time at all, it raised his self-awareness of how dirty he really was. In one motion, he lifted an ungloved hand over his face and up through his hair. Upon his naked fingertips, he felt the brittle beard birthed from his stubble, the oil seeping from pores of his grimy flesh, along with his matted and greasy dirty-blond hair. The shard was stuck in his eyes during the thought. *You're filthy, in more ways than one…*

Suddenly and strangely, like many times before, X'ieth saw the cloak move on its own, peeling itself back to reveal the blade, as if to tempt him. As a reflex, the young knight slammed his hand over the cloak, pounding the table with a loud bam, and pinning the fabric to the tabletop. Instantly, people in the distance looked his way, startled out of their preoccupations, and now curious as to what was happening.

X'ieth deflected their stares by looking down at his hand overtop of the bundle. *Did it really move?* He wondered this each and every time the same thing took place. While he was confident of what he saw, he still had his doubts. And those doubts suggested he were going mad. *Arlem just has you on edge, with the city running short on supplies and luck. You need to go back to Sergros…*

But X'ieth had tried leaving with little luck. Visions suddenly assaulted him, of his failed attempts to secure a horse on the king's credit for his return to Sergros; the stable keepers outright laughed at him. When he tried to acquire a cart mule afterward in the same manner, the outcome was even worse: the merchant laughed him right out of Arlem's square, along with the bystanders, who pointed and heckled him. *Guess you'll have to walk.*

He reached for the mug, grabbed it, and took a long drink of water to wet his throat. After swallowing the water, he wiped his mouth, and sat the mug back on the table. *Walk or ride, it doesn't matter. Just get out…*

Since X'ieth miraculously arrived at Arlem from following the providential black cloud, he had thought a great deal about what he would do. Unfortunately, the path before him was anything but clear, for it seemed despite whatever he could do, there still might be no warm welcome in Sergros. *At least not without another miracle…*

The situation was multi-faceted. To be recognized as the Child of Light, he would at a minimum have to return to Sergros with Esmeralda's head, to prove he had defeated the Child of Darkness. Or alternatively, he would need the Guardsmen to vouch for him. But he neither possessed Esmeralda's head nor the company of his friends, which was easily consternating. *What will you prove by returning to Sergros empty-handed, without your fellow Guardsmen and bearing the black shard?!*

The black shard was the other big problem. For beyond the matter of proving his victory over Darkness, was the matter of needing to bear the white shard, to confirm that he were the Child of Light. But he had a token that confirmed the exact opposite; he had the black shard, not the white. When X'ieth grappled with that especially, it caused him to bury his head in his hand. *What will you do?*

And if it were not enough to have no proof of defeating Esmeralda, and no tokens from the Light Prophecy, there was another thing weighing heavily on him: the gloom had not gone away. Talus was sure that Esmeralda brought the gloom by stealing energies from Karnath; yet stopping her had not lifted the perpetual fog and overcast. *Outside seems as drear as it was, the day you left for your quest…*

Sitting there before the bundle, X'ieth was confronted by these three things. They swarmed his mind, a fury of voices that were distant at first, but soon grew closer and louder, echoing again and again. *There's no proof you defeated the Darkness. There's no evidence that you're the Child of Light. There's no lifting of the gloom.* The voices continued speaking, forcing X'ieth to bring both hands to the sides of his face.

"Stop… Stop it…" he muttered to himself.

There was some distant motion in the pub, as a few patrons turned around, to look at him.

The voices continued barraging X'ieth. *There's no proof that you're the Child of Light. That's only what you think!* The varied voices reached agreement on that point. *Why yes! Yes! Yes, indeed!*

The voices in X'ieth's head continued voicing their agreement, speaking it over and over, until the point where the young knight could not take it any longer.

"Stop it!" he yelled, still with his hands to his face.

Finally, the voices stopped in his head.

Noises sounded as a few more pub goers shifted on their benches or bar stools, to see who had cried out. Once again, X'ieth deflected their stares, rehashing what he blamed for his uneasiness. *Arlem just has you on edge… Things will be better once you leave. And you'll find of way to explain yourself to Talus. You'll find a way…*

Sudden thoughts of Millicent and his newborn child beckoned X'ieth home. He pictured his wife with her bulging belly, exactly as he last saw her at his cottage, with teary blue eyes above tear-stained cheeks. In that moment, X'ieth realized that his family was perhaps more a reason than any other to put off his fears of going to Sergros and simply return, even if Talus would not welcome him in his own country.

Some distant talk in the pub suddenly pulled his attention. X'ieth glanced over to see three men in drab commoner's garb, who sat in the pub's dark corner, talking amongst themselves.

"The king had a feast I hear," one said.

"Aye, it was weeks ago!" another added.

"Since then, there hasn't been a single delivery of supplies or food to Arlem! Me thinks the king runs out!"

"Sounds true to me!"

"I agree," echoed the third man. "Let's see how long it goes before Arlem riots again! There will be protests around Castle Sergros, if this keeps up!"

As their murmuring continued, X'ieth drifted out of the conversation much like he drifted in, his mind endlessly adrift like a wayward vessel, tossed about on life's stormy sea. Despite his own problems, it became clear to him that these were not the only problems in Sergros—even it was tempting to think otherwise.

Feeling more dryness in his throat, X'ieth took another sip of water. But as he lifted it to his lips, a familiar male voice entered his ears.

"It was a pass in the rock that I hardly knew about!"

X'ieth sat down the mug, and jolted up from the bench, to gaze all around the pub.

"I thought none of us would survive."

A different male voice, equally familiar, made X'ieth even more edgy. Something was definitely amiss.

He grabbed the bundle, and moved out from the bench, so quickly that his leg bumped into it and sent a painful pulse through his right calf. Adrenaline started pumping through him, as he walked row after row of tables, studying faces in the crowd like a book from academy. *You know whom you heard... But it can't be, can it?*

But suddenly, interrupting his thoughts was a tapping. It came from behind, on his left shoulder.

X'ieth turned about to see a ghost.

"Lad, you made it!" exclaimed Nathan, standing behind the young knight. "We've been in Arlem now for days, hoping you'd show..."

X'ieth could not believe his eyes, and remained shocked. His jaw quivered and his skin turned pale. He simply did not know how to reply. *Esmeralda's tower fell apart! The Guard was inside, yet... Nathan's alive?!* His mind sputtered thoughts, and his mouth worked no better.

"How did you?! Wh... where did you come from?!" X'ieth stammered, examining Nathan from head-to-toe, as more a specimen than an acquaintance.

X'ieth caught a distant stir in the pub from his periphery. He looked yonder in that direction, beyond Nathan, to see Finnel rise from one of the long tables, with his mug of ale raised to salute the young knight. He scooted out from the bench, and sauntered over to where both he and Nathan stood, on a perfectly healed leg!

"I got to the hospice just in time," Finnel said jokingly, "right before anarchy erupts in Arlem!" He looked right at X'ieth while speaking, from about two cubits away. "This city's on the brink of riot," he said lowly. His blue eyes sparkled in the dim light, being set in a healthy face that apparently had gotten some nourishment since the last time X'ieth saw him.

X'ieth glanced away from Finnel, and shot his gaze back to the spot where Finnel arose, and there sat Hammar and Zeros also, both lifting a hand to show their presence. X'ieth looked back to Finnel, and then to Nathan, finding himself in wild disbelief. *Everyone's alive!*

For a few moments, the disbelief lingered, and X'ieth found himself double-checking his own vision, alternating looks between Nathan, Finnel, and both Hammar with Zeros seated afar. *They're alive! They're all alive!*

Despite his elation, X'ieth remained unspoken, with Nathan and Finnel both grinning at him over his stalled tongue. In that moment, it was hard to say anything just yet, for such joy filled X'ieth at seeing his friends return safely from Esmeralda's tower that it was unspeakable, at first.

"You made it!" he blurted out, looking at Nathan. X'ieth turned to Finnel and stepped closer, before using his free hand to grab Finnel's arm. He pinched its skin to test that he was real.

"It be true... We're here as people, not ghosts!" shouted Nathan with a smile.

X'ieth smiled back warmly, as relief flooded over him. At the back of his mind, he worked through the implications of his friend's wellbeing: *Now you'll have a warmer welcome in Sergros, with friends to corroborate your story!*

Excitedly, X'ieth spewed forth a series of questions.

"So tell me, how did it happen?! How did you escape in time?!" He asked one question after another in hopes of detail, acting like an eager child about to receive a gift. "How did you get out of Liath, when the mountain broke apart?!"

X'ieth recalled the last he saw of the Guard in Esmeralda's tower. With the exception of Zeros, they lied there on the floor, bloody and motionless, while the mountain around the tower shook to bits, just as X'ieth fled on Gremel's back. It occurred to him then, how a bigger miracle than even his own would have needed to happen, for the Guardsmen to be alive and well in Arlem, sharing an ale together!

Nathan lifted his hand. "Be at ease, man! What took place in the tower was a miracle, just like our escape from Saol. None of us could explain it. We awoke from Esmeralda's in a secret pass of Liath, with only flesh wounds and good stories to tell!"

A bit lost for words, X'ieth shook his head.

"That's amazing," he said, at last.

"Well, Zeros knows a bit more than us," Finnel admitted. "A robed youth supposedly appeared in the tower and was fighting Magicia. The last thing he saw was the youth smacking the tower's floor with his staff, before the whole scene turned white, exactly like it did when we ran from the vespers, out of Saol! The next thing any of us knew, we awoke far from the tower in a hidden pass of Liath, only a few hours hike from Forest Saol."

"And Zeros has more than stories," Nathan whispered. "He has your trophy."

X'ieth looked to Nathan, confused. "Eh?"

"The mercenary told me in confidence," Nathan said lowly, "about the king's test for you to bring back the sorceress' head, to prove that you had earned your promotion to the Seventh Order."

X'ieth blinked at Nathan without a word. *How would Zeros know that?!* The young knight had never told Zeros about Talus' test for this particular quest, so what the pack leader now mentioned suggested that the mercenary knew about it all along. And potentially, Zeros knew a bit more about him than X'ieth had even gathered.

At that realization, feelings of mistrust for Zeros awakened in X'ieth. *Who is he really, and what more does he know? What does he want?* The young knight let his gaze wander back over to Zeros, who sat with Hammar sharing a story. The dwarf pounded the table a few times, laughing hysterically with apparent entertainment.

"He had *it* when we awoke upon the pass."

Nathan's words cut into X'ieth's thoughts.

"Had what?"

"Esmeralda's head. It's rotting as we speak in his chamber, ready for you to present personally to Talus. You deserve the honor, for your wit and valor when fighting Esmeralda!"

Coward. Luck. Desire. All in one instant, X'ieth saw himself hide while his friends were in harm's way, and sneak out to luckily slay Esmeralda, all over his desires for the shard. The situation easily made him sick to his stomach. *There's no wit or valor there...*

"If you'll call it that," X'ieth sighed. While he was unhappy about how Nathan framed the victory, having Esmeralda's head and his comrades to back him lifted a heavy weight from his chest. *Talus has to believe you now.*

"What's that?" Finnel asked.

When X'ieth looked his way, he saw the elf suddenly reach his hands for bundle in his arms. He had a knee-jerk reaction, while pulling it away protectively.

"Leave it be!" he hissed, barring his teeth like a threatened animal. His face contorted, his eyes widened, and his heart leaped in his chest, as his partial and unfounded fondness for the shard manifested itself. The black shard of sword had become a thing he grew to both love and hate in the course of his journey— from Liath, through Saol, and to Arlem.

"What is it?" asked Nathan, also with a curious hand. He laid it on the crimson cloak and tugged.

"Don't touch it!" X'ieth roared, deflecting Nathan's hand and ripping the bundle away.

He stared back at them, breathing fiercely through flared nostrils, with his heart pounding in his chest and blood thumping his temple. *What do they want with your shard?! Your shard...*

But while X'ieth looked fierce, and ready to guard the shard with his life, Nathan and Finnel did not look the same. Both of them timidly backed away a few cubits, as if retreating.

X'ieth clutched the bundle all the more tightly, while his mind filled with the recall of Nathan actually touching the bundle. *They can't take it away... No one can!*

When X'ieth detected motion in his periphery, he looked around and took in the background, seeing then how everyone visiting in the tavern had instantly stopped their talking, eating, and drinking, to gawk at the young knight. A few people behind tables eating bowls of thinned soups or porridge leered at X'ieth, with mouths agape and spoons suspended in upraised hands. Drops from their utensils fell back into their dishes with noticeable dripping that strangely was all that could be heard in the pub, which had been brought to a dead silence.

X'ieth screamed at one youngster who stared, open-mouthed and wide-eyed, a spoon held in trembling hand.

"What are you looking at?!"

The young man in simple clothes—a gray tunic and dark trousers fastened with a leather belt—fell off the bench, to stutter from the floor. "I… I was just leaving!"

He ran through the tables and out the door, not looking back. In his departure, the door swung upon its hinges, and X'ieth felt a cold gust rip through the pub. But that coldness seemed not so cold, just as his darkness seemed not so Dark, as it would seem to anyone who was isolated within the world created by their black shard.

The swinging door finally slammed shut with a bang, bringing X'ieth back to the spectacle he created in the pub. All Arlemers stared at him, like he was a crazed lunatic. And perhaps no one, including the pub landlord, was ready to confront a group of Guardsmen in the king's service, raucous or not.

Suddenly, an iron spoon could be heard, rattling a ceramic plate. X'ieth looked in that direction, seeing an elven maiden suddenly rise off her bench and away from her table, and then dart for the door, leaving her meal behind. He watched her move hurriedly through the pub in her sackcloth dress, her locks of black hair bouncing as she went. Just like the young man she exited, and did not look back.

As the door banged shut again, X'ieth felt a bit uncomfortable himself. "A good idea," he said, in reference to the departures, and stomped through the pub himself.

Right before leaving, when halfway out the door, X'ieth sensed a person get up from their bench. He turned to find Zeros standing, the mercenary's features awash with concern.

"Don't follow me!" X'ieth barked.

His words stopped Zeros then and there. For only a moment longer X'ieth made eye contact with the mercenary, before heading out the door and onto Arlem's cobblestone streets, wrestling with a problem way bigger than himself. For the black shard had taken its hold!

Chapter 67
Lye and Blindside

Since that moment in Saol—the one where he turned his heart against Destiny—things got much worse for X'ieth Armstrong. He continued battling fantasies of touching the black shard's grip, as he did from the instant he took the shard from Lucen. But now, he felt resisting those fantasies took much more work, like Karnatha had left him alone to defend against this final rite of passage—the final rite, before the Child of Darkness fought Kayareth at Gallow Cliff.

Since taking the shard, X'ieth had mixed emotions of love and hate for the object that intensified each passing second, into what was becoming absolute insanity. Just like what happened in the pub, he frequently spoke to himself about the bundle and physically wrestled with it, probably appearing to others as a complete loon. His saner half realized this, and realized that if he did not do something soon, something very bad would happen. *The shard will take over your life...*

With that thought, X'ieth stepped out of Arlem's pub and onto the cobblestone, where instantly, a cold wind smacked him in the face. He paid it no heed and stormed through the empty city streets, going without a clear plan, but nevertheless, having a mission.

Visions of pregnant Millicent flashed before his eyes, of her being teary and sad at the cottage, before he left the woman behind for his quest. It brought to mind Lucen's words: *Leave the shard with me, and forget this ever happened. Go back to your plain life in the home with Millicent. Leave now, you can still make your child's birth.*

The idea appealed to his one side that hated the shard, and now, his mission became just that: somehow freeing himself from the shard's hold, and returning his life to what it was, in the interests of his family and job. *Perhaps it's what you should've done from the start...*

X'ieth hastened his step on the cobblestone, thinking of how Arlem's offerings might help him out of his predicament. His mind went back to his initial trip to the city, to his stroll of its business district, wondering if there was anything in the district that could help him. He remembered most of the shops were abandoned or closed, except one: the blacksmith.

The thought literally stopped X'ieth on the streets, bringing his kicking boots to a sudden halt. Slowly, his mind continued churning, thinking next of the poor experience he had in the city, when encountering Arlem's street gangs. The leader's words came to him: *I bet your armor would command a bit of money with the smithy. He's always looking for scrap metal!*

X'ieth returned from the thought, onto the streets of Arlem, and it was there that it slowly occurred to him. *Take the shard to the blacksmith and let him scrap it.* The idea seemed reasonable indeed, and that was exactly what the young knight planned to do.

"I must destroy the shard, or it'll destroy me!"

With those words, he continued moving through Arlem, toward the business district. From what he remembered, the business district was just across the residential district where he was at now. Bearing that in mind, he hurried by row upon row of homes having locked doors and smoking chimneys, keeping his eyes set on the buildings in the distance—the shops.

In a matter of minutes, X'ieth appeared at the center of Arlem's business district, holding the bundle and with a look of developing desperation in his eyes.

"Where is it? Where is it?!" he muttered, scanning the shops one by one, only to find nothing but closed storefronts. Even after a second look, he still did not see the blacksmith. And since the tradesman would not throw open his door to wave the young knight into his shop, X'ieth would have to find it—if it were even there. A wave of fret suddenly crashed over him. *Hopefully he's not closed shop, due to crime or lacking demand!*

He walked along the stores, carefully looking at each one. When he passed the textiles shop, a flashback hit him, of the tall woman's fabric coming undone, without a third and important strand in her threading. He saw himself at the pane, wide-eyed and open-mouthed, as she suddenly disappeared, along with her fabric upon the loom that unraveled into thin air. X'ieth forced himself to stop thinking about what had happened. *Certainly more pressing things are at hand…*

X'ieth became all the more worried when coming to the end of the row and still not finding the blacksmith. The outcome played on his fears and growing desperation over the shard, like somehow the blacksmith was the only one who could deliver him from evil, if and only if he could find the blacksmith's shop. His mind fretted again. *What if ironically, he closed due to lacking materials?!* X'ieth remembered then, how Talus informed him how some Sergrothian miners never returned with the gloom, and in his moment of despair, it seemed applicable.

From his last visit to Arlem, X'ieth recalled the blacksmith shop being at the end of one row of shops. Yet, here he was at the end of one row, and the blacksmith was nowhere in sight! *Where is it?!* His face stretched in bewilderment, and his jaw dropped. *It was right here!*

But then, as if by chance, X'ieth heard a door open, down the adjacent row of shops and on the opposite side. He turned immediately, seeing a middle-aged man leave one shop, with a shiny sword in one hand. This was clearly the blacksmith's shop. X'ieth had clearly recollected the wrong row of shops and the wrong end. *Damn it!*

X'ieth moved past his frustration, and approached the building, which resembled all others in Arlem. It was a structure of gray stone, overhung by a red slate roof that cloaked a chimney billowing puffy, white smoke. At its front was an insulated window. X'ieth stepped up to it and peered inside.

He could see the burly blacksmith toiling away at his anvil, pounding on heated iron that glowed orange. Behind him was a table filled with sundry tools of the trade, an orderly assortment of tools, from chisels to pinchers, from tongs to hammers, many of varied shape and size. On the wall was the forge that flashed red and orange fires; it sat at the foot of a chimney stretching up the inner wall, which connected to the bellows halfway up.

Relief poured over X'ieth at the sight of the smithy still at work. He spun from the window, walked over to the front door, and barged in with his bundled shard. The door creaked open upon its hinges, and instantly, X'ieth was greeted by sounds of metal hitting metal, along with the shop's warmth. A cold wind followed him from behind, prompting him to turn and close the door. It banged shut.

At the noise, the blacksmith looked up briefly. But surprisingly, he quickly turned back to his iron working, as if hoping that his visitor would just go away.

X'ieth spoke up. "Pardon me, sir."

He continued hammering the heated iron.

Clang clang! ... Clang clang!

X'ieth wondered why the blacksmith would ignore him. *Did the smith hear, or does he just act like he didn't?*

"Pardon me, sir. I need some help!"

Clang clang! ... Clang clang! ... Clang CLANG!

"I've much work," said the smithy, not taking his eyes off the anvil. *Clang clang!* "I can't take on much else." *Clang clang! Clang clang!*

The smithy is always looking for scrap metal! With a pause, X'ieth responded, "I need *nothing created*, but rather *something destroyed*. I'm bringing you scrap metal."

The smith stopped pounding the iron, and looked up at the young knight. In that instant, X'ieth could see the perspiration beading the smith's balding head; it caught the forge's light. The smith stood there at his anvil, holding a strip of heated metal with tongs in one gloved hand, its surface orange and aglow. In the smith's other gloved hand, he held a hammer.

In one motion, the smith dropped his hammer, tongs, and worked metal on the anvil, and came over to X'ieth with eager eyes. "I've always a need for scraps. What old metalwork do you need done away with?"

X'ieth stood before the blacksmith, holding his bundle. The part of him loving the shard wanted him to escape out the door with the object, so that he and the shard could still be together. That part of X'ieth wanted him to run, but the young knight's other part insisted. *No. Do it.*

Slowly, and with some reluctance, X'ieth opened his crimson cloak to reveal the black shard. The moment the nightly blade emerged, he looked away so not to tempt himself, keeping his eyes on the smith.

X'ieth watched how at first, the smithy just examined the object closely, as if struggling to place what it was, or how the metal might be used. *Why don't you take a look as well?* Despite his objective of keeping his eyes off the shard, X'ieth found that his own temptations were still there, pressing him. *Why don't you look too? Just a little look...*

As the smithy continued studying the blade, X'ieth could not restrain himself any longer from peeking at it just the same. And so, his eyes fell upon the nightly sword, and the moment they did, he found that indeed it was beautiful to look upon, with its black, mirrored blade reflecting the forge fires in rainbow shimmers. *The black shard...* Part of X'ieth loved the shard, and lusted over it.

"The Dark Prophecy!"

The blacksmith's voice pulled X'ieth from his absorption with the shard. He looked up to the smith, who stared back with a face of sudden worry, as if agitated by the sight. X'ieth watched the blacksmith take off his gloves one by one, and retreat a few steps while muttering something else about the Dark Prophecy. He stood there, with the gloves in his hands.

The smithy paused, which fed X'ieth's hope. But then came the smithy's request, in a calm but firm voice.

"Please leave my shop."

His hopes began dying, and alarms sounded in his head. *No, no... Nooo! He has to help you!* Those alarms were easily enough for X'ieth to fervently plead with Arlem's blacksmith.

"Please, good sir! I must destroy the sword."

X'ieth watched the blacksmith strain to breathe, looking down at the shard again. And the longer the blacksmith looked, the more the object seemed to cause him dread and further agitation.

"Leave now! Go!"

"Please, sir!" X'ieth begged, motivated by the desperation inside him. "I am of the Sergrothian Crimson Guard, having found this sword during the king's quest upon the Mountains of Liath! No one should possess this shard, not I or anyone else, so please help me destroy it!"

He watched the smith scowl at the black blade, clearly not wanting anything to do with it. X'ieth continued talking frantically, as if to continue arguing for the smith's action. "I simply wish to prevent this sword from falling into the wrong hands!" The young knight prayed carelessly, as he spoke. *Please... Just let him try and destroy it.*

"I'll do what I can," the smith said gruffly. With clear reluctance, he gloved his hands once more. "I shouldn't have worked today," the smithy grumbled below his breath. "Hardly a soul in Arlem works, yet foolish me at the forge trying *to earn* a living."

X'ieth watched the smith take up the tongs from the anvil. He turned around and approached the young knight, opening them then pinching them closed, with his eyes on the shard.

During the blacksmith's walk over to him, X'ieth kept his eyes on the tongs, knowing that the smith would use them to pluck the shard from his clutches. And that realization anguished the part of X'ieth that loved the shard— the part of him that never wanted to let it go. Yet X'ieth fought himself to stay in place, and let the blacksmith do what was needed.

As expected, the blacksmith used the tongs to snatch the shard from the young knight's grip. Right when the blacksmith took the sword, spun to the forge, and began walking away, X'ieth extended his hands uncontrollably for the smith's back. His hands trembled and his fingers curled, as one part of him yearned for the shard. *Get it! Take it back!!!* X'ieth struggled to get a hold of himself before the smith could notice. *No...*

X'ieth forced his hands to his sides, told himself to breath slowly, and altogether tried to calm himself. *It's for the best... Your best...* Meanwhile, the smith took the shard to his forge, where the sacred and legendary broken sword was subjected to its flames.

It was less than a minute before the smith jerked the shard out of the flames, bringing it close to his skin but not touching it. From across the room, X'ieth heard the blacksmith remark, "That can't be."

What can't be?! X'ieth swallowed hard, as the smithy turned about with the shard in his tongs. But unlike the metal that the smith previously worked, the sword was not a glowing orange, but rather of ordinary appearance for what it was. It appeared as if it were never even in the fire!

"It heated not," the blacksmith said. "Let me stoke the fires as hot as we can stand!" With hopeful yet concerned eyes, X'ieth followed the blacksmith's arms as he pumped the bellows to stoke the fires hotter. As the process continued, he felt the forge's heat severely increase over time, and watched its flames jump higher. The hotter the flames, and the higher their jump, X'ieth became certain this would make a difference. *Surely, a forge this hot would melt most metals!*

As the fires stoked even hotter, X'ieth sweated in his armor and began to feel woozy. He leaned against the wall for support, wondering how much longer he could tolerate the intense heat. But suddenly then, the blacksmith stopped pumping the bellows, and once again, subjected the shard to the hotter fires.

After what seemed a minute, the blacksmith turned about with the shard in his tongs, still black as usual and without orange glow. The young knight's heart jumped to his throat.

"That's simply not possible!" yelled the blacksmith. "It heats not!"

At the news, X'ieth began to wring his hands nervously. He prayed without care that the shard would melt. *Please, let it be destroyed!*

The smithy sighed heavily in frustration, and for a moment, X'ieth feared that he was on the verge of quitting. But fortunately for the young knight, the blacksmith had another idea.

"Let me try breaking it, with my vice…"

The blacksmith motioned to the vice over on the table with the tools, behind the anvil. He watched the blacksmith scurry over, still carrying the shard in his tongs.

When there, the blacksmith placed the shard in the vice and began turning the crank, so to tighten its grips over the blade and break it. But upon the grips closing, the vice screw popped out and clanged upon the floor, sending a singular thought through X'ieth's mind. *The shard broke his machine!*

The blacksmith shook his head. "It's not possible!"

The blacksmith, appearing somewhat frightened, hurried from his vice over to X'ieth, with the shard outstretched far from body and still pinched in the tongs.

"Here, take it! This doesn't belong here!"

X'ieth received the shard back in his cloak, as the blacksmith released it with the tongs, and then, took several steps back.

Urgently, X'ieth pled with the smith. "No wait! Surely there's something else!"

The blacksmith's face showed of utter terror. His skin seemed pale, like that of a corpse.

"No, there's not!" he replied. "According to legend, that sword was forged in Ires Star. Surely it's indestructible by any forge in Karnath! I was a fool for trying…"

X'ieth watched the blacksmith take another step back, reacting as though a monster entered the shop.

"I know *who* you are," he said in an unsteady voice.   X'ieth suddenly realized where this was going. He protested the association the blacksmith was making. "No, no… I'm not!"

But despite his protests, the blacksmith yelled over him. "You're the Child of Darkness!"

The words damaged X'ieth. He did not expect to hear them again, after Lucen's mistaken proclamation. And so, as a defense, his mind ran over with denial. *No, that's all wrong! This is all wrong! You're the Child of Light!*

The blacksmith shouted at the top of his lungs, "Get from this place, and don't come back!" His eyes were wild, and his demeanor now estranged from the goodwill shown earlier. He wanted the young knight to leave, and to leave immediately.

X'ieth felt helpless. He dropped his head, bundled the shard tight, and went out the door onto the cobblestone street, utterly perplexed by the smith's words. At the back of his mind, beyond his ocean of denial, was the question: *Are you... Kayareth?!* He dared not think it, but just the same, the question was still there.

Outside the blacksmith's shop, X'ieth found himself standing in the middle of Arlem's business district, once again exposed to the cold. He shook his head, and in so doing, tried to shake off two proclamations of bad destiny—one from Lucen, and a second from the smith.

Taking a few steps down Arlem's windy street, he muttered the words repeatedly, "I am the Child of Light... The Child of Light!" He stopped and looked back to the blacksmith shop, cursing beneath his breath. "To the Void with you, smithy..."

The sky was darkening as nightfall descended, just as were the young knight's hopes of being freed from the shard's hold, and all that the shard implied of his character. X'ieth's half that hated the shard, likewise hated the idea of being evil.

In an aside, he cried aloud, "In my heart, I'm the good one who goes to Gallow Cliff and fights Shaizan for the black shard, using the white! I'm the good one!"

X'ieth continued shouting into the streets, "I am the hero!" It rang out loudly and echoed for what seemed an eternity, so surely the whole world knew his true identity now, even Arlem's blacksmith. But as much as the young knight wished to remove his burden of the shard and clear the many suspicions surrounding his seeming identity, alas, he could not.

In his hands, X'ieth held his crimson cloak wrapping the black shard, perhaps stronger evidence of his identity than any other token. It sent his mind spinning with questions regarding why he put himself in this position. *Why did you take the sword from Lucen? Why?!*

But just as he questioned taking the sword, his other side began questioning why he would leave it behind. *Why leave what you can't live without! You need it. Suppose you just open the cloak, to see it one more time... So you can, touch it...*

"No!" X'ieth shouted, shooing the idea from his mind, and again, all that it suggested of him.

Just then, a yell came from behind his shoulder.

"X'ieth!" It was a male voice.

But X'ieth stood there in another world, with his face lowered. He glowered at the bundle, as the person ran up beside him.

"X'ieth!"

The young knight lifted his eyes, and saw Zeros.

"I've been looking all over for you!" he exclaimed.

"I've been looking for me too…"

X'ieth mumbled incomprehensibly, his broken thoughts now poorly strung into spoken words. He began walking past Zeros.

"What happened back there?" Zeros asked, walking alongside X'ieth. From his periphery, he noticed Zeros glancing down at the bundled shard.

"Don't worry; I'm fine." X'ieth muttered, while heading down the street. At the mercenary's question, he recollected his behavior back in the pub, and now, tried to seem much more collected. "I just don't like people touching my stuff."

"Lad, here were are again, with you saying nothing's wrong, when really there's more to it than that."

X'ieth and Zeroes continued walking together. The young knight did not know if he could trust Zeros. Without an invitation, the mercenary had read his mind upon Liath. And in addition to that, the mercenary knew about his poor relationship with Talus, his home life, and potentially other things, yet pretended to know less. *But even so, is there much to lose by trying to tell him your problems?* X'ieth mulled over it for a moment, and eventually decided to try.

"I once expected that I had great purpose in life, but now, I fear that I'm not purposed for anything great at all. And to make matters worse, I fear that I'm purposed to do something horrible!"

At the mention of doing something horrible, thoughts raced through X'ieth's head, of Shaizan at Gallow Cliff in his black armor of god, wielding the nightly shard, with a mob of giants behind him, carrying banners of a gray snake coiled about eclipsing suns. At the mention of doing something horrible, he thought of Shaizan defeating Kayareth to obtain the white shard and bring Eternal Darkness to Karnath through Maken's whole gray blade. While the idea pleased his one part loving the shard, his other part cringed. *That's not your childhood dream!*

X'ieth stopped on the street, and Zeros too. They both met eyes. Icy winds blew around them, and in the background, gray stone buildings loomed with red slate roofs, a constant backdrop for Arlem.

After a long silence, Zero spoke. "No man is meant for the bad destiny of horrible things like hurting others, and neither are you. Also, no man is meant for null destiny, to do nothing without any purpose, and neither are you. But as for good destiny, it's not as black and white. It's gray."

Zeros continued. "Sometimes our greatest expectations can end up being our greatest letdowns. But these broken dreams are as much of our good destiny as any other thing that's meant to be, for to succeed at anything, we must try many things, and in the course of trying many things, we will fail more than once. Failure can be heartbreaking and at times, it seems like enough for us to stop dreaming, but trying and failing before eventually succeeding is what Destiny has ordained, not just giving up. You must not give up on yourself! Believe always you're meant for more than null and bad destinies!"

X'ieth grumbled, being in no mood for a sermon.

"We are all destined to dream gray, and many people often share the same gray dreams. While several people can dream the same dream, sometimes only one person can live it… This is why our gray dreams are uncertain, and for some people, why these dreams are divinely intended to become broken."

In an aside, Zeros turned and spoke to the empty streets. "But despite this truth, some gray dreamers will continue to pursue their dreams, and such can lead to unhappiness or even personal ruin! When dreamers trade enriching relationships with family, friends, and god for sought after things that aren't meant to be, they sacrifice their growth and their potential!"

Zeros faced the young knight again.

X'ieth shook his head, thinking of something radically different than what Zeros described. *It's not that your dreams were uncertain or not meant to be. It's something else…* His mind suddenly filled with Urzel's words. *False premonitions suggest one's web of destiny being re-spun by those acting off their premonitions!* He remembered his flawed premonitions with Taurus and back at his cottage with the unforeseen visitors, and what those flawed premonitions might mean. His mind slowly reached a conclusion. *Someone changed your fate.*

All of a sudden, X'ieth started speaking, saying things that popped into his mind before the ideas had enough time to solidify. "Someone took this from me. Someone has changed how my life is unfolding, how our lives were destined to unfold! All of us on this mission are living rewritten fates! *This* isn't supposed to happen to me! *This* is for someone else to endure!"

"What is *this*? What are you talking about?"

X'ieth continued talking, more to himself than to Zeros, even though he stared the mercenary in the face.

"Yes, that's it. Esmeralda spoke of premonitions about the shard, and for what purpose Magicia would use it! She acted off those premonitions, and thereby changed my future… I shouldn't even be here…"

Zeros appeared lost, as if confused or not even listening, and it angered the young knight. X'ieth turned from Zeros and started walking off, without a glance back.

"Wait," Zeros called. "Don't go."

X'ieth continued walking.

"Wait!"

X'ieth stopped himself and spun around. "What?!"

Zeros stood there, straight-faced with his hand up.

"I don't know how to help you…"

"You can't! No one can help me."

Zeros paused, as if not knowing what to say.

"I'm sorry you feel that way," he replied, finally. "And I'm sorry for everything else that's happened."

As before, X'ieth turned his back to Zeros, and prepared to leave. Nevertheless, Zeros continued speaking to the young knight.

"I'm sorry for reading your mind on Liath. I'm sorry for not telling you the truth about me, and my relationship with Talus. I'm sorry…"

The young knight took a step away.

"X'ieth, there's something I need to tell you! And I'm about to lose the last chance I have…"

X'ieth stopped. Slowly, he turned around and faced the mercenary, with a scowl across his face.

Zeros started talking. "Look, after a drink or two more in Arlem we'll go back to Sergros, and your life will go back to normal, maybe even get better than before you left. My life, however, will not get better. So before I return to the misery I've lived for decades, I need to take this chance to tell you the truth. And I'd best not say it around the others."

X'ieth arched his eyebrows.

"I'll tell you what happened to me," Zeros said. "I'll tell you why my career diverged from that of the respected Garlew Il'therin."

At that, X'ieth did not understand why Zeros was being so secretive. *Couldn't this story be told over ale, back at the pub?* To X'ieth, it made little sense.

"I was charged with treason in the Isles Crusades."

The words stole X'ieth's breath, for this offense was punishable by death in the Triangle Kingdoms, especially in Sergros. He was not expecting to hear this.

"You remember I mentioned Elucid in Saol, asked Zeros, "after the vespers attacked?"

X'ieth nodded silently.

"Well, during the Isles Crusades, Elucid passed from Karnath in my company, and I saw to his ritual burial in the appropriate Hirishin tomb."

Zeros fell silent, and the winds blew, as if taking over the conversation.

"And what of it?" asked X'ieth, growing impatient.

"Well, some of my command sought to rob Elucid's grave. They claimed to be on a mission from Talus, to recover Laotzu's bones. When I found out, I didn't believe them. I… reacted poorly."

"Oh?" X'ieth said. "What did you do?"

X'ieth released the question, wishing he could retract it a moment later. He was not at all sure where it would lead, and if he was ready for its answer.

At the young knight's question, Zeros' countenance darkened like a blue sky that suddenly gave way to tempest clouds. The mercenary's mouth began working, speaking words as coldly as their chilling content.

"I killed them," he said grimly. "I killed them all."

Appalled, X'ieth dropped his jaw. The young knight pulled the bundle closer, in that moment looking at the mercenary a different way. *Zeros, a former Sergrothian commander, killed his command?! He's a monster... A murderer!*

"When I returned to Sergros after the Crusades," Zeros continued, "Talus confirmed that his soldiers Drichal, Hetron, Gambul, and Rystys had a secret assignment of recovering Laotzu's bones, should a suspicious grave be found or a person appearing as icons of the Juniperth king from Old Karnath's legend. I, of course, never believed that. But anyway, what happened became grossly exaggerated with the king, hence my charge of treason."

"How did you avoid the death penalty?" X'ieth asked, with a hint of hesitation.

Zeros became deeply solemn. "Talus still punished me," he said, "in a way more severe than being drawn and quartered."

"What is more severe than death, a cruel one at that?!" asked X'ieth, with strong feelings over the situation. *Zeros should've been punished for what he did!*

"My punishment for treason was permanent exile from Sergros, and separation from my own family."

Zeros stepped closer, his eyes glued to X'ieth's.

"How does this concern me?" asked the young knight, his one leg trembling.

Zeros deflected the question, and talked on. "Many would think this a less severe punishment that being drawn and quartered, but I disagree." In an aside he said, "What is life, if it cannot be enjoyed with the people one loves, or in the places one cherishes?"

"How does this concern me?!" X'ieth asked again, growing bothered now. Winds blew behind his words and afterward too, bridging the talk that intermittently fell silent between him and Zeros.

With much delay and seeming deliberation, Zeros went on. "My punishment has been gradually reduced, as Talus permitted me to regain trust through indentured servitude to Sergros. I've been on the king's service for years now, as a lowly hired hand."

X'ieth became noticeably restless, fidgeting his arm, his leg still atremble. *He's dodging your question.*

"Working for Talus all this time has given me the unfortunate experience to understand your situation."

"Of what consequence is any of this to me?!" X'ieth snapped, a scowl wrinkling his face. Zeros was a silent for a moment, as another wind bridged their conversation, cracking a whip of ice over X'ieth. He shivered, not for the cold, but for his suspense.

"My life has become unbearable with the king's ways," Zeros shared, like not even hearing X'ieth. "He likes to control people with mind games, by getting inside their head. My life took a turn for the worse many years ago when the king began toying with me, as I watched everything I used to live for fade away."

X'ieth listened to the mercenary with complete engagement, dreading what he would disclose. *He dodged your questions. Why?!*

"Talus dangled the reinstatement of my prior life before me, while assigning the most challenging and unpleasant missions to repay a debt that he would never consider settled."

Zeros glanced down momentarily, as if to avoid the young knight's gaze. After a while, he looked up again, having found more words to continue. His face tensed, as he talked more about the king. And the more he talked, the more it became clear to X'ieth how Zeros loathed Talus for not simply killing him.

At a point, X'ieth found the mercenary's gushing about his situation both repetitive and circular. The whole time, the young knight fidgeted nervously, still dreading what would be said. *He dodged your questions, on purpose.*

During the next break in dialogue, X'ieth launched his question again. "Why are you telling me all this?"

There was another long pause, padded by winds.

"X'ieth, I am *not* your father."

Zeros' sudden words hit X'ieth like a club to the head. A remote part of him feared exactly the contrary would be said. *Who then, is Zeros?*

"A father would've been there for you, unlike me. I never acted like your father, though that's who I should have been!"

The words completely floored X'ieth. *No, no... Nooo!* The reality was as bad as he expected. His father was a murderer, a criminal in Sergros, who let him grow up fatherless. *So, you being an adopted son of the king has just been Talus' cover-up for Zeros' dark past, and at the same time, a sadistic ploy to hurt a father by estranging his son?!*

To X'ieth, the answer to his own question was evident. In disbelief he opened his mouth to speak but was rendered speechless, and Zeros, as if oblivious or uncaring to the young knight's feelings, just went on without a stop.

"You are the family I've been separated from all these years."

X'ieth initial reaction was one of self-defense, to invalidate the mercenary's claims, so that those claims could not hurt him. And so eventually, X'ieth found the voice to speak his denial. "I am an orphan without father or mother. I'm not just fatherless. How is *that*?"

Zeros' face turned even sadder.

"You are more than fatherless, and much to my hatred of Talus." At each spoken word, there was a noticeable quiver in Zeros' body from anger. "My separation from your mother was too much for her to bear, and so, she took her life."

The news completely quieted X'ieth and his denial; he was devastated now from an unbeknownst story of tragedy and loss. But as if insensitive to his pains, Zeros kept going on and on, until X'ieth wished that he would become mute.

"I can't make this up to you!" Zeros admitted, at last. "I can't repay years of lacking the audacity to face Talus, who forbid me from ever contacting you! I've missed so much of your life." Tears welled up in Zeros' eyes. "He raised you in the castle, just to spite me!"

X'ieth's illusion of having earned anything in life crumbled, more fissures to his dreams—cracks that multiplied and spread. *Can it be, that your entire childhood was just the king's tactic to manipulate your father, just as the knighthood has become Talus' way of getting to you?!*

The notion of Talus manipulating X'ieth just like Zeros was a worrying pattern that made him uneasy. His mouth went dry, his heart pounded in his chest, and his lungs worked stiffly. Equally distressing was the notion that both of his parents made selfish choices that led to him being an orphan. All in one instant, X'ieth was overwhelmed by negative feelings that so many important people in his life had not genuinely cared for him. It was difficult to accept, but how could he not?

Zeros' voice sliced through his thoughts.

"Talus put me on this assignment with my own son, asking me not to speak with him as a father!" Zeros exclaimed. "Like lye to the skin, he did this to irritate me! Talus loves to keep wounds open, so he can bother them! If he gets into your mind, he controls your life! This whole ordeal shows a darker face of our king!"

Anger built up inside of X'ieth, putting him on the verge of explosion. He was mad that Zeros had lied to him, and even madder about how he would suffer from lye to his own skin, now that he was blindsided by the truth. *And the truth will bother you for years! This will get under your skin and never leave you alone!*

"I'm sorry for not being in your life until now!" Zeros said. "Please know, that I am proud of what you've become—a noble knight, a good husband and, soon, a caring father!"

From his silence, X'ieth suddenly barked at Zeros. "Enough already!" With a pause and a swallow, he continued. "Let's go back to the inn, for I should lie down a while. Some sleep might do me well, to stomach all this."

X'ieth felt inclined to cursing and violence, but restrained himself. He glanced over to Zeros, who nodded reluctantly, as if understanding his son's position. Toward the inn, they both walked quietly, their footsteps a sounding percussion against that uneven stone. In utter silence the two men went—both un-fatherly father and fatherless son—all the way back to the inn, and there, parted ways.

Immediately, and without a single word, X'ieth ventured through the inn to his room for some sleep, whereas Zeros went to the adjacent pub to take a sorrowful drink, considering his confession untimely, foolish, and misplaced.

"IMPOSING ON SMITHY"

Chapter 68
Losing Inhibitions

After bumping into Zeros on Arlem's streets, both X'ieth and the mercenary walked back to the inn, where the young knight went inside to lie down, and Zeros went into the adjacent pub for a drink.

As much as X'ieth wanted to sleep—in order to disconnect his mind from what Zeros disclosed—he could not help himself from reflecting on his own life. And so, instead of falling asleep, X'ieth lied awake in his room upon its bed, with the bundled shard resting atop his chest. He was on his back and staring up at the ceiling, counting the beams supporting the roof, and letting his mind go adrift on a sea of thought.

While lying there, X'ieth imagined himself talking to Zeros on the streets, just as it happened in the last hour. He recalled how the mercenary explained that he was the young knight's long lost father, why X'ieth never had a mother, and why Talus was so cruel with him, especially in the years of his adulthood. Reliving that conversation made X'ieth feel sad, depressed, and angry all at once, for it made him realize that he lacked so many basic things that others enjoyed and likely took for granted.

In the middle of imagining the scene and dwelling on its inappropriateness, an image suddenly wedged itself between X'ieth and his thoughts. It was the shard with its black-mirrored blade, which resplendently sparkled and dazzled him even in his imagination, just as it did from the blacksmith's shop. *Open it, just for a look...*

The words flew through his mind, crashing into thoughts that ranged from Zeros' confession, to others about Millicent and his newborn. These all seemed like matters that should take higher priority than a sword, so X'ieth shut out the images of the shard, pushing them through a door at the back of his mind. But as soon as the door shut, it burst back open, and the images of the shard were there again. In his mind, X'ieth could still see the shard and its tempting grip, and the sight awakened his love for the sword.

The situation repeated itself several times over: X'ieth tried to concentrate on the situation involving Zeros, only to be interrupted by thoughts of the shard. And the more it occurred, the more X'ieth became aware of what was sitting atop of his chest. *The bundle...*

His eyes trailed to his crimson cloak wrapping the shard, and in the moment of eye contact, he was tempted to gaze upon the actual sword. *Open it, just for a look...* In spite of the temptation, X'ieth resisted opening the bundle. *No. Don't do it.*

While he resisted opening it, he could not pry his eyes off the cloak. He just kept staring at it, and as he did, his mind stayed active, challenging his decision. *But why wouldn't you open it? It's right there...* His inner voice raised the question, of why he would not indulge his wants, when the shard was within reach.

X'ieth sat up in his bed with the bundle resting in his hands, and his eyes upon it.

"Touch me," came a whisper.

X'ieth arched an eyebrow, thinking the sword had spoken to him through the cloak. He leaned closer.

"What did you say?"

"Touch me," came the whisper, again.

X'ieth swallowed. His hands began trembling, and he imagined opening the cloak. Once again, the beautiful shard appeared and interrupted his thoughts, calling to him, tempting him. *Touch me.*

In what seemed to be an involuntary movement, X'ieth peeled back one flap of the cloak. *What are you doing?!* said his one part, which hated the shard. *Don't stop!* said the other part, which loved it. Immediately, X'ieth felt conflicted over both proceeding and stopping.

In another involuntary movement, his hand peeled back another flap of the cloak, exposing the nightly blade. Even in the room's low lighting, the black shard struck his eyes as brilliantly prismatic, with speckles of blue, green, yellow, and red dispersed along its mirrored surface. A smile snuck to the corner of his lips, and his eyes sparkled with the lust he felt for the sword.

X'ieth continued staring at the shard, entranced by the light captured in its darkness, an irony yet to be understood. He stared even longer, as minutes flowed into hours, in what became a newfound vacancy of normal wants, wherein the shard completed him and he needed nothing else. He began to feel a strange affection for the shard, one that would have shamed a man committed to his senses, but not X'ieth. For in that moment, gone were the times where his family and job completed him, for these were now at best equals, if not inferiors, to what he gazed upon. *The shard... Your shard...*

In yet another involuntary turn of his hand, X'ieth reached for the shard's grip, a thing that his other part forbid for so long. As before, his fingers trembled as they moved closer and closer, falling just a hair's length from the handle, right before making contact.

In that moment, the sword's darkness captivated his eyes, as did its blade capture light, and X'ieth became spellbound by his own intrigue for the shard. His smile broadened, as the object enamored him more and more, rendering him increasingly obsessive over it. *The shard... Your shard...*

Suddenly, a faint rapping sounded from deep within his mind, a thing that was barely perceptible from his state of absorption with the shard.

Knock knock knock!

X'ieth paid it no heed, and deepened his fixation over the object. His smile stayed in place, he gazed upon it without even blinking, and his body quivered at times. *The shard… Your shard…*

KNOCK KNOCK KNOCK!

The rapping suddenly turned into a loud knocking, and broke his trance with the shard. It came from the door to his inn room, and now, it was obvious that this knocking was never from within his mind.

The sound perturbed X'ieth; it pulled him from a place of meditation on the shard. Instantly, his smile dropped into straight lips and he turned, looking to the entrance of his chamber—a door of wooden planks fastened together with bands of hand-wrought iron.

"What is it?!" he asked angrily.

There was a moment of silence.

"It is I," eventually came a voice through the door, both familiar and unwelcomed. *Zeros.* X'ieth lowered his eyes to the thin space between the door's bottom and its threshold, watching the mercenary's shadow dance as he shifted outside.

There was another moment of silence, in which his mind went awash in memories of talking with Zeros upon Arlem's streets. All in one instant, he remembered how Zeros confessed to being his father, how his mother took her life with Zeros' exile from Sergros, and how Talus was more or less getting back at Zeros through taking him in as an orphan. His straight lips became a frown, and his mind was left to wonder the obvious. *What does Zeros want?!*

"Please, do join us for a celebratory drink, before we return to Sergros."

X'ieth sat there on the corner of his bed, with his mouth devoid of words for Zeros. In his mind though, much went on. There, images arose of Nathan and Hammar grabbing at the bundled shard, back in the pub. An upset voice piped up: *There's little to celebrate with those who intruded upon your shard!* It was true, X'ieth did not like the other knights grabbing at the shard; it was not their property, and they had no right. *If you drink with them, it could happen again.*

X'ieth shook his head, acknowledging the truth in this, while also, realizing how his earlier reaction in the pub was likely viewed as inappropriate by his intruders. *How would you even drink with them, after what happened already?* He paused for a moment, weighing their perceived inappropriateness then, versus the inappropriateness they would perceive now, should he show no camaraderie whatsoever. *Nathan won't take it well if you skip drinking… Ugh.*

"I'll be down shortly," X'ieth said, wishing he had not spoken one moment later. *This will be nothing short of awkward…* His eyes trailed from the door, back to the shard. *Nothing short of distracting…*

The sound of footsteps started moving away from his door; X'ieth listened to them grow fainter by the second. When the footsteps could no longer be heard, he looked down to his hands, where the shard was now strangely cloaked again. As strange as it was, it was far less strange than other things concerning the shard, so X'ieth paid it little heed.

He reclined back on the bed, laying his head atop the pillow and resting the bundle atop his chest, just as before. Once again, he began to count the roof's support beams, and as he did, he let his mind return to the matter of Zeros and what this implied of his dreams.

If his whole experience growing up in Castle Sergros was only part of the king's ploy to punish Zeros, then his want to enter the knighthood was circumstantial, just as his achievement of that dream. In life, seizing each dream might be likened unto climbing the next mountain visible on the horizon, one that's seen from the peak of another mountain already climbed. And for X'ieth, therein lied the problem: he never would have grown up in Castle Sergros and never would have fancied the Guardsmen riding through the castle courts, had Talus not been using him to indirectly punish Zeros. And thereby, his place on a mountain already climbed was superficial, as was his want to climb higher, along with the opportunity to do so.

Cracks formed in his dream of the knighthood, even though it had already come true. And other such dreams formed cracks as well, like meeting Millicent and starting a family with her. *Outside of Castle Sergros and the sphere of Talus' influence, you would have never wed the daughter of once-seeing oracles.* The thought weakened his perception of actually living certain dreams, in that Talus' ulterior motives to hurt Zeros made everything seem fake: earning his knighthood, marrying the woman of his wild fancies, fathering a family.

X'ieth redirected his eyes from the support beams to the bundle on his chest, a thing that threatened his bigger dream of being Kayareth. And it was then the combination of his lived dreams and unlived dreams—his cumulative dream—started to slip into the darkness of his mind, like it was never meant to be and somehow, Karnatha had never divinely intended any of it for his life.

That prospect made X'ieth feel cheated, given the ideas that made him feel entitled to it all. *This life is wholly your good destiny—a destiny that should be divinely intended by the higher powers. Being the hero, a knight, a father, and a husband are all your dreams, and your every dream is meant to be. For it can't be, that you dreamt your dreams merely for them to become broken! Surely god gave you dreams for a reason.*

In the bed, X'ieth turned over to lie on his side, as if again turning away from Destiny, like he did in Forest Saol. In that position, he hugged the bundle in his arms and stared at the room's stone wall. And then, X'ieth began speaking in a metallic voice, with hardness in his heart against Destiny.

"I am the hero," he said, keeping his head above water, in his sea of denial. "And I am a noble knight. I am a husband, and soon will be a father. It's not my fault that spiders are re-spinning my web of destiny; it's not my fault that spiders are trying to change all of this. But I won't have a different life than the one I've dreamed. I won't."

He balled his fists and hugged the bundle tighter, and continued staring at the wall. Through clenched teeth he said, "I am the Child of Light, the good one who lifts Darkness from Karnath. I am he, the one to be called Kayareth, regardless of my re-spun destiny. I am he, regardless of Karnatha's will."

X'ieth shut his eyes and in time, he fell asleep to dream as he did so many times before. He saw himself holding the bundled shard in the middle of his channeling chamber. Fog drifted around him and rolled over the entire room from floor to ceiling, where his Source entry was nowhere to be found.

Immediately, X'ieth felt both cold and Darkness. He looked all around the channeling chamber, and behind him there stood a familiar sight. Once again, the box-like shadow loomed in the distance, just like in his dream—the one had in Forest Saol. It was a dream wherein a vesper spoke to him: *A shard of sword is more than what seems, for shards are those of broken dreams. And just as this, your shard is the choice you make in the wake of dreams breaking, so be careful about the choice you're making.*

X'ieth shivered. Slowly, his gaze drifted downward, to the bundle he held. And even more slowly, he pulled away the cloth, to expose the shard's nighty blade and its handle, which stuck out. Like ore to loadstone, the exposed grip pulled his hands, and his trembling fingers hovered over it. He fought the magnetism, refusing to touch the sword.

And then, breaking his aura of attraction with the shard, a distant stirring brought X'ieth to look up toward the box-like shadow, where the fog parted on both sides as a curtain being drawn. It revealed a set of double wooden doors hung upon a foggy backdrop, which showed carven inlays of thorns. And then, quite abruptly, the doors began to buckle as a strong force hit them from behind.

Boom! Boom!

The sound repeated itself, growing louder.

BOOM! BOOM!

As the doors continued to buckle, X'ieth watched blood flow out the crack, where they came together. It pooled at the base of the double doors, and in a river, it traveled toward his feet.

BOOM! BOOM!

X'ieth began alternating his gaze between the doors, the river of blood, and the shard. When he looked at the shard on one occasion, its aura of attraction was restored, and instantly the sword pulled his hand closer. His fingers trembled as his resistance against the shard weakened, and just as the door, he knees began to buckle.

BOOM! BOOM!

When his fingers were a hair's length from touching the shard's grip, a different loud noise broke his aura of attraction for the shard, making him reflexively look up.

CRACK!!!

X'ieth watched as the buckling doors suddenly burst open, as their locks busted. And behind them was a wave of blood as high as the ceiling, towering over X'ieth and now, crashing down!

In the split second before the crimson wave hit, X'ieth uttered, "Karnatha gave me dreams, because they were meant to be! They were meant to be, not this."

At the last word, the tide of blood struck X'ieth—immersing him, drowning him. And just as the blood washed over the room, otherworldly chimes filled the air, along with the sound of a child's cry, both faint and inconsolable.

KNOCK KNOCK!

A loud rap upon the door awakened X'ieth. He opened his eyes, and found himself hugging the bundle, and staring at the stone wall from his place on the bed. From over his shoulder, he could hear a voice through the door, outside the room.

"Come for a drink?" asked Zeros.

X'ieth blinked several times, a bit shaken by the dream. *Those sounds were heard in Forest Saol—the child crying, the chimes. What do they mean?* His mind pondered the question, which came and went without an answer, and left X'ieth unsettled.

KNOCK KNOCK!

Again came the knocking, breaking his thoughts.

"All right, already!" called X'ieth, irritated with the persistent knock.

He grunted, got up from his bed with the bundle in hand, and went to the door. The young knight undid the lock, and opened it up to see Zeros standing there, in the hallway on the inn's upper floor that led to the other rooms. Although the mercenary appeared exactly the same as before his confession hours ago, X'ieth had trouble seeing things that way. *He looks different now...*

"Let's go," X'ieth said glumly, with little appreciation for drink, meal, or sleep. *Do this for the others, if not yourself.*

Down the stairs the two proceeded, out the inn, and into the adjacent pub. There, all the knights had a spot on a long table, situated in the middle of a space filled with people, warmth, and the clamor of talk. Candles flickered light onto the shadowed patrons sitting beneath, and as typical of pubs in Arlem, the scents of sawdust, fermenting ale, and smoked bakus root filled the air.

X'ieth was seated at the table opposite to Zeros and held the bundled shard. From his seat, he looked across the common room at the pub landlord, a round and pudgy man, whom Nathan engaged with the coin he saved by inquiring of the king's credit throughout their quest. He stood there before the landlord, bouncing a small sack of moneys in his palm; it was tied at the neck and jangled as it bounced.

"Keep those ale coming," Nathan exclaimed, "for all my knights!" While speaking, he motioned to the long table where the others were seated. And after that, the pack leader handed over the coin to the pub landlord, who received it with a grin and hurried off to fetch the first round of ales.

Within a few moments, five iron mugs landed on their table, brimming with foam. And so started X'ieth going through the motions of drinking, without his heart in the act. He lifted his mug at Nathan's recommendation of a toast, and the rest became repetition.

X'ieth abstained from much conversation, simply watched the others have a good time, and on occasion, sipped his ale dispassionately. It was mainly Nathan, Hammar, and Finnel laughing together over their ales, and X'ieth and Zeros remaining stoical, perhaps under the guise of listening.

As conversations ensued, X'ieth was glad that no one brought up what happened earlier concerning Finnel and Nathan attempting to touch the bundle and him exploding. With that in mind, X'ieth leaned his elbows on the table.

"Yeah, fortunate for me," he muttered, looking down dreamily at his prized possession, wrapped in his cloak. *The shard... Your shard...*

X'ieth found himself less repelled by the having the shard with him. In fact, it started to feel comfortable and familiar. But beyond those things, having the shard made X'ieth feel better over his realization that so many things in his life were not as genuine as they seemed. For that realization left a gaping void inside of him, and strangely, the shard was filling it. *The shard... Your shard...*

Distantly, X'ieth could hear Hammar and Finnel jabber on, getting progressively drunk on the ale.

"This was your look then, elf!" the dwarf said rowdily, recounting their fight with the vespers and wearing a silly grimace for Finnel's benefit.

Finnel laughed and slapped the table hard, causing X'ieth to look up, disturbed from the sudden noise and vibrations. Nathan joined in their boisterous, drunken laughs, none of them able to keep a straight face for very long, and all of them swigging ale then wiping their lips when the laughter stopped.

After less than an hour, a dozen empty mugs stood on the table, and the pub landlord was hasty to set down more, brimming with foam. When the landlord left, X'ieth glanced at Zeros, who buried his face into both palms, with elbows upon the table and forearms raised. When the mercenary peeked out, the young knight looked away, bothered by the mere sight of his face.

Suddenly, X'ieth detected some stirring in his periphery. It was a disturbance on the stage along one side of the public room, where clearly a vocstrum got ready to perform. *Just what you need: to hear The Child's Triumph again. You'll have to drink through this one. A good thing you just got fresh ale...*

X'ieth looked into the latest mug of sudsy ale that was set before him, untouched and ready for his lips. He raised the mug and started chugging down the ale, during which he heard the fast strumming of a few practice chords, and then, a young clear voice singing the song.

"The Child of Darkness to Gallow Cliff, the Age of Darkness he shall gift..."

All of a sudden, X'ieth began choking on the ale. He lowered the mug instantly, hacking and coughing. The young knight clumsily grabbed the bundled shard, stood to his feet, and looked at the stage. In its center stood wild-haired Lucen appearing as a vocstrum; he wore green and blue-checkered garb and a pointy hat, while holding a seven-stringed, bowl-backed danar lute.

X'ieth suddenly felt a weight lifted from his arms, as the black shard fell out of his cloak and onto the table, hitting several mugs of ale, which spilled all over! Hammar started laughing at the accident, and seemed unaware that the black shard had made an appearance in Arlem's pub.

X'ieth turned to his left and also his right, hearing nothing but Hammar's raucous laugh overtop of a deathly silence. And sure enough, he saw how every eye in the pub was either upon him or the black shard. In the background, he noticed Lucen upon the stage. When X'ieth made eye contact with the youth, Lucen smiled, winked, tipped his pointy hat, and then vanished into thin air.

The young knight's attention went back to those in the pub. Some people were now standing while others remained seated. Wide eyes, open mouths, and gasping rippled through the crowd.

"It's... it's the black shard," someone finally shouted, over Hammar's laugh.

"He's the one from before," another added, "one of anger, wrath I'd say!"

X'ieth saw an older man stand at his far right, who wore a dusty blue tunic that tied at its neck and gray trousers. His face was smooth and covered in wrinkly skin, dotted by piercing green eyes, and his head was bald, with only a ring of white hair left. With an upraised hand and a pointing finger, he singled out X'ieth.

"This knight from Sergros is Shaizan, the Child of Wrath! He's the Child of Darkness!"

Just as his former proclamations, this one stunned and hurt X'ieth. He could not believe what was happening.

With the man's words, X'ieth witnessed Arlem's pub go into uproar, more people immediately afoot and talking loudly, as prejudice rippled through the crowd, just as shock did a moment sooner. Surely to them, any man of wrathful demeanor possessing the black shard was the worst of bad persons—the

Child of Wrath named Shaizan, a figure lifted from the pages of the Dark Prophecy!

Wasting no time, X'ieth wrapped his cloak about the shard, took up the bundle, and headed for the door. The people between him and the exit cleared from his way immediately, as if he was infected by the plague. As distasteful as the gesture was, it gave the young knight a clear escape and he was not about to protest.

Out from Arlem's pub X'ieth went, as fast as his legs would carry him. As he took to the streets, winds immediately pounded his body, but X'ieth was unfazed. With everything going on, the chill on this cold wintery night was the least of his concerns, by far.

He ran and ran faster, at first hearing only the patter of his feet layered on top of the wind. But in a matter of moments, additional sounds could be heard— the door to Arlem's pub being thrown open, and the sudden scurry of Arlemers on the cobblestone, following X'ieth.

"He went there!" one shouted.

"Don't let him get away!" cried another.

X'ieth kept running, sprinting all the way to Arlem's residential district, beside its well for drinking water. He stood at the well with the bundle in his arms and the wind blowing over him. From a distance he saw floating lanterns and torches, as the Arlemers following him converged on his spot, some already having pitchforks and axes in hand!

You need to run! Get out of here! One part of X'ieth urged him to flee, for his safety's sake. Yet another part of him had a different idea. *Touch the shard...*

There on the cobblestone walk, X'ieth acted without understanding his own actions. He unwrapped the black shard once again, and looked down at the mirrored, nightly blade as the moonlight basked over it, giving the sword a dark brilliance that continued to consume the young knight with deep, unfounded desire.

In that very moment with his prized possession, X'ieth wanted it more than anything else, just like in his room. It had filled a void left vacant by so many things in his life that no longer fulfilled him like they once did. It had done him a favor, and begged his attention. *Touch me.*

He watched the Arlemers stop about ten cubits from him, a number of men and woman varied in age, dwarves and elves too. A glance over his shoulder revealed the same mix from behind, surrounding him on all sides. An angry crowd X'ieth saw, two rows thick carrying assorted tools, lanterns, and torches, all waved in their hands beneath Arlem's hat of red slate rooftops adorned with Karnath's night sky—a sky rent in gloom's cloud and shining star.

There's forty, thought X'ieth, *maybe more.*

"We've got him!" shouted a man at the mob's front, who stepped closer.

"Wait, he's got the shard!" warned another.

"Is this what you want me to do?!" X'ieth shouted, putting his hand close to the shard's handle, as if to gesture touching it.

Gasps rang out from the mob.

"That's what the Dark Prophecy foretold!" a young woman shouted, frantically. "It says he'll touch it!"

"Well, that's what you'll make me do!" snarled X'ieth. "Prejudice can be an awful thing, don't you know?"

"You'll make the choice yourself," Nathan said.

X'ieth turned to see Finnel and Nathan standing there, a bit woozily, with their swords drawn. Zeros lingered behind them, with his weapon left sheathed. Hammar was nowhere to be found, and was perhaps still laughing in the pub, by himself.

"Prejudice can only lead to poor choices, but still one's choices they are!" continued Nathan.

X'ieth swallowed hard, worried where this confrontation would lead. But with his swallow came a strange feeling, a tingling sensation that started in his scalp and ran down to his toes. It sent chills through his entire body, and he shuddered before the mob, still holding the bundled shard. *What's happening to you?!*

As a matter of instinct, X'ieth entered his channeling chamber, only to watch it enlarge from small and ordinary to the size of the space he often saw in his disturbing dreams, where it was robed in fog. His eyes followed the walls and ceiling, which moved outward in an expansion. *How in the Void?! It's like tethering without anyone else!* The ceiling became vaulted and the space grew many times bigger.

X'ieth turned about and saw not his simple Source entry with its loop handle, but rather the double wooden doors from his dreams, featuring carven inlays of thorns. At the sight, he remembered how the doors opened in his latest dream, and a wave of blood crashed over him. He cringed at the memory of being drowned in blood.

He opened his eyes and in so doing, returned to the mob in Arlem. X'ieth felt the phantom sense of cold prickles all over him, from whatever took place. Sudden motion on the red rooftops directed his attention there, where a middle-aged man of brown hair stood, wearing a dark surcoat of obsidian buttons and a nightly cloak flapping behind; it showed three falling white stars.

In an aside the mysterious figure shouted, "I am Sydullus, Lord of Suffering, and live for your pain and that of others! With your chance of entering Arlem comes trial, and by trial comes growth. Now, arise to your awakening!"

When the man disappeared without a word, X'ieth returned his focus to the other knights confronting him, and also the crowd. *You're amid something oddly Dark*, he told himself, *something not understood!*

"Drop the shard!" ordered Finnel. "Only innocent blood will be shed by this!"

X'ieth called out, "This oddness upon me, is not of my doing! How can I be blamed for all that's amiss? You heard the vocstrum's song, did you not?! The Child's Triumph goes much differently!

"No vocstrum has even sang tonight!" said Nathan.

X'ieth was shocked. *Lucen sang from the pub's stage. Didn't anyone hear what he sang?!* The young knight heard gasps and murmuring on his every side.

"He's crazy!" one shouted.

"A dangerous loon!" declared another.

"A monster!" added one more. "Just look at him!"

"Put down the shard, or else!" ordered Finnel.

When he did not comply, X'ieth noticed sudden movement from both Finnel and Nathan: their legs began to run; their arms swung their swords back. He did not want to fight them, but he knew despite that, they would fight him. And so, knowing what he had to do, he went into his enlarged channeling chamber, not knowing what to expect. *Something has happened to you, man. Something strange…*

Inside the room, now enlarged, X'ieth again faced the strange set of double doors. With a turn of his head, he noted how his Source exit showed of similar appearance, from across the enlarged space. He returned his eyes to the Source entry, fearing the imminent act of drawing Nexus. *You'll need magic to protect yourself, even if not to fight them. Just open them…*

Suddenly then, X'ieth heard the same otherworldly voice from Saol echo the channeling chamber. It was garbled and deep in tone. *Darconas!*

"Your shard presents a choice, much like opening a door of ivy or of thorns. It is a choice, just as leaving these doors closed. Doing nothing and something are both choices. And so, you'll awaken to your choice, like everyone in Karnath has awoken to choices in the wake of his or her broken dreams. Renewed spirit, contempt for life, or apathy… All choices…"

X'ieth tracked the voice around his enlarged channeling chamber, but he could not place it. And so, not being able to locate the voice and not understanding these arcane words, he walked to double-door Source entry. He stood there for a moment and sighed, wondering if given the circumstances, this were really a choice at all. *By the chance of everything happening, you have to open these doors.* X'ieth grabbed the handles, preparing himself to pull the doors open.

"Dark on us," said Darconas, from out of nowhere. "You've made your choice as have they. Badness or nullity in exchange for broken dreams is Karnath's barter, with only few finding dreams anew. You too, might feel inclined toward the same, but remember; sometimes what feels natural is actually the wrong choice. Badness and nullity should be avoided, even if life momentarily doesn't offer all that it should."

Strange words from a strange being... Just open these doors, and use the Nexus before its too late. Thoughts pressed him, of Nathan and Finnel's impending attacks.

In one sudden motion, X'ieth used all his might to pull open the doors by their bronze handles. And in so doing, he pulled against his mental restraint. The doors gave way, and as they did, he watched light form all along their edges, right before a torrent of power flooded in over their threshold!

He watched the torrent flow all around him. It flowed and flowed, filling the enlarged room from floor to ceiling, and with it, his aux core. In the chamber now filled with Nexus, a concentrated whorl of energy encircled X'ieth, rising up from the floor and high above his head. It was a sheet of raw Nexus—aqua green in color, surging like lightning, and raging like fire.

This immense power was unlike anything that X'ieth had ever wielded before, and it bestowed confidence to the young knight that he could do whatever was needed. *Even mind control.* And it occurred to X'ieth then that he should do just that. *Use mind control to change their minds. Simply make Nathan and Finnel think differently, and stop their attacks.*

With that idea, X'ieth used the energy all about him to push two distinct streams through his room, to the corresponding spots where Finnel and Nathan stood in Arlem. X'ieth then used a trigger of picturing their heads as a proxy for mind control, and at the very thought, two Source exits of blue energy appeared. *This is where you go, to access their firewalls. It's working!*

Eager to defuse the situation, X'ieth jumped into both Source exits at once and simultaneously traversed separate flows in a bizarre out-of-body experience. It was likened unto going down a winding tube of blue energies, wrought in Nexus.

After traveling the tubes of blue Nexus, X'ieth saw two dams suddenly appear, face-to-face; these symbolized the firewalls of Nathan and Finnel. He glanced down at his own body, but saw no arms or legs. Yet, through sheer will, X'ieth punched and kicked the dams until cracks formed. *Just like my dreams*, he thought, as he widened the fissures with his continued blows, until they gave way to small holes, from which blue energies shot out, and the dams sprayed each other!

X'ieth dove into the opposing sprays, and immediately found himself back at Arlem's well, surrounded by the mob and confronted by Nathan and Finnel, who ran toward him. Zeros stayed behind, with a face full of dread, waving his arms while crying aloud, "Put down the shard!"

With a scowl X'ieth said, "Oh I've wished all along that my fellow knights would think better of me than the commoners! If I could *change your mind*, I would."

X'ieth felt the connection to the minds of Nathan and Finnel, which seemed like he held both knights by the throat and could change their behavior at his whim.

Nathan and Finnel ran closer, and when they were about three to four cubits away by X'ieth's judgment, the young knight spoke in a hushed tone, not much louder than a whisper. "As this shard kills my dreams, perhaps you should suffer the same."

X'ieth watched as Finnel and Nathan stopped running under his mind control, with their eyes rolled up in their head. But immediately after they stopped, both knights threw their swords to the ground, and synchronously fell right upon them!

All in one moment, X'ieth's eyes widened, his eyebrows raised, and his jaw dropped open, as he was aghast over what had happened. He watched in horror as Finnel and Nathan's knees hit the cobblestone at precisely the same time with a deft thud.

His eyes found the crimson swords jutting through their guts and out their backs. His eyes found the blood that flowed all over the streets. His ear found their sounds of death, the gargles and wheezes of brave souls passing from this world. *What have you done?!*

Gasps rang out from the mob.

"What devilry is this?!" exclaimed one.

"That's a terrible sight!" shouted another.

"Shaizan is more a sorcerer than a swordsman!"

"He thought we wanted a monster, and he gave us one for sure!"

As the comments died, so did Finnel and Nathan, toppling over on their sides, in a pool of red.

X'ieth looked up, and saw Zeros with a look of terror behind his eyes. He stepped forward with an upraised hand, seeming cautious. "Don't do this!"

In the young knight's mind, ran a counter encouragement. *Touch me. Touch me. Touch me!*

X'ieth once again looked down at the shard, since it begged for his attention. And upon making eye contact, its aura of attraction was restored. Like many times before, the young knight felt his hand suddenly drawn to the shard's grip, as if the sword was a magnet and he was metal.

"Don't do this, X'ieth!" Zeros pled, yet again.

X'ieth fought with himself, trying hard to avoid touching the shard's grip. But then, something happened inside of him. He realized how he was at a critical juncture, exactly like his father once was. *Zeros forfeited greater purpose than the purpose Destiny affords him now, by killing his command and leaving behind the glory that followed Garlew. Likewise, will you be as pathetic as him, by forfeiting the shard and handing over a greater purpose than the purpose Destiny affords you?*

Visions filled X'ieth's mind, of Shaizan riding a black horse at Gallow Cliff, and there, commanding a host of giants to victory against Kayareth, as was foretold in the Dark Prophecy. While it was certainly not his childhood dream, he started to wonder if this Dark purpose was greater than what his life would otherwise afford him, in the absence of the black shard.

X'ieth stopped fighting the force, and let his hand be drawn to the shard's grip, effectively letting Destiny decide whether he would touch the shard or not.

"What is meant to be, shall be," he said. "So let the cards fall as they may!"

As his fingers came a hair's length from the grip, the Arlemers went wild.

"He's about to touch it!" one said.

"That's the prophecy's fruition!" said another.

X'ieth suddenly let go of the cloak; it fell to the cobblestone and lied at his feet. And then, his fingers made contact with the shard's grip, eliciting gasps and more comments from the crowd.

"No!" screamed Zeros.

"He touched it!" shouted an elf.

At first contact, X'ieth felt nothing special. His life or purpose did not expand, nor did his ego. He had taken the final rite of the Child, leaving the outcome to chance, only to find the deed surprisingly underwhelming.

But then, Lucen's words came to mind: *This shard has a core that no mortal could ever fill with energy, one that is nearly bottomless.* He remembered how Esmeralda accumulated energy in the sword, and X'ieth thought that perhaps a greater destiny would come by just that. And so, he tapped the Nexus.

In his channeling chamber X'ieth pulled open the double doors, and in came a torrent of energy, just like before. This time, however, his Source exit opened on its own, and the energy passed through his chamber and into the shard's core. By this means, torrent after torrent of energy went into the shard. When X'ieth opened his eyes and looked at the nightly blade now ignited green, just as he witnessed in Esmeralda's tower!

Immediately, the crowd's fear could be heard.

"Stay back!" cried a man.

X'ieth looked at where the sound originated, seeing many warding him off with their pitchforks, axes, and hoes.

"You wanted me to be Shaizan?!" shouted X'ieth. "Well, there you have it. I touched the shard. I'm Shaizan."

X'ieth said the words half mockingly, as if a remote part of him doubted the prophecy and questioned the significance of him touching the shard. But when he looked down and inspected his skin, X'ieth became scared. It had reddened all over and his muscles bulged beneath, as blood coursed through enlarged veins on his arms! His heart pounded from within his chest, and he could literally hear its deep throbs.

Thump thump, thump thump, thump thump!

Given what happened, he had to wonder. *Are you Shaizan? Are you Shaizan?!*

X'ieth watched Zeros retreat into the mob of Arlemers—face-forward, his eyes wild with fear. He spoke, while taking each step back.

"What have you become?!"

Then suddenly, Zeros turned about and sprinted through the mob. Some people left the mob and followed him off into the night, dropping whatever they carried and screaming as they went.

"Let's go!"

"Save yourselves!"

X'ieth called out to Zeros. "Resign yourself from problems, father… like you always have!"

Zeros ran away from a big problem indeed—a self-fulfilling prophecy. The Arlemers assumed X'ieth was Shaizan over him merely possessing the black shard, which was unfair, prejudiced, and ultimately influenced his decision to touch the shard and become just what the Arlemers feared.

The young knight shook his head, disgusted by the situation. *Karnath wants to believe a Dark Prophecy more than disbelieve it! The people want you to be Shaizan, more than yourself!* His feelings over these perceived sentiments hurt him deeply, and X'ieth grew so angry that he shut his eyes and imagined fire raining from the sky to consume Arlem. *Just have this city of prejudice go away!*

And then unexpectedly, there was a flash of light behind his eyelids and the sensation of terrible heat.

When X'ieth opened his eyes, he saw fire had erupted upon every rooftop in Arlem, as far as the eye could see! In response, the crowd went crazy, as people turned to push past others, frantically trying to leave.

"He'll destroy the city!" one said, fleeing the well.

Just like the impalement of Finnel and Nathan, the outcome was not want X'ieth wanted. Yet, it was related to what he had thought. And so, not wanting to hurt anyone or damage the city, X'ieth thought how he should not imagine such things anymore. *Just stop it!*

"He's monstrous!" a woman shouted.

"Aye, a monster! Everyone run for your lives!"

The people scattered like straw, running and screaming into the night. It upset X'ieth even more, how they misunderstood him.

X'ieth closed his eyes, wishing that people who did not understand him would just go away. But when he opened his eyes, just that had happened, though perhaps in a way he had never imagined.

The people fleeing the well—perhaps forty or so in number—were all gorily dead, with their mangled bodies strewn throughout the residential district. The cobblestone walk was painted crimson and littered by body parts, as if the people had been torn to pieces.

When X'ieth looked down, he saw that his hands were bloodied and that the black shard was no longer glowing as before. In one sudden instant, his heart skipped a beat and leapt to the top of his throat. His hands trembled, and his mind struggled to work. *How did this happen?! The innocent blood of Arlem is on your hands?!* The reality jarred X'ieth, unlike any experience thus far on his quest.

Now panicky, X'ieth closed his eyes, imagining different, that the people of Arlem would be safe. Yet, upon viewing the streets again, he saw orange glows at the locks of every door, with each glow sourced by its own stream of green energy. He followed one stream backward, and found that it emanated from his own aux core! *No! No!!!*

X'ieth opened his mouth in mixed awe and horror, and watched the locks melt, just before terrible sounds emanated from the doors and windows of homes, below their roofs now ablaze.

All over the residential district, X'ieth could hear a sudden pounding as those trapped behind locked doors within their homes tried to escape. His eyes went from one window to the next, seeing flames dance behind the panes and from within the houses, after the roofs gave way to the fire. And those fires that lit up second-story windows were a preface to yet another horrible scene, where many jumped from the windows to the cobblestone and broke their legs, as told by the cracking of bones and loud wailing that filled the entire corridor. And beneath all the dreadful noise, X'ieth could hear the inconsolable cry of a lone child.

A bit traumatized, X'ieth moved through the streets, listening to more people pound upon their doors from inside their homes and scream at the top of their lungs. He moved through the streets, listening to others wailing from the cobblestone, with broken legs or worse. The sights and sounds were horrific, and made X'ieth hesitant to believe this was really happening, as it seemed more a bizarre nightmare than reality.

"Let us out! Let us out!" many cried, varied voices from the fires. "Let us out!" Those screams filled the night with agony—the incredible pain from burning alive. It was the same had by those climbing higher to touch the sun, only to find that they were only fated to burn. And just as this, many in Arlem were fated to burn, by their own desires of greater purpose than what life afforded them, chasing gray dreams higher and higher until those dreams broke, a thing that ended in Arlemers giving up on ever trying again, and being placated by Sergrothian welfare versus dreams anew.   That placation led to them locking themselves away from the challenges of a life outside, and thereby, that placation led to their demise, turning stone enclosures into graves tonight.

As the young knight continued walking among those Arlemers who fell from above—those hurt and crippled now, still crying aloud—he closed his eyes again, wishing he had never come to Arlem from Saol. But this time, even though withholding his imagination of harming them, X'ieth could not shut out images of himself cutting down the Arlemers in the streets with that shard, like one hewing wood. *Stop it! Stop!* He wanted the images to end, but alas, they would not.

When X'ieth peeled back his eyelids, he saw the carnage wrought from the unwanted images that just went through his mind. Mangled bodies stretched over the cobblestone for his vision's limit, the remnants of people torn asunder. He glanced down at his hands, again bloody. And in his hands was the shard, speckled in blood. *How can this be?!*

His heart pounded all the more in his chest, his breathing quickened, and adrenaline flowed through him. He looked to his hands, again shaking, as was his entire body, both immersed in Arlem's blood. *Have you done this evil?!* he wondered with hysterics. *You're dirtied by the blood of those you swore to protect!*

To both knees X'ieth fell, as did his spirit. With all that had happened, the part of him that hated the shard was now awakened to what it could do in Karnath. Knowing these things pained X'ieth, and he cried out into the Darkness, with his hand outstretched to the Light that he formerly knew. His sea of denial went well above his head, yet he still found the voice to deny the Darkness upon him.

"I'm the Child of Light, not this! I am good!"

A long time passed, and slowly X'ieth stood to his feet with the black shard in hand. A tear streamed from his one eye. *Something has gone wrong with you, man... Why would you do these things?!* He felt terrible inside over potentially serving Fate's Fray to the Arlemers.

"Let Arlem become Baal!"

X'ieth looked over his shoulder and beheld the man in black, watching him as before. Sydullus leered from the rooftops, through dancing flames of orange and yellow. And suddenly then, into his ear wandered a familiar noise.

RAWWWRRR! RAWWWWWWWRRRRRRRR!

From his rear, X'ieth sensed a tall shadow engulf him, taller than any structure in Arlem, even the church with its spire. He turned around, and saw gray scales at his side, those of Gremel!

X'ieth looked up a pair of muscled, scaly legs that extended into her mid-section and chest, where on each side was an arm that bent at its elbow and had a set of large, scythe-like talons at its end. Atop her chest was her head, with a maw lined with razor-sharp teeth and backed by a horned pate. Behind Gremel's shoulders hung two leathery wings. Fire reached up the sides of her snout, and warned of her breath. She stared back at the young knight with her bright yellow eyes, striped by a fang-like pupil.

In the instant of seeing Gremel, X'ieth remembered the last he saw of her, how she fled from her own nest and left her eggs behind after Lucen gravely wounded her using the energized shard. His eyes scanned her body, looking for where the Nexus struck. Upon gazing over her chest, he saw it: a terrible burn, where her scaly flesh had blistered and bubbled.

RAWWWRRR! RAWWWWWWWRRRRRRRR!

X'ieth looked away, and covered his ear with his free hand. When he looked back, he saw Gremel lift one of her claws up to her face; inside her talons wriggled an Arlemer. In one sudden motion, the dragon stuffed the screaming townsperson into her mouth. Noises proceeded of Gremel eating her prey— squishes, sloshing, and snapping bones, all padded by screams.

X'ieth suddenly felt wetness all over him. He looked down, and saw wet blood on his hands and the same on the shard. He gazed back up, and saw how blood rained from Gremel's mouth onto him. And after the dragon finished munching on the Arlemer, flames reached up the side of her snout, a moment before she sprayed fire onto the nearby red slate roofs.

It suddenly did not seem as just coincidence that Gremel bloodied his hands and the shard, along with setting fire to the buildings. It made X'ieth wonder who really did these misdeeds in Arlem. *Was it you, or the dragon?!*

X'ieth faced Gremel on the streets of Arlem, against the backdrop of burning buildings and dead people littering the cobblestone. He brandished the black shard and wore his Guardsmen armor, knowing it was not the best defense against her fires.

And just as the young knight considered that, he heard footsteps on the cobblestone at his right. He directed his attention there, seeing a sinister man walk up from between two buildings. Shadows veiled his face at first, but after a few moments, it emerged into plain sight. He had black hair pulled into a tail, a dark goatee rung about the lips. In his hand was spiky black armor having gray accents. The figure resembled icons of Ma'althan seen throughout Karnath, and mere notion sobered X'ieth. *It can't be Ma'althan… It can't be.*

"Take it," the man said, raising the breastplate for X'ieth to see. "My armor is the armor of god. It protects against elements, giving strength to wield wind and fire…"

X'ieth blinked, and when he opened his eyes, he found the spiky armor on his body! He looked up, back to where the sinister man appeared, seeing no one there.

RAWWWWRRR! RAWWWWWWWWRRRRRRRR!

At the roar, X'ieth turned to Gremel. Once again, she had fire reaching up the sides of her snout. The dragon snorted loudly, and her eyes shined in the night. In the air, the wind swirled burning embers all around X'ieth, reminding him that the dragon would continue destroying the city by fire, if he did not stop her here.

X'ieth went into his channeling chamber, where he ran up to his double-door Source entry, grabbed the bronze handles, and pulled. A torrent of Nexus knocked the doors open, entering the room and going out the Source exit, and into the shard.

When X'ieth returned to the streets, the nightly blade was illuminated green with Nexus energy. He held the shard in both hands, and met Gremel's striking yellow eyes. *Vanquish her then, if you live to do nothing better!*

In balled fists, X'ieth held the shard in front of him, blade up and still glowing green. Reflections of the energy inside jumped about in the young knight's eyes, along with the light from Arlem's fire. The young knight's face grew gnarled like a tree in Saol, showing the anger he felt for the dragon. And then, in one sudden motion, he rushed Gremel with the shard, prepared to deliver death.

While running down the cobblestone, he watched her snout closely, anticipating her to breathe fire at any moment. When Gremel's mouth opened, it was moments before she spewed a stream of fire right at X'ieth! He saw the fire coming, and as a first instinct, ducked and then tried to roll beneath it. But the flames were lower than he judged and despite his efforts, he rolled right into the fire!

X'ieth saw flames all about him and could feel their heat, yet surprisingly he was untouched since the armor fed on them! It glowed red while eating the fire and then returned black, as before.

RAWWWWWWWRRRRRRRR!

X'ieth grunted, slapping his hand to his ear, as he got up from his roll and continued pressing toward Gremel. A few moments was all it took for him to be five cubits away from her feet.

Using all the strength in his legs, he leaped into the air and onto her left thigh, which was somewhat level from her bended knee. And just as his boots touched down on her scaly flesh, X'ieth saw a shadow loom over him; it was her left claw, coming right toward him!

He leaped before the claw crashed down, this time across Gremel's chest and up toward her right arm, aiming to land on its elbow. Amidst his jump, X'ieth saw how she suddenly retracted her talons on the right claw to create a deadly barrier of scythes to block his target—the elbow!

Still midair, X'ieth used magic to launch a fluid offense and strike several of the talons with the shard, having the objective of clearing just enough space for him to clear the claw. And just as planned, his shard moved in a green blur to hit the talons, showering gold and orange sparks, and displacing them just enough for him to pass through the claw, right before landing on the elbow.

RAWWWWWWWRRRRRRRR!

Gremel released a loud roar, and the sound pulsed through X'ieth's head, causing him severe pain. To cope with it, he chomped down his teeth, and blood gushed from his sore gums, greeting his tongue with a metallic taste. X'ieth looked past his pain to the prize: the path up Gremel's arm, to her shoulder, and then her neck. He ran in that direction, not waiting for an invitation.

The young knight dashed onto Gremel's shoulder, and she turned her head, literally eyeing him right as he approached with his illuminated shard. He ran across her shoulder, right before Gremel's neck.

"To the Void with you!" X'ieth cried, as he reared back the sword of legend, blazing green with Nexus energy. And with one deft swing, he slashed through her jugular and sent the energy inside the shard deep into her neck, dealing a cauterized wound that took off the dragon's head! It fell off her body to the ground without even a splat of blood, and only a loud thud.

Without a head, Gremel stumbled and then crashed into a stone building with flames shooting out of its windows and off its roof. As she collided into the structure, X'ieth held onto one of the barbs on Gremel's back for support; it extended up from the barbs on her tail. The impact reached the young knight's ear as loud and deafening.

X'ieth rode the dragon's fall, until he was close enough to the cobblestone, where he jumped off. He landed crouched on the street in front of the building just destroyed, with the black shard in his one hand. His broadsword was sheathed on his belt, and its cased blade touched the ground beside his knee. Embers flurried around his body, as he knelt in place, uncloaked and in Ma'althan's spiky armor that was splattered by Arlem's blood. Fires danced upon the houses that surrounded him, the spectators to his rise to wrath over Gremel, and also, her fall.

Suddenly, the clip-clop of a horse's galloping sounded from the young knight's rear. X'ieth turned around, hearing it continue as he did, only to find someone whom he did not expect to see. *Zeros!* Down the cobblestone street, the mercenary approached him on his horse with both hands on his reins. Arlem's fiery destruction loomed in the background.

When close enough, Zeros stopped and spoke.

"You didn't have to become this..."

Tears formed in X'ieth's eyes, as he recalled leaving the matter of touching the black shard up to Destiny, and his hand went to its handle, without a divine intervention. The outcome defiantly smacked his childhood dream in its face—his dream of becoming Kayareth.

"I was supposed to be the Child of Light," X'ieth snarled, against the crackle and hiss of flames. "I dreamed of it since a boy, not this. But Destiny had other plans..."

"Other plans perhaps, but good plans. Destiny gave us many gray dreams, some unattainable and some not. But even so, gray dreams are meant to inspire us, to make us reach farther than we otherwise would, not to send us into a downward spiral upon their breaking! Yet, upon your gray dream not coming true, you chose the latter…"

Zeros took one hand off his reins, put it to his side, and drew his sword. The steel left its casing with a metallic slide, and it met the air with glimmers from the fire's light.

"You didn't have to become this. You were meant for more, and you could have *chosen* better!"

X'ieth immediately felt conflicted over how many of his choices really led to this outcome. *It seems more of chance than of choice…*

"But despite your choice," Zeros continued, "I'll choose better, by striving to undo what was clearly never meant to be! I'll not have a son who extends my legacy of wrongful murder!"

"I've done no evil," X'ieth contended, "even if my appearance would suggest I'm the evilest of men!" He choked on his next words, being unsure of whom had done what. "It was the ancient dragon Gremel that destroyed Arlem by fire, not me!"

With the black shard, X'ieth motioned in the direction of where the dragon's head fell, a location now veiled by smoke. Zeros glanced over, and looked back with a quizzical face, as if not seeing anything there.

"No dragon testifies to your deeds, only Arlem's dead. And those innocent cry for an avenger!"

With those words, Zeros used his legs to sharply squeeze his horse, and charged X'ieth with his sword.

In that moment of being attacked by his own father in burning Arlem, X'ieth wished all the more that he had not come here. He wished Arlem would become like none of this had ever happened. But unfortunately, the young knight's desires and imagination were intricately linked to an immense power he wielded, a power yet to be entirely understood.

With that thought in mind, X'ieth took the black shard in both hands as Zeros charged him upon the horse, and he let torrent after torrent of Nexus energy pass into the sword, igniting its blade a fiery green. And then, as an expected product of his wish that Arlem would become like none of this ever happened, Arlem would instead become like it never was.

Just when Zeros was about five cubits from X'ieth, almost within striking distance, a fiery whirlwind suddenly emanated from the black shard and formed about the young knight! And that fiery whirlwind spun faster and grew larger and hotter in a single instant, incinerating Zeros along with Gremel's corpse, before sweeping Arlem into a molten mixture, where the entire city became obliterated. The whole time X'ieth was amidst it all, protected by his spiky armor; it grew blood red as it fed off the fiery carnage in Arlem, and as the young knight's imagination and desires did harm to the city and its occupants.

What just happened was the product of X'ieth handling the black shard as he struggled to piece together the shards of his broken dreams. What just happened was a careless act where his future would suffer.

For embracing the black shard caused X'ieth to downplay all his dreams come true, and to feel at lower lows than were real. The black shard distorted his perception of what might be attained tomorrow versus today, limiting his potential. The black shard made him bitter and resentful of god over a present situation, making him lose his Karnathan religion and all of its benefits to come. The black shard broke his relationships with his friends and family, just as it did with Destiny. The black shard was a vice that eroded his self-control and made him weak to the desires of his flesh.

Indeed, via the black shard of his present, X'ieth started to destroy his future by what happened in Arlem. And much like himself, the Arlemers met fiery destruction that day through their own black shards, where dreamer's dawn became dreamer's dusk for many, and their dreams fell short of reality, only to break apart.

"ARLEM BECOMES BAAL"

Chapter 69
The Evangelist Knight

The winds had greeted Sagult as he was leaving Logan, where he had witnessed Kort fulfill the prophecy by bringing a mist over Doj and lifting the village's famine. And ever since sailing out of Logan, the winds had been with him on the sea; they were providence from Destiny, and bolstered his faith in a plan that dramatically departed from his orders of bringing Kort to justice.

Instead, Sagult would ride up and down the Mainland's west coast, proclaiming Kort as the Child of Light and amassing believers who would go to Gallow Cliff and fight in his name, as the Army of Light. It was a plan that he would embrace, in spite of others who refused to believe.

From his position in the ship's quarterdeck, Sagult watched over his crew divided; they were standing upon the main deck, distantly squabbling and bickering. There were two militants going at it, both young males.

"Now see here, I ain't gonna be the one who tells Talus we disobeyed!" said the one militant, with his finger in the other militant's face.

"You can tell Talus whatever you want!" said the other militant, slapping the finger away. "Cause you don't believe Kort's the One of Prophecy, and you'll be back in Sergros by yourself, without us!"

So far, there were only arguments and no violence, so Sagult kept his distance, staying with the captain at the wheel, just hoping that they would not have to deal with a full-on mutiny before they reached the Mainland. And just as he held that hope, there sounded a clunking and clanging from the stairs leading up to the quarterdeck, as two armored knights ascended. *Not again...*

Anticipating another argument with two particular militants, Sagult kept his eyes on the blue sea until whomever was climbing the steps reached their top. During his wait, a gust blew, lifting his cloak and ruffling his overgrown, coppery hair on his head and face. From above, the riggings creaked as more wind swelled in ship's white sails.

When the two knights reached the quarterdeck, Sagult spun around and confirmed his suspicions. *Inklin and Retha, as expected.* The both stood side by side, with the stairs and the quarterdeck's railing behind them, laden with tired ropes and old lanterns.

Inklin was on the left, a middle-aged man of acute features: intense eyes, a sharpened nose, and a bald head showing a tattoo of Sergros' lion. He came with the reinforcements sent from Sergros, being a knight in the *Royal*

Protectorate, an order of lesser nobility than the Crimson Guard, its purpose being to attend Talus during his leaves from Sergros.

Retha was the woman on the right, another human knight in the Protectorate. She wore attire that matched Inklin's, similar to the Crimson Guard's outfit, though with blue instead of crimson accents. Her ears showed of multiple holes, likely for jewelry that she adorned herself with when not in the king's service. At the back of her head hung a tail of brown hair, tied with a string.

"We're going straight to the king," Inklin threatened, in a voice both scratchy and deep.

"Do as you must," replied Sagult, "but just remember to tell of the rice famine in Doj, and how this criminal rode a mighty leviathan to heal the land, exactly as the prophecy foretold of the Child of Light!"

At his words, Sagult noticed how those crewmembers and militants upon the deck who were likeminded with Inklin went to one side, while those likeminded with Sagult went to the other, symbolizing the divide The crew members and militants all looked up, watching and listening to him argue with the knights.

Sagult studied the supporters of Inklin; it was about half a dozen people mixed in gender, age, and race, all of whom were angry over being taken from their families for a mission that Sagult aborted without due cause.

If only they could understand and believe, thought Sagult. *Kort is so much more than a criminal… He's the only chance Karnath has against the Child of Darkness; he's the One of Prophecy!* Sagult's convictions over this never saw a single doubt in his entire trip from the Isles back to the Mainland.

"What even makes you believe?" Retha asked feistily, breaking Sagult's thoughts. He looked at her, seeing her shake her head; her tail of hair flopped about. "Kort merely watered some crops, the same that will be done better on the Mainland in a few years' time."

As his immediate reply, Sagult smiled without a word. He knew how when in academy, Retha joined a scholarly coalition between Sergros and Deardrum, on a project to innovate irrigation systems. After making contributions enough for her graduation, she chose to pursue an elite order of knighthood versus the more common and profitable path, of continuing her studies to be suited for the practice of Sergrothian law.

"You think it simple?" Sagult finally replied, "to have freshwaters of Arzan moved all the way to Doj?"

"I do," she said pointedly and without hesitation.

Inklin bobbed his head in agreement, and the one corner of his lip rose in a smirk.

"Well, I think differently," asserted Sagult. "Not the brightest of mind in Sergros could have done it, nor could the quickest of foot in Juniper, nor Deardrum's strongest of might! What Kort did was no easy thing."

Both Retha and Inklin scowled their disbelief.

Just then, the captain announced land was in sight.

"Breslin's harbor!" he yelled, from the wheel.

Sagult glanced to the horizon, seeing Breslin's pastel fisher homes from afar; they were several hundred spans away, hued in cyan, magenta, yellow, and teal.

"I'll take her to port!" said the captain.

As the ship sailed toward Breslin's port, Sagult anticipated what this news meant. *Change.* He would address the people first in Breslin, which he believed was the very first step in sparking a mass following of Kort upon the Mainland. The mere idea kept a smile on his face, as he turned back to Inklin and Retha.

"You want to know why I'm persuaded to believe?"

"Why's that?" said Inklin brashly, before Retha could even reply.

"Kort was at the right time and place, and did the undoable then." A wind bridged Sagult's comment with his next. "The prophecy names a feat not easily done and a situation not frequent, hence it remained unfulfilled until now. To me, there's little chance that Kort Al'starz is not whom I say."

Another wind interceded with Retha and Inklin still glaring, as if unmoved by the argument.

"So go if you will to Talus," Sagult urged them, "but be sure to spare no details. We all know what we saw. Kort lifted famine and fulfilled the prophecy."

After Sagult's words, Retha and Inklin stood quietly at his rear, and he turned his attention toward Breslin. The sounds of their talking became replaced with background noises—gulls squawking overhead, and the rolling ocean waves. Several minutes elapsed, and the town's distant colorful fisher homes came closer and closer in his sight, going from small to large.

It was not much longer until the ship came into the port, and Sagult looked over at a pier lined with desperate people pushing toward the pier's end, where the vessel would dock. They appeared destitute, with hopelessness in their eyes, speaking of their desire to leave.

Sagult suddenly heard orders from the captain.

"Lower the anchor! Wind the ties!"

For but a moment, Sagult looked away from the droves of townspeople on the piers, seeing the crew scurry across the ship's deck to execute the captain's orders. It was literally moments before the ship would be ported, and Sagult's mission of evangelizing Kort would begin. *Give them one more chance to come along...*

Sagult looked back to Inklin and Retha.

"But I'd rather you join me," he said, his eyes alit with passion and vigor. "It'll take faith to leave your comforts in Sergros, and venture to Gallow Cliff to do more and be more. But it's the opportunity of a lifetime, to fight for good destiny there! And you can make the choice to go if you want, to help the Child of Light save Karnath from Darkness!"

"I know right from wrong," Inklin retorted, "and will uphold the king's request, even when it's not in accord with my own."

"A man's duties to his king and country are there indeed," Sagult said with a nod, "and I shall pay for my choices one day, perhaps in Sergros. Though for a common good, I forsake all requests that deter me from this cause far nobler than even the king's!"

Retha shot back. "For this, you'll see the same punishment as Kort! You, and everyone else aboard this ship who follows in your way!"

"Then that punishment will be endured, for the greater good of Karnath!" Sagult shouted back like a zealot, his eyes fiery and his voice energetic. "I tell you verily, that this elf fallen from knighthood will change the Dark Prophecy! Kort is the Child of Light."

Their conversation lapsed, and soon Sagult could hear the sounds of gulls squawking overhead, waters lapping against the ship, and the distant talk of Breslin's townspeople.

"It's a ship! They don't come often!"

"I hope it can take us away from here…"

"Aye, there isn't much for us in Breslin!"

Sagult knew that these were exactly the people who needed to hear his good news, and he was prepared to deliver it. But before doing so, he would say a final word to Inklin and Retha.

"I've chosen my path, and you yours. The winds have been in my sails for this quick journey back to the Mainland, to tell all who will listen about what was seen! I believe Destiny clearly takes my side, but even so, the best of chance to both of you."

And then, Sagult turned away from Retha and Inklin, to face the people crowded on the pier.

"He's gone mad," Inklin muttered, disrespectfully.

But Sagult would not speak a comeback to those undermining words. Instead, he started his first proclamation of Kort upon the Mainland—the first of many more to come—by opening his mouth.

"People of Breslin, heed my words and trust what I say! I, the commander of Sergrothian soldiers sent to the Isles in search of Kort Al'starz, have great news for you!"

(Days Beforehand, in New Yoke)

Back at New Yoke's port Nym stood, waiting and watching. She fixated on the clouds in particular, staring at them across the rolling waves, with hopes that one of them would suddenly become the billowy white sails of her ship come in. *Not yet...*

Nym still looked for Kort, but was near the boundary of her physical limits with her pregnancy, the very edge of her abilities as a mere mortal. Being closer to delivering the child, she found herself generally uncomfortable, short on breath, and with difficulty walking.

It was easily a situation that challenged her locating Kort upon the Mainland, but despite it, she kept looking. Yet, search as she did for weeks, she could not find Kort in the west coast of the Mainland, and this was where she last saw him. Knowing that the Sergrothian militants had pushed both her and Kort westward on the continent before he disappeared, this outcome led to a startling conclusion: *Perhaps Kort is no longer on the Mainland? Perhaps all this time, he's been in the Isles?*

"Watch it, will ya?!" a young man shouted, from right beside her.

Nym looked over to where the man gestured, at her hand, guessing that she had pinched his skin when carelessly leaning up against the pile in want of comfort.

"My regrets," she said, and moved a footstep or two away from the pile. Immediately, people pushed to fill the space, and lean up against it.

She watched it happen with a sense of misery. *Guess I'll just stand...*

It was hard to lean or sit on the pier, given how crowded it became. Sitting almost certainly meant being stepped on, and leaning against the piles was not guaranteed. There were few piles and many people, and leaning was a pleasure coveted by all.

But in the middle of her discomforts from standing, a gentle wind rejuvenated Nym, serving a reminder that with wind comes change. And that reminder stirred up a number of matters she pondered, since the Forerunners punished her for doing more than interfering on the mortal plane. *They say Kort changed the Game, but can he even bear the burden of Garlew Il'therin?* she wondered. *Would he fulfill the prophecy by lifting famine from Logan?! Maybe that's why he's in the Isles?!*

Like the Forerunners, Nym did not know if Kort could manage as the Child, but regardless of his outcome, Nym would continue to feel deep, unconditional love for him. *I wish to be in his strong arms again, and I'll stop at nothing to place him, even though my strength wanes! If it must be, my dying breath will be in want of his presence and touch...*

While thinking about her wants of Kort, Nym imagined his face and being, and it filled her with heartache that she was so far from him, after searching city upon city and town upon town, after putting her best foot forward, and despite defying the Forerunner's threat of added punishment. Nym kept talking to people and listening, trying to discover information concerning Kort's whereabouts. She even went back to Breslin to search for him there a second time, as she was doing now in New Yoke. *But still, nothing...*

Weeks ago, Nym decided that added punishment or not, she could not give up on searching, for being separated from Kort far exceeded anything that she could possibly suffer now. *What more could the Forerunners do to me? Death?! This chasm between Kort and I is mental and physical torment, a spiritual torture just the same! These are far worse than death...*

Without Kort in her life, Nym felt that part of herself was missing, and she struggled with the vacancy day in and day out, in every breath of her lungs, with every throb of her beating heart! She could not stop searching for Kort, for it would mean to accept a loveless life of lonely heartbreak, and also, damning her child to a fatherless upbringing. *I'll have neither!*

With that resolution, out to the waters she gazed with hopes high but spirits low, wishing and wanting for a ship to take her to the Isles. *Perhaps a thing not destined to be...* she thought despairingly, not having seen a ship to port yet, after days of waiting.

It was a crushing thought, and Nym beseeched Destiny for answers. In an aside, she looked to the heavens and shouted, "Why Destiny, must my immortal's heart bleed so for mortal love? To be without the one I need, is equivalent to endless and unsatisfied want! There's no remedy to this, no getting better, or moving beyond, should I always be apart from him!"

The winds blew gently, the waves rolled, and gulls squawked out their depressing song, but Destiny did not answer. And so, Nym pressed the deity, continuing her grievous lament.

"To be without Kort, is summer and no rain, is spring lacking flowers! To be without him, is winter's cold and no snow, an autumn grimly gray—with no varied color! For me, my unfulfilled want of him is life near unlivable!"

Tears streamed down her face, and stained her soiled dress. The winds stirred her matted, silver hair.

"Life without Kort, is rust to my iron resolve, a stem of only thorns to my love's rose! I'm as restless as I am weary, as hopeful as I am ever let down! Oh Destiny, I am as healed by his memories, as I'm hurt by this life with him not had!"

Nym wept more and more, as her profound and bottomless sadness inside now poured out. But despite her cries to Karnatha, nothing sounded in her ears except the constant ebb and flow of the tide. It was like her life force, slowly and constantly going out of her, in spite of her moving no closer to her goals of finding Kort. And so, Nym mourned much greater than the gulls squawking overhead, which mourned only their lack of food. *Unlike them, I mourn losing everything! My life without Kort is simply not worth living...*

Nym looked around the wharf, seeing dwarves, elves, and humans of varied age and race in an utter state of despair, as they waited for the next ship to port in New Yoke. Upon seeing them, she realized that she had become just like them: hoping for better, though fearing the worst.

While she would to go to the Isles to solve her dilemma of lost love, many would go there to run from the gloom bearing down on New Yoke and Breslin. Though it was not the literal gloom as seen from Castle Sergros, it was of gloom of a different sort with similar effects.

Refugees fled to New Yoke in the wake of the Isles Conspiracy, and the influx of people led to economic stagnation, since they were dependent on others to have their needs met. They were consumers only and not producers through labor, which strained local resources, and created a situation that was exacerbated when provisions stopped coming from Sergros. As a result, crime flourished as the townspeople and refugees alike often just took what they wanted by force, if it was available for the taking. This made for an environment where the actual producers could no longer turn their labor into dreams, and many of the productive became slumped, downtrodden, and beaten by the world in which they lived.

The gloom made the people of New Yoke shadows of their former selves, who now, were on the run from null and bad destinies. In the course of meeting people in town, Nym knew many who fell upon such hard times that they planned to sell their worldly possessions in hopes of sailing to the Isles for an escape from their present perils.

It was a desire for a different way of life, one seen in the eyes of everyone standing on the pier. And Nym met their eyes with compassion, yet sadness for what the New Yokers lacked. For despite these people being hungry for change, nearly everyone lost the will to hunt. Some stayed as long as the handouts came from Sergros, whereas others worked at one job as long as they could, but in the end, everyone gave up and was fleeing a fight for their destiny.

Nym moved her eyes off the needy folk all around, and back onto the sea. In so doing, she returned to her own problems. She sighed wistfully, "Kort, I need you!" And then, she began praying again that a ship would arrive soon.

But as Nym prayed and looked out to the sea, time passed and no ships could be seen or heard. But suddenly then, against the intermittent whisper of winds, a sound came from behind. From over her shoulder, Nym heard the rhythmic thud of steps against the wharf, as someone clearly approached with a steady stride and a short gait. And with that sound came the scrapes of many feet, as people hurried to move out of the way for whomever came!

Nym turned with her eyebrows arched, at first seeing only the blinding sun. Immediately, she raised a hand over her forehead to shield her eyes, and then could see whom the people stepped aside for, a woman unlike most,

Magicia—the most powerful sorceress in all of Karnath, as named by the esteemed Guild of Sorcery.

Nym's eyebrows fell and her mouth dropped, as Magicia approached with gray eyes directed right at her! As she came, Nym looked over Magicia twice, just to confirm her vision was not betrayal. *It's really her...* She appeared as Nym remembered her, with braided red hair, and a green serpent pendant pinned at the neck of her yellow sorceress robe, which strangely was covered in gray dust and had its purple band torn from one sleeve.

Magicia stopped walking when a step away from Nym. "You wait for your ship to come in here, but maybe the *wrong ship*."

Nym's forehead wrinkled. *Does Magicia know of a ship going to the Isles? How does she even know I wait for ship to sail in?*

"What do you mean?" Nym replied slowly, with a mix of anxiety and heightened hope.

"I know whom you seek, and what you intend to do."

Nym's face turned red. It was not the first time she struggled to deal with the humiliation of a mere mortal knowing more than her.

Magicia continued, "And in your search, many choices present themselves, this one being most important."

Humbly, Nym asked for guidance. "Please advise me, oh powerful sorceress. How shall I be wise this day?"

Nym nervously watched Magicia stare back a long while without a word, as if somehow assessing her holistic state of being—in mind, body, heart, and soul. Then, with a pause, she finally spoke. "Waiting for a ship in New Yoke versus Breslin means very different outcomes."

Nym interjected, cutting Magicia off in haste. "I was to Breslin before New Yoke! Neither any ship docked there, nor would any come soon!"

Magicia displayed a warm smile. "Too quickly the traits of mortals mar your array of virtues, for presumption and impatience are coveted only by fools. A ship comes to New Yoke and another to Breslin, each to dock in days."

When Magicia said those words, Nym's face showed surprise and elation. *Two ships! Surely I can find a spot upon one of them!* she thought hopefully, in spite of eyeing so many people trying to leave the Mainland.

"But any voyage to the Isles," Magicia went on, "will make you and Kort pass like two ships in the night."

Nym's features morphed from happy and relieved to those of pensive intrigue. *Could it be*, she thought slowly, *that Magicia means Kort is aboard the vessel coming into the other port?*

"Do you say, that the one I love is aboard Breslin's ship?" Nym finally asked.

A long pause followed, delivered with Magicia's unwavering, unblinking stare. "Of that, I cannot assure you," Magicia said finally, with a smile. "But trust me, you will miss something special, should you choose the former over the latter."

With that, Nym watched Magicia walk away from the pier and back onto the cobblestone street, to leave her behind with mysterious words, and an impetus to risk missing a ship inbound to New Yoke, to catch another one inbound to Breslin.

(Days Later, Evangelism and Mutiny)

"People of Breslin," Sagult said from his ship. "Heed my words and trust what I say! I, the commander of Sergrothian soldiers sent to the Isles in search of the fugitive Kort Al'starz, have great news for you!"

At Sagult's words, those on the pier responded favorably. Eyes lit up. Smiles went all around. Surely many presumed the obvious outcome.

"You've found Kort, haven't you?!"

"Aye, we knew you would. But what took so long?"

Sagult waved his hands to quiet the crowd.

"No no, my friends. I have much better news than that! I have witnessed something that speaks differently to the character of this supposed criminal! Kort is someone who *we've been hoping for*!"

People grew silent, as a stunned look gradually developed upon their faces. But then, positive reactions slowly started forming throughout the crowd. People smiled and some started chatting noisily with the person next to them. It was a renewal of hope in them that Sagult was glad to see, and a renewal of hope that the people needed desperately.

For many in Breslin had lost hopes in their future upon the Mainland, and the mention of hope immediately caught their attention. Among dejected souls, one might not find others more dismayed than these, a whole lot of people with broken dreams, with only poor outlooks on the horizon. And as such, those gathered upon the pier were starving for good news.

Being upon the ship's quarterdeck, Sagult came closer to the crowd, bending over its railing as he addressed the people with an aura of zeal, and a booming voice that carried far. "Everything you've heard about Kort now changes with what I proclaim! Never have I seen such a splendid thing, not in all my life!"

"What is it?!" one shouted.

"Aye, tell us already!" exclaimed another.

Sagult calmed them again with his hands, wearing a smile from ear-to-ear at their eagerness and enthusiasm for what he had to say. Surely, his standing as a Sergrothian knight of high authority aided their expectations.

Sagult stopped waving his hands and for just a moment, surveyed the crowd. Smiling, he looked at clusters of people until a bright light suddenly shined in his eyes, sending a sharp pain through his head. It was a brilliant light, as if reflected off a sheet of silver in the midday sun, causing Sagult to suppress a grimace and divert his stare in the opposite direction. He started talking to avoid the people growing restless.

"Kort Al'starz rode the mythical leviathan to lift a rice famine from the fishing village Doj! And that village has an old port called Logan!"

Gasps rang out through the crowd. Sagult smiled in satisfaction. *Let that sink in!*

Someone from the crowd suddenly exclaimed in a loud voice. "Kort fulfilled the prophecy!"

Another person remarked, "Kort is the Child!"

It was then that Sagult shouted, "The words spoken are true indeed! Kort Al'starz is the Child of Light!" He cupped his hands and bellowed the last phrase, the sounds of his oratory lingering in the open air.

With a broader smile, Sagult watched the crowd go absolutely ecstatic. People hollered and cheered, throwing their hands up as lost hope most evidently flooded their souls. Their hopelessness was replaced with hope that Kort—one previously of poor standing—could somehow change the Dark Prophecy.

"This makes everything different!" a lady exclaimed. People about her echoed their hearty agreement.

"He'll change the Dark Prophecy!" a man said.

"Kort can change everything!" yelled another.

As Sagult listened to them, he smiled and began surveying the crowd again, following people who spoke. Another reflection of silver suddenly hit his eye, and sent pain through his head. Sagult maintained a weak smile and shielded his eyes with one hand, while continuing to look in the same direction. This time, he wanted to see what was causing the light. Beyond the glare, he saw an elven maiden having silver hair; the sunlight reflected off of it.

Sagult redirected his vision and continued.

"Those of faith, those wanting good destiny, I beseech you to sell everything you own and use the proceeds to travel to Gallow Cliff!"

Sagult suddenly jumped onto the railing of the quarterdeck with a bang, to stand even higher. He lifted his hands into the air, and spoke with intense features.

"Take up tools, take up weapons! Let us join the Child of Light at Gallow Cliff, in a battle for good destiny as the Army of Light! The one he confronts seeks to stop time and bring the Age of Darkness upon Karnath, a blight from which the land would never heal!"

The crowd grew excited, and all at once, turned for the pier's exit, and started pushing for it. Some shouted as they went.

"Let us go, and fight with Kort for good destiny!"

"Aye, to Gallow Cliff!"

"I'll give anything to get there!"

The people pushed around a horse-bound man right off the pier, who had been watching Sagult's address from the cobblestone streets. Sagult studied him, as he sat patiently on his horse, stroking the beast's head to calm her, as the people passed. *Does this man wish to talk with me?* He wondered.

When the pier emptied, the rider approached the ported ship. As Sagult followed the man and his horse, another blinding light hit his eyes, again as if reflected off silver, forcing him to momentarily look away. And when Sagult looked back, he saw the elven maiden of silver hair step in front of the rider, being about five cubits away; she had messed hair, tattered clothes, and looked as poor as anyone else. *What is she doing?*

Sagult watched as the rider tried to move around the maiden, but she jumped with surprising speed at the horseman's side, grabbing his arm and dismounting him!

"What are you doing?!" asked the rider, as he tumbled to the pier.

Shocked, Sagult watched with an open mouth and his hand frozen midair, seeing the maiden mount the black horse and gallop away, without looking back. Hoof clops against the cobblestone faded behind the man's voice.

"Thief! Thief!" the rider cried from the pier.

Sagult hopped off the railing, hurried from the quarterdeck, down the stairs, onto the deck, which he ran across to the ship's side that was tied to port. He jumped off and onto the pier, and ran down to the fallen rider. As he went, he shook his head, not understanding why the maiden acted as she did. *Rush to Gallow Cliff, but not like that!* he thought, his smile gone.

When arriving at the rider's side, Sagult reached down his hand, which the horseman took hold of. Sagult helped him to his feet, a young man in drab tunic and trousers, with a gray cloak over his shoulders.

Sagult brushed off the man's clothes as the fellow turned frantically in the direction the maiden left.

"How shall I ride to Castle Sergros!" he said with angst. "My parents expect me there in several days' time!"

"Postpone that trip," suggested Sagult, tugging at the man's sleeve, to get his attention. The horseless horseman turned from the cobblestone, and faced Sagult's brilliant amber eyes. "Follow me instead, for the fight of a lifetime! I'm going along the Mainland's west coast, and then to Gallow Cliff! Didn't you hear the wonderful news! Kort Al'starz, the elf wanted for Garlew's murder, is no worse a person than the Child of Light!"

"Do you mean…?" the rider asked, with excitement clear in his voice and his features alive.

Enthusiastically, Sagult cut him off, "Yes! At Logan's port in the Isles, I saw it with my own eyes—Kort rode the mythical leviathan to water the crops of Doj, a village facing famine! He lifted famine from Logan!"

Sagult watched, as the man's countenance proxied increased elation.

"That's unbelievable!" remarked the rider. "I had caught the tail end of your talk, and was wondering what all the commotion was about. My, that is unbelievable!"

"Unbelievable indeed!" Sagult remarked, patting the young lad on the shoulder before wrapping his own arm around it and taking him up the pier, in the direction of the ported ship where the rest of his evangelists waited.

Upon Sagult and the man taking only a few steps together, Inklin and Retha met them on the pier, wearing scowls. The two knights came to a sudden halt, and their blue cloaks flowing behind them fell still against their backs. Inklin was the first to talk.

"Only for reason of the king's commission, do we engage in insubordination. It wasn't right to have Kort go free without standing trial, regardless of what happened in the Isles."

Retha piped up then. "It's amazing that the people of Breslin didn't break into uproar over your news! If they had Kort in their grips a moment prior, many would exact justice on him before the Sergrothian courts could get the chance." She spoke about these things, as if disappointed.

Retha fell silent. Inklin's eyes sparkled with faint admiration for Sagult.

"My only pleasure here was observing the people's change of heart with your address. You certainly have a way with words."

Sagult took a moment to consider his mission again of evangelizing Kort's name with his fellow supporters. To be successful, they would have to garner a huge amount of influence over the people upon the Mainland.

"May my words continue to have power," Sagult said, with utmost confidence. "May all of our words together have power!" He motioned to his supporters standing tall on the ship deck, up above them. "Let everyone know, of what good Kort Al'starz has done and what good he shall do!"

From the deck, those sharing Sagult's cause threw balled fists into the air and blurted out cheers.

"Kort is change!" one said.

"Aye, change we need!" called out another.

"Let all upon the Mainland know!" yelled a third.

Sagult eyed his loyal few, and called out to them. "Hopefully the king's credit will be honored in Breslin, for us to acquire horses and crude supplies for continued travel. We shall need horses and provisions to ride day and night in the name of Kort, telling one and all that he's the One of Prophecy, being destined for a showdown with Shaizan at Gallow Cliff—in the name of the Light and Karnath's good destiny!"

Sagult smiled as more cheers came from his supporters on the ship deck, beneath the long white sails hanging off the masts. But to that smile, the dissenting Inklin and Retha could only show a bigger frown. In moments, they sighed, turned away, and began murmuring while stomping off.

Before going out of Sagult's earshot, Retha called back, from a distance, "This isn't the last you'll see of us!"

Inklin joined her, "We're right; you're wrong. You'll face your dues in the Sergrothian courts, where your precedent will serve for that of a criminal uncaught! Let's see how well your silver tongue fares there."

With his arm still around the young lad's shoulder, Sagult stood there on the pier and before his ship, watching the two knights fade from view. They disappeared into the townspeople who scurried across the cobblestone in haste to Gallow Cliff, after being galvanized by Sagult's words.

After a moment more of watching them, Sagult turned his attention to the rider, knowing that he, this young man, and his supporters together formed a band of evangelist knights with a common mission.

Sagult flashed a grin to him as they walked up into the ship. He prayed silently, *Destiny, please empower us!* And with that prayer, off he would go with his evangelists, out of Breslin and beyond.

"EVANGELISM AND FERVOR"

Chapter 70
Ledge of Doubts

ort sat on a ledge in the Jezban Mountains with his legs dangling over stretches of the mossy terrain below. From his vantage point, he could see the distant Tai Forest, and beyond that, the land's end where the blue waters of Korinth touched the sands. The sun lowered on the horizon, as nightfall imminently loomed over the land, promising some relief from the scorching heat suffered during the day.

It had been almost a week since Kort rode into Doj upon the leviathan and the monster created a mist over the fields, which saved the last rice crop. Days of celebration followed that event, uniting Doj and Reiju together and filling both villages with songs, dancing, eating, and other festivities. The people believed Kort was the Child of Light; they believed that they were saved from famine, and that Karnath was saved from the Age of Darkness.

But unexpectedly, things reverted to how they were before Kort lifted famine: the sun remained intense, baking the lands, the winds stopped, there was no rain, and by the week, fewer and fewer fish were caught at sea. Both Doj and Reiju viewed the situation as though more was needed than just Kort fulfilling part of the prophecy; everyone knew he needed to take the next step in order to truly heal their lands. And this was what brought him to Jezban and rendered him thoughtful about what to do. *My next step…*

Kort remained seated on the ledge, leaning back on his hands that rested palm-down upon the rock, and still dangling his legs. A voice raced through this mind, the female voice from the crowd of Dojese: *He is the chosen one, the Child of Destiny to restore Light to Karnath! He's the One who shall revert the Dark Prophecy to the Light!*

The person who spoke was a woman, an unexpected visitor from the Mainland who deliberately stirred up both villages to believe that Kort would indeed fight at Gallow Cliff according to the Light Prophecy, as opposed to following Elucid's plan of one shard up Liath. As a result of her doing, Kort was hard pressed over the decision.

Going to Gallow Cliff would betray his commitment to Elucid, and also, left him with reservations about failure and certain death without seeing Nym again. *If part of the Dark Prophecy has come true about me lifting famine, could the rest come true as well?* Kort wondered. On the other hand, going up Liath to destroy the shard would literally let down Doj and Reiju, whose expectations were set by the unexpected visitor.

Kort considered the possibilities. *So, under the pressure of the villagers, I could just disappoint Elucid by going to Gallow Cliff.* An image suddenly popped into his head of himself bloody and dead at the foot of Gallow Cliff with Nym nowhere to be found. He cringed; the idea was unpalatable. *Or, Elucid and I could stick to our original plan. We might even work toward overturning the peoples' expectations...* An image popped into his head of division in the villages by this means, and hostilities over the final choice; he shook his head. Neither option seemed ideal.

Alternative to these options, you might just wait and for now, do nothing... It was the temptation of null destiny hanging over him, being the safest option. But, the drawback to doing nothing was that it was the least effective at doing greater good for Karnath than just lifting famine, and also, appeasing the villagers and Elucid. *Me doing nothing will literally do nothing for everyone... And that's unacceptable.*

Kort sighed. After hours of mulling over the matter on yet another day, he still did not know what to do, and the sun slipped even lower on the horizon. His time was running out.

In a matter of minutes, footsteps sounded at Kort's rear. He looked over his shoulder only to see a familiar face: Genze. When he lifted famine from Doj, it spared rice crops that were thought lost. Needing rice, the people of Reiju were drawn into the village with the saved crop, and Genze was among them. Kort met him days ago, and met him now with a smile. The fisherman's attitude had drastically improved.

"The others are looking for you."

Kort's smile dipped into straight lips. And then, his face showed surprise. "Shouldn't you be looking for me too? I didn't think anyone knew where I was..."

"I didn't know, but a Dojese boy saw you leave the village. He told me you hiked up the mountain."

"Oh." With nothing more than that, Kort looked away from Genze, and off toward the horizon, wondering what his next horizon should be. Going back to the village would be a discussion about just that.

Genze walked closer, and sat down next to Kort on the ledge also letting his legs dangle.

"Tough choices are part of life," he said, looking at the dusk sky. "And it's not an option to avoid the choices, or leave them up to chance..."

Kort nodded his head, agreeing with what was said, but still not knowing how to decide.

"Remember when you stayed with me, in Reiju?"

Kort looked over at Genze. "Of course."

"Remember how comfortable you were there?"

With a smile and a laugh, Kort dropped his gaze.

"Not that comfortable! We were at odds," he said, studying the mossy terrain below.

"But not too uncomfortable to stay for weeks."

Kort's eyes went back to the fisherman.

Genze continued. "But my point is not so much that you stayed, but rather that you left, even though you had been comfortable staying for weeks. That decision took you away from your comforts, yet you made it for the better."

Genze placed a hand on Kort's shoulder.

"And just like that, I know you can make your decision again! C'mon… let's get back before it's dark."

"Aye," Kort said, with a final glance to the horizon.

With that, both he and Genze pulled their legs onto the ledge, stood up, and began hiking down the side of the mossy mountain, through a portion of the stalky Tai Forest, and back to Doj. The trip took more than an hour, and by the time they returned, it was early evening.

Genze led Kort back to Raiden's house, where Kort and Elucid had been having discussions. As Kort walked behind Genze and up to the house, he glanced out to Doj, seeing the distant rows of stilted fisher homes that stood before the rolling sea and docked boats, both at a distance.

The village was lit up, with nearly every window of every home agleam by a flickering candle. The village was alive with the sound of upbeat music, heard against the backdrop of chirping crickets and humming locusts. The villagers continued celebrating, playing their clappers, flutes, and guitars, all instruments of the Dojese made from Tai's stalks, used together to produce a lively tune.

Despite the return of dire circumstances in Doj and Reiju, the villagers still adored Kort. But he knew if his next step was not taken soon, that adoration would be short-lived. And with that realization, Kort went to pull open the sliding door, to go inside. But before he could, Genze called out to him.

"I must return to Reiju, but before I go, know that I believe in you Kort. I believe in you and your judgment, and wish for the best in whatever you decide."

At the comment, Kort smiled and glanced over his shoulder; Genze's type of support was just what he had needed: an attitude that left Kort's destiny in his own hands, and empowered him to make his own choices.

"Thank you for that, friend. If only others could afford me the same."

"Perhaps they will in time, and even if they won't, you might consider coping with that or finding different company! Destiny be with you."

Genze turned away, and started down the dirt road connecting Doj to Reiju.

"And with you as well!" Kort called to him.

Genze did not turn, and just kept walking the path.

With the fisherman gone, Kort entered through the door, and shut it behind him. When he turned around, the first thing he saw was Elucid, standing tall at the far left corner of the room and casting a long shadow over the floor boards. At the center of the room, sat a burning white candle in its dish, with runny wax going down its sides, and a moth flying about its flame. Behind the candle and on the wall, was a sliding door into Raiden's chamber. And several cubits from the candle, toward the far right corner of the room, sat their unexpected visitor: the renowned Magicia, the most powerful sorceress in all of Karnath.

She sat cross-legged on the floor, wearing a dusty yellow robe and her green serpent pendant at the robe's neckline; the robe's sleeves featured colored bands of the Guild, with one band having been torn out. Behind her shoulders fell her long braids of red hair. She had pensive features—pout rosebud lips puckered in contemplation and narrowed gray eyes fixed upon the candle. Even after Kort entered, she did not look away from it.

Kort's eyes caught motion as shadows cast by the moth danced upon the floor. He watched the gray-winged insect, still aflutter about the candle's flame. Again and again, the moth would encircle the candle, veering close and then flying away. The sight struck Kort as an odd phenomenon, where the light drew the moth, and it acted as either not knowing that fire can burn, or willing to take the risk of burning alive to chase the fire's allure.

"Be like the moth."

Kort heard Magicia's voice, though her mouth did not as much as move.

"What?"

"Be like the moth!"

Images entered Kort's mind, of him lying dead and bloody beneath Gallow Cliff. And then, superimposed on that image was the moth chasing the flame. He gasped.

All in one moment, Kort realized that should be go to Gallow Cliff, it was analogous to the flame that the moth chased, which had dangers that he in no way could anticipate when pursing great good to many. And the flame of Gallow Cliff could burn him terribly, for beyond his possible death, it might mean never seeing Nym again.

Yet Kort still chased the flame, and now upon knowing the danger of Gallow Cliff, he had to wonder if his hesitance to just leave with Elucid for Liath was a sign that he was willing to bear risks of death and not seeing Nym, for the best of good destinies—fighting Shaizan in the Battle for Destiny.

"Be like the moth!"

Kort heard Magicia's voice again, but still, her mouth did not as much as move. He shook his head, looking back from the sorceress to the moth meandering about the flame. And then, in an aside, he spoke to the moth about his inner conflict over the matter. "How many mountains shall I climb, only to reach the top and see yet another loftier and distant peak? Will I go yet higher, to even the sun, and burn alive in want of dreams larger than life?! There must be a balance, between the best destiny and bad destiny, wherein all can find the simple good, even one depraved like me! I fear that dreaming of Gallow Cliff is dreaming gray."

Kort looked back to Magicia, and this time, she actually opened her mouth and spoke.

"Have you decided Gallow Cliff?"

Kort's throat worked out a swallow. He was not sure what to do just yet. Even so, Magicia pressed him.

"It's the right choice. Take the shard of sword there. At the cliffs, we will enlist the aide of seroxians from Old Karnath to destroy the Child of Darkness! The seroxians are much more powerful than our legends make them out to be, and that power can help us win!"

Until this point, Elucid had been a silent and stationary mountain of armor in Raiden's house, towering over everyone. And now, that mountain moved and spoke in a boom that startled Kort. He jumped.

"The shard must be taken to Liath and destroyed. Stop insisting otherwise!"

"No!" Magicia shouted. "Follow the prophecy as written! The only thing you should be changing is winning versus losing, and the seroxians can help that cause. Have him go to Gallow Cliff instead of Liath."

Kort's eyes moved back to Elucid. He anticipated another clash from the crimson knight with Magicia, as their argument had been repetitive over days since the prophecy's fulfillment, continuing in bouts off and on. *And I'm stuck in the middle of it... Liath or Gallow Cliff.*

"Trust me instead of the sorceress!"

Elucid spoke to Kort instead of Magicia, and it surprised him. They had largely acted like Kort did not even exist, and merely would follow their end decision.

Kort turned and listened to Elucid.

"What I say is correct, Kort. You should journey to the highest peak in the eastern pass of Liath. At the summit, if you throw the white shard toward Ires Constellation with all your bodily might and all the faith in your heart, Ires Star shall consume the blade and ensure time evermore!"

Magicia piped up. "Everyone at Gallow Cliff will perish if the Child of Light does not join the fight! The seroxians may even turn on the lower races, if the Child is not there! It's part of my agreement with them…"

Elucid fired a quick response. "Let them go then, and face giants. Life is full of giants, especially in one's Battle for Destiny! You talk as though you presume less."

Kort followed the talking heads, back and forth.

Magicia answered, "The seroxians are not my main concern, rather I am concerned about *him*. To *him*, the people of Karnath will surely fall!"

At her statement, Kort had to wonder, *Who is this dangerous man to which Magicia alludes?*

"Then they must rise!" Elucid boomed, breaking Kort's concentration. "Whether they fall to him, or whether they fall to the seroxians, the people of Karnath must rise. Not all battles can be about winning, but all battles must be about fighting 'til the end. Those who have elected to fight at Gallow Cliff have courageously decided what they deem is the right fight, and they must fight with goodwill and for the good cause of their own good destiny! There's no cause greater than that. But likewise, Kort and I have a good destiny that's away from the cliffs, in Liath."

Magicia implored Kort. "Please, follow the prophecy as written; follow me to the cliffs! What Elucid is saying isn't supported by either the Light or Dark Prophecy, so how can any of us trust that?!"

Elucid boomed a response. "This is more Magicia's personal battle than anything else! Prophecy or not, that's why she's really drawn to the cliffs. What she won't tell you is that she finally remembers losing alongside Naketo there, with the seroxians on her side!"

Magicia gasped, as if Elucid had revealed something she had hoped to go unknown.

At the same time, Kort's mind immediately spun with questions over the mention of Naketo at Gallow Cliff. *Raiden's adopted grandchild, Naketo, the son of Garlew… lost at Gallow Cliff?! Lost what?! How even, as Garlew never wed?!* It was perplexing to hear about Naketo at Gallow Cliff, but Kort hardly understood why and kept silent, in hopes of learning by carefully listening.

"Our memories have been stolen from us," Elucid continued. "I, like you, have new premonitions by the day, and learn more and more about the fight we're in. While I don't understand why we've been losing this fight in times no more, I must acknowledge that we have been losing and that we need to fight differently, lest this continue happening! Going to Liath is fighting differently."

Magicia launched a comeback. "I too foresee a future already had, a future laid to waste, but what of it?! For time allows second chances and we can make this right—years before Naketo's maturity! Don't you see, we're in a different age, with different possibilities?!"

"Naketo's maturity? There is no Naketo," Elucid countered, "just like there's nothing to be gained at Gallow Cliff. Only loss and suffering are to be had there, like we've had two times already! Does there really need to be a third loss for us to come to our senses, at an earlier time than this?! "

The conversation turned strange and befuddled Kort; there was talk of different times, and people that could not even exist, so it was confusing for him at best. However, it became clear to him then that his choice was even more challenged, in that he could not understand the big picture concerning the Game. The situation prompted him to pray, while standing there and listening: *Please Destiny... Help me make the right decision in spite of my lack of understanding! For I must decide so that I can finish my course, since like Elucid said, all fights must be finished... I just hope I can see Nym along the way... Please Destiny... Please...*

"If only one shard is destroyed," Elucid boomed, interrupting Kort's meditation. "The two shards can never be melded together again, thus time evermore."

Magicia heatedly interjected. "That's strictly prohibited! I've seen the gatekeeper Wicken at Liath, placed by Destiny to avoid this unfairness for the Darkness. If such were allowed, the Child of Darkness would need *both shards* to stop time, and the Child of Light would only need *one shard* to ensure time could never be stopped with the whole sword."

Elucid's voice suddenly overpowered Magicia's.

"The gatekeeper was removed as a modification to the Game, due to the Gray Child. If you don't know, then refrain from speaking!"

"I know not what you disclose not!" Magicia replied, feistily. "Did you spare that detail about Wicken, when you told me earlier of the immortals' whispering?! Did you suppose I wouldn't support Liath over Gallow Cliff?! Clearly you did."

"Nonsense. You keep arguing against reason, as only your guilt compels you to the cliffs!"

"I am neither predictable," Magicia replied, "nor am I senseless! I know much more than you give me credit for, knight. Tread with care."

"Realize that I'm partly aware of what you're trying to undo," Elucid said. "This force pushes you toward Gallow Cliff to fight *him*, regardless of how many times you lose. You must stop *him*, at any cost. I get that."

Kort could only keep quiet for so long. It was only a matter of time before he asked some questions, in hopes of improved clarity.

"Fight *who*?" he blurted out. "The Child of Darkness? Why are we fighting him more than once?"

Elucid turned slowly from Magicia to look right at Kort, before answering in a booming deep voice that grew yet deeper, as the crimson knight described their foe.

"The man is not entirely the Child of Darkness, and he's much more dangerous than his appearance would suggest. He's a lone man taking many names, someone who works toward another's nefarious end for his own misguided reasons! He's a man who embraces the black shard of another's broken dreams, and who won't let go as time passes, causing us to fight him again and again."

Kort shook his head. *I don't understand...*

"Some things you're better off not knowing."

Kort stared back at Elucid. While he trusted the crimson knight, it became difficult at times when Elucid seemingly guarded information. Whenever this happened, it stirred up the words that Kort was told by the woman in white, echoed by the ghost from Tai Forest—*Trust not the crimson knight.*

Kort shut the idea out and refused to go down that path—not after trusting Elucid through the storm; not after trusting Elucid through his venture into the leviathan's belly; not after lifting famine in the Isles based on Elucid's guidance. But, if the crimson knight were trustworthy and still did not disclose certain things, he had to wonder why. *Maybe, Elucid isn't sure? Maybe, Elucid doesn't know?* On one hand, with Elucid as his wise counsel and his guide, it was a scary prospect. But on the other hand, with Elucid not knowing things versus hiding them, it would be more forgivable if the crimson knight happened to be wrong.

When Magicia piped up again, it broke Kort's concentration, yet again. He looked over.

"After the Child of Darkness is defeated at Gallow Cliff," she said, "the whole gray blade can be destroyed in Ires Star, just like the Light Prophecy mentions. You can do what I want and do what the Dojese expect, and then afterward, you can also do what Elucid wants. Both options are possible, just in a particular order consistent with the prophecy. Bear this in mind!"

Suddenly, Elucid released a booming sigh. Despite it being so hard for Kort to detect emotions from the crimson knight, he sensed what was surely exasperation.

"We forget that our wants must be set aside, sorceress. I fear that these past few days we've made a very important oversight. Our arguments have excluded something essential, *someone* essential."

Kort looked back to Elucid, who paused for emphasis before continuing.

"Whether he goes to Gallow Cliff directly or bypasses the cliffs to journey to the heights of Liath, it's his decision, and his alone. As much as we want either course of action, in the end Kort has to make the choice, and he has to make it on his own."

Magicia shook her head, as if to acknowledge what Elucid said. "Of course," the woman replied. "We're just trying to help him."

The inflection point in the argument was terrifying for Kort. Still, after further discussion, he did not know what the best choice would be. And he had to accept that perhaps remotely, part of him hoped that the decision would be made for him.

Kort looked at Elucid first, and then Magicia. His lips were barred from speaking, and a look of indecisiveness was surely plastered upon his face.

Elucid gave another sigh, and Kort looked over.

"Perhaps we confuse him more than help him."

Magicia nodded and paused, before speaking about something unmentioned as of yet.

"Perhaps a matter of fact should influence his judgments, versus our preferences," Magicia said. "I was hoping to gain his support without this information, because it will likely bias his decision. Yet I must make this admission now, regardless of what bias it may cause."

Slowly, Kort faced Magicia and leaned closer.

"What admission?"

A sinking feeling filled Kort's gut with anticipation. His eyes drifted to the shadows dancing on the floor, about the candle's flame yet flickering, where another moth joined the former. Both of them chased the light together.

"Speak," said Elucid to Magicia, "words untainted by your wishes or mine."

"As you wish."

Magicia's eyes trailed from Elucid to Kort. In that moment, for a reason not really understood, the paradoxical appearance of Magicia's face stood out to him more than usual: its skin evidenced age, while at the same time, her skin seemed as young as that of a maiden just reaching her maturity. Magicia's gray eyes burrowed into Kort's; they were steady, fearless, and lent feelings of transparency to Kort. And given that, he was ready to hear what she had to say, with a listening ear and an open mind.

"When you lifted famine in Doj, it was an amazing deed both foretold in the Light and Dark Prophecies. But your support comes from not only that deed."

Kort raised his eyebrows.

Magicia continued. "Your pursuer Sagult saw you fulfill the prophecy, and it moved him deeply. Now he advocates for you upon the Mainland, to clear the suspicions surrounding your name, and to proclaim you as the One of Prophecy, who was chosen by Destiny to battle with the Child of Darkness at Gallow Cliff."

The words absolutely shocked Kort. *In a huge leap of faith, Sagult goes from pursuing me to endorsing me?! I thought he went back to Sergros after seeing me upon the leviathan, and would do nothing more...* On one hand, Kort counted it flattering to hear that his good deed for Doj befriended a sworn enemy. But on the other hand, he knew Sagult's character and convictions, and it seemed off. *Surely a single deed wouldn't aright my many wrongs in his eyes... How could he move past that?* Kort wondered.

"Up and down the Mainland's west coast, all the way to Gallow Cliff at the south of the continent, he and other knights currently evangelize in your name at the risk of facing the same punishment as you, should they come before the Sergrothian courts."

"Is *that* the admission?" Kort asked.

"No. Remember, I previously mentioned how zealots rallied your name on the Mainland, leaving them anonymous until now. It's been reason enough for me to argue with Elucid that you not attending many followers at Gallow Cliff would put them all in grave danger." Magicia paused before going on. "But there's another compulsive reason to go, one not yet shared."

"Is there?" Kort asked, hating the suspense.

Magicia nodded slowly.

"As a result of Sagult's evangelism, many Mainlandish folk have decided to face Shaizan already, having left behind their worldly possessions to fight for good destiny at Gallow Cliff. *And among those reached is Nym, who carries your child.*"

The words literally floored Kort. His mouth went agape and his knees began to tremble. Although he had entered Raiden's house and stood this whole time, he suddenly felt inclined to sit.

He lowered himself to the floor, letting his legs stretch out before him. And just as he lowered himself, his gut dropped to the bottom of Karnath. He immediately found it difficult to breathe.

Kort began stammering.

"Wh… where was she seen?! How do you know?!"

"In Breslin," Magicia answered, "I'm told she alighted a man from his steed, took the horse, and hurriedly rode to the cliffs, all in hopes of meeting you there."

So many mixed thoughts clashed within Kort's head as he attempted to process the news. *Nym is with child, my child?!* The information caused joy that swelled within him and brought a smile to his lips. But the smile slowly faded as he realized the perils in which Nym and his child would be, should he follow Elucid's beckon to Liath. *Oh no! That would mean her facing the Child of Darkness, without me!*

And then it hit Kort, an epiphany had in pervasive silence. Until this moment, he had embraced choice—to run from Sagult, to go on Korinth, to enter the leviathan. And choice had supposedly enabled him to map out the course of his own destiny. But now, this news about Nym came by chance, and seemed to rob him of making the choice. Magicia was right; there inevitably would be bias in his decision given the news, and that bias was strong!

Kort gasped, feeling as though a rug was pulled out from underneath his feet. *I feel there's no longer any decision here. I simply must go to the cliffs; I must! What decent father would not?!* He swallowed hard, feeling settled over the outcome, but not about the means by which the decision came. *In the moment of choice, I hesitated. And now, I've forfeited choice to chance!*

Sitting upon the floor, with Elucid at his left and Magicia at his right, Kort fixed on the white candle that likewise sat in its iron dish, with even more runny wax dribbling down the sides as the flame continued to burn and allure.

For now, twice as many moths chased the light as before, altogether making four. They fluttered their wings, nearing the flame, again and again.

In an aside, Kort cried out to Destiny.

"Can this really be?"

As usual, silence was his reply.

"As a product of choice and chance, opportunities develop now in my life, giving rise to more instances of either choice or chance that may lead into both, all over again! In this way, destiny seems to be a cycle, where choice and chance intertwine to lead my fate."

He kept his eyes upon the flame and the mothy air about it, and spoke in a voice no more strident than a hush.

"My destiny, fathered by choice, mothered by chance—son of both, a daughter of neither alone!"

In the middle of his aside, Kort paused, letting silence envelope him. He watched the moths, and slowly realized the truth about his life, and about that of everyone else in Karnath.

Sometimes chance dictates one's destiny, whereas at other times, choice decides one's fate. It is not one or the other holding true in a mutually exclusive way, but rather both holding true at distinct moments of one's life. Choice neither decides destiny alone nor does chance, but both choice and chance decide it together! Fate is choice and chance, and I was a fool to think that my choice alone could map out my future!

In his moment of clarity, Kort smiled.

I was a fool to presume this, just as fools who presume their lives are nothing more than chance, for that idea is equally wrong! Life is constantly full of decisions that offer few options, and one must not relinquish influence of their own destiny in defeat, for the choices that can be made should be made, with timeliness, in soundness of mind, and goodness of heart! So it's not that good choices lead into good destiny, but rather that good choices often lead into good chances, and good chances often lead into good choices! Good destiny—the divine purpose had by one and all, as ordained by Karnatha—is nothing more than good choice and good chance, using one's hidden talents and with the right motives!

Kort spoke to the moths in his aside, vocalizing what he had learned from his moment of reflection.

"When choices beset me, I'll choose goodly and hope for good chance! And when chances beset me, I'll hope their product allows me to choose goodly! This is how I shall cope with a fate brought by both choice and chance! This is how I shall pursue my good destiny!"

It was in that moment where Kort began to understand, that in the balance of his own battle for good destiny hung the gap between his ideals and reality. And in that, he would be held accountable for his choices and how they affected others.

Kort looked to Elucid and then to Magicia; they both waited upon him in silence. Kort knew what he had to do, and it conjured up Elucid's words concerning fishers no longer fishing, and doers no longer doing. *I'll put off bias and face this difficult decision, to choose one way or the other! It's what I should've done from the start, and I'll not forfeit choice ever again! Though my urge to go to the cliffs seems overwhelming, I must weigh both options carefully.*

Elucid released another booming sigh; it broke Kort's thoughts.

"Well played, sorceress."

The crimson knight spoke, as if assuming that Kort's decision was final, when in reality it was not even made. But before Kort could communicate that, Elucid lowered his gaze to the floor, and continued.

"Whatever choice you ultimately make, I support it," said Elucid. "Just remember to always do the right thing, the good and wholesome thing in your heart that you feel most sure of, the sound thing lent credence from judgments in your own mind. Balance emotions with critical thinking, to achieve greater ends than from either one alone."

Elucid sighed again, glancing to Magicia.

"I won't be the one to insist that a single shard into Ires Star is the only way to win this Game of Time and Broken Sword. My beliefs do not mean that Gallow Cliff before Liath is necessarily without victory. Perhaps it'll be on all of us to decide whether or not we win, whatever we do and wherever we are."

Kort nodded his head and got up from the floor.

"Forgive me, but it's still a lot for me to consider. Maybe some sleep will clear my mind and give me direction in this matter."

"As you wish," Magicia said. "But do be mindful of the time, for it's upon us if we go to Gallow Cliff. The Child of Darkness already touches the black shard, I fear."

The words made Kort realize that he had not yet touched the white shard. It remained untouched, in the room ahead.

With those words, Kort stepped toward the adjoining chamber where Raiden slept, separated from the main room by a sliding door on the wall between Elucid and Magicia. As he went, his footsteps creaked upon the wood and against the backdrop of crickets and locusts, which still could be heard from outside.

When at the sliding door, Kort looked back when the candle's light suddenly flicked. He beheld a peculiar sight there: the four moths came so close to the fire, where all at once, their wings suddenly caught aflame! He watched them fall damaged, away from the flickering light, to drop wingless a moment later and struggle from the floor, whilst burning alive. It was as if the moths had touched the sun.

Kort's vision went back to the flame, still dancing as before, as the allure it had been all along. He turned away and opened the sliding door; it glided upon its track with hardly a noise. He stepped into Raiden's chamber and closed the door behind him, knowing that isolation, thought, and a little rest would surely lead to his decision.

"AS MOTHS TO FLAMES"

Chapter 71
Chance or Choice

For sometime Kort lied facedown and awake on the mat in Raiden's room, beside the paper lamp that glowed weakly. The mat was on the far wall of the room opposite the sliding door; it had a window above it, which was covered by thin netting. Along the wall on the door's left was the purple cloak; it was stretched over the floor with the white shard of sword laid on top, the grip of which was still untouched.

Kort tossed and turned, unable to sleep. His mind kept spinning about which of the two options would be best: going to Gallow Cliff to confront the Child of Darkness as stated in the prophecy, or instead, climbing Liath to destroy the white shard and prevent the gray blade from ever being formed.

Kort started thinking about what action was intrinsically right given the opportunity that Destiny had bestowed upon him. *Could it be, that just lifting famine isn't my redemption's end? To whom much is given, much will be required. And as one given the opportunity of being the Child of Light, surely I'm required now to stop the Child of Darkness by going to Gallow Cliff! My life might not afford greater redemption than that, for all my wrongdoings...* Kort suddenly realized that going to Gallow Cliff was perfectly aligned with his mission all along: redemption, after leading a life of wrongs. It sobered him.

Kort's mind jumped to a different consideration: the impact on others of not going to Gallow Cliff. If he were not present in the fight, Nym and his supporters would face the Child of Darkness alone. An immediate afterthought followed; he envisioned Nym and many others being slain at the cliffs! Kort literally saw an uncontended, wayward knight in black and spikey armor, slinging the black shard and delivering death to one and all. Kort shook his head. *No, I can't have that. I can't!*

After contemplating it for only moment, Kort realized that Gallow Cliff seemed most befitting for the opportunity he was given, and furthermore, it seemed the best option for those who would actually go to the cliffs.

"Is there really a choice here?" he groaned from the mat, knowing exactly what he needed to do.

Kort swallowed hard, thinking he ought to at least consider the second option. But the more he thought about it, the more he realized that all the second option achieved was appeasing Elucid. It did not follow the prophecy as written; it opposed the expectations of two entire villages and the most powerful sorceress in Karnath; it abandoned those who believed in him, including Nym and his child.

He thought about the latter point, with his face buried in the mat. *Many people, having given up everything and trusted me, would be endangered and let down, immolated for naught! Their wasted sacrifice would be more blood on my hands!* And when considering that, it hit Kort: the second option would potentially continue his Dark past of hurting others. *I can't have that either…*

Time elapsed, and as it did, Kort came to increased contentment with the first option. He eventually fell asleep. In a dream, all he could see was blackness about him, but from the blackness he heard Nym's voice.

"Kort, come to me!"

He looked down, and saw his hands and feet in the black; he saw himself, but nothing else. Kort looked up.

"Nym, where are you?" he cried, his voice breaking, when he heard her again mid-sentence.

"Kort, come to me!"

Then suddenly, the blackness around Kort materialized into a glorious view. He stood atop the chalk white Gallow Cliff, where the strong winds ruffled his clothes underneath a blue cloudless sky. Before him appeared Nym on the rock, adorned in her black robe, and with her silver hair blowing in the winds, just as his own. She welcomed him with a smile and an extended hand.

"Kort, come to me!"

Kort showed a smile ear-to-ear, larger than any he had shown for months, since the night when he left Nym outside Breslin, in fear for her safety. And with that smile, he drew nigh to her, reaching forth his hand to touch her own. But just before their hands made contact, the dream suddenly ended!

Kort opened his eyes, only to find that he had sleepwalked to the place in Raiden's room where the shard lied upon the purple cloak. His hand hovered over its handle; it was the same hand that would have touched Nym's hand in his dream. In that instant, Kort perceived touching the shard's grip and going to Gallow Cliff as reuniting with his love. It was yet another reason to choose the cliffs over Liath.

Not wasting a moment more, Kort grabbed the white shard by its handle, letting the hilt rest upon his thumb and forefinger. In the moment of contact, such calm overcame him, as if touching the grip signified his choice, one that could not be retracted; his decision had been made. He looked at his hand holding the sword, realizing again that this was the best option for everyone involved: for Nym, his child, and his supporters.

Kort stopped himself to consider what the act meant. *As spoken of in the Dark Prophecy, to Gallow Cliff the Child would go, three days after touching the grip. Three days it is then…*

With the white shard in his balled fist, Kort turned, noting the morning light that streamed through the window, pouring over the space where the shard had lied. *I must've slept the night away...*

A sight interrupted any further thoughts on the time. There, on the floor, beyond the purple cloak and basking in the sunlight, were metal objects of shimmer and gleam. Kort stepped closer, keeping his eyes on the objects, until he understood what they were. *Armor.* Though it was not just any ordinary armor; it was a full set of beautiful white armor with gold inlays: from boots and gauntlets, to breastplate and helmet.

Kort stopped himself one footstep from the armor, and studied it more. Images flashed through his mind of icons seen in Karnathan churches, where the Forerunner of Light wore such armor. *This... This couldn't be.*

He reached down to touch the helmet, but when his fingers came near it, a human being suddenly appeared in the empty space beyond the armor! It was a man dressed in a fine white tunic and trousers, who wore pointed white shoes. He was older in age and had snowy hair falling down his shoulders, and also a matching goatee rung about his lips. His gray eyes showed an undying determination; they were piercing and fiery, literally drilling into Kort.

Startled, he jumped back.

"Speak being, of your name and person!"

"Be not alarmed," said the man. "I am Autheos, the Forerunner of Light, the advocate of good destiny in both Old and New Karnath."

Kort swallowed hard. *First the white shard, then the Forerunner, now this...* His eyes trailed again to the armor, finding it hard to believe. *This must be, the armor of god...*

A whirlwind of unbelievable happenings swept Kort into the stories of Karnathan myth, legend, and prophecy. He had witnessed so many amazing things in the past few weeks that it only made sense for him to continue believing with childlike faith. *That's all I can do...*

"It's the armor of god," said Autheos. "It protects against elements, and empowers whoever wears the armor in water and sands. Take it."

With some hesitance, Kort reached for the breastplate and took it up in one hand. He looked it over and judged its quality in his palm. The armor felt extremely durable and well constructed to his touch, the product of otherworldly craftsmanship.

Kort's eyes went back to Autheos.

"You've come so far without aides," the Forerunner continued. "No Servants of Light have acted on your behalf, only on that of Ma'althan's. Despite such odds against you, for a cause deemed greater than yourself you've persevered, and this is all that matters."

Kort suddenly felt a sting from his past. *You're a traitor, a murderer, and a knight who betrayed the common trust of his kingdom. You deserve prison or death!* He hung his head low, feeling so unworthy in the moment of the title he bore. It stirred his mind with thoughts of others far more nobler than him, others who were far more deserving. *Sagult could've easily had this title, or even young X'ieth from the Sixth Order of the Guard! Both of them are more upright! Garlew set a high standard that few could meet, let alone me.*

Autheos surprised Kort with edifying words, as if the Forerunner had read his mind.

"The turn of your spirit from Darkness to Light makes you just as useful as any other of good and noble heart. And for that, Destiny smiles upon you this day!"

Autheos gestured to the armaments on the floor. "Please, wear my armor to Gallow Cliff for your protection. Again I tell you, it's the armor of god, fashioned in the virtues of goodness and the Light."

With those welcoming words, Kort laid the white shard upon the floor, and put the breastplate over his body. He attached it, and then the other pieces, one by one. But after putting on all the armor, he took a few steps across the room, and felt significant spacing between the plating and his body. *It's too big for me!* The armor shifted around him with clings and clangs.

Dejectedly, Kort dropped his head, and so dropped his spirit. He turned from Autheos, and lifted his voice in an aside. "Despite my faith that I'm the Child of Light, surely this large armor is meant for another! Garlew Il'therin could wear it, before me!"

"Be not dismayed," Autheos said calmly. "Negative indicators of one's destiny can betray us all, so use this compass for guidance. Always do good things you feel naturally inclined toward, and things for which you have natural aptitude. Do this, and the rest will fall into place. Know that Gallow Cliff is all these things for you."

Out of Kort's view, the Forerunner blinked, leaving him alone in the room. Kort breathed slowly, looking down at the armor he wore, and the white shard lying on the floor. *I mustn't let the armor's size be my dismay! I've decided Gallow Cliff, and there I must go!*

He bent over and picked up the shard once more. With the sword in hand, he arose and glanced at the mat, seeing the purple cloak crumpled before it. The cloak was too long for him to wear, so Kort left it behind and walked to the room's sliding door. The armor felt awkward with his every step there, clinking and clanging along the way.

When at the door, Kort pulled it open, and emerged into the adjoining chamber. As he stepped out, Elucid met him. Kort looked beyond the crimson knight, seeing an otherwise empty house; Magicia was nowhere to be found.

"I've made my choice of Gallow Cliff," said Kort, emboldened by his careful consideration over the matter.

"As before, I respect your choice," said Elucid. The crimson knight gazed down upon the white shard Kort held and the armor of god Kort wore, studying them as if something were missing. And then, Elucid peered into Raiden's chamber, seeing there the purple cloak, crumpled on the floor and left behind.

"Won't you also wear the purple cloak to Gallow Cliff?" asked Elucid, gesturing to it with a metal hand.

Kort glanced over his shoulder and into Raiden's room. When he saw the cloak left behind, the visual made him remember how it was much too long for him.

"I might trip on that! Surely it's more suited for you than it is for me, given its length," Kort said, smiling.

Elucid stared back in silence for a while, before speaking in a booming voice.

"I was hoping you could wear it." After a pause, Elucid continued. "But one way or another, that cloak must come with us to Gallow Cliff, and I shall wear it if you cannot."

"Why?" Kort asked, curious about the cloak.

Elucid remained silent.

Kort maintained his trust for the crimson knight, and thought back to his earlier consideration. *Elucid doesn't know why he's carrying the cloak, does he? Elucid just knows it's important?* He wondered.

Eventually, Kort just nodded. *The purpose of the cloak matters little, and what's worn to the cliffs is the least of our problems. The outcome at Gallow Cliff is far more important.*

And at that thought, Kort swallowed hard, with the oracles' stark foretelling at the back of his mind: *And this war shall not be without a victor, for that day the one called Shaizan shall defeat Kayareth in a final duel between the Darkness and the Light.*

Kort showed a face of determination.

"Even if it takes my life," he said, "I'll change the Dark Prophecy." He looked to Elucid before continuing. "We'll change the Dark Prophecy together, and the Light Prophecy shall be fulfilled. To Gallow Cliff we go!"

"NYM'S BECKON CALL"

Chapter 72
Seroxians to War

It had been weeks since Merphonox was visited by Darconas in Old Karnath, and after that, the shadow had appeared recently to tell the seroxian king that Magicia would bridge their worlds within three days. But Merphonox had not seen Darconas since; their contact ended suddenly and strangely.

Indeed, this happening seemed odd to Merphonox, and he was beginning to feel as though the shadow were testing him, as to whether he would go into New Karnath on his own or not. But even so, he still intended on rallying the seroxians to his cause of entering New Karnath. To this end, he arranged a meeting with Vaxlan and others tonight at Grotto Tribute, the outcome of which would decide who would follow him into New Karnath.

And so it was, at the appointed time Merphonox stood in the grotto, between two large spirals composed of many acryllum sconces holding burning candles. Behind him was the ellipsoidal monument hung midair, showing the etched names of all the seroxians who had died over a thousand years ago in the Tragedy of Old Karnath. As before, Merphonox wore a two-toned tunic over his muscular chest, with one half black and the other white. Covering his strong lower body were gray leather pants having their legs shoved into knee-high boots.

Seated on the cave floor all around Merphonox were scores of seroxians, male and female alike, many wearing light tunics and trousers, others wearing long flowing robes. In the midst of these seroxians sat Vaxlan, adorned in a maroon hooded robe.

With blue hawk eyes, he peered out of his hood at Merphonox, having a shaven head and face, except for a triangle of hair above his chin, point-down. Tattooed on his left cheek was the crest of Seroxia: progressively eclipsing suns, with a gray serpent coiled about them. A few rows of seroxians behind Vaxlan sat Sithrel and Gibit, two fiery youths that were Merphonox's most loyal supporters and highly skilled sorcerers; both had brown hair, brown eyes, and bronze skin.

The hundreds of flaming candles in each spiral floated to the right and then back to the left, shedding flickers of yellow light on the faces of every seroxian present. A reddish orange dusk sky showed outside the grotto, hung above the dark crag rock and gray fields of Old Karnath. Despite it being near evening, Merphonox continued addressing those in attendance.

"It was wrong of Maken to give the lower races New Karnath after the creator ended the rebellion! It was wrong for us, the innocent bystanders to the rebellion, to suffer loss! It was never our place to dissuade our brother seroxians from rebelling! It was never our place!"

Almost all the seroxians around Merphonox watched on without a noise. However, Gibit and Sithrel voiced their support.

"He's right!"

"Aye, it shouldn't have been on us to stop it! Maken's expectations were unfair!"

Merphonox gestured for them to quiet themselves, and they did. He afterward continued pressing the others.

"We were clearly wronged by Maken's punishment. But let us put the past behind us, and let us enter New Karnath to do good rather than evil. As I've already told you, the Dark Prophecy will come true there, unless we intervene! So we must help the inferiors fight the Child of Darkness! In return, they'll show us the location of the River of Life, which mirrors the one dried up by Maken in Old Karnath! For seroxians, the River is immortality."

Right in the middle of his speech, sudden flashes of Gallow Cliff appeared before Merphonox's eyes. He saw a scene of a grinning young man wearing spikey black armor who wielded a black sword, which was split down its middle, just like the legendary shard. Before the young man was his opponent: a bronze-skinned elf with sooty black hair wearing white armor who wielded the white shard, and behind him, Magicia, a crimson knight, along with a mob of armed seroxians carrying the banners of Seroxia. And among the seroxians, Merphonox saw himself!

Images of the scene kept coming, interrupting his speech and inserting pauses between his every few words.

"So then, we shall enter New Karnath and… triumph over the… Child… the Child of Darkness!" He suddenly saw the young man collide with his opponents at Gallow Cliff, and masterfully use the black shard to separate seroxian after seroxian from the realm of the living, as wheat from the chaff. He saw their blood; he heard their moans of agony, before their deaths beneath the towering cliffs.

Merphonox struggled to continue.

"We shall… win the battle… through an alliance with the inferiors and thereby… find the River!"

Amid his sentence suddenly came another image into his mind, of the young man confronting him at Gallow Cliff; Merphonox imagined himself standing before the youth who held the black shard, wearing the horned armor of his father Penultum, and holding a long lance along with a round shield. And then in one moment, the youth blindingly attacked with his sword, cracking the horned armor with an array of slashes, and sending Merphonox to his knees, moments before the seroxian king slumped over and died in a pool of his own blood!

To Merphonox, the thought struck him as horrifying, shocking, and disturbing, for in this, he saw himself slain by the black shard, just like Eriens had been in the Tragedy. And the mere idea of Merphonox befalling the same fate was enough to rob him of a silver tongue.

"We shall… win," he stammered.

Murmuring rippled through the seated seroxians.

"Did you see that too?" asked one seroxian to another sitting beside him, who nodded affirmatively.

"Aye, I just saw us at the cliffs. And we all died!"

"Me too," a seroxian interjected from behind, looking forward at the other two.

There was a pause, as if everyone in the grotto mulled over what this meant before applying the knowledge. The outbursts were hurried and sudden.

"I'm not going!"

"Aye, nor am I!"

The worried talk continued and continued, until it dawned on Merphonox that everything he saw, was also seen by others in attendance at the grotto. And these premonitions had a devastating effect on the king's speech, in that many seroxians went from potentially supporting Merphonox, to no longer wanting to be involved.

Vaxlan suddenly stood up from the crowd, and lifted his hands to silence everyone.

"Merphonox withholds truth from you all!"

A moment later, Sithrel and Gibit rose, anticipating that Vaxlan was purposely acting as a rabble-rouser to disrupt Merphonox's speech and motivate the seroxians to an opposing cause. Little did they know that the premonitions upon everyone already had done just this.

"How dare he?" Gibit asked, gesturing with his hands to urge the crowd to consider the same of Vaxlan's interruption.

"This is Merphonox's forum to speak, not anyone else's!" said Sithrel, cocking his head. "And as such, this isn't the appropriate time for Vaxlan to talk!"

There was a pause, followed by feedback from the crowd. Seroxians began murmuring amongst themselves, some speaking aloud.

"Let's hear what he has to say!" said one.

"Aye, I want to know what the king withholds!"

A round of "Ayes" came from the group.

Merphonox raised his hands. "That's enough!"

All talked stopped, and all eyes went to him.

Merphonox continued. "Let Vaxlan speak."

Gibit and Sithrel started murmuring to each other.

"My king, are you sure?!" Sithrel asked, a moment later. The burning candles flickered light that littered his face. Outside, a velvet night sky showed as the day ended.

Merphonox extended a reassuring hand.

"Let it be. If the seroxians don't allow free talk in Seroxia, we would be no better than the savage inferiors who likely tolerate much less!"

Despite the reassurance, Sithrel argued.

"I know what he'll say, and it's divisive!"

"I know," snapped Merphonox, "I think many in attendance now know of what he will speak. Even so, let him speak freely here, as he would in any other forum. Free speech has long been our way, and it shall continue to be our way! No kingdom will ever prosper without this."

Merphonox watched Sithrel and Gibit hesitantly back down, as if they questioned the decision of Vaxlan addressing the attendees. Slowly, they took their seats in the crowd; they both sat cross-legged, leaning their heads forward and ready to listen.

"By urging the seroxians to Gallow Cliff in New Karnath, you are ignoring how even our oracles foretell Shaizan winning the Game! And furthermore, you speak either in ignorance of our premonitions or blindness to them! Has Sithrel shared with you my visions, and those of others who sit in our midst?!"

Merphonox glared at Sithrel who nodded shamefully, as if knowing about the premonitions had by the king as well as others, well in advance of this meeting. *Wish I knew this was coming...* he thought, with some disdain for the developing situation.

Vaxlan continued, drawing the king's attention.

"Yes, we've confided in your supporter Sithrel, hoping that you might better understand our premonitions of the future that pertain to your mission. Yet fear of difficult conversations can lead to pursed lips among those lacking the required courage for them."

Vaxlan's eyes trailed to Sithrel for a moment, before going off into the crowd, to reach the seated seroxians.

"Many in this room foresee the seroxians slaughtered at Gallow Cliff in New Karnath! The inferiors' Army of Light and its leader Naketo are killed just as we, by one who acts in the name of Shaizan, a wild one named Lucen!"

Merphonox caught movement across the group of seated seroxians, as many nodded in agreement.

"That's exactly what will happen!" one shouted.

"Aye, I saw it before me eyes!" said another.

Vaxlan lifted his hands and quieted them.

"Silence, please!"

He looked to Merphonox, and let his hands fall. Vaxlan continued standing in the place where he had been seated, amid the crowd of seroxians. All eyes were on him.

"Despite us seroxians having god-like abilities in sword and magic, whoever enters New Karnath is destined to die at the hands of this Lucen!"

Vaxlan suddenly started walking between the seroxians sitting on the cave floor, toward the depth of the grotto where Merphonox was, alongside the monument. When he came close to the seroxian king, he motioned to the monument and the etching upon it.

"Do you want our names to be in stone, as these? Perhaps if we give enough, we can have our names on the placard too, beside that of Hrya!"

The words infuriated Merphonox; Hrya was family.

"Watch your tongue, Vaxlan!" he snarled. "I'll tolerate you speaking freely at my summons, insofar as it's not of my family! Hrya sacrificed more that any of us could."

Vaxlan lowered his hand.

"My purpose is not to agitate, so I'll not pour liquors in what you declare a wound. I mean no offense."

Merphonox relaxed his face, and became silent.

Vaxlan stared back. "My purpose is to avoid another tragedy! The seroxians have a way of life here, beyond the ruin that followed Maken's curse long ago. So let us enjoy what we have, here and now, with no thought of more! Let us live in the present rather than the past, and savor each moment upon us!"

Merphonox stepped up to Vaxlan. The seroxians stared in each other's faces. "Only a fool enjoys his present without sobriety over the past, and without care for the future! Seroxia can live well now, and better to come. Why do you want to limit the future of the seroxian race, by insisting that we raise our children upon cursed land, and live under the shadow of what this monument represents: the Tragedy, and its horrors for the seroxians?!"

"No, you've got it all wrong," Vaxlan said, with contempt in his voice. His blue eyes raged. "I insist on giving mute seroxians a voice, those who won't speak for themselves and would be otherwise swayed by peer pressure to do as you suggest, *with reservations*. If your uncle's sacrifice has proxied sacrifice for the seroxians as a people, I can't have anyone persuaded to sacrifice more."

"What reservations?!"

"Reservations of losing everything held dear—families and friends, homes and lands! Many fear losing good destiny in Seroxia, only for this chance of destiny better. Given my premonitions, I count your plan more a gamble than a sure thing, and many now feel the same."

Vaxlan turned to address the seated seroxians.

"I have greater aspirations in Old Karnath than becoming a corpse under the cliffs in New Karnath, another name on a new memorial! I've greater dreams than causing my sons' future hate for life, and their thirst for my avengement until the day when they themselves bet their families and homes against the same odds, only to lose everything!"

Vaxlan turned to Merphonox.

"Stop this, and save yourself."

He put his hand on Merphonox's shoulder.

Vaxlan went on. "Stop embracing the black shard of Penultum's broken dream! His Fate's Fray of wanting New Karnath—even as he died of illness—is becoming your own!"

Merphonox retorted, "My Fate's Fray is fighting for my good destiny in New Karnath! It's a good destiny for all of us, one that's better than a life in Old Karnath."

"That's what you say, but it's not what you do."

Merphonox raised an eyebrow.

Vaxlan continued. "Thinking of Fate's Fray as only a fight for your destiny is a convenience that avoids the original intent of our elders who penned the Book of Karnatha. What they intended is stark but very real: Fate's Fray is indeed the potential unraveling of what we're meant to be, an unraveling that might be had in our Battle for Destiny—a series of fights over our lives— wherein some fights are lost because of our gray dreams, which break apart into shards of opposing hues."

Vaxlan continued staring Merphonox in his face, without even blinking or looking away for a moment.

"In the wake of our broken gray dreams, we all must choose to embrace one of the hued shards. Embracing the white shard doesn't lead to Fate's Fray; it's rising upon falling, trying again even in failure, or dreaming anew. However, embracing the black shard is not letting go of gray dreams, and this is where Fate's Fray can happen. By not letting go, or by making choices that abandon the future value of our lives without our broken gray dreams, we self-destruct through our black shards. This is what you're doing, by jeopardizing what your life could be in Old Karnath, to chase the gray dream of New Karnath!"

The dormant anger inside Merphonox returned, as Vaxlan's words touched upon his unhealed wounds. He pushed the seroxian's hand off his shoulder.

Vaxlan paid it no heed and turned to the seated seroxians, as if deeming their attention a higher priority.

"Jeopardizing your life here for the dream of a better life there is nothing short of foolish, and it's a gamble where one can lose everything. So like me, don't you all aspire for more than a gamble of better destiny, at the risk of becoming another name on this monument?!"

Merphonox glanced into the crowd, seeing a sea of faces nodding their approval, as if moved by Vaxlan's words. He realized then he had to do something.

"There's nothing wrong with one's appreciation of the simple life," interjected Merphonox, "for the seeming little things are among the biggest!"

Eyes in the crowd went to him.

Merphonox continued. "Nothing in life is better than a family united under one roof and living in harmony, as families should, with greater appreciation for togetherness than other things, material and vain! But do realize that if your natural inclination is for more than this, do not content yourself with less! One can have the simple life, but also purpose beyond the home! In fact, we all can have a purpose beyond the home, a purpose to create the legacy we'll hand down to our children—the means by which they can live dreams bigger than our own! As such, there's a greater purpose to our lives, than just gifting life to our children. Instead of settling for mediocrity, we can do our best to assure that they succeed, prosper, and live fulfilled lives! For if our children are to live in any other way, is it good enough?! I say not."

"It's fine and well if that's your purpose," Vaxlan shot back, "but many here have a different purpose, including me. Our families and maintaining a peaceful life for them is our priority today, not tomorrow. On the other hand, your family and their peace sound like future priorities for you, things you're willing to barter today in exchange for war with Lucen. But that election is an unreasonable imposition to your family, and does no good in Old Karnath or New Karnath, so it can't be your good destiny! In this, you're just being selfish. And should you suggest that it's for a greater good than merely your own, you've deluded yourself as much as you would be tricking your brother seroxians with lies!"

Vaxlan turned to the seated seroxians.

"To leave your families in Old Karnath to war with Lucen in New Karnath isn't good destiny for any of us! Do understand that in the wake of our broken dreams after Maken's punishment, the good destiny we've eventually found in Old Karnath is a dream anew, versus the nightmare that Merphonox proposes. It's not a purpose aligned with our good destiny, and thus is not a purpose worthy of having."

Merphonox watched Vaxlan face him again.

"Starting a war without cause isn't good destiny…"

"That's not what I'm doing, for I implore seroxians to join a noble cause of stopping the Dark Prophecy!"

Blank faces stared back at the seroxian king, as he struggled to gain support from the audience. Slowly, the gears in Merphonox's mind began turning, and he wondered if he would be more successful if he appealed to a different sentiment, one that was deeply rooted in him. *Justice to the seroxians, for Maken's punishment and my uncle's death! Reclaiming New Karnath would be justice, and we have the opportunity to do just that…*

Unbeknownst to him, the king's heart took a worrying turn in the direction of Eriens. His mind immediately flooded with depictions of the violence against his people in the Tragedy; he saw the renderings in churches across Old Karnath, of Magicia killing Eriens and Hrya; he saw her red braided hair and gray eyes, as she stoop overtop a field in New Karnath covered in seroxian blood. It drew contempt to his lips.

Merphonox kept his gaze on those seated.

"I seek justice," he said coldly. "Justice for what my family suffered; justice for what our great race deserves! Thousands of years ago, my father became brother-less when attempting a peaceful entry into New Karnath. The inferiors spilled Hrya's blood needlessly in an act that shamed the seroxians, as we are a much more powerful race! We're faster, stronger, and smarter than they, yet the cursed lower races beguiled my uncle and killed him coldly! And that disgrace was only born from another: Maken cursing our land, and re-creating paradise for the inferiors. If we weren't put in this poor position, the seroxians would never have needed peace with the inferiors to access paradise. For instead, we would be enjoying paradise, as we should for abstaining from the rebellion!"

Merphonox saw many blank stares in the crowd, knowing what he was up against: the people's apathy that grew out of centuries of their separation from past injustices and newer generations that were not directly affected by the Tragedy. Even so, he pressed them, confident that someone here was just as mad as him, about what had happened to the seroxians over the ages.

"The age of seroxians tolerating these injustices is over! Let us take justice into our own hands, by entering New Karnath to battle the inferiors!"

Merphonox saw the people and their hollow stares, some yawning, some whispering with each other, surely about how entering the coveted land would be a loss, per their premonitions. And so, the king's mind spun desperately to reach them before it was too late. *They see Lucen winning, so tell them then that you'll join Lucen in New Karnath, and fight the Child of Light and the inferiors…* It was a crazy idea, but it was the best one Merphonox had.

"We'll win, not be our might in sword and magic," Merphonox said, somewhat hesitantly. "But by joining Lucen against the inferiors! If none of you think we can beat him, well then, let's join him!"

Gasps rang out in the crowd, as the seroxians made a key association: Lucen supposedly fought in the name of Shaizan, and by this, Merphonox suggested the seroxians fight with this person, a believed agent of Darkness!

Merphonox saw Vaxlan face him, and there was an evident fury about the seroxian, seen through his blue eyes.

"So then, your true reason becomes known! You've brought us together by suggesting everyone join you to fight against Lucen in New Karnath. But now, you suggest we join Lucen, so the only constant here seems to be your lust for New Karnath! And there's no noble cause in that."

Merphonox argued differently.

"Is it wrong to refuse letting these disgraces hang over us? I personally cannot live to see these things go unfixed for my children, and my children's children! Perhaps you lost the fire in your belly, but I have not… I believe we were meant for more! Therefore, I believe we must try to be more! I believe in us!"

Vaxlan spun to the seated seroxians.

"To the contrary, Merphonox believes only in himself and in his gray dreams. If you've listened to me tonight and followed my reasoning, you should now be aware that what he proposes is not our good destiny. He says he wants us to be more than we are by reclaiming New Karnath, but in that, he presumes his future life is meant for more than what Destiny affords him in his present!"

Vaxlan's eyes caught the reflections of the fires, as he moved his gaze from one seated seroxian to the next.

"The truth is, if we cannot pursue gray dreams in our present without forfeiting the present value of our future, we ought not to pursue them. And likewise, we ought not to follow Merphonox into New Karnath if it prevents us from living our future lives and meeting our potentials—if we have to give up what we've worked for since the rebellion and the Tragedy! It does. So let us leave this place, and enjoy the goodness of our present more than the fancied goodness of a poorly chanced future!"

Vaxlan pushed past Merphonox and went for the grotto's exit, where he waited with crossed arms. And then, from around the cave, seroxians stood to their feet a few at a time, and made their way to Vaxlan. Before long, nearly everyone in the grotto was heading out. As if not believing what they say, Gibit and Sithrel watched with wonderment, still seated cross-legged on the floor.

Merphonox lifted a hand, and called to those departing. At his word, everyone stopped.

"My sorrows are not your sorrows," Merphonox said, meeting their eyes. "And perhaps, my motivations of revenge and restoring fairness are not something we can share. But what we do have in common, is the desire to do more and be more as a people!"

"We are enough already!" Vaxlan interjected. "Join me if you agree…"

The seroxians resumed departing.

Merphonox called out to them again.

"Wait!" he shouted. This time, only a few turned his way as many others continued leaving, going past Vaxlan and out of the grotto. "Very soon, Old Karnath will be bridged with New Karnath. And in that moment the seroxians will be so close to inheriting a land of promise, one spoken of in our legends for its fertile fields and endless possibilities. It's a land of opportunity we've coveted, a land that had we been born in, we would've done more with its potential than these inferiors did! Let that chance pass you by, only if you're contented with what you have!"

Merphonox gulped, as the seroxians who lingered where they stood paused for a moment before also turning away, to resume departing. The king glanced to the cave floor, where his loyal supporters Sithrel and Gibit still sat, unmoving. His gaze went back to Vaxlan, who stood at the door, as the last few seroxians passed by.

"Destiny be with you," he said.

When Vaxlan turned away, it dawned on Merphonox that no one choose to go with him to New Karnath, except his biased supporters. It was depressing, and put a scowl on his face.

Before leaving, Vaxlan said, "Continue climbing, king… Climb higher to chase after the sun, for you have yet to learn how those with pursuits of more are fated to burn, if their gray dreams break and they can't let go. It might serve you a lesson to be content with the good destiny you have, rather than relentlessly pursuing more."

With that, Vaxlan left.

Merphonox listened to his steps, not really believing what had just happened. All his premonitions told him he would have a host of seroxians join him at Gallow Cliff in New Karnath, not just two. He felt confused. He felt angry.

Merphonox looked out to the dark sky and exclaimed in an aside, "Go seroxians, and walk in the footsteps of your forefathers, but insist not to understand their ways! Go seroxians, and bask also in the shadows of this landmark, seeking refuge from the sun beneath its shade, but care not to understand the significance of this memorial, nor that of any other to come!"

From over his shoulder, Merphonox heard someone stand up. Footsteps rang out in the grotto, in the moments before he felt a hand on his shoulder. The king turned, he and saw Sithrel.

"I'm sorry, my king," Sithrel said in a low voice. "Vaxlan told me of his visions, but I refrained from telling you. I thought his revelation would interfere with your delivery of the rally tonight, had you known beforehand."

Gibit rose and came to Sithrel's side.

"I believe Vaxlan made plans to speak tonight, whether Sithrel told or not. I'm sorry for what occurred."

Merphonox nodded, and Sithrel removed his hand. The king looked over them, watching the candles' light jitter upon their faces.

"Whether we have an army with us or not," Merphonox said, "we must head to Gallow Cliff tonight in Old Karnath. We do not lack a cause, even though we lack support." Vaxlan came to mind, just as Darconas, who had not showed himself for days. Merphonox shook his head.

"Fear not, my king," Gibit said, "we are with you."

Sithrel stated, "All of Seroxia exercises a right to free will tonight, choosing against your mission, but we join your side, your purpose, and your cause!"

Merphonox spoke, "It's good to have companions for this journey. I shall need you both. Let us ready for war, and go to Gallow Cliff this night with a mage, to maintain the bridge into New Karnath while we enter."

Sithrel and Gibit nodded.

With that, Merphonox and his supporters left the grotto and went their separate ways in order to prepare for themselves. And so it was that much later, in the kingdom's armory, Merphonox took up his father's long lance and round shield for combat. Each bore the insignias of Deardrum. He adorned himself also with Penultum's glimmering black armor and decorative mantle, depicting the same insignia, rich in symbolism and meaning.

Before laying the cloak over his shoulders, Merphonox stared at it for a moment; its fabric had stripes of black on a field of gray, which showed three white suns that progressed from a full eclipse to a partial eclipse, and then, to no eclipse at all. A gray serpent coiled itself around the three suns, representing a wise progression from darkness to light. Such was embedded in Deardrumman values: the application of knowledge to gains in even more knowledge, through both research and innovation. *A journey of the mind*, he thought, *from unknowing to knowing.* Merphonox planned to continue that tradition in New Karnath.

This is for father, and for uncle Hrya! With that commitment, Merphonox fastened the cloak's chain about his neck, and left Castle Deardrum for what he deemed as his good destiny: the coveted land. He arrived at Gallow Cliff within an hour, where Sithrel, Gibit, and a mage were already waiting for him.

Merphonox started walking up the tall, rocky incline that went up the back of Gallow Cliff, toward its precipice overlooking the sea. The three seroxians followed behind him, the loud claps of their boots against the chalk cliff perhaps sending an alarm across dimensions, a warning of war to come. The night sky spread over them like a funeral's shroud, moonlit with touches of starlight.

Merphonox hiked and hiked, all the way up to the ledge of Gallow Cliff, where he stood there with the mage. The winds frenzied his graying hair that stuck out of his wickedly curved metal helmet. His mantle likewise flowed behind him, and lent to the silhouette of a mighty warrior in the night.

At the ledge, Merphonox stared into the tossing sea, at the waves crashing on the embankment below, splash upon splash growing all the more furious. It prompted his thought about attacking the inferiors: *Just as we shall furiously come upon them!*

Over the sea gusts, the mage called out.

"How long?"

"Patience," Merphonox said, with his hand upraised, the one that held his shield. His other hand bore the lance at the side of his armored body. "Magicia will place the shard in New Karnath, and when she does, we'll enter and a precipitation of death shall rain upon the inferiors! They are corn, they are wheat, and we the millstone! Let them be crushed into grain and meal, to sift through our hands! May winds scatter the subdued from thence, nevermore to be seen in New or Old Karnath!"

"Ha ha ha," Sithrel laughed, Gibit too.

When the king looked to the evening sky, Merphonox saw the moon and stars resting upon a black tapestry. But then in one moment, he watched the overhead turn blood red, and all the stars fell from heaven in trails of receding light, kissing the night goodbye, never to shine again. Merphonox blinked and blinked, disbelieving this vision seen though not understood. Eventually, he assumed it only spoke of his great victory to come.

"TO RECLAIM PARADISE"

Chapter 73
A Compelling Story

X'ieth opened his eyes from out of sleep, awakening to a gray room. He found himself lying on a crude bed in a chamber of stone, seeing the floor, ceiling, and walls from his resting position. At the room's far end, there was a window between him and the diverse building tops outside, all seated beneath a gloomy overcast. On the wall opposite the window, was a locked door.

He looked to his arms and legs; they were robed in white cottons, and his skin had clearly been bathed. X'ieth sat up in bed, scooted to its corner, and dropped his feet to the floor. During the sudden movements, he felt straw bundles of the bed's mattress shift beneath him. And as his feet met the cold stone, he felt icicles shoot up through his body. At that moment, his mind filled with memories of what happened in Arlem, and the feelings of shifting and coldness suddenly became akin to his guilt moving, along with his conscience freezing over.

Vivid flashbacks of Arlem betook X'ieth: he heard the crackle of fires intermixed with sounds of the dying; he smelled the burnt flesh and ash; he saw immense carnage—blood all over the streets, from people gored. The recollection of sheer tragedy in Arlem drove him to clutch his face in both hands, and shudder in horror. *What have you done?!*

With his hands still on his cheeks, X'ieth threw himself upon both feet and stood there screaming, "What have I done?! What have I done?!" All in one instant, his breathing became rapid and his heart beat faster and faster in his chest.

Memories of Arlem continued stimulating his senses. He saw the blood. He heard the screams. He smelled death. The memories came and came, an unstoppable force that literally brought him to his knees. There, on the floor, he writhed in emotional pains—guilt, sadness, and regret. "No!" X'ieth screamed, refusing to believe it was his fault. "I didn't... I couldn't have!"

Somewhere amid his poor memories, images of Gremel came to his mind; he saw the giant dragon, eating Arlem's townsfolk and showering blood on the city, just before the monster spewed fire over a stretch of red slate rooftops. The images stopped, and he shook his head. "It was her! Gremel did this!"

But as much as X'ieth wanted to believe, when he looked to his hands, he saw blood emerge from their grooves! The blood flowed and flowed, filling his palms, and spilling onto the floor. X'ieth blinked several times, and then suddenly, his hands appeared clean as if they were never stained at all. But despite the troubling vision going away, it perplexed him just the same. For

X'ieth did not know exactly what had happened in Arlem and he feared the worst.

X'ieth glanced to the window, noticing something strange about it. *It has bars.* A bit dumbfounded by the sight of iron bars over the window, the young knight just stared at first, not knowing how to react. But then in one sudden instant, he got off his knees and ran to the window, grabbed the bars, and looked outside, seeing the skyline of Castle Sergros. Outside was freedom, a privilege that he might have lost by one night's doing. The realization made him gasp. *You're in a prison quarters!*

Breathless, X'ieth gazed out the window, beholding gray everywhere, like the mural towers on the far walls that blended in with the gloom, sitting beneath coned hats of black onyx. Beside the towers were square, freestanding keeps of stone, jutting high into the sky, also as gray as the day. Adding to the effect, the walls, towers, and keeps all rose out of a sea of gray cobblestone that spread in all directions. Everything indeed was gray, like a gray dream come to life.

X'ieth angled his head, to see what was at the side of his tower. To the right, he saw adjacent turrets, circular in shape and with corbeled tops. He looked to his left, seeing the same. The appearance outside suggested it was early morning or midday, but it was impossible to know for sure with the gloom.

His eyes fell upon the crisscrossing iron over the casement, long rods that protruded from the stone. With all his strength X'ieth pulled at them, but they would not budge!

He considered ideas for a way out, and all that came to mind was more scenes from Arlem. But it was then that he vaguely recalled thinking things into being there, by a bizarre magical power. With that idea, he closed his eyes and concentrated, imagining that the bars were not even there. Yet, despite how much he focused, when he opened his eyes, the bars were still blocking him from freedom!

He went into his channeling chamber, seeing an enlarged room as he did in Arlem, with a tall double-door Source entry of wood, having carven inlays of thorns. X'ieth ran to the doors, grabbed their bronze handles, and pulled outward. The doors came apart, and along their edges shined a flash of Nexus from beyond the chamber. He pulled more, and the green energy streamed into the room, filling it from floor to ceiling. When the room was full of Nexus, the Source entry slammed shut.

X'ieth turned around, and went for his Source exit with the energy amassed about his body. When he reached the Source exit, he pushed open the door and visualized a fiery destruction on par with Arlem, hoping that the trigger image would be enough for him to blast the barred window to oblivion.

A moment later, X'ieth found himself in the prison quarters and at the window, channeling Nexus where he stood. Green energy arced from his midsection as an underwhelming flame that whooshed over the iron bars, which the young knight still held. The rods conducted the heat, and immediately, X'ieth felt his hands burning!

"Aggrhh!" He let go instantly, suffering a line of burns and blisters across both palms. X'ieth stared at his hands in disbelief, hardly expecting this outcome. It was enough to tell him that his recall of amazing power in Arlem might not be true to his memories.

X'ieth waited some time, and then slowly, he put his hands near the bars. The young knight did not sense heat, and so, he grabbed onto them again, shaking them with all his might. As before, they would not budge.

"I've done nothing wrong!" he yelled, his words breaking under the weight of his own doubts.

Again, X'ieth shook the bars over the window.

"No, no, no!"

Denial surged through him. He could not accept what was happening, or that it was for due cause.

Slowly, X'ieth realized that something was missing. *The shard!* He started searching the room frantically. There was no furniture beside the bed, so he went there and inspected under the mattress, running his hand along its length. *Nothing there...* He pulled off the linen sheets, threw them to the floor, and ran his hands over the top of the bundled straw. *Nothing there...* Next, he looked under the crude bedframe, also finding the same. *Nothing there...*

His mind went wild. *Where's the shard? Where is it?!* All of a sudden, negative feelings surfaced from his one side that loved the shard, his side that had obsessed over the black sword in Arlem. He felt empty. He felt incomplete. He felt desperate.

But following those negative feelings came positive feelings, from his other side that hated the shard and wanted it gone; this was the side of X'ieth that urged him to the blacksmith's shop in Arlem, and kept him there despite a sudden desire to leave. He felt relieved. He felt unbound. He felt free.

And these positive feelings outweighed the negatives, such that X'ieth felt more relieved than empty, more unbound than incomplete, and more free than desperate. His mixed emotions netted to an overall positive feeling that felt wonderful indeed, in the wake of the black shard captivating him and nearly driving him mad, ever since he took it from Lucen in the Mountains of Liath.

"It's gone!" he cheered triumphantly, experiencing a victory over the shard. X'ieth balled his hands into fists and threw his arms into the air. "It's gone!" X'ieth sung to himself and danced in the chamber, elated beyond belief. "The black shard be gone! It be gone!"

The more he danced, sung, and celebrated, the more a burden was lifted from off of his chest. X'ieth carried on like a reveler, with a smile on his face and cheer in his voice. He sucked the air passionately, savoring each breath more than the last, as he savored his life more now than he had with the shard. "It's gone, it's gone, it's gone!" he said repeatedly and happily, giving his farewell to the broken sword that nearly drove him off the edge of Karnath and into the Void, with insanity and obsession.

In the middle of his continued celebration, a distinct click was heard, but it was hardly enough for X'ieth to stop celebrating. Little did he realize though, that the click was the room's door unlatching.

"Ahem…"

Mid-dance, X'ieth froze. Slowly, he turned about, seeing the door to his room now swung open, with guards in a wide stairwell, and an official at the room's entrance. The official was the same man seen in Talus' throne room, the one who escorted X'ieth to a chamber in the eleventh tower, where he slept the night before departing on his quest the next day. Just as then, the man wore a blue tunic above his tight brown pants. But this time, instead of giving a warm welcome he stood there glaring, as if severely bothered by the sight of X'ieth celebrating.

He stared back at the official, with his hands frozen in the air. His face went flush from embarrassment, and X'ieth felt hot all over. In a single moment, the young knight lowered his arms, regained his composure, and stood still, waiting for the man to speak.

With a sigh of disgust, the official said, "Prepare for your summons with the king, to be held not more than one hour from now."

X'ieth watched as the man looked him up and down, with a scowl on his face, his nose upturned, and snorting in even snider manner than before. Then, the official exited, closing the door behind him.

X'ieth heard sounds of latching, followed by those of fading footsteps as the ensemble walked down the stairs. With that, he returned to a state of solitude and the whole encounter pounded a realization through him. *That official just treated you as some sort of criminal!* The treatment was offensive and touched upon his feelings of guilt.

After the official had departed, X'ieth stared at the closed door, feeling some fret over his impending meeting with Talus. His mind filled with worrying questions: *Who would vouch for you? How would you even explain any of this, man? What does Talus know, and what even happened after your blackout?* He stood there defenseless to each and every one of them, unable to answer any.

At the pit of his gut, a sickening sensation developed, as X'ieth realized that after all this, he still might not make it home to see his wife and child. With that in mind, he turned toward the window in hopes of seeing the light of day once more, which soon might become a pleasure taken for granted, should he end up in the Sergrothian dungeons.

However, when X'ieth turned he came face-to-face with Lucen, instead of seeing the barred window! His jaw dropped and his eyes widened.

Immediately, feelings of surprise did combat with those of his anger and frustration.

After a moment of reticence, X'ieth shouted heatedly, "You!"

Lucen stared back without a word. As usual, he flashed his crooked smile and flipped his wild hair. In addition to his gnarled staff, he carried a sack showing blotches of blood.

X'ieth yelled, "I should tear you limb-from-limb!"

"If you must," said Lucen, nonchalantly.

With that taunt, X'ieth lunged and grabbed at Lucen with both hands, but the youth vanished into thin air and reappeared a few cubits behind his shoulder. A few more iterations of this occurred: X'ieth lunged, and Lucen disappeared before being caught, only to reappear at the young knight's rear. And as it was, with X'ieth lunging again and again only to catch air, he tired and eventually had to stop to catch his breath.

Playfully, Lucen asked, "Are we done yet?"

Between his panting, X'ieth spoke out.

"I never… should've trusted you!"

Lucen maintained his smile, and suddenly threw the bloody sack to the young knight. X'ieth showed quick reflexes and snatched it from the air. When he did, he immediately felt its weight in his hands. With fear, he peered down at the bloody sack, seeing the twine fastened about its neck.

"What… what is this?"

Lucen's smile grew even wider.

"It's what you need?" the youth replied.

X'ieth paused. *How can he know what you need?*

"And what do you think that is?"

"Guidance on your story."

X'ieth emitted a blank stare. *Eh?*

Lucen continued. "You have many questions and not many answers, so let me help you avoid patching holes in your story with false memories. Let me guide you."

Lucen gestured for X'ieth to open the sack.

"Go on, consider it a gift."

There was now a tremble in the young knight's hands. The sight of blood stains on the sack warned of artifacts of death inside, and X'ieth wondered if the contents would only amount to a sick play on his self-doubts, guilt, and regret over what had happened in Arlem.

After just a moment of fiddling, X'ieth undid the twine and the sack's neck came open. Almost instantly, the acrid odor of decay filled his nostrils. He gagged and dropped the sack to the floor; it hit with a thud. With horror, he watched Esmeralda's decomposed head roll across the gray stone—a foul smelling thing that had rotted for days. His contorted face as revulsion reached across, and X'ieth turned away heaving, trying to breathe through his mouth. Meanwhile, Lucen cackled away.

"Ha ha ha!"

"What am I to do with that?!" X'ieth asked between heaves, looking up to Lucen again. "That alone might not convince the king…"

Lucen passed his sinister grin.

"Oh, you'd be surprised. The head can make a compelling story for Talus, if you piece together the rest."

X'ieth listened carefully, as Lucen proposed that he tell a story of slaying the evil sorceress, unfortunately after her misdeeds brought the fiery wrath of Gremel upon the entire city of Arlem, where all its occupants perished along with his fellow Guardsmen.

When finished, Lucen laughed aloud.

"Ha ha! Now doesn't that sound like what happened with Pyrus? It's makes the story more believable, in that Esmeralda also drew a dragon's wrath upon the city, and many suffered the consequence!"

X'ieth shook his head. Inside, he wrestled with whether or not the flashbacks of him doing harm to the Arlemers were real, versus those of Gremel doing harm.   "But," X'ieth said hesitantly, "are these events true, as you've spoken?" If he had anything to do with Arlem's destruction, X'ieth would feel terrible over suggesting it had all been due to the dragon. His inner voices held diametric views on the matter, and sparred off against each other. *You have an obligation to speak honestly under morals, man… Just as the oaths of knighthood bind you!* His other side contended, *Speaking about what you're not sure of does no harm…*

Lucen spoke, interrupting his thoughts.

"I implore you to use your better judgments, for if you consider what happened from the beginning of your quest until now, you'll realize it's exactly as I've said, minus a few details…"

X'ieth mulled over what Lucen said, as the youth's argument had its merits. *It did kind of happen that way…*

Lucen came at X'ieth from another angle.

"And beyond your better judgments, perhaps you should ask yourself if you know for sure that you even awoke at all, after lying down at Arlem's inn? Are you confident that you did not dream a nightmare, perhaps in response to a father's misplaced confession?"

How does Lucen know about Zeros? X'ieth could not refrain from wondering. He stared back silently.

"Well?" Lucen asked. "Are you sure?"

X'ieth considered the questions again, and they caught him off-guard, injecting doubts in his heart. *Could it all just be a nightmare?* He wondered.

Despite how farfetched Lucen's suggestion seemed, the young knight did not know how to defend against it.

X'ieth kept silent, and looked at Lucen blankly. As he stood there, his mind swam in possibilities: *You destroyed Arlem. Gremel destroyed Arlem. No one destroyed Arlem, and it was all a dream.* The young knight did not know what to believe, but it occurred to him that under the first two possibilities, he could not prove his innocence if he were suspected of wrongdoing in Arlem. *Then don't say anything, so not to incriminate yourself...* The idea immediately seemed wrong, for if he had absolutely nothing to say, Talus would presume his guilt.

X'ieth continued looking at Lucen, and the more he did, the more he blamed Lucen for putting him in contact with the black shard, which caused whatever problems the young knight faced now. At the thought of him being to blame, X'ieth became upset. His nostrils flared, his breathing became hurried, and his heart pounded in his chest. He still looked at Lucen, and it was not long until the only thing he saw standing before him was fault. *Lucen wanted you to do this, and he's to blame for everything!*

Quite unexpectedly, deep wrath moved X'ieth from standing idly to committing violence. He turned to the nearest stone wall and punched it repeatedly with his fist; dust filled the air, as a piece of it crumbled and fell on the floor. Next, X'ieth ran to the bed and in an uncontrollable rage, he took up its one side, overturning the frame, and hurling it against the wall! Upon making contact, the frame broke into its constituent beams, which clattered noisily across the floor.

"Arrgghhhh!" All of a sudden, X'ieth screamed at the top of his lungs, as his ranting and raving continued running its course. He threw his shoulders back, turned around, and faced Lucen.

The youth stood there with a hand up, as if to fend off the reaction and prevent it from escalating further. X'ieth just leered at Lucen, debating if he should lunge at him again. *Knock that smile right off his face...*

As if reading his mind, Lucen dropped his smile.   "Talus connected you to the black shard, not me." Lucen took a step closer, coming right in X'ieth's face and within the young knight's reach. "Stop running from the destiny of not getting what you want in life. There's nothing wrong or shameful of dying with your dreams, so own that destiny. You're not the Child of Light."

The words damaged X'ieth. As an immediate response, he shook his head. *Don't believe him.* X'ieth could not believe Lucen, for he still held onto the shard of his broken dream and would not let go. *You're the Child... You're Kayareth...*

With some disbelief over Lucen's behavior, X'ieth looked at his once friend, still unable to place why the youth had done this, and if he could be trusted. *Let me guide you.*

X'ieth glanced to the corner of the room, to where Esmeralda's head had rolled. *The head can make a compelling story, if you piece together the rest: Esmeralda angered Gremel. Gremel destroyed Arlem, and everyone in it. Just say, the last thing you remember is trying to stop the dragon, before you ended up here…*

"I've been there for you all along," Lucen said to X'ieth, still withholding his smile. "I saved you from Kort; I warned you of the gang in Arlem; I cued you when to slay Esmeralda; I prevented Gremel from crushing you; and now, I give you a story for Talus that hopefully will get you back home. I'm more of a friend than you think, and I hope our relationship can be as it was, despite what's happened."

Lucen took a step backward, away from X'ieth, before vanishing into thin air.

All alone now, denial raged inside the young knight—denial that he had done anything wrong, denial that he was the person that others had called him. X'ieth felt upset again, and as before, he turned about and threw pieces of the bed about the room; he punched the walls; he screamed.

"I touched not the shard!" he exclaimed. "I'm the hero!" The sound echoed the room's confined space again and again, just like the image that kept resurfacing in his mind: *The image of you as Kayareth…*

A click was heard, behind all of his carrying on. It did not stop him.

"I'm a noble knight of Sergros!" X'ieth declared, hoping all in the world could hear him now, especially Talus who for long knew of his heroism and knightly manner. Maybe all would see, or at least some, like the official who had unlocked the door moments ago and entered the room.

X'ieth was abashed. He turned to the man from another expressive moment, one that surely reflected poorly upon him. At his feet was the destroyed bed—pieces of timber, rope strands, and hay—all strewn about the floor. Dust still hung in the air, just as the echo of his words. *I'm a noble knight.*

"The king will see you now," said the official in a cold voice. The man glared from the entrance in disapproval, with guards behind him in the stairwell.

Slowly, X'ieth nodded. He knew the likely thing was that something bad had happened in Arlem, and he felt the weight of accusations against him already, before any had even been made. Yet, a part of him feared that he deserved whatever charges were coming. He sighed and pushed the thought out of his mind. *Get this over with…*

X'ieth turned from the official, and sighted the sack at his feet along with Esmeralda's head in the corner. For him, seeing the latter conjured up Lucen's words: *The head can make a compelling story, so why not tell it? Maybe.*

With that in mind, X'ieth reached down and picked up the bloodstained sack off the floor. With the sack in hand, he walked over to the room's corner, stooped down, bagged Esmeralda's head, and then tied the sack. He took the head to the room's door, and exited into the stairwell.

X'ieth was immediately surrounded by guards. He looked at them, and they all showed faces as stern as steel, with eyes forward and not even glancing his way. *Your escort to the throne room...*

The official led X'ieth and the guards down the stairs, away from the prison quarters. The young knight followed the man, with soldiers on his every side.

While his wrists were free from the weight of shackles and chains, the same could not be said of his conscience. Fearing he was more involved than what Lucen suggested, X'ieth thought long and hard about what he would say, wrestling with the matter every step to his destination.

(The King and Sergros' Problems)

Talus stood in a second-floor alcove that opened to several bay windows, which overlooked the castle courtyard outside Gawdin's basilica. Over his shoulder, the king glanced back into his main hall. It was a long room, having gray stone walls whereupon burning torches alternated with blue banners that showed the Sergrothian gold lion, and extending to a vanishing point in the adjoining vestibule. The vestibule was an antechamber before the hall, where guests would wait before informal sessions with the king. At the center of the hall was some furniture—a table with a chalice and uncorked wine bottle on top, and a cushioned chair.

More shouts could be heard from outside in the courtyard. It made Talus turn back to the windows.

"Feed your people!" shouted an angry man.

"We cannot work, we cannot do!" said another.

"The gloom prevents us!" yelled a woman.

"Help your citizens, lest we go without!"

Talus gazed into the crowd of Sergrothians from the city, who now, occupied his courtyard. It was literally a disgruntled mob inside Castle Sergros, ironically protesting on the day of thanks. Lines of soldiers held them back.

At the mere sight of the people and hearing what they continued to say, the king's problems hit home. With the gloom, many of his subjects were without work, food, and shelter. He tried to intervene with handouts from the Sergrothian reserves, which now had been depleted, save another few days of provisions for those inside the castle.

Despite his premonitions of the gloom going away and the Guard returning to Sergros, he had the gloom staring him in the face each morning, one Guardsman back in Sergros, and big problems facing one of the oldest yet brightest cities in his province: Arlem. Altogether, it was a disaster, and more and more it seemed like the end. *At this rate, if the Dark Prophecy came true tomorrow, it wouldn't matter much...*

Talus sighed. His head continued to ache from lack of sleep; his eyes were heavy and sore too. A cold draft came through the thin panes of glass in the bay window, rubbing salt in his latest wound: there was only enough firewood to heat half the castle, if that.

"Bring us the king!"

"Aye, let him sleep with us in the streets, and join us to hunt rats for dinner!"

More shouting from outside reminded Talus that firewood was the least of his worries. He sighed again, and prayed silently. *Destiny, where are you?*

Talus continued looking through the window, into the crowds, paying particular attention to the faces of his subjects—a canvas on which misery had been painted. His people were hurting. His people were angry. His people were confused. These were they—people with wants and needs; people that he had tried to help through the gloom, but failed. *Perhaps if I had instead helped them help themselves, things would be different...*

Through everything that had happened, Talus observed how his handouts using the kingdom's reserves had only fostered dependency in his people, and now, they were more inclined to extending an open hand than putting one to the plow. *And all it took for this riot to happen, was the hand that feeds to no longer have food...*

Talus lingered at the pane, watching his restless people, and mulling over how it got to his point. Lessening provisions started it all, and weeks ago, those in the city about Castle Sergros had noticed supplies were running short. As the storeroom got lower and lower, Talus needed to slow the actual delivery of goods to cities in the province, and bought time by having the heralds and royal officials explain delays to the various towns. But when provisions had diminished to a dangerously low level, handouts in the castle walls stopped completely, leading to riots here. And word of this was spreading from the castle, and threatened to descend the entire province into chaos. Arlem had rioted a week ago, and people were leaving Breslin and New Yoke like rats would leave a sinking ship.

This problem facing Sergros was complex, but experts made Talus aware of the root problem: *Too many of my people feel entitled to what's not rightfully theirs. As some received handouts out of true need, others stopped working and extended an open hand, thinking they too deserved the same. For these, it was easier to beg for food than to work for it...*

The king's economic advisors explained how the Sergrothian reserves became depleted much too quickly, via this phenomenon and the non-existence of appropriate measures to limit welfare to citizens of true need. Exacerbating this problem were illegal immigrants from Juniper and the Isles, who fled to the cities where handouts were initially abundant; they were ready to consume but not willing to produce. The king's economic advisors summarized the situation, by describing prosperous economies as a two-way street of consumption balanced with production, completely unlike Sergros now.

Talus knew that there were good intentions at the heart of his provisions to the Sergrothians: shouldering hurt people through a hard time. So he kept to those plans, trusting Destiny to remove the gloom before careless handouts led to problems. Additionally, due to trust issues, he willfully ignored the insights of Cedric and other members of the Senate, committing himself to the simplest way of dealing with the problem, but probably not in his citizens' long-term interest. *A season of hard times becomes a life of hard times for those who prefer to be cared for by others, without a will to move beyond their trying times, to the extent that they really can…*

Bad politics had caught up with Talus, and he estimated that the Senate would try to make him pay for it, with Cedric leading the charge. It was well known in the Senate that the Darxar line had been elected by the people for a very long time, because they managed to win widespread favor with the majority of citizens by re-distributing Sergrothian wealth.

Talus, like his father Elix, figured those who could bear more taxes should pay them, so that others could have more at the expense of the rich. *After all, the rich are only rich by inheritance, extortion, thievery, and such, so those at the top stay at the top for generations, unless a fair king intervenes, such as myself! Because of me, the poor can have better lives!*

By this strategy the king won votes, election cycle after election cycle. And given that success, Talus never would have presumed that Destiny thought poorly of his actions. But now, given Karnatha's silence, he had to wonder about his choices, given the prevailing problems in Sergros and their likely consequences. *Is this Destiny's way, of punishing me for not promoting my people to work? All along, would they have been most happy through hard work and self-sufficiency?* He wondered.

Nervously, Talus drummed his fingers on the casement's frame, glancing to the vestibule again. *How to circumvent this big problem?* he thought, directing his eyes back to the window. *It's too late for the people to work hard now. Perhaps Sergros can borrow its way out of this mess? Perhaps…*

Deardrum had wealth, and had no recent involvement in aiding their allies, so surely they had available resources. Given this, Talus was sure that Thimbraldorf, the King of Deardrum, was in a position to lend, and borrowing would avoid his need to increase taxes further for the wealthiest citizens of Sergros. He grinned at his cunning. *The Senate will be delighted to hear about this! Sergros already has a credit line with Deardrum and the kingdom has some debt with them even now, so what's a little more?* The plan seemed foolproof.

Talus stood at the window musing over the situation, confident that borrowing money would be enough to restart the Sergrothian economy. He loved the idea of borrowing, but hated the idea of making the deal with Thimbraldorf, as it would be a major blow to his pride. *You'll be seen as crawling to the dwarves for help... Ugh.* Talus was well aware how the dwarves could never refrain from pointing out greed and poor stewardship in humans, among other distasteful characteristics. *For sure, I'll face their condescension before I get their help...*

Talus growled at the situation, shook his head, and walked away from the window, out of the alcove, and into the main hall. In the middle of the room was a lavish chair of polished wood with plush blue cushions. Beside it stood a table, bearing a bottle of red wine next to a chalice filled to the brim.

He came before the table, and took hold of the chalice to enjoy what might be some of his last simple pleasures for a while, at least until the dwarves lent the humans some money.

Unlike his binge drinking before, he now sipped his red wine in moderation, while considering the best way to approach Thimbraldorf for aid. *I could write a letter... Takes too long. I could go in person... Maybe. Or, I could save face and just send my best negotiators. Splendid.*

Talus smiled, and the unpalatable images in his mind instantly vanished, of himself kneeling before Thimbraldorf—the burly king of the dwarves, with a huge, frizzy white beard—who mocked him from the throne. *The humans need money from the dwarves, eh?* The voice went as the images—both gone.

Contented with this direction, Talus sat on the chair with his chalice in hand. The cushions shifted under his weight; the chair was far more comfortable than his throne. He started feeling better about things. But with a sigh of pleasure, his mind randomly filled with a misplaced memory that was perhaps related to a previous time where he had premature feelings of relief: the feast he arranged off his premonitions of the Guard's return and the gloom receding, where the ghostly woman appeared.

Recalling the event brought Talus' stupidity to mind. With might, he slammed his chalice onto the table, causing wine to splash out and onto his hand. He let go of it, and wiped his hand on his kingly garb, unafraid of the stains. A voice went through his head: *You might not be in this situation if you hadn't been so confident in your premonitions!*

"Foolish, foolish, foolish!" he yelled at the thought, as the memory made him more than mad. *A good thing my advisors did not mention the feast when explaining why our coffers have emptied; I would've cut out their tongues myself...* The feast had humiliated Talus, even if no one had called him out on its tremendous waste, or his premonitions being wrong.

Talus leaned forward in the chair, folded his hands before his face, and rested his chin on top. He thought about the past for a moment longer, and then pushed the memories from his mind.

"None of that matters now…"

It was clear to him how things would proceed. He would borrow money from Deardrum, create some royal jobs for his citizens to get the Sergrothian economy moving, and all would be well. *In the end, Cedric will be the laughing stock of the Senate, when things go back to order. He'll see…*

Being a devout Karnathan, Talus maintained faith that one way or another, Destiny would ensure he kept his throne, and Destiny would protect his kingdom from Darkness. An image of the ghostly woman popped into his head, and he shut it out. *She's not going to bring down Sergros, nor will Cedric! Destiny will see to my continued rule… Destiny will…*

In an aside, Talus spoke to Karnatha, "How long until Sergros sees a blue sky, bright foliage in Saol, and blooming flowers in Liath? How long, Destiny, until this early winter yields to the brisk autumn that I love, erasing gray with colors many? Or will it be spring that greets us after gloom, with birds soaring and green grass on our fields? How long?"

A scowl formed on the king's face, at sudden thoughts that suggested it would not be today that the gloom lifted from over Sergros. Instead, it would be tomorrow, or the day after. For today Talus had already heard of more gloomy things—vast destruction in the southeast, as told by reports from his scouts.

Indeed, the Sergrothian scouts informed Talus that unexplainably Arlem lied in charred ruins, after their recent survey of the site. *Entire spans around the city have been completely blackened, the stone and slate melted I'm told!* Talus heard that nothing remained of Arlem but debris, a knight with a sword clave to his hand, and the suspicion of unseen misdeeds.

And so, as many times already today, Talus impatiently glanced to the vestibule, anticipating the suspect at any moment. *Now where is he?!*

(The Culprit Speaks)

Accompanied by the guards, X'ieth followed the official down the stairs of the tower, and through many corridors of gray stone in Castle Sergros, to a spiral staircase leading up to a vestibule. The vestibule was a foyer of sorts, with a doorway leading into a hall used for informal meetings with Talus. Both the vestibule and the hall had high ceilings and a regal appearance. All along the way, the young knight saw how the kingdom's former prosperity manifested itself through elaborate statues and tapestries galore, all featuring the lion of Sergros.

He reached the vestibule first, where in passing he noticed a cluster of blue-cushioned seats off the entrance. The room had a hand-woven, royal blue carpet across the floor with a gold lion crest at its center and gold tassels along its edges, two doorways facing each other, and a twin set of tall windows on each wall adjacent to those containing the doors. The windows on his right opened to the sprawling courtyard of Gawdin's basilica. Through the glass panes, X'ieth saw a mob of people on the streets held back by Sergrothian soldiers; their cries reached his ear.

"Feed your people!" shouted an angry man.

"Clothe us!"

"Give us shelter!"

"We deserve better than this!" said another.

The cries continued, desperate and angry.

Behind the official and beset by guards, X'ieth stepped into the main hall from the vestibule. As soon as the space became visible to him, he noticed Talus seated at the room's center, in a cushioned chair. Beside the chair was a table having a wine bottle atop, along with a chalice that was nearly full.

Not more than a moment before X'ieth saw Talus, they both entered a stare down. Even from a distance, the young knight could see dark circles beneath the king's eyes, perhaps telling of his restless nights in the restless city about Castle Sergros.

More noises came to X'ieth through the distant bay windows in the alcove, at the hall's end. The cries were muffled and difficult to make out, yet they were audible and confirmed the pressures bearing down on Talus.

"How is it fair, that you feast on dainties while your people starve!" yelled a man

"Attend to us!" shouted another. "Take care of your subjects, as a king should! Meet our needs!"

As the yelling faded, X'ieth swallowed hard, knowing he stood against more than suspicions, rather a king on the verge of anarchy—a king looking for a scapegoat, and maybe more. His imagination ran wild about what might happen, causing him to swallow again. He gulped fear.

Still staring at Talus, X'ieth found it hard to look away from the king's fiery brown eyes, but eventually he did, glancing briefly at his kingly blue cape and his brow's crown, tokens of a rule held dear. He redirected his eyes to the king's body; he saw Talus hunched with hands folded before his chest and his chin resting atop, as if contemplating a matter deeply.

When before Talus, the official stopped walking and X'ieth stopped as well, along with his guard escort.

"My king, here's X'ieth from the prison quarters."

Talus slowly removed his chin, and with the index finger and thumb on his one hand, he began pinching his beard over and over again. The king enjoyed a few moments of silent beard fiddling, before speaking.

"You may leave us."

X'ieth watched the official nod, and then retreat with the band of guards through the main hall, back toward the vestibule. Before they could reach the antechamber, Talus called out to them, "Soldiers, wait in the foyer for further command."

For just a moment, X'ieth diverted his eyes from Talus to watch the guards pile up in the vestibule; there was about half a dozen or so.

"Ahem…"

X'ieth heard Talus suddenly clear his throat, and it brought the young knight's attention back to the king. The king glared ominously at him. What was once a dulled face, tired and worn, now became a worrying face of coldness and sadism, perhaps the most familiar of his many deemed acquaintances in Castle Sergros.

Under the king's icy gaze, X'ieth squeezed the sack tighter by its neck. He kept a good grip on the burlap, despite his sweaty hands now, and beforehand, an altercation with one solider that tried to take it away at the official's request. For still having it in his possession, he owed the sack's death scent, as the foul odor repelled the guard more than his physical resistance.

From out of the chair, Talus suddenly rose to both feet; he stood nearly half a cubit taller than X'ieth. When the young knight met the king's eyes, Talus snarled harshly. "Kneel before me."

To X'ieth, the command immediately seemed out of place, for this was a hall for informal meetings with the king, outside of the throne room. *So why then, does Talus want formalities?* He wondered.

"Kneel!" Talus shouted gruffly, when X'ieth did not comply. He heard sudden clings and clangs of shifting armor from soldiers in the vestibule, as if some of them stirred, feeling the need to act. It was then that X'ieth realized how there was potential for his situation to worsen, and the prospect reasoned with him. *Just kneel. Don't make this any harder than it already is…*

With that decision, X'ieth went to one knee, perhaps more reluctantly than ever before. When kneeling, he lowered his head and waited for Talus to speak. A few moments passed, and he found himself studying crevices between stone slabs on the floor, which was easily a relief from staring into the king's eyes

"Both knees!" Talus screamed.

X'ieth stopped himself from studying the stone, to ponder why Talus would pointedly assert his authority more than usual. It made little sense to him.

In that moment's pause, X'ieth felt sharp pain in his calf, as Talus kicked his one upraised leg so that he dropped it. *What in the Void?!*

Now upon both knees, X'ieth glared up at Talus, who glowered right back at him.

"You'll show respect, one way or another!"

X'ieth gave a crisp reply. "Kneeling upon both knees has never been customary of Sergrothian knights."

"Many things will be customary now!" retorted Talus. X'ieth watched him turn and grab his chalice of wine, giving it a sip and then keeping it in his hand, while turning back, with brown eyes fiery like a kiln.

"During your goose chase," Talus said, "I've been watching this kingdom fall apart. People are without food, clothing, and shelter, and my politicians keep closed quarters from me each and every day, waiting for the imminent like damned vultures!"

Talus took a seat again. Meanwhile, X'ieth lowered his gaze to the floor, finding momentary refuge from the king's eyes. His hands continued to sweat. His heart raced. His chest felt constricted, and his body was tense. He squeezed the sack even tighter than before.

"Face me," Talus commanded, from the chair.

X'ieth looked up.

"Where are my knights, the Crimson Guard?"

Talus took another sip of wine.

X'ieth paused, seeing flashes of Finnel and Nathan on their knees in Arlem, bleeding out after falling on their swords. *Are they really dead because of you?!*

"Well?!" Talus asked again, impatiently.

X'ieth paused again, keeping silent.

"Should I consider," Talus went on, "that…"

Mid-sentence, X'ieth interposed, "They're dead." He watched the king's countenance darken, like waters of the deep. Though Talus said nothing immediately, X'ieth knew the sight of contemplation when he saw it. This was it.

"What do you mean?!" Talus asked. "How?!"

Hesitate and he'll think the worst, so out with it, man! With this understanding, X'ieth hurried his reply.

"Lewes and Tol died in Saol, to vespers with magical swords."

Shock plastered Talus' face. X'ieth noted the sharp movements of his facial muscles, contouring his skin as he reacted to the news.

"The others perished in Arlem," X'ieth continued, "before the city was destroyed by dragon fire."

Talus fell silent, and started thinking again. It was only a matter of time before the shock left the king's face and it relaxed. Talus resumed fiddling with his beard, this time twisting it between a pair of fingers.

"And how did *that* happen?" he asked suddenly.

Like lightning, X'ieth brought his reply.

"Esmeralda drew Gremel's wrath by destroying the forest and mountain, and the dragon followed us to Arlem."

X'ieth proceeded to tell how a grueling fight broke out in Arlem, from which the others perished but he was fortunate enough to stay alive. In the dragon's visit to the city, it became decimated by fire. He told the story confidently, yet inside, he felt unsure about if it were true.

The story drove Talus into a deeper coma of thought, where minutes of silence passed, before the king eventually emerged.

"And how can you prove this?" he asked, stabbing the young knight with dagger eyes.

X'ieth maintained his gaze, not blinking.

"I cannot."

In response to that admission, Talus sat there for a while longer. Silence ensued, and eventually the king raised his chalice to chug down his wine, an intense guzzle where it ran from the corners of his lips over his clothes. X'ieth saw a new stain form on the king's garb beside an older stain. Talus wiped his mouth clean with his sleeve.

"So you come back with nothing?!" the king asked pointedly. "With none of the Guard to back your story, Arlem burnt to ashes, and the gloom staring me in the face each morning?!"

BAM!

Talus slammed his chalice on the table, and the noise startled X'ieth. The slam resonated through the hall. The king abruptly stood from his chair, and towered over the young knight. X'ieth discerned a guard begin running from the antechamber, as if feeling the need to intervene. Immediately, Talus yelled at the soldier.

"Go back, imbecile… I'll call you when needed!"

Sounds could then be heard, of the guard's retreat. Talus' eyes followed him, as if to make sure the man did as told, and did so without delay.

"Ahem…" X'ieth cleared his throat.

Talus looked back.

"You challenged me to slay the sorceress," he said, having the king's attention. "Here…"

X'ieth tossed the bloodstained bag to the king's feet; it landed on the stone floor with a dull thud.

Talus curiously leaned forward, and took up the sack. He began untying it. At that moment, X'ieth discerned some soldiers stirring in the vestibule, as if about to come to the king's aid.

Talus raised a hand, to keep them at bay.

"It's unneeded. Stay where you are."

When Talus undid the twine, he peeked into the bag. Almost instantly, it emitted the deathly stench of decaying flesh, which sent the king into a hacking spell. *Cough! Hack! Cough!*

And though the acrid smell reached X'ieth's nostrils, the young knight quickly breathed through his mouth, refrained from gagging, and let a smile curve his lips, as wide as could be.

At the king's coughing, guards rushed from the vestibule. Talus lifted a straightened hand, palm-out.

"Stay at ease! I said it's unneeded."

Talus tossed the sack aside, and slumped into his chair with a look of ongoing recovery upon his face. X'ieth enjoyed the sight thoroughly. *No words are needed to put a naysayer in their place. The results speak for themselves.*

Moments later, X'ieth observed Talus stand up from the chair again; as before, he towered over the young knight. X'ieth hid his smile as the king glared down, with a look never crosser.

"You think bringing me this rotten head does you any good?! There are more questions here than answers, and you remain the primary suspect in Arlem!"

X'ieth's jaw dropped, and at that, a smile formed across the king's lips.

"Did anyone tell you," Talus asked, "that so far no dragon droppings have been found in Arlem's ruins? Such makes your story a bit implausible, so even as we meet, my finest diggers conduct an ongoing investigation of the site, and they shall reveal the truth very shortly."

X'ieth knew a thing or two about criminal convictions in Sergros. *There has to be evidence of wrongdoing presented, which influences judgments at a trial. And there isn't any such evidence here…*

"So currently," X'ieth asked, "you cannot deduce more than a terrible fire consumed all of Arlem? You have no evidence against me, is that right?"

The remark agitated Talus considerably, prompting him to growl as he slunk back into his chair. A long while, the king grumbled while drumming a few fingers against the chair's armrest, clearly mulling over the situation.

Talus started thinking out loud. "Cedric might think it's a weak case but, nonetheless, I'm king and can have anyone jailed for just about anything, without evidence."

From the chair, Talus stood once again, putting both hands together. *Clap clap clap!* X'ieth found the noise loud and irritating in his ear.

"Scribes, scribes… Someone call my scribes!" From the vestibule, arose sounds of scurrying feet.

Not knowing what was happening, X'ieth wondered, *Why does he need scribes?* It seemed unnecessary.

A few moments passed, and X'ieth saw a middle-aged scribe enter the chamber, his yellow, feathered hat bouncing with every hurried step. The scribe's greenish vesture showed an embroidered quill pen between two lions of Sergros that faced each other. X'ieth glanced down, noticing pointy shoes of brown leather upon his feet.

"Come hither," Talus said, motioning for the scribe. "And take record of these forthcoming edicts."

X'ieth watched Talus stare him in the eyes, while speaking to the scribe.

"For being suspected of wrongdoing in Arlem, the knighthood of X'ieth Armstrong is hereby removed until the investigation finishes, and he's found free of guilt in the Sergrothian courts!" The scribe began scribbling.

"What?!" X'ieth asked from his knees, with exasperation. The fissure widened, and suddenly his dream of remaining a knight broke apart, shattering now into a million pieces. In Arlem, X'ieth suffered depression over what Zeros shared and how it might have influenced his success in life. As a result, he felt at lower lows than were real, by doubting the circumstances for his knighthood and his marriage. But now, the unreal low of not meritoriously earning his knighthood became a real low of his stripped knighthood, and the reality crushed him.

Satisfaction ran across Talus' face, true to the king's sadistic nature, as if the young knight's sorrow pleased him. He continued talking, making the wound a little bit deeper.

"With my decision, his Guardsmen sword and armor—as found on him in Arlem—have been taken back to the Sergrothian armory, and his line of credit in the king's service has been cancelled as of today."

Behind the king's words, the scribe scribbled away, furiously inking everything onto parchment.

For X'ieth, his feelings of loss grew greater as his dream of the knighthood shattered right before his eyes, into shards of opposing hue—white and black. And with those feelings, his eyes widened in disbelief, his heart throbbed in his chest from anger, and he could feel his skin redden and become extremely hot.

"Because he's suspected of the same crime as Pyrus," Talus continued, "imprisonment seems befitting until the investigation completes."

"What?!" X'ieth protested again, unable to believe what he heard. *There's been no trial. There's no evidence. Therefore, you can't be treated as a criminal!* His conversation with Talus had transitioned from shocking to simply unbelievable, and now, altogether unconscionable.

"If Pyrus, the dragon hunter, had been captured during your last mission, he would have seen the same punishment until trial."

X'ieth realized where this was going, and what the consequences would be. *You've a wife with child at home, possibly a child not even born!*

X'ieth protested, "I have a family who needs me—a family who won't see me, if I'm unlawfully detained at Castle Sergros and prevented from going home!"

Talus shrugged. "That's not my concern."

His calloused reply increased the young knight's rage seven fold. His heart throbbed harder, his breathing grew fiercer, and his skin became redder.

"This is no way of treating a loyal subject of the king, and a noble knight such as me! I…" X'ieth shouted, talking so fast that spit flew from his mouth.

A dire thought suddenly crossed the young knight's mind, cutting him off mid-sentence and rendering him speechless. *What goes on now between you and the king, is exactly what Zeros described… Talus separated him from his family and exploited him, just like the king plans to do with you!*

Outraged at the thought, X'ieth rose from off his knees, and in so doing, he would stand up to Talus as he vowed to do before leaving Sergros on his quest. *Have your word! Take action! Don't tolerate abuse!*

"How dare you deem my words false without proof," X'ieth continued, upon his feet. "And how dare you speak of separating me from my family?! How dare you be cruel with me like this, as you've been, lo these many years I've spent in the Crimson Guard!"

The scribe scribbled a final note on the scroll, and dashed away before the situation could worsen. As the scribe exited, the young knight saw two unarmed soldiers quickly enter from the vestibule.

X'ieth raised his fists and waited with ready hands for the pair of soldiers to converge on his location. When the first of them came near, he grabbed the man by the hand and elbow, hurling him into the oncoming soldier. Like two tin cans from the tin-maker, he watched them bang together and then fall to the floor with a clang. There, he saw the soldiers struggle to stand again, their armor clattering noisily against the stone while they did.

When X'ieth turned from the soldiers to Talus, he saw the king staring with an open mouth and wide eyes, as if he were extremely afraid of something he beheld. X'ieth continued watching, not knowing what went on, and seeing Talus step backward, before falling into his cushioned chair. Against the backrest, Talus leaned and pressed his head, while clenching his garb in white-knuckled fists. From that position, he spoke in a shaky voice.

"You… You found the black shard upon Liath, didn't you?!"

Startled by the question, X'ieth felt his gut sink.

"What do you mean?!" he asked.

"I see you now," Talus gasped, "with the black shard! When we found you, this sword you had not, only your own sword!"

Talus suddenly recoiled with estranged eyes, as if bewildered by visions before him. He continued speaking.

"I see you with that sword now," he muttered terrified, "and you look like the Child who wields it in the Dark Prophecy." The king swallowed hard. "You appear as him! You… You are…"

X'ieth watched Talus continue to push back in the chair, until it fell right over! With a loud bang the chair tumbled back first and hit the floor. The king scooted rearward, over its backrest. The whole time, he stared forward with a hand lifted before his face, as if to shield himself from X'ieth.

"The visions of you overlay with images of the youth from the basilica that I saw weeks ago!" Talus said the words, now pointing a shaking finger at X'ieth. The young knight stepped back. "Y… You… You're the Darkness upon this kingdom, the one who caused this gloom! You're… *him.*"

The words damaged X'ieth more than anything that he had heard yet, from anyone; Talus alluded that he was someone Dark, and was somehow responsible for what ailed all of Sergros!

"All this time," Talus continued, "the Child of Darkness hunted an innocent sorceress! You're the Child of Darkness, aren't you?!"

X'ieth suddenly found it very difficult to breathe, like a vice was suddenly clasped about his chest. In his own skin, he felt uncomfortable then, as the king's allusion became something far more concrete.

The two soldiers who had fell were now afoot once more. In addition to them, X'ieth heard more soldiers pile into the main hall from the antechamber, as if it became clear to every guard that a situation escalated there. The sound of their feet rose noticeably in the hall.

Still scooting back, further away from the chair, Talus suddenly proclaimed, "X'ieth… is the Child of Darkness! He's Shaizan!"

X'ieth stood before his dream of being the hero, which since Arlem, had showed a large crack—large and right down its center. *First Lucen called you the Child of Darkness, second was Arlem's people, and now Talus does it a third time!* With the king's latest proclamation, the fissure widened even more, and the king's words echoed his mind: *You're the Child of Darkness.* This time, unlike before, there was no inner voice of denial from X'ieth, just silence and the start of his acceptance.

His jaw aquiver, Talus barked orders to the guards, "Take him to the prisons, to await execution!"

From all sides, X'ieth saw soldiers close in, and it was moments before they took hold of him. In their clutches, he threw his arms and struggled to free himself. *No, no, no!* Of all the things lost—his honor and knighthood, his dream of being the hero—he thought then about lost freedom in the dungeons, about being away from Millicent and his child, and that thought devastated him.

"Unhand him!" came a sudden voice, piercing the developing situation. "Unhand him, and seize the king!"

Still wrestling with the soldiers, X'ieth looked over his shoulder. From the vestibule, he perceived High Chancellor Cedric enter with upraised hands. Confusion showed on the faces of those who had seized him.

Talus yelled at Cedric. "I'm still king, and should have you hauled down there instead of the boy. Aged meat would be a delicacy for the dungeon rats!"

Given the politician's entrance and words, X'ieth did not know what to expect. But suddenly then, he felt the soldiers loosen their grip on him. When they did, he turned for a better view of the politician: a man in beige garb with balding head and balled nose, holding a parchment in one hand showing many scribbled signatures along with the royal seal.

"Here's the order signed unanimously by the other chancellors, to try you for crimes against Sergros, with your repeated poor rulings of the kingdom."

"Absurd!" said Talus, with eyes on the parchment.

"You brought only poverty, instability, and despair to the citizens of Sergros amid this gloom," replied Cedric. "So soldiers, seize your dethroned king!"

Astonished, X'ieth felt the soldiers let go of him, only to take hold of Talus instead! When the king was in their clutches, he squirmed. While struggling, Talus shouted repeatedly, "You're all making a big mistake!"

In the middle of his wriggling, Talus broke one arm free and pointed a shaking finger at X'ieth.

"There, he's the Child of Darkness! I had a vision that told me he's Shaizan!"

Cedric shook his head. "Sure he is, just like Esmeralda was. Guards, take him to the prison quarters… to await trial!"

X'ieth watched the soldiers work together and haul Talus away from the main hall, and through the vestibule. Along the way he kicked and screamed, and before going out of sight, he said his final words to X'ieth:

"You'll be held accountable for all of your Dark deeds, to a power much higher than the throne of Sergros! Remember, that any decent person having a conscience will remember to honor their family first, then Destiny, and finally their country in all they do! You though, have dishonored all three."

The words struck X'ieth poorly, like those spoken by a complete hypocrite. *How has there been any honor in how he treated you, and how he's ruled his kingdom?!* Indeed, it did not seem like Talus had honored his father Elix, the deity Karnatha, or his kingdom Sergros by a reckless rule of wild accusations and careless spending.

By the time X'ieth had finished his thought, Talus was gone and the room fell silent. In the hall, he saw Cedric face him with an apologetic look about him.

"I'm sorry for that." Rolling his eyes, the politician muttered to himself, "Now Talus accuses his own knights as being the Child of Darkness. It's absolute madness…"

Cedric sighed. "Go home to your wife and child. Your service to Sergros is much appreciated."

A huge sense of relief flooded X'ieth over evading the dungeons. He nodded, with a deep breath.

"Regarding Arlem," Cedric told X'ieth, "should the investigation warrant any further information from you, your presence would be required back in Sergros for more questioning. But we won't know anything else for days."

X'ieth shook his head. "Understood."

After his reply, a silence developed in the hall.

Cedric gestured to the doorway into the vestibule.

"I assume you know the way out. You'll find a carriage awaiting you in the gate courtyard, leading out of the castle, into the city."

X'ieth flashed a weak smile. "Thank you."

He turned and began walking away, but before he could leave the hall, Cedric's voice was heard.

"Oh, there's one more thing…"

X'ieth stopped instantly, and his heart jumped in his chest. Slowly, he spun about to face Cedric.

"Yes?"

"On Millicent's behalf," Cedric said, "you asked Talus months ago for an oracle to attend your child's birth. The king withheld this from you for control, just as so many other things. Knowing the right thing to do, I requested Lady Lyda of Juniper to make an appearance at your home, without consulting Talus."

In his mind, X'ieth thought of Millicent's wants and needs, and the news put excitement in his voice.

"So, the oracle will come?!"

Cedric lifted his hand with its palm out, as if to slow the young knight's expectations.

"Well, she hasn't yet written back but…"

Cedric sighed thoughtfully and dropped his hand.

"Do have your wife set her hopes on Lady Lyda's attendance. Sergros will see to this thing, as it's the least the kingdom should do for a knight who's sacrificed so much."

X'ieth flashed another smile.

"Thank you for everything."

Just then, X'ieth had a bizarre thought that whatever vision betook Talus might just overcome Cedric, if he waited around for it. *Better leave now, before he changes his mind!* The smile on his face became weaker. He gulped.

With that in mind X'ieth turned, walked a bit, and ducked through the doorway into the vestibule. Familiar with this part of the castle, he went out of the vestibule to a spiral staircase leading down. He took the steps all the way to a first-floor annex that connected the building to other buildings of the castle, through winding corridors of stone. He followed the length of the corridors to an exit doorway, which opened to the gate courtyard. The whole journey was far from thoughtless for X'ieth; he could not stop rehashing the encounter with

Talus, especially the poorer moments. *He kicked you into kneeling, much like a despicable man kicks a dog when angry!*

The cold air bit X'ieth as he stepped outside and into the courtyard; it was the same area seen from the barred window of his prison quarters. A sea of gray cobblestone spread out in all directions, ending in gray stone walls, off of which hung mural towers, pointing into the sky with cone-like, onyx tops. Beside the towers were square, freestanding keeps, also of gray stone. At the far end of the space, was a portcullis gate that separated the castle courtyard from the city streets that was not seen before from the window.

X'ieth redirected his eyes to the middle of the courtyard, where a horse-drawn carriage stayed, manned by a lone driver up top. The driver was an elderly man who wore a floppy diamond-shaped granite-colored hat, and was bundled in a thick gray coat above his long, black trousers, with a dark woolen scarf wrapped about his neck. Reins extended from the driver's gloved hands to a harnessed black horse, which looked dejectedly at the cobblestone, considerably thinned and lacking muscle mass.

X'ieth stopped walking about ten cubits from the coach, and just stood silently. In that moment, a distant part of him felt empty. It was part of him that he hardly understood; a part of him that was most difficult to place; a part of him that loved what his other part hated.

His eyes trailed to the enclosing ramparts and battlements of Castle Sergros, to their round turrets with corbeled tops and onyx-hatted mural towers, to the square keeps jutting high from the ground. It was a place of immense familiarity—a place he often missed and felt incomplete without—yet a place that now left something to be desired, beyond his pardon and release.

"Are ya comin', boy?!" the man called.

X'ieth met the driver's impatient glare.

"Aye," he replied, flatly.

X'ieth sighed from a heavy heart, and walked to the coach, wrestling with his feelings of emptiness as he went.

The young knight estimated that some of it came from Talus' final exercise of authority—the rescinding of his knighthood—something that Cedric did not undo.

When at the coach door, he pulled its handle toward him. The door opened, revealing a dark cabin inside where a window shed light on a blue-cushioned seat that was made of wood and bolted to the carriage bottom. And on the cushions was something he did not expect to see, something that one part of him feared seeing but another part rejoiced in seeing: it was his crimson cloak, wrapped about a long, obvious object.

Like ore to loadstone, it attracted X'ieth upon him making the sight. Unable to resist, he climbed into the coach, closed the door behind him, and took a spot on the seat beside the bundle.

Slowly, he lifted the bundle in his hands, feeling the outline of the broken sword through the cloak's fabric. In recent days, he felt most conflicted about the shard, oscillating from love to hate for it, but now, back again to love. And that love for the black shard filled the emptiness inside him, the vacancy born from his broken dreams—a space that can be used for good, evil, or nothing at all.

X'ieth stared at the bundle, and it was only a matter of time until his hands slowly peeled back the cloak to reveal the shard's blade. It was black and nightly, reflecting the light in prismatic glimmers of red, green, yellow, and blue. A smile went to his lips and his heart beat faster, as he stared at the shard without even blinking.

X'ieth stared and stared at the shard, getting lost in its Darkness, and hardly noticing when the coach jerked into motion and began rolling down the cobblestone streets. When one carriage wheel suddenly went over a bump, the carriage abruptly jolted him and broke his concentration.

It was then that the young knight looked out the window, as the coach whipped him past crowds of people protesting throughout the city.

"Give us food!"

"Give us clothes!"

"Give us shelter!"

"Meet our needs!"

Their voices fell on his ears, but he cared little for the cares of others, being drawn once again to the shard.

Uninhibited now and with his cloak peeled back, X'ieth focused again on the smooth black blade, not quite understanding by what fortune the shard came back to him, or if that fortune was really misfortune.

But in time, the shard allayed his worries. His body calmed with the shard back in his possession, and his heartbeats slowed inside his chest, like the slow and steady beats of a funeral drum. Once again, X'ieth felt that he was amidst something much larger than himself—a matter not navigable alone, making need for guidance.

As the carriage took him out of the city surrounding Castle Sergros, his mind filled with the image of Lucen's face. *Let me guide you.* X'ieth gripped the shard tighter through the cloak, and swallowed hard. In all likelihood, that was exactly what would happen.

"CHILD OF DARKNESS"

Chapter 74
The Belabored

illicent's scream came shrilly, at the top of her lungs, "You caused this!"

X'ieth shrunk back from the main space of his own cottage, where his wife lied upon their bed. The bed had been dragged from their bedchamber and sat beside a table with two chairs pushed in, one on each end. The table stood against a windowed wall, with a lone burning candle atop, flickering orange light into the dim space.

At the moment of her words, X'ieth made eye contact with Millicent. And in so doing, he witnessed her many discomforts, and internalized massive guilt for getting her pregnant in the first place. There she lied, bedridden on the straw mattress, with her face and forearms glistening in sweat, and her blonde hair frazzled more than usual. Her blue eyes spoke of pain, and possibly, regret. Her face showed the fatigues of child labor, as she started having contractions several hours ago.

"Now, now, you mustn't go after him just yet!" said the handmaid, who was at Millicent's side, rubbing her arm in a soothing way. "Save your strength for pushing!"

X'ieth looked to the handmaid, an elderly woman who assisted with the pregnancy. She had arrived a few days before him. At his glance, she looked his way and gave a weak smile, which wrinkled her face a bit more than it already was. Half her teeth were missing but she was a happy soul, with gray hair telling of her age and soft, brown eyes that sent impressions of empathy. She stood half a cubit beneath the young knight's chin, and was adorned in a simple, gray dress.

"He caused this!" Millicent said to the handmaid.

X'ieth looked back, and she stared right at him.

In the wake of her accusation, he found himself without a word to say. She appeared beyond angry, drilling into him with her blue eyes, once soft and lovely like a serene sea, though now, cold and steely.

"You caused this!"

X'ieth dropped his head, still unspoken.

A few moments later he looked up, and Millicent was still glaring at him. He found a moment's relief by glancing away, seeing the fire pit behind her and at her left, the table and chairs on the windowed wall. The same wall extended to a tired, wooden door behind him, for entering and exiting the cottage.

From outside, a fierce wind suddenly blew and shook the door noisily; X'ieth heard the latch struggle to hold the thing in place. For a moment, he looked over his shoulder and in the direction of the door, literally watching it, as if half expecting the door to open up on its own, like it had weeks ago with the winds, shortly before the Guardsmen first arrived at his cottage. Either that, or Galwin barging through, as his servant currently chopped wood for the fire pit, just as before.

Perhaps it was X'ieth's way of thinking his experiences at home would not change much, which had become a natural expectation. After departing Sergros, X'ieth arrived home within a few hours, and since then, it was like nothing had even changed from before his departure. While the timing of his return was spectacular, as Millicent had just gone into labor, contention mounted instantly with her, just as always.

She was upset about her pregnancy, even though she had been pregnant for months. She was upset about him leaving on his quest, even though he came back and would be there for the birth. She was upset about the oracle, even though Cedric had essentially promised that Lady Lyda would be there. Despite the circumstances, it seemed that she was always upset about something out of this time, like her present mattered little and all her anger and frustrations were in the immutable past or the foreseeable future.

X'ieth sighed, and looked back to Millicent. Despite his best efforts to simultaneously lead both a fulfilling career and marriage, her attitude made for a painstaking realization: *There's nothing you can do to please her in the present. It's as if she's mad about past choices, like merely being pregnant or that you went on your quest. It's as if she's mad about uncertainty in her future, since Lady Lyda hasn't arrived yet. Given this, how can Millicent's problems be fixed? If I could go back to another age and change time, would it make a difference?* He wondered.

"You caused this!"

The words sliced through his thoughts, as Millicent angrily accused him again. He focused on her once more, the woman he loved, who perhaps felt differently toward him now. If only he could know.

"I'm sorry," he said, gently.

"I don't need sorry!" she cried, with tears running down her cheeks. "I need this to be over!"

The handmaid calmed her, rubbing her arm again in a soothing way. "Just push, and soon, it all will be over…"

Recovering from her distraction, Millicent focused and began pushing, grunting as she did. Meanwhile, the handmaid met eyes with X'ieth, and used a hand to shoo him from the room, silently lipping the word 'go'.

X'ieth dropped his head, turned about, and walked over to the space of the door, where he began pacing.

After a short while, the handmaid was heard clearing her throat.

"Ahem."

X'ieth continued pacing but looked in her direction, and when he did, she lipped the words 'out of sight'.

The young knight sighed, as he wished to keep in the main space with Millicent, to avoid his own distractions. But as the situation was, he walked beyond the area where the door was, into a hallway off the right of the door, which led deeper into the cottage. And upon stepping into the hallway, he found himself stopped by the sight of what was in the room up ahead.

Down the hallway and across cubits of dusty stone flooring, he saw it well: the corner of his crimson cloak, as it had been spread across the floor in the back room. He immediately saw flashes of the black shard before his eyes, which bent the corners of his lips into a smile. As if the shard emitted certain magnetism, his feet were pulled down the hall, one after the other. As he came closer, more of the crimson cloak became visible, and with it, the shard lying atop could be seen. His smile widened.

"Push! Push!"

Sounds arose of Millicent grunting.

"Push! More!"

Millicent let out an exasperated sigh.

"I cannot do anymore!"

The handmaid replied, "Yes, you can!"

"I cannot!" Millicent screamed.

Weeping could be heard, up the hall.

The sudden development broke the shard's hold over X'ieth. Immediately, he turned around as Millicent continued sobbing, and stepped up the hall until the handmaid and his wife came into his view. From the house's shadows, he peered at them, seeing the handmaid try to comfort Millicent, again with a soothing hand. But she caustically deflected it.

"Don't you understand?! I can't do more!"

Compelled to exert himself, X'ieth ran up the hall and into the main space. Millicent kept sobbing, acting as if she hated the ordeal of childbirth. She seemed unaware of her husband's appearance.

"But you can do more, just as you always have."

Millicent, still with tears flowing, looked to X'ieth.

"I can't do more!" she hissed, clenching her teeth.

"But you can!" X'ieth said, lifting a hand and stepping closer. "Every time I go away, it's unbearable for you to endure, yet you find the strength to manage for a greater good—the good of my return and our togetherness!"

He came to the bed, and took her hands in his own.   X'ieth continued. "And just like this, you can and must manage again for a greater good—our child!"

"I can't do this anymore!" she protested, pushing away X'ieth by his hands. "Every time I push myself further, I've already pushed too far. It's too hard. Don't you get that?!"

"If not for anything else," chimed in the handmaid. "Push more, so to finish what you've started!"

X'ieth glanced over. *That probably won't help.*

He looked back to Millicent, with intentions to act. Seldom was X'ieth an emotionally intelligent man, but this time perhaps he would be, realizing then that he had to be more than just another voice lecturing his wife. Instead, he would have to be invested in the moment, for Millicent needed attention; she needed a listener; she needed her husband to hold her. And so he did.

X'ieth embraced his wife, kissed her on the forehead, held her, and readied himself to listen.

"I can't do this!" she shouted, trying hard to free herself from his hold. But X'ieth would not let go. He met her blue eyes under the candlelight.

"Why can't you, my love? Tell me."

Millicent sighed, as if frustrated over her husband yet again not understanding her.

"Time," she declared.

"Time?" he asked. "There's plenty of time…"

"No," she replied. "I'm out of time to work more, to try any harder! Can't you see that I'm spent?!"

X'ieth internalized the comment, realizing the childbirth must be much harder than he realized—firstly as a bystander, and secondly, as a man.

"There is only the time we make for things," X'ieth said, softly. "And we make time for special things that are worthwhile. Given that truth, I beg you, to make more time for this, for surely there is nothing more worthwhile than our child!"

Millicent pouted, puffing out her lower lip, moments before pushing her husband away.

"I've never known such pain that is inside!"

She paused, and started crying again.

"I hate you for doing this to me! I hate you!"

X'ieth dropped his jaw and showed wide eyes. Her words injured him, as he loved his wife and had never thought that she would feel any less. His love for her was unwavering, but too often the reciprocal of that love did waver in deeds, but now, it wavered in words. *Did she really mean that?!* He wondered, dreadfully.

"I love you," X'ieth said to her with a delay, hoping that it was just her pregnancy talking.

The handmaid motioned for X'ieth to leave. He hung his head low, and began walking away. As he went, he caught the tail end of the handmaid's talk with Millicent.

"Like he said, we only have the time we make for worthwhile things, so just give this more time."

Millicent shouted, "There's not more time I can give, only time no more!"

In the hallway again, X'ieth stopped where he was, as the comment overpowered him. Suddenly, images from the Karnathan church icons entered his head, those of Kayareth fighting Shaizan at Gallow Cliff. The images focused on the red-haired warrior, zooming in on the nightly warrior and his nightly sword, until it centered on Shaizan's face, which disturbingly became his own! It was then that the entire scene came apart, like threads unwoven from a garment, each frayed into twine with the twine dissolving into air!

Exhaling deeply, X'ieth emerged from the vision, which seemed to him a worrying premonition of something to come. And just as he did, he heard Millicent grunting again, as she resumed her pushing.

"That's it, just push, one at a time!" the handmaid said. "Push and then break, push and then break!"

"Come out!" Millicent pled, between grunts. "Come out, please come out!"

The grunting went on in the background, as X'ieth once again turned his attention to the distant room, where like before, the corner of his crimson cloak was visible on its floor. He stepped closer, and as he did, the shard came into view. The smile returned to his lips, as did the magnetism pulling him down the hall.

X'ieth came all the way to the room's entrance, and peered inside. From where he stood, he saw his vacant bedchamber now emptied of its bed, an object that had been replaced instead by the shard. The black sword rested on the crimson cloak, dazzling its beholders with sparkling allure. For even in the dim light, its blade gleamed in prismatic shimmers of blue, red, yellow, and green.

With eyes widened by desire, X'ieth looked over the blade from top to bottom, starting at the mirror-like black blade. It was long and slender, extending to a silver hilt. Below the hilt was the shard's grip, wrapped in sable leather.

In the moment his eyes settled upon the shard, images flashed through his mind of himself wielding it in Arlem, drawing torrent after torrent of Nexus energy through his channeling chamber and into the sword, which glowed a luminous green. The picture was glorious, and it made his smile even bigger.

Knock knock knock!

Entranced by the shard, X'ieth did not hear a sound. He just stared and stared, having the dance of that prismatic light along the blade trapped inside his pupils. It was then that X'ieth imagined himself as the Child whom he had never dreamed of being as a lad, yet it was someone very important in the stories of old. *Shaizan...*

Knock knock! ... KNOCK KNOCK!

A strident noise broke his absorption with the shard. X'ieth snapped out of his trance, hearing a loud knock at the front door of his cottage. *The oracle!*

Instantly, his mind traveled to daring places—the mere notion that Millicent might somehow be elated, should this be the oracle that had arrived! And with that joyous thought, to the front door of the cottage X'ieth went, with high hopes of his wife's favor.

"ZEROS AND THE CONFESSION"

nxiously, X'ieth went up the hallway and to the front door of his cottage, after hearing a knock. When he came to the door, his hand was jittery with excitement, causing him to fiddle with the latch. Millicent's happiness was stuck in his head from the moment he heard the knock, and he hoped it was more than wishful thinking. *The wife has never been easy to please, but maybe she'll be pleased with the oracle!*

Upon opening the door, X'ieth was met by fierce winds and the gloom, along with someone there, though not the oracle. Rather, it was smiling Lucen in his traveler's robe, holding a gnarled staff in his hand. His blue eyes sparkled in the night, and a gust blew his wild hair over his face; he flipped it back with a toss of the head.

X'ieth was extremely ambivalent over seeing Lucen; his anger and frustration did wrestle with his needs for friendship and guidance. The mere sight of Lucen conjured up the youth's words, as said in Castle Sergros: *I hope our relationship can be as it was. Let me guide you.*

Not knowing what to do, X'ieth just stood there with the door open, staring at Lucen who stared right back. During this whole time, cold seeped into his cottage, carried by the freezing winds.

There was a sudden break in Millicent's grunts.

"Shut the door already!" she screamed. "Lady Lyda is not coming, nor is anyone else!"

"Worry not about him," shouted the handmaid, "just focus and push!"

With the door still open, X'ieth turned in the direction of Millicent, seeing the fire pit at her rear, where the flames cowered to the barging winds. The sight of the weakening fire reminded him of his weakening marriage, where even until now, shortcomings in both a husband and a wife prevented their mutual understanding, making compromises, and ultimately having peace.

But also weakening like the fire were his dreams. *Your knighthood is gone, and you being the hero is questionable...* The thought sorrowed him and he stood there dejected, with the door wide open and winds ravaging his unattended fire. He literally watched its embers lose glow, just as he lost zest for his life. In this, the fire told his whole intimate story, without a single word.

X'ieth turned from Millicent and the fire, back to the door. Lucen lingered there without a word, standing silently in the cold. Slowly then, and with some hesitation, he closed the door right in his face!

He redid the latch and secured the door, hearing the winds howl on the other side. Literally a moment later, regret started to well up within X'ieth. *You have the shard, but haven't a clue what to do with it! You need guidance!*

His inner voice pressed him, but just as he did, Millicent could be heard, struggling in her labor. He sighed. *It's not the time or the place, is it?* It was a difficult thing for him to acknowledge, for from the moment he happened upon the shard in his carriage ride back home, he felt attraction for it and craved guidance on what to do. And as such, the shard inappropriately distracted him from his wife, skewing his priorities.

But what will you do with the shard? At the thought, images of the black sword and its nightly blade flashed before his eyes, and X'ieth began to feel foolish. *You need guidance! There's no other way out of this.*

Yet, despite that realization, X'ieth had shut the door on Lucen and potentially had shut out the possibility of getting his help. Being frustrated with the situation, X'ieth leaned against the door and started to bang his head against it. At every impact, he felt the door vibrate with a bam, and the same happened to his skull. *Stupid. Stupid. Stupid.*

Of all his hazy memories of Arlem, two things seemed concrete to X'ieth: with the black shard he lost control, and the shard was capable of destroying futures. Visions betook him then, of his cottage in burning rubble just like the buildings of Arlem; the visual was sobering. A remote part of him feared what the black shard might do in his own home, and that factored into his want of guidance. *You should've let him in!*

Motivated by his fears, X'ieth decided against his first impulse and opened the door, to welcome Lucen inside. But this time, he stared at an empty space at his doorstep, containing only fog and the winds!

Feeling some despair over not finding him there, X'ieth went out into the cold and peered about in hopes of seeing Lucen. But the gloom enveloped him, filling his vision only with gray. Through the fog, the fierce winds beat him mercilessly, and his warmth started to leave him through his thin tunic and trousers. He shivered.

After only a few moments, X'ieth retreated into the cottage through the door, which had been left wide open. As he entered, he heard Millicent's yell.

"Destiny damn you, X'ieth Armstrong! She's not coming, I said!"

"Focus and push!" the handmaid replied. "Don't be distracted like him!"

He shut the door behind him and re-latched it. As his hands went through the motions, he felt bad inside, as if he had passed up an important opportunity to get Lucen's help—an opportunity that perhaps he could not afford to lose. *What if you give in to the shard here, and lose control like you did in Arlem? What if your family suffers?* He shook his head. *It won't come to that… It can't, can it?*

X'ieth turned, and unexpectedly came face-to-face with Lucen. Surprise reached across his face—all at once, his lips parted, his eyes widened, and his brow raised. They stared at each other before the cottage door, with sounds arising from Millicent in her continued labor.

"Ugh! Arghh!"

"Push more!" said the handmaid.

"I fear that I can't!"

"You can! Just a little more…"

The voices and grunting went on in the background, leaving X'ieth to his encounter with Lucen. Once again, though by a strange means, the young knight and the youth were united under one roof. But given all that had happened, X'ieth remained silent, not knowing what exactly he should say.

X'ieth kept quiet so long that finally Lucen diverted his eyes, and veered off to the right, down the hallway that led into the cottage's depths.

X'ieth hastened after him, likewise going into the hallway and following the train of Lucen's brown traveler's robe, which floated behind the youth, as he walked toward the room ahead, wherein the shard did lie.

Millicent's labor remained ongoing, still heard in the background.

"I'm pushing! I'm pushing!"

"Then push more!" responded the handmaid. "You can do this, but you must not give up!"

Lucen stepped inside the room. X'ieth came up behind him, and stayed at the entrance. From his vantage point, he watched the youth sit down cross-legged right before the shard. A smile reached Lucen's lips, and his eyes were immediately glued on the black sword.

"You enter just like that?" X'ieth asked. "Without even an invitation?"

Lucen replied after a few moments of silence, without even looking back. "Who needs an invitation, when already welcome?"

X'ieth fell silent, and Lucen paused.

"So, when are you going to Gallow Cliff?" he asked, finally.

The mere suggestion sent fluttery wriggles through X'ieth, felt first in the belly. He suddenly saw his same premonition, where the icon of Shaizan came to life, showing a face that became his own. Recollecting that made him shudder, and he banished the idea from his mind. Instead, he chose to think of Millicent and her giving birth. *Being here for her should be your priority, not Gallow Cliff. He can't be serious.*

X'ieth sighed and shook his head.

"My wife yelps as we speak," he said, "suffering immense pains to deliver an unwilling child into this world! How dare you suggest I leave her side?! I must be here, for what reasonable husband would not be? You can't be serious about me going…"

She wailed just then, emphasizing his very point.

"I look serious, do I not?" Lucen said. "You touched the shard's grip once, and we both know what follows. To Gallow Cliff you must go."

X'ieth shook his head, again.

"You must be crazed," he replied. "*My place* is here with Millicent, and to attend the birth of my child."

"Oh, that sounds like *the place* of a family man. Is that really all your destiny affords you?"

At that question, X'ieth instantly felt his yearnings for a destiny greater than an ordinary life—the same yearning that he felt before leaving for his quest, and many times before that. In his mind, he saw the icon of Shaizan come alive, who stood at Gallow Cliff having the Army of Darkness behind him, with their weapons raised and their serpent banners streaming. The scene was perhaps the epitome of unordinary, a prophecy of an important figure doing something that would prove legendary. *Is this the greatness you're destined for?* He wondered, free from the denial or protests of his inner voice.

Lucen's voice suddenly interrupted his thoughts.

"Before the oracles would proclaim a child," he said, "it's typical that the father would always know the child's name in his heart, though not the child's gender. Do you know of this phenomenon?"

X'ieth arched his eyebrows. "No."

Lucen turned with a smile. "Of course not."

"Eh?" asked the young knight.

Lucen smiled even more.

"That's right, you don't value this tradition as your wife does. So how then would you care to know what's typical? In any event, I wager if you know the name beforehand, you'll lose interest in the birth."

X'ieth said, "And what does *that* mean?!"

There was a pause, and filling the space in their conversation was Millicent's grunting, along with the handmaid's coaxing.

Lucen finally replied, "Well, knowing the child's name might bring mixed feelings for you. Remember the background story of *The Unwholesome Inheritance*?"

The youth paused, keeping a constant smile.

X'ieth meanwhile stared back, inquisitively.

"As the story goes, there was a grand feast in Old Karnath, one involving all seven kingdoms. It was held to celebrate vast reconstruction after Maken's punishment. At dinner, an oracle brought great shame to Eriens' wife Mildred by proclaiming her child's name *as Kilwroth*."

"I'm not ashamed of my child," X'ieth interjected.

"Well, Mildred was," Lucen shot back. "Over that name, she wished herself dead at the feast, and ironically, she later died in childbirth. Eriens went mad over it."

Before Lucen had the chance to elaborate on the story, a series of loud knocks emanated from the door.

KNOCK KNOCK!

X'ieth looked away from Lucen, up the hall. And just as he did, it happened again.

KNOCK KNOCK!

Without waiting on Lucen, X'ieth ran up the hallway and all the way to the cottage's door. Like before, his hopes for Millicent's happiness soared, making him so excited that he fiddled anxiously with the latch. *Please let it be her, Destiny! Please, for my wife…*

X'ieth swung open the door, and any icy wind punched him in the face. He squinted and stared into the gloom as fog wafted into the cottage. Barely discernable to him was a black cloak floating away; it was that of whoever had knocked on the door. *They're leaving!*

At the thought, X'ieth hurried into the cold, not bothering to shut the door behind him. By the time he left the cottage, the black cloak had already disappeared from his sight, now absorbed by the gloom. Nevertheless, he ran in the direction it was last seen, seeing before him only a cubit or two, and beyond that, a field of gray. As he went, he shielded his eyes and kept his face forward.

After running a little, he watched the black cloak appear again. X'ieth caught up with it, and put a hand on the person's shoulder.

"Wait! Please, don't go."

The cloak stopped moving, and the figure turned about. It was a man bundled up to his nose, with a gray scarf wrapped about his neck. Through the fog, X'ieth could still make out the man's long coat that fell to his knees, which was embroidered with gold lions: the crest of his own kingdom. This was a Sergrothian royal official.

"Go?! We just came from Juniper!"

The mention of Juniper played on X'ieth's excitement. *It's Lady Lyda!*

"Juniper is days from Sergros, but we're here so swiftly because Lady Lyda started her journey already, after receiving Cedric's summons. She had been slowed because her carriage busted a wheel north of Sergros, but we found her just in time and brought her here!"

Given his elation, X'ieth hardly could pay attention to the background story. *It's Lady Lyda! Millicent will be so happy!* He smiled at the thought.

"Come with me," the official said, waving for X'ieth to follow him. Together, they walked through the fog against the freezing winds. The young knight shivered, as he still wore only his tunic and trousers, and was without a coat. In a matter of moments, the silhouette of a horse-drawn carriage appeared.

X'ieth kept on the official's tail, all the way to the carriage door. There, the official reached forth a gloved hand, took hold of the door handle, and opened it. And out stepped Lady Lyda, a female elf from Juniper of the most elegant appearance.

From half a cubit away, X'ieth could see her well, as the carriage's body obstructed the winds and swirling fog, giving him a clear view. Lady Lyda wore a black fanciful gown, with a green cloak upon her shoulders, over which fell her radiantly blonde hair, being gold like the sun. She had eyes of jade green like the Jezban Mountains, and with merely her stare, she sent impressions of wisdom and knowledge. Altogether, her very presence spoke of inordinate greatness.

The official ran to her, taking both of her hands so to help her down. When she planted her feet on the ground, she let go of his hands and practically ignored the official, getting right to business by approaching X'ieth.

"You are the father, so tell me now: do you have faith that I can name your child, proclaim the gender, and thus speak to his or her purpose in life?"

Up until now, X'ieth had scoffed at the idea of oracles naming children, but upon seeing Lady Lyda in person, his faith underwent a radical transformation. It was perhaps the bizarre nature of her chanced arrival—despite his initial request being withheld by Talus, despite Millicent's naysaying—that changed everything and gave him childlike faith in the oracles and their abilities. *It's a miracle that Lady Lyda is here, and that she's here now!*

"Yes, I believe," replied X'ieth, immediately.

And with his sincere belief, the child's name entered his heart, just like Lucen described. But at the name, X'ieth stopped. His whole world stopped in one singular moment, as if the freezing winds ceased blowing and the swirling fog swirled no more. There was a sliver of calm, absolute and complete, allowing for him to ponder the name. *How... how is this possible?!*

At the conclusion of his thought, the winds resumed howling, pounding X'ieth like a juggernaut. He continued shivering in his tunic and trousers, suffering from the elements, but suffering more from the child's name that came upon him.

With a face stricken by confusion, astonishment, and perhaps even fear, X'ieth turned from Lady Lyda, and began stumbling through the fog, back toward the cottage. With his every other step through the gloom, he denied the viability of the child's name that had settled in his heart. *It's not possible; it's not!*

Walking a short distance brought X'ieth back to the cottage; he barely saw it through the gloom, a silhouette of a home with its window faintly aglow. Without delay, he went to the closed door; it had been shut after he left. His near frozen hands pushed against its surface.

As the door moved inward, X'ieth was barraged by the relative warmth of the cottage compared to the gloom's cold, along with sounds of Millicent grunting and the handmaid continuing to edify her.

"Ugh! Arghh!"

"Push more, just a little more!"

Without even waiting for Lady Lyda to enter, X'ieth slammed the door behind him and veered right, down the hallway. Bearing the child's name in mind, he walked cautiously toward the end room, wherein Lucen had stayed behind with the shard. *It's not possible…*

When reaching the hall's end, X'ieth stopped before the entrance to his bedchamber and looked inside. Just as he left him, Lucen still sat upon the floor, caressing the shard's blade with his bare fingers.

As if sensing X'ieth, the youth glanced back.

"So, how does it feel to know the name of your forthcoming child?"

A chilling grin marked Lucen's face.

With rock-hard features, X'ieth barked, "This was never funny, and I'm certainly not humored now!"

X'ieth stepped through the entrance and closer to Lucen. He stooped down, lowering himself closer to the youth's face. And likewise, he lowered his voice.

"Tell me what it means; my child's name is *Lucen*."

At his admission, Lucen's eyes sparkled.

X'ieth studied him where he sat, and knew that this supposed reality was anything but possible. For Lucen was a young man, likely a few years younger than himself, and therefore could not be his child!

In the background, X'ieth suddenly heard the front door open then close, followed by the sounds of Lady Lyda addressing Millicent and the handmaid.

"I've come from Juniper, as fast as I could."

"Lady Lyda! Thank Destiny you've arrived!" said the handmaid. "Her faith had dwindled!"

"It's her?!" Millicent asked.

"Yes, it's Lady Lyda. She's here!"

X'ieth maintained his stare at Lucen as the conversation between the ladies continued, without him.

Lucen laughed, "You might not presume anything, until Lady Lyda proclaims your child's name. For until then, how do you know this name is truly from her, and not contrived of your own mind?"

"I trusted her," X'ieth said plainly, "and when I did, the knowledge entered my heart. So explain that!"

"If that's enough to sway you, so be it. Believe then, whatever you see fit."

After a long break, X'ieth chided Lucen; it seemed that the youth somehow understood the mystery about what was happening, and derived pleasure from his reactions.

"Don't make light of this thing!" X'ieth yelled. "It's neither jest nor folly!"

Suddenly and surprisingly, X'ieth heard unexpected news from up the hallway. It was Lady Lyda's voice.

"Come, for the vision is upon me!"

Without a second thought for his talk with Lucen, and without further hesitation over the mysterious child's name, X'ieth ran up the hallway and into the main area. He saw Lady Lyda standing beside the bed in which Millicent lied, laying a hand on her forehead as she labored, as if to draw a vision of the child's future from her mind.

At the sight, X'ieth came to an abrupt stop, and stood in place, several cubits before the bed. He silently watched Lady Lyda stand still, keeping her hand placed over Millicent's brow. She closed her green eyes, and meditated deeply and fervently, whispering things that the young knight could not hear. The cycle of Lady Lyda's meditation and Millicent's labor repeated for some time, and X'ieth grew nervous as the process went on.

After what seemed forever, X'ieth beheld Lady Lyda open her eyes. Rays of light protruded from their sockets and around her face, illuming the otherwise dim chamber. And when this happened, Lady Lyda spoke in a booming and powerful female voice.

"Your child is among us, having a clouded future."

The rays of light continued shining from Lady Lyda's eyes, and the rays became suddenly thicker, just as the light about her face grew abruptly more intense. The sight of her countenance terrified X'ieth, and his heart beat faster in his chest at the oracle's every word; his breathing was stiff and strained.

"From this clouded future," Lady Lyda continued, "whether the child's deeds are in the Dark or the Light cannot be ascertained. But the child's character should be clear from the child's name!"

As Lady Lyda faced him, X'ieth swallowed hard. The thick beams of light still shot from her eyes, and her face glowed like the moon. But suddenly then, something different started happening to her, as the vision continued its course: her head jerked back and forth, and the light somehow grew even more intense!

X'ieth shielded his eyes at the development, growing all the more fearful. In a firm voice, he pled with the oracle to deliver her news.

"Speak the child's name, and end my torment!"

But even with his request, there was silence. Lady Lyda continued jerking back and forth, and her lighted countenance became yet brighter. But after some time, long and agonizing for X'ieth to endure, she turned to him, took her hand off Millicent's forehead, and said the following words in a low, trembling voice.

"The name of your child is…"

"THE PRONOUNCEMENT"

After a brief pause, Lady Lyda took her hand off Millicent's forehead and turned to X'ieth. She leaned toward him, still with her face glowing like the moon and thick beams of light shooting from her eyes. She lowered her voice and shared with him what she foresaw, of his child's name and gender.

"The name of your son is… Shaizan."

Given what he learned previously, X'ieth expected to hear the name 'Lucen' instead. But this news rendered him completely shocked. In the instant of hearing the name 'Shaizan', his mouth dropped open, and his legs began to tremble, along with his entire body.

At exactly the same time, Lady Lyda fainted. In a single moment, her lit face became extinguished like a quenched flame, and she fell from off her feet and onto the stone floor, hitting it with a pronounced thud. X'ieth watched her lie there with her chest swelling slightly, as her lungs worked out shallow breaths, indicating that she was still alive.

The young knight continued trembling in place, impaired from acting. In the background, he heard the handmaid urge Millicent, who had stopped pushing with apparent frustration over the situation.

"Keep pushing!"

"Wait, what did she say?! I heard not a thing!"

"Lady Lyda fainted," the handmaid replied, "before speaking the name!"

"But why?!" asked Millicent, being upset.

"It matters not! Speak with her later. Now push!"

The voices faded, as X'ieth became absorbed with a disturbing issue: the mismatch between the name in his heart, and what Lady Lyda now shared. *Your child can't be two different people!* To him, that apparent truth made the mismatched names seem nonsensical.

But then, as if to make matters more baffling for X'ieth, both named persons seemed equally preposterous. It was clear that Lucen was too old to be his child. It was also clear that the foregoing proclamations from Lucen, the Arlemers, and Talus had suggested Shaizan was none other than him. *How can the revealed names be of people who can't be your child?* He wondered, but the situation was anything but clear.

X'ieth felt somewhat settled after mulling over the situation and taking a few deep breaths. He stopped trembling. Now as still as a statue, he stood there in the main area facing the bed, where his wife lied. In a single look, he took in

Millicent resuming her pushing, the handmaid resuming her coaching, and Lady Lyda sprawled out unconscious upon the floor.

But above the sounds of his wife grunting, and above the sounds of the handmaid talking, was a stirring down the hallway, one that emanated from his bedchamber. The sound prompted X'ieth to consider the person waiting there, who likely could provide clarity on the mismatched names, the names themselves, and maybe even more.

In one sudden motion, X'ieth bolted out of the main area and down the hallway, with his heart racing faster than his legs. The room's entrance quickly came into his view, and X'ieth stopped at the threshold. He peered into the chamber, finding Lucen standing beside the crimson cloak spread out on the floor. In his right hand, the youth held the black shard by its blade and stared at it.

X'ieth watched Lucen clench the blade so tightly that its edge cut his hand, causing blood to flow from his fist and down one side of his forearm, all the way to his elbow. But strangely, at Lucen's elbow the blood reversed direction and ran up the opposite side of his forearm, flowing back into the youth's wound, which afterward healed! Lucen looked away from the shard and back to X'ieth, flashing a sinister smile.

"Tell me what goes on!" demanded X'ieth.

Lucen replied with laughter. "Aha ha ha!"

X'ieth grew enraged with the youth's act. All in one motion, he rotated his torso to the right, reached across his chest with his left arm, and punched the wall. A shock ran up his arm as his fist contacted the gray stone. The wall cracked when his knuckles collided with its grainy surface, and chunks of rock crumbled to the floor.

"Tell me now what happens," X'ieth shouted, "for I know you know!"

Despite his violent reaction over Lucen's laughter, X'ieth somehow elicited more laughter from the youth. Lucen cackled on for some time, near uncontrollably.

"Aha ha ha! Aha ha ha, ha ha ha ha!"

The laughter seemed cold and sadistic.

X'ieth stood there at the threshold, with his fist balled and his knuckles bleeding. He wanted to trust Lucen, and he needed the youth's guidance. Yet, he detested how Lucen acted now, like the whole ordeal was somehow an inside joke, one that X'ieth simply did not understand.

Lucen stopped laughing, and finally spoke.

"I felt the same way when my child was named Shaizan, in a future we'll never see."

X'ieth was dumbfounded at the comment, which temporarily stunned him. "What?"

Lucen showed another chilling smile.

"That's right. What happens to you now also happened to me. My son too, was proclaimed Shaizan."

X'ieth went from confused to severely confused.

"You said I was Shaizan. But the oracles said my son was Shaizan. And now, you're saying the oracles proclaimed your son as Shaizan, in the future? Surely, Shaizan cannot be three persons; it makes no sense! So again I'm asking you, what goes on?!"

Lucen kept a constant smile.

"You know a little magic, about tethering and chaining, so therefore you know enough to understand what's happening to us."

X'ieth stared back confused.

"What is a chain," Lucen asked, "a chain of iron?"

X'ieth paused. "A collection of iron links fitted together, with each link connected to one or two others. How does that explain anything?"

"By itself, it doesn't explain much. The answer to your question lies in the analogy. Think of Shaizan as the chain, and our spirits as the links across time, putting him in multiple ages."

X'ieth did not understand. *What does that mean?*

As if inferring his confusion, Lucen assured him it did not matter. "Don't worry if it's puzzling today, for tomorrow you'll be living what I've mentioned, and there's no better way to learn than by application!"

He smiled and laughed. "Aha ha ha!"

X'ieth shook his head, still not understanding.

"Why is this happening to me?"

Lucen dropped his smile and grew serious.

"Why don't you ask Karnatha? Why don't you ask her, about why chance has dictated your destiny instead of choice? Surely, no man would choose a poor fate, yet by chance it comes upon us, with our children being named Shaizan!"

X'ieth swallowed hard, as Lucen's statement resonated with him. *That's you, man… That's exactly you… You've been a good person until now, and have done little wrong to warrant bad destiny… Yet, you lost your knighthood after serving your king. Yet, you possess the black shard, despite dreaming of being the hero since a boy.* To X'ieth, the situation seemed very unfair, given all the good choices he had made throughout his life, given all the good intentions he had, in his heart. In the end, it was exactly as Lucen just said—poor chance.

Lucen smiled. "I guess that means whatever happens just happens, right? Bad things sometimes happen to good people, not by their choice but by poor chance. I feel among them, don't you?"

X'ieth saw Lucen take a step closer. In response, the young knight backed away, also by one step. He was now in the hallway, and Lucen stood at the entrance to the bedchamber.

"Yes, you do feel among them, even if you won't admit it. And for that reason, I'm sure you can commiserate with me. Allow me to share my little story about bad things happening to good people. It goes like this…"

And with that, Lucen began telling X'ieth his background story, which supposedly took place decades from today, in a future that they would never see. He was the son of a lowly Sergrothian knight, who would later grow up to become a blacksmith in Winsdor—the best in the village. And he would marry just like his father, an oracle's daughter, whose parents later proclaimed their first child as Shaizan, at birth.

As the story went, Lucen and his family became ostracized in Winsdor due to the peoples' prejudice over the child's name. And the situation worsened each passing year, becoming the worst in Shaizan's early adulthood, where he found the black shard when hiking in the Mountains of Liath. When Shaizan returned home, the villagers saw him carrying the sword and they reacted by beating him to near death. And then, they dragged him through the streets to the village's end, before throwing him out with the warning that his return would mean his demise. After that happened, Lucen lost ties with his son and was never the same.

"It was hardly the life that I wanted, one where my family's misery came from something so simple—a name."

X'ieth listened in silence, not speaking once.

"How do you suppose that made me feel?" Lucen asked crisply. "To have the oracles name my son as the hated one from the Dark Prophecy? To have my family likewise be hated, without them committing a crime against anyone? Do you have any idea how that feels?"

"You likely felt how I did in Arlem," X'ieth replied. "I accidentally revealed the black shard in a pub, a few hours after displaying anger with my fellow knights in the very same place. The peoples' prejudices about an angry man carrying around the black shard made them instantly conclude I was Shaizan, regardless of reality. It didn't matter if I was a good person or not; all that mattered was what they thought…"

"Precisely, and for the victim of prejudice, what a negative feeling that is! But through it all, just remember that this is how you're meant to feel—how you're destined to feel! Think of it, your poor outcome, just like that of anyone else, was ordained by powers greater than either of us—powers that served you poor chance. So we all should ask Destiny why our lives didn't turn out like we wanted—why our dreams ended up breaking, instead of coming true! For some reason, Destiny ordained many of us to have poor chance and to be less than our dreams would have. So again, perhaps we all should ask why."

Lucen's words immediately ushered a flashback upon X'ieth, of his lonely passage through Forest Saol. He remembered himself feeling the cold in his bones, as he stumbled across spans and spans of gnarled trees with leafless, tangled branches, which stood lifeless in the foggy woods. He recalled crying out to Destiny for help as he went. He felt trapped by the black shard. He felt hurt by what it betokened, given how it betrayed his dreams of being the hero. He felt so far away from his family, and unable to get back. Yet cried as he did, Karnatha remained deaf and mute, only putting a black cloud on his horizon—a black cloud that he eventually sat under in Arlem.

"Perhaps we shouldn't ask," X'ieth replied to Lucen's comment, with hardness in his voice. "For Destiny doesn't speak." He resented Karnatha for her silence. *She should've helped you; she owed you better…*

Millicent's grunt carved through his thoughts.

"Arrrrgggggghhh!"

"Keep pushing!" exclaimed the handmaid. "You're almost there! I think I can see the baby!"

The noises faded, leaving X'ieth to his confrontation with Lucen in the bedchamber. The predicament kept him away from his wife, but despite wanting to leave Lucen to be with her, a number of forces held him in place. He wanted answers. He wanted the shard. He wanted guidance.

"You're catching on. Asking god for answers is pointless, but that's where the journey begins for one of broken dreams—the search for understanding and closure. You won't get either from god, but what you will get is bitterness over your life's poor outcome from its poor chances, with no insight from above. Yet, it's our bitterness that enables us to act, in order to aright life's many wrongs. For you, acting is Gallow Cliff."

X'ieth did not understand the proposition.

"My life fell short of what I wanted, but how will Gallow Cliff change any of that? If I take the shard and go with you, surely it would only add time's end to my broken dreams, making things even worse."

"Oh, it wouldn't be as crushing as you think…"

X'ieth looked at Lucen quizzically. "Huh?"

"Well, just think of what time's end might mean."

X'ieth raised an eyebrow. "Without time, would existence just… continue indefinitely? Would it be… free from the effects of aging and deterioration?"

X'ieth shook his head and gave a wry laugh.

"Well, perhaps Karnath would adore me for that blessing in disguise," he muttered to himself. "Guess it's not too late for me to do something good with my life. Who would've thought it would be this way…"

Lucen interrupted X'ieth.

"Your joking aside, you believe the same about stopping time as Shaizan did, in the first walk. He thought stopping time would extend the age indefinitely into the future, which seems logical at first, but ends up being wrong. *Time's end in any age, triggers the age's end. And back at the finish of the second walk, when the thread of causality had still stitched the ages' weaves together, ending any age would have caused the end of all ages thereafter—the unraveling of multiple weaves from the fabric of creation! This is the cause effect, now no more ever since Karnatha slashed the thread of causality."*

Not understanding, X'ieth looked blankly at Lucen.

Lucen went on. *"Time is the energy that pushes Karnath forward.* It was the Nexus with which Karnatha dressed her distaff, when spinning the threads of creation from strands of energy, life, and matter."

He went on, against the backdrop of Millicent grunting and the handmaid yelling.

"But it's the most essential strand, the fiber that no thread in the weaves can do without. Each age's weave is constructed from threads having strands of life and matter, along with strands of time for a given era. And when the strand of time is removed from threads in a weave, the weave unravels... "

Lucen's words ignited a flashback for X'ieth, born in his mind from a trail of blinding light. He saw the front window of Arlem's textile mill, where a tall and middle-aged woman attempted to spin together threads on her distaff from three strands. One of the three suddenly disappeared, and without it, the remaining strands would not intertwine. As a result, her weave unraveled because it had been made from threads that were now incomplete.

"That was no woman at all!" said Lucen, as if reading X'ieth's mind. "That was Karnatha herself, puzzled by the fray of her fabric, just like she's puzzled over the fray of our fates. Ever since ether started being withheld in the Void, Karnatha has been confused over how slaying time unravels the fabric of creation, or why that unraveling has already begun! She doesn't remember that the Game has been played two times already! She doesn't remember why unraveled weaves are hurting her! She can't remember, because Saora has held most of her memories captive, since the first walk."

Questions swarmed X'ieth's mind. *The fabric of creation is unraveling?! What does that mean?!*

"The fabric of creation has started unraveling, because weaves of the fabric have been unraveled! And the fabric will continue unraveling with more unraveled weaves, since without causality, the fabric has become merely a bundle of separate weaves for different ages. The weaves in the fabric used to be stitched together with the thread of causality, but like I said, no more."

X'ieth shut out his questions and kept silent, realizing that Lucen was answering some of them as he talked. And so, he refocused his attention and tried to absorb every bizarre detail like a sponge. *Let him speak...*

"Repeated play of the Game is the reason for the unraveling of creation's fabric, but in that, it's important to remember why the Game is being played at all. Long ago, Maken created the worlds and the seroxians, and creation was good. But Karnatha, the creator of Maken, foresaw all of the seroxians finding

Darkness and bad destiny in their future; someone who called himself Shaizan had led them to it. Karnatha feared that the seroxians were not strong enough to overpower Shaizan's influence and seize their destiny in the battle between good and evil, and so, she intervened…"

Lucen began describing how Karnatha acted, so to give creation what she thought was an equal chance at a future destiny of either good or evil, and an opportunity to avoid the seroxians endlessly fighting a fight that she believed they could never win for the good. She mixed her blood with that of the seroxians, which gave rise to the Children of Destiny and their descendants, who would play a simple game that would decide Karnath's fate: eternal Darkness or eternal Light. The former would be assured through a curse upon creation, the latter would be assured through a spell.

"Karnatha believed her own Children would be better suited than the seroxians for a fair fight to decide the prevailing destiny in Karnath. And thus the Game was formed, involving the Children of Destiny, a sword that can slay time, and the fate of time itself. Through creating the Game, Karnatha transferred the Battle for Destiny from the seroxians to her own Children, removing the need for any seroxian to fight for their destiny, should he or she choose not to. Her intention was that her Children, being stronger than the seroxians, would always fight the Battle for Destiny, regardless of whether anyone else joined in the fight. This would make the Battle for Destiny fair, but at the same time, would not preclude those seroxians wanting a greater stake in their fate from joining the Children at Gallow Cliff, and taking a specific side."

X'ieth tried to hold back his looks of confusion. The background story that Lucen shared was the very foundation of Karnathan teachings, which explained how the Game was devised to fairly decide how the scale of destiny would tip in Karnath. However, this telling seemed completely disconnected from Lucen's claim that the Game was somehow unraveling the fabric of creation. *Lucen says the age's time is energy, a strand that no thread in the fabric's weaves can do without? When the strand is removed, the age's weave unravels, but how? Maybe he's getting to it. Just keep listening…*

Lucen paused, and smiled, as if reaching part of the explanation that he loved sharing.

"This story must sound familiar, as you know the Karnathan accounts well. But keep in mind that what you've learned is not the whole story! Indeed, there's another conflict in Karnath behind the conflict of the Game. And the truth to that statement will explain why the Game is being played repeatedly, how creation's fabric is unraveling, and to what end these things are being done."

Lucen continued. "Some theologians in Karnath believe that Destiny and the Void have been at war since Destiny broke from the Void. Their conjecture of war is correct, but their thoughts on the war's timing and motive are not. The Void was not angry because Destiny broke away from it at the beginning of time, to use spent energy to empower doing from out of its state of nothingness. Rather, Saora became upset at Karnatha for introducing the Game at the start of the second walk, whereby destiny was stolen from the people."

The mention of Saora made X'ieth's skin crawl. She infrequently was mentioned in the Book of Karnatha as the persona of the Void—the antithesis of Karnatha. She was said to be similar in appearance to Karnatha, though with a body that jittered in the world of spent energy, eyes that burned of truth, and a mouth that spoke its light.

"And for that reason, Saora seeks to undo the Game, by undoing everything that Destiny achieved in the world of spent energy."

Lucen's statement struck X'ieth as bizarre and implausible. There were core Karnathan principles pertaining to spent and unspent energies and how those energies could interact, and these suggested that Saora could not step into Karnatha's realm to do or undo anything. X'ieth understood that unspent energy resided in the Void; it was held in reserve and without a destined use. On the other hand, he knew spent energy resided in Destiny, which went into all things created that had a destined purpose. *The two energies are separate*, he thought. *They can't intermingle!*

X'ieth could not keep silent any longer.

"How can Saora do anything here?" he blurted out. "We are in the realm of *spent* energy, but the Saora is *unspent* energy, as the manifestation of the Void!"

"Are you so sure of that?" Lucen asked. "Even others in Sergros disagree, some proposing theories about *voiding* and the like, where spent energies can end up as unspent energies in the Void."

X'ieth shook his head. *The whole idea of voiding is baseless nonsense...*

Lucen's eyes sparkled as he spoke on.

"Well, you won't have to exercise your faith by believing otherwise, for there are a few people in Karnath who are willing to aid the Void's objective of ending the Game. These people have been empowered by Saora through a form of ether, better known to you as premonitions. This ether gives them knowledge."

"Knowledge for... what?" X'ieth asked, with his eyebrow raised.

"Knowledge on how to use the Game to destroy itself, and thereby resolve its injustice to one and all! Every time Darkness wins the Game, time is stopped, which unravels another weave. Eventually, with enough wins, all the weaves can be unraveled! Without the weaves, the fabric of creation cannot exist. Ending the Game by this means is what Saora wants, and two people were given the knowledge to do this."

That statement was the start of Lucen sharing yet another story of how in the future, at the end of something he called *the second walk of existence*, Shaizan would enjoy a romance with the powerful sorceress Magicia, who later would persuade him to work with her toward Saora's goal of ending the Game.

Together, Shaizan and Magicia led a backtracking expedition through time, to do just that. Their motivations were very different, and something that Lucen described with glee.

Supposedly, at the end of *the first walk of existence*, Shaizan acted without Magicia to extend Karnath's final age into the future, given how Karnatha became too weak to weave another age, due to the peoples' null destiny in the Age of Light. He attempted doing this by ending time, which unraveled the final age and sent all of its accumulated ether into the Void. This happened before the Void went to war with Destiny, and it was literally the backstory of Shaizan that would factor into his future willingness to help Magicia, for his initial aims of stopping time were actually good.

Saora released the ether of Shaizan's deed back into Destiny's world and it moved the time marker all the way back to Maken's creation of the world, where the memories struck Karnatha as premonitions of bad destiny entering Karnath, sometime in its future. As a reaction, she invented the Game and started its play, at the start of this second walk of existence. This Game deliberately involved only her own Children and no longer required the seroxians to fight their own Battle for Destiny, since they could not be trusted to keep bad destiny from entering the world. This is why the Void became angry at Destiny, and waged a holy war to stop the Game and return destiny to all seroxians—cursed and un-cursed alike.

Saora needed a messenger, and Magicia ended up being just that when she was affected by the Game. Hrya died upon Eriens betraying her trust, which caused Magicia to become bent on revenge against Destiny for having the Game. Empowered by knowledge of how to stop the Game, she enlisted Shaizan's help in their future romance, where his own premonitions of stopping time at the first walk's end, persuaded him to help.

"Little did Shaizan and Magicia know," Lucen said, "that the Game wouldn't end until existence itself ended!"

All of the information, especially this, perplexed X'ieth to no end and was incredibly bizarre; he simply could not understand most of it, even though he knew the Karnathan teachings well, and was able to follow some talk of Shaizan and the Game. But many things spoken were hard to grasp, like existence having multiple *walks of a time marker*, Shaizan trying to save the world from Karnatha's last age in the first walk, Magicia and Shaizan being romantically involved in the second, and them helping Saora unravel creation one age at a time through some crazy plot, which X'ieth was somehow caught in the middle of.

X'ieth felt anxious, like with all of this information, he was losing sight of what he really needed to understand: whom his child would be, and why going to Gallow Cliff was in his future. He wanted clarity, but perhaps the aim of clarity was mistaken, given how convoluted Lucen's telling had become. *Chew the meat; spit out the bones… Listen.*

"So," X'ieth began a question, with his head spinning, "Magicia and Shaizan allied with Saora in the future, against Karnatha and her Game? You speak of this like it happens years from now, not like it's about to happen. How am I Shaizan then, or even my son? How does this future you describe have any consequence to my present?!"

Behind his own words, X'ieth heard Millicent grunting in her labor. The handmaid continued yelling.

"Push! Push! Push!"

Lucen spoke, pulling back X'ieth's attention.

"Would you believe that the sins of a son could visit his father? The opposite is common superstition in Karnath, so I'll understand if you find this suggestion strange."

"What do you mean?" asked X'ieth.

Lucen chortled, "Well, Saora would have the Game end, if the Game is to rob people of their Battle to Destiny, for she believes we all must fight for our fate! And to this end, a son's sins come to the father, like how Shaizan came to me and led me to Gallow Cliff, and now, I come to you. It's happening through a simple consequence of the *weave effect* when ages unravel."

He continued. "The *weave effect* happens whenever a future weave unravels, and all its accumulated ether enters the Void, which Saora can later release to the earlier weaves in the fabric's bundle. The earliest released ether in a given age pulls back *the age's time marker* to that point in the age."

X'ieth could not help letting his mouth drop open, and showing a blank stare. *Each age's time marker?!* The comment defied his notion of time being one continuum, on which a time marker was at his present, before his future, and ahead of his past. Yet, Lucen described something truly bizarre, as if time were this fragmented thing—weaves in a bundle, based on how history had already been written in previous walks of a single time marker—where the past did not affect the present, nor did the present affect the future, and multiple times were being lived simultaneously, in different ages. It was unbelievably mind-boggling for him to comprehend. *Don't even try. Instead, get what you need to know from him.*

"Ether? Time markers?" X'ieth asked. "What are you even talking about?! And like I asked before, how does this pertain to me?!"

"Ah, that's right," Lucen kept going, as if not hearing X'ieth's protests. "You don't know about ether yet. Ether is a few things, such as peoples' memories from a future age. Their memories fall between the weaves when the age unravels, to be reborn as premonitions in the past ages. This is the most common consequence of the weave effect, but there are others that you'll learn of later."

X'ieth started to get annoyed by how the conversation took so many directions, and seemed to purposefully stray from his questions.

"Why do you keep avoiding my questions?!" he snapped. "How does any of this pertain to me?!"

"Oh, you're very much in the process of finding that out, firsthand. What I'm sharing with you is future information, part of my experience and part of my premonitions. And learning of the future is akin to how Magicia used the weave effect to her advantage. She asked Saora to release all of Shaizan's memories from the first walk, those about him stopping time. It turned out that Shaizan having these memories in the second walk motivated him to stop time again. And now, here in the third walk, Shaizan's memories fell to me and led me to do the same. Just as Shaizan, I stopped time in the future, decades from now. And you… you're about to follow in my footsteps."

The comment hit X'ieth, like a rock to his skull. *Lucen says the Game is being played over and over again, to somehow unravel creation. Shaizan did it, two times? Lucen did it, once? And now, he suggests you go to Gallow Cliff and do the same!*

"That's…" he said, not knowing how to continue.

Lucen interjected, "That's what you'll do?"

X'ieth paused and just looked at Lucen, taken off guard yet again by the suggestion. Images suddenly flashed through his head, of red-haired Shaizan at Gallow Cliff gripping the black shard and wearing dark armor. He stood before a host of giants that brandished weapons, having their serpent banners streaming under a starlit sky, in the ocean breeze. The chalky cliff walls loomed as an aweing backdrop. It was a scene that transcended a simple life. It was extraordinary. It would become legendary.

"It's not the time," X'ieth said, looking down the hallway. Sounds reached to him of Millicent grunting, and the handmaid still shouting. *You should be there, not here.*

X'ieth stepped up the hall, but Lucen grabbed him by the arm, keeping him where he stood.

"Don't you see that our work isn't over?"

X'ieth looked back at Lucen, shaking his arm free.

"Magicia and Shaizan chose to start Saora's work, but for poor reasons. I've done much better than my son in this respect, for I have cause to continue playing the Game, one that even trumps the reasons that Saora has!"

X'ieth sighed. One half of him felt like he should go to Millicent, but his other half wanted to stay. *Listen to him.*

Lucen continued. "My goal is no different than Saora's; we'll play the Game over and over, the Darkness will win over and over, and creation's fabric will unravel, one weave at a time. But my motive differs from that of Saora's, for instead of just ending the Game, I wish to avenge our broken dreams, which I'll do by stealing destiny from the Children, as well as from everyone else! That way, no one gets want they want out of life! No one's dreams will ever come true again."

Lucen leaned forward; he smiled. "You see, *the lifeblood of good destiny is time well spent*, and Destiny foolishly had strands of its life force embedded in the fabric of creation. In this, Karnatha invested herself in a world full of people who, throughout the ages, have squandered their time away with null destiny, or wasted it with bad destiny! Wasting time voids spent energy and in this, Destiny itself voids, being the well of spent energies across time. This is why Karnatha is dying, with every age unraveled!"

Lucen's entire face lit up with enthusiasm.

"I say, give the fool Destiny a quick death versus a slow one. Saora's fiendish plot is called *Time No More* and like she wanted, it ends the Game. But Time No More does far more than that in my opinion. As the Game is played over and over, as long the Darkness wins, time dies and along with it, Destiny does too! *Time no more, is therefore destiny no more*!"

The comment choked X'ieth. Lucen was not just going along with Saora's plot. He was motivated by Destiny's death, to avenge his own broken dreams, and those of others!

X'ieth could not believe what he was hearing.

"How is this even possible?!"

Lucen laughed evilly now.

"Remember, Destiny's lifeblood is time, and time is the strand of energy that's the essential fiber for every thread in the fabric of creation. When time is voided, weaves unravel, and Destiny loses life force."

X'ieth had the same flashback, born in his mind from a trail of blinding light. As before, he saw the front window of Arlem's textile mill, where a tall and middle-aged woman attempted to spin together threads on her distaff from three strands. One of the three suddenly disappeared, and without it, the remaining strands would not intertwine. As a result, her weave unraveled because it had been made from threads that were now incomplete.

"But… but how, can this be? How is time voided?"

"*The gray sword of legend, assembled from the black and white shards, is the conduit between the Void and Destiny…* It bridges the wells of spent energies and unspent energies! At Gallow Cliff, there's a well of spent energy reserved for the destines of those in Karnath; it's the age's time that must be voided to unravel the age itself!"

With a pause, Lucen threw his head back and cackled, "Mwha ha ha ha, Mwha ha ha ha, Ha ha ha!"

Somewhere deep within X'ieth, a wholesome, good part of him awakened. It had a voice and spoke to him, at first sounding foreign, like something he had never heard before. *No… No. Say that word to him. No.*

X'ieth took a step back. "N… no," he stammered, as his tongue struggled to articulate his resistance. "That's not right… it's not right at all!"

Lucen took a step forward. X'ieth was in the hallway, literally up against the wall. The youth was not far from his face.

X'ieth started thinking, and his mind ran wild. He thought concisely of what Lucen shared, how Darkness winning the Game would void the age's time and unravel the current weave, slowly killing Destiny. *In that, Lucen would steal the peoples' time and their fates; he would rob them of good destiny!* It was a whopping conclusion that brought accusations against Lucen to his lips.

"You," X'ieth muttered slowly, "you're the thief of people's time, and by stealing *that* you rob them of their good destiny! You're getting back at Karnatha for your broken dreams, through everyone in Karnath!"

Lucen replied, "And what's so wrong with that? Those who dream have become weak—too weak to find good destiny. For when the dreams break apart, so do the people. Stifled then, they waste their time, the very essence of their precious lives!"

Lucen continued. "Those who dream are fools. They dream too big, and live a life of null destiny when finding these dreams were only destined to break."

At those words, all of the things that X'ieth grew up believing about dreams swelled inside his head, like a bubble. *Dreams are sacred, and there's joy in dreaming! Whether dreams are likely or poorly chanced, whether they are great or small, dreams should still be had! They are unique to the person, and tell of his or her defining character! Dreams are wonderful…*

But in the middle of thinking those things, the bubble suddenly popped for X'ieth. He saw himself in Forest Saol, shaking his fist and screaming at Karnatha while holding the black shard, on the verge of bad destiny and having his life's dream inverted. X'ieth wondered then, if Lucen's words were true. *You dreamt too big, and look at what happened! You lost your knighthood, and stand to lose more…* The thought floored him.

Lucen continued. "Few in Karnath dream again after enough broken dreams. The product of broken dreams is disappointment, which leads people to either null destiny or bad destiny. A legendary example was Eriens, who tended toward bad destiny when he didn't get what he wanted out of life. His child was given a title telling only of wrath and death, his wife died, and as a seroxian in Old Karnath, he lacked New Karnath! Given all of that, he betrayed Magicia's trust of a peaceful entry into New Karnath, and waged war on the inferiors. There will likely be many to follow in his way."

Lucen spoke on. "Now, isn't embracing bad destiny like Eriens worse than what I'm doing? For in essence, I'm merely speeding up null destiny by stealing time from people who will likely stop dreaming and do nothing, once they become disappointed."

"No, it's the same!" X'ieth shouted. His conscience spoke to him. *Lucen is making a choice for others that's not his to make; it will hurt people... Say it.* "You've found bad destiny just like Eriens, by hurting others in the wake of your broken dreams! This... this is..."

The following words went through X'ieth's mind: *This is the worst thing anyone can do; it's the worst of bad destinies! Now, say that.* But as he had the thought, images flashed before his eyes, of death and fiery destruction in Arlem. He saw the people bloody and gored. He saw their lives' work, burning up, and their Dreamer's Dawn becoming Dreamer's Dusk. *You hurt people... You did wrong.* The realization stalled his tongue from saying anything more of Lucen's deeds.

Lucen continued. "This is what? Changing little? Perhaps. Taking time away from those who won't use it changes little. The reality of their apathy for life is testified by the lack of useful premonitions in Karnath. Do you know why so many things have happened similarly, in three walks of existence?"

X'ieth stared back blankly, wondering if it were a trick question. Lucen did not wait for a reply.

"It's because people have largely ceased from doing, and many preclude themselves from both failure and success by giving up on life. After one big broken dream, the people of Karnath forgot that failure is part of success, and they simply stopped trying! Due to exactly this, dreamers dream less and less, by the day."

Lucen's face grew firm, as he talked more.

"What can be learned from premonitions of a future, without failure or success? Nothing, I say."

In an aside, Lucen turned to the bedchamber and bellowed to its four walls. "How many times will ages be rewritten, with people not rewriting their own destiny?! Premonitions provide no feedback for people to correct their failed outcomes, because the future shows them living in a way that doesn't promote growth, positive change, and betterment! Everyone's life is a portion of the age's weave, but spots on the fabric are tired and worn without change. In this, those in Karnath forfeit choices for a better life and cause their own Fate's Fray, the unraveling of what they were meant to be!"

X'ieth watched Lucen turn from the bedchamber, facing him again, with the cottage's dim light casting shadows over his face. The young knight met his blue eyes, wanting so desperately then to speak his mind. *Tell him that what he describes is awful! Tell him that time must be the peoples', to spend as they will! Tell him, it's not his right to take way anyone's time or destiny, let alone all of Karnath!* But like before, X'ieth found his tongue stalled.

"All the people of Karnath deserve to lose their time, their destiny, and their dreams, because they forfeit opportunities daily, so narrowly focused on one failed outcome in their life that they overlook potential. Assuming that their initial defeats are defining, they throw away their time through null destiny. It's a slow trickle of spent energy into the Void, and I grow tired of waiting! So let the dam be bust when time is ended at Gallow Cliff, and all the spent energy for this age become a flood of unused potential, voided and forever gone!"

After Lucen fell silent, X'ieth stared at him intently. In that moment, he had to question everything that Lucen had done for him, as it seemed now that all along, Lucen had a motive. His words in the prison quarters came to mind: *I saved you from Kort; I cued you when to slay Esmeralda, I prevented Gremel from crushing you; I gave you a story for Talus.*

"Is this why you saved me?" X'ieth asked, his mind awash in the memories of Lucen's help. "To go to Gallow Cliff, and be part of this?!"

X'ieth had wanted to trust Lucen; he needed guidance. But now, he felt as if their friendship was not genuine as it should be, as if this whole time he had been misled into thinking it was.

"I saved you countless times, for your own good."

"What does that mean?" X'ieth asked.

"Everyone in Karnath has a neglected purpose, and without me, you would have neglected yours. This is it."

Suddenly, the handmaid's shout was heard.

"I see the head! The baby is finally coming!"

Millicent continued grunting, clearly pushing.

X'ieth looked up the hallway, but Lucen cackled then, bringing back his attention.

"Mwha ha ha ha! One age at a time, I will make Karnath the *Land of Broken Dreams*, to the eventual death of time and Destiny!"

During that statement, X'ieth noticed a certain lust in Lucen's familiar eyes, present all along though escaping him until now. And with that, he saw Lucen step closer, getting right in his face.

"Through the weave effect, those who live in multiple ages will find themselves in the past, without a future, and with their premonitions as haunting memories of what will never be! I only give people the drear reality which they've earned, through giving up in the wake of their broken dreams."

X'ieth felt like moving away from Lucen, up the hall and back toward the cottage's main area. But instead of doing so, he stayed in place, just looking at him, not knowing what to believe or what to do. And his indecision continued for a few moments, up until the point where Millicent's grunting ended in a blood-curdling scream!

Without a thought, X'ieth stormed up the hall and into the cottage's main area. He looked in the direction of the bed, seeing Lady Lyda still at its foot and on the floor, unconscious. He directed his eyes up, seeing the handmaid with her back turned, facing the window and rocking a bundle in her arms. He looked over to the bed, where Millicent was, lying limp with her eyes wide open and glossed over.

The sight filled X'ieth with despair, for it seemed like something more than Millicent fainting had happened. Slowly then, he approached her in a bit of disbelief, his jaw atremble and his body shaking.

"Millicent, my love?" he called, watching her lie.

X'ieth came closer now to the bed, a cubit away, seeing the motionless body there, its face staring up at the roof in death's gaze. Every moment he saw her without life was torment, and before long, tears poured furiously from his eyes, hot and runny, wetting his skin as they fell.

Inside the grief choked him, seizing his throat with an unseen hand. X'ieth struggled to breathe, while in that moment he questioned the worth of another, as it became obvious that she had taken her last.

"Millicent, my love!" he whispered amid tears, shuddering at the sight of her lifelessness, shuddering more at the trace of his warm fingers against her skin cold.

Millicent, my love! he anguished, unable to cope.

In that moment of X'ieth's immeasurable loss, the voice of his conscience fell silent again, as gone from him went more of his good destiny, and gone from him went more of his goodwill. Millicent's death was devastating for him to endure, as she was the only woman that he had ever loved; it ripped his spirit asunder—never to be mended, and nevermore to be whole. All he could do was writhe in his many regrets of what he did not accomplish with her, in the time that they had.

You never learned how to communicate effectively with her, how to make compromises with her and keep them, how to live with her in a way that honored your marriage vows! And now it's too late, for the opportunity to choose differently has come and past. She's gone! She is gone, and never to return!

He stayed there at the bedside, and eventually his tears stopped flowing; they began drying on his face, but the same could not be said of his tears within. For his heart continued to cry over what had happened, and for him, that inward sorrow might never end.

Time elapsed, and with it, his mind began pondering. *Millicent gave birth, yet there's no sound of a child crying! Where is my son?! Where is he?!*

Frantically, X'ieth gazed back to the handmaid, still standing with her back turned, and facing the window before the table and chairs. He walked toward her, extending his right hand, so to touch her on the shoulder. But before the young knight could come close enough, the handmaid turned around, and it was clear from her wrinkled face and the tearstained front of her blue dress that she, too, had been crying. In her arms was a child in swaddling cloths, as motionless as Millicent.

"The child came like this," she said, in sorrow.

X'ieth saw the handmaid approach him, and when near enough, she handed over the child.

"I'm sorry," she whispered. "I'm so sorry."

With a seized heart, X'ieth took hold of his baby boy in one arm. Using his opposite hand, he traced a fingertip along his child's face. The skin seemed lifeless, cold to his touch. In this, he was immediately haunted by memories of grazing Millicent's face moments ago.

At first glance, grief smote X'ieth hard, but it elicited no external reaction from him, only inward pain that fueled his resentment toward Destiny, for his life given. *So many dear ones taken, and for what?! Karnatha should've prevented this; she owed you better...*

With the lifeless baby in his arms, X'ieth pressed the swaddling clothes firmly against his chest. Soon his eyes gushed with tears, as he could not refrain from crying again. And in that moment of colossal sorrow, his grief kindled a fiery anger in the depths of his soul at a sudden and terrible realization: *You lost everything.*

X'ieth stood in his cottage, a day after his knighthood was rescinded, cubits away from his wife who just died at childbirth, holding his lifeless son, and with the black shard in the back room, suggesting the poorest of titles a man could wear. His every dream literally crumbled around him—he was not the hero; he was no longer a knight or husband, nor a father.

To one knee, X'ieth fell with his lifeless son, weeping more and more in a pervasive heartache that literally stung his soul. In an aside, he lamented, "This is too much to bear! Why would Destiny will for me to shoulder such heavy weights?! Fettered now am I, chained to bitterness, anger, and contempt! Never will I recover from this and cannot be held liable, for what man could endure such woe without a lasting, negative effect?"

From behind him, X'ieth heard soft footsteps coming closer from up the hallway, sounds that spoke of Lucen's approach. And it was only a matter of moments, before the young knight felt a force on his shoulder, strange and unlike a human touch.

Looking over, X'ieth saw it was Lucen's hand; the youth held the black shard in his other arm by its blade, which reflected the candlelight in rainbow shimmers. The young knight pushed Lucen away, refusing any semblance of comfort. For X'ieth, contact with Lucen was again a strange force, and not like a human touch.

"You want to know who your son is?" asked Lucen. "Then believe he's standing right beside you."

X'ieth kept his eyes down, staring at his lifeless son in complete heartbreak. *Your child, born dead... Your wife, died giving birth... Why? Why?!* He would never ever understand all the dimensions of his latest tragedy.

Lucen spoke, despite X'ieth being taken by grief, and continuing to weep.

"I may not have grown up like you wanted, father… But I'm still your son. Your child's life is in me, for *I am ether that fell from the future's unraveled weave*. It may not be clear now, but more than memories fall between the weaves. Just know that things must be this way."

After some time, X'ieth stopped crying. He turned to the handmaid; she lingered where she was, by the table and chairs, before the window. He walked there, away from Lucen and the shard.

"Here," he said, handing over the swaddled corpse. "Give my boy the ritual Karnathan burial for a miscarried child. Make the grave. Pray the prayers."

The handmaid took it.

"Will you… not be there?" she asked, delicately.

"I cannot."

"Then… what shall be his epitaph?" asked the handmaid, again delicately.

"*Here lies Lucen,*" he replied in a solemn tone, his tears drying. "*Son of X'ieth, Died at Birth [2035 A.R.]*"

After giving up his son's body, X'ieth lowered his eyes to the floor, and waited for the sounds of the handmaid's departure to come and go. He soon heard the door open, and then close.

Left there with Lucen, X'ieth felt the aftereffects of his own broken dreams, the inability to dream again, strangely as Lucen had described. He was never the hero and no longer a knight, husband, or father. And with that, he acknowledged a sad truth: *There's no good destiny left for you, perhaps only bad destiny at Gallow Cliff…*

Images suddenly flashed through his head, of red-haired Shaizan at Gallow Cliff gripping the black shard and wearing dark armor. He stood before a host of giants that brandished weapons, having their serpent banners streaming under a starlit sky, in the ocean breeze. The chalky cliff walls loomed as an aweing backdrop. And then the images ceased, all in one moment.

X'ieth looked up from the floor, around his quiet cottage, seeing Millicent lie as she was, and behind her, the fire dying in the pit. With only a glance, it served a retelling of his most intimate story.

Lucen came to his side, still holding the shard.

"Life is filled with heartache, for those who can't let go of black shards from their broken dreams. Such is your life, but even so, the greatness of making legends awaits you in your black shard, at Gallow Cliff. You're the One meant to fulfill the Dark Prophecy this age."

At the last word, X'ieth glanced down and watched Lucen push the shard toward him. He held it by the blade, with its grip up, being less than half a cubit away. Suddenly, X'ieth felt the attraction; he felt the magnetism; he felt tempted by his natural urges to wield the sword.

His hands had fallen to his sides, and the one closest to the shard began trembling, as if yearning to hold the sword. But at the same time, images flashed before his eyes of himself wielding it in Arlem, followed by those of death and fiery destruction. He saw the people bloody and gored. He saw the buildings in burning rubble. *No, don't. Don't touch it.*

X'ieth's hand was immediately drawn to the shard, but showing some restraint, he stopped it from moving any closer by exerting a force equal and opposite to the sword's attraction. His hand hung midair, as he exchanged looks between the sword and his own fingers, still trembling, in seeming want of touching the black shard, as if having a will of their own.

"But what are you even fighting for?" asked Lucen, who glanced at the young knight's hand. "All the ages after this one have been voided; there's no moving forward. And the *Age of Darkness* from Shaizan's future victory *is a curse among the ether*, which has fallen to this weave. It's the very gloom ripping Sergros apart right now—the very gloom disrupting life in the Isles! Given this, there's nothing left in your present life to savor. So again, what are you fighting for?"

To that, X'ieth was left speechless and without a comeback. *It's true.* In silence, he lowered his head and closed his eyes, unable to envision his own future beyond Gallow Cliff. *You lost everything, and now only have the shards of your broken dream. Why not as Eriens, let the black shard of your dreams, be the black shard of sword?*

X'ieth, still holding his hand back from the shard, suddenly felt inclined to stop fighting—a feeling that had many factors. His bitterness against Destiny was one. The sum total of all his losses, crushing defeats, and disappointments was another. He felt hurt. He felt sad. He felt upset. He felt emptiness. And it was then, that his cumulative feeling inside turned to hatred and malice, consuming him wholly to the point where no longer was he, a person fit for life.

At that, he stopped fighting, and let his hand move toward the shard's grip. He closed his eyes, and let the blackness envelope him. In moments, he felt the shard's grip in his hand. And then, X'ieth opened his eyes, viewing the world through a prism of pure rage, contempt, and malice. It burned within him, growing and growing in fury, until at last the anger inside rented his soul from top to bottom, and he became the Child of Wrath mentioned in the Dark Prophecy!

He clenched his fists, the shard in one, and looked to his body, watching the veins pulse underneath his skin, like vines that winded up his muscled arms, which bulged like large tree trunks. His skin also reddened in hue, as if enflamed by his deep-rooted wrath.

Lucen looked X'ieth up and down. He smiled.

"Weeks ago, you never lived in the wake of a broken dream, but now we find differently. Today, your reveries die, and with that haunted look you attend the requiems. You're haunted by the memories of dreams had, though now gone. *People often die with their broken dreams, long before their physical death. No different are you.* Again, let me say, there is no shame in dying with your dreams, as most of Karnath does already. There is only injustice of those few who get what they want, among a whole lot of defeated dreamers."

Without a counter claim, X'ieth just listened. He gripped the shard tighter in his hand.

"If you cannot have your dreams, no one else should either. Together, let's make Karnath the Land of Broken Dreams this age, to the death of time and Destiny!"

X'ieth stood there, holding the shard, and looking to Lucen. Into his head pranced the same images, of Shaizan at Gallow Cliff, backed by the Army of Darkness. It was more than the simple life. It was extraordinary. It would prove legendary. *You need that, not this. You've needed that greatness all along...* After a moment's delay, the young knight nodded, in an instant of his life that he never anticipated living.

"Let's..." he whispered.

With that, X'ieth went into his enlarged channeling chamber and pulled open the same double wooden doors, having carven inlays of thorns. The doors parted with a blast of Nexus along their edges, and then, a stream of energy flooding into the chamber. His Source exit opened on its own, and torrents of Nexus began flowing through the entry and out the exit.

X'ieth returned to his cottage, were the black shard in his hand now glowed a luminous green. His midsection glowed green as well, as the Nexus entered his core.

X'ieth started channeling complex flows of green energy, all about the cottage's main area. At the same time, he maintained a parallel process of pushing torrents of Nexus into the shard, and letting trigger images of fiery destruction surge through his mind.

Suddenly, he watched the energy flows continue to arc from the shard and take multiple paths across the cottage's main space; they drifted below its thatched roof and between its gray stone walls. The flows shed droplets of Nexus that hung in the air, all of teardrop form, which suddenly erupted into roaring green flames! He could immediately feel the immense heat.

It was moments before a deep rumble was heard, and the entire house started shaking. Straw fell from above, off the thatched roof, and onto the floor. X'ieth gazed down, seeing cracks and hairline fissures spread along the house's stone foundation. He looked up, and saw Millicent lying lifeless in their bed. The sight made him angrier than he already was.

"Arrrrgggghhhhhhh!" he screamed, beyond mad.

The sound of his cry echoed the space, and it was heard above the ongoing, deep rumble. He clenched his teeth, and continued thinking of Arlem's destruction.

At that, the cottage shook all the more violently, and the vibrations increased in frequency and magnitude, causing the cracks in the flooring and walls to widen and multiply. The green flames became black, and then, abruptly burst into orange color. The heat intensified inside the cottage.

X'ieth succumbed to a ravaging anger in his heart—an anger that affected his body. He looked down to see his white tunic split open, exposing his pectoral. His chest throbbed, as his heart beat steadily and strongly beneath, pushing Ma'althan's blood through his veins. The sights shocked him, and defied certain norms he had for himself; he never saw himself, as this. Yet, X'ieth came to accept what he was, and so, he gave himself a reminder. *You're the Child of Darkness.*

X'ieth felt the cottage continue to shake, and saw the energy continue to arc from the shard and through the main area, upsetting the interior. Pots and kitchen implements fell from the cupboards and banged discordantly; spice jars fell off the shelf and smashed; the candle dish clattered off his nearby table. He watched it all happening before his eyes, thinking it was befitting and exactly what he wanted. *Let it all fall apart, just like your broken dreams!*

With that thought, he flung out his left arm and pinched his fingers together on its hand. He watched as the motion folded a nearby Nexus arc through his table and his set of chairs. Under the energy field, the wood furniture abruptly splintered into bits with a series of loud snaps. Likewise, every object in the house rattled, crashed, and broke. There was cracking stone; there was groaning, snapping wood; there was shattering ceramic and glass; there was the clings and clangs of metal. It was nothing but offensive noise to his ear, which foreshadowed the complete and utter destruction of the place where he had made a life, for years.

And then, under its great duress, X'ieth watched as his cottage fell apart! Its walls gave way, bringing the thatched roof down upon him, Lady Lyda, and the lifeless Millicent. But before being crushed by stone, wood, and hay, he held the debris back with only an upraised hand, palm-out. That single motion was enough to control the remaining arcs of Nexus from the shard, for that purpose.

With the shard in hand, X'ieth stayed at the center of where his cottage once stood; pieces of the house floated in the air before him, suspended by Nexus. Beyond the debris and at his right, he saw Galwin standing a ways from the site with an armful of firewood, his eyes wide, and his mouth open. The servant dropped everything, turned around, and ran in terror, soon disappearing into the gloom.

"Mwha ha ha ha, Mwha ha ha ha, Ha ha ha!"

X'ieth heard a laughter, and looked to his left, beyond the floating debris. Lucen stood there, holding his staff with his arms stretched at each side and his head thrown back. With joy, he seemed to study the destruction.

"Every warp and weft, unraveled will be. From time's end to start, all the weaves! Mwha ha ha, Ha ha ha!"

X'ieth looked back to the floating remains of his cottage, still suspended by Nexus and dancing about him, just as the shards of his broken dreams did dance in his forlorn eyes. It was then that he felt at his lowest low, like all of his good choices that brought him this far were for naught—like his entire life was meaningless.

For a moment, X'ieth thought about everything that had happened to him. In his mind, he saw Millicent dead. He saw his lifeless child. He saw his knightly armor back in the armory. *It's been a life of hurt. Make it go away...*

With that thought alone, X'ieth watched the debris go into the gray sky, hurled by Nexus. It was absorbed by clouds, disappeared, and not to be seen again. The action used all the Nexus he had pulled, and emptied his core. The shard's blade turned black again.

"Ha ha ha! Ha ha ha!"

Still with the shard in hand, X'ieth looked back to the field where he stood, now without the floating debris around him. Lucen still stood where he was, but now, in the place where Galwin had appeared, was the same man of dark hair and dark goatee from Arlem—the one matching icons in Karnathan churches throughout the Mainland. He held his spiky, black armor in both hands, as was given to X'ieth before.

The man kept silent, but he spoke in X'ieth's mind.

Take my armor, the armor of god; it protects against elements, and will let you wield wind and fire...

X'ieth watched the man toss the black armor to him. When the armor came about a cubit away, each piece sped to his body and automatically fastened itself, with its latches latching, and its straps strapping. X'ieth had the same exact experience in Arlem, and it felt familiar. And given his familiarity with what was happening, he gave himself another reminder. *You're the Child of Darkness.*

The man turned, and disappeared into the gloom.

Lucen looked to X'ieth, with his usual smile.

"Onward to Gallow Cliff," he said, motioning to the westward sky, "for our reckoning with time and Destiny!"

Again, in an instant of his life that he never anticipated living, X'ieth nodded. With that, he pulled more energy into his channeling chamber, pushing torrent after torrent through the shard. The young knight's core sparked green, and so did the shard's blade, burning brighter and brighter.

With hollow eyes and an empty heart, X'ieth imagined himself in the sky, going to Gallow Cliff. And just like that, orange flames roared all about him like a torch shroud, and he jumped into the horizon becoming immediately airborne—a ball of fire in flight, riding the winds to bad destiny at the cliffs.

"FORESHADOWING"

Chapter 77
Missing Ether

(2075 A.R., Over forty years after Lucen arrived...)

[Second Walk of Existence]

Shaizan demanded to know.

"How do you think that makes me feel?!"

His scream carried through the dismal grounds of the Sergrothian graveyard outside Winsdor—weathered stone, weedy grass, and twisted trees, overlaid with a thick fog and siting beneath the blackest sky. The night was gloomy, cold, and dark, where only a sliver of crescent moon peaked out from the clouds overhead, barely visible though still shedding pale light.

Shaizan glared at Magicia, the most powerful sorceress in Karnath, whom he had courted for some time now; she leaned casually against a tombstone, currently yawning. In this, she continued to act coldly about his plight, as if instead of being his love, she were just another frigid wind, with the sole purpose of chilling him to the bone. Given Magicia's cold feelings these past few hours, Shaizan became increasingly suspicious that her behavior indicated she knew something of what had happened, or had even planned it. Whatever the case, it was an ugly, unseen side of Magicia.

From her face, he looked again to the tombstone against which she leaned, and the sight infuriated him. For etched thereon was the epitaph: *Here lies Kayareth, Son of Naketo, Died at Birth [2054 A.R.]*

He gazed longer upon the grave, and his anger increased more and more the longer he looked, until the point where it summoned words to his lips.

"This tombstone mocks my battered body!"

Shaizan's scream hung in the air, as dull pains coursed through his body, the lingering reminder of what had just happened in Winsdor. He returned to his village after hiking the Mountains of Liath, where he had been looking for Magicia. But instead of finding her, he only found a bundle upon the path—a cloak wrapped around a long object. And that was where his problems started.

Curious by nature, Shaizan undid the bundle, only to find that it contained the black shard of sword, something that was supposedly lost since Eriens entered New Karnath to war with the inferiors, over a thousand years ago.

767

Shaizan took the bundle with him, thinking the black shard could end up in the wrong hands, should he leave it on the mountain trail.

Being that Shaizan long confided in his father Lucen, he hoped that his father could provide advice on what to do. And with that aim, Shaizan returned to his village, but before getting home, the shard unfortunately became unbundled in Winsdor's square by a rude youth, who displayed the peoples' longstanding mistrust for his family. This young man literally knocked Shaizan's bundle from his hands and to the streets, and then tugged the cloak so that whatever was inside, fell out.

It was the worst thing that could happen to an innocent man named Shaizan, especially when the oracles recently proclaimed the Dark Prophecy. Needless to say, everyone in Winsdor's square saw that Shaizan had the black shard in his possession and immediately reacted. They gasped. They showed wide eyes. They murmured. And then, they closed in on Shaizan and began beating on him. In this way, he learned the hard way that the village would automatically presume the wrong hands for the sword were his own.

After a thorough tousling, the villagers dragged Shaizan to the Winsdor's end, and threw him out, along with his bundle. He tumbled to the ground hard, in the field on which the village stood. Hurting all over, he slowly leaned onto his hands, and got to his feet. He was bruised and dirty. He was bloody. He was bleeding. Shaizan looked back to Winsdor, seeing men waving upraised fists at him, and yelling that should he come back, he would be dead. And as the villagers went back to their homes and families, leaving Shaizan where he was, Magicia coincidentally walked up to him through the fields with perfect timing, like she had been waiting there all along and knew what would happen.

The poor experience in Winsdor separated Shaizan from his family, and made him question if Magicia was somehow involved. The villagers acted on the perceived connection between Shaizan and the Dark prophecy, without having more of a basis for their beliefs than loose associations. And the insult to his injuries was staring him in the face: the tombstone, which suggested that the Dark Prophecy could not even come true, if the Child of Light was somehow already dead.

"This tombstone mocks my battered body!"

Shaizan shouted it again for good measure, unbelievably frustrated over being beaten up over the oracles' lie. *At least they didn't kill you...*

Shaizan's red hair was matted and a mess. His skin was soiled, bruised, and showed of crusted blood. His gray tunic had been ripped along its sleeves and down its front from being dragged over the cobblestone; his black trousers were torn on one leg, from the same. The holes in his clothing showed his muscled arms, chest, and thigh. At his sides dangled his arms, with one hand holding the black shard—a token to what had become his nightmare.

The freezing winds blew hard, further messing his hair and lashing his body with a whip of ice. Shaizan stood before the tombstone of Kayareth, on which Magicia kept leaning, continuing her uncomely behavior of carelessness and apathy to his plight.

With continued frustration for the situation, Shaizan spun from the tombstone and shouted in an aside.

"If Shaizan beats Kayareth at Gallow Cliff and ends time, then clearly he beats a dead man! And the Dark Prophecy has no more life than he! It's a dead forecast—untrue, worthless lies—the oracles' deceit! As such, I was hurt for no good reason! I was hurt, for naught."

Turning back to the tombstone, Shaizan saw Magicia leaning up against it, sending another icy stare, her pretty features not so soft now. Seeing her that way offended him; he looked down at the black shard.

The sword was beautiful to look upon, with rainbow glimmers running up its blade. The sword was wonderful to hold, having an excellent feel unlike any sword his father had ever forged as a blacksmith. Shaizan found the sword amazing, both to his touch and to his sight. He found the sword strangely magnetic, and something that he could not easily put down.

In his hand, Shaizan suddenly began flipping the black shard around his forearm; for some time, he watched its mirrored blade rotate into the night. Wielding the sword for him was a pleasantry, but at the same time, it brought to mind how it was the very reason for what had happened.

Shaizan suddenly stopped flipping the blade about his forearm, and raised it before his face, bringing his eyes up to Magicia's. Just looking at her past the shard played upon his suspicions that she knew something about what had happened.

"*This* is why they believe," he told Magicia, referring to the sword. "The damned black shard… in my possession. Deep inside, I knew they really wanted me to touch it, if only to prove themselves right. Well, I did! "

At his statement, Magicia momentarily looked away. Her face went flush, and it reaffirmed Shaizan's suspicions. *She certainly knows more than you give her credit for…* His mind began inventing things she might be withholding from him. *Perhaps, she knew you would find that shard in Liath, instead of her… Perhaps, she conspired with the villagers, and told them ahead of time of what you had found…*

Shaizan's thoughts suddenly felt wrong, as they clashed with his deep feelings of love and adoration for Magicia. And so, he pushed them far from his mind. *You love her unconditionally, so does it matter? No.*

With that, Shaizan pivoted from his suspicions.

"But beyond the shard, surely the name I bear strengthens their beliefs!" he said. "My father and mother mustn't have cared much for me! Surely they knew from the Light Prophecy how the Children were named. Yet, they didn't think for me with the oracle's title. They could've given me a different name, but they didn't!"

Shaizan lowered the shard, walked to where Magicia leaned, and extended the sword, letting its blade bump into Kayareth's headstone, literally a slab of stone jutting from the ground.

Shaizan balled his free hand into a fist, and raised it to the level of his chest. In a low voice he spoke to himself, as the freezing winds continued to blow and rile him.

"Did my father hate me so, and did my mother hate me more?! To allow the oracle's name upon me?!"

He squeezed the shard's grip and removed the shard's blade from the tombstone.

"No parent loving me would've done such a thing!"

In that moment, the harsh, embittered voice of Shaizan triumphed over the mournful, howling gusts.

He looked up then and met Magicia's gray eyes.

"Tell me why, the villagers in Winsdor beat me, dragged me through the streets, and threw me out as a pauper to the cold?! Men and women of Sergros, those I've known my whole life, some who cared for me as a child, now forsake me! No one offers me shelter or help; no one believes in me anymore!"

Feeling contempt for life, Shaizan lowered his eyes and viewed the frost-crowned weeds around Kayareth's tombstone. He spoke to himself angrily.

"My accusers are hypocrites, those who long shunned the Light Prophecy and now embrace the Dark Prophecy, to mindlessly tarnish the name and body of an innocent man through their prejudice! To them, there's more proof in my living flesh than *his* dead bones! Don't they remember burying him here?!"

Using the shard, Shaizan tapped the tombstone, as if to accentuate his point. After doing it a few times, he stopped and looked up from the tombstone, to the gloomy sky overhead. He bellowed into the night's darkness.

"Indeed there's no greater truth than what I now profess. For today, the whole world turns its back on me, and I am truly alone! Every friend has become my enemy, men once of praise now my scoffers, and those once of care now careless for me! I presently fight so much more than just myself."

From her quiet, Magicia spoke. "You're not alone."

Shaizan looked over to where she leaned, his face showing surprise, as if a rock had come to life after eons of silence and suddenly wanted to have a conversation.

"I've been here with you all this time, and I know this path you walk."

Magicia stopped leaning on the tombstone, and took a few steps away, to stand beside it.

Shaizan shook his head in disagreement; he did not feel Magicia's support was as strong as he needed. But then, before being able to reflect any more on her remark, he noted motion in his periphery.

He looked to the side, out into the graves dotting the dreary landscape, where he saw a silhouette of a figure approaching in the background, over Magicia's shoulder. *Likely someone from Winsdor who wants to beat on you more. Wonder how well they'd do it, with a sword stuck between their ribs!*

Shaizan flipped the black shard again, about his forearm, watching its blade as it twirled.

"When losing everything," Magicia said.

Shaizan stopped flipping the sword, as her words grabbed his attention. He gazed her way.

Magicia continued. "When losing everything, people are often robbed of their decorum. The hour of irreparable loss tears the very fiber of their decency! It did for me, and it's happening to you. A man of broken dreams blames himself, others, and Destiny for what destroys him. And in the end, Destiny alone is truly at fault."

Shaizan felt a strong, frigid wind suddenly blow against him then, like a brute beating him down further with an ice club, in a moment not understood—a moment lacking clarity and so utterly dark.

"Do you love me?" asked Magicia, over the wind.

"Yes," he replied, not giving it a second thought. "I'm baffled though, by your behavior."

The gust died with his words.

"And I'm baffled by yours," she responded. "You doubt me already, without a basis. It is the same, for those of Winsdor to doubt you, over loose associations when you're still a man free from guilt. It was wrong of them, and also, it's wrong of you."

More motion in Shaizan's periphery directed his attention to the rows of tombstones that extended out to the graveyard's end, a backdrop full of twisted trees and contorted branches. There, in the distance, the figure could still be seen approaching.

Magicia stepped across Shaizan's field of vision. He turned to watch her go back to Kayareth's tombstone, where she stooped down to trace the headstone's etching with her fingers.

"There's a belief in Karnath, that children who die at birth are without a spirit," she said. "It seems that Kayareth was among them. You're a victor already."

He arched an eyebrow. *Huh? What does that mean?*

Shaizan watched Magicia lower her head and shut her eyes, while stooping before the grave. And then, in one motion, she raised her head, opened her eyes, and stood tall. She faced him.

"Know that I'll stand by you through this, as I have stood by you through all other things. Stop doubting me. Start trusting me!"

She paused, before launching a question.

"Now, do you trust me?"

The words made Shaizan feel conflicted. On one hand, he trusted that Magicia loved him, and would never purposely hurt him. Yet, he knew that she might have bore the risk of hurting him, toward a specific goal that he did not understand. She was the most powerful sorceress in Karnath, and to him, it seemed possible that her goals might wedge their way between them. *Can you trust that this hasn't happened?* He wondered, with doubts.

After a delay, Shaizan responded. "Yes."

"Then you won't mistrust me, whatever I say?"

Shaizan swallowed. "Yes..."

He suddenly grew scared, not sure of where her question or his affirmation might lead.

"Then I'll speak. Kayareth was born in the same year as you, some two decades ago," she said quietly. "He died at birth, so according to the prophecy you're a victor already, without an opponent. You've won the Game."

The comment momentarily paralyzed Shaizan; he could not even react. He just kept staring at Magicia, who stared right back without a word. Slowly, his mind started to process what she said. *Magicia proposes you actually go to Gallow Cliff, and do what everyone in Winsdor feared you would do?! You touched the shard to prove them right, but would you really do that?!* He was not so sure he could, or would.

She continued. "Don't you see, you're destined to win?! You must've already beaten Kayareth sometime in the future. That explains why the oracles foresee your victory—why they've predicted you to win!"

With those words, Shaizan's paralysis came back. It took a few moments before his mind could even begin working. *The Game hasn't even been started... Why would she say that? What exactly does she know that you don't?*

As Shaizan silently pondered her words, Magicia grew excited. Her cold face suddenly came alive with a smile on her lips and light in her eyes. She took Shaizan's hands in her own.

"Don't you see," Magicia continued, "it's finally happening! The Game and Destiny are finally ending, a thing that I've prayed so long for!"

Shaizan looked confused. *Where is this coming from?!* He looked into Magicia's gray eyes, searching desperately for her there—the woman he grew to love; the woman that he knew. His mind considered what or with whom Magicia was meddling.

"Who... whom did you pray to?!" Shaizan asked.

Her face stayed enthused, as she replied.

"Saora, the Maiden of the Void!"

A certain terror gripped Shaizan in that, for Saora was the one mentioned in the Book of Karnatha who was supposedly at war with Destiny. Few in Karnath even knew of her, and of those who did, even fewer believed in her.

"Saora?!" he replied. "Why did you pray to her?!"

"I needed vengeance against Destiny for the Game."

"But why?!" Shaizan asked. "Why do this?!"

"Karnatha took something from me."

Shaizan paused. "And what was that?"

"It's an old wound. One's that healed."

"So why seek vengeance?!" he exclaimed.

Shaizan and Magicia stared at each other. Her lips trembled, as if in want of speaking, but they stayed shut like she held something back. But then, after a long delay, she managed to tell Shaizan why. Her first love died in a conflict that arose from the Game.

The admission pained Shaizan, and his mind buzzed with questions. *Why does Magicia still seek vengeance?! Does she still love him?! Does she really love you?!*

Shaizan released Magicia's hands and turned from both her and tombstone, with a mix of hurt and doubt stricken across his face. A cold wind lashed his back, sending chills down his spine. He felt the urge to shiver but shrugged it off, knowing that he could not get any colder than Magicia's words and deeds had already made him feel. He stood silent long enough, until he felt a gentle hand on his shoulder.

"What is it, Shaizan?" she asked, softly.

He paused, looking for the right words to say.

"You wouldn't still need vengeance, if he was a thing of the past. I fear he's your first and only love, and you've never had a second love, or any other."

"No," she said, caressing his shoulder. "That's not true. I love you, I do."

"Do you?!" he asked, pulling away from Magicia's hand, still having his back to her.

Shaizan heard a patter of feet as Magicia ran around his side, and took his hands. In the gloom, she met his blue eyes with her own. The winds ravaged them more, but it was easily ignored given what hung in the balance: them.

"Then you don't need to avenge a past love!" Shaizan said. "I should be enough for you to forget him and what happened. I should be enough…"

"No one will be enough for me to forget the death of someone innocent! Not you, nor an exact copy of him. Wrongs are wrongs, and must be made right."

Magicia let go of Shaizan's hands and turned from him to row after row of graves, the twisted trees, and the gloomy night. She spoke in an aside.

"Since Hrya's death, I have died each day! Since Hrya's death, I cannot see my future beyond his past! Since Hrya's death, I can't see my life, when it is overhung by the shadow of his death! My first love saw bad destiny, for just a chance at mankind's good destiny through the Game. And there's injustice in that barter—injustice for which Karnatha must pay! Nothing good can become of her Game, not now or ever! It must end."

Shaizan saw Magicia turn back to him. She took his hands. She met his eyes. She connected, emotionally.

"Please understand, I feel certain wrongs must be made right," she said. "And please understand that you are the only one who can help me aright this terrible wrong! You stopped time in the future, and are meant to do it again. You are the one that Saora promised to me—the chosen one to end the Game and Destiny!"

Magicia explained Saora's promise, how during the final age, the chosen one would come to Karnath and help her end time. It was a deed that would unravel the final age, so that everyone and their memories fell to the previous age, and that the previous age became a new final age. Then, in this new final age, Saora said that time must be unraveled again so that the process could be repeated in yet another age. She promised Magicia that if she kept playing the Game backward in time with the chosen one and winning it for the Darkness so to unravel more weaves, the Game would eventually end, and along with it, Destiny. Supposedly, there would come a day in a past age, where time would not have to be unraveled anymore, and Destiny and the Game would be no more. For Magicia, it was perfect. It would be vengeance, and it would bring peace.

But it did not seem so perfect to Shaizan. Alarms went off in his head, while Magicia spoke on about Saora and her promises. It seemed crazy. It seemed dangerous. It seemed divisive. He wondered how he could trust her, and how their relationship could continue, given this information.

But then, as Magicia entered a silence and waited on Shaizan's reply, his mind began to consider their exchange, had moments ago. *You won't mistrust me, whatever I say? Yes...* With that mere recollection, he realized his present thoughts betrayed the trust Magicia had placed in him for honesty and transparency, and this realization easily made him feel awful.

He stood there facing her, silent as the headstones, feeling this way until a gradual development took place: an inner voice began to reason with him: *Consider if, this first love of hers had been you. Wouldn't you want to be avenged, if you had died wrongfully because of the Game? You would, wouldn't you? So open yourself to her...*

Shaizan became stoic, weighing these things carefully for some time. He transposed himself into Magicia's unnamed love, and into Magicia herself, trying hard to understand what was just, and what was best. This went on for minutes, where Shaizan stood with Magicia in the graveyard, holding her hands and staring into her eyes. She remained silent, as if to allow him distance from her inputs and time to consider matters on his own.

Inwardly, Shaizan confronted his Karnathan faith and furthermore, how Magicia's present aims and meddling conflicted with that. His father had raised him as a firm believer, exactly as his own father had brought him up. In accordance with how he was taught, Shaizan took vain prayers and vain practice of religion very seriously; these were blasphemy against Karnatha and worship redirected to the Void. He avoided these acts, and other such things, wanting nothing to do with the Void. But now, Magicia went against his convictions and would force a tradeoff between his love and his religion. *But given how Karnatha has forsaken you now in your time of need, is your religion worth keeping? Why not trade?* The prospect was tempting.

He finally sighed and broke the silence, speaking then from his heart.

"It's hard for me to believe that Saora's promises could really lead to good destiny for Karnath. You're telling me that she wants us to go to Gallow Cliff, and win the Game for the Darkness? And afterward, she wants us to keep doing it, in earlier times? Surely it will bring the curse of Eternal Darkness upon Karnath…"

"If Saora's promise is true, our action can end Karnatha's awful Game once and for all! If Saora's promise is true, we can kill an evil god who only brings war, death, and suffering to Karnath!"

Shaizan's concerns about the curse of Eternal Darkness remained, and he could not see beyond them, regardless of the arguments that Magicia made in favor of Gallow Cliff. *Given the curse, this plan would mean bad destiny for Karnath, forever! And it might be, regardless of whether Saora's promises are true. You can't have that…*

"Please," Magicia begged.

Shaizan detected sudden motion in his periphery. He spun from Magicia, to the distant graveyard scene, seeing the silhouette of the approaching figure grow larger, being almost upon their spot. The person walked between the tombstones, right toward them.

"What is it?" Magicia asked.

"Wait," Shaizan replied. "Someone's followed us."

Shaizan watched the figure emerge from the gloom and come right up to them, stopping several cubits away. It was a magical knight from Tekkneo, in a suit of crimson armor. The knight wore a purple cloak over its shoulders, and in the knight's one hand was the legendary white shard.

"Who are you?!" Shaizan asked.

He watched the knight stand tall among the shadows cast by the leaning headstones, towering about two cubits above his head. The knight stayed quiet, and at first, only the howling winds served as Shaizan's reply.

"Who are you?!"

"It's perhaps the ghost of Kayareth," said Magicia, coming up to Shaizan's side. "The white shard suggests that much."

A booming, powerful voice came from the armor.

"I am Elucid."

Shaizan looked at Magicia, puzzled. "Who?"

Magicia shrugged. "I don't know."

"I mean neither of you any harm."

The crimson knight raised a metal hand, as if to deflect misconstrued intentions.

"Then what do you mean to us?" Magicia asked.

Elucid looked to Shaizan and started explaining.

"The legendary Game is on the eve of being played at Gallow Cliff, clearly between us both. I've come to you three days in advance of us being there, in hopes of changing your mind."

"Don't you dare!" Magicia yelled, clearly upset by a proposition that ran counter to her interests.

"I've learned," Elucid said, "to let people make their own way, and choose their own choices. And with him, I plan to do the same."

"His choice is made!" snapped Magicia.

Shaizan looked at her crossly. "Oh, it is?"

Magicia stared back, sullen and silent.

"Every choice has consequences, and it's important that Shaizan understands the consequences of this one."

Shaizan stood there with his blue eyes on Elucid. The pale moonlight anointed the knight's glimmering armor, and the icy winds swirled the purple cloak behind Elucid. In the knight's gauntlet was the white shard, and Shaizan began to question if Elucid even planned to fight with it at all.

Magicia spoke. "There are consequences to the Game continuing indefinitely without a victor, as it has for thousands of years; it needs to end! There are consequences for Destiny putting the innocent at risk, with reckless plans for sealing creation's destiny; I've suffered these already!"

"But you must understand, the consequences are greater for you to go to Gallow Cliff and start your mission for Saora, backward in time! I am told that we're at the end of the second walk now, and what she wants is a third walk unlike the others, where the time marker doesn't make a full walk from the beginning of time, overwriting history. Instead, Saora will lead Karnatha to slash causality's thread and create many time markers, one in each isolated age. The third walk will be backward, from the last isolated age to the first, disintegrating time by its ages."

Shaizan looked at Magicia. This was more or less what she described to him, a thing allegedly with no consequences. He looked back to Elucid, and sought clarification.

"And what are the bigger consequences of that?"

Elucid paused before replying.

"With Saora's plan, there's no stopping point, as she's promised. There won't come a day in a past age, where time won't have to be unraveled anymore, where the Game will stop, and where Destiny will cease to exist. I'm afraid that Saora wants you both to start a process that will gain momentum, and wipe clean all history of the Game, destroying time and existence!"

The comment seemed to anger Magicia.

"That's not true!" she exclaimed. "Saora's plan will restore good destiny in Karnath. I know firsthand that Karnatha can't be trusted for that; she's given me bad destiny already with her Game."

"Well, that's not what I've come to find…"

Shaizan listened, as Elucid shared how Saora had been misleading both him and Magicia about playing the Game at Gallow Cliff, through premonitions that did not present the whole truth. In this, Magicia would arrive to Gallow Cliff with the Child of Darkness, and Elucid would represent the Child of Light there. But unbeknownst to them, their fight would start an epic battle across time, where the future would start falling into the past and existence itself would ultimately end.

"Saora hates the Game, and she'll undo it by re-writing history!"

"Impossible," Magicia muttered.

"It's true. The Game, Destiny, and existence are linked together by time. When one ends, they all end."

Shaizan saw Magicia shake her head.

"If you go to Gallow Cliff and fight with Shaizan, I'm afraid he'll win, for there's presently not a force strong enough to stop him! And Shaizan's victory will be the first among many victories that will lead to Karnath being no more. It will lead into a fiendish cycle by which your loved ones, like Esmeralda, will ultimately be erased from time, where they suffer in each isolated age until time's end. Is that what you want?!"

Magicia swallowed. Her eyes appeared moist.

"I don't believe it. I won't."

"You should, because I've learned Saora's secrets. Ethers that she wished to keep secret from us have been leaked to me, so I know things that you don't. We have a chance to stop this before it starts!"

"I don't believe you!"

Elucid paused, as if hitting a wall with Magicia.

"You don't have to believe, but he should."

With that, Elucid looked to Shaizan and continued.

"Following Magicia to the cliffs this age starts a war across time, one to be waged by your father and your father's father, until your first ancestor at the dawn of creation—Kilmar. In this age, the Armies of Light and Darkness are but an army of one, for only we shall fight at Gallow Cliff, should you so choose. But in earlier ages, many will join the conflict and the carnage will be more putrefying than if all the oceans of Karnath were blood, baking beneath the hot sun."

Shaizan's arched his eyebrows.

"What do you propose, if not the cliffs?"

"No!" Magicia pled with Shaizan. "Don't do it!"

Shaizan raised his hand, as if to quell her.

Elucid continued. "Follow me to Liath, where we must fight Wicken the Wicked and climb its highest peak. There we can meld the shards into the whole gray sword, and destroy the blade in Ires Star. The Game will end, even if its history and the pain it's caused shall remain."

Magicia protested. "No! Don't listen to this!"

Shaizan turned to her.

"We can't trust what is overly suspicious! This knight talks of winning the Game for the Light, which is what Karnatha wanted all along. The Book of Karnatha explains how Destiny wanted a fair means of deciding destiny for Karnath, yet ironically, Karnatha devised the Game based on premonitions of the seroxians finding bad destiny in their future! So Karnatha has been biased toward the Light all along, and this Elucid is likely an agent of Karnatha! So, we must not do as the knight says!"

At her insistence, thoughts started racing through Shaizan's mind. *Wouldn't a victory for the Light be best for Karnath? What is good destiny, if not this? Can it be that Magicia somehow sees bad destiny, as good?* He wondered about these things, now confused over what to do, and being pulled from two sides.

The situation for Shaizan became a tugging match, when Magicia walked a distance from him and settled at about the same length as Elucid had, though at his opposite side. Magicia stood in the direction of Gallow Cliff, and Elucid stood in the direction of Liath.

"You must choose to follow one of us."

In that moment, the winds blew hard, as if to emphasize the hard decision. Shaizan weighted the options, and tried to rightly decide what was really good destiny for Karnath. *Magicia says that Karnatha is really evil, a god who must perish with her Game, at the risk of Eternal Darkness for Karnath. Elucid says that Saora is tricking them both, and that the Game must be won for the Light, without being punitive to Karnatha...*

Shaizan spent only a few moments thinking, but it was strangely enough time for him to find Elucid's argument more compelling than Magicia's. The knight did not want to fight Shaizan and sought a victory for the Light, to end the Game once and for all. It seemed straightforward, avoided trust in Saora, avoided the curse of eternal Darkness, and promoted good destiny in Karnath. *Is there really a decision?* He wondered.

But just as Shaizan had the thought, he felt opposing pressures of not complying with what Magicia wanted. They were romantically involved, and it was natural for him to strive toward making the woman happy, and to the extent possible, aligning his goals with her own. *But is her goal no longer to an extant possible?*

Shaizan mulled over the matter for a while longer. As he did, the winds beat upon him, and Magicia's patience waned beneath the night sky. Time was short for a decision, or at least so she thought. Nevertheless, he took more time to think, being in hopes of peace over his eventual choice. But as much time as he spent, and as hard as he thought, Shaizan still felt torn between the options and came to a point where he felt the best he could do was acting off his instincts of right and wrong.

Slowly, and with some hesitation, Shaizan stepped in the direction of Elucid.

Magicia gasped. "How dare you! What about us?!"

Shaizan swallowed. He held his breath, and prepared to take another step toward the knight. But before he could lift his foot off the ground, his body went awash in unspeakable pain. Deep aches throbbed through his head, and down through his extremities, as information began surging through his mind. It sent him to his knees.

As the pain continued, he thrashed wildly, alternating between pounding the ground, beating his chest, and pulling his hair. As the pain continued, the sound of his agony filled the entire gravesite, and lingered above the harsh winds.

The whole time, visions furiously popped into Shaizan's head, life experiences from out of nowhere, ones that concerned him at Gallow Cliff with Kayareth. They seemed as events from another walk of his own life—events that until now, he did not recall living.

What's... happening... to me?!

**** Shaizan's Recall – End of the Age of Light ****

[First Walk of Existence]

Shaizan stood on the embankment beneath Gallow Cliff, his bare feet touching the cool waters under the ashen moon; it was hung high in the sky, on the horizon over the rolling sea. Gusty ocean winds lifted his red hair, also his white Servant's robe with gold tassels.

In an aside, he bellowed into the night sky, about his frustrations over Karnatha.

"How can this be, that time will be no more?! How can it be, that Karnatha won't weave again?!" Enraged, he balled both fists, unable to rest

with the idea of this age being Karnath's last. Karnatha was supposedly too weak to weave another.

Shaizan was beyond upset at her, and ready to take action against Destiny's will, so to prevent Karnath from reaching its end point in time. As the guardian between the path between wells of spent energies and unspent energies, he was prepared to do what was needed to halt time this age, in order to keep Karnath where it was, indefinitely.

From the shore suddenly came a familiar voice, over the rhythmic splashing tide.

"Don't let this get the best of you!" Kayareth shouted. "I know why you're here, and what you're planning to do."

"Why do you care?" Shaizan called back.

He heard Kayareth start to wade through the water, approaching him from off the shore. Shaizan did not even bother to turn around. Instead, he stared into the horizon, focusing on what he needed to do.

"You've nothing to lose!" Shaizan said, wryly. "Karnatha choose you over me to be lifted from the weave… You'll have immortality in a matter of days! So leave mortals to worry about the affairs of life and death!"

"I'm sorry," Kayareth said. "She should've picked you instead."

"I'm sorry too, but not for her choice…"

With his reply, Shaizan began pulling Nexus. Immediately, his midsection shined of radiant green light.

"What then, causes you sorrow?!" asked Kayareth.

"Your apathy, and that of the other Servants of the Light! We've preserved Light in this world our entire lives, and for what?! Karnath isn't supposed to end like this! Karnath is meant for more than this!"

While talking, Shaizan kept channeling Nexus, pulling against every sensed mental restraint. Then suddenly, a different sort of energy entered his aux core—the power of time well spent, the driver of good destiny. His midsection shined a brilliant white.

"What are you doing?!" Kayareth yelled. "Don't forsake your oath to Karnatha! You're the guardian of this well for spent energy, not the thief!"

"I'll pull this energy 'til I die!" Shaizan replied. "I'll risk my own life, if it's enough for this age to continue without time! If I achieve that, I'll count my life well spent, just as this energy was intended! Existence is about people finding good destiny…"

Shaizan suddenly felt Kayareth's hand on his shoulder, and he turned about to punch his friend in the face, practically assuming Kayareth's intervention. Shaizan kept channeling the whole time.

There was a splash as Kayareth fell into the waters at the blow. Shaizan turned back, and refocused on what he was doing.

In only a few moments, he heard Kayareth pull himself up out of the water. Shaizan glanced back, seeing his friend stare at him with wide eyes and a bloody lip curled by anger. Kayareth's blond hair was soaked, just as his Servant's robe with gold tassels; both clung to his body. In the waters, Shaizan and Kayareth stood staring at each other, with the waves crashing down.

Then suddenly, Shaizan saw the wound on Kayareth's lip heal, and his friend lunged to take hold of him. Within moments, Shaizan felt Kayareth's hands on his shoulders, and the two started grappling in the sea, with more waves breaking over them.

"I'm warning you... just leave!" Shaizan shouted.

But Kayareth did not listen; he continued to wrestle.

Meanwhile, Shaizan felt the energy burning him as his core reached capacity. He knew then he needed a larger vessel for the energy of time. And so, he forced a tether with Kayareth and began pushing tremendous Nexus into his friend's core.

Shaizan saw Kayareth's eyes widen, as if he noticed what was happening and knew of its inherent dangers. Shaizan felt his struggle become fiercer, as if Kayareth began struggling for his life.

"You'll kill us both!" Kayareth exclaimed.

"I told you to leave, and now, you're going to be part of this, like it or not. We'll both die to see Karnath continue indefinitely!"

Shaizan fought with Kayareth even harder, forcing his friend to stay in place.

"You fool! We'll die and our spirits will go into the Void! You don't even know if stopping time will do what you think!"

"It's worth a try, so cooperate with me!" Shaizan said. "I need to put the age's time somewhere, and right now, there's no better place than you and me!"

Shaizan continued, "Karnatha entrusted me with the path between the wells of spent and unspent energies; she commended me with Karnath's potential! And so, I'm abusing that trust for a greater cause: a life without time is surely my good destiny, and that of the whole world's!"

Together, the aux cores of Shaizan and Kayareth filled with the energy of time well spent, and their midsections grew whiter and yet whiter, until the blinding light was all that could be seen, by anyone near or far.

****

"Shaizan!" screamed Magicia.

She rushed to Shaizan, and kneeled beside him.

Shaizan's torment ended as soon as it started. He suddenly found himself kneeling in the Sergrothian graveyard, with his pain now gone, and only double vision and a ringing upon both ears. Within moments, his vision and hearing returned to normal, and all that he could sense were the freezing winds and Magicia's embrace.

"Are you all right?!"

Woozily, Shaizan struggled to his feet, and Magicia rose with him.

"I believe so… Visions strangely came upon me!"

Shaizan looked to Magicia. She swallowed.

"That was ether. Saora has sent you ether…"

Shaizan grew quiet at the comment, wary of Saora sending him anything. But beyond that feeling, he reflected on his new memories about what seemed to be the future, where he stopped time for a good cause. *You were a Servant of the Light, those spoken of in Karnathan myth as the immortal protectors of Karnath, bestowed with skills and virtues. And as a Servant, you stopped time to protect Karnath from Karnatha being too weak to weave again.*

In the middle of Shaizan's thoughts, what Magicia said to him earlier began to resonate. *You must've already beaten Kayareth sometime in the future. That explains why the oracles foresee your victory—why they've predicted you to win!* It was then that it occurred to him. *This was it. You just remembered stopping time, and for good cause.*

Both Shaizan and Magicia stood side by side, cubits away from Elucid. Magicia stepped away from him, and went back to where she was. He looked over, and watched her glare icily his way, as cold as the frigid winds. She rested her hands on her hips, as if impatiently waiting.

"You must choose to follow one of us!"

His decision point became obvious again. Before the ether had struck, Shaizan had begun walking toward Elucid, though now, things seemed different. His mind took a radical turn and started to equate stopping time with doing good, whereby his former thoughts about Magicia became inverted. *Can it be that Magicia somehow sees bad destiny, as good? No, it's not. She sees good destiny!*

Shaizan turned from Elucid, and took a step toward Magicia. Her eyes lit up as before, and a smile instantly snuck to her lips.

"Saora poisons you," Elucid said.

The comment stopped Shaizan. He looked back.

"No doubt she sent you ether, of a time no more—a time that's been unraveled. Was your ether from the Age of Light, at a point in time where Karnatha was too weak to weave? Was your ether from the Age of Light, where the peoples' null destiny slowly squandered the energy of time and Karnatha's life force over the ages, rendering her weak? Was your ether from the Age of Light, where you murdered Kayareth trying to stop Karnath's end from ever happening?"

Shaizan was shocked. "How did you know?!"

Elucid stared back silently.

"It doesn't matter how," the knight said at last, "all that matters now is that you use your good heart to make good judgments. You made bad judgments then. In that future, there was only null destiny in the world, a thing that slowly drained life force from Karnatha. But you introduced bad destiny then, by killing your friend!"

Shaizan shook his head. "No, I didn't!"

"Yes," Elucid said, "you did. And Karnatha knew about it then, before you ended time. Saora sent Karnatha's memories back to her at the beginning of time in the second walk, to see how she would react to foreknowledge of bad destiny in Karnath, to try her and see if she were biased toward preferences for one of the two hues. So indirectly, what you did made her start the Game."

"Lies!" Shaizan sneered. "This isn't my fault!"

"It is," Elucid replied, "but you can choose differently, and stop the Game here and now! Over the Game, there may have been conflict on the mortal and immortal planes ages! Over the Game, there may have been many mortals who were hurt! But even so, you can end all of that now."

Shaizan shook his head again, still in disbelief.

"C'mon!" Magicia shouted. "Let's go."

Shaizan looked her way; she still stood as she was, in the direction of Gallow Cliff, with hands on her hips and sending an icy glare. Behind her, the night sky began yielding to dawn.

Elucid called to him from the other side.

"Don't go! Don't become what she'll have you be—a man bound to bad destiny!"

It was in that moment that Shaizan felt at his lowest low. He was beset by the peoples' prejudice, which had labeled him as a nobody his whole life, and now, labeled him as the villain, before he had committed any wrong. He was beset by the suggestions of others, that he could only achieve null destiny or bad destiny, but never good destiny.

And then, he saw it—an image in his head, of himself at Gallow Cliff, as depicted in the icons within Karnathan churches throughout the Mainland. He wore black, spikey armor and wielded the black shard on the white sands beneath a tall, white cliff. The wind stirred his long red hair into motion, just as the scene stirred his spirit with excitement. For it transcended his awful life, one afflicted by prejudice; and it seemed the best of good destinies for others, in disguise! *That's what you need…*

Shaizan took a step toward Magicia, and stopped.

"Everyone can overcome prejudice!" Elucid said. "Everyone can be better than what others expect! The words of others need not be your end; they need not become your bad destiny!"

He took another step toward Magicia, and stopped.

"Would it persuade you to know my name, to know whom you're really talking to?"

"C'mon!" Magicia shouted, as if frustrated that Shaizan was not already by her side. "Let's go already!"

Shaizan did not turn around or answer the knight.

"I am Laotzu, a king without a kingdom. Elucid is only my alias, as my whole life, I've sought to elucidate people, even until now."

Shaizan lowered his eyes upon the weedy grass.

"Do you know why I'm a king without a kingdom?"

"Why's that?" Shaizan asked, in a steely voice.

"Long before the rebellion against Maken and Maken's punishment, I begged my own people of Kingdom Juniper to repent! But alas, no one trusted me then, as you mistrust me now! So I ask, how can I persuade you?"

Visions of grandeur filled Shaizan's head. Going to the cliffs would start an epic battle across time, which would play out exactly as Saora had promised Magicia. An evil god would die, her horrible Game would end, and there would be peace. *And you'll be the hero who brings that good destiny to Karnath, immortalized by legend!* It was a lofty thought, for a man who had hit an abysmal low.

"Please, how can I persuade you?!"

"You can't," Shaizan said, not turning back.

And with that, he walked all the over to Magicia's side. She smiled and took his hand in her own. Together, Shaizan and Magicia walked off, in the direction of Gallow Cliff. The dawn had now broken the night sky with brilliant color; it was a sheet of golden orange.

When Shaizan and Magicia were only a few cubits away from Elucid, the knight called out.

"Magicia…"

Shaizan was surprised when Magicia stopped walking. Like her, he also stopped. She turned around and looked to Elucid, and Shaizan followed suit.

"What?" she asked, coldly.

"You'll find much too late that Saora merely makes Karnatha's Game her own. The energies of times past will flow to the Void, overwriting Karnath's history with pains much greater than anything the land has ever known!"

Elucid fell silent, and a cold wind blew. The knight continued talking momentarily.

"One day, I predict you'll join me, but it may be too late. By then, you'll have found Shaizan is a force stronger than both of us! By then, you'll have found that Shaizan's power is unmatched in this age, and many before it! The mightiest of seroxians will go to Gallow Cliff to fight him—cursed and un-cursed alike, male and female, young and old—and they will all fall."

Shaizan looked between Elucid and the lonely gravesite of Kayareth, pondering what these words meant.

"If not a matched opponent," he asked the knight, "then what are you?"

Another gust swept over them, swirling Elucid's purple cloak and pulling at Shaizan's hair. And save that wind, there was no response to his question.

"C'mon!" Magicia said, back to her impatience. "What this knight says is of little importance. It was to those of Juniper long ago, and now, it's unimportant to us."

With that, Shaizan and Magicia turned, and walked out of the Sergrothian graveyard, past rows of gnarled and leafless trees upon the site, and into the orange horizon, toward Gallow Cliff. It was the same direction Elucid would take three days from now—a direction away from Liath, and toward meeting Shaizan again and again, across time itself.

(Awakening from Magicia's Dream)

Magicia opened her eyes, awakening from her dream to the white sands below Gallow Cliff, a tall chalky rock that loomed over the rolling blue sea. It was night, and she saw the stars shined above in the night sky, along with the moon. Noises of the tide fell upon her ears, and she could smell the scent of salts in the air. Her senses confirmed where she was and for what reason. *The Battle for Destiny!*

Magicia sat up and leaned back on her hands; she felt the sand conform around her fingers. The moonlight poured over her little spot on the shore, shedding light on the distant sands where Kort and Nym lied together. Seeing them there made her smile. *We have the Gray Child. It will be enough to beat Shaizan; it has to be! It has to be...*

Suddenly, scenes from Magicia's dream overwhelmed her in a blur of images that went through her mind. Like so many times before she had seen Shaizan in her dreams, but this dream was different. This dream was special, because it was exactly what Magicia had asked Saora for: to remember Shaizan as he was, before any of this happened. And Saora delivered.

Magicia sighed. She pulled her knees to her chest and threw her arms around them. She felt chilly winds blow off the sea, making her shiver in her dusty sorceress' robe. Her braids of red hair followed them, dusty like her robe.

A deep, booming voice could be heard.

"Saora kept to her promise."

Magicia looked to her left, in the opposite direction of Nym and Kort, seeing the crimson knight standing with its arms crossed. *Elucid...*

"You've had the dream too?" Magicia asked.

There was a long pause.

"I did," Elucid replied. "It was the close of existence's second walk, shortly before Karnatha slashed the thread of causality. I knew she would do it, like so many other things back then, when Saora's memories had been leaked to me. Now, I know so much less."

Elucid sighed, and then continued.

"We all know so much less now…"

Magicia kept her eyes on the sea, not bothering to look back. Like Elucid, she sighed deeply, wishing so much for an end. *Please let us win, Destiny… I'm so sorry for my poor choices. Elucid was right, and I was a fool for not listening to him. By losing Shaizan, I've lost everything…*

"But as little as we know, your time for lost love has come to an end," Elucid said, as if presuming Magicia's occupation was with Shaizan.

Magicia held her tongue, letting the next wind pass.

"For every loss, there's a time to move on…"

With her words, another wind blew over them, and the stars and moon continued to watch from above.

When the wind died, Elucid spoke.

"The time for love ends now, and is replaced with a time for war. You wanted the cliffs over Liath, so ready yourself. Tomorrow we fight."

Magicia nodded, and the scene faded to black.

"CHOOSE A SIDE"

Chapter 78
Enigmas and Expansions

(797 A.R., Over a thousand years ago...)

Condemnation from the seroxians of Windsor drove Kilwroth to the sea. Bruised and beaten, he stared face-to-face at the crashing waves, with his back turned to the towering walls of Gallow Cliff, and also, the night. The full moon and the starry sky watched over him, wondering what, if anything, he would do.

I should throw myself into the waters... In that moment, it occurred to Kilwroth that his life might not hold a better option than simply being taken out to sea by the current. That way he would just drown, and end the torment to which Old Karnath had subjected him for years. Or maybe, a green portal would open for him in the sea, just like it did for Laotzu when he left Kilwroth and went back into New Karnath, as shown to Kilwroth in premonitions. That way, the inferiors could take his life, much like they did with his father Eriens. Either way, Destiny could decide his fate.

A sudden wind pulled at Kilwroth's tunic, trousers, and his purple cloak. It blew his long black hair around the sides of his face; some of it got in his eyes. With one hand, he removed the strands to continue staring into the sea, fixating on how this could be his end, if he were just courageous enough to take the plunge.

All the negatives in Kilwroth's life stacked up, as a giant mountain that he was no longer willing to climb. It was not so much the mountain of bad things that made him feel this way, but merely one additional bad thing on top of everything else. In particular, it was what just happened to him in the nearest village outside the dilapidated stone walls of Castle Malgun—Winsdor.

It all started when Kilwroth ventured there in order to get out of the castle and prevent himself from going crazy over his premonitions. The premonitions started in the last week, on the day of his seventeenth birthday, and they were very strange. They showed someone showing up randomly to Castle Malgun who claimed to be Laotzu, took Eriens' purple cloak, and departed through a portal back into New Karnath, with final remarks about a war across time that had to be fought in the future. But even more strangely and more to Kilwroth's despair, his premonitions suggested Laotzu and him had become close friends, and friendships were something he was missing all of these years. No family. No friends. He was by himself in his father's crumbling castle, an outcast in society over Eriens' deeds, and oh so lonely.

Kilwroth thought that Winsdor would be a good way of feeling less isolated and getting his mind off of his premonitions. As most places on the Mainland, he knew he would not be well received there, but planned on concealing his face to avoid problems with the villagers. For someone like him, it was a risky thing to do, but in his opinion it was a risk worth taking, for the intrinsic benefits of seeing others socialize and mingle. For this was how he idealized that life should be lived, and Kilwroth wanted to see what he was missing.

And with that plan he went, concealing himself when inside Windsor, but still unable to keep himself far from trouble. For by sheer coincidence, he ended up being in the wrong place at the wrong time, by happening upon a surprising and mysterious meeting that took place far from the village center.

On the outskirts of Windsor, off the dirt road into town, stood a derelict brown shack that leaned to the side on a plot of weedy grass. It had a dingy, old semblance, with its dark, wooden exterior—weather beaten and tired— with shingles hanging off a roof that had apparently seen one too many storms, and its windows staring back as hollow eyes from the body of a deceased.

At first, he stopped just to marvel at how the thing even remained upright. Surely the house was unlived in, or so he thought, at least until hearing multiple voices coming from within. Some were loud, as if yelling.

His first instinct was to leave and just go to the village center, as planned. But somewhere deep inside, a voice nudged him to go closer, to see what or who was inside the shack. *Go check it out…*

And with that prompting, he walked off the dirt road that led into Windsor, past a foreboding, gnarled tree, onto the grass littered by dead leaves, and toward the shack, having one particular window in view. When reaching the dusty pane he peered inside, seeing what appeared to be a vacant home, its space largely emptied of furnishings and forfeited to spiders, which repurposed it to their webs.

Voices suddenly sounded, bringing Kilwroth's attention to the lower corner on the window, where he could see a hallway inside the shack that ended in a staircase leading down to a cellar. And upon the staircase were several male seroxians, talking amongst each other.

"I'm destined to rule Old Karnath!"

A male seroxian spoke. He had blond hair and blue eyes, and in his hand, an object bundled in a burlap sack, which he raised high for all to see.

"This means I'm the Child, and destined to rule!"

"Aye," replied one seroxian with him.

"A shard can't mean anything else," said another.

The seroxians with him nodded their heads, as if in complete agreement with his claims.

"If you're with me then, I propose anarchy! Let us raise an army and overthrow the Kingdom of Deardrum to the north, ruled by Penultum! If I'm the Child, then Destiny is with me and anyone who joins my side."

"Count me in!" replied one of the seroxians, without the slightest delay.

"Aye, me too!" said another.

Further agreement ripped through everyone on the stairs talking.

Hearing these things stirred Kilwroth to action. He turned away from the window and left the shack without staying a moment longer. Once back on the dirt road, he went straight to the village center, and informed the authorities of what he had heard.

In so doing, Kilwroth revealed himself to the villagers, who immediately gathered that they spoke with Eriens' troubled child, whose inheritance was something presumably Darker than just a crumbling kingdom. Their reaction was poor and prompt; the authorities banded together some male seroxians of Windsor, and dragged Kilwroth through the streets, before casting him out.

"Neither you nor anyone of your cursed seed will ever do good in Karnath! Your father was the reason we never secured the coveted land, and you're no better!"

Their last comment stayed between his ears, and resonated with him of what other seroxians had demonstrated to him his whole life, by their deeds. Kilwroth was a young seroxian, only seventeen years old. Yet the seroxians of Old Karnath ostracized him, emphasized that he was fatherless and damaged, and made him feel unable to do anything good for himself or others. Even now, he tried to warn those of Windsor of anarchy on the horizon, of a force that would oppose an entire kingdom, and threaten peace in Old Karnath. Yet, the seroxians choose to embrace their prejudices of him and his father more than his warnings. And by that, they invalidated and nullified his good deed.

The starry sky lingered overtop Kilwroth's head, along with the full moon staring down; all of heaven held its breath as he contemplated the situation, and whether his life was worth anything to Old Karnath, or whether it was just worth taking. But suddenly—distracting him from his thoughts and his decision on that matter—were three falling stars that descended through the night, against the backdrop of other stars still in their place.

Kilwroth turned his attention to the falling stars, studying them and the phenomenon of stars falling among so many others still hung in the sky and shining bright. But as he watched them, a sudden flashback came upon him of a memory that surely he was too young to remember, but nonetheless, of a memory awakened within him.

**** Kilwroth's Flashback—Eve of Eriens' Betrayal ****

(780 A.R.)

[Second Walk of Existence]

A young maiden rocked the wooden crib of a baby seroxian, and thankfully the child eventually fell asleep. She had been caring for Kilwroth non-stop since his birth weeks ago, given the untimely death of his mother Mildred; she was the wife of Eriens.

The child Kilwroth going to sleep meant a moment where the maiden could finally rest. Smiling, she turned away from the sleeping baby to the open window in the nursery; it was one of many windows in the cliff-top fortress—a portal to the outside world that stimulated her senses. Sounds of the rolling tide entered, along with the touch of winds off the sea at the cliff's foot, bringing with them the delightful smell of salts. And also there was starlight, pouring through the window from the sky above, strewn with celestial wonder.

When a single star suddenly fell through the sky, the maiden turned her attention to it. She followed the star as it streaked down through the heavens, with a tail behind it. Her mouth parted when the falling star enlarged in her sight, and seemingly became noticeably bigger than the surrounding stars. And it continued growing larger and brighter as it fell, to the point where it was so large and so bright that the maiden reflexively looked away. But in that moment, a blinding light flooded the room and she was forced to shut her eyes!

A child's sudden crying brought the maiden to look up. She turned to the crib, seeing its wood charred and burning, its linens singed! The stone around the crib appeared the same, blackened and sooty, as if the falling star struck Kilwroth! She ran there and peered down at the baby, who cried and threw his arms, but seemed unhurt.

Even so, she took Kilwroth up and rocked him in her arms, trying to soothe the crying child but to no avail. The child cried and cried—inconsolably— until the point where she hurried out to Eriens' study, to tell him of what had happened.

****

Kilwroth exited the flashback, still staring into the night sky and watching the three falling stars. But before his mind could even ponder the vision, yet another distraction emerged from the night.

All around the falling stars, the other stars started jittering about the moon. Two pockets of stars moved above the moon, one of its left and another on its right, like two eyes above a large mouth. And then, the moon's pale surface started to burn brightly, just as fires of the sun, right before the sky started talking to Kilwroth!

"Right now, your inheritance is less wholesome than theirs. But in the end, it's perhaps bigger than that of all others'."

It was the ghostly woman from Kilwroth's dreams, now born of the stars and moon. In times past and just as now, she came to him, and told him of his great purpose. But in the midst of all that had happened in Windsor—being beaten and cast out for warning the seroxians of war to come—Kilwroth now had his doubts. Clearly no one in Old Karnath thought he was meant for any purpose other than trouble, and he was starting to believe the same.

"You keep telling me I'm a rising star, but I feel as though I'm falling, like those three…" Kilwroth pointed to the three falling stars, on the ghostly woman's far left.

"A rising star is one who dreams gray, and at one time, those three were just that…"

"Just what?" Kilwroth asked, not understanding.

"Falling stars are the ghosts of rising stars. Falling stars are ethers, the remnants of broken dreams. They're the curse of dreaming gray and aspiring big, of things larger than life… They're the memories of failing on the way to success… They're the tormented souls of those who never persisted in failure until success… Three stars fall before you now, and likewise, there are three ethers, of which I have spoken."

"Am I destined for the same?"

"No, you're destined for far greater, if you will fight and if you will wait! Just as those in Karnath, I too have dreamt gray, and you are the one who gets to live my dream. *Both of you.*"

"What do you mean?!" Kilwroth asked, again removing his hair from his eyes amid another wind. The waves crashed before him, as his discussion ensued with the talking sky.

"You are one of two centerpieces in my Game of Broken Time and Sword, and one of the main benefactors to my cause. Yet you, far more than *him*, have the power to change this Game when the time comes. You can end it. You can continue it. Whichever you decide…"

"What do you mean?!" Kilwroth asked, perplexed as the woman's answers only deepened his pit of missing knowledge and understanding.

"Though I've expanded on many things, there's no time to expand on this. You see, your time is at hand!"

Above sounds of the sea and the night breezes, Kilwroth suddenly heard clamor behind him, from a distance. He turned, seeing torchlight and what seemed like all the seroxians of Windsor piling onto the embankment!

"There he is! Get him." The blond seroxian shouted, the one who Kilwroth heard proclaiming himself as the Child in the shack on the village's outskirts.

Kilwroth turned, and Saora continued talking.

"The anarchy you wanted to stop has contaminated all of Windsor, and it will spread like wildfire across much of Old Karnath, leading to a civil war where Deardrum will fall, and King Penultum and Prince Merphonox will perish. In Windsor's embrace of the Child's supposed rise to power through overthrowing seroxian governments, they have decided to find you and kill you, before you can warn any others of what is to come!"

The news shocked Kilwroth. He turned away from the sea and the talking sky, back to the cliff and the embankment. On the horizon, he saw Castle Malgun, reminding him of whom he was, and what the world thought that he could do. On the embankment, he saw the crowd converging on him—an angry mob with torches and farm tools—ready to take his life. The blond-haired seroxian at the front lifted the broken shard of sword with one hand. Though Kilwroth could not see its color in the dark of night, it occurred to him then who the seroxian was. *Can this be Kayareth?!*

The Light Prophecy of Old Karnath slithered through Kilwroth's mind, and its implications for him since he was now at Gallow Cliff, being confronted by a blond-haired, shard-wielding warrior. He turned back to the talking sky, after pondering this.

Before he could delve the matter more, the three falling stars above suddenly merged into one, which grew bigger and brighter in the sky, just like in his flashback; the sight distracted him from the matter of his identity. The one larger star streaked through the sky, and suddenly, a blinding light forced him to shut his eyes! And moments later, he sensed intense heat and an impact on the embankment, as the star suddenly struck down!

Kilwroth opened his eyes and turned about. Before him, on a stretch of charred rock, was a shard of sword. In color, it was neither white nor black in his eyes, because it burned bright orange from the star's fires.

"What is this?!" he asked.

The sky responded, from behind his back.

"It's the shard of a broken gray dream—the ethers."

"What?!"

"Don't question what; don't question anything. Just take it up, and defend yourself against the Child."

"But what does this mean, of me and my purpose?!"

"You're a Child also. A special Child, unlike him."

"How?! This makes little sense."

"Something is inside you, Kilwroth. Ether from a future time—from the first walk—struck you as an infant. It made you cry for what lied in store, something you understood then, but now, stand to learn as an adult."

Kilwroth saw the crowd close in on him from the embankment; they were maybe twenty cubits away.

"Kill him!" yelled the blond-haired seroxian.

I should throw myself into the waters... At that thought, Kilwroth glanced back to the waters, remembering the sea could be his end. But then, he returned his gaze to the oncoming seroxians and thought differently. *I should fight for a greater destiny than null destiny.*

The two options wrestled with each other in Kilwroth's mind. Slowly, the seroxian began to realize that he—perhaps like many in Old Karnath—had undervalued the meaning of his own life by contemplating suicide. But all this time, the ghostly woman had hinted that he was meant for more, and maybe that were true. *I just hope that by more, she doesn't mean that I'm Shaizan!*

To Kilwroth, fighting for more than a life of nothingness seemed well worth the risk of fighting the blond-haired seroxian. And so, he leaned down to the rock and picked up the glowing shard in one hand. In that moment, it felt heavy and unsure in his grip, and he could feel the heat radiating from the energized blade, betokening of a power inside that surely would be unordinary and estranged for any seroxian. Yet, despite these forewarnings, he knew he had to use the blade, and so, he would.

From over his shoulder the sky spoke again.

"The spirit of Kayareth resides within you for this fight. Likewise, in the future, Shaizan's spirit dwells within a warrior who will be uncontended for a season. But in time, you'll both meet and you'll both be matched. Until then, there will be many victories not leaving much to savor. Even so, on with your fight, and give me a show."

"WAKE OF BROKEN DREAMS"

Chapter 79
To Gallow Cliff

Kort fell to his knees at the top of Gallow Cliff, several hundred cubits away from its ledge. The impact clanked his suit of armor, despite being padded by the grass, causing a few stones to tumble out his hands. He had gathered an armful of them from the surrounding area to continue building his pile.

Tears flowed down his cheeks, as Kort heaped the armful of stones on top of those already stacked. And then, he collected the fallen stones that escaped his arms, and began putting them onto the pile as well. The whole time, the blue sky loomed over his shoulders, dotted by puffy white clouds and the golden sun, which baked him inside his armor. He felt uncomfortable, even in the moments the ocean sent its cool breezes.

For Kort, there would be no relief and no rest, not after what had just happened. And so, he continued working and he continued crying. Just like him, Nym cried from where she stood at his rear, casting a long shadow on the ground. Elucid stood by her side, casting an even longer shadow. Overhead, gulls circled and squawked mournfully, as if they too knew the pains felt in aching hearts, on a day that was far from perfect for both Kort and Nym.

Only yesterday, Kort learned that Nym had ridden non-stop to meet him at Gallow Cliff, and like Magicia had told him in Doj, she indeed was pregnant with his child. But soon after her arrival to the cliffs, they both learned horrible news: she had miscarried! It was awful. It was devastating. It was so utterly sad. And neither of them would ever recover.

After placing the last few stones, Kort leaned back and surveyed the mound of smooth rocks. This was the grave for his child, and the sight alone drove grief through him. *Why did this happen? Why, Destiny? Why?!*

He received no answer but the wind, as an ocean breeze listed just then, filling his nose with a whiff of salt.

All of a sudden, Nym's crying became immense, and before Kort could even turn, he saw her throw herself right before him, over the mound! And then, in the same motion, she began removing the stones with hands that literally shook from heartache.

Kort leaned forward and embraced her before she could uncover their child. She instantly struggled to break free of his hold, but despite that, he held her all the more tightly. She lamented and wept in his arms, trying to pull away even harder.

"I've been a stranger to death for so long!" she cried. "And I cannot bear the effects of death any more!"

Kort did not know what to say. He remained silent, and ran his fingers through her matted silver hair, still containing her.

"I can't bear it," she sobbed. "I just can't!"

Kort pulled his head closer to her ear.

"Nor can I," he whispered. "But we must."

Kort watched Nym face him, and finally, she received his embrace. In his arms, she shuddered with grief, pain, and disbelief. She cried and wept, even more.

Kort held her there, crying too, never wanting to let go. As much as he desired to be her support, he did not know the right words to say. Surely anything that he could say or do would not help much. *But shouldn't I at least try?*

"We will never know why Destiny has allowed this," he whispered, finally. "But we must bear it, for if we cannot, all we have endured is for waste. And all that is before us is at stake!"

Into Kort's mind popped terrible images—of him serving in the Guard as a spy, of him going through Baal in search of Taurus, and of him ultimately killing Garlew instead. But then, into his mind popped other images, of him riding out the storm on Korinth, of him journeying deep inside the leviathan, of him saving crops in Doj and Reiju. And finally, into his mind popped more images—envisioned things—of him going to Gallow Cliff to defeat of the Child of Darkness, of him seizing the black shard, of him climbing up Liath to destroy the gray blade and save Karnath from the Age of Darkness.

The images connected his past into his present and his present into his future. He realized then that if his child's death would be his permanent downfall—something from which he could not move past—his whole life's journey had been for naught. He had to rise. He had to go on. He had to keep fighting. He realized that life would inevitably get him down, but he would have to get himself back up. *Do it. Rise.*

Kort looked beyond Nym to his child's grave. It had become a place in his life from which he did not want to turn away—a place from which it was difficult to turn away! Part of him wanted to start removing the stones, just as Nym had. But he stopped himself, knowing it would not change anything, and only stood to jeopardize more. *Rise.*

"Let's get up, and take our sorrow from here."

Kort whispered the words to Nym, and then stood with her. She limply leaned into him, as if defeated by the turn of events. She continued crying too, tears that wet her hair, which had now fallen into her eyes.

And then Kort watched, as from out of her deep sadness, Nym looked up with tears drying upon her cheeks. He took the moment to peer inside her eyes, as if they had become gray portals into the depths of this now mortal's soul—

panes of a brilliant looking glass that told all: Nym loved him dearly, just as much as she loved the future she envisioned with him, and all that she presumed it would hold, such as a family.

"I must confess," Kort said to her. "I thought you wouldn't come. I thought… you had stopped loving me."

Kort's voice cracked at the mere suggestion.

Nym stared back silently, plain-faced. After a long delay, she answered over the winds.

"Well, you thought wrong, for I never stopped loving you! Months ago, I loved you enough to give up my immortality, and now, I loved you enough to come to the cliffs, despite the risks!"

Her reply made Kort remember how Nym had shared with him that she was indeed a powerful being as he suspected, in fact one of the fabled immortals. Because of her love for him, she lost per powers, which made it all the more difficult for her to reunite with him.

"I know now," Kort replied.

He brushed her damp hair away from her eyes.

"It was all my fault; I should've never of left you outside of Breslin, like I did. I'll never leave you again; I promise. Please forgive me."

"It was never a wrong," Nym replied, flashing a weak smile. "And it doesn't need forgiveness. You left to protect me."

With that, Kort and Nym embraced. Being slightly taller than she, he lowered his head to her own, and kissed her on the lips.

After the kiss, Kort watched Nym glance to the grave and then back to him. "Our love has always endured misgivings, and this too shall pass!"

At her comment, Kort went ice cold. His face looked suddenly grim, and a lump rose to the top of his throat. Nym's words agreed exactly with those from his nightmare at Raiden's house, where he killed her. Images of death ran through this mind; he saw Nym's eyes go lifeless, as he stood face-to-face with her, while holding the handle of bloody Hirishin sword that he had thrust through her belly!

He shut out the images from his mind, and returned to Nym on the cliff top. But in that moment, he could not refrain from glancing back to the mound of rocks, as Nym had already done. It was the resting place for his nameless son, and represented a death that strangely coincided with his dream. In this, he could not help himself from thinking that somehow this nightmare was partly a foreshadowing of things to come. He gulped fear. *Destiny keep us…*

Kort let go of Nym, and when he did, she stepped up to the grave. He watched her bow her head, and whisper a prayer for the child:

"Please Destiny, keep the life energy gone from him inside the world of doing. Please keep the energy from slipping… into the Void."

Kort reverentially lowered his eyes to the grass, bearing in mind how what Nym did now was a Karnathan ritual done for children who died at birth: praying that their lost life force would not slip into the Void—that their life would not be in vain.

Raising his eyes, Kort looked to Nym. She had started crying again. A strong wind blew, pulling the tears across her cheeks and off her face, as if Destiny were taking away her sadness.

Kort turned from Nym and looked to the sky. He stood there, wearing the armor of Autheos with the sheathed white shard hung from his belt. The winds blew, pulling his lengthy soot black hair into his sharp, brown eyes. His face contorted and he raised his gauntleted fist into the air at Karnatha, feeling mad at her because she had not taken away his sadness. It remained.

"Why, Destiny? Why?!" he asked. "Life was not in my son at birth, so I ask, was I not to enjoy life with him?! Was he never meant to live?! Was he only part of my punishment, for my life of wrongs?!"

There was no reply, and in that quiet, Kort eventually felt less redeemed than he had felt before, upon lifting famine from Doj. *Have I truly repaid anything at all?* He wondered, despairingly.

There was a series of heavy steps, as Elucid walked up behind Kort. He turned around, and looked at the crimson knight. They stood about one cubit apart.

Elucid placed a metal hand on Kort's shoulder, with the other holding the purple cloak.

"I'm sorry for what happened…"

Kort found himself struggling to believe; Elucid's armor emitted little in terms of emotion.

Elucid continued. "But believe me, this is not your punishment from Destiny. And you are already redeemed."

Kort's eyes fell to the grass.

Elucid squeezed his shoulder. He looked back up.

"This day affords one of small stature the opportunity to stand above all others. This day affords one who has faltered his entire life, the opportunity to further right his wrongs. Let not this poor chance deprive you of doing great good. This wasn't your fault."

"I'm ready."

Kort heard Nym suddenly talk.

A moment afterward, he saw her come up behind Elucid. He acknowledged her with a brief nod.

"Aye, let's go."

With that, Kort, Elucid, and Nym walked together toward the ledge. As they went, Kort focused on the cliff's end ahead and the opening expanse of the sea, spans below. He could hear the sounds of ocean waves crashing against the large rocks, which jutted from the waters before the shore. The tide rolled in as the day died, and gulls still soared overhead in the azure sky, squawking a dirge.

The grass peeled back to the cliff rock, and it was not long until Kort reached the area about ten cubits from the ledge. When there, he stepped out closer to the precipice.

From over his shoulder, Elucid spoke.

"Magicia went down to the shore. Before she left us, she said the seroxians expect a Sink about now. So raise the shard, and their mage's Nexus will find it from the other side."

Kort lowered his hand to the shard's grip at his belt, and just then, a bit of apprehension slithered through him over the seroxians. He remembered depictions of them in books of myth and lore, showing the beings as many times larger than humans and slightly taller than giants. In that, the idea of meeting the seroxians seemed scary. *Even so, we need their help...*

Kort nodded, acknowledging Elucid and agreeing that their need of help was real. He drew the white shard from its scabbard. The blade glided from its casing with a metallic song, ringing out clearly despite the muffling winds and the crashing waves.

As recommended, Kort held the blade high over the precipice of Gallow Cliff, angled toward the heavens. Within moments, a stream of green energy appeared from out of thin air, from over the ledge. He watched the energy travel to the shard's tip and down its entire length in a blazing spark, illuminating the shard green!

Kort was surprised by the immediacy of seeing it. *Here, just like that?* He had trouble accepting that the connection from the seroxians' realm had already been made. With some disbelief, his eyes followed the energy in the shard's blade out to where it had emanated from. It was what appeared to be an opening portal over the ledge and hung upon the blue sky, currently about a cubit in diameter and slowly growing.

Kort continued holding the shard and energy continued flowing into its blade, from out of the sky. After a while, his arms tired under the sword's weight and quivered every so slightly. And when the shard shifted just as slightly, the flow of energy broke for a moment.

"Keep the shard steady," boomed Elucid. "The bridge can't be established between Old and New Karnath, unless constant force is applied across the dimension's seams, in order to pull them back. When the sword moves, it disrupts that force."

Kort nodded, now more mindful of his movements. He held the shard steady for a few minutes, being able to defend against the fatigue in his arms by witnessing progress. Before his eyes, the portal continued to grow, now having a diameter twice as big as before.

Suddenly, Kort sensed a flash of light from behind his shoulder, as sometimes would happen when Elucid mediated through the Nexus. *Magicia?* He wondered if she had done the same.

"Well, well… you ended up here after all," came a young, taunting voice. "If my recollection serves me well, I wasn't to be so sure of that."

"You know that I had a different course in mind, *Lucen*. But getting one's way is not always possible when working together with others. On the other hand, that's not something you know much about…"

Kort listened as Elucid clearly was having a conversation with a person who just randomly appeared on the cliff top. *Who is this Lucen?!* He wondered, anxiously.

"I'm most pleased to see both Kort and Nym reunited for such a special occasion. For me, this will simply be a repeat of a time no more, a new age that soon we'll never see again! Ha ha ha!"

Lucen seemed chipper and laughed hysterically, as if entertained by the situation. The behavior made Kort feel the same way as he did when in Raiden's house, with Magicia and Elucid bickering over things he could hardly understand. He felt anxious. He felt helpless. He felt like whatever was happening was way over his head. *Repeat of a time no more? What?!*

Lucen continued. "While the setting is always the same, the faces change time and time again! I wager Kort will put up less of a fight, than Garlew's son *Naketo*."

When that name entered Kort's ears, he lowered the glowing shard. With that, his link with the mage in Old Karnath was immediately broken, and the portal off the ledge began to shrink.

"What are you doing?!" asked Elucid, sharply. "Concentrate on your task, and ignore his banter. Lucen only seeks to incite us. He's our enemy."

At the reprimand, Kort grumbled and he placed the shard again. Within seconds, its blade surged green as the connection with Old Karnath was established. The portal stopped shrinking and began growing, as it was before.

"On second thought," Lucen went on, "a direct comparison isn't even impossible now, for a child cannot be conceived without a father."

The banter suddenly crossed a line for Kort. Lucen referred to him killing Garlew Il'therin and how this event consequently prevented Naketo from ever being born. This was knowledge that seemed extremely unordinary for most people, let alone someone of such a young age. *Just who is this Lucen?!*

Still holding the shard at the precipice, Kort glanced over his shoulder, seeing a robed traveler beside Euclid and Nym. He held a gnarled staff, had smooth youthful skin on his face, and had wild hair on his head that blew wildly in the winds. The green light from the portal danced in his blue eyes.

"Stay focused!" boomed Elucid.

Kort looked back to the portal, seeing that his movements disrupted the link to Old Karnath, yet again.

Lucen continued. "What's most amusing, is that Kort can only blame himself for what happened. Because Taurus had premonitions that Kort would betray him, he did not leave the Isles immediately during the Conspiracy as Nym had instructed. This ultimately put Garlew in harm's way when Kort tried to topple the Isles Conspiracy. So, if Kort had never attempted to do this good deed, Sergros would still have a hero! What a pity…"

"Silence!" Nym snapped, issuing harsh words that suggested Lucen had struck more a nerve with her, than with anyone else on the cliff.

Lucen paused. "Well, it seems like this is a sour topic. How about we change it? I'll direct a question to Elucid, one asked *every* age before it's erased."

Lucen continued. "What are you even fighting for?"

The winds blew then, but Elucid remained silent.

Kort squinted as the gusts whipped him, hardly believing Elucid kept quiet, for their bluster was a pathetic answer to Lucen's loaded question. Through his mind went various ideas about how he would answer, if asked the same. *I'd tell Lucen, I'm fighting for good destiny! I'd tell him, I'm fighting for Karnath… and for Nym!*

Lucen continued. "Tell me, why do you still fight, already knowing that the next age is gone and everything beyond it! Karnath is almost out of time this age too, and once more your failure shall witness my success."

Kort got annoyed with Elucid's silence. Kort got further annoyed with Lucen's instigation, and all of this enigmatic talk of things to come, and things already passed.

"What's he talking about?!"

Kort arched his eyebrows and extended the shard before the growing portal, waiting on the crimson knight.

"Well?!" he pressed Elucid.

"Never mind his taunts! Lucen wants to distract us! Like I said, he's our enemy more than our friend."

Lucen laughed, "Oh, you haven't told him yet?! I hope he likes surprises as much as me!"

"What surprise? Elucid?!"

Kort looked back with wide eyes. With his movement, the link broke again, the shard extinguished, and the portal started shrinking, once again.

"Keep yourself centered! Trust me, all of this is too difficult for you to understand! Just know that the outcome is bad should he win, and let that be your motivation to fight *everyone* on his side!"

At Elucid's reply, Kort focused again on the shard, reestablishing the link within moments. As he turned back and held the sword, his mind spun. Kort wondered what Lucen was speaking about, and if it were true that the crimson knight had not disclosed everything. *Destiny only knows… Just trust him.*

"I guess you're without a comeback too," said Lucen, going back to his question: what Elucid was fighting for. "You're without a comeback, just like X'ieth."

Kort nearly lost his focus and broke the link, again.

X'ieth? Why does he mention X'ieth? What does X'ieth have to do with any of this?! The situation became increasingly mysterious to Kort, with one question after another, each without an answer.

Lucen laughed wildly like a jackal, as if contented by having had the last word. Or perhaps, he laughed because of the sudden appearance of an orange fireball on the horizon, heading right toward the cliff!

"Ha ha ha! Ha ha ha ha!"

"Danger comes from above!" shouted Nym.

Kort glanced over his shoulder, and saw her pointing a finger to the oncoming threat.

He turned back, watching the ball of fire get closer and closer. It had a man's silhouette inside.

"Lower the shard!" Nym said. "It's the Child of Darkness, and you'll have to fight him!"

Kort lowered the shard, breaking the link. He took his eyes off the fireball for a moment to watch the sword extinguish, the energy stop flowing, and the portal's diameter—now three cubits—get smaller. He suddenly felt immense heat that made him sweat inside his armor. It prompted him to look up, where he perceived the orange ball of fire about twenty cubits off the ledge! *Get ready…*

At the precipice and still holding his sword, Kort assumed a strong defensive stance, setting his right foot forward and his left to the side. He straightened his back and waited upon bended knee, holding the white shard over his head.

All of a sudden, the fireball dropped out of the air and into the sea. In the same moment, Kort's jaw dropped open and his eyes widened with surprise. The fireball and the man inside it were gone from sight, as quickly as they first were seen!

But then, a second or so after the fireball had fallen, a thunderous splash could be heard from the sea. Kort kept his face of surprise and Nym as well, when suddenly a sheet of water rose up above the ledge, being higher than Gallow Cliff itself!

The wave's tall crest cast a shadow over Kort, reminding him of the storm on Korinth. He doubled back, and screamed to Nym, "Come to me, now!"

Kort took a few steps away from the precipice, and Nym hurried to his side. Instantly, he felt her grab onto him at the waist. He peered over his shoulder, and observed Elucid and Lucen look at each other for a moment, before vanishing into the air, like ghosts.

Kort directed his attention forward, to the frightening wave that towered over the cliff rock. It was a speeding wall of water, which directly faced both him and Nym, moving closer by the second! It literally filled his field of view from left to right, and soon blotted out the day's light, submerging the couple in inky darkness.

"What will we do?!? Nym cried.

"I'm not sure yet!" Kort replied.

But despite lacking surety, he hand an image of a shield in his mind; he imagined protection. In a split second, Kort closed his eyes and found himself in his enlarged channeling chamber. From its center, he saw its expansive stone walls, floor, and vaulted ceilings all around him. At the far end of the space was his Source entry, a set of double wooden doors having carven inlays of ivy. He ran there, and pulled on its bronze handles.

At first, the doors cracked open with green light along their edges, and then they opened wider, allowing multiple streams of energy to flow in, past Kort's waist. Behind him, the Source exit opened on its own, allowing torrents of energy to flow through, without being limited by the chamber's size. They swirled into the chamber, like a vortex.

Kort snapped back to the cliff top, where his midsection shined with a brilliant green light, just as the shard's blade, with an arc of energy linking the two.

From his left to his right, and going all around him, Kort saw a protective aura come into being—a dome of green energy that emanated from the glowing shard. And the shield formed just in time, right before the waters crashed down from the wave's crest and splashed upon the cliffs!

Kort felt Nym squeeze him tighter, as the wave collided with the dome and ran all over it. Standing together, they watched the mighty waters through a transparent shield of raw energy. The waters continued to flow and flow, for well over a minute. The whole time, Kort continued pushing and pulling Nexus continuously, channeling it in then out of the shard, while keeping the trigger image of a shield present in his mind.

When the waters finally subsided, Kort stopped channeling. The Nexus dome disappeared, leaving Kort and Nym where they stood. He fell into her, exhausted from wielding magic to fend off the wave. It took a few moments for him to recuperate. In the background were the sounds of rolling waves, and water dripping off the ledge. The cliff top was thoroughly wet.

"Are you all right?" Nym asked, with worry.

"I'm fine," Kort panted. With every breath, he could feel the noticeable spacing between his chest and the oversized breastplate. From Nym, he turned and looked to the ledge, suspecting that whoever caused this could likely be confronted there.

"I must go to the ledge. Please, stay at a distance and be safe!"

Kort sensed Nym release him, and he moved from her then, toward the cliff precipice ten cubits before him, where waters still dripped over its side. Behind him, Nym walked off the cliff rock, and back onto the grass.

With Kort's steps closer to the precipice, a retelling of the Dark Prophecy went on inside his mind: *And this war shall not be without a victor, for on that day the one called Shaizan shall defeat Kayareth in a final duel between the Darkness and the Light.*

With a hard swallow, Kort stepped up to the ledge. He stared down upon the embankment. The sheer cliff fell for over a span to the sea, white and chalky, with streaks of granite. From the deadly heights, he marveled over Maken's creation; it was amazing how tall the cliff was, and how the ledge appeared identical to cliff wall. *Get closer, so you can see the embankment…*

With some reservation, Kort stepped a bit further out, unsure of where exactly the ledge was. It looked like the cliff wall, and it suddenly seemed reasonable how some men might trip to their death, in an attempt to do exactly what he needed to do: get a closer view. *Where's the ledge?*

Kort stopped himself after a few steps. He could now see the shoreline assaulted by the tide, surrounded by rocks protruding from the waters. Upon one of those rocks below, Kort saw a man standing there with fiery red skin, holding the black shard and wearing nightly armor, being of wicked curves and spikes. *The Child of Darkness!*

"I challenge you come down and see if the Dark Prophecy is true!"

Being all the way up on the cliff top, Kort could still hear the man's call; it was booming and powerful. Kort swallowed, not wanting to forsake his place on the cliff, never wishing to leave Nym again.

"Come here," Kort yelled, "if you wish to see for yourself!"

Kort returned a cold glare, as the man on the rock just looked up at him. And then, after a long while, Kort saw the man nod, sheath the black sword, and begin leaping up the cliff face, right his way!

With a boom, the man's feet touched the straight cliff wall for a moment, and in the very next moment, he jumped again to a place yet higher on the rock, sounding off another boom. The man repeated his bounds, which produced a series of similar sounds.

Boom boom! … Boom boom! … Boom boom!

From Kort's perspective, it seemed as though the man in black armor ran up the cliff wall at him! And so, Kort backpedaled from the precipice a few cubits, just before the figure made a final leap up the wall to hover over the cliff's ledge. In that moment, he unsheathed the black shard midair and using both hands, drew it back behind his head. A crimson cloak swirled behind him.

Kort assumed his defensive stance again, setting his right foot forward and his left to the side. He straightened his back and waited upon bended knee, holding the white shard over his head.

Like lightning, Kort watched the man strike with the black shard, and he felt the impact a moment later, as the black shard hit the white! The broken swords met with a shower of yellow sparks, and Kort's boots skidded back on the cliff top, two whole cubits. The motion displaced loose rocks, which clattered over the ledge.

Kort could not believe his sight, as he stared into the hazel eyes of his former comrade in the Sixth Order of the Guard. *It's X'ieth Armstrong!* The realization was jarring, and his next thought was even more jarring: *It should be you in that armor, not him. It should be you…*

"You?!" shouted X'ieth, heatedly. "You, the murderer of Garlew, are the Child of Light,?! If this irony is what chance now buys me, then surely there's no justice left in Karnath!"

"This title came not to me not by chance," replied Kort, "but by choice. I ran from Sagult in hopes of redemption greater than punishment in Sergros, which took me out onto the waters of Korinth. There, I fought a terrible storm to stay alive, suffered through weeks of starvation, even the death of my friend, and finally saved a leviathan, who in turn helped me save Doj from famine! I made good choices to help others, and Destiny blessed me for it!"

"And I haven't made good choices to help others?!" X'ieth asked. His eyes were fiery and wide, and spit flew from his mouth as he yelled. "I've already helped more people than you ever will! I embarked on the king's noble quest to end the gloom for an entire kingdom, and that has entailed hardships that you will never know! Weary and cold, I rode through the night to Arlem, got lost in Saol only to fight and defeat a legion of vespers there."

X'ieth continued. "And then, by Destiny's providence, I was able to leave Saol and climb Liath to confront the evil sorceress Esmeralda who caused the gloom! I beheaded her, but not soon enough to prevent Gremel from retaliating to the sorceress' misdeeds by turning Arlem into Baal. But in the face of her destruction, I confronted the dragon and slayed her by serving Esmeralda's very fate!"

Kort showed a face of disbelief. They both had just exchanged epic stories, but X'ieth's story seemed more epic than his own! It was amazing. It was incredible. It was exactly what the Child of Darkness would do, per the Dark Prophecy!

Kort's incredulity prompted X'ieth to respond.

"Yes, that's right. I beheaded Gremel and thereby avenged an entire city, in the pursuit of good destiny for an entire kingdom! Yet, despite my good deeds, only evil awaited me upon my return to Sergros: Talus stripped me of my knighthood, my wife died giving birth to a miscarried child, and now this! Does that seem fair?!"

As the two stood off, face-to-face and separated by clashed swords, Kort felt X'ieth push him back before lunging at him with the black shard. Kort wielded the white shard and met the weapon's blade, causing more sparks to buffet the air.

"Grrr!" X'ieth growled, as if mad over so many things, from his many poor chances to seeing a criminal wear the armor of Autheos, which perhaps he deemed himself more worthy of wearing.

Kort realized that X'ieth was very angry, so angry that it might impair his ability to fight. It was something that perhaps could be his advantage. *Whatever he'll say and whatever he'll do, just try to stay calm... If you stay calm, it'll be your advantage, not his... Remember, calm.*

Kort silently stared back at X'ieth, who seemed to be increasingly provoked by the quiet. He watched the young knight's eyes grow wide, moments before X'ieth tightened his grip on the black shard and leaned into it more, pushing Kort back by another cubit.

His feet skidded on the cliff top, and in that moment, Kort saw the young knight preparing to lunge, as he did before. But instead of waiting around to block the attack, Kort had a different idea. He instead stepped aside as X'ieth lunged, and whipped around his right leg in a surprise kick!

Smack! Kort's flying foot hit the young knight in his head. He watched X'ieth fall to the ground, sprawled out and clutching the shard from where he lied.

As Kort lowered his leg, he felt the loose breastplate bounce on his chest. He watched X'ieth slowly sit up, while clasping his head in his hand. Kort just stood there holding the white shard, waiting for X'ieth to speak. But the young knight stayed quiet, just rubbing his head and holding his sword.

Kort's sight fell upon X'ieth's hand, which gripped the black shard tightly. The scene was enough to stir up Magicia's request: *Do whatever you can to take his mind off the shards...* Though Magicia did not tell Kort what she was planning or why she wanted this, he trusted her. And so, Kort realized that this might be the opportune time to taunt X'ieth into becoming distracted from the black shard.

"Has your combat really become *this* bad?!"

X'ieth immediately looked up at Kort, showing a cross face that appeared hard like a rock, with eyes that burned like fire. In the same motion, he took his hand off his head, reached across his chest, and pulled back the chain mail covering his opposite arm.

As far as Kort could tell, X'ieth did this to purposely reveal a mark upon his bicep, one that he knew the young knight had. It was a ring made up of five separate rings, each one intersecting two others: the insignia of the *Five-Banded*

Fists. This was a symbol indicating mastery of an ancient fighting style that involved defensive moves more than offensive, such as grappling, throws, and holds. X'ieth clearly had earned the mark through demonstrating his skill.

"My combat bad? No, you took a cheap shot."

Kort stopped himself from giving a comeback. It was clear that X'ieth was annoyed about being kicked in the skull, and perhaps wanted a chance to demonstrate his skills in hand-to-hand combat.

"Why don't we fight without shards?"

Kort said the words after a delay, and went silent, waiting on X'ieth's response. He watched the young knight sit on the cliff top, with legs stretched out before him, still holding the shard while showing his mark. His mouth parted ever so slightly, and Kort could tell the suggestion caught him off guard.

"Or, are you afraid of meeting your match?"

With that, Kort reached across his chest, pulled up the mail over his opposite arm with his free hand, and revealed his own mark of skill: it was the dreaded *Three-Arced Lashing*, formed by two arcs bending from opposing sides and meeting at a point, with a third between them, overlaying the same spot.

Beneath a sky that now darkened in early evening, Kort watched X'ieth inspect his upper arm, as if to study the emblem branded upon his flesh. He imagined the challenge that the young knight felt, for if X'ieth had studied the Five-Banded Fists, surely he knew of its counter style. Being an opposing form, the Three-Arced Lashing was offensive in nature, characterized by many moves that involved brutal combinations of punches, kicks, and other blows, along with stunning acrobatics. No doubt X'ieth was aware how masters of this art were quick, nimble, and deadly. And for that reason, Kort estimated that his opponent would find this challenge hard to turn down.

Kort saw X'ieth smile, before letting go of his mail and using his free hand to push himself up from the ground, while keeping his other hand on the black shard.

"For so long I found myself unwilling to touch the shard," he said, with eyes on Kort. "I wanted to, but had my doubts about *what* this sword could do."

"The point being?" asked Kort in a steely tone. "Do you accept my challenge, or not?"

"My point," X'ieth sneered, "is that I now know the shard's power. Yet, despite knowing it, I accept your challenge, merely to prove that I am more powerful than you, even without my shard."

X'ieth sheathed his shard in the casing on his belt.

Kort nodded and followed suit, sheathing his too.

"So then, we fight limb-to-limb."

"Magic too," X'ieth added. "That should make things interesting…"

X'ieth laughed haughtily before going on.

"Ha ha ha… Whether I beat you with a broken sword or my bare hands, just know that however I win, I'll meld together your white shard with my black shard, and stop time!"

The words pierced Kort like a spear to his side. They hung in the air like a snow flurry, and haunted him like a ghost, more than any words that Sagult had ever told him. They sparked another retelling: *And this war shall not be without a victor, for that day the one called Shaizan shall defeat Kayareth in a final duel between the Darkness and the Light.*

The retelling continued inside Kort's head, until he could not stand it any longer. He shuddered.

"The shard you'll take not," Kort snarled back, shaking off the feelings of defeat. "And time shall continue forevermore! Now on to the fighting, and less of the taunt!"

Kort put his hands together, fist in palm, cracking his knuckles in preparation. Likewise, from side to side he tilted his neck, cracking his upper vertebrae. He saw X'ieth hold open his hands at waist-level, assuming a strong stance of the art, as if to welcome the first attack.

Kort raised both of his forearms, holding them equidistant and parallel to his chest. He pulled Nexus into his aux core, a torrent that filled his enlarged channeling chamber. It welled within him, accumulating at his center as a mass of energy.

Kort closed his eyes, concentrating further on channeling the Source. Every muscle in his body became tense; his veins became pronounced all along his extremities. He opened his eyes, just in time to see X'ieth swallow, no doubt with some fear for what lied in store.

Without giving X'ieth notice, Kort rushed toward him, throwing punches and uppercuts with both arms—one after the other, and then twirling about with jump kicks. With each attack he pushed Nexus out; energy flowed from his aux core, into his fists and feet, and out into the air, forming glowing arcs of raw energy behind X'ieth that would cause his pain, if he touched them. These were shock fields that faded over time, meant to snare him.

As Kort attacked, he watched X'ieth carefully backpedal, avoiding the energy arcs while dodging every one of his strikes. Suddenly, Kort saw the young knight stop backpedaling and run up beside him. The next thing Kort knew, he felt X'ieth grab him by his right wrist and the elbow of the same arm, before spinning and throwing him into the nearest energy arcs!

In but an instant, Kort's body impacted a series of the shock fields. Upon contact, a loud crack sounded in his ears, and extreme pain coursed through his entire body, feeling like lightning daggers stabbing him all over. He gritted his teeth and shut his eyes, as the shock fields knocked him around in his loose armor.

Kort hit the rock hard, still tumbling. He opened his eyes and saw a few more of the energy arcs, only cubits away! In an attempt to slow himself, Kort entered his channeling chamber. Once inside, he ran to his Source entry, pulled open the doors, and a stream of energy entered, filling his aux core.

He snapped back to the cliff top, where he skidded across the cliff top. Kort pushed the Nexus on both of his thighs to slow himself. The energy barely brought him to a stop, less than a cubit before the remaining arcs! The shock fields began to fade, ironically as he settled before them.

Kort found himself now just as X'ieth was, seated on the rock with about twenty cubits between them. The situation was easily humbling. *This might be harder than I expected...*

In that moment, Kort's eyes trailed to the white shard, a source of power greater than his own. The look elicited some banter from his opponent.

"Reconsidering already, are we?" asked X'ieth.

"Not a chance!" Kort said.

He rolled on his back and swung his legs over his head, building momentum before suddenly throwing his entire body upright. Once on both feet, Kort did not hesitate in mounting another attack. He began sprinting toward X'ieth, and with every stride, he could hear the oversized armor rattling on his body.

Clang clang! Clang clang! Clang clang!

Kort kept his eyes on X'ieth, watching as his opponent prepared for a frontal attack in yet another defensive stance. *But is he really prepared, for this?*

When within striking distance, Kort kicked one foot into X'ieth's lower chest. With a smirk, the young knight grabbed at Kort's appendage, as if expecting to easily counter the attack. *Think again!*

The words went through his head, just as Kort anchored himself onto X'ieth's breastplate with his one foot set, bringing his other foot up to execute a kick-flip off his opponent's face!

Kort kicked X'ieth's head and flipped off, with his feet going over his head. As he flipped, he caught glimpses of sky and the young knight staggering back, hand-to-brow. He pulled Nexus into his core while airborne, having yet another surprise in store.

Using the energy, Kort maneuvered himself higher through the Nexus field, out of the flip, and above X'ieth! From above, he watched his foe; the young knight looked all around on the cliff top, not seeing Kort anywhere. It was the perfect moment to strike.

Kort immediately stopped channeling, pushed the remaining energy into his feet, pulled them together, and came down in a head stomp, right toward the young knight's head!

A moment before hitting X'ieth, Kort saw him look up with surprise before spryly moving away, just in time for him to miss his mark. With a boisterous crack, Kort's feet slammed down hard on the rock, sending loose fragments of the cliff into flight.

Immediately, Kort saw X'ieth forsake his defensive position by running up and grabbing at him. Kort parried again and again, evading the first few lunges, but eventually the young knight latched onto his left arm.

Kort felt a sudden pull forward, as X'ieth fell onto his back while tugging his arm and wedging a foot between them. At that moment, Kort was certain he would be thrown, and it was definitely too late to counter. *Just take it, and recover...*

As expected, Kort's entire body flew over the young knight's head, as X'ieth released Kort's arm and kicked him off. While flying through the air, Kort rotated his body, tucked his appendages forward, and gracefully landed into a crouch on the cliff. Over his shoulder and about ten cubits away was X'ieth, who now, stood on his feet once again.

Instantly, Kort sprung up, turned around, and charged X'ieth. When within striking distance, he opened his legs like a scissors, pivoted upon one heel, and whirled around his appendage in a wide kick.

From the corner of his eye, Kort watched X'ieth duck beneath his flying leg. Then suddenly, he felt roughly taken to the rock as X'ieth tackled him at the waist! Kort went down under the young knight's weight, hitting the cliff hard. Pain pounded into his back, and throughout his entire body. He clenched his teeth, and a tear ran from the corner of his left eye.

Kort viewed X'ieth overtop of him by half a cubit; the young knight lifted a balled fist, and was about to strike him in the face. *Don't let that happen!*

Quickly, Kort leaned up and head-butted X'ieth. He heard X'ieth grunt, and felt the young knight roll off of him, undoubtedly with a ringing head. He gathered that much from his own head, for it was ringing sorely.

Kort sat up, holding his head in his hand; it throbbed and ached. He turned to X'ieth, seeing the young knight still doing the same, his face red from noticeable anger and frustration.

Kort turned away, figuring they both would spend a moment to recompose themselves. But then, a flash of green light made him reconsider. It stirred Kort to action when he saw it in his periphery, getting him on both feet without delay. His immediate instinct was to face X'ieth, and when he did, he saw the young knight standing and ready to fight. This time, though, he would apparently strike with magic.

Beneath the early evening sky, Kort watched X'ieth now afoot once more and with his back to the ledge, having the sea behind him and his crimson cloak astir in the winds. Nexus emanated from the young knight's midsection in a ball of green light, from which energies flowed out on every side, into the black armor. The energies flowed and flowed, lending the nightly armor a green pulsating luster, seen clearly in the descending darkness.

Suddenly, Kort felt the cliff begin shaking, as from X'ieth's black armor those energies went to his feet and seeped into the rock. The cliff quaked so hard that Kort lost his balance, and in the distance, he saw the same happen to Nym on the grass. *What's going on?!*

He met eyes with her, and held the shaking cliff.

"Be careful!" Nym yelled.

From his peripheral vision, Kort noted the cliff's rock split underneath him at his left, revealing rays of orange light. Not knowing exactly what would happen, Kort pulled Nexus and filled his aux core, readying himself for a counter. And just as he did, the rock erupted into a fountain of molten rock, summoned up from the depths of Karnath, far below!

At the sight of danger, Kort glimpsed Nym run further away onto the grass. As she kept far from danger, he acted on his own behalf by holding the Nexus in his core, and back-flipping tens of cubits away, in order to put himself at a safe distance from the lava. In a split second, he had to wonder how this came to be. *What manner of magic is this?! It's like he's connected to fires in the heart of Karnath!*

From a safer distance, Kort released his Nexus and studied what was happening. Geysers of lava rock had sprung up on his left, forming a fiery wall that forced him to retreat in the opposite direction. The lava was still so close that he could feel its immense heat. Sweat beaded from his skin.

As the lava geysers came closer, Kort continued backing away from them, seeing more and more fountains explode on his left. X'ieth still stood in the distance, straight ahead of Kort and at the precipice, channeling more energy through the black armor and into the rock.

"Fair is fair!" shouted X'ieth. "I only wield magic, the awesome power of fire!"

Kort suddenly felt immense heat at his right. He spun around and confronted additional lava geysers there, spewing molten rock like the others, and making for a sheet of fire that walled his escape, on yet another side!

X'ieth remained before Kort on a straight line, being tens of cubits away and with his back to the ledge, having a wall of lava geysers on each side of the path between them. But in that moment, Kort thought of Nym. *Run to her, for you're stronger together. He's too powerful! Go!*

With that idea, Kort turned in the opposite direction of X'ieth, averting his previous plans of fighting for the option of regrouping with Nym. He would still have to run along a corridor of molten lava, but it seemed like a better option than confronting X'ieth alone.

But suddenly then, before he could take a single step, more lava geysers broke from the rock cubits behind him! Kort gasped. It made the path to X'ieth and the ledge the only one possible. Then and there, he found himself in a position where he had to confront the Child, or die.

But what about Nym?! Kort looked at his rear, across the lava fountains, seeing her safe on the grass. They made eye contact, and suddenly Nym started running toward the cliff edge and around the geysers, as if sensing Kort needed help. This sent alarms off in Kort's head, as it seemed like she were running into danger.

"No! Stay there! I don't need help!"

Despite his pleas, she was already gone, running around the lava fountains and toward the cliff's edge.

Sounds of the geysers pulled back Kort's attention. He whipped around, seeing them continue to erupt. They closed in on Kort's left, right and rear, creating a narrowing path to X'ieth, who still stood tens of cubits away, at the ledge. The longer Kort waited, the hotter he felt, as the lava came nearer and nearer. *I can't wait any longer*, he thought. *Confront him now, or Nym will instead!*

The thought made Kort swallow his fear. He suddenly did not care about the lava, pain, or death. He cared about Nym. He cared about others. *Keep them from danger, by keeping X'ieth away… Send him into the sea!*

Kort imagined himself running up the corridor of lava fountains to X'ieth at the ledge, pulling Nexus, and punching the cliff rock with his magical might, to break off the ledge and send X'ieth into the waters below. It made for a splendid thought. *Do it!*

With that idea, Kort darted toward X'ieth, up the corridor of lava fountains. At his every side—except straight ahead—the geysers kept erupting, spewing molten rock and narrowing the path to his target. To avoid being burnt or worse, Kort leaped, juked, front-flipped, and cartwheeled his way up the path. As he ran, his nostrils filled with smoke and ash, sending visions of Baal through his mind. *Not the time!* He shut them out, and stayed focused.

Kort flipped and ran, all the way to the very end of the fiery corridor, where he executed a final flip to leave it and confront X'ieth. The young knight waited for Kort as he had been, with both eyes shut, and green fires burning overtop of his open palms held at his waist, turned up and facing the sky. A ball of Nexus burned at his center, feeding the flames. As before, the young knight's crimson cloak swirled behind him.

During that final flip up the corridor, Kort's hands touched the cliff top, a moment before his legs went up over his head, and then back to the rock. When his feet touched down, he was five cubits away from X'ieth, facing him head-on.

"Come to me!" X'ieth snarled. "Give me the best you have!" The young knight opened his hazel eyes, and they burned with anger.

Kort entered his channeling chamber, ran to his Source entry, and pulled open the double doors. Streams of Nexus surged through it, all around his body in a swirling vortex. The energy flowed and flowed, soon filling the room from floor to ceiling.

Back on the cliff, Kort's gauntleted fists ignited with Nexus; the energy flowed in arcs from a sudden ball of brilliant green light at his midsection. His fists grew brighter and brighter as he channeled more Nexus there, and in one instant, he slammed his flaming fists into the cliff rock between him and X'ieth!

"Arrrrgghhhhh!" Kort screamed.

Crack, CRACK CRACK!

Abruptly, a series of deafening cracks could be heard, as the ledge separated from the cliff, cubits behind Kort, with both the young knight and ex-knight upon it!

A sinking feeling immediately filled Kort's gut, as he fell with X'ieth toward the waters on a support of crumbling rock. At the very beginning of his descent, he saw Nym run to the edge of the cliff from out of nowhere, reaching out her hand.

"Kort!" she screamed in terrible anguish, as if spans had now formed between her and her love.

Like Nym, Kort extended his hand up toward her, and reciprocated her call, "Nym!"

But despite their protests, the broken ledge took Kort further and further away, toward the sea and toward a probable demise.

"BATTLE FOR DESTINY"

Chapter 80
Fall from Grace

As the Child of Darkness, X'ieth was a powerhouse, wreaking havoc now upon Gallow Cliff. With his back to its ledge, he stood under the descending darkness of night, his crimson cloak flapping in the winds, his body adorned in Ma'althan's armor, its surface black though now tinted with a green luster, as energies fell off the armor to his feet, and seeped into the cliff rock to bring absolute chaos to Kort and his company.

Through his mind danced visions of fiery destruction, and that was exactly what was happening: lava had already spewed up in geysers from Karnath's center. The geysers formed all around Kort, displacing Kort's companion from her place of safety, and giving Kort no other option but a head-on confrontation with X'ieth. And that was exactly what he wanted. *Kort must fight you... He must fight you, and as the prophecy goes, he will lose.* The thought brought a smile to his lips.

When X'ieth saw Kort start running toward him, down a corridor on the cliff top lined with lava fountains, he closed his eyes and concentrated on wielding more Nexus to Kort's demise: X'ieth planned to greet him upon his exit from the corridor, with a strong blast of magic that would obliterate him completely!

X'ieth let his hands drop to the level of his waist, where he held them turned up toward heaven, with green fires flaming overtop. Likewise, a ball of Nexus burned at his center, feeding the flames in arcs of energy. He listened carefully, to the sounds of Kort's approach, intermixed with the sounds of erupting geysers. *He's getting closer...*

X'ieth waited like this until he knew Kort neared the end of the corridor. When he was sure that Kort was close enough, he opened his eyes and taunted his opponent.

"Come to me! Give me the best you have!"

And apparently Kort would.

X'ieth saw him emerge from the corridor with flaming fists, instantly slamming them down into the cliff rock, causing a series of loud cracks to proceed.

Crack, CRACK CRACK!

Before X'ieth could even attack, he felt a sudden sinking sensation, as the ledge abruptly detached from the cliff, behind the point where Kort had struck! It led to both he and Kort falling from Gallow Cliff, upon a long piece of rock that started crumbling apart, midair!

X'ieth was not happy about his surprise. *It stopped your plan. It will require you to plan differently. It could threaten your success...* He found the last thought infuriating, something that he would not accept. *Never!*

Upon both feet, he braced himself on the long slab of rock, as the sinking feeling remained in his gut, and now, air currents flowed all over his face and body, exacerbating his descent. X'ieth peered up the slab with squinted eyes to his opponent Kort, who now stood with his back turned, reaching up to his companion that remained upon the cliffs—a silver haired elf.

"Kort!" she cried, extending her hand to him.

"Nym!" he shouted back, doing the same.

X'ieth stared contemptuously at their love, something that a cruel life had taken away from him. Through his mind pranced images of Millicent dead upon their bed, and it called upon his rage. *This fight must go on!*

As they fell together on the slab of rock, X'ieth ran up to Kort with a growl, and grabbed his opponent by the gauntleted hand. Kort spun about to deliver a face full of punches, which caused X'ieth to release Kort's hand, duck, and then jump back. In so doing, he managed to dodge each strike, and when he did, X'ieth lunged forward and skillfully hooked his arms in those of Kort's, and then used his hip for leverage to take him off both feet and down onto the rock.

There, X'ieth loomed over Kort and pinned him on his back, holding his arms down by pinning their elbows with his own. He interleaved his fingers on both hands and pressed them over Kort's throat, slowly choking him. As X'ieth watched his opponent struggle and gasp, his eyes widened with unsavory rage and through his mind went the same disbelief. *It's impossible that Kort's the Child of Light! Impossible! It should've been you instead...*

X'ieth pushed his interleaved hands harder and harder over Kort's throat, surely pushing is opponent closer to defeat. But then, unexpectedly, X'ieth saw Kort float away through the night sky, on a piece of rock! The supporting slab beneath them had just broken into bits.

All of a sudden, X'ieth felt in free-fall, and flailed his arms amid the rocks that descended alongside him. He threw himself over one, feeling its hard surface against his chest through the armor.

Upon hearing a series of claps, X'ieth looked to his left. In the distance, he beheld other rocks falling and Kort jumping among them, from one crumbled piece to the next, coming right toward him! X'ieth lifted himself all the way up on the small rock, barely having enough room to stand. The sinking feeling stayed constant in his gut, and the winds molested his body and hair. *Focus...*

X'ieth closed his eyes, and went to his enlarged channeling chamber, where his Source entry sat at a distance—a set of double doors with carven inlays of thorns. He ran up and pulled them open by their bronze handles, causing the doors to part with a blast of brilliant green light along their edges. And then, the doors opened wider, and multiple flows of energy surged in, swirling about X'ieth in a vortex that began filling the room, from floor to ceiling. He ran to his Source exit with the energy around him, and used the trigger image of fiery destruction, swept into a windstorm.

X'ieth opened his eyes, and returned from his very brief moment of concentration. He still stood on a piece of rock, plummeting to the sea with increasing velocity. His eyes detected motion in the darkness; he could still see Kort bouncing closer, being only three rocks away from his own. *Execute your counter*, he thought. *Your armor gives the strengths of wind and fire, and you've only shown him one so far!* With that, X'ieth waited for Kort to leap to the nearest rock, and to come within striking distance. When Kort was there, the young knight saw him spring off the rock instantly, mounting a jump kick right at his head!

In that moment, X'ieth connected to the air currents through his armor. *What if they swirled, like this?* He twisted the fingers on his right hand and swept the air in Kort's vicinity into a tornado that sucked his opponent out of his jump kick and inside!

X'ieth continued swirling the air currents, putting himself at the eye of the tornado, from which Ma'althan's armor protected him. Happily, he watched Kort spin around and around the twister, with a winced expression upon his face. *Kort should've known not to meddle with you!*

A few moments after X'ieth started the tornado, the young knight's plummet from the cliff top ended abruptly with a forceful landing upon the embankment. To his surprise, his feet hit the rock and the impact rippled up through his legs; he absorbed it using the remaining Nexus in his core, letting the tornado die.

"Graahhh!" X'ieth grunted, as he landed hard, watching pieces of the ledge fall into the water, all around him. Large splashes hit him in his face, blurring his sight. When his vision un-blurred, X'ieth saw a watery hurricane spinning right at him, tens of cubits tall with Kort at its center! He rubbed his eyes; hardly believing that what he saw was real.

X'ieth looked back up to Kort, noticing flows of green energy emanating from his armor and into the hurricane. He had used water from the sea, and converted the twister into a new storm of his own. It occurred to X'ieth then, how this was a counter element to fire. *He's using the power of water...*

But even so, X'ieth would take back what was his. He flashed a crooked smile, and began channeling Nexus again. When the hurricane was right overtop of him, the thought of fiery destruction stoked in his mind, and from out of his armor stoked terrible orange fires, all around him! As a human torch, X'ieth leapt into the hurricane, pushing Kort out of the storm's center, and waiting as his flames turned the hurricane's waters into steam.

Kort fell onto one of the rocks on the embankment. A small stretch of sea stood between him and the shore.

"This is mine now!" X'ieth screamed, as the hurricane turned into a cyclone of hot air.

He moved it toward Kort, who jumped from rock to rock on the embankment, and then jumped over the waters and onto the white sands beneath Gallow Cliff. X'ieth followed after Kort who ran away, along the shore and the towering cliff walls.

"There's no escaping, Kort!" X'ieth screamed, then laughing sadistically. "Ha ha ha, Ha ha ha!"

X'ieth continued channeling Nexus for fire, and soon after he left the sea in his pursuit of Kort, the cyclone changed back, from one of hot air to one of fire.

Tens of cubits off the ground, at the eye of a fiery twister and literally riding this storm, X'ieth gleefully watched Kort flee on the shore. *One can only run from death for so long!* he thought.

X'ieth moved the tornado forward to relentlessly pursue Kort, and each moment, he gained on the ex-knight a little. But then in one instant, Kort stopped running; he turned around and faced X'ieth, seeming confident and audacious. *You fool…*

"One should never stop running!" yelled X'ieth, from the cyclone. "Yet you have, so now, get your due!"

X'ieth moved his twister inferno closer to Kort. Visions danced before his eyes, of incinerating him with the fiery tornado, his armor clunking to the sands atop a pile of charred bones, and that leaving X'ieth the spoils of victory: the white shard. It made his smile.

With victory in mind, X'ieth drove the tornado even closer, but moments before it collided with Kort, he saw his opponent's mid-section spark green, and flows of Nexus suddenly emanated therefrom, to the cliff wall overhead and into the besetting sea. *What's he doing?!*

Not knowing, X'ieth continued driving the twister right at Kort, but just before impact, Kort smashed his own fists together. In less than a blink of an eye, the motion brought a gigantic portion of the cliff face crumbling down into a hand and a large expanse of the sea taking the same form, both of which sped from opposite sides toward X'ieth and his cyclone! The sudden and terrifying sight sent alarms off in X'ieth: *No! That's not supposed to happen!*

The sea and the cliff literally sandwiched X'ieth and his fiery tornado, and in much the same way he received a knuckle sandwich from massive fists— one composed of water, and the other of sand. Being counter elements to his wind and fire, the two-way strike was explosive, and immediately neutralized the spinning twister that X'ieth had created!

He felt a sudden impact, which hurled him from his position in the tornado's eye—tens of cubits in the air—and onto the shore. X'ieth hit it hard with a series of loud bangs. All around him, charred, dampened rock crashed along with shattered glass, the latter of which formed from heated sands.

Ma'althan's armor absorbed it all, and X'ieth rattled inside as his body rolled across the shore to an eventual stop, where his face slid into the white sands, bleeding and flecked with crystalline bits. The tide washed up against him, soaking his dirty-blond hair and inflaming his flesh wounds. Lying there, X'ieth reached his hand down to his belt, feeling the black shard still within its sheath. Knowing it was there relieved him. *Whew...*

All over, his limbs and extremities ached, and his muscles felt sore beneath his spiky suit of armor. X'ieth did not want to get up, and perhaps he could not get up. But then, from out of nowhere, a gauntleted hand reached down to him, offering him help. It was Kort.

Reluctantly, X'ieth took Kort's hand and used his support, as he sluggishly got afoot. He stood there, feeling woozy and about to fall over, stumbling from side to side. The sound of the ocean waves seemed muffled inside his head, and he proceeded to pound sand from his one ear. He coughed, feeling it also in his lungs. Meanwhile, Kort began walking away, following the cliff wall up the shore. It was not long before Kort started jogging. *You'll catch up. Just a moment longer...*

From his cut and bleeding cheek, X'ieth pulled a few bloody pieces of glass, and dropped them to the white sands; they stained red. He coughed again and sucked in the clean ocean air, while glancing over the shore where the fiery twister met sand, parts of it now smooth and clear, just like the glass he withdrew from his face; it sparkled in the darkness, catching the twinkle of stars above that shined in the night sky.

Above the winds and the waves, X'ieth could still hear the pat of Kort's feet. He redirected his eyes then, discerning him running further up the shore, along the pristine white walls of Gallow Cliff; it was overhung by a starry, velvet sky of royal blue.

In that moment, X'ieth felt the wind blow right in his face, carrying salty scents to his nostrils and stimulating his senses, sending a reminder to not let his destiny escape him, not on a cliffy seaside or anywhere else. *Don't let Kort get away! You're meant for more.*

"Grrr!" growled X'ieth, as he forced his hurting body into motion and ran up the shore, after Kort. *You'll catch up to him, if it's the last thing you do!* X'ieth sprinted after the ex-knight, keeping him in sight with every stride forward. He felt cramps in his legs, but continued running nonetheless. *Don't stop, man! Don't stop for anything!*

X'ieth ran and ran after Kort, who looked back over his shoulder, as if hearing his approach. When they made eye contact, Kort ran all the faster. But

X'ieth had longer legs, and he increased his own speed, managing to gain on Kort. *You'll catch up. You have to.*

X'ieth continued running and he continued gaining, to the point where about forty cubits of shoreline stretched between him and Kort. He huffed and puffed, running as fast as he could, which made his armor clang about his body. As he went, he watched his opponent up ahead, still following the shore as it wrapped around the cliff, which now, bent the right.

At one point, X'ieth heard a distant rumble, yet he continued sprinting after Kort. But soon, that distant rumble came closer and closer, growing in magnitude until it was a loud thunder. And it was then that X'ieth saw them, as the cliff face rolled back to reveal an expanse of shoreline around the bend. It was an army, hundreds of cubits away, and running right for them!

X'ieth surveyed the force that came at him and Kort, hardly believing his own eyes. It was a host of the most diverse composition, tens of hundreds of elves, humans, and dwarves—most on foot, though some riding horses. On their tongues, was the *The Child's Triumph*, sung by a motley army adorned in white, having their countenances emboldened by their cause: defeating the Child of Darkness. And in their hands, some carried the banners of Sergros, a gold lion on a field of blue, blending seamlessly into the night sky. He saw others holding tools and weapons of sundry sort, ready for war. There was bearded woodsmen with worn axes, old farmers with rusty pitchforks, and gamey hunters of nocked bows and quivers of goose-feathered arrows.

They were far away, but X'ieth could still see them well. He looked across the sea of intense faces, seeing diversity beyond race alone. From simple to sophisticated folk, from young to old, from big to small, and from male to female, peoples from the Hirishin Isles and the west coast of the Mainland, joined together now in what had become the most unusual following. For these folk of varied trade and country accounted for those who believe Kort Al'starz had become the Child of Light; those who believed he would alter the prophetic doom, and stop the Age of Darkness from befalling Karnath!

The sight injured X'ieth and he quickly protected himself from its implications. *So many believe in Kort*, he thought to himself when seeing the Army of Light, *and just as many will be disappointed! Kort will die, as will they!*

X'ieth continued gaining on Kort, not slowing himself after seeing the Army. He headed right toward the approaching throng, ready to fight anything and anyone for a destiny greater than his former simple life. And such as this, the sound of their advance did not worry him for, as it grew louder in his ear, it sounded as a call to something he was always fated for—something that would laugh in the face of his Fate's Fray. *You should've been in Kort's boots, but Destiny decided otherwise, and so, these boots will be worn on your journey to glory!* The thought raptured X'ieth with grand visions of his victory and his place in Karnath's books of legends, bringing a smile to his face.

As he continued pressing toward Kort and the Army of Light, X'ieth witnessed something peculiar indeed. From the Army's front line, which streamed in the lion banners of Sergros, emerged an armored man upon a sable horse, lanky and bearded, having hair of coppery hue. His pointed nose, slender jawbone, and amber eyes marked him well. *Sagult?! He brought the Army here?! But why?! How?!* Questions went round and round in X'ieth's mind about Sagult's involvement, dizzying him, all without an answer. *Doesn't matter*, he concluded. *Just fight them!*

Still hundreds of cubits away, X'ieth watched Sagult ride from the front lines of the Army, as if he had just seen Kort. He rode ahead of his fellow riders on horse, with columns of many more marching from behind.

"The Child of Light to Gallow Cliff, shall smite the Dark and its Age will lift!" they sang and sang.

X'ieth watched, as in a single instant, Sagult drew his broadsword and pointed it at Kort, rallying those in his command with lofty words:

"Let us fight with Kort this day! He lifted famine from Logan, and now, he'll lift gloom from Karnath!"

At that, the mighty host behind Sagult pressed on with even more energy. They shouted. They cheered. They sang louder. They raised weapons and banners, even higher, from on horse and foot alike.

Just as the sight of the Army had injured X'ieth, this one did too. But this time, he could not keep a rocky face as hard as the cliffs. This time, he could not hold back his sadness. It stole the smile right off his lips, and his eyes showed of less determination than before. *They believe… All of them believe… in Kort… as the Child! It's like your very dream, stolen by another!* With that realization, X'ieth found sorrow, and replacing the determination in his eyes were tears, now welling up at their corners. He fought them off and kept running.

Breath after hurried breath, X'ieth sucked in the air, still sprinting after Kort whom he lagged behind, now by only ten cubits. His eyes detected a ball of green light further up the sands, between Kort and the Army. It was strange, and made him want to stop and look, so to understand exactly what it was. *Don't stop. Keep running.*

And so he did. Under the towering cliff wall, X'ieth continued up the shore, still on Kort's tail. But in only a few strides more, X'ieth could better discern the green light up ahead, without stopping and gawking. It was a portal, from which energy emanated into a glowing shard of sword, stuck nearby between two rocks! The portal appeared exactly as described in *The Story of Old Karnath*, where a portal opened up a path between worlds, whereby Maken exiled the cursed seroxians into New Karnath.

X'ieth saw Kort slow down when sufficiently near the spot, and he did too. The young knight panted freely with the ex-knight there, shaking his head back and forth, with his eyes stuck on the glowing shard.

"How… is… this possible?"

Between his struggled breaths, the words could barely escape his mouth. X'ieth was winded, just like Kort.

"As described… in legend," Kort said, huffing and puffing. "Only the shards… permit the seams… to be pulled back… those of the dimension."

"We have them," replied X'ieth, dropping his hand to his belt and feeling the shard. It was still there.

"I had mine."

It was then that panic filled X'ieth. He looked down from Kort's face, to the belt around his waist, where an empty sheath hung. The mere sight filled him with anxiety that while he was distracted from their shards with hand-to-hand combat, someone had used the white shard to his detriment. *Who would do this?! Why?!*

And with that thought, X'ieth beheld Magicia appear unexpectedly from thin air; she wore her yellow sorceress robe covered in Liath's dust.

"What trickery is this?!"

X'ieth snarled through clenched teeth.

Magicia and Kort smiled back.

"Let's see how you win," she said, "against the Gray Child, the Army of Light, and soon… the seroxians."

At her words, X'ieth felt a sudden tightness in his chest and his heart began racing. His mind filled with images of Kort, Magicia, the Army, and a band of legendary giants confronting him. Suddenly, his odds of winning seemed poor, regardless of what the Dark Prophecy foretold.

His eyes fell upon the glowing white shard. *Why not win the fight before it's fought?* X'ieth had the idea, as it dawned on him that the white shard was all that he was fighting for, yet it sat there unguarded, right in front of his face. *So take it now, before this fight!*

With blinding speed, X'ieth ran around Kort and Magicia, bound for the shard in the rock, hoping to run fast enough to avoid any mishap. As he went, his peripheral vision told him that from the portal, three tall beings suddenly emerged. The figure at the front was clad in black, horned armor, carried a large lance and a round shield, and stood over seven cubits in stature!

But X'ieth dismissed what had happened and focused on the white shard before him, knowing that victory was just a few cubits away. *Grab that shard, meld together the gray blade, and end time!* The thought hastened his step.

But while the tall figures emerging from the portal looked similar to giants, with the faces and features of humans, those looks deceived X'ieth. For while the beings appeared as oversized humans, it would be proven momentarily how they were much stronger in might and magic, than any of the so-called inferiors. The fabled seroxians would now debunk their place in Karnath's lore!

Chapter 81
Worlds Collide

X'ieth ran toward the white shard, not taking his lusting eyes off its brilliant green light. The sword was literally twenty cubits away, wedged between two rocks surrounded by sands, its blade aglow with Nexus. The ocean waves rolled up against the shore, a little ways off.

With every stride forward, his lips upturned more and more in a smile. The shard was so close that X'ieth could almost touch it, and in that, he could almost touch his dazzling future. Within a few footsteps were literally his victory, his destiny, and his legacy.

When about five cubits from the shard, X'ieth suddenly felt a strange force pull his arms to the side! And then, the same force lifted his legs right off the ground! Midair, X'ieth hovered in place, on a field of energy that bound him from behind. He glanced down to his body, seeing green bands of energy about his arms and legs! *What's happening?!*

X'ieth tried to touch the Nexus, but he felt no connection! Immediately, he went to his enlarged channeling chamber—an expansive space surrounded by stone walls, floors, and vaulted ceilings—where he stood at its center. At the far end of the room was his Source entry, a set of large double doors with carven inlays of thorns and bronze handles. He ran up to them and pulled the doors; they creaked open, but no light shined along their edges, and no streams of energy flowed out. *There's nothing!*

X'ieth snapped back to the shore, somewhat overwhelmed by feelings of hopelessness. He found himself as he was, struggling in the Nexus binds, which now, started pulling him further and further away from the shard. He literally saw the sword slipping away from him, and with it, his future, his destiny, and his place in the books of legend. *No, no… No!!!*

The act of X'ieth being pulled away from his dreams awakened his initial thoughts about his own Fate's Fray—how Millicent and Talus caused his divine purpose to unravel into something far less palatable than being the Child of Light. Millicent's unfairness and Talus' challenges inverted his good deeds as a Guardsman into poorly motivated ones, earning him little with Destiny. *They held you back, from being Kayareth…* And now, X'ieth was being held back from doing what he would, as Shaizan.

In just a few moments, the bands of Nexus took X'ieth back to where he last stood on the shore, before running off toward the shard. In an instant, he felt the energy about him dissipate, dropping him to the sands. He landed on his feet, facing the glowing sword wedged between the two rocks, and behind it, the cliffs. As he stood, his back was turned to Magicia, Kort, and whoever emerged from the portal, and so, he whipped about immediately while lowering a hand to his sheathed shard.

In the instant of his turning, X'ieth saw Kort standing beside Magicia next to the green portal, and the three large seroxians. The backdrop showed the Army of Light charging up the shore, the rolling sea on the left, and cliff rock looming high at the right.

His focus centered on the male seroxian standing at the front of the portal, with the silhouettes of two others behind him. The seroxian was over ten cubits tall, muscled, and mighty, with a face chiseled like a rock, having the semblance of a mountain covered in black armor, curvy and horned. He held a long lance and a round shield. Graying hair reached out of his helmet, blowing in the winds, just like the decorative mantle around his shoulders, striped in blacks and grays. The portal's light and the moon shined upon him, accentuating his features in the night.

Just as X'ieth touched the shard's grip at his side, a bolt of green lightning shot from the hands of a seroxian behind the frontmost warrior, being wrought in Nexus! In a split second, that bolt struck the sands at his feet, marking the spot black and leaving it smoking. X'ieth froze and his jaw dropped. *What power!*

Suddenly, in the space at the right of the portal, X'ieth watched Lucen and a crimson knight appear. The crimson knight wore a tall metal demon, standing a few cubits beneath the seroxians. X'ieth saw Lucen and the crimson knight look to each other with a nod, and then begin channeling Nexus.

From their centers flowed streams of blue and green energies into a lattice hung midair, between the seroxians and the inferiors, reminiscent in appearance to what X'ieth beheld in Esmeralda's abode. *Perhaps this is the same magic, by which Magicia spoke with Gremel?* X'ieth wondered.

With his hand resting on the shard's hilt, X'ieth stood there sizing up the seroxian before him, a few head heights above his own, heavily muscled, and seeming ancient; not only did the figure appear as solid as mountain, but also, he appeared as old.

In the background, X'ieth still saw the Army of Light approach. But now, looks of dread and worry spread across their faces, as some reacted to the seroxians before them, a sight taken right out of Karnathan mythology.

"Are those the seroxians?!" one asked from the Army, her worry clear.

"They're as big as the legends tell," gasped a man.

"Maybe larger!" shouted another.

X'ieth watched Sagult circle back from his place twenty cubits ahead of the Army. On his sable horse that snorted and reared its head, he faced them, waving his broadsword before pointing it down to the sands.

"Army of Light, stop here!" Sagult said in a loud voice, one that carried over the shore.

His command rippled through the Army of Light; they began halting, some distance away from the seroxians, perhaps three hundred cubits by X'ieth's judgment. People at the front slowed first, and then those behind them, and then, those even further behind.

Their murmuring still went on.

"They're massive!" one said.

"Like giants, but bigger!" said another.

Sagult yelled, "Be at ease, everyone! Be at ease!"

The murmuring quieted some, but still continued.

"I can't believe it. The seroxians!"

The comments went on, now less than before.

Other riders at the front joined Sagult, making for five total. They conversed among themselves on horseback, surely about how they would engage the seroxians. Meanwhile, the Army kept talking, and soon, some new ideas arose among them.

"It's just three seroxians and the Child," said one.

"Is that all the Army of Darkness is?!" said another.

"We can take them!"

"Aye!" shouted a man.

More "Ayes" sounded from rows of the Army, indicating a newfound confidence in its ranks, and perhaps, a development that would alter Sagult's command and throw the Army into chaos. It was enough to break the huddle of the horsemen at its lead. Without delay, Sagult rode closer to the Army's front line, as the four other riders went down the Army's length, two on the left and two on the right, all of them carrying a message.

"Wait where you are," Sagult yelled, "until commanded differently!"

"Be still, everyone! Let us wait!" called the others.

The four riders reiterated their message, riding along the shore. They rode the Army's length, and then circled back, rejoining Sagult at the front.

X'ieth watched the development, not understanding what was happening or what would become of it. As he looked between Kort and Magicia, the seroxians, and the Army, he once again felt daunted by the forces against him.

When sensing motion in his periphery, X'ieth looked over to see Kort walk to the white shard that was still glowing and wedged between the rocks on the shore. In one motion, he removed it, discharged the Nexus into the sands, and dropped the extinguished shard into his sheath. The portal into Old Karnath started shrinking, behind the seroxians.

He heard a sudden gallop. X'ieth faced the Army, still being about three hundred cubits away, watching Sagult canter to a closer spot, less than fifty cubits off.

A startling boom was heard, a loud voice uttering strange words, and then, understandable ones in Mainlandish. "I am Merphonox…"

The seroxian had spoken through the magical filter.

X'ieth turned in the direction of the shrinking portal. He saw the seroxian there, the green light flickering over him, as before.

"I am Merphonox, King of Deardrum in Old Karnath. And I do not come in peace, unless everyone in New Karnath submits to my power!"

Magicia spoke. "Per my agreement reached with Darconas, only the Child of Darkness should suffer the seroxians' wrath, none else!"

Her Mainlandish words entered the filter, and then, after a delay, came out in seroxian.

Merphonox showed a cold and uncaring gaze, as if the king did not care about breaking a promise that Darconas had struck with the inferiors.

Magicia insisted. "Please help us!"

Her voice went from serious to pleading, hinting of desperation. "The spinoff of my vengeance must be stopped; Shaizan cannot do this… not again!"

"Darconas and his promises are no good for you, especially if they're no good for me!" Merphonox snarled, suggesting a troubled relationship with his grandfather. "And besides, what deals struck with mere men will seroxians actually honor!"

Merphonox paused and then shouted, "None!"

He smote the ground hard with his lance, as if to accentuate the point.

"But," Magicia said softly, "I foresaw you helping me… in my premonitions! You helped us and the Army of Light, perhaps in a time no more!"

"Your fancies are much different than reality," Merphonox replied. "The seroxians gain nothing but risk from entering New Karnath to help you undo the oracles' Dark Prophecy. I have premonitions too, and they tell me the Army of Light loses this fight! Know that we—the seroxians—are not on the losing side!"

X'ieth watched Merphonox's eyes trail to Lucen. The king studied the youth a long while, as if contemplating a distant familiarity.

Magicia pled, "You fight not just to undo the prophecy but for a cause much greater, as I have unleashed Darkness in Karnath of which you might not understand! You would fight to preserve New Karnath in this age, and it's a land big enough to share! Your entrance does not have to be in bloodshed…"

X'ieth watched sudden anger spread across Merphonox's face, like an epidemic. His chiseled features became all the more toughened and his fiery gray eyes widened with visceral rage, hinting at a deep resentment that consumed him.

"The blood of my ancestors cries from these fields to mock your words," yelled Merphonox, "so think carefully before lying to me! I am not as easily beguiled by your sweet talk and empty promises, as was Eriens!"

Merphonox continued. "Hrya, brother to my father Penultum, the son of Darconas, died in New Karnath through the Tragedy of Old Karnath! And my premonitions tell me if the seroxians join you inferiors, a similar fate lies in store for us!"

Magicia countered. "Do you forget too quickly, how Eriens died here as well? He spilled my peoples' blood along with his own, when betraying my trust! Had he entered New Karnath in peace, things would've gone differently. I loved Hrya and never wanted him to be harmed, let alone die!"

X'ieth could hear sorrow in Magicia's voice.

Merphonox replied. "Being a cursed seroxian yourself—one who lived through the rebellion—makes you all the more partial to these humans! For that reason, you cannot be trusted!"

Merphonox's words were loud, and they lingered in the open air, with waves crashing behind them.

He went on. "Perhaps amid our entry now and our imminent conquest of your land, you argue the case of Hrya to deceive the seroxians for the humans' gain of New Karnath! How can we even trust that you loved Hrya, as you say? How can we trust you at all?!"

X'ieth saw Magicia lower her ageless face to the sands, as if searching for words to say. After a few moments, filled with winds and waves, she looked back up and spoke.

"I cannot convince you that my story of Hrya is true, nor can I convince you that the lower races didn't take his life! But I urge you to look past these hard feelings in good faith! See beyond a past that cannot be altered to realize that New Karnath is a land of promise, to be enjoyed by more than only one race!"

In an aside, Magicia shouted to the starry sky, "Let what remains of time be spent in peace rather than war!"

Despite Magicia's pleas and despite her polished words, X'ieth saw the seroxians unmoved in heart and mind, precursors to what would be a continued staunchness toward their own causes.

Merphonox insisted on the same. "Our affairs are very different from yours, hence we remain the enemy of the Children of Light and Darkness, and the lower races as well! The seroxians will not choose any side, but the winning!"

Slowly then, Magicia took bold steps toward the seroxian king. X'ieth's eyes followed her every move on the white sands, captivated by the sight of her delicate skin bathed in pallid moonlight from above. When a cubit or two away from Merphonox, she stopped herself and with her hand, removed the Guild's serpent pendant from her neckline, holding it up for all to see.

"Then let not this symbol confuse you, for I'm taking my side! Before sundown after the Children touch each shard's grip, the Army of Darkness as a *Serpent* shall fight the Army of Light as a *Lion*. If you're not for us, you're against us."

And with that paraphrase of the Dark Prophecy, Magicia hurled the pendant into the sea, making clear her side was with the Child of Light, even if Merphonox would not take it.

Silence fell over everyone on the shore—the seroxians, Kort and Magicia, X'ieth, Sagult and his Army, along with Lucen and the crimson knight.

Then suddenly, there was movement. X'ieth watched Lucen slowly approach Merphonox. The moonlight poured over him just as Magicia, making him look like a ghost. He settled before the king.

"Have your premonitions already acquainted you with me?" he asked. "Have they spoken to my accolades and victories in a future, never more to be seen?

X'ieth witnessed how, as before, a haunted look occupied Merphonox, as if he pondered a distant familiarity about Lucen, unexplained and odd, though certainly acknowledged.

Merphonox studied Lucen's face.

"It's… it's you."

He paused.

"You're indeed the one from my premonitions, but without your black armor and your black sword."

Lucen smiled, "It's not my age to fight, so I wear neither. But still, I represent the winning side. And this presents a problem for you since, as you stated, you wish to not join the Child of Darkness."

Merphonox looked back without a word.

Lucen motioned to X'ieth, and continued.

"The Child of Darkness here and myself are on the same side. If you help neither Child, this makes for two enemies versus one. If you help neither Child, this pins you against me. Of all enemies, am I one that you want?!"

Just then, the winds blew hard.

Merphonox swallowed. To X'ieth, he appeared bothered by a mere human threatening him.

"By looks alone," Merphonox sneered defensively, "you're someone any seroxian could squash like a bug."

Lucen countered. "Yet, from your premonitions, you know better? Before, I bested both the seroxians and the Army of Light, along with Naketo… And if you want, our fight can become a repeat of that. Surely my future success predicts my past success…"

Lucen flashed a wide smile.

He continued. "The real question you must ask yourself, is whether you truly want to be on the winning side? I give you the opportunity to ally with the Child of Darkness and me. I give you the opportunity… to win."

"At what gain?!" hissed Merphonox.

"New Karnath."

A wind served as a soulful intermission to their exchange. X'ieth still stood there with his hand on shard's hilt, eyeing the blackened sand where the lightning struck moments prior. He wanted to act; he wanted to attack. But he held himself back. *Let Lucen negotiate this. You might not have to fight the seroxians after all…*

Lucen elaborated. "We have interests that complement your own, king. For as your prophecy even states, the Child of Darkness only wishes to best the opposing hue, seize the whole gray blade, and stop time."

"At what gain?!" hissed Merphonox again, clearly irritated at the non-response. "How would New Karnath do us any good, if time is stopped?!"

"Well," Lucen said with a smile, "if you aid us, then you will not only have this land in our victory, but also, you'll have it forever! Imagine New Karnath as an ageless paradise, where no seroxian ever grows old, where no one shadows… like your grandfather did."

The crimson knight spoke suddenly.

"The youth is lying! Time ending in this age causes existence to end at this point in time! If you help Lucen end time now, you'll only find yourself in the past, without New Karnath, still having these unlived dreams! Not to mention, Maken's curse of Old Karnath comes now to New Karnath from the future, corroding the good here!"

X'ieth saw Kort's face change. It showed surprise.

Lucen lifted a hand, denouncing the statement.

"All these things that Elucid just said must sound as sheer fantasy, a Dark dream maybe, but certainly not reality! Do you see a curse to these pristine shores, the blue waters beset by sands white, overhung by cliffs whiter? No, none of us behold a curse! Elucid is the one who's lying. So put these words behind you and join me, to get what the seroxians deserve—intransient and un-cursed paradise."

X'ieth's mouth dropped at Lucen's mention of the crimson knight as Elucid. The comment resonated with him of the account Zeros gave in Forest Saol, about a large man in the Hirishin Isles possessing a blood-red metal demon, having the very same name. It easily became mind-boggling how so many seemingly isolated events were somehow interrelated. *Could it be, that this crimson knight is the Elucid of which Zeros spoke? It must be.*

"This is not going as planned," Magicia whispered to Elucid. "I'm sorry… I'm sorry for not supporting Liath."

"And I too," Elucid said. "Though in all honesty, I'm not sure why. 'Tis my missing ethers…"

The whispers died, as did all of the conversation upon the shore, leaving everyone in another swath of quiet.

Eventually, Merphonox broke the silence.

"Do you promise that the land would be ours? Answer carefully, inferior! For if you lie, the wrath of Seroxia will be upon you."

The seroxian words went through the filter, coming out in Mainlandish.

Lucen responded with a straight face.

"Indeed you shall have New Karnath, if the seroxians will aid only the Dark, and none else."

Merphonox pounded his lance handle upon the ground, as if to indicate a decision made.

"So be it then," Merphonox said, "upon your very life! We fight with you, at your command."

Lucen smiled at Magicia.

"Now then," said the youth, "I guess your sweet talk did little good, as your seroxians now fight with me!"

"How did you know?!" she asked, surprised.

"I didn't, but figured upon this happening. Chance has always been on my side…"

X'ieth watched Magicia glower at Lucen, which led to Lucen's increased satisfaction.

From the right of the portal, Elucid walked up, one metal foot after another.

Lucen grinned, "It'll be difficult for any force lacking a cause to unify and fight against Darkness! Can you even answer my question now? What, if anything, are you even fighting for?"

Elucid boomed a reply, "I know why, and will tell."

"Oh," said Lucen, "I'll be delighted to hear!"

X'ieth heard Sagult gallop even closer. He came about twenty-five cubits away and spoke.

"And so will we!" he shouted, with enthusiasm. "Please tell us, and in so doing, rally the Army of Light!"

Another wind ran over X'ieth's short hair. He looked from Sagult back to Lucen, seeing the youth smile again. Lucen raised his hand to Merphonox, as if to suspend their wrath until Elucid was done.

"Fine then. Let them have their rally."

D own the shore, beyond the shrinking portal and the two stones where the white shard was wedged, a large rock towered over the entire Army of Light; it jutted from out of the sands, nearly fifteen cubits high and perhaps being a place where Elucid could be heard and seen by everyone. With that intention, the crimson knight jumped there; comets of green Nexus trailed from the metal demon's boots as it flew through the air.

With a single leap, Elucid settled onto the rock, having the purple cloak in one hand, and a curved Hirishin blade slung over the back. Winds swirled the white cloak around Elucid's shoulders into motion. From that spot, the crimson knight was able to survey everyone. Elucid saw Kort and Magicia, Lucen and X'ieth, the three seroxians, and the Army of Light—a sea of faces in need of the same. *Karnath needs a call to its good destiny! All people need to hear the call, even our enemies.*

Now standing upon the rock, Elucid stopped to take in the collective scene, before speaking to the assembled host. Past the Army were stretches of white sands dotted here and there by black rocks, beset by the chalky cliffs on the left and the moving sea on the right, where waves rolled in from Korinth in the tide's ebb and flow. Glory's crown to the Army was heavens aglow with reams of stars and the ashen moon, both sending gentle streams of light through a velvet sky of royal blue.

To Elucid, these sights were familiar, reminding the crimson knight of Naketo and battles lost at Gallow Cliff. Inside, Elucid still felt uncertainty about any cause other than Liath, but would support Kort nonetheless. *Believe it just as the others: the Gray Child can change everything! Destiny, help me speak to them uplifting words, despite my internal struggle! Destiny, please let me encourage them and not hinder these ones, in search of good destiny!*

Elucid finished the prayer, and continued looking over the needy spectators. In that moment, the crimson knight felt the obligations to guide. And Elucid would, unhooking the white cloak and replacing it with the purple mantle, before releasing the white cloak to the winds. It floated away, over the sea. As the purple cloak became secured about Elucid's shoulders, it flapped in every gust. *It's time. Address them.*

"Let not Lucen—nor any other man—make you think we lack a cause, for we have found a great one from within! I, along with the Child of Light, and also this Army, share a common cause—noble and great! We fight for *the remainder of time*, to be used with purpose and enjoyed!"

Elucid motioned to Lucen, X'ieth, and Merphonox.

"This opposing force thinks we're already beaten. According to them, we are people without a future and destined to be stuck in a time before this one, haunted by memories of what could be, but never will be! According to them, we have no future, and this prospect is enough to draw upon our hopelessness!"

Elucid passed narrow eye slits face-after-face in the crowd, trying to connect with the entire Army.

"Even if it's true that there will come a time no more, it mustn't mean we should forfeit the choice and chance our lives afford today, or tomorrow either! Letting anything or anyone put you in that place of forfeiture now, is Time No More!"

Elucid continued. "Surely for everyone there will come a time no more, but it's not yet upon us! For we have time that remains, and what matters most is how we use it. We were meant to use our time for good versus evil, to heal instead of hurt, and to grow instead of stunt! Our remaining time is sufficient for us to find good destiny and to help others find it too! Our remaining time can always lead us to a destiny greater than badness and waste!"

Elucid's words were powerful, resonating down the shore and along the cliff walls, an echo to be heard over and over in the minds of those who were listening. Elucid's words were empowering, building an upwelling emotion in the people, causing some to chime in.

"Whatever time we have left counts!" shouted one.

"Aye, for good destiny!" said another.

Elucid nodded. "Yes, we stand united in this. We, the Army of Light, stand united for those who dare to dream with goodness and virtue in their hearts, and those of noble and worthwhile pursuit who persist in arduous times for their dreams, to the greater good of Karnath!"

The Army gave more cheers, Kort and Magicia too.

Elucid continued. "We fight one who seeks to end time, one who says our potential has already run out through our broken dreams, with life's letdowns being our end! But we can achieve better than this with the time that remains, and in such we find great cause! This Army battles for today; it fights for *tomorrow*! For in both are realms of good possibilities, for every one of you!"

Shouts of agreement rippled through the Army, in a great upsurge of emotion and spirit. People connected with what Elucid was saying, and they agreed.

"Even though some suffer and are afflicted," Elucid boomed, "though some are poor and destitute, in want and needy, and others sickly too, with tomorrow comes hope for opportunity and a better life, even to those who are presently without!"

Elucid paused, as these choice words struck a chord within the people, and stirred their voices into what became a collective roar of enthusiasm! They shouted. They hollered. They cheered. They all were excited.

Elucid continued. "We fight for the balance of time, and our right to use it toward embracing the white shard of our broken dreams. Though we fall, we rise! Though we fail, we try again! Though we may eventually give up, we dream anew! This is positive coping—the white shard…"

Elucid's words galvanized the Army. They clapped and cheered, lifting their weapons high. Shouts erupted from the crowd.

"There's life beyond broken dreams!" said an elf from Sergros, a few rows back.

"From our shattered dreams to new dreams!" cried a dwarf, from Deardrum.

And then, from the very front, Kort asserted, "Being at the cliffs now *is* my dream!"

"Being here," Magicia said, "is a dream come true for us all! We're all dreaming anew!"

The momentum of Elucid's words carried through the crowd, rousing everyone to hopes greater than the dismal life many knew before coming here, to hopes in what goodness the remainder of their lives might entail. The choices and chances of the future meant a world of good possibilities for all present, to seize varied and unique good destinies, and bring good into Karnath.

Elucid suddenly drew the Hirishin sword from its casing, lifting its gleaming blade high to the heavens.

"In this, I salute those hurting most among the ranks of the Army of Light. To those who are just as shattered as their broken dreams, be encouraged in good doing! For only by doing comes achievement, and only by doing shall the Army of Light triumph over these fallen few, these ones succumbing to negative emotions from the deferred hopes of yesterday!"

Elucid glanced to Lucen, pointing the sword there.

"While these ones have lost to the gloom, you all have overcome your gloom today by choosing to fight for your futures, despite life getting you down! This is our Battle for Destiny! This is our Fate's Fray! So let us fight this day our war for tomorrow, and employ in it all our heart, soul, and might!"

The Army burst into charismatic cheer, a thunder that now quaked the foot of Gallow Cliff. Elucid was quick to perceive how the Army's enthusiasm considerably affected the Army of Darkness. Lucen showed indignant eyes; he clenched his gnarled staff in his fist and glowered. But on the other hand, X'ieth's once hardened face now softened quite a bit, as if something went on inside him—perhaps a subtle movement of the heart.

Elucid watched as Lucen suddenly left the side of X'ieth and the seroxians, and came to Army's front line.

"You've had many words," said Lucen. "Isn't that enough to rally your force to great cause? Perhaps not, so let me speak freely about the real point of this gathering—Time No More."

With seeming spite for Elucid's edification, Lucen went on, a certain devilry in his piercing blue eyes.

"As the *Lord of Broken Dreams*," he said, "I am the *aftereffects of your broken dreams*, the disappointment and heartache that breeds your contempt for life! I am the *end of your time and destiny*, the reason that prevents you from doing, and limits you to being! When I unravel yet another weave, you'll find yourself in the past, without a future, and haunted by visions of what [you] may never be!"

Lucen's face lit up. He grinned and continued.

"Because of me, you won't constructively cope with your past to plan a better future! Opportunity will pass everyone by, when I erase your time—the spent energy that everyone should've used to seize their good destiny!"

But despite Lucen's interruption, the Army of Light remained unshaken—a thing that gradually marred his countenance. His eyes became all the more indignant and fiery, his forehead scrunched, and his lips curled.

"And even if somehow you think that your broken dreams won't get the best of you, just remember that *who you are*, will. In the end, *you are the lower races*, those who are *inferior* to the seroxians. Even with all your confidence, you don't stand a chance against them!"

Lucen's comment quieted the Army considerably. Many now leered at Merphonox and suddenly there were no more energetic shouts, only the peoples' silence and fear. And in this, Elucid realized an intervention was needed. *Say something! Lucen is making everyone feel inadequate compared to the seroxians over their race, which in the end, must matter little! For all seroxians were created equal, cursed and un-cursed alike!*

"You all face fears," Elucid told the Army, interrupting their worry. "You face fears of the seroxian king, fears of yourself failing! Lucen here dubs you as the *lower races* compared to Merphonox, to have you feel inferior, to have you feel weak! And if you believe that your race *is* inferior because of his words alone, then he has beaten you, long before your battle even starts!"

Elucid paused. The crimson knight's stare drifted through the assembled mass, visiting those showing faces of fear and consternation.

Elucid looked first to those from Sergros.

"Humans of varied virtue, both men and woman!"

Elucid then locked eyes with some from Deardrum.

"Dwarves, of both ingenuity and might!"

And finally, Elucid turned to those of Juniper.

"Elves, fairness and strength follow you, with love for nature! Combined, your subtle differences to humans make you one of a kind!"

Elucid continued, collectively addressing everyone.

"People here, know now that the superb crafts of Merphonox are distributed among you! Know it that when allied together, we are just as strong, as he!"

Elucid shouted those last words, while pointing the curved Hirishin blade at the distant seroxians. With that gesture, the Army beneath the rock at the foot of Gallow Cliff burst into ecstatic cheer. It was a moving tribute to the lower races, esteeming them higher with praises of equality.

Many beat upraised weapons and shields against their chests, just as many howled and hooted alike. Their combined spirit for a shared mission blended together into one strong sound, a harmonious thunder that surely upset Lucen's confidence, as well as his companions—the Army of Darkness.

As expected, Elucid witnessed exactly this with Lucen, who still lingered at the Army's front, near Magicia, Kort, and Sagult. He dropped his face and scowled at his feet, while walking all the way back to the seroxians and X'ieth, acting as if beaten before the fight.

When there, Lucen looked up, meeting X'ieth's hazel eyes. "Get ready for war!" he shouted.

At his command, Lucen flashed a wide smile and extended his staff with one hand. Elucid watched Nexus spark down its length, right before Lucen fashioned the staff into a sword of green fire! The sight prompted an immediate realization: *Lucen has always fought in the ages after this, and this age, he has yet to be beaten. So knowing that, ready the Army to their cause!*

Elucid looked away from Lucen and back to the Army, raising the Hirishin sword and saying this last thing:

"The oracles foresaw this day ending in a victory for Darkness at Gallow Cliff, but let it be known that this is the age of rewritten fates, of good destinies contrived in good hearts that can be seized through hard work, perseverance, and favorable chance! Little do you all know, your choices made upon premonitions and inclinations have overwritten your fates in a former walk of life, never more to be seen! Such as this, the Dark Prophecy shall be overwritten as well! This day shall go down in infamy as one where a spirited folk set to do good, overcame the word of prophets and the deeds of the Child of Darkness!"

Elucid saw Sagult ride to the Army's front, lifting his broadsword to the sky with a shout, "These words spoken are true, so onward to our fight, to your prophecy's change, and to the Age of Light!"

Sagult pointed the sword at Merphonox. "Attack!"

Once again, cheers erupted from the Army.

"For time!" shouted some.

"For destiny!" yelled others.

A third cry rang out, from Kort first and then echoed by so many others in the charge: "For dreams!"

With those sentiments, the Army of Light rushed toward the Army of Darkness, as their Battle for Destiny unfolded now at Gallow Cliff, just as described in the Dark Prophecy, though hopefully with its victor to change.

Chapter 83
Battle for Destiny

After Elucid's rally, X'ieth watched as Sagult commanded the Army of Light to attack the seroxians. The host rushed forward, with those at its front moving first, before those at its middle and those at its rear. The Army bypassed X'ieth and converged on the area before Merphonox, swarming the seroxians like ants would swarm a much larger threat.

While this was happening, X'ieth saw Lucen fashion his staff into a flaming green blade and face off directly with Elucid, in what was the most intense and fanciful swordplay that he had ever seen. They both were extremely skilled, flowing into form after form with stunning precision and speed—Fire's Breath, Lightning Impedes, Geyser's Fount, and many others. *Maybe they're more skilled than any swordsman of the Waning Crescent, in the Mainland or the Isles!* He wondered. Meanwhile, multi-colored sparks showered from their whirling blades, as the two exchanged strike for parry in a dizzying blur.

X'ieth turned and saw Kort staring right at him, from a distance of about ten cubits. They both drew their shards at the same exact time, their blades singing a metallic harmony while sliding from their scabbards. The sounds were superimposed upon those of war developing all around them; the young knight could hear a thunderous clash of steel, as the Army met the seroxians and Lucen met Elucid.

Seeing Kort as Kayareth was motivation enough for X'ieth to do the same. He charged his former comrade at full speed, swung his sword, and their shards likewise clashed when Kort blocked.

X'ieth swung again; Kort blocked. X'ieth swung yet again, and as before, Kort blocked. Their shards met with flashy glint and metallic song, swing after swing. Every strike, X'ieth released his anger over the situation. He was mad to begin with, but now, even more so after hearing Elucid's motivational talk. It made him angry over being Shaizan instead of Kayareth—over being a force that stood for people breaking after their broken dreams and never recovering. As much as he wanted to be someone legendary, Shaizan's identity was starting to not sit well with him. He wanted to be good; he wanted to be better than this. *But, perhaps what Shaizan stands for, describes you better than Kayareth...*

When Kort blocked another strike, X'ieth kept his shard against Kort's, peeling back his lips, showing clenched teeth, and growling. Past their crisscrossed blades, X'ieth looked into Kort's brown eyes, and as he did, the anger grew inside of him. Images flashed in his mind—of Talus taking his knighthood, of his wife dying in childbirth, of his son being born lifeless, and of him holding the black shard versus the white. These were the broken dreams of X'ieth Armstrong that had broken this young knight, and these were broken dreams from which he might never recover or move beyond.

"Grrrrgggghhhhh!" X'ieth growled again.

Kort stared back without a word, glancing away to the Army in the background, where the fight against Merphonox was becoming a massacre of the lower races. There were sounds of a metallic chatter, followed by shrieking and sprays of blood.

X'ieth suddenly felt Kort push him back with the white shard, before his opponent ran off into the fray. His feet skidded back two cubits on the stand, and X'ieth braced himself, barely stopping himself from falling. He looked up, just in time to see the back of Kort's armor.

"Face me, coward!" he yelled.

X'ieth stood there with his fist raised, holding the black shard in his other hand, with its tip touching the sands. He watched Kort keep running right in the direction of Merphonox, as if having a greater interest in that fight versus the one with the young knight.

X'ieth looked beyond Kort, up the sands, past scores of humans, dwarves, and elves brave enough to confront the seroxians—some already being injured or dead—all the way to Merphonox, who stood at a distance with his two sorcerers behind him. The sorcerers filled their aux cores with Nexus, causing their midsections to shine green. Merphonox likewise pulled Nexus and his midsection shined as well. He already started channeling the energy into his lance; the weapon glowed greener and greener each moment, from tip to handle.

Wails and groans rose from all over the shore, redirecting X'ieth's attention; he looked away from Merphonox and back to the injured humans, elves, and dwarves surrounding the seroxian king. Many had fallen to the sands, which now, were stained crimson; their flesh had been ripped open, and they bled profusely onto the shore, while vocalizing utter agony. Those closest to Merphonox were the most injured, but some further back were also injured as well.

Before, X'ieth had glossed over this sight when looking to Merphonox, but now, upon refocusing on the carnage all around him, he felt differently. It was appalling. It was shocking. It was saddening. These were his fellow Sergrothians and allies, literally being slaughtered right in front of him, by some unknown means. *How did this even happen?!* He wondered, not understanding the source of their grave injuries.

X'ieth looked back to Merphonox, seeing the standing fighters nearest the king back off, perhaps warned of his power by the gulf of dying and dead inferiors between them. These were tens of humans, elves and dwarves who stepped back defensively, raising their weapons before fearful and horror-stricken faces. From a few rows back, the hunters launched waves of arrows at Merphonox, but the sorcerers behind the king raised Nexus shields to deflect every single projectile. The arrows hit the shield with showers of yellow sparks, before their shafts broke and they fell to the sands, bent.

X'ieth redirected his vision back a few heads, seeing Kort reach the Army's rear—the start of a huge cluster of people. He began navigating his way through the crowd closer to Merphonox.

Angered, X'ieth taunted again, "Coward!"

Kort did not stop, turn, or even glance back.

X'ieth stepped toward the fray, but his legs instantly froze, preventing him from taking a step further. Visions of all the slain bombarded his eyes, driving a realization through him: *Another step more, and that could be you...* He suddenly felt like the true coward.

There was a sudden clamor near Merphonox, and X'ieth looked there, seeing the closest standing fighters now accompanied by several horseman. Of them, Sagult was there, pointing his sword at Merphonox.

"Ready yourselves!"

"No, don't!" Kort yelled, from the middle of the Army. He started quickly pushing toward Sagult, moving faster than before.

"Attack!" Sagult cried.

He, and several riders on Merphonox's opposite flank, suddenly rushed the seroxians, along with a group of fighters on foot. As they approached, Merphonox kept channeling more energy into his lance, while the sorcerers behind him continued pulling Nexus into their cores. All of their midsections still blazed with green light.

X'ieth watched the engagement unfold. Those of the Army leaped over the injured and slain, to a place several cubits before Merphonox, nearly within striking distance. Sagult and the other horsemen rode beside them, with their weapons raised to deal blows against the seroxian king. Kort pushed even closer, breaking through the front line, and being separated from Sagult and the others by the fallen. And then, it happened.

Merphonox's glowing lance disappeared into thin air. At first notice, the sight dumbfounded X'ieth. *It's gone... But where did it go?* He wondered, searching all around with curious eyes. As he did, the sorcerers behind Merphonox used their Nexus to form an energy shield over all three of them—a green dome.

Moments later, X'ieth witnessed black specks fly over those confronting Merphonox, appearing as a swarm of locusts! To the eye, it seemed like these black specks were tiny shards of the lance, bits of metal that chattered noisily as they moved.

Tat tat tat! Tat tat tat! Tat tat tat! Tat tat tat!

X'ieth watched the black specks move through the fighters, drawing blood and death along the way. There was squishing. There was snapping. Abruptly, footmen were no longer afoot, now fallen to the sands, stained red as they bled with pain, from wounds all over. Their flesh was torn and their bones were broken, causing their loud screams, the sounds of which were dreadful. *What… is… that?!*

At the horrid sight, X'ieth felt even more heartbreak over his fellow Sergrothians and allies being killed by the seroxians. Then and there, he battled with himself over doing something, and more than once, he took a step closer to the danger, only to retract his foot a moment later. *Can you really let this happen, man?!* He literally asked himself the question, but his mind gave no reply. Yet, his stationary body was a better answer to that question than any words he could contrive. Again, he felt like the true coward.

Aghast with horror, X'ieth followed the black specks in the air, as suddenly, they swarmed Sagult and other horsemen who rode to attack Merphonox. Just like the fighters on foot, blood immediately erupted from the horses and men, and Sagult was no exception.

From the Army's front line, Kort emerged, jumping over the fallen and running up beside Sagult's horse, just as the evangelist knight began to slide from his saddle, in the direction opposite of Kort. Sagult had suffered grave wounds, and was already loosing much blood.

"No!" shouted Kort, with an upraised hand.

X'ieth watched how in one fluent motion, Kort sheathed his shard, placed his foot into the stirrup that Sagult's foot left, and climbed onto the side of the running horse! And then, before Sagult could fall out of the saddle, Kort reached across and caught the evangelist knight by his elbow. The horse ran away from Merphonox and around the Army, with both Sagult and Kort upon it.

X'ieth lifted his hand to his mouth, as the swarm of black specks followed Kort and Sagult. But just as the specks came upon them, a field of green energy shielded them and the horse, one shaped like a dome. The specks bounced off the barrier with an array of sparks—yellow, red, and orange in color. Wafting from the dome was a stream of green energy, which X'ieth traced to Magicia, who was standing at a safe distance from Merphonox's lance attack.

Lowering his hand from his mouth, X'ieth watched on, seeing Kort take the reins of Sagult's horse, steering it to safety at the Army's rear. Kort glanced over his shoulder, as if looking for the other riders and any of the fighters on foot.

"Rally to me! Rally to me!" he cried.

Joining Kort just then were two riders of the four others, both of which took the same escape route and managed to flee from Merphonox, but like Sagult, had been badly scathed.

Rally to me! Rally to me! The words Kort shouted made X'ieth recollect his daydream of becoming Kayareth. He saw himself wearing white armor and riding a white horse in polished barding, over white sands beneath whiter cliffs, shouting the same words to the Army of Light at his rear, waving the lion banners under a perfect sky.

But suddenly, that image in his mind shattered into a million pieces before disappearing into a consuming blackness. And then, in the wake of his fond memory was only grief. Immediately, X'ieth felt his eyes go heavy, and tears welled up at their corners, ready to roll off, down his cheeks and into a bottomless well of sorrow.

Unlike before, X'ieth could not fight them back, and he wept profoundly. Tear rivulets gushed from his eyes, streamed down his face, around the corners of his chapped lips, and into his dry mouth, tasting just as bitter as his grief. The young knight had experienced sadness many times since acquiring the black shard, and in those experiences, he was able to better contain himself. But now, as someone lived out his biggest gray dream exactly as he had dreamed it himself, he found himself defenseless to the tears. He was crushed that his dreams went unlived, while they were being lived by someone else—someone who seemed so unworthy.

In an aside, X'ieth looked to the starlit sky, and spoke of his heartache. "Can it be, that these dreams of mine have been thieved away from me? Or is it rather, that not all my gray dreams are meant to be?"

X'ieth experienced a sudden recall of Zeros' words in Arlem—words that he had dismissed at the time, but nevertheless, words that had still sunken in: *We are all destined to dream gray, and many people often share the same gray dreams. While several people can dream the same dream, sometimes only one person can live it... This is why, for some people, certain dreams are divinely intended to become broken.*

X'ieth stood on the shores of Gallow Cliff, with his face full of tears, as he watched Kort help Sagult get down to the sands, before the horse collapsed and became motionless. In that moment, X'ieth's life suddenly seemed like a natural mix of dreams unbroken and broken, where some broken dreams could be put back together, but some were never even meant to be fixed! *Being the Child of Light is just that. It was a title that surely many coveted, but the reality was always the same: there could be only one Kayareth. It wasn't you. It wasn't them. And it's not unfair.*

Winds blew over X'ieth as he stared at Kort tending to Sagult, who lied in the shore; in the background, Merphonox launched another attack, filled with metallic chatter, squishes, and screaming. It was more of the bloodshed that Kort had tried to stop, and realizing that made X'ieth dissatisfied with himself. *Unlike you, Kort prioritized the Army of Light's battle over a legendary fight! Unlike you, Kort valorously faced Merphonox without fear and at risk of his own life! And unlike you, this criminal is deserving of a hero's title for what he's done today... Kort is indeed the Child of Light, but even so, you don't have to be the Child of Darkness...*

X'ieth continued watching Kort, as the battle ensued behind him and the tears dried upon his cheeks. It was then that it hit him: *You didn't have to become this... Yet, you let selfishness lead you here!* X'ieth saw himself in the weeks before Gallow Cliff, distanced from mending his relationships with an unsupportive wife and a difficult king, all in favor of chasing a gray dream that was not meant to be, which in the end, effectively turned his life upside down. He lost his religion. He lost his career. He lost his family. And he ultimately lost his morals—all for the black shard of his broken dream.

X'ieth felt pained by his actions, and in another aside, he continued talking to the sea. "Though dreams break, dreams broken need not become nightmares! That's what this has become, the worst nightmare I could ever imagine!"

Amid that backdrop of chaos—screams of the dying, screams of those still fighting—X'ieth looked down with great disgust to the spikey armor of Ma'althan and the black shard in his hand, feeling differently then. He would rather bear no shard at all, if it were not the white shard. He would rather go naked, than wear black armor to protect a Dark heart from the battlements of the Light. He would rather have a good and ordinary life, than one that was evil and legendary.

"This isn't me," he whispered to himself, still looking at Ma'althan's armor. "This didn't have to be me either. I did this. I let my guard down and made the wrong choices, something that in the end, has only added to my broken dreams!" X'ieth glanced to the carnage all around him, referring to just that.

He continued. "Fate's Fray was indeed my Battle for Destiny, a battle we all fight our entire lives, one full of victories but some defeats. For me, it was a defeat when my gray dream of becoming Kayareth did not see reality, and in this, I allowed my good destiny to unravel! It happened by *a Fate's Fray within my Fate's Fray*, where I encountered this broken dream of being the Child during my Battle for Destiny, took up its black shard, and forsook the positive sources of growth and enrichment in my life over it, thereby unraveling my very future!"

There on the shore, visions pulled X'ieth to his knees. He saw himself, forsaking opportunities in his own home to be a better husband to Millicent, forsaking opportunities in Castle Sergros to be a better knight with Talus, and forsaking opportunities in Forest Saol to be a better Karnathan with Destiny— again, all over the black shard of his gray dream, which was broken and destined ever to be. *This was wrong! You were wrong, for doing these things! Your priorities were so skewed...*

Again, tears flowed from X'ieth's eyes as he stayed where he was, kneeling on the sands. He dropped the black shard and it fell on the shore, right in front of him.

"Destiny, forgive me!" he cried out. "Please, forgive me for all of these wrongs I've committed, and how my actions have hurt so many others along the way! I was selfish to chase my gray dream, when it was no longer worthwhile and started hurting those in my life! I was wrong in doing so! Please, I ask you to forgive me…"

X'ieth cried and cried more, sending his prayer of heartfelt contrition on the winds, and hopefully, into Karnatha's ears. She heard.

Immediately upon his prayer, a great peace found its way into X'ieth's heart, and he felt forgiven. And in the moment following that peace, the young knight came upon a realization whereby he might be redeemed:

"My broken dreams don't mean I can't dream again," he said to himself, his tears drying. "I can dream new dreams, like saving the Army of Light and stopping this! *I don't need to be the hero in order to be heroic.*"

The epiphany was perhaps sent from above; it jerked his eyes back to the losing Army of Light, to the swarming black specks that again wreaked havoc on anyone getting too close to Merphonox. *Help save them.*

X'ieth got up off his knees, grabbed the black shard and sheathed it, and looked around until he saw Kort afar, still tending to Sagult. Magicia stood over them, shaking her head as she spoke lowly with Kort.

Having newfound courage, X'ieth left his place on the shore that was at a safe distance from Merphonox's lance attacks. In so doing, he went into the fray and literally happened upon so much carnage, for which he felt directly responsible. *This is your fault entirely, so you must stop it before everyone perishes! You must…*

X'ieth kept his eyes on Kort, Sagult, and Magicia ahead, jumping over bodies of the dead and darting around the wounded. When about ten cubits from Magicia and Kort, he could overhear their talk.

"I can't heal him," said Magicia, despondently. "He's too far gone! And I got here too late. I'm sorry…"

"Can't you try?!" asked Kort.

Sagult, covered in his own blood, and with flesh wounds all over, spoke in a weak voice from the sands.

"If you change the Dark Prophecy… that'll be well worth… my life or yours."

Sagult closed his eyes and drifted off.

X'ieth watched him die, and the sight increased his profound sadness. Sagult was his former comrade in the Sixth Order, a family man, and a man of righteousness, one like X'ieth had never seen before in Sergros. And he was dead because of the young knight's misdeeds, grieving X'ieth even more. *Sagult… No! No!!!*

When X'ieth looked away from Sagult, he saw Kort staring right at him with fiery, indignant eyes. The ex-knight instantly sprung up and wielded the white shard against his opponent.

X'ieth jumped back, not even drawing the black shard to defend himself. He raised a hand, and protested the attack. "No, wait! I don't want to fight!"

X'ieth saw Kort advance on him. He retreated a step, and tripped on a fighter's corpse, causing him to fall to the sands with a dull thud. There were more corpses all around him.

From his place among the dead on the shore, X'ieth looked up, seeing Kort loom over him with the white shard in both hands. Kort held its grip at the level of his breastplate, putting one hand over the other, with the shard's tip pointed down, and ready to be plunged into the young knight's heart.

X'ieth protested again from the sands. "No! Don't!"

But Kort seemed done with reasoning. As if not even listening, he raised the white shard up and then plunged it down, with the point aimed at the young knight's chest. But before it could reach X'ieth, Magicia released a blood-curdling scream.

"Do not this thing!"

Kort barely stopped himself, freezing with the shard mid-plunge, to look over his shoulder at her. X'ieth glanced up, seeing Magicia shouting from Kort's rear with an extended hand, palm-out.

"There is hope for evil men!" she exclaimed. "We must give them second chances, for we have all have made mistakes ourselves! So let not the death of this young knight be another mistake among your own!"

"I don't want to fight you!" said X'ieth.

Kort turned, with cynicism written across his face.

X'ieth met his eyes and continued. "Please, believe me! I won't fight you. Instead, we must fight on the same side, lest the whole Army of Light perish before us!"

"How can we trust you?!" Kort asked, arching an eyebrow and curling his lip, still holding the shard with its point over the young knight's chest.

"You'll have to find a way!" X'ieth answered.

"Yes, we must!" Magicia chimed in.

Kort looked to her again, nodded, lowered the white shard and sheathed it. "So be it…"

Magicia continued. "We must trust him! Not only do we need his help, but also, I can relate to his position as one damaged! I started something very bad for Karnath, something I'm trying to undo, even as we speak! Likewise, he has done the same by joining Lucen and the seroxians as the Army of Darkness, and allowing war to reach the Army of Light! This wasn't supposed to happen like this, and the seroxians must be stopped!"

X'ieth slowly got to his feet, and Kort stepped back. As more shrieks arose, he turned in the direction of Merphonox, where he saw another group of nearby fighters being injured or killed by the lance attack. The air turned crimson as Merphonox's lance disappeared and the black specks swarmed the Army, beclouding spans of the shore with sprays of the inferiors' blood. The wave of fighters was struck down with immediacy and gore, their flesh ripped asunder.

X'ieth turned to Magicia.

"What is that?!" he asked, assuming that she had the answer, being more knowledgeable than he.

Magicia faced X'ieth, showing a serious face.

"Merphonox's lance is made from the same material as my transition stone, which I use to mediate through the Nexus. Just like my stone enables me to mediate through energy fields, the weapon can do the same in fractions of a second, delivering omnipresent strikes for the length of Merphonox's locus of control!"

X'ieth looked back to Merphonox, who still was protected by the Nexus shields created by the sorcerers at his rear. And then suddenly, those shields disappeared and the swarm of black specks ravaging the fighters abruptly changed directions and went back to Merphonox, where they coalesced into a lance in the king's hand, with a burst of green light! Unprotected, the sorcerers and Merphonox started pulling Nexus again, causing their midsections to glow green, as well as the king's lance. Meanwhile, the Army kept their distance from the seroxians, with the wounded unable to attack, and the unwounded too afraid.

"That's when a strike can be made," said Kort.

X'ieth shook his head. "But we need to be close." He estimated how long the seroxians took to pull more Nexus for the next attack; it was a few moments.

"Our strikes would have to be very fast," said Kort.

"We can tether to perform integrated sword and magic," replied X'ieth. "Perhaps that'll give us enough speed to strike when the seroxians replenish their cores."

X'ieth and Kort paused, looking to each other.

"But what will happen to us during the attack?"

X'ieth found himself rendered silent by Kort's question. *What would happen to us?* He saw images of Sagult, who looked like a piece of raw meat in armor, and the thought made him shudder.

Magicia interjected herself.

"I can protect you during Merphonox's attack. My locus of control is greater than his, so from a safe distance, I could shield you both."

X'ieth imagined the cyclical dynamic of the seroxians' attack, from the two sorcerers protecting Merphonox while the lance strikes were underway, to the attack ending, the shields lowering, and their recharge starting with no protection. He saw him and Kort shielded from the lance attack, and striking in the moment the seroxians pulled Nexus to recharge their cores.

"It should work," he muttered.

But as X'ieth looked back at the Army and surveyed the carnage wrought from Merphonox's magical lance—the dying people littering the sands, their cries ringing out against the ocean waves—it instilled a very different thought in him: *It has to work.*

X'ieth glanced back, finding Kort in dismay.

"The seroxians fill their cores so fast; will we really have enough time to strike? I… I don't hold the Crescent."

Doubts flowed from Kort, as the Army died.

X'ieth's disdain increased over the situation.

"We can waste time speculating," he said, looking at Kort. "We can waste time fearing, or we can simply try our plan… Some things in life are worth taking risks. To me, this is one such thing."

Sounds arose of chatter, squishing, and cries.

X'ieth looked to Merphonox, seeing hordes of elves, humans, and dwarves falling before the king with much gore. He stood there watching, entranced by the immense bloodshed and death. In that instant, the young knight knew that doing nothing was simply not an option.

He looked back to Kort, who still seemed doubtful.

"If you don't join me," X'ieth said, "I'll attempt the plan with Magicia's help."

With those words, X'ieth gazed her way, wondering if Magicia binding him by spell long ago—at his induction into the Guard—made his desires to protect innocent blood less than genuine. But even so, he trusted that somewhere deep within, he had changed for the better. *No man's destiny must be bad by necessity, as if by nature, for there is always a choice! And just like this, you're making a choice to pursue good destiny after the bad.*

"I'm more for it than against it," replied Kort, from over his shoulder.

X'ieth turned to Kort, and Magicia faced them both.

He nodded. "We three of broken dreams, can seize this dream anew. Let's ally to save the Army…"

He addressed Magicia then.

"Do stay safe, and protect us from the lance!"

He talked to Kort next, with a sparkle in his eyes.   "And let us fight the king together!"

"Run into position," Magicia said, "I've cover you."

X'ieth faced Kort. "Ready?"

"Aye," he replied. "Let's do this!"

Without further delay, X'ieth and Kort unsheathed their shards and ran toward Merphonox, clad in the armors of god and prepared to fight. As they went, X'ieth saw the seroxian king and his sorcerers up ahead, beyond stretches of his fellow Sergrothians and allies, bleeding from the ground, being maimed or already dead. There were many elves and dwarves among them, but mostly humans.

Interspersed with the wounded and casualties, X'ieth beheld some fighters still standing. All of them were deathly afraid of confronting Merphonox now, perhaps after seeing what the king could do; they kept outside of Merphonox's locus of control, so not to be harmed by the king's lance attacks.

While running, X'ieth saw the wounded and unwounded littering the scarlet sands beneath Gallow Cliff, where the winds still blew off the sea and its waves still crashed. The sky was a deep blue lit by stars and moon, and the night was far from over.

X'ieth and Kort jumped hurdles of the slain and continued running toward Merphonox, who once again, held a glowing lance with his sorcerers behind him pulling Nexus, all of them being unprotected.

"Now's the perfect time for our first strike!"

X'ieth nodded to Kort while running; he could not agree more with him.

With that idea as their motivation, they ran all the faster toward Merphonox, both of them keeping pace with each other, literally sprinting neck-to-neck. But when about twenty cubits from the king, it happened: Merphonox's lance disappeared!

The next thing X'ieth knew, the swarm of black specks sped at him and Kort, chattering metallically along the way! It conjured up his thoughts about the sounds that had always followed—melons smashing, sticks snapping, and shrieks. These were the sounds of agony and death: squishing flesh and cracking bones. In his mind, he saw Sagult after being wounded; it was the image of a piece of meat in armor. And now, it might be his turn!

When the black specks descended upon X'ieth and Kort, sparks flew off their armor. They kept their eyes up and they kept running, but could not help but worry over the sensations they felt. In particular, X'ieth swore he was burning and blood suddenly trickled down the side of his face. It was in the moment before a green dome appeared out of nowhere, going overtop him and Kort, and shielding them from Merphonox's lance. *Magicia's protection!*

X'ieth and Kort ran together under the Nexus shield, with the black specks overtop of them, with more yellow sparks flying off and the same zapping sounds as metal collided with the energy field. The Children went all the way to about twenty cubits before Merphonox, outside the king's physical reach. X'ieth assumed position at one flank of Merphonox, and Kort at the opposite flank.

When they settled before the seroxian king, the black specks came back, forming a lance in his hand. As before, he and his sorcerers began to channel Nexus, causing their midsections and the lance to glow green.

When X'ieth and Kort confronted Merphonox, it elicited the king's laughter at first, and then, archaic words.

"Venire ad te, ut uterque moreretur?" asked Merphonox in his native tongue. "Et erit in aeternum, aede recepit, in Novus Karnath, et filii qui, ut seroxian."

X'ieth had no idea what that meant, but he knew that it could not be good. Despite the perceived language barrier, he announced their purpose in Mainlandish.

"Your words won't save you or your sorcerers, Merphonox! This carnage stops here!"

Kort chimed in. "You've taken one too many lives this day, and I'll aim that you take not another!"

"Fools, I speak your simple tongue," replied Merphonox. "Hearing Lindenburg from Tekkneo for but an afternoon was enough for me to learn…"

X'ieth took his eyes off Merphonox, to watch the energy arc from the king's aux core into the lance, which continued to pulse with luminous green light.

Kort suddenly budged, as if to attack.

X'ieth yelled to him. "Stop! Fill your core first."

Kort stopped, with a quizzical look about him.

X'ieth finished the thought. "We need speed."

"Right," Kort said, stepping back. "I remember."

With that, X'ieth and Kort began filling their cores.

Merphonox addressed them. "Simple inferiors, I asked if you came to die among the others? I shall be enshrined forevermore in New Karnath, as the seroxian who killed both Children and ensured neither Light nor Dark Prophecy came true! I told the robed youth to tread carefully, and being confronted by two Children versus one easily counts as his betrayal!"

With that, Merphonox reminded X'ieth and Kort why they would need speed, for within only a few moments of recharging themselves, his lance disappeared, the sorcerers raised the Nexus shield over all three of them, and the seroxian attack commenced, yet again. Black specks swarmed X'ieth and Kort, but right as they did, Magicia formed a green shield over them, and the specks bounced off with multi-colored sparks and zapping sounds.

Despite what was happening, X'ieth and Kort focused on pulling Nexus into their enlarged channeling chambers. As they did, their midsections glowed brilliantly green, and they drew energy until it burned them. X'ieth found the sight of their blazing aux cores akin to Merphonox's intense gray eyes, fiery and ablaze with the king's desire for New Karnath. When X'ieth recognized that he, Kort, and Magicia reckoned with the seroxians' immense power, it was a sobering realization that easily made him prayerful. *Destiny, please help us! Please…*

"Tether with me!" X'ieth yelled.

Kort looked over, and nodded. "Aye!"

In the next instant, X'ieth went back to his channeling chamber, where he stood at its center. He ran to his Source exit and pushed a flow out, and just as he did, a flow came in through his Source entry. He merged them.

In the moment X'ieth did this, a rumble sounded. From his spot near his Source exit, he gazed around the room, watching as the walls and ceiling of his channeling chamber began to shake and move! With a rumble, they expanded and expanded, making the room bigger and bigger. This went on for a few moments, until finally, the walls and ceiling came to a complete stop.

X'ieth looked across his channeling chamber, and it was vast, now having combined with Kort's! In size, it was perhaps likened unto Magicia's chamber, being larger than the cumulative space of their two chambers in isolation, for X'ieth and Kort were stronger together. X'ieth saw Kort appear at the center of the vast channeling chamber, being only partially filled by the energy that they had pulled.

"Now!" hollered X'ieth, pushing the exit open.

He and Kort snapped back to the shores of Gallow Cliff, with their minds moving magic, and magic propelling their bodies, as far as their accumulated Nexus would take them. But as X'ieth and Kort sped toward Merphonox with their shards drawn, they suddenly found themselves stopped and out of Nexus! Kort had used far more energy than was needed for what he was attempting to do: integrated sword and magic.

On Merphonox's opposite flanks they stood, as sitting ducks on still waters, less than ten cubits from the seroxian king, and now, within their foe's striking distance! Merphonox had long arms and an even longer lance.

X'ieth looked at the glowing lance in Merphonox's hand, half expecting it to disappear, as before. But this time it did not vanish; it was wielded instead! X'ieth glanced up, seeing Merphonox glare down with fiery eyes upon both him and Kort, as the king now swung his weapon!

Fear turned X'ieth's stomach, as he raised his shard to block the lance. His block was successful and black shard met the lance with sparks, in an impact that sent X'ieth to the sands and tumbling away from Merphonox. The king quickly arced the lance over to his opposite side, batting it at Kort, who nimbly ducked beneath it, and started running. Meanwhile, X'ieth got afoot.

"Retreat!" he yelled to Kort, who backed away.

X'ieth did the same, going back to a safe distance.

Just as both Children removed themselves from Merphonox's physical reach, another lance attack commenced. A green dome formed over Merphonox and his sorcerers, and the black specks swarmed X'ieth and Kort. But before the lance particulate could do them any damage, Magicia's shield formed overtop of them, and the specks bounced off with yellow sparks and zaps.

Through the Nexus barrier X'ieth peered, seeing Magicia at a distance, maybe thirty cubits in the sky; she hovered upon a field of Nexus through the air with her aux core aglow in green light, pushing the energy to protect him and Kort. *Thank Destiny for her help…*

As Merphonox's lance attack continued, X'ieth reflected on what just happened. Even with a tether, he and Kort did not have enough Nexus to rush the seroxian king during his recharging. And furthermore, if they could not rush Merphonox during that short time and attack him blindingly fast, they were both at risk to direct strikes with the lance. X'ieth would not wager over who was stronger or more skilled at melee of him and Kort versus Merphonox, for the king's advantage was clear.

"Remember, we need to channel!" Kort yelled.

X'ieth nodded to acknowledge it.

With that, X'ieth and Kort pulled Nexus into their combined core without a clear sense of how they could even use it to speed up to Merphonox.

Merphonox's lance attack ended. The sorcerers lowered their Nexus shield and began recharging. Meanwhile, the black specks returned to Merphonox and materialized as the lance in his hand. He, too, started channeling, pushing Nexus into it for another attack.

X'ieth looked to Kort. "Ready to try again?!"

A few steps were suddenly heard at his rear.

"No, don't!" said a female voice.

X'ieth turned, seeing a few unwounded fighters from the Army approach, now having entered Merphonox's locus of control, and the danger zone.

"You don't have enough magic!" shouted a woman.

X'ieth saw her, a plain maiden with freckles, big brown eyes, and long brown hair that reached out of her kettle helm, oversized and slipping off her head, just like the pieces of armor she wore. She held a makeshift spear.

Images flashed before his eyes of Sagult, superimposed on those of the maiden. X'ieth knew she was in danger and saw her just as his deceased friend— a raw and bloody piece of meat, in armor.

"You're too close!" X'ieth exclaimed. "Stay back!"

"But you don't have enough magic!" she argued.

"And we can help!" said an elven lad, joining her side. He was unarmored, wearing black boots, along with a simple white tunic and brown trousers tied at the waist. His skin was tan, like that of the sorcerers with Merphonox. In his hands was a pitchfork.

"We need their help!" Kort said.

X'ieth spun to him.

"They can link to us and send us more Nexus!"

X'ieth thought about it for a moment. *He's right.*

The young knight looked back to the fighters. Even more piled behind them, making for half a dozen or so, with the other fighters still keeping their distance, not being as brave as these. With concerned faces, they watched on from up the shore, having opened mouths and wide eyes. All around them were the dead and the maimed, with the latter moaning over their wounds.

"You may die if you stay here," X'ieth warned, meeting the maiden's brown eyes. "But if you're willing to risk your life, link to us and send us Nexus! With your help, we'll have enough Nexus to strike the seroxian king!" He looked to the others, to include them in his request.

"Some things are worth taking a risk, and this is one such thing!" the maiden replied, fearlessly.

Her words resonated with those of the young knight, said earlier. *It is worth it. Use their help.*

At that statement, the midsections of the half dozen fighters shined green as they all pulled Nexus. The fighters pushed the energy to the nearest sensed mental restraint, and began filling the combined core of X'ieth and Kort.

Merphonox's lance attack started. The sorcerers raised their Nexus shield and a dome formed over the seroxians, after the black specks flew from the lance in Merphonox's hand and into the air, about to go on another path of destruction.

X'ieth and Kort felt pressure from the links formed with the fighters, and now, even more streams of Nexus flooded in through their Source entry of their combined channeling chamber. It was a large set of double doors, wooden, though without carven inlays of thorns or ivy.

X'ieth stood with Kort at the Source exit, pulling his own stream of Nexus through the entry, just as his comrade. He looked back through the vast channeling chamber, seeing the fighters present. The maiden with brown hair stood at its center, alongside others of the half dozen. And in one moment, there were the sudden sounds of metallic chatter, smashing melons, and snapping sticks in the room, and the fighters were jarringly afflicted with grave wounds! The elven lad and the maiden bled, both having ripped flesh.

Out of his channeling chamber, X'ieth snapped back to the shores of Gallow Cliff, where he saw Magicia's Nexus barrier protecting both him and Kort from the black specks, which swarmed over the nearby fighters. The sights and sounds were the same as those sensed before, and just as they were horrible then, they remained the same now. X'ieth watched the fighters suffering Merphonox's wrath, and he wished he could change places. *It should be you suffering, not them! Others have suffered enough...*

When Merphonox's lance attack ended, the sorcerers lowered their Nexus shield and the dome overtop the seroxians disappeared. In that moment, the king and his minions began recharging, and there were only the sounds of the sea, the winds, and people hurting.

"Attack!" Kort yelled.

X'ieth realized the fighters had sacrificed themselves for this moment, and it was upon them. He engaged himself, and as before, used his mind to move Nexus, which moved his body across a stretch of twenty cubits in the blink of an eye. Both him and Kort sped up to Merphonox in a green blur, and given the additional Nexus from the fighters, they had energy left over. X'ieth and Kort channeled it into their shards, before attacking Merphonox from opposite flanks.

As he wielded his now glowing shard against Merphonox's round shield, X'ieth looked away, right before there were scrapes, blinding light, and many sparks. In his periphery, he could sense the same happening from Kort's strike to the shield.

When the light and sparks faded, X'ieth inspected Merphonox's shield; it was smoking and dented from the impact the shards had made, which over time, seemed like it would surely weaken the shield.

Magicia flew into X'ieth's sight, hovering as she was before on a field of Nexus, thirty cubits in the air, where she charged her core to make the protective barrier.

"Get back!" she cried.

Just then, X'ieth could sense the lance's shadow overtop of him. He turned and rolled forward, evading the weapon right before it crashed down on him. The lance hit the shore, shaking the ground and sending sand flying on all sides of X'ieth's back. He could feel the vibrations of the impact through his legs.

Where's Kort?! He glanced over, seeing him at about twenty cubits from Merphonox, safely standing at the king's opposite flank. The sight relieved him.

Just then, more fighters joined the spot where the half dozen others were dead or maimed from the last attack. X'ieth saw them arrive in their clinking armor, stopping beside the elven lad who whimpered from the sands, along with the maiden of brown hair and eyes. Where exposed, their skin was ripped apart and bleeding, and some of their bones were broken. To make matters worse, the woman's armor had been badly dented, and likely squeezed her.

X'ieth was amazed, as the lad and the maiden pushed themselves up, as if prepared for another round. These ones were more than brave, now showing that they would rise upon falling, and try again.

X'ieth shook off his negative feelings about the Army sacrificing themselves in this way and just went to his channeling chamber, knowing that he merely needed to honor their sacrifice with doing his part. As before, the fighters linked to him and Kort, while both of them also pulled Nexus, filling as much of the vast channeling chamber with energy as they could, while the seroxians finished recharging.

X'ieth pulled and pulled Nexus, praying for another successful strike. *Please, Destiny... Help us win...* In his channeling chamber, X'ieth could see

Kort and the other fighters, working hard toward that end. He hoped that their effort would be enough.

X'ieth saw the fighters in the channeling chamber suddenly show grave wounds, and outside the chamber, he could hear the metallic chatter, the smashing melons, and the snapping sticks. Merphonox's lance attack had started.

X'ieth snapped back to the shore, where the dark sky spread overtop of them like a funeral shroud. Before his eyes was the barrier of Nexus, protecting him and Kort from Merphonox's lance, while the fighters were exposed to the seroxians' attack. *No!* It grieved the young knight tremendously, how they were being hurt to spare him from the same.

The black specks ravaged the fighters, and occasionally, they hit the barrier shielding X'ieth and Kort, mixing together the sounds of zapping with those of death. With little patience, X'ieth watched yellow sparks fly into the air as the lance particulate bounced off; he remained eager for the attack to end on the fighters. *C'mon…*

When Merphonox's lance attack ended, like before, the sorcerers lowered their Nexus shield. Merphonox and the sorcerers started recharging.

"Attack!" X'ieth shouted, as his mind moved the Nexus, and his Nexus moved his body in a green blur. Kort rushed to Merphonox from the opposite side. By the time they got there, they had excess Nexus in their combined core, which they channeled into their shards. Together, in a coordinated crisscross slash, they executed a joint blow to Merphonox with more bangs, bright light, and sparks. A thud sounded, as Merphonox's shield was sliced in half, and its scraps fell to the sands.

"He has no protection now!" Kort exclaimed.

X'ieth added, "Let him weaken with every strike."

Merphonox grumbled, at the sight of his father's shield, now broken.

"This means nothing!" the king hissed.

Merphonox swiped at Kort with his lance, as they ran away. And suddenly, there was the sudden sound of someone falling to the ground.

Mid-run, X'ieth spun about, not yet out of Merphonox's physical reach. To his surprise, he saw that Kort had tripped and was now on the shore, as Merphonox reared the lance, as if preparing to skewer the fallen ex-knight.

"Move!" X'ieth yelled, as he ran there.

Merphonox thrust the lance at Kort before X'ieth could arrive, but Kort rolled to the side, avoiding it.

"Grrrhhh!" growled Merphonox, raising the weapon and trying to smash Kort with it, after his dodge.

As the lance came down, X'ieth deflected it with his shard, causing the sharp noise of metal on metal. He reached down, and helped Kort to his feet.

"Go!" X'ieth shouted to him, as the shadow of Merphonox's lance rose over them both. They turned and ran. As they went, the young knight could sense the lance crash down behind him, causing more sand to fly, along with more vibrations.

"Thanks to you!" Kort said, while running.

X'ieth did not reply. *Thanks be to Destiny...*

When X'ieth and Kort got out of Merphonox's physical reach, they saw even more fighters come into the king's locus of control, ready to help. Of the fighters already there, some were unfortunately dead, including the elven lad. But of those who were injured and maimed, like the maiden of brown eyes and hair, they rose upon falling and continued to help, as they could.

X'ieth went to his channeling chamber, where he saw Kort and the fighters with him. He stood with Kort at the Source exit, as some fighters were at the room's center, and others of them were clustered about the room's Source entry. Its two doors were open, and everyone pulled streams of Nexus into the chamber, filling it as much as they could in the time that remained.

"Keep pulling!" X'ieth called out to them.

"We can do this!" shouted Kort.

As before, and ever so sadly, the fighters in the channeling chamber showed grave wounds, and those horrid sounds arose of metallic chatter, smashing melons, and breaking sticks.

X'ieth snapped back to the shores, seeing Magicia's barrier protecting him and Kort from the black specks. From behind a shield of Nexus, he sadly watched the lance particulate ravage the fighters, with many of them dying. Waiting for the attack to end was torturous for him to endure, yet during that time, X'ieth pulled as much Nexus as he could just like Kort, praying that they could deal another blow to Merphonox, and bring this battle closer to being over.

When the lance attack ended, the sorcerers lowered the shield around the seroxians and began recharging their cores. As before, Merphonox channeled energy into his lance, perhaps judging that his attack would eventually prove viable when Magicia tired, and could no longer protect them.

"You'll never win!" snarled Merphonox, with his core glowing bright green. "Never! We're seroxians!"

"We'll see about that!" Kort shouted.

"Attack, now!" X'ieth said.

Both he and Kort sped toward Merphonox in a train of green Nexus energy. And when upon the king, they coordinated a crisscross slash of Merphonox's horned armor with their shards blazing. The strike was powerful and damaged the armor, leaving it dented and smoking.

"It's working!" Kort said.

"Aye, let's do it again!" replied X'ieth

With that plan, their last strike become one of many more to come, the many that would be needed until the seroxians' defeat. And over hours, the night gave way to morning light, as the remaining fighters of the Army gained courage and joined their comrades in the danger zone, helping Kort and X'ieth continue their attacks. In so doing, Army slowly thinned in numbers, from hundreds to tens of the willing. And in so doing, many fell and many rose, just as many sacrificed and many died. The whole time, Magicia was able to protect X'ieth and Kort, and any estimate that Merphonox had made of her endurance was very wrong; her powers lasted through the fight.

"Arrghhhh!" shouted Merphonox at last, under the burgeoning morning light. Tired and panting, X'ieth looked back after the sparks stopped, seeing how a final crisscross slash with Kort served the seroxian king his fatal wound.

Merphonox fell down to his knees as his horned black armor split open, exposing his gaping wounds that now bled upon the scarlet shore. In an aside, he shouted, "The path of Eriens was not right after all! For my end reveals this walk to destruction!"

Merphonox wobbled on his knees, about to fall over. All around the seroxian king was extreme carnage, stack and stacks of inferiors, some four bodies high. Only few twitched, moaned, or showed other signs of life, while so many others had died—a fate that Merphonox would now share with them.

At the sight of Merphonox on his knees and nearing death, X'ieth did not double back after his strike, and neither did Kort. Together they stood, clad in their bloody armors of god and breathing hard, both of them with their eyes upon the seroxian king, who in the next moment, dropped his lance and crumbled upon his face with a loud thud. His two sorcerers ran scared, down the shore and far away, disappearing into the morning light, as did the night. The seroxian king had fallen, and the battle was over.

When Merphonox died, the dozen or so remaining fighters of the Army of Light cheered.

"We did it!" shouted some.

Others exclaimed, "It worked!"

"Praise be to Destiny!"

And like this, more joyous things were said.

Weary from the fight, X'ieth turned to Lucen and Elucid. The youth and the crimson knight had come to a standstill in their fast-paced sword duel, and now, lent their attention to X'ieth and Kort. Joining them was Magicia, who floated forward on a field of Nexus, settling down beside Kort, for the conclusion of the real fight near dawn—their Fate's Fray.

After the battle with Merphonox was over, the exhausted X'ieth Armstrong stood on the shores beneath Gallow Cliff, clad in the bloodstained armor of Ma'althan, dirtied from the blood of so many who fell, of the Army of Light. At his sides, his tired arms dangled; the black shard was in his right hand, with its tip touching the scarlet sands.

Panting, he looked up from Merphonox's corpse, and surveyed the carnage all around him, beneath the early morning light. The sands at the cliff foot were painted red, with bodies of the slain scattered about and only a dozen fighters left standing. Among them were Kort, Magicia, Lucen, and Elucid.

For X'ieth, helping Kort and Magicia slay the seroxian king provided little in terms of redemption. All of the guilt he felt before returned, and despite his change of heart, he saw himself as no better of a person. Visions flashed before his eyes, of him killing in Arlem, of him bringing his cottage down and killing the unconscious Lady Lyda, and of him joining the Army of Darkness at Gallow Cliff to bring even more killing, as confirmed by the deceased all around him, as far as the eye could see. *The good you've done by slaying Merphonox, is not enough...*

X'ieth met Lucen's blue eyes. The youth stood about ten cubits off, holding a flaming green blade in his hand, which just then, became a gnarled staff again. Lucen glanced over his shoulder to the young knight, as his body was facing Elucid's. In that moment, the winds off the sea stirred his wild hair into a wilder mess, as the tide rolled in against the shore, a short distance from where everyone gathered. The crimson knight towered over Lucen, bearing that curved Hirishin sword in one hand, its blade gouged along its length from the intense swordplay with Lucen. The purple cloak flapped from Elucid's shoulders, taken by the gusts.

"This is not me," X'ieth said to Lucen, banging on the black breastplate over his chest with a free hand, referring to himself and what he had become. "This is not any man by nature, only those who make poor choices."

"What has gotten into you?!" Lucen snapped.

X'ieth sighed as his answer. And then, piece by piece, he began to compulsively pull off Ma'althan's armor, littering the shore with it. Repeated clangs and dull thuds filled the air when metal hit sand, as he unlatched the armor's latches and unstrapped its straps.

"What are you doing?!" asked Lucen.

He turned his body to X'ieth, and stepped closer.

Meanwhile, X'ieth continued removing Ma'althan's armor, until the last plate was off and he stood in the tunic and trousers that he wore underneath. By then, X'ieth had the youth right in his face.

"This can't happen!" yelled Lucen.

X'ieth looked back quietly at Lucen. Over his shoulder was the clear blue sea, separated from them both by a gulf of bloodied sand and corpses.

"This can't happen!" he yelled again. "What are you waiting for?! Finish this!"

"What do you mean?" asked X'ieth, plain-faced.

"It won't end here like this. So what are you waiting for?! Slay the Army of Light, and also this Child!"

Lucen pointed at Kort while talking.

He continued. "Your destiny is right there, mocking you from his hands. So seize the white shard already! Form the gray sword! End time!"

Lucen gestured to the blood-streaked white shard in Kort's possession. Its blade touched the sands, dangled from his limp arm.

Despite how Lucen grew fanatical, X'ieth remained silent and composed, just watching him.

To that continued quiet, Lucen's face wrinkled in anger. He irately demanded an answer.

"To my words, what say you? What say you?!"

The visual of the distant carnage slapped X'ieth in the face; there was nothing to say but his admittance of guilt in this matter. The sight of the dead continued making X'ieth feel so bad over what had happened. It was wrong. It was evil. It was bad destiny for his people. *And it's all your fault*, he told himself, shaking his head.

At the back of his mind, he wondered if his change of heart were somehow a delayed effect of Magicia binding him by spell long ago, to protect innocent blood. In this, not only did X'ieth feel guilt, but also, he doubted the authenticity of his own contrition.

His eyes trailed to Magicia; she stood on the bloody sands in her dusty yellow sorceress robe, showing determined gray eyes, and with her locks of braided red hair lifted by the winds. Seeing her there slowly reminded X'ieth of what she had mentioned to him and Kort: Magicia supposedly had started something very bad in Karnath, and she was doing all she could to stop it. She could not alter time and undo her wrongs, but in her time that remained, she would do all that was possible to right them through living better. *And for you, that's all that matters now. Just do all you can to live better and to make your wrongs right. There's nothing more to do.*

X'ieth looked back to Lucen and spoke.

"Enough innocent blood has been shed this day, and no more shall be spilled for my sake."

At this, Lucen went wide-eyed and protested.

"You reneged on your word! Your intentions are poor, your sayings deceitful!"

X'ieth paused thoughtfully. A wind blew then.

He replied, "To the contrary, my intentions are good. For I've realized now that Shaizan's bad destiny was never anyone's to be had! Because of prejudice he chose bad destiny, but other men need not do the same!"

Another wind blew; the tide rolled to the shore.

X'ieth continued. "While Shaizan decided poorly, I won't. And while others decide poorly, I won't. In the end, every man has his choice to do good or evil, and so do I! Such as this, fulfilling the Dark Prophecy is Shaizan's doing, but it cannot be mine!"

X'ieth felt inspired by the words of Elucid; they changed his perspective on time, and he would stand for what he believed in. With his shoulders straight and his chin up, X'ieth said aloud, "I choose to share the Army's cause, to battle for the remainder of time so that it can be used with purpose and enjoyed!"

X'ieth smiled. His face showed joy, yet conviction.

He continued. "It does not matter if time will end, for all that matters is the time remaining—that it be used for good versus evil—that with it, we help instead of hurt each other!"

X'ieth saw Magicia look to him and smile.

He went on. "Whether by the bindings of spell or not, I'm glad to do right in my end, for all those who dwell in Karnath. Men come and go from this world, and in their passing some are remembered for good, others for evil. Those remembered beyond their death enjoy immortality for their choices and chances in life. Just as this, my poor choices and chances 'til now shall earn me mention, long after my dying breath!"

X'ieth gazed around, to Kort, Magicia, Lucen, Magicia, and the fighters. All eyes were on him; they were listening. And on top of that, Lucen was glowering.

"I am ashamed," X'ieth admitted, "for taking the wrong side. Some elect to take no sides, which only suits battles not worth fighting. But should a man deem a battle worthy, he ought to take a side, though let it be the right one. This battle was worthy of being fought, yet I took the wrong side. But that was yesterday, and this is today…"

Lucen glowered even more.

"You can't just change your mind like that!" he hissed through barred teeth, with his lips curled. Lucen's blue eyes were fire. His hair remained wild in the wind, and his face grew as gnarled as his staff.

X'ieth ignored Lucen's reaction, and went on. "This day I choose the right side," he said. "This day I take good over evil, and new dreams instead of the broken! This day I find good destiny after bad destiny, after no destiny at all! Let it be known that my fate or that of any other man mustn't be this Dark, by neither choice nor chance I say! All men can choose good, and from evil turn away!"

"Less of the talk, and more of the show!" Lucen shouted. "You can't change your destiny by words alone!"

X'ieth replied, "Indeed a show is due, thus a show I shall render to you. But before I do, here's your answer. For you asked, what say I?"

After his last word, X'ieth allowed quiet.

Winds blew, waves rolled on the shore, gulls squawked overhead, and suspense built up in Lucen. He appeared edgy and quivered from anger.

"Out with it already!" Lucen shouted.

X'ieth turned from him, and gazed to the morning sky that birthed a sunrise, showing hints of orangey red that tinted the edge of every cloud in sight.

X'ieth spun back to Lucen. "*This* say I."

And then, in a loud voice—one that filled every corner and crevice of the towering white cliff, and every span of the white-sanded shores—X'ieth proclaimed, "Upon this day that decides the Game, let the Child of Darkness be remembered for good rather than evil! Let the Child of Darkness be remembered for choosing the right side, and helping them beat you!"

As his last word rang out, X'ieth saw Lucen just smirk, as if failing to suppress his own haughtiness.

"Do what you will," Lucen barked. "It's in vain."

"Is it?" X'ieth replied. "Is that because you presume your cycle can't be broken?"

"That's right, you can't stop me! No one has yet!"

X'ieth said, "Every cycle can be broken. I'm not sure how all of this has happened, but I've gathered enough to surmise that Shaizan involved you in Time No More, and now you're involving me. But if you're stopped here, this can't go on! If you're stopped here, this can't continue backward in time, unraveling enough weaves to kill time and Destiny!"

"As far as I can tell," Lucen replied, "you just continue talking. And it seems that's all you are: talk."

"A show is due," X'ieth said. "As promised, I'll give you more than words."

"But what will you do?!" Lucen asked.

X'ieth paused. All eyes stayed on him.

"Break the cycle!"

In one fluent, sudden motion, X'ieth tossed up the black shard, caught the point of its blade, letting its handle hit the sands. And then, he threw himself forward while guiding the sword's tip to his gut, causing the shard to impale him! He fell to his knees.

In a single moment, the shard's tip pierced his abdomen wall, its blade went through his body, and then, the bloody sword emerged out of his back! As it happened, X'ieth felt a jolt of blinding pain, and he saw his whole life flash before his eyes: visions of his treasured childhood filled with Karnath's olden stories and dreams of being Kayareth; visions of graduating academy, being knighted in the Crimson Guard, and marrying Millicent. He saw it all, in a split second.

The next moment, X'ieth found himself back on the shores of Gallow Cliff, on his knees and hunching over with the black shard jutting out of his back, with much blood. He lifted his hand from his gut—the same hand he had guided the sword with—and saw his palm stained crimson. *You did it... You did it!*

Weakly, X'ieth laughed, as the life faded from him. He looked up to Kort, Magicia, Lucen, and the remaining fighters, all of them stunned with shock, having their mouths agape. The crimson knight was there too, but emitted no emotions.

"Why?!" Kort blurted out, as if not understanding the reason X'ieth took his life.

Wheezing, X'ieth slowly answered in rasps.

"Without a father, there can be no son… I am Lucen's father… And Lucen is Shaizan's father... So if I die… it breaks the cycle. Things must be this way."

Magicia hurried to X'ieth. She kneeled beside him.

She confessed, "My spell upon the Guard never bound you to protect innocent blood. All along, you chose right on your own inclination, a thing every man can do! Often many forget that doing right is a choice…"

X'ieth felt more blood leak from him, and he felt faint, about to fall over. Magicia caught him before it happened. Leaning up against her, he started to feel cold and his world swirled around, as wine in a chalice before the sniff. *It's almost over… You did it.*

In his ear, X'ieth heard Magicia talk excitedly, as she turned over her shoulder and addressed the others.

"He did it," she said. "He broke Saora's cycle!"

There was a moment of calm. Winds blew. Waves crashed. Gulls squawked. X'ieth shut his eyes as he leaned against Magicia, and waited to die. *You did it.*

But out of nowhere, Lucen's sadistic cackles arose.

"Ha ha ha, Ha ha ha, Mwha ha ha ha!"

The sounds punched X'ieth into a state of alertness; he opened his eyes, and could see Lucen still standing there. He was not fading into thin air as a child never born, nor did Lucen seem concerned that such a thing might happen. *Something's wrong... Something is very wrong!*

X'ieth mustered his strength to speak.

"Wh... why... aren't you... dying?" he stammered.

The winds, waves, and gulls gave a seaside interlude, and then, there was another bout of Lucen's laughter. "Ha ha ha... Ha ha ha... Mwha ha ha ha!"

Lucen laughed, "Now I've seen everything. You expect me to simply disappear by that age-old play on causality?"

He continued, "Don't you get it, *between the ages there is no cause effect*! Karnatha cut the thread of causality, so I can exist in this age independent of you! I came here and already absorbed the ether of your child. And now, you're next..."

X'ieth pushed Magicia away, and fell forward onto his hands, hunching over. Pain shot throughout his body in sharp pulses, and he felt colder and colder. The black shard still ran through him, and he bled out. He felt engulfed by a shadow, as Magicia rose up from the sands, to her feet.

Lucen went on. "Now you learn the subtleties of the weave effect, for more than one thing can move from one voided age to the earlier ages. *Memories, curses, and spirits are ethers that fall between the weaves*! I am ether from the future, unaffected by the causality in this age or any other!"

Lucen chortled, louder and fuller this time.

"Ha ha ha, Mwha ha ha ha!"

X'ieth continued hunching over and with his lips parted in disbelief, and the life flowing from him. *You did this to yourself... for naught.* In that moment, X'ieth realized that Lucen was still a very real threat that needed to be fought, but he had weakened himself considerably. As if to demonstrate just that, a wind blew then, almost knocking him to his face. *No, don't give in to death.*

It was tempting for X'ieth to fall over and let death take its hold, but he fought it. He could discern the distinct steps and gait of Lucen, as the youth walked closer.

"I am the spirit of Lucen *from the future*, and have consumed Lucen's spirit *in this age*! That's why your son was born dead... Imprisoned inside of me is the angry spirit of my son Shaizan! My traversal up the Dark Lineage will lead to the spirits of descendants imprisoned in the spirits of ancestors, until every age is voided in our wrath! Destiny and time will surely perish! Ha ha ha... Aha ha ha ha!"

In an aside, Lucen turned to the sea and spoke.

"May every dream in Karnath evaporate as fumes!" he said. "Those who have wasted the spent energy reserved for their good destines now receive their due, for I shall send that energy to the Void! Ha ha ha!"

Magicia lamented. "No, no... this ought to be different! He should have disappeared into thin air!"

"Don't do this, Lucen!" said Elucid, over her despairing voice, as if somehow the like had happened before, and the crimson knight knew about it.

X'ieth looked up, watching Lucen's sandaled foot come nearer and nearer, until the point where the youth stood only a cubit or so away. Through his mind, sounded a voice, begging him to not stay down. *Get up! Get up!*

X'ieth raised one knee, and as he moved, acute pains shot through his body.

Meanwhile, Elucid continued reasoning with Lucen.

"Stop this! There's a design for people's time, just as creation itself! Everyone in Karnath has a purpose! Destiny means for everyone to find hidden talents and do good in their time that remains, to their fulfillment and for their livelihood! The people of Karnath deserve another chance to use their time to find good destiny! The people of Karnath deserve the opportunity, to transform time into dreams anew! Don't take that away from them!"

Using a hand, X'ieth pushed himself up from his one raised knee, to a standing position. The motion tolled him with more sharp pains in his gut and his back. He grinded his teeth hard, and another broke from the gum line, filling his mouth with blood and his head with throbbing aches. He spit out the tooth onto the sands.

With much effort, X'ieth had risen upon falling. He now stood upon his feet, though feeling woozy and about to fall over. But before he could, Lucen caught him. To the young knight, the contact felt like a powerful force had intercepted him, unlike a person with a physical body.

"Worry not," he said to X'ieth. "I have you, father."

Lucen leaned close to his head and whispered in his ear. "If Shaizan can only fulfill the Dark Prophecy, then Shaizan you shall become!"

In his ear, X'ieth suddenly heard hurried steps with a large gait. He glanced over, just in time to see Elucid rushing Lucen, with a purple cloak flowing behind the metal demon, and that gouged Hirishin sword clave in the knight's metal hand!

X'ieth continued watching, sensing Lucen turn suddenly and fling out one of his hands, causing Elucid to abruptly collapse mid-run, when about two or so steps away! The crimson knight hit the red sands, clutching the metal demon's helmet, as if writhing in unspeakable agony. The gouged sword fell from the knight's hand.

"Arrrgghhhh!" boomed Elucid.

X'ieth stood with Lucen, who still held him up.

"Your missing ether," Lucen said to Elucid. "Delivered happily by Saora in a way to excruciate you, physically as well as mentally!"

X'ieth felt an immediate lack of support, when Lucen no longer propped him up! The young knight fell hard to his knees, with the shard still running through him. He looked up, to see Lucen's sandaled feet move away from him, and over to the now fallen Elucid. Behind the knight was Magicia, also on the sands with hands to her head, as if she, too, had received ether.

X'ieth watched as Lucen came up to the crimson knight, reached under the plum cloak to the metal demon's back, and pulled out a glowing stone. It was a glass ball of glowing green energy, a perfect sphere. Lucen held it up in his hand with a smile, as in moments the metal demon fell into its constituent pieces of armor, from which a shadow spilled forth! To X'ieth, it looked exactly as the shadow Darconas that appeared in his dream—a tall, two-dimensional silhouette having breadth and height, but not having depth.

X'ieth was dumbfounded. Kort gasped.

"Laotzu's shadow," said Kort. "It's true…"

Lucen grinned, "Elucid is nothing more than that!"

Feeling colder and weaker, X'ieth looked to the sand again. It was only a moment before Lucen's sandaled feet appeared beneath his nose, and a strange hand fell on his shoulder, seeming as the ghost of a touch. Through his mind, sounded the same voice, begging him to not stay down. *Get up! Get up!*

X'ieth raised his knee as before, trying to stand.

Lucen knocked it down with his staff.

The impact made him unstable; X'ieth toppled to the side, seeing the sands get closer and closer to his face. But abruptly, he felt caught again by the same force: Lucen.

X'ieth felt pulled to his feet from under his arms. He saw Lucen grabbing him there, taking him up so that once again, they stared face-to-face. It was then that X'ieth felt helpless, and he grew prayerful. *Please Destiny, I forsook you once but now find my faith again, albeit in a trying time! See past this, and help me stop Lucen!*

In that moment, X'ieth went to his enlarged channeling chamber. He saw himself there, with the same gut wound. Being injured, the young knight struggled across the room to his Source entry, and pulled open the double doors. Weak light shined along their edges, and then, streams of Nexus entered, some of them being just as weak, like his health. But suddenly, additional flows gushed in through the Source entry—stronger flows. X'ieth turned from the doors to see Kort standing at the center of the room, pulling Nexus then pushing it his way. Streams of energy flowed from the ex-knight's glowing midsection, to the young knight.

"Nexus to you, friend!" Kort yelled. "Let us ally once more against Lucen!"

X'ieth nodded, again weakly.

And then, he saw streams of Kort's energy surge through the double doors, and swirl around him in a vortex of green Nexus. To X'ieth, it seemed like a feat of integrated sword and magic might be their last chance to attack Lucen together. He imagined somehow grabbing the black shard, withdrawing its blade from his body, and slaying Lucen with Kort, in a magic-powered blur. *Please Destiny... Let our attack be enough to send Lucen's spirit back to the Void!*

Energy continued swirling around X'ieth, as it flowed into the channeling chamber through the Source entry, gradually filling the room from the floor to his waist.

"You think there's some way out, don't you?!"

Surprised at hearing the young voice, X'ieth turned from the Source entry, seeing Lucen at Kort's side, holding his gnarled staff. His smile turned sinister.

"Well, think again!" shouted Lucen.

X'ieth watched the youth raise his staff high, one hand over the other, and turn it into a lightning bolt! And then, in a quick motion, Lucen slammed the lightning bolt into the waist-high Nexus. Immediately, the energy became like the bolt—electricity! It jolted and jittered, and a shock jumped through X'ieth, a deep pulse felt from head-to-toe that knocked him off his feet. As his body tumbled back in the room, he saw Kort suffering the same.

X'ieth popped right out of his channeling chamber, back to the shore beneath Gallow Cliff, with his attempt of wielding Nexus now failed. He was face-to-face with Lucen, being supported as before, from under his arms. Still with his grave injury to the gut, X'ieth felt weak and cold. He breathed shallowly and his eyelids frequently shut; each time, he fought them back open.

In the distance, X'ieth saw Kort on both knees, breathing heavily from Lucen's magical counter. Beyond Kort, stood Magicia beside the unsuited crimson knight, a hovering shadow about to fade away into the morning light. Behind Laotzu and Magicia was the Army's remnant, standing amid the backdrop of immense carnage that stained these white sands. The gulls had already started feeding off the flesh of the dead.

Kort got afoot, and shouted.

"Let's not stay idle, but let us attack!"

X'ieth watched Kort and the dozen remaining fighters run, leaping over the slain as they went, to charge Lucen. But unexpectedly, X'ieth felt Lucen tuck his shoulder under his arm, before turning to smite the sands with the gnarled staff. In X'ieth's legs was a sudden tremor, which propagated from the spot where he and Lucen stood, and took Kort and the fighters off their feet! With a thud, they all hit the sands hard, some of them groaning.

Lucen laughed, "Ha ha ha!"

Sad for them X'ieth looked away, feeling cold all over, as if about to pass from Karnath. In his mind, he entered his channeling chamber once more, seeing the double doors before him, both of wood and showing carven inlays of thorns. He stood right at them, leaning against the pair, his hands open and palms pressed to the wood's grain. A glance down revealed the black shard protruding from his stomach. For him, the shard had always been a self-inflicted wound, and now, it was one that would not heal.

In that moment, X'ieth wondered if he had the strength to pull open his Source entry one more time. *You want to, so try...* He felt so incredibly weak, but nonetheless, he slid his hands over the door's wooden surface, all the way to the twin bronze handles. When feeling them, he moved his body over and took hold of them, one in each hand.

X'ieth squeezed the bronze handles tight and pulled as hard as he could. In his weakened state, the act was immense exertion for him; it felt as if his flesh were being torn apart. He winced. He grit his teeth. He growled. It was awful to endure, yet he continued pulling, until the doors opened and his watchful eyes detected light along their edges. His muscles flexed as he continued pulling, straining to open up the doors, even further.

"By my black shard I am damaged, just as I've damaged others." The words came off his lips with a grunt, as he pulled more. "But my white shard is like Kort's... a comeback in the wake of my broken dreams."

Just then, the doors opened wider, and X'ieth watched the thorn inlays on his Source entry morph into ivy, and its wood turned a lighter grain. The change easily made him smile. His eyes picked up more light shining through the doorway now, more than had shined along the doors' edges.

"In our comeback after broken dreams," he whispered, "we've won..."

He panted, going on as he did. "We've won our battle, even though I haven't seen victory here..."

X'ieth pulled as hard as he could, and the Source entry came all the way open. "Arrggh!"

The very next moment, he basked in an aura of green light, which was the Nexus behind the doors, representing an individual's connection to the Source.

Immediately, the words of Thorin Krails came to mind: *The Nexus is a closed system, wherefrom life energy flows at birth, and to where it returns at death.* With that thought, X'ieth knew he was going back into the Nexus, and he faced the prospect without worry.

"It is well," he whispered. "It is well."

With that, X'ieth threw himself through the Source entry with all his might, toward the distant green light. After tumbling across the threshold, the light zoomed toward him and engulfed his entire sight!

Immediately, he felt the sensation of falling through the light. As he fell, it became brighter and brighter, so bright that it outshined the brightest of fallen stars. X'ieth descended deeper into the light, seemingly without a stop or without an end. In his eyes, the light all around him suddenly took the form of Millicent, and X'ieth saw her reaching out to him. She plummeted through the light, alongside his body.

"X'ieth…"

"Millicent, my love!" he replied. "I thought I'd never get another chance to tell you, that you were the good destiny I've overlooked all of these years! Through the black shard of my broken dreams, I've overlooked the finer things in my life, for what was never meant to be!"

While falling together through the light, X'ieth took hold of her hand in his own and met her blue eyes, connecting with her more then, than in years of their troubled marriage. And in that moment, the young knight felt sudden contentment only moments before hearing his Source entry suddenly slam shut! *BANG!!!*

It was a sound that came from out of nowhere—a sound that jolted him back to the foot of Gallow Cliff. X'ieth blinked his eyes open, and saw Lucen's face again. They stood on the stands, with Lucen propping him up. He could feel the youth's shoulder under his arm, feeling as an otherworldly force, and completely unlike a human touch. And it was then, that X'ieth reached his weakest point, and gasped a dying breath with a grin.

"It is well, he said.

With those words, X'ieth saw blackness, felt extreme cold, and also, an indwelling by the force.

(Transition to Kort)

Kort got up from the sands, with his unbelieving eyes fixed on Lucen, unsure of what he just saw. It appeared like the youth just walked into X'ieth, robe and all! *Did that really happen?!*

Kort held the white shard in one limp arm; its blade fell and its tip poked the sands. Behind him, he sensed the remaining fighters slowly rise. All of them had been sent to the shore when Lucen pounded the sands with his gnarled staff, and now, this had happened. And little did Kort know that even stranger things were about to take place.

In continued disbelief Kort watched as, seemingly with renewed strength, X'ieth stood on the bloody sands, looking right at him with his hands at his sides. His feet were spaced at shoulder width, planted on the bloody sands amidst corpses of the slain from which gulls perched and tore flesh; in the background was the rolling blue sea and the looming sky of morning, now a baby blue.

And then, all in one instant, Kort saw X'ieth's blond hair show alternating streaks of scarlet red, and his eyes turn sapphire blue! When detecting motion, Kort's vision fell to X'ieth's gut, where the young knight grabbed the black shard's blade by both hands and slowly began removing it from his belly. Those hands worked and worked, until the entire sword was withdrawn, the black shard fell to the sands, and then, the young knight's wound healed, as if it were never there! In the next moment, X'ieth stooped down and picked up the black shard, got to his feet with the weapon in hand, and looked Kort in the eyes.

The sight filled Kort with dread of abnormal proportions. What happened now topped all of his Dark encounters in Baal with mages, giants, and undercover soldiers—opponents who he presumed were aided by a supernatural force, yet were opponents that could be defeated. On the other hand, given X'ieth's healing that he had just witnessed, it seemed like this foe might not die!

Kort saw X'ieth continue to glare at him from about ten cubits away, knowing that their confrontation was imminent. Magicia and the shadow were behind him.

Kort turned over his shoulder, and yelled to Laotzu.

"What's happening?! Why aren't we winning?!"

To Kort, the outcome flew in the face of all that Elucid and Magicia had hoped for, prior to reaching the cliffs. Despite their disagreement over Gallow Cliff, they both had wished to change the Dark Prophecy versus see it come true, as seemed to be happening now.

With much hesitation Laotzu replied, "My missing ether tells me more about Liath than I knew before!"

"This is no time for puzzles!" Kort shouted. "Why aren't we winning? Why are we struggling to change the Dark Prophecy?!"

"Because," Laotzu said, "my presumption was wrong. I was wrong."

"About?!" Kort asked, looking back to X'ieth.

"Kayareth's spirit. At Gallow Cliff, the *Lord of Constant Dream* was meant to battle the *Lord of Broken Dreams* in a Battle for Destiny fought in the hearts of men! This is what Karnatha foresaw when designing the Game, but it was merely her premonition of something that happened in the first walk. Yet, because of Saora's intervention, Shaizan fighting Kayareth wouldn't happen right away in Karnatha's Game!"

Kort looked back. "What do you mean?!"

Laotzu continued. "When the first walk ended, the final age unraveled and among the ethers that went into the Void were the spirits of Kayareth and Shaizan. Shaizan's spirit went to the future, to the age before the last. But Kayareth's spirit was sent to an earlier age, hundreds of years after the rebellion, and over a thousand years before our time! Their spirits are destined to meet in time…"

Kort glanced back at X'ieth, not understanding what, if anything, Laotzu was getting at. The ex-knight stood there looking near identical to Kayareth in the Karnathan icons, adorned in the armor of Autheos and wielding the white shard. Given this, Kort grew annoyed with the shadow over the situation's lack of clarity.

"What does that mean?!" he asked.

"It means, I'm not the Lord of Constant Dream, nor are you! Kilwroth, son of Eriens, is Kayareth. As such, we have no chance at victory, as we don't have the spirit to win! We lack Kayareth's spirit…"

The comment triggered a series of flashbacks in Kort's mind, interspersed with bursts of light. He saw Elucid offering him the purple cloak. *I was hoping you could wear it.* He saw Elucid on Raiden's boat, disclosing interests in Liath versus Gallow Cliff. *I foresee going to Liath as the [only] way to win this Game.* And he saw the lips of the woman in white, speaking the words: *Trust not, the crimson knight.* The last words echoed repeatedly in his head, filling him with regret as he drew an obvious conclusion: *Elucid knew about this all along!*

Kort swallowed, while looking over his shoulder again. He saw Magicia staring at X'ieth, her face frozen over in fear, as if she had just seen a ghost. Beside her was the shadow of Laotzu spilled from Elucid's armor, hovering in the air as just that—a ghost.

"You knew!" shouted Kort. His face went numb.

"I knew not," answered Laotzu. "My premonitions made me unsettled about coming here. *The Unwholesome Inheritance*, the purple cloak, and promptings for Liath amid so many remembered failures at these cliffs… Saora was playing a game with us all—her own game, where she played both sides. But we overlooked her hints. I'm sorry."

"You knew," insisted Kort, again. He felt cold.

"I didn't," swore Laotzu. "She withheld my ether."

Strong winds blew just then, and Kort looked back to X'ieth. The young knight stood before him, and was clearly a powerful opponent. But now, Laotzu postulated that X'ieth was even more powerful than Kort had presumed, being indwelled by Shaizan's spirit, which made him a force that could not beat by anyone lacking Kayareth's spirit.

Hearing this was punishing for Kort to endure, for he was now at Gallow Cliff in the armor of Autheos and holding the white shard, with a heart full of dreams that supposedly, were never his to live! *Laotzu says the dream of being Kayareth is not yours to live, but Kilwroth's!* The mere idea devastated him.

Visions tore through Kort then, of Nym reaching to him from the cliff top as he fell to the shores with X'ieth, of her miscarrying the child, of his redemption through a hero's title. It occurred to him then, that if what Laotzu said was true, his second separation from Nym was for naught, as was his child dying! And on top of that, his feelings of redemption betrayed the truth! *If what Laotzu says is true, it's nothing more than an ensemble of broken dreams! No.*

Kort looked straightway to X'ieth, refusing to believe. He shook his head. He told himself 'no'. This could not be happening.

"I'm sorry," said Magicia, from his rear. "I let you come here, with no way to win! Age after age, I keep falling into the same trap that Saora has placed."

Kort continued his denial. *No... No.*

"She withholds my memories, and I can't remember this will happen until it's too late!" Magicia added.

Kort still refused to believe. *No. You're Kayareth.*

"Where's Kayareth?" he asked, calmly.

There was silence, save the rolling waves and blowing winds. It incited him.

"Where's Kayareth?!" he screamed.

The words echoed, said at the top of his lungs.

"Like I said, Kayareth is gone from this age," Laotzu responded, softly but firmly. "My ether now tells me that Liath was the only real choice, for coming here meant fighting Shaizan alone!"

Kort gulped, looking back at X'ieth again. He was being told something that he rejected—that his opponent was stronger than him, that he could not win, and that he did not have the spirit for it. These ideas came from those who fought on his side, and for that reason, they terrified him. Kort gulped, his body now awash in numbness, with the sensation of pins and needles pricking his face and extremities.

Laotzu rambled, as if trying to right a situation that had gone wrong.

"Saora told me all this in the future, right after Lucen bested Naketo! She hinted at how the moving time markers would have you re-author your fate, and through the endowment become the Child! Saora predicted how Karnatha would respond to her continued upsets of Destiny's Game, through removing Wicken from Liath and having the Servants of Light turn to Darkness! But you must understand, this ether was withheld from me!"

Kort shook his head, insisting differently.

"Where's Kayareth?!" he screamed.

"Gone," Magicia said. "I'm sorry. We're sorry."

"No!" Kort shot back. "I'll not accept this, and I'm disappointed that you already have! I'll tell you where Kayareth is—he's here. He's with us, and we can win!"

With that, Kort charged X'ieth up ahead. But despite his courage, Magicia stayed where she was, as did the other fighters, perhaps being demoralized by Laotzu's news. For surely the spoken things were dissuading, but nonetheless, they were not enough to stop Kort from seizing a hero's title. *You're Kayareth. You're Kayareth!*

Kort met X'ieth and their shards clashed, releasing sounds to wed those of the ocean gusts and the gentle sea.

Across their blades, Kort heard X'ieth speak.

"I and Shaizan are one! The combined essence of both Lucen and Shaizan overpowers me. I am Shaizan, and today, Karnath's Dark Prophecy will be fulfilled."

"And I am Kayareth!" Kort shouted. "The only part of the Dark Prophecy that shall come true in Karnath is what's happened already! The rest shall be my victory, glory, and legacy… when I change that prophecy!"

Kort's eyes burned with a desire far Darker than his motives before Laotzu had spoken. And all around him were the unspoken witnesses, the dead spectators being eaten by the gulls, who would attest to Kort changing now for the worst, if only they were still alive. Kort was suffering the very same downfall, as X'ieth had suffered himself, when not becoming the Child of Light!

Kort pushed X'ieth back with the white shard, causing his opponent's feet to skid on the bloody sands. He charged X'ieth again, striking repeatedly as his opponent blocked. Kort took a fierce offensive, while X'ieth assumed a leisurely defensive.

"Ha ha ha… Ah ha ha ha…" X'ieth laughed. "Is this all you have? Is this it?!"

Enduring the taunt, Kort flowed through all the sword forms he knew—Fire's Breath, Lightning Impedes, Geyser's Fount, and many more, one after the other. X'ieth blocked them all, gracefully and with skill. In response, Kort flowed into different forms, those of Endo Najatsu—a form of Hirishin swordplay—dealing out forms like Blossomed Flower, Budding Rose, Death Harvester, and more. Again, X'ieth blocked, without even breaking a sweat. Kort on the other hand, was sweating profusely.

Given the situation, Kort extended himself. He began inventing new sword forms, literally blending Mainlandish and Hirishin swordplay together like an artist, attacking X'ieth in ways that few could anticipate or contrive. And yet, despite the novelty of his offensives, X'ieth countered each one with shadowed defensives, as if coming to a mastery of combat that could only happen perfecting an art over multiple generations. X'ieth had become a synthesis of himself, Lucen, and Shaizan in one person, and increased in power and in skill from his descendants—descendants on the outermost branch of his family tree, the Dark Lineage.

About ten cubits away from each other, Kort and X'ieth faced off, with their shards held in both hands, extended in front of their faces. Kort was clad in the armor of god, and X'ieth wore only his tunic and trousers. A sea of dead filled the shores of Gallow Cliff—corpses on top of each other, contorted and with frozen faces of dread. Kort feared he might be among them. *Don't give up. Never do it!*

Kort glanced beyond X'ieth's shoulder, and from how their combat had repositioned them on the shore, he could see Magicia and Laotzu's shadow in the distance. The remaining fighters stood behind them. Everyone was watching and waiting for the fight's end.

"I never… should've trusted you," Kort panted, with his eyes on the shadow. "Why… didn't you tell me?!"

Laotzu replied, "I've been trustworthy all along. Ultimately, it was your choice to come here, and this outcome makes you question why. But in the wake of another broken dream, you forget that the white shard is never a guarantee against new dreams breaking!"

Kort saw himself as Kayareth. In his mind, he filled the white armor, he wielded the white shard, he commanded the Army of Light, and he would become legendary for changing the Dark Prophecy. *That's what you're meant to do. After all your wrongs, it must be!* But as Elucid suggested, his new dream of being Kayareth was now shattering into pieces.

"You can't win!" called out Laotzu.

"We must wait for Kilwroth," Magicia said, shaking her head. "There's no other way… With our missing ethers, we understand this now."

"There is!" Kort yelled, still breathing hard. "I'll show you… who can win, and who cannot! I'll show you… who is Kayareth, and who is not!"

He charged X'ieth again, with a face wrinkled in unholy rage, and his white shard out, thrust at his foe. When he came near, X'ieth stepped to the side, avoiding the weapon. Kort took one hand off the shard, and whipped its elbow into X'ieth's sternum and rotated his forearm up into his opponent's nose. Their was a sudden explosion of blood from the young knight's face.

"Ha ha ha… Mwha ha ha ha…" X'ieth laughed. "Is that it? Is that all you've got?!"

Again, Kort engaged in swordplay with the young knight, who stood there in the moment prior, holding the black shard with blood all over his face. Their shards met again and again with sparks, as they exchanged strikes for blocks. But this time, X'ieth moved from a defensive position into an offensive one, slashing at Kort repeatedly.

Kort watched X'ieth's arms blur, as he rapidly wielded the black shard with a train of Nexus behind his body; it was integrated sword and magic, and Kort struggled to keep pace. The attacks were so fast, he retreated tens of cubits down the bloody shore, stepping over bodies of the slain as he went. Magicia, Laotzu, and the fighters just watched without helping, as if already assuming defeat.

With a few more strikes, Kort felt the white shard abruptly knocked right out of his hands! It sailed through the air over his shoulder, as he stared at the grinning X'ieth, now being unarmed and vulnerable. But to Kort's surprise, instead of attacking him, X'ieth pushed past him and ran for the white shard. He turned, seeing it had landed on the sands over ten cubits away.

In the split second that Kort watched X'ieth's back as he ran by, thoughts went through his head about what Laotzu and Magicia had said. *You can't win. You're not Kayareth. Wait for Kilwroth; there's no other way.*

The words damaged Kort, and his natural defense mechanism was denial. It surged through him the very moment X'ieth had passed, and Kort would not stand idle. *No. You're Kayareth! Show them that you are!*

Kort pulled Nexus into his aux core, and with it, he raced to the back of X'ieth, right as the young knight happened upon the white shard and was a moment away from lifting the weapon off the sands. As X'ieth's hand fell to the shard resting upon the shore, Kort reared back on one leg and raised his other leg high, preparing to deliver a fatal axe kick. In that moment, Kort knew that if he allowed his opponent to get both shards, all of his sacrifice and that of others would be for naught—almost dying on Korinth, Nym's miscarriage, the Army of Light being slaughtered—all for naught. *If X'ieth gets both shards, all is lost. For time will be ended, and with it, my dreams!*

Kort brought his leg down with enough force to break a giant's back, slamming the edge of his foot into X'ieth's vertebrae, right as the young knight took hold of the white shard in addition to the black, which he was already holding. Upon that unexpected and powerful impact, X'ieth went face first into the sands, dropping the black shard, but still holding onto the white.

Kort saw the black shard on the sands. The morning light fell upon its dark blade and prismatically reflected off in rainbow shimmers. With a bizarre magnetism, the shard pulled at his hands, just as it pulled at the corners of his lips, raising them up into a smile. The shard's image was also stuck in his desiring eyes. *Take it! Take it! Take it!*

Without a second thought, Kort took the black shard in his hand, and in the moment of contact, the sword seemed like the most important thing in Karnath to him. It was a close match for how he felt about being Kayareth, in spite of what Laotzu had shared.

In the corner of his eye, Kort saw X'ieth wriggle upon the shore from where he lied, as the waters washed up against the sands, the sounds of which were heard, behind his groans. An inner voice sounded inside his head. *Let him be. Just let him be.* Kort ignored it.

In a sudden and quick motion, Kort drove the black shard through X'ieth's back. Upon making the wound, the young knight yelped in sure pain, and his body convulsed, before going completely still. *He died... He died!*

Having had witnessed Lucen stepping into X'ieth, and the healing of his grave gut wound, Kort was surprised at what appeared to be the young knight's death. He stooped down, and looked at his opponent's face, seeing X'ieth's hollow eyes. They were frozen upon the white shard in his hand, as if that were the last thing the young knight desired, before leaving Karnath.

Kort turned to the distant others, with the black shard in his own hand, now being only a few cubits from the water. Magicia, Laotzu, and the fighters all came forth, everyone but the shadow with wide smiles upon their faces.

"He did it!" a man exclaimed, among the fighters.

"I didn't think he could," admitted Magicia, perhaps having the biggest grin. "But you did! You broke Saora's cycle, Kort! I should've never have doubted you. After all, you are the Gray Child!"

With her last word, Kort saw a flash in the corner of his eye. He turned back to X'ieth's corpse, where indeed there was light, a ball of white light burning over his back. The sight dropped Kort's jaw, right in the moment before the white light jumped from the young knight and into him, through his core! In that moment, Kort felt indwelled by a force of unspeakable power, and all he could see was white.

(Transition to Magicia)

Magicia put her hand to her mouth, as she watched the ball of white light enter Kort, and his eyes suddenly became sapphire blue just as streaks of red became interspersed with his black hair! *Kort just became Shaizan!* she thought with dread. *But how?!*

"Oh no," Laotzu said, despondently. "We should have known this might happen."

Magicia turned, her mouth agape. "What is it?!"

The shadow faced her and spoke. A sliver in the being's dark head moved as it did; the sliver was placed below its two dots for eyes.

"There's been another endowment. What's happened now is exactly how Kort came to bear Garlew's burden. It's a spiritual transfer, whereby both the Light and Dark Lineages are now on the Gray Lineage!"

Magicia gasped. "No… It ought not to be."

Yet, as much as she denied it, Kort was standing before her as Shaizan, exactly like X'ieth had become. Her eyes felt suddenly heavy, and tears formed in them. *No...*

Laotzu continued. "Life is never all that we want, but still, we must rise upon falling, we must dream new dreams. This is what Karnath ought to do, and what we shall do in an earlier weave…"

Magicia snarled, "This isn't over yet, but yet, we're acting like it is! We're acting like this battle is hopeless! Well, this act I can no longer act, and this talk I can no longer talk! Let us not be hypocrites, and do what we can in our time that remains!"

Magicia turned from Laotzu just in time to witness Kort retrieve the white shard from X'ieth's corpse. In the very next moment, she saw him channel Nexus into both shards simultaneously—the white in his left hand, the black in his right. The blades glowed greener and greener, and when showing of blinding light, he put them both together! The action caused them to meld into one sword with a blast of luminous yellow, now forming Maken's whole gray sword! The sight set off alarms in Magicia's head: *He'll end time! Destiny let me stop this!*

With the gray sword in hand, Kort looked out to the sea. He threw his head back, and laughed.

"Mwha ha ha ha!!! Mwha ha ha ha!!!"

Magicia ran up from behind him, and was maybe fifteen cubits away. As she went, she stepped into her vast channeling chamber to prepare her attack. She found herself in a vast channeling chamber, before an enormous set of double doors—her Source entry. She pulled against every mental restraint she could sense, and the doors flew open, causing Nexus to begin flooding in. It flowed and flowed, until at the level of Magicia's waist, where suddenly, the strong flow became a weak trickle!

Magicia was alarmed. *What's happening?!* She pulled against her mental restraints, but the trickle remained. She pulled harder, with the same outcome: her strong stream of Nexus was gone. And then unexpectedly, her Source entry slammed closed, leaving her in the vast channeling chamber, filled with Nexus to her waist but no higher. And after the doors closed, it happened.

Magicia watched as from the pool of energy all around her, a mop of hair suddenly arose, drenched and hanging over a women's face. The head kept rising as the woman stood from her place of submergence. She loomed over Magicia, still with the hair over her face.

"Who… who are you?!" Magicia asked.

Light shined from behind the hair covering the woman's face, in the moment before she pulled back the hair to reveal a mouth and eyes of gold light, shining bright. Magicia gasped. *Saora! Destiny be with me…*

"Destiny is not with you now!" cackled Saora.

Magicia's heart began beating mightily. She snapped from her moment of concentration in her channeling chamber, and back to the shore, where still, she ran to confront Kort. *I can't let Saora do this again! You were a fool for thinking this was over before it was! It's not, so do what you can in the time that you have!*

With that thought, Magicia pushed her remaining Nexus from her aux core and out to her palms; they went alit with green energy. In her eyes, Kort appeared closer with each and every step. But then, when Magicia was at his heels, she saw him turn quickly with an extended hand, clasping her about the neck!

Immediately, Magicia felt her body lifted right off the sands by Kort's muscled arm. Unable to breathe, she clawed at him with her energized hands. She put them on his breastplate, and pushed the energy out into fire, but the element was counteracted by Autheos' armor. Even so, Magicia pushed out more and more energy, draining her channeling chamber, to produce more fire. Just as the last attack, it had no adverse effect on Kort and she tired.

"Remember how you loved me," Kort asked, staring into her eyes, as he clenched her throat with one hand. Her feet dangled and kicked over the sands, as she struggled.

Kort continued. "Remember how you loved me before we overwrote that fate with a new story of bitter rivalry? Do you remember?"

Magicia stared back into his blue eyes. At the question, her mind went awash with memories of Shaizan, to which Kort was but a proxy. She remembered how both of them were together in a time no more; they were a couple deeply in love. *I remember…*

And then, Magicia felt Kort's fingers loosen about her neck for but a moment, giving her a single breath.

"I… still… love you," she admitted, using it up.

With that, Magicia felt Kort tighten his grip once more about her neck, squeezing harder and harder, to choke the life from her. With her steely gray eyes, she peered into his own; they spoke of coldness—of a love long gone.

Laotzu, the shadow, watched Kort drop Magicia's limp body to the sands below Gallow Cliff, her dying words destined to outlive this doing, her voice to transcend time and wander endlessly through the Void.

(Transition to Laotzu)

"Everyone has a conscience; why are you no longer listening to yours?" Laotzu asked Kort, without any answer besides the breezy winds and the lolling tide.

Laotzu stood with the remaining fighters of the Army of Light, all of them spellbound by the turn of events, only able to observe the Dark Prophecy unfold before them.

Kort held the gray sword up in one hand, and into its blade, he drew immense power from the field of Nexus all around Gallow Cliff—from the sands, the cliff rock, and the sea. Energies flowed to Kort's uplifted hand from each source, converging upon the sword from all directions, in thick streams of green energy. These were the energies of time well spent that had been stored at Gallow Cliff, those meant for everyone's good destiny, which were about to be channeled to the Void.

Unable to stop what was happening, Laotzu watched on, as the gray sword's blade grew extremely bright, each moment more luminescent that presumed possible in the last, as energy accumulated there.

In an aside, Laotzu spoke in a despondent voice, "This again, is on my hands!"

Looking to Kort, the shadow cried aloud. "Surely you know this plot to kill Destiny cannot go prior to Kilwroth Etharus Falington, the son of Eriens, King of Malgun. Surely you know!"

Kort responded, "We shall see if Destiny can survive Time No More! Ha ha ha… Mwha ha ha ha ha!"

As the blade's light grew even more intense, Laotzu saw the remaining fighters shield their eyes, as Kort continued the very deed foretold. The gray sword's core created a Sink having the strongest attractor in all of Karnath, which drew the special Nexus that moved the world forward—the spent energy of time dedicated for people's destines—from the well at Gallow Cliff.

And in the very next instant, Kort turned to the sea, discharged the blade's energy into the heavens, and thereby voided the energy of time in the current weave! Laotzu looked up, as the blast blanketed the morning sky in a transient, though dazzling light. In that very moment, spent energies flowed over the bridge, into the Void. *Another age is gone!* thought the shadow in despair. *And you couldn't stop it, much like you couldn't stop Juniper from rebelling!*

At that exact moment, time itself stopped. In Tekkneo, clocks designed to perpetually run seized for their first occasion ever; elsewhere hourglasses broke freeing their sands; and where the sun shined in Karnath, its gaze upon dials remained fixed and unchanging. Throughout all of New and Old Karnath, the people suddenly could hear nothing but an eerie ringing in their ears, growing louder and louder. People in all walks of life, everywhere far and wide, ceased from doing, and just existed for life's season. Time itself had stopped.

Beneath Gallow Cliff, the sun hung in the morning sky and Laotzu could see a silhouette there of a female persona, none other than Karnatha herself. And then, beside Laotzu appeared a ghostly woman of jittering skin, with blotches of gold light for her eyes and mouth; it was Saora.

Saora spoke to Karnatha up above.

"She who forgets will be destined to remember. Here are your memories, Karnatha. Here are your memories, so you know how to pray… Pray that you find a way to end this Game, before it ends you! Pray you find how to sew your weaves back together, as the time markers move independently to rewrite Karnath's history, now non-causal and without apparent seams! Aha ha ha! Ha ha ha!"

With that, a blast of light emanated from Saora's hand, and flew up into the sky toward the sun, as if intended for Karnatha herself. It was much like the light that jumped from X'ieth's corpse into Kort. It was ether.

(Transition to Nym)

Shaizan stood as he was, facing the sea and with the gray sword raised overhead.

"Stop!" came a female voice.

Nym ran up the shore from behind Shaizan, as fast as she could, being about twenty cubits away. She saw his red hair flowing down his shoulders as he looked out to the sea, holding the gray sword. He was strangely wearing white armor, but even still, she came closer. *Almost there! You must stop him from doing this...*

She kept running, fearing that she had already waited too long. Nym just saw Shaizan discharge the light from the gray blade into the sky. *If you wait any longer, time will end! Act, now!*

Fifteen cubits from Shaizan, she stopped running and dropped three throwing knives into her palm.

"Shaizan!" she called. "Face me!"

Shaizan turned, and as he did, she hurled the blades at his head. But instead of Shaizan, Nym saw Kort turned around instead!

"Nym… You came back!"

Horrified, she watched the blades twist toward their target. *Splash! Splash! Thunk!*

One of Nym's blades had missed its mark, going off into the sea. The second blade took off one of Kort's pointy ears and like the first, also went into the sea. But the third blade did Kort serious harm; it nicked the side of his neck, hitting an artery. He bled profusely, clasping a gauntlet to his neck, and applying pressure. Blood spurted out.

"Kort!" Nym screamed.

He slowly fell to his knees, there on the shore.

She ran to him, catching him in her arms before he fell completely. Nym looked into Kort's eyes; they were blue, and no longer brown. She looked at his hair, seeing the red streaks alternating with his black locks. *He became Shaizan... But how?! Why?!* She did not know.

Nym heard Kort gasp for air; blood spurted out of his gauntlet, as it could not be pressed tightly over his neck. She moved his glove aside, and quickly replaced it with her hand, applying pressure. Blood still spurted out between her fingers from the wound, but less than before.

Pain wrenched Nym's heart; just as Kort, she bled, but from the inside. Tears poured from her eyes and down her cheeks, over what she beheld: Kort was dying, and she had invoked his death. To her, this was the worst consequence of mortality that was even possible.

"Kort!" she said. "I never meant to hurt you…"

"Nym," Kort gasped, looking into her eyes. "Our love has always endured misgivings. This too… will pass."

Blood continued spurting between her fingers, and as he lost more blood, Kort was slipping away. Nym's tears increased; they become hot and heavy.

"Kort, don't leave me!" she pled, torn by grief.

"This is a time no more," he said. "It's gone."

"What do you mean?" Nym sobbed.

"I stopped… time. This age… is gone."

The realization smacked her. Nym realized that Kort had become Shaizan, and that light discharged into the sky moments ago, was time. *Kort stopped time, but what will that mean?* To her, the consequences were anything but obvious.

"Our memories," Kort gasped, "and our spirits… will come again… to Karnath. At an earlier time… they'll come again. And maybe… we'll be together again…"

Nym saw Kort's eyes gloss over in death's stare, and when that happened, she felt dead herself and wanted nothing more of life. She pulled Kort's face close to her own, and she cried uncontrollably on him over what had just transpired. Nym cried out her deep and bottomless sadness. *For my love, time has run out!*

Nym removed her bloody hand from Kort's neck, and now, only some leaked out without as much force as before. And then, all of a sudden, as she kneeled on the sands with Kort in her arms, an intense burning developed in her head.

As the terrible pain continued, Nym let go of Kort's body and clutched her head in both hands, in a reflex reaction to the sensation of fire entering her ears and setting her entire mind ablaze! She shut her eyes. She grit her teeth. She bit down hard. But tried as she did, nothing seemed to help. Nym could not compensate.

While her pain went on, a series of images flashed through Nym's mind, imparting knowledge from memories of the past and the future. Kort's memories were there, but also, those from X'ieth, Lucen, and Shaizan. And from this combination of memories, Nym came to understand the cycle of Time No More, and what Saora planned through the *Unwholesome Inheritance*. In particular, visions flooded her of what Lucen knew, of Kilwroth fighting for times in the past up until the Middle Age, and of Shaizan fighting for times in the future back until the same Middle Age. The Middle Age was not a special era, but rather, just a point where Kilwroth and Shaizan were destined meet at the crossroads of time, per Saora's plan.

When the burning finally stopped so did the images, and Nym found herself as she was, kneeling on the shore with her hands about her head. Instant relief came over her; she dropped her hands and exhaled slowly, seeing Kort who still lied there on the sands, now deceased. The winds dried the tears on her face, but she still felt her tears wet and flowing from within.

Nym leaned down to Kort, and gazed upon his lifeless face. His eyes were hollow, and his lips parted.

"Kilwroth is coming," she said. "But before he does, we will meet again."

Nym shut her eyes, and kissed Kort on the lips.

When she opened her eyes a moment later, Nym saw a ball of white light over Kort's core. She sensed light from the corners of her eyes, and looked around, seeing the same all over the bloody shores of Gallow Cliff. Indeed, the piles upon piles of the dead showed the same, with every corpse upon the sands also having a similar ball of light!

To Nym, the sight was mesmerizing: literally a sea of lights forming over spans of sand before the blue seas, like a field of glowing cotton! She watched with wonderment, as these lights grew brighter, before they started shooting up from the bodies, into the air, where they disappeared within the light morning sky. Curiously, Nym stared at them as this happened. *Where are they going?* She wondered.

On the next wind would be her answer, for it brought to Nym's ears the sound of otherworldly chimes, with each note melding into the next, transient though intransient, gone in a moment but lingering forever. And with those sounds, the sky turned a shade of blood red, allowing her to see exactly where the lights went.

Upon the heavens, she saw one luminous streak, then another, and then one more, shooting together, right beside one another. The scene resembled the three falling stars on her cloak. And just like these, were the remaining lights from all over the shore, shooting up into the sky, to fall as stars through the red heavens.

Nym gasped. "Ethers…"

She was literally witnessing the memories, spirits, and curses of the current age leave the world and enter the sky, perhaps bound for the next age. *These are the ethers, of a time no more!*

Right then, the ball of light over Kort's core joined the others in the red sky, adding one more falling star to the hundreds upon hundreds that filled the heavens. In the background the chimes kept playing, and Nym could do nothing but listen and watch, keeping her eye on Kort's ether. So badly, we wished that she could become as one of those stars, to join him in the sky.

And then, out of nowhere, Nym heard the chimes become an eerie voice.

"Falling stars are the ghosts of rising stars. Falling stars are ethers, the remnants of broken dreams. They're the curse of dreaming gray and aspiring big, of things larger than life… They're the memories of failing on the way to success… They're the tormented souls of those who never persisted in failure until success… Three stars fell before you, and likewise, there are three ethers…"

Despite the voice of chimes, Nym kept her eyes on Kort's ether, continuing to envy a position among the stars. *Please, whoever can hear this, let me be with Kort. Please.*

"Am I destined for the same?" Nym asked. "After all, I am the Fallen Servant. Can I not fall among them?!"

The voice replied, "Yes."

Then suddenly, Nym glanced down, and the same ball of light shined over her core. The next thing she knew, she was shooting through the air and into the sky, as another ether among the rest. Now with the stars, Nym found Kort's ether up there, and together they were again.

Those ethers sailed the blood red skies into the higher heavens, onto the prior age and those before it, in a journey that they had taken many times before. For this very thing occurred in Karnath ironically prior to Shaizan, prior to Lucen, and prior to X'ieth, when people killed their time each day, long before its death now. Too few realized that time was there to balance failures with successes, serving as a medium for progress. Instead, time became a medium to the wasteful existence of many, those who chose to be without purpose—a thing that Destiny never intended for anyone!

And so in this age, as in other times no more, Fate's Fray befell Karnath that was not any different from what the people already suffered. Curious minds may wonder, of what consequence was stopping time for a world where it was regarded an inconvenience of sorts, consequently squandered with the peoples' poor stewardship and excess frivolity? What would become, of stopping time?

The answer to the question would be revealed with Karnath's plight. For even when time stopped, the people of the land could still blink. And upon opening their eyes, they found themselves in the past and without a future, left with haunting visions of what would never be. In this, those born to earlier ages soon found themselves in the previous weave, with only some ether from this age unraveled, which now, was a weave never to be.

Just like this, the very first unraveling happened only because too many in Karnath would not use their time well. Instead, they chose to trade their good destiny for a heart's hollow, their apathy being to blame. Perhaps if enough people in Karnath had felt differently about their time, Karnatha would have never weakened, and Shaizan would not have become what he eventually became.

Now, the only hope for Karnath would be the peoples' new destiny coming forth in another age, one where Shaizan simply could not prevail and people would envisage dreams anew. But here rests the real problem: too many in Karnath have grown complacent to once again have the same Fate's Fray as of yesterday, the day before yesterday, and before that even—back to a broken dream, where in life some experienced, Time No More.

High above the full moon that filled a blood-red sky, and even higher above the stars of heaven, Karnatha wept bitterly for Karnath. And with her tears fell all the stars from space in a trail of receding light; they kissed the night goodbye, never to shine again.

The falling stars plummeted to Karnath, bathing the Children of Destiny in brilliant fire, the pair who fought the Battle for Destiny at the foot of Gallow Cliff. Amid her crying, Karnatha offered up this prayer for those who dwell in Old and New Karnath, in hopes that their fate might be changed:

Karnatha's Prayer (2035 A.R.)

With this deed, yet again all is gone. Oh Karnath weeps in this end, and I too for chaos never ordained of Destiny! Shaizan's doing has brought forth great loss, from which this land may never recover. What a reproach to Destiny and all of creation!

Zeros and Raiden, time depends on you just as the natural course of history! I pray you find a way to overcome the circumstances you shall face, and rise above this malady that unfortunately has become your destiny. May conscience be your guide, and may Destiny be with you both in a quest for the restoration of order!

Chapter 85
Across Time

In the last few moments leading up to another age's end, Karnatha was given back her ether and enlightened as to how the *world of doing* was literally slipping into the Void, across time. And with that knowledge she prayed that her Children at an earlier time would make different decisions in order to break the cycle of Time No More, for it stood to erase Karnath's history as well as Karnath's god.

All of Karnatha's prayers concerned someone rising to meet his or her potential in the matter of Time No More and them reverting chaos back to order. And just like any prayer said, her prayers would go somewhere to help a troubling situation, even back thousands of years to a time from which her help would eventually come.

It could not be the age that X'ieth and Kort lived in, nor could it be that of Lucen and Naketo, nor that of Shaizan and Kayareth. For in these ages, everything had already been lost for Destiny, Karnath, and its people. But even though losses occurred in those ages, it would not preclude victories from occurring in others, just as time well spent would see an endless struggle to balance failure with success. Such as this, Kilwroth would need to balance the future's losses to Shaizan against his own past victories, as part of an unwholesome inheritance: bearing the burden upon Kayareth's shoulders, or being crushed by it.

Kilwroth Etharus Falington inherited a war across time from his father Eriens, who bartered with Saora for peace of mind to leave behind his motherless child and selfishly enter New Karnath to war with the inferiors. In the moment that Eriens enjoyed peace, Kilwroth was indwelt by Kayareth's spirit, which had been imprisoned in the Void since the first walk of existence. And since that moment, Kilwroth's fate had changed forever: he was to save both time and Destiny.

The year was 898 A.R., and once again, Kilwroth enjoyed victory at Gallow Cliff in Old Karnath, just as he had enjoyed it in earlier ages. This particular age, he sat at the cliff's ledge, with his feet dangling over the seawaters below, where the tide mounted its vicious assault against the shore. The winds lifted the purple cloak around Kilwroth's shoulders and stirred his lengthy black hair, putting strands in his rugged face, which now, was as worn as the embankment at cliff's foot.

The war across time had tired Kilwroth; it started in the age just before Laotzu visited him in the second walk, in which his childhood was coming to an end. Since then, the war had taken Kilwroth forward a century into his adulthood; he was now a hundred and eighteen years old, older and wiser than he was when saving his first age. And with him saving another age today, he grew stronger and more experienced too.

Kilwroth continued sitting there on the ledge, as the night gave way to morning and a sliver of sun rose on the horizon; his silver armor reflected its light, being embellished with accents matching his plum cloak. At the rock on his right, the whole gray sword lied there with his hand resting over its grip; it had been melded together from the shards and was destined for destruction in Ires Star.

At Kilwroth's left, was a glowing green portal that led into New Karnath, being hung midair and off the cliff's edge. It was portal through which the Army of Light and Laotzu had entered to help him fight; they gathered on the cliff top behind him with their weapons lowered, now sharing a moment of silence for their fallen foe.

In the Army's midst lied the dead Child of Darkness: *Wrath Herrs of Malgun.* Wrath was a former member of his father's kingdom, who found the black shard and led an insurgence to overthrow Merphonox's throne. But Kilwroth had stopped it from ever happening.

Like the Army, Kilwroth had a moment of silence. He felt sad over Wrath's misdeeds. He felt sad over taking life, knowing that life had sanctity. He felt sad over this happening over and over again, until he could meet Shaizan at the crossroads of time. It was enough for him to hang his head low, but nevertheless this was his destiny.

In his moment of solidarity, Kilwroth felt thankful once again for the Army of Light, knowing that his victory came not by his efforts alone. He relied on them, a host of varied people, tens of thousands in number. They were neither mighty seroxians of Old Karnath nor were they warriors of New Karnath, but it did not matter. For Kilwroth and the Army of Light had something in common—something much larger than race, religion, gender, or creed. It was a will to do good and to dream on, even after broken dreams.

Suddenly, from over his shoulder, Kilwroth heard steps at his rear. They were slow but constant, and had the most familiar gait. *Laotzu...* Kilwroth smiled as Laotzu settled behind him, both of them being right at the cliff's ledge. And then, Kilwroth heard him speak, above sounds of the gulls overhead, the lolling tide, and the constant winds of change.

"Defeating Wrath was a major step in your journey to the Middle Age, but your work isn't over yet. You must still go to the Mountains of Liath and destroy the gray sword, so that this age will be safe, just as the others you've already saved."

Kilwroth considered the words, and then nodded.

"I know; we've been here many times before. Since we've just started an age, the cause effect *within this weave* will propagate the event of the sword's destruction to its end. And that outcome will remain, regardless of how the age's time marker tracks ether from the future; there's no rewriting the sword's destruction this age, once it's done."

Kilwroth spoke of what had been done so far at the conclusion of battles at Gallow Cliff: destroying the sword in Ires Star, so that the Battle for Destiny could not be fought again in the age. And just like this, he knew what to expect when Ires Star consumed the sword: he would see a brilliant flash of white light, before finding himself blasted into the next age, where he would appear as he was now, without the shards and with only a new battle to be won.

Using his left hand, Kilwroth helped himself up from the ledge while grabbing the sword with his right hand. Slowly, he turned about and saw Laotzu standing there and smiling warmly, his friend who was aging gracefully with slight wrinkles in his face and touches of gray in his brown hair. He glanced down at Laotzu's shimmering silver armor, which had yellow accents, being in the same color of Kingdom Juniper.

Kilwroth looked beyond Laotzu where the Army of Light stood—humans, elves, and dwarves from New Karnath. The young and the old, the big and the small, the male and the female alike, were all among their ranks, smiling back and with weapons in hand, some carrying banners of Sergros showing a lion.

Kilwroth made a wide gesture to the whole Army, and then set his eyes upon Laotzu.

"What a privilege," he said, "to be aided by so many people inclined to do great good—those with the will to dream on even after dreams shatter! These few have defeated *him* by merely arriving at Gallow Cliff to fight. Facing giants courageously and rising upon falling make people victors, with or without victory."

Laotzu shook his head in agreement.

"They have done it, but those ahead of them will struggle. We must carry this golden age forward into the future, for I sense much is lost within the people of ages to come! In future times, those who lose wars will fail to realize they're either fighting the wrong battle, or they merely stopped fighting the right one. And amid their momentary failures, they'll forget how in the past, they won more than they lost."

Kilwroth replied, "It's possible to carry our age of dreams forward, but such may prove difficult. Enough people must arrive at Gallow Cliff to fight their own Battle for Destiny, before being able to join the larger struggle."

Kilwroth's eyes trailed again to the Army of Light.

"It's the difference between men and women finding the will to dream again, versus whole nations. Individuals must win their Battle for Destiny, prior to Karnath being triumphant in the same."

After his comment, Kilwroth turned away from the Army and Laotzu, to the stunning vistas seen from the cliff's top, where he beheld the most majestic sunrise ever witnessed in Old Karnath. The sky was a canvas streaked by violet hues and brushed by gold-dipped feathers, strewn across the blue sea—an artistry of nature to celebrate the moment's achievement: another fraction of time had been well spent. He watched the sky for some time, and after a while, Laotzu began speaking again.

"We all have a part to play in the conflict. Let us focus on ours, and they upon theirs. If we all do what we must, the roaring fire in this land of opportunity can be rekindled in another age. For long it has been snuffed out."

With that, silence reigned over the group at Gallow Cliff, and only after a long while, Kilwroth turned from the awing sunrise to face Laotzu and the Army of Light. Then from the quiet, he spoke, his voice ringing out with power and surety.

"As disappointments collide with our dreams, likewise one day I shall collide with Shaizan. And as our dreams may shatter upon the impact of disappointments, my body may shatter upon fighting him. Like two coaches speeding toward each other from opposite directions—I from the past, he from the future—our epic clash in time is imminent!"

A strong wind blew then, just as silence replaced Kilwroth's words; it served an intermission that rejuvenated those upon the cliff, lifting spirits much higher than they already soared. Kilwroth looked to Laotzu, and the Army watched on intently, as if everyone awaited his wise words.

Kilwroth continued. "No matter what happens, I am sure what resides in me will continue on to the next age, and the age after that, until the end of time. The spirit of Kayareth will persist, even if I die. And just as this, the will to dream on shall persist in some when dreams break. Though badness and malady linger in the world, the will to do good shall prevail over the will to do evil, whether by me or by the next one of both choice and chance!"

Kilwroth lowered his head, and said in humility, "I'm no one special. All that Destiny requires is that a person be willing, and Destiny shall make those who are willing, able as well."

With his words, Kilwroth unfastened the chain of his purple cloak, took it off his shoulders, and extended it to Laotzu in his hand.

"Take my mantle, and fight in times when I can't."

Kilwroth let go, just as Laotzu grabbed it.

"I shall do my best."

"In the second walk, when you came to me in Castle Malgun," Kilwroth said. "I trusted you with my mantle, not knowing what you would do with it. But now I understand that there are future times in which I won't be present to face Shaizan, and you'll need to fight my fight for me, to either win or die trying."

"Those ages are numbered," Laotzu replied with a smile. "The Middle Age is coming, in which you and Shaizan meet again. I hope to be with you then, as I am with you now."

Kilwroth smiled back. With only a moment more, he stared past Laotzu and the Army of Light, to the Mountains of Liath on the northeast horizon. In so doing, Kilwroth faced his destiny, far from Gallow Cliff. His periphery told him that Laotzu joined him in the stare.

"The next step in your journey awaits."

Kilwroth turned. He saw Laotzu using his arm to gesture to the trail going down the cliff and toward Liath, a deed to perhaps source his reminiscence when leading others in ages to come. He nodded, and showed a smile.

"My story is not without a sequel, but that sequel is perhaps without a writer," Kilwroth said. "For a good sequel to any story should live on in the hearts of men and be practiced in their words and deeds, rather than being bound in a book. You've taught me this much already…"

Weary in body but strong of heart, Kilwroth slowly stepped from his spot with the gray blade in hand. He set his eyes upon Liath and steered his thoughts toward the sword's destruction in Ires Star, as these were the callings of a hero, and he was the new hero of Karnath—the prophesized Child of Light.

All at once, Kilwroth heard the Army of Light burst into song, singing praises to the champion who slayed the Child of Darkness and brought Light to Karnath. By the handful, they threw rainbow confetti into the air, a flurry of colors that lingered there. Some of it fell on Kilwroth's face and hair.

"The Child of Light to Gallow Cliff," they sang. "Did smite the Dark and its age did lift!"

While marching through the crowd of people, Kilwroth kept the gray sword at his side and raised his other hand high, as the rainbow confetti showered over him. The whole time, he kept both eyes fixed on Liath's distant peak, his goal from which he would not look back. As he went, his boots clapped the white rock one after the other, ringing out to proclaim his victory over Darkness.

Kilwroth continued marching forward, with his eyes straightway. He could heard the crowd's cheers mix together with the crowd's song, as trumpets sounded and drums played, heralding a hero to his destiny in Liath, where only a dangerous journey up the mountain awaited. Ovation shook Old Karnath then, as the Army venerated the Child of Light over a deed that would live on with infamy throughout the ages, to be immortalized in legend forevermore.

For Kilwroth, there was no white horse, no Castle Sergros, no kings, lords, or ladies in attendance. Yet, his celebration was exactly the reverie that X'ieth Armstrong would dream of, over a thousand years from now, upon one dark night in Forest Saol. Indeed, Kilwroth's celebration was exactly what X'ieth would come to want.

Suddenly then, Laotzu's potent voice rose over all of the celebratory noise. "One more thing, Lord of Constant Dream."

Kilwroth stopped, his attention now drawn, though he did not look back.

"Destiny be with you," said Laotzu.

Kilwroth's face lit up with a smile. "Destiny be with us both, for choice and chance pave our way…"

And with that remark, Kilwroth walked down the trail toward Liath, and Laotzu threw the purple cloak around his shoulders and fastened its clasp, before heading through the portal and back into New Karnath. They were both ready to repeat a winning fight in the past and a losing fight in the future, all over again, until the Middle Age.

THE END

"CLASH OF THE NULLEN SERVANTS"

About the Author

James Arthur Tocksworth is a published academic author with a somewhat colorful and inspirational past, which interestingly connects him to the world of fantasy fiction. At the age of 11, Tocksworth led a mundane childhood, being the overweight kid at school who no one particularly liked. One day after the bus dropped him off from school, he walked on the shoulder of the road across the street from his house, where he unexpectedly became involved in a pedestrian accident: an automobile collided into him at high-speed!

The accident left Tocksworth with traumatic brain injury (TBI), and palsy of his third cranial nerve, which gave him a droopy eyelid, double vision, and weaker eyesight in one eye. After three months of physical rehabilitation, he went back to grade school, not being well treated due to a physical blemish and some behavioral antics that were common post-TBI. As a coping mechanism he put on even more weight, to weigh in at an all-time high of nearly 250 lb.

Despite his difficulties reading, Tocksworth found fantasy fiction to be very inspirational after his accident. He felt uplifted by immersive stories that came in a variety of formats, such as books, anime, and video games. Some of his favorites then were the Lord of the Rings and Wheel of Time series (books), Final Fantasy (games), and Hakkenden: Legend of the Dog Warriors (anime). In these vivid stories, he admired how characters decisively navigated through difficult situations and overcame huge obstacles. He could not help drawing a parallel to his own life, and purposed to improve his course, partly as a result of these positive influences.

Since that resolution, life has not been without challenges for Tocksworth, but indeed it has changed for the better. In his senior year of high school, he lost all his excess weight and has never gained it back. Though behind a year of school from his accident, he managed to catch up and graduate a year early from high school. Being seventeen years old, he enrolled immediately at a university in Philadelphia, where he majored in mathematics and finished his four-year BS degree in only three years. While working in industry in complex systems integration, he earned a PhD degree in engineering. In the area of advanced controls, he has published several journal and conference papers as lead author, and is co-author of a book chapter as well. Tocksworth currently works in risk management at a large bank. When not crunching numbers, he enjoys travel, distance running, lifting weights, and creative writing.

Fantasy fiction profoundly inspired Tocksworth to change his own life, and he is convinced that the genre still has that same power today. If interested, please see the Afterword to understand the author's particular inspirations for this work. Thanks for reading, and all the best to you!

Afterword

Memorable books in the epic fantasy genre often have immersive worlds with detailed peoples and cultures, a unique magic system, gripping plot, likeable characters, non-stop action and, of course, conflict between good and evil. This work tends to focus upon plot, characters, and action versus other aspects that can make fantasy fiction all the more fantastical. The reason for this mix is to provide the reader an interesting read while not compromising his or her ability to relate to the story on a personal level. After all, Fate's Fray is an allegory with many positive keynotes meant to challenge readers.

This novel derives from several experiences the author has had in life, with particular emphasis on the past ten years. A decade of time put Tocksworth amid many competing interests related to family, work, and personal pursuits. While these problems are boring, typical, and ever-present in parts of the developed world, for him it became literally a battle for his own destiny. On more occasions than one, he found himself fighting desperately against the odds to get what he wanted out of life, often to have dreams break upon the impact of disappointments after constant efforts to succeed. It can be hard to get back on one's feet after failures, and some people stop dreaming with enough broken dreams or negatively cope with their disappointments. Both actions can lead people to less purposeful lives than they would have otherwise lived. Fate's Fray addresses this hypothetical situation by fitting the common struggle of chasing dreams into an epic story about a Battle for Destiny, where good and evil fight each other using shards of a broken dream, where both sides hope to put the pieces back together again, though for different causes.

This story involves a lot of characters, but mainly follows X'ieth, a young knight with bigger dreams than just having an ordinary life that entails a family and career. Instead, he wants to be Karnath's hero. His belief of being meant for more than the ordinary owes to the story's Karnathan religion, which in general, makes Karnathans feel their future lives are meant for more than what their present lives have afforded them. In this vein, X'ieth is convinced that his true destiny is larger than life, but fears his future might unravel over negativities with his family and career; he considers this unraveling as his possible Fate's Fray, and believes his wife and the king are getting in the way of his greatness. Within the first few chapters of the book, X'ieth is pulled into a quest that indulges his lofty aspirations, and without challenges to his way of thinking, he continues believing the same thing well into the story.

However, in the middle of X'ieth's adventure, his comrade Zeros urges him to consider Fate's Fray differently, as a battle for what he wants out of life, where he blames no one more than himself for not achieving his biggest dreams. Despite this input, X'ieth continues believing the same way, and on top of that, starts thinking that he is entitled to everything for which he aspires. As the story progresses, X'ieth encounters sizeable disappointments on a few fronts, and through enduring them, comes to the conclusion that chasing dreams is only healthy for any individual up until the point where one does not compromise the positive influences that factor into the potential of his or her own life.

Embracing the black shard of sword, which symbolizes negative coping over a broken dream, allegorically represents the point where a person throws away his or her future. The story suggests that broken dreams can be the path to no longer dreaming, self-destructing through repressed anger or substance abuse, and forsaking positive relationships with family, friends, and god. All of these things can undercut one's potential, and also, may destroy the potential of those around them.

There is a societal ill of people having skewed priorities and undervaluing what should matter most in life in order to chase after big dreams. People neglect important relationships with family, friends, and god in the pursuit of more, and as a result, hurt their own future. Relationships matter and are key to your development and realizing your full potential; don't throw them away over broken dreams or chasing gray dreams. There's nothing wrong with dreaming, and there's nothing wrong with dreaming big. But individuals should realize that the benefits of dreaming big have costs to one's self, as well as other people in one's life. Everyone should question if the benefits of dreaming big justify the costs. What impositions do big dreams place upon family and friends? How much effort will big dreams require of you? If your dreams don't come true, can you cope with that outcome in a way that preserves the future value and potential of your own life? Dream responsibly.

Besides the aforementioned message, this novel sends other positive messages. It was written to encourage doers in good doing—those stuck in their past, with no progress toward their desired future, who are haunted by visions of construed success that presumably might never be. Remember that when failure comes, to rise upon falling and try again, for goodness often awaits those who commit themselves to worthwhile causes! If failure persists despite trying and trying again, remember how new dreams lie in the wake of broken dreams! There's something that everyone is meant to do in his or her life, and it's just a matter of finding it. So despite momentary or continued failures, keep fighting for your good destiny; we owe ourselves better than a crushing defeat, along with owing the same to those who invested in us. Never give up on yourself. Confront giant challenges. Rise upon falling. Don't be afraid of trying new things. It's important to make positive differences in the world. We all can do good deeds today, regardless of our mistakes yesterday.

In addition to the allegorical aspects of the novel, its story has some bizarre elements of a complete fictional nature. Since this is fantasy fiction as opposed to science fiction, much of what goes on does not relate well to hard sciences. However, the explanation for certain twists in the story has some technical underpinnings that might be unobvious without a note from the author. The book presents the unraveled weaves as a mechanism for the information structure to change arbitrarily in earlier ages, and *Stochastic Processes* largely inspires this idea. Also, there is a poly-furcation mentioned in the story that leads into chaos as the premonitions move time markers in multiple ages, the weak influence here being *Chaos Theory and Non-Linear Dynamics*. Together these ideas give the effect of history evolving like *Monte Carlo Simulation*, where each occasion the time marker moves sees an entirely random path, forged by those decisive and lucky enough to act upon their premonitions before others. Together, these mechanisms make the characters' futures a function of choice and chance, which parallels the human experience.